BERNARD CORNWELL was born
South Essex. Having graduated f
he worked for BBC TV for seven years, mostly as a producer on the *Nationwide* programme, before taking charge
of the Current Affairs department for the BBC in Northern
Ireland. In 1978 he became editor of Thames Television's
Thames at Six. He is married to an American and lives in
the USA.

SHARPE'S FORTRESS

Richard Sharpe and
the Siege of Gawilghur,
December 1803

BERNARD CORNWELL

HarperCollins*Publishers*

HarperCollins*Publishers*
77–85 Fulham Palace Road,
Hammersmith, London w6 8jb

www.**fire**and**water**.com

Published by HarperCollins*Publishers* 1999
1 3 5 7 9 8 6 4 2

Copyright © Bernard Cornwell 1999

The Author asserts the moral right to
be identified as the author of this work

A catalogue record for this book
is available from the British Library

ISBN 0 00 225930 3

Maps by Ken Lewis

Set in Postscript Monotype Baskerville and Linotype Meridien by
Rowland Phototypesetting Ltd, Bury St Edmunds, Suffolk

Printed and bound in Great Britain by
Caledonian International Book Manufacturing Ltd, Glasgow

All rights reserved. No part of this publication may be
reproduced, stored in a retrieval system, or transmitted,
in any form or by any means, electronic, mechanical,
photocopying, recording or otherwise, without the prior
permission of the publishers.

Sharpe's Fortress is for
Christine Clarke,
with many thanks

AFGHANISTAN

RAJPUTANA

Indus

DELHI ■

MAHRATTA

Gawilghur ●
✕ ● Argaum
✕ ● Assaye BERAR

BOMBAY ■

● Ahmednuggur

HYDERABAD

MYSORE

Seringapatam
●

■ MA

CEYLO

KEN LEWIS

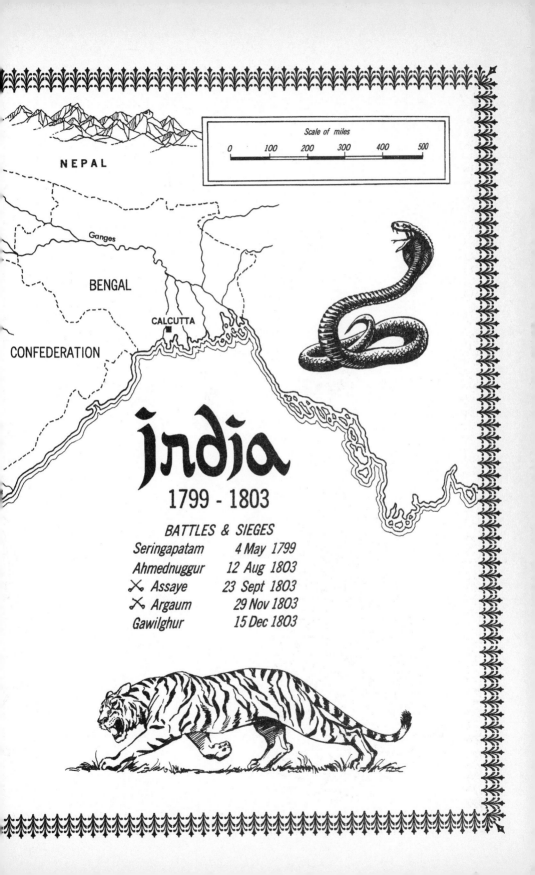

NEPAL

Scale of miles

| 0 | 100 | 200 | 300 | 400 | 500 |

Ganges

BENGAL

CALCUTTA

CONFEDERATION

india
1799 - 1803

BATTLES & SIEGES

Seringapatam	4 May 1799
Ahmednuggur	12 Aug 1803
✕ Assaye	23 Sept 1803
✕ Argaum	29 Nov 1803
Gawilghur	15 Dec 1803

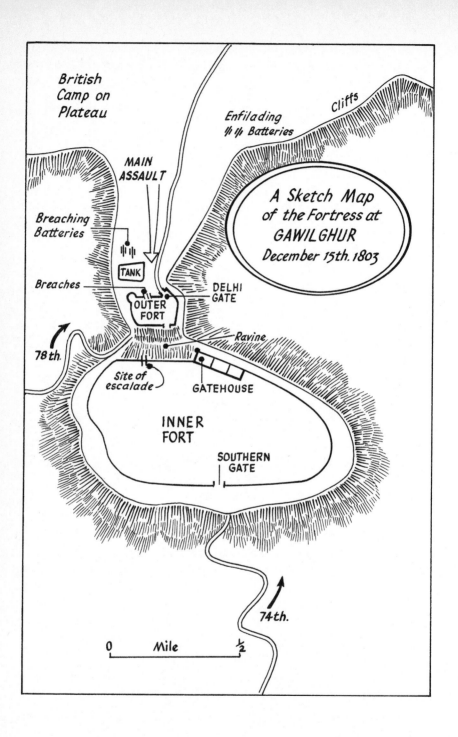

British
Camp on
Plateau

Cliffs

Enfilading
◊ ◊ Batteries

MAIN
ASSAULT

A Sketch Map
of the Fortress at
GAWILGHUR
December 15th. 1803

Breaching
Batteries

TANK

Breaches

DELHI
GATE

OUTER
FORT

Ravine

78 th.

Site of
escalade

GATEHOUSE

INNER
FORT

SOUTHERN
GATE

74 th.

0   Mile   ½

CHAPTER 1

Richard Sharpe wanted to be a good officer. He truly did. He wanted it above all other things, but somehow it was just too difficult, like trying to light a tinderbox in a rain-filled wind. Either the men disliked him, or they ignored him, or they were over-familiar and he was unsure how to cope with any of the three attitudes, while the battalion's other officers plain disapproved of him. You can put a racing saddle on a carthorse, Captain Urquhart had said one night in the ragged tent which passed for the officers' mess, but that don't make the beast quick. He had not been talking about Sharpe, not directly, but all the other officers glanced at him.

The battalion had stopped in the middle of nowhere. It was hot as hell and no wind alleviated the sodden heat. They were surrounded by tall crops that hid everything except the sky. A cannon fired somewhere to the north, but Sharpe had no way of knowing whether it was a British gun or an enemy cannon.

A dry ditch ran through the tall crops and the men of the company sat on the ditch lip as they waited for orders. One or two lay back and slept with their mouths wide open while Sergeant Colquhoun leafed though his tattered Bible. The Sergeant was short-sighted, so had to hold the book very close to his nose from which drops of sweat fell onto the pages. Usually the Sergeant read quietly, mouthing the words and sometimes frowning when he came across a difficult name, but today he was just slowly turning the pages with a wetted finger.

'Looking for inspiration, Sergeant?' Sharpe asked.

'I am not, sir,' Colquhoun answered respectfully, but somehow managed to convey that the question was still impertinent. He dabbed a finger on his tongue and carefully turned another page.

So much for that bloody conversation, Sharpe thought. Somewhere ahead, beyond the tall plants that grew higher than a man, another cannon fired. The discharge was muffled by the thick stems. A horse neighed, but Sharpe could not see the beast. He could see nothing through the high crops.

'Are you going to read us a story, Sergeant?' Corporal McCallum asked. He spoke in English instead of Gaelic, which meant that he wanted Sharpe to hear.

'I am not, John. I am not.'

'Go on, Sergeant,' McCallum said. 'Read us one of those dirty tales about tits.'

The men laughed, glancing at Sharpe to see if he was offended. One of the sleeping men jerked awake and looked about him, startled, then muttered a curse, slapped at a fly and lay back. The other soldiers of the company dangled their boots towards the ditch's crazed mud bed that was decorated with a filigree of dried green scum. A dead lizard lay in one of the dry fissures. Sharpe wondered how the carrion birds had missed it.

'The laughter of fools, John McCallum,' Sergeant Colquhoun said, 'is like the crackling of thorns under the pot.'

'Away with you, Sergeant!' McCallum said. 'I heard it in the kirk once, when I was a wee kid, all about a woman whose tits were like bunches of grapes.' McCallum twisted to look at Sharpe. 'Have you ever seen tits like grapes, Mister Sharpe?'

'I never met your mother, Corporal,' Sharpe said.

The men laughed again. McCallum scowled. Sergeant Colquhoun lowered his Bible and peered at the Corporal. 'The Song of Solomon, John McCallum,' Colquhoun said, 'likens a woman's bosom to clusters of grapes, and I have no doubt it refers to the garments that modest women wore in the Holy Land. Perhaps their bodices possessed balls of knotted wool as decoration? I cannot see it is a matter for your merriment.' Another cannon fired, and this time a round shot whipped through the tall plants close to the ditch. The stems twitched violently, discharging a cloud of dust and small birds into the cloudless sky. The birds flew about in panic for a few seconds, then returned to the swaying seedheads.

'I knew a woman who had lumpy tits,' Private Hollister said. He was a dark-jawed, violent man who spoke rarely. 'Lumpy like a coal sack, they were.' He frowned at the memory, then shook his head. 'She died.'

'This conversation is not seemly,' Colquhoun said quietly, and the men shrugged and fell silent.

Sharpe wanted to ask the Sergeant about the clusters of grapes, but he knew such an enquiry would only cause ribaldry among the men and, as an officer, Sharpe could not risk being made to look a fool. All the same, it sounded odd to him. Why would anyone say a woman had tits like a bunch of grapes? Grapes made him think of grapeshot and he wondered if the bastards up ahead were equipped with canister. Well, of course they were, but there was no point in wasting canister on a field of bulrushes. Were they bulrushes? It seemed a strange thing for a farmer to grow, but India was full of oddities. There were naked sods who claimed to be holy men, snake-charmers who whistled up hooded horrors, dancing bears draped in tinkling bells, and contortionists draped in bugger all, a right bloody circus. And the clowns ahead would have canister. They would wait till they saw the redcoats, then load up the tin cans that burst like duckshot from the gun barrels. For what we are about to receive among the bulrushes, Sharpe thought, may the Lord make us truly thankful.

'I've found it,' Colquhoun said gravely.

'Found what?' Sharpe asked.

'I was fairly sure in my mind, sir, that the good book mentioned millet. And so it does. Ezekiel, the fourth chapter and the ninth verse.' The Sergeant held the book close to his eyes, squinting at the text. He had a round face, afflicted with wens, like a suet pudding studded with currants. '"Take thou also unto thee wheat, and barley,"' he read laboriously, '"and beans, and lentils, and millet, and fitches, and put them in one vessel, and make thee bread thereof."' Colquhoun carefully closed his Bible, wrapped it in a scrap of tarred canvas and stowed it in his pouch. 'It pleases me, sir,' he explained, 'if I can find everyday things in the scriptures. I like to see things, sir, and imagine my Lord and Saviour seeing the selfsame things.'

'But why millet?' Sharpe asked.

'These crops, sir,' Colquhoun said, pointing to the tall stems that surrounded them, 'are millet. The natives call it *jowari*, but our name is millet.' He cuffed the sweat from his face with his sleeve. The red dye of his coat had faded to a dull purple. 'This, of course,' he went on, 'is pearl millet, but I doubt the scriptures mention pearl millet. Not specifically.'

'Millet, eh?' Sharpe said. So the tall plants were not bulrushes, after all. They looked like bulrushes, except they were taller. Nine or ten feet high. 'Must be a bastard to harvest,' he said, but got no response. Sergeant Colquhoun always tried to ignore swear words.

'What are fitches?' McCallum asked.

'A crop grown in the Holy Land,' Colquhoun answered. He plainly did not know.

'Sounds like a disease, Sergeant,' McCallum said. 'A bad dose of the fitches. Leads to a course of mercury.' One or two men sniggered at the reference to syphilis, but Colquhoun ignored the levity.

'Do you grow millet in Scotland?' Sharpe asked the Sergeant.

'Not that I am aware of, sir,' Colquhoun said ponderously, after reflecting on the question for a few seconds, 'though I daresay it might be found in the Lowlands. They grow strange things there. English things.' He turned pointedly away.

And sod you too, Sharpe thought. And where the hell was Captain Urquhart? Where the hell was anybody for that matter? The battalion had marched long before dawn, and at midday they had expected to make camp, but then came a rumour that the enemy was waiting ahead and so General Sir Arthur Wellesley had ordered the baggage to be piled and the advance to continue. The King's 74th had plunged into the millet, then ten minutes later the battalion was ordered to halt beside the dry ditch while Captain Urquhart rode ahead to speak with the battalion commander, and Sharpe had been left to sweat and wait with the company.

Where he had damn all to do except sweat. Damn all. It was a good company, and it did not need Sharpe. Urquhart ran it well, Colquhoun was a magnificent sergeant, the men were as content as soldiers ever were, and the last thing the company needed was a brand new officer, an Englishman at that, who, just two months before, had been a sergeant.

The men were talking in Gaelic and Sharpe, as ever, wondered if they were discussing him. Probably not. Most likely they were talking about the dancing girls in Ferdapoor, where there had been no mere clusters of grapes, but bloody great naked melons. It had been some sort of festival and the battalion had marched one way and the half-naked girls had writhed in the opposite direction and Sergeant Colquhoun had blushed as scarlet as an unfaded coat and shouted at the men to keep their eyes front. Which had been a pointless order, when a score of undressed *bibbis* were bobbling down the highway with silver bells tied to their wrists and even the officers were staring at them like starving men seeing a plate of roast beef. And if the men were not discussing women, they were probably grumbling about all the marching they had done in the last weeks, criss-crossing the Mahratta countryside under a blazing sun without a sight or smell of the enemy. But whatever they were talking about they were making damn sure that Ensign Richard Sharpe was left out.

Which was fair enough, Sharpe reckoned. He had marched in the ranks long enough to know that you did not talk to officers, not unless you were spoken to or unless you were a slick-bellied crawling bastard looking for favours. Officers were different, except Sharpe did not feel different. He just felt excluded. I should have stayed a sergeant, he thought. He had increasingly thought that in the last few weeks, wishing he was back in the Seringapatam armoury with Major Stokes. That had been the life! And Simone Joubert, the Frenchwoman who had clung to Sharpe after the battle at Assaye, had gone back to Seringapatam to wait for him. Better to be there as a sergeant, he reckoned, than here as an unwanted officer.

No guns had fired for a while. Perhaps the enemy had packed up and gone? Perhaps they had hitched their painted cannon to their ox teams, stowed the canister in its limbers and buggered off northwards? In which case it would be a quick about-turn, back to the village where the baggage was stored, then another awkward evening in the officers' mess. Lieutenant Cahill would watch Sharpe like a hawk, adding tuppence to Sharpe's mess bill for every glass of wine, and Sharpe, as the junior officer, would have to propose the loyal toast and pretend not to see when half the bastards wafted their mugs over their canteens. King over the water. Toasting a dead Stuart pretender to the throne who had died in Roman exile. Jacobites who pretended George III was not the proper King. Not that any of them were truly disloyal, and the secret gesture of passing the wine over the water was not even a real secret, but rather was intended to goad Sharpe into English indignation. Except Sharpe did not give a fig. Old King Cole could have been King of Britain for all Sharpe cared.

Colquhoun suddenly barked orders in Gaelic and the men picked up their muskets, jumped into the irrigation ditch where they formed into four ranks and began trudging northwards. Sharpe, taken by surprise, meekly followed. He supposed he should have asked Colquhoun what was happening, but he did not like to display ignorance, and then he saw that the rest of the battalion was also marching, so plainly Colquhoun had decided number six company should advance as well. The Sergeant had made no pretence of asking Sharpe for permission to move. Why should he? Even if Sharpe did give an order the men automatically looked for Colquhoun's nod before they obeyed. That was how the company worked; Urquhart commanded, Colquhoun came next, and Ensign Sharpe tagged along like one of the scruffy dogs adopted by the men.

Captain Urquhart spurred his horse back down the ditch. 'Well done, Sergeant,' he told Colquhoun, who ignored the praise. The Captain turned the horse, its hooves breaking through the ditch's crust to churn up clots of dried mud. 'The rascals are waiting ahead,' Urquhart told Sharpe.

'I thought they might have gone,' Sharpe said.

'They're formed and ready,' Urquhart said, 'formed and ready.' The Captain was a fine-looking man with a stern face, straight back and steady nerve. The men trusted him. In other days Sharpe would have been proud to serve a man like Urquhart, but the Captain seemed irritated by Sharpe's presence. 'We'll be wheeling to the right soon,' Urquhart called to Colquhoun, 'forming line on the right in two ranks.'

'Aye, sir.'

Urquhart glanced up at the sky. 'Three hours of daylight left?' he guessed. 'Enough to do the job. You'll take the left files, Ensign.'

'Yes, sir,' Sharpe said, and knew that he would have nothing to do there. The men understood their duty, the corporals would close the files and Sharpe would simply walk behind them like a dog tied to a cart.

There was a sudden crash of guns as a whole battery of enemy cannon opened fire. Sharpe heard the round shots whipping through the millet, but none of the missiles came near the 74th. The battalion's pipers had started playing and the men picked up their feet and hefted their muskets in preparation for the grim work ahead. Two more guns fired, and this time Sharpe saw a wisp of smoke above the seedheads and he knew that a shell had gone overhead. The smoke trail from the burning fuse wavered in the windless heat as Sharpe waited for the explosion, but none sounded.

'Cut his fuse too long,' Urquhart said. His horse was nervous, or perhaps it disliked the treacherous footing in the bottom of the ditch. Urquhart spurred the horse up the bank where it trampled the millet. 'What is this stuff?' he asked Sharpe. 'Maize?'

'Colquhoun says it's millet,' Sharpe said, 'pearl millet.'

Urquhart grunted, then kicked his horse on towards the front of the company. Sharpe cuffed sweat from his eyes. He wore an officer's red tail coat with the white facings of the 74th. The coat had belonged to a Lieutenant Blaine who had died at Assaye and Sharpe had purchased the coat for a shilling in the auction of dead officers' effects, then he had clumsily sewn up the bullet hole in the left breast, but no amount of scrubbing had rid the coat of Blaine's blood which stained the faded red weave black. He wore his old trousers, the ones issued to him when he was a sergeant, red leather riding boots that he had taken from an Arab corpse in Ahmednuggur, and a tasselled red officer's sash that he had pulled off a corpse at Assaye. For a sword he wore a light cavalry sabre, the same weapon he had used to save Wellesley's life at the battle of Assaye. He did not like the sabre much. It was clumsy, and the curved blade was never where you thought it was. You struck with the sword, and just when you thought it would bite home, you found that the blade still had six inches to travel. The other officers carried claymores, big, straight-bladed, heavy and lethal, and Sharpe should have equipped himself with one, but he had baulked at the auction prices.

He could have bought every claymore in the auction if he had wished, but he had not wanted to give the impression of being wealthy. Which he was. But a man like Sharpe was not supposed to have money. He was up from the ranks, a common soldier, gutter-born and gutter-bred, but he had hacked down a half-dozen men to save Wellesley's life and the General had rewarded Sergeant Sharpe by making him into an officer, and Ensign Sharpe was too canny to let his new battalion know that he possessed a king's fortune. A dead king's fortune: the jewels he had taken from the Tippoo Sultan in the blood and smoke-stinking Water Gate at Seringapatam.

Would he be more popular if it was known he was rich? He doubted it. Wealth did not give respectability, not unless it was inherited.

Besides, it was not poverty that excluded Sharpe from both the officers' mess and the ranks alike, but rather that he was a stranger. The 74th had taken a beating at Assaye. Not an officer had been left unwounded, and companies that had paraded seventy or eighty strong before the battle now had only forty to fifty men. The battalion had been ripped through hell and back, and its survivors now clung to each other. Sharpe might have been at Assaye, he might even have distinguished himself on the battlefield, but he had not been through the murderous ordeal of the 74th and so he was an outsider.

'Line to the right!' Sergeant Colquhoun shouted, and the company wheeled right and shook itself into a line of two ranks. The ditch had emerged from the millet to join a wide, dry riverbed, and Sharpe looked northwards to see a rill of dirty white gunsmoke on the horizon. Mahratta guns. But a long way away. Now that the battalion was free of the tall crops Sharpe could just detect a small wind. It was not strong enough to cool the heat, but it would waft the gunsmoke slowly away.

'Halt!' Urquhart called. 'Face front!'

The enemy cannon might be far off, but it seemed that the battalion would march straight up the riverbed into the mouths of those guns. But at least the 74th was not alone. The 78th, another Highland battalion, was on their right, and on either side of those two Scottish battalions were long lines of Madrassi sepoys.

Urquhart rode back to Sharpe. 'Stevenson's joined.' The Captain spoke loud enough for the rest of the company to hear. Urquhart was encouraging them by letting them know that the two small British armies had combined. General Wellesley commanded both, but for most of the time he split his forces into two parts, the smaller under Colonel Stevenson, but today the two small parts had combined so that twelve thousand infantry could attack together. But against how many? Sharpe could not see the Mahratta army beyond their guns, but doubtless the bastards were there in force.

'Which means the 94th's off to our left somewhere,' Urquhart added loudly, and some of the men muttered their approval of the news. The 94th was another Scottish regiment, so today there were three Scottish battalions attacking the Mahrattas. Three Scottish and ten sepoy battalions, and most of the Scots reckoned that they could have done the job by themselves. Sharpe reckoned they could too. They may not have liked him much, but he knew they were good soldiers. Tough bastards. He sometimes tried to imagine what it must be like for the Mahrattas to fight against the Scots. Hell, he guessed. Absolute hell. 'The thing is,' Colonel McCandless had once told Sharpe, 'it takes twice as much to kill a Scot as it does to finish off an Englishman.'

Poor McCandless. He had been finished off, shot in the dying moments of Assaye. Any of the enemy might have killed the Colonel, but Sharpe had convinced himself that the traitorous Englishman, William Dodd, had fired the fatal shot. And Dodd was still free, still fighting for the Mahrattas, and Sharpe had sworn over McCandless's grave that he would take vengeance on the Scotsman's behalf. He had made the oath as he had dug the Colonel's grave, getting blisters as he had hacked into the dry soil. McCandless had been a good friend to Sharpe and now, with the Colonel deep buried so that no bird or beast could feast on his corpse, Sharpe felt friendless in this army.

'Guns!' A shout sounded behind the 74th. 'Make way!'

Two batteries of six-pounder galloper guns were being hauled up the dry riverbed to form an artillery line ahead of the infantry. The guns were called gallopers because they were light and were usually hauled by horses, but now they were all harnessed to teams of ten oxen so they plodded rather than galloped. The oxen had painted horns and some had bells about their necks. The heavy guns were all back on the road somewhere, so far back that they would probably be too late to join this day's party.

The land was more open now. There were a few patches of tall millet ahead, but off to the east there were arable fields and Sharpe watched as the guns headed for that dry grassland. The enemy was watching too, and the first round shots bounced on the grass and ricocheted over the British guns.

'A few minutes before the gunners bother themselves with us, I fancy,' Urquhart said, then kicked his right foot out of its stirrup and slid down beside Sharpe. 'Jock!' He called a soldier. 'Hold onto my horse, will you?' The soldier led the horse off to a patch of grass, and Urquhart jerked his head, inviting Sharpe to follow him out of the company's earshot. The Captain seemed embarrassed, as was Sharpe, who was not accustomed to such intimacy with Urquhart. 'D'you use a cigar, Sharpe?' the Captain asked.

'Sometimes, sir.'

'Here.' Urquhart offered Sharpe a roughly rolled cigar, then struck a light in his tinderbox. He lit his own cigar first, then held the box with its flickering flame to Sharpe. 'The Major tells me a new draft has arrived in Madras.'

'That's good, sir.'

'It won't restore our strength, of course, but it'll help,' Urquhart said. He was not looking at Sharpe, but staring at the British guns that steadily advanced across the grassland. There were only a dozen of the cannon, far fewer than the Mahratta guns. A shell exploded by one of the ox teams, blasting the beasts with smoke and scraps of turf, and Sharpe expected to see the gun stop as the dying beasts tangled the traces, but the oxen trudged on, miraculously unhurt by the shell's violence. 'If they advance too far,' Urquhart murmured, 'they'll become so much scrap metal. Are you happy here, Sharpe?'

'Happy, sir?' Sharpe was taken aback by the sudden question.

Urquhart frowned as if he found Sharpe's response unhelpful. 'Happy,' he said again, 'content?'

'Not sure a soldier's meant to be happy, sir.'

'Not true, not true,' Urquhart said disapprovingly. He was as tall as Sharpe. Rumour said that Urquhart was a very rich man, but the only sign of it was his uniform which was cut very elegantly in contrast to Sharpe's shabby coat. Urquhart rarely smiled, which made it difficult to be easy in his company. Sharpe wondered why the Captain had sought this conversation, which seemed untypical of the unbending Urquhart. Perhaps he was nervous about the imminent battle? It seemed unlikely to Sharpe after Urquhart had endured the cauldron of fire at Assaye, but he could think of no other explanation. 'A fellow should be content in his work,' Urquhart said with a flourish of his cigar, 'and if he ain't, it's probably a sign that he's in the wrong line of business.'

'Don't have much work to do, sir,' Sharpe said, wishing he did not sound so surly.

'Don't suppose you do,' Urquhart said slowly. 'I do see your meaning. Indeed I do.' He shuffled his feet in the dust. 'Company runs itself, I suppose. Colquhoun's a good fellow, and Sergeant Craig's showing well, don't you think?'

'Yes, sir.' Sharpe knew he did not need to call Urquhart 'sir' all the time, but old habits died hard.

'They're both good Calvinists, you see,' Urquhart said. 'Makes 'em trustworthy.'

'Yes, sir,' Sharpe said. He was not exactly sure what a Calvinist was, and he was not going to ask. Maybe it was the same as a freemason, and there were plenty of those in the 74th's mess, though Sharpe again did not really know what they were. He just knew he was not one of them.

'Thing is, Sharpe,' Urquhart went on, though he did not look at Sharpe as he spoke, 'you're sitting on a fortune, if you follow me.'

'A fortune, sir?' Sharpe asked with some alarm. Had Urquhart somehow smelt out Sharpe's hoard of emeralds, rubies, diamonds and sapphires?

'You're an ensign,' Urquhart explained, 'and if you ain't happy you can always sell your commission. Plenty of fine fellows in Scotland who'll pay you for the rank. Even some fellows here. I gather the Scotch Brigade has some gentlemen rankers.'

So Urquhart was not nervous about the coming fight, but rather about Sharpe's reaction to this conversation. The Captain wanted to be rid of Sharpe, and the realization made Sharpe even more awkward. He had wanted to be made an officer so badly, and already he wished he had never dreamed of the promotion. What had he expected? To be slapped on the back and welcomed like a long-lost brother? To be given a company of troops? Urquhart was watching him expectantly, waiting for a response, but Sharpe said nothing.

'Four hundred pounds, Sharpe,' Urquhart said. 'That's the official rate for an ensign's commission, but between you and me you can squeeze at least another fifty. Maybe even a hundred! And in guineas. But if you do sell to a ranker here, then make damn sure his note is good.'

Sharpe said nothing. Were there really gentlemen rankers in the 94th? Such men could afford to be officers, and had an officer's breeding, but until a commission was vacant they served in the ranks, yet ate in the mess. They were neither fish nor fowl. Like Sharpe himself. And any one of them would snap at the chance to buy a commission in the 74th. But Sharpe hardly needed the money. He possessed a fortune already, and if he wanted to leave the army then all he needed to do was resign his commission and walk away. Walk away a rich man.

'Of course,' Urquhart went on, oblivious of Sharpe's thoughts, 'if the note's written on a decent army agent then you won't have any worries. Most of our fellows use John Borrey in Edinburgh, so if you see one of his notes then you can place full trust in it. Borrey's an honest fellow. Another Calvinist, you see.'

'And a freemason, sir?' Sharpe asked. He was not really sure why he asked, but the question just got blurted out. He supposed he wanted to know if it was the same thing as a Calvinist.

'I really couldn't say.' Urquhart frowned at Sharpe and his voice became colder. 'The point is, Sharpe, he's trustworthy.'

Four hundred and fifty guineas, Sharpe thought. It was not to be spat on. It was another small fortune to add to his jewels, and he felt the temptation to accept Urquhart's advice. He was never going to be welome in the 74th, and with his plunder he could set himself up in England.

'Coins on the barrel-head,' Urquhart said. 'Think on it, Sharpe, think on it. Jock, my horse!'

Sharpe threw away the cigar. His mouth was dry with dust and the smoke was harsh, but as Urquhart mounted his horse he saw the scarcely smoked cigar lying on the ground and gave Sharpe an unfriendly look. For a second it seemed as if the Captain might say something, then he pulled on the reins and spurred away. Bugger it, Sharpe thought. Can't do a thing right these days.

The Mahratta cannon had got the range of the British galloper guns now and one of their round shot landed plumb on a carriage. One wheel splintered, tipping the six-pounder gun onto its side. The gunners leaped off the limber, but before they could detach the spare wheel, the ox team bolted. They dragged the broken gun back towards the sepoys, leaving a vast plume of dust where the axle boss dragged through the dry soil. The gunners ran to head the oxen off, but then a second team panicked. The beasts had their painted horns down and were galloping away from the bombardment. The Mahratta guns were firing fast now. A round shot slashed into another gun team, spurting ox blood bright into the sky. The enemy guns were big brutes, and with a much longer range than the small British six-pounders. A pair of shells exploded behind the panicked oxen, driving them even faster towards the sepoy battalions on the right of Wellesley's line. The limbers were bouncing frantically on the uneven ground and every lurch sent shot tumbling or powder spilling. Sharpe saw General Wellesley turn his horse towards the sepoys. He was doubtless shouting at them to open ranks and so allow the bolting oxen to pass through the line, but instead, quite suddenly, the men themselves turned and ran. 'Jesus!' Sharpe said aloud, earning himself a reproving look from Sergeant Colquhoun.

Two battalions of the sepoys were fleeing. Sharpe saw the General riding among the fugitives, and he imagined Wellesley shouting at the frightened men to stop and re-form, but instead they kept running towards the millet. They had been panicked by the oxen and by the weight of enemy shot that beat the dry grassland with dust and smoke. The men vanished in the high stalks, leaving nothing behind but a scatter of embarrassed officers and, astonishingly, the two panicked gun teams which had inexplicably stopped short of the millet and now waited patiently for the gunners to catch them.

'Sit yourselves down!' Urquhart called to his men, and the company squatted in the dry riverbed. One man took a stump of clay pipe from his pouch and lit it with a tinderbox. The tobacco smoke drifted slowly in the small wind. A few men drank from their canteens, but most were hoarding their water against the dryness that would come when they bit into their cartridges. Sharpe glanced behind, hoping to see the *puckalees* who brought the battalion water, but there was no sign of them. When he turned back to the north he saw that some enemy cavalry had appeared on the crest, their tall lances making a spiky thicket against the sky. Doubtless the enemy horsemen were tempted to attack the broken British line and so stampede more of the nervous sepoys, but a squadron of British cavalry emerged from a wood with their sabres drawn to threaten the flank of the enemy horsemen. Neither side charged, but instead they just watched each other. The 74th's pipers had ceased their playing. The remaining British galloper guns were deploying now, facing up the long gentle slope to where the enemy cannon lined the horizon. 'Are all the muskets loaded?' Urquhart asked Colquhoun.

'They'd better be, sir, or I'll want to know why.'

Urquhart dismounted. He had a dozen full canteens of water tied to his saddle and he unstrung six of them and gave them to the company. 'Share it out,' he ordered, and Sharpe wished he had thought to bring some extra water himself. One man cupped some water in his hands and let his dog lap it up. The dog then sat and scratched its fleas while its master lay back and tipped his shako over his eyes.

What the enemy should do, Sharpe thought, is throw their infantry forward. All of it. Send a massive attack across the skyline and down towards the millet. Flood the riverbed with a horde of screaming warriors who could add to the panic and so snatch victory.

But the skyline stayed empty except for the guns and the stalled enemy lancers.

And so the redcoats waited.

Colonel William Dodd, commanding officer of Dodd's Cobras, spurred his horse to the skyline from where he stared down the slope to see the British force in disarray. It looked to him as though two or more battalions had fled in panic, leaving a gaping hole on the right of the redcoat line. He turned his horse and kicked it to where the Mahratta warlord waited under his banners. Dodd forced his horse through the aides until he reached Prince Manu Bappoo. 'Throw everything forward, sahib,' he advised Bappoo, 'now!'

Manu Bappoo showed no sign of having heard Dodd. The Mahratta commander was a tall and lean man with a long, scarred face and a short black beard. He wore yellow robes, had a silver helmet with a long horse-tail plume, and carried a drawn sword that he claimed to have taken in single combat from a British cavalry officer. Dodd doubted the claim, for the sword was of no pattern that he recognized, but he was not willing to challenge Bappoo directly on the matter. Bappoo was not like most of the Mahratta leaders that Dodd knew. Bappoo might be a prince and the younger brother of the cowardly Rajah of Berar, but he was also a fighter.

'Attack now!' Dodd insisted. Much earlier in the day he had advised against fighting the British at all, but now it seemed that his advice had been wrong, for the British assault had dissolved in panic long before it reached musket range. 'Attack with everything we've got, sahib,' Dodd urged Bappoo.

'If I throw everything forward, Colonel Dodd,' Bappoo said in his oddly sibilant voice, 'then my guns will have to cease fire. Let the British walk into the cannon fire, then we shall release the infantry.' Bappoo had lost his front teeth to a lance thrust, and hissed his words so that, to Dodd, he sounded like a snake. He even looked reptilian.

Maybe it was his hooded eyes, or perhaps it was just his air of silent menace. But at least he could fight. Bappoo's brother, the Rajah of Berar, had fled before the battle at Assaye, but Bappoo, who had not been present at Assaye, was no coward. Indeed, he could bite like a serpent.

'The British walked into the cannon fire at Assaye,' Dodd growled, 'and there were fewer of them and we had more guns, but still they won.'

Bappoo patted his horse which had shied away from the sound of a nearby cannon. It was a big, black Arab stallion, and its saddle was encrusted with silver. Both horse and saddle had been gifts from an Arabian sheik whose tribesmen sailed to India to serve in Bappoo's own regiment. They were mercenaries from the pitiless desert who called themselves the Lions of Allah and they were reckoned to be the most savage regiment in all India. The Lions of Allah were arrayed behind Bappoo: a phalanx of dark-faced, white-robed warriors armed with muskets and long, curved scimitars. 'You truly think we should fight them in front of our guns?' Bappoo asked Dodd.

'Muskets will kill more of them than cannon will,' Dodd said. One of the things he liked about Bappoo was that the man was willing to listen to advice. 'Meet them halfway, sahib, thin the bastards out with musket fire, then pull back to let the guns finish them with canister. Better still, sahib, put the guns on the flank to rake them.'

'Too late to do that,' Bappoo said.

'Aye, well. Mebbe.' Dodd sniffed. Why the Indians stubbornly insisted on putting guns in front of infantry, he did not know. Daft idea, it was, but they would do it. He kept telling them to put their cannon between the regiments, so that the gunners could slant their fire across the face of the infantry, but Indian commanders reckoned that the sight of guns directly in front heartened their men. 'But put some infantry out front, sahib,' he urged.

Bappoo thought about Dodd's proposal. He did not much like the Englishman who was a tall, ungainly and sullen man with long yellow teeth and a sarcastic manner, but Bappoo suspected his advice was good. The Prince had never fought the British before, but he was aware that they were somehow different from the other enemies he had slaughtered on a score of battlefields across western India. There was, he understood, a stolid indifference to death in those red ranks

23

that let them march calmly into the fiercest cannonade. He had not seen it happen, but he had heard about it from enough men to credit the reports. Even so he found it hard to abandon the tried and tested methods of battle. It would seem unnatural to advance his infantry in front of the guns, and so render the artillery useless. He had thirty-eight cannon, all of them heavier than anything the British had yet deployed, and his gunners were as well trained as any in the world. Thirty-eight heavy cannon could make a fine slaughter of advancing infantry, yet if what Dodd said was true, then the red-coated ranks would stoically endure the punishment and keep coming. Except some had already run, which suggested they were nervous, so perhaps this was the day when the gods would finally turn against the British. 'I saw two eagles this morning,' Bappoo told Dodd, 'outlined against the sun.'

So bloody what? Dodd thought. The Indians were great ones for auguries, forever staring into pots of oil or consulting holy men or worrying about the errant fall of a trembling leaf, but there was no better augury for victory than the sight of an enemy running away before they even reached the fight. 'I assume the eagles mean victory?' Dodd asked politely.

'They do,' Bappoo agreed. And the augury suggested the victory would be his whatever tactics he used, which inclined him against trying anything new. Besides, though Prince Manu Bappoo had never fought the British, nor had the British ever faced the Lions of Allah in battle. And the numbers were in Bappoo's favour. He was barring the British advance with forty thousand men, while the redcoats were not even a third of that number. 'We shall wait,' Bappoo decided, 'and let the enemy get closer.' He would crush them with cannon fire first, then with musketry. 'Perhaps I shall release the Lions of Allah when the British are closer, Colonel,' he said to pacify Dodd.

'One regiment won't do it,' Dodd said, 'not even your Arabs, sahib. Throw every man forward. The whole line.'

'Maybe,' Bappoo said vaguely, though he had no intention of advancing all his infantry in front of the precious guns. He had no need to. The vision of eagles had persuaded him that he would see victory, and he believed the gunners would make that victory. He imagined dead red-coated bodies among the crops. He would avenge Assaye and prove that redcoats could die like any other enemy. 'To your men, Colonel Dodd,' he said sternly.

Dodd wheeled his horse and spurred towards the right of the line where his Cobras waited in four ranks. It was a fine regiment, splendidly trained, which Dodd had extricated from the siege of Ahmednuggur and then from the panicked chaos of the defeat at Assaye. Two disasters, yet Dodd's men had never flinched. The regiment had been a part of Scindia's army, but after Assaye the Cobras had retreated with the Rajah of Berar's infantry, and Prince Manu Bappoo, summoned from the north country to take command of Berar's shattered forces, had persuaded Dodd to change his allegiance from Scindia to the Rajah of Berar. Dodd would have changed allegiance anyway, for the dispirited Scindia was seeking to make peace with the British, but Bappoo had added the inducement of gold, silver and a promotion to colonel. Dodd's men, mercenaries all, did not care which master they served so long as his purse was deep.

Gopal, Dodd's second-in-command, greeted the Colonel's return with a rueful look. 'He won't advance?'

'He wants the guns to do the work.'

Gopal heard the doubt in Dodd's voice. 'And they won't?'

'They didn't at Assaye,' Dodd said sourly. 'Damn it! We shouldn't be fighting them here at all! Never give redcoats open ground. We should be making the bastards climb walls or cross rivers.' Dodd was nervous of defeat, and he had cause to be for the British had put a price on his head. That price was now seven hundred guineas, nearly six thousand rupees, and all of it promised in gold to whoever delivered William Dodd's body, dead or alive, to the East India Company. Dodd had been a lieutenant in the Company's army, but he had encouraged his men to murder a goldsmith and, faced with prosecution, Dodd had deserted and taken over a hundred sepoys with him. That had been enough to put a price on his head, but the price rose after Dodd and his treacherous sepoys murdered the Company's garrison at Chasalgaon. Now Dodd's body was worth a fortune and William Dodd understood greed well enough to be fearful. If Bappoo's army collapsed today as the Mahratta army had disintegrated at Assaye, then Dodd would be a fugitive on an open plain dominated by enemy cavalry. 'We should fight them in the hills,' he said grimly.

'Then we should fight them at Gawilghur,' Gopal said.

'Gawilghur?' Dodd asked.

'It is the greatest of all the Mahratta fortresses, sahib. Not all the

25

armies of Europe could take Gawilghur.' Gopal saw that Dodd was sceptical of the claim. 'Not all the armies of the world could take it, sahib,' he added earnestly. 'It stands on cliffs that touch the sky, and from its walls men are reduced to the size of lice.'

'There's a way in, though,' Dodd said, 'there's always a way in.'

'There is, sahib, but the way into Gawilghur is across a neck of high rock that leads only to an outer fortress. A man might fight his way through those outer walls, but then he will come to a deep ravine and find the real stronghold lies on the ravine's far side. There are more walls, more guns, a narrow path, and vast gates barring the way!' Gopal sighed. 'I saw it once, years ago, and prayed I would never have to fight an enemy who had taken refuge there.'

Dodd said nothing. He was staring down the gentle slope to where the red-coated infantry waited. Every few seconds a puff of dust showed where a round shot struck the ground.

'If things go badly today,' Gopal said quietly, 'then we shall go to Gawilghur and there we shall be safe. The British can follow us, but they cannot reach us. They will break themselves on Gawilghur's rocks while we take our rest at the edge of the fortress's lakes. We shall be in the sky, and they will die beneath us like dogs.'

If Gopal was right then not all the king's horses nor all the king's men could touch William Dodd at Gawilghur. But first he had to reach the fortress, and maybe it would not even be necessary, for Prince Manu Bappoo might yet beat the redcoats here. Bappoo believed there was no infantry in India that could stand against his Arab mercenaries.

Away on the plain Dodd could see that the two battalions that had fled into the tall crops were now being brought back into the line. In a moment, he knew, that line would start forward again. 'Tell our guns to hold their fire,' he ordered Gopal. Dodd's Cobras possessed five small cannon of their own, designed to give the regiment close support. Dodd's guns were not in front of his white-coated men, but away on the right flank from where they could lash a murderous slanting fire across the face of the advancing enemy. 'Load with canister,' he ordered, 'and wait till they're close.' The important thing was to win, but if fate decreed otherwise, then Dodd must live to fight again at a place where a man could not be beaten.

At Gawilghur.

*   *   *

The British line at last advanced. From east to west it stretched for three miles, snaking in and out of millet fields, through pastureland and across the wide, dry riverbed. The centre of the line was an array of thirteen red-coated infantry battalions, three of them Scottish and the rest sepoys, while two regiments of cavalry advanced on the left flank and four on the right. Beyond the regular cavalry were two masses of mercenary horsemen who had allied themselves to the British in hope of loot. Drums beat and pipes played. The colours hung above the shakos. A great swathe of crops was trodden flat as the cumbersome line marched north. The British guns opened fire, their small six-pound missiles aimed at the Mahratta guns.

Those Mahratta guns fired constantly. Sharpe, walking behind the left flank of number six company, watched one particular gun which stood just beside a bright clump of flags on the enemy-held skyline. He slowly counted to sixty in his head, then counted it again, and worked out that the gun had managed five shots in two minutes. He could not be certain just how many guns were on the horizon, for the great cloud of powder smoke hid them, but he tried to count the muzzle flashes that appeared as momentary bright flames amidst the grey-white vapour and, as best he could guess, he reckoned there were nearly forty cannon there. Forty times five was what? Two hundred. So a hundred shots a minute were being fired, and each shot, if properly aimed, might kill two men, one in the front rank and one behind. Once the attack was close, of course, the bastards would switch to canister and then every shot could pluck a dozen men out of the line, but for now, as the redcoats silently trudged forward, the enemy was sending round shot down the gentle slope. A good many of these missed. Some screamed overhead and a few bounced over the line, but the enemy gunners were good, and they were lowering their cannon barrels so that the round shot struck the ground well ahead of the redcoat line and, by the time the missile reached the target, it had bounced a dozen times and so struck at waist height or below. Grazing, the gunners called it, and it took skill. If the first graze was too close to the gun then the ball would lose its momentum and do nothing but raise jeers from the redcoats as it rolled to a harmless stop, while if the first graze was too close to the attacking line then the ball would bounce clean over the redcoats. The skill was to skim the ball low enough to be certain of a hit, and all along the line the round shots were taking their toll. Men were plucked back with shattered hips and legs. Sharpe passed one spent cannonball that was sticky with blood and thick with flies, lying twenty paces from the man it had eviscerated. 'Close up!' the sergeants shouted, and the file-closers tugged men to fill the gaps. The British guns were firing into the enemy smoke cloud, but their shots seemed to have no effect, and so the guns were ordered farther forward. The ox teams were brought up, the guns were attached to the limbers, and the six-pounders trundled on up the slope.

'Like ninepins.' Ensign Venables had appeared at Sharpe's side. Roderick Venables was sixteen years old and attached to number seven company. He had been the battalion's most junior officer till Sharpe joined, and Venables had taken it on himself to be a tutor to Sharpe in how officers should behave. 'They're bowling us over like ninepins, eh, Richard?'

Before Sharpe could reply a half-dozen men of number six company threw themselves aside as a cannonball bounced hard and low towards them. It whipped harmlessly through the gap they had made. The men laughed at having evaded it, then Sergeant Colquhoun ordered them back into their two ranks.

'Aren't you supposed to be on the left of your company?' Sharpe asked Venables.

'You're still thinking like a sergeant, Richard,' Venables said. 'Pig-ears doesn't mind where I am.' Pig-ears was Captain Lomax, who had earned his nickname not because of any peculiarity about his ears, but because he had a passion for crisply fried pig-ears. Lomax was easy-going, unlike Urquhart who liked everything done strictly according to regulations. 'Besides,' Venables went on, 'there's damn all to do. The lads know their business.'

'Waste of time being an ensign,' Sharpe said.

'Nonsense! An ensign is merely a colonel in the making,' Venables said. 'Our duty, Richard, is to be decorative and stay alive long enough to be promoted. But no one expects us to be useful! Good God! A junior officer being useful? That'll be the day.' Venables gave a hoot of laughter. He was a bumptious, vain youth, but one of the few officers in the 74th who offered Sharpe companionship. 'Did you hear a new draft has come to Madras?' he asked.

'Urquhart told me.'

'Fresh men. New officers. You won't be junior any more.'

28

Sharpe shook his head. 'Depends on the date the new men were commissioned, doesn't it?'

'Suppose it does. Quite right. And they must have sailed from Britain long before you got the jump up, eh? So you'll still be the mess baby. Bad luck, old fellow.'

Old fellow? Quite right, Sharpe thought. He was old. Probably ten years older than Venables, though Sharpe was not exactly sure for no one had ever bothered to note down his birth date. Ensigns were youths and Sharpe was a man.

'Whoah!' Venables shouted in delight and Sharpe looked up to see that a round shot had struck the edge of an irrigation canal and bounced vertically upwards in a shower of soil. 'Pig-ears says he once saw two cannonballs collide in mid-air,' Venables said. 'Well, he didn't actually see it, of course, but he heard it. He says they suddenly appeared in the sky. Bang! Then flopped down.'

'They'd have shattered and broken up,' Sharpe said.

'Not according to Pig-ears,' Venables insisted. 'He says they flattened each other.' A shell exploded ahead of the company, whistling scraps of iron casing overhead. No one was hurt and the files stepped round the smoking fragments. Venables stooped and plucked up a scrap, juggling it because of the heat. 'Like to have keepsakes,' he explained, slipping the piece of iron into a pouch. 'I'll send it home for my sisters. Why don't our guns stop and fire?'

'Still too far away,' Sharpe said. The advancing line still had half a mile to go and, while the six-pounders could fire at that distance, the gunners must have decided to get really close so that their shots could not miss. Get close, that was what Colonel McCandless had always told Sharpe. It was the secret of battle. Get close before you start slaughtering.

A round shot struck a file in seven company. It was on its first graze, still travelling at blistering speed, and the two men of the file were whipped backwards in a spray of mingling blood. 'Jesus,' Venables said in awe. 'Jesus!' The corpses were mixed together, a jumble of splintered bones, tangled entrails and broken weapons. A corporal, one of the file-closers, stooped to extricate the men's pouches and haversacks from the scattered offal. 'Two more names in the church porch,' Venables remarked. 'Who were they, Corporal?'

'The McFadden brothers, sir.' The Corporal had to shout to be heard over the roar of the Mahratta guns.

'Poor bastards,' Venables said. 'Still, there are six more. A fecund lady, Rosie McFadden.'

Sharpe wondered what fecund meant, then decided he could guess. Venables, for all his air of carelessness, was looking slightly pale as though the sight of the churned corpses had sickened him. This was his first battle, for he had been sick with the Malabar Itch during Assaye, but the Ensign was forever explaining that he could not be upset by the sight of blood because, from his earliest days, he had assisted his father who was an Edinburgh surgeon, but now he suddenly turned aside, bent over and vomited. Sharpe kept stolidly walking. Some of the men turned at the sound of Venables's retching.

'Eyes front!' Sharpe snarled.

Sergeant Colquhoun gave Sharpe a resentful look. The Sergeant believed that any order that did not come from himself or from Captain Urquhart was an unnecessary order.

Venables caught up with Sharpe. 'Something I ate.'

'India does that,' Sharpe said sympathetically.

'Not to you.'

'Not yet,' Sharpe said and wished he was carrying a musket so he could touch the wooden stock for luck.

Captain Urquhart sheered his horse leftwards. 'To your company, Mister Venables.'

Venables scuttled away and Urquhart rode back to the company's right flank without acknowledging Sharpe's presence. Major Swinton, who commanded the battalion while Colonel Wallace had responsibility for the brigade, galloped his horse behind the ranks. The hooves thudded heavily on the dry earth. 'All well?' Swinton called to Urquhart.

'All well.'

'Good man!' Swinton spurred on.

The sound of the enemy guns was constant now, like thunder that did not end. A thunder that pummelled the ears and almost drowned out the skirl of the pipers. Earth fountained where round shot struck. Sharpe, glancing to his left, could see a scatter of bodies lying in the wake of the long line. There was a village there. How the hell had he walked straight past a village without even seeing it? It was not much of a place, just a huddle of reed-thatched hovels with a few patchwork gardens protected by cactus-thorn hedges, but he had still walked clean past without noticing its existence. He could see no one there. The villagers had too much sense. They would have packed their few pots and pans and buggered off as soon as the first soldier appeared near their fields. A Mahratta round shot smacked into one of the hovels, scattering reed and dry timber, and leaving the sad roof sagging.

Sharpe looked the other way and saw enemy cavalry advancing in the distance, then he glimpsed the blue and yellow uniforms of the British 19th Dragoons trotting to meet them. The late-afternoon sunlight glittered on drawn sabres. He thought he heard a trumpet call, but maybe he imagined it over the hammering of the guns. The horsemen vanished behind a stand of trees. A cannonball screamed overhead, a shell exploded to his left, then the 74th's Light Company edged inwards to give an ox team room to pass back southwards. The British cannon had been dragged well ahead of the attacking line where they had now been turned and deployed. Gunners rammed home shot, pushed priming quills into touch-holes, stood back. The sound of the guns crashed across the field, blotting the immediate view with grey-white smoke and filling the air with the nauseous stench of rotted eggs.

The drummers beat on, timing the long march north. For the moment it was a battle of artillerymen, the puny British six-pounders firing into the smoke cloud where the bigger Mahratta guns pounded at the advancing redcoats. Sweat trickled down Sharpe's belly, it stung his eyes and it dripped from his nose. Flies buzzed by his face. He pulled the sabre free and found that its handle was slippery with perspiration, so he wiped it and his right hand on the hem of his red coat. He suddenly wanted to piss badly, but this was not the time to stop and unbutton breeches. Hold it, he told himself, till the bastards are beaten. Or piss in your pants, he told himself, because in this heat no one would know it from sweat and it would dry quickly enough. Might smell, though. Better to wait. And if any of the men knew he had pissed his pants he would never live it down. Pisspants Sharpe. A ball thumped overhead, so close that its passage rocked Sharpe's shako. A fragment of something whirred to his left. A man was on the ground, vomiting blood. A dog barked as another tugged blue guts from an opened belly. The beast had both paws on the corpse to give its tug purchase. A file-closer kicked the dog away, but as soon as the man was gone the dog ran back to the body. Sharpe wished he could have a good wash. He knew he was lousy, but then everyone was lousy.

Even General Wellesley was probably lousy. Sharpe looked eastwards and saw the General spurring up behind the kilted 78th. Sharpe had been Wellesley's orderly at Assaye and as a result he knew all the staff officers who rode behind the General. They had been much friendlier than the 74th's officers, but then they had not been expected to treat Sharpe as an equal.

Bugger it, he thought. Maybe he should take Urquhart's advice. Go home, take the cash, buy an inn and hang the sabre over the serving hatch. Would Simone Joubert go to England with him? She might like running an inn. The Buggered Dream, he could call it, and he would charge army officers twice the real price for any drink.

The Mahratta guns suddenly went silent, at least those that were directly ahead of the 74th, and the change in the battle's noise made Sharpe peer ahead into the smoke cloud that hung over the crest just a quarter-mile away. More smoke wreathed the 74th, but that was from the British guns. The enemy gun smoke was clearing, carried northwards on the small wind, but there was nothing there to show why the guns at the centre of the Mahratta line had ceased fire. Perhaps the buggers had run out of ammunition. Some hope, he thought, some bloody hope. Or perhaps they were all reloading with canister to give the approaching redcoats a rajah's welcome.

God, but he needed a piss and so he stopped, tucked the sabre into his armpit, then fumbled with his buttons. One came away. He swore, stooped to pick it up, then stood and emptied his bladder onto the dry ground. Then Urquhart was wheeling his horse. 'Must you do that now, Mister Sharpe?' he asked irritably.

Yes, sir, three bladders full, sir, and damn your bloody eyes, sir. 'Sorry, sir,' Sharpe said instead. So maybe proper officers didn't piss? He sensed the company was laughing at him and he ran to catch up, fiddling with his buttons. Still there was no gunfire from the Mahratta centre. Why not? But then a cannon on one of the enemy flanks fired slantwise across the field and the ball grazed right through number six company, ripping a front rank man's feet off and slashing a man behind through the knees. Another soldier was limping, his leg deeply pierced by a splinter from his neighbour's bone. Corporal McCallum, one of the file-closers, tugged men into the gap while a piper ran across to bandage the wounded men. The injured would be left where they fell until after the battle when, if they still lived, they would be carried to the surgeons. And if they survived the knives and saws they would be shipped home, good for nothing except to be a burden on the parish. Or maybe the Scots did not have parishes; Sharpe was not sure, but he was certain the buggers had workhouses. Everyone had workhouses and paupers' graveyards. Better to be buried out here in the black earth of enemy India than condemned to the charity of a workhouse.

Then he saw why the guns in the centre of the Mahratta line had ceased fire. The gaps between the guns were suddenly filled with men running forward. Men in long robes and headdresses. They streamed between the gaps, then joined together ahead of the guns beneath long green banners that trailed from silver-topped poles. Arabs, Sharpe thought. He had seen some at Ahmednuggur, but most of those had been dead. He remembered Sevajee, the Mahratta who fought alongside Colonel McCandless, saying that the Arab mercenaries were the best of all the enemy troops.

Now there was a horde of desert warriors coming straight for the 74th and their kilted neighbours.

The Arabs came in a loose formation. Their guns had decorated stocks that glinted in the sunlight, while curved swords were scabbarded at their waists. They came almost jauntily, as though they had utter confidence in their ability. How many were there? A thousand? Sharpe reckoned at least a thousand. Their officers were on horseback. They did not advance in ranks and files, but in a mass, and some, the bravest men, ran ahead as if eager to start the killing. The great robed mass was chanting a shrill war cry, while in its centre drummers were beating huge instruments that pulsed a belly-thumping beat across the field. Sharpe watched the nearest British gun load with canister. The green banners were being waved from side to side so that the silk trails snaked over the warriors' heads. Something was written on the banners, but it was in no script that Sharpe recognized.

'74th!' Major Swinton called. 'Halt!'

The 78th had also halted. The two Highland battalions, both under strength after their losses at Assaye, were taking the full brunt of the Arab charge. The rest of the battlefield seemed to melt away. All Sharpe could see was the robed men coming so eagerly towards him.

'Make ready!' Swinton called.

'Make ready!' Urquhart echoed.

'Make ready!' Sergeant Colquhoun shouted. The men raised their muskets chest high and pulled back the heavy hammers.

Sharpe pushed into the gap between number six company and its left-hand neighbour, number seven. He wished he had a musket. The sabre felt flimsy.

'Present!' Swinton called.

'Present!' Colquhoun echoed, and the muskets went into the men's shoulders. Heads bowed to peer down the barrels' lengths.

'You'll fire low, boys,' Urquhart said from behind the line, 'you'll fire low. To your place, Mister Sharpe.'

Bugger it, Sharpe thought, another bloody mistake. He stepped back behind the company where he was supposed to make sure no one tried to run.

The Arabs were close. Less than a hundred paces to go now. Some had their swords drawn. The air, miraculously smoke-free, was filled with their blood-chilling war cry which was a weird ululating sound. Not far now, not far at all. The Scotsmen's muskets were angled slightly down. The kick drove the barrels upwards, and untrained troops, not ready for the heavy recoil, usually fired high. But this volley would be lethal.

'Wait, boys, wait,' Pig-ears called to number seven company. Ensign Venables slashed at weeds with his claymore. He looked nervous.

Urquhart had drawn a pistol. He dragged the cock back, and his horse's ears flicked back as the pistol's spring clicked.

Arab faces screamed hatred. Their great drums were thumping. The redcoat line, just two ranks deep, looked frail in front of the savage charge.

Major Swinton took a deep breath. Sharpe edged towards the gap again. Bugger it, he wanted to be in the front line where he could kill. It was too nerve-racking behind the line.

'74th!' Swinton shouted, then he paused. Men's fingers curled about their triggers.

Let them get close, Swinton was thinking, let them get close.

Then kill them.

Prince Manu Bappoo's brother, the Rajah of Berar, was not at the village of Argaum where the Lions of Allah now charged to destroy the heart of the British attack. The Rajah did not like battle. He liked the idea of conquest, he loved to see prisoners paraded and he craved the loot that filled his storehouses, but he had no belly for fighting.

Manu Bappoo had no such qualms. He was thirty-five years old, he had fought since he was fifteen, and all he asked was the chance to go on fighting for another twenty or forty years. He considered himself a true Mahratta; a pirate, a rogue, a thief in armour, a looter, a pestilence, a successor to the generations of Mahrattas who had dominated western India by pouring from their hill fastnesses to terrorize the plump princedoms and luxurious kingdoms in the plains. A quick sword, a fast horse and a wealthy victim, what more could a man want? And so Bappoo had ridden deep and far to bring plunder and ransom back to the small land of Berar.

But now all the Mahratta lands were threatened. One British army was conquering their northern territory, and another was here in the south. It was this southern redcoat force that had broken the troops of Scindia and Berar at Assaye, and the Rajah of Berar had summoned his brother to bring his Lions of Allah to claw and kill the invader. This was not a task for horsemen, the Rajah had warned Bappoo, but for infantry. It was a task for the Arabs.

But Bappoo knew this was a task for horsemen. His Arabs would win, of that he was sure, but they could only break the enemy on the immediate battlefield. He had thought to let the British advance right up to his cannon, then release the Arabs, but a whim, an intimation of triumph, had decided him to advance the Arabs beyond the guns. Let the Lions of Allah loose on the enemy's centre and, when that centre was broken, the rest of the British line would scatter and run in panic, and that was when the Mahratta horsemen would have their slaughter. It was already early evening, and the sun was sinking in the reddened west, but the sky was cloudless and Bappoo was anticipating the joys of a moonlit hunt across the flat Deccan Plain. 'We shall gallop through blood,' he said aloud, then led his aides towards his army's right flank so that he could charge past his Arabs when they had finished their fight. He would let his victorious Lions of Allah pillage the enemy's camp while he led his horsemen on a wild victorious gallop through the moon-touched darkness.

And the British would run. They would run like goats from the tiger. But the tiger was clever. He had only kept a small number of horsemen with the army, a mere fifteen thousand, while the greater part of his cavalry had been sent southwards to raid the enemy's long supply roads. The British would flee straight into those men's sabres.

Bappoo trotted his horse just behind the right flank of the Lions of Allah. The British guns were firing canister and Bappoo saw how the ground beside his Arabs was being flecked by the blasts of shot, and he saw the robed men fall, but he saw how the others did not hesitate, but hurried on towards the pitifully thin line of redcoats. The Arabs were screaming defiance, the guns were hammering, and Bappoo's soul soared with the music. There was nothing finer in life, he thought, than this sensation of imminent victory. It was like a drug that fired the mind with noble visions.

He might have spared a moment's thought and wondered why the British did not use their muskets. They were holding their fire, waiting until every shot could kill, but the Prince was not worrying about such trifles. In his dreams he was scattering a broken army, slashing at them with his *tulwar*, carving a bloody path south. A fast sword, a quick horse and a broken enemy. It was the Mahratta paradise, and the Lions of Allah were opening its gates so that this night Manu Bappoo, Prince, warrior and dreamer, could ride into legend.

CHAPTER 2

'Fire!' Swinton shouted.

The two Highland regiments fired together, close to a thousand muskets flaming to make an instant hedge of thick smoke in front of the battalions. The Arabs vanished behind the smoke as the redcoats reloaded. Men bit into the grease-coated cartridges, tugged ramrods that they whirled in the air before rattling them down into the barrels. The churning smoke began to thin, revealing small fires where the musket wadding burned in the dry grass.

'Platoon fire!' Major Swinton shouted. 'From the flanks!'

'Light Company!' Captain Peters called on the left flank. 'First platoon, fire!'

'Kill them! Your mothers are watching!' Colonel Harness shouted. The Colonel of the 78th was mad as a hatter and half delirious with a fever, but he had insisted on advancing behind his kilted Highlanders. He was being carried in a palanquin and, as the platoon fire began, he struggled from the litter to join the battle, his only weapon a broken riding crop. He had been recently bled, and a stained bandage trailed from a coat sleeve. 'Give them a flogging, you dogs! Give them a flogging.'

The two battalions fired in half companies now, each half company firing two or three seconds after the neighbouring platoon so that the volleys rolled in from the outer wings of each battalion, met in the centre and then started again at the flanks. Clockwork fire, Sharpe called it, and it was the result of hours of tedious practice. Beyond the battalions' flanks the six-pounders bucked back with each shot, their wheels jarring up from the turf as the canisters ripped apart at the muzzles. Wide swathes of burning grass lay under the cannon smoke. The gunners were working in shirtsleeves, swabbing, ramming, then ducking aside as the guns pitched back again. Only the gun commanders, most of them sergeants, seemed to look at the enemy, and then only when they were checking the alignment of the cannon. The other gunners fetched shot and powder, sometimes heaved on a handspike or pushed on the wheels as the gun was relaid, then swabbed and loaded again. 'Water!' a corporal shouted, holding up a bucket to show that the swabbing water was gone.

'Fire low! Don't waste your powder!' Major Swinton called as he pushed his horse into the gap between the centre companies. He peered at the enemy through the smoke. Behind him, next to the 74th's twin flags, General Wellesley and his aides also stared at the Arabs beyond the smoke clouds. Colonel Wallace, the brigade commander, trotted his horse to the battalion's flank. He called something to Sharpe as he went by, but his words were lost in the welter of gunfire, then his horse half spun as a bullet struck its haunch. Wallace steadied the beast, looked back at the wound, but the horse did not seem badly hurt. Colonel Harness was thrashing one of the native palanquin bearers who had been trying to push the Colonel back into the curtained vehicle. One of Wellesley's aides rode back to quieten the Colonel and to persuade him to go southwards.

'Steady now!' Sergeant Colquhoun shouted. 'Aim low!'

The Arab charge had been checked, but not defeated. The first volley must have hit the attackers cruelly hard for Sharpe could see a line of bodies lying on the turf. The bodies looked red and white, blood against robes, but behind that twitching heap the Arabs were firing back to make their own ragged cloud of musket smoke. They fired haphazardly, untrained in platoon volleys, but they reloaded swiftly and their bullets were striking home. Sharpe heard the butcher's sound of metal hitting meat, saw men hurled backwards, saw some fall. The file-closers hauled the dead out of the line and tugged the living closer together. 'Close up! Close up!' The pipes played on, adding their defiant music to the noise of the guns. Private Hollister was hit in the head and Sharpe saw a cloud of white flour drift away from the man's powdered hair as his hat fell off. Then blood soaked the whitened hair and Hollister fell back with glassy eyes.

'One platoon, fire!' Sergeant Colquhoun shouted. He was so short-sighted that he could barely see the enemy, but it hardly mattered. No one could see much in the smoke, and all that was needed was a steady nerve and Colquhoun was not a man to panic.

'Two platoon, fire!' Urquhart shouted.

'Christ Jesus!' a man called close to Sharpe. He reeled backwards, his musket falling, then he twisted and dropped to his knees. 'Oh God, oh God, oh God,' he moaned, clutching at his throat. Sharpe could see no wound there, but then he saw blood seeping down the man's grey trousers. The dying man looked up at Sharpe, tears showed at his eyes, then he pitched forward.

Sharpe picked up the fallen musket, then turned the man over to unstrap the cartridge box. The man was dead, or so near as to make no difference.

'Flint,' a front rank man called. 'I need a flint!'

Sergeant Colquhoun elbowed through the ranks, holding out a spare flint. 'And where's your own spare flint, John Hammond?'

'Christ knows, Sergeant.'

'Then ask Him, for you're on a charge.'

A man swore as a bullet tore up his left arm. He backed out of the ranks, the arm hanging useless and dripping blood.

Sharpe pushed into the gap between the companies, put the musket to his shoulder and fired. The kick slammed into his shoulder, but it felt good. Something to do at last. He dropped the butt, fished a cartridge from the pouch and bit off the top, tasting the salt in the gunpowder. He rammed, fired again, loaded again. A bullet made an odd fluttering noise as it went past his ear, then another whined overhead. He waited for the rolling volley to come down the battalion's face, then fired with the other men of six company's first platoon. Drop the butt, new cartridge, bite, prime, pour, ram, ramrod back in the hoops, gun up, butt into the bruised shoulder and haul back the doghead, Sharpe did it as efficiently as any other man, but he had been trained to it. That was the difference, he thought grimly. He was trained, but no one trained the officers. They had bugger all to do, so why train them? Ensign Venables was right, the only duty of a junior officer was to stay alive, but Sharpe could not resist a fight. Besides, it felt better to stand in the ranks and fire into the enemy's smoke than stand behind the company and do nothing.

The Arabs were fighting well. Damned well. Sharpe could not remember any other enemy who had stood and taken so much concentrated platoon fire. Indeed, the robed men were trying to advance, but they were checked by the ragged heap of bodies that had been their

39

front ranks. How many damned ranks had they? A dozen? He watched a green flag fall, then the banner was picked up and waved in the air. Their big drums still beat, making a menacing sound to match the redcoats' pipers. The Arab guns had unnaturally long barrels that spewed dirty smoke and licking tongues of flame. Another bullet whipped close enough to Sharpe to bat his face with a gust of warm air. He fired again, then a hand seized his coat collar and dragged him violently backwards.

'Your place, Ensign Sharpe,' Captain Urquhart said vehemently, 'is here! Behind the line!' The Captain was mounted and his horse had inadvertently stepped back as Urquhart seized Sharpe's collar, and the weight of the horse had made the Captain's tug far more violent than he had intended. 'You're not a private any longer,' he said, steadying Sharpe who had almost been pulled off his feet.

'Of course, sir,' Sharpe said, and he did not meet Urquhart's gaze, but stared bitterly ahead. He was blushing, knowing he had been reprimanded in front of the men. Damn it to hell, he thought.

'Prepare to charge!' Major Swinton called.

'Prepare to charge!' Captain Urquhart echoed, spurring his horse away from Sharpe.

The Scotsmen pulled out their bayonets and twisted them onto the lugs of their musket barrels.

'Empty your guns!' Swinton called, and those men who were still loaded raised their muskets and fired a last volley.

'74th!' Swinton shouted. 'Forward! I want to hear some pipes! Let me hear pipes!'

'Go on, Swinton, go on!' Wallace shouted. There was no need to encourage the battalion forward, for it was going willingly, but the Colonel was excited. He drew his claymore and pushed his horse into the rear rank of number seven company. 'Onto them, lads! Onto them!' The redcoats marched forward, trampling through the scatter of little fires started by their musket wadding.

The Arabs seemed astonished that the redcoats were advancing. Some drew their own bayonets, while others pulled long curved swords from scabbards.

'They won't stand!' Wellesley shouted. 'They won't stand.'

'They bloody well will,' a man grunted.

'Go on!' Swinton shouted. 'Go on!' And the 74th, released to the kill, ran the last few yards and jumped up onto the heaps of dead before slashing home with their bayonets. Off to the right the 78th were also charging home. The British cannon gave a last violent blast of canister, then fell silent as the Scots blocked the gunners' aim.

Some of the Arabs wanted to fight, others wanted to retreat, but the charge had taken them by surprise and the rearward ranks were still not aware of the danger and so pressed forward, forcing the reluctant men at the front onto the Scottish bayonets. The Highlanders screamed as they killed. Sharpe still held the unloaded musket as he closed up on the rear rank. He had no bayonet and was wondering whether he should draw his sabre when a tall Arab suddenly hacked down a front rank man with a scimitar, then pushed forward to slash with the reddened blade at the second man in the file. Sharpe reversed the musket, swung it by the barrel and hammered the heavy stock down onto the swordsman's head. The Arab sank down and a bayonet struck into his spine so that he twisted like a speared eel. Sharpe hit him on the head again, kicked him for good measure, then shoved on. Men were shouting, screaming, stabbing, spitting, and, right in the face of number six company, a knot of robed men were slashing with scimitars as though they could defeat the 74th by themselves. Urquhart pushed his horse up against the rear rank and fired his pistol. One of the Arabs was plucked back and the others stepped away at last, all except one short man who screamed in fury and slashed with his long curved blade. The front rank parted to let the scimitar cut the air between two files, then the second rank also split apart to allow the short man to come screaming through on his own, with only Sharpe in front.

'He's only a lad!' a Scottish voice shouted in warning as the ranks closed again.

It was not a short man at all, but a boy. Maybe only twelve or thirteen years old, Sharpe guessed as he fended off the scimitar with the musket barrel. The boy thought he could win the battle single-handed and leaped at Sharpe, who parried the sword and stepped back to show he did not want to fight. 'Put it down, lad,' he said.

The boy spat, leaped and cut again. Sharpe parried a third time, then reversed the musket and slammed its stock into the side of the boy's head. For a second the lad stared at Sharpe with an astonished look, then he crumpled to the turf.

'They're breaking!' Wellesley shouted from somewhere close by. 'They're breaking!'

Colonel Wallace was in the front rank now, slicing down with his claymore. He hacked like a farmer, blow after blow. He had lost his cocked hat and his bald pate gleamed in the late sunlight. There was blood on his horse's flank, and more blood spattered on the white turnbacks of his coat tails. Then the pressure of the enemy collapsed and the horse twisted into the gap and Wallace spurred it on. 'Come on, boys! Come on!' A man stooped to rescue Wallace's cocked hat. Its plumes were blood-soaked.

The Arabs were fleeing. 'Go!' Swinton shouted. 'Go! Keep 'em running! Go!'

A man paused to search a corpse's robes and Sergeant Colquhoun dragged the man up and pushed him on. The file-closers were making sure none of the enemy bodies left behind the Scottish advance were dangerous. They kicked swords and muskets out of injured men's hands, prodded apparently unwounded bodies with bayonets and killed any man who showed a spark of fight. Two pipers were playing their ferocious music, driving the Scots up the gentle slope where the big Arab drums had been abandoned. Man after man speared the drum-skins with bayonets as they passed.

'Forward on! Forward on!' Urquhart bellowed as though he were on a hunting field.

'To the guns!' Wellesley called.

'Keep going!' Sharpe bellowed at some laggards. 'Go on, you bastards, go on!'

The enemy gun line was at the crest of the low rise, but the Mahratta gunners dared not fire because the remnants of the Lions of Allah were between them and the redcoats. The gunners hesitated for a few seconds, then decided the day was lost and fled.

'Take the guns!' Wellesley called.

Colonel Wallace spurred among the fleeing enemy, striking down with the claymore, then reined in beside a gaudily painted eighteen-pounder. 'Come on, lads! Come on! To me!'

The Scotsmen reached the guns. Most had reddened bayonets, all had sweat streaks striping their powder-blackened faces. Some began rifling the limbers where gunners stored food and valuables.

'Load!' Urquhart called. 'Load!'

'Form ranks!' Sergeant Colquhoun shouted. He ran forward and tugged men away from the limbers. 'Leave the carts alone, boys! Form ranks! Smartly now!'

Sharpe, for the first time, could see down the long reverse slope. Three hundred paces away were more infantry, a great long line of it massed in a dozen ranks, and beyond that were some walled gardens and the roofs of a village. The shadows were very long for the sun was blazing just above the horizon. The Arabs were running towards the stationary infantry.

'Where are the galloper guns?' Wallace roared, and an aide spurred back down the slope to fetch the gunners.

'Give them a volley, Swinton!' Wellesley called.

The range was very long for a musket, but Swinton hammered the battalion's fire down the slope, and maybe it was that volley, or perhaps it was the sight of the defeated Arabs that panicked the great mass of infantry. For a few seconds they stood under their big bright flags and then, like sand struck by a flood, they dissolved into a rabble.

Cavalry trumpets blared. British and sepoy horsemen charged forward with sabres, while the irregular horse, those mercenaries who had attached themselves to the British for the chance of loot, lowered their lances and raked back their spurs.

It was a cavalryman's paradise, a broken enemy with nowhere to hide. Some Mahrattas sought shelter in the village, but most ran past it, throwing down their weapons as the terrible horsemen streamed into the fleeing horde with sabres and lances slicing and thrusting.

'*Puckalees*!' Urquhart shouted, standing in his stirrups to look for the men and boys who brought water to the troops. There was none in sight and the 74th was parched, the men's thirst made acute by the saltpetre in the gunpowder which had fouled their mouths. 'Where the . . . ?' Urquhart swore, then frowned at Sharpe. 'Mister Sharpe? I'll trouble you to find our *puckalees*.'

'Yes, sir,' Sharpe said, not bothering to hide his disappointment at the order. He had hoped to find some loot when the 74th searched the village, but instead he was to be a fetcher of water. He threw down the musket and walked back through the groaning, slow-moving litter of dead and dying men. Dogs were scavenging among the bodies.

'Forward now!' Wellesley called behind Sharpe, and the whole long line of British infantrymen advanced under their flags towards the village. The cavalry was already far beyond the houses, killing with abandon and driving the fugitives ever farther northwards.

Sharpe walked on southwards. He suspected the *puckalees* were still back with the baggage, which would mean a three-mile walk and, by the time he had found them, the battalion would have slaked its thirst from the wells in the village. Bugger it, he thought. Even when they gave him a job it was a useless errand.

A shout made him look to his right where a score of native cavalrymen were slicing apart the robes of the dead Arabs in search of coins and trinkets. The scavengers were Mahrattas who had sold their services to the British and Sharpe guessed that the horsemen had not joined the pursuit for fear of being mistaken for the defeated enemy. One of the Arabs had only been feigning death and now, despite being hugely outnumbered, defied his enemies with a pistol that he dragged from beneath his robe. The taunting cavalrymen had made a ring and the Arab kept twisting around to find that his tormentor had skipped away before he could aim the small gun.

The Arab was a short man, then he turned again and Sharpe saw the bruised, bloody face and recognized the child who had charged the 74th so bravely. The boy was doomed, for the ring of cavalrymen was slowly closing for the kill. One of the Mahrattas would probably die, or at least be horribly injured by the pistol ball, but that was part of the game. The boy had one shot, they had twenty. A man prodded the boy in the back with a lance point, making him whip round, but the man with the lance had stepped fast back and another man slapped the boy's headdress with a *tulwar*. The other cavalrymen laughed.

Sharpe reckoned the boy deserved better. He was a kid, nothing more, but brave as a tiger, and so he crossed to the cavalrymen. 'Let him be!' he called.

The boy turned towards Sharpe. If he recognized that the British officer was trying to save his life he showed no sign of gratitude; instead he lifted the pistol so that its barrel pointed at Sharpe's face. The cavalrymen, reckoning this was even better sport, urged him to shoot and one of them approached the boy with a raised *tulwar*, but did not strike. He would let the boy shoot Sharpe, then kill him. 'Let him be,' Sharpe said. 'Stand back!' The Mahrattas grinned, but did not move. Sharpe could take the single bullet, then they would tear the boy into sabre-shredded scraps of meat.

The boy took a step towards Sharpe. 'Don't be a bloody fool, lad,' Sharpe said. The boy obviously did not speak English, but Sharpe's tone was soothing. It made no difference. The lad's hand was shaking and he looked frightened, but defiance had been bred into his bone. He knew he would die, but he would take an enemy soul with him and so he nerved himself to die well. 'Put the gun down,' Sharpe said softly. He was wishing he had not intervened now. The kid was just distraught enough and mad enough to fire, and Sharpe knew he could do nothing about it except run away and thus expose himself to the jeers of the Mahrattas. He was close enough now to see the scratches on the pistol's blackened muzzle where the rammer had scraped the metal. 'Don't be a bloody fool, boy,' he said again. Still the boy pointed the pistol. Sharpe knew he should turn and run, but instead he took another pace forward. Just one more and he reckoned he would be close enough to swat the gun aside.

Then the boy shouted something in Arabic, something about Allah, and pulled the trigger.

The hammer did not move. The boy looked startled, then pulled the trigger again.

Sharpe began laughing. The expression of woe on the child's face was so sudden, and so unfeigned, that Sharpe could only laugh. The boy looked as if he was about to cry.

The Mahratta behind the boy swung his *tulwar*. He reckoned he could slice clean through the boy's grubby headdress and decapitate him, but Sharpe had taken the extra step and now seized the boy's hand and tugged him into his belly. The sword hissed an inch behind the boy's neck. 'I said to leave him alone!' Sharpe said. 'Or do you want to fight me instead?'

'None of us,' a calm voice said behind Sharpe, 'wants to fight Ensign Sharpe.'

Sharpe turned. One of the horsemen was still mounted, and it was this man who had spoken. He was dressed in a tattered European uniform jacket of green cloth hung with small silver chains, and he had a lean scarred face with a nose as hooked as Sir Arthur Wellesley's. He now grinned down at Sharpe.

'Syud Sevajee,' Sharpe said.

'I never did congratulate you on your promotion,' Sevajee said, and leaned down to offer Sharpe his hand.

Sharpe shook it. 'It was McCandless's doing,' he said.

'No,' Sevajee disagreed, 'it was yours.' Sevajee, who led this band of horsemen, waved his men away from Sharpe, then looked down at the boy who struggled in Sharpe's grip. 'You really want to save that little wretch's life?'

'Why not?'

'A tiger cub plays like a kitten,' Sevajee said, 'but it still grows into a tiger and one day it eats you.'

'This one's no kitten,' Sharpe said, thumping the boy on the ear to stop his struggles.

Sevajee spoke in quick Arabic and the boy went quiet. 'I told him you saved his life,' Sevajee explained to Sharpe, 'and that he is now beholden to you.' Sevajee spoke to the boy again who, after a shy look at Sharpe, answered. 'His name's Ahmed,' Sevajee said, 'and I told him you were a great English lord who commands the lives and deaths of a thousand men.'

'You told him what?'

'I told him you'd beat him bloody if he disobeys you,' Sevajee said, looking at his men who, denied their entertainment, had gone back to looting the dead. 'You like being an officer?' he asked Sharpe.

'I hate it.'

Sevajee smiled, revealing red-stained teeth. 'McCandless thought you would, but didn't know how to curb your ambition.' Sevajee slid down from his saddle. 'I am sorry McCandless died,' the Indian said.

'Me too.'

'You know who killed him?'

'I reckon it was Dodd.'

Sevajee nodded. 'Me too.' Syud Sevajee was a high-born Mahratta, the eldest son of one of the Rajah of Berar's warlords, but a rival in the Rajah's service had murdered his father, and Sevajee had been seeking revenge ever since. If that revenge meant marching with the enemy British, then that was a small price to pay for family pride. Sevajee had ridden with Colonel McCandless when the Scotsman had pursued Dodd, and thus he had met Sharpe. 'Beny Singh was not with the enemy today,' he told Sharpe.

Sharpe had to think for a few seconds before remembering that Beny Singh was the man who had poisoned Sevajee's father. 'How do you know?'

'His banner wasn't among the Mahratta flags. Today we faced Manu Bappoo, the Rajah's brother. He's a better man than the Rajah, but he refuses to take the throne for himself. He's also a better soldier than the rest, but not good enough, it seems. Dodd was there.'

'He was?'

'He got away.' Sevajee turned and gazed northwards. 'And I know where they're going.'

'Where?'

'To Gawilghur,' Sevajee said softly, 'to the sky fort.'

'Gawilghur?'

'I grew up there.' Sevajee spoke softly, still gazing at the hazed northern horizon. 'My father was killadar of Gawilghur. It was a post of honour, Sharpe, for it is our greatest stronghold. It is the fortress in the sky, the impregnable refuge, the place that has never fallen to our enemies, and Beny Singh is now its killadar. Somehow we shall have to get inside, you and I. And I shall kill Singh and you will kill Dodd.'

'That's why I'm here,' Sharpe said.

'No.' Sevajee gave Sharpe a sour glance. 'You're here, Ensign, because you British are greedy.' He looked at the Arab boy and asked a question. There was a brief conversation, then Sevajee looked at Sharpe again. 'I have told him he is to be your servant, and that you will beat him to death if he steals from you.'

'I wouldn't do that!' Sharpe protested.

'I would,' Sevajee said, 'and he believes you would, but it still won't stop him thieving from you. Better to kill him now.' He grinned, then hauled himself into his saddle. 'I shall look for you at Gawilghur, Mister Sharpe.'

'I shall look for you,' Sharpe said.

Sevajee spurred away and Sharpe crouched to look at his new servant. Ahmed was as thin as a half-drowned cat. He wore dirty robes and a tattered headdress secured by a loop of frayed rope that was stained with blood, evidently where Sharpe's blow with the musket had caught him during the battle. But he had bright eyes and a defiant face, and though his voice had not yet broken he was braver than many full-grown men. Sharpe unslung his canteen and pushed it into the boy's hand, first taking away the broken pistol that he tossed away. 'Drink up, you little bugger,' Sharpe said, 'then come for a walk.'

The boy glanced up the hill, but his army was long gone. It had vanished into the evening beyond the crest and was now being pursued by vengeful cavalry. He said something in Arabic, drank what remained of Sharpe's water, then offered a grudging nod of thanks.

So Sharpe had a servant, a battle had been won, and now he walked south in search of *puckalees*.

Colonel William Dodd watched the Lions of Allah break, and spat with disgust. It had been foolish to fight here in the first place and now the foolery was turning to disaster. 'Jemadar!' he called.

'Sahib?'

'We'll form square. Put our guns in the centre. And the baggage.'

'Families, sahib?'

'Families too.' Dodd watched Manu Bappoo and his aides galloping back from the British advance. The gunners had already fled, which meant that the Mahrattas' heavy cannon would all be captured, every last piece of it. Dodd was tempted to abandon his regiment's small battery of five-pounders which were about as much use as pea-shooters, but a soldier's pride persuaded him to drag the guns from the field. Bappoo might lose all his guns, but it would be a cold day in hell before William Dodd gave up artillery to an enemy.

His Cobras were on the Mahratta right flank and there, for the moment, they were out of the way of the British advance. If the rest of the Mahratta infantry remained firm and fought, then Dodd would stay with them, but he saw that the defeat of the Arabs had demoralized Bappoo's army. The ranks began to dissolve, the first fugitives began to run north and Dodd knew this army was lost. First Assaye, now this. A goddamn disaster! He turned his horse and smiled at his white-jacketed men. 'You haven't lost a battle!' he shouted to them. 'You haven't even fought today, so you've lost no pride! But you'll have to fight now! If you don't, if you break ranks, you'll die. If you fight, you'll live! Jemadar! March!'

The Cobras would now attempt one of the most difficult of all feats of soldiering, a fighting withdrawal. They marched in a loose square, the centre of which gradually filled with their women and children. Some other infantry tried to join the families, but Dodd snarled at his men to beat them away. 'Fire if they won't go!' he shouted. The last thing he wanted was for his men to be infected by panic.

Dodd trailed the square. He heard cavalry trumpets and he twisted

48

in his saddle to see a mass of irregular light horsemen come over the crest. 'Halt!' he shouted. 'Close ranks! Charge bayonets!'

The white-jacketed Cobras sealed the loose square tight. Dodd pushed through the face of the square and turned his horse to watch the cavalrymen approach. He doubted they would come close, not when there were easier pickings to the east and, sure enough, as soon as the leading horsemen saw that the square was waiting with levelled muskets, they sheered away.

Dodd holstered his pistol. 'March on, Jemadar!'

Twice more Dodd had to halt and form ranks, but both times the threatening horsemen were scared away by the calm discipline of his white-coated soldiers. The red-coated infantry was not pursuing. They had reached the village of Argaum and were content to stay there, leaving the pursuit to the horsemen, and those horsemen chased after the broken rabble that flooded northwards, but none chose to die by charging Dodd's formed ranks.

Dodd inclined to the west, angling away from the pursuers. By nightfall he was confident enough to form the battalion into a column of companies, and by midnight, under a clear moon, he could no longer even hear the British trumpets. He knew that men would still be dying, ridden down by cavalry and pierced by lances or slashed by sabres, but Dodd had got clean away. His men were tired, but they were safe in a dark countryside of millet fields, drought-emptied irrigation ditches and scattered villages where dogs barked frantically when they caught the scent of the marching column.

Dodd did not trouble the villagers. He had sufficient food, and earlier in the night they had found an irrigation tank that had yielded enough water for men and beasts. 'Do you know where we are, Jemadar?' he asked.

'No, sahib.' Gopal grinned, his teeth showing white in the darkness.

'Nor do I. But I know where we're going.'

'Where, sahib?'

'To Gawilghur, Gopal. To Gawilghur.'

'Then we must march north, sahib.' Gopal pointed to the mountains that showed as a dark line against the northern stars. 'It is there, sahib.'

Dodd was marching to the fortress that had never known defeat. To the impregnable fastness on the cliff. To Gawilghur.

*　　*　　*

49

Dawn came to the millet fields. Ragged-winged birds flopped down beside corpses. The smell of death was already rank, and would only grow worse as the sun rose to become a furnace in a cloudless sky. Bugles called reveille, and the picquets who had guarded the sleeping army around Argaum cleared their muskets by loosing off shots. The gunfire startled birds up from corpses and made the feasting dogs growl among the human dead.

Regiments dug graves for their own dead. There were few enough to bury, for no more than fifty redcoats had died, but there were hundreds of Mahratta and Arab corpses, and the lascars who did the army's fetching and carrying began the task of gathering the bodies. Some enemies still lived, though barely, and the luckiest of those were despatched with a blow of a mattock before their robes were rifled. The unlucky were taken to the surgeons' tents.

The enemy's captured guns were inspected, and a dozen selected as suitable for British service. They were all well made, forged in Agra by French-trained gunsmiths, but some were the wrong calibre and a few were so overdecorated with writhing gods and goddesses that no self-respecting gunner could abide them. The twenty-six rejected guns would be double-shotted and exploded. 'A dangerous business,' Lieutenant Colonel William Wallace remarked to Sharpe.

'Indeed, sir.'

'You saw the accident at Assaye?' Wallace asked. The Colonel took off his cocked hat and fanned his face. The hat's white plumes were still stained with blood that had dried black.

'I heard it, sir. Didn't see it,' Sharpe said. The accident had occurred after the battle of Assaye when the enemy's captured cannon were being destroyed and one monstrous piece, a great siege gun, had exploded prematurely, killing two engineers.

'Leaves us short of good engineers,' Wallace remarked, 'and we'll need them if we're going to Gawilghur.'

'Gawilghur, sir?'

'A ghastly fortress, Sharpe, quite ghastly.' The Colonel turned and pointed north. 'Only about twenty miles away, and if the Mahrattas have any sense that's where they'll be heading.' Wallace sighed. 'I've never seen the place, so maybe it isn't as bad as they say, but I remember poor McCandless describing it as a brute. A real brute.

Like Stirling Castle, he said, only much larger and the cliff's twenty times higher.'

Sharpe had never seen Stirling Castle, so had no real idea what the Colonel meant. He said nothing. He had been idling the morning away when Wallace sent for him, and now he and the Colonel were walking through the battle's litter. The Arab boy followed a dozen paces behind. 'Yours, is he?' Wallace asked.

'Think so, sir. Sort of picked him up yesterday.'

'You need a servant, don't you? Urquhart tells me you don't have one.'

So Urquhart had been discussing Sharpe with the Colonel. No good could come of that, Sharpe thought. Urquhart had been nagging Sharpe to find a servant, implying that Sharpe's clothes were in need of cleaning and pressing, which they were, but as he only owned the clothes he wore, he could not really see the point in being too finicky. 'I hadn't really thought what to do with the lad, sir,' Sharpe admitted.

Wallace turned and spoke to the boy in an Indian language, and Ahmed stared up at the Colonel and nodded solemnly as though he understood what had been said. Perhaps he did, though Sharpe did not. 'I've told him he's to serve you properly,' Wallace said, 'and that you'll pay him properly.' The Colonel seemed to disapprove of Ahmed, or maybe he just disapproved of everything to do with Sharpe, though he was doing his best to be friendly. It had been Wallace who had given Sharpe the commission in the 74th, and Wallace had been a close friend of Colonel McCandless, so Sharpe supposed that the balding Colonel was, in his way, an ally. Even so, Sharpe felt awkward in the Scotsman's company. He wondered if he would ever feel relaxed among officers. 'How's that woman of yours, Sharpe?' Wallace asked cheerfully.

'My woman, sir?' Sharpe asked, blushing.

'The Frenchwoman, can't recall her name. Took quite a shine to you, didn't she?'

'Simone, sir? She's in Seringapatam, sir. Seemed the best place for her, sir.'

'Quite, quite.'

Simone Joubert had been widowed at Assaye where her husband, who had served Scindia, had died. She had been Sharpe's lover and, after the battle, she had stayed with him. Where else, she asked, was she to go? But Wellesley had forbidden his officers to take their wives on the campaign, and though Simone was not Sharpe's wife, she was white, and so she had agreed to go to Seringapatam and there wait for him. She had carried a letter of introduction to Major Stokes, Sharpe's friend who ran the armoury, and Sharpe had given her some of the Tippoo's jewels so that she could find servants and live comfortably. He sometimes worried he had given her too many of the precious stones, but consoled himself that Simone would keep the surplus safe till he returned.

'So are you happy, Sharpe?' Wallace asked bluffly.

'Yes, sir,' Sharpe said bleakly.

'Keeping busy?'

'Not really, sir.'

'Difficult, isn't it?' Wallace said vaguely. He had stopped to watch the gunners loading one of the captured cannon, a great brute that looked to take a ball of twenty or more pounds. The barrel had been cast with an intricate pattern of lotus flowers and dancing girls, then painted with garish colours. The gunners had charged the gaudy barrel with a double load of powder and now they rammed two cannonballs down the blackened gullet. An engineer had brought some wedges and a gunner sergeant pushed one down the barrel, then hammered it home with the rammer so that the ball would jam when the gun was fired. The engineer took a ball of fuse from his pocket, pushed one end into the touch-hole, then backed away, uncoiling the pale line. 'Best if we give them some space,' Wallace said, gesturing that they should walk south a small way. 'Don't want to be beheaded by a scrap of gun, eh?'

'No, sir.'

'Very difficult,' Wallace said, picking up his previous thought. 'Coming up from the ranks? Admirable, Sharpe, admirable, but difficult, yes?'

'I suppose so, sir,' Sharpe said unhelpfully.

Wallace sighed, as though he was finding the conversation unexpectedly hard going. 'Urquhart tells me you seem' – the Colonel paused, looking for the tactful word – 'unhappy?'

'Takes time, sir.'

'Of course, of course. These things do. Quite.' The Colonel wiped a hand over his bald pate, then rammed his sweat-stained hat back into place. 'I remember when I joined. Years ago now, of course, and I was only a little chap. Didn't know what was going on! They said turn left, then turned right. Damned odd, I thought. I was arse over elbow for months, I can tell you.' The Colonel's voice tailed away. 'Damned hot,' he said after a while. 'Damned hot. Ever heard of the 95th, Sharpe?'

'95th, sir? Another Scottish regiment?'

'Lord, no. The 95th Rifles. They're a new regiment. Couple of years old. Used to be called the Experimental Corps of Riflemen!' Wallace hooted with laughter at the clumsy name. 'But a friend of mine is busy with the rascals. Willie Stewart, he's called. The Honourable William Stewart. Capital fellow! But Willie's got some damned odd ideas. His fellows wear green coats. Green! And he tells me his riflemen ain't as rigid as he seems to think we are.' Wallace smiled to show he had made some kind of joke. 'Thing is, Sharpe, I wondered if you wouldn't be better suited to Stewart's outfit? His idea, you should understand. He wrote wondering if I had any bright young officers who could carry some experience of India to Shorncliffe. I was going to write back and say we do precious little skirmishing here, and it's skirmishing that Willie's rogues are being trained to do, but then I thought of you, Sharpe.'

Sharpe said nothing. Whichever way you wrapped it up, he was being dismissed from the 74th, though he supposed it was kind of Wallace to make the 95th sound like an interesting sort of regiment. Sharpe guessed they were the usual shambles of a hastily raised wartime battalion, staffed by the leavings of other regiments and composed of gutter rogues discarded by every other recruiting sergeant. The very fact they wore green coats sounded bad, as though the army could not be bothered to waste good red cloth on them. They would probably dissolve in panicked chaos in their first battle.

'I've written to Willie about you,' Wallace went on, 'and I know he'll have a place for you.' Meaning, Sharpe thought, that the Honourable William Stewart owed Wallace a favour. 'And our problem, frankly,' Wallace continued, 'is that a new draft has reached Madras. Weren't expecting it till spring, but they're here now, so we'll be back to strength in a month or so.' Wallace paused, evidently wondering if he had softened the blow sufficiently. 'And the fact is, Sharpe,' he resumed after a while, 'that Scottish regiments are more like, well, families!

53

Families, that's it, just it. My mother always said so, and she was a pretty shrewd judge of these things. Like families! More so, I think, than English regiments, don't you think?'

'Yes, sir,' Sharpe said, trying to hide his misery.

'But I can't let you go while there's a war on,' Wallace continued heartily. The Colonel had turned to watch the cannon again. The engineer had finished unwinding his fuse and the gunners now shouted at everyone within earshot to stand away. 'I do enjoy this,' the Colonel said warmly. 'Nothing like a bit of gratuitous destruction to set the juices flowing, eh?'

The engineer stooped to the fuse with his tinderbox. Sharpe saw him strike the flint then blow the charred linen into flame. There was a pause, then he put the fuse end into the small fire and the smoke fizzed up.

The fuse burned fast, the smoke and sparks snaking through the dry grass and starting small fires, then the red hot trail streaked up the back of the gun and down into the touch-hole.

For a heartbeat nothing happened, then the whole gun just seemed to disintegrate. The charge had tried to propel the double shot up the wedged barrel, but the resistance was just big enough to restrict the explosion. The touch-hole shot out first, the shaped piece of metal tearing out a chunk of the upper breach, then the whole rear of the painted barrel split apart in smoke, flame and whistling lumps of jagged metal. The forward part of the barrel, jaggedly torn off, dropped to the grass as the gun's wheels were splayed out. The gunners cheered. 'One less Mahratta gun,' Wallace said. Ahmed was grinning broadly. 'Did you know Mackay?' Wallace asked Sharpe.

'No, sir.'

'Captain Mackay. Hugh Mackay. East India Company officer. Fourth Native Cavalry. Very good fellow indeed, Sharpe. I knew his father well. Point is, though, that young Hugh was put in charge of the bullock train before Assaye. And he did a very good job! Very good. But he insisted on joining his troopers in the battle. Disobeyed orders, d'you see? Wellesley was adamant that Mackay must stay with his bullocks, but young Hugh wanted to be on the dance floor, and quite right too, except that the poor devil was killed. Cut in half by a cannonball!' Wallace sounded shocked, as though such a thing was an outrage. 'It's left the bullock train without a guiding hand, Sharpe.'

Christ, Sharpe thought, but he was to be made bullock master!

'Not fair to say they don't have a guiding hand,' Wallace continued, 'because they do, but the new fellow don't have any experience with bullocks. Torrance, he's called, and I'm sure he's a good fellow, but things are likely to get a bit more sprightly from now on. Going deeper into enemy territory, see? And there are still lots of their damned horsemen at large, and Torrance says he needs a deputy officer. Someone to help him. Thought you might be just the fellow for the job, Sharpe.' Wallace smiled as though he was granting Sharpe a huge favour.

'Don't know anything about bullocks, sir,' Sharpe said doggedly.

'I'm sure you don't! Who does? And there are dromedaries, and elephants. A regular menagerie, eh? But the experience, Sharpe, will do you good. Think of it as another string to your bow.'

Sharpe knew a further protest would do no good, so he nodded. 'Yes, sir,' he said.

'Good! Good! Splendid.' Wallace could not hide his relief. 'It won't be for long, Sharpe. Scindia's already suing for peace, and the Rajah of Berar's bound to follow. We may not even have to fight at Gawilghur, if that's where the rogues do take refuge. So go and help Torrance, then you can set a course for England, eh? Become a Greenjacket!'

So Ensign Sharpe had failed. Failed utterly. He had been an officer for two months and now he was being booted out of a regiment. Sent to the bullocks and the dromedaries, whatever the hell they were, and after that to the green-coated dregs of the army. Bloody hell fire, he thought, bloody hell fire.

The British and their allied cavalry rode all night, and in the dawn they briefly rested, watered their horses, then hauled themselves into their saddles and rode again. They rode till their horses were reeling with tiredness and white with sweat, and only then did they give up the savage pursuit of the Mahratta fugitives. Their sabre arms were weary, their blades blunted and their appetites slaked. The night had been a wild hunt of victory, a slaughter under the moon that had left the plain reeking with blood, and the sun brought more killing and wide-winged vultures that flapped down to the feast.

The pursuit ended close to a sudden range of hills that marked the northern limit of the Deccan Plain. The hills were steep and thickly wooded, no place for cavalry, and above the hills reared great cliffs, dizzyingly high cliffs that stretched from the eastern to the western horizon like the nightmare ramparts of a tribe of giants. In places there were deep re-entrants cut into the great cliff and some of the British pursuers, gaping at the vast wall of rock that barred their path, supposed that the wooded clefts would provide a path up to the cliff's summit, though none could see how anyone could reach the highland if an enemy chose to defend it.

Between two of the deep re-entrants a great promontory of rock jutted from the cliff face like the prow of a monstrous stone ship. The summit of the jutting rock was two thousand feet above the horsemen on the plain, and one of them, scrubbing blood from his sabre blade with a handful of grass, glanced up at the high peak and saw a tiny puff of whiteness drifting from its crest. He thought it a small cloud, but then he heard a faint bang of gunfire, and a second later a round shot dropped vertically into a nearby patch of millet. His captain pulled out a telescope and trained it high into the sky. He stared for a long time, then gave a low whistle.

'What is it, sir?'

'It's a fortress,' the Captain said. He could just see black stone walls, shrunken by distance, poised above the grey-white rock. 'It's hell in the bloody sky,' he said grimly, 'that's what it is. It's Gawilghur.'

More guns fired from the fortress, but they were so high in the air that their shots lost all their forward momentum long before they reached the ground. The balls fell like nightmare rain and the Captain shouted at his men to lead their horses out of range. 'Their final refuge,' he said, then laughed, 'but it's nothing to do with us, boys! The infantry will have to deal with that big bastard.'

The cavalrymen slowly moved southwards. Some of their horses had lost shoes, which meant they had to be walked home, but their night's work was well done. They had ravaged a broken army, and now the infantry must cope with the Mahrattas' final refuge.

A sergeant shouted from the right flank and the Captain turned westwards to see a column of enemy infantry appearing from a grove of trees just over a mile away. The white-coated battalion still possessed their artillery, but they showed no sign of wanting a fight. A crowd of civilians and several companies of fugitive Mahrattas had joined the regiment which was heading for a road that twisted into the hills beneath the fort, then zigzagged its way up the face of the rock promontory. If that road was the only way into the fort, the cavalry Captain thought, then God help the redcoats who had to attack Gawilghur. He stared at the infantry through his telescope. The white-coated troops were showing small interest in the British cavalry, but it still seemed prudent to quicken his pace southwards.

A moment later and the cavalry was hidden behind millet fields. The Captain turned a last time and gazed again at the fortress on the soaring cliffs. It seemed to touch the sky, so high it stood above all India. 'Bastard of a place,' the Captain said wonderingly, then turned and left. He had done his job, and now the infantry must climb to the clouds to do theirs.

Colonel William Dodd watched the blue-coated cavalrymen walk their tired horses southwards until they vanished beyond a field of standing millet. The subadar in charge of the regiment's small cannon had wanted to unlimber and open fire on the horsemen, but Dodd had refused his permission. There would have been no point in attacking, for by the time the guns were loaded the cavalrymen would have walked out of range. He watched a last salvo of round shot plummet to earth from the fort's high guns. Those cannon were of little use, Dodd thought, except to overawe people on the plain.

It took Dodd's regiment over seven hours to climb to the fort of Gawilghur, and by the time he reached the summit Dodd's lungs were burning, his muscles aching and his uniform soaked with sweat. He had walked every step of the way, refusing to ride his horse, for the beast was tired and, besides, if he expected his men to walk up the long road, then he would walk it as well. He was a tall, sallow-faced man with a harsh voice and an awkward manner, but William Dodd knew how to earn his men's admiration. They saw that he walked when he could have ridden, and so they did not complain as the steep climb sapped their breath and stole their strength. The regiment's families, its baggage and its battery of cannon were still far below on the twisting, treacherous track that, in its last few miles, was little more than a ledge hacked from the cliff.

Dodd formed his Cobras into four ranks as they approached Gawilghur's southern entrance where the great metal-studded gates were being swung open in welcome. 'March smartly now!' Dodd called to his men. 'You've nothing to be ashamed of! You lost no battle!' He pulled himself up into his saddle and drew his gold-hilted sword to salute the flag of Berar that flapped above the high gate-tower. Then he touched his heels to the mare's flanks and led his undefeated men into the tower's long entrance tunnel.

He emerged into the afternoon sun to find himself staring at a small town that was built within the stronghold's ramparts and on the summit of Gawilghur's promontory. The alleys of the town were crammed with soldiers, most of them Mahratta cavalrymen who had fled in front of the British pursuit, but, twisting in his saddle, Dodd saw some infantry of Gawilghur's garrison standing on the firestep. He also saw Manu Bappoo who had outridden the British pursuit and now gestured to Dodd from the gate-tower's turret.

Dodd told one of his men to hold his horse, then climbed the black walls to the top firestep of the tower where he stopped in awed astonishment at the view. It was like standing at the edge of the world. The plain was so far beneath and the southern horizon so far away that there was nothing in front of his eyes but endless sky. This, Dodd thought, was a god's view of earth. The eagle's view. He leaned over the parapet and saw his guns struggling up the narrow road. They would not reach the fort till long after nightfall.

'You were right, Colonel,' Manu Bappoo said ruefully.

Dodd straightened to look at the Mahratta prince. 'It's dangerous to fight the British in open fields,' he said, 'but here . . . ?' Dodd gestured at the approach road. 'Here they will die, sahib.'

'The fort's main entrance,' Bappoo said in his sibilant voice, 'is on the other side. To the north.'

Dodd turned and gazed across the roof of the central palace. He could see little of the great fortress's northern defences, though a long way away he could see another tower like the one on which he now stood. 'Is the main entrance as difficult to approach as this one?' he asked.

'No, but it isn't easy. The enemy has to approach along a narrow strip of rock, then fight through the Outer Fort. After that comes a ravine, and then the Inner Fort. I want you to guard the inner gate.'

Dodd looked suspiciously at Bappoo. 'Not the Outer Fort?' Dodd reckoned his Cobras should guard the place where the British would attack. That way the British would be defeated.

'The Outer Fort is a trap,' Bappoo explained. He looked tired, but the defeat at Argaum had not destroyed his spirit, merely sharpened his appetite for revenge. 'If the British capture the Outer Fort they will think they have won. They won't know that an even worse barrier waits beyond the ravine. That barrier has to be held. I don't care if the Outer Fort falls, but we must hold the Inner. That means our best troops must be there.'

'It will be held,' Dodd said.

Bappoo turned and stared southwards. Somewhere in the heat-hazed distance the British forces were readying to march on Gawilghur. 'I thought we could stop them at Argaum,' he admitted softly.

Dodd, who had advised against fighting at Argaum, said nothing.

'But here,' Bappoo went on, 'they will be stopped.'

Here, Dodd thought, they would have to be stopped. He had deserted from the East India Company's army because he faced trial and execution, but also because he believed he could make a fortune as a mercenary serving the Mahrattas. So far he had endured three defeats, and each time he had led his men safe out of the disaster, but from Gawilghur there would be no escape. The British would block every approach, so the British must be stopped. They must fail in this high place, and so they would, Dodd consoled himself. For nothing imaginable could take this fort. He was on the world's edge, lifted into the sky, and for the redcoats it would be like scaling the very heights of heaven.

So here, at last, deep inside India, the redcoats would be beaten.

Six cavalrymen in the blue and yellow coats of the 19th Light Dragoons waited outside the house where Captain Torrance was said to be billeted. They were under the command of a long-legged sergeant who was lounging on a bench beside the door. The Sergeant glanced up as Sharpe approached. 'I hope you don't want anything useful out of the bastards,' he said acidly, then saw that the shabby-uniformed Sharpe, despite wearing a pack like any common soldier, also had a sash and a sabre. He scrambled to his feet. 'Sorry, sir.'

Sharpe waved him back down onto the bench. 'Useful?' he asked.

'Horseshoes, sir, that's all we bleeding want. Horseshoes! Supposed to be four thousand in store, but can they find them?' The Sergeant spat. 'Tells me they're lost! I'm to go to the *bhinjarries* and buy them!

I'm supposed to tell my captain that? So now we have to sit here till Captain Torrance gets back. Maybe he knows where they are. That monkey in there' – he jerked his thumb at the house's front door – 'doesn't know a bloody thing.'

Sharpe pushed open the door to find himself in a large room where a half-dozen men argued with a harried clerk. The clerk, an Indian, sat behind a table covered with curling ledgers. 'Captain Torrance is ill!' the clerk snapped at Sharpe without waiting to discover the new-comer's business. 'And take that dirty Arab boy outside,' the clerk added, jerking his chin at Ahmed who, armed with a musket he had taken from a corpse on the battlefield, had followed Sharpe into the house.

'Muskets!' A man tried to attract the clerk's attention.

'Horseshoes!' an East India Company lieutenant shouted.

'Buckets,' a gunner said.

'Come back tomorrow,' the clerk said. 'Tomorrow!'

'You said that yesterday,' the gunner said, 'and I'm back.'

'Where's Captain Torrance?' Sharpe asked.

'He's ill,' the clerk said disapprovingly, as though Sharpe had risked the Captain's fragile health even by asking the question. 'He cannot be disturbed. And why is that boy here? He is an Arab!'

'Because I told him to be here,' Sharpe said. He walked round the table and stared down at the ledgers. 'What a bleeding mess!'

'Sahib!' The clerk had now realized Sharpe was an officer. 'Other side of the table, sahib, please, sahib! There is a system here, sahib. I stay this side of the table and you remain on the other. Please, sahib.'

'What's your name?' Sharpe asked.

The clerk seemed affronted at the question. 'I am Captain Tor-rance's assistant,' he said grandly.

'And Torrance is ill?'

'The Captain is very sick.'

'So who's in charge?'

'I am,' the clerk said.

'Not any longer,' Sharpe said. He looked up at the East India Company lieutenant. 'What did you want?'

'Horseshoes.'

'So where are the bleeding horseshoes?' Sharpe asked the clerk.

'I have explained, sahib, I have explained,' the clerk said. He was a middle-aged man with a lugubrious face and pudgy ink-stained fingers that now hastily tried to close all the ledgers so that Sharpe could not read them. 'Now please, sahib, join the queue.'

'Where are the horseshoes?' Sharpe insisted, leaning closer to the sweating clerk.

'This office is closed!' the clerk shouted. 'Closed till tomorrow! All business will be conducted tomorrow. Captain Torrance's orders!'

'Ahmed!' Sharpe said. 'Shoot the bugger.'

Ahmed spoke no English, but the clerk did not know that. He held his hands out. 'I am closing the office! Work cannot be done like this! I shall complain to Captain Torrance! There will be trouble! Big trouble!' The clerk glanced at a door that led to the inner part of the house.

'Is that where Torrance is?' Sharpe asked, gesturing at the door.

'No, sahib, and you cannot go in there. The Captain is sick.'

Sharpe went to the door and pushed it open. The clerk yelped a protest, but Sharpe ignored him. A muslin screen hung on the other side of the door and entangled Sharpe as he pushed into the room where a sailor's hammock hung from the beams. The room seemed empty, but then a whimper made him look into a shadowed corner. A young woman crouched there. She was dressed in a sari, but she looked European to Sharpe. She had been sewing gold braid onto the outer seams of a pair of breeches, but now stared in wide-eyed fright at the intruder. 'Who are you, Ma'am?' Sharpe asked.

The woman shook her head. She had very black hair and very white skin. Her terror was palpable. 'Is Captain Torrance here?' Sharpe asked.

'No,' she whispered.

'He's sick, is that right?'

'If he says so, sir,' she said softly. Her London accent confirmed that she was English.

'I ain't going to hurt you, love,' Sharpe said, for fear was making her tremble. 'Are you Mrs Torrance?'

'No!'

'So you work for him?'

'Yes, sir.'

'And you don't know where he is?'

'No, sir,' she said softly, looking up at Sharpe with huge eyes. She was lying, he reckoned, but he guessed she had good reason to lie, perhaps fearing Torrance's punishment if she told the truth. He considered soothing the truth out of her, but reckoned it might take too long. He wondered who she was. She was pretty, despite her terror, and he guessed she was Torrance's *bibbi*. Lucky Torrance, he thought ruefully. 'I'm sorry to have disturbed you, Ma'am,' he said, then he negotiated the muslin curtain back into the front room.

The clerk shook his head fiercely. 'You should not have gone in there, sahib! That is private quarters! Private! I shall be forced to tell Captain Torrance.'

Sharpe took hold of the clerk's chair and tipped it, forcing the man off. The men waiting in the room gave a cheer. Sharpe ignored them, sat on the chair himself and pulled the tangle of ledgers towards him. 'I don't care what you tell Captain Torrance,' he said, 'so long as you tell me about the horseshoes first.'

'They are lost!' the clerk protested.

'How were they lost?' Sharpe asked.

The clerk shrugged. 'Things get lost,' he said. Sweat was pouring down his plump face as he tentatively tried to tug some of the ledgers away from Sharpe, but he recoiled from the look on the Ensign's face. 'Things get lost,' the clerk said again weakly. 'It is the nature of things to get lost.'

'Muskets?' Sharpe asked.

'Lost,' the clerk admitted.

'Buckets?'

'Lost,' the clerk said.

'Paperwork,' Sharpe said.

The clerk frowned. 'Paperwork, sahib?'

'If something's lost,' Sharpe said patiently, 'there's a record. This is the bloody army. You can't have a piss without someone making a note of it. So show me the records of what's been lost.'

The clerk sighed and pulled one of the big ledgers open. 'Here, sahib,' he said, pointing an inky finger. 'One barrel of horseshoes, see? Being carried on an ox from Jamkandhi, lost in the Godavery on November 12th.'

'How many horseshoes in a barrel?' Sharpe asked.

'A hundred and twenty.' The long-legged cavalry Sergeant had come into the office and now leaned against the doorpost.

'And there are supposed to be four thousand horseshoes in store?' Sharpe asked.

'Here!' The clerk turned a page. 'Another barrel, see?'

Sharpe peered at the ill-written entry. 'Lost in the Godavery,' he read aloud.

'And here.' The clerk stabbed his finger again.

'Stolen,' Sharpe read. A drop of sweat landed on the page as the clerk turned it back. 'So who stole it?'

'The enemy, sahib,' the clerk said. 'Their horsemen are everywhere.'

'Their bloody horsemen run if you so much as look at them,' the tall cavalry Sergeant said sourly. 'They couldn't steal an egg from a chicken.'

'The convoys are ambushed, sahib,' the clerk insisted, 'and things are stolen.'

Sharpe pushed the clerk's hand away and turned the pages back, looking for the date when the battle had been fought at Assaye. He found it, and discovered a different handwriting had been used for the previous entries. He guessed Captain Mackay must have kept the ledger himself, and in Mackay's neat entries there were far fewer annotations reading 'stolen' or 'lost'. Mackay had marked eight cannonballs as being lost in a river crossing and two barrels of powder had been marked down as stolen, but in the weeks since Assaye no fewer than sixty-eight oxen had lost their burdens to either accidents or thieves. More tellingly, each of those oxen had been carrying a scarce commodity. The army would not miss a load of round shot, but it would suffer grievously when its last reserve of horseshoes was gone. 'Whose handwriting is this?' Sharpe had turned to the most recent page.

'Mine, sahib.' The clerk was looking frightened.

'How do you know when something is stolen?'

The clerk shrugged. 'The Captain tells me. Or the Sergeant tells me.'

'The Sergeant?'

'He isn't here,' the clerk said. 'He's bringing a convoy of oxen north.'

'What's the Sergeant's name?' Sharpe asked, for he could find no record in the ledger.

'Hakeswill,' the cavalry Sergeant said laconically. 'He's the bugger we usually deal with, on account of Captain Torrance always being ill.'

'Bloody hell,' Sharpe said, and pushed the chair back. Hakeswill! Obadiah bloody Hakeswill! 'Why wasn't he sent back to his regiment?' Sharpe asked. 'He isn't supposed to be here at all!'

'He knows the system,' the clerk explained. 'Captain Torrance wanted him to stay, sahib.'

And no bloody wonder, Sharpe thought. Hakeswill had worked himself into the army's most profitable billet! He was milking the cow, but making sure it was the clerk's handwriting in the ledger. No flies on Obadiah. 'How does the system work?' he asked the clerk.

'Chitties,' the clerk said.

'Chitties?'

'An ox driver is given a chitty, sahib, and when he has delivered his load the chitty is signed and brought here. Then he is paid. No chitty, no money. It is the rule, sahib. No chitty, no money.'

'And no bloody horseshoes either,' put in the lean Sergeant of the 19th.

'And Sergeant Hakeswill pays the money?' Sharpe asked.

'If he is here, sahib,' the clerk said.

'That doesn't get me my damned horseshoes,' the Company Lieutenant protested.

'Or my buckets,' the gunner put in.

'The *bhinjarries* have all the essentials,' the clerk insisted. He made shooing gestures. 'Go and see the *bhinjarries*! They have necessaries! This office is closed till tomorrow.'

'But where did the *bhinjarries* get their necessaries, eh? Answer me that?' Sharpe demanded, but the clerk merely shrugged. The *bhinjarries* were merchants who travelled with the army, contributing their own vast herds of pack oxen and carts. They sold food, liquor, women and luxuries, and now, it seemed, they were offering military supplies as well, which meant that the army would be paying for things that were normally issued free, and doubtless, if bloody Hakeswill had a finger in the pot, things which had been stolen from the army in the first place. 'Where do I go for horseshoes?' Sharpe asked the clerk.

The clerk was reluctant to answer, but he finally spread his hands and suggested Sharpe ask in the merchants' encampment. 'Someone will tell you, sahib.'

'You tell me,' Sharpe said.

'I don't know!'

'So how do you know they have horseshoes?'

'I hear these things!' the clerk protested.

Sharpe stood and bullied the clerk back against the wall. 'You do more than hear things,' he said, leaning his forearm against the clerk's neck, 'you know things. So you bloody well tell me, or I'll have my Arab boy chop off your goolies for his breakfast. He's a hungry little bugger.'

The clerk fought for breath against the pressure of Sharpe's arm. 'Naig.' He offered the name plaintively when Sharpe relaxed his arm.

'Naig?' Sharpe asked. The name rang a distant bell. A long-ago bell. Naig? Then he remembered a merchant of that name who had followed the army to Seringapatam. 'Naig?' Sharpe asked again. 'A fellow with green tents?'

'The very one, sahib.' The clerk nodded. 'But I did not tell you this thing! These gentlemen are witnesses, I did not tell you!'

'He runs a brothel!' Sharpe said, remembering, and he remembered too how Naig had been a friend to Sergeant Obadiah Hakeswill four years before. Sharpe had been a private then and Hakeswill had trumped up charges that had fetched Sharpe a flogging. 'Nasty Naig' had been the man's nickname, and back then he had sold pale-skinned whores who travelled in green-curtained wagons. 'Right!' Sharpe said. 'This office is closed!' The gunner protested and the cavalry Sergeant looked disappointed. 'We're going to see Naig,' Sharpe announced.

'No!' the clerk said too loud.

'No?' Sharpe asked.

'He will be angry, sahib.'

'Why should he be angry?' Sharpe demanded. 'I'm a customer, ain't I? He's got horseshoes, and we want horseshoes. He should be delighted to see us.'

'He must be treated with respect, sahib,' the clerk said nervously. 'He is a powerful man, Naig. You have money for him?'

'I just want to look at his horseshoes,' Sharpe said, 'and if they're army issue then I'll ram one of them down his bloody throat.'

The clerk shook his head. 'He has guards, sahib. He has *jettis*!'

'I think I might let you go on your own,' the East India Company Lieutenant said, backing away.

'*Jettis?*' The light dragoon Sergeant asked.

'Strongmen,' Sharpe explained. 'Big buggers who kill you by wringing your neck like a chicken.' He turned back to the clerk. 'Where did Naig get his *jettis*? From Seringapatam?'

'Yes, sahib.'

'I killed enough of the buggers,' Sharpe said, 'so I don't mind killing a few more. Are you coming?' he asked the cavalry Sergeant.

'Why not?' The man grinned.

'Anyone else?' Sharpe asked, but no one else seemed to want a fight that afternoon.

'Please, sahib,' the clerk said weakly.

Sharpe ignored him and, followed by Ahmed and the cavalryman, went back into the sunlight. 'What's your name?' Sharpe asked the Sergeant.

'Lockhart, sir. Eli Lockhart.'

'I'm Dick Sharpe, Eli, and you don't have to call me "sir", I'm not a proper bleeding officer. I was made up at Assaye, and I wish the buggers had left me a sergeant now. They sent me to be a bloody bullock driver, because I'm not fit for anything else.' He looked at Lockhart's six troopers who were still waiting. 'What are they doing here?'

'Didn't expect me to carry the bloody horseshoes myself, did you?' Lockhart said, then gestured at the troopers. 'Come on, boys. We're going to have a scrap.'

'Who said anything about a scrap?' Sharpe asked.

'He's got horseshoes,' Lockhart explained, 'but we don't have money. So there's only one way to get them off him.'

'True,' Sharpe said, and grinned.

Lockhart suddenly looked oddly shy. 'Was you in the Captain's quarters, sir?'

'Yes, why?'

The tough-looking Sergeant was actually blushing now. 'You didn't see a woman there, did you, sir?'

'Dark-haired girl. Pretty?'

'That's her.'

'Who is she?'

'Torrance's servant. A widow. He brought her and her husband out from England, but the fellow died and left her on her own. Torrance won't let her go.'

66

'And you'd like to take her off his hands, is that it?'

'I've only ever seen her at a distance,' the Sergeant admitted. 'Torrance was in another regiment, one of the Madrassi's, but we camped together often enough.'

'She's still there,' Sharpe said drily, 'still alive.'

'He keeps her close, he does,' Lockhart said, then kicked a dog out of his path. The eight men had left the village and entered the sprawling encampment where the merchants with their herds, wagons and families were camped. Great white oxen with painted horns were hobbled by pegs, and children scurried among the beasts collecting their dung which they slapped into cakes that would be dried for fuel. 'So tell me about these *jettis*,' Lockhart asked.

'Like circus strongmen,' Sharpe said, 'only it's some kind of religious thing. Don't ask me. None of it makes bleeding sense to me. Got muscles like mountains, they have, but they're slow. I killed four of the buggers at Seringapatam.'

'And you know Hakeswill?'

'I know bloody Hakeswill. Recruited me, he did, and he's been persecuting me ever since. He shouldn't even be with this army, he's supposed to be with the Havercakes down south, but he came up here with a warrant to arrest me. That didn't work, so he's just stayed, hasn't he? And he's working the bleeding system! You can wager your last shilling that he's the bastard who supplies Naig, and splits the profit.' Sharpe stopped to look for green tents. 'How come you don't carry your own spare horseshoes?'

'We do. But when they've gone you have to get more from the supplies. That's how the system's supposed to work. And yesterday's pursuit left half the hooves wrecked. We need shoes.'

Sharpe had seen a cluster of faded green tents. 'That's where the bastard is,' he said, then looked at Lockhart. 'This could get nasty.'

Lockhart grinned. He was as tall as Sharpe and had a face that looked as though it had survived a lifetime of tavern brawls. 'Come this far, ain't I?'

'Is that thing loaded?' Sharpe nodded at the pistol at Lockhart's belt. A sabre also hung there, just like the one at Sharpe's hip.

'It will be.' Lockhart drew the pistol and Sharpe turned to Ahmed and mimed the actions of loading the musket. Ahmed grinned and pointed to the lock, indicating that his weapon was already charged.

'How many of the buggers will be waiting for us?' Lockhart asked.

'A dozen?' Sharpe guessed.

Lockhart glanced back at his six men. 'We can deal with a dozen buggers.'

'Right,' Sharpe said, 'so let's bloody well make some trouble.' He grinned, because for the first time since he had become an officer he was enjoying himself.

Which meant someone was about to get a thumping.

CHAPTER 3

Major General Sir Arthur Wellesley rode northwards among a caval-cade of officers whose horses kicked up a wide trail of dust that lingered in the air long after the horsemen had passed. Two troops of East India Company cavalry provided the General's escort. Manu Bappoo's army might have been trounced and its survivors sent skeltering back into Gawilghur, but the Deccan Plain was still infested with Mahratta cavalry ready to pounce on supply convoys, wood-cutting parties or the grass-cutters who supplied the army's animals with fodder and so the two troops rode with sabres drawn. Wellesley set a fast pace, revelling in the freedom to ride in the long open country. 'Did you visit Colonel Stevenson this morning?' he called back to an aide.

'I did, sir, and he's no better than he was.'

'But he can get about?'

'On his elephant, sir.'

Wellesley grunted. Stevenson was the commander of his smaller army, but the old Colonel was ailing. So was Harness, the commander of one of Wellesley's two brigades, but there was no point in asking about Harness. It was not just physical disease that assaulted Harness, for the Scotsman's wits were gone as well. The doctors claimed it was the heat that had desiccated his brains, but Wellesley doubted the diagnosis. Heat and rum, maybe, but not the heat alone, though he did not doubt that India's climate was bad for a European's health. Few men lived long without falling prey to some wasting fever, and Wellesley was thinking it was time he left himself. Time to go back home before his health was abraded and, more important, before his existence was forgotten in London. French armies were unsettling all Europe and it could not be long before London despatched an army to fight the old foe, and Wellesley wanted to be a part of it. He was

69

in his middle thirties and he had a reputation to make, but first he had to finish off the Mahrattas, and that meant taking Gawilghur, and to that end he was now riding towards the great rampart of cliffs that sealed off the plain's northern edge.

An hour's ride brought him to the summit of a small rise which offered a view northwards. The plain looked dun, starved of water by the failed monsoon, though here and there patches of millet grew tall. In a good year, Wellesley guessed, the millet would cover the plain from horizon to horizon, a sea of grain bounded by the Gawilghur cliffs. He dismounted on the small knoll and took out a telescope that he settled on his horse's saddle. It was a brand new glass, a gift from the merchants of Madras to mark Wellesley's pacification of Mysore. Trade now moved freely on India's eastern flank, and the telescope, which had been specially ordered from Matthew Berge of London, was a generous token of the merchants' esteem, but Wellesley could not get used to it. The shape of the eyepiece was less concave than the one he was used to, and after a moment he snapped the new telescope shut and pulled out his old glass which, though lower powered, was more comfortable. He stared for a long time, gazing at the fort which crowned the rock promontory. The black stone of the fortress walls looked particularly sinister, even in the sunlight. 'Good God,' the General muttered after a while. Fail up there, he thought, and there would be no point in going home. He could go to London with some victories under his belt, and men would respect him even if the victories had not been against the French, but go with a defeat and they would despise him. Gawilghur, he thought sourly, had the look of a career-breaker.

Colonel Wallace, Wellesley's healthy brigade commander, had also dismounted and was inspecting the fortress through his own glass. 'Devil of a place, Sir Arthur,' Wallace said.

'How high is it, Blackiston?' Wellesley called to one of his aides, an engineer.

'I took a triangulation yesterday, sir,' Blackiston said, 'and discovered the fortress walls are eighteen hundred feet above the plain.'

'Is there water up there?' Colonel Butters, the chief engineer, asked.

'We hear there is, sir,' Blackiston said. 'There are tanks in the fort; huge things like lakes.'

'But the water level must be low this year?' Butters suggested.

'I doubt it's low enough, sir,' Blackiston murmured, knowing that Butters had been hoping that thirst might defeat the garrison.

'And the rascals will have food, no doubt,' Wellesley commented.

'Doubtless,' Wallace agreed drily.

'Which means they'll have to be prised out,' the General said, then bent to the glass again and lowered the lens to look at the foothills below the bluff. Just south of the fort was a conical hill that rose almost halfway up the flank of the great promontory. 'Can we get guns on that near hill?' he asked.

There was a pause while the other officers decided which hill he was referring to. Colonel Butters flinched. 'We can get them up there, sir, but I doubt they'll have the elevation to reach the fort.'

'You'll get nothing bigger than a twelve-pounder up there,' Wallace said dubiously, then slid the telescope's view up the bluff to the walls. 'And you'll need bigger shot than twelve-pounders to break down that wall.'

'Sir Arthur!' The warning call came from the officer commanding the East India Company cavalry who was pointing to where a group of Mahratta horsemen had appeared in the south. They had evidently been following the lingering dust cloud left by the General's party and, though the approaching horsemen only numbered about twenty men, the sepoy cavalry wheeled to face them and spread into a line.

'It's all right,' Wellesley called, 'they're ours. I asked them to meet us here.' He had inspected the approaching horsemen through his telescope and now, waving the sepoy cavalry back, he walked to greet the *silladars*. 'Syud Sevajee,' Wellesley acknowledged the man in the shabby green and silver coat who led the cavalrymen, 'thank you for coming.'

Syud Sevajee nodded brusquely at Wellesley, then stared up at Gawilghur. 'You think you can get in?'

'I think we must,' Wellesley said.

'No one ever has,' Sevajee said with a sly smile.

Wellesley returned the smile, but slowly, as if accepting the implied challenge, and then, as Sevajee slid down from his saddle, the General turned to Wallace. 'You've met Syud Sevajee, Wallace?'

'I've not had that pleasure, sir.'

Wellesley made the introduction, then added that Syud Sevajee's father had been one of the Rajah of Berar's generals.

71

'But is no longer?' Wallace asked Sevajee.

'Beny Singh murdered him,' Sevajee said grimly, 'so I fight with you, Colonel, to gain my chance to kill Beny Singh. And Beny Singh now commands that fortress.' He nodded towards the distant promontory.

'So how do we get inside?' Wellesley asked.

The officers gathered around Sevajee as the Indian drew his *tulwar* and used its tip to draw a figure eight in the dust. He tapped the lower circle of the eight, which he had drawn far larger than the upper. 'That's what you're looking at,' he said, 'the Inner Fort. And there are only two entrances. There's a road that climbs up from the plain and goes to the Southern Gate.' He drew a squiggly line that tailed away from the bottom of the figure eight. 'But that road is impossible. You will climb straight into their guns. A child with a pile of rocks could keep an army from climbing that road. The only possible route into the Inner Fort is through the main entrance.' He scratched a brief line across the junction of the two circles.

'Which will not be easy?' Wellesley asked drily.

Sevajee offered the General a grim smile. 'The main entrance is a long corridor, barred by four gates and flanked by high walls. But even to reach it, Sir Arthur, you will have to take the Outer Fort.' He tapped the small upper circle of the figure eight.

Wellesley nodded. 'And that, too, is difficult?'

'Again, two entrances,' Sevajee said. 'One is a road that climbs from the plain. You can't see it from here, but it twists up the hills to the west and it comes to the fort here.' He tapped the waist of the figure eight. 'It's an easier climb than the southern road, but for the last mile of the journey your men will be under the guns of the Outer Fort. And the final half-mile, General, is steep.' He stressed the last word. 'On one side of the road is a cliff, and on the other is a precipice, and the guns of the Outer Fort can fire straight down that half-mile of road.'

Colonel Butters shook his head in gloomy contemplation of Sevajee's news. 'How come you know all this?' he asked.

'I grew up in Gawilghur,' Sevajee said. 'My father, before he was murdered, was killadar of the fortress.'

'He knows,' Wellesley said curtly. 'And the main entrance of the Outer Fort?'

'That,' Sevajee said, 'is the fortress's weakest point.' He scratched a line that pierced the uppermost curve of the small circle. 'It's the only level approach to the fortress, but it's very narrow. On one side' – he tapped the eastern flank of the line – 'the ground falls steeply away. On the other side is a reservoir tank. So to reach the fort you must risk a narrow neck of land that is swept by two ramparts of guns, one above the other.'

'Two walls?' Wallace asked.

'Set on a steep hill,' Sevajee said, nodding. 'You must fight uphill across both walls. There is an entrance, but it's like the Inner Fort's entrance: a series of gates with a narrow passage leading from one to the other, and men above you on both sides hurling down rocks and round shot.'

'And once we've captured the Outer Fort,' Wellesley asked, 'what then?'

Sevajee offered a wolfish smile. 'Then your troubles are just beginning, Sir Arthur.' He scuffed out the diagram he had made in the dust and scratched another, this one showing two circles, one large and one small, with a space between them. 'The two forts are not connected. They are separated here' – he tapped the space between the circles with his *tulwar* – 'and that is a ravine. A deep ravine. So once you have the Outer Fort, you still have to assault the Inner Fort, and its defences will be untouched. It has a wall which stands at the top of the ravine's cliff, and that is where your enemy will be taking refuge; inside the wall of the Inner Fort. My father reckoned no enemy could ever capture Gawilghur's Inner Fort. If all India should fall, he said, then its heart would still beat at Gawilghur.'

Wellesley walked a few paces north to stare at the high promontory. 'How big is the garrison?'

'Normally,' Sevajee said, 'about a thousand men, but now? It could be six or seven times that many. There is room inside for a whole army.'

And if the fort did not fall, Wellesley thought, then the Mahrattas would take heart. They would gather a new army and, in the new year, raid southwards again. There would be no peace in western India till Gawilghur fell. 'Major Blackiston?'

'Sir?'

'You'll make an exploration of the plateau.' The General turned to

73

Sevajee. 'Will you escort Major Blackiston up into the hills? I want sketches, Blackiston, of the neck of land leading to the main entrance. I want you to tell me where we can place breaching batteries. I need to know how we can get guns up to the tops of the hills, and I need to know it all within two days.'

'Two days?' Blackiston sounded appalled.

'We don't want the rascals to take root up there, do we? Speed, Blackiston, speed! Can you leave now?' This question was directed at Sevajee.

'I can,' Sevajee answered.

Wellesley waved Blackiston on his way. 'Two days, Major! I want you back tomorrow evening!'

Colonel Butters frowned at the far hills. 'You're taking the army to the top?'

'Half the army,' Wellesley said, 'the other half will stay on the plain.' He would need to hold Gawilghur between his redcoats like a nut, and hope that when he squeezed it was the nut, and not the nutcracker, that broke. He pulled himself back into the saddle, then waited as the other officers mounted. Then he turned his mare and started back towards the camp. 'It'll be up to the engineers to get us onto the heights,' he said, 'then a week's hard carrying to lift the ammunition to the batteries.' The thought of that job made the General frown. 'What's the problem with the bullock train?' he demanded of Butters. 'I'm hearing complaints. Over two thousand muskets stolen from convoys, and Huddlestone tells me there are no spare horseshoes; that can't be right!'

'Torrance says that bandits have been active, sir,' Butters said. 'And I gather there have been accidents,' he added lamely.

'Who's Torrance?' Wellesley asked.

'Company man, sir, a captain. He took over poor Mackay's duties.'

'I could surmise all that for myself,' the General said acidly. 'Who is he?'

Butters blushed at the reproof. 'His father's a canon at Wells, I think. Or maybe Salisbury? But more to the point, sir, he has an uncle in Leadenhall Street.'

Wellesley grunted. An uncle in Leadenhall Street meant that Torrance had a patron who was senior in the East India Company, someone to wield the influence that a clergyman father might not have. 'Is he as good as Mackay?'

Butters, a heavy-set man who rode his horse badly, shrugged. 'He was recommended by Huddlestone.'

'Which means Huddlestone wanted to be rid of him,' Wellesley snapped.

'I'm sure he's doing his best,' Butters said defensively. 'Though he did ask me for an assistant, but I had to turn him down. I've no one to spare. I'm short of engineers already, sir, as you well know.'

'I've sent for more,' Wellesley said.

Wallace intervened. 'I gave Torrance one of my ensigns, Sir Arthur.'

'You can spare an ensign, Wallace?'

'Sharpe, sir.'

'Ah.' Wellesley grimaced. 'Never does work out, does it? You lift a man from the ranks and you do him no favours.'

'He might be happier in an English regiment,' Wallace said, 'so I'm recommending he exchanges into the Rifles.'

'You mean they're not particular?' Wellesley asked, then scowled. 'How the devil are we to fight a war without horseshoes?' He kicked back at the mare, angry at the predicament. 'My God, Butters, but your Captain Torrance must do his job!' Wellesley, better than anyone, knew that he would never take Gawilghur if the supply train failed.

And Gawilghur had never been taken.

Dear God, Wellesley thought, but how was it ever to be done?

'Big buggers,' Sergeant Eli Lockhart murmured as they neared the two green tents. The cavalryman was speaking of the guards who lolled in chairs outside Naig's tents. There were four in view, and two of them had bare, oiled chests that bulged with unnatural muscle. Their hair was never cut, but was instead coiled around their heads. They were keeping guard outside the larger of the tents, the one Sharpe guessed was Naig's brothel. The other tent might have been the merchant's living quarters, but its entrance was tightly laced, so Sharpe could not glimpse inside.

'The two greasy fellows are the *jettis*,' Sharpe said.

'Big as bloody beeves, they are,' Lockhart said. 'Do they really wring your neck?'

'Back to front,' Sharpe said. 'Or else they drive a nail into your

75

skull with their bare hand.' He swerved aside to go past the tents. It was not that he feared to pick a fight with Naig's guards, indeed he expected a scrap, but there was no point in going bald-headed into battle. A bit of cleverness would not go amiss. 'I'm being canny,' he explained to Lockhart, then turned to make sure that Ahmed was keeping up. The boy was holding Sharpe's pack as well as his musket.

The four guards, all of them armed with firelocks and *tulwars*, watched the British soldiers walk out of sight. 'They didn't like the look of us,' Lockhart said.

'Mangy buggers, they are,' Sharpe said. He was glancing about the encampment and saw what he wanted just a few paces away. It was some straw, and near it was a smouldering campfire, and he screwed a handful of the straw stalks into a spill that he lit and carried to the rear of the smaller tent. He pushed the flaming spill into a fold of the canvas. A child watched, wide-eyed. 'If you say anything,' Sharpe told the half-naked child, 'I'll screw your head off back to front.' The child, who did not understand a word, grinned broadly.

'You're not really supposed to be doing this, are you?' Lockhart asked.

'No,' Sharpe said. Lockhart grinned, but said nothing. Instead he just watched as the flames licked at the faded green canvas which, for a moment or two, resisted the fire. The material blackened, but did not burn, then suddenly it burst into fire that licked greedily up the tent's high side. 'That'll wake 'em up,' Sharpe said.

'What now?' Lockhart asked, watching the flame sear up the tent's side.

'We rescue what's inside, of course.' Sharpe drew his sabre. 'Come on, lads!' He ran back to the front of the tent. 'Fire!' he shouted. 'Fire! Fetch water! Fire!'

The four guards stared uncomprehendingly at the Englishman, then leaped to their feet as Sharpe slashed at the laces of the small tent's doorway. One of them called a protest to Sharpe.

'Fire!' Lockhart bellowed at the guards who, still unsure of what was happening, did not try to stop Sharpe. Then one of them saw the smoke billowing over the ridge of the tent. He yelled a warning into the larger tent as his companions suddenly moved to pull the Englishman away from the tent's entrance.

'Hold them off!' Sharpe called, and Lockhart's six troopers closed on the three men. Sharpe slashed at the lacing, hacking down through the tough rope as the troopers thumped into the guards. Someone swore, there was a grunt as a fist landed, then a yelp as a trooper's boot slammed into a *jetti*'s groin. Sharpe sawed through the last knot, then pushed through the loosened tent flaps. 'Jesus!' He stopped, staring at the boxes and barrels and crates that were stacked in the tent's smoky gloom.

Lockhart had followed him inside. 'Doesn't even bother to hide the stuff properly, does he?' the Sergeant said in amazement, then crossed to a barrel and pointed to a 19 that had been cut into one of the staves. 'That's our mark! The bugger's got half our supplies!' He looked up at the flames that were now eating away the tent roof. 'We'll lose the bloody lot if we don't watch it.'

'Cut the tent ropes,' Sharpe suggested, 'and push it all down.'

The two men ran outside and slashed at the guy ropes with their sabres, but more of Naig's men were coming from the larger tent now. 'Watch your back, Eli!' Sharpe called, then turned and sliced the curved blade towards a *jetti*'s face. The man stepped back, and Sharpe followed up hard, slashing again, driving the huge man farther back. 'Now bugger off!' he shouted at the vast brute. 'There's a bloody fire! Fire!'

Lockhart had put his attacker on the ground and was now stamping on his face with a spurred boot. The troopers were coming to help and Sharpe let them deal with Naig's men while he cut through the last of the guy ropes, then ran back into the tent and heaved on the nearest pole. The air inside the tent was choking with swirling smoke, but at last the whole heavy array of canvas sagged towards the fire, lifting the canvas wall behind Sharpe into the air.

'Sahib!' Ahmed's shrill voice shouted and Sharpe turned to see a man aiming a musket at him. The lifting tent flap was exposing Sharpe, but he was too far away to rush the man, then Ahmed fired his own musket and the man shuddered, turned to look at the boy, then winced as the pain in his shoulder struck home. He dropped the gun and clapped a hand onto the wound. The sound of the shot startled the other guards and some reached for their own muskets, but Sharpe ran at them and used his sabre to beat the guns down. 'There's a bloody fire!' he shouted into their faces. 'A fire! You want everything to burn?' They did not understand him, but some realized that the fire threatened

77

their master's supplies and so ran to haul the half-collapsed burning canvas away from the wooden crates.

'But who started the fire?' a voice said behind Sharpe, and he turned to see a tall, fat Indian dressed in a green robe that was embroidered with looping fish and long-legged water-birds. The fat man was holding a half-naked child by the hand, the same small boy who had watched Sharpe push the burning straw into a crease of the canvas. 'British officers,' the fat man said, 'have a deal of freedom in this country, but does that mean they can destroy an honest man's property?'

'Are you Naig?' Sharpe asked.

The fat man waved to his guards so that they gathered behind him. The tent had been dragged clear of the crates and was burning itself out harmlessly. The green-robed man now had sixteen or seventeen men with him, four of them *jettis* and all of them armed, while Sharpe had Lockhart and his battered troopers and one defiant child who was reloading a musket as tall as himself. 'I will give you my name,' the fat man said unpleasantly, 'when you tell me yours.'

'Sharpe. Ensign Sharpe.'

'A mere ensign!' The fat man raised his eyebrows. 'I thought ensigns were children, like this young man.' He patted the half-naked boy's head. 'I am Naig.'

'So perhaps you can tell me,' Sharpe said, 'why that tent was stuffed full of our supplies?'

'Your supplies!' Naig laughed. 'They are my goods, Ensign Sharpe. Perhaps some of them are stored in old boxes that once belonged to your army, but what of that? I buy the boxes from the quartermaster's department.'

'Lying bastard,' Sergeant Lockhart growled. He had prised open the barrel with the number 19 incised on its side and now flourished a horseshoe. 'Ours!' he said.

Naig seemed about to order his guards to finish off Sharpe's small band, but then he glanced to his right and saw that two British officers had come from the larger tent. The presence of the two, both captains, meant that Naig could not just drive Sharpe away, for now there were witnesses. Naig might take on an ensign and a few troopers, but captains carried too much authority. One of the captains, who wore the red coat of the Scotch Brigade, crossed to Sharpe. 'Trouble?' he asked. His revels had plainly been interrupted, for his trousers were still unbuttoned and his sword and sash were slung across one shoulder.

'This bastard, sir, has been pilfering our supplies.' Sharpe jerked his thumb at Naig then nodded towards the crates. 'It's all marked as stolen in the supply ledgers, but I'll wager it's all there. Buckets, muskets, horseshoes.'

The Captain glanced at Naig, then crossed to the crates. 'Open that one,' he ordered, and Lockhart obediently stooped to the box and levered up its nailed lid with his sabre.

'I have been storing these boxes,' Naig explained. He turned to the second captain, an extraordinarily elegant cavalryman in Company uniform, and he pleaded with him in an Indian language. The Company Captain turned away and Naig went back to the Scotsman. The merchant was in trouble now, and he knew it. 'I was asked to store the boxes!' he shouted at the Scotsman.

But the infantry Captain was staring down into the opened crate where ten brand new muskets lay in their wooden cradles. He stooped for one of the muskets and peered at the lock. Just forward of the hammer and behind the pan was an engraved crown with the letters GR beneath it, while behind the hammer the word Tower was engraved. 'Ours,' the Scotsman said flatly.

'I bought them.' Naig was sweating now.

'I thought you said you were storing them?' the Scotsman said. 'Now you say you bought them. Which is it?'

'My brother and I bought the guns from *silladars*,' Naig said.

'We don't sell these Tower muskets,' the Captain said, hefting the gun that was still coated with grease.

Naig shrugged. 'They must have been captured from the supply convoys. Please, sahib, take them. I want no trouble. How was I to know they were stolen?' He turned and pleaded again with the Company cavalry Captain who was a tall, lean man with a long face, but the cavalryman turned and walked a short distance away. A crowd had collected now and watched the drama silently, and Sharpe, looking along their faces, suspected there was not much sympathy for Naig. Nor, Sharpe thought, was there much hope for the fat man. Naig had been playing a dangerous game, but with such utter confidence that he had not even bothered to conceal the stolen supplies. At the very least he could have thrown away the government issue boxes and tried to file the lock markings off the muskets, but Naig must have believed he had powerful friends who would protect him. The cavalryman seemed to be one of those friends, for Naig had followed him and was hissing in his ear, but the cavalryman merely pushed the Indian away, then turned to Sharpe. 'Hang him,' he said curtly.

'Hang him?' Sharpe asked in puzzlement.

'It's the penalty for theft, ain't it?' the cavalryman insisted.

Sharpe looked to the Scottish Captain, who nodded uncertainly. 'That's what the General said,' the Scotsman confirmed.

'I'd like to know how he got the supplies, sir,' Sharpe said.

'You'll give the fat bastard time to concoct a story?' the cavalryman demanded. He had an arrogance that annoyed Sharpe, but everything about the cavalryman irritated Sharpe. The man was a dandy. He wore tall, spurred boots that sheathed his calves and knees in soft, polished leather. His white breeches were skin tight, his waistcoat had gold buttons, while his red tail coat was clean, uncreased and edged with gold braid. He wore a frilled stock, a red silk sash was draped across his right shoulder and secured at his left hip by a knot of golden braid, his sabre was scabbarded in red leather, while his cocked hat was plumed with a lavishly curled feather that had been dyed pale green. The clothes had cost a fortune, and clearly his servants must spend hours on keeping their master so beautifully dressed. He looked askance at Sharpe, a slight wrinkle of his nostrils suggesting that he found Sharpe's appearance distressing. The cavalryman's face suggested he was a clever man, but also that he despised those who were less clever than himself. 'I don't suppose Sir Arthur will be vastly pleased when he hears that you let the fellow live, Ensign,' he said acidly. 'Swift and certain justice, ain't that the penalty for theft? Hang the fat beast.'

'That is what the standing orders say,' the Scotch Brigade Captain agreed, 'but does it apply to civilians?'

'He should have a trial!' Sharpe protested, not because he was so committed to Naig's right to a hearing, but because he feared the whole episode was getting out of hand. He had thought to find the supplies, maybe have a mill with Naig's guards, but no one was supposed to die. Naig deserved a good kicking, but death?

'Standing orders apply to anyone within the picquet lines,' the cavalry Captain averred confidently. 'So for God's sake get on with it! Dangle the bastard!' He was sweating, and Sharpe sensed that the elegant cavalryman was not quite so confident as he appeared.

'Bugger a trial,' Sergeant Lockhart said happily. 'I'll hang the bastard.' He snapped at his troopers to fetch a nearby ox cart. Naig had tried to retreat to the protection of his guards, but the cavalry Captain had drawn a pistol that he now held close to Naig's head as the grinning troopers trundled the empty ox cart into the open space in front of the pilfered supplies.

Sharpe crossed to the tall cavalryman. 'Shouldn't we talk to him, sir?'

'My dear fellow, have you ever tried to get the truth out of an Indian?' the Captain asked. 'They swear by a thousand gaudy gods that they'll tell the truth, then lie like a rug! Be quiet!' Naig had begun to protest and the cavalryman rammed the pistol into the Indian's mouth, breaking a tooth and gashing Naig's gum. 'Another damned word, Naig, and I'll castrate you before I hang you.' The cavalryman glanced at Sharpe, who was frowning. 'Are you squeamish, Ensign?'

'Don't seem right, sir. I mean I agree he deserves to be hung, but shouldn't we talk to him first?'

'If you like conversation so much,' the cavalryman drawled, 'institute a Philosophical Society. Then you can enjoy all the hot air you like. Sergeant?' This last was to Lockhart. 'Take the bastard off my hands, will you?'

'Pleasure, sir.' Lockhart seized Naig and shoved him towards the cart. One of the cavalry troopers had cut a length of guy rope from the burnt remnants of the tent and he now tied one end to the tip of the single shaft that protruded from the front of the ox cart. He made a loop in the rope's end.

Naig screamed and tried to pull away. Some of his guards started forward, but then a hard voice ordered them back and Sharpe turned to see that a tall, thin Indian in a black and green striped robe had come from the larger tent. The newcomer, who looked to be in his forties, walked with a limp. He crossed to the cavalry Captain and spoke quietly, and Sharpe saw the cavalryman shake his head vehemently, then shrug as if to suggest that he was powerless. Then the Captain gestured to Sharpe and the tall Indian gave the Ensign a look of such malevolence that Sharpe instinctively put his hand on his sabre's hilt. Lockhart had pulled the noose over Naig's head. 'Are you sure, sir?' he asked the cavalry Captain.

'Of course I'm sure, Sergeant,' the cavalryman said angrily. 'Just get on with it.'

'Sir?' Sharpe appealed to the Scots Captain, who frowned uncertainly, then turned and walked away as though he wanted nothing more to do with the affair. The tall Indian in the striped robe spat into the dust, then limped back to the tent.

Lockhart ordered his troopers to the back of the cart. Naig was attempting to pull the noose free of his neck, but Lockhart slapped his hands down. 'Now, boys!' he shouted.

The troopers reached up and hauled down on the backboard so that the cart tipped like a seesaw on its single axle and, as the troopers pulled down, so the shaft rose into the air. The rope stretched and tightened. Naig screamed, then the cavalryman jumped up to sit on the cart's back and the shaft jerked higher still and the scream was abruptly choked off. Naig was dangling now, his feet kicking wildly under the lavishly embroidered robe. None of the crowd moved, none protested.

Naig's face was bulging and his hands were scrabbling uselessly at the noose which was tight about his neck. The cavalry officer watched with a small smile. 'A pity,' he said in his elegant voice. 'The wretched man ran the best brothel I ever found.'

'We're not killing his girls, sir,' Sharpe said.

'That's true, Ensign, but will their next owner treat them as well?' The cavalryman turned to the big tent's entrance and took off his plumed hat to salute a group of sari-clad girls who now watched wide-eyed as their employer did the gallows dance. 'I saw Nancy Merrick hang in Madras,' the cavalryman said, 'and she did the jig for thirty-seven minutes! Thirty-seven! I'd wagered on sixteen, so lost rather a lot of tin. Don't think I can watch Naig dance for half an hour. It's too damned hot. Sergeant? Help his soul to perdition, will you?'

Lockhart crouched beneath the dying man and caught hold of his heels. Then he tugged down hard, swearing when Naig pissed on him. He tugged again, and at last the body went still. 'Do you see what happens when you steal from us?' the cavalry Captain shouted at the crowd, then repeated the words in an Indian language. 'If you steal from us, you will die!' Again he translated his words, then gave Sharpe a crooked grin. 'But only, of course, if you're stupid enough to be caught, and I didn't think Naig was stupid at all. Rather the reverse. Just how did you happen to discover the supplies, Ensign?'

'Tent was on fire, sir,' Sharpe said woodenly. 'Me and Sergeant Lockhart decided to rescue whatever was inside.'

'How very public-spirited of you.' The Captain gave Sharpe a long, speculative look, then turned back to Lockhart. 'Is he dead, Sergeant?'

'Near as makes no difference, sir,' Lockhart called back.

'Use your pistol to make sure,' the Captain ordered, then sighed. 'A shame,' he said. 'I rather liked Naig. He was a rogue, of course, but rogues are so much more amusing than honest men.' He watched as Lockhart lowered the shaft, then stooped over the prostrate body and put a bullet into its skull. 'I suppose I'll have to find some carts to fetch these supplies back where they belong,' the Captain said.

'I'll do that, sir,' Sharpe said.

'You will?' The Captain seemed astonished to discover such willingness. 'Why on earth would you want to do that, Ensign?'

'It's my job, sir,' Sharpe said. 'I'm Captain Torrance's assistant.'

'You poor benighted bastard,' the Captain said pityingly.

'Poor, sir? Why?'

'Because I'm Captain Torrance. Good day to you, Ensign.' Torrance turned on his heel and walked away through the crowd.

'Bastard,' Sharpe said, for he had suddenly understood why Torrance had been so keen to hang Naig.

He spat after the departed Captain, then went to find some bullocks and carts. The army had its supplies back, but Sharpe had made a new enemy. As if Hakeswill were not enough, he now had Torrance as well.

The palace in Gawilghur was a sprawling one-storey building that stood on the highest point within the Inner Fort. To its north was a garden that curled about the largest of the fortress's lakes. The lake was a tank, a reservoir, but its banks had been planted with flowering trees, and a flight of steps led from the palace to a small stone pavilion on the lake's northern shore. The pavilion had an arched ceiling on which the reflections of the lake's small waves should have rippled, but the season had been so dry that the lake had shrunk and the water level was some eight or nine feet lower than usual. The water and the exposed banks were rimed with a green, foul-smelling scum, but Beny

Singh, the Killadar of Gawilghur, had arranged for spices to be burned in low, flat braziers so that the dozen men inside the pavilion were not too offended by the lake's stench.

'If only the Rajah was here,' Beny Singh said, 'we should know what to do.' Beny Singh was a short, plump man with a curling moustache and nervous eyes. He was the fortress commander, but he was a courtier by avocation, not a soldier, and he had always regarded his command of the great fortress as a licence to make his fortune rather than to fight the Rajah's enemies.

Prince Manu Bappoo was not surprised that his brother had chosen not to come to Gawilghur, but had instead fled farther into the hills. The Rajah was like Beny Singh, he had no belly for a fight, but Bappoo had watched the first British troops creep across the plain beneath the fort's high walls and he welcomed their coming. 'We don't need my brother here to know what we must do,' he said. 'We fight.' The other men, all commanders of the various troops that had taken refuge in Gawilghur, voiced their agreement.

'The British cannot be stopped by walls,' Beny Singh said. He was cradling a small white lap dog which had eyes as wide and frightened as its master's.

'They can, and they will,' Bappoo insisted.

Singh shook his head. 'Were they stopped at Seringapatam? At Ahmednuggur? They crossed those city walls as though they had wings! They are – what is the word your Arabs use? – *djinns!*' He looked about the gathered council and saw no one who would support him. 'They must have the *djinns* on their side,' he added weakly.

'So what would you do?' Bappoo asked.

'Treat with them,' Beny Singh said. 'Ask for *cowle.*'

'*Cowle?*' It was Colonel Dodd who intervened, speaking in his crude, newly learned Marathi. 'I'll tell you what terms Wellesley will offer you. None! He'll march you away as a prisoner, he'll slight these walls and take away the Rajah's treasures.'

'There are no treasures here,' Beny Singh said, but no one believed him. He was soothing the little dog which had been frightened by the Englishman's harsh voice.

'And he'll give your women to his men as playthings,' Dodd added nastily.

Beny Singh shuddered. His wife, his concubines and his children were all in the palace, and they were all dear to him. He pampered them, worshipped them and adored them. 'Perhaps I should remove my people from the fort?' he suggested hesitantly. 'I could take them to Multai? The British will never reach Multai.'

'You'd run away?' Dodd asked in his harsh voice. 'You bloody won't!' He spoke those three words in English, but everyone understood what they meant. He leaned forward. 'If you run away,' he said, 'the garrison loses heart. The rest of the soldiers can't take their women away, so why should you? We fight them here, and we stop them here. Stop them dead!' He stood and walked to the pavilion's edge where he spat onto the green-scummed bank before turning back to Beny Singh. 'Your women are safe here, Killadar. I could hold this fortress from now till the world's end with just a hundred men.'

'The British are *djinns*,' Beny Singh whispered. The dog in his arms was shivering.

'They are not *djinns*,' Dodd snapped. 'There are no demons! They don't exist!'

'Winged *djinns*,' Beny Singh said in almost a whimper, 'invisible *djinns*! In the air!'

Dodd spat again. 'Bloody hell,' he said in English, then turned fast towards Beny Singh. 'I'm an English demon. Me! Understand? I'm a *djinn*, and if you take your women away I'll follow you and I'll come to them at night and fill them with black bile.' He bared his yellowed teeth and the Killadar shuddered. The white dog barked shrilly.

Manu Bappoo waved Dodd back to his seat. Dodd was the only European officer left in his forces and, though Bappoo was glad to have the Englishman's services, there were times when Colonel Dodd could be tiresome. 'If there are *djinns*,' Bappoo told Singh, 'they will be on our side.' He waited while the Killadar soothed the frightened dog, then he leaned forward. 'Tell me,' he demanded of Beny Singh, 'can the British take the fortress by using the roads up the hill?'

Beny Singh thought about those two steep winding roads that twisted up the hill beneath Gawilghur's walls. No man could survive those climbs, not if the defenders were raining round shot and rocks down the precipitous slopes. 'No,' he admitted.

'So they can only come one way. Only one way! Across the land bridge. And my men will guard the Outer Fort, and Colonel Dodd's men will defend the Inner Fort.'

'And no one,' Dodd said harshly, 'no one will get past my Cobras.' He still resented that his well-trained, white-coated soldiers were not defending the Outer Fort, but he had accepted Manu Bappoo's argument that the important thing was to hold the Inner Fort. If, by some chance, the British did capture the Outer Fort, they would never fight past Dodd's men. 'My men,' Dodd growled, 'have never been defeated. They never will be.'

Manu Bappoo smiled at the nervous Beny Singh. 'You see, Killadar, you will die here of old age.'

'Or of too many women,' another man put in, provoking laughter.

A cannon sounded from the Outer Fort's northern ramparts, followed a few seconds later by another. No one knew what might have caused the firing and so the dozen men followed Manu Bappoo as he left the pavilion and walked towards the Inner Fort's northern ramparts. Silver-furred monkeys chattered at the soldiers from the high branches.

Arab guards stood at the gate of the Rajah's garden. They were posted to stop any common soldiers of the garrison going to the paths beside the tank where the Killadar's women liked to stroll in the cool of the evening. A hundred paces beyond the garden gate was a steep-sided rock pit, about twice as deep as a man stood high, and Dodd paused to look down into its shadowed depths. The sides had been chiselled smooth by stone-workers so that nothing could climb up from the floor that was littered with white bones. 'The Traitor's Hole,' Bappoo said, as he paused beside Dodd, 'but the bones are from baby monkeys.'

'But they do eat men?' Dodd asked, intrigued by the shadowed blackness at the foot of the hole.

'They kill men,' Bappoo said, 'but don't eat them. They're not big enough.'

'I can't see any,' Dodd said, disappointed, then suddenly a sinuous shadow writhed swiftly between two crevices. 'There!' he said happily. 'Don't they grow big enough to eat men?'

'Most years they escape,' Bappoo said. 'The monsoon floods the pit and the snakes swim to the top and wriggle out. Then we must find new ones. This year we've been saved the trouble. These snakes will grow bigger than usual.'

Beny Singh waited a few paces away, clutching his small dog as though he feared Dodd would throw it down to the snakes. 'There's a bastard who ought to be fed to the snakes,' Dodd said to Bappoo, nodding towards the Killadar.

'My brother likes him,' Bappoo said mildly, touching Dodd's arm to indicate that they should walk on. 'They share tastes.'

'Such as?'

'Women, music, luxury. We really do not need him here.'

Dodd shook his head. 'If you let him go, sahib, then half the damned garrison will want to run away. And if you let the women go, what will the men fight for? Besides, do you really think there's any danger?'

'None,' Bappoo admitted. He had led the officers up a steep rock stairway to a natural bastion where a vast iron gun was trained across the chasm towards the distant cliffs of the high plateau. From here the far cliffs were almost a mile away, but Dodd could just see a group of horsemen clustered at the chasm's edge. It was those horsemen, all in native robes, who had prompted the Outer Fort's gunners to open fire, but the gunners, seeing their shots fall well short of the target, had given up. Dodd drew out his telescope, trained it, and saw a man in the uniform of the Royal Engineers sitting on the ground a few paces from his companions. The engineer was sketching. The horsemen were all Indians. Dodd lowered the telescope and looked at the huge iron gun. 'Is it loaded?' he asked the gunners.

'Yes, sahib.'

'A *haideri* apiece if you can kill the man in the dark uniform. The one sitting at the cliff's edge.'

The gunners laughed. Their gun was over twenty feet long and its wrought-iron barrel was cast with decorations that had been painted green, white and red. A pile of round shot, each over a foot in diameter, stood beside the massive carriage that was made from giant baulks of teak. The gun captain fussed over his aim, shouting at his men to lever the vast carriage a thumb's width to the right, then a finger's breadth back, until at last he was satisfied. He squinted along the barrel for a second, waved the officers who had followed Bappoo to move away from the great gun, then leaned over the breach to dab his glowing portfire onto the gun's touch-hole.

The reed glowed and smoked for a second as the fire dashed down to the charge, then the vast cannon crashed back, the teak runners sliding up the timber ramp that formed the lower half of the carriage.

Smoke jetted out into the chasm as a hundred startled birds flapped from their nests on the rock faces and circled in the warm air.

Dodd had been standing to one side, watching the engineer through his glass. For a second he actually saw the great round shot as a flicker of grey in the lower right quadrant of his lens, then he saw a boulder close to the engineer shatter into scraps. The engineer fell sideways, his sketch pad falling, but then he picked himself up and scrambled up the slope to where his horse was being guarded by the cavalrymen.

Dodd took a single gold coin from his pouch and tossed it to the gunner. 'You missed,' he said, 'but it was damned fine shooting.'

'Thank you, sahib.'

A whimper made Dodd turn. Beny Singh had handed his dog to a servant and was staring through an ivory-barrelled telescope at the enemy horsemen. 'What is it?' Bappoo asked him.

'Syud Sevajee,' Singh said in a small voice.

'Who's Syud Sevajee?' Dodd asked.

Bappoo grinned. 'His father was once killadar here, but he died. Was it poison?' he asked Beny Singh.

'He just died,' Singh said. 'He just died!'

'Murdered, probably,' Bappoo said with amusement, 'and Beny Singh became killadar and took the dead man's daughter as his concubine.'

Dodd turned to see the enemy horsemen vanishing among the trees beyond the far cliff. 'Come for revenge, has he? You still want to leave?' he demanded of Beny Singh. 'Because that fellow will be waiting for you. He'll track you through the hills, Killadar, and slit your throat in the night's darkness.'

'We shall stay here and fight,' Beny Singh declared, retrieving the dog from his servant.

'Fight and win,' Dodd said, and he imagined the British breaching batteries on that far cliff, and he imagined the slaughter that would be made among the crews by this one vast gun. And there were fifty other heavy guns waiting to greet the British approach, and hundreds of lighter pieces that fired smaller missiles. Guns, rockets, canister, muskets and cliffs, those were Gawilghur's defences, and Dodd reckoned the British stood no chance. No chance at all. The big gun's smoke drifted away in the small breeze. 'They will die here,' Dodd said, 'and we shall chase the survivors south and cut them down like dogs.' He turned and looked at Beny Singh. 'You see the chasm? That is where their demons will die. Their wings will be scorched, they will fall like burning stones to their deaths, and their screams will lull your children to a dreamless sleep.' He knew he spoke true, for Gawilghur was impregnable.

'I take pleasure, no, Dilip, make that I take humble pleasure in reporting the recovery of a quantity of stolen stores.' Captain Torrance paused. Night had just fallen and Torrance uncorked a bottle of arrack and took a sip. 'Am I going too fast for you?'

'Yes, sahib,' Dilip, the middle-aged clerk, answered. 'Humble pleasure,' he said aloud as his pen moved laboriously over the paper, 'in reporting the recovery of a quantity of stolen stores.'

'Add a list of the stores,' Torrance ordered. 'You can do that later. Just leave a space, man.'

'Yes, sahib,' Dilip said.

'I had suspected for some time,' Torrance intoned, then scowled as someone knocked on the door. 'Come,' he shouted, 'if you must.'

Sharpe opened the door and was immediately entangled in the muslin. He fought his way past its folds.

'It's you,' Torrance said unpleasantly.

'Me, sir.'

'You let some moths in,' Torrance complained.

'Sorry, sir.'

'That is why the muslin is there, Sharpe, to keep out moths, ensigns and other insignificant nuisances. Kill the moths, Dilip.'

The clerk dutifully chased the moths about the room, swatting them with a roll of paper. The windows, like the door, were closely screened with muslin on the outside of which moths clustered, attracted by the candles that were set in silver sticks on Torrance's table. Dilip's work was spread on the table, while Captain Torrance lay in a wide hammock slung from the roof beams. He was naked. 'Do I offend you, Sharpe?'

'Offend me, sir?'

'I am naked, or had you not noticed?'

'Doesn't bother me, sir.'

'Nudity keeps clothes clean. You should try it. Is the last of the enemy dead, Dilip?'

'The moths are all deceased, sahib.'

'Then we shall continue. Where were we?'

'"I had suspected for some time,"' Dilip read back the report.

'Surmised is better, I think. I had surmised for some time.' Torrance paused to draw on the mouthpiece of a silver-bellied hookah. 'What are you doing here, Sharpe?'

'Come to get orders, sir.'

'How very assiduous of you. I had surmised for some time that depredations – I can spell it if you cannot, Dilip – were being made upon the stores entrusted to my command. What the devil were you doing, Sharpe, poking about Naig's tents?'

'Just happened to be passing them, sir,' Sharpe said, 'when they caught fire.'

Torrance gazed at Sharpe, plainly not believing a word. He shook his head sadly. 'You look very old to be an ensign, Sharpe?'

'I was a sergeant two months ago, sir.'

Torrance adopted a look of pretended horror. 'Oh, good God,' he said archly, 'good God alive. May all the spavined saints preserve us. You're not telling me you've been made up from the ranks?'

'Yes, sir.'

'Sweet suffering Jesus,' Torrance said. He lay his head back on the hammock's pillow and blew a perfect smoke ring that he watched wobble its way up towards the ceiling. 'Having confidential information as to the identity of the thief, I took steps to apprehend him. You will notice, Sharpe, that I am giving you no credit in this report?'

'No, sir?'

'Indeed I am not. This report will go to Colonel Butters, an appallingly bombastic creature who will, I suspect, attempt to take some of the credit for himself before passing the papers on to Arthur Wellesley who, as you may know, is our commander. A very stern man, our Arthur. He likes things done properly. He plainly had a very stern governess in his nursery.'

'I know the General, sir.'

'You do?' Torrance turned his head to look at Sharpe. 'Socially, perhaps? You and he dine together, do you? Pass the time of day, do you? Hunt together, maybe? Drink port? Talk about old times? Whore together, perhaps?' Torrance was mocking, but there was just an edge of interest in his voice in case Sharpe really did know Sir Arthur.

'I mean I've met him, sir.'

Torrance shook his head as though Sharpe had been wasting his time. 'Do stop calling me "sir". It may be your natural subservience, Sharpe, or more likely it is the natural air of superiority that emanates from my person, but it ill becomes an officer, even one dredged up from the ranks. A search of his tents, Dilip, secured the missing items. I then, in accordance with general orders, hanged the thief as an example. I have the honour to be, et cetera, et cetera.'

'Two thousand muskets are still missing, sir,' Sharpe said. 'Sorry, sir. Didn't mean to call you "sir".'

'If it pleases you to grovel, Sharpe, then do so. Two thousand muskets still missing, eh? I suspect the bugger sold them on, don't you?'

'I'm more interested in how he got them in the first place,' Sharpe said.

'How very tedious of you,' Torrance said lightly.

'I'd suggest talking to Sergeant Hakeswill when he gets back,' Sharpe said.

'I won't hear a word spoken against Obadiah,' Torrance said. 'Obadiah is a most amusing fellow.'

'He's a lying, thieving bastard,' Sharpe said vehemently.

'Sharpe! Please!' Torrance's voice was pained. 'How can you say such wicked things? You don't even know the fellow.'

'Oh, I know him, sir. I served under him in the Havercakes.'

'You did?' Torrance smiled. 'I see we are in for interesting times. Perhaps I should keep the two of you apart. Or perhaps not. Brick!' The last word was shouted towards a door that led to the back of the commandeered house.

The door opened and the black-haired woman slipped past the muslin. 'Captain?' she asked. She blushed when she saw Torrance was naked, and Torrance, Sharpe saw, enjoyed her embarrassment.

'Brick, my dear,' Torrance said, 'my hookah has extinguished itself. Will you attend to it? Dilip is busy, or I would have asked him. Sharpe? May I have the honour of naming you to Brick? Brick? This is Ensign Sharpe. Ensign Sharpe? This is Brick.'

'Pleased to meet you, sir,' the woman said, dropping a brief curtsey before she stooped to the hookah. She had clearly not told Torrance that she had met Sharpe earlier.

'Ma'am,' Sharpe said.

'Ma'am!' Torrance said with a laugh. 'She's called Brick, Sharpe.'

'Brick, sir?' Sharpe asked sourly. The name was utterly unsuited to the delicate-featured woman who now deftly disassembled the hookah.

'Her real name is Mrs Wall,' Torrance explained, 'and she is my laundress, seamstress and conscience. Is that not right, little Brick?'

'If you say so, sir.'

'I cannot abide dirty clothes,' Torrance said. 'They are an abomination unto the Lord. Cleanliness, we are constantly told by tedious folk, is next to godliness, but I suspect it is a superior virtue. Any peasant can be godly, but it is a rare person who is clean. Brick, however, keeps me clean. If you pay her a trifle, Sharpe, she will doubtless wash and mend those rags you are pleased to call a uniform.'

'They're all I've got, sir.'

'So? Walk naked until Brick has serviced you, or does the idea embarrass you?'

'I wash my own clothes, sir.'

'I wish you would,' Torrance said tartly. 'Remind me why you came here, Sharpe?'

'Orders, sir.'

'Very well,' Torrance said. 'At dawn you will go to Colonel Butters's quarters and find an aide who can tell you what is required of us. You then tell Dilip. Dilip then arranges everything. After that you may take your rest. I trust you will not find these duties onerous?'

Sharpe wondered why Torrance had asked for a deputy if the clerk did all the work, then supposed that the Captain was so lazy that he could not be bothered to get up early in the morning to fetch his orders. 'I get tomorrow's orders at dawn, sir,' Sharpe said, 'from an aide of Colonel Butters.'

'There!' Torrance said with mock amazement. 'You have mastered your duties, Ensign. I congratulate you.'

'We already have tomorrow's orders, sahib,' Dilip said from the table where he was copying a list of the recovered stores into Torrance's report. 'We are to move everything to Deogaum. The pioneers' stores are to be moved first, sahib. The Colonel's orders are on the table, sahib, with the chitties. Pioneers' stores first, then everything else.'

'Well, I never!' Torrance said. 'See? Your first day's work is done, Sharpe.' He drew on the hookah which the woman had relit. 'Excellent, my dear,' he said, then held out a hand to stop her from leaving. She crouched beside the hammock, averting her eyes from Torrance's naked body. Sharpe sensed her unhappiness, and Torrance sensed Sharpe's interest in her. 'Brick is a widow, Sharpe,' he said, 'and presumably looking for a husband, though I doubt she's ever dared to dream of marrying as high as an ensign. But why not? The social ladder is there to be climbed and, low a rung as you might be, Sharpe, you still represent a considerable advancement for Brick. Before she joined my service she was a mop-squeezer. From mop-squeezer to an officer's wife! There's progress for you. I think the two of you would suit each other vastly well. I shall play Cupid, or rather Dilip will. Take a letter to the chaplain of the 94th, Dilip. He's rarely sober, but I'm sure he can waddle through the marriage ceremony without falling over.'

'I can't marry, sir!' Sharpe protested.

Torrance, amused at himself, raised an eyebrow. 'You are averse to women? You dislike dear Brick? Or you've taken an oath of celibacy, perhaps?'

Sharpe blushed. 'I'm spoken for, sir.'

'You mean you're engaged? How very touching. Is she an heiress, perhaps?'

Sharpe shrugged. 'She's in Seringapatam,' he said lamely. 'And we're not engaged.'

'But you have an understanding,' Torrance said, 'with this ravishing creature in Seringapatam. Is she black, Sharpe? A black *bibbi*? I'm sure Clare wouldn't mind, would you? A white man in India needs a *bibbi* or two as well as a wife. Don't you agree, Brick?' He turned to the woman, who ignored him. 'The late Mister Wall died of the fever,' Torrance said to Sharpe, 'and in the Christian kindness of my heart I continue to employ his widow. Does that not speak well of my character?'

'If you say so, sir,' Sharpe said.

'I see my attempt to play Cupid is not meeting with success,' Torrance said. 'So, Sharpe, to business. Tomorrow morning I suggest you go to Deogaum, wherever the hell that is.'

'With the bullocks, sir?'

Torrance raised his eyebrows in exasperation. 'You are an officer, Sharpe, not a bullock driver. You don't prod rumps, you leave that to the natives. Go early. Ride there at dawn, and your first duty will be to find me quarters.'

'I don't have a horse,' Sharpe said.

'You don't have a horse? Don't have a horse? Good God alive, man, what bloody use are you? You'll just have to bloody well walk then. I shall find you in Deogaum tomorrow afternoon and God help you if you haven't found me decent quarters. A front room, Sharpe, where Dilip can conduct business. A large room for me, and a hole for Brick. I would also like to have a walled garden with adequate shade trees and a small pool.'

'Where is Deogaum?' Sharpe asked.

'Northwards, sahib,' Dilip answered. 'Close to the hills.'

'Beneath Gawilghur?' Sharpe guessed.

'Yes, sahib.'

Sharpe looked back to Torrance. 'Can I ask a favour of you, sir?'

Torrance sighed. 'If you insist.'

'At Gawilghur, sir, I'd like permission to join the assault party.'

Torrance stared at Sharpe for a long time. 'You want what?' he finally asked.

'I want to be with the attack, sir. There's a fellow inside, see, who killed a friend of mine. I want to see him dead.'

Torrance blinked at Sharpe. 'Don't tell me you're enthusiastic! Good God!' A sudden look of terror came to the Captain's face. 'You're not a Methodist, are you?'

'No, sir.'

Torrance pointed the hookah's mouthpiece towards a corner of the room. 'There is a linen press, Sharpe, d'you see it? Inside it are my clothes. Amidst my clothes you will find a pistol. Take the pistol, remove yourself from my presence, apply the muzzle to your head and pull the trigger. It is a much quicker and less painful way of dying.'

'But you won't mind if I join the attack?'

'Mind? You're not, surely, labouring under the misapprehension that I care about your existence? You think I might mourn you, even after such a short acquaintance? My dear Sharpe, I fear I shall not miss you at all. I doubt I'll even remember your name once you're dead. Of course you can join the assaulting party. Do what you like! Now I suggest you get some sleep. Not here, though, I like my privacy.

Find a tree, perhaps, and slumber beneath its sheltering branches. Good night to you, Sharpe.'

'Good night, sir.'

'And don't let any moths in!'

Sharpe negotiated the muslin and slipped out of the door. Torrance listened to the footsteps go away, then sighed. 'A tedious man, Dilip.'

'Yes, sahib.'

'I wonder why he was made an officer?' Torrance frowned as he sucked on his hookah, then shook his head. 'Poor Naig! Sacrificed to a mere ensign's ambition. How did that wretched Sharpe even know to look in Naig's tent? Did he talk to you?'

'Yes, sahib,' Dilip admitted.

Torrance stared at him. 'Did you let him look at the ledgers?'

'He insisted, sahib.'

'You're a bloody fool, Dilip! A bloody, bloody fool. I should thrash you if I wasn't so tired. Maybe tomorrow.'

'No, sahib, please.'

'Oh, just bugger away off, Dilip,' Torrance snarled. 'And you can go too, Brick.'

The girl fled to the kitchen door. Dilip collected his ink bottle and sand-sprinkler. 'Shall I take the chitties now, sahib, for the morning?'

'Go!' Torrance roared. 'You bore me! Go!' Dilip fled to the front room, and Torrance lay back in the hammock. He was indeed bored. He had nothing to do and nowhere to go. Most nights he would go to Naig's tents and there drink, gamble and whore, but he could hardly visit the green pavilion this night, not after stringing Naig up by the neck. Damn it, he thought. He glanced at the table where a book, a gift from his father, lay unopened. The first volume of *Some Reflections on Paul's Epistle to the Ephesians* by the Reverend Courtney Mallison, and it would be a frigid day in the devil's house before Torrance read that turgid tome. The Reverend Mallison had been Torrance's childhood tutor, and a vicious beast he had been. A whipper, that was Mallison. Loved to whip his pupils. Torrance stared at the ceiling. Money. It was all down to money. Everything in the damned world was down to money. Make money, he thought, and he could go home and make Courtney Mallison's life a misery. Have the bastard on his knees. And Mallison's daughter. Have that prim bitch on her back.

There was a knock on the door. 'I said I didn't want to be disturbed!'

Torrance shouted, but despite his protest the door opened and the muslin billowed inward, letting in a flutter of moths. 'For Christ's sake,' Torrance cursed, then fell abruptly silent.

He fell silent, for the first man through the door was a *jetti*, his bare torso gleaming with oil, and behind him came the tall man with a limp, the same man who had pleaded for Naig's life. His name was Jama, and he was Naig's brother, and his presence made Torrance acutely aware of his nudity. He swung off the hammock and reached for his dressing gown, but Jama twitched the silk garment off the chair back. 'Captain Torrance,' he said with a bow.

'Who let you in?' Torrance demanded.

'I expected to see you in our small establishment tonight, Captain,' Jama said. Where his brother had been plump, noisy and a braggart, Jama was lean, silent and watchful.

Torrance shrugged. 'Maybe tomorrow night?'

'You will be welcome, Captain, as always.' Jama took a small sheaf of papers from his pocket and fanned his face with them. 'Ten thousand welcomes, Captain.'

Ten thousand rupees. That was the value of the papers in Jama's hand, all of them notes signed by Torrance. He had signed far more, but the others he had paid off with supplies filched from the convoys. Jama was here to remind Torrance that his greatest debts remained unpaid. 'About today . . .' Torrance said awkwardly.

'Ah, yes!' Jama said, as though he had momentarily forgotten the reason for his visit. 'About today, Captain. Do tell me about today.' The *jetti* said nothing, just leaned against the wall with folded arms, his oiled muscles shining in the candlelight and his dark eyes fixed immovably on Torrance.

'I've already told you. It wasn't of my doing,' Torrance said with as much dignity as a naked man could muster.

'You were the one who demanded my brother's death,' Jama said.

'What choice did I have? Once the supplies were found?'

'But perhaps you arranged for them to be found?'

'No!' Torrance protested. 'Why the hell would I do that?'

Jama was silent a moment, then indicated the huge man at his side. 'His name is Prithviraj. I once saw him castrate a man with his bare hands.' Jama mimed a pulling action, smiling. 'You'd be astonished at how far a little skin can stretch before it breaks.'

'For God's sake!' Torrance had gone pale. 'It was not my doing!'

'Then whose doing was it?'

'His name is Sharpe. Ensign Sharpe.'

Jama walked to Torrance's table where he turned the pages of *Some Reflections on Paul's Epistle to the Ephesians*. 'This Sharpe,' he asked, 'he was not obeying your orders?'

'Of course not!'

Jama shrugged. 'My brother was careless,' he admitted, 'over confident. He believed that with your friendship he could survive any enquiry.'

'We were doing business,' Torrance said. 'It was not friendship. And I told your brother he should have hidden the supplies.'

'Yes,' Jama said, 'he should. And so I told him also. But even so, Captain, I come from a proud family. You expect me to watch my brother killed and do nothing about it?' He fanned out the notes of Torrance's debts. 'I shall return these to you, Captain, when you deliver Ensign Sharpe to me. Alive! I want Prithviraj to take my revenge. You understand?'

Torrance understood well enough. 'Sharpe's a British officer,' he said. 'If he's murdered there'll be an enquiry. A real enquiry. Heads will be broken.'

'That is your problem, Captain Torrance,' Jama said. 'How you explain his disappearance is your affair. As are your debts.' He smiled and pushed the notes back into the pouch at his belt. 'Give me Sharpe, Captain Torrance, or I shall send Prithviraj to visit you in the night. In the meantime, you will please continue to patronize our establishment.'

'Bastard,' Torrance said, but Jama and his huge companion had already gone. Torrance picked up *Some Reflections on Paul's Epistle to the Ephesians* and slammed the heavy book down on a moth. 'Bastard,' he said again. But on the other hand it was Sharpe who would suffer, not him, so it did not really matter. And what was Sharpe anyway? Nothing but an upstart from the ranks, so who would care if he died? Torrance killed another moth, then opened the kitchen door. 'Come here, Brick.'

'No, sir, please?'

'Shut up. And come here. You can kill these damn moths while I get drunk.'

Filthy drunk, he reckoned, for he had been scared today. He knew he had very nearly got caught when Sharpe had stripped the tent away from the purloined supplies, but by killing Naig quickly Torrance had protected himself, and now the price of his continued survival was Sharpe's death. Arrange that, he thought, and all his troubles would be past. He forced Brick to drink some arrack, knowing how she hated it. Then he drank some himself. Damn Sharpe to hell, he thought, damn the interfering bastard to hell, which was where Sharpe was going anyway so Torrance drank to that happy prospect. Farewell, Mister Sharpe.

CHAPTER 4

Sharpe was not sure how far away Deogaum was, but guessed it was close to twenty miles and that was at least a seven-hour journey on foot, and so it was long before dawn when he stirred Ahmed from his sleep beside the smouldering remains of a bullock-dung fire, then set off under the stars. He tried to teach Ahmed some English. 'Stars,' Sharpe said, pointing.

'Stars,' Ahmed repeated dutifully.

'Moon,' Sharpe said.

'Moon,' Ahmed echoed.

'Sky.'

'Moon?' Ahmed asked, curious that Sharpe was still pointing to the sky.

'Sky, you bugger.'

'Skyoobugger?'

'Never mind,' Sharpe said. He was hungry, and he had forgotten to ask Captain Torrance where he was supposed to draw rations, but their northward route took them through the village of Argaum where the fighting battalions of the army were bivouacked. Unburied bodies still littered the battlefield, and scavenging wild dogs growled from the dark stench as Sharpe and Ahmed walked past. A picquet challenged them at the village, and Sharpe asked the man where he would find the cavalry lines. He could not imagine taking Ahmed to the 74th's mess for breakfast, but Sergeant Eli Lockhart might be more welcoming.

The reveille had sounded by the time Sharpe came to the gully where the horses were picketed and the troopers' campfires were being restored to life. Lockhart scowled at the unexpected visitor through the smoky dawn gloom, then grinned when he recognized Sharpe.

'Must be some fighting to do, lads,' he announced, 'the bleeding infantry's here. Good morning, sir. Need our help again?'

'I need some breakfast,' Sharpe admitted.

'Tea, that'll start you off. Smithers! Pork chops! Davies! Some of that bread you're hiding from me. Look lively now!' Lockhart turned back to Sharpe. 'Don't ask me where the chops come from, sir. I might have to lie.' He spat in a tin mug, scoured its interior with the end of his blanket, then filled it with tea. 'There you are, sir. Does your boy want some? Here you are, lad.' Lockhart, a mug of tea in his own hand, then insisted on taking Sharpe to the picketed horses. 'See, sir?' He lifted a horse's leg to show off the new horseshoe. 'My guvnor's beholden to you. I might introduce you after breakfast.'

Sharpe assumed that Lockhart was talking of his troop commander, but once the pork chops and bread had been eaten, the Sergeant led Sharpe across to the lines of the native cavalry, and then to the tent of the 7th Native Cavalry's commanding officer who, it seemed, was in charge of all the army's cavalry. 'He's called Huddlestone,' Lockhart said, 'and he's a decent fellow. He'll probably offer us another breakfast.'

Colonel Huddlestone did indeed insist that both Lockhart and Sharpe join him for a breakfast of rice and eggs. Sharpe was beginning to see that Lockhart was a useful man, someone who was trusted by his officers and liked by his troopers, for Huddlestone greeted the Sergeant warmly and immediately plunged into a conversation about some local horses that had been purchased for remounts and which Huddlestone reckoned would never stand the strain of battle, though Lockhart seemed to feel that a few of them would be adequate. 'So you're the fellow who smoked out Naig?' Huddlestone said to Sharpe after a while.

'Didn't take much doing, sir.'

'No one else did it, man! Don't shy away from credit. I'm damned grateful to you.'

'Couldn't have done it without Sergeant Lockhart, sir.'

'Damned army would come to a stop without Eli, ain't that so?' the Colonel said, and Lockhart, his mouth full of egg, just grinned. Huddlestone turned back to Sharpe. 'So they gave you to Torrance?'

'Yes, sir.'

'He's a lazy bugger,' Huddlestone said vengefully. Sharpe, astonished at the open criticism, said nothing. 'He's one of my own officers,' Huddlestone went on, 'and I confess I wasn't sorry when he asked to be given duty with the bullock train.'

'He asked, sir?' Sharpe found it curious that a man would prefer to be with the baggage when he could be in a fighting unit.

'His uncle is grooming him for a career in the Company,' Huddlestone said. 'An uncle in Leadenhall Street. Know what Leadenhall Street is, Sharpe?'

'Company offices, sir?'

'The very same. The uncle pays him an allowance, and he wants Torrance to get some experience in dealing with *bhinjarries*. Got it all planned out! A few years in the Company's army, another few trading in spices, then home to inherit his uncle's estate and his seat in the Court of Directors. One day we'll all be tugging our forelocks to the lazy bugger. Still, if he wants to run the baggage train it's no skin off our bums, Sharpe. No one likes the job, so Torrance is welcome to it, but my guess is that you'll be doing most of his work.' The Colonel frowned. 'He arrived in India with three English servants! Can you believe it? It ain't as if servants are hard to find here, but Torrance wanted the cachet of white scullions. Two of 'em died of the fever, then Torrance had the nerve to say that one of them hadn't earned the cost of the voyage out and so he's forcing the widow to stay on and pay the debt!' Huddlestone shook his head, then gestured for his servant to pour more tea. 'So what brings you here, Ensign?'

'On my way to Deogaum, sir.'

'He really came to beg his breakfast, Colonel,' Lockhart put in.

'And I've no doubt the Sergeant fed you before you came to steal my victuals?' Huddlestone asked, then grinned. 'You're in luck, Ensign. We're moving up to Deogaum today. You can ride with us.'

Sharpe blushed. 'I've no horse, sir.'

'Eli?' Huddlestone looked at Lockhart.

'I've got a horse he can ride, sir.'

'Good.' Huddlestone blew on his tea. 'Welcome to the cavalry, Sharpe.'

Lockhart found two horses, one for Sharpe and the other for Ahmed. Sharpe, ever uncomfortable on horseback, struggled into the saddle under the cavalry's sardonic gaze, while Ahmed jumped up and kicked back his heels, revelling in being back on a horse.

They went gently northwards, taking care not to tire the horses. Sharpe, as he rode, found himself thinking about Clare Wall, and that made him feel guilty about Simone Joubert, the young French widow who waited for him in Seringapatam. He had sent her there with a southbound convoy and a letter for his friend Major Stokes, and doubtless Simone was waiting for Sharpe to return when the campaign against the Mahrattas was over, but now he needed to warn her that he was being posted back to England. Would she come with him? Did he want her to come? He was not sure about either question, though he felt obscurely responsible for Simone. He could give her a choice, of course, but whenever Simone was faced by a choice she tended to look limp and wait for someone else to make the decision. He had to warn her, though. Would she even want to go to England? But what else could she do? She had no relatives in India, and the nearest French settlements were miles away.

His thoughts were interrupted at mid-morning when Eli Lockhart spurred alongside his horse. 'See it?'

'See what?'

'Up there!' Lockhart pointed ahead and Sharpe, peering through the dust haze thrown up by the leading squadrons, saw a range of high hills. The lower slopes were green with trees, but above the timber line there was nothing but brown and grey cliffs that stretched from horizon to horizon. And at the very top of the topmost bluff he could just see a streak of dark wall broken by a gate-tower. 'Gawilghur!' Lockhart said.

'How the hell do we attack up there?' Sharpe asked.

The Sergeant laughed. 'We don't! It's a job for the infantry. Reckon you're better off attached to that fellow Torrance.'

Sharpe shook his head. 'I have to get in there, Eli.'

'Why?'

Sharpe gazed at the distant wall. 'There's a fellow called Dodd in there, and the bastard killed a friend of mine.'

Lockhart thought for a second. 'Seven hundred guineas Dodd?'

'That's the fellow,' Sharpe said. 'But I'm not after the reward. I just want to see the bugger dead.'

'Me too,' Lockhart said grimly.

'You?'

'Assaye,' Lockhart said brusquely.

'What happened?'

'We charged his troops. They were knocking seven kinds of hell out of the 74th and we caught the buggers in line. Knocked 'em hard back, but we must have had a dozen troopers unhorsed. We didn't stop, though, we just kept after their cavalry and it wasn't till the battle was over that we found our lads. They'd had their throats cut. All of them.'

'That sounds like Dodd,' Sharpe said. The renegade Englishman liked to spread terror. Make a man afraid, Dodd had once told Sharpe, and he won't fight you so hard.

'So maybe I'll go into Gawilghur with you,' Lockhart said.

'Cavalry?' Sharpe asked. 'They won't let cavalry into a real fight.'

Lockhart grinned. 'I couldn't let an ensign go into a fight without help. Poor little bugger might get hurt.'

Sharpe laughed. The cavalry had swerved off the road to pass a long column of marching infantry who had set off before dawn on their march to Deogaum. The leading regiment was Sharpe's own, the 74th, and Sharpe moved even farther away from the road so that he would not have to acknowledge the men who had wanted to be rid of him, but Ensign Venables spotted him, leaped the roadside ditch, and ran to his side. 'Going up in the world, Richard?' Venables asked.

'Borrowed glory,' Sharpe said. 'The horse belongs to the 19th.'

Venables looked slightly relieved that Sharpe had not suddenly been able to afford a horse. 'Are you with the pioneers now?' he asked.

'Nothing so grand,' Sharpe said, reluctant to admit that he had been reduced to being a bullock guard.

Venables did not really care. 'Because that's what we're doing,' he explained, 'escorting the pioneers. It seems they have to make a road.'

'Up there?' Sharpe guessed, nodding towards the fortress that dominated the plain.

'Captain Urquhart says you might be selling your commission,' Venables said.

'Does he?'

'Are you?'

'Are you making an offer?'

'I've got a brother, you see,' Venables explained. 'Three actually. And some sisters. My father might buy.' He took a piece of paper from a pocket and handed it up to Sharpe. 'So if you go home, why not see my pater? That's his address. He reckons one of my brothers should join the army. Ain't any good for anything else, see?'

'I'll think on it,' Sharpe said, taking the paper. The cavalry had stretched ahead and so he clapped his heels back, and the horse jerked forward, throwing Sharpe back in the saddle. For a second he sprawled, almost falling over the beast's rump, then he flailed wildly to catch his balance and just managed to grasp the saddle pommel. He thought he heard laughter as he trotted away from the battalion.

Gawilghur soared above the plain like a threat and Sharpe felt like a poacher with nowhere to hide. From up there, Sharpe reckoned, the approaching British army would look like so many ants in the dust. He wished he had a telescope to stare at the high, distant fortress, but he had been reluctant to spend money. He was not sure why. It was not that he was poor, indeed there were few soldiers richer, yet he feared that the real reason was that he felt fraudulent wearing an officer's sash, and that if he were to buy the usual appurtenances of an officer – a horse and a telescope and an expensive sword – then he would be mocked by those in the army who claimed he should never have been commissioned in the first place. Nor should he, he thought. He had been happier as a sergeant. Much happier. All the same, he wished he had a telescope as he gazed up at the stronghold and saw a great billow of smoke jet from one of the bastions. Seconds later he heard the fading boom of the gun, but he saw no sign of the shot falling. It was as though the cannonball had been swallowed into the warm air.

A mile short of the foothills the road split into three. The sepoy horsemen went westwards, while the 19th Light Dragoons took the right-hand path that angled away from the domineering fortress. The country became more broken as it was cut by small gullies and heaped with low wooded ridges – the first hints of the tumultuous surge of land that ended in the vast cliffs. Trees grew thick in those foothills, and Deogaum was evidently among the low wooded hills. It lay east of Gawilghur, safely out of range of the fortress's guns. A crackle of musketry sounded from a timbered cleft and the 19th Dragoons, riding ahead of Sharpe, spread into a line. Ahmed grinned and made sure his musket was loaded. Sharpe wondered which side the boy was on.

Another spatter of muskets sounded, this time to the west. The Mahrattas must have had men in the foothills. Perhaps they were stripping the villages of the stored grain? The sepoys of the East India Company cavalry had vanished, while the horsemen of the 19th were filing into the wooded cleft. A gun boomed in the fort, and this time Sharpe heard a thump as a cannonball fell to earth like a stone far behind him. A patch of dust drifted from a field where the shot had plummeted, then he and Ahmed followed the dragoons into the gully and the leaves hid them from the invisible watchers high above.

The road twisted left and right, then emerged into a patchwork of small fields and woods. A large village lay beyond the fields – Sharpe guessed it must be Deogaum – then there were shots to his left and he saw a crowd of horsemen burst out of the trees a half-mile away. They were Mahrattas, and at first Sharpe thought they were intent on charging the 19th Light Dragoons, then he realized they were fleeing from the Company cavalry. There were fifty or sixty of the enemy horsemen who, on seeing the blue-and-yellow-coated dragoons, swerved southwards to avoid a fight. The dragoons were turning, drawing sabres and spurring into pursuit. A trumpet sounded and the small fields were suddenly a whirl of horses, dust and gleaming weapons.

Sharpe reined in among a patch of trees, not wanting to be at the centre of a Mahratta cavalry charge. The enemy horse pounded past in a blur of hooves, shining helmets and lance points. The Company cavalry was still a quarter-mile behind when Ahmed suddenly kicked back his heels and shot out of the hiding place to follow the Mahratta cavalry.

Sharpe swore. The little bastard was running back to join the Mahrattas. Not that Sharpe could blame him, but he still felt disappointed. He knew he had no chance of catching Ahmed who had unslung his musket and now rode up behind the rearmost enemy horseman. That man looked round, saw Ahmed was not in British uniform, and so ignored him. Ahmed galloped alongside, then swung his musket by its barrel so that the heavy stock cracked into the Mahratta's forehead.

The man went off the back of his horse as though jerked by a rope. His horse ran on, stirrups flapping. Ahmed reined in, turned and jumped down beside his victim. Sharpe saw the flash of a knife. The sepoy cavalry was closer now, and they might think Ahmed was the enemy, so Sharpe shouted at the boy to come back. Ahmed scrambled back into his saddle and kicked his horse to the trees where Sharpe waited. He had plundered a sabre, a pistol and a leather bag, and had a grin as wide as his face. The bag held two stale loaves of flat bread, some glass beads and a small book in a strange script. Ahmed gave one loaf to Sharpe, threw away the book, draped the cheap beads about his neck and hung the sabre at his waist, then watched as the dragoons cut into the rearward ranks of the fugitives. There was the blacksmith's sound of steel on steel, two horses stumbled in flurries of dust, a man staggered bleeding into a ditch, pistols banged, a lance shivered point downwards in the dry turf, and then the enemy horse was gone and the British and sepoy cavalry reined in.

'Why can't you be a proper servant?' Sharpe asked Ahmed. 'Clean my boots, wash my clothes, make my supper, eh?'

Ahmed, who did not understand a word, just grinned.

'Instead I get some murderous urchin. So come on, you bugger.' Sharpe kicked his horse towards the village. He passed a half-empty tank where some clothes lay to dry on bushes, then he was in the dusty main street which appeared to be deserted, though he was aware of faces watching nervously from dark windows and curtain-hung door-ways. Dogs growled from the shade and two chickens scratched in the dust. The only person in sight was a naked holy man who sat cross-legged under a tree, with his long hair cascading to the ground about him. He ignored Sharpe, and Sharpe ignored him. 'We have to find a house,' Sharpe told the uncomprehending Ahmed. 'House, see? House.'

The village headman, the *naique*, ventured into the street. At least Sharpe assumed he was the *naique*, just as the *naique* assumed that the mounted soldier was the leader of the newly arrived cavalrymen. He clasped his hands before his face and bowed to Sharpe, then clicked his fingers to summon a servant carrying a small brass tray on which stood a little cup of arrack. The fierce liquor made Sharpe's head feel suddenly light. The *naique* was talking ten to the dozen, but Sharpe quietened him with a wave. 'No good talking to me,' he said, 'I'm nobody. Talk to him.' He pointed to Colonel Huddlestone who was leading his Indian cavalrymen into the village. The troopers dis-mounted as Huddlestone talked to the headman. There was a squawk as the two chickens were snatched up. Huddlestone turned at the sound, but his men all looked innocent.

High above Sharpe a gun banged in the fortress. The shot seared out to fall somewhere in the plain where the British infantry marched.

The dragoons came into the village, some with bloodied sabres, and Sharpe surrendered the two horses to Lockhart. Then he searched the street to find a house for Torrance. He saw nothing which had a walled garden, but he did find a small mud-walled home that had a courtyard and he dropped his pack in the main room as a sign of ownership. There was a woman with two small children who shrank away from him. 'It's all right,' Sharpe said, 'you get paid. No one will hurt you.' The woman wailed and crouched as though expecting to be hit. 'Bloody hell,' Sharpe said, 'does no one in this bleeding country speak English?'

He had nothing to do now until Torrance arrived. He could have hunted through the village to discover paper, a pen and ink so he could write to Simone and tell her about going to England, but he decided that chore could wait. He stripped off his belt, sabre and jacket, found a rope bed, and lay down.

Far overhead the fortress guns fired. It sounded like distant thunder. Sharpe slept.

Sergeant Obadiah Hakeswill tugged off his boots, releasing a stench into the room that caused Captain Torrance to close his eyes. 'Good God,' Torrance said weakly. The Captain felt ill enough already. He had drunk the best part of a bottle of arrack, had woken in the night with gripes in the belly, and then slept unevenly until dawn when someone had scratched at his door and Torrance had shouted at the pest to go away, after which he had at last fallen into a deeper sleep. Now he had been woken by Hakeswill who, oblivious of the stench, began to unwrap the cloths that bound his feet. It smelt, Torrance thought, like rotted cheese that had been stored in a corpse's belly. He shifted his chair slightly towards the window and pulled his dressing gown tighter about his chest. 'I'm truly sorry about Naig,' Torrance said. Hakeswill had listened in disbelief to the tale of Naig's death and seemed genuinely saddened by it, just as he had been shocked by the news that Sharpe was now Torrance's assistant.

'The bleeding Scotch didn't want him, sir, did they?' Hakeswill said. 'Never thought the Scotch had much sense, but they had wits enough to get rid of Sharpie.' Hakeswill had uncovered his right foot and Torrance, barely able to endure the stink, suspected there was black fungus growing between the Sergeant's toes. 'Now you've got him, sir,' Hakeswill went on, 'and I pities you, I does. Decent officer like you, sir? Last thing you deserved. Bleeding Sharpie! He ain't got no right to be an officer, sir, not Sharpie. He ain't a gentleman like your good self, sir. He's just a common toad, like the rest of us.'

'So why was he commissioned?' Torrance asked, watching as Hakeswill tugged at the crusted cloth on his left foot.

'On account of saving the General's life, sir. Leastwise, that's what is said.' Hakeswill paused as a spasm made his face twitch. 'Saved Sir Arthur's life at Assaye. Not that I believe it, sir, but Sir Arthur does, and the result of that, sir, is that Sir Arthur thinks bloody Sharpie is a blue-eyed boy. Sharpie farts and Sir Arthur thinks the wind's turned southerly.'

'Does he now?' Torrance asked. That was worth knowing.

'Four years ago, sir,' Hakeswill said, 'I had Sharpie flogged. Would have been a dead 'un too, he would, like he deserved, only Sir Arthur stopped the flogging after two hundred lashes. Stopped it!' The injustice of the act still galled the Sergeant. 'Now he's a bleedin' officer. I tells you, sir, the army ain't what it was. Gone to the dogs, it has.' He pulled the cloth from his left foot, then frowned at his toes. 'I washed them in August,' he said in wonderment, 'but it don't look like it, does it?'

'It is now December, Sergeant,' Torrance said reprovingly.

'A good sluice should last six months, sir.'

'Some of us engage in a more regular toilet,' Torrance hinted.

'You would, sir, being a gentleman. Thing is, sir, I wouldn't normally take the toerags off, only there's a blister.' Hakeswill frowned. 'Haven't had a blister in years! Poor Naig. For a blackamoor he wasn't a bad sort of fellow.'

Naig, Torrance believed, had been as evil a creature as any on the surface of the earth, but he smiled piously at Hakeswill's tribute. 'We shall certainly miss him, Sergeant.'

'Pity you had to hang him, sir, but what choice did you have? Between the devil and a deep blue buggeration, that's where you were, sir. But poor Naig.' Hakeswill shook his head in sad remembrance. 'You should have strung up Sharpie, sir, more's the pity you couldn't. Strung him up proper like what he deserves. A murdering bastard, he is, murdering!' And an indignant Hakeswill told Captain Torrance how Sharpe had tried to kill him, first by throwing him among the Tippoo's tigers, then by trapping him in a courtyard with an elephant trained to kill by crushing men with its forefoot. 'Only the tigers weren't hungry, see, on account of being fed? And as for the elephant, sir, I had me knife, didn't I? I jabbed it in the paw, I did.' He mimed the stabbing action. 'Right in its paw, deep in! It didn't like it. I can't die, sir, I can't die.' The Sergeant spoke hoarsely, believing every word. He had been hanged as a child, but he had survived the gallows and now believed he was protected from death by his own guardian angel.

Mad, Torrance thought, bedlam-mad, but he was nevertheless fascinated by Obadiah Hakeswill. To look at, the Sergeant appeared the perfect soldier; it was the twitch that suggested something more interesting lay behind the bland blue eyes. And what lay behind those childish eyes, Torrance had decided, was a breathtaking malevolence, yet one that was accompanied by an equally astonishing confidence. Hakeswill, Torrance had decided, would murder a baby and find justification for the act. 'So you don't like Mister Sharpe?' Torrance asked.

'I hates him, sir, and I don't mind admitting it. I've watched him, I have, slither his way up the ranks like a bleeding eel up a drain.' Hakeswill had taken out a knife, presumably the one which he had stabbed into the elephant's foot, and now cocked his right heel on his left knee and laid the blade against the blister.

Torrance shut his eyes to spare himself the sight of Hakeswill performing surgery. 'The thing is, Sergeant,' he said, 'that Naig's brother would rather like a private word with Mister Sharpe.'

'Does he now?' Hakeswill asked. He stabbed down. 'Look at that, sir. Proper bit of pus. Soon be healed. Ain't had a blister in years! Reckon it must be the new boots.' He spat on the blade and poked the blister again. 'I'll have to soak the boots in vinegar, sir. So Jama wants Sharpe's goolies, does he?'

'Literally, as it happens. Yes.'

'He can join the bleeding queue.'

'No!' Torrance said sternly. 'It is important to me, Sergeant, that Mister Sharpe is delivered to Jama. Alive. And that his disappearance occasions no curiosity.'

'You mean no one must notice?' Hakeswill's face twitched while he thought, then he shrugged. 'Ain't difficult, sir.'

'It isn't?'

'I'll have a word with Jama, sir. Then you can give Sharpie some orders, and I'll be waiting for him. It'll be easy, sir. Glad to do it for you.'

'You are a comfort to me, Sergeant.'

'That's my job, sir,' Hakeswill said, then leered at the kitchen door where Clare Wall had appeared. 'Sunshine of my life,' he said in what he hoped was a winning tone.

'Your tea, sir,' Clare said, offering Torrance a cup.

'A mug for the Sergeant, Brick! Where are your manners?'

'She don't need manners,' Hakeswill said, still leering at the terrified Clare, 'not with what she's got. Put some sugar in it, darling, if the Captain will spare me some.'

'Give him sugar, Brick,' Torrance ordered.

Hakeswill watched Brick go back to the kitchen. 'A proper little woman, that, sir. A flower, that's what she is, a flower!'

'No doubt you would like to pluck her?'

'It's time I was married,' Hakeswill said. 'A man should leave a son, sir, says so in the scriptures.'

'You want to do some begetting, eh?' Torrance said, then frowned as someone knocked on the outer door. 'Come!' he called.

An infantry captain whom neither man recognized put his head round the door. 'Captain Torrance?'

'That's me,' Torrance said grandly.

'Sir Arthur Wellesley's compliments,' the Captain said, his acid tone suggesting that the compliments would be remarkably thin, 'but is there any reason why the supplies have not moved northwards?'

Torrance stared at the man. For a second he was speechless, then he cursed under his breath. 'My compliments to the General,' he said, 'and my assurances that the bullock train will be on its way immediately.' He waited until the Captain had gone, then swore again.

'What happened, sir?' Hakeswill asked.

'The bloody chitties!' Torrance said. 'Still here. Dilip must have come for them this morning, but I told him to bugger off.' He swore again. 'Bloody Wellesley will pull my guts out backwards for this.'

Hakeswill found the chitties on the table and went to the door, leaving small bloody marks on the floor from his opened blister. 'Dilly! Dilly! You black bastard heathen swine! Here, take these. On your way!'

'Damn!' Torrance said, standing and pacing the small room. 'Damn, damn, damn.'

'Nothing to worry about, sir,' Hakeswill said.

'Easy for you to say, Sergeant.'

Hakeswill grinned as his face was distorted by twitches. 'Just blame someone else, sir,' he said, 'as is usually done in the army.'

'Who? Sharpe? You said yourself he's Wellesley's blue-eyed boy. I'm supposed to blame him? Or you, perhaps?'

Hakeswill tried to calm the Captain down by giving him his cup of tea. 'Blame Dilly, sir, on account of him being a heathen bastard as black as my new boots.'

'He'll simply deny everything when questioned!' Torrance protested.

Hakeswill smiled. 'Won't be in a position to deny anything, sir, will he? On account of being . . .' He paused, stuck his tongue out, opened his eyes wide and made a choking noise.

'Good God, Sergeant,' Torrance said, shuddering at the horrid picture suggested by Hakeswill's contorted face. 'Besides, he's a good clerk! It's damned difficult to replace good men.'

'It's easy, sir. Jama will give us a man. Give us a good man.' Hakeswill grinned. 'It'll make things much easier, sir, if we can trust the clerk as well as each other.'

Torrance flinched at the thought of being in league with Obadiah Hakeswill, yet if he was ever to pay off his debts he needed the Sergeant's cooperation. And Hakeswill was marvellously efficient. He could strip the supplies bare and not leave a trace of his handiwork, always making sure someone else took the blame. And doubtless the Sergeant was right. If Jama could provide a clerk, then the clerk could provide a false set of accounts. And if Dilip was blamed for the late arrival of the pioneers' stores, then Torrance would be off that particularly sharp and nasty hook. As ever, it seemed as though Hakeswill could find his way through the thorniest of problems.

'Just leave it to me, sir,' Hakeswill said. 'I'll look after everything, sir, I will.' He bared his teeth at Clare who had brought his mug of tea. 'You're the flower of womanhood,' he told her, then watched appreciatively as she scuttled back to the kitchen. 'Her and me, sir, are meant for each other. Says so in the scriptures.'

'Not till Sharpe's dead,' Torrance said.

'He'll be dead, sir,' Hakeswill promised, and the Sergeant shivered as he anticipated the riches that would follow that death. Not just Clare Wall, but the jewels. The jewels! Hakeswill had divined that it had been Sharpe who had killed the Tippoo Sultan in Seringapatam, and Sharpe who must have stripped the ruler's body of its diamonds and emeralds and sapphires and rubies, and Sharpe, Hakeswill reckoned, was still hiding those stones. From far away, dulled by the heat of the day, came the sound of artillery firing. Gawilghur, Hakeswill thought, where Sharpe should not reach, on account of Sharpe being Hakeswill's business, and no one else's. I will be rich, the Sergeant promised himself, I will be rich.

Colonel William Dodd stood on the southernmost battlements of Gawilghur with his back against the parapet so that he was staring down into a palace courtyard where Beny Singh had erected a striped pavilion. Small silver bells that tinkled prettily in the small breeze were hung from the pavilion's fringed hem, while under the canopy a group of musicians played the strange, long-necked stringed instruments which made a music that, to Dodd's ears, sounded like the slow strangulation of cats. Beny Singh and a dozen pretty creatures in saris were playing some form of Blind Man's Buff, and their laughter rose to the ramparts, making Dodd scowl, though if truth were told he was inordinately jealous of Beny Singh. The man was plump, short and timid, yet he seemed to work some magical spell on the ladies, while Dodd, who was tall, hard and scarred to prove his bravery, had to make do with a whore.

Damn the Killadar. Dodd turned sharply away and stared over the heat-baked plain. Beneath him, and just far enough to the east to be out of range of Gawilghur's largest guns, the edge of the British encampment showed. From this height the rows of dull white tents looked like speckles. To the south, still a long way off, Dodd could see the enemy baggage train trudging towards its new encampment. It was odd, he thought, that they should make the oxen carry their burdens through the hottest part of the day. Usually the baggage marched just after midnight and camped not long after dawn, but today the great herd was stirring the dust into the broiling afternoon air and it looked, Dodd thought, like a migrating tribe. There were thousands of oxen in the army's train, all loaded with round shot, powder, tools, salt beef, arrack, horseshoes, bandages, flints, muskets, spices, rice, and with them came the merchants' beasts and the merchants' families, and the ox herdsmen had their own families and they all needed more beasts to carry their tents, clothes and food. A dozen elephants plodded in the herd's centre, while a score of dromedaries swayed elegantly behind the elephants. Mysore cavalry guarded the great caravan, while beyond the mounted picquets half-naked grass-cutters spread into the fields to collect fodder that they stuffed into nets and loaded onto yet more oxen.

Dodd glanced at the sentries who guarded the southern stretch of Gawilghur's walls and he saw the awe on their faces as they watched the enormous herd approach. The dust from the hooves rose to smear the southern skyline like a vast sea fog. 'They're only oxen!' Dodd growled to the men. 'Only oxen! Oxen don't fire guns. Oxen don't climb walls.' None of them understood him, but they grinned dutifully.

Dodd walked eastwards. After a while the wall ended, giving way to the bare lip of a precipice. There was no need for walls around much of the perimeters of Gawilghur's twin forts, for nature had provided the great cliffs that were higher than any rampart a man could make, but Dodd, as he walked to the bluff's edge, noted places here and there where an agile man could, with the help of a rope, scramble down the rock face. A few men deserted Gawilghur's garrison every day, and Dodd did not doubt that this was how they escaped, but he did not understand why they should want to go. The fort was impregnable! Why would a man not wish to stay with the victors?

He reached a stretch of wall at the fort's southeastern corner and there, high up on a gun platform, he opened his telescope and stared down into the foothills. He searched for a long time, his glass skittering over trees, shrubs and patches of dry grass, but at last he saw a group of men standing beside a narrow path. Some of the men were in red coats and one was in blue.

'What are you watching, Colonel?' Prince Manu Bappoo had seen Dodd on the rampart and had climbed to join him.

'British,' Dodd said, without taking his eye from the telescope. 'They're surveying a route up to the plateau.'

Bappoo shaded his eyes and stared down, but without a telescope he could not see the group of men. 'It will take them months to build a road up to the hills.'

'It'll take them two weeks,' Dodd said flatly. 'Less. You don't know how their engineers work, sahib, but I do. They'll use powder to break through obstacles and a thousand axemen to widen the tracks. They'll start their work tomorrow and in a fortnight they'll be running guns up to the hills.' Dodd collapsed the telescope. 'Let me go down and break the bastards,' he demanded.

'No,' Bappoo said. He had already had this argument with Dodd who wanted to take his Cobras down into the foothills and there harass the road-makers. Dodd did not want a stand-up fight, a battle of musket line against musket line, but instead wanted to raid, ambush and scare the enemy. He wanted to slow the British work, to dishearten the sappers and, by such delaying tactics, force Wellesley to send forage parties far into the countryside where they would be prey to the Mahratta horsemen who still roamed the Deccan Plain.

Bappoo knew Dodd was right, and that the British road could be slowed by a campaign of harassment, but he feared to let the white-coated Cobras leave the fortress. The garrison was already nervous, awed by the victories of Wellesley's small army, and if they saw the Cobras march out of the fort then many would think they were being abandoned and the trickle of deserters would become a flood.

'We have to slow them!' Dodd snarled.

'We shall,' Bappoo said. 'I shall send *silladars*, Colonel, and reward them for every weapon they bring back to the fort. But you will stay here, and help prepare the defences.' He spoke firmly, showing that the subject was beyond discussion, then offered Dodd a gap-toothed smile and gestured towards the palace at the centre of the Inner Fort. 'Come, Colonel, I want to show you something.'

The two men walked through the small houses that surrounded the palace, past an Arab sentry who protected the palace precincts, then through some flowering trees where monkeys crouched. Dodd could hear the tinkle of the bells where Beny Singh was playing with his women, but that sound faded as the path twisted deeper into the trees. The path ended at a rock face that was pierced by an arched wooden door. Dodd looked up while Bappoo unlocked the door and saw that the great rock slab formed the palace foundations and, when Bappoo thrust back the creaking door, he understood that it led into the palace cellars.

A lantern stood on a shelf just inside the door and there was a pause while Bappoo lit its wick. 'Come,' Bappoo said, and led Dodd into the marvellous coolness of the huge low cellar. 'It is rumoured,' Bappoo said, 'that we store the treasures of Berar in here, and in one sense it is true, but they are not the treasures that men usually dream of.' He stopped by a row of barrels and casually knocked off their lids, revealing that the tubs were filled with copper coins. 'No gold or silver,' Bappoo said, 'but money all the same. Money to hire new mercenaries, to buy new weapons and to make a new army.' Bappoo trickled a stream of the newly minted coins through his fingers. 'We have been lax in paying our men,' he confessed. 'My brother, for all his virtues, is not generous with his treasury.'

Dodd grunted. He was not sure what virtues the Rajah of Berar did possess. Certainly not valour, nor generosity, but the Rajah was fortunate in his brother, for Bappoo was loyal and evidently determined to make up for the Rajah's shortcomings.

'Gold and silver,' Dodd said, 'would buy better arms and more men.'

'My brother will not give me gold or silver, only copper. And we must work with what we have, not with what we dream of.' Bappoo put the lids back onto the barrels, then edged between them to where rack after rack of muskets stood. 'These, Colonel,' he said, 'are the weapons for that new army.'

There were thousands of muskets, all brand new, and all equipped with bayonets and cartridge boxes. Some of the guns were locally made copies of French muskets, but several hundred looked to Dodd to be of British make. He lifted one from the racks and saw the Tower mark on its lock. 'How did you get these?' he asked, surprised.

Bappoo shrugged. 'We have agents in the British camp. They arrange it. We meet some of their supply convoys well to the south and pay for their contents. It seems there are traitors in the British army who would rather make money than seek victory.'

'You buy guns with copper?' Dodd asked scathingly. He could not imagine any man selling a Tower musket for a handful of copper.

'No,' Bappoo confessed. 'To buy the weapons and the cartridges we need gold, so I use my own. My brother, I trust, will repay me one day.'

Dodd frowned at the hawk-faced Bappoo. 'You're using your money to keep your brother on the throne?' he asked and, though he waited for an answer, none came. Dodd shook his head, implying that

Bappoo's nobility was beyond understanding, then he cocked and fired the unloaded musket. The spark of the flint flashed a sparkle of red light against the stone ceiling. 'A musket in its rack kills no one,' he said.

'True. But as yet we don't have the men to carry these muskets. But we will, Colonel. Once we have defeated the British the other kingdoms will join us.' That, Dodd reflected, was true enough. Scindia, Dodd's erstwhile employer, was suing for peace, while Holkar, the most formidable of the Mahratta monarchs, was staying aloof from the contest, but if Bappoo did win his victory, those chieftains would be eager to share future spoils. 'And not just the other kingdoms,' Bappoo went on, 'but warriors from all India will come to our banner. I intend to raise a *compoo* armed with the best weapons and trained to the very highest standard. Many, I suspect, will be sepoys from Wellesley's defeated army and they will need a new master when he is dead. I thought perhaps you would lead them?'

Dodd returned the musket to its rack. 'You'll not pay me with copper, Bappoo.'

Bappoo smiled. 'You will pay me with victory, Colonel, and I shall reward you with gold.'

Dodd saw some unfamiliar weapons farther down the rack. He lifted one and saw it was a hunting rifle. The lock was British, but the filigree decoration on the stock and barrel was Indian. 'You're buying rifles?' he asked.

'No better weapon for skirmishing,' Bappoo said.

'Maybe,' Dodd allowed grudgingly. The rifle was accurate, but slow to load.

'A small group of men with rifles,' Bappoo said, 'backed up by muskets, could be formidable.'

'Maybe,' Dodd said again, then, instead of putting the rifle back onto the rack, he slung it on his shoulder. 'I'd like to try it,' he explained. 'You have ammunition?'

Bappoo gestured across the cellar, and Dodd went and scooped up some cartridges. 'If you've got the cash,' he called back, 'why not raise your new army now. Bring it to Gawilghur.'

'There's no time,' Bappoo said, 'and besides, no one will join us now. They think the British are beating us. So if we are to make our new army, Colonel, then we must first win a victory that will ring through India, and that is what we shall do here at Gawilghur.' He spoke very confidently, for Bappoo, like Dodd, believed Gawilghur to be unassailable. He led the Englishman back to the entrance, blew out the lantern and carefully locked the armoury door.

The two men climbed the slope beside the palace, passing a line of servants who carried drinks and sweetmeats to where Beny Singh whiled away the afternoon. As ever, when Dodd thought of the Killadar, he felt a surge of anger. Beny Singh should have been organizing the fortress's defences, but instead he frittered away his days with women and liquor. Bappoo must have divined Dodd's thoughts, for he grimaced. 'My brother likes Beny Singh. They amuse each other.'

'Do they amuse you?' Dodd asked.

Bappoo paused at the northern side of the palace and there he gazed across the ravine to the Outer Fort which was garrisoned by his Lions of Allah. 'I swore an oath to my brother,' he answered, 'and I am a man who keeps my oaths.'

'There must be those,' Dodd said carefully, 'who would rather see you as Rajah?'

'Of course,' Bappoo answered equably, 'but such men are my brother's enemies, and my oath was to defend my brother against all his enemies.' He shrugged. 'We must be content, Colonel, with what fate grants us. It has granted me the task of fighting my brother's wars, and I shall do that to the best of my ability.' He pointed to the deep ravine that lay between the Outer and the Inner Forts. 'And there, Colonel, I shall win a victory that will make my brother the greatest ruler of all India. The British cannot stop us. Even if they make their road, even if they haul their guns up to the hills, even if they make a breach in our walls and even if they capture the Outer Fort, they must still cross that ravine, and they cannot do it. No one can do it.' Bappoo stared at the steep gorge as if he could already see its rocks soaked in enemy blood. 'Who rules that ravine, Colonel, rules India, and when we have our victory then we shall unlock the cellar and raise an army that will drive the redcoats not just from Berar, but from Hyderabad, from Mysore and from Madras. I shall make my brother Emperor of all southern India, and you and I, Colonel, shall be his warlords.' Bappoo turned to gaze into the dust-smeared immensity of the southern sky. 'It will all belong to my brother,' he said softly, 'but it will begin here. At Gawilghur.'

And here, Dodd suddenly thought, it would end for Bappoo. No man who was willing to endure a feeble wretch like Beny Singh, or protect a cowardly libertine like the Rajah, deserved to be a warlord of all India. No, Dodd thought, he would win his own victory here, and then he would strike against Bappoo and against Beny Singh, and he would raise his own army and use it to strike terror into the rich southern kingdoms. Other Europeans had done it. Benoît de Boigne had made himself richer than the kings of all Christendom, while George Thomas, an illiterate Irish sailor, had risen to rule a princedom for his widowed mistress. Dodd saw himself as a new Prester John. He would make a kingdom from the rotting scraps of India, and he would rule from a new palace in Gawilghur that would be like no other in the world. He would have roofs of gold, walls of white marble and garden paths made from pearls, and men from all India would come to pay him homage. He would be Lord of Gawilghur, Dodd thought, and smiled. Not bad for a miller's son from Suffolk, but Gawilghur was a place to stir dreams for it lifted men's thoughts into the heavens, and Dodd knew that India, above all the lands on God's earth, was a place where dreams could come true. Here a man was either made rich beyond all desire, or else became nothing.

And Dodd would not be nothing. He would be Lord of Gawilghur and the terror of India.

Once the redcoats were defeated.

'Is this the best you could manage, Sharpe?' Torrance enquired, looking about the main room of the commandeered house.

'No, sir,' Sharpe said. 'There was a lovely house just up the road. Big shady courtyard, couple of pools, a fountain and a gaggle of dancing girls, but I thought you might prefer the view from these windows.'

'Sarcasm ill becomes an ensign,' Torrance said, dropping his saddle-bags on the earthen floor. 'Indeed, very little becomes ensigns, Sharpe, except a humble devotion to serving their betters. I suppose the house will have to suffice. Who is that?' He shuddered as he stared at the woman whose house he was occupying.

'She lives here, sir.'

'Not now, she doesn't. Get rid of the black bitch, and her foul children. Brick!'

Clare Wall came in from the sunlight, carrying a sack. 'Sir?'

'I'm hungry, Brick. Find the kitchen. We made a late start, Sharpe,' Torrance explained, 'and missed dinner.'

'I imagine that's why the General wants to see you, sir,' Sharpe said. 'Not because you missed dinner, but because the supplies weren't here on time.'

Torrance stared at Sharpe in horror. 'Wellesley wants to see me?'

'Six o'clock, sir, at his tent.'

'Oh, Christ!' Torrance threw his cocked hat across the room. 'Just because the supplies were a little late?'

'Twelve hours late, sir.'

Torrance glared at Sharpe, then fished a watch from his fob. 'It's half past five already! God help us! Can't you brush that coat, Sharpe?'

'He don't want to see me, sir. Just you.'

'Well, he's bloody well going to see both of us. Clean uniform, Sharpe, hair brushed, paws washed, face scrubbed, Sunday best.' Torrance frowned suddenly. 'Why didn't you tell me you saved Wellesley's life?'

'Is that what I did, sir?'

'I mean, good God, man, he must be grateful to you?' Torrance asked. Sharpe just shrugged. 'You saved his life,' Torrance insisted, 'and that means he's in your debt, and you must use the advantage. Tell him we don't have enough men to run the supply train properly. Put in a good word for me, Sharpe, and I'll repay the favour. Brick! Forget the food! I need a clean stock, boots polished, hat brushed. And give my dress coat a pressing!'

Sergeant Hakeswill edged through the door. 'Your 'ammock, sir,' he said to Torrance, then saw Sharpe and a slow grin spread across his face. 'Look who it isn't. Sharpie!'

Torrance wheeled on the Sergeant. 'Mister Sharpe is an officer, Hakeswill! In this unit we do observe the proprieties!'

'Quite forgot myself, sir,' Hakeswill said, his face twitching, 'on account of being reunited with an old comrade. Mister Sharpe, ever so pleased to see you, sir.'

'Lying bastard,' Sharpe said.

'Ain't officers supposed to observe the properties, sir?' Hakeswill demanded of Torrance, but the Captain had gone in search of his native servant who had charge of the luggage. Hakeswill looked back to Sharpe. 'Fated to be with you, Sharpie.'

'You stay out of my light, Obadiah,' Sharpe said, 'or I'll slit your throat.'

'I can't be killed, Sharpie, can't be killed!' Hakeswill's face wrenched itself in a series of twitches. 'It says so in the scriptures.' He looked Sharpe up and down, then shook his head ruefully. 'I've seen better things dangling off the tails of sheep, I have. You ain't an officer, Sharpie, you're a bleeding disgrace.'

Torrance backed into the house, shouting at his servant to drape the windows with muslin, then turned and hurried to the kitchen to harry Clare. He tripped over Sharpe's pack and swore. 'Whose is this?'

'Mine,' Sharpe said.

'You're not thinking of billeting yourself here, are you, Sharpe?'

'Good as anywhere, sir.'

'I like my privacy, Sharpe. Find somewhere else.' Torrance suddenly remembered he was speaking to a man who might have influence with Wellesley. 'If you'd be so kind, Sharpe. I just can't abide being crowded. An affliction, I know, but there it is. I need solitude, it's my nature. Brick! Did I tell you to brush my hat? And the plume needs a combing.'

Sharpe picked up his pack and walked out to the small garden where Ahmed was sharpening his new *tulwar*. Clare Wall followed him into the sunlight, muttered something under her breath, then sat and started to polish one of Torrance's boots. 'Why the hell do you stay with him?' Sharpe asked.

She paused to look at Sharpe. She had oddly hooded eyes that gave her face an air of delicate mystery. 'What choice do I have?' she asked, resuming her polishing.

Sharpe sat beside her, picked up the other boot and rubbed it with blackball. 'So what's he going to do if you bugger off?'

She shrugged. 'I owe him money.'

'Like hell. How can you owe him money?'

'He brought my husband and me here,' she said, 'paid our passage from England. We agreed to stay three years. Then Charlie died.' She paused again, her eyes suddenly gleaming, then sniffed and began to polish the boot obsessively.

Sharpe looked at her. She had dark eyes, curling black hair and a long upper lip. If she was not so tired and miserable, he thought, she would be a very pretty woman. 'How old are you, love?'

She gave him a sceptical glance. 'Who's your woman in Seringapatam, then?'

'She's a Frenchie,' Sharpe said. 'A widow, like you.'

'Officer's widow?' Clare asked. Sharpe nodded. 'And you're to marry her?' Clare asked.

'Nothing like that,' Sharpe said.

'Like what, then?' she asked.

'I don't know, really.' Sharpe said. He spat on the boot's flank and rubbed the spittle into the bootblack.

'But you like her?' Clare asked, picking the dirt from the boot's spur. She seemed embarrassed to have posed the question, for she hurried on. 'I'm nineteen,' she said, 'but nearly twenty.'

'Then you're old enough to see a lawyer,' Sharpe said. 'You ain't indentured to the Captain. You have to sign papers, don't you? Or make your mark on a paper. That's how it was done in the foundling home where they dumped me. Wanted to make me into a chimney sweep, they did! Bloody hell! But if you didn't sign indenture papers, you should talk to a lawyer.'

Clare paused, staring at a sad tree in the courtyard's centre that was dying from the drought. 'I wanted to get married a year back,' she said softly, 'and that's what Tom told me. He were called Tom, see? A cavalryman, he was. Only a youngster.'

'What happened?'

'Fever,' she said bleakly. 'But it wouldn't have worked anyway, because Torrance wouldn't ever let me marry.' She began polishing the boot again. 'He said he'd see me dead first.' She shook her head. 'But what's the point in seeing a lawyer? You think a lawyer would talk to me? They like money, lawyers do, and do you know a lawyer in India that ain't in the Company's pocket? Mind you' – she glanced towards the house to make sure she was not being overheard – 'he hasn't got any money either. He gets an allowance from his uncle and his Company pay and he gambles it all away, but he always seems to find more.' She paused. 'And what would I do if I walked away?' She left the question hanging in the warm air, then shook her head. 'I'm miles from bleeding home. I don't know. He was good to me at first. I liked him! I didn't know him then, you see.' She half smiled. 'Funny, isn't it? You think because someone's a gentleman and the son of a clergyman that they have to be kind? But he ain't.' She vigorously brushed the boot's tassel. 'And he's been worse since he met that Hakeswill. I do hate him.' She sighed. 'Just fourteen months to go,' she said wearily, 'and then I'll have paid the debt.'

'Hell, no,' Sharpe said. 'Walk away from the bugger.'

She picked up Torrance's hat and began brushing it. 'I don't have family,' she said, 'so where would I go?'

'You're an orphan?'

She nodded. 'I got work as a house girl in Torrance's uncle's house. That's where I met Charlie. He were a footman. Then Mr Henry, that's his uncle, see, said we should join the Captain's household. Charlie became Captain Torrance's valet. That was a step up. And the money was better, only we weren't paid, not once we were in Madras. He said we had to pay our passage.'

'What the devil are you doing, Sharpe?' Torrance had come into the garden. 'You're not supposed to clean boots! You're an officer!'

Sharpe tossed the boot at Torrance. 'I keep forgetting, sir.'

'If you must clean boots, Sharpe, start with your own. Good God, man! You look like a tinker!'

'The General's seen me looking worse,' Sharpe said. 'Besides, he never did care what men looked like, sir, so long as they do their job properly.'

'I do mine properly!' Torrance bridled at the implication. 'I just need more staff. You tell him that, Sharpe, you tell him! Give me that hat, Brick! We're late.'

In fact Torrance arrived early at the General's tent and had to kick his heels in the evening sunshine. 'What exactly did the General say when he summoned me?' he asked Sharpe.

'He sent an aide, sir. Captain Campbell. Wanted to know where the supplies were.'

'You told him they were coming?'

'Told him the truth, sir.'

'Which was?'

'That I didn't bloody well know where they were.'

'Oh, Christ! Thank you, Sharpe, thank you very much.' Torrance twitched at his sash, making the silk fall more elegantly. 'Do you know what loyalty is?'

Before Sharpe could answer the tent flaps were pushed aside and Captain Campbell ducked out into the sunlight. 'Wasn't expecting you, Sharpe!' he said genially, holding out his hand.

Sharpe shook hands. 'How are you, sir?'

'Busy,' Campbell said. 'You don't have to go in if you don't want.'

'He does,' Torrance said.

Sharpe shrugged. 'Might as well,' he said, then ducked into the tent's yellow light as Campbell pulled back the flap.

The General was in his shirtsleeves, sitting behind a table that was covered with Major Blackiston's sketches of the land bridge to Gawilghur. Blackiston was beside him, travel-stained and tired, while an irascible-looking major of the Royal Engineers stood two paces behind the table. If the General was surprised to see Sharpe he showed no sign of it, but instead looked back to the drawings. 'How wide is the approach?' he asked.

'At its narrowest, sir, about fifty feet.' Blackiston tapped one of the sketches. 'It's wide enough for most of the approach, two or three hundred yards, but just here there's a tank and it squeezes the path cruelly. A ravine to the left, a tank to the right.'

'Fall to your death on one side,' the General said, 'and drown on the other. And doubtless the fifty feet between is covered by their guns?'

'Smothered, sir. Must be twenty heavy cannon looking down the throat of the approach, and God knows how much smaller metal. Plenty.'

Wellesley removed the inkwells that had been serving as weights so that the drawings rolled up with a snap. 'Not much choice, though, is there?' he asked.

'None, sir.'

Wellesley looked up suddenly, his eyes seeming very blue in the tent's half light. 'The supply train is twelve hours late, Captain. Why?' He spoke quietly, but even Sharpe felt a shiver go through him.

Torrance, his cocked hat held beneath his left arm, was sweating. 'I . . . I . . .' he said, too nervous to speak properly, but then he took a deep breath. 'I was ill, sir, and unable to supervise properly, and my clerk failed to issue the chitties. It was a most regrettable occurrence, sir, and I can assure you it will not happen again.'

The General stared at Torrance in silence for a few seconds. 'Colonel Wallace gave you Ensign Sharpe as an assistant? Did Sharpe also fail to obey your orders?'

'I had sent Mister Sharpe ahead, sir,' Torrance said. The sweat was now pouring down his face and dripping from his chin.

'So why did the clerk fail in his duties?'

'Treachery, sir,' Torrance said.

The answer surprised Wellesley, as it was meant to. He tapped his pencil on the table's edge. 'Treachery?' he asked in a low voice.

'It seemed the clerk was in league with a merchant, sir, and had been selling him supplies. And this morning, sir, when he should have been issuing the chitties, he was employed on his own business.'

'And you were too ill to detect his treachery?'

'Yes, sir,' Torrance said almost pleadingly. 'At first, sir, yes, sir.'

Wellesley gazed at Torrance for a few silent seconds, and the Captain had the uncomfortable feeling that the blue eyes saw right into his soul. 'So where is this treacherous clerk now, Captain?' Wellesley asked at last.

'We hanged him, sir,' Torrance said and Sharpe, who had not heard of Dilip's death, stared at him in astonishment.

The General slapped the table, making Torrance jump in alarm. 'You seem very fond of hanging, Captain Torrance?'

'A necessary remedy for theft, sir, as you have made plain.'

'I, sir? I?' The General's voice, when he became angry, did not become louder, but more precise and, therefore, more chilling. 'The general order mandating summary death by hanging for thievery, Captain, applies to men in uniform. King's and Company men only. It does not apply to civilians. Does the dead man have family?'

'No, sir,' Torrance said. He did not really know the answer, but decided it was better to say no than to prevaricate.

'If he does, Captain,' Wellesley said softly, 'and if they complain, then I shall have no choice but to put you on trial, and depend upon it, sir, that trial will be in the civilian courts.'

'I apologize, sir,' Torrance said stiffly, 'for my over-zealousness.'

The General stayed silent for a few seconds. 'Supplies were missing,' he said after a while.

'Yes, sir,' Torrance agreed weakly.

'Yet you never reported the thefts?' Wellesley said.

'I did not believe you wished to be troubled by every mishap, sir,' Torrance said.

'Mishap!' Wellesley snapped. 'Muskets are stolen, and you call that a mishap? Such mishaps, Captain Torrance, lose wars. In future you will inform my staff when such depredations are made.' He stared at

Torrance for a few seconds, then looked at Sharpe. 'Colonel Huddlestone tells me it was you, Sharpe, who discovered the missing supplies?'

'All but the muskets, sir. They're still missing.'

'How did you know where to look?'

'Captain Torrance's clerk told me where to buy supplies, sir.' Sharpe shrugged. 'I guessed they were the missing items, sir.'

Wellesley grunted. Sharpe's answer appeared to confirm Torrance's accusations, and the Captain gave Sharpe a grateful glance. Wellesley saw the glance and rapped the table, demanding Torrance's attention. 'It is a pity, Captain, that we could not have questioned the merchant before you so summarily executed him. May I presume you did interrogate the clerk?'

'My sergeant did, sir, and the wretch confessed to having sold items to Naig.' Torrance blushed as he told the lie, but it was so hot in the tent and he was sweating so heavily that the blush went unnoticed.

'Your sergeant?' Wellesley asked. 'You mean your havildar?'

'Sergeant, sir,' Torrance said. 'I inherited him from Captain Mackay, sir. Sergeant Hakeswill.'

'Hakeswill!' the General said in astonishment. 'What's he still doing here? He should be back with his regiment!'

'He stayed on, sir,' Torrance said, 'with two of his men. His other two died, sir, fever. And he had no alternative orders, sir, and he was too useful to let go, sir.'

'Useful!' Wellesley said. He had been the commanding officer of the 33rd, Hakeswill's regiment, and he knew the Sergeant well. He shook his head. 'If you find him useful, Torrance, then he can stay till Gawilghur's fallen. But then he returns to his regiment. You'll make sure of that, Campbell?'

'Yes, sir,' the aide said. 'But I believe some of the 33rd are on their way here, sir, so the Sergeant can return with them.'

'The 33rd coming here?' Wellesley asked in surprise. 'I ordered no such thing.'

'Just a company, sir,' Campbell explained. 'I believe headquarters detailed them to escort a convoy.'

'Doubtless we can make use of them,' the General said grudgingly. 'Is it awkward for you, Sharpe? Serving with Hakeswill?' Officers who were promoted from the ranks were never expected to serve with their old regiments, and Wellesley was plainly wondering whether Sharpe found his old comrades an embarrassment. 'I daresay you'll get by,' the General said, not waiting for an answer. 'You usually do. Wallace tells me he's recommended you for the Rifles?'

'Yes, sir.'

'That could suit you, Sharpe. Suit you very well. In the meantime, the more you learn about supplies, the better.' The cold eyes looked back to Torrance, though it appeared the General was still talking to Sharpe. 'There is a misapprehension in this army that supplies are of small importance, whereas wars are won by efficient supply, more than they are won by acts of gallantry. Which is why I want no more delays.'

'There will be none, sir,' Torrance said hastily.

'And if there are,' Wellesley said, 'there will be a court martial. You may depend upon that, Captain. Major Elliott?' The General spoke to the engineer who until now had been a spectator of Torrance's discomfiture. 'Tell me what you need to build our road, Major.'

'A hundred bullocks,' Elliott said sourly, 'and none of your spavined beasts, Torrance. I want a hundred prime Mysore oxen to carry timber and road stone. I'll need rice every day for a half-battalion of sepoys and an equivalent number of pioneers.'

'Of course, sir,' Torrance said.

'And I'll take him' – Elliott stabbed a finger at Sharpe – 'because I need someone in charge of the bullocks who knows what he's doing.'

Torrance opened his mouth to protest, then sensibly shut it. Wellesley glanced at Sharpe. 'You'll attach yourself to Major Elliott, Sharpe. Be with him at dawn tomorrow, with the bullocks, and you, Captain Torrance, will ensure the daily supplies go up the road every dawn. And I want no more summary hangings.'

'Of course not, sir.' Torrance, relieved to be let off so lightly, ducked his head in an awkward bow.

'Good day to you both,' the General said sourly, then watched as the two officers left the tent. He rubbed his eyes and stifled a yawn. 'How long to drive the road, Elliott?'

'Two weeks?' the Major suggested.

'You've got one week. One week!' The General forestalled Elliott's protest. 'Good day to you, Elliott.'

The engineer grumbled as he ducked out into the fading light. Wellesley grimaced. 'Is Torrance to be trusted?' he asked.

'Comes from a good family, sir,' Blackiston said.

'So did Nero, as I recall,' Wellesley retorted. 'But at least Torrance has got Sharpe, and even if Sharpe won't make a good officer, he's got the makings of a decent sergeant. He did well to find those supplies.'

'Very well, sir,' Campbell said warmly.

Wellesley leaned back in his chair. A flicker of distaste showed on his face as he recalled the terrible moment when he had been unhorsed at Assaye. He did not remember much of the incident for he had been dazed, but he did recall watching Sharpe kill with a savagery that had astonished him. He disliked being beholden to such a man, but the General knew he would not be alive if Sharpe had not risked his own life. 'I should never have given Sharpe a commission,' he said ruefully. 'A man like that would have been quite content with a fiscal reward. A fungible reward. That's what our men want, Campbell, something that can be turned into rum or arrack.'

'He appears to be a sober man, sir,' Campbell said.

'Probably because he can't afford the drink! Officers' messes are damned expensive places, Campbell, as you well know. I reward Sharpe by plunging him into debt, eh? And God knows if the Rifles are any cheaper. I can't imagine they will be. He needs something fungible, Campbell, something fungible.' Wellesley turned and rummaged in the saddlebags that were piled behind his chair. He brought out the new telescope with the shallow eyepiece that had been a gift from the merchants of Madras. 'Find a goldsmith in the camp followers, Campbell, and see if the fellow can replace that brass plate.'

'With what, sir?'

Nothing too flowery, the General thought, because the glass was only going to be pawned to pay mess bills or buy gin. 'In gratitude, AW,' he said, 'and add the date of Assaye. Then give it to Sharpe with my compliments.'

'It's very generous of you, sir,' Campbell said, taking the glass, 'but perhaps it would be better if you presented it to him?'

'Maybe, maybe. Blackiston! Where do we site guns?' The General unrolled the sketches. 'Candles,' he ordered, for the light was fading fast.

The shadows stretched and joined and turned to night around the British camp. Candles were lit, lanterns hung from ridge-poles and fires fed with bullock dung. The picquets stared at shadows in the darkness, but some, lifting their gaze, saw that high above them the tops of the cliffs were still in daylight and there, like the home of the gods, the walls of a fortress showed deadly black where Gawilghur waited their coming.

CHAPTER 5

The first part of the road was easy enough to build, for the existing track wound up the gentler slopes of the foothills, but even on the first day Major Elliott was filled with gloom. 'Can't do it in a week!' the engineer grumbled. 'Man's mad! Expects miracles. Jacob's ladder, that's what he wants.' He cast a morbid eye over Sharpe's bullocks, all of them prime Mysore beasts with brightly painted horns from which tassels and small bells hung. 'Never did like working with oxen,' Elliott complained. 'Bring any elephants?'

'I can ask for them, sir.'

'Nothing like an elephant. Right, Sharpe, load the beasts with small stones and keep following the track till you catch up with me. Got that?' Elliott hauled himself onto his horse and settled his feet in the stirrups. 'Bloody miracles, that's what he wants,' the Major growled, then spurred onto the track.

'Elliott!' Major Simons, who commanded the half-battalion of sepoys who guarded the pioneers building the road, called in alarm. 'I haven't reconnoitred beyond the small hillock! The one with the two trees.'

'Can't wait for your fellows to wake up, Simons. Got a road to build in a week. Can't be done, of course, but we must look willing. Pinckney! I need a havildar and some stout fellows to carry pegs. Tell 'em to follow me.'

Captain Pinckney, the officer in charge of the East India Company pioneers, spat onto the verge. 'Waste of bloody time.'

'What is?' Sharpe asked.

'Pegging out the route! We follow the footpath, of course. Bloody natives have been scurrying up and down these hills for centuries.' He turned and shouted at a havildar to organize a party to follow Elliott up the hill, then set the rest of his men to loading the oxen's panniers with small stones.

The road made good progress, despite Elliott's misgivings, and three days after they had begun the pioneers cleared a space among the trees to establish a makeshift artillery park where the siege guns could wait while the rest of the road was forged. Sharpe was busy and, because of that, happy. He liked Simons and Pinckney, and even Elliott proved affable. The Major had taken Wellesley's demands that the road be made in a week as a challenge, and he pressed the pioneers hard.

The enemy seemed to be asleep. Elliott would ride far ahead to reconnoitre the route and never once saw a Mahratta. 'Stupid fools,' Elliott said one night beside the fire, 'they could hold us here for months!'

'You still shouldn't ride so far ahead of my picquets,' Simons reproved the Major.

'Stop fussing, man,' Elliott said, and next morning, as usual, he rode out in front to survey the day's work.

Sharpe was again bringing stones up the road that morning. He was walking at the head of his ox train on the wooded stretch above the newly made artillery park. The day's heat was growing and there was little wind in the thick woods of teak and cork trees that covered the low hills. Groups of pioneers felled trees where they might obstruct a gun carriage's progress, and here and there Sharpe saw a white-washed peg showing where Elliott had marked the track. Shots sounded ahead, but Sharpe took no notice. The upland valleys had become a favourite hunting ground for the *shikarees* who used nets, snares and ancient matchlocks to kill hares, wild pigs, deer, quail and partridge that they sold to the officers, and Sharpe assumed a party of the hunters was close to the track, but after a few seconds the firing intensified. The musketry was muffled by the thick leaves, but for a moment the sound was constant, almost at battle pitch, before, as suddenly as it had erupted, it stopped.

His bullock drivers had halted, made nervous by the firing. 'Come on!' Sharpe encouraged them. None of them spoke English, and Sharpe had no idea which language they did speak, but they were good-natured men, eager to please, and they prodded their heavily laden bullocks onwards. Ahmed had unslung his musket and was peering ahead. He suddenly raised the gun to his shoulder, and Sharpe pushed it down before the boy could pull the trigger. 'They're ours,' he told the lad. 'Sepoys.'

A dozen sepoys hurried back through the trees. Major Simons was with them and, as they came closer, Sharpe saw the men were carrying a makeshift stretcher made from tree branches and jackets. 'It's Elliott.' Simons paused by Sharpe as his men hurried ahead. 'Bloody fool got a chest wound. He won't live. Stupid man was too far forward. I told him not to get ahead of the picquets.' Simons took a ragged red handkerchief from his sleeve and wiped the sweat from his face. 'One less engineer.' Sharpe peered at Elliott who was blessedly unconscious. His face had gone pale, and pinkish blood was bubbling at his lips with every laboured breath. 'He won't last the day,' Simons said brutally, 'but I suppose we should get him back to the surgeons.'

'Where are the enemy?' Sharpe asked.

'They ran,' Simons said. 'Half a dozen of the bastards were waiting in ambush. They shot Elliott, took his weapons, but ran off when they saw us.'

Three *shikarees* died that afternoon, ambushed in the high woods, and that night, when the road-builders camped in one of the grassy upland valleys, some shots were fired from a neighbouring wood. The bullets hissed overhead, but none found a target. The picquets blazed back until a havildar shouted at them to hold their fire. Captain Pinckney shook his head. 'I thought it was too good to last,' he said gloomily. 'It'll be slow work now.' He poked the fire around which a half-dozen officers were sitting.

Major Simons grinned. 'If I was the enemy,' he said, 'I'd attack Mister Sharpe's oxen instead of attacking engineers. If they cut our supply line they'd do some real damage.'

'There's no point in shooting engineers,' Pinckney agreed. 'We don't need Royal Engineers anyway. We've been making roads for years. The fellows in the blue coats just get in the way. Mind you, they'll still send us another.'

'If there are any left,' Sharpe said. The campaign had been fatal for the engineers. Two had died blowing up the enemy guns at Assaye, another three were fevered and now Elliott was either dying or already dead.

'They'll find one,' Pinckney grumbled. 'If there's something the

King's army doesn't need then you can be sure they've got a healthy supply of it.'

'The Company army's better?' Sharpe asked.

'It is,' Major Simons said. 'We work for a sterner master than you, Sharpe. It's called book-keeping. You fight for victories, we fight for profits. Leadenhall Street won't pay for fancy engineers in blue coats, not when they can hire plain men like us at half the cost.'

'They could afford me,' Sharpe said. 'Cheap as they come, I am.'

Next morning Simons threw a strong picquet line ahead of the work parties, but no Mahrattas opposed the pioneers who were now widening the track where it twisted up a bare and steep slope that was littered with rocks. The track was ancient, worn into the hills by generations of travellers, but it had never been used by wagons, let alone by heavy guns. Merchants who wanted to carry their goods up the escarpment had used the road leading directly to the fortress's Southern Gate, while this track, which looped miles to the east of Gawilghur, was little more than a series of paths connecting the upland valleys where small farms had been hacked from the jungle. It was supposed to be tiger country, but Sharpe saw none of the beasts. At dawn he had returned to Deogaum to collect rice for the sepoys, and then spent the next four hours climbing back to where the pioneers were working. He was nervous at first, both of tigers and of an enemy ambush, but the worst he suffered was a series of drenching rainstorms that swept up the mountains.

The rain stopped when he reached the working parties who were driving the road through a small ridge. Pinckney was setting a charge of gunpowder that would loosen the rock and let him cut out a mile of looping track. His servant brought a mug of tea that Sharpe drank sitting on a rock. He stared southwards, watching the veils of grey rain sweep across the plain.

'Did Wellesley say anything about sending a new engineer?' Major Simons asked him.

'I just collected the rice, sir,' Sharpe said. 'I didn't see the General.'

'I thought you were supposed to be a friend of his?' Simons observed sourly.

'Everyone thinks that,' Sharpe said, 'except him and me.'

'But you saved his life?'

Sharpe shrugged. 'I reckon so. Either that or stopped him getting captured.'

'And killed a few men doing it, I hear?'

Sharpe looked at the tall Simons with some surprise, for he had not realized that his exploit had become common knowledge. 'Don't remember much about it.'

'I suppose not. Still,' Simons said, 'a feather in your cap?'

'I don't think Wellesley thinks that,' Sharpe said.

'You're a King's officer now, Sharpe,' Simons said enviously. As an East India Company officer he was trapped in the Company's cumbersome system of promotion. 'If Wellesley thrives, he'll remember you.'

Sharpe laughed. 'I doubt it, sir. He ain't the sort.' He turned southwards again because Ahmed had called a warning in Arabic. The boy was pointing downhill and Sharpe stood to see over the crown of the slope. Far beneath him, where the road passed through one of the lush valleys, a small party of horsemen was approaching and one of the riders was in a blue coat. 'Friends, Ahmed!' he called. 'Looks like the new engineer,' Sharpe said to Simons.

'Pinckney will be delighted,' Simons said sarcastically.

Pinckney came back to inspect the approaching party through a telescope, and spat when he saw the blue coat of the Royal Engineers. 'Another interfering bastard to teach me how to suck eggs,' he said. 'So let's blow the charge before he gets here, otherwise he'll tell us we're doing it all wrong.'

A crowd of grinning sepoys waited expectantly about the end of the fuse. Pinckney struck a light, put it to the quickmatch, then watched the sparks smoke their way towards the distant charge. The smoke trail vanished in grass and it seemed to Sharpe that it must have extinguished itself, but then there was a violent coughing sound and the small ridge heaved upwards. Soil and stone flew outwards in a cloud of filthy smoke. The sepoys cheered. The explosion had seemed small to Sharpe, but when the smoke and dust cleared he could see that the ridge now had a deep notch through which the road could climb to the next high valley.

The pioneers went to shovel the loosened earth away and Sharpe sat again. Ahmed squatted beside him. 'What am I going to do with you?' Sharpe asked.

'I go to England,' Ahmed said carefully.

'You won't like it there. Cold as buggery.'

'Cold?'

'Freezing.' Sharpe mimicked a shiver, but plainly it meant nothing to the Arab boy.

'I go to England,' Ahmed insisted.

A half-hour later the new engineer appeared just beneath Sharpe. He wore a wide-brimmed straw hat, rode a grey horse and was trailed by three servants who led pack mules laden with luggage amongst which Sharpe could see a tripod, a surveyor's level and a vast leather tube that he guessed held a telescope. The engineer took off his hat and fanned his face as he rounded the last bend. ''Pon my soul,' he said cheerfully, 'but thank God the horse does the climbing and not me.'

Pinckney had come back to greet the engineer and held out his hand as the blue-coated Major slid from his saddle. 'Captain Pinckney, sir,' he introduced himself.

'Pinckney, eh?' the white-haired engineer said cheerfully. 'I knew a Pinckney in Hertfordshire. He made ploughshares, and damn fine ones too.'

'My uncle Joshua, sir.'

'Then you must be Hugh's boy, yes? An honour!' He shook Pinckney's hand vigorously. 'Major John Stokes, at your service, though I don't suppose you need me, do you? You must have built more roads than I ever did.' Major Stokes looked towards Sharpe who had stood and was now smiling. 'Good God in His blessed heaven,' Stokes said, 'it can't be! But it is! My dear Sharpe! My dear Mister Sharpe. I heard all about your commission! Couldn't be more pleased, my dear Sharpe. An officer, eh?'

Sharpe smiled broadly. 'Only an ensign, sir.'

'Every ladder has a first rung, Sharpe,' Stokes said in gentle reproof of Sharpe's modesty, then held out his hand. 'We shall be mess mates, as they say in the Navy. Well, I never! Mess mates, indeed! And with a Pinckney too! Hugh Pinckney forges mill gears, Sharpe. Never seen a man make better-toothed wheels in all my life.' He clasped Sharpe's hand in both of his. 'They grubbed me out of Seringapatam, Sharpe. Can you believe that? Told me all the other engineers had the pox, and summoned me here just in time to discover that poor Elliott's dead.

I suppose I shouldn't complain. It's awfully good for my promotion prospects.' He let go of Sharpe's hand. 'Oh, and by the way, I travelled north with some of your old comrades! Captain Charles Morris and his company. Not the most charming creature, is he?'

'Not one of my favourites, sir,' Sharpe admitted. Good God! Bloody Morris was here? First Hakeswill, then Morris!

'He didn't want to come,' Stokes said, 'but higher powers deemed that I had to be protected from the ungodly, so they insisted on an infantry escort.' He turned as a rattle of gunfire sounded higher up the escarpment. 'Bless my soul! Is that musketry?'

'Picquet line, sir,' Pinckney explained. 'The enemy harasses us, but they're not thrusting home.'

'They should, they should. A battalion of skirmishers in these hills could keep us at bay for a month! Well, I never, Sharpe! An ensign!' The Major turned back to Pinckney. 'Sharpe and I ran the armoury at Seringapatam for four years.'

'You ran it, sir,' Sharpe said. 'I was just your sergeant.'

'Best sergeant I ever had,' Stokes told Pinckney enthusiastically. 'And it's not "sir"' – he turned to Sharpe – 'but John.' He grinned at Sharpe. 'They were four good years, eh? Best we'll ever have, I daresay. And here you are now, an officer! My dear fellow, I couldn't be more overjoyed.' He sniffed the air. 'Been blowing things up, Pinckney?'

'Cutting through that ridge, sir. I trust you don't mind that we didn't wait for you?'

'Mind? Why should I mind? You go ahead, dear fellow. I'm sure you know your business better than I do. God knows why they need an engineer here at all! Probably to be decorative, eh? Still, I'll make myself useful. I thought I might map the escarpment. Hasn't been done, you see. Of course, Pinckney, if you need advice, just ask away, but I'll probably be at sixes and sevens groping for an answer.' He beamed at the delighted Pinckney, then looked at the rough country through which the road led. 'This is fine landscape, isn't it? Such a relief after the plains. It reminds me of Scotland.'

'There are tigers here, Major,' Sharpe said.

'And there's all kinds of fierce things in Scotland too, Sharpe. I was once posted to Fort William and might as well have been in darkest China! It was worse than Newfoundland. And speaking of America, Sharpe, that young lady you sent me has travelled there. Extraordinary thing to do, I thought, and I advised her to abandon the whole wretched idea. There are bears, I told her, fierce bears, but she wouldn't be persuaded.'

'Simone, sir?' Sharpe asked, at first not believing his ears, then feeling a dreadful premonition.

'A charming creature, I thought. And to be widowed so young!' Stokes tutted and shook his head. 'She went to a fortune teller, one of those naked fellows who make funny faces in the alley by the Hindu temple, and says she was advised to go to a new world. Whatever next, eh?'

'I thought she was waiting for me, sir,' Sharpe said.

'Waiting for you? Good Lord, no. Gone to Louisiana, she says. She stayed in my house for a week – I moved out, of course, to stop any scandal – and then she travelled to Madras with Mrs Pennington. Remember Charlotte Pennington? The clergyman's widow? I can't think the two of them will get along, but your friend said the fortune teller was adamant and so she chose to go.' The Major was eager to give Sharpe the rest of the news from Seringapatam. The armoury was closing down, he said, now that the frontier of the British-held territory was so much farther north, but Stokes had kept himself busy dismantling the town's inner fortifications. 'Very ill made, Sharpe, disgraceful work, quite disgraceful. Walls crumbled to the touch.'

But Sharpe was not listening. He was thinking of Simone. She had gone! By now she was probably in Madras, and maybe already on board a ship. And she had taken his jewels. Only a few of them, true, but enough. He touched the seam of his jacket where a good many of the Tippoo's other jewels were hidden.

'Did Madame Joubert leave any message?' he asked Stokes when the Major paused to draw breath. What did he hope, Sharpe wondered, that Simone would want him to join her in America?

'A message? None, Sharpe. Too busy to write, I daresay. She's a remarkably wealthy woman, did you know? She bought half the raw silk in town, hired a score of bearers and off she went. Every officer in town was leaving a card for her, but she didn't have the time of day for any of them. Off to Louisiana!' Stokes suddenly frowned. 'What is the matter, Sharpe? You look as if you've seen a ghost. You're not sickening, are you?'

'No, no. It's just I thought she might have written.'

'Oh! I see! You were sweet on her!' Stokes shook his head. 'I feel for you, Sharpe, 'pon my soul, I do, but what hope could you have? A woman with her sort of fortune doesn't look at fellows like us! 'Pon my soul, no. She's rich! She'll marry high, Sharpe, or as high as a woman can in French America.'

Her sort of fortune indeed! Simone had no fortune, she had been penniless when Sharpe met her, but he had trusted her. God damn the Frog bitch! Stolen a small fortune. 'It doesn't matter,' he told Stokes, but somehow it did. Simone's betrayal was like a stab to the belly. It was not so much the jewels, for he had kept the greater part of the plunder, but the broken promises. He felt anger and pity and, above all, a fool. A great fool. He turned away from Stokes and stared down the track to where a dozen oxen escorted by two companies of sepoys were trudging towards him. 'I've got work coming,' he said, not wanting to discuss Simone any further.

'I passed those fellows on my way,' Stokes said, 'carrying powder, I think. I do like blowing things up. So just what do you do here, Sharpe?'

'I keep the pioneers supplied with material, sir, and sign in all the convoys.'

'Hope it leaves you time to help me, Sharpe. You and me together again, eh? It'll be like the old days.'

'That'd be good, sir,' Sharpe said with as much enthusiasm as he could muster, then he walked down the track and pointed to where the ox-drivers should drop their barrels of gunpowder. The men crowded about him with their chitties, and he pulled out a pencil and scrawled his initials in the corner of each one, thus confirming that they had completed and were owed for one journey.

The last man also handed Sharpe a sealed paper with his name written in a fine copperplate hand. 'From the clerk, sahib,' the man said, the phrase plainly much practised for he spoke no other English.

Sharpe tore the seal off as he walked back up the hill. The letter was not from the clerk at all, but from Torrance. 'Bloody hell!' he cursed.

'What is it?' Stokes asked.

'A man called Torrance,' Sharpe complained. 'He's in charge of the bullocks. He wants me back at Deogaum because he reckons there are forged chitties in the camp.'

'In the far south of India,' Stokes said, 'they call them *shits*.'

Sharpe blinked at the Major. 'Sorry, sir?'

'You mustn't call me "sir", Sharpe. 'Pon my soul, yes. I had a Tamil servant who was forever asking me to sign his *shits*. Had me all in a dither at first, I can tell you.'

Sharpe crumpled Torrance's note into a ball. 'Why the hell can't Torrance sort out his own *shits*?' he asked angrily. But he knew why. Torrance was scared of another meeting with Wellesley, which meant the Captain would now follow the rules to the letter.

'It won't take long,' Stokes said, 'not if you take my horse. But keep her to a steady walk, Richard, because she's tired. And have her rubbed down and watered while you're sorting out the *shits*.'

Sharpe was touched by Stokes's generosity. 'Are you sure?'

'What are friends for? Go on, Richard! On horseback you'll be home for supper. I'll have my cook brew up one of those *mussallas* you like so much.'

Sharpe left his pack with Stokes's baggage. The big ruby and a score of other stones were in the pack, and Sharpe was half tempted to carry it to Deogaum and back, but if he could not trust Stokes, who could he trust? He tried to persuade Ahmed to stay behind and keep an eye on the baggage, but the boy refused to be parted from Sharpe and insisted on trotting along behind the horse. 'Stokes won't hurt you,' Sharpe told Ahmed.

'I'm your havildar,' Ahmed insisted, hefting his musket and peering about the deserted landscape for enemies. There was none in sight, but Ahmed's gesture reminded Sharpe of Elliott's death and he wondered if he should have waited for the ox convoy to return to Deogaum, for the convoys all had escorts of sepoys or mercenary horsemen. He was tempted to kick the horse into a trot, but he resisted the impulse.

The danger was more acute once he reached the lower hills, for Mahratta horsemen were forever probing the perimeter of the British camp and being chased away by cavalry patrols. Twice he saw horsemen in the distance, but neither group took any notice of Sharpe who was ready to haul Ahmed up onto the horse and then ride for his life if he was threatened. He did not relax until he met a patrol of Madrassi cavalry under the command of a Company lieutenant who escorted him safely to the encampment.

Deogaum was now surrounded by a great spread of tents and makeshift booths, homes to soldiers and camp followers. A dancing bear was performing for a crowd of infantrymen and the animal reminded Sharpe of Major Stokes's words about America. Simone! It was his own damn fault. He should never have trusted the woman. The thought of his own foolishness plunged Sharpe into a black mood that was not helped by the sight of two redcoat privates lounging on a bench outside Torrance's quarters. Neither man moved as Sharpe slid from the horse. He gave the reins to Ahmed and mimed that the boy should rub the grey mare down with straw and then water her.

The two redcoats shifted slightly as if acknowledging Sharpe's presence, but neither man stood. He knew both of them; indeed, not so very long ago he had marched in the same ranks as these two men whose coats had the red facings of the 33rd. Kendrick and Lowry, they were called, and two worse characters it would have been hard to find in any light company. Both were cronies of Hakeswill's, and both had been among the small party Hakeswill had brought north in his failed attempt to arrest Sharpe. 'On your feet,' Sharpe said.

Kendrick glanced at Lowry, who looked back at Kendrick, and the two made faces at each other as though they were surprised by Sharpe's demands. They hesitated just long enough to make their insolence plain, but not quite long enough to make it punishable, then stood to attention. 'Is that your 'orse, Mister Sharpe?' Kendrick asked, stressing the 'mister'.

Sharpe ignored the question and pushed into the house to find a new clerk sitting behind the table. He was a young, good-looking Indian with oiled hair and a very white robe. He wore an apron to protect the robe from ink spots. 'You have business, sahib?' he asked brusquely.

'With Captain Torrance.'

'The Captain is ill.' The Indian, whose English was very good, smiled.

'He's always bloody ill,' Sharpe said and walked past the protesting clerk to push open the inner door.

Torrance was in his hammock, smoking his hookah, and dressed in an Indian gown embroidered with dragons while Sergeant Hakeswill was sitting at a small table counting a pile of coins. 'Sharpe!' Torrance sounded surprised. Hakeswill, looking equally surprised, sullenly stood to attention. 'Wasn't expecting you till this evening,' Torrance said.

'I'm here,' Sharpe said unnecessarily.

'So it is apparent. Unless you're a spectre?'

Sharpe had no time for small talk. 'You've got a problem with chitties?' he asked abruptly.

'Tiresome, isn't it?' Torrance seemed uncomfortable. 'Very tiresome. Sergeant, you have business elsewhere?'

'I've got duties, sir!' Hakeswill snapped.

'Attend to them, dear fellow.'

'Sir!' Hakeswill stiffened, turned to the right, then marched from the room.

'So how are you, Sharpe? Keeping busy?' Torrance had swung himself off the hammock and now scooped the coins into a leather bag. 'I hear poor Elliott died?'

'Shot, sir.'

Torrance shuddered as if the news was personal. 'So very sad,' he sighed, then retied the belt of his elaborate gown. 'I never did thank you, Sharpe, for being so supportive with Sir Arthur.'

Sharpe had not thought he had been supportive at all. 'I just told the truth, sir.'

'My father would be proud of you, and I'm deeply grateful to you. It seems Dilip was in league with Naig.'

'He was?'

Torrance heard the disbelief in Sharpe's voice. 'No other explanation, is there?' he said curtly. 'Someone must have been telling Naig which convoys carried the vital supplies, and it had to be Dilip. I must say I thought Wellesley was damned obtuse! There really is no point in having scruples about hanging natives. There isn't exactly a shortage of them, is there?' He smiled.

'There's something wrong with the chitties?' Sharpe demanded rudely.

'So there is, Sharpe, so there is. Our new clerk discovered the discrepancies. He's a smart young fellow. Sajit!'

The young clerk came into the room, clasped his hands and offered Torrance a slight bow. 'Sahib?'

'This is Ensign Sharpe, Sajit. He's by way of being my deputy and thus as much your sahib as I am.'

Sajit offered Sharpe a bow. 'I am honoured, sahib.'

'Perhaps you could show Mister Sharpe the problematical chitties, Sajit?' Torrance suggested.

Sajit went back to the outer room and returned a moment later with a pile of the grubby paper slips. He placed them on the table, then invited Sharpe to inspect them. All the chitties had Sharpe's initials in the bottom right-hand corner, most of them in pencil, but some had been initialled in ink and Sharpe set those aside. 'I didn't sign any of those,' he said confidently. 'I don't have a pen and ink.'

'You were right, Sajit!' Torrance said.

'You honour me, sahib,' Sajit said.

'And every chitty is a stolen anna,' Torrance said, 'so we have to discover which bullock men gave us the false ones. That's the problem, Sharpe.'

'They've got names on them,' Sharpe said, pointing at the slips of paper. 'You hardly needed to drag me down here to tell you who they were issued to!'

'Please don't be tedious, Sharpe,' Torrance said plaintively. 'Ever since the General put a shot across our bows I am forced to be particular. And the names mean nothing! Nothing! Look' – he scooped up the chitties – 'at least a dozen are assigned to Ram, whoever Ram is. There are probably a dozen Rams out there. What I want you to do, Sharpe, is go round the encampment with Sajit and point out which men have visited the road. Sajit can then identify which bullock men are submitting false claims.'

Sharpe frowned. 'Why doesn't Sajit just identify which men were ordered up the mountain? They must have got their chitties from him?'

'I want to be sure, Sharpe, I want to be sure!' Torrance pleaded.

'My testimony, sahib, would not be believed,' Sajit put in, 'but no one would doubt the word of an English officer.'

'Bloody hell,' Sharpe said. The last thing he felt like doing was wandering about the bullock camp identifying drivers. He was not sure he could do it anyway. 'So why not summon the bullock men here?' he demanded.

'The bad ones would run away, sahib, rather than come,' Sajit said.

'Best to ambush them in their encampment, Sharpe,' Torrance said.

'I'll do my best,' Sharpe grunted.

'I knew you would!' Torrance seemed relieved. 'Do it now, Sharpe, and perhaps you could join me for a late dinner? Say at half past one?'

Sharpe nodded, then went back into the sunlight to wait for Sajit. Kendrick and Lowry had vanished, presumably with Hakeswill. Ahmed had found a bucket of water and Stokes's mare was drinking greedily. 'You can stay here, Ahmed,' Sharpe said, but the boy shook his head. 'You're my bleeding shadow,' Sharpe grumbled.

'Shadow?'

Sharpe pointed to his own shadow. 'Shadow.'

Ahmed grinned, all white teeth in a grubby face. He liked the word. 'Sharpe's shadow!' he said.

Sajit emerged from the house with a pink silk parasol that he offered to Sharpe. Sharpe refused, and the clerk, who had discarded his apron, gratefully shaded himself from the fierce midday sun. 'I am sorry to be troublesome to you, sahib,' he said humbly.

'No trouble,' Sharpe said dourly, following the clerk. Ahmed came behind, leading the Major's mare.

'The boy need not come,' Sajit insisted, glancing behind at the horse which seemed to alarm him.

'You tell him that,' Sharpe said, 'but don't blame me if he shoots you. He's very fond of shooting people.'

Sajit hurried on. 'I think I know, sahib, which is the bad man who is cheating us. He is a fellow from Mysore. He gave me many chitties and swore you signed them in front of him. If you would be so kind as to confirm or deny his story, we shall be finished.'

'Then let's find the bugger and be done with it.'

Sajit led Sharpe through the bullock lines where the wealthier herds-men had erected vast dark and sagging tents. Women slapped bread dough beside small ox-dung fires, and more piles of the fuel dried in the sun beside each tent entrance. Sharpe looked for Naig's big green tents, but he could not see them and he assumed that whoever had inherited Naig's business had packed up and gone.

'There, sahib, that is the bad man's tent.' Sajit nervously led Sharpe towards a brown tent that stood slightly apart from the others. He stopped a few paces from the entrance and lowered his voice. 'He is called Ranjit, sahib.'

'So fetch the bugger,' Sharpe said, 'and I'll tell you if he's lying or not.'

Sajit seemed nervous of confronting Ranjit for he hesitated, but then plucked up his courage, collapsed the parasol and dropped to the ground to crawl into the tent which sagged so deeply that the doorway was scarce higher than a man's knee. Sharpe heard the murmur of voices, then Sajit backed hurriedly out of the low fringed entrance. He slapped at the dust on his white robes, then looked at Sharpe with a face close to tears. 'He is a bad man, sahib. He will not come out. I told him a sahib was here to see him, but he used rude words!'

'I'll take a look at the bastard,' Sharpe said. 'That's all you need, isn't it? For me to say whether I've seen him or not?'

'Please, sahib,' Sajit said, and gestured at the tent's entrance.

Sharpe took off his hat so it would not tangle with the canvas, hoisted the tent's entrance as high as he could, then ducked low under the heavy brown cloth.

And knew instantly that it was a trap.

And understood, almost in the same instant, that he could do nothing about it.

The first blow struck his forehead, and his vision exploded in streaks of lightning and shuddering stars. He fell backwards, out into the sunlight and someone instantly grabbed one of his ankles and began pulling him into the deep shadow. He tried to kick, tried to push himself against the tent's sides, but another hand seized his second leg, another blow hammered the side of his skull and, mercifully, he knew nothing more.

'He's got a thick skull, our Sharpie,' Hakeswill said with a grin. He prodded Sharpe's prone body and got no reaction. 'Fast asleep, he is.' The Sergeant's face twitched. He had hit Sharpe with the heavy brass-bound butt of a musket and he was amazed that Sharpe's skull was not broken. There was plenty of blood in his black hair, and he would have a bruise the size of a mango by nightfall, but his skull seemed to have taken the two blows without splintering. 'He always was a thick-headed bugger,' Hakeswill said. 'Now strip him.'

'Strip him?' Kendrick asked.

'When his body is found,' Hakeswill explained patiently, 'if it is found, and you can't rely on bleeding blackamoors to do a proper job and hide it, we don't want no one seeing he's a British officer, do we? Not that he is an officer. He's just a jumped-up bit of muck. So strip him, then tie his hands and feet and cover his eyeballs.'

Kendrick and Lowry jerked and tugged Sharpe's coat free, then handed the garment to Hakeswill who ran his fingers along the hems. 'Got it!' he exulted when he felt the lumps in the cloth. He took out a knife, slit the coat and the two privates stared in awe as he eased the glittering jewels out of the tightly sewn seam. It was dark in the shadowed tent, but the stones gleamed bright. 'Get on with it!' Hakeswill said. 'The rest of his clothes off!'

'What are you doing?' Sajit had sidled into the tent and now stared at the jewels.

'None of your bleeding business,' Hakeswill said.

'You have jewels?' Sajit asked.

Hakeswill slid out his bayonet and stabbed it at Sajit, checking the lunge a fraction before the blade would have punctured the clerk's neck. 'The jewels ain't your business, Sajit. The jewels are my business. Your business is Sharpie, got it? I agreed to give him to your bleeding uncle, but I gets what he carries.'

'My uncle will pay well for good stones,' Sajit said.

'Your Uncle Jama's a bleeding monkey who'd cheat me soon as fart at me, so forget the bleeding stones. They're mine.' Hakeswill thrust the first handful into a pocket and started searching the rest of Sharpe's clothes. He slit open all the seams, then cut Sharpe's boots apart to discover a score of rubies hidden in the folded boot-tops. They were small rubies, scarce bigger than peas, and Hakeswill was looking for one large ruby. 'I saw it, I did. The bloody Tippoo had it on his hat. Large as life! Look in his hair.'

Kendrick obediently ran his fingers through Sharpe's blood-encrusted hair. 'Nothing there, Sarge.'

'Turn the bugger over and have a look you know where.'

'Not me!'

'Don't be so bloody squeamish! And tie his hands. Fast now! You don't want the sod waking up, do you?'

The clothes and boots yielded sixty-three stones. There were rubies, emeralds, sapphires and four small diamonds, but no large ruby. Hakeswill frowned. Surely Sharpe would not have sold the ruby? Still, he consoled himself, there was a fortune here, and he could not resist putting all the stones together on a mat and staring at them. 'I do like a bit of glitter,' he breathed as his fingers greedily touched the jewels. He put ten of the smaller stones in one pile, another ten in a second, and pushed the two piles towards Kendrick and Lowry. 'That's your cut, boys. Keep you in whores for the rest of your lives, that will.'

'Perhaps I will tell my uncle about your stones,' Sajit said, staring at the jewels.

'I expect you will,' Hakeswill said, 'and so bleeding what? I ain't as dozy as Sharpie. You won't catch me.'

'Then maybe I shall tell Captain Torrance.' Sajit had positioned himself close to the entrance so that he could flee if Hakeswill attacked him. 'Captain Torrance likes wealth.'

Likes it too much, Hakeswill thought, and if Torrance knew about the stones he would make Hakeswill's life hell until he yielded a share. The Sergeant's face juddered in a series of uncontrollable twitches. 'You're a bright lad, Sajit, ain't you?' he said. 'You might be nothing but a bleeding heathen blackamoor but you've got more than bullock dung for brains, ain't you? Here.' He tossed Sajit three of the stones. 'That keeps your tongue quiet, and if it don't, I'll cut it out and have a feed on it. Partial to a plate of tongue, I am. Nice piece of tongue, knob of butter and some gravy. Proper food, that.' He pushed the rest of the stones into his pocket, then stared broodingly at Sharpe's naked trussed body. 'He had more,' Hakeswill said with a frown, 'I know he had more.' The Sergeant suddenly clicked his fingers. 'What about his pack?'

'What pack?' Lowry asked.

'The bleeding pack he carries, which he shouldn't, being an officer, which he ain't. Where's his pack?'

The privates shrugged. Sajit frowned. 'He had no pack when he came to the Captain's house.'

'You're sure?'

'He came on a horse,' Lowry said helpfully. 'It were a grey horse, and he didn't have no pack.'

'So where's the horse?' Hakeswill demanded angrily. 'We should look in its saddlebags!'

Lowry frowned, trying to remember. 'A bleeding kid had it,' he said at last.

'So where's the kid?'

'He ran off,' Sajit said.

'Ran off?' Hakeswill said threateningly. 'Why?'

'He saw you hit him,' Sajit said. 'I saw it. He fell out of the tent. There was blood on his face.'

'You shouldn't have hit him till he was right inside the tent,' Kendrick said chidingly.

'Shut your bloody face,' Hakeswill said, then frowned. 'So where did the kid run?'

'Away,' Sajit said. 'I chased him, but he climbed onto the horse.'

'Kid don't speak English,' Kendrick said helpfully.

'How the hell do you know that?'

''Cos I talked to him!'

'And who's going to believe a heathen black kid what don't speak English?' Lowry asked.

Hakeswill's face was racked by a quick series of twitches. He suspected he was safe. Lowry was right. Who would believe the kid? Even so the Sergeant wished that Jama's men were coming earlier to fetch Sharpe. Jama himself had gone away from the camp, reckoning that if he was going to murder a British officer then it was best done a long way from the British army. Hakeswill had warned Jama not to expect Sharpe until the evening, and now he had to guard him until dusk. 'I told you to put a bandage on his eyes,' Hakeswill snapped. 'Don't want him to see us!'

'It don't matter if he does,' Kendrick said. 'He ain't going to see the dawn, is he?'

'Got more lives than a basketful of bleeding cats, that one,' Hakeswill said. 'If I had any sense I'd slit his throat now.'

'No!' Sajit said. 'He was promised to my uncle.'

'And your uncle's paying us, yes?'

'That too is agreed,' Sajit said.

Hakeswill stood and walked to Sharpe's unconscious body. 'I put those stripes on his back,' he said proudly. 'Lied through my teeth, I did, and had Sharpie flogged. Now I'll have him killed.' He remembered how Sharpe had flung him among the tigers and his face twitched as he recalled the elephant trying to crush him to death, and in his sudden rage he kicked at Sharpe and went on kicking until Kendrick hauled him away.

'If you kill him, Sarge,' Kendrick said, 'then the blackies won't pay us, will they?'

Hakeswill let himself be pulled away. 'So how will your uncle kill him?' he asked Sajit.

'His *jettis* will do it.'

'I've seen them bastards at work,' Hakeswill said in a tone of admiration. 'Just make it slow. Make it slow and make it bleeding painful.'

146

'It will be slow,' Sajit promised, 'and very painful. My uncle is not a merciful man.'

'But I am,' Hakeswill said. 'I am. Because I'm letting another man have the pleasure of killing Sharpie.' He spat at Sharpe. 'Dead by dawn, Sharpie. You'll be down with Old Nick, where you ought to be!'

He settled against one of the tent poles and trickled jewels from one palm to the other. Flies crawled among the crusting blood in Sharpe's hair. The Ensign would be dead by dawn, and Hakeswill was a rich man. Revenge, the Sergeant decided, was sweet as honey.

Ahmed saw Sharpe fall back from the tent entrance, saw blood bright on his forehead, then watched as hands seized Sharpe and dragged him into the deep shadows.

Then Sajit, the clerk with the pink umbrella, turned towards him. 'Boy,' he snapped, 'come here!'

Ahmed pretended not to understand, though he understood well enough that he was a witness to something deeply wrong. He backed away, tugging Major Stokes's mare with him. He let the musket slip down from his shoulder and Sajit, seeing the threat, suddenly rushed at him, but Ahmed was even faster. He jumped up to sprawl across the saddle and, without bothering to seat himself properly, kicked the horse into motion. The startled mare leaped away as Ahmed hauled himself onto her back. The stirrups were too long for him, but Ahmed had been raised with horses and could have ridden the mare bareback, blindfolded and back to front. He swerved southwards, galloping between tents, fires and grazing bullocks, and leaving Sajit far behind. A woman shouted a protest as he nearly galloped over her children. He slowed the mare as he reached the edge of the encampment and looked back to see that he had left Sajit far behind.

What the hell should he do? He knew no one in the British camp. He looked up at the high summit where Gawilghur just showed. He supposed his old comrades in Manu Bappoo's Lions of Allah were up there, but his uncle, with whom he had travelled from Arabia, was dead and buried in Argaum's black earth. He knew other soldiers in the regiment, but he also feared them. Those other soldiers wanted Ahmed to be their servant, and not just to cook for them and clean their weapons. Sharpe alone had shown him friendliness, and Sharpe now needed help, but Ahmed did not know how to provide it. He thought about the problem as he knotted the stirrup leathers.

The plump, red-faced and white-haired man in the hills had been friendly, but how was Ahmed to talk to him? He decided he ought to try and so he turned the horse, planning to ride her all about the camp perimeter and then back up the road into the hills, but an officer of the camp picquets saw him. The man was riding a horse and he spurred it close to Ahmed and noted the British saddle cloth. 'What are you doing, boy?' he asked. The officer presumed Ahmed was exercising the horse, but Ahmed took fright at the challenge and kicked back.

'Thief!' the officer shouted and gave chase. 'Stop! Thief!'

A sepoy turned with his musket and Ahmed nudged the horse so that she ran the man down. There was a group of houses close by and Ahmed turned towards them, jumped a garden wall, thumped through some beds of vegetables, jumped another wall, ducked under some fruit trees, jumped a hedge and splashed through a muddy pond before kicking the horse up a bank and into some trees. The officer had not dared follow him through the gardens, but Ahmed could hear the hue and cry beyond the houses. He patted the mare's neck as she threaded through the trees, then curbed her at the wood's edge. There was about a half-mile of open country, then more thick woods that promised safety if only the tired mare could make the distance without faltering. 'If Allah wills it,' Ahmed said, then kicked the horse into a gallop.

His pursuers were well behind, but they saw him break cover and now a dozen horsemen were chasing him. Someone fired at him. He heard the musket shot, but the ball went nowhere near him. He leaned over the mane and just let the horse run. He looked back once and saw the pursuers bunching in his path, and then he was in the trees and he twisted northwards, cut back west, then went north again, going ever deeper into the woods until at last he slowed the blowing horse so that the sound of her thumping hooves would not betray him.

He listened. He could hear other horses blundering through the leaves, but they were not coming any closer, and then he began to wonder if it would not be better to let himself be caught after all, for surely someone among the British would speak his language? Maybe if he went all the way to where the men were making the road in the hills he would be too late to help Sharpe. He felt miserable, utterly unsure what he should do, and then he decided he must go back and find help within the encampment and so he turned the horse back towards his pursuers.

And saw a musket pointing straight at his throat.

The man holding the musket was an Indian and had one of the spiralling brass helmets that the Mahrattas wore. He was a cavalryman, but he had picketed his horse a few yards away and had crept up on Ahmed on foot. The man grinned.

Ahmed wondered if he should just kick the tired mare and risk his luck, but then another Mahratta stepped from the leaves, and this one held a curved *tulwar*. A third man appeared, and then more men came, all mounted, to surround him.

And Ahmed, who knew he had panicked and failed, wept.

It seemed to Dodd that Prince Manu Bappoo's policy of rewarding freebooters with cash for weapons captured from the British was failing miserably. So far they had fetched in three ancient matchlocks that must have belonged to *shikarees*, a broken musket of local manufacture, and a fine pistol and sword that had been taken from an engineer officer. No scabbard for the sword, of course, but the two trophies, so far as Dodd was concerned, were the only evidence that the Mahrattas had tried to stop the British approach. He pestered Manu Bappoo, pleading to be allowed to take his Cobras down to where the pioneers were driving the road, but the Rajah's brother adamantly refused to let Dodd's men leave the fortress.

Dodd himself was allowed to leave, but only to exercise his horse, which he did each day by riding west along the brink of the plateau. He did not go far. There was a tempting price on his head, and though no enemy cavalry had been seen on the plateau since the engineer had made his reconnaissance, Dodd still feared that he might be captured, and so he only rode until he could see the British works far beneath him. Then, protected by a handful of Bappoo's horsemen, he would stare through a telescope at the ant-like figures labouring so far below. He watched the road widen, and lengthen, and one morning he saw that two battalions of infantry had camped in one of the high valleys, and next day he saw the beginnings of an artillery park: three guns, a forage cart, a spare wheel wagon and four ammunition limbers.

He cursed Bappoo, knowing that his Cobras could destroy that small park and hurl the British into dazed confusion, yet the Prince was content to let the enemy climb the escarpment unopposed. The road was being remade, yet even so it was still steep enough in places to need a hundred men to haul one gun. Yet day by day Dodd saw the number of guns increase in the artillery park, then inch up the hill and he knew it would not be long before the British reached the plateau and their besieging forces would seal off the narrow isthmus of rock that led from the cliffs to the great fortress.

And still Manu Bappoo made no proper effort to harry the redcoats. 'We shall stop them here,' the Prince told Dodd, 'here,' and he would gesture at Gawilghur's walls, but William Dodd was not so sure that the redcoats would be stopped so easily. Bappoo might be convinced of the fortress's strength, but Bappoo knew nothing of modern siege craft.

Each morning, as he returned from his excursion along the cliff top, Dodd would dismount as he reached the isthmus and give his horse to one of his escort so that he could walk the attackers' route. He tried to see the fortress as the redcoats would see it, tried to anticipate where their attack would come and how it would be made.

It was, he had to admit, a brutal place to attack. Two great walls protected the Outer Fort, and though the British could undoubtedly breach those walls with cannon fire, the two ramparts stood on a steep slope so that the attackers would need to fight their way uphill to where the defenders would be waiting among the ruins of the breaches. And those breaches would be flanked by the massive round bastions that were too big to be collapsed by the twelve- or eighteen-pounder guns Dodd expected the British to deploy. The bastions would spit round shot, musket balls and rockets down into the British who would be struggling towards the nearer breach, their approach route getting ever narrower until it was finally constricted by the vast tank of water that blocked most of the approach. Dodd walked the route obsessively and could almost feel sorry for the men who would have to do it under fire.

A hundred paces from the fort, where the defenders' fire would be most lethal, the attackers would be squeezed between the reservoir and the cliff edge, compressed into a space just twenty paces wide. Dodd stood in that space each day and stared up at the double walls and counted the artillery pieces. Twenty-two cannon were pointing at him and when the redcoats came those barrels would be loaded with canister, and besides those heavy guns there was a mass of smaller weapons, the murderers and spitfires that could be held by one man and which could blast out a fistful of stone scraps or pistol balls. True, the British would have destroyed some of the larger guns, but the barrels could be mounted on new carriages and resited behind the vast bastions so that the attackers, if they even succeeded in climbing up to the breach, would be enfiladed by cannon fire. And to reach that far they would need to fight uphill against Bappoo's Arabs, and against the massed musketry of the garrison.

It was a prospect so daunting that Prince Manu Bappoo expected most of the attackers would sheer away from the breaches and run to the Delhi Gate, the Outer Fort's northern entrance. That gate would undoubtedly have been shattered by British cannon fire, but once inside its arch the attackers would find themselves in a trap. The road inside the gate curled up beside the wall, with another great wall outside it, so that anyone on the cobbles was dwarfed by the stone ramparts on either side, and those would be lined with men firing down or else throwing the great rocks that Bappoo had ordered piled onto the firesteps. Inch by bloody inch the redcoats would fight their way up the narrow road between the walls, only to turn the corner to see an even greater gate standing in front of them, and one, moreover, that could not be reached by the besiegers' cannon fire. Thus, Bappoo reckoned, the British assault would be thwarted.

Dodd was not so sure. The Prince was right in thinking that there was no way in through the Delhi Gate, but Dodd suspected the breaches would be less formidable. He had begun to see weaknesses in the ancient walls, old cracks that were half hidden by weeds and lichen, and he knew the skill of the British gunners. The wall would break easily, and that meant the breaches would be big and wide, and Dodd reckoned the British would fight their way through. It might be a hard fight, but they would win it. And that meant the British would capture the Outer Fort.

But Dodd did not express that opinion to Bappoo, nor did he urge the Prince to build an earthen glacis outside the wall to soak up the fire of the breaching batteries. Such a glacis would delay the British for days, even weeks, but Dodd encouraged the Prince to believe that the Outer Fort was impregnable, for in that misapprehension lay Dodd's opportunity.

Manu Bappoo had once told Dodd that the Outer Fort was a trap. An enemy, if they captured the Outer Fort, would think their battle won, but then they would come to Gawilghur's central ravine and find a second, even greater fort, waiting on its far side. But for Dodd the Outer Fort was Manu Bappoo's trap. If Manu Bappoo lost the Outer Fort then he, like the enemy, would have to cross the ravine and climb to the Inner Fort, and it was there that Dodd commanded and, try as Dodd might, he could see no weaknesses in the Inner Fort's defences. Neither Manu Bappoo nor the British could ever cross the ravine, not if Dodd opposed them.

The Inner Fort was quite separate from the Outer. No wall joined them, only a track that dropped steeply to the bed of the ravine and then climbed, even more steeply, to the intricate gateway of the Inner Fort. Dodd used that track each day, and he tried to imagine himself as an attacker. Twenty more guns faced him from the Inner Fort's single wall as he descended the ravine, and none of those guns would have been dismounted by cannon fire. Muskets would be pouring their shot down into the rocky ravine and rockets would be slashing bloodily through the British ranks. The redcoats would die here like rats being pounded in a bucket, and even if some did survive to climb the track towards the gate, they would only reach Gawilghur's last horror.

That horror was the entrance, where four vast gates barred the Inner Fort, four gates set one after another in a steep passage that was flanked by towering walls. There was no other way in. Even if the British breached the Inner Fort's wall it would not help, for the wall was built on top of the precipice which formed the southern side of the ravine, and no man could climb that slope and hope to survive. The only way in was through the gate, and Wellesley, Dodd had learned, did not like lengthy sieges. He had escaladed Ahmednuggur, surprising its defenders by sending men with ladders against the unbreached walls, and Dodd was certain that Wellesley would similarly try to rush the Inner Fort. He could not approach the wall, perched on its cliff, so he would be forced to send his men into the ghastly entrance that twisted as it climbed, and for every steep step of the way, between each of the four great gates, they would be pounded by muskets, crushed by stones, blasted by cannon and savaged by rockets dropped from the parapets. It could not be done. Dodd's Cobras would be on the firesteps and the redcoats would be beneath them, and the redcoats would die like cattle.

Dodd had no great opinion of Indian rockets, but he had stockpiled more than a thousand above the Inner Fort's murderous entrance, for within the close confines of the walled road the weapons would prove lethal. The rockets were made of hammered tin, each one about sixteen inches long and four or five inches in diameter, with a bamboo stick the height of a man attached to each tin cylinder that was crammed with powder. Dodd had experimented with the weapon and found that a lit rocket tossed down into the gate passage would sear and bounce from wall to wall, and even when it finally stopped careering madly about the roadway, it went on belching out a torch of flame that would scorch trapped men terribly. A dozen rockets dropped between two of the gates might kill a score of men and burn another score half to death. Just let them come, Dodd prayed as he climbed each morning towards the Inner Fort. Let them come! Let them come and let them take the Outer Fort, for then Manu Bappoo must die and the British would then come to Dodd and die like the Prince.

And afterwards the fugitives of their beaten army would be pursued south across the Deccan Plain. Their bodies would rot in the heat and their bones whiten in the sun, and the British power in India would be broken and Dodd would be Lord of Gawilghur.

Just let the bastards come.

That evening Sergeant Hakeswill pushed aside the folds of muslin to enter Captain Torrance's quarters. The Captain was lying naked in his hammock where he was being fanned by a bamboo punkah that had been rigged to a ceiling beam. His native servant kept the punkah moving by tugging on a string, while Clare Wall trimmed the Captain's fingernails. 'Not too close, Brick,' Torrance said. 'Leave me enough to scratch with, there's a good girl.' He raised his eyes to Hakeswill. 'Did you knock, Sergeant?'

'Twice, sir,' Hakeswill lied, 'loud and clear, sir.'

'Brick will have to ream out my ears. Say good evening to the Sergeant, Brick. Where are our manners tonight?'

Clare lifted her eyes briefly to acknowledge Hakeswill's presence and mumbled something barely audible. Hakeswill snatched off his hat. 'Pleasure to see you, Mrs Wall,' he said eagerly, 'a proper pleasure, my jewel.' He bobbed his head to her and winked at Torrance, who flinched.

'Brick,' Torrance said, 'the Sergeant and I have military matters to discuss. So take yourself to the garden.' He patted her hand and watched her leave. 'And no listening at the window!' he added archly. He waited until Clare had sidled past the muslin that hung over the kitchen entrance, then leaned precariously from the hammock to pick up a green silk robe that he draped over his crotch. 'I would hate to shock you, Sergeant.'

'Beyond shock, sir, me, sir. Ain't nothing living I ain't seen naked, sir, all of 'em naked as needles, and never once was I shocked, sir. Ever since they strung me up by the neck I've been beyond shock, sir.'

And beyond sense, too, Torrance thought, but he suppressed the comment. 'Has Brick left the kitchen?'

Hakeswill peered past the muslin. 'She's gone, sir.'

'She's not at the window?'

Hakeswill checked the window. 'On the far side of the yard, sir, like a good girl.'

'I trust you've brought me news?'

'Better than news, sir, better than news.' The Sergeant crossed to the table and emptied his pocket. 'Your notes to Jama, sir, all of them. Ten thousand rupees, and all paid off. You're out of debt, sir, out of debt.'

Relief seared through Torrance. Debt was a terrible thing, a dreadful thing, yet seemingly inescapable if a man was to live to the full. Twelve hundred guineas! How could he ever have gambled that much away? It had been madness! Yet now it was paid, and paid in full. 'Burn the notes,' he ordered Hakeswill.

Hakeswill held the notes into a candle flame one by one, then let them shrivel and burn on the table. The draught from the punkah disturbed the smoke and scattered the little scraps of black ash that rose from the small fires. 'And Jama, sir, being a gentleman, despite being an heathen bastard blackamoor, added a thankee,' Hakeswill said, putting some gold coins on the table.

'How much?'

'Seven hundred rupees there, sir.'

'He gave us more, I know that. You're cheating me, Sergeant.'

'Sir!' Hakeswill straightened indignantly. 'On my life, sir, and I speak as a Christian, I ain't ever cheated a soul in my life, sir, not unless they deserved it, in which case they gets it right and proper, sir, like it says in the scriptures.'

Torrance stared at Hakeswill. 'Jama will be back in the camp in a day or two. I can ask him.'

'And you will find, sir, that I have treated you foursquare and straight, sir, on the nail, sir, on the drumhead, as one soldier to another.' Hakeswill sniffed. 'I'm hurt, sir.'

Torrance yawned. 'You have my sincerest, deepest and most fervent apologies, Sergeant. So tell me about Sharpe.'

Hakeswill glanced at the punkah boy. 'Does that heathen speak English, sir?'

'Of course not.'

'Sharpie's no more, sir.' Hakeswill's face twitched as he remembered the pleasure of kicking his enemy. 'Stripped the bastard naked, sir, gave him a headache he won't ever forget, not that he's got long to remember anything now on account of him being on his way to meet his executioner, and I kept him trussed up till Jama's men came to fetch him. Which they did, sir, so now he's gone, sir. Gone for bleeding ever, just as he deserves.'

'You stripped him?' Torrance asked, puzzled.

'Didn't want the bastards dropping off a body all dressed up in an officer's coat, sir, even though the little bleeder should never have worn one, him being nothing more than a jumped-up dribble of dried toad-spittle, sir. So we stripped him and burned the uniform, sir.'

'And nothing went wrong?'

Hakeswill's face twitched as he shrugged. 'His boy got away, but he didn't make no trouble. Just vanished. Probably went back to his mummy.'

Torrance smiled. All was done, all was solved. Even better, he could resume his trade with Jama, though perhaps with a little more circumspection than in the past. 'Did Sajit go with Sharpe?' he asked, knowing he would need an efficient clerk if he was to hide the treacherous transactions in the ledger.

'No, sir. He's with me, sir, outside, sir.' Hakeswill jerked his head towards the front room. 'He wanted to go, sir, but I gave him a thumping on account of us needing him here, sir, and after that he was as good as gold, sir, even if he is an heathen bit of scum.'

Torrance smiled. 'I am vastly in your debt, Sergeant Hakeswill,' he said.

'Just doing my duty, sir.' Hakeswill's face twitched as he grinned and gestured towards the garden window. 'And hoping for a soldier's reward, sir.'

'Brick, you mean?' Torrance asked.

'Me heart's desire, sir,' Hakeswill said hoarsely. 'Her and me, sir, made for each other. Says so in the scriptures.'

'Then the fruition of the prophecy must wait a while,' Torrance said, 'because I need Brick to look after me, and your duty, Sergeant, is to assume Mister Sharpe's responsibilities. We shall wait till someone notices that he's missing, then claim that he must have been ambushed by Mahrattas while on his way here. Then you'll go up the mountain to help the engineers.'

'Me, sir?' Hakeswill sounded alarmed at the prospect of having to do some real work. 'Up the mountain?'

'Someone has to be there. You can't expect me to do it!' Torrance said indignantly. 'Someone must stay here and shoulder the heavier responsibilities. It won't be for long, Sergeant, not for long. And once the campaign is over I can assure you that your heart's desires will be fully met.' But not, he decided, before Hakeswill paid him the money Clare owed for her passage out from England. That money could come from the cash that Jama had given Hakeswill this night which, Torrance was sure, was a great deal more than the Sergeant had admitted. 'Make yourself ready, Sergeant,' Torrance ordered. 'Doubtless you will be needed up the road tomorrow.'

'Yes, sir,' Hakeswill said sullenly.

'Well done, good and faithful Hakeswill,' Torrance said grandly. 'Don't let any moths in as you leave.'

Hakeswill went. He had three thousand three hundred rupees in his pocket and a fortune in precious stones hidden in his cartridge box. He would have liked to have celebrated with Clare Wall, but he did not doubt that his chance would come and so, for the moment, he was a satisfied man. He looked at the first stars pricking the sky above

Gawilghur's plateau and reflected that he had rarely been more content. He had taken his revenge, he had become wealthy, and thus all was well in Obadiah Hakeswill's world.

CHAPTER 6

Sharpe knew he was in an ox cart. He could tell that from the jolting motion and from the terrible squeal of the ungreased axles. The ox carts that followed the army made a noise like the shrieking of souls in perdition.

He was naked, bruised and in pain. It hurt even to breathe. His mouth was gagged and his hands and feet were tied, but even if they had been free he doubted he could have moved for he was wrapped in a thick dusty carpet. Hakeswill! The bastard had ambushed him, stripped him and robbed him. He knew it was Hakeswill, for Sharpe had heard the Sergeant's hoarse voice as he was rolled into the rug. Then he had been carried out of the tent and slung into the cart, and he was not sure how long ago that had been because he was in too much pain and he kept slipping in and out of a dreamlike daze. A nightmare daze. There was blood in his mouth, a tooth was loose, a rib was probably cracked and the rest of him simply ached or hurt. His head throbbed. He wanted to be sick, but knew he would choke on his vomit because of the gag and so he willed his belly to be calm.

Calm! The only blessing was that he was alive, and he suspected that was no blessing at all. Why had Hakeswill not killed him? Not out of mercy, that was for sure. So presumably he was to be killed somewhere else, though why Hakeswill had run the terrible risk of having a British officer tied hand and foot and smuggled past the picquet line Sharpe could not tell. It made no sense. All he did know was that by now Obadiah Hakeswill would have teased Sharpe's gems from their hiding places. God damn it all to hell. First Simone, now Hakeswill, and Hakeswill, Sharpe realized, could never have trapped Sharpe if Torrance had not helped.

But knowing his enemies would not help Sharpe now. He knew he had as much hope of living as those dogs who were hurled onto the mud flats beside the Thames in London with stones tied to their necks. The children used to laugh as they watched the dogs struggle. Some of the dogs had come from wealthy homes. They used to be snatched and if their owners did not produce the ransom money within a couple of days, the dogs were thrown to the river. Usually the ransom was paid, brought by a nervous footman to a sordid public house near the docks, but no one would ransom Sharpe. Who would care? Dust from the rug was thick in his nose. Just let the end be quick, he prayed.

He could hear almost nothing through the rug. The axle squealing was the loudest noise, and once he heard a thump on the cart's side and thought he heard a man laugh. It was night-time. He was not sure how he knew that, except that it would make sense, for no one would try to smuggle a British officer out in daylight, and he knew he had lain in the tent for a long time after Hakeswill had hit him. He remembered ducking under the tent's canvas, remembered a glimpse of the brass-bound musket butt, and then it was nothing but a jumble of pain and oblivion. A weight pressed on his waist, and he guessed after a while that a man was resting his feet on the rug. Sharpe tested the assumption by trying to move and the man kicked him. He lay still again. One dog had escaped, he remembered. It had somehow slipped the rope over its neck and had paddled away downstream with the children shrieking along the bank and hurling stones at the frightened head. Did the dog die? Sharpe could not remember. God, he thought, but he had been a wild child, wild as a hawk. They had tried to beat the wildness out of him, beat him till the blood ran, then told him he would come to a bad end. They had prophesied that he would be strung up by the neck at Tyburn Hill. Dick Sharpe dangling, pissing down his legs while the rope burned into his gullet. But it had not happened. He was an officer, a gentleman, and he was still alive, and he pulled at the tether about his wrists, but it would not shift.

Was Hakeswill riding in the cart? That seemed possible, and suggested the Sergeant wanted somewhere safe and private to kill Sharpe. But how? Quick with a knife? That was a forlorn wish, for Hakeswill was not merciful. Perhaps he planned to repay Sharpe by putting him beneath an elephant's foot and he would scream and writhe until the great weight would not let him scream ever again and his bones would crack and splinter like eggshells. Be sure your sin will find you out. How many times had he heard those words from the Bible? Usually thumped into him at the foundling home with a blow across the skull for every syllable, and the blows would keep coming as they chanted the reference. The Book of Numbers, chapter thirty-two, verse twenty-three, syllable by syllable, blow by blow, and now his sin was finding him out and he was to be punished for all the unpunished offences. So die well, he told himself. Don't cry out. Whatever was about to happen could not be worse than the flogging he had taken because of Hakeswill's lies. That had hurt. Hurt like buggery, but he had not cried out. So take the pain and go like a man. What had Sergeant Major Bywaters said as he had thrust the leather gag into Sharpe's mouth? 'Be brave, boy. Don't let the regiment down.' So he would be brave and die well, and then what? Hell, he supposed, and an eternity of torment at the hands of a legion of Hakeswills. Just like the army, really.

The cart stopped. He heard feet thump on the wagon boards, the murmur of voices, then hands seized the rug and dragged him off. He banged hard down onto the ground, then the rug was picked up and carried. Die well, he told himself, die well, but that was easier said than done. Not all men died well. Sharpe had seen strong men reduced to shuddering despair as they waited for the cart to be run out from under the gallows, just as he had seen others go into eternity with a defiance so brittle and hard that it had silenced the watching crowd. Yet all men, the brave and the cowardly, danced the gallows dance in the end, jerking from a length of Bridport hemp, and the crowd would laugh at their twitching antics. Best puppet show in London, they said. There was no good way to die, except in bed, asleep, unknowing. Or maybe in battle, at the cannon's mouth, blown to kingdom come in an instant of oblivion.

He heard the footsteps of the men who carried him slap on stone, then heard a loud murmur of voices. There were a lot of voices, all apparently talking at once and all excited, and he felt the rug being jostled by a crowd and then he seemed to be carried down some steps and the crowd was gone and he was thrown onto a hard floor. The voices seemed louder now, as if he was indoors, and he was suddenly possessed by the absurd notion that he had been brought into a cock-fighting arena like the one off Vinegar Street where, as a child, he had earned farthings by carrying pots of porter to spectators who were alternatively morose or maniacally excited.

He lay for a long time. He could hear the voices, even sometimes a burst of laughter. He remembered the fat man in Vinegar Street, whose trade, rat-catching, took him to the great houses in west London that he reconnoitred for his thieving friends. 'You'd make a good snaffler, Dicky,' he'd say to Sharpe, then he would clutch Sharpe's arm and point to the cockerels waiting to fight. 'Which one'll win, lad, which one?' And Sharpe would make a haphazard choice and, as often as not, the bird did win. 'He's a lucky boy,' the rat-catcher would boast to his friends as he tossed Sharpe a farthing. 'Nipper's got the luck of the devil!'

But not tonight, Sharpe thought, and suddenly the rug was seized, unwound, and Sharpe was spilt naked onto hard stones. A cheer greeted his appearance. Light flared in Sharpe's eyes, dazzling him, but after a while he saw he was in a great stone courtyard lit by the flames of torches mounted on pillars that surrounded the yard. Two white-robed men seized him, dragged him upright and pushed him onto a stone bench where, to his surprise, his hands and feet were loosed and the gag taken from his mouth. He sat flexing his fingers and gasping deep breaths of humid air. He could see no sign of Hakeswill.

He could see now that he was in a temple. A kind of cloister ran around the courtyard and, because the cloister was raised three or four feet, it made the stone-paved floor into a natural arena. He had not been so wrong about the cock-fighting pit, though Vinegar Street had never aspired to ornately carved stone arches smothered with writhing gods and snarling beasts. The raised cloister was packed with men who were in obvious good humour. There were hundreds of them, all anticipating a night's rare entertainment. Sharpe touched his swollen lip and winced at the pain. He was thirsty, and with every deep breath his bruised or broken ribs hurt. There was a swelling on his forehead that was thick with dried blood. He looked about the crowd, seeking one friendly face and finding none. He just saw Indian peasants with dark eyes that reflected the flame light. They must have come from every village within ten miles to witness whatever was about to happen.

In the centre of the courtyard was a small stone building, fantastically carved with elephants and dancing girls, and crowned by a stepped tower that had been sculpted with yet more gods and animals painted red, yellow, green and black. The crowd's noise subsided as a man showed at the doorway of the small shrine and raised his arms as a signal for silence. Sharpe recognized the man. He was the tall, thin, limping man in the green and black striped robe who had pleaded with Torrance for Naig's life, and behind him came a pair of *jettis*. So that was the sum of it. Revenge for Naig, and Sharpe realized that Hakeswill had never intended to kill him, only deliver him to these men.

A murmur ran through the spectators as they admired the *jettis*. Vast brutes, they were, who dedicated their extraordinary strength to some strange Indian god. Although Sharpe had met *jettis* before and had killed some in Seringapatam, he did not fancy his chances against these two bearded brutes. He was too weak, too thirsty, too bruised, too hurt, while these two fanatics were tall and hugely muscled. Their bronze skin had been oiled so that it gleamed in the flame light. Their long hair was coiled about their skulls, and one had red lines painted on his face, while the other, who was slightly shorter, carried a long spear. Each man wore a loincloth and nothing else. They glanced at Sharpe, then the taller man prostrated himself before a small shrine. A dozen guards came from the courtyard's rear and lined its edge. They carried muskets tipped with bayonets.

The tall man in the striped robe clapped his hands to silence the crowd's last murmurs. It took a while, for still more spectators were pushing into the temple and there was scarce room in the cloister. Somewhere outside a horse neighed. Men shouted protests as the newcomers shoved their way inside, but at last the commotion ended and the tall man stepped to the edge of the stone platform on which the small shrine stood. He spoke for a long time, and every few moments his words would provoke a growl of agreement, and then the crowd would look at Sharpe and some would spit at him. Sharpe stared sullenly back at them. They were getting a rare night's amusement, he reckoned. A captured Englishman was to be killed in front of them, and Sharpe could not blame them for relishing the prospect. But he was damned if he would die easy. He could do some damage, he reckoned, maybe not much, but enough so that the *jettis* remembered the night they were given a redcoat to kill.

The tall man finished his speech, then limped down the short flight of steps and approached Sharpe. He carried himself with dignity, like a man who knows his own worth to be high. He stopped a few paces from Sharpe and his face showed derision as he stared at the Englishman's sorry state. 'My name,' he said in English, 'is Jama.'

Sharpe said nothing.

'You killed my brother,' Jama said.

'I've killed a lot of men,' Sharpe said, his voice hoarse so that it scarcely carried the few paces that separated the two men. He spat to clear his throat. 'I've killed a lot of men,' he said again.

'And Naig was one,' Jama said.

'He deserved to die,' Sharpe said.

Jama sneered at that answer. 'If my brother deserved to die then so did the British who traded with him.'

That was probably true, Sharpe thought, but he said nothing. He could see some pointed helmets at the back of the crowd and he guessed that some of the Mahratta horsemen who still roamed the Deccan Plain had come to see his death. Maybe the same Mahrattas who had bought the two thousand missing muskets, muskets that Hakeswill had supplied and Torrance had lied about to conceal the theft.

'So now you will die,' Jama said simply.

Sharpe shrugged. Run to the right, he was thinking, and grab the nearest musket, but he knew he would be slowed by the pain. Besides, the men on the cloister would jump down to overpower him. But he had to do something. Anything! A man could not just be killed like a dog.

'You will die slowly,' Jama said, 'to satisfy the debt of blood that is owed to my family.'

'You want a death,' Sharpe asked, 'to balance your brother's death?'

'Exactly so,' Jama said gravely.

'Then kill a rat,' Sharpe said, 'or strangle a toad. Your brother deserved to die. He was a thief.'

'And you English have come to steal all India,' Jama said equably. He looked again at Sharpe's wounds, and seemed to get satisfaction from them. 'You will soon be pleading for my mercy,' he said. 'Do you know what *jettis* are?'

'I know,' Sharpe said.

'Prithviraj,' Jama said, gesturing towards the taller *jetti* who was bowing before the small altar, 'has castrated a man with his bare hands. He will do that to you and more, for tonight I have promised these people they will see the death of a hundred parts. You will be torn to pieces, Englishman, but you will live as your body is divided, for that is a *jetti*'s skill. To kill a man slowly, without weapons, tearing him piece by piece, and only when your screams have assuaged the pain of my brother's death will I show you mercy.' Jama gave Sharpe one last look of disdain, then turned and walked back to the shrine's steps.

Prithviraj leaned forward and rang a tiny handbell to draw the god's attention, then put his hands together and bowed his head a last time. The second *jetti*, the one with the spear, watched Sharpe with an expressionless face.

Sharpe forced himself to stand. His back ached and his legs were weak so that he tottered, making the crowd laugh at him. He took a step to his right, but the closest guard just edged away. A carved stool had been fetched from the shrine and Jama was now sitting at the top of the steps. A huge bat flickered in and out of the torchlight. Sharpe walked forward, testing his legs, and was amazed he could stand at all. The crowd jeered his faltering gait, and the sound made Prithviraj turn from his devotions. He saw that Sharpe posed no danger and so turned back to the god.

Sharpe staggered. He did it deliberately, making himself look weaker than he really was. He swayed, pretending that he was about to fall, then took some slurred sideways steps to get close to one of the guards. Seize a musket, he told himself, then ram its muzzle into Jama's face. He swayed sideways again, and the closest guard just stepped back and levelled the bayonet at Sharpe. The dozen sentries plainly had orders to keep Sharpe inside the *jetti*'s killing ground. Sharpe measured the distance, wondering if he could get past the bayonet to seize the musket, but a second guard came to reinforce the first.

Then Prithviraj stood.

He was a bloody giant, Sharpe thought, a giant with an oiled skin and upper arms as thick as most men's thighs. The crowd murmured in admiration again, and then Prithviraj undid his loincloth and let it fall so that he was naked like Sharpe. The gesture seemed to imply that he sought no advantage over his opponent, though as the huge man came down from the shrine the second *jetti* took care to stay close beside him. Two against one, and the second had a spear, and Sharpe had nothing. He glanced at the burning torches, wondering if he could seize one and brandish it as a weapon, but they were mounted too high. Christ, he thought, but do something! Anything! Panic began to close in on him, fluttering like the bat which swooped into the flame light again.

He backed away from the *jettis* and the crowd jeered him. He did not care. He was watching Prithviraj. A slow-moving man, too musclebound to be quick, and Sharpe guessed that was why the second *jetti* was present. His job would be to herd Sharpe with the glittering spear, and afterwards to hold him still as Prithviraj tore off fingers, toes and ears. So take the spearman first, Sharpe told himself, put the bastard down and take his weapon. He edged to his left, circling the courtyard to try and position himself closer to the spear-carrying *jetti*. The crowd sighed as he moved, enjoying the thought that the Englishman would put up a fight.

The spear followed Sharpe's movements. He would have to be quick, Sharpe thought, desperately quick, and he doubted he could do it. Hakeswill's kicking had slowed him, but he had to try and so he kept on circling, then abruptly charged in to attack the spearman, but the weapon was jabbed towards him and Prithviraj was much faster than Sharpe had expected and leaped to catch him, and Sharpe had to twist awkwardly away. The crowd laughed at his clumsiness.

'Accept your death,' Jama called. A servant was fanning the merchant's face.

Sweat poured down Sharpe's cheeks. He had been forced towards that part of the courtyard nearest the temple's entrance where there were two stone flights of stairs leading up to the cloister. The steps, jutting into the yard, formed a bay in which Sharpe suddenly realized he was trapped. He moved sideways, but the spear-carrying *jetti* covered him. The two men knew he was cornered now and came slowly towards him and Sharpe could only back away until his spine touched the cloister's edge. One of the spectators kicked him, but with more malice than force. The *jettis* came on slowly, wary in case he suddenly broke to right or left. Prithviraj was flexing his huge fingers, making them supple for the night's work. Scraps of smouldering ash whirled away from the torches, one settling on Sharpe's shoulder. He brushed it off.

'Sahib?' a voice hissed from behind Sharpe. 'Sahib?'

Prithviraj looked calm and confident. No bloody wonder, Sharpe thought. So kick the naked bugger in the crotch. He reckoned that was his last chance. One good kick, and hope that Prithviraj doubled over. Either that or run onto the spear and hope the blade killed him quickly.

'Sahib!' the voice hissed again. Prithviraj was turning sideways so that he would not expose his groin to Sharpe, then he beckoned for the other *jetti* to close in on the Englishman and drive him out from the wall with his spear. 'You bugger!' the voice said impatiently.

Sharpe turned to see that Ahmed was on hands and knees among the legs of the spectators, and what was more the child was pushing forward the hilt of the *tulwar* he had captured at Deogaum. Sharpe leaned on the cloister edge and the crowd, seeing him rest against the stone, believed he had given up. Some groaned for they had been anticipating more of a fight, but most of the watching men just jeered at him for being a weakling.

Sharpe winked at Ahmed, then reached for the *tulwar*. He seized the handle, pushed away from the stone and turned, dragging the blade from the scabbard that was still in Ahmed's grasp. He turned fast as a striking snake, the curved steel silver-red in the courtyard's flame light, and the *jettis*, thinking he was a beaten man, were not prepared. The man with the spear was closest, and the curved blade slashed across his face, springing blood, and he instinctively clutched his eyes and let the spear drop. Sharpe moved to the right, scooped up the fallen spear, and Prithviraj at last looked worried.

The guards raised their muskets. Sharpe heard the clicks as the dogheads were hauled back. So let them shoot him, he thought, for that was a quicker death than being dismembered and gelded by a naked giant. Jama was standing, one hand in the air, reluctant to let his guards shoot Sharpe before he had suffered pain. The wounded *jetti* was on his knees, his hands clutched to his face which was streaming blood.

Then a musket fired, its sound unnaturally loud in the confines of the courtyard's carved walls. One of the guards flinched as the musket ball whipped past his head to chip a flake of stone from one of the decorated arches. Then a voice shouted from the cloister by the temple entrance. The man spoke in an Indian language, and he spoke to Jama who was staring appalled as a group of armed men pushed their way to the very front of the crowd.

It was Syud Sevajee who had fired, and who had spoken to Jama, and who now grinned down at Sharpe. 'I've told him it must be a fair fight, Ensign.'

'Me against him?' Sharpe jerked his chin at Prithviraj.

'We came for entertainment,' Syud Sevajee said, 'the least you can do is provide us with some.'

'Why don't you just shoot the bugger and have done with it?'

Sevajee smiled. 'This crowd will accept the result of a fair fight, Ensign. They might not like it if I simply rescue you. Besides, you don't want to be in my debt, do you?'

'I'm in your debt already,' Sharpe said, 'up to my bloody eyeballs.' He turned and looked at Prithviraj who was waiting for a sign from Jama. 'Hey! Goliath!' Sharpe shouted. 'Here!' He threw the *tulwar* at the man, keeping the spear. 'You want a fair fight? So you've got a weapon now.'

The pain seemed to have vanished and even the thirst had gone away. It was like that moment at Assaye when he had been surrounded by enemies, and suddenly the world had seemed a calm, clear-cut place full of delicious opportunity. He had a chance now. He had more than a chance, he was going to put the big bastard down. It was a fair fight, and Sharpe had grown up fighting. He had been bred to it from the gutter, driven to it by poverty and inured to it by desperation. He was nothing if he was not a fighter, and now the crowd would get the bloody sport they wanted. He hefted the spear. 'So come on, you bastard!'

Prithviraj stooped and picked up the *tulwar*. He swung it in a clumsy arc, then looked again at Jama.

'Don't look at him, you great ox! Look at me!' Sharpe went forward, the spear low, then he raised the blade and lunged towards the big man's belly and Prithviraj made a clumsy parry that rang against the spear blade. 'You'll have to put more strength into it than that,' Sharpe said, pulling back the spear and standing still to tempt the *jetti* forward. Prithviraj stepped towards him, swung the blade and Sharpe stepped back so that the *tulwar*'s tip slashed inches from his chest.

'You have to be quick,' Sharpe said, and he feinted right, spun away and walked back to the left leaving Prithviraj off balance. Sharpe turned and lunged with the spear, pricking the big man's back and leaving a trickle of blood. 'Ain't the same, is it, when the other fellow's got a weapon?' He smiled at the *jetti*. 'So come on, you daft pudding. Come on!'

The crowd was silent now. Prithviraj seemed puzzled. He had not expected to fight, not with a weapon, and it was plain he was not accustomed to a *tulwar*. 'You can give up,' Sharpe said. 'You can kneel down and give up. I won't kill you if you do that, but if you stay on your feet I'll pick you apart like a joint of bloody meat.'

Prithviraj did not understand a word, but he knew Sharpe was dangerous and he was trying to work out how best to kill him. He glanced at the spear, wishing he had that weapon instead of the *tulwar*, but Sharpe knew the point should always beat the edge, which was why he had kept the spear. 'You want it quick or slow, Sevajee?' Sharpe called.

'Whichever you prefer, Ensign,' Sevajee said, smiling. 'It is not for the audience to tell the actors how the play should go.'

'Then I'll make it quick,' Sharpe said, and he pointed at Prithviraj with his free hand and motioned that the *jetti* could kneel down. 'Just kneel,' he said, 'and I'll spare you. Tell him that, Sevajee!'

Sevajee called out in an Indian language and Prithviraj must have decided the offer was an insult, for he suddenly ran forward, *tulwar* swinging, and Sharpe had to step quickly aside and parry one of the cuts with the spear's staff. The blade cut a sliver of wood from the shaft, but went nowhere near Sharpe.

'No good doing that,' Sharpe said. 'You're not making hay, you great pudding, you're trying to stay alive.'

Prithviraj attacked again, but all he could think to do was make great swings with the blade, any one of which might have slit Sharpe into two, but the attacks were clumsy and Sharpe backed away, always circling around to the middle of the courtyard so that he was not trapped against its edges. The crowd, sensing that Prithviraj might win, began to urge him on, but some noticed that the Englishman was not even trying to fight yet. He was taunting the *jetti*, he was evading him and he was keeping his spear low.

'I thought you said it would be quick,' Sevajee said.

'You want it over?' Sharpe asked. He crouched, raising the spear blade, and the motion checked Prithviraj who stared at him warily. 'What I'm going to do,' Sharpe said, 'is cut your belly open, then slit your throat. Are you ready?' He went forward, jabbing the spear, still low, and Prithviraj backed away, trying to parry the small lunges, but Sharpe dragged the spear back each time before the parry could connect, and Prithviraj frowned. He seemed hypnotized by the shining blade that flickered like a snake's tongue, and behind it Sharpe was grinning at him and taunting him, and Prithviraj tried to counter-attack once, but the spear slashed up to within an inch of his face and he went on stepping backwards. Then he backed into the blinded *jetti* who still crouched on the flagstones and Prithviraj staggered as he lost his balance.

Sharpe came up from the crouch, the spear lancing forward and the wild parry came far too late and suddenly the blade was punching and tearing through the skin and muscle of the *jetti*'s stomach. Sharpe twisted the leaf-shaped steel so that it did not get trapped in the flesh and then he ripped it out, and blood washed across the temple floor and Prithviraj was bending forward as if he could seal the pain in his belly by folding over, and then the spear sliced from the side to slash across his throat.

The crowd sighed.

Prithviraj was on the stones now, curled up with blood bubbling from his sliced belly and pulsing from his neck.

Sharpe kicked the *tulwar* from the *jetti*'s unresisting hand, then turned and looked at Jama. 'You and your brother did business with Captain Torrance?'

Jama said nothing.

Sharpe walked towards the shrine. The guards moved to stop him, but Sevajee's men raised their muskets and some, grinning, jumped down into the courtyard. Ahmed also jumped down and snatched the *tulwar* from the flagstones. Prithviraj was on his side now, dying.

Jama stood as Sharpe reached the steps, but he could not move fast with his limp and suddenly the spear was at his belly. 'I asked you a question,' Sharpe said.

Jama still said nothing.

'You want to live?' Sharpe asked. Jama looked down at the spear blade that was thick with blood. 'Was it Torrance who gave me to you?' Sharpe asked.

'Yes,' Jama said.

'If I see you again,' Sharpe said, 'I'll kill you. If you go back to the British camp I'll hang you like your brother, and if you so much as send a message to Torrance, I'll follow you to the last corner on God's earth and I'll castrate you with my bare hands.' He jabbed the spear just enough to prick Jama's belly, then turned away. The crowd was silent, cowed by Sevajee's men and by the ferocity they had witnessed in the temple courtyard. Sharpe tossed away the spear, pulled Ahmed towards him and patted the boy's head. 'You're a good lad, Ahmed. A bloody good lad. And I need a drink. By Christ, I'm thirsty.'

But he was also alive.

Which meant some other men would soon be dead.

Because Sharpe was more than alive. He was angry. Angry as hell. And wanting revenge.

Sharpe borrowed a cloak from one of Sevajee's men, then pulled himself up behind Ahmed onto Major Stokes's horse. They rode slowly away from the village where the torches guttered in the temple towards the smear of red light that betrayed where the British encampment lay some miles to the west. Sevajee talked as they rode, telling Sharpe how Ahmed had fled straight into the arms of his men. 'Luckily for you, Ensign,' the Indian said, 'I recognized him.'

'Which is why you sent for help, isn't it?' Sharpe asked sarcastically. 'It's why you fetched some redcoats to get me out of that bloody tent.'

'Your gratitude touches me deeply,' Sevajee said with a smile. 'It took us a long time to make sense of what your boy was saying, and I confess we didn't wholly believe him even then, and by the time we thought to take him seriously, you were already being carried away. So we followed. I thought we might fetch some entertainment from the evening, and so we did.'

'Glad to be of service, sahib,' Sharpe said.

'I knew you could beat a *jetti* in a fair fight.'

'I beat three at once in Seringapatam,' Sharpe said, 'but I don't know as it was a fair fight. I'm not much in favour of fair fights. I like them to be unfair. Fair fights are for gentlemen who don't know any better.'

'Which is why you gave the sword to the *jetti*,' Sevajee observed drily.

'I knew he'd make a bollocks of it,' Sharpe said. He was tired suddenly, and all the aches and throbs and agony had come back. Above him the sky was brilliant with stars, while a thin sickle moon hung just above the faraway fortress. Dodd was up there, Sharpe thought, another life to take. Dodd and Torrance, Hakeswill and his two men. A debt to be paid by sending all the bastards to hell.

'Where shall I take you?' Sevajee asked.

'Take me?'

'You want to go to the General?'

'Christ, no.' Sharpe could not imagine complaining to Wellesley. The cold bugger would probably blame Sharpe for getting into trouble. Stokes, maybe? Or the cavalry? Sergeant Lockhart would doubtless welcome him, but then he had a better idea. 'Take me to wherever you're camped,' he told Sevajee.

'And in the morning?'

'You've got a new recruit,' Sharpe said. 'I'm one of your men for now.'

Sevajee looked amused. 'Why?'

'Why do you think? I want to hide.'

'But why?'

Sharpe sighed. 'D'you think Wellesley will believe me? If I go to Wellesley he'll think I've got sunstroke, or he'll reckon I'm drunk. And Torrance will stand there with a plum in his bloody mouth and deny everything, or else he'll blame Hakeswill.'

'Hakeswill?' Sevajee asked.

'A bastard I'm going to kill,' Sharpe said. 'And it'll be easier if he doesn't know I'm still alive.' And this time, Sharpe vowed, he would make sure of the bastard. 'My only worry,' he told Sevajee, 'is Major Stokes's horse. He's a good man, Stokes.'

'That horse?' Sevajee asked, nodding at the grey mare.

'You reckon a couple of your fellows could return it to him in the morning?'

'Of course.'

'Tell him I got thrown from the saddle and snatched up by the enemy,' Sharpe said. 'Let him think I'm a prisoner in Gawilghur.'

'And meanwhile you'll be one of us?' Sevajee asked.

'I've just become a Mahratta,' Sharpe said.

'Welcome,' said Sevajee. 'And what you need now, Sharpe, is some rest.'

'I've had plenty of rest,' Sharpe said. 'What I need now are some clothes, and some darkness.'

'You need food too,' Sevajee insisted. He glanced up at the sliver of moon above the fort. It was waning. 'Tomorrow night will be darker,' he promised, and Sharpe nodded. He wanted a deep darkness, a shadowed blackness, in which a living ghost could hunt.

Major Stokes was grateful for the return of his horse, but saddened over Sharpe's fate. 'Captured!' he told Sir Arthur Wellesley. 'And my own fault too.'

'Can't see how that can be, Stokes.'

'I should never have let him ride off on his own. Should have made him wait till a group went back.'

'Won't be the first prison cell he's seen,' Wellesley said, 'and I daresay it won't be the last.'

'I shall miss him,' Stokes said, 'miss him deeply. A good man.'

Wellesley grunted. He had ridden up the improved road to judge its progress for himself and he was impressed, though he took care not to show his approval. The road now snaked up into the hills and one more day's work would see it reach the edge of the escarpment. Half the necessary siege guns were already high on the road, parked in an upland meadow, while bullocks were trudging up the lower slopes with their heavy burdens of round shot that would be needed to break open Gawilghur's walls. The Mahrattas had virtually ceased their raids on the road-makers ever since Wellesley had sent two battalions of sepoys up into the hills to hunt the enemy down. Every once in a while a musket shot would be fired from a long distance, but the balls were usually spent before they reached a target. 'Your work won't end with the road,' Wellesley told Stokes, as the General and his staff followed the engineer on foot towards some higher ground from where they could inspect the fortress.

'I doubted it would, sir.'

'You know Stevenson?'

'I've dined with the Colonel.'

'I'm sending him up here. His troops will make the assault. My men will stay below and climb the two roads.' Wellesley spoke curtly, almost offhandedly. He was proposing to divide his army into two again, just as it had been split for most of the war against the Mahrattas. Stevenson's part of the army would climb to the plateau and make the main assault on the fortress. That attack would swarm across the narrow neck of land to climb the breaches, but to stop the enemy from throwing all their strength into the defence of the broken wall Wellesley proposed sending two columns of his own men up the steep tracks that led directly to the fortress. Those men would have to approach unbroken walls up slopes too steep to permit artillery to be deployed, and Wellesley knew those columns could never hope to break into Gawilghur. Their job was to spread the defenders thin, and to block off the garrison's escape routes while Colonel Stevenson's men did the bloody work. 'You'll have to establish Stevenson's batteries,' Wellesley told Stokes. 'Major Blackiston's seen the ground' – he indicated his aide – 'and he reckons two eighteens and three iron twelves should suffice. Major Blackiston, of course, will give you whatever advice he can.'

'No glacis?' Stokes directed the question to Blackiston.

'Not when I was there,' Blackiston said, 'though of course they could have made one since. I just saw curtain walls with a few bastions. Ancient work, by the look of it.'

'Fifteenth-century work,' Wellesley put in and, when he saw that the two engineers were impressed by his knowledge, he shrugged. 'Syud Sevajee claims as much, anyway.'

'Old walls break fastest,' Stokes said cheerfully. The two big guns, with the three smaller cannon, would batter the wall head on to crumble the ancient stone that was probably unprotected by a glacis of embanked earth to soak up the force of the bombardment, and the Major had yet to find a fortress wall in India that could resist the strike of an eighteen-pounder shot travelling half a mile every two seconds. 'But you'll want some enfilading fire,' he warned Wellesley.

'I'll send you some more twelves,' Wellesley promised.

'A battery of twelves and an howitzer,' Stokes suggested. 'I'd like to drop some nasties over the wall. There's nothing like an howitzer for spreading gloom.'

'I'll send an howitzer,' Wellesley promised. The enfilading batteries would fire at an angle through the growing breaches to keep the enemy from making repairs, and the howitzer, which fired high in the air so that its shells dropped steeply down, could bombard the repair parties behind the fortress ramparts. 'And I want the batteries established quickly,' Wellesley said. 'No dallying, Major.'

'I'm not a man to dally, Sir Arthur,' Stokes said cheerfully. The Major was leading the General and his staff up a particularly steep patch of road where an elephant, supplemented by over sixty sweating sepoys, forced an eighteen-pounder gun up the twisting road. The officers dodged the sepoys, then climbed a knoll from where they could stare across at Gawilghur.

By now they were nearly as high as the stronghold itself and the profile of the twin forts stood clear against the bright sky beyond. It formed a double hump. The narrow neck of land led from the plateau to the first, lower hump on which the Outer Fortress stood. It was that fortress which would receive Stokes's breaching fire, and that fortress which would be assailed by Stevenson's men, but beyond it the ground dropped into a deep ravine, then climbed steeply to the much larger second hump on which the Inner Fortress with its palace and its lakes and its houses stood. Sir Arthur spent a long time staring through his glass, but said nothing.

'I'll warrant I can get you into the smaller fortress,' Stokes said, 'but how do you cross the central ravine into the main stronghold?'

It was that question that Wellesley had yet to answer in his own mind, and he suspected there was no simple solution. He hoped that the attackers would simply surge across the ravine and flood up the second slope like an irresistible wave that had broken through one barrier and would now overcome everything in its path, but he dared not admit to such impractical optimism. He dared not confess that he was condemning his men to an attack on an Inner Fortress that would have unbreached walls and well-prepared defenders. 'If we can't take it by escalade,' he said curtly, collapsing his glass, 'we'll have to dig breaching batteries in the Outer Fortress and do it the hard way.'

In other words, Stokes thought, Sir Arthur had no idea how it was to be done. Only that it must be done. By escalade or by breach, and by God's mercy, if they were lucky, for once they were into the central ravine the attackers would be in the devil's hands.

It was a hot December day, but Stokes shivered, for he feared for the men who must go up against Gawilghur.

Captain Torrance had enjoyed a remarkably lucky evening. Jama had still not returned to the camp, and his big green tents with their varied delights stood empty, but there were plenty of other diversions in the British camp. A group of Scottish officers, augmented by a sergeant who played the flute, gave a concert, and though Torrance had no great taste for chamber music he found the melodies were in tune with his jaunty mood. Sharpe was gone, Torrance's debts were paid, he had survived, and he had strolled on from the concert to the cavalry lines where he knew he would find a game of whist. Torrance had succeeded in taking fifty-three guineas from an irascible major and another twelve from a whey-cheeked ensign who kept scratching his groin. 'If you've got the pox,' the Major had finally said, 'then get the hell to a surgeon.'

'It's lice, sir.'

'Then for Christ's sake stop wriggling. You're distracting me.'

'Scratch on,' Torrance had said, laying down a winning hand. He had yawned, scooped up the coins, and bid his partners a good night.

'It's devilish early,' the Major had grumbled, wanting a chance to win his money back.

'Duty,' Torrance had said vaguely, then he had strolled to the merchant encampment and inspected the women who fanned themselves in the torrid night heat. An hour later, well pleased with himself, he had returned to his quarters. His servant squatted on the porch, but he waved the man away.

Sajit was still at his candle-lit desk, unclogging his pen of the soggy paper scraps that collected on the nib. He stood, touched his inky hands together and bowed as Torrance entered. 'Sahib.'

'All well?'

'All is well, sahib. Tomorrow's chitties.' He pushed a pile of papers across the desk.

'I'm sure they're in order,' Torrance said, quite confident that he spoke true. Sajit was proving to be an excellent clerk. He went to the door of his quarters, then turned with a frown. 'Your uncle hasn't come back?'

'Tomorrow, sahib, I'm sure.'

'Tell him I'd like a word. But not if he comes tonight. I don't want to be disturbed tonight.'

'Of course not, sahib.' Sajit offered another bow as Torrance negotiated the door and the muslin screen.

The Captain shot the iron bolt, then chased down the few moths that had managed to get past the muslin. He lit a second lamp, piled the night's winnings on the table, then called for Clare. She came sleepy-eyed from the kitchen.

'Arrack, Brick,' Torrance ordered, then peeled off his coat while Clare unstoppered a fresh jar of the fierce spirit. She kept her eyes averted as Torrance stripped himself naked and lay back in his hammock. 'You could light me a hookah, Brick,' he suggested, 'then sponge me down. Is there a clean shirt for the morning?'

'Of course, sir.'

'Not the darned one?'

'No, sir.'

He turned his head to stare at the coins which glittered so prettily in the smoky lamplight. In funds again! Winning! Perhaps his luck had turned. It seemed so. He had lost so much money at cards in the last month that he had thought nothing but ruin awaited him, but now the goddess of fortune had turned her other cheek. Rule of halves, he told himself as he sucked on the hookah. Save half, gamble the other half. Halve the winnings and save half again. Simple really. And now that Sharpe was gone he could begin some careful trading once more, though how the market would hold up once the Mahrattas were defeated he could not tell. Still, with a slice of luck he might make sufficient money to set himself up in a comfortable civilian life in Madras. A carriage, a dozen horses and as many women servants. He would have an harem. He smiled at the thought, imagining his father's disgust. An harem, a courtyard with a fountain, a wine cellar deep beneath his house that should be built close to the sea so that cooling breezes could waft through its windows. He would need to spend an hour or two at the office each week, but certainly not more for there were always Indians to do the real work. The buggers would cheat him, of course, but there seemed plenty of money to go around so long as a man did not gamble it away. Rule of halves, he told himself again. The golden rule of life.

The sound of singing came from the camp beyond the village. Torrance did not recognize the tune, which was probably some Scottish song. The sound drifted him back to his childhood when he had sung in the cathedral choir. He grimaced, remembering the frosty mornings when he had run in the dark across the close and pushed open the cathedral's great side door to be greeted by a clout over the ear because he was late. The choristers' cloudy breath had mingled with the smoke of the guttering candles. Lice under the robes, he remembered. He had caught his first lice off a counter-tenor who had held him against a wall behind a bishop's tomb and hoisted his robe. I hope the bastard's dead, he thought.

Sajit yelped. 'Quiet!' Torrance shouted, resenting being jarred from his reverie. There was silence again, and Torrance sucked on the hookah. He could hear Clare pouring water in the yard and he smiled as he anticipated the soothing touch of the sponge.

Someone, it had to be Sajit, tried to open the door from the front room. 'Go away,' Torrance called, but then something hit the door a massive blow. The bolt held, though dust sifted from crevices in the plaster wall either side of the frame. Torrance stared in shock, then twitched with alarm as another huge bang shook the door, and this time a chunk of plaster the size of a dinner plate fell from the wall. Torrance swung his bare legs out of the hammock. Where the devil were his pistols?

A third blow reverberated round the room, and this time the bracket holding the bolt was wrenched out of the wall and the door swung in onto the muslin screen. Torrance saw a robed figure sweep the screen aside, then he threw himself over the room and pawed through his discarded clothes to find his guns.

A hand gripped his wrist. 'You won't need that, sir,' a familiar voice said, and Torrance turned, wincing at the strength of the man's grip. He saw a figure dressed in blood-spattered Indian robes, with a *tulwar* scabbarded at his waist and a face shrouded by a head cloth. But Torrance recognized his visitor and blanched. 'Reporting for duty, sir,' Sharpe said, taking the pistol from Torrance's unresisting grip.

Torrance gaped. He could have sworn that the blood on the robe was fresh for it gleamed wetly. There was more blood on a short-bladed knife in Sharpe's hand. It dripped onto the floor and Torrance gave a small pitiful mew.

'It's Sajit's blood,' Sharpe said. 'His penknife too.' He tossed the wet blade onto the table beside the gold coins. 'Lost your tongue, sir?'

'Sharpe?'

'He's dead, sir, Sharpe is,' Sharpe said. 'He was sold to Jama, remember, sir? Is that the blood money?' Sharpe glanced at the rupees on the table.

'Sharpe,' Torrance said again, somehow incapable of saying anything else.

'I'm his ghost, sir,' Sharpe said, and Torrance did indeed look as though a spectre had just broken through his door. Sharpe tutted and shook his head in self-reproof. 'I'm not supposed to call you "sir", am I, sir? On account of me being a fellow officer and a gentleman. Where's Sergeant Hakeswill?'

'Sharpe!' Torrance said once more, collapsing onto a chair. 'We heard you'd been captured!'

'So I was, sir, but not by the enemy. Leastwise, not by any proper enemy.' Sharpe examined the pistol. 'This ain't loaded. What were you hoping to do, sir? Beat me to death with the barrel?'

'My robe, Sharpe, please,' Torrance said, gesturing to where the silk robe hung on a wooden peg.

'So where is Hakeswill, sir?' Sharpe asked. He had pushed back his head cloth and now opened the pistol's frizzen and blew dust off the pan before scraping at the layer of caked powder with a fingernail.

'He's on the road,' Torrance said.

'Ah! Took over from me, did he? You should keep this pistol clean, sir. There's rust on the spring, see? Shame to keep an expensive gun so shabbily. Are you sitting on your cartridge box?'

Torrance meekly raised his bottom to take out his leather pouch which held the powder and bullets for his pistols. He gave the bag to Sharpe, thought about fetching the robe himself, then decided that any untoward move might upset his visitor. 'I'm delighted to see you're alive, Sharpe,' he said.

'Are you, sir?' Sharpe asked.

'Of course.'

'Then why did you sell me to Jama?'

'Sell you? Don't be ridiculous, Sharpe. No!' The cry came as the pistol barrel whipped towards him, and it turned into a moan as the barrel slashed across his cheek. Torrance touched his face and winced at the blood on his fingers. 'Sharpe –' he began.

'Shut it, sir,' Sharpe said nastily. He perched on the table and poured some powder into the pistol barrel. 'I talked to Jama last night. He tried to have me killed by a couple of *jettis*. You know what *jettis* are, sir? Religious strongmen, sir, but they must have been praying to the wrong God, for I cut one's throat and left the other bugger blinded.' He paused to select a bullet from the pouch. 'And I had a chat with

Jama when I'd killed his thugs and he told me lots of interesting things. Like that you traded with him and his brother. You're a traitor, Torrance.'

'Sharpe –'

'I said shut it!' Sharpe snapped. He pushed the bullet into the pistol's muzzle, then drew out the short ramrod and shoved it down the barrel. 'The thing is, Torrance,' he went on in a calmer tone, 'I know the truth. All of it. About you and Hakeswill and about you and Jama and about you and Naig.' He smiled at Torrance, then slotted the short ramrod back into its hoops. 'I used to think officers were above that sort of crime. I knew the men were crooked, because I was crooked, but you don't have much choice, do you, when you've got nothing? But you, sir, you had everything you wanted. Rich parents, proper schooling.' Sharpe shook his head.

'You don't understand, Sharpe.'

'But I do, sir. Now look at me. My ma was a whore, and not a very good one by all accounts, and she went and died and left me with nothing. Bloody nothing! And the thing is, sir, that when I go to General Wellesley and I tells him about you selling muskets to the enemy, who's he going to believe? You, with your proper education, or me with a dead frow as a mother?' Sharpe looked at Torrance as though he expected an answer, but none came. 'He's going to believe you, sir, isn't he? He'd never believe me, on account of me not being a proper gentleman who knows his Latin. And you know what that means, sir?'

'Sharpe?'

'It means justice won't be done, sir. But, on the other hand, you're a gentleman, so you knows your duty, don't you?' Sharpe edged off the table and gave the pistol, butt first, to Torrance. 'Hold it just in front of your ear,' he advised Torrance, 'or else put it in your mouth. Makes more mess that way, but it's surer.'

'Sharpe!' Torrance said, and found he had nothing to say. The pistol felt heavy in his hand.

'It won't hurt, sir,' Sharpe said comfortingly. 'You'll be dead in the blink of an eyelid.' He began scooping the coins off the table into Torrance's pouch. He heard the heavy click as the pistol was cocked, then glanced round to see that the muzzle was pointing at his face. He frowned and shook his head in disappointment. 'And I thought you were a gentleman, sir.'

'I'm not a fool, Sharpe,' Torrance said vengefully. He stood and took a pace closer to the Ensign. 'And I'm worth ten of you. Up from the ranks? You know what that makes you, Sharpe? It makes you a brute, a lucky brute, but it don't make you a real officer. You're not going to be welcome anywhere, Sharpe. You'll be endured, Sharpe, because officers have manners, but they won't welcome you because you ain't a proper officer. You weren't born to it, Sharpe.' Torrance laughed at the look of horrified outrage on Sharpe's face. 'Christ, I despise you!' he said savagely. 'You're like a dressed-up monkey, Sharpe, only you can't even wear clothes properly! I could give you lace and braid, and you'd still look like a peasant, because that's what you are, Sharpe. Officers should have style! They should have wit! And all you can do is grunt. You know what you are, Sharpe? You're an embarrassment, you're . . .' He paused, trying to find the right insult, and shook his head in frustration as the words would not come. 'You're a lump, Sharpe! That's what you are, a lump! And the kindest thing is to finish you off.' Torrance smiled. 'Goodbye, Mister Sharpe.' He pulled the trigger.

The flint smashed down on the steel and the spark flashed into the empty pan.

Sharpe reached out in the silence and took the pistol from Torrance's hand. 'I loaded it, sir, but I didn't prime it. On account of the fact that I might be a lump, but I ain't any kind of fool.' He pushed Torrance back into the chair, and Torrance could only watch as Sharpe dropped a pinch of powder into the pan. He flinched as Sharpe closed the frizzen, then shuddered as Sharpe walked towards him.

'No, Sharpe, no!'

Sharpe stood behind Torrance. 'You tried to have me killed, sir, and I don't like that.' He pressed the pistol into the side of the Captain's head.

'Sharpe!' Torrance pleaded. He was shaking, but he seemed power-less to offer any resistance, then the muslin curtain from the kitchen was swept aside and Clare Wall came into the room. She stopped and stared with huge eyes at Sharpe.

'Clare!' Torrance pleaded. 'Fetch help! Quickly now!' Clare did not move. 'Fetch help, my dear!' Torrance said. 'She'll be a witness against you, Sharpe.' Torrance had turned to look at Sharpe and was babbling now. 'So the best thing you can do is to put the gun down. I'll say nothing about this, nothing! Just a touch of fever in you, I expect. It's all a misunderstanding and we shall forget it ever happened. Maybe we could share a bottle of arrack? Clare, my dear, maybe you could find a bottle?'

Clare stepped towards Sharpe and held out her hand.

'Fetch help, my dear,' Torrance said, 'he's not going to give you the gun.'

'He is,' Sharpe said, and he gave Clare the pistol.

Torrance breathed a great sigh of relief, then Clare clumsily turned the gun and pointed it at Torrance's head. The Captain just stared at her.

'Eyes front, Captain,' Sharpe said, and turned Torrance's head so that the bullet would enter from the side, just as it might if Torrance had committed suicide. 'Are you sure?' he asked Clare.

'God help me,' she said, 'but I've dreamed of doing this.' She straightened her arm so that the pistol's muzzle touched Torrance's temple.

'No!' he called. 'No, please! No!'

But she could not pull the trigger. Sharpe could see she wanted to, but her finger would not tighten and so Sharpe took the gun from her, edged her gently aside, then pushed the barrel into Torrance's oiled hair. 'No, please!' the Captain appealed. He was weeping. 'I beg you, Sharpe. Please!'

Sharpe pulled the trigger, stepping back as a gush of blood spouted from the shattered skull. The sound of the pistol had been hugely loud in the small room that was now hazed with smoke.

Sharpe knelt and pushed the pistol into Torrance's dead hand, then picked up the pouch with its gold and thrust it into Clare's hands. 'We're going,' he told her, 'right now.'

She understood the haste and, without bothering to fetch any of her belongings, followed him back into the outer room where Sajit's body lay slumped over the table. His blood had soaked the chitties. Clare whimpered when she saw the blood. 'I didn't really mean to kill him,' Sharpe explained, 'then realized he'd be a witness if I didn't.' He saw the fear on Clare's face. 'I trust you, love. You and me? We're the same, aren't we? So come on, let's get the hell out of here.'

Sharpe had already taken the three jewels from Sajit and he added those to the pouch of gold, then went to the porch where Ahmed stood guard. No one seemed to have been alarmed by the shot, but it was not wise to linger. 'I've got you some gold, Ahmed,' Sharpe said.

'Gold!'

'You know that word, you little bugger, don't you?' Sharpe grinned, then took Clare's hand and led her into the shadows. A dog barked briefly, a horse whinnied from the cavalry lines, and afterwards there was silence.

CHAPTER 7

Dodd needed to practise with the rifle and so, on the day that the British reached the top of the high escarpment, he settled himself in some rocks at the top of the cliff and gauged the range to the party of sepoys who were levelling the last few yards of the road. Unlike a musket, the rifle had proper sights, and he set the range at two hundred yards, then propped the barrel in a stone cleft and aimed at a blue-coated engineer who was standing just beneath the sweating sepoys. A gust of wind swept up the cliffs, driving some circling buzzards high up into the air. Dodd waited until the wind settled, then squeezed the trigger.

The rifle slammed into his shoulder with surprising force. The smoke blotted his view instantly, but another billow of wind carried it away and he was rewarded by the sight of the engineer bent double. He thought he must have hit the man, but then saw the engineer had been picking up his straw hat that must have fallen as he reacted to the close passage of the spinning bullet. The engineer beat dust from the hat against his thigh and stared up at the drifting patch of smoke.

Dodd wriggled back out of view and reloaded the rifle. It was hard work. The barrel of a rifle, unlike a musket, had spiralling grooves cast into the barrel to spin the bullet. The spin made the weapon extraordinarily accurate, but the grooves resisted the rammer, and the resistance was made worse because the bullet, if it was to be spun by the grooves, had to fit the barrel tightly. Dodd wrapped a bullet in one of the small greased leather patches that gave the barrel purchase, then grunted as he shoved the ramrod hard down. One of the Mahratta cavalrymen who escorted Dodd on his daily rides shouted a warning, and Dodd peered over the rock to see that a company of sepoy infantry was scrambling to the top of the slope. The first of them were already on the plateau and coming towards him. He primed the rifle, settled it on the makeshift firestep again and reckoned that he had not allowed for the effect of the wind on the last bullet. He aimed at the sepoys' officer, a man whose small round spectacles reflected the sun, and, letting the barrel edge slightly windwards, he fired again.

The rifle hammered back onto his shoulder. Smoke billowed as Dodd ran to his horse and clambered into the saddle. He slung the rifle, turned the horse and saw that the red-coated officer was on the ground with two of his men kneeling beside him. He grinned. Two hundred paces!

A wild volley of musketry followed the Mahratta horsemen as they rode westwards towards Gawilghur. The balls rattled on rocks or whistled overhead, but none of the cavalrymen was touched. After half a mile Dodd stopped, dismounted and reloaded the rifle. A troop of sepoy cavalry was climbing the last few yards of the road, the men walking as they led their horses around the final steep bend. Dodd found another place to rest the rifle, then waited for the cavalry to approach along the cliff's edge.

He kept the sights at two hundred yards. He knew that was very long range, even for a rifle, but if he could hit at two hundred yards then he was confident of killing at a hundred or at fifty.

'Sahib!' The commander of his escort was worried by the more numerous sepoy cavalry who had now mounted and were trotting towards them.

'In a minute,' Dodd called back. He picked his target, another officer, and waited for the man to ride into the rifle's sights. The wind was fitful. It gusted, blowing dust into Dodd's right eye and making him blink. Sweat trickled down his face. The approaching cavalry had sabres drawn and the blades glittered in the sun. One man carried a dusty pennant on a short staff. They came raggedly, twisting between the rocks and low bushes. Their horses kept their heads low, tired after the effort of climbing the steep hill.

The officer curbed his horse to let his men catch up. The wind died to nothing and Dodd squeezed the trigger and flinched as the heavy stock slammed into his bruised shoulder.

'Sahib!'

'We're going,' Dodd said, and he put his left foot into the stirrup and heaved himself into the saddle. A glance behind showed a riderless horse and a score of men spurring forward to take revenge. Dodd laughed, slung the rifle, and kicked his horse into a canter. He heard a shout behind as the sepoy cavalry were urged into the pursuit, but Dodd and his escort were mounted on fresh horses and easily outstripped the sepoys.

Dodd curbed his horse on the neck of rocky land that led to Gawilghur's Outer Fort. The walls were thick with men who watched the enemy's approach, and the sight of those spectators gave Dodd an idea. He threw the rifle to the commander of his escort. 'Hold it for me!' he ordered, then turned his horse to face the pursuing horsemen. He waved his escort on towards the fortress and drew his sword. It was a beautiful weapon, European made, then sent to India where craftsmen had given it a hilt of gold shaped like an elephant's head. The escort commander, charged with protecting Dodd's life, wanted to stay, but Dodd insisted he ride on. 'I'll join you in five minutes,' he promised.

Dodd barred the road. He glanced behind him once, just to check that the Outer Fort's ramparts were crowded with men, then he looked back to the approaching cavalry. They slowed as they reached the rock isthmus. They could have kept galloping, and Dodd would then have turned his horse and outrun them, but instead they curbed their sweating horses and just stood watching him from a hundred paces away. They knew what he wanted, but Dodd saluted them with his sword just to make certain they understood his challenge. A havildar urged his horse forward, but then an English voice summoned him back and the man reluctantly turned.

The English officer drew his sabre. He had lost his hat in the gallop along the edge of the cliff and had long fair hair that was matted with sweat and dirt. He wore a black and scarlet jacket and was mounted on a tall bay gelding that was white with sweat. He saluted Dodd by holding his sabre up, hilt before his face, then he touched the gelding's flanks with the tips of his spurs and the horse walked forward. Dodd spurred his own horse and the two slowly closed. The Englishman went into a trot, then clapped his heels to drive his horse into a canter and Dodd saw the puffs of dust spurting from the gelding's hooves. He kept his horse at a walk, only touching it into a trot at the very last second as the Englishman stood in his stirrups to deliver a scything cut with the sabre.

Dodd tweaked the rein and his horse swerved to the left, then he was turning it back right, turning it all the way, and the sabre had missed his head by a scant two inches and he had not even bothered to parry with his sword. Now he spurred the horse on, following the officer who was trying to turn back, and the Englishman was still half turned, still tugging on the reins, as Dodd attacked. The sabre made an awkward parry that just managed to deflect the sword's thrust. Dodd hacked back as he passed, felt the blade thump home, then he hauled on the reins and was turning again, and the Englishman was also turning so that the two horses seemed to curl around each other, nose to tail, and the sabre and sword rang together. Dodd was taller than his opponent, but the young Englishman, who was a lieutenant and scarce looked a day over eighteen, was strong, and Dodd's blow had hardly broken the weave of his coat. He gritted his teeth as he hacked at Dodd, and Dodd parried, parried again and the two blades locked, hilt against hilt, and Dodd heaved to try and throw the young man off balance.

'You're Dodd, aren't you?' the Lieutenant said.

'Seven hundred guineas to you, boy.'

'Traitor,' the young Englishman spat.

Dodd heaved, then kicked the Lieutenant's horse so that it moved forward and he tried to slash back with his disengaged sword, but the Lieutenant turned the horse in again. The men were too close to fight properly, close enough to smell each other's breath. The Lieutenant's stank of tobacco. They could hit their opponent with their sword hilts, but not use the blades' lengths. If either horse had been properly schooled they could have been walked sideways away from the impasse, but the horses would only go forward and Dodd was the first to take the risk by using his spurs. He used them savagely, startling his horse so that it leaped ahead, and even so he flinched from the expected slash as the sabre whipped towards his spine, but the Lieutenant was slow and the blow missed.

Dodd rode twenty paces up the track towards the watching sepoys, then turned again. The Lieutenant was gaining confidence and he grinned as the tall man charged at him. He lowered the sabre, using its point like a spearhead, and urged his weary gelding into a trot. Dodd also had his sword at the lunge, elbow locked, and the two horses closed at frightening speed and then, at the very last second,

Dodd hauled on his rein and his horse went right, to the Lieutenant's unguarded side, and he brought the sword back across his body and then cut it forward in one fluid motion so that the blade raked across the Lieutenant's throat. The sabre was still coming across to the parry when the blood spurted. The Lieutenant faltered and his horse stopped. The young man's sword arm fell, and Dodd was turning. He came alongside his opponent whose jacket was now dark with blood, and he rammed the sword into the Lieutenant's neck a second time, this time point first, and the young man seemed to shake like a rat in a terrier's jaws.

Dodd hauled his sword free, then scabbarded it. He leaned over and took the sabre from the dying man's unresisting hand, then pushed the Lieutenant so that he toppled from the horse. One of his feet was trapped in a stirrup, but as Dodd seized the gelding's rein and hauled it round towards the fortress, the boot fell free and the young man was left sprawling amidst his blood on the dusty road as Dodd led his trophy homewards.

The Indians on the ramparts cheered. The sepoys spurred forward and Dodd hurried ahead of them, but the Madrassi cavalrymen only rode as far as their officer's body where they dismounted. Dodd rode on, waving the captured sabre aloft.

A gun fired from the fort and the ball screamed over the rocky isthmus to crash home among the cavalrymen gathered about their officer. A second gun fired, and suddenly the British cavalry and their riderless horses were running away and the cheers on the wall redoubled. Manu Bappoo was on the big buttress close to the gatehouse and he first pointed an admonitory finger at Dodd, chiding him for taking such a risk, then he touched his hands together, in thanks for Dodd's victory, and finally raised his arms above his head to salute the hero. Dodd laughed and bowed his head in acknowledgement and saw, to his surprise, that his white coat was red with the Lieutenant's blood. 'Who would have thought the young man had so much blood in him?' he asked the leader of his escort at the fortress gate.

'Sahib?' the man answered, puzzled.

'Never mind.' Dodd took the rifle back, then spurred his horse into Gawilghur's Delhi Gate. The men on the ramparts that edged the paved entranceway cheered him home.

He did not pause to speak to Manu Bappoo, but instead rode through the Outer Fortress and out of its southern gate, then led his captured horse down the steep path which slanted across the face of the ravine. At the bottom the path turned sharply to the left before climbing to the Inner Fort's massive gateway. The four heavy gates that barred the entranceway were all opened for him, and the hooves of his two horses echoed from the high walls as he clattered up the winding passage. One by one the gates crashed shut behind and the thick locking bars were dropped into their brackets.

His groom waited beyond the last gate. Dodd swung down from his horse and gave both reins to the man, ordering him to water the captured horse before he rubbed it down. He handed his sword to his servant and told him to clean the blood from the blade and only then did he turn to face Beny Singh who had come waddling from the palace garden. The Killadar was dressed in a green silk robe and was attended by two servants, one to hold a parasol above Beny Singh's perfumed head and the other clasping the Killadar's small white lap dog. 'The cheering,' Beny Singh asked anxiously, 'what was it? The guns were firing?' He stared in horror at the blood soaked into Dodd's coat. 'You're wounded, Colonel?'

'There was a fight,' Dodd said, and waited while one of the servants translated for the Killadar. Dodd spoke a crude Marathi, but it was easier to use interpreters.

'The *djinns* are here!' Beny Singh wailed. The dog whimpered and the two servants looked nervous.

'I killed a *djinn*,' Dodd snarled. He reached out and took hold of Beny Singh's plump hand and forced it against his wet coat. 'It isn't my blood. But it is fresh.' He rubbed the Killadar's hand into the gory patch, then raised the plump fingers to his mouth. Keeping his eyes on Beny Singh's eyes, he licked the blood from the Killadar's hand. 'I am a *djinn*, Killadar,' Dodd said, letting go of the hand, 'and I lap the blood of my enemies.'

Beny Singh recoiled from the clammy touch of the blood. He shuddered, then wiped his hand on his silk robe. 'When will they assault?'

'A week?' Dodd guessed. 'And then they will be defeated.'

'But what if they get in?' Beny Singh asked anxiously.

'Then they will kill you,' Dodd said, 'and afterwards rape your wife, your concubines and your daughters. They'll line up for the pleasure, Killadar. They'll rut like hogs,' and Dodd grunted like a pig and jerked his groin forward, driving Beny Singh back.

'They won't!' the Killadar declared.

'Because they won't get in,' Dodd said, 'because some of us are men, and we will fight.'

'I have poison!' Beny Singh said, not comprehending Dodd's last words. 'If they look like winning, Colonel, you'll send me word?'

Dodd smiled. 'You have my promise, sahib,' he said with a pretended humility.

'Better my women should die,' Beny Singh insisted.

'Better that you should die,' Dodd said, 'unless you want to be forced to watch the white *djinns* take their pleasure on your dying women.'

'They wouldn't!'

'What else do they want in here?' Dodd asked. 'Have they not heard of the beauty of your women? Each night they talk of them around their fires, and every day they dream of their thighs and their breasts. They can't wait, Killadar. The pleasures of your women pull the redcoats towards us.'

Beny Singh fled from the horrid words and Dodd smiled. He had come to realize that only one man could command here. Beny Singh was the fortress commander and though he was a despicable coward he was also a friend of the Rajah's, and that friendship ensured the loyalty of much of Gawilghur's standing garrison. The rest of the fortress defenders were divided into two camps. There were Manu Bappoo's soldiers, led by the remnants of the Lions of Allah and loyal to the Prince, and Dodd's Cobras. But if only one of the three leaders was left, then that man would rule Gawilghur, and whoever ruled Gawilghur could rule all India.

Dodd touched the stock of the rifle. That would help, and Beny Singh's abject terror would render the Killadar harmless. Dodd smiled and climbed to the ramparts from where, with a telescope, he watched the British heave the first gun up to the edge of the plateau. A week, he thought, maybe a day more, and then the British would come to his slaughter. And make his wildly ambitious dreams come true.

'The fellow was using a rifle!' Major Stokes said in wonderment. 'I do declare, a rifle! Can't have been anything else at that range. Two hundred paces if it was an inch, and he fanned my head! A much underestimated weapon, the rifle, don't you think?'

'A toy,' Captain Morris said. 'Nothing will replace muskets.'

'But the accuracy!' Stokes declared.

'Soldiers can't use rifles,' Morris said. 'It would be like giving knives and forks to hogs.' He twisted in the camp chair and gestured at his men, the 33rd's Light Company. 'Look at them! Half of them can't work out which end of a musket is which. Useless buggers. Might as well arm the bastards with pikes.'

'If you say so,' Stokes said disapprovingly. His road had reached the plateau and now he had to begin the construction of the breaching batteries, and the 33rd's Light Company, which had escorted Stokes north from Mysore, had been charged with the job of protecting the sappers who would build the batteries. Captain Morris had been unhappy with the orders, for he would have much preferred to have been sent back south rather than be camped by the rock isthmus that promised to be such a lively place in these next few days. There was a chance that Gawilghur's garrison might sally out to destroy the batteries, and even if that danger did not materialize, it was a certainty that the Mahratta gunners on the Outer Fort's walls would try to break down the new works with cannon fire.

Sergeant Hakeswill approached Stokes's tent. He looked distracted, so much so that his salute was perfunctory. 'You heard the news, sir?' He spoke to Morris.

Morris squinted up at the Sergeant. 'News,' he said heavily, 'news? Can't say I have, Sergeant. The enemy has surrendered, perhaps?'

'Nothing so good, sir, nothing so good.'

'You look pale, man!' Stokes said. 'Are you sickening?'

'Heart-sick, sir, that's what I am in my own self, sir, heart-sick.' Sergeant Hakeswill sniffed heavily, and even cuffed at a non-existent tear on his twitching cheek. 'Captain Torrance,' he announced, 'is dead, sir.' The Sergeant took off his shako and held it against his breast. 'Dead, sir.'

'Dead?' Stokes said lightly. He had not met Torrance.

'Took his own life, sir, that's what they do say. He killed his clerk with a knife, then turned his pistol on himself.' The Sergeant demonstrated the action by pretending to point a pistol at his own head and pulling the trigger. He sniffed again. 'And he was as good an officer as ever I did meet, and I've known many in my time. Officers and gentlemen, like your own good self, sir,' he said to Morris.

Morris, as unmoved by Torrance's death as Stokes, smirked. 'Killed his clerk, eh? That'll teach the bugger to keep a tidy ledger.'

'They do say, sir,' Hakeswill lowered his voice, 'that he must have been unnatural.'

'Unnatural?' Stokes asked.

'With his clerk, sir, pardon me for breathing such a filthy thing. Him and the clerk, sir. 'Cos he was naked, see, the Captain was, and the clerk was a handsome boy, even if he was a blackamoor. He washed a lot, and the Captain liked that.'

'Are you suggesting it was a lovers' tiff?' Morris asked, then laughed.

'No, sir,' Hakeswill said, turning to stare across the plateau's edge into the immense sky above the Deccan Plain, 'because it weren't. The Captain weren't ever unnatural, not like that. It weren't a lovers' tiff, sir, not even if he was naked as a needle. The Captain, sir, he liked to go naked. Kept him cool, he said, and kept his clothes clean, but there weren't nothing strange in it. Not in him. And he weren't a man to be filthy and unnatural. He liked the *bibbis*, he did. He was a Christian. A Christian gentleman, that's what he was, and he didn't kill himself. I knows who killed him, I do.'

Morris gave Stokes a shrug, as if Hakeswill's maunderings were beyond understanding.

'But the nub of the thing is, sir' – Hakeswill turned back to face Morris and stood to attention – 'that I ain't with the bullocks no more, sir. I've got orders, sir, to be back with you where I belongs, sir, seeing as some other officer has got Captain Torrance's duties and he didn't want me no more on account of having his own sergeant.' He replaced his shako, then saluted Morris. 'Under orders, sir! With Privates Kendrick and Lowry, sir. Others have taken over our bullocking duties, sir, and we is back with you like we always wanted to be. Sir!'

'Welcome back, Sergeant,' Morris said laconically. 'I'm sure the company will be overjoyed at your return.'

'I knows they will, sir,' Hakeswill said. 'I'm like a father to them, sir, I am,' Hakeswill added to Stokes.

Stokes frowned. 'Who do you think killed Captain Torrance, Sergeant?' he asked, and when Hakeswill said nothing, but just stood with his face twitching, the Major became insistent. 'If you know, man, you must speak! This is a crime! You have a duty to speak.'

Hakeswill's face wrenched itself. 'It were him, sir.' The Sergeant's eyes widened. 'It were Sharpie, sir!'

Stokes laughed. 'Don't be so absurd, man. Poor Sharpe is a prisoner! He's locked away in the fortress, I've no doubt.'

'That's what we all hear, sir,' Hakeswill said, 'but I knows better.'

'A touch of the sun,' Morris explained to Stokes, then waved the Sergeant away. 'Put your kit with the company, Sergeant. And I'm glad you're back.'

'Touched by your words, sir,' Hakeswill said fervently, 'and I'm glad to be home, sir, back in me own kind where I belong.' He saluted again, then swivelled on his heel and marched away.

'Salt of the earth,' Morris said.

Major Stokes, from his brief acquaintance with Hakeswill, was not sure of that verdict, but he said nothing. Instead he wandered a few paces northwards to watch the sappers who were busy scraping at the plateau's thin soil to fill gabions that had been newly woven from green bamboo. The gabions, great wicker baskets stuffed with earth, would be stacked as a screen to soak up the enemy gunfire while the battery sites were being levelled. Stokes had already decided to do the initial work at night, for the vulnerable time for making batteries close to a fortress was the first few hours, and at night the enemy gunfire was likely to be inaccurate.

The Major was making four batteries. Two, the breaching ones, would be constructed far down the isthmus among an outcrop of great black boulders that lay less than a quarter-mile from the fortress. The rocks, with the gabions, would provide the gunners some protection from the fortress's counter-fire. Sappers, hidden from the fort by the lie of the land, were already driving a road to the proposed site of the breaching guns. Two other batteries would be constructed to the east of the isthmus, on the edge of the plateau, and those guns would enfilade the growing breaches.

There would be three breaches. That decision had been made when Stokes, early in the dawn, had crept as close to the fortress as he had dared and, hidden among the tumbled rocks above the half-filled tank, had examined the Outer Fort's wall through his telescope. He had stared a long time, counting the gun embrasures and trying to estimate how many men were stationed on the bastions and firesteps. Those were details that did not really concern him for Stokes's business was confined to breaking the walls, but what he saw encouraged him.

There were two walls, both built on the steep slope which faced the plateau. The slope was so steep that the base of the inner wall showed high above the parapet of the outer wall, and that was excellent news, for making a breach depended on being able to batter the base of a wall. These walls, built so long ago, had never been designed to stop artillery, but to deter men. Stokes knew he could lay his guns so that they would hammer both walls at once, and that when the ancient stonework crumbled, the rubble would spill forward down the slope to make natural ramps up which the attackers could climb.

The masonry seemed to have stayed largely unrepaired since it had been built. Stokes could tell that, for the dark stones were covered with grey lichen and thick with weeds growing from the gaps between the blocks. The walls looked formidable, for they were high and well provided with massive bastions that would let the defenders provide flanking fire, but Stokes knew that the dressed stone of the two walls' outer faces merely disguised a thick heart of piled rubble, and once the facing masonry was shattered the rubble would spill out. A few shots would then suffice to break the inner faces. Two days' work, he reckoned. Two days of hard gunnery should bring the walls tumbling down.

Stokes had not made his reconnaissance alone, but had been accompanied by Lieutenant Colonel William Kenny of the East India Company who would lead the assault on the breaches. Kenny, a lantern-jawed and taciturn man, had lain beside Stokes. 'Well?' he had finally asked after Stokes had spent a silent five minutes examining the walls.

'Two days' work, sir,' Stokes said. If the Mahrattas had taken the trouble to build a glacis it would have been two weeks' work, but such was their confidence that they had not bothered to protect the base of the outer wall.

Kenny grunted. 'If it's that easy, then give me two holes in the inner wall.'

'Not the outer?' Stokes asked.

'One will serve me there,' Kenny said, putting an eye to his own telescope. 'A good wide gap in the nearer wall, Stokes, but not too near the main gate.'

'We shall avoid that,' the Major said. The main gate lay to the left so that the approach to the fortress was faced by high walls and bastions rather than by a gate vulnerable to artillery fire. However, this gate was massively defended by bastions and towers, which suggested it would be thick with defenders.

'Straight up the middle,' Kenny said, wriggling back from his viewpoint. 'Give me a breach to the right of that main bastion, and two on either side of it through the inner wall, and we'll do the rest.'

It would be easy enough to break down the walls, but Stokes still feared for Kenny's men. Their approach was limited by the existence of the great reservoir that lay on the right of the isthmus. The water level was low, and scummed green, but the tank still constricted the assault route so that Kenny's men would be squeezed between the water and the sheer drop to the left. That slender space, scarce more than fifty feet at its narrowest, would be furious with gunfire, much of it coming from the firesteps above and around the main gate that flanked the approach. Stokes had already determined that his enfilading batteries should spare some shot for that gate in an attempt to unseat its cannon and unsettle its defenders.

Now, under the midday sun, the Major wandered among the sappers filling the gabions. He tested each one, making certain that the sepoys were ramming the earth hard into the wicker baskets, for a loosely filled gabion was no use. The finished gabions were being stacked on ox carts, while other carts piled with powder and shot waited nearby. All was being done properly, and the Major stared out across the plateau where the newly arrived troops were making their camp. The closest tents, ragged and makeshift, belonged to a troop of Mahratta horsemen who had allied themselves with the British. Stokes, watching the robed guards who sat close to the tents, decided it would be best if he locked his valuables away and made sure his servant kept an eye on the trunk. The rest of the Mahratta horsemen had trotted north-wards, going to seek springs or wells, for it was dry up here on the plateau. Dry and cooler than on the plain, though it was still damned hot. Dust devils whirled between the farther tent rows where muskets were stacked in neat tripods. Some shirt-sleeved officers, presumably from the East India Company battalions, were playing cricket on a smoother stretch of turf, watched by bemused sepoys and men from the Scotch Brigade.

'Not their game, sir, is it, sir?' Hakeswill's voice disturbed Stokes.

The Major turned. 'Eh?'

'Cricket, sir. Too complicated for blackamoors and Scotchmen, sir, on account of it being a game that needs brains, sir.'

'Do you play, Sergeant?'

'Me, sir? No, sir. No time for frittering, sir, being as I'm a soldier back to front, sir.'

'It does a man good to have a pastime,' Stokes said. 'Your Colonel, now, he plays the violin.'

'Sir Arthur does, sir?' Hakeswill said, plainly not believing Stokes. 'He's never done it near me, sir.'

'I assure you he does,' Stokes said. He was irritated by Hakeswill's presence. He disliked the man intensely, even though Hakeswill had spent only a short time as Sharpe's substitute. 'So what is it, Sergeant?'

Hakeswill's face twitched. 'Come to be of use to you, sir.'

The reply puzzled Stokes. 'I thought you'd been returned to company duties?'

'That I am, sir, and not before time. But I was thinking of poor Sharpie, sir, as you tell me he languishes in the heathens' jail, sir, which I did not know, sir, until you told me.'

Stokes shrugged. 'He's probably being fairly treated. The Mahrattas aren't renowned for being unduly cruel to prisoners.'

'I was wondering if he left his pack with you, sir?'

'Why would he do that?' Stokes asked.

'I was just wondering, sir. Officers don't like carrying their baggage everywhere, sir, not if they want to keep their dignity, and if he did leave his pack with you, sir, then I thought as how we might relieve you of the responsibility, sir, seeing as how Mister Sharpe was a comrade of ours for so long. That's what I was thinking, sir.'

Stokes bridled, but was not certain why. 'It isn't a heavy responsibility, Sergeant.'

'Never thought it was, sir, but it might be a nuisance to you, sir, seeing as how you're charged with other duties, and I would relieve you of the responsibility, sir.'

Stokes shook his head. 'As it happens, Sergeant, Mister Sharpe did leave his pack with me, and I promised him I would keep it safe, and I'm not a man to break promises, Sergeant. I shall keep it.'

'As you chooses, sir!' Hakeswill said sourly. 'Just thought it was a Christian act, sir.' He turned and marched away. Stokes watched him, then shook his head and turned back to gaze at the growing encampment.

Tonight, he thought, tonight we shall make the batteries, and tomorrow the big guns will be hauled forward. Another day to fill the magazines with powder and shot and then the stone-breaking could begin. Two days of battering, of dust and rubble and smoke, and then the cricketers could lead the charge across the isthmus. Poor men, Stokes thought, poor men.

'I hate night actions,' Captain Morris complained to Hakeswill.

'Because of Serry-apatam, sir? A right dog's mess, that was.' The battalion had attacked a wood outside Seringapatam by night and the companies had become separated, some became lost, and the enemy had punished them.

Morris attached his scabbard to its slings and pulled his hat on. It was dark outside, and soon the oxen would drag the gabions forward to the position Stokes had chosen for the breaching batteries. It would be a prime moment for the enemy to sally out of the fortress, so Morris and his company must form a picquet line ahead of the proposed batteries. They must watch the fortress and, if an attack was made, they must resist it, then slowly fall back, protecting the sappers until the reserve troops, a battalion of sepoys, could be brought forward from the plateau. With any luck, Morris fervently hoped, the enemy would stay in bed.

'Evening, Morris!' Major Stokes was indecently cheerful. 'Your lads are ready?'

'They are, sir.'

Stokes led Morris a few yards from his tent and stared towards the fortress that was nothing but a dark shape in the night beyond the closer blackness of the rocks. 'The thing is,' Stokes said, 'that they're bound to see our lanterns and must hear the carts, so they're liable to unleash a pretty furious artillery barrage. Maybe rockets as well. But take no heed of it. Your only job is to watch for infantry coming from the gate.'

'I know, sir.'

'So don't use your muskets! I hear musket fire, Captain, and I think infantry. Then I send for the Madrassi lads, and the next moment the whole place is swarming with redcoats who can't tell who's who in the dark. So no firing, you understand? Unless you see enemy infantry. Then send a message to me, fight the good fight and wait for support.'

Morris grunted. He had been told this twice already, and did not need the instructions a third time, but he still turned to the company which was paraded and ready. 'No one's to fire without my express permission, you understand?'

'They understands, sir,' Hakeswill answered for the company. 'One musket shot without permission and the culprit's earned himself a skinned back, sir.'

Morris took the company forward, following the old road that led directly to the gateway of the Outer Fort. The night was horribly dark, and within a few paces of leaving the engineers' encampment, Morris could hardly see the road at all. His men's boots scuffed loud on the hard-packed stones. They went slowly, feeling their way and using what small light came from the merest sliver of moon that hung like a silver blade above Gawilghur.

'Permission to speak, sir?' Hakeswill's hoarse voice sounded close to Morris.

'Not too loud, Sergeant.'

'Like a mouse, sir, quiet I will be, but, sir, if we're here, does that mean we'll be joining the assault on the fort, sir?'

'God, no,' Morris said fervently.

Hakeswill chuckled. 'I thought I should ask, sir, on account of making a will.'

'A will?' Morris asked. 'You need a will?'

'I have some wealth,' Hakeswill said defensively. And soon, he reckoned, he would have even more, for he had cleverly confirmed his surmise that Sharpe's missing pack was in Major Stokes's keeping.

'You have some wealth, do you?' Morris asked sarcastically. 'And who the hell will you leave it to?'

'Your own self, sir, if you'll forgive me, sir. No family, apart from the army, sir, which is mother's milk to me.'

'By all means make your will,' Morris said. 'Connors can draw one up for you.' Connors was the company clerk. 'I trust, of course, that the document proves redundant.'

'Whatever that means, sir, I hopes the same.'

The two men fell silent. The dark loom of the fortress was much closer now, and Morris was nervous. What was the point of this futile exercise anyway? He would be damned if he would be able to see any enemy infantrymen, not in this pitch black, unless the fools decided to carry a lantern. Some lights showed in Gawilghur. There was a glow above the Outer Fort that must have been cast by the fires and lights in the Inner Fort, while closer Morris could see a couple of flickering patches where fires or torches burned inside the nearer defences. But those scattered lights would not help him see an enemy force debouching from the gate.

'Far enough,' he called. He was not really sure if he had gone close enough to the fort, but he had no fancy to go further, and so he stopped and hissed at Hakeswill to spread the men westwards across the isthmus. 'Five paces between each pair of men, Sergeant.'

'Five paces it is, sir.'

'If anyone sees or hears anything, they're to pass the message back here to me.'

'They'll do so, sir.'

'And no fool's to light a pipe, you hear me? Don't want the enemy spraying us with canister because some blockhead needs tobacco.'

'Your orders is noted, sir. And where would you want me, sir?'

'Far end of the line, Sergeant.' Morris was the sole officer with the company, for both his lieutenant and ensign had the fever and so had stayed in Mysore. But Hakeswill, he reckoned, was as good as any lieutenant. 'You can order men to fire if you're certain you see the enemy, but God help you if you're wrong.'

'Very good, sir,' Hakeswill said, then hissed at the men to spread out. They vanished into the blackness. For a moment there was the sound of boots, the thump of musket stocks hitting rocks and the grunts as the redcoats settled, but then there was silence. Or near silence. The wind sighed at the cliff's edge while, from the fort, there drifted a plangent and discordant music that rose and fell with the wind's vagaries. Worse than bagpipes, Morris thought sourly.

The first axle squeals sounded as the oxen dragged the gabions forward. The noise would be continuous now and, sooner or later, the enemy must react by opening fire. And what chance would he have of seeing anything then, Morris wondered. The gun flashes would blind him. The first he would see of an enemy would be the glint of starlight on a blade. He spat. Waste of time.

'Morris!' a voice hissed from the dark. 'Captain Morris!'

'Here!' He turned towards the voice, which had come from behind him on the road back to the plateau. 'Here!'

'Colonel Kenny,' the voice said, still in a sibilant whisper. 'Don't mind me prowling around.'

'Of course not, sir.' Morris did not like the idea of a senior officer coming to the picquet line, but he could hardly send the man away. 'Honoured to have you, sir,' he said, then hissed a warning to his men. 'Senior officer present, don't be startled. Pass the word on.'

Morris heard Kenny's footsteps fade to his right. There was the low murmur of a brief conversation, then silence again, except for the demonic squeal of the ox-cart axles. A moment later a lantern light showed from behind the rocks where Stokes was making one of his main batteries. Morris braced himself for the enemy reaction, but the fortress stayed silent.

The noise grew louder as the sappers heaved the gabions from the carts and manhandled them up onto the rocks to form the thick bastion. A man swore, others grunted and the great baskets thumped on stone. Another lantern was unmasked, and this time the man carrying it stepped up onto the rocks to see where the gabions were being laid. A voice ordered him to get down.

The fort at last woke up. Morris could hear footsteps hurrying along the nearer firestep, and he saw a brief glow as a linstock was plucked from a barrel and blown into red life. 'Jesus,' he said under his breath, and a moment later the first gun fired. The flame stabbed bright as a lance from the walls, its glare momentarily lighting all the rocky isthmus and the green-scummed surface of the tank, before it was blotted out by the rolling smoke. The round shot screamed overhead, struck a rock and ricocheted wildly up into the sky. A second gun fired, its flame lighting the first smoke cloud from within so that it seemed as if the wall of the fort was edged with a brief vaporous luminance. The ball struck a gabion, breaking it apart in a spray of earth. A man groaned. Dogs were barking in the British camp and inside the fortress.

Morris stared towards the dark gateway. He could see nothing, because the guns' flames had robbed him of his night vision. Or rather he could see wraithlike shapes which he knew were more likely to be his imagination than the approach of some savage enemy. The guns were firing steadily now, aiming at the small patch of lantern light, but then more lights, brighter ones, appeared to the west of the isthmus, and some of the gunners switched their aim, not knowing that Stokes had unveiled the second lights as a feint.

Then the first rockets were fired, and they were even more dazzling than the guns. The fiery trails seemed to limp up from the fort's bastions, seething smoke and sparks, then they leaped up into the air, wobbling in their flight, to sear over Morris's head and slash north towards the camp. None went near their targets, but their sound and the flaming exhausts were nerve-racking. The first shells were fired, and they added to the night's din as they cracked apart among the rocks to whistle shards of shattered casing over the struggling sappers. The firing was deliberate as the gun captains took care to lay their pieces before firing, but still there were six or seven shots every minute, while the rockets were more constant. Morris tried to use the brightness of the rocket trails to see the ground between his hiding place and the fort, but there was too much smoke, the shadows flickered wildly, and his imagination made movement where there was none. He held his fire, reckoning he would hear the gate open or the sound of enemy footsteps. He could hear the defenders shouting on the wall, either calling insults to the enemy hidden in the dark or else encouraging each other.

Hakeswill, at the very right-hand end of the line, cowered among the rocks. He had been sheltering with Kendrick and Lowry, but the enemy cannonade had driven him still further right to where there was a deep cleft. He knew he was safe there, but even so every screaming rocket made him flinch, while the sound of the shells exploding and the round shots cracking against stone made him draw his knees up into his chest. He knew there was a senior officer visiting the picquet line because the message telling of the Colonel's presence had been passed down the line. Kenny's visit struck Hakeswill as a daft thing for any man with gold braid on his coat to do, but when the Colonel hissed his name aloud he kept silent. At least he assumed it was the visiting officer, for the summons was insistent and authoritative, but Hakeswill ignored it. He did not want to draw attention to himself in case the heathen blackamoor gunners aimed their cannon at him. Let the officer hiss away, he decided, and a moment later the man went away.

'Who are you?' a low voice asked Private Kendrick just a few yards from Hakeswill's hiding place.

'Kendrick, sir.'

'To me, Private. I need your help.'

Kendrick slipped back towards the voice. Bastard interfering officer, he thought, but he had to obey. 'Where are you, sir?' he asked.

'Here, man! Hurry, now, hurry!'

Kendrick slipped on a slanting stone and sat down with a bump. A rocket slashed overhead, spewing fire and sparks, and in its brief light he saw a shadow above him, then felt a blade at his throat. 'One noise,' the voice hissed, 'and you're dead.'

Kendrick went very still. He did not make any noise at all, but he still died.

A lucky shell struck a pair of oxen, disembowelling the beasts that lowed pitifully as they collapsed onto the road. 'Get them out of the way!' a voice roared, and sepoys struggled with the massive animals, cutting their harnesses and pulling the dying beasts into the rocks. Other men ran the empty cart back to the encampment, making way for the next wagon to drag more gabions forward. 'Kill them!' the officer ordered. 'Use your bayonets! No musket fire!' The sepoys finished off the oxen, stabbing again and again into their thick necks while the bloody hooves thrashed violently. Another shell landed nearby, slicing its fragments among the rocks. The road was slippery with spilled guts over which the next cart rolled impassively, its axle screeching like a demon.

'All well, soldier?' a voice asked Private Lowry.

'Yes, sir.'

'I'm Colonel Kenny,' the man said, dropping down beside Lowry.

'Yes, sir,' Lowry acknowledged nervously.

'See anything?'

'Nothing, sir,' Lowry said, then gasped as he felt a blade at his throat.

'Where's Hakeswill?' the voice hissed in his ear, and Lowry suddenly knew this was not Colonel Kenny who had him in a tight grip.

'Dunno, sir,' Lowry said, then began to cry out, but the cry was cut off as the blade sawed deep into his gullet.

A ball, fired low, struck plumb on the great boulder that sheltered Hakeswill and the Sergeant whimpered as he tried to wriggle deeper into the cleft. A rocket landed thirty paces behind him and began to chase its tail, whirling about on the turf, scattering sparks, until it finally lodged against a rock and burned itself out in a display of small blue flames. Another round shot hammered into the gabions, but now they were well stacked and the ball's impact was soaked up by the tight-packed soil.

A whistle blew from the battery site, then blew twice more. Morris, relieved by the sound, called to the men to his right. 'Back to the road! Pass it on! Back to the road!' Thank God the worst of the ordeal was over! Now he was supposed to withdraw to the battery, ready to protect it through the remaining hours of the dark night, but Morris knew he would feel a good deal safer once he was behind the gabions, just as he knew that the cessation of the work would probably persuade the Mahrattas to cease fire. 'Close on me!' he called to his company. 'Hurry!'

The message was passed along the picquet line and the men ran at a crouch back to where Morris waited. They bumped into each other as they gathered, then squatted as Morris called for Hakeswill.

'Not here, sir,' Sergeant Green finally decided.

'Count the men, Sergeant,' Morris ordered.

Sergeant Green numbered the men off. 'Three missing, sir,' he reported. 'Hakeswill, Lowry and Kendrick.'

'Damn them,' Morris said. A rocket hissed up from the gatehouse, twisted in the night to leave a crazy trail of flame-edged smoke, then dived down to the left, far down, plunging into the ravine that edged the isthmus. The light of the exhaust flashed down the steep cliffs, finally vanishing a thousand feet below Morris. Two guns fired together, their balls hammering towards the fake lanterns. The battery lanterns had vanished, evidence that the sappers had finished their work.

'Take the men to the battery,' Morris ordered Green. 'Garrard? You stay with me.'

Morris did not want to do anything heroic, but he knew he could not report that he had simply lost three men, so he took Private Tom Garrard west across the tumbled ground where the picquet line had been stretched. They called out the names of the missing men, but no reply came.

It was Garrard who stumbled over the first body. 'Don't know who it is, sir, but he's dead. Bloody mess, he is.'

Morris swore and crouched beside the body. A rocket's bright passage showed him a slit throat and a spill of blood. It also revealed that the man had been stripped of his coat which lay discarded beside the corpse. The sight of the gaping throat made Morris gag.

'There's another here, sir,' Garrard called from a few paces away.

'Jesus!' Morris twisted aside, willing himself not to throw up, but the bile was sour in his throat. He shuddered, then managed to take a deep breath. 'We're going.'

'You want me to look for the other fellow, sir?' Garrard asked.

'Come on!' Morris fled, not wanting to stay in this dark charnel house.

Garrard followed.

The gunfire died. A last rocket stitched sparks across the stars, then Gawilghur was silent again.

Hakeswill cowered in his hiding place, shuddering as the occasional flare of an exploding shell or passing rocket cast lurid shadows into the narrow cleft. He thought he heard Lowry call aloud, but the sound was so unexpected, and so quickly over, he decided it was his nerves. Then, blessedly, he heard the whistle that signalled that the sappers were done with their work, and a moment later he heard the message being called along the line. 'Back to the road! Back to the road!'

The rockets and guns were still battering the night, so Hakeswill stayed where he was until he sensed that the fury of the fire was diminishing, then he crept out of his cleft and, still keeping low, scuttled eastwards.

'Hakeswill!' a voice called nearby.

He froze.

'Hakeswill?' The voice was insistent.

Some instinct told the Sergeant that there was mischief in the dark, and so Hakeswill crouched lower still. He heard something moving in the night, the scrape of leather on stone, the sound of breathing, but the man did not come close to Hakeswill who, petrified, edged on another pace. His hand, feeling the ground ahead of him, suddenly found something wet and sticky. He flinched, brought his fingers to his nose and smelt blood.

'Jesus,' he swore under his breath. He groped again, and this time found a corpse. His hands explored the face, the open mouth, then found the gaping wound in the neck. He jerked his hand back.

It had to be Lowry or Kendrick, for this was about where he had left the two privates, and if they were dead, or even if only one of them was dead, then it meant that Captain Torrance's death had been no lovers' tiff. Not that Hakeswill had ever believed it was. He knew who it was. Bloody Sharpe was alive. Bloody Sharpe was hunting his enemies, and three, maybe four, were already dead. And Hakeswill knew he would be next.

'Hakeswill!' the voice hissed, but farther away now.

A gun fired from the fort and in its flash Hakeswill saw a cloaked shape to his north. The man was crossing the skyline, not far from Hakeswill, but at least he was going away. Sharpe! It had to be Sharpe! And a terror grew in Hakeswill so that his face twitched and his hands shook.

'Think, you bugger,' he told himself, 'think!'

And the answer came, a sweet answer, so obvious that he wondered why he had taken so long to find it.

Sharpe was alive, he was not a prisoner in Gawilghur, but haunting the British camp, which meant that there was one place that would be utterly safe for Hakeswill to go. He could go to the fortress, and Sharpe would never reach him there for the rumour in the camp was that the assault on Gawilghur was likely to be a desperate and bloody business. Likely to fail, some men said, and even if it did not, Hakeswill could always pretend he had been taken prisoner. All he wanted at this moment was to be away from Sharpe and so he sidled southwards, down the hill, and once he reached the flatter ground, he ran towards the now dark walls of the fort through the drifting skeins of foul-smelling powder smoke.

He ran past the tank, along the approach road, and round to the left where the great gatehouse loomed above him in the dark. And once there he pounded on the massive, iron-studded doors.

No one responded.

He pounded again, using the butt of his musket, scared witless that the sound would bring an avenging horror from the dark behind, and suddenly a small wicket gate in the larger door was pulled open to flood flame light into the night.

'I'm a deserter!' Hakeswill hissed. 'I'm on your side!'

Hands seized him and pulled him through the small doorway. A smoking torch burned high on the wall to show Hakeswill the long, narrow entranceway, the dark ramparts, and the dark faces of the men who had him prisoner. 'I'm on your side!' he shouted as the gate was closed behind him and his musket was snatched away. 'I'm on your side!'

A tall, hawk-faced man strode down the stone road. 'Who are you?' he asked in English.

'I'm someone willing to fight for you, sir. Willing and able, sir. Old soldier, sir.'

'My name is Manu Bappoo,' the man said in a sibilant voice, 'and I command here.'

'Very good, sir. Sahib, I mean, very good.' Hakeswill bobbed his head. 'Hakeswill, sir, is my name. Sergeant Obadiah Hakeswill.'

Manu Bappoo stared at the redcoat. He disliked deserters. A man who deserted his flag could not be trusted under any other flag, but the news that a white soldier had run from the enemy ranks could only hearten his garrison. Better, he decided, to leave this man alive as a witness to the enemy's crumbling morale than shoot him out of hand. 'Take him to Colonel Dodd,' he ordered one of his men. 'Give him back his firelock. He's on our side.'

So Hakeswill was inside Gawilghur and among the enemy. But he was safe from the terror that had turned his life to sudden nightmare. He was safe from Sharpe.

CHAPTER 8

The sappers who had emplaced the gabions were too excited to go to sleep and instead were milling about a pair of smoky fires. Their laughter rose and fell on the night wind. Major Stokes, pleased with their work, had produced three jars of arrack as a reward, and the jugs were being passed from hand to hand.

Sharpe watched the small celebration and then, keeping to the shadows among Syud Sevajee's encampment, he went to a small tent where he stripped off his borrowed Indian robes before crawling under the flap. In the dark he blundered into Clare who, kept awake by the sound of the bombardment and then by the voices of the sappers, put up a hand and felt bare flesh. 'You're undressed!' She sounded alarmed.

'Not quite,' Sharpe said, then understood her fear. 'My clothes were soaking,' he explained, 'so I took them off. Didn't want to wet the bed, eh? And I've still got my shirt on.'

'Is it raining? I didn't hear it.'

'It was blood,' he said, then rummaged under the blanket he had borrowed from Syud Sevajee and found Torrance's pouch.

Clare heard the rattle of stones. 'What is it?'

'Just stones,' he said, 'pebbles.' He put the twenty jewels he had retrieved from Kendrick and Lowry into the pouch, stowed it safe under the blanket, then lay down. He doubted he had found every stone, but he reckoned he had retrieved most of them. They had been loose in the two privates' pockets, not even hidden away in their coat seams. God, he felt tired and his body had still not recovered from Hakeswill's kicking. It hurt to breathe, the bruises were tender and a tooth was still loose.

'What happened out there?' Clare asked.

'The engineers put the gabions in place. When it's light they'll scrape the gun platform and make the magazines, and tomorrow night they'll bring up the guns.'

'What happened to you?' Clare amended her question.

Sharpe was silent for a while. 'I looked up some old friends,' he said. But he had missed Hakeswill, damn it, and Hakeswill would be doubly alert now. Still, a chance would come. He grinned as he remembered Morris's scared voice. The Captain was a bully to his men and a toadie to his superiors.

'Did you kill someone?' Clare asked.

'Two men,' he admitted, 'but it should have been three.'

'Why?'

He sighed. 'Because they were bad men,' he said simply, then reflected it was a true answer. 'And because they tried to kill me,' he added, 'and they robbed me. You knew them,' he went on. 'Kendrick and Lowry.'

'They were horrid,' Clare said softly. 'They used to stare at me.'

'Can't blame them for that, love.'

She was silent for a while. The laughter of the sappers was subsiding as men drifted towards their tents. The wind gusted at the tent's entrance and brought the smell of burnt powder from the rocky isthmus where patches of grass still flamed around the exhausted rocket tubes. 'Everything's gone wrong, hasn't it?' Clare said.

'It's being put right,' Sharpe replied.

'For you,' she said.

Again she was silent, and Sharpe suspected she was crying. 'I'll get you home to Madras,' he said.

'And what'll happen to me there?'

'You'll be all right, lass. I'll give you a pair of my magic pebbles.'

'What I want,' she said softly, 'is to go home. But I can't afford it.'

'Marry a soldier,' Sharpe said, 'and be carried home with him.' He thought of Eli Lockhart who had been admiring Clare from a distance. They would suit each other, Sharpe thought.

She was crying very softly. 'Torrance said he'd pay my way home when I'd paid off the debt,' she said.

'Why would he make you work for one passage, then give you another?' Sharpe asked. 'He was a lying bastard.'

'He seemed so kind at first.'

'We're all like that,' Sharpe said. 'Soft as lights when you first meet a woman, then you get what you want and it changes. I don't know. Maybe not every time.'

'Charlie wasn't like that,' Clare said.

'Charlie? Your husband?'

'He was always good to me.'

Sharpe lay back. The light of the dying fires flickered in the tent's loose weave. If it rained, he thought, the cloth would leak like a pepper pot. 'There are good men and bad,' he said.

'What are you?' Clare asked.

'I think I'm good,' he said, 'but I don't know. All the time I get into trouble, and I only know one way out. I can fight. I can do that all right.'

'Is that what you want? To fight?'

'God knows what I want.' He laughed softly. 'I wanted to be an officer more than I'd wanted anything in my life! I dreamed of it, I did. I wanted it so bad that it hurt, and then the dream came true and it woke me up and I wondered why I'd wanted it so much.' He paused. Syud Sevajee's horses stamped their feet softly behind the tent. 'Some buggers are trying to persuade me to leave the army. Sell the commission, see? They don't want me.'

'Why not?'

'Because I piss in their soup, lass.'

'So will you leave?'

He shrugged. 'Don't want to.' He thought about it. 'It's like a club, a society. They don't really want me, so they chuck me out, and then I have to fight my way back in. But why do I do it if they don't want me? I don't know. Maybe it'll be different in the Rifles. I'll try 'em, anyway, and see if they're different.'

'You want to go on fighting?' Clare asked.

'It's what I'm good at,' Sharpe said. 'And I do enjoy it. I mean I know you shouldn't, but there ain't any other excitement like it.'

'None?'

'Well, one.' He grinned in the dark.

There was a long silence, and he thought Clare had fallen asleep, but then she spoke again. 'How about your French widow?'

'She's gone,' Sharpe said flatly.

'Gone?'

'She buggered off, love. Took some money of mine and went. Gone to America, I'm told.'

Clare lay in silence again. 'Don't you worry about being alone?' she asked after a while.

'No.'

'I do.'

He turned towards her, propped himself on an elbow and stroked her hair. She stiffened as he touched her, then relaxed to the gentle pressure of his hand. 'You ain't alone, lass,' Sharpe said. 'Or only if you want to be. You got trapped, that's all. It happens to everyone. But you're out now. You're free.' He stroked her hair down to her neck and felt warm bare skin under his hand. She did not move and he softly stroked farther down. 'You're undressed,' he said.

'I was warm,' she said in a small voice.

'What's worse?' Sharpe asked. 'Being warm or being lonely?'

He thought she smiled. He could not tell in the dark, but he thought she smiled. 'Being lonely,' she said very softly.

'We can look after that,' he said, lifting the thin blanket and moving to her side.

She had stopped crying. Somewhere outside a cock crowed and the eastern cliffs were touched with the first gold of the day. The fires on the rocky neck of land flickered and died, their smoke drifting like patches of thin mist. Bugles called from the main encampment, summoning the redcoats to the morning parade. The night picquets were relieved as the sun rose to flood the world with light.

Where Sharpe and Clare slept.

'You abandoned the dead men?' Wellesley growled.

Captain Morris blinked as a gust of wind blew dust into one of his eyes. 'I tried to bring the bodies in,' he lied, 'but it was dark, sir. Very dark. Colonel Kenny can vouch for that, sir. He visited us.'

'I visited you?' Kenny, lean, tall and irascible, was standing beside the General. 'I visited you?' he asked again, his inflection rising to outrage.

'Last night, sir,' Morris answered in plaintive indignation. 'On the picquet line.'

'I did no such thing. Sun's gone to your head.' Kenny glowered at Morris, then took a snuff box from a pocket and placed a pinch on his hand. 'Who the devil are you, anyway?' he added.

'Morris, sir. 33rd.'

'I thought we had nothing but Scots and sepoys here,' Kenny said to Wellesley.

'Captain Morris's company escorted a convoy here,' Wellesley answered.

'A light company, eh?' Kenny said, glancing at Morris's epaulettes. 'You might even be useful. I could do with another company in the assault party.' He snorted the snuff, stopping one nostril at a time. 'It cheers my boys up,' he added, 'seeing white men killed.' Kenny commanded the first battalion of the 11th Madrassi Regiment.

'What's in your assault unit now?' Wellesley asked.

'Nine companies,' Kenny said. 'The grenadiers and two others from the Scotch Brigade, the flankers from my regiment and four others. Good boys, all of them, but I daresay they won't mind sharing the honours with an English light company.'

'And I've no doubt you'll welcome a chance to assault a breach, Morris?' Wellesley asked drily.

'Of course, sir,' Morris said, cursing Kenny inwardly.

'But in the meantime,' Wellesley went on coldly, 'bring your men's bodies in.'

'Yes, sir.'

'Do it now.'

Sergeant Green took a half-dozen men down the neck of land, but they only found two bodies. They were expecting three, but Sergeant Hakeswill was missing. The enemy, seeing the redcoats among the rocks above the reservoir, opened fire and the musket balls smacked into stones and ricocheted up into the air. Green took a bullet in the heel of his boot. It did not break the skin of his foot, but the blow hurt and he hopped on the short, dry grass. 'Just grab the buggers and drag them away,' he said. He wondered why the enemy did not fire their cannon, and just then a gun discharged a barrel of canister at his squad. The balls hissed all about the men, but miraculously none was hit as the soldiers seized Kendrick and Lowry by their feet and ran back towards the half-completed battery where Captain Morris waited. Both the dead men had slit throats.

Once safe behind the gabions the corpses were treated more decorously by being placed on makeshift stretchers. Colonel Kenny intercepted the stretcher-bearers to examine the corpses which were already smelling foul. 'They must have sent a dozen cut-throats out of the fort,' he reckoned. 'You say there's a sergeant missing?'

'Yes, sir,' Morris answered.

'Poor fellow must be a prisoner. Be careful tonight, Captain! They'll probably try again. And I assure you, Captain, if I decide to take a stroll this evening, it won't be to your picquet line.'

That night the 33rd's Light Company again formed a screen in front of the new batteries, this time to protect the men dragging up the guns. It was a nervous night, for the company was expecting throat-slitting Mahrattas to come silently through the darkness, but nothing stirred. The fortress stayed silent and dark. Not a gun fired and not a rocket flew as the British cannon were hauled to their new emplacements and as powder charges and round shot were stacked in the newly made ready magazines.

Then the gunners waited.

The first sign of dawn was a grey lightening of the east, followed by the flare of reflected sun as the first rays lanced over the world's rim to touch the summit of the eastern cliffs. The fortress walls showed grey-black. Still the gunners waited. A solitary cloud glowed livid pink on the horizon. Smoke rose from the cooking fires inside the fortress where the flags hung limp in the windless air. Bugles roused the British camp which lay a half-mile behind the batteries where officers trained telescopes on Gawilghur's northern wall.

Major Stokes's job was almost finished. He had made the batteries, and now the gunners must unmake the walls, but first Stokes wanted to be certain that the outermost breach would be made in the right place. He had fixed a telescope to a tripod and now he edged it from side to side, searching the lichen-covered stones just to the right of a bastion in the centre of the wall. The wall sloped back slightly, but he was sure he could see a place where the old stones bulged out of alignment, and he watched that spot as the sun rose and cast a hint of shadow where the stones were not quite true. Finally he screwed the telescope's mount tight shut, so that the tube could not move, then summoned the gun captain of the battery's eighteen-pounder. A major actually commanded this battery, but he insisted that his sergeant go to the spyglass. 'That's your target,' Stokes told the Sergeant.

The Sergeant stooped to the telescope, then straightened to see over the glass, then stooped again. He was chewing a wad of tobacco and had no lower front teeth so that the yellow spittle ran down his chin in a continuous dribble. He straightened, then stooped a third time. The telescope was powerful, and all he could see in the glass circle was a vertical joint between two great stones. The joint was some four feet above the wall's base, and when it gave way the wall would spill forward down the slope to make the ramp up which the attackers could swarm. 'Smack on the joint, sir?' the Sergeant asked in a Northumbrian accent so pronounced that Stokes did not at first understand him.

'Low on the joint,' Stokes said.

'Low it is, sir,' the Sergeant said, and stooped to squint through the glass once more. 'The joint gapes a bit, don't it?'

'It does,' Stokes said.

The Sergeant grunted. For a while, he reckoned, the battering would drive the stones in, sealing the gap, but there was pressure there and the wall must eventually give way as the battered stones weakened. 'That bugger'll burst like an abscess,' the Sergeant said happily, straightening from the telescope. He returned to his gun and barked at his men to make some minute adjustments to its trail. He himself heaved on the elevating screw, though as yet the gun was still masked by some half-filled gabions that blocked the embrasure. Every few seconds the Sergeant climbed onto the trail to see over the gabions, then he would demand that the gun was shifted a half-inch left or a finger's breadth to the right as he made another finicky adjustment to the screw. He tossed grass in the air to gauge the wind, then twisted the elevation again to raise the barrel a tiny amount. 'Stone cold shot,' he explained to Stokes, 'so I'm pointing her a bit high. Maybe a half turn more.' He hammered the screw with the heel of his hand. 'Perfect,' he said.

The *puckalees* were bringing water which they poured into great wooden tubs. The water was not just to slake the gunners' thirst and soak the sponges that cleaned out the barrels between shots, but was also intended to cool the great weapons. The sun was climbing, it promised to be a searing hot day, and if the huge guns were not drenched intermittently with water they could overheat and explode the powder charges prematurely. The Sergeant was choosing his shot now, rolling two eighteen-pounder balls up and down a stretch of bare earth to judge which was the more perfect sphere. 'That one,' he said, spitting tobacco juice onto his chosen missile.

Morris's Light Company trailed back up the road, going to the camp where they would sleep. Stokes watched them pass and thought of Sharpe. Poor Sharpe, but at least, from wherever he was imprisoned inside the fortress, he would hear the siege guns and know that the redcoats were coming. If they got through the breach, Stokes thought gloomily, or if they ever managed to cross the fortress's central ravine. He tried to suppress his pessimism, telling himself that his job was simply to make the breach, not win the whole victory.

The chosen shot was rolled into the gun's muzzle, then rammed down onto the canvas bags of powder. The Sergeant took a length of wire that hung looped on his belt and rammed it through the cannon's touch-hole, piercing the canvas bag beneath, then selected a priming tube, a reed filled with finely milled powder, and slid it down into the powder charge, but leaving a half-inch of the reed protruding above the touch-hole. 'Ready when you are, sir,' he told the Major commanding the battery who, in turn, looked at Stokes.

Stokes shrugged. 'I imagine we wait for Colonel Stevenson's permission.'

The gunners in the second breaching battery which lay fifty yards west of the first had trained their telescopes over the gabions to watch where the first shot fell. The scar it left in the wall would be their aiming mark. The two enfilading batteries also watched. Their work would begin properly when the first of the three breaches was made, but till then their twelve-pounders would be aimed at the cannon mounted on Gawilghur's ramparts, trying to dismount them or tumble their embrasures into rubble.

'That wall won't last long,' the battery Major, whose name was Plummer, opined. He was staring at the wall through Stokes's telescope.

'We'll have it opened up today,' Stokes agreed.

'Thank God there ain't a glacis,' Plummer said.

'Thank God, indeed,' Stokes echoed piously, but he had been thinking about that lack and was not so sure now that it was a blessing. Perhaps the Mahrattas understood that their real defence was the great central ravine, and so were offering nothing but a token defence of the Outer Fort. And how was that ravine to be crossed? Stokes feared that he would be asked for an engineering solution, but what could he do? Fill the thing with soil? That would take months.

Stokes's gloomy presentiments were interrupted by an aide who had been sent by Colonel Stevenson to enquire why the batteries were silent. 'I suspect those are your orders to open fire, Plummer,' Stokes said.

'Unmask!' Plummer shouted.

Four gunners clambered up onto the bastion and manhandled the half-filled gabions out of the cannon's way. The Sergeant squinted down the barrel a last time, nodded to himself, then stepped aside. The other gunners had their hands over their ears. 'You can fire, Ned!' Plummer called to the Sergeant, who took a glowing linstock from a protective barrel, reached across the gun's high wheel and touched the fire to the reed.

The cannon hammered back a full five yards as the battery filled with acrid smoke. The ball screamed low across the stony neck of land to crack against the fort's wall. There was a pause. Defenders were running along the ramparts. Stokes was peering through the glass, waiting for the smoke to thin. It took a full minute, but then he saw that a slab of stone about the size of a soup plate had been chipped from the wall. 'Two inches to the right, Sergeant,' he called chidingly.

'Must have been a puff of wind, sir,' the Sergeant said, 'puff of bloody wind, 'cos there weren't a thing wrong with gun's laying, begging your pardon, sir.'

'You did well,' Stokes said with a smile, 'very well.' He cupped his hands and shouted at the second breaching battery. 'You have your mark! Fire on!' A billow of smoke erupted from the fortress wall, followed by the bang of a gun and a howl as a round shot whipped overhead. Stokes jumped down into the battery, clutching his hat. 'It seems we've woken them up,' he remarked as a dozen more Mahratta guns fired. The enemy's shots smacked into the gabions or ricocheted wildly along the rocky ground. The second British battery fired, the noise of its guns echoing off the cliff face to tell the camp far beneath that the siege of Gawilghur had properly begun.

Private Tom Garrard of the 33rd's Light Company had wandered to the edge of the cliff to watch the bombardment of the fortress. Not that there was much to see other than the constantly replenished cloud of smoke that shrouded the rocky neck of land between the batteries and the fortress, but every now and then a large piece of stone would fall from Gawilghur's wall. The fire from the defences was furious, but it seemed to Garrard that it was ill aimed. Many of the shots bounced over the batteries, or else buried themselves in the great piles of protective gabions. The British fire, on the other hand, was slow and sure. The eighteen-pound round shots gnawed at the wall and not one was wasted. The sky was cloudless, the sun rising ever higher and the guns were heating so that after every second shot the gunners poured buckets of water on the long barrels. The metal hissed and steamed, and sweating *puckalees* hurried up the battery road with yet more skins of water to replenish the great vats.

Garrard was sitting by himself, but he had noticed a ragged Indian was watching him. He ignored the man, hoping he would go away, but the Indian edged closer. Garrard picked up a fist-sized stone and tossed it up and down in his right hand as a hint that the man should go away, but the threat of the stone only made the Indian edge closer. 'Sahib!' the Indian hissed.

'Bugger off,' Garrard growled.

'Sahib! Please!'

'I've got nothing worth stealing, I don't want to buy anything, and I don't want to roger your sister.'

'I'll roger your sister instead, sahib,' the Indian said, and Garrard twisted round, the stone drawn back ready to throw, then he saw that the dirty robed man had pushed back his grubby white head cloth and was grinning at him. 'You ain't supposed to chuck rocks at officers, Tom,' Sharpe said. 'Mind you, I always wanted to, so I can't blame you.'

'Bloody hell!' Garrard dropped the stone and held out his right hand. 'Dick Sharpe!' He suddenly checked his outstretched hand. 'Do I have to call you "sir"?'

'Of course you don't,' Sharpe said, taking Garrard's hand. 'You and me? Friends from way back, eh? Red sash won't change that, Tom. How are you?'

'Been worse. Yourself?'

'Been better.'

Garrard frowned. 'Didn't I hear that you'd been captured?'

'Got away, I did. Ain't a bugger born who can hold me, Tom. Nor you.' Sharpe sat next to his friend, a man with whom he had marched in the ranks for six years. 'Here.' He gave Garrard a strip of dried meat.

'What is it?'

'Goat. Tastes all right, though.'

The two sat and watched the gunners at work. The closest guns were in the two enfilading batteries, and the gunners were using their twelve-pounders to systematically bring down the parapets of the ramparts above Gawilghur's gate. They had already unseated a pair of enemy guns and were now working on the next two embrasures. An ox-drawn limber had just delivered more ammunition, but, on leaving the battery, the limber's wheel had loosened and five men were now standing about the canted wheel arguing how best to mend it. Garrard pulled a piece of stringy meat from between his teeth. 'Pull the broken wheel off and put on a new one,' he said scornfully. 'It don't take a major and two lieutenants to work that out.'

'They're officers, Tom,' Sharpe said chidingly, 'only half brained.'

'You should know.' Garrard grinned. 'Buggers make an inviting target, though.' He pointed across the plunging chasm which separated the plateau from the Inner Fort. 'There's a bloody great gun over there. Size of a bloody hay wain, it is. Buggers have been fussing about it for a half-hour now.'

Sharpe stared past the beleaguered Outer Fort to the distant cliffs. He thought he could see a wall where a gun might be mounted, but he was not sure. 'I need a bloody telescope.'

'You need a bloody uniform.'

'I'm doing something about that,' Sharpe said mysteriously.

Garrard slapped at a fly. 'What's it like then?'

'What's what like?'

'Being a Jack-pudding?'

Sharpe shrugged, thought for a while, then shrugged again. 'Don't seem real. Well, it does. I dunno.' He sighed. 'I mean I wanted it, Tom, I wanted it real bad, but I should have known the bastards wouldn't want me. Some are all right. Major Stokes, he's a fine fellow, and there are others. But most of them? God knows. They don't like me, anyway.'

'You got 'em worried, that's why,' Garrard said. 'If you can become an officer, so can others.' He saw the unhappiness on Sharpe's face. 'Wishing you'd stayed a sergeant, are you?'

'No,' Sharpe said, and surprised himself by saying it so firmly. 'I can do the job, Tom.'

'What job's that, for Christ's sake? Sitting around while we do all the bloody work? Having a servant to clean your boots and scrub your arse?'

'No,' Sharpe said, and he pointed across the shadowed chasm to the Inner Fort. 'When we go in there, Tom, we're going to need fellows who know what the hell they're doing. That's the job. It's beating hell out of the other side and keeping your own men alive, and I can do that.'

Garrard looked sceptical. 'If they let you.'

'Aye, if they let me,' Sharpe agreed. He sat in silence for a while, watching the far gun emplacement. He could see men there, but was not sure what they were doing. 'Where's Hakeswill?' he asked. 'I looked for him yesterday, and the bugger wasn't on parade with the rest of you.'

'Captured,' Garrard said.

'Captured?'

'That's what Morris says. Me, I think the bugger ran. Either ways, he's in the fort now.'

'You think he ran?'

'We had two fellows murdered the other night. Morris says it were the enemy, but I didn't see any of the buggers, but there was some fellow creeping round saying he was a Company colonel, only he weren't.' Garrard stared at Sharpe and a slow grin came to his face. 'It were you, Dick.'

'Me?' Sharpe asked straight-faced. 'I was captured, Tom. Only escaped yesterday.'

'And I'm the king of bloody Persia. Lowry and Kendrick were meant to arrest you, weren't they?'

'It was them who died?' Sharpe asked innocently.

Garrard laughed. 'Serve them bloody right. Bastards, both of them.' An enormous blossom of smoke showed at the distant wall on the top of the cliffs. Two seconds later the sound of the great gun bellowed all around Sharpe and Garrard, while the massive round shot struck the stalled limber just behind the enfilading battery. The wooden vehicle shattered into splinters and all five men were hurled to the ground where they jerked bloodily for a few seconds and then were still. Fragments of stone and wood hissed past Sharpe. 'Bloody hell,' Garrard said admiringly, 'five men with one shot!'

'That'll teach 'em to keep their heads down,' Sharpe said. The sound of the enormous gun had drawn men from their tents towards the plateau's edge. Sharpe looked round and saw that Captain Morris was among them. The Captain was in his shirtsleeves, staring at the great cloud of smoke through a telescope. 'I'm going to stand up in a minute,' Sharpe said, 'and you're going to hit me.'

'I'm going to do what?' Garrard asked.

'You're going to thump me. Then I'm going to run, and you're going to chase me. But you're not to catch me.'

Garrard offered his friend a puzzled look. 'What are you up to, Dick?'

Sharpe grinned. 'Don't ask, Tom, just do it.'

'You are a bloody officer, aren't you?' Garrard said, grinning back. 'Don't ask, just do it.'

'Are you ready?' Sharpe asked.

'I've always wanted to clobber an officer.'

'On your feet then.' They stood. 'So hit me,' Sharpe said. 'I've tried to pinch some cartridges off you, right? So give me a thump in the belly.'

'Bloody hell,' Garrard said.

'Go on, do it!'

Garrard gave Sharpe a half-hearted punch, and Sharpe shoved him back, making him fall, then he turned and ran along the cliff's edge. Garrard shouted, scrambled to his feet and began to pursue. Some of the men who had gone to fetch the five bodies moved to intercept Sharpe, but he dodged to his left and disappeared among some bushes. The rest of the 33rd's Light Company was whooping and shouting in pursuit, but Sharpe had a long lead on them and he twisted in and out of the shrubs to where he had picketed one of Syud Sevajee's horses. He pulled the peg loose, hauled himself into the saddle and kicked back his heels. Someone yelled an insult at him, but he was clear of the camp now and there were no mounted picquets to pursue him.

A half-hour later Sharpe returned, trotting with a group of native horsemen coming back from a reconnaissance. He peeled away from them and dismounted by his tent where Ahmed waited for him. While Sharpe and Garrard had made the diversion the boy had been thieving and he grinned broadly as Sharpe ducked into the hot tent. 'I have every things,' Ahmed said proudly.

He had taken Captain Morris's red coat, his sash and his sword-belt with its sabre. 'You're a good lad,' Sharpe said. He needed a red coat, for Colonel Stevenson had given orders that every man who went into Gawilghur with the attackers must be in uniform so that they were not mistaken for the enemy. Syud Sevajee's men, who planned to hunt down Beny Singh, had been issued with some threadbare old sepoys' jackets, some of them still stained with the blood of their previous owners, but none of the jackets had fitted Sharpe. Even Morris's coat would be a tight fit, but at least he had a uniform now. 'No trouble?' Sharpe asked Ahmed.

'No bugger saw me,' the boy said proudly. His English was improving every day, though Sharpe worried that it was not quite the King's English. Ahmed grinned again as Sharpe gave him a coin that he stuffed into his robes.

Sharpe folded the jacket over his arm and stooped out of the tent. He was looking for Clare and saw her a hundred paces away, walking with a tall soldier who was dressed in a shirt, black trousers and spurred boots. She was deep in conversation, and Sharpe felt a curious pang of jealousy as he approached, but then the soldier turned round, frowned at Sharpe's ragged appearance, then recognized the man under the head cloth. He grinned. 'Mister Sharpe,' he said.

'Eli Lockhart,' Sharpe said. 'What the hell are the cavalry doing here?' He jerked his thumb towards the fort that was edged with white smoke as the defenders tried to hammer the British batteries. 'This is a job for real soldiers.'

'Our Colonel persuaded the General that Mister Dodd might make a run for it. He reckoned a dozen cavalrymen could head him off.'

'Dodd won't run,' Sharpe said. 'He won't have space to get a horse out.'

'So we'll go in with you,' Lockhart said. 'We've got a quarrel with Mister Dodd, remember?'

Clare was looking shy and alarmed, and Sharpe reckoned she did not want Sergeant Lockhart to know that she had spent time with Ensign Sharpe. 'I was looking for Mrs Wall,' he explained to Lockhart. 'If you can spare me a few minutes, Ma'am?'

Clare shot Sharpe a look of gratitude. 'Of course, Mister Sharpe.'

'It's this jacket, see?' He held out Morris's coat. 'It's got red facings and turnbacks, and I need white ones.' He took off his head cloth. 'I wondered if you could use this. I know it's a bit filthy, and I hate to trouble you, Ma'am, but I don't reckon my sewing's up to making turnbacks, cuffs and collars.'

'You could take that captain's badge off while you're about it, love,' Lockhart suggested to Clare, 'and the skirmisher's wings. Don't reckon Mister Sharpe wants that coat's real owner to recognize it.'

'I'd rather he didn't,' Sharpe admitted.

Clare took the coat, gave Sharpe another grateful look, then hurried towards Sevajee's tents. Lockhart watched her go. 'Been wanting a chance to talk to her for three years,' he said wonderingly.

'So you found it, eh?'

Lockhart still watched her. 'A rare-looking woman, that.'

'Is she? I hadn't really noticed,' Sharpe lied.

'She said you'd been kind to her,' Lockhart said.

'Well, I tried to help, you know how it is,' Sharpe said awkwardly.

'That bloody man Torrance killed himself and she had nowhere to go. And you found her, eh? Most officers would try to take advantage of a woman like that,' Lockhart said.

'I'm not a proper officer, am I?' Sharpe replied. He had seen the way that Clare looked at the tall cavalryman, and how Lockhart had stared at her, and Sharpe reckoned that it was best to stand aside.

'I had a wife,' Lockhart said, 'only she died on the voyage out. Good little woman, she was.'

'I'm sorry,' Sharpe said.

'And Mrs Wall,' Lockhart went on, 'lost her husband.' Widow meets widower. Any minute now, Sharpe thought, and the word fate would be used. 'It's destiny,' Lockhart said in a tone of wonderment.

'So what are you going to do about her?' Sharpe asked.

'She says she ain't got a proper home now,' Lockhart said, 'except the tent you lent her, and my Colonel won't mind me taking a wife.'

'Have you asked her?'

'More or less,' Lockhart said, blushing.

'And she said yes?'

'More or less,' Lockhart said again, blushing more deeply.

'Bloody hell,' Sharpe said admiringly, 'that's quick!'

'Real soldiers don't wait,' Lockhart said, then frowned. 'I heard a rumour you'd been snaffled by the enemy?'

'Got away,' Sharpe said vaguely. 'Buggers were careless.' He turned and watched as an errant rocket from the fort soared up into the cloudless sky to leave a thickening pile of smoke through which, eventually, it tumbled harmlessly to earth. 'Are you really joining the attack?' he asked Lockhart.

'Not in the front rank,' Lockhart said. 'I ain't a fool. But Colonel Huddlestone says we can go in and look for Dodd. So we'll wait for you boys to do the hard work, then follow.'

'I'll look out for you.'

'And we'll keep an eye on you,' Lockhart promised. 'But in the meantime I'll go and see if someone needs a needle threaded.'

'You do that,' Sharpe said. He watched the cavalryman walk away, and saw, at the same time, that Ahmed had been evicted from Clare's tent with Sharpe's few belongings. The boy looked indignant, but Sharpe guessed their exile from the tent would not last long, for Clare would surely move to the cavalryman's quarters before nightfall. Ding dong, he thought, wedding bells. He took the pouch with its jewels from Ahmed, then, while his uniform was being tailored, he went to watch the guns gnaw and batter at the fort.

The young horseman who presented himself at the gate of Gawilghur's Inner Fort was tall, arrogant and self-assured. He was dressed in a white silk robe that was tied at the waist with a red leather belt from which a golden-hilted *tulwar* hung in a gem-encrusted scabbard, and he did not request that the gates be opened, but rather demanded it. There was, in truth, no good reason to deny his orders, for men were constantly traversing the ravine between the two forts and Dodd's Cobras were accustomed to opening and closing the gates a score of times each day, but there was something in the young man's demeanour that annoyed Gopal. So he sent for Colonel Dodd.

Dodd arrived a few moments later with the twitching English Sergeant at his side. The horseman rounded on Dodd, shouting at him to punish Gopal, but Dodd just spat, then turned to Hakeswill. 'Why would a man be riding a horse out of this gate?'

'Wouldn't know, sir,' Hakeswill said. The Sergeant was now dressed in a white coat that was crossed with a black sash as a sign of rank, though quite what rank the sash denoted was uncertain.

'There's nowhere to exercise a horse,' Dodd said, 'not unless he plans to ride through the Outer Fort into the English camp. Ask him his business, Gopal.'

The young man refused to answer. Dodd shrugged, drew his pistol and aimed it at the horseman's head. He cocked the gun and the sound of the hammer engaging echoed loudly from the ramparts. The young man blanched and shouted at Gopal.

'He says, sahib, that he is on an errand for the Killadar,' Gopal explained to Dodd.

'What errand?' Dodd demanded. The young man plainly did not want to answer, but Dodd's grim face and the levelled pistol persuaded him to take a sealed packet from the pouch that hung from his belt. He showed Dodd the Killadar's seal, but Dodd was not impressed by the red wax with its impression of a snake curled about a knife blade. 'Who is it addressed to?' he demanded, gesturing that the young man turn the package over.

The horseman obeyed and Dodd saw that the packet was addressed to the commanding officer of the British camp. It must have been written by a clerk who was unfamiliar with the English language, for it was atrociously spelt, but the words were unmistakable and Dodd stepped forward and seized the horse's bridle. 'Haul him out of the saddle, Gopal,' Dodd ordered, 'hold him in the guardroom and send a man to fetch Manu Bappoo.'

The young man attempted a momentary resistance, even half drawing his *tulwar* from its precious scabbard, but a dozen of Dodd's men easily overpowered him. Dodd himself turned away and climbed the steps to the rampart, motioning Hakeswill to follow him. 'It's obvious what the Killadar is doing,' Dodd growled. 'He's trying to make peace.'

'I thought we couldn't be defeated here, sir,' Hakeswill said in some alarm.

'We can't,' Dodd said, 'but Beny Singh is a coward. He thinks life should be nothing but women, music and games.'

Which sounded just splendid to Obadiah Hakeswill, but he said nothing. He had presented himself to Dodd as an aggrieved British soldier who believed the war against the Mahrattas was unfair. 'We ain't got no business here, sir,' he had said, 'not in heathen land. It belongs to the blackamoors, don't it? And there ain't nothing here for a redcoat.'

Dodd had not believed a word of it. He suspected Hakeswill had fled the British army to avoid trouble, but he could hardly blame the Sergeant for that. Dodd himself had done the same, and Dodd did not care about Hakeswill's motives, only that the Sergeant was willing to fight. And Dodd believed his men fought better when white men gave them orders. 'There's a steadiness about the English, Sergeant,' he had told Hakeswill, 'and it gives the natives bottom.'

'It gives them what, sir?' Hakeswill had asked.

Dodd had frowned at the Sergeant's obtuseness. 'You ain't Scotch, are you?'

'Christ no, sir! I ain't a bleeding Scotchman, nor a Welshman. English, sir, I am, through and through, sir.' His face twitched. 'English, sir, and proud of it.'

So Dodd had given Hakeswill a white jacket and a black sash, then put him in charge of a company of his Cobras. 'Fight well for me here, Sergeant,' he told Hakeswill when the two men reached the top of the rampart, 'and I'll make you an officer.'

'I shall fight, sir, never you mind, sir. Fight like a demon, I will.'

And Dodd believed him, for if Hakeswill did not fight then he risked being captured by the British, and God alone knew what trouble he would then face. Though in truth Dodd did not see how the British could penetrate the Inner Fort. He expected them to take the Outer Fort, for there they had a flat approach and their guns were already blasting down the breaches, but they would have a far greater problem in capturing the Inner Fort. He showed that problem now to Hakeswill. 'There's only one way in, Sergeant, and that's through this gate. They can't assault the walls, because the slope of the ravine is too steep. See?'

Hakeswill looked to his left and saw that the wall of the Inner Fort was built on an almost sheer slope. No man could climb that and hope to assail a wall, even a breached wall, which meant that Dodd was right and the attackers would have to try and batter down the four gates that barred the entranceway, and those gates were defended by Dodd's Cobras. 'And my men have never known defeat, Sergeant,' Dodd said. 'They've watched other men beaten, but they've not been outfought themselves. And here the enemy will have to beat us. Have to! But they can't. They can't.' He fell silent, his clenched fists resting on the firestep. The sound of the guns was constant, but the only sign of the bombardment was the misting smoke that hung over the far side of the Outer Fort. Manu Bappoo, who commanded there, was now hurrying back towards the Inner Fort and Dodd watched the Prince climb the steep path to the gates. The hinges squealed as, one after the other, the gates were opened to let Bappoo and his aides in. Dodd smiled as the last gate was unbarred. 'Let's go and make some mischief,' he said, turning back to the steps.

Manu Bappoo had already opened the letter that Gopal had given to him. He looked up as Dodd approached. 'Read it,' he said simply, thrusting the folded paper towards the Colonel.

'He wants to surrender?' Dodd asked, taking the letter.

'Just read it,' Bappoo said grimly.

The letter was clumsily written, but intelligible. Beny Singh, as Killadar of the Rajah of Berar's fortress of Gawilghur, was offering to yield the fort to the British on the sole condition that the lives of all the garrison and their dependants were spared. None was to be hurt, none was to be imprisoned. The British were welcome to confiscate all the weaponry in the fort, but they were to allow Gawilghur's inhabitants to leave with such personal property as could be carried away on foot or horseback.

'Of course the British will accept!' Manu Bappoo said. 'They don't want to die in the breaches!'

'Has Beny Singh the authority to send this?' Dodd asked.

Bappoo shrugged. 'He's Killadar.'

'You're the general of the army. And the Rajah's brother.'

Bappoo stared up at the sky between the high walls of the entranceway. 'One can never tell with my brother,' he said. 'Maybe he wants to surrender? But he hasn't told me. Maybe, if we lose, he can blame me, saying he always wanted to yield.'

'But you won't yield?'

'We can win here!' Bappoo said fiercely, then turned towards the palace as Gopal announced that the Killadar himself was approaching.

Beny Singh must have been watching his messenger's progress from the palace, for now he hurried down the path and behind him came his wives, concubines and daughters. Bappoo walked towards him, followed by Dodd and a score of his white-coated soldiers. The Killadar must have reckoned that the sight of the women would soften Bappoo's heart, but the Prince's face just became harder. 'If you want to surrender,' he shouted at Beny Singh, 'then talk to me first!'

'I have authority here,' Beny Singh squeaked. His little lap dog was in his arms, its small tongue hanging out as it panted in the heat.

'You have nothing!' Bappoo retorted. The women, pretty in their silk and cotton, huddled together as the two men met beside the snake pit.

'The British are making their breaches,' Beny Singh protested, 'and tomorrow or the day after they'll come through! We shall all be killed!' He wailed the prophecy. 'My daughters will be their playthings and my wives their servants.' The women shuddered.

'The British will die in the breaches,' Bappoo retorted.

'They cannot be stopped!' Beny Singh insisted. 'They are *djinns*.'

Bappoo suddenly shoved Beny Singh back towards the rock pit where the snakes were kept. The Killadar cried aloud as he tripped and fell backwards, but Bappoo had kept hold of Beny Singh's yellow silk robe and now he held on tight so that the Killadar did not fall. Hakeswill sidled to the pit's edge and saw the monkey bones. Then he saw a curving, flickering shape slither across the pit's shadowed floor and he quickly stepped back.

Beny Singh whimpered. 'I am the Killadar! I am trying to save lives!'

'You're supposed to be a soldier,' Bappoo said in his hissing voice, 'and your job is to kill my brother's enemies.' The women screamed, expecting to see their man fall to the pit's floor, but Manu Bappoo kept a firm grip on the silk. 'And when the British die in the breaches,' he said to Beny Singh, 'and when their survivors are harried south across the plain, who do you think will get the credit for the victory? The Killadar of the fort, that is who! And you would throw that glory away?'

'They are *djinns*,' Beny Singh said, and he looked sideways at Obadiah Hakeswill whose face was twitching, and he screamed. 'They are *djinns*!'

'They are men, as feeble as other men,' Bappoo said. He reached out with his free hand and took hold of the white dog by the scruff of its neck. Beny Singh whimpered, but did not resist. The dog struggled in Manu Bappoo's grip. 'If you try to surrender the fortress again,' Manu Bappoo said, 'then this will be your fate.' He let the dog drop. It yelped as it fell into the pit, then howled piteously as it struck the rock floor. There was a hiss, a scrabble of paws, a last howl, then silence. Beny Singh uttered a shriek of pity for his dog before babbling that he would rather give his women poison to drink than risk that they should become prey to the terrible besiegers.

Manu Bappoo shook the hapless Killadar. 'Do you understand me?' he demanded.

'I understand!' Beny Singh said desperately.

Manu Bappoo hauled the Killadar safely back from the pit's edge. 'You will go to the palace, Beny Singh,' he ordered, 'and you will stay there, and you will send no more messages to the enemy.' He pushed the Killadar away, then turned his back on him. 'Colonel Dodd?'

'Sahib?'

'A dozen of your men will make certain that the Killadar sends no messages from the palace. If he does, you may kill the messenger.'

Dodd smiled. 'Of course, sahib.'

Bappoo went back to the beleaguered Outer Fort while the Killadar slunk back to the hilltop palace above its green-scummed lake. Dodd detailed a dozen men to guard the palace's entrance, then went back to the rampart to brood over the ravine. Hakeswill followed him there. 'Why's the Killadar so scared, sir? Does he know something we don't?'

'He's a coward, Sergeant.'

But Beny Singh's fear had infected Hakeswill who imagined a vengeful Sharpe come back from the dead to pursue him through the nightmare of a fortress fallen. 'The bastards can't get in, sir, can they?' he asked anxiously.

Dodd recognized Hakeswill's fear, the same fear he felt himself, the fear of the ignominy and shame of being recaptured by the British and then condemned by a merciless court. He smiled. 'They will probably take the Outer Fort, Sergeant, because they're very good, and because our old comrades do indeed fight like *djinns*, but they cannot cross the ravine. Not if all the powers of darkness help them, not if they besiege us for a year, not if they batter down all these walls and destroy the gates and flatten the palace by gunfire, because they will still have to cross the ravine, and it cannot be done. It cannot be done.'

And who rules Gawilghur, Dodd thought, reigns in India.

And within a week he would be Rajah here.

*   *   *

Gawilghur's walls, as Stokes had guessed, were rotten. The first breach, in the outer wall, took less than a day to make. In mid-afternoon the wall had still been standing, though a cave had been excavated into the dusty rubble where Stokes had pointed the guns, but quite suddenly the whole rampart collapsed. It slid down the brief slope in a cloud of dust which slowly settled to reveal a steep ramp of jumbled stone leading into the space between the two walls. A low stub of the wall's rear face still survived, but an hour's work served to throw that remnant down.

The gunners changed their aim, starting the two breaches in the higher inner wall, while the enfilading batteries, which had been gnawing at the embrasures to dismount the enemy's guns, began firing slantwise into the first breach to dissuade the defenders from building obstacles at the head of the ramp. The enemy guns, those which survived, redoubled their efforts to disable the British batteries, but their shots were wasted in the gabions or overhead. The big gun which had inflicted such slaughter fired three times more, but its balls cracked uselessly into the cliff face, after which the Mahratta gunners mysteriously gave up.

Next day the two inner breaches were made, and now the big guns concentrated on widening all three gaps in the walls. The eighteen-pounder shots slammed into rotten stone, gouging out the wall's fill to add to the ramps. By evening the breaches were clearly big enough and now the gunners aimed their pieces at the enemy's remaining cannon. One by one they were unseated or their embrasures shattered. A constant shroud of smoke hung over the rocky neck of land. It hung thick and pungent, twitching every time a shot whipped through. The enfilading twelve-pounders fired shells into the breaches, while the howitzer lobbed more shells over the walls.

The British guns fired deep into dusk, and minute by minute the enemy response grew feebler as their guns were wrecked or thrown off the firesteps. Only as black night dropped did the besiegers' hot guns cease fire, but even now there would be no respite for the enemy. It was at night that the defenders could turn the breaches into deathtraps. They could bury mines in the stony ramps, or dig wide trenches across the breach summits or make new walls behind the raw new openings, but the British kept one heavy gun firing throughout the darkness. They loaded the eighteen-pounder with canister and, three times an hour, sprayed the area of the breaches with a cloud of musket balls to deter any Mahratta from risking his life on the rubbled slopes.

Few slept well that night. The cough of the gun seemed unnaturally loud, and even in the British camp men could hear the rattle as the musket balls whipped against Gawilghur's wounded walls. And in the morning, the soldiers knew, they would be asked to go to those walls and climb the tumbled ramps and fight their way through the shattered stones. And what would wait for them? At the very least, they suspected, the enemy would have mounted guns athwart the breaches to fire across the attack route. They expected blood and pain and death.

'I've never been into a breach,' Garrard told Sharpe. The two men met at Syud Sevajee's tents, and Sharpe had given his old friend a bottle of arrack.

'Nor me,' Sharpe said.

'They say it's bad.'

'They do,' Sharpe agreed bleakly. It was supposedly the worst ordeal that any soldier could face.

Garrard drank from the stone bottle, wiped its lip, then handed it to Sharpe. He admired Sharpe's coat in the light of the small campfire. 'Smart bit of cloth, Mister Sharpe.'

The coat had been given new white turnbacks and cuffs by Clare Wall, and Sharpe had done his best to make the jacket wrinkled and dusty, but it still looked expensive. 'Just an old coat, Tom,' he said dismissively.

'Funny, isn't it? Mister Morris lost a coat.'

'Did he?' Sharpe asked. 'He should be more careful.' He gave Garrard the bottle, then climbed to his feet. 'I've got an errand, Tom.' He held out his hand. 'I'll look for you tomorrow.'

'I'll look out for you, Dick.'

Sharpe led Ahmed through the camp. Some men sang around their fires, others obsessively honed bayonets that were already razor sharp. A cavalryman had set up a grinding stone and a succession of officers' servants brought swords and sabres to be given a wicked edge. Sparks whipped off the stone. The sappers were doing their last job, making ladders from bamboo that had been carried up from the plain. Major Stokes supervised the job, and his eyes widened in joy as he saw Sharpe approaching through the firelight. 'Richard! Is it you? Dear me, it is!

Well, I never! And I thought you were locked up in the enemy's dungeons! You escaped?'

Sharpe shook Stokes's hand. 'I never got taken to Gawilghur. I was held by some horsemen,' he lied, 'but they didn't seem to know what to do with me, so the buggers just let me go.'

'I'm delighted, delighted!'

Sharpe turned and looked at the ladders. 'I didn't think we were making an escalade tomorrow?'

'We're not,' Stokes said, 'but you never know what obstacles have to be overcome inside a fortress. Sensible to carry ladders.' He peered at Ahmed who was now dressed in one of the sepoy's coats that had been given to Syud Sevajee. The boy wore the red jacket proudly, even though it was a poor, threadbare and bloodstained thing. 'I say,' Stokes admired the boy, 'but you do look like a proper soldier. Don't he just?' Ahmed stood to attention, shouldered his musket and made a smart about-turn. Major Stokes applauded. 'Well done, lad. I'm afraid you've missed all the excitement, Sharpe.'

'Excitement?'

'Your Captain Torrance died. Shot himself, by the look of things. Terrible way to go. I feel sorry for his father. He's a cleric, did you know? Poor man, poor man. Would you like some tea, Sharpe? Or do you need to sleep?'

'I'd like some tea, sir.'

'We'll go to my tent,' Stokes said, leading the way. 'I've still got your pack, by the way. You can take it with you.'

'I'd rather you kept it another day,' Sharpe said, 'I'll be busy tomorrow.'

'Busy?' Stokes asked.

'I'm going in with Kenny's troops, sir.'

'Dear God,' Stokes said. He stopped and frowned. 'I've no doubt we'll get through the breaches, Richard, for they're good breaches. A bit steep, perhaps, but we should get through, but God only knows what waits beyond. And I fear that the Inner Fort may be a much bigger obstacle than any of us have anticipated.' He shook his head. 'I ain't sanguine, Sharpe, I truly ain't.'

Sharpe had no idea what sanguine meant, though he did not doubt that Stokes's lack of it did not augur well for the attack. 'I have to go into the fort, sir. I have to. But I wondered if you'd keep an eye on

Ahmed here.' He took hold of the boy's shoulder and pulled him forward. 'The little bugger will insist on coming with me,' Sharpe said, 'but if you keep him out of trouble then he might survive another day.'

'He can be my assistant,' Stokes said happily. 'But, Richard, can't I persuade you to the same employment? Are you ordered to accompany Kenny?'

'I'm not ordered, sir, but I have to go. It's personal business.'

'It will be bloody in there,' Stokes warned. He walked on to his tent and shouted for his servant.

Sharpe pushed Ahmed towards Stokes's tent. 'You stay here, Ahmed, you hear me? You stay here!'

'I come with you,' Ahmed insisted.

'You bloody well stay,' Sharpe said. He twitched Ahmed's red coat. 'You're a soldier now. That means you take orders, understand? You obey. And I'm ordering you to stay here.'

The boy scowled, but he seemed to accept the orders, and Stokes showed him a place where he could sleep. Afterwards the two men talked, or rather Sharpe listened as Stokes enthused about some fine quartz he had discovered in rocks broken open by the enemy's counter-battery fire. Eventually the Major began yawning. Sharpe finished his tea, said his good night and then, making certain that Ahmed did not see him go, he slipped away into the dark.

He still could not sleep. He wished Clare had not gone to Eli Lockhart, although he was glad for the cavalryman that she had, but her absence made Sharpe feel lonely. He walked to the cliff's edge and he stood staring across the great gulf towards the fortress. A few lights showed in Gawilghur, and every twenty minutes or so the rocky isthmus would be lit by the monstrous flame of the eighteen-pounder gun. The balls would rattle against stone, then there would be silence except for the distant sound of singing, the crackle of insects and the soft sigh of the wind against the cliffs. Once, when the great gun fired, Sharpe distinctly saw the three ragged holes in the two walls. And why, he wondered, was he so intent on going into those deathtraps? Was it revenge? Just to find Hakeswill and Dodd? He could wait for the attackers to do their work, then stroll into the fort unopposed, but he knew he would not choose that easy path. He would go with Kenny's men and he would fight his way into Gawilghur for no other reason than pride. He was failing as an officer. The 74th had rejected him, the Rifles did not yet know him, so Sharpe must take a reputation back to England if he was to stand any chance of success.

So tomorrow he must fight. Or else he must sell his commission and leave the army. He had thought about that, but he wanted to stay in uniform. He enjoyed the army, he even suspected he was good at the army's business of fighting the King's enemies. So tomorrow he would do it again, and thus demonstrate that he deserved the red sash and the sword.

So in the morning, when the drums beat and the enemy guns beat even harder, Sharpe would go into Gawilghur.

CHAPTER 9

At dawn there was a mist in Deogaum, a mist that sifted through the rain trees and pooled in the valleys and beaded on the tents. 'A touch of winter, don't you think?' Sir Arthur Wellesley commented to his aide, Campbell.

'The thermometer's showing seventy-eight degrees, sir,' the young Scotsman answered drily.

'Only a touch of winter, Campbell, only a touch,' the General said. He was standing outside his tent, a cup and saucer in one hand, staring up through the wisps of mist to where the rising sun threw a brilliant light on Gawilghur's soaring cliffs. A servant stood behind with Wellesley's coat, hat and sword, a second servant held his horse, while a third waited to take the cup and saucer. 'How's Harness?' the General asked Campbell.

'I believe he now sleeps most of the time, sir,' Campbell replied. Colonel Harness had been relieved of the command of his brigade. He had been found ranting in the camp, demanding that his Highlanders form fours and follow him southwards to fight against dragons, papists and Whigs.

'Sleeps?' the General asked. 'What are the doctors doing? Pouring rum down his gullet?'

'I believe it is tincture of opium, sir, but most likely flavoured with rum.'

'Poor Harness,' Wellesley grunted, then sipped his tea. From high above him there came the sound of a pair of twelve-pounder guns that had been hauled to the summit of the conical hill that reared just south of the fortress. Wellesley knew those guns were doing no good, but he had stubbornly insisted that they fire at the fortress gate that looked out across the vast plain. The gunners had warned the General that the weapons would be ineffective, that they would be firing too far and too high above them, but Wellesley had wanted the fortress to know that an assault might come from the south as well as across the rocky isthmus to the north, and so he had ordered the sappers to drag the two weapons up through the entangling jungle and to make a battery on the hill top. The guns, firing at their maximum elevation, were just able to throw their missiles to Gawilghur's southern entrance, but by the time the round shot reached the gate it was spent of all force and simply bounced back down the steep slope. But that was not the point. The point was to keep some of the garrison looking southwards, so that not every man could be thrown against the assault on the breaches.

That assault would not start for five hours yet, for before Lieutenant Colonel Kenny led his men against the breaches, Wellesley wanted his other attackers to be in place. Those were two columns of redcoats that were even now climbing the two steep roads that twisted up the great cliffs. Colonel Wallace, with his own 74th and a battalion of sepoys, would approach the Southern Gate, while the 78th and another native battalion would climb the road which led to the ravine between the forts. Both columns could expect to come under heavy artillery fire, and neither could hope to break into the fortress, but their job was only to distract the defenders while Kenny's men made for the breaches.

Wellesley drained the tea, made a wry face at its bitter taste and held out the cup and saucer for the servant. 'Time to go, Campbell.'

'Yes, sir.'

Wellesley had thought about riding to the plateau and entering the fortress behind Kenny, but he guessed his presence would merely distract men who had enough problems to face without worrying about their commander's approval. Instead he would ride the steep southern road and join Wallace and the 74th. All those men could hope for was that the other attackers got inside the Inner Fort and opened the Southern Gate, or else they would have to march ignominiously back down the hill to their encampment. It was all or nothing, Wellesley thought. Victory or disgrace.

He mounted, waited for his aides to assemble, then touched his horse's flank with his spurs. God help us now, he prayed, God help us now.

*   *   *

Lieutenant Colonel Kenny examined the breaches through a telescope that he had propped on a rock close to one of the breaching batteries. The guns were firing, but he ignored the vast noise as he gazed at the stone ramps which his men must climb. 'They're steep, man,' he grumbled, 'damned steep.'

'The walls are built on a slope,' Major Stokes pointed out, 'so the breaches are steep of necessity.'

'Damned hard to climb though,' Kenny said.

'They're practical,' Stokes declared. He knew the breaches were steep, and that was why the guns were still firing. There was no hope of making the breaches less steep, the slope of the hill saw to that, but at least the continued bombardment gave the attacking infantry the impression that the gunners were attempting to alleviate the difficulties.

'You've made holes in the walls,' Kenny said, 'I'll grant you that. You've made holes, but that don't make them practical holes, Stokes. They're damned steep.'

'Of necessity,' Stokes repeated patiently.

'We ain't monkeys, you know,' Kenny complained.

'I think you'll find them practical, sir,' Stokes said emolliently. He knew, and Kenny knew, that the breaches could not be improved and must therefore be attempted. Kenny's grumbling, Stokes suspected, was a disguise for nerves, and Stokes could not blame the man. He would not have wanted to carry a sword or musket up those rugged stone slopes to whatever horrors the enemy had prepared on the other side.

Kenny grunted. 'I suppose they'll have to suffice,' he said grudgingly, snapping his telescope shut. He flinched as one of the eighteen-pounders roared and billowed smoke all about the battery, then he strode into the acrid cloud, shouting for Major Plummer, the gunner officer.

Plummer, powder-stained and sweating, loomed out of the smoke. 'Sir?'

'You'll keep your pieces firing till we're well on the breaches?'

'I will, sir.'

'That should keep their damned heads down,' Kenny said, then fished a watch from his fob. 'I make it ten minutes after nine.'

'Eight minutes after,' Plummer said.

'Exactly nine o'clock,' Stokes said, tapping his watch to see if the hands were stuck.

'We'll use my timepiece,' Kenny decreed, 'and we'll move forward on the strike of ten o'clock. And remember, Plummer, keep firing till we're there! Don't be chary, man, don't stop just because we're close to the summit. Batter the bastards! Batter the bastards!' He frowned at Ahmed who was staying close to Stokes. The boy was wearing his red coat which was far too big for him, and Kenny seemed on the point of demanding an explanation for the boy's odd garb, then abruptly shrugged and walked away.

He went to where his men crouched on the track that led to the fortress gate. They were sheltered from the defenders by the lie of the land, but the moment they advanced over a small rocky rise they would become targets. They then had three hundred yards of open ground to cross, and as they neared the broken walls they would be squeezed into the narrow space between the tank and the precipice where they could expect the fire of the defenders to be at its fiercest. After that it was a climb to the breaches and to whatever horrors waited out of sight.

The men sat, trying to find what small shade was offered by bushes or rocks. Many were half drunk, for their officers had issued extra rations of arrack and rum. None carried a pack, they had only their muskets, their ammunition and bayonets. A few, not many, prayed. An officer of the Scotch Brigade knelt bare-headed amongst a group of his men, and Kenny, intrigued by the sight, swerved towards the kneeling soldiers to hear them softly repeating the twenty-third psalm. Most men just sat, heads low, consumed by their thoughts. The officers forced conversation.

Behind Kenny's thousand men was a second assault force, also composed of sepoys and Scotsmen, which would follow Kenny into the breach. If Kenny failed then the second storming party would try to go farther, but if Kenny succeeded they would secure the Outer Fort while Kenny's troops went on to assault the Inner. Small groups of gunners were included in both assault groups. Their orders were to find whatever serviceable cannon still existed in the Outer Fort and turn them against the defenders beyond the ravine.

An officer wearing the white facings of the 74th picked his way up the track between the waiting troops. The man had a cheap Indian sabre at his waist and, unusually for an officer, was carrying a musket and cartridge box. Kenny hailed him. 'Who the devil are you?'

'Sharpe, sir.'

The name rang a bell in Kenny's mind. 'Wellesley's man?'

'Don't know about that, sir.'

Kenny scowled at the evasion. 'You were at Assaye, yes?'

'Yes, sir,' Sharpe admitted.

Kenny's expression softened. He knew of Sharpe and he admired a brave man. 'So what the devil are you doing here, Sharpe? Your regiment is miles away! They're climbing the road from Deogaum.'

'I was stranded here, sir,' Sharpe said, deciding there was no point in trying to deliver a longer explanation, 'and there wasn't time to join the 74th, sir, so I was hoping to go with my old company. That's Captain Morris's men, sir.' He nodded up the track to where the 33rd's Light Company was gathered among some boulders. 'With your permission of course, sir.'

'No doubt Morris will be glad of your help, Sharpe,' Kenny said, 'as will I.' He was impressed by Sharpe's appearance, for the Ensign was tall, evidently strong and had a roguish fierceness about his face. In the breach, the Colonel knew, victory or defeat as often as not came down to a man's skill and strength, and Sharpe looked as if he knew how to use his weapons. 'Good luck to you, Sharpe.'

'And the best to you, sir,' Sharpe said warmly.

He walked on, his borrowed musket heavy on his shoulder. Eli Lockhart and Syud Sevajee were waiting with their men among the third group, the soldiers who would occupy the fort after the assault troops had done their work, if, indeed, the leading two thousand men managed to get through the walls. A rumour was spreading that the breaches were too steep and that no one could carry a weapon and climb the ramps at the same time. The men believed they would need to use their hands to scramble up the stony piles, and so they would be easy targets for any defenders at the top of the breaches. The gunners, they grumbled, should have brought down more of the wall, if not all of it, and the proof of that assertion was the guns' continual firing. Why would the guns go on gnawing at the wall if the breaches were already practical? They could hear the strike of round shot on stone, hear the occasional tumble of rubble, but what they could not hear was any fire from the fortress. The bastards were saving their fire for the assault.

Sharpe edged among sepoys who were carrying one of Major Stokes's bamboo ladders. The dark faces grinned at him, and one man offered Sharpe a canteen which proved to contain a strongly spiced arrack. Sharpe took a small sip, then amused the sepoys by pretending to be astonished by the liquor's fierceness. 'That's rare stuff, lads,' Sharpe said, then walked on towards his old comrades. They watched his approach with a mixture of surprise, welcome and apprehension. When the 33rd's Light Company had last seen Sharpe he had been a sergeant, and not long before that he had been a private strapped to the punishment triangle; now he wore a sword and sash. Although officers promoted from the ranks were not supposed to serve with their old units, Sharpe had friends among these men and if he was to climb the steep rubble of Gawilghur's breaches then he would rather do it among friends.

Captain Morris was no friend, and he watched Sharpe's approach with foreboding. Sharpe headed straight for his old company commander. 'Good to see you, Charles,' he said, knowing that his use of the Christian name would irritate Morris. 'Nice morning, eh?'

Morris looked left and right as though seeking someone who could help him confront this upstart from his past. Morris had never liked Sharpe, indeed he had conspired with Obadiah Hakeswill to have Sharpe flogged in the hope that the punishment would end in death, but Sharpe had survived and had been commissioned. Now the bastard was being familiar, and there was nothing Morris could do about it. 'Sharpe,' he managed to say.

'Thought I'd join you, Charles,' Sharpe said airily. 'I've been stranded up here, and Kenny reckoned I might be useful to you.'

'Of course,' Morris said, conscious of his men's gaze. Morris would have liked to tell Sharpe to bugger a long way off, but he could not commit such impoliteness to a fellow officer in front of his men. 'I never congratulated you,' he forced himself to say.

'No time like the present,' Sharpe said.

Morris blushed. 'Congratulations.'

'Thank you, Charles,' Sharpe said, then turned and looked at the company. Most grinned at him, but a few men avoided his gaze. 'No Sergeant Hakeswill?' Sharpe asked guilelessly.

'He was captured by the enemy,' Morris said. The Captain was staring at Sharpe's coat which was not quite big enough and looked, somehow, familiar.

Sharpe saw Morris frowning at the jacket. 'You like the coat?' he asked.

'What?' Morris asked, confused by his suspicions and by Sharpe's easy manner. Morris himself was wearing an old coat that was disfigured by brown cloth patches.

'I bought the coat after Assaye,' Sharpe said. 'You weren't there, were you?'

'No.'

'Nor at Argaum?'

'No,' Morris said, stiffening slightly. He resented the fact that Sharpe had survived those battles and was now suggesting, however delicately, that the experience gave him an advantage. The truth was that it did, but Morris could not admit that any more than he could admit his jealousy of Sharpe's reputation.

'So what are our orders today?' Sharpe asked.

Morris could not accustom himself to this confident Sharpe who treated him as an equal and he was tempted not to answer, but the question was reasonable and Sharpe was undoubtedly an officer, if merely an ensign. 'Once we're through the first wall,' Morris answered unhappily, 'Kenny's going to attack the left-hand upper breach and he wants us to seal off the right upper breach.'

'Sounds like a decent morning's work,' Sharpe said happily, then raised a hand to Garrard. 'How are you, Tom?'

'Pleased you're here, sir.'

'Couldn't let you babies go into a breach without some help,' Sharpe said, then held out his hand to Sergeant Green. 'Good to see you, Sergeant.'

'Grand to see you too, sir,' Green said, shaking Sharpe's hand. 'I heard you'd been commissioned and I hardly dared believe it!'

'You know what they say about scum, Sergeant,' Sharpe said. 'Always floats to the top, eh?' Some of the men laughed, especially when Sharpe glanced at Morris who had, indeed, expressed that very opinion not long before. Others scowled, for there were plenty in the company who resented Sharpe's good fortune.

One of them, a dark-faced man called Crowley, spat. 'You always were a lucky bastard, Sharpie.'

Sharpe seemed to ignore the remark as he stepped through the seated company and greeted more of his old friends, but when he was behind Crowley he turned abruptly and pushed out the butt of his slung musket so that the heavy stock thumped into the private's head. Crowley let out a yelp and turned to see Sharpe standing above him. 'The word, Crowley,' Sharpe said menacingly, 'is "sir".'

Crowley met Sharpe's gaze, but could not hold it. 'Yes, sir,' he said meekly.

'I'm sorry I was careless with the musket, Crowley,' Sharpe said.

There was another burst of laughter, making Morris scowl, but he was quite uncertain of how to deal with Sharpe and so he said nothing. Watson, a Welsh private who had joined the regiment rather than face an assize court, jerked a thumb towards the fort. 'They say the breaches are too steep, Mister Sharpe.'

'Nothing to what you Welsh boys climb every day in the mountains,' Sharpe said. He had borrowed Major Stokes's telescope shortly after dawn and stared at the breaches, and he had not much liked what he had seen, but this was no time to tell the truth. 'We're going to give the buggers a right bloody thrashing, lads,' he said instead. 'I've fought these Mahrattas twice now and they don't stand. They look good, but press home on the bastards and they turn and run like jack rabbits. Just keep going, boys, keep fighting, and the buggers'll give up.'

It was the speech Morris should have made to them, and Sharpe had not even known he was going to make any kind of speech when he opened his mouth, but somehow the words had come. And he was glad, for the men looked relieved at his confidence, then some of them looked nervous again as they watched a sepoy coming up the track with a British flag in his hands. Colonel Kenny and his aides walked behind the man, all with drawn swords. Captain Morris drank deep from his canteen, and the smell of rum wafted to Sharpe.

The guns fired on, crumbling the breaches' shoulders and filling the air with smoke and dust as they tried to make the rough way smooth. Soldiers, sensing that the order to advance was about to be given, stood and hefted their weapons. Some touched rabbits' feet hidden in pockets, or whatever other small token gave them a fingerhold on life.

239

One man vomited, another trembled. Sweat poured down their faces.

'Four ranks,' Morris said.

'Into ranks! Quick now!' Sergeant Green snapped. An howitzer shell arced overhead then plummeted towards the fort trailing its wisp of fuse smoke. Sharpe heard the shell explode, then watched another shell follow. A man dashed out of the ranks into the rocks, lowered his trousers and emptied his bowels. Everyone pretended not to notice until the smell struck them, then they jeered as the embarrassed man went back to his place. 'That's enough!' Green said.

A sepoy drummer with an old-fashioned mitred shako on his head gave his drum a couple of taps, while a piper from the Scotch Brigade filled his bag then settled the instrument under his elbow. Colonel Kenny was looking at his watch. The guns fired on, their smoke drifting down to the waiting men. The sepoy with the flag was at the front of the forming column, and Sharpe guessed the enemy must be able to see the bright tip of the colour above the rocky crest.

Sharpe took the bayonet from his belt and slotted it onto the musket. He was not wearing the sabre that Ahmed had stolen from Morris, for he knew the weapon would be identifiable, and so he had a *tulwar* that he had borrowed from Syud Sevajee. He did not trust the weapon. He had seen too many Indian blades break in combat. Besides he was used to a musket and bayonet.

'Fix bayonets!' Morris ordered, prompted by the sight of Sharpe's blade.

'And save your fire till you're hard in the breach,' Sharpe added. 'You've got one shot, lads, so don't waste it. You won't have time to reload till you're through both walls.'

Morris scowled at this unasked-for advice, but the men seemed grateful for it, just as they were grateful that they were not in the front ranks of Kenny's force. That honour had gone to the Grenadier Company of the 94th who thus formed the Forlorn Hope. Usually the Hope, that group of men who went first into a breach to spring the enemy traps and fight down the immediate defenders, was composed of volunteers, but Kenny had decided to do without a proper Forlorn Hope. He wanted to fill the breaches quickly and so overwhelm the defences by numbers, and thus hard behind the Scotch Brigade's grenadiers were two more companies of Scots, then came the sepoys and Morris's men. Hard and fast, Kenny had told them, hard and fast.

Leave the wounded behind you, he had ordered, and just get up the damned breaches and start killing.

The Colonel looked at his watch a last time, then snapped its lid shut and put it into a pocket. He took a breath, hefted his sword, then shouted one word. 'Now!'

And the flag went forward across the crest and behind it came a wave of men who hurried towards the walls.

For a few seconds the fortress was silent, then the first rocket was fired. It seared towards the advancing troops, trailing its plume of thick smoke, then abruptly twisted and climbed into the clear sky.

Then the guns began.

Colonel William Dodd saw the errant rocket twist into the sky, falter amidst a growing tumult of its own smoke, then fall. Manu Bappoo's guns began to fire and Dodd knew, though he could not see over the loom of the Outer Fort, that the British attack was coming. 'Gopal!' he called to his second in command.

'Sahib?'

'Close the gates.'

'Sahib?' Gopal frowned at the Colonel. It had been agreed with Manu Bappoo that the four gates that barred the entranceway to the Inner Fort would be left open so that the defenders of the Outer Fort could retreat swiftly if it was necessary. Dodd had even posted a company to guard the outermost gate to make sure that no British pursuers could get in behind Manu Bappoo's men, yet now he was suggesting that the gates should be shut? 'You want me to close them, sahib?' Gopal asked, wondering if he had misheard.

'Close them, bar them and forget them,' Dodd said happily, 'and pull the platoon back inside the fort. I have another job for them.'

'But, sahib, if –'

'You heard me, Jemadar! Move!'

Gopal ran to do Dodd's bidding, while the Colonel himself walked along the firestep that edged the entranceway to make certain that his orders were being obeyed. He watched, satisfied, as the troops guarding the outer gate were brought back into the fortress and then as, one by one, the four vast gates were pushed shut. The great locking bars, each as thick as a man's thigh, were dropped into their metal brackets. The Outer Fort was now isolated. If Manu Bappoo repelled the British then it would be a simple matter to open the gates again, but if he lost, and if he fled, then he would find himself trapped between Dodd's Cobras and the advancing British.

Dodd walked to the centre of the firestep and there climbed onto an embrasure so that he could talk to as many of his men as possible. 'You will see that I have shut the gates,' he shouted, 'and they will stay shut! They will not be opened except by my express permission. Not if all the maharajahs of India stand out there and demand entrance! The gates stay shut. Do you understand?'

The white-coated soldiers, or at least those few who spoke some English, nodded while the rest had Dodd's orders translated. None showed much interest in the decision. They trusted their Colonel, and if he wanted the gates kept closed, then so be it.

Dodd watched the smoke thicken on the far side of the Outer Fort. A grim struggle was being waged there, but it was nothing to do with him. He would only begin to fight when the British attacked across the ravine, but their attacks would achieve nothing. The only way into the Inner Fort was through the gates, and that was impossible. The British might batter down the first gate with cannon fire, but once through the arch they would discover that the entranceway turned sharply to the left, so their gun could not fire through the passage to batter down the three other doors. They would have to fight their way up the narrow passage, try to destroy the successive gates with axes, and all the while his men would be pouring slaughter on them from the flanking walls.

'Sahib?' Gopal called, and Dodd turned to see that the Jemadar was pointing up the path that led to the palace. Beny Singh had appeared on the path, flanked by a servant carrying a parasol to protect the Killadar from the hot sun.

'Send him up here, Jemadar!' Dodd shouted back.

Dodd felt a quiet exaltation at the neatness of his tactics. Manu Bappoo was already cut off from safety, and only Beny Singh was now left as a rival to Dodd's supremacy. Dodd was tempted to cut the Killadar down here and now, but the murder would have been witnessed by members of the garrison who were still loyal to Beny Singh, and so instead Dodd greeted the Killadar with a respectful bow. 'What's happening?' Beny Singh demanded. He was breathing hard from the effort of climbing to the firestep, then he cried out in dismay because the guns on the southern wall of the Outer Fort, those guns that overlooked the ravine, had suddenly opened fire to pump gouts of grey-white smoke.

'I fear, sahib,' Dodd said, 'that the enemy are overwhelming the fort.'

'They're doing what?' The Killadar, who was dressed for battle in a clean white robe girdled by a red cummerbund and hung with a jewelled scabbard, looked horrified. He watched the smoke spread across the ravine. He was puzzled because it was not at all clear what the nearer guns were firing at. 'But the enemy can't get in here!'

'There are other British soldiers approaching, sahib,' Dodd said, and he pointed to the smoke cloud above the ravine. The guns on the near side of the Outer Fort, most of them small three- and five-pounder cannon, were aiming their pieces westwards, which meant that British troops must be approaching up the steep road which led from the plain. Those troops were still out of Dodd's sight, but the gunnery from the Outer Fort was eloquent proof of their presence. 'There must be redcoats coming towards the ravine,' Dodd explained, 'and we never foresaw that the British might assault in more than one place.' Dodd told the lie smoothly. 'I have no doubt they have men coming up the southern road too.'

'They do,' the Killadar confirmed.

Dodd shuddered, as though the news overwhelmed him with despair. 'We shall do our best,' he promised, 'but I cannot defend everything at once. I fear the British will gain the victory this day.' He bowed to the Killadar again. 'I am so very sorry, sahib. But you can gain an immortal reputation by joining the fight. We might lose today's battle, but in years to come men will sing songs about the defiance of Beny Singh. And how better for a soldier to die, sahib, than with a sword in his hand and his enemies dead about his feet?'

Beny Singh blanched at the thought. 'My daughters!' he croaked.

'Alas,' Dodd said gravely, 'they will become soldiers' toys. But you should not worry, sahib. In my experience the prettiest girls usually find a soldier to defend them. He is usually a big man, crude and forceful, but he stops the other men from raping his woman, except his friends, of course, who will be allowed some liberties. I am sure your wives and daughters will find men eager to protect them.'

Beny Singh fled from Dodd's reassurances. Dodd smiled as the

Killadar ran, then turned and walked towards Hakeswill who was posted in the bastion above the innermost gate. The Sergeant had been issued with a sword to accompany his black sash. He slammed to attention as Dodd approached him. 'Stand easy, Mister Hakeswill,' Dodd said. Hakeswill relaxed slightly. He liked being called 'Mister', it somehow seemed appropriate. If that little bastard Sharpe could be a mister and wear a sword, then so could he. 'I shall have a job for you in a few minutes, Mister Hakeswill,' Dodd said.

'I shall be honoured, sir,' Hakeswill replied.

Dodd watched the Killadar hurry up the path towards the palace. 'Our honoured commander,' he said sarcastically, 'is taking some bad news to the palace. We must give the news time to take root there.'

'Bad news, sir?'

'He thinks we're going to lose,' Dodd explained.

'I pray not, sir.'

'As do I, Mister Hakeswill, as do I. Fervently!' Dodd turned to watch the gunners in the Outer Fort and he saw how puny their small cannon were and he reckoned that such fire would not hold up the redcoats for long. The British would be in the ravine in half an hour, maybe less. 'In ten minutes, Mister Hakeswill, you will lead your company to the palace and you will order the Arab guards to come and defend the walls.'

Hakeswill's face twitched. 'Don't speak their heathen language, sir, begging your pardon, sir.'

'You don't need their language. You've got a musket, use it. And if anyone questions your authority, Mister Hakeswill, you have my permission to shoot them.'

'Shoot them, sir? Yes, sir. With pleasure, sir.'

'Anyone at all, Mister Hakeswill.'

Hakeswill's face twitched again. 'That fat little bugger, sir, him what was just here with the curly moustache . . .'

'The Killadar? If he questions you . . .'

'I shoot the bugger, sir.'

'Exactly.' Dodd smiled. He had seen into Hakeswill's soul and discovered it was black as filth, and perfect for his purposes. 'Do it for me, Mister Hakeswill, and I shall gazette you as a captain in the Cobras. Your havildar speaks some English, doesn't he?'

'A kind of English, sir,' Hakeswill said.

'Make sure he understands you. The palace guards are to be despatched to the walls.'

'They will, sir, or else they'll be dead 'uns.'

'Very good,' Dodd said. 'But wait ten minutes.'

'I shall, sir. And good day to you, sir.' Hakeswill saluted, about-turned and marched down the ramparts.

Dodd turned back to the Outer Fort. Rockets seared out of the smoke cloud above which Manu Bappoo's flag still hung. Faintly, very faintly, Dodd could hear men shouting, but the sound was being drowned by the roar of the guns which unsettled the silver-grey monkeys in the ravine. The beasts turned puzzled black faces up towards the men on the Inner Fort's walls as though they could find an answer to the noise and stink that was consuming the day.

A day which, to Dodd's way of thinking, was going perfectly.

The 33rd's Light Company had been waiting a little to the side of the track and Captain Morris deliberately stayed there, allowing almost all of Kenny's assault troops to go past before he led his men out of the rocks. He thus ensured that he was at the rear of the assault, a place which offered the greatest measure of safety.

Once Morris moved his men onto the fort's approach road he deliberately fell in behind a sepoy ladder party so that his progress was impeded. He walked at the head of his men, but turned repeatedly. 'Keep in files, Sergeant!' he snapped at Green more than once.

Sharpe walked alongside the company, curbing his long stride to the slow pace set by Morris. It took a moment to reach the small crest in the road, but then they were in sight of the fortress and Sharpe could only stare in awe at the weight of fire that seemed to pour from the battered walls.

The Mahrattas' bigger guns had been unseated, but they possessed a myriad of smaller cannon, some little larger than blunderbusses, and those weapons now roared and coughed and spat their flames towards the advancing troops so that the black walls were half obscured behind the patchwork of smoke that vented from every embrasure. Rockets added to the confusion. Some hissed up into the sky, but others seared into the advancing men to slice fiery passages through the ranks.

The leading company had not yet reached the outer breach, but was hurrying into the narrow space between the precipice to the east and the tank to the west. They jostled as their files were compressed, and then the gunfire seemed to concentrate on those men and Sharpe had an impression of blood misting the air as the round shot slammed home at a range of a mere hundred paces. There were big round bastions on either flank of the breach, and their summits were edged with perpetual flame as the defenders took turns to blast muskets down into the mass of attackers. The British guns were still firing, their shots exploding bursts of dust and stone from the breach, or else hammering into the embrasures in an effort to dull the enemy's fire.

An aide came running back down the path. 'Hurry!' he called. 'Hurry!'

Morris made no effort to hasten his pace. The leading Scots were past the tank now and climbing the gentle slope towards the walls, but that slope became ever steeper as it neared the breach. The man with the flag was in front, then he was engulfed by Highlanders racing to reach the stones. Kenny led them, sword in hand. Muskets suddenly flamed from the breach summit, obscuring it with smoke, and then an eighteen-pounder shot churned up the smoke and threw up a barrowload of broken stone amidst which an enemy musket wheeled. Sharpe quickened his pace. He could feel a kind of rage inside, and he wondered if that was fear, but there was an excitement too, and an anxiety that he would miss the fight.

He could see the fight clearly enough, for the breach was high above the approach road and the Scots, scrambling up using their hands, were clearly visible. The British gunners were still firing, hammering round shot just inches over the Scotsmen's heads to keep the summit of the breach clear of the enemy, and then, abruptly, the guns stopped and the redcoats climbed into the dust that hung thick above the shattered stones. A mass of Arabs climbed the breach's inner slope, coming to oppose the Scots, and scimitars rang against bayonets. The red coats of the attackers were turned pink by the stone dust. Colonel Kenny was in the front rank, straddling a chunk of masonry as he parried a scimitar. He lunged, piercing an enemy's throat, then stepped forward, downwards, knowing he was across the summit and oblivious of the muskets that flamed above him from the upper wall. The British gunners, their weapons relaid, started to fire at the upper wall, driving the defenders away from the firestep. The Scots rammed their bayonets forward, kicked the dead off the blades, stepped over the corpses and followed Kenny down to the space inside the walls. 'This way!' Kenny shouted. 'This way!' He led the rush of men to the left, to where the inner breach waited, its slope twitching as the round shot slammed home. Some Arabs, fleeing the Scotsmen's snarling rage, died as they tried to climb the inner breach and were struck by the cannonballs. Blood spattered across the inner wall, smeared the ramp, then was whitened by the dust.

Kenny glanced behind to make sure that the column was close behind him. 'Keep them coming,' he shouted to an aide who stood on the summit of the first breach. 'Keep them coming!' Kenny spat a mouthful of dust, then shouted at the Scots to start the ascent of the second breach.

'Hurry! Hurry!' Kenny's aides who were still outside the walls urged on the column. The rearmost ranks of the Colonel's assault party were stringing out, and the second storming group was not far behind. 'Close up!' the aides urged the laggards. 'Close up!'

Morris reluctantly quickened. The sepoys carrying the ladders were running down the slight slope which led to the narrow space beside the tank where the enemy's guns were aimed. All along Gawilghur's walls the smoke jetted, the flames spat and the rockets blasted out in gouts of smoke and streams of sparks. Even arrows were being fired. One clattered on a rock near Sharpe, then spun into the grass.

The Scots were climbing the inner breach now, and a stream of men was vanishing over the rocky summit of the outer breach. No mines had awaited the attackers, and no cannon had been placed athwart the breach to blast them as they flooded through the wall. Sepoys scrambled up the stones.

'Hurry!' the aides shouted. 'Hurry!'

Sharpe ran down the slope towards the tank. His canteen and haversack thumped on his waist, and sweat poured down his face. 'Slow down!' Morris shouted at him, but Sharpe ignored the call. The company was breaking apart as the more eager of the men hurried to catch up with Sharpe and the others dallied with Morris. 'Slow down, damn you!' Morris called to Sharpe again.

'Keep going!' Kenny's aides shouted. Two of them had been posted beside the tank and they gestured the men on. The round shot of the breaching batteries hammered above their heads making a noise like great barrels rolling across floorboards, then cracked into the smoke-rimmed upper wall. A green and red flag waved there. Sharpe saw an Arab aim a musket, then smoke obscured the sight. A small cannonball struck a sepoy, throwing him back and smearing the stony road with blood and guts. Sharpe leaped the sprawling body and saw he had reached the reservoir. The water was low and scummed green. Two Scots and a sepoy lay on the sun-baked mud, their blood seeping into the cracks that crazed the bank. A musket ball hammered into the mud, then a small round shot lashed into the rear of Morris's company and bowled over two men. 'Leave them!' an aide shouted. 'Just leave them!' A rocket smashed close by Sharpe's head, enveloping him in smoke and sparks. A wounded man crawled back beside the road, trailing a shattered leg. Another, blood oozing from his belly, collapsed on the mud and lapped at the filthy water.

Sharpe half choked on the thick smoke as he stumbled up the rising ground. Big black round shot lay here, left from the cannonade that had made the first breach. Two redcoat bodies had been heaved aside, three others twitched and called for help, but Kenny had posted another aide here to keep the troops moving. Dust spurted where musket balls lashed into the ground, then Sharpe was on the breach itself, half lost his balance as he climbed the ramp, and then was pushed from behind. Men jostled up the stones, clambered up, hauled themselves up with one hand while the other gripped their musket. Sharpe put his hand on a smear of blood. The dusty rubble was almost too hot to touch, and the ramp was much longer than Sharpe had anticipated. Men shouted hoarsely as they climbed, and still the bullets thudded down. An arrow struck and quivered in a musket stock. A rocket crashed into the flood of men, parting it momentarily as the carcass flamed madly where it had lodged between a boulder and a cannonball. Someone unceremoniously dumped a dead Scotsman on top of the hissing rocket and the press of men clambered on up over the corpse.

Once at the summit the attackers turned to their left and ran down the inside of the breach to the dry grass that separated the two walls. A fight was going on in the left-hand breach, and men were bunching behind it, but Sharpe could see the Scots were gradually inching up the slope. By God, he thought, but they were almost in! The British guns had ceased firing for fear of hitting their own men.

Sharpe turned right, going to the second inner breach that Morris's company was supposed to seal off. High above him, from the firestep of the inner wall, defenders leaned over to fire down into the space between the ramparts. Sharpe seemed to be running through a hail of bullets that magically did not touch him. Smoke wreathed about him, then he saw the broken stones of the breach in front and he leaped onto them and clambered upwards. 'I'm with you, Dick!' Tom Garrard shouted just behind, then a man appeared in the smoke above Sharpe and heaved down a baulk of wood.

The timber struck Sharpe on the chest, throwing him back onto Garrard who clutched at him as the two men fell on the stones. Sharpe swore as a fusillade of musket fire came down from the breach summit. A handful of men was with him, maybe six or seven, but none seemed to be hit. They crouched behind him, waiting for orders. 'No farther!' Morris shouted. 'No farther!'

'Bugger him,' Sharpe said, and he picked up his musket. Just then the British guns, seeing that the right-hand breach was still occupied by the Mahrattas, opened fire again and the balls hammered into the stones just a few feet over Sharpe's head. One defender was caught smack in the belly by an eighteen-pounder shot and it seemed to Sharpe that the man simply disintegrated in a red shower. Sharpe ducked as the blood poured down the stones, trickling past him and Garrard in small torrents. 'Jesus,' Sharpe said. Another round shot slammed into the breach, the sound of the ball's strike as loud as thunder. Shards of stone whipped past Sharpe, and he seemed to be breathing nothing but hot dust.

'No farther!' Morris said. 'Here! To me! Rally! Rally!' He was crouched under the inner wall, safe from the defenders on the breach, though high above him, on the undamaged firestep, Arab soldiers still leaned out to fire straight down. 'Sharpe! Come here!' Morris ordered.

'Come on!' Sharpe shouted. Bugger Morris, and bugger all the other officers who said you could put a racing saddle on a carthorse, but the beast would not go quick. 'Come on!' he shouted again as he clambered up the stones, and suddenly there were more men to his right, but they were Scots, and he saw that the leading men of the second assault group had reached the fortress. A red-haired lieutenant led them, a claymore in his hand.

The Lieutenant was climbing the centre of the breach, while Sharpe was trying to clamber up the steeper flank. The Highlanders went past

Sharpe, screaming at the enemy, and the sight of their red coats made the British gunners cease fire, and immediately the breach summit filled with robed men who carried curved swords with blades as thick as cleavers. Swords clashed, muskets crashed, and the red-haired Lieutenant shook like a gaffed eel as a scimitar sliced into his belly. He turned and fell towards Sharpe, dropping his claymore. A line of defenders was now firing down the breach, while a huge Arab, who looked seven feet tall to Sharpe, stood in the centre with a reddened scimitar and dared any man to challenge him. Two did, and both he threw back in a shower of blood. 'Light Company!' Sharpe shouted. 'Give those bastards fire! Fire!'

Some muskets banged behind him and the row of defenders seemed to stagger back, but they closed up again, rallied by the huge man with the bloodstained scimitar. Sharpe had his left hand on the broken shoulder of the wall and he used it to haul himself up, then twisted aside as the closest Arabs turned and fired at him. The balls whiplashed past as a flaming lump of wadding struck Sharpe on the cheek. He let go of the wall and fell backwards as a grinning man tried to stab him with a bayonet. Dear God, but the breach was steep! His cheek was burnt and his new coat scorched. The Scots tried again, surging up the centre of the breach to be met by a line of Arab blades. More Arabs came from inside the fortress and poured a volley of musket fire down the face of the ramp. Sharpe aimed his musket at the tall Arab and pulled the trigger. The gun hammered into his shoulder, but when the smoke cleared the big man was still standing and still fighting. The Arabs were winning here, they were pressing down the face of the breach and chanting a blood-curdling war cry as they killed. A man rammed a bayonet at Sharpe, he parried it with his own, but then an enemy grasped Sharpe's musket by the muzzle and tugged it upwards. Sharpe cursed, but held on, then saw a scimitar slashing towards him and so he let go of the musket and fell back again. 'Bastards,' he swore, then saw the dead Scottish Lieutenant's claymore lying on the stones. He picked it up and swept it at the ankles of the Arabs above him, and the blade bit home and threw one man down, and the Scots were charging up the breach again, climbing over their own dead and screaming a raw shout of hate that was matched by the Arabs' cries of victory.

Sharpe climbed again. He balanced on the steep stones and hacked with the claymore, driving the enemy back. He scrambled up two more feet, wreathed in bitter smoke, and reached the spot where he could grip the wall at the edge of the breach. All he could do now was hold onto the stone with his left hand and thrust and swing with the sword. He drove men back, but then the big Arab saw him and came across the breach, bellowing at his comrades to leave the redcoat's death to his scimitar. He raised the sword high over his head, like an executioner taking aim, and Sharpe was off balance. 'Push me, Tom!' he shouted, and Garrard put a hand on Sharpe's arse and shoved him hard upwards just as the scimitar started downwards, but Sharpe had let go of the wall and reached out to hook his left hand behind the tall man's ankle. He tugged hard and the man shouted in alarm as his feet slid out from under him and as he bumped down the breach's flank. 'Now kill him!' Sharpe bellowed and a half-dozen redcoats attacked the fallen man with bayonets as Sharpe hacked at the Arabs coming to the big man's rescue. His claymore clashed with scimitars, the blades ringing like blacksmith's hammers on anvils. The big man was twisting and twitching as the bayonets stabbed again and again through his robes. The Scots were back, thrusting and snarling up the centre, and Sharpe forced himself up another step. Garrard was beside him now, and the two were only a step from the summit of the breach. 'Bastards! Bastards!' Sharpe was panting as he hacked and lunged, but the Arabs' robes seemed to soak up the blows, then suddenly, almost miraculously, they backed away from him. A musket fired from inside the fortress and one of the Arabs crumpled down onto the breach's inner ramp, and Sharpe realized that the men who had fought their way through the left-hand breach must have turned and come to attack this breach from the inside. 'Come on!' he roared, and he was on the summit at last and there were Scots and Light Company men all about him as they spilt down into the Outer Fortress where a company of the Scotch Brigade waited to welcome them. The defenders were fleeing to the southern gate which would lead them to the refuge of the Inner Fort.

'Jesus,' Tom Garrard said, leaning over to catch his breath.

'Are you hurt?' Sharpe asked.

Garrard shook his head. 'Jesus,' he said again. Some enemy gunners, who had stayed with their weapons till the last minute, jumped down from the firestep, dodged past the tired redcoats scattered inside the wall and fled southwards. Most of the Scots and sepoys were too breathless to pursue them and contented themselves with some musket shots. A dog barked madly until a sepoy kicked the beast into silence.

Sharpe stopped. It seemed suddenly quiet, for the big guns were silent at last and the only muskets firing were from the Mahrattas defending the gatehouse. A few small cannon were firing to the south, but Sharpe could not see them, nor guess what their target was. The highest part of the fort lay to his right, and there was nothing on the low summit but dry grassland and a few thorny trees. No defenders gathered there. To his left he could see Kenny's men assaulting the gatehouse. They were storming the steps to the parapet where a handful of Arabs were making a stand, though they stood no chance, for over a hundred redcoats now gathered under the wall and were firing up at the firestep. The defenders' robes turned red. They were trapped now between the musket balls and the bayonets of the men climbing the steps, and though some tried to surrender, they were all killed. The other Mahrattas had fled, gone over the high ground in the centre of the Outer Fort to the ravine and to the larger fort beyond.

A vat stood in an embrasure of the wall and Sharpe heaved himself up and found, as he had hoped, that the barrel contained water for the abandoned guns. They were very small cannon, mostly mounted on iron tripods, but they had inflicted a hard punishment on the men crammed along the fort's approach. The dead and wounded had been pushed aside to make way for the stream of men approaching the breaches. Major Stokes was among them, Ahmed at his side, and Sharpe waved to them, though they did not see him. He dipped his hands in the water, slung it over his face and hair, then stooped and drank. It was filthy stuff, stagnant and bitter with powder debris, but he was desperately thirsty.

A cheer sounded as Colonel Kenny's men hoisted the British flag above the captured Delhi Gate. Manu Bappoo's flag was being folded by an aide, to be carried back to Britain. A squad of Scotsmen unbarred the big inner gate, then the outer one, to let even more redcoats into the fort that had fallen so quickly. Exhausted men slumped in the wall's shade, but Kenny's officers were shouting at them to find their units, to load their muskets and move on south.

'I think our orders are to guard the breach,' Morris suggested as Sharpe jumped down from the firestep.

'We go on,' Sharpe said savagely.

'We –'

'We go on, sir,' Sharpe said, investing the 'sir' with a savage scorn.

'Move, move, move!' a major shouted at Morris. 'The job ain't done yet! Move on!' He waved southwards.

'Sergeant Green,' Morris said reluctantly, 'gather the men.'

Sharpe walked up the hill, going to the high spot in the fort, and once there he stared southwards. Beneath him the ground fell away, gently at first, then steeply until it disappeared in a rocky ravine that was deep in shadow. But the far slope was sunlit, and that slope was a precipitous climb to an unbreached wall, and at the wall's eastern end was a massive gatehouse, far bigger than the one that had just been captured, and that far gatehouse was thick with soldiers. Some had white coats, and Sharpe knew those men. He had fought them before. 'Bloody hell,' he said softly.

'What is it?'

Sharpe turned and saw Garrard had followed him. 'Looks bloody nasty to me, Tom.'

Garrard stared at the Inner Fort. From here he could see the palace, the gardens and the defences, and suddenly those defences were blotted out by smoke as the guns across the ravine opened fire on the redcoats who now spread across the Outer Fort. The round shot screamed past Sharpe and Garrard. 'Bloody hell,' Sharpe said again. He had just fought his way through a breach to help capture a fort, only to find that the day's real work had scarcely begun.

Manu Bappoo had hoped to defend the breaches by concentrating his best fighters, the Lions of Allah, at their summits, but that hope had been defeated by the British guns that had continued to fire at the breaches until the redcoats were almost at the top of the ramps. No defender could stand in the breach and hope to live, not until the guns ceased fire, and by then the leading attackers were almost at the summit and so the Lions of Allah had been denied the advantage of higher ground.

The attackers and defenders had clashed amidst the dust and smoke at the top of the breach and there the greater height and strength of the Scotsmen had prevailed. Manu Bappoo had raged at his men, he had fought in their front rank and taken a wound in his shoulder, but his Arabs had retreated. They had gone back to the upper breaches, and there the redcoats, helped by their remorseless cannon, had prevailed again, and Bappoo knew the Outer Fort was lost. In itself that was no great loss. Nothing precious was stored in the Outer Fort, it was merely an elaborate defence to slow an attacker as he approached the ravine, but Bappoo was galled by the swiftness of the British victory. For a while he swore at the redcoats and tried to rally his men to defend the gatehouse, but the British were now swarming over the breaches, the gunners on the walls were abandoning their weapons, and Bappoo knew it was time to pull back into the stronghold of the Inner Fort. 'Go back!' he shouted. 'Go back!' His white tunic was soaked in his own blood, but the wound was to his left shoulder and he could still wield the gold-hilted *tulwar* that had been a gift from his brother. 'Go back!'

The defenders retreated swiftly and the attackers seemed too spent to pursue. Bappoo waited until the last, and then he walked backwards, facing the enemy and daring them to come and kill him, but they simply watched him go. In a moment, he knew, they would reorganize themselves and advance to the ravine, but by then he and his troops would be safely locked within the greater fortress.

The last sight Bappoo had of the Delhi Gate was of an enemy flag being hauled to the top of the pole that had held his own flag, then he dropped down the steep slope and was hustled through the south gate by his bodyguard. The path now ran obliquely down the steep side of the ravine before turning a hairpin bend to climb to the Inner Fort. The first of his men were already scrambling up that farther path. The gunners on the southern wall, who had been trying to stop the redcoats approaching on the road from the plain, now abandoned their small cannon and joined the retreat. Bappoo could only follow them with tears in his eyes. It did not matter that the battle was not lost, that the Inner Fort still stood and was likely to stand through all eternity, he had been humiliated by the swiftness of the defeat. 'Hurry, sahib,' one of his aides said.

'The British aren't following,' Bappoo said tiredly, 'not yet.'

'Those British,' the aide said, and pointed west to where the road from the plain climbed to the ravine. And there, at the bend where the road disappeared about the flank of the steep slope, was a company of redcoats. They wore kilts, and Bappoo remembered them from

Argaum. If those men hurried, they might cut off Bappoo's retreat and so he quickened his pace.

It was not till he reached the bottom of the ravine that he realized something was wrong. The leading groups of his men had reached the Inner Fort, but instead of streaming into the gate they were milling about on the slope beneath. 'What's happening?' he asked.

'The gates are shut, sahib,' his aide said in wonderment.

'They'll open any minute,' Bappoo said, and turned as a musket bullet whistled down from the slope behind him. The British who had captured the Outer Fort had at last advanced to the edge of the ravine and beneath them they saw the mass of retreating enemy, so they began to fire down. 'Hurry!' Bappoo shouted, and his men pushed on up the hill, but still the gates did not open.

The British fire became heavier. Redcoats were lining the hilltop now and pouring musket fire into the ravine. Bullets ricocheted from the stone sides and flicked down into the press of men. Panic began to infect them, and Bappoo shouted at them to be calm and return the fire, while he pushed through the throng to discover why the Inner Fort's gates were closed. 'Dodd!' he shouted as he came close. 'Dodd!'

Colonel Dodd's face appeared above the rampart. He looked quite calm, though he said nothing.

'Open the gate!' Bappoo shouted angrily.

Dodd's response was to raise the rifle to his shoulder.

Bappoo stared up into the muzzle. He knew he should run or twist away, but the horror of fate kept him rooted to the path. 'Dodd?' he said in puzzlement, and then the rifle was blotted out by the smoke of its discharge.

The bullet struck Bappoo on the breastbone, shattering it and driving scraps of bone deep into his heart. The Prince took two shuddering breaths and then was dead.

His men gave a great wail as the news of their Prince's death spread, and then, unable to endure the plunging fire from the Outer Fort, and denied entrance to the Inner, they fled west towards the road which dropped to the plain.

But the road was blocked. The Highlanders of the 78th were nearing its summit and they now saw a great panicked mass surging towards them. The Scotsmen had endured the artillery fire of the Outer Fort during their long climb, but now those guns had been abandoned. To their right the cliffs soared up to the Inner Fort, while to their left was a precipice above a dizzying gorge.

There was only room for twelve men to stand abreast on the road, but Colonel Chalmers, who led the 78th, knew that was space enough. He formed his leading half-company into three ranks with the front row kneeling. 'You'll fire by ranks,' he said quietly.

The panicked defenders ran towards the kilted Highlanders, who waited until every shot could kill. 'Front rank, fire!' Chalmers said.

The muskets started, and one by one the three ranks fired, and the steady fusillade tore into the approaching fugitives. Some tried to turn and retreat, but the press behind was too great, and still the relentless fire ripped into them, while behind them redcoats came down from the Outer Fort to attack their rear.

The first men jumped off the cliff, and their terrible screams faded as they plunged down to the rocks far beneath. The road was thick with bodies and running with blood.

'Advance twenty paces!' Chalmers ordered.

The Highlanders marched, halted, knelt and began firing again. Bappoo's survivors, betrayed by Dodd, were trapped between two forces. They were stranded in a hell above emptiness, a slaughter in the high hills. There were screams as men tumbled to their deaths far beneath and still the fire kept coming. It kept coming until there was nothing left but quivering men crouching in terror on a road that was rank with the stench of blood, and then the redcoats moved forward with bayonets.

The Outer Fort had fallen and its garrison had been massacred.

And William Dodd, renegade, was Lord of Gawilghur.

CHAPTER 10

Mister Hakeswill was not sure whether he was a lieutenant in William Dodd's eyes, but he knew he was a Mister and he dimly apprehended that he could be much more. William Dodd was going to win, and his victory would make him ruler of Gawilghur and tyrant of all the wide land that could be seen from its soaring battlements. Mister Hakeswill was therefore well placed, as Dodd's only white officer, to profit from the victory and, as he approached the palace on Gawilghur's summit, Hakeswill was already imagining a future that was limited only by the bounds of his fancy. He could be a rajah, he decided. 'I shall have an harem,' he said aloud, earning a worried look from his Havildar. 'An harem I'll have, all of me own. *Bibbis* in silk, but only when it's cold, eh? Rest of the time they'll have to be naked as needles.' He laughed, scratched at the lice in his crotch, then lunged with his sword at one of the peacocks that decorated the palace gardens. 'Bad luck, them birds,' Hakeswill told the Havildar as the bird fled in a flurry of bright severed feathers. 'Bad luck, they are. Got the evil eye, they do. Know what you should do with a peacock? Roast the bugger. Roast it and serve it with 'taters. Very nice, that.'

'Yes, sahib,' the Havildar said nervously. He was not certain he liked this new white officer whose face twitched so compulsively, but Colonel Dodd had appointed him and the Colonel could do no wrong as far as the Havildar was concerned.

'Haven't tasted a 'tater in months,' Hakeswill said wistfully. 'Christian food, that, see? Makes us white.'

'Yes, sahib.'

'And I won't be sahib, will I? Your highness, that's what I'll be. Your bleeding highness with a bedful of bare *bibbis*.' His face twitched as a bright idea occurred to him. 'I could have Sharpie as a servant.

Cut off his goolies first, though. Snip snip.' He bounded enthusiastically up a stone staircase, oblivious of the sound of gunfire that had erupted in the ravine just north of the Inner Fort. Two Arab guards moved to bar the way, but Hakeswill shouted at them. 'Off to the walls, you scum! No more shirking! You ain't guarding the royal pisspot any longer, but has to be soldiers. So piss off!'

The Havildar ordered the two men away and, though they were reluctant to abandon their post, they were overawed by the number of bayonets that faced them. So, just like the guards who had stood at the garden gate, they fled. 'So now we look for the little fat man,' Hakeswill said, 'and give him a bloodletting.'

'We must hurry, sahib,' the Havildar said, glancing back at the wall above the ravine where the gunners were suddenly at work.

'God's work can't be hurried,' Hakeswill answered, pulling at one of the latticed doors that led into the palace, 'and Colonel Dodd will die of old age on that wall, sonny. Ain't a man alive who can get through that gate, and certainly not a pack of bleeding Scotchmen. Bugger this door.' He raised his right foot and battered down the locked lattice with his boot.

Hakeswill had expected a palace dripping with gold, festooned with silk and paved with polished marble, but Gawilghur had only ever been a summer refuge, and Berar had never been as wealthy as other Indian states, and so the floors were common stone, the walls were painted in limewash and the curtains were of cotton. Some fine furniture of ebony inlaid with ivory stood in the hallway, but Hakeswill had no eye for such chairs, only for jewels, and he saw none. Two bronze jars and an iron cuspidor stood by the walls where lizards waited motionless, while a brass poker, tongs and fire shovel, cast in Birmingham, mounted on a stand and long bereft of any hearth, had pride of place in a niche. The hallway had no guards, indeed no one was in sight and the palace seemed silent except for a faint sound of choking and moaning that came from a curtained doorway at the far end of the hall. The noise of the guns was muffled. Hakeswill hefted his sword and edged towards the curtain. His men followed slowly, bayonets ready, eyes peering into every shadow.

Hakeswill swept the curtain aside with the blade, and gasped.

The Killadar, with a *tulwar* slung at his side and a small round shield strapped to his left arm, stared at Hakeswill above the bodies of his wives, concubines and daughters. Eighteen women were on the floor. Most were motionless, but some still writhed as the slow pain of the poison worked its horrors. The Killadar was in tears. 'I could not leave them for the English,' he said.

'What did he say?' Hakeswill demanded.

'He preferred they should die than be dishonoured,' the Havildar translated.

'Bleeding hell,' Hakeswill commented. He stepped down into the sunken floor where the women lay. The dead had greenish dribbles coming from their mouths and their glassy eyes stared up at the lotuses painted on the ceiling, while the living jerked spasmodically. The cups from which they had drunk the poison lay on the tiled floor. 'Some nice *bibbis* here,' Hakeswill said ruefully. 'A waste!' He stared at a child, no more than six or seven. There was a jewel about her neck and Hakeswill stooped, grasped the pendant and snapped the chain. 'Bleeding waste,' he said in disgust, then used his sword blade to lift the sari of a dying woman. He raised the silk to her waist, then shook his head. 'Look at that!' he said. 'Just look at that! What a bleeding waste!'

The Killadar roared in anger, drew his *tulwar* and ran down the steps to drive Hakeswill from his women. Hakeswill, alarmed, backed away, then remembered he was to be a rajah and could not show timidity in front of the Havildar and his men, so he stepped forward again and thrust the sword forward in a clumsy lunge. It might have been clumsy, but it was also lucky, for the Killadar had stumbled on a body and was lurching forward, his *tulwar* flailing as he sought his balance, and the tip of Hakeswill's blade ripped into his throat so that a spray of blood pulsed onto the dead and the dying. The Killadar gasped as he fell. His legs twitched as he tried to bring the *tulwar* round to strike at Hakeswill, but his strength was going and the Englishman was above him now. 'You're a *djinn*!' the Killadar said hoarsely.

The sword stabbed into Beny Singh's neck. 'I ain't drunk, you bastard,' Hakeswill said indignantly. 'Ain't seen a drop of mother's milk in three years!' He twisted the sword blade, fascinated by the way the blood pulsed past the steel. He watched until the blood finally died to a trickle, then jerked the blade free. 'That's him gone,' Hakeswill said. 'Another bloody heathen gone down to hell, eh?'

The Havildar stared in horror at Beny Singh and at the corpses drenched with his blood.

'Don't just stand there, you great pudding!' Hakeswill snapped. 'Get back to the walls!'

'The walls, sahib?'

'Hurry! There's a battle being fought, or ain't you noticed? Go on! Off with you! Take the company and report to Colonel Dodd as how the fat little bugger's dead. Tell him I'll be back in a minute or two. Now off with you! Quick!'

The Havildar obeyed, taking his men back through the hallway and out into the sunlight that was being hazed by the smoke rising from the ravine. Hakeswill, left alone in the palace, stooped to his work. All the dead wore jewellery. They were not great jewels, not like the massive ruby that the Tippoo Sultan had worn on his hat, but there were pearls and emeralds, sapphires and small diamonds, all mounted in gold, and Hakeswill busied himself delving through the bloodied silks to retrieve the scraps of wealth. He crammed the stones into his pockets where they joined the gems he had taken from Sharpe, and then, when the corpses were stripped and searched, he roamed the palace, snarling at servants and threatening scullions, as he ransacked the smaller rooms. The rest of the defenders could fight; Mister Hakeswill was getting rich.

The fight in the ravine was now a merciless massacre. The garrison of the Outer Fort was trapped between the soldiers who had captured their stronghold and the kilted Highlanders advancing up the narrow road, and there was no escape except over the precipice, and those who jumped, or were pushed by the panicking mass, fell onto the shadowed rocks far below. Colonel Chalmers's men advanced with bayonets, herding the fugitives towards Kenny's men who greeted them with more bayonets. A thousand men had garrisoned the Outer Fort, and those men were now dead or doomed, but seven thousand more defenders waited within the Inner Fort and Colonel Kenny was eager to attack them. He tried to order men into ranks, tugging them away from the slaughter and shouting for gunners to find an enemy cannon that could be fetched from the captured ramparts and dragged to face the massive gate of the Inner Fort, but the redcoats had an easier target in the huddled fugitives and they enthusiastically killed the helpless enemy, and all the while the guns of the Inner Fort fired down at the redcoats while rockets slammed into the ravine to add to the choking fog of powder smoke.

The slaughter could not endure. The beaten defenders threw down their guns and fell to their knees, and gradually the British officers called off the massacre. Chalmers's Highlanders advanced up the road that was now slippery with blood, driving the few prisoners in front of them. Wounded Arabs crawled or limped. The survivors were stripped of their remaining weapons and sent under sepoy guard back up to the Outer Fort, and for every step of their way they suffered from the fire that flamed and crackled from the Inner Fort. Finally, exhausted, they were taken out through the Delhi Gate and told to wait beside the tank. The parched prisoners threw themselves at the green-scummed water and some, seeing that the sepoy guards were few in number, slipped away northwards. They went without weapons, masterless fugitives who posed no threat to the British camp, which was guarded by a half-battalion of Madrassi sepoys.

The northern face of the ravine, which looked towards the uncon-quered Inner Fort, was now crowded with some three thousand red-coats, most of whom did nothing but sit in whatever small shade they could find and grumble that the *puckalees* had not fetched water. Once in a while a man would fire a musket across the ravine, but the balls were wild at that long range, and the enemy fire, which had been heavy during the massacre on the western road, gradually eased off as both sides waited for the real struggle to begin.

Sharpe was halfway down the ravine, seated beneath a stunted tree on which the remnants of some red blossom hung dry and faded. A tribe of black-faced, silver-furred monkeys had fled the irruption of men into the rocky gorge, and those beasts now gathered behind Sharpe where they gibbered and screamed. Tom Garrard and a dozen men of the 33rd's Light Company had gathered around Sharpe, while the rest of the company was lower down the ravine among some rocks. 'What happens now?' Garrard asked.

'Some poor bastards have to get through that gate,' Sharpe said.

'Not you?'

'Kenny will call us when he needs us,' Sharpe said, nodding towards the lean Colonel who had at last organized an assault party at the bottom of the track which slanted up towards the gate. 'And he bloody will, Tom. It ain't going to be easy getting through that gate.' He touched the scorch mark on his cheek. 'That bloody hurts!'

'Put some butter on it,' Garrard said.

'And where do I get bleeding butter here?' Sharpe asked. He shaded his eyes and peered at the complex ramparts above the big gate, trying to spot either Dodd or Hakeswill, but although he could see the white jackets of the Cobras, he could not see a white man on the ramparts. 'It's going to be a long fight, Tom,' he said.

The British gunners had succeeded in bringing an enemy five-pounder cannon to the edge of the ravine. The sight of the gun provoked a flurry of fire from the Inner Fort, wreathing its gatehouse in smoke as the round shot screamed across the ravine to plunge all around the threatening gun. Somehow it survived. The gunners rammed it, aimed it, then fired a shot that bounced just beneath the gate, ricocheted up into the woodwork, but fell back.

The defenders kept firing, but their smoke obscured their aim and the small captured cannon had been positioned behind a large low rock that served as a makeshift breastwork. The gunners elevated the barrel a trifle and their next shot struck plumb on the gates, breaking a timber. Each successive shot splintered more wood and was greeted by an ironic cheer from the redcoats who watched from across the ravine. The gate was being demolished board by board, and at last a round shot cracked into its locking bar and the half-shattered timbers sagged on their hinges.

Colonel Kenny was gathering his assault troops at the foot of the ravine. They were the same men who had gone first into the breaches of the Outer Fort, and their faces were stained with powder burns, with dust and sweat. They watched the destruction of the outer gate of the Inner Fort and they knew they must climb the path into the enemy's fire as soon as the gun had done its work. Kenny summoned an aide. 'You know Plummer?' he asked the man.

'Gunner Major, sir?'

'Find him,' Kenny said, 'or any gunner officer. Tell them we might need a light piece up in the gateway.' He pointed with a reddened sword at the Inner Fort's gatehouse. 'The passage ain't straight,' he explained to the aide. 'Get through the gate and we turn hard left. If our axemen can't deal with the other gates we'll need a gun to blow them in.'

The aide climbed back up to the Outer Fort, looking for a gunner. Kenny talked to his men, explaining that once they were through the shattered gate they would find themselves faced by another and that the infantry were to fire up at the flanking firesteps to protect the axemen who would try to hack their way through the successive obstacles. 'If we put up enough fire,' Kenny said, 'the enemy'll take shelter. It won't take long.' He looked at his axemen, all of them huge sappers, all carrying vast-bladed axes that had been sharpened to wicked edges.

Kenny turned and watched the effect of the five-pounder shots. The gate's locking bar had been struck plumb, but the gate still held. A badly aimed shot cracked into the stone beside the gate, starting up dust, then a correction to the gun sent a ball hammering into the bar again and the thick timber broke and the remnants of the gates fell inwards. 'Forward!' Kenny shouted. 'Forward!'

Four hundred redcoats followed the Colonel up the narrow track that led to the Inner Fort. They could not run to the assault, for the hill was too steep; they could only trudge into the fury of Dodd's fusillade. Cannon, rockets and muskets blasted down the hill to tear gaps in Kenny's ranks.

'Give them fire!' an officer on the ravine's northern side shouted at the watching redcoats, and the men loaded their muskets and fired at the smoke-masked gatehouse. If nothing else, the wild fire might keep the defenders' heads down. Another cannon had been fetched from the Outer Fort, and now added its small round shots to the fury that beat audibly on the gatehouse ramparts. Those ramparts were thick with the powder smoke gouted by the defenders' cannon and muskets and it was that smoke which protected Kenny's men as they hurried up the last few yards to the broken gate. 'Protect the sappers!' Kenny shouted and then, his sword in his hand, he clambered over the broken timbers and led his attackers into the entrance passage.

Facing Kenny was a stone wall. He had expected it, but even so he was astonished by the narrowness of the passage that turned sharply to his left and then climbed steeply to the second unbroken gate. 'There it is!' he shouted, and led a surge of men up the cobbled road towards the iron-studded timbers.

And hell was loosed.

The firesteps above the gateway passage were protected by the outer wall's high rampart, and Dodd's men, though they could hear the musket balls beating against the stones, were safe from the wild fire that lashed across the deep ravine. But the redcoats beneath them, the men following Colonel Kenny into the passage, had no protection. Musket fire, stones and rockets slashed into a narrow space just twenty-five paces long and eight wide. The leading axemen were among the first to die, beaten down by bullets. Their blood splashed high on the walls. Colonel Kenny somehow survived the opening salvo, then he was struck on the shoulder by a lump of stone and driven to the ground. A rocket slashed past his face, scorching his cheek, but he picked himself up and, sword in numbed hand, shouted at his men to keep going. No one could hear him. The narrow space was filled with noise, choking with smoke in which men died and rockets flared. A musket ball struck Kenny in the hip and he twisted, half fell, but forced himself to stand and, with blood pouring down his white breeches, limped on. Then another musket ball scored down his back and threw him forward. He crawled on blood-slicked stones, sword still in his hand, and shuddered as a third ball hit him in the back. He still managed to reach the second gate and reared up to strike it with his sword, and then a last musket ball split his skull and left him dead at the head of his men. More bullets plucked at his corpse.

Kenny's surviving men tried to brave the fire. They tried to climb the slope to the second gate, but the murderous fire did not cease, and the dead made a barrier to the living. Some men attempted to fire up at their tormentors on the firestep, but the sun was high now and they aimed into a blinding glare, and soon the redcoats began to back down the passage. The weltering fire from above did not let up. It flayed the Scotsmen, ricocheted between the walls, struck dead and dying and living, while the rockets, lit and tossed down, seared like great comets between the stone walls and filled the space with a sickening smoke. The dead were burned by rocket flames which exploded their cartridge boxes to pulse gouts of blood against the black walls, but the smoke hid the survivors who, under its cover, stumbled back to the hill outside the fortress. They left a stone-walled passage filled with the dying and the dead, trickling with blood, foul with smoke and echoing with the moans of the wounded.

'Cease fire!' Colonel Dodd shouted. 'Cease fire!'

The smoke cleared slowly and Dodd stared down at a pit of carnage in which a few bodies twitched. 'They'll come again soon,' Dodd warned his Cobras. 'Fetch more stones, make sure your muskets are loaded. More rockets!' He patted his men on the shoulders, congratulating them. They grinned at him, pleased with their work. It was like killing rats in a barrel. Not one Cobra had been hit, the first enemy assault had failed and the others, Dodd was certain, would end in just the same way. The Lord of Gawilghur was winning his first victory.

Major Stokes had found Sharpe shortly before Kenny made his assault, and the two men had been joined first by Syud Sevajee and his followers, then by the dozen cavalrymen who accompanied Eli Lockhart. All of them, Stokes, Sevajee and Lockhart, had entered the Outer Fort after the fight for the breaches was finished, and now they stood watching the failure of Kenny's assault. The survivors of the attack were crouching just yards from the broken entrance that boiled with smoke, and Sharpe knew they were summoning the courage to charge again. 'Poor bastards,' he said.

'No choice in the matter,' Stokes said bleakly. 'No other way in.'

'That ain't a way in, sir,' Sharpe said dourly, 'that's a fast road to a shallow grave.'

'Overwhelm them,' Stokes said, 'that's the way to do it. Overwhelm them.'

'Send more men to be killed?' Sharpe asked angrily.

'Get a gun over that side,' Stokes suggested, 'and blast the gates down one after the other. Only way to prise the place open, Sharpe.'

The covering fire that had blazed across the ravine died when it was obvious the first attack had failed, and the lull encouraged the defenders to come to the outer embrasures and fire down at the stalled attackers.

'Give them fire!' an officer shouted from the bed of the ravine, and again the muskets flared across the gorge and the balls spattered against the walls.

Major Stokes had levelled his telescope at the gate where the thick smoke had at last dissipated. 'It ain't good,' he admitted. 'It opens onto a blank wall.'

'It does what, sir?' Eli Lockhart asked. The cavalry Sergeant was looking aghast at the horror across the ravine, grateful perhaps that the cavalry was never asked to break into such deathtraps.

'The passage turns,' Stokes said. 'We can't fire straight up the entranceway. They'll have to drag a gun right into the archway.'

'They'll never make it,' Sharpe said. Any gun positioned in the outer arch would get the full fury of the defensive fire, and those defenders were protected by the big outer wall. The only way Sharpe could see of getting into the fortress was by battering the whole gatehouse flat, and that would take days of heavy cannon fire.

'The gates of hell,' Stokes said softly, staring through his glass at the bodies left inside the arch.

'Can I borrow the telescope, sir?' Sharpe asked.

'Of course.' Stokes cleaned the eyepiece on the hem of his jacket. 'It ain't a pretty sight though.'

Sharpe took the glass and aimed it across the ravine. He gave the gatehouse a cursory glance, then edged the lens along the wall which led westwards from the besieged gate. The wall was not very high, perhaps only twelve or fifteen feet, much lower than the great ramparts about the gatehouse, and its embrasures did not appear to be heavily manned. But that was hardly a surprise, for the wall stood atop a precipice. The defences straight ahead were not the wall and its handful of defenders, but the stony cliff which fell down into the ravine.

Stokes saw where Sharpe was aiming the glass. 'No way in there, Richard.'

Sharpe said nothing. He was staring at a place where weeds and small shrubs twisted up the cliff. He tracked the telescope from the bed of the ravine to the base of the wall, searching every inch, and he reckoned it could be climbed. It would be hard, for it was perilously steep, but if there was space for bushes to find lodgement, then a man could follow, and at the top of the cliff there was a brief area of grass between the precipice and the wall. He took the telescope from his eye. 'Has anyone seen a ladder?'

'Back up there.' It was Ahmed who answered.

'Where, lad?'

'Up there.' The Arab boy pointed to the Outer Fort. 'On the ground,' he said.

Sharpe twisted and looked at Lockhart. 'Can you boys fetch me a ladder?'

'What are you thinking of?' Lockhart asked.

'A way in,' Sharpe said, 'a bloody way in.' He gave the telescope to Stokes. 'Get me a ladder, Sergeant,' he said, 'and I'll fix those buggers properly. Ahmed? Show Sergeant Lockhart where you saw the ladder.'

'I stay with you,' the boy said stubbornly.

'You bloody don't.' Sharpe patted the boy on the head, wondering what Ahmed made of the slaughter that had been inflicted on his countrymen in the ravine, but the boy seemed blessedly unaffected. 'Go and help the Sergeant,' he told Ahmed.

Ahmed led the cavalrymen uphill. 'What are you doing, Richard?' Stokes asked.

'We can climb up to the wall,' Sharpe said, pointing to where the trail of weeds and bushes snaked up the other side of the ravine. 'Not you, sir, but a light company can do it. Go up the ravine, send a ladder up and cross the wall.'

Stokes trained the telescope and stared at the opposing cliff for a long while. 'You might get up,' he said dubiously, 'but then what?'

Sharpe grinned. 'We attack the gatehouse from the back, sir.'

'One company?'

'Where one company can go, sir, another can follow. Once they see we're up there, other men will come.' He still held the great claymore which was too big to fit into the scabbard of his borrowed sword, but now he discarded that scabbard and shoved the claymore into his belt. He liked the sword. It was heavy, straight-bladed and brutal, not a weapon for delicate work, but a killer. Something to give a man confidence. 'You stay here, sir,' he told Stokes, 'and look after Ahmed for me. The little bugger would love to get in a fight, but he ain't got the sense of a louse when it comes to a scrap and he's bound to get killed. Tom!' he called to Garrard, then beckoned that he and the rest of the 33rd's Light Company should follow him down to where Morris sheltered among the rocks. 'When Eli gets here with the ladder, sir,' he added to Stokes, 'send him down.'

Sharpe ran down the ravine's steep side into the smoke-reeking shadows where Morris was seated under a tree making a meal out of bread, salt beef and whatever liquor was left in his canteen. 'Don't have enough food for you, Sharpe,' he said.

'Not hungry,' Sharpe lied.

'You're sweating, man,' Morris complained. 'Why don't you find yourself some shade? There's nothing we can do until the gunners knock that bloody gatehouse flat.'

'There is,' Sharpe said.

Morris cocked a sceptical eye up at Sharpe. 'I've had no orders, Ensign,' he said.

'I want you and the Light Company, sir,' Sharpe said respectfully. 'There's a way up the side of the ravine, sir, and if we can get a ladder to the top then we can cross the wall and go at the bastards from the back.'

Morris tipped the canteen to his mouth, drank, then wiped his lips. 'If you, twenty like you and the Archangel Gabriel and all the bloody saints asked me to climb the ravine, Sharpe, I would still say no. Now for Christ's sake, man, stop trying to be a bloody hero. Leave it to the poor bastards who are under orders, and go away.' He waved a hand.

'Sir,' Sharpe pleaded, 'we can do it! I've sent for a ladder.'

'No!' Morris interrupted loudly, attracting the attention of the rest of the company. 'I am not giving you my company, Sharpe. For God's sake, you're not even a proper officer! You're just a bumped-up sergeant! A bloody ensign too big for your boots and, allow me to remind you, Mister Sharpe, forbidden by army regulations to serve in this regiment. Now go away and leave me in peace.'

'I thought you'd say that, Charles,' Sharpe said ruefully.

'And stop calling me Charles!' Morris exploded. 'We are not friends, you and I. And kindly obey my order to leave me in peace, or had you not noticed that I outrank you?'

'I had noticed. Sorry, sir,' Sharpe said humbly and he started to turn away, but suddenly whipped back and seized Morris's coat. He dragged the Captain back into the rocks, going so fast that Morris was momentarily incapable of resistance. Once among the rocks, Sharpe let go of the patched coat and thumped Morris in the belly. 'That's for the flogging you gave me, you bastard,' he said.

'What the hell do you think you're doing, Sharpe?' Morris asked, scrambling away on his bottom.

Sharpe kicked him in the chest, leaned down, hauled him up and thumped him on the jaw. Morris squealed with pain, then gasped as Sharpe backhanded him across the cheek, then struck him again. A group of men had followed and were watching wide-eyed. Morris turned to appeal to them, but Sharpe hit him yet again and the Captain's eyes turned glassy as he swayed and collapsed. Sharpe bent over him. 'You might outrank me,' he said, 'but you're a piece of shit, Charlie, and you always were. Now can I take the company?'

'No,' Morris said through the blood on his lips.

'Thank you, sir,' Sharpe said, and stamped his boot hard down on Morris's head, driving it onto a rock. Morris gasped, choked, then lay immobile as the breath scraped in his throat.

Sharpe kicked Morris's head again, just for the hell of it, then turned, smiling. 'Where's Sergeant Green?'

'Here, sir.' Green, looking anxious, pushed through the watching men. 'I'm here, sir,' he said, staring with astonishment at the immobile Morris.

'Captain Morris has eaten something that disagreed with him,' Sharpe said, 'but before he was taken ill he expressed the wish that I should temporarily take command of the company.'

Sergeant Green looked at the battered, bleeding Captain, then back to Sharpe. 'Something he ate, sir?'

'Are you a doctor, Sergeant? Wear a black plume on your hat, do you?'

'No, sir.'

'Then stop questioning my statements. Have the company paraded, muskets loaded, no bayonets fixed.' Green hesitated. 'Do it, Sergeant!' Sharpe roared, startling the watching men.

'Yes, sir!' Green said hurriedly, backing away.

Sharpe waited until the company was in its four ranks. Many of them looked at him suspiciously, but they were powerless to challenge his authority, not while Sergeant Green had accepted it. 'You're a light company,' Sharpe said, 'and that means you can go where other soldiers can't. It makes you an elite. You know what that means? It means you're the best in the bloody army, and right now the army needs its best men. It needs you. So in a minute we'll be climbing up there' – he pointed to the ravine – 'crossing the wall and carrying the fight to the enemy. It'll be hard work for a bit, but not beyond a decent light company.' He looked to his left and saw Eli Lockhart leading his men down the side of the ravine with one of the discarded bamboo ladders. 'I'll go first,' he told the company, 'and Sergeant Green will go last. If any man refuses to climb, Sergeant, you're to shoot the bugger.'

'I am, sir?' Green asked nervously.

'In the head,' Sharpe said.

Major Stokes had followed Lockhart and now came up to Sharpe. 'I'll arrange for some covering fire, Sharpe,' he said.

'That'll be a help, sir. Not that these men need much help. They're the 33rd's Light Company. Best in the army.'

'I'm sure they are,' Stokes said, smiling at the seventy men who, seeing a major with Sharpe, supposed that the Ensign really did have the authority to do what he was proposing.

Lockhart, in his blue and yellow coat, waited with the ladder. 'Where do you want it, Mister Sharpe?'

'Over here,' Sharpe said. 'Just pass it up when we've reached the top. Sergeant Green! Send the men in ranks! Front rank first!' He walked to the side of the ravine and stared up his chosen route. It looked steeper from here, and much higher than it had seemed when he was staring through the telescope, but he still reckoned it was climbable. He could not see the Inner Fort's wall, but that was good, for neither could the defenders see him. All the same, it was bloody steep. Steep enough to give a mountain goat pause, yet if he failed now then he would be on a charge for striking a superior officer, so he really had no choice but to play the hero.

So he spat on his bruised hands, looked up one last time, then started to climb.

The second assault on the Inner Fort's gatehouse fared no better than the first. A howling mass of men charged through the wreckage of the shattered gate, stumbled on the dead and dying as they turned up the passage, but then the killing began again as a shower of missiles, rockets and musket fire turned the narrow, steep passage into a charnel house. An axeman succeeded in reaching the second gate and he stood above Colonel Kenny's scorched body to sink his blade deep into the timber, but he was immediately struck by three musket balls and dropped back, leaving the axe embedded in the dark, iron-studded wood. No one else went close to the gate, and a major, appalled at the slaughter, called the men back. 'Next time,' he shouted at them, 'we designate firing parties to give cover. Sergeant! I want two dozen men.'

'We need a cannon, sir,' the Sergeant answered with brutal honesty.

'They say one's coming.' The aide whom Kenny had sent to fetch a cannon had returned to the assault party. 'They say it'll take time, though,' he added, without explaining that the gunner officer had declared it would take at least two hours to manhandle a gun and ammunition across the ravine.

The Major shook his head. 'We'll try without the gun,' he said.

'God help us,' the Sergeant said under his breath.

Colonel Dodd had watched the attackers limp away. He could not help smiling. This was so very simple, just as he had foreseen. Manu Bappoo was dead and the Havildar had returned from the palace with the welcome news of Beny Singh's murder, which meant that Gawilghur had a new commander. He looked down at the dead and dying redcoats who lay among the small flickering blue flames of the spent rockets. 'They've learned their lesson, Gopal,' he told his Jemadar, 'so next time they'll try to keep us quiet by firing bigger volleys up at the firesteps. Toss down rockets, that'll spoil their aim.'

'Rockets, sahib.'

'Lots of rockets,' Dodd said. He patted his men on their backs. Their faces were singed by the explosions of the powder in their muskets' pans, they were thirsty and hot, but they were winning, and they knew it. They were his Cobras, as well trained as any troops in India, and they would be at the heart of the army that Dodd would unleash from this fortress to dominate the lands the British must relinquish when their southern army was broken.

'Why don't they give up?' Gopal asked Dodd. A sentry on the wall had reported that the bloodied attackers were forming to charge again.

'Because they're brave men, Jemadar,' Dodd said, 'but also stupid.'

The furious musket fire had started again from across the ravine, a sign that a new attack would soon come into the blood-slick gateway. Dodd drew his pistol, checked it was loaded, and walked back to watch the next failure. Let them come, he thought, for the more who died here, the fewer would remain to trouble him as he pursued the beaten remnant south across the Deccan Plain. 'Get ready!' he called. Slow matches burned on the firestep and his men crouched beside them with rockets, waiting to light the fuses and toss the terrible weapons down into the killing place.

A defiant cheer sounded, and the redcoats came again to the slaughter.

*   *   *

The cliff face was far steeper than Sharpe had anticipated, though it was not sheer rock, but rather a series of cracks in which plants had taken root, and he found that he could pull himself up by using stony outcrops and the thick stalks of the bigger shrubs. He needed both hands. Tom Garrard came behind, and more than once Sharpe trod on his friend's hands. 'Sorry, Tom.'

'Just keep going,' Garrard panted.

It became easier after the first ten feet, for the face now sloped away, and there was even room for two or three men to stand together on a weed-covered ledge. Sharpe called for the ladder and it was pushed up to him by the cavalrymen. The bamboo was light and he hooked the top rung over his right shoulder and climbed on upwards, following a jagged line of rocks and bushes that gave easy footing. A line of redcoats trailed him, muskets slung. There were more bushes to Sharpe's left, shielding him from the ramparts, but after he had climbed twenty feet those bushes ended and he prayed that the defenders would all be staring at the beleaguered gatehouse rather than at the precipice below. He pulled himself up the last few feet, cursing the ladder that seemed to get caught on every protrusion. The sun beat off the stone and the sweat poured down him. He was panting when he reached the top, and now there was nothing but steep, open ground between him and the wall's base. Fifty feet of rough grass to cross and then he would be at the wall.

He crouched at the edge of the cliff, waiting for the men to catch up. Still no one had seen him from the walls. Tom Garrard dropped beside him. 'When we go, Tom,' Sharpe said, 'we run like bloody hell. Straight to the wall. Ladder up, climb like rats and jump over the bloody top. Tell the lads to get over fast. Bastards on the other side are going to try and kill us before we can get reinforced, so we're going to need plenty of muskets to fend the buggers off.'

Garrard peered up at the embrasures. 'There's no one there.'

'There's a few there,' Sharpe said, 'but they ain't taking much notice. Dozy, they are,' he added, and thank God for that, he thought, for a handful of defenders with loaded muskets could stop him dead. And dead is what he had better be after striking Morris, unless he could cross the ramparts and open the gates. He peered up at the battlements as more men hauled themselves over the edge of the cliff. He guessed the wall was lightly manned by little more than a picquet line, for no one would have anticipated that the cliff could be climbed, but he also guessed that once the redcoats appeared the defenders would quickly reinforce the threatened spot.

Garrard grinned at Sharpe. 'Did you thump Morris?'

'What else could I do?'

'He'll have you court-martialled.'

'Not if we win here,' Sharpe said. 'If we get those gates open, Tom, we'll be bloody heroes.'

'And if we don't?'

'We'll be dead,' Sharpe said curtly, then turned to see Eli Lockhart scrambling onto the grass. 'What the hell are you doing here?' Sharpe demanded.

'I got lost,' Lockhart said, and hefted a musket he had taken from a soldier below. 'Some of your boys ain't too keen on being heroes, so me and my boys are making up the numbers.'

And it was not just Lockhart's cavalrymen who were climbing, but some kilted Highlanders and sepoys who had seen the Light Company scrambling up the cliff and decided to join in too. The more the merrier, Sharpe decided. He counted heads and saw he had thirty men, and more were coming. It was time to go, for the enemy would not stay asleep for long. 'We have to get over the wall fast,' he told them all, 'and once we're over, we form two ranks.'

He stood and hefted the ladder high over his head, holding it with both hands, then ran up the steep grass. His boots, which were Syud Sevajee's cast-offs, had smooth soles and slipped on the grass, but he stumbled on, and went even faster when he heard an aggrieved shout from high above him. He knew what was coming next and he was still thirty feet from the walls, a sitting target, and then he heard the bang of the musket and saw the grass flatten ahead of him as the gases from the barrel lashed downwards. Smoke eddied around him, but the ball had thumped into one of the ladder's thick uprights, and then another musket fired and he saw a fleck of turf dance up.

'Give them fire!' Major Stokes roared from the bottom of the ravine. 'Give them fire!'

A hundred redcoats and sepoys blasted up at the walls. Sharpe heard the musket shots clatter on the stone, and then he was hard under the rampart and he dropped the leading end of the ladder and rammed it into the turf and swung the other end up and over. A bloody escalade, he thought. A breach and an escalade, all in one day, and he pulled the claymore out from his belt and pushed Garrard away from the foot of the ladder. 'Me first,' he growled, and began to climb. The rungs were springy and he had the terrible thought that maybe they would break after the first few men had used the ladder, and then a handful of soldiers would be trapped inside the fortress where they would be cut down by the Mahrattas, but there was no time to dwell on that fear, just to keep climbing. The musket balls rattled the stones to left and right in a torrent of fire that had driven the defenders back from the parapet, but at any second Sharpe would be alone up there. He roared a shout of defiance, reached the top of the ladder and extended his free hand to grip the stone. He hauled himself through the embrasure. He paused, trying to get a sense of what lay beyond, but Garrard shoved him and he had no option but to spring through the embrasure.

There was no firestep! Jesus, he thought, and jumped. It was not a long jump down, maybe eight or ten feet, for the ground was higher on the inner side of the wall. He sprawled on the turf and a musket bullet whipped over his back. He rolled, got to his feet, and saw that the defenders had low wooden platforms that they had been using to peer over the top of the wall. Those defenders were running towards him now, but they were few, very few, and already Sharpe had five redcoats on his side of the wall, and more were coming. But so was the enemy, some from the west and more from the east. 'Tom! Look after those men.' Sharpe pointed westwards, then he turned the other way and dragged three men into a crude rank. 'Present!' he called. The muskets went up into their shoulders. 'Aim low, boys,' he said. 'Fire!'

The muskets coughed out smoke. A Mahratta slid on the grass. The others turned and ran, appalled at the stream of men now crossing the wall. It was a curious mix of English skirmishers, Highland infantry, sepoys, cavalrymen and even some of Syud Sevajee's followers in their borrowed red jackets. 'Two ranks!' Sharpe shouted. 'Quick now! Two ranks! Tom! What's happening behind me?'

'Buggers have gone, sir.'

'Two ranks!' Sharpe shouted again. He could not see the gatehouse from here because the hill inside the wall bulged outwards and hid the great ramparts from him, but the enemy was forming two hundred paces eastwards. The wall's defenders, in brown jackets, were joining a company of white-coated Cobras who must have been in reserve and those men would have to be defeated before Sharpe could hope to advance on the gatehouse. He glanced up the hill and saw nothing there except a building half hidden by trees in which monkeys gibbered. No defenders there, thank God, so he could ignore his right flank.

A Scottish sergeant had shoved and tugged the men into two ranks. 'Load!' Sharpe said, though most of the men were already loaded. 'Sergeant?'

'Sir?'

'Advance along the wall. No one's to fire till I give the word. Sergeant Green?' Sharpe called, waited. 'Sergeant Green!' Green had evidently not crossed the wall yet, or maybe he had not even climbed the cliff. 'Sergeant Green!' Sharpe bellowed again.

'Why do you need him?' a voice called.

It was a Scottish captain. Christ, Sharpe thought, but he was out-ranked. 'To bring the next group on!'

'I'll do it,' the Scotsman said, 'you go!'

'Advance!' Sharpe shouted.

'By the centre!' the Sergeant shouted. 'March!'

It was a ragged advance. The men had no file-closers and they spread out, but Sharpe did not much care. The thing was to close on the enemy. That had always been McCandless's advice. Get close and start killing, because there's bugger all you can do at long range, though the Scottish Colonel would never have used that word. This is for you, McCandless, Sharpe thought, this one's for you, and it struck him that this was the first time he had ever taken troops into formal battle, line against line, muskets against muskets. He was nervous, and made even more nervous by the fact that he was leading a makeshift company in full view of the thousands of redcoats on the ravine's northern slope. It was like being trapped on stage in a full theatre; lose here, he thought, and all the army would know. He watched the enemy officer, a tall man with a dark face and a large moustache. He looked calm and his men marched in three tight ranks. Well trained, Sharpe thought, but then no one had ever said William Dodd could not whip troops into shape.

The Cobras stopped when the two units were a hundred paces apart.

They levelled their muskets and Sharpe saw his men falter. 'Keep going!' he ordered. 'Keep going!'

'You heard the man!' the Scottish Sergeant bellowed. 'Keep going!'

Sharpe was at the right-hand flank of his line. He glanced behind to see more men running to catch up, their equipment flapping as they stumbled over the uneven ground. Christ, Sharpe thought, but I'm inside! We're in! And then the Cobras fired.

And Sharpe, ensign and bullock driver, had a battle on his hands.

The redcoats stormed the gatehouse a third time, this attempt led by two squads who hugged the walls either side of the passage and then turned their muskets up to blast the defenders on the opposite firestep. The tactic seemed to work, for they ripped off their first volley and under its cover a third squad comprised of axemen charged over the dead and dying and scrambled up the steep stone path towards the second gate.

Then the lit rockets began to drop from on high. They struck the bodies and then flamed into life and ricocheted madly about the confined space. They tore into the two musket squads, flamed among the axemen, choked men with their smoke, burned them with flame and exploded to strew the carnage with more blood and guts. The axemen never even reached the gate. They died under the musket fire that followed the rockets, or else, wounded, they tried to crawl back through the thick smoke. Rocks hurtled down from the flanking firesteps, pulping the dead and the living into horror. The survivors fled, defeated again.

'Enough!' Colonel Dodd shouted at his men. 'Enough!' He peered down into the stone chamber. It looked like something from hell, a place where broken things twitched in blood beneath a reeking pall of smoke. The rocket carcasses still burned. The wounded cried for help that was not coming, and Dodd felt an elation sear through him. It was even easier than he had dared to hope.

'Sahib!' Gopal said urgently. 'Sahib?'

'What?'

'Sahib, look!' Gopal was pointing westwards. There was smoke and the crackling sound of a musket fight. The noise and smoke were coming from just beyond the curve of the hill so Dodd could not see what was happening, but the sound was enough to convince him that a considerable fight had broken out a quarter-mile away, and that might not have mattered, except that the smoke and the noise came from inside the wall.

'Jesus!' Dodd swore. 'Find out what's happening, Gopal. Quick!' He could not lose. He must not lose. 'Where's Mister Hakeswill?' he shouted, wanting the deserter to take over Gopal's responsibilities on the firestep, but the twitching Sergeant had vanished. The musketry went on, but beneath Dodd there were only moans and the smell of burning flesh. He stared westwards. If the damned redcoats had crossed the wall then he would need more infantry to drive them out and seal whatever place they had found to penetrate the Inner Fort. 'Havildar!' He summoned the man who had accompanied Hakeswill to the palace. 'Go to the Southern Gate and tell them to send a battalion here. Quick!'

'Sahib,' the man said, and ran.

Dodd found that he was shaking slightly. It was just a small tremor in his right hand which he stilled by gripping the gold elephant-shaped hilt of his sword. There was no need to panic, he told himself, everything was under control, but he could not rid himself of the thought that there would be no escape from this place. In every other fight since he had defected from British service he had made certain of a route along which he could retreat, but from this high fortress on its soaring bluff there was no way out. He must win, or else he must die. He watched the smoke to the west. The firing was constant now, suggesting that the enemy was inside the fort in force. His hand twitched, but this time he did not notice as, for the first time in weeks, the Lord of Gawilghur began to fear defeat.

The volley from the company of white-coated Cobras hammered towards Sharpe's men, but because they were spread more widely than usual many of the balls wasted themselves in the gaps between the files. Some men went down, and the rest instinctively checked, but Sharpe shouted at them to keep marching. The enemy was hidden in smoke, but Sharpe knew they would be reloading. 'Close the files, Sergeant,' he shouted.

'Close up! Close up!' the Scots Sergeant called. He glanced at Sharpe, suspecting that he was taking the small company too close to the enemy. The range was already down to sixty yards.

Sharpe could just see one of the Indians through the smoke. The man was the left flanker of the front rank, a small man, and he had bitten off his cartridge and was pouring the powder down the muzzle of his musket. Sharpe watched the bullet go in and the ramrod come up ready to plunge down into the barrel. 'Halt!' he called.

'Halt!' the Sergeant echoed.

'Present!'

The muskets came up into the men's shoulders. Sharpe reckoned he had about sixty men in the two ranks, fewer than the enemy's three ranks, but enough. More men were running up from the ladder all the time. 'Aim low,' he said. 'Fire!'

The volley slammed into the Cobras who were still loading. Sharpe's men began to reload themselves, working fast, nervous of the enemy's next volley.

Sharpe watched the enemy bring their muskets up. His men were half hidden by their own musket smoke. 'Drop!' he shouted. He had not known he was going to give the order until he heard himself shout it, but it suddenly seemed the sensible thing to do. 'Flat on the ground!' he shouted. 'Quick!' He dropped himself, though only to one knee, and a heartbeat later the enemy fired and their volley whistled over the prostrate company. Sharpe had slowed his men's loading process, but he had kept them alive and now it was time to go for the kill. 'Load!' he shouted, and his men climbed to their feet. This time Sharpe did not watch the enemy, for he did not want to be affected by their timing. He hefted the claymore, comforted by the blade's heaviness.

'Prepare to charge!' he shouted. His men were pushing their ramrods back into their musket hoops, and now they pulled out their bayonets and twisted them onto blackened muzzles. Eli Lockhart's cavalrymen, some of whom only had pistols, drew their sabres.

'Present!' Sharpe called, and the muskets went up into the shoulders again. Now he did look at the enemy and saw that most of them were still ramming.

'Fire!' The muskets flamed and the scraps of wadding spat out after the bullets to flicker their small flames in the grass. 'Charge!' Sharpe shouted, and he led the way from the right flank, the claymore in his hand. 'Charge!' he shouted again and his small company, sensing that they had only seconds before the enemy's muskets were loaded, ran with him.

Then a blast of musketry sounded to Sharpe's right and he saw that the Scottish Captain had formed a score of men on the flank and had poured in a volley that struck the Cobras just before Sharpe's charge closed the gap.

'Kill them!' Sharpe raged. Fear was whipping inside him, the fear that he had mistimed this charge and that the enemy would have a volley ready just yards before the redcoats struck home, but he was committed now, and he ran as hard as he could to break into the white-coated ranks before the volley came.

The Havildar commanding the Cobra company had been appalled to see the redcoats charging. He should have fired, but instead he ordered his men to fix their own bayonets and so the enemy was still twisting the blades onto their muskets when the leading redcoats burst through the smoke. Sharpe hacked his heavy sword at the front rank, felt it bite and slide against bone, twisted it free, lunged, kicked at a man, and suddenly Eli Lockhart was beside him, his sabre slashing down, and two Highlanders were stabbing with bayonets. Sharpe hacked with the sword two-handed, fighting in a red rage that had come from the nervousness that had assailed him during the charge. A sepoy trapped the Cobras' Havildar, feinted with the bayonet, parried the *tulwar*'s counter-lunge, then stabbed the enemy in the belly. The white coats were running now, fleeing back towards the smoke that boiled up from the gatehouse which lay beyond the bulge of the hill. Tom Garrard, his bayonet bloodied to the hilt, kicked at a wounded man who was trying to aim his musket. Other men stooped to search the dead and dying.

The Scottish Captain came in from the flank. He had the winged epaulettes of a light company. 'I didn't know the 74th were up here,' he greeted Sharpe, 'or is it the 33rd?' He peered at Sharpe's coat, and Sharpe saw that Clare's newly sewn facings had been torn in the climb, revealing the old red material beneath.

'I'm a lost sheep, sir,' Sharpe said.

'A very welcome lost sheep,' the Captain said, holding out his hand. 'Archibald Campbell, Scotch Brigade. Brought my company up here, just in case they got bored.'

'Richard Sharpe, 74th,' Sharpe said, shaking Campbell's hand, 'and bloody glad to see you, sir.' Sharpe suddenly wanted to laugh. His force, which had pierced the Inner Fort's defences, was a ragged mix of Indians and British, cavalrymen and infantry. There were kilted Highlanders from the 78th, some of Campbell's men from the 94th, maybe half of the 33rd's Light Company, and a good number of sepoys.

Campbell had climbed one of the low timber platforms that had let the defenders peer over the firestep, and from its vantage point he stared at the gatehouse which lay a quarter-mile eastwards.

'Are you thinking what I'm thinking, Mister Sharpe?' he asked.

'I'm thinking we should take the gatehouse,' Sharpe said, 'and open the gates.'

'Me too.' He shifted to make room for Sharpe on the small platform. 'They'll no doubt be trying to evict us soon, eh? We'd best make haste.'

Sharpe stared at the gatehouse where a great smear of smoke showed above the ramparts that were thick with white-coated Cobras. A shallow flight of stone stairs led from inside the fortress to the firestep, and the gates could not be opened until that firestep was cleared of the enemy. 'If I take the firestep,' he suggested to Campbell, 'you can open the gates?'

'That seems a fair division of labour,' Campbell said, jumping down from the platform. He had lost his hat and a shock of curly black hair hung over his narrow face. He grinned at Sharpe. 'I'll take my company and you can have the rest, eh?' Campbell strode up the hill, shouting for his own Light Company to form in a column of three ranks.

Sharpe followed Campbell off the platform and summoned the remaining men into line. 'Captain Campbell's going to open the gates from the inside,' he told them, 'and we're going to make it possible by clearing the parapets of the bastards. It's a fair distance to the gate, but we've got to get there fast. And when we get there, the first thing we do is fire a volley up at the firestep. Clean some of the buggers off before we go up there. Load your muskets now. Sergeant Green!'

Green, red-faced from the effort of climbing up the ravine and running to join Sharpe, stepped forward. 'I'm here, sir, and sir –'

'Number off twenty men, Green,' Sharpe ordered the panting Sergeant. 'You'll stay down below and provide covering fire while we climb the steps, understand?'

'Twenty men, sir? Yes, sir, I will, sir, only it's Mister Morris, sir.' Green sounded embarrassed.

'What about him?' Sharpe asked.

'He's recovered, sir. His tummy, sir, it got better' – Green managed to keep a straight face as he delivered that news – 'and he said no one else was to climb the cliff, sir, and he sent me to fetch the men what had climbed it back down again. That's why I'm here, sir.'

'No, you're not,' Sharpe said. 'You're here to number off twenty men who'll give the rest of us covering fire.'

Green hesitated, looked at Sharpe's face, then nodded. 'Right you are, sir! Twenty men, covering fire.'

'Thank you, Sergeant,' Sharpe said. So Morris was conscious again, and probably already making trouble, but Sharpe could not worry about that. He looked at his men. They numbered seventy or eighty now, and still more Scotsmen and sepoys were coming up the cliff and crossing the wall. He waited until they all had loaded muskets and their ramrods were back in their hoops. 'Just follow me, lads, and when we get there kill the bastards. Now!' He turned and faced east. 'Come on!'

'At the double!' Campbell called to his company. 'Forward!'

The fox was in the henhouse. Feathers would fly.

CHAPTER 11

The 74th, climbing the road that led from the plain to Gawilghur's Southern Gate, could hear the distant musketry sounding like a burning thorn grove. It crackled, flared up to a crescendo, then faded again. At times it seemed as though it would die altogether and then, just as sweating men decided the battle must be over, it rattled loud and furious once more. There was nothing the 74th could do to help. They were still three hundred feet beneath the fortress and from now on they would be within killing range of the guns mounted on Gawilghur's south-facing ramparts. Those guns had been firing at the 74th for over an hour now, but the range had been long and the downward angle steep, so that not a ball had struck home. If the 74th had had their own artillery, they could have fired back, but the slope was too steep for any gun to fire effectively. The gunners would have had to site their cannon on a steep upwards ramp, and every shot would have threatened to turn the guns over. The 74th could go no farther, not without taking needless casualties, and so Wellesley halted them. If the defenders on the southern wall looked few he might contemplate an escalade, but the sepoys carrying the ladders had fallen far behind the leading troops so no such attack could be contemplated yet. Nor did the General truly expect to try such an assault, for the 74th's task had always been to keep some of the fort's defenders pinned to their southern walls while the real attack came from the north. That purpose, at least, was being accomplished, for the walls facing the steep southern slope looked thick with defenders.

Sir Arthur Wellesley dismounted from his horse and climbed to a vantage point from which he could stare at the fortress. Colonel Wallace and a handful of aides followed, and the officers settled by some rocks from where they tried to work out what the noise of the battle meant. 'No guns,' Wellesley said after cocking his head to the distant sound.

'No guns, sir?' an aide asked.

'There's no sound of cannon fire,' Colonel Wallace explained, 'which surely means the Outer Fort is taken.'

'But not the Inner?' the aide asked.

Sir Arthur did not even bother to reply. Of course the Inner Fort was not taken, otherwise the sound of fighting would have died away altogether and fugitives would be streaming from the Southern Gate towards the muskets of the 74th. And somehow, despite his misgivings, Wellesley had dared to hope that Kenny's assault would wash over both sets of ramparts, and that by the time the 74th reached the road's summit the great Southern Gate would already have been opened by triumphant redcoats. Instead a green and gold flag hung from the gate-tower which bristled with the muskets of its defenders.

Wellesley now wished that he had ridden to the plateau and followed Kenny's men through the breaches. What the hell was happening? He had no way of reaching the plateau except to ride all the way down to the plain and then back up the newly cut road, a distance of over twenty miles. He could only wait and hope. 'You'll advance your skirmishers, Colonel?' he suggested to Wallace. The 74th's skirmishers could not hope to achieve much, but at least their presence would confirm the threat to the southern walls and so pin those defenders down. 'But spread them out,' Wellesley advised, 'spread them well out.' By scattering the Light Company across the hot hillside he would protect them from cannon fire.

Beyond the southern ramparts, far beyond, a pillar of smoke smeared the sky grey. The sound of firing rose and fell, muted by the hot air that shimmered over the fort's black walls. Wellesley fidgeted and hoped to God his gamble would pay off and that his redcoats, God alone knew how, had found a way into the fort that had never before fallen.

'Give them fire!' Major Stokes roared at the men on the ravine's northern side. 'Give them fire!' Other officers took up the call, and the men who had been watching the fight across the ravine loaded their firelocks and began peppering the gatehouse with musket balls.

Stokes had climbed back up the northern side of the ravine so that he could see across the farther wall, and he now watched as the two small groups of redcoats advanced raggedly over the hillside. A column was farthest away, while the nearer men were in a line, and both advanced on the strongly garrisoned gatehouse which had just repelled yet another British attack through the broken gate. Those defenders would now turn their muskets on the new attackers and so Stokes roared at men to fire across the ravine. The range was terribly long, but any distraction would help. The gunners who had smashed down the gate fired at the parapets, their shots chipping at stone. 'Go, man, go!' Stokes urged Sharpe. 'Go!'

Captain Morris, his mouth swollen and bleeding, and with a bruise blackening one eye and another disfiguring his forehead, staggered up the hillside. 'Major Stokes!' he called petulantly. 'Major Stokes.'

Stokes turned to him. His first reaction was that Morris must have been wounded trying to cross the wall, and he decided he must have misjudged the man who was not, after all, such a coward. 'You need a surgeon, Captain?'

'That bloody man, Sharpe! He hit me! Hit me! Stole my company. I want charges levelled.'

'Hit you?' Stokes asked, bemused.

'Stole my company!' Morris said in outrage. 'I ordered him to go away, and he hit me! I'm telling you, sir, because you're a senior officer. You can talk to some of my men, sir, and hear their story. Some of them witnessed the assault, and I shall look for your support, sir, in the proceedings.'

Stokes wanted to laugh. So that was how Sharpe had found the men! 'I think you'd better forget bringing charges against Mister Sharpe,' the engineer said.

'Forget bringing charges?' Morris exclaimed. 'I will not! I'll break the bastard!'

'I doubt it,' Stokes said.

'He hit me!' Morris protested. 'He assaulted me!'

'Nonsense,' Stokes said brusquely. 'You fell over. I saw you do it. Tripped and tumbled. And that's precisely what I'll allege at any court martial. Not that there'll be a court martial. You simply fell over, man, and now you're suffering from delusions! Maybe it's a touch of the sun, Captain? You should be careful, otherwise you'll end up like poor

Harness. We shall ship you home and you'll end your days in bedlam with chains round your ankles.'

'Sir! I protest!' Morris said.

'You protest too much, Captain,' Stokes said. 'You tripped, and that's what I shall testify if you're foolish enough to bring charges. Even my boy saw you trip. Ain't that so, Ahmed?' Stokes turned to get Ahmed's agreement, but he had vanished. 'Oh, God,' Stokes said, and started down the hill to find the boy.

But sensed he was already too late.

The first hundred paces of Sharpe's advance were easy enough, for the sun-baked ground was open and his men were still out of sight of the gatehouse. The few defenders who had manned the wall above the ravine had fled, but as soon as the redcoats breasted the slope of the hill to see the gatehouse ahead, the enemy musketry began. 'Keep running!' Sharpe shouted, though it was hardly a run. They staggered and stumbled, their scabbards and haversacks banging and flapping, and the sun burned down relentlessly and the dry ground spurted puffs of dust as enemy musket balls flicked home. Sharpe was dimly aware of a cacophony of musketry from his left, the fire of the thousands of redcoats on the other side of the ravine, but the gatehouse defenders were sheltered by the outer parapet. A group of those defenders was manhandling a cannon round to face the new attack. 'Just keep going!' Sharpe called, the breath rasping in his throat. Christ, but he was thirsty. Thirsty, hungry and excited. The gatehouse was fogged by smoke as its defenders fired their muskets at the unexpected attack that was coming out of the west.

Off to his right Sharpe could see more defenders, but they were not firing, indeed they were not even formed in ranks. Instead they bunched beside a low wall that seemed to edge some gardens and supinely watched the confrontation. A building reared up beyond that, half obscured by trees. The place was huge! Hilltop after hilltop lay within the vast ring of Gawilghur's Inner Fort, and there had to be a thousand places for the enemy to assemble a force to attack Sharpe's open right flank, but he dared not worry about that possibility. All that mattered now was to reach the gatehouse and kill its defenders and so let a torrent of redcoats through the entrance.

The cannon fired from the gatehouse. The ball struck the dry ground fifty yards ahead of Sharpe and bounced clean over his head. The smoke of the gun spread in front of the parapet, spoiling the aim of the defenders, and Sharpe blessed the gunners and prayed that the smoke would linger. He had a stitch in his side, and his ribs still hurt like hell from the kicking that Hakeswill had given him, but he knew they had surprised this enemy, and an enemy surprised was already half beaten.

The smoke thinned and the muskets flamed from the wall again, making more smoke. Sharpe turned to shout at his men. 'Come on! Hurry!' He was crossing a stretch of ground where some of the garrison had made pathetic little lodges of thin branches propped against half dead trees and covered with sacking. Ash showed where fires had burned. It was a dumping ground. There was a rusting iron cannon carriage, a stone trough that had split in two and the remains of an ancient windlass made of wood that had been sun-whitened to the colour of bone. A small brown snake twisted away from him. A woman, thin as the snake and clutching a baby, fled from one of the shelters. A cat hissed at him from another. Sharpe dodged between the small trees, kicking up dust, breathing dust. A musket ball flicked up a puff of fire ash, another clanged off the rusting gun carriage.

He blinked through the sweat that stung his eyes to see that the gate passage's inner wall was lined with white-coated soldiers. The wall was a good hundred paces long, and its firestep was reached by climbing the flight of stone steps that led up beside the innermost gate. Campbell and his men were running towards that gate and Sharpe was now alongside them. He would have to fight his way up the stairs, and he knew that it would be impossible, that there were too many defenders, and he flinched as the cannon fired again, only this time it belched a barrelful of canister that threw up a storm of dust devils all about Sharpe's leading men.

'Stop!' he shouted. 'Stop! Form line!' He was close to the wall, damned close, not more than forty paces. 'Present!' he shouted, and his men raised their muskets to aim at the top of the wall. Smoke still hid half the rampart, though the other half was clear and the defenders were firing fast. A Scotsman staggered backwards and a sepoy folded over silently and clutched his bleeding belly. A small dog yapped at the soldiers. The smoke was clearing from the mouth of the cannon. 'You've got one volley,' Sharpe called, 'then we charge. Sergeant

Green? I don't want your men to fire now. Wait till we reach the top of the steps, then give us covering fire.' Sharpe wanted to lash out with his boot at the damned dog, but he forced himself to show calm as he paced down the front of the line. 'Aim well, boys, aim well! I want that wall cleared.' He stepped into a space between two files. 'Fire!'

The single volley flamed towards the top of the wall and Sharpe immediately ran at the steps without waiting to see the effect of the fire. Campbell was already at the innermost gate, lifting its heavy bar. He had a dozen men ready to enter the passageway, while the rest of his company faced back into the fort's interior to fight off any of the garrison who might come down from the buildings on the hill.

Sharpe took the steps two at a time. This is bloody madness, he thought. Suicide in a hot place. Should have stayed in the ravine. The sun beat off the stones so that it was like being in an oven. There were men with him, though he could not see who they were, for he was only aware of the top of the stairs, and of the men in white who were turning to face him with bayonets, and then Green's first volley slammed into them, and one of the men spun sideways, spurting a spray of blood from his scalp, and the others instinctively twitched away from the volley and Sharpe was there, the claymore slashing in a haymaker's sweep that bounced off the wounded man's skull to drive a second man over the wall's unprotected edge and into the passageway.

Where the innermost gate was opening, scraping on the stone and squealing on its huge hinges as Campbell's men heaved on the vast doors.

A bayonet lunged at Sharpe, catching his coat, and he hammered the hilt of the claymore down onto the man's head, then brought up his knee. Lockhart was beside him, fighting with a cold-blooded ferocity, his sabre spattering drops of blood with every cut or lunge. 'Over there!' Lockhart shouted to his men, and a half-dozen of the cavalrymen ran across the top of the archway to challenge the defenders on the outer walkway. Tom Garrard came up on Sharpe's right and plunged his bayonet forward in short, disciplined strokes. More men ran up the stairs and pushed at those in front so that Sharpe, Lockhart and Garrard were shoved forward against the enemy who had no space to use their bayonets. The press of men also protected Sharpe from the enemy's muskets. He beat down with the heavy sword, using his height to dominate the Indians who were keening a high-pitched war cry. A bayonet hit Sharpe plumb on his hip bone and he felt the steel grind on bone and he slammed the claymore's hilt down onto the man's head to crumple his shako, then down again to beat the man to the ground. The bayonet fell away and Sharpe climbed over the stunned man to slash at another defender. A musket banged close by him and he felt the scorch of the barrel flame on his burnt cheek. The press of men was thick, too thick to make progress, even though he beat at them with the sword which he cut downwards with both hands. 'Throw them over the bloody side!' Lockhart shouted, and the tall cavalryman slashed his sabre, just missing Sharpe, but the hissing blade drove the enemy frantically back and two of them, caught on the edge of the firestep, screamed and fell to where they were beaten to death by the musket butts of Campbell's Highlanders. Campbell himself was running to the next gate. Two more gates to unbar and the way would be open, but the Cobras were thick on the walls and Dodd was screaming at them to shoot into the press of men, attackers and defenders alike, and so throw back the impudent handful of red-coats who had turned his rear.

Then the attackers outside the fort, who had despaired of making another charge into the smoke- and blood-stinking alley where so many had died, heard the fight on the ramparts and so they came back, flooding into the shadow of the arch and there aiming up at the firesteps. The muskets hammered, more men came, and the Cobras were assailed from in front and from below. 'Rockets!' Dodd shouted, and some of his men lit the missiles and tossed them down into the passageway, but they were nervous of the attackers coming along the top of the rampart. Those attackers were big men, crazed with battle, slashing with swords and bayonets as they snarled their way along the wall. Sergeant Green's men fired from below, picking off defenders and forcing others to duck.

'Fire across! Fire across!' Captain Campbell, down in the passage-way, had seen the defenders thickening in front of the men attacking along the tops of the walls and now he cupped his hands and shouted at the men behind the front ranks of the attackers. 'Fire across!' He pointed, showing them that they should angle their fire over the pass-ageway to strike the defenders on the opposite wall and the men, understanding him, loaded their muskets. It took a few seconds, but at last the crossfire began and the pressure in front of Sharpe gave way. He swung the huge sword backhanded, half severing a man's head, twisted the blade, thrust it into a belly, twisted it again, and suddenly the Cobras were backing away, terrified of the bloody blades.

The second gate was opened. Campbell was the first man through and now there was only one gate left. His sergeant had brought a score of men into the passageway and those Scotsmen began to fire up at the walls, and the Cobras were crumbling now because there were redcoats below them on both sides, and more were hacking their way along the rampart, and the defenders were pinned in a small place with nowhere to go. The only steps to the gateway's firestep were in redcoat hands, and Dodd's men could either jump or surrender. A piper had started playing, and the mad skirl of the music drove the attackers to a new fury as they closed on the remnants of Dodd's Cobras. The redcoats were screaming a terrible war cry that was a compound of rage, madness and sheer terror. Sharpe's tattered white facings were now so soaked in blood that it looked as if he wore the red-trimmed coat of the 33rd again. His arm was tired, his hip was a great aching sore, and the wall was still not clear. A musket ball snatched at his sleeve, another fanned his bare head, and then he snarled at an enemy, cut again, and Campbell had the last bar out of its brackets and his men were heaving on the gate, and the attackers who had come from outside the fort were pulling on it, while beyond the outermost arch, on the slope above the ravine, an officer beckoned to all the troops waiting to the north.

A cheer sounded, and a flood of redcoats ran down into the ravine and up the track towards the Inner Fort. They smelt loot and women. The gates were open. The fortress in the sky had fallen.

Dodd was the last man on Sharpe's wall. He knew he was beaten, but he was no coward, and he came forward, sword in hand, then recognized the bloody man opposing him. 'Sergeant Sharpe,' he said, and raised his gold-hilted sword in an ironic salute. He had once tried to persuade Sharpe to join him in the Cobras, and Sharpe had been tempted, but fate had kept him in his red coat and brought him to this last meeting on Gawilghur's ramparts.

'I'm Mister Sharpe now, you bastard,' Sharpe said, and he waved Lockhart and Garrard back, then jumped forward, cutting with the claymore, but Dodd parried it easily and lunged at Sharpe, piercing his coat and glancing the sword point off a rib. Dodd stepped back, flicked the claymore aside, and lunged again, and this time the blade cut into Sharpe's right cheek, opening it clean up to the bone beside his eye.

'Marked for life,' Dodd said, 'though I fear it won't be a long life, Mister Sharpe.' Dodd thrust again and Sharpe parried desperately, deflecting the blade more by luck than skill, and he knew he was a dead man because Dodd was too good a swordsman. McCandless had warned him of this. Dodd might be a traitor, but he was a soldier, and a good one.

Dodd saw Sharpe's sudden caution, and smiled. 'They made an officer out of you, did they? I never knew the British army had that much sense.' He advanced again, sword low, inviting an attack from Sharpe, but then a redcoat ran past Sharpe, sabre swinging, and Dodd stepped fast back, surprised by the sudden charge, although he parried it with an instinctive skill. The force of the parry knocked the redcoat off balance and Dodd, still with a smile, lunged effortlessly to skewer the redcoat's throat. It was Ahmed, and Sharpe, recognizing the boy, roared with rage and ran at Dodd who flicked the sword back, blood streaming from its tip, and deflected the claymore's savage cut, turned his blade beneath it and was about to thrust the slim blade into Sharpe's belly when a pistol banged and Dodd was thrown hard back, blood showing on his right shoulder. His sword arm, numbed by the pistol bullet, hung low.

Sharpe walked up to him and saw the fear in Dodd's eyes. 'This is for McCandless,' he said, and kicked the renegade in the crotch. Dodd gasped and bent double. 'And this is for Ahmed,' Sharpe said, and swept the claymore up so that its heavy blade ripped into Dodd's throat, and Sharpe, still holding the sword double-handed, pulled it hard back and the steel sawed through sinew and muscle and gullet so that the firestep was suddenly awash with blood as the tall Dodd collapsed. Eli Lockhart, the long horse pistol still smoking in his hand, edged Sharpe aside to make certain Dodd was dead. Sharpe was stooped by Ahmed, but the boy was dying. Blood bubbled at his throat as he tried to breathe. His eyes looked up into Sharpe's face, but there was no recognition there. His small body heaved frantically, then was still. He had gone to his paradise. 'You stupid bastard,' Sharpe said, tears trickling to dilute the blood pouring from his cheek. 'You stupid little bastard.'

Lockhart used his sabre to cut the ropes holding the flag above the gatehouse and a roar of triumph sounded from the ravine as the flag came down. Then Lockhart helped Sharpe strip Ahmed of his red jacket and, lacking a British flag to hoist, they pulled the faded, blood-reddened coat up to the top of the pole. Gawilghur had yielded.

Sharpe cuffed tears and blood from his face. Lockhart was grinning at him, and Sharpe forced a smile in return. 'We did it, Eli.'

'We bloody did.' Lockhart held out a hand and Sharpe gripped it.

'Thank you,' Sharpe said fervently, then he let go of the cavalryman's hand and kicked Dodd's corpse. 'Look after that body, Eli. It's worth a fortune.'

'That's Dodd?'

'That's the bastard. That corpse is worth seven hundred guineas to you and Clare.'

'You and me, sir,' Lockhart said. The Sergeant looked as ragged and bloody as Sharpe. His blue jacket was torn and bloodstained. 'We'll share the reward,' he said, 'you and me, sir.'

'No,' Sharpe said, 'he's all yours. I just wanted to see the bastard dead. That's reward enough for me.' Blood was pouring from his cheek to add to the gore on his coat. He turned to Garrard who was leaning against the parapet, gasping for air. 'Look after the boy for me, Tom.'

Garrard, seeing that Ahmed was dead, frowned in puzzlement.

'I'm going to give him a proper burial,' Sharpe explained, then he turned and walked down the wall where exhausted redcoats rested among the dead and dying Cobras, while beneath them, in the passage that Campbell had opened, a stream of soldiers poured unopposed into the fort.

'Where are you going?' Garrard shouted after Sharpe.

Sharpe did not answer. He just walked on. He had another enemy to hunt, and an even richer reward to win.

The defenders were hunted down and killed. Even when they tried to surrender, they were killed, for their fortress had resisted and that was the fate of garrisons that showed defiance. Blood-maddened redcoats, fed on arrack and rum, roamed the vast stronghold with bayonets and greed both sharpened. There was little enough loot, but plenty of women, and so the screaming began.

Some defenders, knowing Gawilghur's geography, slipped to those parts of the perimeter where no wall faced outwards and dangerously narrow paths led down the cliffs. They streamed like ants down the rock, going to oblivion. Some hid, knowing that the rage of the attackers would soon enough be exhausted. Those who could not escape or find a hiding place died.

Flies buzzed in the palace where the dead were already stinking in the heat. Officers wandered the rooms, marvelling at their poverty. They had expected to find another mansion like the Tippoo Sultan's palace, a glittering trove of gems, gold, ivory and silk, but the Rajah of Berar had never been rich. Some discovered the cellars and they noted the great armoury, but were more interested in the barrels of cash, though when they saw the coins were all of copper they spat in disgust. A company of sepoys found some silver plate that they cut apart with their bayonets. Syud Sevajee had found his enemy, his father's murderer, but Beny Singh was already dead and Sevajee could do little more than spit on his corpse.

Beneath the palace, redcoats splashed in the lake, slaking their thirst. Some had discarded their red jackets, hanging them from the trees, and a ragged man, who had slipped unseen from the palace, stole one of the coats and pulled it on before limping towards the captured gatehouse. He was a white man, and wore a pair of dirty trousers and a ragged shirt, while a white coat and a black sash were bundled under one arm. His hair was lank, his skin filthy, and his face twitched as he shuffled along the path. No one took any notice of him, for he looked like any other redcoat who had found his small scrap of loot, and so Obadiah Hakeswill slunk northwards with a fortune in jewels concealed in his shabby clothes. He reckoned he had only to get through the gate, and across the Outer Fort, and then he would run. Where? He did not know. Just run. He was rich now, but he would still need to steal a horse. There would be plenty of officers' horses in the camp, and maybe he would be lucky and find a dead man's horse so that the loss would not be noticed for days. Then he would ride southwards. South to Madras, and in Madras he could sell the jewels, buy proper clothes and become a gentleman. Obadiah Hakeswill, Gent. Then he would go home. Home to England. Be a rich gentleman there.

He ignored the redcoats. The buggers had won, and it was not fair. He could have been a rajah, but at least he was as rich as any rajah, and so he sidled down the dusty path and the gatehouse was not very far away now. An officer was ahead, standing with a drawn claymore beside the snake pit and staring down into its horror, and then he turned and walked towards Hakeswill. The officer was hatless, bloody-faced, and Obadiah limped off the track, praying that he would not be noticed. The officer went safely past and Hakeswill breathed a silent prayer of thanks and swerved back to the track. Only a trickle of men came through the gate now, and most of them were too intent on joining the plundering to care about a single man limping the other way. Hakeswill grinned, knowing he would get away. He would be a gentleman.

Then a sword point pricked his spine and Hakeswill froze.

'I've been looking for you for days, Obadiah,' a hated voice said, and Hakeswill turned to look up into Sharpe's face, but the face was half hidden by blood, which was why he had not recognized the officer standing beside the snake pit.

'I was a prisoner,' Hakeswill whined, 'a prisoner.'

'You're a bloody liar.'

'For the love of God, help me.' Obadiah pretended not to recognize Sharpe, pretended to be mad. He twitched and moaned, let spittle dribble from his mouth and twisted his hands in submission. 'Locked me up,' he said, 'the heathen bastards locked me up. Ain't seen daylight in days.'

Sharpe leaned forward and snatched the coat that was bundled under Hakeswill's arm. Hakeswill stiffened, and Sharpe smiled as he saw the flash of anger in the Sergeant's eyes. 'Want the coat back, Obadiah? So fight me for it.'

'I was a prisoner,' Hakeswill insisted, no longer moaning like a mad thing.

Sharpe shook the coat open. 'So why's the jacket white, Obadiah? You're a bleeding liar.' He felt the coat's pockets, felt the hard lumps and knew his jewels were safe again. Hakeswill's eyes glinted with a terrible and frustrated rage. 'Go on, Obadiah,' Sharpe said, 'fight me.'

'I was a prisoner,' Hakeswill said, and he glanced to his right, hoping he could make a run for it, for though he might have lost the jewels in the coat, he had others in his trousers. And Sharpe, he now saw, had a wound in the hip. Perhaps Sharpe could not run. So run now, he told himself, and then the flat of the claymore's blade struck him hard across the scalp. He yelped, then went still as the sword point pricked at his throat.

'You sold me to Jama, didn't you?' Sharpe said. 'But that was a mistake, Obadiah, because I beat his *jettis* into pulp. I'll do that to you now. But take your clothes off first.'

'You can't do this to me!' Hakeswill shouted, hoping to attract attention. His face twitched. 'You can't do this! 'Gainst regulations, it is!'

'Strip, Obadiah,' Sharpe said.

'There are rules! Regulations! Says so in the scriptures!'

The claymore's point jabbed at Hakeswill's throat, drawing blood from the scar that had been left when they had tried to hang the young Obadiah. The pain quietened the Sergeant, and Sharpe smiled. 'I half beat Captain Morris to death, Sergeant, so do you think it worries me that there are rules which say I mustn't touch you? Now you've got a choice. You can strip naked, or you can let me strip your corpse naked. I don't care which it is. I don't care if they bloody hang me for your murder. It'd be worth it. So shut the hell up, and get your bloody clothes off.'

Hakeswill looked for help, but there was none in sight, and the sword point twisted in his broken skin and he gabbled that he was undressing himself, and he scrabbled at the rope belt on his trousers, and tore the buttons out of his shirt. 'Don't kill me!' he shouted. 'I can't be killed! I can't die!' He pulled off the shirt, tugged off his boots and pulled down his trousers.

'Now the foot cloths,' Sharpe said.

Hakeswill sat and unwrapped the filthy strips and so was left white and naked under the terrible sun. Sharpe used the sword's tip to pull the clothes into a pile. He would search them, extract the gems, then leave them.

'On your feet now, Obadiah,' he said, encouraging the naked man with the sword's reddened tip.

'I can't die, Sharpie!' Hakeswill pleaded, his face racked by twitches. 'I can't! You tried! The tigers wouldn't eat me and the elephant wouldn't kill me. You know why? Because I can't die! I've got an angel, I do, my own soul's angel and she looks after me.' He shouted the words, and all the while he was being pressed backwards by the sword tip, and he danced on the rocks because they were so hot and his feet were bare. 'You can't kill me. The angel looks after me. It's Mother, Sharpie, that's who the angel is, it's Mother all white and shiny. No, Sharpie, no! I can't die!' And the sword stabbed at his belly and Hakeswill jumped back, and jumped back again when the tip slashed at his scrawny ribs. 'They tried to hang me but they couldn't!' he declared. 'I dangled and I danced, and the rope wouldn't kill me, and here I am! I cannot die!' And then he screamed, because the sword had stabbed one last time and Hakeswill had stepped back to avoid the lunge, only this time there was no rock behind him, only a void, and he screamed as he fell into the shadows of the snake pit.

He screamed again as he hit the stone floor with a thump. 'I can't die!' he shouted triumphantly, and stared up at the black shape of his enemy. 'I can't die!' Hakeswill called again, then something sinuous and shadowy flickered to his left and he had no time to worry about Sharpe. He screamed, because the snakes were staring at him with hard flat eyes. 'Sharpie!' he shouted. 'Sharpie!'

But Sharpe had gone to collect the pile of rags.

And Hakeswill was alone with the serpents.

Wellesley heard the distant cheers, but could not tell whether it was his own men who celebrated or the enemy who was making the noise. The smoke cloud that had hung so thick and constant beyond the fortress faded.

He waited.

The defenders on the south wall still fought. They fired their cannon at the 74th's skirmish line which, because it was well spread out and sheltered by the rocks on the steep hillside, survived the sporadic cannonade. The smoke of the guns hung by the walls. Wellesley looked at his watch. Four o'clock. If the fort had not fallen, then it would soon be too late. Night would come and he would have to retreat ignominiously to the plain below. The intermittent crackle of muskets from the north told him that something was still happening, but whether it was men looting, or the sound of the defenders firing at defeated attackers, he could not tell.

Then the guns on the south wall fell silent. Their smoke lingered, then drifted away in the hot wind. Wellesley waited, expecting the cannon to fire again, but they remained quiet. 'Maybe they've run,' he said. The green and gold flag still hung over the gate-tower, but Wellesley could see no defenders there.

'If the fortress has fallen, sir,' Wallace pointed out, 'then why aren't they running out of this gate?'

'Because they know we're here,' Wellesley said, and took out his telescope. By mistake he had brought the new glass, the one he intended to give to Sharpe which had been engraved with the date of Assaye, and he put it to his eye and examined the southern wall. The embrasures were empty. The guns were still there, their blackened muzzles just showing, but no men. 'I think we shall advance, Wallace,' Wellesley said, snapping the glass shut.

'It could be a trap, sir.'

'We shall advance,' Wellesley said firmly.

The 74th marched with colours flying, drummers beating and pipers playing. A battalion of sepoys followed, and the two regiments made a brave sight as they climbed the last stretch of the steep road, but still the great Southern Gate of Gawilghur was closed before them. Wellesley spurred ahead, half expecting the defenders to spring a surprise and appear on the ramparts, but instead it was a redcoat who suddenly showed there and Wellesley's heart leaped with relief. He could sail home to England with another victory in his pocket.

The redcoat on the wall slashed at the flag's halyard and Wellesley watched as the green and gold banner fluttered down. Then the redcoat turned and shouted to someone inside the fortress.

Wellesley spurred his horse. Just as he and his aides came into the shadow of the gatehouse, the great gates began to open, hauled back by dirty-looking redcoats with stained faces and broad grins. An officer stood just beyond the arch and, as the General rode into sight, the officer brought his sword up in salute.

Wellesley returned the salute. The officer was drenched in blood, and the General hoped that was not a reflection of the army's casualties. Then he recognized the man. 'Mister Sharpe?' He sounded puzzled.

'Welcome to Gawilghur, sir,' Sharpe said.

'I thought you'd been captured?'

'I escaped, sir. Managed to join the attack.'

'So I see.' Wellesley glanced ahead. The fort seethed with jubilant redcoats and he knew it would take till nightfall to restore order. 'You should see a surgeon, Mister Sharpe. I fear you're going to carry a scar on your face.' He remembered the telescope, but decided he would give it to Sharpe later and so, with a curt nod, he rode on.

Sharpe stood and watched the 74th march in. They had not wanted him, because he was not a gentleman. But, by God, he was a soldier, and he had opened the fort for them. He caught Urquhart's eye, and Urquhart looked at the blood on Sharpe's face and at the crusting scabs on Sharpe's sword, then looked away. 'Good afternoon, Urquhart,' Sharpe said loudly.

Urquhart spurred his horse.

'Good afternoon, Sergeant Colquhoun,' Sharpe said.

Colquhoun marched doggedly on.

Sharpe smiled. He had proved whatever he had set out to prove, and what was that? That he was a soldier, but he had always known that. He was a soldier, and he would stay a soldier, and if that meant wearing a green jacket instead of a red, then so be it. But he was a soldier, and he had proved it in the heat and blood of Gawilghur. It was the fastness in the sky, the stronghold that could not fall, and now it was Sharpe's fortress.

Historical Note

I have done the 94th, sometimes known as the Scotch Brigade, and their Light Company which was led by Captain Campbell, a great disservice, for it was they, and not Sharpe, who found the route up the side of the ravine and then across the Inner Fort's wall at Gawilghur, and who then assailed the gatehouse from the inside and, by opening the succession of gates, allowed the rest of the attacking force into the fortress. Fictional heroes steal other men's thunder, and I trust the Scots will forgive Sharpe. The Captain Campbell whose initiative broke Gawilghur's defence was not the same Campbell who was one of Wellesley's aides (and who had been the hero at Ahmednuggur).

The 33rd's Light Company was not at Gawilghur; indeed the only British infantry there were Scottish regiments, the same Scotsmen who shocked Scindia's army into rout at Assaye and took the brunt of the Arab attack at Argaum. Wellesley's war against the Mahrattas, which ended in complete victory at Gawilghur, was thus won by Madrassi sepoys and Scottish Highlanders, and it was an extraordinary victory.

The battle of Assaye, described in *Sharpe's Triumph*, was the engagement which destroyed the cohesion of the Mahratta Confederation. Scindia, the most powerful of the princes, was so shocked by the defeat that he sued for peace, while the Rajah of Berar's troops, deserted by their allies, fought on. Undoubtedly their best strategy would have been an immediate retreat to Gawilghur, but Manu Bappoo must have decided that he could stop the British and so decided to make his stand at Argaum. The battle happened much as described in this novel; it began with an apparent Mahratta advantage when the sepoys on the right of Wellesley's line panicked, but the General calmed them, brought them back, then launched his line to victory. The Scots, just as they had been at Assaye, were his shock troops, and they destroyed the Arab regiment that was the best of Bappoo's infantry. There were no Cobras in Bappoo's army, and though William Dodd existed, and was a renegade fugitive from the East India Company army, there is no record of his having served Berar. The survivors of Argaum retreated north to Gawilghur.

Gawilghur is still a mightily impressive fortress, sprawling over its vast headland high above the Deccan Plain. It is deserted now, and was never again to be used as a stronghold after the storming on 15 December 1803. The fort was returned to the Mahrattas after they made peace with the British, and they never repaired the breaches which are still there, and, though much overgrown, capable of being climbed. No such breaches remain in Europe, and it was instructive to discover just how steep they are, and how difficult to negotiate, even unencumbered by a musket or sword. The great iron gun which killed five of the attackers with a single shot still lies on its emplacement in the Inner Fort, though its carriage has long decayed and the barrel is disfigured with graffiti. Most of the buildings in the Inner Fort have vanished, or else are so overgrown as to be invisible. There is, alas, no snake pit there. The major gatehouses are still intact, without their gates, and a visitor can only marvel at the suicidal bravery of the men who climbed from the ravine to enter the twisting deathtrap of the Inner Fort's northern gate. Defeat would surely have been their reward, had not Campbell and his Light Company found a way up the side of the ravine and, with the help of a ladder, scaled the wall and so attacked the gates from the inside. By then Beny Singh, the Killadar, had already poisoned his wives, lovers and daughters. He died, like Manu Bappoo, with his sword in his hand. Manu Bappoo almost certainly died in the breaches and not, as the novel says, in the ravine, though that was where most of his men died, trapped between the attackers who had captured the Outer Fort and the 78th who were climbing the road from the plain. They should have found refuge within the Inner Fort, and bolstered its defences, but for reasons that have never been explained, the Inner Fort's gates were fast shut against the survivors of the Outer Fort's garrison.

Elizabeth Longford, in *Wellington, The Years of the Sword*, quotes the late Jac Weller as saying of Gawilghur, 'three reasonably effective troops of Boy Scouts armed with rocks could have kept out several times their number of professional soldiers'. It is difficult to disagree.

Manu Bappoo and Beny Singh made no effort to protect the Outer Fort's walls with a glacis, which was their primary mistake, but their real stronghold was the Inner Fort, and it fell far too swiftly. The supposition is that the defenders were thoroughly demoralized, and the few British casualties (about 150), most of them killed or wounded in the assault on the gatehouse, testify to the swiftness of the victory. A hundred and fifty sounds like a small 'butcher's bill', and so it is, but that should not hide the horror of the fight for the Inner Fort's gatehouse where Kenny died. That fight occurred in a very small space and, for a brief while, must have been as ghastly as, say, the struggle for Badajoz's breaches nine years later. Campbell's escalade up the precipice saved an enormous number of lives and cut a nasty fight blessedly short. Indeed, the victory was so quick, and so cheaply gained, that a recent biography of the Duke of Wellington (in 1803 he was still Sir Arthur Wellesley) accords the siege less than three lines, yet to the redcoat who was sweating up the hill to the plateau and who was expected to carry his firelock and bayonet across the rocky isthmus to the breaches in the double walls it was a significant place and his victory remarkable.

The real significance of Gawilghur lay in the future. Sir Arthur Wellesley had now witnessed the assault of the breach at Seringapatam, had escaladed the walls of Ahmednuggur and swept over the great defences of Gawilghur. In Portugal and Spain, confronted by even greater defences manned by determined French soldiers, it is claimed that he underestimated the difficulties of siege work, having been lulled into complacency by the ease of his Indian victories. There may be truth in that, and at Ciudad Rodrigo, Badajoz, Burgos and San Sebastian he took dreadful casualties. My own suspicion is that he did not so much underestimate the ability of defences to withstand him, as overestimate the capacity of British troops to get through those defences and, astonishingly, they usually lived up to his expectations. And it was Scotsmen who gave him those high expectations: the Scots who used four ladders to capture a city at Ahmednuggur and one ladder to bring down the great fortress of Gawilghur. Their bravery helped disguise the fact that sieges were terrible work, so terrible that the troops, regardless of their commander's wishes, regarded a captured stronghold as their own property, to destroy and violate as they wished. This was their revenge for the horrors that the defenders had inflicted on them, and there was undoubtedly a vast slaughter inside Gawilghur once the victory was gained. Many of the defenders must have escaped down the steep cliffs, but perhaps half of the seven or eight thousand died in an orgy of revenge.

And then the place was forgotten. The Mahrattas were defeated, and even more of India came under British rule or influence. But Sir Arthur Wellesley was done with India, it was time to sail home and look for advancement against the more dangerous and nearer enemy, France. It will be four years before he sails from England to Portugal and to the campaign that will raise him to a dukedom. Sharpe will also go home, to a green instead of a red jacket, and he too will sail to Portugal and march from there into France, but he has a snare or two waiting on his path before he reaches the peninsula. So Sharpe will march again.

792.8092 NIJ A03708
£15.99

Richard Buckle was born in Warcop, Westmorland, in 1916 and educated at Marlborough and Balliol College, Oxford. After a period as an art student in London and Paris he founded the magazine *Ballet* in 1939, which he revived and edited from 1946–52. He served in the Scots Guards from 1939–1946. He wrote several plays, two of which were produced, and in 1954–5 designed and directed the now legendary Diaghilev Exhibition in Edinburgh and London. He has organized exhibitions of ballet, film, theatre, sculpture, painting and photography both in Britain and abroad.

From 1948–55 he was ballet critic of the *Observer*, and from 1959–75 ballet critic for the *Sunday Times*. Richard Buckle helped to found the Theatre Museum now in Covent Garden. He is currently writing his memoirs (1965–1997).

A03708

By the same author

The Adventures of a Ballet Critic
In Search of Diaghilev
The Prettiest Girl in England
Dancing for Diaghilev (with Lydia Sokolova)
Jacob Epstein, Sculptor
U and Non-U Revisited (editor)
Self-Portrait with Friends: Diaries of Cecil Beaton (editor)
Diaghilev
Buckle at the Ballet
The Most Upsetting Woman: Autobiography (vol. 1)
In the Wake of Diaghilev: Autobiography (vol. 2)
George Balanchine: Ballet Master (in collaboration with John Taros)

RICHARD BUCKLE

Nijinsky

PHOENIX
GIANT

A PHOENIX GIANT PAPERBACK

First published in Great Britain by Weidenfeld & Nicolson in 1971
Revised 1975 and 1980
This paperback edition published in 1998 by Phoenix, a division of Orion Books Ltd,
Orion House, 5 Upper St Martin's Lane, London WC2H 9EA

Copyright © Richard Buckle, 1971

The right of Richard Buckle to be identified as the author of
this work has been asserted by him in accordance with the
Copyright, Designs and Patents Act 1988.

All rights reserved. No part of this publication may be
reproduced, stored in a retrieval system, or transmitted, in
any form or by any means, electronic, mechanical,
photocopying, recording or otherwise, without the prior
permission of the copyright owner.

A CIP catalogue record for this book is available from the
British Library.

ISBN: 1 85799 984 3

Printed and bound in Great Britain by
Butler & Tanner Ltd, Frome and London

CITY AND ISLINGTON
SIXTH FORM COLLEG
283-309 GOSWELL ROAD
LONDON
EC1
TEL 020 7520 0652

To Cecil Beaton,
enlivening neighbour, encouraging friend

CONTENTS

PLATES

18. Nijinsky in 'Petrushka' (close-up). *Photo Dover Street Studio.*
19a. Tamara Karsavina and Nijinsky in 'Petrushka'. Drawing by Valentine Gross. *Theatre Museum, London, Gross-Hugo donation.*
19b. Nijinsky in 'Petrushka'. Drawing by Valentine Gross. *Theatre Museum, London, Gross-Hugo donation.*
20. Nijinsky in 'Le Dieu bleu'. *Photo Bert.*
21a. Nijinsky in 'Narcisse'. *Photo Balogh, courtesy of Sotheby & Co.*
21b. Nijinsky in 'Les Orientales' (close-up). *Photograph in collection of Theatre Museum, London, Gross-Hugo donation.*
22. Nijinsky in 'L'Après-midi d'un faune'. *Photo Bert. Theatre Museum, London, Gross-Hugo donation.*
23a. Nijinsky in 'L'Après-midi d'un faune'. *Photo Baron de Meyer, reproduced by courtesy of Mr John O'Brien from a copy of Meyer's very rare book of photographs of 'L'Après-midi'.* This book has been handsomely reprinted by Dance Books, London.
23b. Nijinsky, Lydia Nelidova and five of the other six Nymphs in 'L'Après-midi d'un faune'. *Photo Baron de Meyer, reproduced by courtesy of Mr John O'Brien from Meyer's book.*
24a–f. Tamara Karsavina, Ludmilla Schollar and Nijinsky in 'Jeux'. Pastels by Valentine Gross. *Collection Harvard College Library.*
25a–d. Tamara Karsavina, Ludmilla Schollar and Nijinsky in 'Jeux'. *Photos Gerschel, the first reproduced from a 'Comoedia Illustré' programme of the Ballets Russes for 1913, courtesy of Mme Schollar.*
26a–c. Three male dancers in 'Le Sacre du printemps'.
26d. Six female dancers in 'Le Sacre du printemps'; Julitska, Ramberg (Marie Rambert), Jejerska, Boni, Boniecka, Faithful. *Reproduced from a 'Comoedia Illustré' programme of the Ballets Russes for 1913.*
27a. Group from 'Le Sacre du printemps', Act I. Pastel by Valentine Gross. *Theatre Museum, London, Gross-Hugo donation.*
27b. Group from 'Le Sacre du printemps', Act II. Pastel by Valentine Gross. *Theatre Museum, London, Gross-Hugo donation.*
28a. Josefina Kovalevska, Miriam Ramberg (Marie Rambert), Ekaterina Oblokova and Sophie Pflanz on the *Avon. Photograph, courtesy of Dame Marie Rambert, enlarged by Astrid Zydower.*
28b. Romola and Vaslav Nijinsky at the Majestic Hotel, Buenos Aires, after their wedding. *Photograph from a scrapbook made by Lady Juliet Duff, collection of Mr Richard Davies and Mr David Dougill.*
29a. Romola and Vaslav Nijinsky in their car, New York, 1916.
29b. Romola and Vaslav Nijinsky at Virginia Water, Surrey, 1949. *Photo-*

LINE DRAWINGS

Line Drawings

ACKNOWLEDGEMENTS

The author wishes to express his gratitude to Mme Romola Nijinsky for having kindly granted permission for extensive quotations from her books entitled *Nijinsky* and *The Last Days of Nijinsky*, published by Victor Gollancz Ltd, and from her book entitled *The Diary of Vaslav Nijinsky*, published by Jonathan Cape Ltd.

He is also grateful to Mr Vitale Fokine for permission to quote extracts from his father's memoirs, for the information which Mr Fokine gave him about the details discovered by the researchers working on the Russian edition of the book, and also for Mr Fokine's own opinions.

He would like to thank the following publishers for allowing him to use copyright material: Constable & Co. Ltd (*The Diaghilev Ballet 1909–1929* by Grigoriev); Chatto & Windus Ltd (*Memoirs*, Vol. II by Benois); Putnam & Co. Ltd (*Reminiscences of the Russian Ballet* by Benois).

ILLUSTRATIONS

Sources for all the illustrations are acknowledged on pp. ix–xiv.

NOTE ON SPELLING AND DATES

An attempt has been made at consistency in spelling Russian names. Russian spelling is phonetic, however, and to be really consistent one would write 'Benua' for 'Benois' and 'Burman' for 'Bourman', which would seem freakish.

Dates are given New Style, that is, according to the Western (Grigorian) Calendar.

PRINCIPAL CHARACTERS

ASTRUC, GABRIEL. French-Jewish music publisher, later founder of the Comité International de Patronage Artistique; impresario who made possible the triumph of the Russian Ballet in the west.

BAKST, LEON (born Rosenberg). Painter and stage designer, close friend of Diaghilev and designer of several of his most celebrated ballets.

BENOIS, ALEXANDRE. St Petersburg painter, art historian and stage designer. Originally Diaghilev's mentor, he later designed a number of ballets for him, notably 'Petrushka'.

BOLM, ADOLF. Principal character dancer of the Diaghilev Ballet from 1909 till 1917.

BOURMAN, ANATOLE. Classmate of Nijinsky; member of Diaghilev's company from 1911. Later married to Klementovitch. Wrote with Dorothy Lyman a life of Nijinsky.

CECCHETTI, ENRICO (MAESTRO). Milanese dancer and ballet master, established in Petersburg on and off from 1890 to 1909, later ballet master of Diaghilev's company and teacher of Nijinsky.

CHALIAPINE, FEODOR. Russian singer, foremost bass of his day. First presented in the west by Diaghilev in 'Boris'.

COCTEAU, JEAN. French writer, author of the libretto of 'Le Dieu bleu'.

DEBUSSY, CLAUDE. French composer, whose 'L'Après-midi' was used by Nijinsky and from whom Diaghilev commissioned 'Jeux'.

DIAGHILEV, SERGEI PAVLOVITCH. Russian nobleman, who brought Russian painting, music, opera and ballet for the first time to western Europe. The lover of Nijinsky.

DUFF, LADY JULIET. Daughter of Lady Ripon; one of the Russian Ballet's warmest English supporters.

DUNCAN, ISADORA. American pioneer of a free form of dance to music of great composers.

FOKINE, MICHEL. St Petersburg dancer and innovating choreographer of most of Nijinsky's roles from 'Le Pavillon d'Armide' (1907) to 'Daphnis et Chloë' (1912). With the Diaghilev Ballet from 1909 to 1914 with a gap in 1913.

GREFFUHLE, COMTESSE. Celebrated beauty and queen of Paris society: President of Les Concerts de Paris and the earliest patron of Diaghilev in the west.

GRIGORIEV, SERGEI. Member of the Diaghilev Ballet and its *régisseur* from 1909 to 1929. Husband of Lubov Tchernicheva.

GUNSBOURG, BARON DMITRI DE. Russian-Jewish financier and art patron. A backer of the Diaghilev Ballet.

HAHN, REYNALDO. French composer, commissioned to write 'Le Dieu bleu' for Diaghilev.

KARSAVINA, TAMARA. St Petersburg ballerina, member of the Diaghilev Ballet from 1909 to 1914 and again later. Nijinsky's partner in most works.

KCHESSINSKAYA, MATILDA. St Petersburg ballerina, mistress of Nicholas II when Tsarevitch, then of various Grand Dukes. Friend and enemy of Diaghilev, she appeared briefly with his company in the west in 1911 and 1912.

LVOV, PRINCE PAVEL DMITRIEVITCH. St Petersburg dilettante, patron of sportsmen and artists. Nijinsky's first male admirer. Introduced him to Diaghilev.

MARKUS, EMILIA. Hungary's most famous actress. Mother of Romola de Pulszky.

MASSINE (born MIASSINE), LEONIDE. Moscow dancer, successor of Nijinsky in Diaghilev's affections and as choreographer.

MORRELL, LADY OTTOLINE. Bloomsbury hostess and friend of Diaghilev and Nijinsky.

NIJINSKA, BRONISLAVA FOMINICHNA. Third child and only daughter of Thomas and Eleonora Nijinsky. Member of Diaghilev's company. Later married to Kotchetovsky.

NIJINSKAYA, ELEONORA NICOLAIEVNA. Polish-born, *née* Bereda. Dancer at the Warsaw Opera until her marriage to Thomas Nijinsky. Mother of Stanislav, Vaslav and Bronislava.

NIJINSKY, THOMAS. Polish-born dancer and choreographer. Husband of Eleonora Bereda and father of Stanislav, Vaslav and Bronislava Nijinsky. Toured Russia with his own ballet troupe.

NIJINSKY, VASLAV FOMITCH. Second son of Thomas and Eleonora Nijinsky.

PAVLOVA, ANNA. St Petersburg ballerina, only for two brief periods a member of the Diaghilev Ballet.

PULSZKY, ROMOLA DE. Hungarian born, an enthusiast for the arts. Later wife of Nijinsky.

RAMBERT, MARIE (born MIRIAM RAMBERG). Russo-Polish dancer, briefly a member of the Russian Ballet and friend of Nijinsky.

RIPON, THE MARCHIONESS OF. The first English supporter of the Russian Ballet.

SERT, MISIA. Born Godebska, married in turn Thadée Natanson, Alfred Edwards and José-Maria Sert. Close friend and patron of Diaghilev from 1908.

STRAVINSKY, IGOR. Russian composer launched by Diaghilev, who commissioned from him 'L'Oiseau de feu', 'Petrushka', 'Le Sacre', etc.

VLADIMIR ALEXANDROVITCH, GRAND DUKE OF RUSSIA. Brother of Alexander III and eldest uncle of Nicholas II. The only member of the Imperial Family to support Diaghilev's enterprises in the west.

INTRODUCTION
TO THE FIRST EDITION

This book is very much the result of teamwork. When I began it I thought that the most I should be able to do would be to collate the many memoirs and articles by the collaborators of Diaghilev and Nijinsky which had appeared since Romola Nijinsky's life of her husband in 1933. The job of sifting truth from falsehood and putting the evidence in order alone seemed to justify another biography. I could not guess to what a marvellous extent I should have the co-operation of so many people who had lived or worked with Nijinsky.

Some of my conversations with Nijinsky's friends, relations, colleagues or successors took place near home, some in distant lands. My talks with Dame Marie Rambert took place in Kew Gardens, in Holland Park and in her own home on Campden Hill. Those with Mme Karsavina were held in her pretty house in Hampstead. Mr Massine gave me his recollections over dinner on two successive evenings at the Falcon Hotel in Stratford-upon-Avon. I was shown the setting of Nijinsky's early studies in Petersburg by Mme Natalia Dudinskaya, who now rules the school where he worked. I discussed him with M. Pierre Vladimirov in the offices of the School of American Ballet in New York and with Mme Ludmilla Schollar in William Christensen's Ballet School in San Francisco. When I met Mme Bronislava Nijinska for the first time, in her little house perched on a beetling crag at Pacific Palisades near Los Angeles, I felt I had really come to the ends of the earth as well as to the ultimate repository of truth about Nijinsky. Mme Bronislava's second husband had died ten days before, her hearing was poor and her English non-existent – besides which she had long been writing a book of her own about her brother. Nevertheless, she gave up two afternoons to answer my questions and to tell me things I did not know. Her daughter, Irina Nijinska-Raetz, to whom my friend Tamara Toumanova had introduced me a day or two before – thus making the interviews possible – acted as interpreter.

It was the dauntless Mme Irina who, two years later, while her mother was staging a ballet in Florence for the Maggio Musicale, read the whole 200,000 words of my book aloud – very loud – to Mme Bronislava, translating it into Russian as she went along. This took place mostly at night in a hotel bedroom, with people banging on the wall. I then met Mmes Bronislava and Irina in Paris, and in another hotel bedroom, with David Dougill taking notes, received their comments and corrections. It was Mme Irina who sensibly suggested that as technical descriptions of dancing could not be fuller in a book of this nature they should be omitted altogether; and I took her advice as far as I was able and cut them down to the minimum.

Mme Romola Nijinsky had already read my book with devoted diligence during a week spent at the Cavendish Hotel, Jermyn Street, when, on the afternoon the horse Nijinsky won the Two Thousand Guineas, she arrived at my flat in Covent Garden bursting with excitement about the race (which she had watched on colour television at Television House, near the Waldorf Hotel, where her husband had spent his first nights in England), to give me her detailed comments on the typescript. All her suggestions and corrections I accepted. Some months later, during the summer of 1970, I had further talks with Mme Romola Nijinsky, Mme Bronislava Nijinska and Mme Irina Nijinska-Raetz at the Cavendish Hotel: these led to extensive rewriting. Mme Romola Nijinsky later read through the final draft of the book again and approved it.

Through Mr Robert Craft, Mr Stravinsky answered a series of questionnaires and checked many points. He also read certain chapters and offered suggestions. Mr Grigoriev answered many detailed questionnaires, his answers being transcribed by his wife Mme Tchernicheva. To my great regret both Mr Stravinsky and Mr Grigoriev died while the book was in preparation.

To these helpful friends, Nijinsky's colleagues, his partner, the composer of his 'Sacre du printemps', the chief guardian of classical tradition at his old school, his sister, niece and wife, I am more grateful than I can say.

Other members of the Diaghilev Ballet who gave their time to help me or answered letters were Mme Doubrovska, Mme Sokolova, Mme Lopokhova, the late Hilda Bewicke (Mrs Arfa), Miss Maria Chabelska, Mr Idzikovsky, Mr Dolin and that wonderful *chef d'orchestre*, the late Ernest Ansermet.

If I had known twenty years ago that I was going to write Nijinsky's life how much more evidence I could have gathered from illustrious people who have died in that period! What questions I should have asked Alexandre Benois and Jean Cocteau! But I did enjoy the friendship of Lady Juliet Duff, and I have drawn on my memories of conversations with her, as well as on an essay she wrote on Diaghilev which was unpublished at the time of her death.

I never met Mme Valentine Hugo (*née* Gross), who died in 1968, but through the courtesy of M. Jean Hugo, whose first wife she was, a mass of notes and sketches were made available to me. Apart from being the most assiduous of artists in recording Nijinsky in all his roles, she planned to write a life of him. This never materialized, and I hope she would approve of this book which has been made with her posthumous help.

I owe an immense debt of gratitude to my old friend Mr Erich Alport, who invited me to go with him to Russia before I even knew I was to write the book, thus enabling me, as it turned out, to describe aspects of Leningrad at first hand. To the insistence, enthusiasm and generosity of Mr Lincoln Kirstein I owe a trip to the United States, which included my visit to California and the discovery of the Astruc papers in the Museum and Library of Performing Arts at Lincoln Center, New York.

Gabriel Astruc, the most enlightened and daring of musical impresarios, made possible the early triumphs of the Russian Ballet in Paris – and paid for this dearly. The survival of his correspondence with Diaghilev at Lincoln Center, of which I should have been unaware without Mr Kirstein's prompting, clarified a number of important points, helped towards exact dating, and proved the most valuable single group of documents for the study of the Russian Ballet's history. Mlle Lucienne Astruc, daughter of the impresario, has been a friend since the days of the Diaghilev Exhibition, and she has given me many precious documents which will one day find their way to our London Museum of Theatre Arts.

A number of dancers have helped me give some account of the choreography of certain ballets. Mme Karsavina described, mimed and danced for me passages of 'Le Pavillon d'Armide', and Mme Schollar and Mr Wilzak helped me with the same ballet. Miss Amanda Knott of Ballet Rambert corrected my description of 'L'Après-midi d'un faune', as did Mr Vassili Trunoff of Festival Ballet my account, made from memory only, with the aid of a gramophone record, of 'Schéhérazade'.

M. Jean Hugo gave me helpful information about Paris society in the early years of the Diaghilev Ballet. Mme Jean Hugo took much trouble to find out who the person was whose collection of Gauguin paintings excited Nijinsky. M. Philippe Jullian was kind enough to help identify a number of people listed as being present at the first famous *répétition générale* in 1909.

I thank these friends in France most sincerely. Mme Natalia Dudinskaya supplied me with a list of Nijinsky's roles at the Mariinsky, as well as the old photograph of Theatre Street, and I am so grateful for her help.

At the suggestion of Mme Bronislava Nijinska I got in touch with the distinguished ballet historian Mme Vera Krasovskaya, who read my chapter about Nijinsky's early years and provided facts from Leningrad sources to which I should not otherwise have had access. Besides making many useful comments, invaluable in that they expressed a Russian point of view, she went to great trouble to find out the truth about certain specific events – such as Nijinsky's pre-graduation appearance in 'Don Giovanni' – so that, thanks to her, valuable information can be published for the first time. My debt to her is considerable, and so is my gratitude.

Not only must I express my warm gratitude to Miss Genevieve Oswald, Curator of the Dance Collection of the New York Public Library at the Museum and Library of Performing Arts, and her staff, but also the Libraries and staff of the Bibliothèque Nationale, the Bibliothèque de l'Arsenal and the Bibliothèque de l'Opéra, Paris, and of the British Museum Reading Room, the BM Newspaper Library, Colindale, and the Royal Opera House, Covent Garden.

The research in America was begun by me and concluded by Mr Brian Blackwood, who also did all the research in Paris. Mr David Dougill did all the London research. These two colleagues expedited work on the book and were of incalculable service to the cause.

Mr Blackwood was first called in, however, in his capacity as a musician. He is himself preparing a book on the musical side of the Diaghilev Ballet, and was able during 1969 and 1970 to give me part of his time to make good the deficiencies of my technical knowledge of music. Once I had decided that it was desirable to give wherever possible some sort of choreographic account of the ballets Nijinsky danced or invented, it seemed a pity not to supply also some parallel notes on the music. We therefore together set about working out our descriptions. It was very hard to decide how far to go, because this is not a musical text-book any more than it is a book on ballet technique. Mr Blackwood, if this were his own book, could and no doubt would go into far more detail, and I must take the blame if the reader finds that we have stopped short in 'describing' a score, just as I must be held responsible for any descriptive phrases which to a musician may seem fanciful and imprecise. Mr Blackwood played over for me, at the Music Library of the Senate House, London University, the piano scores of certain almost forgotten ballets, such as 'Le Pavillon d'Armide' and 'Le Dieu bleu', which have never been recorded.

xxiv

In the case of 'Le Sacre du printemps' – far the most important score dealt with, and the hardest to describe – Mr Blackwood prepared the first analysis, I injected a few of my own thoughts, then cut the piece by half. Mr Stravinsky and Mr Craft read the draft, made certain comments and approved at least one specific phrase. But I was far from satisfied, and in the absence of Mr Blackwood, with my neighbour in the country, the composer Thomas Eastwood, I played over a record of the ballet again, two evenings running, and together we concocted a fuller description. So, some of the phrases are Mr Blackwood's, some Mr Eastwood's and some mine. This draft was then sent back for comment to Mr Stravinsky and Mr Craft.

It was my colleague Mr Desmond Shawe-Taylor who played me a record of Liszt's 14th Rhapsody one Sunday afternoon in Dorset, and with him and Mr John Bryson, a collaborator on my Diaghilev and Shakespeare Exhibitions, I discussed what kind of a ballet Diaghilev would have made of it, if he had got it on.

So many friends made helpful suggestions or provided small pieces of information: the late Antonio Gandarillas; Mr Alexander Tcherepnine; Mr Philip Dyer, who as a child was patted on the head by Diaghilev, who was my assistant on the Diaghilev Exhibition and who is now Wardrobe Master to our incipient Museum of Theatre Arts; my colleague Mr Felix Aprahamian; Mme Nadia Lacoste, Directrice du Centre de Presse, Principauté de Monaco; Baroness Budberg; Mr Miklos de Szakats, former husband of Nijinsky's younger daughter; Lady Diana Cooper; Baron Tassilo von Watzdorf; Mr Ronald Crichton; Mr Nigel Gosling; Mr H. S. Ede; Mr Harold Rosenthal; Mr Raymond Mander and Mr Joe Mitchenson; Mr Richard Davies; Mr John Peter; Mr Stuart Nicol of Royal Mail Lines, Ltd; Mr Duncan Grant; Mr Boris Kochno.

Much of this book was written at a remote cottage in Wiltshire, and at times, when writing it, I would see no one but the postman for several days at a stretch. If it were not that a few kind neighbours cheered me up and entertained me in the evenings I might have fallen into a melancholy and broken off the work; so I take pleasure in thanking for their continued hospitality Mr and Mrs John Arundell (she being the great-granddaughter of Lady Ripon and grand-daughter of Lady Juliet Duff) and their children; Mr and Mrs Julian Bream; Mr and Mrs Thomas Eastwood; Mrs Edmund Fane; and Mr Cecil Beaton, who spurred on my work with his enthusiasm and inspired me with his industry.

Mr David Dougill patiently typed and retyped many versions of every chapter, copying endless insertions and corrections in quintuplicate. As our task drew to a close, and after we had overstepped several deadlines, he prepared the whole of the first draft of the penultimate chapter, incorporating details and press notices of the Ballet's North American tours which have not been published before. He also worked with me on the Notes, and I really do not believe I should have had the courage to complete these without him. (I had so many sources of information that I had forgotten what some of them were.) Finally, Mr Dougill crowned his labours by making the Index single-handed.

In January and February 1970, which was the period of what would have been our final spurt, Mr Blackwood, Mr Dougill and I, working in adjacent rooms in my flat in Covent Garden, had the pleasure and honour of being joined, in a fourth room, by Mrs Margaret Power, who came, out of friendship to me and devotion to Nijinsky's memory, to type, insert and correct and indeed to criticize and improve. A *doyenne* of balletomanes in this country, she became, at the end of the last war, a good friend to the Nijinskys in Vienna. She later helped to care for Nijinsky in England, and after his death continued as a friend to his widow. In more than one sense she was a blessing to our work.

I say 'what would have been our final spurt' because I had intended to end the book with Nijinsky's illness. At the request of Mr Anthony Godwin of Weidenfeld & Nicolson, I added one more chapter bringing the story up to Nijinsky's death: this was written during the summer of 1970.

At the time of Nijinsky's second funeral in Paris in summer, 1953, I was collecting material for the Diaghilev Exhibition, which was to be held at the 1954 Edinburgh Festival to commemorate the twenty-fifth anniversary of Diaghilev's death. I had been asked to do this simply because I was a critic of ballet known to be interested in Nijinsky and the Diaghilev period, and nothing much was expected of me except to assemble a number of designs and portraits and hang them on a wall: but as I became more and more engrossed in the detective work and correspondence necessary for this collection – and I was helped by many old friends and collaborators of Diaghilev, such as Lady Juliet Duff and Alexandre Benois – I began to devise techniques of display which were considered novel at the time, with the result that I found myself landed with a second career – that of an exhibition designer. The sales in 1968 and 1969 of the Diaghilev Wardrobe, which I catalogued for Sotheby's, led directly to the foundation of a Museum of Theatre Arts* in London, with sections devoted to drama, opera and ballet, which I hope will soon find a home in the

---

*The museum is called 'The Theatre Museum', and it is a department of the Victoria and Albert Museum. (1979).

neighbourhood of Covent Garden. Our Museum, for which we have collected some of Nijinsky's own costumes, portraits of him, action studies by Valentine Gross, and the costumes of his great ballet 'Le Sacre du printemps' – still fresh because worn so little during all those years – should prove the most lasting result of a chain of events which can be traced back to my first sight of the photograph of Nijinsky in 'Le Spectre de la rose' on the jacket of his wife's biography, at Liverpool Street Station half a lifetime ago.

INTRODUCTION
TO THE SECOND EDITION

This paperback edition of my biography contains a little new material and many corrections. I was extremely fortunate in the reviewers of my first edition. Some of them – I am thinking in particular of Dame Rebecca West and Sir Sacheverell Sitwell – even produced reminiscences of Nijinsky, which I have incorporated gratefully in the new edition. Sir Sacheverell also (but in a letter) pointed out to me the only mistake I have ever become aware of in the books of Alexandre Benois: namely that the baroque architecture which Diaghilev took Nijinsky to see when they were planning the Bach ballet at Baden-Baden in 1913 must have been at Vierzehnheiligen, not at Einsiedeln, which is in Switzerland. Strangers have been helpful as well as reviewers. A young man came up to me in Piccadilly and said 'Surely it was Eugène Lami, not Ciceri, who designed Taglioni's costume in "La Sylphide"'. Of course it was. Thanks, friend. From Mr Oleg Kerensky's *Pavlova*, published in 1973, I learned that I was wrong in thinking Pavlova's mother was Jewish: it was her unacknowledged father. I have corrected this mistake. Mr Lincoln Kirstein reread my book in January 1974 and gave me a number of useful notes.

There were some serious criticisms which I took to heart. In the *Dancing Times* Miss Mary Clarke (in the course of a very generous review) complained of my lengthy descriptions of ballets. 'There is no task less rewarding than trying to put on paper the action of a ballet and an account of the accompanying music.' I agree. Having written these descriptions, I wanted to cut most of them: but my publisher wouldn't let me. 'People can always skip them,' he said, 'but they make the book more complete.'

I thought of relegating them to an Appendix in the Penguin edition, but decided that this would be cheating. I have tried, however, to abbreviate some of them.

Another criticism was that there was too much about Diaghilev. I agree. I had wanted to call the book 'Diaghilev and Nijinsky' but was prevented. That I got carried away and included an excess of material from the Astruc papers in the Museum and Library of Performing Arts, I also agree: but it was so fascinating. Being historically minded, I suppose I have come to think that in certain books an accumulation of documentary material takes precedence over artistic perfection of form. Some critics thought that there was not enough about Nijinsky in the book. To this I can only say that I put in all I could find. As my friend Alexander Bland pointed out in a fine article in *The Observer*, the enigma of Nijinsky is still unsolved. He is indeed a mystery and likely to remain one. Some critics thought I had given a complete picture of Nijinsky as a dancer, while failing to portray him as a man; while others, notably John Percival of *The Times*, thought the reverse. I expect both judgements were right. Nevertheless I have written an extra paragraph about the kind of dancer I think Nijinsky was, and have quoted in it both Rebecca West, who saw Nijinsky, and Alexander Bland, who didn't but who understands very well what makes dancers tick (p. 389 *et seq.*).

Mr Oleg Kerensky's appetite for sexological research prompted him to complain in the *Guardian* that I related 'with whom he did it, but not what he did'. I rather incline to Mrs Patrick Campbell's well-known attitude to these matters.

Nijinsky's younger daughter Tamara Weninger reviewed my book in the *Arizona Republicer*. She remembered her 'smiling dear father' and wondered why I had not consulted her or her elder sister Kyra. I had thought that as she was only born after Nijinsky's illness she would not have much to offer, but I agree that I should at least have consulted Mme Kyra Nijinsky, and am now proud to include some words by her in this edition.

Sir Geoffrey Keynes, brother of the great Maynard who married Lydia Lopokhova, mentioned, in a letter to me about *Nijinsky*, that he had gone with Rupert Brooke to see him dance. I thought this small piece of information was worth including (although I had been taxed by Dale Harris in the New York *Saturday Review* with my gossipy approach). Then, lunching one day in the country with Sir Cecil Beaton (to whom my book was dedicated), I was enchanted to meet Miss Cathleen Nesbitt. She told me how *she* had gone to the Russian Ballet with Rupert Brooke, and recalled what he said about Nijinsky afterwards. I am so grateful to be able to include her reminiscence too. I am also indebted to Mr Costa Achillopoulos for a reminiscence of Nijinsky's last recital at St Moritz. Mr John Geissler kindly sent me the translation of an interview Nijinsky gave in Cologne.

Here are some of the principal additions: more letters from Hugo von Hofmannsthal to Richard Strauss about the 'Orestes' ballet which he did not compose for Diaghilev and about the 'Joseph' ballet which he did; a fuller account of the action of 'Jeux' and its relation to the score, written by Brian Blackwood, whose book on the music of Diaghilev's Ballet from 1909 to 1914 has now been completed, though not published; some new thoughts about Nijinsky's wedding and Diaghilev's reaction to it. These 'new thoughts' were the result of my noticing – having been blind enough to overlook it before – that the date on the invitation to the wedding breakfast in Buenos Aires (lent me by Mme Sokolova and reproduced in the hard-back edition) was September 19, whereas the wedding and the wedding breakfast actually took place on September 10. I rang up Mme Sokolova. It was clear to us both that after the invitations were printed somebody had had second thoughts and put forward the date of the marriage, presumably announcing the change on the call-board of the theatre. This discovery gave rise to further reflections on Diaghilev's reaction to the news. To my great sorrow Mme Sokolova died shortly after this conversation.

It would be boastful to mention the names of some of the distinguished people who overwhelmed me with their praise of the biography, but I cannot resist quoting two compliments. Mme Romola Nijinsky wrote: 'I know Vaslav would have loved it.' Then, on a Christmas card, shortly before her death, Mme Bronislava Nijinska called the book 'wonderful'. Such encouragement gives one the determination to do better next time.

Shortly before sending this new edition to press I was given to read by Mme Irina Nijinska-Raetz the Memoirs of her mother, the late Mme Bronislava Nijinska. In these the boyhood and early travels of Nijinsky, which, through ignorance, I have disposed of in a few conjectural sentences at the foot of p. 4 and the head of p. 5, are covered in extraordinary and fascinating detail. As this remarkable book will obviously be published before long, I have resisted the temptation to borrow from it to enrich my own.

INTRODUCTION
TO THE THIRD EDITION

Although I had revised my book for Penguin's first paperback edition I had still overlooked a few wrong dates; these I have now corrected.

During the past year (1978) I finished my life of Diaghilev; and Romola Nijinsky died. Igor Markevitch, who was Diaghilev's last protégé and whose first wife was Nijinsky's daughter Kyra, had given me precious information about Diaghilev at the end of his life. In May 1978, when I came out of the Salisbury General Infirmary after a thigh operation, I had a telephone call from Markevitch's secretary in Switzerland. She told me that Romola Nijinsky was dying in a Paris hotel, and that Igor Markevitch, who was himself in a Swiss hospital, appealed to me to help her. The idea that I, who knew so few people in Paris compared with the celebrated *maestro*, should be able to give moral, medical or financial assistance from my cottage in Wiltshire – apart from being on crutches and waited on hand and foot by my 86-year-old mother (which of course Markevitch could not know) – seemed to me particularly fantastic; but I was evidently destined to be involved with the Nijinsky family. I telephoned Boris Kochno; he was out of Paris. There was no question of approaching Serge Lifar, who had been at some pains to ensure that Romola should not be buried in the plot beside Nijinsky which he had reserved most incongruously for himself. Romola Nijinsky died before I could be of any use.

During Romola's life nobody had been allowed access to the famous Nijinsky Diaries, which were widely regarded as an almost sacred text. I was able to tell Markevitch, who was one of her executors, that Romola had recently sent the manuscript of these to be sold by Christie's, the London auctioneers. Because of her death, the sale was naturally postponed.

Nijinsky's sister, Bronislava, whom I came to love and admire at the end of her life, told me she thought she could spot which parts of the published 'Diary' were by her brother and which were faked. I had not been able to print this during Romola's lifetime. As I could not go to London at the time I asked Christie's to send me an English translation of the original manuscript, so that I could, if necessary, emend passages in my Diaghilev book. Although Markevitch, as executor, gave me a letter of authority, the auctioneers were unco-operative. Markevitch subsequently transferred the Diaries to Sotheby's, who sold them on 24 July 1979 for £45,000. I have still not seen them. It appears that Romola suppressed a great deal.

Bronislava told me that Romola had written her life of Nijinsky in the 1930s with the intention of having it made into a film. She hoped to earn a lot of money. Who can blame her? She had to look after her sick husband. But her lurid portrait of Diaghilev and much of her sensational story were intended to satisfy the demands of the film industry. How strange that, in spite of her talent, drive and will-power, and although she sold the rights to more than one studio, the longed-for film was never made in her lifetime. Yet perhaps it was not so strange, for if a film had been made it would have had to satisfy so many of the exigent Romola's requirements; and if anyone had dared to make the film without her approval she would have been hell-bent on litigation. Going to law was her favourite amusement.

At the end of Nijinsky's life, Romola put about the story that he was cured and fit for work again. This was because she wanted a permit for him to enter the United States, a country which does not admit the mentally sick. Nijinsky may have become calmer, but he was neither normal nor intelligent. The selfless and devoted Margaret Power, who died in October 1977, told me that during all the time she visited Nijinsky and helped to care for him, in Vienna, at Schloss Mittersill, and in England – although Vaslav was fond of her, and although she loved him – he never once spoke a word to her. They used to play pointless ping-pong together, and Vaslav liked to pile up things, then knock them down. Margaret bought him some hollow coloured bricks. He also liked throwing things about and would not always stop. It was Margaret (as I have related) who had to identify Nijinsky's body when Lifar had it dug up, and it was she who travelled with it to Paris, watching faithfully by the coffin. She found that when she arrived at the Gare du Nord Lifar had made no arrangements to meet her; but he was much in evidence on the following day, posing and orating with ministers before the television cameras. Romola cabled from America promising to pay all Margaret's costs, and asking her to throw red roses into the grave (though in fact the coffin was never lowered in Margaret's presence). Margaret, as usual, obeyed instructions – at her own expense.

Flamboyant as she was – and, by the way, predominantly homosexual – Romola Nijinsky cared for her sick husband for many, many years. But the faithful, disinterested Margaret Power should not be forgotten.

CHAPTER ONE

1898–1908

August 1898–December 1908

On 20 August 1898, Eleonora Nicolaievna Nijinskaya, a pretty middle-aged Polish woman, took her nine-year-old younger son to the Imperial School of Ballet in Petersburg, hoping that he might be accepted as a pupil. Her elder son was simple-minded and she had a seven-year old daughter. Since her husband had left her, life was not easy; but if the State took over the maintenance of her boy, it would be easier. It was not only a question of bread, however: in her mind were thoughts of art and glory. She had been a fine dancer herself, but had left the stage to look after her family. Her husband Thomas, also a Pole, was a superb dancer, but he had never appeared in the Imperial Theatres of Moscow or Petersburg. He might have done if he had wanted to, even though not a graduate of the Imperial Schools, but he enjoyed a wandering life and made more money on the road.[1] Very little of this found its way to Eleonora.

Poles were slightly underprivileged subjects of the Russian Empire. The last Emperor but one, the liberal-minded Alexander II, who had emancipated the serfs in 1861, had been assassinated twenty years later by a Pole. The present Emperor was extremely conservative.

If the boy Vaslav became a pupil of the Imperial School he would have his foot on the lowest rung of the ladder of the Civil Service: he would be the equivalent of a junior officer cadet. After seven or eight years, if he graduated to the company of the Mariinsky Theatre, he would climb from *corps de ballet* to *coryphé*, from *coryphé* to second *soliste*, from second *soliste* to first *soliste*, from first *soliste* to *premier danseur*. As a leading dancer Vaslav could attain fame and fortune. In Russia the whole structure of society was a graded pyramid cul-

I

minating in the Tsar. If you were not a member of the Civil Service you were in limbo and outer darkness – you were nothing. Ninety per cent of the Tsar's subjects were nothing.

Teatralnaya Ulitsa (Theatre Street), to which mother and son had come, was built by the Italian architect, Rossi; it is one of the most beautiful streets in the world and certainly the most regular. Two identical blocks of buildings nearly two hundred yards long confront each other to form the street, which terminates at its northern end in the splendid pile of the Alexandrinsky Theatre (where drama is performed) and at the other in an open space on the quay of the Fontanka, one of the curving rivers and canals which bring an element of unruly romanticism to the regulated vistas of classical Petersburg, much as the Water of Leith does to the New Town of Edinburgh or, less obviously the old Indian trail of Broadway to the ordered canyons of Manhattan. The arcading of the ground floors of these 'terraces' is repeated above by taller arches which frame not only the big windows of the *piano nobile*, but the semi-circular windows of the second floor, linked by decorative plaster panels in relief; these upper arches being separated by pairs of engaged Doric columns supporting the double cornice. The monotony is imperceptibly broken by projecting bays four arches away from either end of the blocks, their first-floor windows having triangular pediments. Like most of the late eighteenth- and early nineteenth-century buildings in Petersburg, Rossi's blocks are painted a warm pinkish ochre, and against this consoling colour the white columns and decorations stand out. But this is not a street of ostentation, a parade, a *boulevard* or *corso*. Because the Alexandrinsky Theatre presents its *back* to it, blocking its end rather awkwardly, the visitor is aware of a monastic university atmosphere, as in the quadrangle of an Oxford college, or in Jefferson's serene enclosure at Charlottesville. This is a place of training and research. The left-hand building as you looked north housed the Ministry of Education: the right-hand, students of the theatre and ballet schools.

The mother and son paused at the arched entry of the Ballet School, and, no doubt, as I did when I followed in their historic footsteps a few years ago, inquired the way of a uniformed porter, to be directed diagonally half-left across a courtyard to a corner door.

Inside it, even then, was there a crone-like *concierge*, and were there plants and plaques on the wall at the foot of the marble stairs? Herds of fearful, expectant children, fathers and mothers were pouring in – between a hundred and a hundred and fifty boys[2] with one or both parents. From the crowded office at the top of the stairs they would be directed to the rehearsal room, where usually only the senior girls had their classes.

It was (and is) a cheerful big room, because through the tall windows which ran down both sides there were glimpses of trees. The floor had a ramp corresponding to that of the Mariinsky stage so that students could get used to dancing on a slight slope before they graduated to the Imperial company. The wall at the 'deep end' was covered with mirrors. As in all ballet class-rooms a *barre*, on which dancers must support themselves with one hand to perform their preliminary exercises, ran round the other three sides. There was a gallery all round the top, and there were portraits of the Emperor and of old ballerinas and celebrated teachers on the walls.[3]

The boys lined up to be inspected by the staff of teachers, doctors and ballet-masters, the chief of all being the eighty-three-year-old Swede, Christian Johannsen, who had been in his youth the pupil of the Danish choreographer, August Bournonville, who had been the pupil of the Franco-Italian Auguste Vestris, who had been taught by his father, Gaetano Vestris, who had studied under the Swiss-French Jean-Georges Noverre, who had given dancing-lessons during her youth in Vienna to Queen Marie Antoinette and collaborated later in Paris on the production of 'Iphigénie en Tauride' with Gluck.

Because of Thomas's fame the name of Nijinsky was not unknown to the examiners, but there was no question of admitting pupils on any consideration other than merit. Vaslav was backward at his lessons and a real mother's boy. Luckily, the teacher of the senior boys' class, Nicolas Legat, noticed him.[4] 'The first impression he produced on the examining commission was an unfavourable one, for he appeared awkward in manner and delicate in health. But at the doctor's examination I was struck by the formation of his thigh muscles . . . I told Nijinsky to move a few paces away and jump. His

3

leap was phenomenal. "That youngster can be made into a fine dancer," I said, and passed him without further ado.'

Happy mother and son! The gates of life were flung open. Although of fifteen boys chosen about ten were due to be eliminated at the end of the first two years' training, Eleonora had to have faith that her boy would prevail. Of the six boys eventually left in the 1898 class, five were destined to come to a tragic end – Iliodor Lukiano poisoned by his own hand at twenty-one, George Rosaï dead of pneumonia at twenty-one, Grigori Babitch killed by a jealous husband at twenty-three, Mikhail Feodorov dead of tuberculosis at twenty-six,[5] Nijinsky insane at thirty-one. Only Anatole Bourman would survive to write a bad book about his great schoolfellow for the bafflement of future biographers.

Eleonora was the daughter of a Warsaw cabinet-maker.[6]* She followed her elder sister into the ballet school of the Warsaw theatre and became a member of the company. There was no tradition of dancing either in her family or in that of her husband.† Thomas Nijinsky's father had fought as a patriot and guerrilla in the Polish insurrection of 1863 and lost his small property in consequence.[7] Thomas was handsome in the extreme. An outstanding dancer in both classical and character roles, he was also a gifted choreographer and had his own troupe of dancers. After their marriage, Thomas and Eleonora toured the length and breadth of Russia, and their three children, Stanislav, Vaslav and Bronislava, born within six years, toured with them. Vaslav was born in Kiev on 12 March, New Style (28 February, Old Style) 1888,[8] but not baptized until two years, four months later, in Warsaw in the Catholic faith, his mother post-dating his birth for reasons connected with military service. Not many children are christened four hundred miles from where they were born. Bronislava was baptized at the same time. There can have been few such travelled children in the whole of that immense land which divided the West from the East and stretched from the dark Arctic wastes to the sun-drenched vineyards of the Caspian Sea. We can imagine them, like a family of Picasso's acrobats of the 'blue period', alone in a cold and empty landscape, but, in fact, life was

*It is not true that he was of gentle birth or that he shot himself.
†The statement that Thomas came of a line of dancers is false.

4

more boisterous and colourful than that. The children watched their parents in Protean disguises from the wings of theatres and even sometimes appeared with them. Although their life was spent moving from one small-town cheap hotel to another, they saw, heard and smelt the landscape and the people of Russia. Such was the background of Vaslav and Bronislava, who were destined to produce to the music of Stravinsky two of the elemental Russian epics of our time, 'Le Sacre du printemps' and 'Les Noces'.

Perhaps Stanislav would have grown up to be a dancer and choreographer too, but one day in Warsaw, when he was six, he fell out of a window, struck his head on the pavement and became mentally retarded. Eleonora had an idea that this insanity might have been latent, because, shortly before he was born, the family had been attacked by bandits in a mountain village in the Caucasus and the shock to her had been so great that she had lost the power of speech for three days.[9] There was no tradition of madness on either side of the family. Thomas, however, was subject to fits of uncontrollable passion, during which he appeared to be out of his mind. These rages Vaslav inherited.[10]

From his father Vaslav also inherited his high cheekbones and slanting eyes, which, in spite of the Nijinskys' Polish nationality, would seem to be indications of Tartar blood. From Thomas too came the extraordinary jump. Not only Vaslav and Bronislava, but also their daughters, were to have both the jump and the Tartar face. From his mother Vaslav inherited his gentle affectionate nature. Eleonora was 'a genius of a mother'.[11]

Thomas was too attractive to be faithful to his wife. When his mistress Rumiantseva joined the troupe and Thomas started another family, Eleonora renounced the stage, took her children off and settled in Petersburg (but she and Thomas were never divorced).[12] It was also easier for her to have medical attention for Stanislav in the western capital. The boy was briefly apprenticed to a watchmaker, but could not concentrate on the work. His mother reconciled herself to the fact that he would never be able to earn a living. He got worse and was eventually confined in a State asylum. Eleonora and Bronislava used to visit him every Sunday. Vaslav feared to go.

Thomas Nijinsky came back to Petersburg to see his wife and

children at least once, when Vaslav was six or seven. Father and son went bathing on the Neva, and Thomas threw Vaslav into the water thinking that this would teach him to swim. Vaslav sank to the bottom, but managed to save himself by catching hold of a rope.[13]

The Nijinsky family moved into a flat in Mokhovaya Street, which ran north-south between the long Serguevskaya Street (parallel with and not far from the Neva) and the Simeonovsky Bridge over the Fontanka. They were little more than five minutes' walk from the delightful Summer Garden, planted by Peter the Great, in which the opening scene of Tchaikovsky's 'Queen of Spades' takes place. It was an aristocratic neighbourhood, but in Petersburg many princely façades conceal a hinterland of subsidiary courtyards and tenements. The Stieglitz Museum was nearby, and on wet days Eleonora took her children there or to the Alexander III Museum, or to see the Imperial treasures of the Hermitage, which adjoined Rastrelli's red Winter Palace.[14]

In the 1890s Russia consisted of a small nineteenth-century intelligentsia in a seventeenth-century population. The Greek-Orthodox religion was Byzantine, and so were the despotism of the Tsar and the ignorance of the people. But for a century thoughts of liberty had been budding, and these were not unconnected with a slow revolution in the world of art. It is significant that Pushkin, the father of Russian culture, whose poems and plays not only inspired the writers who came after him, but so many musicians who made them into operas and ballets, should have been exiled to the Caucasus for expressing his liberal ideas.

Between the accession in 1825 of Nicholas I, the oppressor of Pushkin, and the abdication in 1917 of Nicholas II, the opponent of Diaghilev, there took place a renaissance in the arts, which may be said to have reached its height in a series of performances staged not in Russia but in Paris and Western Europe during the last decade of the period, and of which Vaslav Nijinsky was the supreme ornament.

Between the death of Gogol in 1852 and the end of the century there appeared Turgenev's *Fathers and Sons*, Tolstoy's *War and Peace*, *Anna Karenina* and *The Kreutzer Sonata*, Dostoyevsky's *Crime and Punishment*, *The Idiot*, *The Devils* and *The Brothers*

Karamazov, and Chekhov's *The Seagull* and *Uncle Vanya*. During the same period Glinka would die; Balakirev would compose his songs and symphonies; Borodin 'Prince Igor'; Mussorgsky 'Boris Godounov' and 'Khovanshchina'; Rimsky-Korsakov nearly all his operas and symphonic poems and Tchaikovsky his complete works. In the 'eighties and 'nineties there was a reaction against the dominant school of painters known as Peredvijniki or Peripatetics,* whose academism had a pervasive moralistic and nationalist tone: the new wave of artists, less ready to suppress their personalities for a cause, inclined towards the doctrine of Art for Art's Sake, and were labelled Decadents. From the former group stood out the illustrious figure of Ilya Repine, a painter of real distinction, excelling in historical scenes, *genre* and portraiture, who turned gradually from academism and story-telling towards more Impressionist ideals. His pupil Valentin Serov, son of the composer of 'Judith' and other operas, formed a link between the Peredvijniki and the Decadents: in his work we can find something of Manet, Sargent and even Whistler. The landscapes of Isaak Levitan appear as a bridge between Constable and the Impressionists; he has been compared to Corot and Boudin. Two younger Moscow landscapists, Alexandre Golovine and Konstantin Korovine, were the first painters to be drawn to work for the theatre. Mikhail Vrubel, who, like the latter, used paint with a freedom approaching frenzy, was a completely original painter of Russian life, an expressionist before the word was invented. In the Western capital Alexandre Benois, who, with the Beardsley-influenced Leon Bakst, would play a leading role in the sphere of theatrical design, was a gentler minor talent, specializing in evocative landscapes and townscapes, particularly of Petersburg and its surrounding country palaces, and of Versailles. His friend Konstantin Somov also had a nostalgia for the past – he might be called the Russian Conder; while Nicolas Roerich's unrealistic images and archaeological dreams, coupled with the love of pure colour he had in common with both Somov and Bakst, may be seen as parallel to the symbolism of Gauguin.

At the Imperial Ballet School the school year, which was eight

* Because of their travelling exhibitions.

months long, began in September, on the day when the Imperial Theatres reopened after the four months' summer recess. For the first two years, until it was decided which children should be accepted as permanent members of the Imperial School, they lived at home. Vaslav walked to school and back: it took him twenty minutes.[15]

The new day-boys were only issued with caps: these were like an officer cadet's, with patent leather peaks and the Imperial eagle in silver. They must have looked with envy at their seniors and determined to work hard in order to earn the full uniform. The boarders had three uniforms: a black one for every day, a dark blue for holidays and a grey linen for the summer. The tunics were embroidered on either side of the military collar with silver lyres framed in palms and surmounted by a crown. The two overcoats, one for winter with an astrakhan collar, the other for summer, were also of military cut, double-breasted, ankle-length and with silver buttons. There were boots, shoes and six changes of underwear. When Vaslav had earned this wardrobe he would really see himself as a person of consequence.

For ballet classes the boys wore white shirts and black trousers. Vaslav was not entirely a beginner: he had already learnt from his parents the five positions of classical ballet and a few basic steps.[16] From the start it was clear to his companions that this Pole had stolen a march on them. His happiest hours were during the morning class, for all children enjoy best what they do best, and he was behind the others in the afternoon lessons of French, History and Mathematics. Day-boys brought their lunch with them, but Vaslav did not look forward to lunch-time and recreation time because he was treated as an outcast by the other boys. He was despised for being Polish, silent, bad at expressing himself and apparently slow-witted; and he was laughed at for his Tartar or Mongolian features and nicknamed 'Japonczek' – the little Japanese. Vaslav did not submit to his classmates' bullying in silence. He was always quick to defend himself, had many fights and punched many noses. His marks for behaviour were invariably very low. When there was any trouble Rosaï, Bourman, Babitch and the others always tried to put the blame on Vaslav, and as he never told tales he was often punished. Throughout his eight years at school he never made a friend.[17]

His masters, however, were aware of his potentialities. He was quickly promoted from the class of the good-looking, amusing and popular Sergei Legat to that of his elder brother Nicolas, who had spotted Vaslav's jump at the entrance examination.[18] Legat used to have all the windows in the classroom open until a minute before the lesson began. The boys lined up along the *barre* and their teacher accompanied them on his violin. 'In ten minutes,' wrote Bourman,* 'our blood tingled! We had to work to keep warm – and we worked until the heat from our bodies created an aura of steam around us while our breath made us look as though we held white plumes between our teeth. I have often remembered how cold it was, and thought of Legat, unable to exercise as we did, patiently teaching us, now shouting excited orders at us, now counting sharply to emphasize the tempo that he set by plucking the strings of his violin. Always happy and smiling, he made his lessons a joy, and loved us both as a friend and a teacher.'[19]

The Legat brothers were, after Pavel Gerdt, the principal male dancers at the Mariinsky. They were clever caricaturists and had published an album of water-colours of their fellow artists which amazed Petersburg. For classes in mime the boys went to Gerdt. This famous man had been a *premier danseur* for thirty-two years: he was equally renowned for his classical dancing, his partnering and his mime, and had played Prince Désiré in the original 'Sleeping Beauty', or rather 'La Belle au bois dormant', eight years before. Its composer, Tchaikosvky, was dead, but its choreographer, Marius Petipa, still reigned supreme over the ballet of the Mariinsky Theatre, for which he had staged over sixty ballets by himself and

---

*I must explain my policy with regard to Anatole Bourman's book *The Tragedy of Nijinsky* which came out three years after Romola Nijinsky's successful life of her husband. People who write books usually do it because they need money, so we must not judge Bourman too severely for allowing his collaborator, Miss D. Lyman, to work up his reminiscences into as sensational a tale as possible. It was necessary for her purpose to present Bourman as a much closer friend of Nijinsky's than he was, and to make him the eye-witness of all the crucial events in Nijinsky's life. The dancer's most recent (1957) biographer, Mme Françoise Reiss, accepted Bourman's story as the truth, and was thus able to enliven her narrative with some lurid anecdotes. I have Mme Bronislava Nijinska's assurance that a number of episodes are pure invention. Yet Bourman could not help telling the truth sometimes. I have had to use my discernment and have been readier in crediting unsensational details of school life, which it would have been hard for Miss Lyman to invent, than any other parts of the book.

others since his arrival in Petersburg from France over half a century ago.

The boys' classrooms and the boarders' dormitories were on the top floor. The girls lived and worked down below, secluded as nuns, under the strict eye of their headmistress, Varvara Ivanovna Lihosherstova. Boys and girls were not allowed to speak to each other even when they joined in lessons of ballroom dancing and were waltzing together.

During the last few years a kind of revolution had been taking place in Russian ballet dancing.[20] The Petersburg school had always prided itself on its style and artistry – the Moscow artists went in more for bravura and dramatic effect: then, during the eighties and nineties a series of Italian guest-artists at the Mariinsky had dazzled Petersburg with their strength and acrobatic feats. Prominent among these were Enrico Cecchetti, who had been the original Bluebird in 'The Sleeping Beauty', Carlotta Brianza, who had been Aurora, and Pierina Legnani, whose thirty-two *fouettés* – a step with which a female dancer whips herself into spinning like a top, rising and falling on the toes of one foot which remains on the same spot throughout – had taken the town by storm. All the Russian dancers became eager to learn the Italian tricks, and the day when the celebrated Matilda Kchessinskaya, who had been the Tsar's mistress before his marriage, and was the favourite of several Grand Dukes, accomplished this *tour de force*, was the occasion for patriotic rejoicing. In 1898 the school had engaged Cecchetti to hold a 'parallel class of perfection' for the dancers of the company in addition to – or as an alternative to – Johannsen's class. The marriage of Italian strength and Russian style was to be the special glory of the rising generation of dancers: and of these Nijinsky would be the brightest star.

For two years Vaslav walked to school every morning and home every evening. If he liked he could walk by the Fontanka river almost the whole way. Down Mokhovaya, sharp right, and he was by the Simeonovsky Bridge. He could either follow the curve of the river to the right, passing the Anichkov Bridge by the Anichkov Palace where the Dowager Empress lived, and on to the Chernishev Bridge, which was just at the bottom of Theatre Street; or when he came to the

Anichkov Bridge with its bronze horse-tamers, he could turn right up the endless Nevsky Prospekt and then left through the gardens in front of the Alexandrinsky Theatre, past Mikeshin's statue of Catherine the Great. This was a little shorter. But if, pausing at the bottom of Mokhovaya before crossing the road towards the river, he happened to glance left, he would have seen on the corner of Simeonovskaya and the Liteiny Prospekt a building in which was living the man who would guide him to his future triumphs. In the top-floor flat Diaghilev, with his friends Benois, Bakst and Nouvel, all Nijinsky's future collaborators, were planning their magazine *Mir Iskustva*, 'The World of Art'.

Born in the Selistchev Barracks in the province of Novgorod in 1872, Sergei Pavlovitch Diaghilev lost his mother a few days after his birth; but his father, an officer in the Imperial Guard, took as his second wife a kind and cultivated woman, Elena Panaeva, and Diaghilev's childhood in Petersburg and later in Perm was spent in a lively and music-loving circle of step-brothers and cousins. Although by 1898 he had assumed the leadership of the group of friends who were going to play so historic a role, the man around whom they had all first collected was Alexandre Nicolaievitch Benois, who was two years older.

Benois was one of those Russians without a drop of Russian blood. On his father's side French and German, on his mother's Venetian, he was to prove the ideal interpreter in paint and words of Peter's west-looking capital, and the chronicler of its treasures. His father and maternal grandfather were both architects and had collaborated on the building of the Mariinsky Theatre. Benois was a gentle, studious, amusing man, devoted to all forms of art and applied art. In 1898 he had been married for four years and had known Diaghilev for eight. He describes his first meeting with the latter:

It was at the beginning of the summer of 1890 that I met Diaghilev; I was twenty and he was eighteen. He had just left school at Perm and was in St Petersburg to matriculate at the University at the same time as his cousin, Dima Filosofov, Valetchka Nouvel and myself. We three had also just finished our studies at the K. May school. Dima had already left for the country; but before going he had asked Nouvel and myself to look after his cousin, who was to be in St Petersburg for a few days on his way to the Filosofovs' country house. We plunged into intimacy at this first meeting, and before the end of the evening were calling each other 'thou'. What chiefly struck Nouvel and me about the newcomer was his air of well-being, his full face, fresh complexion and the big mouth which revealed, when he smiled, teeth of a dazzling whiteness. Dima's cousin was smiling all the time, and as often as not his smile would herald a burst of loud, infectious laughter. In sum, Serge struck us as being a good fellow, though a bit simple and provincial: and if we received him on intimate terms from the very beginning it was only because he was a close relation of the Filosofov family. How amazed we should have been to know that we had just welcomed the one who was to become in so few years captain of our team, the man who would help us to realize all our dreams in the varied fields of art! For we all dreamed of nothing less than striving to bring about a renaissance of art in Russia!

Serge Diaghilev, then, was admitted to our circle, but he only really became one of us by gradual stages. We were all rather sedate young men, real mothers' boys, keen on attending lectures, mad about the theatre: we seemed older than we were. Dima's cousin, on the other hand, was a little childish and showed a certain tendency to violent action: he never stopped hitting us, for instance, and would even challenge us to fight – an offer we should never have dreamt of accepting . . . Anyway, we knew we stood no chance against 'big Serge', who was so much stronger than we were.

Diaghilev's real nature was that of a fighter. So that as all traces of his youthful naïveté vanished and our friendship grew deeper, a kind of struggle became manifest in our relations. In the early years of our friendship I was Serge's chief mentor; and the avidity with which he pounced on whatever information struck him as valuable delighted me and flattered my pedagogic instinct. Even then, however, his attitude would often change with the greatest ease from that of a peaceable and submissive disciple to one of pugnacity, in which he took pleasure in landing well-directed and demoralizing blows. The pupil would suddenly grow arrogant and his studious apprenticeship turn to cynical exploitation. Quarrels would follow which often seemed final. I sometimes wrote him indignant letters, only to receive vague excuses in reply. But all would end in a touching reconciliation and tears from Serge – for, besides being a fighter, and essentially a man of action, Diaghilev was sentimental, and quarrels with his friends upset him greatly.

It was music first of all that brought us together. Without being professionals or virtuosos, we were all passionate lovers of music; but Serge

dreamed of devoting himself entirely to the art. All the time he was studying law along with us, he took singing lessons with Cotogni, the famous
baritone of the Italian Opera; while for musical theory, which he wanted
to master completely so as to rival Moussorgsky and Tchaikovsky, he
went to the very source and studied with Rimsky-Korsakov. However,
our musical tastes were not always the same. The quality our group
valued most was what the Germans call *Stimmung*, and besides this, the
power of suggestion and dramatic force. The Bach of the Passions, Gluck,
Schubert, Wagner and the Russian composers – Borodin in 'Prince Igor',
Rimsky and, above all, Tchaikovsky, were our gods. Tchaikovsky's
'Queen of Spades' had just been performed for the first time at the Opera
of St Petersburg, and we were ecstatic about its Hoffmannesque element,
notably the scene in the old Countess's bedroom. We liked the composer's
famous Romances much less, finding them insipid and sometimes trivial.
These Romances, however, were just what Diaghilev liked. What he
valued most was broad melody, and in particular whatever gave a singer
the chance to display the sensuous qualities of his voice. During the years
of his apprenticeship he bore our criticisms and jokes with resignation, but
as he learned more about music – and about the history of art in general –
he gained in self-confidence and found reasons to justify his predilections.
There came a time when not only did he dare to withstand our attacks but
went on to refute our arguments fiercely.

His attitude towards the plastic arts was quite different. He had no
creative ambitions in the direction of painting, sculpture or architecture,
not having tried his hand at any of them, so he contented himself with the
role of dilettante; and the opinions of those people he acknowledged as
authorities (particularly Bakst, Serov and myself) were accepted as Gospel
truth. Yet even over these matters Diaghilev managed to surprise us, for
he would leap from indifference to enthusiasm, from total ignorance to
unusual expertise. It was in this way that we saw him become in the course
of a few months the historian of Russian eighteenth-century art, untiring
in his researches in the State archives and museums, as well as in private
collections, working with the zest he put into any task he took to heart.

One could certainly call Diaghilev a creative genius, although it is not
easy to analyse the nature of his creative gift. He practised neither painting
not sculpture, nor was he a professional writer; for his few critical essays,
remarkable as they were as proofs of his taste and judgement, did not
amount to much – and anyway Serge hated the business of writing. He
even lost faith before long in any vocation he may have felt for music,
which was his real speciality. In no branch of art did he become an execu-

tant or a creator: and yet one cannot deny that his whole activity was *creative*. It is impossible to believe that the painters, musicians and choreographers who gave birth to the movement known as *Mir Iskustva*, 'The World of Art', from the paper we published, would have worked to such good effect had not Diaghilev placed himself at their head and taken command of them. There was one thing lacking in the artists of that generation who have since become world-famous; they lacked the spirit to fight and impose themselves. This spirit Diaghilev possessed in the highest degree, so that we can say he too had his unique speciality, namely *will-power* ... This powerful manipulator of men obliged creative artists to become the obedient executants of their own ideas under his despotic sway.[21]

Benois's meeting, at the house of his brother Albert, with Leon Bakst, whose real name was Rosenberg, dates from a few months earlier:

On entering Albert's upstairs studio one day in March 1890 I came upon a young man I did not know. Albert introduced his new acquaintance to me as a gifted artist; I took but little notice of this as it was Albert's usual way of introducing any painter. Mr Rosenberg's exterior was in no way remarkable. The rather regular features were spoilt by his short-sighted eyes, his bright red hair and a thin moustache which straggled over his curved lips. His shy and at the same time ingratiating manner seemed to me, if not off-putting, at least unpleasing. Mr Rosenberg smiled very often and laughed too much. It was clear that he was most happy at having been received in the house of such a famous painter as my brother was at that time ...

Our friendly feelings for Levushka Rosenberg were mixed with some pity. He told Valetchka Nouvel and me how hard his life was. He had been left without any means of subsistence after the sudden death of his father, a well-to-do man (a stockbroker, I believe) who had only had time to provide his children with a good elementary education. Levushka had been obliged to find the means to keep not only himself but also his mother, his grandmother, two sisters and a very young brother. Moreover he did not want to leave the Academy of Arts, which he attended as an external student. His work at the Academy took up much of his time and he lacked the means to buy the materials necessary for his artistic work.[22]

Other members of the group of friends – and these had all been at school with Benois – were the painter Konstantin Somov, Walter Nouvel, whose speciality among the arts was music, and Diaghilev's cousin, Dmitri Filosofov, whose interests were more abstract and metaphysical. Diaghilev, Filosofov and Nouvel were homosexual.

The first two had been on grand tours of Western Europe together. Diaghilev had made a point of meeting celebrated painters such as Lenbach and Liebermann, of hearing Wagner's operas, of seeing the treasures of Florence and Venice, and of buying pictures and antique furniture. He dreamed of founding a museum: at least for the meanwhile he intended to live in style.

The brotherhood called each other by their diminutive or *petits noms*: Serioja for Sergei, Levushka for Leon, Shoura for Alexandre, Dima for Dmitri, Valetchka for Walter, Kostia for Konstantin.

In 1898–9, with the backing of Sava Mamontov, the Moscow millionaire and patron of the Moscow Arts Theatre, and Princess Tenisheva, a collector of pictures on a large scale, Diaghilev and his friends founded the periodical *Mir Iskustva*. This was something entirely new in Russia. Possibly inspired by *The Yellow Book* and *The Savoy*, it was luxuriously produced with half-tone blocks on art paper and decorations in line in the text, but it differed from the English publications (a link with which was provided by an article commissioned from D. S. McColl on Aubrey Beardsley) in that it published no poetry or fiction. It was a mouthpiece for the group of friends through which they would voice their views on ancient and modern Russian art and architecture, foreign art, music, literature, philosophy and the theatre. Not that their views always coincided. Benois, who was in Paris when the first number was produced, was horrified by the importance Diaghilev gave to the neo-archaistic architect and ikon painter Vaznetzov. As the years went on – and although the first backers withdrew after a year and had to be replaced, publication continued until 1904 – the slightly mystical influence of Filosofov on Diaghilev was gradually replaced by that of the more 'visual' Benois. The music section was run by Alfred Nourok and was serious rather than brilliant – among articles of interest were those by Grieg on Mozart and by Nietzsche on Wagner at Bayreuth. *Mir Iskustva* stirred up many controversies and earned the friends the epithet of 'decadent'. Repine, for instance, broke with them completely, but this did not prevent Diaghilev devoting a number to his work some months later. By and large, every Russian critic of note contributed to the periodical and the work of every important Russian painter was reproduced in it. The *Mir*

Iskustva group also arranged exhibitions of Russian, Finnish, German and English paintings at various museums in Petersburg between 1899 and 1901.

The editorial office of the *World of Art* was Sergei Diaghilev's apartment on the top floor of a big house at the corner of the Liteiny Prospekt and the Simeonevskaya Street ... The place of honour was occupied by three portraits by Lenbach (obtained in 1895), two drawings by Menzel, some water-colours by Hans Herrman and Bartels, a pastel portrait by Puvis de Chavannes and several sketches by Dagnan-Bouveret.

The Jacobean chairs stood ... in Serioja's dining-room. The drawing-room, which served our editor as study, contained, besides the Blüthner piano, several heavy, gilded, velvet-covered armchairs, a large velvet ottoman and some small antique Italian cupboards on which stood an excellent copy of Donatello's bust of Niccolò da Uzzano, several casts of Pompeian bronzes and numerous photographs of artists, authors and musicians, all autographed for Diaghilev. Here stood in close proximity Gounod and Zola, Menzel and Massenet. These were the trophies of 1895 when the young Diaghilev had found it necessary to convey his respects to a number of celebrities ...

A handsome, large, black, sixteenth-century table served as the 'editor's desk'. It had been brought by Serioja from Italy, and was said to have aroused the envy of Wilhelm von Bode himself. Serioja sat at the head in a very imposing armchair upholstered in old velvet. In front of him lay writing materials and among them a pot of glue and a large pair of scissors which served as a favourite distraction for him – Diaghilev was passionately fond of cutting out photographs from which reproductions were made in the review ... The rooms overlooking the yard were dull and dark and really rather resembled one's idea of a business office. Here were heaps of papers, kept in order by poor Dima Filosofov, who had voluntarily taken upon himself the ungrateful jobs of being simultaneously office manager, chief of staff, tutor and general secretary who had to receive all visitors. The large packages of reproductions sent from abroad were unpacked in these back rooms, where it was again Filosofov who sorted and numbered them before putting them away in the cupboards. It was here also that our other martyr – the next victim of Serioja's despotism – Levushka Bakst spent whole days in inventing elegant titles for the drawings and retouching the photographs, in an attempt to give them a more artistic character. Sometimes the good-natured, easy-going Levushka would have sudden fits of rebellion and indignation, but more often he willingly – and, oh, how artistically! – spent his time manipulating Indian ink and Paris white.

This work also helped him to earn something, for he was still in rather difficult circumstances.

The meetings of the editorial staff invariably took place in the dining-room, but they were entirely unlike those of other papers. The mere fact that they took place during tea-time, to the accompaniment of the hissing samovar, gave them a very homely unofficial character. Serioja's old nurse, who had taken the place of his mother during the first years of his life and was sincerely and tenderly loved by him, usually poured out tea. It was the custom for each of us to approach her and shake hands; I myself usually kissed her, for I had a real feeling of love for this venerable old woman with her faded and somewhat sorrowful face. His love for her did not prevent Serioja from treating her in the 'traditional rather masterly way'. Without, however, really hurting her feelings, he used to scold and shout at her in fun; this she easily forgave, indeed, she was ready to forgive her favourite far graver pranks than those. How delighted the old woman would be when her former charge would suddenly begin hugging and pulling her about during one of his teasing moods. The nanny never took part in our conversation, and she probably couldn't make out what these noisy young people were up to, who disputed ceaselessly and sometimes laughed so unrestrainedly. What could she, an illiterate peasant woman understand about painting, music, religion, philosophy or aesthetics? Nevertheless, it was clear that in her own way she really enjoyed being with us. She enjoyed seeing that Serioja had so many friends and she probably felt that he was gradually becoming a person of importance, almost as important as his papa, the General Diaghilev. Tea was always served with *krendeli* and *soushki** and lemon cut in rounds. On the very rare occasions that Diaghilev entertained ladies, sandwiches of minced salt beef – *spécialité de la maison* – would be added to the usual fare, but nothing else was considered necessary. Diaghilev seldom took his meals at home and never invited his friends to lunch or dinner. If he found it necessary to entertain anyone, he invited them to a restaurant, for in St Petersburg's French restaurants one could eat and drink exceedingly well.

Besides the old nanny, there was yet another figure who was a characteristic part of Diaghilev's household, his manservant Vassili Zhuikov ... Vassili's appearance was not as picturesque as nanny's. He was small, and had an ordinary but rather clever face, to which a black moustache gave a rather military air not quite proper in a servant. Yet Vassili was what one might call the *perfect* servant; not that he was servile towards his master or

Krendeli: biscuits in a figure-of-eight shape; *soushki*: biscuits, shaped in rings, and made of a different dough, strung on a stick.

other people in general; on the contrary, Vassili was very independent in his attitude and even, at times, verged on impertinence. Vassili's 'professional' talent expressed itself in unlimited devotion to his master, a capacity that Diaghilev perceived at once, for he possessed a wonderful gift of detecting all kinds of talent. He immediately understood that Vassili was just the servant he needed, although from the purely decorative point of view he was not quite the thing.[23]

In 1899 a friend of Diaghilev's, the charming and cultivated Prince Sergei Volkonsky, was appointed Director of the Imperial Theatres, and at once set about employing the group of friends. Diaghilev became a junior assistant to the Director. Filosofov was appointed to the Repertory Committee at the Alexandrinsky. Benois was to design a production of Taneev's opera 'Cupid's Revenge' at the Hermitage Theatre; Bakst was given a French play *Le Cœur de la Marquise;* Somov designed programmes. Diaghilev's first task was to edit the year-book of the Imperial Theatres; and in 1900 this usually dull and colourless publication was transformed into a magnificent volume with articles on the work of the late Director Vsevolojsky, on the eighteenth-century designer Gonzago and on the architecture of the Alexandrinsky Theatre. Even the Tsar approved.

The friends, however, had bigger ideas than this. They planned a new production of Delibes's 'Sylvia', with Benois supervising and designing the first act, Korovine the second and Benois's nephew Eugene Lanceray the third. Bakst was to design the costumes except for one which would be by Serov. Preobrajenskaya and the Legat brothers would dance the principal parts.[24]

The Mariinsky Theatre was over a mile from the school, but from the beginning of their eight years of study the ballet students took part in performances of ballet or opera there, swelling a crowd or standing in the background to lend perspective, so that the theatre was part of their lives. They were conveyed to and from it by horse-drawn vehicles known as Noah's Arks. Ballet performances were on Wednesdays and Sundays – the latter being the *chic* night – and rehearsals for them usually on Fridays. Climbing to their dressing-room on the fifth floor, the boys were dressed and made-up, to emerge on the vast stage in its blazing lights to face the blue and silver auditorium filled with the Court and Society. On this stage their friendly teachers, Gerdt, Nicolas and Sergei Legat, were transformed into princes and heroes, and there they beheld them partnering the fabled ballerinas and sharing their acclamations.

In December 1900 Pavel Gerdt had a benefit night, dancing with Kchessinskaya in Petipa's 'Bayadère'. In January 1901 Legnani gave her farewell performance and was, with one exception, the last of the Italian guest-artists to appear in Petersburg. In February there was a scandal, but it is unlikely that any word of it reached the ears of the second-year students.

Volkonsky had got into trouble over the production of 'Sylvia' with his heads of departments, who told him that he should not entrust the supervision of such a large-scale work to a junior colleague. Trying to please everybody, the unfortunate director asked Diaghilev to share the honours of the show with the senior officials, but promised that this would only be a matter of form and that artistically everything would go on just as before. Diaghilev was headstrong and refused. He thought he could force Volkonsky's hand, and threatened to discontinue editing the Annual of the Imperial Theatres. The mild prince suddenly lost his temper and ordered Diaghilev to continue his editorial duties. Diaghilev rushed back to his flat, where the friends were working on their 'Sylvia' sketches, and broke the news. Consternation set in. Korovine, the Moscow artist attached to the Imperial Theatres, became scared of losing his job, and Serov, older and wiser than the others, grew silent, evidently disapproving of Diaghilev's intransigence; but Filosofov and Benois wrote letters of protest to the director. Diaghilev wrote confirming his refusal to edit the Annual.

Volkonsky did all he could to heal the breach, even coming round to Diaghilev's flat with his Moscow colleague Teliakovsky and spending two hours discussing the matter with the friends. But Diaghilev was adamant. One reason for his attitude was that the Grand Duke Sergei Mikhailovitch, Kchessinskaya's lover, was backing him up. Both the Grand Duke and the ballerina hated Volkonsky. That day the Grand Duke took the train to Tsarskoe Selo to put in a word with the Emperor. The following day, however, the Tsar signed the order for Diaghilev's dismissal. Two days later Diaghilev opened the *Government Gazette*, hoping to find Volkonsky had resigned, only to read that he himself had been dismissed 'under Article 3' which only applied to rare cases of disgraceful behaviour. This was a shattering blow. His hopes of guiding the destiny of the Russian theatre vanished into air. The consequences to the world outside Russia would be great. [25]

There was a sequel. In April Kchessinskaya was to dance for the first time the role of La Camargo in Petipa's ballet of that name to the music of Minkus, taken over from the departed Legnani, and, as she was so small, did not want to wear the eighteenth-century hooped skirt which was appropriate to the role. When, against orders she appeared in a short *tutu*, she was fined a small sum, which was the normal consequence of any breach of regulations. The announcement of her fine, pinned on the call-board, was too much for the powerful lady. She appealed through the Grand Duke to the Tsar. The fine was remitted. Volkonsky resigned in July.[26]

That spring there had been a State visit from the French President, and Kchessinskaya danced 'Le Lac des Cygnes' in a theatre in the park of Tsarskoe Selo. The evening was later described by a girl pupil who took part in it just before her graduation:

> The gala performance took place in the Chinese theatre of Tsarskoe Selo, which stood in the Chinese Village, a graceful whim of Catherine the Great. Built in 1778, the theatre was kept in good repair. It stood among ancient pagoda-like fir trees. Inside, it was of rare charm – lacquer panels ornamenting the boxes, red and gold rococo chairs, bronze chandeliers with porcelain flowers – all the precious *chinoiseries* of the eighteenth century. All through the evening there was no applause. The bejewelled audience remained mute, passive as a *tableau vivant* in the light of innumerable candles. The Imperial Family and the Court were present. Every artist afterwards received a present from the Emperor, as was always the case with Imperial performances.[27]

The observant girl was destined in a few years' time to be Nijinsky's partner, and like him one of the glories of the age. Tamara Platonovna Karsavina, the daughter of a dancer and of a lady of gentle birth descended from Byzantine Emperors, was to develop many wonderful qualities seldom united in one woman, for besides being beautiful, she was also intelligent and good. She had an ivory pallor and huge dark eyes, and she had a sense of humour. Within the next few weeks she passed her examinations and made her début at the Mariinsky before it closed for the summer recess in a *pas de deux* danced with Michel Fokine, called 'Le Pêcheur et la perle'.

Fokine was five years older than Karsavina, handsome and intellectual and with a searching mind, already dissatisfied with the traditional artificialities of the classical ballet and dreaming of new forms. He and Karsavina fell in love. She herself described him thus:

Michel Fokine began his career on the stage of the Mariinsky Theatre in 1898. For some years before his graduation he was fondly watched by the elder members of the profession – a remarkable dancer in the making. Prodigious leap, virile execution, most expressive arms, the head of a young Byron.

The inflammable hearts of the girl pupils as well were all a-flutter. Many a bad mark for behaviour did we catch for sneaking into a forbidden passage that bridged our quarters with the artists' studio, to peep at him practising. And the amount of fond names we bestowed on him! When my master told me Fokine consented to partner me at my début I could hardly believe my luck. Four years of seniority meant a lot in our hierarchy. So, during my first year on the stage, I felt flattered when he used to settle by my side with his tea in the lunch interval. Munching sandwiches, we talked of art – or rather, he talked and I listened, enchanted and a little frightened by his daring views. He would see me home, carrying my bag for me – miles out to a distant part of the town. We thought the walk was too short. We spoke of art – mostly ... On the way, he sometimes took me to a museum to show me his favourite pictures: at that time he studied painting and music. Storms – and how frequent! – interrupted our brief idyll. Impetuous by nature, he had in his youth a strain of fanatical intolerance.[28]

During the autumn and winter of 1901 Carlotta Zambelli, the Milanese star of the Paris Opéra, came to give several performances of 'Coppélia', 'Giselle' and 'Pakhita' at the Mariinsky. There were complaints that at the end of the first ballet she only did eight *fouettés en attitude* and only on *demi-pointe* instead of on the tips of her toes, and she was conscious of an adverse clique among the balletomanes and the 'court' of Kchessinskaya, but she earned praise from the critic Svetlov for her lightness, elevation and elegance. She studied the role of Giselle under Cecchetti, but was surprised to find it was the custom in Russia for each ballerina to insert a brilliant variation of her own choice from a different ballet and with music by a different composer. Petipa, the old expatriate, came to watch her practise, sitting with a rug over his knees, and saying 'Well, show me how they dance in Paris.' Old Johannsen in an interview in the *Petersburg Gazette* compared her unfavourably with Taglioni. But to be compared with Taglioni at all must have been rather flattering, one would think. Zambelli was offered a large salary to return in the following season, but refused; and she was the last of the foreign guest-artists.[29]*

Nijinsky was transferred in about 1902, a year or more after he was accepted as a boarder, to the class of Mikhail Obukhov, who was to watch so proudly over his development, while doing what he could to protect him from the jealousy and cruelty of the other boys. Bourman wrote:

Obukhov was also extremely outspoken, remaining a firm disbeliever in praise during the years we spent with him. I never heard him grow enthusiastic. 'Pretty good!' was the acme of approval from his lips. His marking betrayed the same tendency. Twelve was the maximum to be acquired, but Obukhov never gave more than an eight or a nine, except to Vaslav, who was once honoured by an eleven, though even he failed to achieve a twelve. 'Why should I mark any of you with a twelve?' the master would fume. 'Perhaps there is some school in the world better than this, and some dancer who may deserve the highest mark. Here none are perfect!' Nevertheless, he recognized Nijinsky's genius with the highest grade he ever gave and he perceived Nijinsky's need with far more penetration than his mark indicated.[30]

At the beginning of 1902 Gorsky's version of 'Don Quichotte' was given at the Mariinsky, which was the first sign of the new director, Teliakovsky's, reaction against the reign of Petipa. In this Karsavina had the small part of a Cupid. Although the designer of this spectacle was Korovine, a contributor to *Mir Iskustva* and a friend of Benois, the latter wrote a harsh review of it in the magazine, which now set about attacking Teliakosvky and all his works.

There had been rumours that the Moscow production of the old ballet 'Don Quichotte' was a masterpiece, and that its producer, the ballet-

*Kchessinskaya in her memoirs omits to mention Zambelli's visit, and writes that Legnani, who retired in January 1901, was the last guest-artist from abroad.

master Gorsky, had revealed new horizons. This proved to be untrue. Gorsky's new vision was vitiated by the abhorrent lack of organization that is typical of amateur performances. His 'novelties' consisted of making the crowds on the stage bustle and move about fitfully and aimlessly. As regards the action, the dramatic possibilities and the dancers themselves were depressed to a uniformly commonplace level. 'Don Quichotte' had never been an adornment to the Imperial Stage; now it had become something unworthy of it and almost disreputable.[31]

In spite of the declared editorial policy of Diaghilev and the presumed acquiescence to it of his collaborators Benois and Bakst, the latter did not refuse employment by the director of the Imperial Theatres. Benois accepted to design 'Die Götterdämmerung' and Bakst did not withdraw his collaboration in two Greek plays *Hippolytus* and *Oedipus* for the Alexandrinsky Theatre, or in a small ballet called 'Die Puppenfee' or 'The Fairy Doll' for a Court performance at the Hermitage.

By inviting them Teliakovsky indicated that he was in sympathy with their outlook, though determined not to be run by their domineering colleague and editor. Diaghilev was most indignant at their 'treachery'; and his branding of them in his mind as traitors – though he remained determined to get the best work out of them he could – may have been the cause of his frequently high-handed treatment of them in later years. Not that he was not ruthless by nature when artistic questions were at stake. In 1901 Diaghilev moved to a flat at 11 Fontanka, next to the house of Countess Panina and opposite that of Count Sheremetev; and the headquarters of *Mir Iskustva* moved with him.[32]

Matilda Kchessinskaya, who, after the Tsar's marriage, had been, as we have seen, the friend of the Grand Duke Sergei Mikhailovitch, had met, shortly after her tenth anniversary gala in 1900, his first cousin once removed, the ten-year-younger Grand Duke Andrei Vladimirovitch. After an Italian journey with him in the autumn of 1901, she found she was pregnant. In January 1902 she danced in Gorsky's 'Don Quichotte' at the Mariinsky and in February she appeared at the little Hermitage Theatre in 'Les Élèves de Monsieur Dupré', trying not to show herself in profile lest it become too obvious to her ex-lover, the Tsar, who was sitting very close to her

23

in the front row, that she was pregnant by one or the other of his cousins.[33]

The Hermitage Theatre was approached from the picture gallery by a bridge, inside which there was a long ante-room in the Chinese rococo style designed by Quarenghi. Its windows along both sides looked down on the little canal connecting the Neva and the Moika, into which Lisa threw herself in Tchaikovsky's 'Queen of Spades'.* The theatre itself was semi-circular, classical and exquisitely pretty, with pink marbled columns against white walls. Intimate as it was, and used only for performances before the Imperial Family and the Court, the stage was spacious and deep, and at the back of it was a wide sloping road up which elaborate machinery could be dragged or companies of soldiers marched from the street below.† Karsavina gives a description of what the audience looked like from the stage on one of these special performances, which took place only two or three times a year and which, like the evenings at the Mariinsky, came to be a regular, if more exceptional, feature of Vaslav's life, making him feel part of the Imperial hierarchy.

It was the night of a fancy-dress ball, when the entire Court wore historical Russian dresses. That of the Empress Alexandra Feodorovna was the genuine saraphan of Tsaritza Miloslavskaya. Being on that night only one of the *corps de ballet*, where comparatively little concentration was required, I was entirely taken up with the splendour of all that I could see in front of me. I strained my eyes trying to distinguish figures in the semi-obscurity of the audience. Those three in front, the Tsar and both Tsaritzas one could see distinctly. The young Empress, in a heavy tiara, put on over a gauze kerchief entirely concealing her hair, looked like an ikon of rigid beauty; she held her head very stiff, and I could not help feeling it would be difficult for her to bend over her plate at supper. I had a better view of her in the interval while peeping through the hole in the curtain, for which there was great competition; her dress of heavy brocade was sewn over with jewels.[34]

Kchessinskaya's part in 'La Bayadère' contained a dramatic solo in which the heroine, Nikia, disappointed in her faithless lover, is bitten

*She did not do this in Pushkin's story.

†On 4 October 1967, Erich Alport and I were shown this theatre, as yet incompletely restored, by Professor Kraminsky, the learned and inspired renovator of war-scarred Leningrad, and I gazed in amazement down this dark slope into the nether regions.

by a snake and dances until she falls dead. It was now taken over by a girl who had graduated from the school four years before and was already attracting considerable attention. Anna Pavlova's life had been a struggle. She was the illegitimate daughter of a laundress married to a soldier, Matvey Pavlov; her real father is believed to have been Lazar Poliakov, a wealthy Jew of distinguished family.[35] She suffered from poor health. However, her very special qualities of ethereal lightness, her delicately arched instep, her lyrical *port de bras* and the extraordinary passion of her acting, soon made her stand out among her contemporaries. Having known the extreme of poverty, it was understandable that she should consolidate her position by what means she could. She attached herself first to the stage manager of the Mariinsky, a nephew of the director, Teliakovsky, and later to the critic Valerien Svetlov, whose praises helped to enhance her reputation.[36]

Vaslav was dancing in such ballets as 'Casse-noisette', 'Le Talisman' and 'Koniok-gorbunok' or 'The Little Hump-backed Horse', one of the first ballets to have as its subject a Russian fairy story. In 'Pakhita', with fifteen other boys and sixteen girl partners, he was to dance the Polish mazurka.[37] For this they rehearsed in the big classroom on the first floor where the girls' class of perfection was usually held;[38] and it was a matter of some excitement to work with their secluded neighbours. Most of the boys pretended to be in love with one or other of the girls, though it was rare that they were able to exchange a word with her.

Varvara Ivanovna Lihosherstova, directress of the Girls' School, was the inevitable cloud. She always discovered something wrong! Her discipline was as unbending as court etiquette. If one boy spoke too often to his partner, if another laughed, Varvara Ivanovna would dart a piercing glance in his direction, and desserts were lost for a week or visiting privileges were gone in the twinkling of an eye, for she protected her girls with the jealousy of a hen with one chick. She prohibited flirting or joking between boys and girls, and no excuse for transgressions was acceptable, punishment was certain, and there could be no quarter expected.[39]

There were nevertheless times when a puckish sense of mischief showed through Vaslav's shyness and reserve. Someone had pointed out to him Teliakovsky's second-in-command, Krupensky, as the 'evil genius' of the theatre. On an evening when the boys were to impersonate demons in 'Tannhäuser' and Vaslav was completely disguised by a grotesque make-up, whenever he passed Krupensky in the wings he wiggled his forefingers over his ears, making horns, and put out his tongue. After the opera Krupensky had all the boys called on the stage and asked, 'Which was the boy who put out his tongue?' There was a silence; Vaslav was afraid to own up. So the whole class was punished and missed a holiday. Vaslav confessed to his tutor, 'It was I who did it.' The tutor said, 'I know.'[40]

One day the boys were playing at jumping over an iron music-stand and when it was Nijinsky's turn to jump Rosaï screwed it up to an impossible height, so that Vaslav fell, was badly injured and had to be in hospital for several weeks. On another occasion, because of a brawl, Vaslav was actually suspended for a period and sent home.[41]

The teachers gave their pupils very individual supervision and devoted themselves to bringing out their latent talents. Vaslav was not particularly fond of reading, but he took to music and learned the piano – which he played more by ear than sight-reading – the flute, the balalaika and the accordion. His mother did not like him playing the accordion as she thought it common.[42]

A Catholic priest occasionally came to visit Vaslav,[43] but this did not prevent him attending the Orthodox services in the school chapel and being on friendly terms with the school priest, Father Vassili.[44] One day the Catholic priest introduced talk of Russo-Polish politics in the confessional; Vaslav was disgusted and gave up going to confession.[45]

In 1903 Tamara Karsavina was given her first leading role in 'Le Réveil de Flore'.

I set to work with a joyous heart. There was no dramatic plot in this ballet, the part being purely a dancing one requiring a certain amount of technical virtuosity of a higher level than I had hitherto attempted. A year of Johannsen's rebukes had not been spent in vain. I could now master considerable difficulties. Being spring, the smart season was over. That consideration didn't worry me; my spirits were always higher in the spring . . . Marius Petipa was pleased. '*Très bien, ma belle*,' he said. All went well; that is, till the very rehearsal. I must have overworked myself by that time; my toes were blistered, and my strength began failing me. The approach

of the performance brought a sickening fear, a frame of mind due, perhaps, to the fact that my friends on the stage wanted to impress me with
the importance of success; some, less well-disposed, said it was much too
early for me to have a responsible part. Both encouragement and dis-
couragement were equally pernicious to my mental balance. Once the
idea of possible failure had been put into my head, it began working
ravages with my self-control. It hypnotized me . . . By the evening I was
in a wretched state; there was a lump in my throat. I came on, feeling I
was on my trial. All was dizzy before my eyes; I was unsteady, couldn't get
my balance, and my legs shook. At the end applause roared, and bouquets
filled the stage. It didn't cheer me up; I had sentenced myself as a failure.
One hope lurked in my mind – perhaps the audience had not noticed my
slips; they were cheering me so.[46]

Karsavina's stern teacher, old Johannsen, died that year.

Change was in the air. Teliakovsky cut down the subscribers'
nights at the Mariinsky when only the hereditary box-owners could
sit in the lower part of the theatre, and there was a growing middle-
class audience for the ballet. This audience was more liberal-minded
than the aristocratic traditionalists and it began to find fault with the
repertory of Marius Petipa productions.[47] Teliakovsky had already
brought from Moscow the painters Golovine and Korovine, the first
easel-painters to design scenery for opera and ballet. He tried to
promote the work of Russian composers, who, apart from Tchaikovsky, were the laughing-stock of the aristocracy. Now he planned to
replace Petipa with Gorsky from Moscow, who was already teaching
in the school. The old ballet master was to celebrate his fiftieth
anniversary as choreographer to the Imperial Ballet with a new work,
'The Magic Mirror', with music by Koreshchenko and – a sign of
the new order – settings by Golovine, at a gala performance on 9
February 1903.

All seats in the theatre were sold out [wrote Teliakovsky in his diary] for
the new ballet, about which people talked for almost two years, the testi-
monial performance for the famous Petipa. Tales about the forthcoming
novel spectacle interested everybody. The Imperial box was filled by
members of the Imperial family. At eight o'clock sharp the Dowager
Empress Maria Feodorovna and the Tsar with the young Empress arrived.
The ministerial box was also filled with invited persons of high society.
They came to greet their bard who had served three Emperors, to see

another song dedicated to 'grandeur of autocracy', to 'be treated to' a tempting novelty. ('Well, with what will you treat us tonight?' asked the Minister of the Court.)

And suddenly, instead of an ecstatic roar there were whistles, shouts and noise in the audience: in the intermissions there were stormy scenes. The noise did not abate during the entire act. Some people began to shout 'Curtain'. The greatest celebration turned into a loud scandal and this decided the fate of the production. The Imperial box was definitely dissatisfied with the ballet. The Minister also did not like the ballet.

Petipa fell . . . In hostile circles a new candidate was already being discussed, and the newspaper *Birjevye Vyedomosti* printed the following sensational announcement: 'The ballet company will have to get used to a new ballet master, A. Gorsky. He will stage his own versions of "The Hump-backed Horse" and "Swan Lake". He stages both ballets entirely differently and in a much more original manner.'[48]

Although they had begun to arrange choreography at the Mariinsky, the brothers Legat were surprised to find themselves invited to stage a ballet at the Hermitage Theatre.[49] This was 'The Fairy Doll', which had been planned two years before. Nicolas and Sergei were two pierrots, with Kchessinskaya as a doll; and Bakst designed an attractive toyshop set.

About this Benois wrote:

His enthusiasm and love for our native city, St Petersburg, and personal recollections of his childhood, gave Bakst the happy idea of transferring the action to the St Petersburg Arcade, known to every St Petersburg child because of the toyshops that were concentrated there . . .

Our friend was in love with a young widow – Lubov Pavlovna Gritzenko, the daughter of the famous Russian patron of art, P. M. Tretiakov – and his feeling was reciprocated. Their meetings usually took place in studios of the Mariinsky Theatre under the curious pretext of Bakst having chosen to paint his beloved in these strange surroundings. The result of these seances was still more curious. Bakst really did paint Lubov Pavlovna, but the 'portrait' proved to be one of the dolls in the toyshop, and this doll was suspended from the ceiling, among all sorts of other toys, drums, hoops, carriages, clowns, etc. The Imperial Family had noticed this detail during the performance at the Hermitage Theatre and indeed it was impossible not to notice it, for 'Lubov Pavlovna', smiling gracefully, was dangling in the very foreground. Later, when the ballet was transferred to the Mariinsky Theatre, those who were initiated into the mystery of the

strange doll in the black Paris dress and huge hat, so out of place among
the other toys, were tremendously amused at the infatuated artist's invention. Lubov Pavlovna's brother-in-law our great friend S. S. Botkine,
was the one who especially enjoyed the joke. 'Look, look at Luba dangling
there!' he would repeat choking and almost weeping with laughter. Soon
after this, we learnt that the lovers would be united. After many complications from both sides, the wedding took place. Lubov Pavlovna had to
overcome the indignant resistance of all her purely Muscovite relations at
the idea of her marrying a Jew, while Levushka could not make up his
mind to change the faith of his fathers, as was demanded by the Russian
law of that time of Jews who married Christians.[50]

1904 began with the outbreak of the Russo-Japanese war, which no
one took seriously at first, but which was to end after a few months so
ignominiously for the Russians, providing appalling proof of the cor-
ruption and inefficiency of the State. In January Matilda Kchessinskaya gave her 'Farewell Performance' dancing in 'La Fille mal
gardée' and 'Le Lac des Cygnes':[51] but this may only have been due
to a policy of *reculer pour mieux sauter*, as she would be returning to
the stage on and off for another decade.*

The Tsar and Tsarina had only had daughters, but in August the
Empress gave birth to a son and heir and there was great rejoicing
and a holiday granted to the ballet school. This was the pretty
Tsarevitch to whose christening a wicked fairy brought the gift of
haemophilia as a final curse on the doomed Romanov dynasty.

It was a time of scarcity caused by the mobilization of peasant
workers, a time of unemployment and a time of strikes. Murmurs
of political unrest hardly penetrated the walls of the ballet school.
But on Sunday, 8 January 1905, the priest Father Gapon, who was
the founder of a workers' union, led a deputation, which was followed
by an immense crowd, to present a petition to the Tsar at the
Winter Palace. The Tsar was at Tsarskoe Selo, twenty miles away,
which was his usual residence. Troops fired on the workers. This
was the massacre of Bloody Sunday.

Vaslav was on his way home from school to visit his mother,
carrying some books. Coming out of the Alexandrinsky Gardens he
got caught up in the crowd pouring up the Nevsky Prospekt and was

---

*And indeed I saw her in a Russian dance at a Gala at Covent Garden in 1936.

swept along towards the Winter Palace. There was a charge of mounted Cossacks with lead-weighted knouts, and he was struck on the forehead so that the blood flowed down his face. The hungry subjects of the Tsar were falling and dying around him. He managed to escape. His colleague Babitch's pretty seventeen-year-old sister was among the missing.[52] At dusk, returning by sleigh to his home on the Vassilievsky Island, Benois was nearly beaten up by an angry crowd. 'What do you think you are doing? Running people over?'[53]

That night was Preobrajenskaya's Benefit at the Mariinsky. Karsavina, who was not dancing that evening, watched from the stalls the performance of 'Les Caprices du papillon' in which the charming little ballerina excelled. 'Towards the last act, alarming rumours ran in the theatre – riots had broken out in the town; the mob were on their way ... they had already broken into the Alexandrinsky and stopped the performance. Panic spread. The theatre emptied quickly. On the stage the performance never so much as flickered'...[54]

Next morning Vaslav went out with Bourman, Rosaï and Babitch to search for the body of Babitch's sister, but it was never found.[55]

Valentin Serov, who had painted the Tsar's portrait in 1900, was one of many intellectuals shocked by the massacre. The Grand Duke Vladimir, the Tsar's eldest uncle, who commanded the Petersburg garrison, was also President of the Academy of Fine Arts, of which Serov was a member. The painter wrote him an open letter of protest. This was not published; and Serov resigned.

To avoid mass demonstrations it was decreed that the many dead should be buried before dawn. According to Isadora Duncan, she met the endless funeral cortège as she arrived from Berlin. If her train had not been twelve hours late, she wrote, she would not have had this experience which she felt was a turning-point in her life.

There was no one at the station to meet me. When I descended from the train the temperature was ten degrees below zero. I had never felt such cold. The padded Russian coachmen were hitting their arms with their gloved fists to keep the blood flowing in their veins. I left my maid with the baggage, and, taking a one-horse cab, directed the driver to the Hotel Europa. Here I was in the black dawn of Russia, quite alone, on the way to the hotel, when suddenly I beheld a sight equal in ghastliness to any in the imagination of Edgar Allan Poe. It was a long procession that I saw from a distance. Black and mournful it came. There were men laden and bent under their loads – coffins – one after another. The coachman slowed his horse to a walk, and bent and crossed himself. I looked on in the indistinct dawn, filled with horror. I asked him what this was. Although I knew no Russian, he managed to convey to me that these were the workmen shot

Isadora Duncan dancing to Schubert.
Drawing by José Clara.

down before the Winter Palace the day before . . . because, unarmed, they had come to ask the Tsar for help in their distress – for bread for their wives and children. I told the coachman to stop. The tears ran down my face and were frozen on my cheeks as this sad, endless procession passed me. But why buried at dawn? Because later in the day it might have caused more revolution. The sight of it was not for the city in the day-time . . . With boundless indignation I watched these poor grief-stricken workmen carrying their martyred dead.[56]

31

There is something wrong with this story, however, because Isadora had arrived in Petersburg in December 1904, a week or two before.[57] Of course she may have seen the procession from her window at the Europa Hotel. Isadora, the young American who despised ballet and had evolved a new way of dancing naturally which was wonderfully expressive and appeared deceptively simple, had in the last two or three years subjugated Western Europe, and had arrived to extend her conquests in Russia. What was just as extraordinary as her dancing barefoot in flimsy draperies was that she danced not to 'dance music' but to the compositions of the great masters. Her first appearance was in the Hall of Nobles on 26 December before a surprised and elegant audience.

How strange it must have been to those dilettantes of the gorgeous ballet, with its lavish decorations and scenery, to watch a young girl, clothed in a tunic of cobweb, appear and dance before a simple blue curtain to the music of Chopin! Yet even for the first dance there was a storm of applause. My soul that yearned suffered the tragic notes of the Preludes; my soul that aspired and revolted to the thunder of the Polonaises; my soul that wept with righteous anger, thinking of the martyrs of that funeral procession of the dawn; this soul awakened in that wealthy, spoilt, and aristocratic audience a response of stirring applause. How curious!

The next day Isadora received a visit from 'a most charming little lady, wrapped in sables, with diamonds hanging from her ears, and her neck encircled with pearls'. It was Kchessinskaya.

That evening a magnificent carriage, warmed and filled with expensive furs, conducted me to the opera, where I found a first-tier box, containing flowers, bonbons, and three beautiful specimens of the *jeunesse dorée* of Petersburg. I was still wearing my little white tunic and sandals . . . I am an enemy of the ballet . . . but it was impossible not to applaud the fairy-like figure of Kchessinskaya as she flitted across the stage, more like a lovely bird or butterfly than a human being.

Isadora also went to see Pavlova in 'Giselle' and had supper afterwards at her flat, where she sat between Bakst and Benois. Bakst told her fortune and she had an ardent discussion about dancing with Diaghilev.[58]

Diaghilev was about to celebrate his most spectacular triumph to date, an Exhibition of Russian Historical Portraits. All through the previous summer he had travelled about Russia, visiting country houses and unearthing long-hidden or even forgotten paintings, rummaging in attics and playing on the fears of landowners, persuading them to lend their ancestors on the grounds that in time of revolution they would be safer in the capital.[59] The huge exhibition of three thousand portraits represented the past of Russia. Statesmen, princes, ecclesiastics and court beauties were grouped in the echoing immensity of the Tauride Palace, around full-length portraits, under canopies, of the monarchs they had served – imperious Peter, intelligent Catherine, mad Paul and idealistic Alexander I. In the centre a columned sculpture hall was decorated by Bakst as a trellised winter garden. 'There was something oppressive,' Benois thought, 'in this multi-coloured assembly of magnates in gold-embroidered coats, those dressed-up ladies, all this Necropolis, this *Vanitas Vanitatum*, which doubled the pleasure of relaxing in the greenery among the white marble busts.'[60] Years later Diaghilev told Sacheverell Sitwell of the 'alarm and foreboding caused by the room of portraits of the mad Tsar Paul, with his crown worn tilted to one side'.[61]

There were rumours of a general strike, and the Benois family left for Versailles before the official opening of the exhibition by the Emperor.

Later I heard from eye-witnesses and my correspondents about the opening ceremony. It followed the traditional pattern: the Tsar arrived, accompanied by members of his family, and walked slowly past the endless rows of his ancestors. Diaghilev, the Grand Duke Nicolai Mikhailovitch and Prince Dashkov provided explanations. At the end of this review, which lasted for about two hours, Nicholas II thanked his uncle, Diaghilev and Dashkov, but not by a single word did he reveal his personal attitude to all he had seen, although it was all so closely related to his person; everything in it spoke of the past of the Russian monarchy, of his predecessors on the throne and of their collaborators and associates. It was known that the Tsar was interested in history and it might have been expected that this magnificent spectacle would make some kind of impression on him. Perhaps his attitude was due to an emotional paralysis which rendered him inarticulate; or he might have seen in the faces of his ancestors bitter reproaches and terrible warnings of approaching disaster.[62]

But Diaghilev, who had assembled this apotheosis of the Russian past – and most of the portraits were due for destruction – was sworn to the future. At a banquet given in his honour in the Tauride Palace which had been built by Patiomkin, the favourite of Catherine the Great, after his conquest of the Caucasus, Diaghilev spoke the following words:

There is no doubt that every tribute is a summing-up, and every summing-up is an ending. Far from me the thought that tonight's banquet is in any sense the end of the aims for which we have lived up to now. I think you will agree with me that thoughts of summing-up and ending come to one's mind more and more in these days. That is the question that struck me the whole time I was working. Don't you feel that this long gallery of portraits of big and small people that I brought to live in the beautiful halls of the Palais Tauride is only a grandiose summing-up of a brilliant, but, alas! dead period of our history? . . . I have earned the right to proclaim this loudly, because with the last breath of the summer breezes I ended my long travels across the immensity of Russia. It was just after those acquisitive expeditions that I became convinced that the time to sum up was before us. I saw that not only in the brilliant portraits of those ancestors, so far removed from us, but more vividly from their descendants, who were ending their lives. The end of a period is revealed here, in those gloomy dark palaces, frightening in their dead splendour, and inhabited to-day by charming mediocre people who could no longer stand the strain of bygone parades. Here are ending their lives not only people, but pages of history . . .

We are witnesses of the greatest moment of summing-up in history, in the name of a new and unknown culture, which will be created by us, and which will also sweep us away. That is why, with fear or misgiving, I raise my glass to the ruined walls of the beautiful palaces, as well as to the new commandments of a new aesthetic. The only wish that I, an incorrigible sensualist, can express, is that the forthcoming struggle should not damage the amenities of life, and that the death should be as beautiful and as illuminating as the resurrection.[63]

Thus spoke Petronius Arbiter – but with a touch of Spartacus.

If artists and intellectuals tended to fall immediately under Isadora's sway, it was understandable that young ballet dancers should be shocked by her lack of virtuosity.[64] She came to watch classes in Theatre Street and gave a demonstration. Taken aback at

34

first, Vaslav later came to admire her greatly. Her most immediate influence, however, was on Michel Fokine.[65] For several years he had been dreaming of new forms and here was a goddess moving to sublime music. It was his moment of release – of explosion. For the pupils' display in April he was asked to arrange a ballet. He went to the Public Library in search of Greek subject matter, and the aged, white-bearded Vladimir Vasilievitch Stassov, the Director, who was a celebrated critic of art and music, was so impressed that a ballet dancer should have these interests that he took particular trouble to produce the relevant documentation. In the theatre library Fokine found the libretto of an old ballet made by Lev Ivanov in 1896, 'Acis and Galatea', with music by Kadletz: but the inspector of the school would not allow him to discard the conventional ballet style.

I did not try to prove that between the classic and the Greek art there could be a bridge. I realized that I had been carried away by my ideas. Sadly I left the Inspector's office. However, I still managed to produce the ballet not exactly as customary. The girls danced on their toes, but the costumes were a hybrid between the ballet styles and the Greek. Here and there was also a hint of a different, non-balletic plastique. The groupings were unusual, asymmetrical; some performers were placed on different levels, on mounds, tree stubs, trees; others on the floor (it was intended to be grass) – thus avoiding the usual horizontal line grouping. The Dance of the Fauns seemed to be entirely new. Here I had my freedom. The fauns resembled beasts. They performed no ballet steps and, at the end of the ballet dance, did some tumbling, which was not in accordance with the classical school but corresponded very well with the mood of an animal dance.

The boys played a subsidiary part in Fokine's production, as the little ballet was only intended to show off the prowess of Fokine's female pupils. One boy, however, he found 'outstanding for elevation and effort'. Fokine asked him, 'What is your name?' 'Nijinsky,' he answered. It was the meeting of a man and a boy who would make each other famous. 'Acis' was the first of many Fokine ballets Nijinsky was to dance in. For the same performance the choreographer arranged a spectacular 'Polka' for Elena Smirnova and George Rosaï.[66]

Fokine and Karsavina had parted company. He had begged and

35

begged her to marry him. But her mother did not want her to throw herself away on a dancer. Michel then implored Tamara to run away with him. She loved him, but she obeyed her mother.[67] She had become ill, and was sent to Italy where she took classes in Milan. Fokine transferred his affection to one of his pupils, Vera Antonova, a dark girl with an oval face, who adored him. They were married in 1905.

At last the spirit of revolt spread to the ballet. The dancers signed a petition demanding autonomy.

The autumn of 1905 [wrote Karsavina] I remember even now as a nightmare. A cruel October wind from the sea, chill, sleet, sinister hush in the town. For several days trams had not been running, the strike gaining rapidly. I chose a roundabout way, avoiding pickets. Though they let one pass unquestioned, my heart sank every time I came across their encampments. My thin shoes let in water; my feet were numb. A glimmer of hope that I might catch a severe cold to free me from an impending ordeal was my only comfort. I was going to Fokine's flat to take part in what seemed a conspiracy to me ... The light was cut off that night in the whole town. ... A resolution of the meeting was being elaborated ... when I came in ... One by one the belated members arrived, bringing some fresh information. The Railways had stopped; to prevent a meeting of workmen on the Vassilievsky Ostrov [island] the bridges had been raised. Fokine picked up a receiver to see if the telephone was still working. No reply from the exchange ... Two little dancers, mere boys, came in all flushed and excited; they constituted themselves scouts. Their honest admiration for our actions would not allow them to keep quiet. 'We saw some detectives outside,' they bubbled, interrupting each other, 'must be detectives, both in pea-green overcoats and goloshes.' At all times the obviousness of our secret police, their goloshes in all weathers were everybody's joke ... The next step was to try and prevent the matinée performance at the Mariinsky. 'The Queen of Spades' was being given; a considerable number of dancers appeared in it. My duty was to go round the ladies' dressing-rooms and call the dancers off. The task was distasteful to me, and my eloquence not of the most persuasive. A few left the theatre; the majority refused to strike. Within the next few days the circular of the Minister of the Court was made known to the troupe. Our action was qualified as a breach of discipline; all who wished to remain loyal were to sign a declaration. The great majority signed, leaving us, their chosen delegates, in the lurch.[68]

The abortive strike had tragic consequences. Sergei Legat, Vaslav's former teacher, who had been prevailed on to sign the original petition, felt himself a traitor to the Tsar. His anguish was further heightened by unhappy relations with Marie Petipa, with whom he had been living. After a night of raving he cut his throat.[69]

On 13 October the first Soviet of deputies of the workers of Petersburg was formed. This, together with a strike which had brought Russian railways to a standstill, as well as continued risings among the peasants, compelled the Tsar to give out on 17 October that an elected Council or Duma would be established to serve under a Council of Ministers. Russia was to have its first Parliament, with Count Witte as its first 'Prime Minister'. The Duma would meet at the Tauride Palace, the site of Diaghilev's exhibition.

Having given Russia a glimpse of its own history, Diaghilev's next move was to take a huge representative exhibition of two centuries of Russian painting and sculpture to Paris in 1906. In the halls of the Salon d'Automne in the Petit Palais he hung ikons, the eighteenth-century portraits and scenes of Levitsky and Borovikovsky, the neo-classical compositions of Brullov and a great number of works by artists of the 'World of Art', Vrubel, Serov, Bakst, Benois, Somov, Anisfeld, Dobujinsky, Roerich, Korovine, Maliavin and Larionov. The ikons were hung by Bakst on gold brocade, which Benois thought made it difficult to look at them, although the effect was striking in a typical Diaghilev way. Sculpture, as at the Tauride Palace, was shown in a winter garden. Benois also thought the exhibition was not truly representative because Diaghilev had excluded the Peredvijiniki and any painters who did not interest him.[70] Diaghilev's committee was headed by the Grand Duke Vladimir.

Another member of the committee was the rich and handsome Comtesse Greffuhle, queen of Paris Society, President of the Société Musicale, which had been founded by the brilliant and imaginative music-publisher Gabriel Astruc that year. When Diaghilev first went to see her, she had thought there was something odd about him and feared he might be nothing but a social climber. But he impressed her with his remarks about her pictures and when he sat down at the piano and played some Russian songs 'the music was so fresh, so altogether wonderful and lovely', that when he explained that he intended organizing a festival of Russian music in the coming year she was unhesitantly enrolled in his support and the foundation of the future Russian seasons was laid.[71]

Nijinsky had now been eight years at the ballet school and was a senior student. He was still as quiet and self-effacing as ever, still slow at book-learning, still happiest in class. Music attracted him far more than literature, but he sometimes lost himself in a book; he and Bronislava read *David Copperfield* together in a Russian translation, and even had a go at *Don Quixote*, attracted by its handsome red and gold binding. His favourite composers were Rimsky-Korsakov and Wagner; and he could play a piano arrangement of the overture of 'Tannhäuser' without a single mistake. His sight-reading was still weak, but if someone struck a chord he could tell without looking what notes it was composed of.[72] Because of his exceptional ability he might have been allowed to pass out of the school after only six years – if only he could have got through the examinations in subjects other than dancing and music. He was always gentle and friendly with younger students and never addressed even the newest of them as 'thou', which was customary among senior boys, but always 'you', treating them as equals.[73]

The staff and pupils of the ballet school were aware that they had a remarkable dancer in their midst. *How* remarkable, they could not yet know. And of course it was not only his technical virtuosity they were proud of, for technique was second nature to them – it was the manner and style and expression he put into his dancing. In Petersburg technique was never an end in itself.[74]

Nobody was prouder of Vaslav than his teacher Obukhov.

One morning [wrote Karsavina] I came up earlier than usual; the boys were just finishing their practice. I glanced casually, and could not believe my eyes; one boy in a leap rose far above the heads of the others and seemed to tarry in the air. 'Who is that?' I asked Michael Obukhov, his master. 'It is Nijinsky; the little devil never comes down with the music.' He then called Nijinsky forward by himself and made him show me some steps. A prodigy was before my eyes. He stopped dancing, and I felt it was all unreal and could not have been; the boy looked quite unconscious of his achievement, prosy and even backward. 'Shut your mouth,' were his master's parting words. 'You fly-swallower.' 'Off with you all now.' Like peas falling out of a bag, the boys rushed off, their patter a hollow re-percussion in the vaulted passage. In utter amazement I asked Michael why nobody spoke of this remarkable boy, and he about to finish. 'They will soon,' chuckled Michael, 'Don't you worry.'[75]

Obukhov decided to show his prize pupil to the public. Hitherto Nijinsky had appeared only as an inconspicuous figure in *ensembles* at the Mariinsky. It cannot have been without difficulty that his teacher arranged that a boy who had not graduated should take part in a dance with leading members of the company. This was to be a *pas de huit** inserted into Mozart's opera 'Don Giovanni'. The other dancers were Preobrajenskaya, Trefilova, Vaganova, Egorova, Andrianov, Bolm and Leontiev; and it was Trefilova whom Nijinsky supported.[76] The performance took place on 31 January 1906. It was impossible that the young student should not leap higher and turn more *pirouettes* than the other men. So he stood for the first time to hear the world's applause.[77] On 6 February the *pas de huit* was re-peated, but with Pavlova replacing Trefilova.[78] The two great dancers appeared together for the first time.

Fokine's success with 'Acis and Galatea' had one unexpected result. He was invited by Alexander Akimovich Sanine, the producer at the Alexandrinsky Theatre, to arrange a dance of buffoons and jesters in Alexis Tolstoi's play *The Death of Ivan the Terrible*. He was delighted, but told Sanine that as he was not officially a ballet master, the direction of the Imperial Theatres would probably insist on Nicolas Legat doing the job. Sanine undertook to arrange matters; but sure enough, the dreaded Alexander Dmitrievitch Krupensky, assistant director of the Imperial Theatres and head of the production department, told him that he had no business to choose his collaborators without the approval of the office. To the amazement of everybody, Sanine resigned and sent the story to the newspapers.[79]

Shortly after this, in April 1906, Fokine arranged for a charity per-formance a ballet called 'La Vigne' to music of Anton Rubinstein, in which Kyasht, Marie Petipa, Karsavina, Fokina, Pavlova and him-

---

*Bourman records the appearance in 'Don Giovanni', but makes it a *pas de quatre* with Kyasht, Legat and Obukhov. He makes Obukhov lead Nijinsky forward to receive the applause. It is possible that he emerged from the wings to do this.

self impersonated various types of wine. After this he was thrilled to receive the accolade of old Marius Petipa in the form of a visiting-card inscribed with the words

> *Cher camarade Fokine*
> *Enchanté de vos compositions.*
> *Continuez vous deviendrez*
> *un bon maître de ballet*
> *Tout à vous.*[80]*

Fokine was next invited by Victor Dandré, a member of the City Council who later became manager and perhaps the husband of Anna Pavlova†, to stage a whole evening's programme at the Mariinsky at a benefit for the Society of the Prevention of Cruelty to Children. For this he chose to make a two-act ballet, 'Eunice', on a subject taken from Sienkievitch's Roman novel *Quo Vadis*, and a ballet to Chopin orchestrated by Glazunov, called 'Chopiniana'. The music for the former work by Shtcherbashev contained some un-Roman waltzes, which rather discouraged the choreographer, and it was unthinkable that he should be allowed to have barefoot dancers on the Imperial stage, but he tried to make the best of a bad job and produce something as classical-Roman and as un-classical-ballet as possible. He contrived dances without point work, *pirouettes, entrechats* or *battements*; and on the dancers' white tights Bronislava Nijinska painted toe-nails and rosy heels and knees.[81] The ageing but handsome Gerdt impersonated Petronius, Kchessinskaya was the slave Eunice, and Pavlova as Acte performed a Dance of the Seven Veils. There was also a dance with wineskins, a spectacular dance with lighted torches, and an Egyptian *pas de trois* in which Vera Fokina, Julia Siedova and Rutkovskaya sacrificed themselves by darkening their bodies and elongating their eyes in order to become in clinging draperies the first 'Egyptians' not to wear ballet *tutus* on the Imperial stage.[82] Nijinsky had a small part.

Before the performace, which took place on 23 February 1907, Fokine had run into a little trouble with the *doyen* of the balletomanes,

---

*In the English-language edition of Fokine's book (p. 92) the message is quoted slightly inaccurately.

†There is some doubt whether they actually married. Their relationship was primarily a business one.

Nicolas Mikhailovitch Besobrasov, whose rank as full State Councillor entitled him to the honorary rank of general. This kind, portly, white-haired old gentleman exercised considerable power in the ballet world, was thought the final arbiter of quality in *pirouettes* and was a specialist in organizing the seating at benefit nights for dancers in such a way as to make the smartest audience pay the maximum amount of money for their seats. He thought Fokine's reforms were going too far too quickly. 'Continue your experiments at first with the *corps de ballet*. It is impossible to bring the ballerina out on stage without her *tutu*.' The young choreographer listened respectfully, then continued to work exactly as before: but after the performance Besobrasov was one of the first to offer his congratulations.[83]

In the Chopin ballet, the Waltz in C Sharp Minor was danced by Pavlova and Obukhov. Fokine wrote:

The choreography differed from all other *pas de deux* in its total absence of spectacular feats. There was not a single *entrechat*, turn in the air, or *pirouette*. There was a slow turn of the ballerina, holding her partner's hand, but this could not be classified as a *pirouette* because the movement was not confined to the turn but was used for a change of position and grouping. When composing, I placed no restrictions on myself; I simply could not conceive of any spectacular stunts to the accompaniment of the poetic, lyrical Waltz of Chopin. I was totally unconcerned whether this romantic duet would bring applause or satisfy the audience or the ballerina, for I did not think of success at all. That is probably why I was rewarded with one of the greatest successes which has fallen to any of my compositions.[84]

Simple as it appeared this dance was extremely hard to execute correctly. Other numbers in the ballet were the majestic Polonaise in Polish costumes, a nocturne in which Chopin, impersonated by the mime Alexis Bulgakov, was haunted by ghostly monks and consoled by the vision of his beloved, a mazurka in which Siedova as the young bride of an old bridegroom elopes with her true love, and a tarantella led by Vera Fokina in which Michel used steps they had observed together during their honeymoon in Capri.[85]

Some years before, when he was still on good terms with Teliakovsky, Benois had conceived the idea for a ballet based on a story of Théophile Gautier, to be called 'Le Pavillon d'Armide'. He suggested to his nephew by marriage, Nicolas Tcherepnine, a pupil of Rimsky's, that he should write the music, and together they went to see the director about it. 'Are there any waltzes? It is most important to have waltzes!' Teliakovsky had said. And although waltzes were provided and Benois was even paid a fee for his libretto, it was shortly after this that he and the director quarrelled and the project was dropped.[86] Now, early in 1907, Fokine heard a suite from the ballet, which Tcherepnine had arranged, played at a concert and went backstage to seek out the composer. Tcherepnine was pleased that the choreographer liked his music; and shortly afterwards, with costumes borrowed from the Mariinsky wardrobe, the suite was arranged as a one-act ballet and given on 28 April 1907, under the title of 'Le Gobelins animé' – 'The Gobelins tapestry which came to life' – at a school performance. This production was, more or less, the central *divertissement* of the future ballet in three scenes,* and the great hit was the dance of jesters led by George Rosaï.[87] Surprisingly, the formidable Krupensky saw the ballet, liked it and arranged that the whole work as planned by Benois and Tcherepnine – though slightly abbreviated – should be staged at the Mariinsky in the autumn.

At his graduation performance, which took place the night after, 29 April 1907, at the Mariinsky Theatre, Nijinsky performed in a variety of numbers, dancing, according to the critic of the *Petersburg Gazette*, 'the whole evening'.[88] Koslyanninov, the critic of *Theatre and Music*, records him as dancing the variation called 'Lightning' from Petipa's 'Magic Mirror' and also a dance from 'Pakhita',[89] which was probably the famous *pas de trois*. The critics were extremely enthusiastic.[90] Mme Schollar recalls appearing with Nijinsky in an effective *pas de deux* called 'The Prince Gardener' arranged by Klavdia Kulichevska, one of her teachers. Her costume was sewn with spangles, so that in supporting her *pirouettes* Vaslav's hands were cut between thumb and forefinger and her dress was covered in blood – which was considered a bad omen.[91] Mme Bronislava Nijinska remembers her brother dancing in the *divertissement* of 'Le Pavillon d'Armide' with Smirnova, Schollar and Elisaveta Gerdt (daughter of Pavel), who was not to graduate till the following year.[92]

*A fuller description will be found in Chapter Two.

He may have danced all these numbers and more, but the only printed record is of the two dances mentioned in *Theatre and Music*.

The great Kchessinskaya came to congratulate Nijinsky and said she wished to have him as her partner. This meant that although he would officially be only an ill-paid member of the *corps de ballet* he would never dance in the *corps*, but start as a soloist: it was as much as to say his fortune was made.[93]

Then came the other dreaded exams; and Nijinsky failed in history. Authority connived. He was to have another test three days later, set by his own teacher, who gave him warning of the questions. This time he passed. [94] His schooldays were over – not that a dancer's schooling is ever done.

Meanwhile, Diaghilev was back in Paris, and his five Russian concerts took place at the Opéra between 16–30 May. Works by every Russian composer of note from Glinka to Scriabine were performed, Rimsky, Rachmaninov and Glazunov conducting their own. Nikisch and Blumenfeld also conducted; and the singers included Litvinne, Chaliapine, Cherkasskaya, Zbroueva, Petrenko and Smirnov. It was an amazing programme. Even so, as Diaghilev recalled in later years, the first concert ended in a scandal.

The last but one number of the programme was the Prince Galitzky scene from 'Prince Igor', Act I, in which Chaliapine was making his Paris *début*. This was so extraordinarily successful that the applause went on and on and there seemed no limit to the number of times the excited public would recall Chaliapine. Nikisch, who was conducting, made ready to begin Glinka's 'Kamarinskaya', which was the last item on the programme. Several times Nikisch raised his arms ready to start, but the public, by now quite out of hand, refused to be silenced. Then, mortally offended, Nikisch threw down his baton, walked out of the orchestra pit, and left the public stranded. People began to drift out. Upstairs in the gallery the din continued, when, in a sudden hush, we heard a deep bass voice thundering out from the remote heights of the house, in Russian, the words 'Ka-ma-rinska-ya! Get stuffed!' Grand Duke Vladimir, who was sitting beside me in the box, got up and said to the Grand Duchess, 'Well, I think it's time we went home.'[95]

Benois and his family had been for over two years living mostly in Paris and Versailles. Besides painting, Benois had written a book, *The Russian School of Painting*, catalogued the Alexander III

Museum of Russian pictures in the Mikhailovsky Palace, and contributed articles to various journals. Now Tcherepnine, in Paris for the concerts, told him that their ballet 'Le Pavillon d'Armide' was to be performed; and of course Benois was to design it.[96]

Immediately on his admission to the Imperial Ballet, Nijinsky had been sent on holiday: but his summer was not entirely idle. In June came the awaited summons of Kchessinskaya: Vaslav was to be her partner at performances during the army manoeuvres at Krasnoe Selo. These shows, presented in a wooden theatre seating only eight hundred, for the army officers and their families, had an informal picnic atmosphere despite the frequent attendance of Grand Dukes and the Emperor himself. It had been during the Krasnoe Selo 'season', in fact, that Kchessinskaya's romance with Nicolas II, then Tsarevitch, had flowered thirteen years before.[97]

If Vaslav was to dance with Kchessinskaya it could be safely assumed that there would be no more money worries. The family decided to rent a cottage near the Lake of Duderhof, which was in the neighbourhood of Krasnoe Selo, and the Nijinskys settled down to enjoy the summer. One day, unexpected and uninvited, Vaslav's old classmate, Bourman, who had also just graduated, arrived to stay. Knowing that Kchessinskaya was attracted to Nijinsky, he hoped to profit by the connection.[98] Eleonora strongly disapproved of him. Bourman's uncle was some kind of baron, but his father had been disowned by the family because of drink and gambling and he played the piano in a second-rate restaurant. Anatole took after his father. He did not, as he claims in his book, stay the whole summer – he stayed a week:[99] but while discounting most of the sensational stories he propagated, we may take his word for the pleasant way the household passed their time in the country. 'We laughed all day, we ran over the grass with wings on our heels. We read scores of books, and talked and talked, while Mother Nijinsky cooked marvellous Polish dinners for us . . . When Mother Nijinsky stood in the sunshine shouting "Tola! Bronia! Vatzo!" we ran like children, racing and tumbling in to destroy every vestige of a perfect repast, while she smiled benignly at us . . .'[100] Bronislava, on the other hand, disliked Bourman for his lying and boasting of success with women, thought him dirty and kept out of his way as much as possible.[101] It was at this time that Vaslav read Dostoyevsky's *The Idiot*,[102] and perhaps identified himself in a vague way with Prince Myshkin, the Christ-like simpleton, the meek, instinctively understanding, all-forgiving, ridiculous, long-suffering lover, friend and philanthropist, whom children turned to, who foretold in Russia the humbling of princes, and thought mankind could be redeemed by beauty.

Bourman's Dostoyevskian characteristic was that he shared the writer's passion for cards. One day he told Vaslav that he must have five hundred roubles for a gambling debt or he would kill himself. Nijinsky said he could not produce such a sum. Bourman asked him to borrow it. Nijinsky said he could not borrow money to pay such a thing as a gambling debt. 'Then, can't you pawn something?' urged his shameless friend.[103]

The weeks of entertaining the troops at Krasnoe Selo passed gaily, with excursions into the surrounding country and parties at the restaurant opposite the rustic theatre, at which Nijinsky and Bourman were the guests of Kchessinskaya and her attendant Grand Dukes. For dancing a solo before the Emperor, Nijinsky along with all the other dancers was awarded the coveted gold watch with Imperial cypher (which was believed to exempt the owner from arrest in Petersburg); and by the end of the summer he had saved over two thousand roubles.[104]

Thomas Nijinsky, whom his wife and children had not seen for years, heard of his son's growing reputation as a dancer and wrote to ask Vaslav to visit him at Nijni-Novgorod.* Eleonora, who had not forgiven her husband his desertion, was reluctant to let Vaslav go. Her son, however, was suddenly anxious to see his father and he persuaded her.

In Nijni-Novgorod the handsome Thomas, now nearing forty, was waiting. Father and son made friends and danced for each other. On his return home Vaslav would tell his family that Thomas was a greater dancer than himself: his father had shown him steps which he found it impossible to execute. Thomas gave him some cuff-links and promised to come and see him dance in Petersburg: but in fact they never met again.[105]

*Not at Kazan, as stated by Mme Romola Nijinsky. According to his sister, Vaslav never travelled on the Volga, though he longed to.

The Nijinskys had moved more than once since Vaslav had walked to school from the flat in Mokhovaya. Now, on their return from the country, Eleonora celebrated her new affluence by taking a much larger apartment in Ulitsa Bolshoi Konyushennya, the street of the Big Stables, which was a commercial thoroughfare turning off the north side of Nevsky Prospekt, near the Moika Canal and the Hermitage. The flat was over a shop which sold up-to-date Swedish furniture, and it was to be Vaslav's last home in Petersburg.[106]

Whereas the senior boy pupils in the school went to Obukhov for their lessons, the men in the company went to Nicolas Legat. But Cecchetti, who had left the Imperial School in 1902 to pass a few years as ballet master in Poland and Italy, had recently returned. He was shortly to open his own school in Petersburg, but for the time being Pavlova claimed his services and he gave her lessons at her flat in Torgovaya Street near the Mariinsky. Vaslav was anxious to study with the Italian *maestro* rather than with Legat, and Pavlova allowed him to share her private class.[107]

There was another reason not to go to Legat. He was now regarded in the Nijinsky family if not as an enemy, at least as a rival. Legat was jealous of his right to be Kchessinskaya's partner, which Vaslav was beginning to usurp. He was also jealous of a flirtation Vaslav was carrying on with a dancer called Antonina Tchumakova. Legat had formerly had an affair with her elder sister Olga; now he was in love with Antonina, and Nijinsky was a rival twenty years younger.[108]*

Another friend of Nijinsky's was Inna Niesloukhovska, who had graduated at the same time as himself. She was a well-educated girl with pretty eyes, the daughter of the *régisseur* at the Alexandrinsky Theatre, whose house was an intellectual centre. One day, when Vaslav was present at a party there, Inna spoke out in admiration of Isadora, saying that hers was the true art of dancing. Nijinsky was so shocked that he dropped the girl from that moment.† To Bronia he

---

*Antonina subsequently became Legat's (first) wife; and their daughter was the mother of Tatiana Legat of the Kirov Ballet, who is married to that wonderful dancer Yuri Soloviev.

†Niesloukhovska went to Paris with Diaghilev's company in his first 1909 season. She later married a Comte de Chevigné, secretary of the French Embassy in Petersburg and

said 'How can I have anything to do with someone who understands nothing about my work?' Bronia used to tell him when she thought a girl was attracted to him and she noticed that this would prompt him to take the initiative and pay court to her.[109]

Even at this stage of his career Nijinsky's name was beginning to be spoken in Petersburg; and one result was that the young prodigy was in demand to give dancing lessons to the children of well-to-do people. A naïve millionaire miller called Sinyagin wrote to ask if he would give ballroom-dancing classes to his boy and girl. He taught them quadrilles, galops, waltzes, polkas and mazurkas. Nijinsky demanded a hundred roubles an hour – and got it. Bourman went along as accompanist.

The family was typical of the Russian merchant class. We were met [by] our host and hostess bowing crudely . . . The children were a boy of eight and a girl of nine . . .* During the lesson, given in a spacious hall, the whole family and all the servants congregated. Madame Sinyagin, whose face was beautiful, even if she was fat and had short podgy fingers covered with diamonds, the aunts and cousins, the cook, the grooms, the dish-washers, the laundresses and the coachmen – they were all there to watch the Sinyagin hopefuls at their dancing . . . After the lesson we would be ushered into a huge dining-room and placed in seats of honour while every-thing expensive was heaped upon us . . .[110]

Other houses in which Nijinsky gave lessons were more aristocratic. He began to see how the rich lived. Nijinsky never gave lessons in classical ballet to amateurs.[111]

The Mariinsky season began in September. Although Vaslav was still only a member of the *corps de ballet*, paid sixty-five roubles a month, because of the patronage of Kchessinskaya and because his reputation was already so great the management wanted to make the best use of him they could, and he was given solo roles. On 1 October he danced a *pas de deux* from 'Pakhita' with Lydia Kyasht; on the 7th a *pas de deux* in 'La Fille mal gardée' with Elena Smirnova; and in October a *pas de deux* in 'Giselle' – probably the first act 'peasant'

---

a relation of the Comtesse de Chevigné who would be one of Diaghilev's chief supporters (and who was immortalized as the Duchesse de Guermantes by Proust).

*Bourman says they were fat and clumsy but Mme Bronislava Nijinska, who con-firms his story in general, says Nijinsky would not have accepted them as pupils if they were.

dance, of which the music is by Burgmüller, not Adam – with Karsavina.[112] The rehearsal for this was the occasion of a painful scene, which the ballerina never forgot:

The first time we danced before the whole company was at a theatre rehearsal; I was aware of the intense interest of all the artists; I felt a scrutiny, not unkind, round us both, and was more nervous than at a performance. We finished; the company clapped. From a group in the first wing, a sanctum reserved only for primas, an infuriated figure rushed up to me. 'Enough of your brazen impudence. Where do you think you are, to dance quite naked? . . .' I couldn't realize what had happened. It appeared that the strap of my bodice had slipped off and my shoulder had become uncovered, which I was not conscious of during my dance. I stood in the middle of the stage dumb-founded, helpless against volleys of coarse words hurled at me from the same cruel mouth. The *régisseur* came on and led off the Puritan. By this time a dense crowd of sympathizers had surrounded me; my chronic want of handkerchiefs necessitated the use of my tarlatan skirt to wipe away the tears. Preobrajenskaya stroked my head, repeating, 'Sneeze on the viper, sweetheart. Forget her, and think only of those beautiful *pirouettes* of yours.' The scandal spread rapidly, and an ovation met me at the next performance.[113]

The viper was Pavlova, whose jealousy of Karsavina was to follow her throughout her career.[114]

On 10 November Nijinsky danced again in 'La Fille mal gardée' and – for the first time at the Mariinsky with Kchessinskaya – in the number called 'The Prince Gardener', which he had done on his graduation night with Schollar, and which the latter now taught the *prima ballerina*.[115] On 27 December, Nijinsky danced with Siedova a *pas de deux* in 'Le Roi Candaule', in which he had to black his face and appear as a mulatto, crowned with feathers.[116]

Back from Paris, Benois was introduced to Krupensky in his office in the Square of the Alexandrinsky Theatre, at the end of Theatre Street. His first impression of the Assistant Director was favourable. 'He was a young, pleasant and rather portly man with a dark Assyrian beard.' It was soon clear that the ambitious Krupensky regarded 'Le Pavillon d'Armide' as his own particular show-piece which was going to bring him credit. A scene-painting studio in Alexeyevskaya Street was assigned to Benois and he was lent the assistants of the theatre's principal scenic artist, Oreste Allegri.[117]

The collaborators who were to make history were drawing together. Back from his holiday, Fokine came to the studio and Benois met him for the first time.

What appealed to me at once was his gaiety [Benois recorded]. There was absolutely no affectation or pose about him, no pretence of being a genius; on the contrary, he possessed the simplicity and a certain youthful charm that I consider to be the undoubted sign of real talent. One could see that he was captivated by the problem entrusted to him. We agreed with each other at once. He told me about the way he had produced Armide's dances for the performance in the Theatre School and all his ideas fell in with mine. It became clear that I could trust and depend on him.[118]

Now in September 1907, Fokine took Benois to watch a rehearsal in the ballet school. The painter was overcome by the new experience.

I must confess that when I was taken into the rehearsal hall of the Theatre School I was almost dumbfounded. I had often been present at stage rehearsals and was acquainted with many dancers, and this should have been a guarantee against any surprise. But the sight that now presented itself to my eyes was something entirely unexpected. The daylight, streaming through the tall windows on either side of the hall, seemed to make the sea of tarlatan dresses even more ethereal, transparent, foamy. These young women, maidens and little girls, made no use whatsoever of cosmetics, and their youthful bodies and faces were radiant with health and vigour. It made an unusual picture, infinitely more attractive than those which Degas loved to paint. The atmosphere in Degas's ballet pictures is always somewhat gloomy; the dancers, caught unawares during their exercises, which are often far from graceful, seem to be tormented martyrs. Here, on the contrary, everything seemed gay and carefree and, in spite of the masses of people, one breathed freely. The male and female dancers, who sat along the walls in groups or walked about the hall waiting for the rehearsal to begin, did not in the least look like martyrs or 'victims of their profession'.

Fokine led me in and presented me to the company. My bow was answered by a mass curtsey performed by all the rules of court etiquette. Only after this ritual did I proceed to greet the artists I knew, of whom Gerdt, Kchessinskaya and Solianikov were engaged in the principal parts ... Some of them I was seeing for the first time at so close a range and they looked charming in the delightful and becoming costumes, invented during the period of 1830, that were compulsory for rehearsals. Kchessinskaya, who did not conform to rules, was the only dancer to appear in a *tutu* – much shorter than the regulation ones.

The boys of the school stood in a separate group and they, too, wore their working dress and ballet shoes. When I passed them they bowed so deeply that I was embarrassed. A youth . . . was standing with them. I would not have noticed him had not Fokine presented him to me as the artist for whom he had especially composed the part of Armide's slave, so as to give him a chance to display his remarkable talent. Fokine counted on amazing the public by the unusual height of his *sauts* and *vols*, which the youth performed without any visible effort. I must confess that I was rather surprised when I saw this wonder face to face. He was a short, rather thick-set little fellow with the most ordinary, colourless face. He was more like a shop assistant than a fairy-tale hero. But this was – Nijinsky! Little did I expect then, as I shook his hand, that in two years' time he was to gain world renown and end his short but entirely fantastic career crowned with the halo of genius.

Soon silence was ordered. Tcherepnine sat down next to the pianist, the artists took their places and the rehearsal began. The rehearsal was that of the second scene – the coming to life of the Gobelins.

It is impossible to describe the excitement which took possession of me. The performance I had invented and dreamed of was unfolding itself to the music which had, so to say, been made to order for it, had been composed in accordance with my wishes and been actually sanctioned by me. What happiness it was to see my ideas realized *precisely* as I had wished, clothed in the stylish pomposity with which I had endeavoured to express my infatuation for eighteenth-century art, but instinct, at the same time, with the 'Hoffmannish' atmosphere of mystery that had delighted me since my youth. On this memorable day I experienced that very rare feeling – not unmixed, somehow, with pain – that occurs only when something long wished for has at last been accomplished . . . The faces of the dancers, too, seemed to be shining with happiness. The whole company, with very few exceptions, worshipped Fokine, feeling that in him they had a leader who would bring them, by a new path, to unparalleled triumphs.

But there was trouble in store. For reasons unknown Krupensky turned against the ballet and began to raise difficulties. He started to treat Benois arrogantly, and the painter 'saw red'. Diaghilev came to watch a rehearsal at the Mariinsky and after half an hour was politely but firmly asked to leave by a police officer. Benois thought that after this humiliating incident he must have sworn revenge on the Imperial Theatres. 'Certainly he could not have invented a better way than to create his own, world-famous theatre.'

Next Kchessinskaya, perhaps hoping to please the directorate and put a stop to the production, gave up her role. There was an hour of despondency. Benois and Fokine were discussing the crisis in the director's box when Pavlova rushed in, flushed with excitement, and, sitting on the edge of the box with her back to the theatre, offered to dance Armida. Then Gerdt tried to get out of his role, saying he was too old, and had to be persuaded. Krupensky refused to allow the expense of real ostrich feathers for the fans carried by Nubian attendants. At the dress rehearsal the dancers could not recognize each other in unfamiliar costumes and everything was chaos; Fokine lost his temper. Clearly another dress rehearsal was necessary, but the direction said the first night could not be cancelled at forty-eight hours' notice, and the programmes had already been printed. Benois resorted to desperate measures. He went to the telephone and rang up Bakst's brother, Isaiah Rosenberg, who contributed a column to the *Petersburg Gazette*, and told him how badly he and Fokine had been treated. Rosenberg made Benois write the article himself. It appeared next day and was a bombshell. The directorate gave in and 'Le Pavillon d'Armide' was postponed by a week.

The first performance of Benois's ballet took place on 25 November 1907, following the whole of 'Le Lac des Cygnes' and ending at one in the morning. It was a great success. After Pavlova, Gerdt, Nijinsky and the other soloists had made their bows, Benois, Tcherepnine and Fokine were called on the stage. For the painter it was the first time he had enjoyed this 'vainglorious pleasure'; and Pavlova, with her arms full of flowers, kissed him.[119]

That winter Nijinsky began to dance more small roles at the Mariinsky. He appeared in the *grand pas hongrois* in 'Raimonda', the *pas d'action* in 'La Bayadère', the *pas de trois* in 'Pakhita', and a *pas de deux* in 'The Little Hump-backed Horse.'[120]

On 21 March 1908, at a charity performance for the Administration of Imperial Theatres, Fokine proved his versatility by arranging an Egyptian ballet, 'Une Nuit d'Égypte', to music of Arensky, and a second version of 'Chopiniana'. In the former, although he was not allowed new scenery and had to make do with a set from 'Aida', he carried further his reform of ballet costume and insistence on correct period style. The principal roles were taken by Pavlova and Gerdt, while Nijinsky had the honour of being paired with the ballerina Preobrajenskaya in a dance for two slaves. The Chopin ballet drew its inspiration from the C Sharp Minor Waltz in the earlier version, and this number was retained while the other pieces for the new solos and *ensembles* were orchestrated by Maurice Keller. Gone were the ballroom, Chopin and the monks. In their place were a poet and a *corps* of sylphs. With extreme economy Fokine had adapted the longest skirts he could find from old ballets to recreate the image of Taglioni, as Bakst had done with the costume he had designed for Pavlova in the original 'Chopiniana'. At last Fokine had completely banished the *tutu*. The white-clad sylphs, all with hair parted in the middle, were led by Pavlova, Preobrajenskaya and Karsavina. Nijinsky in his black velvet tunic was the poet: this was a testing role, in which virtuosity counted for less than the ability to sustain a mood, which he did throughout the ballet with great success.[121]* Rather oddly, Chopin's 'Polonaise Militaire' was played as an overture.

Between its first performance at the Mariinsky Theatre in 1874 and Mussorgsky's death in alcoholic poverty in 1881, at the age of forty-two, his opera 'Boris Godounov' had been performed fifteen times.[122] It was then dropped from the repertory. In the early years of the twentieth century Rimsky-Korsakov rearranged the work, reorchestrating certain passages and eliminating many of the 'barbaric' elements. 'Boris' was revived for Chaliapine. In Petersburg, however, it was seldom given more than once a year, and Chaliapine's scenes were the only ones greeted with applause. It was the most unpopular opera in the repertory and the revolutionary implications of the Forest scene with the mob of peasants and the false Dmitri were not approved by the Establishment. The Court and Society stayed away from performances of 'Boris', which were only supported by a small group of liberal intellectuals known as *koutchkisti*.

*Fuller descriptions of 'Une Nuit d'Égypte' (revised as 'Cléopâtre') and the second 'Chopiniana' (as 'Les Sylphides') will be found in Chapter II.

Diaghilev loved Mussorgsky's 'Boris Godounov'. He remembered as a child hearing his aunt Panaeva, great grand-daughter of the poet Panaev and a delightful singer, saying to her servants 'I'm going to sing today, so don't forget to send for Mussorgsky.' The composer was her regular accompanist, although naturally it was never his own music he was asked to play. The words 'Don't forget to send for Mussorgsky' haunted Diaghilev all his life. He decided to take a production of 'Boris Godounov' to Paris in the summer of 1908.

First there arose the question of the score. Towards the end of his life Diaghilev wrote:

Certain incidents attendant on the first staging of 'Boris' in 1874 are well known; such as that the scenes in Pimen's cell and the revolutionary scene with the Innocent were banned, and that the direction of the Imperial Theatres insisted on Mussorgsky's adding the Polish scenes to the opera. In the autograph score of Mussorgsky, which has never been recopied and of course never published [in 1927] – the score used in the earliest productions of the opera, before the editing of Rimsky-Korsakov – the scene in Pimen's cell is not included: but I found it among Rimsky-Korsakov's papers. Much has been said about Mussorgsky's inspired idea of ending the opera not with the death of Boris, but with the scene of revolution and the Innocent's song, as was published in the first edition of Rimsky's version. But in Mussorgsky's manuscript the opera ends with the death of Boris, and on the last page the composer wrote 'End of the opera.'

When I came to put on 'Boris' in Paris Rimsky-Korsakov restored certain numbers which had been suppressed from the start, including the famous peal of bells, which was to cause a sensation in Paris. I was terrified of the opera's length and worried about the running order. My friends and I had endless discussions with Rimsky-Korsakov about transposing certain scenes. Among other questions we considered whether we could place the coronation after Pimen's cell, so as to separate the two crowd scenes and end [the act] with the coronation – which was chronologically possible* and theatrically a great improvement. The first year in Paris I gave neither the inn scene nor the scene in Marina's bedroom, so afraid was I of dragging out the opera – which, anyway, most people said the French would never understand! On top of his other alterations I persuaded Rimsky-Korsakov to revise the coronation scene, which struck me

*Benois did not agree with this. (*Memoirs* II, p. 252.)

as too short, and to complete and elaborate some of the carillons. He threw himself excitedly into this work; and the last word I had from him just before his death was a telegram to Paris from Russia asking me 'How do my new bits sound?'[123]

Feeling that the old Russia before Peter the Great and the Moscow oriental style of architecture were not in his line, Benois refused to undertake the décor. He contented himself with designing the more European Polish scene. The Moscow painters Korovine and Golo-vine also refused to design the opera, probably through fear of offending their patron Teliakovsky, who would have nothing to do with Diaghilev: but Golovine agreed to contribute certain general ideas for other artists to elaborate.[124]

Bilibine, an expert on Russian history and ikons, was called in to design and advise on the costumes. Following his indications, Diaghilev and Benois went hunting in the Tartar and Jewish shops of the Petersburg markets for silk, brocade, old head-dresses and tradi-tional costumes.[125] Furthermore, Diaghilev sent Bilibine to search the northern provinces, where he travelled from village to village, 'buying up from the peasants a mass of beautiful old hand-woven sarafans, which had been hoarded in chests for centuries'.[126] These treasures from the past were displayed on the stage of the little Hermitage Court Theatre (where Benois painted his Polish scene) for the inspection of the Grand Duke Vladimir, whose patronage Diaghilev had secured for the enterprise, as for his concerts in the previous year.[127]

Vladimir, second of the five sons of Alexander II, and uncle of the Tsar, was a big, loud-voiced, convivial man, but nevertheless the one committed patron of art among the twenty-seven Grand Dukes. Ranking after the four-year-old Tsarevitch and the Tsar's only surviving brother Michael Alexandrovitch, he was the fourth man in the Empire. He was sixty. His cousin, Grand Duke Alexander Mikhailovitch, who married the Tsar's sister Xenia, describes him thus:

Grand Duke Vladimir collected ancient ikons, he visited Paris twice a year, and he adored to give elaborate parties at his splendid palace in Tsarskoe Selo. A kind-hearted man, he fell victim to his eccentricities. A stranger meeting Grand Duke Vladimir Alexandrovitch was certain to be taken aback by the toughness and by the shouting voice of this Grand Seigneur of Russia. He treated the younger grand dukes with a maximum of contempt. None of us could have engaged him in conversation unless prepared to discuss subjects of art or the finesses of French cooking . . .[128]

The Grand Duke had little in common with his devious, reticent nephew, Tsar Nicholas II: conversely, we may guess that much of the latter's secretiveness and lack of frankness may have been assumed after his premature accession as a defence against the big, overbearing, booming uncles. The Grand Duke's wife, Marie Pavlovna, born a princess of Mecklenburg, was a vivacious, intelligent and brilliant woman, who flung herself into the job of being a leader of society as much as the Empress backed out of hers. Her Court was far more the centre of social and artistic life than that of the cold, proud and shy Tsarina, whom both she and her husband disliked. The Grand Duke Vladimir complained that when he was in the company of the Empress Alexandra Feodorovna he was driven to the desperate expedient of making a genealogical mistake in quoting the Almanach de Gotha in order to arouse his niece to break her silence.[129]

Grand Duke Vladimir was the father of Grand Duke André, Kchessinskaya's friend who was later to marry her. Since first seeing Tamara Karsavina dance, when she was still a pupil in the school, he had prophesied a great future for her and his fatherly interest had continued through the years. He had once caused a flutter in the ballet school by asking Varvara Ivanovna to send him the young Karsavina's photograph. The headmistress, while obliged to obey, was afraid of making her pupil conceited by singling her out, and after anxious consultations with the staff it had been decided to have a photograph taken of every girl in the school.[130]

When the Dowager Empress heard that Diaghilev was taking 'Boris' to Paris she said, 'Couldn't you find anything more boring to give them?'[131]

The Imperial Theatres gave us every possible help on this occasion [wrote Diaghilev. Such was the advantage of having Grand Duke Vladimir behind him]. The chorus was lent by the Bolshoi Theatre, Moscow, our singers were the best available: namely, Chaliapine, Smirnov, Yougina, Zbroueva and Petrenko. A team of stage mechanics came from Moscow under the leadership of K. F. Valz, the supreme technical wizard of his time. Our conductor was F. M. Blumenfeld.

We had come to an agreement with the Paris Opera that they should place their theatre at our disposal for the performance of 'Boris' on condition afterwards that the whole production with its sets and dresses should become their property. The intention was to add the opera to the Paris repertoire and sing it in French. (As the Opera directors subsequently sold the production to the Metropolitan in New York, this never happened; and after my Paris season 'Boris' was given in the United States before being seen again in Europe.)

So we set off for Paris, where a curious and expectant public awaited us. But we ran into incredible difficulties with the hidebound bureaucracy of the Opéra officials. We were told on arrival that it was out of the question to mount an opera as complicated as 'Boris' in the short time allowed for; that the Theatre's own repertory was more than filling the available rehearsal time, and that there was no possibility of rehearsing the singers on stage or of setting up such elaborate scenery. Whatever I asked for I received the same answer. 'Unheard of! Impossible!'

When at last we began to rehearse with the orchestra – and we were only allowed two or three rehearsals – the stage-hands set up such a din on the stage that I had to have a twenty-franc gold piece ready in my hand to tip them when Chaliapine or another principal came on to sing. This was the only way to make them stop their hammering and go off for a drink. Three days before we were due to open they told us that we could only hang our sets on the day of the first performance – and there were seven sets.[132]

Benois remembered this emergency rather differently and recorded Diaghilev's immediate reaction, which Diaghilev did not.

On the day of the semi-official rehearsal, forty-eight hours before the *répétition générale*, Petroman sprang a surprise on us and announced that a mistake had occurred for which we were to blame – that the décor had not the necessary dimensions, did not reach the floor, and that there was much repair work to be done which would take three or four days. Here Diaghilev showed his real self and saved the situation. He declared, quite calmly, that he would not put off the show and was ready to produce the opera without décor. Petroman was so terrified of a scandal that the impossible was done . . .

But even after this, we were still not sure that the dress rehearsal could take place ... some of the chorus singing had not been sufficiently re-hearsed and the only try-out with extras had taken place at midnight and turned into an uncontrollable orgy. This made another unforgettable im-pression: the huge stage of the Opéra, illuminated by only one candle, and crowding on to it a mass of two hundred filthy, stinking people from the street, with false beards awry, and hastily pulled-on boyar fur coats and caps. No wonder that, surprised at their own appearance, these hungry casual 'actors' decided to have some fun, and began to sing and dance, impervious to all calls to order. A catastrophe seemed inevitable and even our fearless Diaghilev took fright.

Then another theatrical miracle took place. Diaghilev decided to ar-range a supper at Larue and hold a council of war to decide whether to give the performance the next day or not. The whole team was summoned, the minor 'props' as well as the artists and the make-up man, a stammerer whom Chaliapine trusted above everybody else. Diaghilev must have been scared to have recourse to such a democratic method![133]

In Diaghilev's words: 'I called a meeting of my collaborators ... Everyone was there, including our Russian technicians. The most vociferous speaker was Valz, backed up by his stage mechanics and by the wig-maker Feodor Grigorievitch Zaika, who always reminded me of Hoffmann's Drosselmeyer. They worked themselves into a frenzy, declaring that postponement would mean the ruin of our enterprise. I decided to take the risk and let the show go on.'

On the night before 'Boris' opened everyone went to bed late. In the early hours Diaghilev heard a knock at his door in the Hôtel Mirabeau.

'Who is it?'

'Can I come in? It is I, Chaliapine.'

'What's the matter, Feodor Ivanovitch?'

'Is there a settee in your room? I can't bear to be alone.'

'So that giant,' wrote Diaghilev, 'spent the night in my room, sleeping fitfully, curled up on a tiny sofa.'[134]

Benois wrote:

The coronation, the polonaise, the revolution were rehearsed three times in the afternoon under Diaghilev's supervision. The chief artists rehearsed their parts with the piano, the painter gave the last touch to banners and ikons, and thirty seamstresses sewed, mended and ironed, I dashed up and down like a madman (there were no lifts or telephones), Diaghilev was reading the proofs of the magnificent programme.[135]

The polonaise was to be danced by dancers of the Opéra ballet, but led by two artists from Petersburg. These were Alexandra Vassilieva, a lady no longer young, who was the companion of the balletomane Besobrasov, and Mikhail Alexandrov, a handsome, vain fellow who believed himself to be an illegitimate son of Alexander II,[136]* and who, as we shall shortly see, was perhaps to play a decisive role in Nijinsky's life.

At last Diaghilev and his friends were able to see the sets, which had been painted in Russia, hung up, put together and lit for the first time. Huge crowds of noblemen, archers, peasants and priests in costumes of such colour and splendour as Paris had never seen, moved before them. The production was ready a few minutes before the performance began.

I hardly had time to change before the curtain went up [wrote Diaghilev]. By the end of the first scene the public were beginning to enjoy themselves. Pimen's cell, with unseen choirs of monks singing in the wings, caused a sensation, and during the coronation scene we realized that 'Boris' was going to be a triumph. I hardly saw this scene as I was superintending the entry of processions of supers. During the second interval when the stage-hands, thunderstruck by our success, saw me in my tail-coat and white gloves moving on some hedges and placing benches for the Polish garden scene, they ran to help me. I had been refused any water for the fountain – all available water, apparently, being reserved exclusively for the firemen – but this did not diminish the success of the Polish scene. French ladies, infatuated with Smirnov, were soon to be heard trilling *O povtori, povtori, Marina!* sounding their guttural r's. The impression made by Chaliapine in the scene of Boris's madness was really overwhelming, and the audience went wild. In the scene of revolution, which I presented in deep snow, the episode of the Innocent, the passing of the imposter Dmitri standing upright in his sleigh and the grand ensembles of the chorus, who brandished torches as they sang, impressed the public most favourably. The only setback in the whole performance was the length of the last intermission, caused by the insistence of Valz on hanging some huge and enormously heavy chandeliers in the set representing the Great Hall of the Kremlin.

*According to Kchessinskaya, a son of Prince Dolgoroukov, the brother of Alexander II's second (morganatic) wife Princess Yurievskaya. Mme B. Nijinska also thought this might be correct.

At this point the audience grew restless and began to stamp. But the scene of Boris's death, when the ascetic monks came on with tall candles and when Boris spoke his last words to his children, was a knockout. The future of Russian opera in the west was assured.

That night, after the opera, Chaliapine strode beside me along the *grands boulevards*, saying over and over again, 'We've done something tonight. I don't know what, but we've really done something!'[137]

Years later Benois still recalled the excitement of that night.

I remember so vividly returning to our hotels at dawn, arm in arm with Diaghilev reluctant to part, and on reaching the Place Vendôme looking up with a challenge at that other conqueror standing on the column!* Even when we reached our rooms we began calling out to each other across the yards, I from my Hôtel de l'Orient to Diaghilev's Hôtel Mirabeau. The sun was already high in the sky when Diaghilev's cousin, Paffka, also rather tipsy, came to my room, and, hearing that we could communicate with Diaghilev through the window, he too started calling out. Finally people were peering out of their windows, indignant at being disturbed, and the porter knocked at our door. I had great trouble in dragging Paffka away from the window and putting him to sleep on a sofa in my room.[138]

Diaghilev wrote:

To show how dubious our whole undertaking had been considered in Russia I must admit that even the Grand Duke Vladimir Alexandrovitch, who was so fond of me, had not dared to come to Paris for our first performance. It was only when he was bombarded with telegrams announcing the triumph of 'Boris' that he and the Grand Duchess made up their minds to take the Nord-Express as it were straight to the theatre. The Grand Duke was genuinely happy and proud that this project which he had been almost the only one to encourage, which he had thrown himself into heart and soul, and which he had helped me to bring off, should have met with so outstanding a success. He was amazed at the high standard of our performance; and at a party he gave at his hotel, the Continental, for the whole company and stage staff he told them in the course of a little speech 'It isn't thanks to me or Diaghilev that "Boris" is such a success – it's all *your* doing. We only planned it: you made it come true.' The chorus misunderstood these words and thought the Grand Duke was dissatisfied with me.

*Napoleon I.

Before he went back to Petersburg the Grand Duke asked me, 'Is it true that you are down 20,000 roubles? Tell me the truth and I'll ask the Emperor to make it up.' I told him it was not true. He smiled and said, 'Perhaps you'd rather notify me in writing?' I insisted that there was not a word of truth in the story. Getting up and coming over to me, he raised his arm, made the sign of the cross and said 'May this blessing preserve you from all evil intrigues!' Then he embraced me.[139]

One result of the Russian opera's success in Paris was that Diaghilev met a woman who was to become one of his dearest friends. Misia, born Godebska, half Polish, half Belgian, was a vivacious, attractive woman in her early twenties, who had been the friend of Mallarmé, Lautrec, Renoir, Bonnard and Vuillard (the last four of whom had painted her) and who was at this time married to the rich proprietor of *Le Matin*, Alfred Edwards, though soon to exchange him for José-Maria Sert.

Misia declared that 'Boris Godounov' was her second love: Debussy's 'Pelléas' had been her first.

For the first night I had invited a few friends into the big box between the pillars. But in the middle of the first act I was so moved by the music that I made my way to the gallery and remained sitting there on a step till the end . . . The stage streamed with gold. Chaliapine's voice rose powerful and magnificent above Mussorgsky's overwhelming music . . . I left the theatre stirred to the point of realizing that something had been changed in my life. The music was with me always . . . I made incessant propaganda for this work and dragged to it all the people I loved . . . Not satisfied with attending every performance, I ordered that all the unsold seats should be brought to me, so that no place remained unsold and Diaghilev had the encouraging illusion of financial success.

Some of this may be exaggerated, but Misia was to prove indeed a staunch supporter of Diaghilev.

It was shortly after the first night [she wrote], that, dining one evening at Prunier's with Sert, I saw Diaghilev.* Sert knew him, and introduced

*According to Benois, who is almost always accurate, it was after the first night of 'Boris' that 'we' – by which I take it he means Diaghilev, possibly Chaliapine, Diaghilev's cousin Pavel Koribut-Kubitovitch and himself – 'celebrated our success quite intimately with Misia Edwards and Mme Bénardaky in the Café de la Paix'. (*Memoirs* II, p. 252.) Yet it would seem that Misia Sert had heard 'Boris' before meeting Diaghilev (M. Sert: *Two or Three Muses*, pp. 111, 112).

him to me. The fervour of my enthusiasm for 'Boris' very soon opened the doors of his heart for me. We remained until five in the morning, and found it intolerable to have to part. The next day he came to see me, and our friendship ended only with his death.[140]

The Serts were destined to prove their friendship in a particular way, for they more than once came to the rescue of Diaghilev's ballet company in times of stress.

According to Bourman, there was a man in the ballet employed as a pimp by rich members of Petersburg society, introducing them to girl dancers who would subsequently appear at the theatre wearing expensive jewels.[141] Although Bourman gives him a different name, there is evidence that he was Alexandrov, who had led the polonaise in 'Boris'.[142] He and an accomplice invited Nijinsky and Bourman to meet a friend at dinner. Why they invited Bourman is not clear, unless they thought Nijinsky would be too shy to come without him. The dinner was at Cubat, one of the best restaurants, overlooked from above by a gallery off which opened the private rooms. The host was Prince Pavel Dmitrievitch Lvov.*

This prince was the artistic member of an old family which would contribute a president to the third (reactionary) Duma of 1912. He was thirty, tall, good-looking, with big blue eyes and a monocle. He had seen Nijinsky dance and was fascinated by him; but learning from the two pimps that the young dancer was sexually naïve – had not 'learnt the score' – he hit upon an ingenious ruse (if we are to believe Bourman) to try him out. He said that his cousin – a beautiful princess, of whom he produced a miniature – was in love with Nijinsky and wanted to buy him a ring. Any young man would have been intrigued by such a romantic situation. The dinner led to a visit to Fabergé; this led to more dinners, visits to night-clubs – such as The Aquarium, where the American Negro Claude Hopkins demonstrated tap-dancing for the first time in Petersburg – more presents and more parties during which 'Vaslav and the Prince would retire to discuss the merits of the unknown princess.'[143]

*Bourman, who calls Alexandrov 'Vasilev', and gives his accomplice the name of 'Guttmann', when there is reason to believe he was a friend of Kchessinskaya's called Baron Gotch, calls Lvov 'Prince Michail-Dmitri'.

Such is Bourman's lurid account. The fact remains that Lvov, a great patron of sportsmen, was a good friend to the whole Nijinsky family, whom he helped financially. Eleonora liked him; and when Bronia had a poisoned foot he took her to a doctor and perhaps saved her career.[144]

Affairs between men were accepted as quite natural in Petersburg society[145] – which was not the case in Paris in those days, and even less in London. It seems safe to state, from his sister's evidence, and in the light of after events, that physically Nijinsky preferred women, even if emotionally, lacking a father, he needed the protective love of an older man.

Nijinsky had never before had such smart clothes, eaten or drunk so well, or been at home in such luxurious houses. To judge from photographs taken at this time, the Prince's admiration brought out in him an inherent vein of feminine provocation. Just as, when dancing, he had the instinctive knowledge of the pattern his limbs were forming without the need to correct his poses in a mirror as other dancers did,[146] so was he conscious that his high cheek-bones and mysterious faun-like look, half voluptuous, half mocking, which it was easy to assume, could make up for the lack of high spirits and brilliant conversation. He kept trying out different ways of doing his hair: a fringe, a slanting parting, a straight parting slightly right of centre, with the fine hair brushed up at the sides.[147]

Was Pavel Dmitrievitch disappointed in Nijinsky offstage? Did he find after the first weeks of their friendship that the dancer was not quite his type? Nijinsky was small in a part where size is usually admired.[148] It was, incidentally, at the house of Lvov that he had what was probably his first sexual experience with a woman. She was a *cocotte* and Vaslav was frightened and put off.*

The relationship lasted a few months but the Prince, apparently, did not fall in love. At least, he was not jealous enough to wish to keep Nijinsky to himself, for he introduced him to the immensely rich Pole, Count Tishkievitch. Nijinsky, however, apparently loved Lvov. In his *Diary* of 1918, which, admittedly, we have to 'interpret', he wrote 'One day I met a Russian prince who introduced me to a

---

*So he told his wife. His sister does not believe the experiment, which she knew about, took place under Lvov's roof.

Polish count . . . This count bought me a piano: I did not love him. I loved the prince and not the count.'[149] According to Mme Bronislava Nijinska it was Lvov, not Tishkievitch, who bought Nijinsky the piano. She remembers the Count as a married man with four children who had known her parents years before in Vilna, who bored her with his lectures on morals and did not approve of girls using scent.[150] Her memories, presumably accurate, cast doubt on the exactitude of her brother's *Diary* or, perhaps, on that of its editor.

Then came the meeting which was to be as fruitful for the future of ballet throughout the world as another famous encounter – that of the Emperor and Empress with Rasputin three years before – would prove disastrous to the House of Romanov.

Diaghilev – who at that time was having an affair with a young man called Alexis Mavrine, employed as his secretary – had of course seen Nijinsky on stage before and since his graduation: Nijinsky knew of Diaghilev's reputation as a champion of Russian art. According to Bourman their very first meeting was during an interval at the Mariinsky. Nijinsky was walking up and down with Prince Lvov in the big hall with mirrors, where to this day Soviet citizens circulate on the long carpets which run beside the walls, leaving empty the polished parquet in the middle; and Lvov introduced him to Diaghilev. The two men must have presented an exceptional contrast. The elder with his big head and imposing manner, with the celebrated white streak in his dark hair which had earned him the nickname 'Chinchilla', and the unnecessary monocle, seemed taller than he was. The younger, five foot four inches in height, in spite of his slanting eyes and the long muscular neck which rose from narrow, sloping shoulders, was essentially private-looking and appeared smaller beside him. Later that evening Diaghilev is said to have joined Lvov and Nijinsky at a party *chez* Cubat. Bourman's account of the conversation at this party, of Diaghilev's boasting of the glorious productions he would show to Europe and Nijinsky's tirade on the superiority of the Petersburg to the Moscow school of ballet, is inherently improbable – we know, for instance, that Nijinsky did not express himself in long speeches: yet one detail recorded by Bourman makes it seem likely that a meeting or meetings of this nature did occur in a restaurant (perhaps he telescoped two parties together).

Bourman remembers Diaghilev taking offence at being described as an *entrepreneur*, with the result that he bore Bourman a grudge and did not sign him up until his third season in Western Europe. This does not seem to be the kind of detail which is invented.[151]

In Nijinsky's own words:

> Lvov* introduced me to Diaghilev, who asked me to come to the Europa Hotel where he lived. I disliked him for his too self-assured voice, but went to seek my luck. I found my luck. At once I allowed him to make love to me. I trembled like a leaf. I hated him, but pretended, because I knew that my mother and I would die of hunger otherwise . . .[152]

Now let us interpret. We realize that as the *Diary* was written during the critical period when Nijinsky's mind was breaking down, it might *all* be a fantasy, without a word of truth in it: but we know from corroborative evidence of many of the incidents which he records that this is not the case. We do not look for logic in the *Diary*, and we notice that within a few lines the writer can utterly reverse his point of view. For instance, a 'letter' of accusation to Diaghilev beginning 'I cannot name you because I have no name for you' ends touchingly 'I am a tender being and want to write you a cradle song . . . a lullaby . . . sleep peacefully, sleep, sleep peacefully.' (The editor, Mme Nijinsky, here appends a footnote: 'The lullaby is written in verse and its translation is not possible.'[153]) Rightly or wrongly, in 1918, the sick Nijinsky felt betrayed by Diaghilev, who, besides, had transferred his love to Massine. Most of the passages relating to Diaghilev sound the bitter recriminatory note of a lovers' quarrel and remind us of certain terrible pages in that famous letter – of which only the more Christian part was published under the name of *De Profundis* – written in Reading Gaol. I'm good: you're bad. I'm right: you're wrong. The self-pity, also reminiscent of a lovers' quarrel, which makes Nijinsky introduce several times in his *Diary* the dying-of-hunger theme, here leads him, as it were, to put the blame on Diaghilev for the privations of his childhood. In 1908, of course, there was no conceivable danger of his not being able to support his mother in comfort. So I interpret: 'I was depressed when I

---

*In the published version of *The Diary of Vaslav Nijinsky* the translator or the editor has misread 'Lvov' as 'Ivor'.

found that my friendship with Prince Lvov, whom I was fond of and found attractive, could not be permanent. At least this new life brought me smart clothes and a piano. When I was introduced to Diaghilev I was becoming used to the idea of being passed around, and imagined that this was the way of the world and such was to be my fate. Diaghilev was exactly twice my age. His voice and overbearing manner rather put me off, but I knew he might be helpful in my career. Our first attempt at making love in the hotel room was not very successful.'

Perhaps we should here add, on Nijinsky's behalf and in fairness to Diaghilev even though it means anticipating a later phase of our story, 'I could not foresee that the sexual aspect of our relationship would sink into unimportance beside the fact that Diaghilev's tuition and encouragement would make me the greatest performer of the age, the most wonderful dancer who ever lived. How could I guess in that hotel bedroom that I should come to depend on Diaghilev as much as any one man ever depended on another?'

Such, in November or December 1908, was the first encounter of two men whose friendship was to become the most notorious since that of Oscar Wilde* and Alfred Douglas in the previous decade. Their union could produce no children, but it would give birth to masterpieces – and change the history of the dance, of music and of painting throughout the world.

*Diaghilev had met Wilde in Paris in 1898. The exiled poet wrote about him to Smithers, his last publisher – and Beardsley's – : 'Have you a copy of Aubrey's drawing of Mlle de Maupin? There is a young Russian here, who is a great amateur of Aubrey's art, who would love to have one. He is a great collector, and rich. So you might send him a copy and name a price, and also deal with him for drawings by Aubrey. His name is Serge de Diaghilew, Hôtel St James, Rue St Honoré, Paris.' (*The Letters of Oscar Wilde*, p. 734.)

CHAPTER TWO

1909

What decided Diaghilev to bring the Russian Ballet to the West?

It could be argued that the existence of the superb Mariinsky company, headed by the celebrated Kchessinskaya, with young artists of genius such as Pavlova, Karsavina and the twenty-one-year-old Nijinsky, made a Paris season inevitable; or that the new ideas of Fokine were bound to find a new public outside Russia; or that Bakst and Benois, the most imaginative stage-designers to have appeared for a century, were inevitably destined for international fame. Yet what ballet company, apart from small groups of character dancers, had ever gone abroad before? In fact two: the Milanese had presented Manzotti's 'Excelsior' in Paris and London in the 1880's,* and during the summer of 1908 Pavlova and Bolm had led a small troupe on a tour of Sweden, Denmark and Germany. Furthermore, what proof was there that Paris, which had seen the flowering of ballet in the Romantic period and its decadence in the age of Degas, could still be persuaded to take an interest in this *démodé* art? Kchessinskaya had made some guest appearances at the Opéra in 1907 and 1908 without sensational acclaim. Then it must be remembered that Bakst and Benois had so far given in Russia only a hint of the marvels they were now on the brink of creating.

Romola Nijinsky wrote that Nijinsky persuaded Diaghilev 'in the early winter of 1909' to present the ballet in Western Europe.[1] Dandré relates how he and Pavlova, at a luncheon in Petersburg in the winter of 1908, 'tried to take advantage of this opportunity [the formation of a committee for the presentation of opera in Paris] to

*Enrico Cecchetti was *premier danseur*.

show the ballet as well' and that '[Diaghilev] was terrified at our suggestion.'[2] Fokine had received, during his 1908 summer holiday in Switzerland, which he partly spent giving lessons to the rich amateur Ida Rubinstein, a letter from Benois revealing that he 'had the idea of persuading Sergei Pavlovitch Diaghilev to take the ballet company to Paris' and to present 'Le Pavillon d'Armide' and other Fokine ballets.[3] Astruc, of the Société Musicale, the promoter of the Parisian concerts, whose interests now extended to Russian opera and ballet, describes how it was he who begged Diaghilev, during the season of 'Boris Godounov', to bring the Russian Ballet in the following year.[4]

Nijinsky, Pavlova, Benois and Astruc may all have been quite correct in recalling these conversations and individually quite justified in believing that he or she had been the deciding factor in the history of the Russian Ballet. But Diaghilev had a way of testing people's reactions, of pretending to be opposed to a course he really favoured, of planting the seed of an idea in a colleague's mind, so that the colleague found himself initiating proposals and persuading Diaghilev to embark on a course of action to which he was already in his heart committed.* Certainly it had been Benois who first persuaded him to take seriously the art of ballet, but once Diaghilev had observed the reforms of Fokine being realized on the Mariinsky stage, once he had seen in 'Le Pavillon d'Armide' that a new unity and expressiveness were possible, and once he had realized that in Pavlova and Nijinsky there were ready at hand two artists of genius to interpret the new ballets, he decided that new kinds of triumph could be enjoyed in the West which – with Teliakovsky in command of the Imperial Theatres – would be impossible in Russia. Two of the essential elements were Pavlova and Nijinsky and it was a feat of diplomacy to make both dancers think that they had talked him into exporting the ballet. The third essential was Fokine, and since he had already worked with Benois and got along well with him, it was for Benois to bring him in. The fourth element, Astruc, was indispensable at the Paris end.

---

*An example of this is Diaghilev's reaction to Benois' proposal to present 'Giselle' in Paris. (See p. 137.) I here draw my own conclusions: but Mme Sokolova, when she read this passage, exclaimed 'Just like the old man!'

The idea of taking Russian ballet to the West had in fact been for some years at the back of Diaghilev's mind. In Moscow in 1906 he had told the French music critic Robert Brussel that in three years he would bring the Russian Ballet to Paris.[5] After the first production of 'Le Pavillon d'Armide' at the Mariinsky in November 1907 Diaghilev told Benois 'This must be shown to Europe'.[6] Suddenly, after the success of 'Boris' these vague thoughts and plans crystallized: the moment had come.

Gabriel Astruc, who had put on the Russian concerts, describes how over dinner *chez* Paillard in summer 1908 he persuaded Diaghilev that Paris must be shown the glories of the Russian dance. This is how Astruc remembered the conversation. He mentioned how he had admired the dancing in the Polish scene of 'Boris', for which Alexandra Vassilieva had come from Petersburg to teach the Opéra dancers – and lead them in – a polonaise.

'You seem so fond of dancing,' said Diaghilev, 'you ought to come to St Petersburg to see our Imperial Ballet. You, in France, do not honour dancing any longer, and the art is incomplete as you show it today. You possess fine ballerinas but you have no idea what a male dancer can be. Our male dancers are stars in Russia. Nothing can give you an idea of how fine our Vaslav is* – I believe that nothing like him has been seen since Vestris.'

'Does he dance alone?'

'Yes – but sometimes with a partner who is almost his equal, la Pavlova. She is the greatest ballerina in the world, excelling both in classicism and character. Like a Taglioni she doesn't dance, but floats; of her, also, one might say that she could walk over a cornfield without bending an ear.'

'But you must have great producers and *maîtres de ballet* to use all those fine talents.'

'We have. There is the old Cecchetti, master of us all, who carries the torch of classicism. Then there is a true genius, Michel Fokine, a descendant of the greatest *maîtres de ballet* of all time.'

'Nijinsky, Fokine and Pavlova must come to Paris – next year.'

'But Paris will never come to see whole evenings of dancing.'[7]

Diaghilev knew perfectly well that he could hold Paris enthralled with whole evenings of Russian ballet – Russian ballet as *he* would

---

*I have quoted Astruc's text of this conversation exactly; but Diaghilev had no personal acquaintance with Nijinsky at the time.

present it – but he wanted Astruc to enjoy the illusion of persuading him.

This conversation took place on 2 June 1908, and Astruc preserved in his files the scribbled notes he made at the dinner table. On a double sheet of writing-paper headed 'Paillard, 2 Chaussée d'Antin, Paris' we can see the birth of the Ballets Russes.[8]

First Astruc wrote the names of ballets Diaghilev proposed to give: 'Le Pavillon d'Armide de Chérepnine avec La Pawlowa – dec et livret Benoist [*sic*]. 2 actes. Sylvia – Léo Delibes. 3 tableaux.' But 'Sylvia' is crossed out. Then 'Giselle . . . . 2 actes.' It was evidently intended that the evenings of ballet should alternate with opera, as indeed they did in the first Russian season, for next is written 'Mozart et Salieri de Rimsky Korsakoff – Anselmi & Chaliapine'. And the theatre Astruc proposed for this season was not the Opéra but 'Théâtre Sarah Bernhardt. Mai 1909.'

Next Astruc made a list, partly no doubt dictated by Diaghilev, of possible patrons for the season: 'S. A. la Princesse Murat – Mse de Ganay – Csse de Chevigné – Csse Ed de Pourtalès – Csse de Hohen-felsen – Psse de Polignac – Grand Duc Cyrille – Csse Jean de Castel-lane – Bnne? de Rothschild.'

Opposite, Astruc totted up costs – 265,000 francs including 50,000 for himself as impresario. Sixteen performances, estimated to take 20,000 francs each, totalled 320,000 francs. At the top of the first page where there was a little space left alongside the letter-heading he then wrote the names of proposed ballerinas: 'Pawlowa II. Préobrajen-skaia. Gelzer. Trefilowa. Sedowa. Kiakcht.' Finally, in the shallow space above the engraved word 'Paillard' he wrote: 'Nijinsky, Kos-low, Mordkine, Andrianow, Bolm, Fokin.'

On 4 June[9] Astruc broached the subject of a season of ballet and opera with the Grand Duchess Vladimir (Marie Pavlovna) at a party of Princesse Edmond de Polignac's. She approved of the idea. Diaghilev and Astruc had further talks, and although the nature of the repertory and the composition of the company remained fluid until almost a month before the Russians came to Paris in the follow-ing May, a contract was signed.

In the contract it was stated that Diaghilev accepted entire financial responsibility for the Russian Season, while Astruc undertook the administration, the publicity and the sale of tickets, for which he was to receive only 2½ per cent of the takings, Diaghilev having induced him to accept half his usual fee.[10] Astruc was Diaghilev's sponsor with the Parisian press, a guarantee of good relations. In France the distinction between editorial matter and advertising is not as sharp as in English-speaking countries, and a sum was set aside for the purpose of commissioning articles from distinguished critics. In fact, Astruc would exert himself in a number of ways not specified in the contract, such as dealing with the decorators and upholsterers who were to renovate the shabby old Châtelet Theatre – for it was at the enormous Châtelet, the home of popular spectacle, and not at the Sarah Bernhardt opposite, that the Russian season was to be held.

Diaghilev made himself responsible not only for financing the season and for presenting the artists of the Imperial Theatres in their own décors and costumes, but for establishing a committee of patrons made up of the leaders of Parisian society and headed by the Grand Duke and Grand Duchess Vladimir.

Returning to Petersburg from his annual holiday in Venice, Diaghilev set about planning his repertory for Paris and engaging dancers. Throughout Petersburg the double windows were screwed into position for the winter; the ice grew thicker on the Neva; the carriages, droshkies and a few cars sped through the snowy streets beneath endless façades of palaces; the gold spire of the yellow and white Admiralty and the gold dome of the adjacent St Isaac's could be seen for miles, while across the river the even higher gold needle of the church within the dread Petropavlovsky Fortress – whose gun daily proclaimed noon – pierced the frozen sky.

Diaghilev's latest flat in Zamiatin Pereúlok, off the English Quay, between the Horse Guards Barracks and the Neva, five minutes' walk south-west of the Admiralty, was to be the centre of this winter season of planning which the planners, who were to take part in the conquest of Europe by the Russian Ballet in the following spring, would remember with such pride and pleasure for the rest of their lives. It was a ground-floor flat, of a pattern common in Petersburg. The principal rooms faced the street, and the servants' quarters, kitchen and bathroom looked on to an inner courtyard. The drawing-room had paper with grey and beige stripes; there were the pictures by Lenbach, Repine and others, and a grand piano. Next door was the slightly smaller dining-room with an oval table covered by a cloth: the Jacobean chairs had not survived from the old flat on the Fontanka. It was here that meetings of the artistic committee were held. In Diaghilev's simple bedroom a light burned before an ikon. Diaghilev's old nurse was now dead and he was looked after only by Vassili Zuikov.[11]

The former colleagues of the 'World of Art' days assembled to plan the first joint season of opera and ballet. Bakst, dapper and scented, in *pince-nez*, with upturned reddish moustache, always busy with a sketch pad; Benois, bearded, also spectacled, enthusiastic, gentle and persuasive, with a slight stoop and twinkling eyes; little cynical Walter Nouvel, with a tendency to pour cold water on the more flamboyant schemes. The group was sometimes augmented by Valerien Svetlov, the critic, with his quiff of white hair;[12] by Prince Argutinsky-Dolgoroukov, a diplomat and collector of paintings and Russian porcelain;[13] by Besobrasov, the bluff old balletomane, who could drink an infinite number of cups of tea;[14] by the quiet Valentin Serov, after Repine the most distinguished living Russian painter, the only man whose word Diaghilev obeyed;[15] by the tall, lanky Tcherepnine; and by the genial Dr Sergei Botkine, who had a beautiful house near the Tauride Palace full of Peter the Great furniture,[16] and was married to the sister-in-law of Bakst.*

Then Benois introduced Fokine to the group's session: he was the one man they could not do without. The young choreographer felt the charm and power of Diaghilev's personality. He was delighted to hear that it was intended to include his 'Pavillon d'Armide' and 'Chopiniana' in the Paris repertory. Diaghilev asked him to think over some Russian themes. They needed a third ballet. Benois suggested Fokine's 'Egyptian Nights', and Diaghilev was interested, but thought Arensky's music too feeble to be given in Paris.[17]

The company, to be composed of artists borrowed from the Imperial Theatres during their vacation, would need a *régisseur*, a manager. After two unsuccessful attempts had been made to employ officials of the Mariinsky, Fokine suggested his friend Grigoriev,

*He was not the Dr Botkine (whose name was Eugene) who attended the Tsar and died with him in Ekaterinburg. Grigoriev confuses the two men.

who had helped him stage several ballets in the last few years; and the big, devoted and imperturbable Sergei Leonidovitch Grigoriev, who, like Atlas, was to support the whole administration of the Ballets Russes on his shoulders for twenty years, was drawn into the enterprise.

I went to see Diaghilev in a great state of excitement. Eight years had gone by since I had first seen him and heard his name ... I rang the bell of his flat with a certain trepidation ... A man with a little beard asked me to come in and said that Diaghilev would like me to wait for him. I was rather glad of the delay, which gave me the chance to calm down ... Diaghilev came in, and after shaking hands, asked me to sit down. Our interview was very brief. He said that Fokine had recommended me as a *régisseur*; that if I agreed he would pay me so much; and that my first duty would be to sign contracts with the artists. I agreed to the terms and he handed me the contracts... He gave me a curiouss mile; his mouth alone smiled, the rest of his face remaining entirely serious ... On leaving him I felt happy: our meeting, his offer to me, and the coming visit to Paris, had completely changed my life. For the moment everything seemed interesting, eventful and full of meaning.[18]

A week later Grigoriev accompanied Fokine to a meeting of the artistic committee.

They were sitting in the dining-room ... on the table to Diaghilev's right stood a samovar, and his valet Vassili poured out tea. There were biscuits and jam on the table, and several plates of Russian sweets. In front of every member of the company lay a sheet of paper and a pencil. Diaghilev had a large exercise book in front of him. He presided over the meeting. Fokine and I were introduced to everybody... The only person I knew was Benois.

Grigoriev describes Bakst, Besobrasov, Svetlov and Nouvel. 'There was one more person, a young man, modest and attractive. His name was Mavrine: he was Diaghilev's secretary ...'[19]

Everyone who attended these meetings smoked except Diaghilev, Benois, Fokine and Grigoriev.[20]

Diaghilev said he wished to change the name of 'Chopiniana' to 'Les Sylphides'. Fokine argued, but gave in. At the Mariinsky, the ballet was preceded by the 'Polonaise Militaire', a survival from the days before it had become an abstract *ballet blanc*, which was clearly out of keeping. Diaghilev wished to replace this by a prelude, and everyone agreed. The Chopin pieces were also to be reorchestrated.* Benois was to design the scenery and costumes (the latter being imitated from old lithographs of Taglioni).

Another week passed and the committee assembled again. This time Diaghilev announced startling decisions about 'Egyptian Nights', which was to be called 'Cléopâtre'. Arensky's overture was to be replaced by Taneev's from the opera 'Oresteia'. Cleopatra's entrance was to be made to music from Rimsky's 'Mlada'. The Bacchanale would be danced to 'Autumn' from Glazunov's 'Seasons'. The orgy-*divertissement* was to end with the dance of the Persian girls from 'Khovanshschina.'

He paused here for a moment, looking at our astonished faces, then smiled and continued: 'Then the end of the ballet is banal. It must be changed. The youth poisoned by Cleopatra, instead of coming to life again must be killed for good, and his bride must sob over his lifeless body as the curtain falls. And since we have no music for such a dramatic scene, I will, ask our dear Nikolai Nikolayevitch [Tcherepnine] to write this music for us.' Tcherepnine was astounded . . . we all sat silent, till at last Fokine spoke. 'Well,' he said, 'with so many changes – it will be an entirely new ballet!' 'That does not matter', said Diaghilev, 'what I want to know is whether you like the idea.' We all said yes, and he continued, 'As for you Lyovushka [Bakst], you will have to paint us a lovely *décor*.' Lyovushka instantly began tracing the plan of the scene as he visualized it and describing it in his curious guttural accent. 'There will be a huge temple on the banks of the Nile. Columns; a sultry day; the scent of the East and a great many lovely women with beautiful bodies . . .' Diaghilev shook his head, as if at an incorrigible child; and we all laughed . . . Diaghilev asked us all to go into the next room, where he sat at the piano with Nouvel next to him and asked us to listen to the altered score. I did not know that Diaghilev could play the piano and watched him doing so. He played very well, biting his tongue the whole time, especially when he came to difficult bits. He would frequently stop and explain to Fokine the passages in the score that had been altered. Fokine sat holding the score and marking them. When the playing was over, everyone started talking and going into the details of the ballet. Nouvel laughed in his peculiar way, remarking that

*By Stravinsky, Grigoriev adds: but Diaghilev did not meet the composer until 6 February 1909.

what we had just heard was just a mediocre *salade russe*. Diaghilev replied that this was unavoidable; he required a third ballet; and this was the only music available. He dismissed Nouvel's criticism almost without considering it.[21]

Nouvel, of course, was right: 'Cléopâtre' was a hotch-potch, yet it would be the cause of several of the big sensations of the Paris season. It is curious to reflect that the fastidious Diaghilev presented three ballets in his 1909 season with music which was in some way unsatisfactory. 'Cléopâtre' was this astonishing *mélange* by six different composers; Tcherepnine's score for 'Le Pavillon d'Armide' was old-fashioned and derivative; and while Chopin's mazurkas, valses and preludes used in 'Les Sylphides' were music of a high order they lost their special quality when orchestrated. Even at this stage, about four months before the Paris opening, Diaghilev was predominantly interested in the operas he was going to present, and regarded the ballet merely as an additional *bonne bouche*.

Before the principal dancers could be signed up it was necessary to decide what roles there were for whom. It was inconceivable that Matilda Kchessinskaya should be left out of the expedition, as she was not only the principal ballerina of the Mariinsky, but also one of the most influential women in Russia: yet she was a dancer in the traditional style, too set in her mould to adapt herself to Fokine's new plasticity of movement, and the choreographer objected to her participation. At length, Diaghilev persuaded him to accept her in 'Le Pavillon d'Armide', which was after all a *pastiche* (however imaginatively worked out) and not a revolutionary work; but he refused to have her in 'Les Sylphides'. Anna Pavlova would be ideal for the latter; and could also dance the dramatic role of the abandoned bride, Ta-hor, in 'Cléopâtre'. Who was to be Cleopatra?

Fokine said he had a private pupil, Ida Rubinstein. 'She is tall, beautiful and plastic in her movements; and I consider her most suitable for the part.' Bakst, who knew Ida Rubinstein well, shared Fokine's opinion; and the rest of the committee were inclined to agree, except His Excellency General Besobrasov. Being a very strict balletomane, he considered that no one except professionals should be admitted into the company . . . He was not convinced and went on grumbling for some time.[22]

Fokine himself would be the hero, Vicomte de Beaugency, in 'Le

Pavillon d'Armide' and Amoun in 'Cléopâtre'. Nijinsky would again have the small dance of Armida's Favourite Slave in the former ballet and be given a similar role in the latter. Diaghilev also wanted him for the poet in 'Les Sylphides'. Adolf Bolm was to lead the dance of Polovtsian warriors in the opera 'Prince Igor'; and Pavel Gerdt (soloist to His Imperial Majesty) was to be the old Marquis-magician in 'Le Pavillon'.

We have seen that Bakst and Botkine had married two sisters, the daughters of Prince Tretiakov: a third sister was the wife of Alexander Siloti, who sponsored a series of concerts which bore his name and which he conducted himself. At the Siloti Concert on 6 February 1909, Diaghilev heard an orchestral piece by a young composer, whose 'Feu d'artifice' (Fireworks) and 'Chant Funèbre' had been played respectively at the Conservatoire in the previous year and at the Rimsky memorial concert on 31 January, on both of which occasions Diaghilev may have been present. The new piece was the Fantastic Scherzo by Igor Stravinsky. Unlike the bibulous and unpleasant Glazunov, whose comment was 'No talent, only dissonance', Diaghilev was thrilled with the new music, foresaw future collaborations over ballets and hastened to introduce himself to the composer. Stravinsky was a small man with a big nose, who had been a devoted pupil of Rimsky's. He and Diaghilev at once became friends; and the first of many commissions Diaghilev gave Stravinsky was the orchestration of Chopin's Valse Brillante for 'Les Sylphides'.

Stravinsky went with Diaghilev to visit Benois on Vassilievsky Island; and he was amused by the sight of Diaghilev making an entrance at the Leiner Restaurant on Nevsky Prospekt (where Tchaikovsky drank the glass of water which was supposed to have given him cholera), 'bowing to people right and left like Baron de Charlus'.* After a concert they would dine 'in a little sawdust delicatessen, on marinated fish, caviar, Black Sea oysters and the most delicious mushrooms in the world'.[23]

Diaghilev left for Moscow to recruit more dancers. He engaged the ballerina Vera Karalli, the fiery character dancer little Sophie

*But of course Proust had not yet invented Charlus. He did so in the course of that year.

Feodorova, her good-looking sister Olga – who will be seen to play a small part in the *private* history of the Russian Ballet – the handsome Mikhail Mordkine and others. He then travelled to Paris to make final arrangements for the season of opera and ballet. While he was away, on 22 February 1909, the Grand Duke Vladimir Alexandrovitch died.

The Paris season had been entirely dependent on the subsidy of 100,000 roubles which the Grand Duke had been promised from the Imperial purse. Kchessinskaya's influence had also been counted on, but in recent conversations with Diaghilev she had been shocked to learn that Armida was to be her only role. Now she decided not to appear with his company in Paris. 'I could not intercede on behalf of a project in which I was no longer taking part. I therefore asked that my requests for a subsidy should not be followed up. All Diaghilev's efforts to obtain that subsidy by other means failed.'[24] Gerdt also left the sinking ship.

When Diaghilev assembled the committee again he had to tell them that he had received a letter from the Imperial Secretariat cancelling the subsidy. After reading out the letter he banged the table and cried 'I am most indignant that the Emperor should act in such a way!'[25] He told his friends that he would try to find a solution to the problem and asked them to come back in a few days' time.

Diaghilev immediately returned to Paris and told Astruc that unless backing could be raised at his end the Russian season could not take place. He told him that he had a private subsidy of 50,000 francs in Russia,[26] but it is likely that he was anticipating this and lying optimistically. In the event, whatever money he did raise in Russia went to pay for the scenery and costumes. Undaunted, the French impresario applied to several financiers for help and secured the promise of 50,000 francs, only to be drawn on if the average receipts of the season fell below 25,000 francs a performance. The backers were later called upon to sign a form of *abonnement* promising either 'a full share' of 10,000 francs, which is what Basil Zaharoff subscribed, or 'a half-share' of 5,000 which is the sum subscribed by Henri de Rothschild, Nicolai de Bénardaky and Max Lyon. In return they were entitled to one stall at *répétitions générales*, one at first performances, admission to the theatre (presumably to stand) at all twenty performances, admission to the *foyer de la danse*, and 25 per cent of the profits, if any.[27]

Diaghilev never discussed his financial difficulties with Nijinsky (or in later years with Massine);[28] nor did he take Grigoriev into his confidence at this time. Even Benois was bothered as little as possible with talk about money; and probably the only friend to know the whole financial story was Nouvel. Even he did not know all that went on in Diaghilev's mind. Back in Petersburg Diaghilev told his committee that Comtesse Greffuhle and Mme Edwards had come to his support, not mentioning that the underwriting had all been done by Astruc's Jewish friends.[29] At this meeting, according to Grigoriev,

Diaghilev arrived looking very spry and animated ... In view of the reduced budget, we should only be able to give one opera in its entirety, namely 'Ivan the Terrible', and only one act of each of the two others, 'Russlan and Liudmila' and 'Prince Igor'. Each of these acts would be given on separate nights, and each followed by two ballets ... But since we had only three ballets decided on so far, we were still one short. What he had in mind to complete three programmes was a *grand divertissement*. We all welcomed this decision except Nouvel, who said that since we could not show the operas as intended, and since the ballet would not really impress Paris sufficiently, it would be better to give up the whole season. Diaghilev got very angry with him at this and said he had signed too many contracts in Petersburg, Moscow and Paris itself. If Nouvel was not satisfied, perhaps he would raise enough backing for us to carry out the scheme as originally planned. This argument silenced Nouvel. Besides, no one took his objection seriously. We all thought Diaghilev was getting out of his difficulties brilliantly and rejoiced on his behalf.[30]

Diaghilev's enemies had not finished with him. On 18 March the Grand Duke André Vladimirovitch wrote to his cousin the Emperor:

Dear Nicky,

As was to be expected, your telegram wrought havoc in the whole Diaghilev business, and now in his attempt to save his beastly affair he is resorting to every subterfuge, from the vilest flatteries to absolute falsehoods. According to information given me, Boris, who will be in attendance on you tomorrow, has been got at on behalf of Diaghilev, and sympathizes with his grievances. He therefore means to ask you not to restore your patronage, for that the latter no longer desires, but to allow him to continue to use the Hermitage for rehearsals, and to borrow the décor and costumes used in the Mariinsky theatre for the season in Paris. We very much hope you will not take the bait, which, let me warn you, will be cast very cleverly, nor grant permission for either the use of the Hermitage or the settings. It would only be conniving at a most unsavoury business which sullies the memory of dear Father.[31]

Permission to use the scenery and costumes of the Imperial Theatres for Diaghilev's operas was withdrawn. (The ballets and the danced and sung act of 'Prince Igor' were all having new décors.) Diaghilev's immediate reaction was to cable Astruc on 12 March asking him to find out whether the Opéra would sell back to him last year's production of 'Boris Godounov'.[32] The answer being 'No', two days later we find him telegraphing, 'If sale absolutely impossible try hiring.'[33] Not until the third week of March did he resign himself to the fact that 'Boris' could not be included in the repertory. His operas would all have to have new sets and costumes. The season was due to open in two months' time.

Through the Grand Duke Vladimir's intercession the little Hermitage Theatre, where Benois had painted his Polish scene for 'Boris', had been placed at the disposal of Diaghilev for rehearsals of the ballet. Benois adored working there.

I had grown to look upon the Hermitage Theatre, which formed part of the great Winter Palace, as something of 'my own' . . . It was entered from the famous Picture Gallery, by crossing the Venetian Bridge over the Winter Canal. As I was almost an *habitué* of the gallery, and was at that time compiling a guide-book of the pictures, I visited it daily. Crossing over, *de plein pied*, from the gallery where I worked as an historian of art, to the delightful rooms where I became a theatrical painter, had a peculiar charm for me. I delighted in the theatre itself – a *chef d'œuvre* of Quarenghi; admiring its ideal proportions, I tried to imagine what it looked like in the days when the great Empress was enthroned there, surrounded by her magnates and friends.[34]

In later years Karsavina remembered how tea and chocolate would be served to the dancers, when they rehearsed there, by court flunkeys.[35]

A fortnight after the Tsar received his cousin's letter, on 2 April, Benois arrived through the snow, full of anticipation, to attend a rehearsal at the Hermitage Theatre.

The artists were already in their dressing-rooms; the dressers, their arms full of foaming tulle skirts, were hurrying along the labyrinths of corridors ... But here I was suddenly accosted by Diaghilev's secretary, Mavrine, who imparted to me the astounding news that we were to collect all our belongings and leave the premises immediately ... Fortunately, half an hour later Mavrine had comforting news for us: our indefatigable leader had rushed all over the town to find some suitable rehearsing hall and had already something in view. Shortly after this came a telephone message inviting us all to a certain Catherine Hall on the Yekaterinsky Canal. I shall never forget that romantic exodus. Mavrine and I headed the procession in one cab, all our artists, dressers with their baskets and stage hands followed behind in others. The long procession stretched across the whole town. The day was dismal and dull but luckily dry. The atmosphere of adventure – almost of a picnic – seemed to soften our slight feeling of shame at having been 'turned out', and when we reached the little-known Catherine Hall we liked it so much that our spirits rose immediately. It was the newly decorated building of a German Club with an impressive entrance and monumental staircase overlooked by an excellent full-length portrait of Catherine ii. This seemed to us a good omen. We had just been turned out of *her* Hermitage and here she was meeting us in the new place with her famous gracious smile, full of intelligence and benevolence.[36]

Grigoriev recorded:

On 2 April at four o'clock in the afternoon there took place the first, and what may justly be called historic, rehearsal of the Diaghilev Ballet.* The entire committee were present. After I had introduced every member of the company† to Diaghilev, he addressed them in the following words, 'It gives me great pleasure to make your acquaintance. I trust that we are going to work together in harmony. I am delighted to be showing Paris the Russian Ballet for the first time. Ballet, to my mind, is one of the most lovely arts and it exists nowhere else in Europe. It will depend on you all to make it a success, and I greatly hope that you will do so.' The speech was applauded; and Diaghilev was surrounded by the members of the company, eager to ask questions.[37]

The first ballet to be rehearsed was the Polovtsian Dances from 'Prince Igor'. Fokine, realizing nothing was known about the remote

*The companies assembled by Diaghilev could not accurately be described as 'Diaghilev Ballet' until 1911.

†But Pavlova and Rubinstein did not rehearse with the company at the Catherine Hall. Grigoriev confirmed this.

Polovtsi tribe, had been reluctant to undertake this choreography, but Diaghilev had told him 'You will do it perfectly, Mikhail Mikhailovitch.' 'On other occasions,' wrote Fokine, 'I began to compose after I absorbed historical, ethnographical, musical and literary material. This time I came to the rehearsals with Borodin's music under my arm. This comprised my total armament.'[38]

Fokine worked at great speed and had almost plotted out the mass groupings of the Polovtsian girls and boys, the dance of the captive women and the charges of the Polovtsian warriors at the first rehearsal. At the end the company crowded round and applauded him.[39] Confident in their heroic employer, Diaghilev, who survived every disaster and inspired their utmost confidence, proud to be involved in the creation of Fokine's novel works of art, conscious that with artists like Benois and Bakst they would be presented to the best possible advantage to the most critical public in the world, the whole company was full of hope and joy.

Meanwhile Diaghilev had been arranging through Astruc that the Paris firm of Fontanes should redecorate the proscenium arch and the six different levels of the Châtelet, and that the firm of Belsacq should re-upholster most of the seats.[40] Astruc was clamouring for photographs of the singers and dancers to be used for publicity.[42]

Calm and confident as he appeared in the presence of his company, Diaghilev was inwardly full of doubts as to how much of his enterprise was feasible or whether it was possible at all. He failed to secure the patronage of the Grand Duke Boris and felt at times that he had so many enemies that the success of the season would be jeopardized if Astruc even mentioned his name in the publicity.[42] He veered between optimism and pessimism. Whereas on 31 March he had telegraphed to Astruc in reply to a query about the size of the company 'A hundred walkers-on. Eighty singers. Seventy dancers. Thirty soloists,'[43] by 6 April, within a few hours of agreeing to the estimate of Fontanes and promising to send him an advance of 5,000 francs the next day, he had come to the conclusion that it would not be possible to give opera at all in Paris. He cabled, 'No opera this year. Bringing brilliant ballet company, eighty strong, best soloists, 15 performances. Repertory can be enlarged if you think necessary to take series of bookings. We shall be able to give three ballets per programme. Have we the right to mount Adam's Giselle? Start big publicity . . .'[44] Not knowing of the weight of Diaghilev's troubles in Russia, Astruc must have thought he was drunk. His refusal to dispense with opera decided Diaghilev to go to Paris as soon as possible to discuss the matter with Astruc and if possible Chaliapine. The very day after his announcement that there would be no opera, he telegraphed to ask whether it would be possible for Geraldine Farrar to sing Marguerite in Boito's 'Mefistofele'.[45] This opera, though not Russian, would provide a role for Chaliapine: it was in fact not given during the Saison Russe.

Back in Petersburg again, Diaghilev had the pleasure of watching the new ballets of Fokine take shape at the Catherine Hall. The windowless auditorium was like that of an ordinary theatre, with rows of theatre seats, but was unusual in being on the first floor.[46] During rehearsals, Diaghilev would order meals to be served for the dancers: these were laid on a long table which was carried in and placed to the left of the orchestra stalls. He himself joined the company at these collations. It was then that Nijinsky was first observed by his fellow artists to be on friendly terms with the great man.[47]

Benois wrote:

I think that the happy atmosphere in which we prepared for our first Paris season had much to do with its subsequent success. It gave the whole company fresh vitality. From ballet-master and *premiers danseurs* to the last dancer in the *corps de ballet*, everyone seemed to unfold and become utterly devoted to the art . . . The ballet-master's spirit must indeed have been delighted and refreshed by the *happiness* of his contact with the company. Those of us who sat watching the work from the stalls were equally happy; here, we felt something was maturing that would amaze the world.[48]

Happy or not, Diaghilev faced a new problem every day. He was dissatisfied with the publicity Astruc had secured him in the French press, suspected a hostile campaign and grew abusive in his telegrams. On 23 April he authorized Astruc to spend another 3,000 francs. There was trouble in Russia over the authors' rights in some of the operas to be performed and he pulled strings to have the question reviewed in the Duma and then brought before the Imperial Council. As late as 27 April he arranged to add two acts of Serov's opera 'Judith' to the repertory, the orgy scene and the final hymn, with Litvinne, Chaliapine, Smirnov and Zbroueva. This necessitated other changes of programme. On the 28th he was able to announce that besides Tcherepnine there would be an additional *chef d'orchestre* in the person of Emile Cooper. A second telegram on the same day gave instructions for alterations in the publicity circular. A third gave the insurance of 'Judith' at 15,000 francs. The next day he cabled about the hire of a scene-painting studio; in a second cable he refused to allow Litvinne to take part in a concert arranged by a rival management; in a third he dealt with Astruc's apprehensions that 'a certain person' should be consulted over the poster, which Diaghilev was resolved to settle without interference from anyone, in consultation with Astruc alone.[49]

The Mariinsky season ended on 1 May. Karsavina had an engagement to fulfil in Germany and was to travel to Paris from there.[50] Pavlova too was on tour and would follow in a week or two. On 2 May, under the command of 'General' Besobrasov, Nijinsky and the rest of the Russian invaders set off for the French capital. Vaslav, who had travelled all over Russia in his youth, had never been outside it before.[51]

Following a day later, Diaghilev was met at the Gare du Nord by Gabriel Astruc, to whom he announced that he had arrived without a *sou* in his pockets, that all the Russian money had been spent on scenery and costumes, and that he relied entirely upon Astruc to pay the company.

Astruc replied that he could not undertake the responsibility of paying out money he had received in subscriptions and advance bookings, because if the theatre caught fire or there was a strike or if Chaliapine was ill he would be obliged to reimburse it within twenty-four hours.

'In that case,' said Diaghilev, 'there can be no Russian season.'[52] But, of course, a compromise had to be reached.

To the Russians Paris was synonymous with Paradise: none of the Mariinsky dancers had ever been there before. Karsavina, who came from Prague a day or two after the others had arrived from Petersburg, described her emotions at the thought of the French capital. 'Paris to me was a city of eternal pleasure, dissipation and sin. So exaggerated had been my ideas of its extreme elegance that in my heart of hearts I expected the streets to be like ballroom floors and to be peopled exclusively with smart ladies, walking along with a frou-frou of silk petticoats ... Above all, I dreaded that I should be too provincial for Paris.'[53] She was staying at the Hôtel Normandie in the rue de l'Echelle, off the Avenue de l'Opéra.[54] Diaghilev and Nijinsky were at the Hôtel de Hollande nearby.[55] Grigoriev and most of the dancers lodged just across the river from the theatre, in various small hotels in the Quartier Latin. Grigoriev too described the feelings Paris aroused in him:

At Petersburg the weather had been cold and damp; the spring had been late; and we were quite surprised to find the sun warm in Paris and the trees in leaf. I took a room in a small hotel in the Boulevard Saint-Michel; and when I came out into the street and looked about, a wonderful feeling of happiness came over me, which was always to remain connected in my memory with this first visit of mine to Paris. I stopped for a few minutes at the corner of the street, gazing across a neighbouring garden. I could scarcely believe that my dream of seeing Paris had come true.[56]

Eleonora Nijinsky had come to Paris to see her children dance – for Bronia too was in the company – and mother and daughter stayed on the Left Bank.[57]

Since 1900 Benois, when he was in Paris, had always stayed at a quiet *maison meublée* in the rue Cambon (now occupied by Chanel's *maison de couture*) and he used to eat at Weber's in the rue Royale: now he became so entranced by the creative fever of the Russian encampment and so delighted with the company of the dancers that he could not tear himself away from them or stir far from the theatre. The restaurant Zimmer was actually part of the theatre building; either there or in humbler restaurants of the neighbourhood, the Bouillon Duval or Bouillon Boulant, he would join a group of dancers, along with Svetlov or Besobrasov or Alexis Mavrine. Three months before, at the Metropole Hotel in Moscow, Diaghilev had pointed out to Benois the good-looking younger sister of Sophie Feodorova as 'the *only* woman he could ever fall in love with'. Now Benois observed to his amusement during these lunches in the shadow of the Châtelet Theatre, where a 'melodrama with shipwreck' called 'Les Aventures de Gavroche' had just been running,[58] that Mavrine,

Diaghilev's boy-friend, had fallen in love with the same lady – which gave him food for thought about the theory of elective affinities.[59]

The Russians had just over a fortnight to prepare their season. The Moscow dancers who arrived two days after the Petersburg troupe had to be taught Fokine's ballets, scenery had to be painted and hung and the productions had to be fitted on to the Châtelet stage. The theatre itself had to be redecorated and the front five rows of stalls removed to allow for the large orchestra. Finally, the legend of the Russians had to be spread round the town. Diaghilev's special method of publicity was to bring his fashionable friends – those who could be counted on to talk in drawing-rooms – to rehearsals; this was particularly liable to enrage Fokine, and there were explosions.[60]

The Châtelet [wrote Karsavina] was well-nigh shaken to its foundations . . . The stage-hands, gruff as they only can be in Paris, the administration pedantic and stagnant, regarded us as lunatics . . . At the back of the stage a party of workmen hammered and sawed, making a new trap-door for Armida's canopied couch. In the auditorium a larger gang out-hammered them. 'I don't like the pit, I will have boxes instead,' decided Diaghilev. Hemmed between the rival gangs, we rehearsed. At times the din drowned the feeble tinkle of the piano. Fokine, in a white frenzy, would call out in the dark: 'Sergei Pavlovitch, for mercy's sake, I cannot work with that blasted noise.' A voice from the dark promised that all would be quiet, and entreated us to carry on. We carried on till a new interruption.[61]

When the opera singers gained possession of the stage the dancers were banished to a stifling studio under the roof.[62]

As the fatal day drew nearer, it seemed more than ever improbable that everything would be ready in time. Fokine grew thinner and thinner. There was no longer time to go out for meals. 'Our troupe remained at the theatre all day long,' recalled Karsavina. 'Diaghilev gave orders – roast fowls, pâtés, salads speedily arrived from a restaurant. Empty packing-cases made quite good tables. Picnic feeling, excellent food, young appetite – in themselves a joy . . .'[63]

So much time was needed for rehearsals that no daily classes were held – an extremely unusual omission in the routine of a ballet company.[64] The dancers would do their warming-up by themselves, holding on to any chairback or piece of scenery which was the right height to support them while they did their *pliés* and *battements*. Nijinsky never failed to go through a complete class by himself, and from time to time Karsavina would walk over to him to practise supported *pirouettes*.[65] Behind the backcloth there strayed a flock of sheep, needed for the last scene of 'Le Pavillon d'Armide.'[66]

Serov had made a delicate drawing in charcoal and white chalk on blue-grey paper of Pavlova in 'Les Sylphides', and although the ballerina was only to appear a fortnight after the opening of the Saison Russe this was enormously enlarged to become the Russians' first poster. Pavlova, wearing the long tulle Taglioni dress designed by Benois, and crowned with white roses, was shown in profile, head held back on the swan-like neck, with arms raised before her as if pressing back the air, drifting forward on the very front of her pointed toes. This was the first sign of the Russian ballet to burgeon on the walls of Paris.*

The Paris season was in full swing. Today we cannot but see it through the eyes of Proust. Some of the people on whom he based his principal characters were Diaghilev's warmest supporters. The great novel, however, which had been conceived during the same winter as the Ballets Russes, would only be begun in the coming summer.[67] Mme de Chevigné (born Laure de Sade), with her bird-like nose and peasant speech, was to become the Duchesse de Guermantes. The old Duc de Gramont (whose third wife, Maria Ruspoli, had a son on 30 April) would contribute to the Duc de Guermantes, as Guiche, the son of his second marriage to Marguerite de Rothschild and husband of Mme Greffuhle's daughter, would to Saint-Loup.[68] Mme Greffuhle (born Elizabeth de Chimay), so rich, vain and resplendent, would be the Princesse de Guermantes, and her cousin Robert de Montesquiou, that hysterical peacock, the Baron de Charlus.[69] One of the guarantors of Diaghilev's season was the Russian expatriate Nicolai de Bénardaky, who would contribute

---

*Very few copies of this poster exist. There is one in the Paris Opéra Museum; I saw one in Legat's studio in Hammersmith in 1939; there is one in the Edinburgh College of Art, given by Lady Juliet Duff to commemorate our Diaghilev Exhibition, which was held there in 1954. I saw one very battered copy in the Theatre Museum in Leningrad, at the corner of Alexandrinsky Square and Theatre Street; and I have a copy, given me by Lucienne Astruc, the daughter of Gabriel Astruc, which is at present on loan to the Royal Ballet School in Richmond Park and is destined for our new Theatre Museum.

something to the character of Swann, just as would his wife, who had a *salon*, to that of Odette; and their daughter Marie, Proust's childish love, would live for ever as Gilberte.[70]

Paris was full of noble Russians, but many of these held aloof from Diaghilev, knowing of the Tsar's disapproval. The King of England arrived from Naples in a grey-green suit and brown boots. The Etienne de Beaumonts had a dinner-party. Isadora began rehearsals with the Colonne Orchestra at the Gaieté-Lyrique. The sister of her lover the American millionaire Paris Singer, Princesse Edmond de Polignac, sent out invitations to a pink and white ball on 8 June. Sarah Bernhardt was playing at her theatre, just opposite the Châtelet, and Réjane at hers; Lucien Guitry was at the Renaissance.[71]

Sales of tickets for the Saison Russe were so good that on 10 May Astruc announced extra performances.[72] While Astruc sold tickets and Diaghilev went his rounds and the world of society gave its *réceptions*, its *bals très restreints*, its *matinées de comédie*, its *soirées musicales*, its *quatre-à-sept*, innocent of coming immortality in Proust's pages, Fokine worked with the dancers.

Robert Brussel, the music critic, in an article in *Figaro*, described the preparations at the Châtelet and the meeting of Petersburg and Moscow dancers a few days before.

The whole company has assembled at the theatre today – the ladies from Moscow, who work in short tunics of red or green Liberty silk and those from Petersburg, who are already in *tutus*. They have not met for years, some of them since they were children or at the dancing school together, so there is kissing, gossip, reminiscing, secret confidences, laughter and exclamations mixed up with *pirouettes*. The men, who hold themselves so well, kiss the hands of the ballerinas.

The thin, highly-strung young man who looks like a fencing master in his cotton tunic is Michel Fokine, ballet-master and reformer of the Russian Ballet. This dark, slender girl with almond eyes and an ivory complexion, who evokes dreams of the gorgeous east, is Vera Karalli from Moscow. This blonde, so smart and supple in her movements, is Alexandra Baldina. That one in walking dress but with red boots, who is trying out a *Czardas* for 'Le Festin' with Michel Mordkine, is Sophie Feodorova. This elusive, thoughtful beauty who seems wafted by infinite grace is Tamara Karsavina . . . Among the men there is the extraordinary Nijinsky, a kind of modern Vestris, but whose dazzling technique is allied to a plastic feeling and a distinction of gesture which are certainly unequalled any-where.

Fokine claps his hands, the talking stops, the dancers take up their positions. They are going to rehearse Tcherepnine's 'Pavillon d'Armide'. Alexandre Benois, author of the libretto and designer of the sets, has something to say. The pianist Pomeranzev sight-reads an unfamiliar score, and plunges into a giddy dance with incredible skill.

They rehearse the *pas de trois* with la Karsavina, la Baldina and Nijinsky. Nijinsky dances his solo and displays his incredible elevation. The grace-ful Karsavina brings to the following variation a suggestion of gentle reserve. Then the imperious Karalli performs the dance of Armida. Last the stage fills with men; and in the Buffoons' dance prodigies are per-formed, while the exuberant Rosaï displays his fantastic steps.

All the dances are rehearsed once more, the slightest error of taste – there are no errors of technique – being the subject of severe reprimands and long digressions. Fokine's sharp eye misses nothing. Watchful, stimulating, he restrains exaggerations, demonstrates, mimes, shows everyone his steps, darts from pianist to dancer and from dancer to pianist . . .[73]

Brussel, a charming little man in his thirties, fell in love with Kar-savina and could not keep away from rehearsals at the Châtelet.[74] Fokine resented having to work in front of all Diaghilev's Paris friends, some of whom, such as the poet Anna de Noailles, Proust's 'princess from the East', Jean Cocteau, Proust's Octave, and Misia Edwards, Proust's Princess Yourbeletieff, were non-stop talkers. Diaghilev asked Grigoriev to keep an eye on these and other visitors and to see they did not interrupt the dancers' work. This he found by no means easy. Young Cocteau wanted to talk to Nijinsky, who fascinated him, Robert Brussel to Karsavina. It was on Brussel that Fokine's wrath fell. There may have been an element of jealousy in this, because although Fokine was now married to Vera, anyone who had loved Karsavina once must love her for ever. Fokine flew into a rage and ordered Brussel out of the theatre. Brussel, highly offended, complained to Diaghilev, but the latter made light of the affair, giving the soft answer that turneth away wrath. 'Evidently the people in charge of the rehearsal,' he said, 'did not realize that M. Brussel had special permission to distract the dancers.'[75]*

*The French word '*distraire*' has the double meaning of 'to divert the attention of' and 'to amuse'.

Another music critic, M. D. Calvocoressi, who had written a book on Mussorgsky, attached himself to the company, and ran errands for the girls.[76]

On 16 May the Moscow orchestra, who were to play for the Saison Russe under their conductor Emile Cooper, arrived in Paris.[77] The *répétition générale* would be on the 19th, so time for orchestral rehearsals was short.

The two newspapers Proust read every morning were *Le Figaro* and *Le Gaulois* – the latter being the local paper of the Faubourg and even more right-wing than the former.[78] On 18 May in *Le Figaro*'s column called 'Courrier des Théâtres' he would have read the announcement:

Au Théâtre du Châtelet à 8 h. ½ très précises, soirée de gala pour la répétition générale du premier spectacle de la 'Saison russe' ... La toilette de soirée sera rigoureusement exigée à toutes les places du théâtre ... On n'entrera plus dans la salle après le lever du rideau.

The composition of the audience by Astruc and Diaghilev was in itself a work of art. Apart from the necessary drama, art and music critics, they had assembled the editors of all the principal papers and journals. Careful for the future Diaghilev had made sure of the presence of several impresarios and directors of Opera Houses. There were Broussan of the Opéra, Albert Carré of the Opéra Comique, Camille Blanc and Raoul Guinsbourg from Monte Carlo, Gatti-Casazza and Dippel from the Metropolitan, New York, Henry Russell from Boston.

Politics and the foreign service were well-represented. In the centre box Pichon, the Foreign Minister, and Nelidov, the Russian Ambassador, sat together with their wives. Also present were MM Barthou, Minister of Works (who would be assassinated with King Alexander of Yugoslavia) with his wife; Doumergue, Minister of Education; Caillaux, Finance Minister, with his wife (who was to kill Calmette, the editor of *Figaro*, in 1914); Dujardin-Beaumetz, Under-Secretary of State for the Fine Arts, who established the Conservatoire in the rue de Madrid; and d'Estournelles de Constant, who had played a part in the Franco-Russian trade pact of 1903.

In the boxes were Mme Greffuhle, who had given a dinner for the company at the Hôtel Crillon a few nights before, Mme de Chevigné and her daughter Mme Bischoffsheim, Mme Madeleine Lemaire, who had a *salon*, painted roses and was to be partly Proust's Mme Verdurin and partly Mme de Villeparisis, Princesse Alexandre de Chimay, Proust's dear friend and sister of Anna de Noailles, and the blue-stocking Mme Bulteau, the latter's great friend, who also had a literary *salon*.

Couture was represented by Mmes Caron and Paquin and M. Doeillet; literature by Jean Richepin, Georges Cain, Léon and Lucien Daudet, Daniel Lesueur (the lady novelist) and Octave Mirbeau; painting and caricature by Paul Helleu, Jacques-Emile Blanche, Sem, and Jean-Louis Forain, whose work Diaghilev had reproduced in *Mir Iskustva* years before; sculpture by Rodin; music by Lalo, Fauré, Saint-Saëns, Ravel and Edouard Colonne; opera by Litvinne, Farrar, Bréval, Cavalieri, Chaliapine, de Reszke and Henri Simon; the theatre by the playwrights Francis de Croisset, Caillavet, Coolus and Henri de Rothschild ('André Pascal') – also a backer, by Clarétie, director of the Comédie Française, by Cécile Sorel, Yvette Guilbert, Jane Marnac, Louise Balthy and Rachel Boyer.

The distinction between actresses and *demi-mondaines* was not in 1909 always clear, but it is interesting to note that Louise de Morn-and, whom Proust loved, was present, as also was Madeleine Carlier, one of the only three women in Cocteau's life and whom he made the heroine of 'Le Grand Ecart'.

There were four celebrated but very different dancers present – the revolutionary Isadora Duncan, Carlotta Zambelli, the current star of the Opéra, who had danced 'Coppelia' in Petersburg eight years before, Rosita Mauri, the former ballerina of the Opéra, and Mariquita, who had played at the Funambules in Deburau's day (1845) and was at this time Ballet Mistress of the Opéra Comique.[79]

There were, however, many more dancers in the house and many more actresses than those named above, for Astruc had had the admirable idea of placing only good-looking young women in the front row of the dress-circle, and to this end distributed tickets among the *danseuses* of the Opéra and the actresses of the Comédie Française. Not a tail-coat, not a bald head to break the lustrous semicircle: only beauty, diamonds and bare shoulders. Blondes alternated with brunettes. This dazzling vision, like a basket of hot-house flowers, made such an impression on *le tout Paris* that in all theatres built after that time the dress-circle was called not *le balcon* but *la corbeille*.[80]

The new red cloth with which Diaghilev had covered the walls of the auditorium, the passages and even some of the floors, thus trans-forming the shabby old theatre into a bright new box, heightened the expectation of the audience.

Meanwhile, backstage, Nijinsky was in the process of becoming Armida's Favourite Slave, the inhabitant of another planet whose laws he instinctively understood and obeyed. Benois had noticed how he gave little proof at rehearsals of what he would be in per-formance. 'Nijinsky performed everything with unfailing precision, but there was something mechanical and automatic in his execution. At the final rehearsals he seemed to awaken from a sort of lethargy; he began to think and feel.'[81]

Nijinsky had arrived at the Châtelet between half-past six and seven. He changed into practice clothes and went through a class by himself at the back of the stage. Then he washed and put on his make-up, which took him half an hour. Order ruled in the dressing-room, where costumes were hung just so, and the sticks of make-up were lined up on the dressing-table with military precision. Finally, Vassili helped Nijinsky into his costume; he put on his white turban; and Maria Stepanovna, the wardrobe mistress, came to see if any-thing needed stitching.[82] Benois described how

the final metamorphosis took place when he put on his costume, about which he was always very particular, demanding that it should be an exact copy of the sketch made by the artist. At these moments the usually apathetic Vaslav became nervous and capricious . . . He gradually began to change into another being, the one he saw in the mirror. He became reincarnated and actually *entered into* his new existence as an exceptionally attractive and poetical personality. The fact that Nijinsky's metamorphosis was predominantly subconscious is in my opinion the very proof of his genius. Only a genius – that is to say, a phenomenon that has no adequate natural explanation – could incarnate the choreographic essence of the rococo period as did Nijinsky in 'Le Pavillon d'Armide' – especially in the Paris version of my ballet.[83]

To *le tout Paris*, seething with expectancy on the other side of the red curtains, Nijinsky gave no thought.

The programme was to open with Benois's ballet, conducted not by Emile Cooper but by its composer Tcherepnine. There were several changes in 'Le Pavillon d'Armide' since the Petersburg production. A quarter of an hour had been cut, and some numbers had been rearranged to form a new *pas de trois* for Karsavina, Baldina and Nijinsky. Benois considered that he had greatly improved the sets and costumes, which, since the withdrawal of Imperial support, had all been made anew for the Paris season. 'In the St Petersburg version I had been worried by the proximity of lilac, pink and yellow, and by the somewhat motley details of the décor for the second scene. These defects I now corrected.' The perspective of topiary in Armida's garden leading to a baroque *tempietto* at the top of a splendid staircase had in Petersburg been seen at an angle: it was now presented full-on and this enabled Valz, the wizard-stage-manager from Moscow, to contrive two gigantic water pyramids on either side.[84] The *tempietto* was replaced by a distant palace 'bosom'd high in tufted trees'.[85]

Pavlova would not arrive in Paris for a fortnight, owing to her European tour, and Armida was to be danced on this night and on the night following by Karalli, whom Benois thought 'a good technician and a very beautiful woman, but a pale performer lacking personality'.[86] Mordkine, likewise from Moscow, took Gerdt's part as René de Beaugency. 'He was far too strong and vigorous a dancer for the part and lacked the poetical tenderness which should be a fundamental quality of my hero. But in Paris my ballet gained from the change in the part of the Marquis which was taken by Bulgakov, in the place of Solianikov. In the latter part of the role, where the ancient Marquis is transformed into the magnificent wizard Hydraot, Bulgakov's interpretation was particularly successful.'[87] The imperfect casting of the hero and heroine made no difference to the success of the ballet, for, as we shall see, the greatest triumphs were not scored by them.

Benois had conceived his ballet as a glorification of 'that most French of epochs, the eighteenth century': he, the descendant of French, Germans and Venetians, and bearing a French name, took pride in showing Parisians that he understood the *style noble* of Versailles better than they did.

Those who were used to the sickly sweetness invariably used in Paris theatres to characterize the Rococo epoch (as for instance the production of 'Manon' at the Opéra Comique) found our colours too vivid and the grace of our dancers too pretentious. But to those who really understood Versailles, the Sèvres china, the tapestries, the gilt apartments of the palaces and the architectural parks, our 'Pavillon d'Armide' was a revelation. Among our most enthusiastic friends were Robert de Montesquiou and Henri de Régnier* himself.[88]

To be exact, 'Le Pavillon' mixed the baroque and rococo styles, Louis XIV and Louis XV, seventeenth and eighteenth centuries – but so, in the course of time, had Versailles itself.

The Russian element in the production consisted in the free way the scenery was painted, Russian designers and scene-painters having caught an element of vigour from the Impressionists before their counterparts at the Opéra and the Opéra Comique. This vigour corresponded to the suppressed passion contained in the Russian dancers' use of the classical vocabulary. Classical dancing at the Paris Opéra in 1909 consisted of a little Italian virtuosity tricked out with a lot of French *coquetterie*. Then, of course, there were Russian elements in the music of 'Le Pavillon', and a real Russian character dance for the Buffoons.

Yet a further enrichment of this classical ballet was its romanticism. This was the original, paradoxical and typically Benois element. The story which had given the painter the idea for his ballet had been Théophile Gautier's *Omphale*, and though this was set in a rococo pavilion and dealt with an animated Beauvais tapestry,† it was romantic and Hoffmannesque: it was a mysterious and rather erotic ghost story. One other element removed Benois's work from the conventional ballet of the period and related it to literature, or rather to the drama: there was no dancing, except the Dance of the Hours, in the first scene and none at all in the last. A mime-play combining mystery

---

* The Parnassian poet, son-in-law of Hérédia, had published his poems about Versailles, 'La Cité des eaux', seven years before.

†For reasons of his own Benois changed Beauvais to Gobelins.

and humour in the manner of 'The Magic Flute' encased the choreography.

Tcherepnine mounts his rostrum.[89] There is a ghostly roll on the kettle-drums and the clarinet and strings begin a mysterious introduction. Dark chords played *pianissimo* bring up the curtain on the dimly lit interior of a baroque pavilion. 'Tall windows with an ornate *œil-de-bœuf* over each of them alternate with columns of polished marble, while the plaster modelling above the central niche represents allegorical figures resting on clouds and supporting a sumptuous canopy adorned with feathers which overhangs the magic Gobelins.'[90] In front of the latter stands a giant ormolu clock, with the figures of Time and Love, impersonated by motionless dancers. To the right, a bed in a curtained alcove and a dressing-table. Lanterns are seen through the windows and lackeys open up the pavilion, preceding the entrance of the sinister old Marquis and his benighted guest, Vicomte René, who is accompanied by his valet, carrying luggage. With old-fashioned and exaggerated courtesy the host, who is dressed in the fashion of the last years of Louis XIV, welcomes young René, whose clothes proclaim the date of the action to be nearer the end of the century. René removes his caped overcoat and shakes the rain off it. The servants bring candelabra, the valet (played by Grigoriev) unpacks. The Marquis takes one of the candlesticks and shows René the tapestry. Without using the old conventional sign language (Fokine's anathema) he mimes that the lady represented in the Gobelins, who sits sadly holding a scarf, surrounded by her attendants, is his daughter dead long since, for love of whom three men took their lives. René is struck by her beauty. The host bows his way out and René disappears into the alcove to go to bed. Moonlight floods the room. At first, fascinated by the tapestry, René remains wakeful, but he sleeps at last. The figure of Time (or Saturn) on the clock reverses his hour-glass, and in a brief mime-scene is overcome by Love (Cupid). Midnight strikes, the twelve hours (girls dressed as boys) step down from the clock and dance a mechanical *andantino* punctuated by chords on harp and celesta. A chromatic theme is heard. This awakens René, who gets up, looks at the tapestry, then returns to bed. The theme sounds again. René is afraid. He considers running away but is reluctant to make a fool

93

of himself. The Gobelins rolls up into its frame, and a living image of the Marquis's daughter, in fact the sorceress Armida, in the same pose with the scarf, surrounded by her courtiers, is seen behind it. Armida places her scarf round the neck of an imaginary Rinaldo, then starts on realizing that her lover is not there. Pitifully she asks the women on her left where he is gone. They reply with sad hopeless gestures. She asks the men on her right the same question and receives the same negative answer. To a sobbing tune, whose rising and falling represents alternate hope and despair, Armida comes down from her frame, seems to see Rinaldo, then shakes her head in disappointment. She tells her ladies to play their harps, and the lament ends with her falling mournfully on one knee.

Meanwhile René, clutching his dressing-gown about him, has crept stealthily around behind Armida. Now comes the big moment. As she sinks on her knee he stretches out his arms to raise her from the ground. She starts, recognizes in him her long-lost Rinaldo and greets him with rapture. René's night clothes are whisked down a trap, and he is revealed in periwig and heroic 'Roman' costume of the Louis XIV period, his whole form suddenly imbued by the baroque style, so that he stands gesturing towards Armida like a splendid statue. At the same time, to a mounting frenzy in the orchestra the walls of the pavilion disappear and we are out-of-doors in brilliant sunlight. Framed by a natural arch of boskage – the only romantic-rococo-pastoral element in the décor, suggestive of Fragonard or Hubert Robert – rears up the splendid symmetry of Armida's garden. It is an essay in curves and obelisks. The dancing-area is defined by a semicircle of dark topiary, while Armida's palace, rising from undulant woods in the distance, is circular behind its portico, and recalls in its fantasy the Piedmontese palaces of Juvara – particularly as it is backed by Alps. The palace is topped by an obelisk or spire, like Sacharov's Admiralty in Petersburg; the topiary looms into obelisks like Tiepolo's idea of pyramids; and the two tall fountains on either side of the stage (fed from the nearby Seine), whose splashing mingles with the music, rise in a similar pointed form. It is Versailles with a difference.

At the top of the steps at the back stands a magnificent figure, the old Marquis transformed into a potent magician, King Hydraot. He wears a long frogged golden mantle and a towering mitred headdress surmounted by blue ostrich feathers. He waves his tall staff in indication that it is he who has effected this magic transformation and comes slowly down the steps. Armida leads Rinaldo across the stage. More courtiers appear and form circular groups. It is Fokine's and Benois's intention that the predominantly pink- and green-clad court – best seen from high up in the theatre – should suggest the pattern of an Aubusson carpet. A further piled-up group of dancers comes up out of the ground. This includes Nubians with tall feather fans. Armida herself wears a Nattier-blue mantle sewn with jewels and trimmed with gold tassels, opening over a plain white muslin skirt. Her white and gold turban is bound with pearls. The Court marches in procession and the enchantress conducts her lover to a dais on the left, from which they will watch the *divertissement*.

The dances which follow include a Brahmsian Valse Noble for eight men and eight women, a grotesque Oriental Bacchanale for eight women (including Fokina, Bronislava Nijinska, Schollar and Tchernicheva), with interjections on the xylophone, and a comic dance in which six limping and hideous monsters discover some beautiful masks, with ringlets made of wood shavings, and with whose aid they delude some young attractive witches to take part in a rather formal Sabbath and go off quite happy. These numbers are varied by processions crossing the stage, one of which stately regroupings is accompanied by solemn Handelian measures for strings, with trumpet calls.

The most spectacular number, however, is the *pas de trois* danced by two of Armida's Confidantes, Karsavina and Baldina, and her Favourite Slave, Nijinsky. His white, yellow and silver costume trimmed with festoons of silk, lace ruffles and ermine tails is a simplified form of the courtly male dancing costume of the eighteenth century, such as Boquet designed, with a *tonnelet* or wired skirt – an exaggerated development of the kilt worn under the stylized Roman armour of dancers in the time of Louis XIV – and kneebreeches. On his head he wears a white silk turban with an ostrich feather: round his neck, high up under the chin, a jewelled band. The two ladies wear yellow and gold. 'It is a marvellous moment [to quote Geoffrey Whitworth] when Nijinsky makes his first and curiously modest

95

entrance into that wonderful scene of pink and green and blue . . .'[91] The opening section of the *pas de trois* when all three dance together is performed to a lilting tune on the plaintive cor anglais; and the Parisians are suddenly aware as the dancers rise, fall, beat and spin that they have never seen dancing of this calibre before. There is a growing murmur of admiration. At the end of this number the dancers leave the stage, Nijinsky being the last to exit, before re-appearing for his solo. Tonight, excited by the warmth of the public's reaction, instead of walking he chooses to leap off. He soars up and up as if he were flying into the tree-tops, and no one sees him be-ginning to come down. No living Parisian has ever beheld such a leap. The gasps of incredulity turn to a thunder of applause.[92] Vestris has returned to France.

The tune for Nijinsky's solo is banal, a typical male variation, scored for full orchestra, *allegro risoluto*. He begins by rising on half point and leaping sideways across the stage. These high jumps alter-nate with *pirouettes*. Then he performs a simpler but peculiarly elegant movement (which is later to be much copied) of inclining forward and stroking his left leg with his right hand, while his left arm is extended behind him. These stylized *révérences*, repeated twice in different directions, alternate with *cabrioles*. As Nijinsky dances he hears an unfamiliar disturbance in the audience, and is afraid. The noise grows louder. At the end of his dance the cheering breaks out.[93]

The role of the Favourite Slave is a dancing one, inserted by Fokine into his ballet to show off Nijinsky's virtuosity: it is not de-veloped dramatically and plays no part in the story of the subjected René, yet by the projection of some intensity of feeling Nijinsky transforms the whole scene. To quote Geoffrey Whitworth again:

The vivid radiant boy is also the hierophant of mysteries, and in the glamour of his presence 'Armide' comes to seem not merely a matchless display of lovely form in lovely motion, but also a type of the supreme functioning of a state of being most strange and utterly alien from our own. The court of Armide, one believes, is part of a definite and settled polity, with its own laws, its own customs and its own business from day to day . . . The secret of this effect . . . partly lies in . . . the conviction of *aloofness* which Nijinsky brings to his rendering . . . [94]

There follows a solo for Baldina, which begins stately and accelerates towards the end, her music being punctuated by brief pauses which allow her to hold striking attitudes.[95]

Karsavina's dance is a gay little *allegro* with celesta and bells (like the Sugar Plum Fairy's solo in 'Casse-noisette') and the combination of her nimble foot-work, her poetic *port de bras*, her lustrous exotic beauty and a magic smile which lights up her whole face, makes an instantaneous impression on the susceptible public of *le tout Paris*. *Pirouettes* – arms held open, one up, one down, with the head tilted back towards the upheld arm; then the arms and *épaulement* are reversed; and finally the arms come together *en couronne*, tellingly tilted – the whole miniature turned into a masterpiece by the marriage of expression and *épaulement*, which casts a spell. She finishes with a *diagonale* of tripping steps, looking down mischievously with raised eyebrows at her hands held at waist level in front of her, finger-tips almost touching; and comes to rest in an eighteenth-century pose.* Once more Tcherepnine has to wait for the applause to subside before he can begin the coda.[96]

Nijinsky leaps on to a swinging tune on clarinets and strings. The two girls take over at a slower pace, then all three join together for the brilliant conclusion of the *pas de trois*, accompanied by the full orchestra *fortissimo*.

The audience has been spellbound by the spectacle and astonished by the revelation of what classical dancing can be. Before the end of the scene they have still one more surprise in store – their first sight of Russian character dancing. The dance of Buffoons, with which the *divertissement* ends, is a high-speed eccentric number to a jerky comic tune, whose rhythm is marked by the tambourine and triangle; and, according to Fokine, it is the most difficult dance, technically, he ever invented. This is led by Nijinsky's old class-mate Rosaï, who performs the cobbler's step, spins in a crouched position, leaps high in the air while he does *entrechats* with his knees, then lands on one knee. The other six boys execute a movement which seems equally improbable, crashing to the floor with crossed legs *à la Turque*, then instantaneously rebounding to catch each other by the feet as they

*Mme Karsavina's demonstration of this dance, seated as she was in a chair, was one of the most expressive pieces of abstract dance the author ever saw.

turn in the air.[97] Coming as a climax to what has gone before this excites the public to frenzy and Rosaï enjoys an acclamation as great as Nijinsky's.*

Karalli comes down from her throne to dance a graceful *allegretto* with flute and harp accompaniment and chiming bells. This is her *pas d'écharpe*, her duet with the magic golden scarf. In the ensuing *pas de deux* to a noble tune she completes her spell by looping the scarf round René. After a waltz of the whole Court Armida and Rinaldo have long trains hung on their shoulders, and with these borne behind them by little pages they walk in solemn procession, as if celebrating their union, to a stately tune with harp *glissandi.*

There has been 'a lot of beautiful walking'[98] throughout this scene; now, as the lights dim and the scene changes back to the interior of the pavilion, Karalli and Mordkine mount the staircase at the back, which is now concealed by the walls of the pavilion and step, together with a few courtiers, into the frame of the Gobelins. The group formed within the frame is the same as that at the beginning, except that Armida's gold scarf enfolds her lover. As the light grows even dimmer, the true 'Gobelins' descends to hide them. In this painted composition, of course, there is no Rinaldo.

The stage, with its curtained alcove in which René is supposed to be sleeping, but in which Mordkine is in fact changing back into his travelling clothes, is now almost empty for three minutes, while Tcherepnine's Sunrise and Pastoral, which amounts to an interlude, is played. First, horn calls and chords on flute and oboe create, as it were, a perspective of landscape as in Delibes's 'Sylvia', suggesting that the pavilion is *au fond des bois*. There are sudden arpeggios on the harp, which get quicker and louder until, with a clash of cymbals and bells, the sun rises. The shepherd's pipe is heard, and the texture of the music thickens as the shepherd himself with his shepherdess drive their flock past outside the windows; the piece closes with a *diminuendo* as they disappear into the distance. Tcherepnine's well-orchestrated number looks backward to the Pastoral Symphony

---

*Fokine claimed it was greater. But of course the more obvious virtuosity of character dancing is often more loudly applauded than the artistry of classical dancing. (This was Mme Bronislava Nijinska's comment.)

and the last act of 'Tristan', and forward to 'Daphnis et Chloë' (whose composer is in the audience).

Now the drama is to be concluded. The bustle of the servants coming to speed René on his way, represented by violins *tremolando*, is rendered sinister by the perversion on bass clarinet and cello of a tune heard earlier, which represents the old Marquis. The latter

Jean Cocteau.
Drawing by Leon Bakst.

greets René, who is still under the influence of what he believes to be a dream. Thèn the Marquis points out the golden scarf hanging on the clock. Aghast, René realizes he is now in fact the slave of the witch Armida. He strikes his brow; and to crashing chromatics, with dominant brass, he falls dead at the old man's feet.

When the curtain came down on 'Le Pavillon d'Armide' there was a storm of applause, and the acclamations continued for some minutes. Mordkine led forward Karalli, and Nijinsky led forward

99

Karsavina and Baldina. Men never took a call without their partners. When the house lights went up, the gentlemen in the stalls, as was usual, rose to their feet, snapped open their silk hats, put them on, lifted their opera-glasses to quiz the ladies in the boxes and raised their hats to those whose eyes they caught.[99] The caricaturist Sem moved down to the front row of the dress-circle to talk to one of the sixty-three beauties assembled there, but Astruc had given orders that no member of the male sex should mar the unity of his diamond horseshoe, and Sem was politely requested to move on by a *garde municipal*.[100] Not every member of this audience, as Jean-Louis Vaudoyer remembered in later years, was carried away by the Russians,[101] and we can imagine that certain dancers of the Opéra on the one hand, and Isadora Duncan on the other, had their reservations. But to the majority it had been revealed that ballet was a serious art, as it had been in the days of Taglioni, and that a male dancer could be a supreme artist. Robert de Montesquiou extolled the perfection of the Russians in his loud falsetto voice, waving his gold-topped cane,[102] the sceptre with which he ruled Paris society. Jean Cocteau moved from box to box, preaching the gospel according to Diaghilev. Mme de Chevigné, wearing her diamond dog-collar, held court.*

If we did not know that Diaghilev's repertory for this season was less the result of careful planning than making do with existing works and embellishing them, we should salute the placing of the Polovtsian act of the opera 'Prince Igor' after 'Le Pavillon' as a master-stroke of programme-building: no two works could be more different or more calculated to display the range of the Russians. The public was transported on a magic carpet from the splendours of a fairy-tale Versailles to the remote solitudes of the Asiatic steppes.

To give an effect of immensity and desolation Nicholas Roerich has abolished wings and painted his scene on a curved canvas.

---

*Cocteau, still comparatively unknown in Paris society, had not yet been introduced to Mme de Chevigné, though they lived in the same house. He was longing to meet this bluff lady, who although she had no money and had never opened a book, was somehow a dominant figure in the Faubourg; a few months after the Russian season he lay in wait for her on the staircase of their house. As she came downstairs he snatched up her poodle and began caressing it effusively. Mme de Chevigné was equal to the occasion: she barked out 'Take care or your powder will come off all over him!' But they became friends later. (Told to me by Jean Hugo.)

Although Gordon Craig deals in verticals rather than horizontals, there is something Craigish about the simplicity and power of Roerich's scene. It is nearly all sky – a mottled golden sky barred with pink clouds. Against this are silhouetted some low rolling grey-green hills, parted by a broad meandering river, and half-hidden by the russet beehive tents of the Polovtsi. As an evocation of the desolate heart of a vast continent it is superb.

From the moment the curtain rises the audience are seized by a sense of the utter strangeness of this unknown land between Persia, Tartary and China, sparsely populated by warring tribes. The oriental colour of Borodin's music is evident from the languorous opening song of the girls attendant on Khontchakovna, the Khan's daughter. There are dancing girls as well as singing girls, and, led by Sophie Feodorova, these perform a contrasting *presto* number, the only dance which will occur until Fokine's choreographic frenzies are let loose at the end of the act. Khontchakovna, sung by Petrenko, delivers her love-starved *cavatina* 'Now the daylight dies'. Some Russian prisoners are led by, returning from labour. Khontchakovna orders her women to give them a drink, and they sing their thanks. There is a patrol of Polovtsian soldiers. Night falls. Now appears Vladimir, Prince Igor's son, a tenor role sung by Smirnov. He and the Polovtsian princess are in love. His aria 'Daylight is fading' is followed by their passionate duet. They part, and Prince Igor comes on to lament his captivity – this is the baritone Charonov. The wheedling Ovlour offers to help him escape, but he refuses. Now follows the entry of the great Khan Khontchak himself in the person of the bass Zaparojetz, and a heroic dialogue ensues in which the Tartar chieftain offers to grant any wish which will make his prisoner's captivity more tolerable, while the Russian declares that he lacks nothing but liberty. This too the Khan is willing to grant Igor if the latter will swear to make war against him no more. Igor cannot promise this and his honourable frankness spurs the Khan to summon his tribesmen, their children and captive slaves to provide for Igor the danced diversion which in Fokine's arrangement will reverberate through Europe and America for many years to come. A barbaric crowd invades the stage. 'Ferocious of aspect, their faces smeared with soot and mud, their coats green and mottled red and ochre, their trousers striped in bright hues, one is reminded of a lair of wild beasts rather than a camp of human beings.'[103]

First the oriental slave girls undulate with their crimson and purple veils to the languid, voluptuous tune on the oboe and cor anglais, which is taken up by the violins and has woodwind and harp accompaniment. After a quicker dance of wild tribesmen, pounding timpani bring on the Khan's warriors, led by Bolm, who charge and leap, brandishing their bows, to the sound of chorus and full orchestra. Starting on a breathless off-beat their music climbs the scale until the top note screams out on strings and woodwind playing in their highest register. The slave girls hover and at the end of their number the warriors fling them over their shoulders. There is a jaunty dance of boys, who have wooden cups attached above their knees and wooden clappers on their hands, which they strike together as they leap and run on the spot and kick up their legs behind them: this builds up to a second entry of the warriors, again matched by the chorus. From now on boys, girls, slaves and warriors, with their appropriate melodies, alternate in swift succession. The singers, praising the Khan, provide a sustaining bourdon to the rapid rhythms of the dancers, and the scene ends with an overpowering climax of movement and sound. At the head of his warriors Bolm charges at the audience, spins in the air and crashes to the ground on one knee, aiming his bow.

In the following interval the audience launched a counter-invasion. 'I realized,' Karsavina recalled, 'something unusual was happening to me and around me: something to which I could give no name, so unexpected, so enormous as to frighten almost. My senses were all blurred that night. The familiar barriers between the stage and the audience were broken. The side doors with their ingenious locks and stern notices – of no avail . . . The stage was so crowded with spectators that there was hardly room to move.'[104] Karsavina and Nijinsky had had a full hour – the duration of the second act of 'Prince Igor' – to change their costumes for the final *divertissement*. 'To perform our usual rite of practising our steps and lifts before going on, Nijinsky and I had to dodge. Hundreds of eyes followed us about . . . "He is a prodigy" and awed whispers "C'est elle!" '[105] In the middle of the hubbub Reynaldo Hahn ran into

Lucien Daudet, and lisped, with calculated absurdity, 'C'est joli, ces danses du Poitou.'[106]

'Le Festin' is only a *divertissement*, but the Russian music – although by various composers – and the fact that it is made up of character or national dances – with the exception of one *pas de deux* – give it a certain unity. Since it is pretending to be a ballet (and for all the Paris public knows it may be the traditional finale of every performance in Petersburg or Moscow) Fokine will not allow his dancers to take calls after the individual numbers. The setting of 'Le Festin' is Korovine's first act of 'Russlan', designed for the Mariinsky and painted afresh for Paris – a medieval Russian banqueting hall. The costumes are by Bakst, Benois, Bilibine and Korovine. First the company process on stage to Rimsky's march from the last act of 'Coq d'or'. Then follows the Georgian Lesghinka from 'Russlan' adapted by Fokine from Petipa, danced by Fokina and ten men. Next comes the *pas de deux* for Karsavina and Nijinsky, which Kchessinskaya would have danced if she had come to Paris and which is curiously entitled 'L'Oiseau de feu',* and which was really Petipa's Blue Bird number from the last act of 'La Belle au bois dormant'.

The fantastic costumes of Bakst obligingly turn Karsavina into the bird (whereas it is really the man who is the Blue Bird in Petipa's *divertissement*) with flaming ostrich feathers on headdress and skirt, and Nijinsky into a turbaned prince with a mustard, lime-green and gold tunic sewn with pearls and topaz. The dazzling choreography creates an immediate impression, which Michael, the company's courier, is to describe afterwards in his own vivid way: 'But when those two came on, Good Lord! I have never seen such a public. You would have thought their seats were on fire.'[107] So Karsavina balances and spins and flutters in *pas de bourrée* and Nijinsky swings through the wonderful *diagonale* of *cabrioles* and *brisés volés*. Difficult indeed to obey the orders of the ruthless Fokine and not to acknowledge the ovation which follows this dance.

*I do not believe that this was, as Fokine thought, because Diaghilev had announced a ballet called 'L'Oiseau de feu' which was not ready. I do not think he had announced it, nor did he commission it successively from Liadov and Stravinsky until the end of 1909.

A Czardas by Gorsky arranged to music of Glazunov is danced by the fiery Sophie Feodorova with Mordkine. Olga Feodorova and Kremnev lead a Hopak of Mussorgsky from 'The Fair at Sorochinsk'; and a Glinka Mazurka from 'A Life of the Tsar' is danced by four couples. Rosaï scores for the second time in the evening with a solo Trepak to the music of the Buffoons' Dance from 'Casse-noisette'. Karalli and Mordkine lead the celebrated Grand Pas Classique Hongrois, in which Nijinsky dances a subordinate role, from Glazunov's 'Raimonda', invented by Petipa. The Finale is danced to the march from Tchaikovsky's Second Symphony; and the programme is over.

But the evening was not over. Karsavina wrote:

All was happy confusion; crowds again, somebody exquisitely dressed staunched the blood trickling down my arm with a cobwebby handkerchief – I had cut myself against Nijinsky's jewelled tunic; Diaghilev picking his way through groups of people, calling 'Where is she? – I must embrace her.' From that day he always called us his children. Somebody was asking Nijinsky if it was difficult to stay in the air as he did while jumping; he did not understand at first, and then very obligingly: 'No! No! not difficult. You have to just go up and then pause a little up there.'[108]

Nijinsky took off his costume, removed his make-up; and went out to supper and fame.

Next morning dawned hot and beautiful, and *Le Figaro* exclaimed about the size and brilliance of the audience at the Châtelet and the transformation of the theatre, comparing the occasion to a *fête* at Versailles in the days of the Empire:[109] but criticism was postponed until after the official première on the 19th, which was only marred by Rosaï hurting his leg in the Buffoons' Dance and having to be replaced in the Trepak. Thursday the 20th was Ascension Day and there was no performance. Karsavina describes how a gruff and cynical old man called Oneguine, a political exile to whom she had been sent an introduction and who had taken her under his wing, brought her the newspapers.

He sat with me as I had my coffee, himself refusing to share the meal. I wore the wrap of double usage, that of opera cloak and dressing-gown, and, as usual, darned stockings. Both items memorable through Oneguine's sneers. I learned amazing things about myself this morning, and that I was 'La Karsavina'. There was quite an extemporaneous feeling of wonder in me as at suddenly perceiving my double . . . [110]

Brussel's article in *Le Figaro* was mostly about the music: but he found room to refer to 'Mme Karsavina, whose subtle technique and marvellous sense of music are combined with expressive grace and poetic feeling and whose success in "L'Oiseau de feu" stopped the show . . .' He went on to praise Nijinsky's extraordinary suppleness and dizzy technique.[111] Other writers called Nijinsky 'Vestris', 'God of the dance', 'prodigy'.[112] One critic, coached by Diaghilev perhaps, became so technical as to describe how Nijinsky could execute *entrechat-dix* and *triples tours en l'air*.[113] In *Commedia* Henri Gauthier-Villars (the husband of Colette) wrote:

The blond and queenly Baldina, Mlle Karsavina of the irresistible charm, the magic of the Feodorovas – I would celebrate them all if I did not feel bound above all to proclaim my admiration for the dancer Nijinsky, wonder of wonders, breaker of the record in *entrechats* . . . Yesterday when he took off so slowly and elegantly, describing a trajectory of $4\frac{1}{2}$ metres and landing noiselessly in the wings an incredulous *Ah!* burst from the ladies. It was truly *le Bond des Soupirs*.[114]*

Once the *répétition générale* and the première were over, although there were two other ballets to be rehearsed, it was possible for the company to look around them and enjoy Paris. Nijinsky did a full class every morning alone by himself, rehearsed and had a late lunch. Then he would either go with Diaghilev to the Louvre, drive in the Bois with Bakst or Nouvel, have a massage or sleep. After the performance Diaghilev usually entertained his committee of friends at Larue or Viel – Benois, Bakst, Roerich, Nouvel, Besobrasov, Svetlov, Argutinsky – and Nijinsky began to appear at these gatherings, listening in silence while the older men discussed the season and planned new projects.[115]

Meanwhile, two elopements took place which changed the history of the Russian Ballet. Karalli ran off with the tenor Sobinov and Mavrine ran off with Olga Feodorova. Whether Karalli's disappearance had something to do with Karsavina's success we can only

---

*Pun on *Le Pont des Soupirs* – the Bridge of Sighs.

surmise. There is reason to believe she was jealous of her[116] – and, after all, one can have an affair with a tenor without breaking one's contract. Karsavina became the company's star and on 25 May, six days before Pavlova arrived, she danced the role of Armida opposite Bolm, who had been much scolded by Fokine for his clumsiness in partnering during rehearsal. She was replaced in the *pas de trois* by Fokine's sister-in-law, Alexandra Feodorova: but in the role of Armida she was allowed to retain her old solo from the *pas de trois*, because it suited her and she considered it the most effective choreography in the ballet; and Feodorova danced something else. Mavrine had more reason to take himself off, as it was clearly awkward to continue as Diaghilev's official friend while enjoying a passionate romance with the one woman who had ever attracted Diaghilev. The latter was already more interested in Vaslav than Alexis, but his pride was hurt at his favourite's treachery. He later forgave him, and was to employ Olga Feodorova again.

Paris, that magic season between spring and summer, the triumph of Russian art and the adulation in which the dancers basked – everything was intoxicating: so that even if one did not fall in love and elope one felt unusually light-headed and bought, perhaps, an expensive hat. Valz, the *chef machiniste* and miracle worker from Moscow, who was an elderly lady-killer with dyed moustache and high heels, gave an extravagant dinner for twenty, including all his favourite *danseuses*, at Le Doyen in the Champs-Elysées.[117] It is a curious fact that in this sort of highly charged atmosphere, in which love flourishes, a man's passion can just as well be directed towards one person as another. Where all seems delightful and desirable there is an element of chance in whom we fall for. Although Diaghilev was more than ever attracted to the withdrawn and serious-minded Nijinsky, he was also a bit in love with Karsavina, his new star, whose intelligence appealed to him as well as her beauty.[118] One sunny morning she was practising alone on the dark and empty stage, when Diaghilev appeared and said 'We are all living in the witchery of Armida's groves. The very air round the Russian season is intoxicated.'[119]

Dr Botkine drove Karsavina to Versailles. It was in the Bosquet d'Apollon that the ballerina learned a lesson. 'The sun, merciless in the clipped walks of the formal avenues, here only dappled the marble of the fountain through the thick foliage.' Karsavina, virtuous herself in spite of all her adorers, had been worried about Diaghilev's homosexuality, a side of life she had only recently become aware of. Botkine said, 'It is a cruel misjudgement to give an ugly name to what is, after all, but a freak of nature.' From his wide experience of human beings, he gave her examples of homosexuals who had lived good lives. 'Botkine made me see that it was the quality of love that makes it beautiful, no matter who the object. The quality of Diaghilev's affections was single-hearted, true and deep, bury them as he would beneath his blasé mask.'[120]

Apart from such functions as an official party given for the company by Briand at the Quai d'Orsay, and at which they performed Russian dances, Ida Rubinstein, Karsavina and Nijinsky were the only dancers who went out in society. Montesquiou became Ida's devoted knight and carried her off to his Pavillon at Neuilly. Karsavina's life was overcrowded with admiration. When she was not being driven to Fontainebleau by Robert Brussel in a hired car filled with all the cushions from his flat, another beau was escorting her to a party at Misia Edwards's house on the Quai Voltaire, from which Proust, shy, polite and green as a ghost, would drive her home. Nor was Karsavina excluded by Diaghilev from gatherings predominantly male. At one of these she observed Nijinsky enthralled by Emmanuel Bibesco's collection of paintings by Gauguin. 'Look at that strength!' he said.[121] Vaslav at once felt an affinity with the painter of Polynesian mysteries, and Gauguin's influence was to mould his thought when he became a choreographer in later years.

Because the success of the Russians was partly due to the new miracle of male dancing, there was something scandalous about it. Since the Romantic period it had been the woman, the Muse, the diva, the ballerina who had been worshipped: to admire a man for his grace and beauty was unheard of and in some circles unthinkable.[122] The scandal of Count Eulenberg's disgrace at the Kaiser's court in the previous year was fresh in people's minds, and it was only nine years since Oscar Wilde had come to an appropriately bad end in Paris. In 1838 Théophile Gautier, deploring the nasty muscular male dancers of his period, intruders in the fairy paradise of the ballet he loved, had disliked them for their excessive masculinity.[123] What would he have thought of the more epicene apparition of Nijinsky in the ballet inspired by his short story? As a matter of fact, if there was a homosexual conspiracy in the air to seduce the public by male charms – and Diaghilev had become overnight a leading figure of the Paris homosexual set, and it rather went to his head[124] – a conspiracy to exalt the male dancer – or rather, Nijinsky, with whom Diaghilev was now in love – at the expense of the ballerina, Gautier cannot be wholly cleared of collusion. In his story *Omphale*, which gave Benois the idea for 'Armida', the Beauvais tapestry represents a long-since-dead Marquis and Marquise in the guise of Hercules and Omphale. Now, Hercules was condemned by the oracle to three years' hard labour, and he chose to be the servant of Omphale. In order to please his lovely mistress – or, as some think, himself – he performed his duty in female attire. It made a change, no doubt, from that lion-skin and club. In the tapestry imagined by Gautier the Marquis-Hercules is decked in silk *panniers*, his neck festooned with ribbons, rosettes and ropes of pearls. He is spinning flax, his little finger 'cocked with peculiar grace'. When the Marquise steps out of the tapestry at night to teach the facts of life to the youth who has been accommodated in the pavilion, he asks her, 'But what will your husband say?' and she replies, laughing, 'Nothing . . . He's the most understanding of husbands!' From this and from the Marquis's decision to be depicted *en travesti*, with pearls, we are meant by Gautier to understand that his inclinations are distinctly *rococo*. Then, surely when a role was inserted in the existing ballet scenario of 'Armida' simply to show off Nijinsky, must it not have been a memory, conscious or unconscious, of Gautier's girlish and domesticated Hercules that prompted Benois to call the new character 'Armida's Favourite *Slave*'? And was not the costume Benois then designed for Nijinsky related to that of the Marquis which Gautier painted only in words? One final proof of a mysterious conspiracy, into which even such heterosexual gentlemen as Gautier and Benois were drawn in spite of themselves! Which old master does Benois draw most like? Tiepolo. Among the frescoes adorning the Villa Valmarana near Vicenza, which Benois had certainly seen, are two depicting the story of Rinaldo and Armida. Although Tiepolo's

Rinaldo is meltingly feminine, it is Armida who wears the necklace. Benois took Armida's pearls and gave them to Nijinsky, adding a few diamonds for good measure. We know it is the same necklace because it is worn as high as it will go, right under the chin. (It started a fashion: Cartier copied it.) Nijinsky's very first entry on the stage of the Châtelet, because of his equivocal personality, because of his allure, because he combined the strength of a man with the grace of a woman, because of his frilled and skirted costume, and because of his jewelled choker, had sped this most homosexual of centuries on its vertiginous course.

After all the trials he had gone through, Diaghilev had reason to be delighted with the success of the Russian season. In spite of the Russian Court's intrigues against him, in spite of the enmity of the Tsar and the Grand Dukes, in spite of the opposition of Kchessinskaya, in spite of the withdrawal of subsidies and the struggle to raise funds, he had proved what Petersburg had refused to believe possible – that the new ballet as conceived by Benois, Bakst, Fokine and himself, was the art-form of the moment and a wonder of the world. He had scored off the Emperor of all the Russias. So he was the greatest man in the world! And it was in this glorious light – or something like it – that Nijinsky would now regard him. Can admiration grow into love and can love live without physical desire?

Eleonora Nijinsky came every night to the theatre. Karsavina was touched to see Vaslav go dutifully up to kiss his mother and say 'Dobra noc', and amused that the mother, who had come to Paris to chaperone her daughter,* would go quietly off with Bronia, while her son went off with Diaghilev.[125]

Chaliapine, who made his first appearance of the season in Rimsky's 'Pskovitianka', renamed by Diaghilev 'Ivan le Terrible', on 25 May, had naturally been counted on by Astruc as the chief attraction of the Saison Russe – and he was paid almost as much as the rest of the company put together – but though his success was great that of the ballet as a whole was to prove greater. 'Ivan' was, of course, the only full-length opera in Diaghilev's season, and there was no dancing in

---

*This was Mme Karsavina's phrase: but Mme Bronislava Nijinska commented 'She never was a chaperone because she believed a good girl will always know how to behave. It was Vaslav and Diaghilev who "chaperoned" me!'

it. Here it is necessary to correct certain errors propagated by previous writers. It may seem impertinent for one who was not present in Paris in 1909 to question facts stated in print by those who were, but the entire French press cannot have conspired to lie. Chaliapine did not, as we have seen, sing in 'Prince Igor', as Grigoriev describes him doing, at the opening of the season: he did not sing in it at all that season. Pavlova and Fokine did not dance in 'Armide' at the première as he states. Pavlova had not arrived and Karalli danced with Mordkine not only at the *répétition générale*, described above, but also at the première.[126] It is interesting that Karsavina thought Pavlova could have arrived before, but waited to see how the ballet was received in Paris.[127] If this is so, she made a mistake which affected the history of ballet – one might say, of the whole world of art – because Karsavina was acclaimed in the press and became the toast of Paris a fortnight before Pavlova (who was already a *prima ballerina* in Russia – which Karsavina was not) ever showed her face at all. From so redolent a book as *Theatre Street* one does not expect exactitude over boring dates and numbers, but Mme Karsavina is wrong in saying 'Pavlova made but a fleeting appearance and left us after a couple of performances',[128] because once Pavlova had arrived she stayed till the end of the season and danced six times, performing in 'Armide' as well as 'Les Sylphides' and 'Cléopâtre'. Had Mme Karsavina remembered the small fact that Pavlova's delayed arrival enabled herself, Karsavina, to conquer Paris – and Diaghilev's good opinion – she might have found it easier to explain certain unpleasant incidents in later years. But Pavlova had always been and always would be jealous of her – which was absurd, as they were such different artists and Pavlova was an ethereal divinity. Indeed, it seems possible that had Pavlova appeared at the beginning of the season to gather the first fruits of acclamation she might never have been impelled to part with Diaghilev and form her own company.*

On 2 June was given the *répétition générale* of the second mixed programme of opera and ballet, and on 4 June this programme comprising the first act of 'Russlan and Liudmila', 'Les Sylphides' and

*Possible, but not probable. As Dame Marie Rambert has pointed out, Pavlova had to be her own master, and knew it.

'Cléopâtre' received its first public performance in Paris. It was Benois who had urged Diaghilev to include in the Paris repertory the second version of Fokine's 'Chopiniana', renamed by Diaghilev; and the latter, constitutionally unable to leave any score alone, had ordered new orchestrations of the Chopin piano pieces from Liadov, Glazunov, Taneev, Sokolov and Stravinsky. Benois had designed a romantic setting of a ruined Gothic church in a moonlit glade which called up memories of Sir Walter Scott, just as his drifting white dresses were reminders of those designed by Eugène Lami for Taglioni in 'La Sylphide' and for Grisi in Gautier's 'Giselle'. The painter was not quite happy about the costume he had created for Nijinsky.

It seemed to me to be a trifle comic when I saw it on the stage. It consisted of a black velvet jacket, a collar *à l'enfant*, a light tie, long curls and white legs. And yet, his slightly caricatured appearance made the artist more like a figure from some old beaded *réticule* or painted lampshade. It was just such funny improbable troubadours who formed the dreams of our own grandmothers, the creators of the embroidered *réticules* and painted lampshades.[129]

Yet as so often happened with Nijinsky, a marvellous and inexplicable instinct made him bend the costume to the service of the role he was to dance. He understood the costume in relation to the choreography and his part in it, he became one with it and he ended by making it seem inevitable.

For the dress rehearsal of this programme 'the house was packed . . . and people were sitting on the steps of the balcony and in the aisles of the stalls. Everyone was bursting with curiosity. When the curtain went up . . . the whole house gasped with admiration and surprise . . . the dancers were like blue pearls . . .'[130]

Like the middle act of 'Armide', Fokine's 'Les Sylphides' was a series of dances – yet how different! While the first portrayed the formal splendours of Versailles where classical ballet was born, the second evoked the tormented dreams of the 1830s. In the former technical virtuosity was essential: in the latter it was utterly out of place. 'Les Sylphides', which, as we have seen, was first given in its final form at the Mariinsky in Petersburg in the previous year, was totally unlike anything seen on the ballet stage before. Dance melted into dance, group into group, and although traditional *pas* were used all formality was taken out of the *port de bras*, all virtuoso steps were omitted. The object was not to display technique but to create a mood. All the same, it was extremely hard to dance and the sustained poses called for considerable strength and experience.

Never before had principal dancers been so merged with the *corps de ballet*; never before had a dancer turned her back on the audience; never before had a male solo contained no double turns in the air or failed to end with a *préparation* and a series of *pirouettes*. An example of how instinctively Fokine breathed the air of a new age (inaugurated by Isadora) is that without his even planning it, each solo that he arranged ended differently. In the first Valse Karsavina finished with a *pirouette* and stopped on her toes with her back to the audience; in the first Mazurka Pavlova ran off the stage; in the second Mazurka Nijinsky, after a jump, fell on one knee, stretching out his right hand as towards a vision; in the Prelude Baldina froze on her toes facing the audience, hand to lips, as if catching the sound of a distant nightingale – or, as Fokine put it, 'imploring the orchestra to play still more softly.'[131]

It is too easy to write poetically about 'Les Sylphides'. The male dancer is a poet, or he is Chopin, which comes to the same thing. But the three principal girl dancers and the *corps de ballet* of sixteen are anything but dancers although all they do is dance. They are fairies or figments of the poet's imagination; they have been compared to water, trees, clouds, mist, festoons of flowers. In his 'Ode to Melancholy' Keats has an epithet which is apposite: 'cloudy trophies' – 'And be among her cloudy trophies hung'. Indeed, if melancholy is the dominant mood of 'Les Sylphides', though there are bursts of joy in it, we might do worse than take as a motto for the ballet another line from the same poem, 'Joy, whose hand is ever at his lips, bidding adieu.' Yearning, hope, disappointment, regret.

The short Prelude (Op. 28, no. 7) which is the most contemplative of the Chopin pieces used, is played before the curtain rises. As the sweet Nocturne (Op. 32, no. 2) begins the first group is revealed, with Pavlova and Karsavina leaning their heads on Nijinsky's shoulders, the *corps* and Baldina reclining at their feet. Some of the *corps* are lined up on either side of the central group, leaning inwards. Others are at the sides. Almost immediately they begin to move, running forward. Throughout the ballet the patterns and motions of the *corps* are as important as the dancing of any one principal; and the fact that they will often regroup themselves in silence between numbers gives the work a gentle continuity, removes it from the old-fashioned *divertissement* and discourages applause.* During the opening Nocturne, while Nijinsky lifts Pavlova and supports her in *arabesque* or stands poised, suspended on his toes, his arms looped like a garland above his head, or kneels yearning, and while Baldina runs through the arch formed by Pavlova's and Nijinsky's arms, hopping and curtseying, the *corps* dip and kneel, their backs to the audience, with undulating arms, tiptoe, rotate, scoop the air with their arms, form into parallel lines and finally into a semicircle.

Karsavina's is the first solo, the Valse (Op. 70, no. 1), and to receive her the *corps*, who at the end of the Nocturne were like festoons, move into two lines at right angles to the audience. This is an ecstatic solo which Fokine thinks Karsavina executes with 'rare romanticism'.[132] To a tripping rhythm, she leaps on, runs backwards *sur les pointes*, flutters her arms, drifts, hand to mouth, as if calling up the 'horns of elfland', then makes a spreading open gesture of both hands as if parting the curtains of the air. She turns *en attitude*, arms *en couronne*, makes a sweeping gesture towards her foot, circles the stage and ends with back turned, arms drifting, looking over her right shoulder.

In silence the *corps* form three sides of a square to prepare for the first Mazurka (Op. 33, no. 2). This is a kind of *perpetuum mobile* and Pavlova, with sylphlike indecision, makes three diagonal entries, as the *corps* do *port de bras* in different directions before forming a semicircle, alternate girls standing and kneeling, with an arch in the middle through which the ballerina will be satisfied to make her fourth entry and begin to dance. With swirling arms she hops in *relevé*, like 'a maenad at the centre of a calm night',[133] pausing to

---

* According to Dame Marie Rambert (who was with the company in 1913 during the absence of Fokine) Nijinsky then acknowledged applause after his solo in 'Les Sylphides'. (Mary Clarke: *Dancers of Mercury*, p. 64.)

hold an *arabesque* before running off – apparently to continue dancing
to another air in another place. In silence the *corps* with their arms
speed her on her way, then form a solid group in the centre.

As the curved melody of the slower Mazurka (Op. 67. no. 3)
begins, Nijinsky 'seems to cast himself loose upon the music's tide'.
He diagonals forward with slow *jetés* and sweeping gestures, crosses
the front of the stage with *cabrioles* and turns, backs with *entrechats*.
'He is the sport and plaything of the flood of melody; dancing not to
it, but with it or by it – almost, indeed, *on* it.'[134] At last he kneels with
rapt gaze, his right arm yearning forward, while with the back of his
left hand he brushes aside a lock of hair. He rises and runs off. The
corps turn their backs, forming an espalier on three sides of a square.
Then they move into three groups, each made up of four kneeling
girls with one standing in the centre.

Now the *andantino* of the Prelude is repeated as Baldina swoops
without jumping and twirls with drifting arms. She makes the
sweeping hand-to-toe gesture and poses *en arabesque penchée*, with
hands crossed on her chest. She stalks forward and poses on tiptoe,
hand to lips, hearing voices. The *corps* form a semicircle, the girls in
pairs, leaning confidentially together.

The next Valse (Op. 64, no. 2) is the *pas de deux* danced by Pavlova
and Nijinsky, and to the first long note the ballerina, who has been
lifted off-stage, appears to descend – with pointed toe visible through
her long diaphanous skirt – from the trees. This choreography fits the
shape of the music very closely. She trips, he yearns. He lifts her
through the air, supports her *en arabesque*, turns her *en attitude*, kneels
and receives her hand on his shoulder. Dancing quicker, he jumps
and turns inside out as she trips after him. He lifts her *en arabesque*
first to one side, then to the other. By now, the *corps*, who were in
two lines, facing each other in pairs, are reclining, hand to chin.
Pavlova runs backwards, half drawn by Nijinsky's magnetism as he
barely touches her wrists. They dance to and fro and as he runs off
he pauses, suspended, on one foot, before he follows her with right
arm raised in appeal and longing.

To the final Valse Brillante, orchestrated by Stravinsky, the *corps*
canter in circles. Two lines advance and retire, then turn diagonally. To a stirring, swinging tune Nijinsky jumps on between the

groups, and draws Pavlova off. The *corps* dance with round drifting arms. A sinuous questioning melody leads to a reprise of the opening music. Everyone stops, then to a faster tempo they charge round and the ballet ends with a re-forming of the opening group. Nijinsky stands at the back with the two ballerinas leaning their heads on his shoulders. A line of dancers run forward to recline in the foreground as the curtain falls.

'Les Sylphides' was the first abstract ballet. 'Cléopâtre', which followed, was as much of a contrast to it as 'Prince Igor' had been to 'Armide'. There had been publicity about a mysterious society woman of striking beauty who would appear in the title role – this was, of course, Ida Rubinstein; and the public had reason to be curious. Rubinstein was to be carried on in a sarcophagus, wrapped up like a mummy. This idea had come to Benois while he listened to Rimsky's music for 'Mlada'. 'I suddenly visualized the Queen's journey through the sands of the desert in this closed coffin, and it logically followed that she should be swathed like a mummy to prevent the least grain of sand penetrating through the covering to blemish her divine body.'[135] Benois found Rubinstein lying like a corpse in her coffin in the wings of the Châtelet, and said, 'Well, Ida Lvovna, how are you feeling?' 'All right, thank you,' she replied, 'but I can't move.'[136]

'Cléopâtre', with its melodramatic theme and its six different composers, sounds rather absurd to us today, but it was nothing of the kind in 1909. In it Fokine was able to realize more than ever before his ideals of a dance-drama divorced from the conventions of the old ballet. 'Cléopâtre' was not a ballet: nobody in it wore point shoes or stood in one of the five positions or executed classical *port de bras*. The novelty of this cannot be overstated. Benois, however, was perfectly aware of the absurdities.

Egyptian young gentlemen never paid court to the temple slaves and never shot arrows with love-letters to the feet of the queen. The daughters of Pharaoh would not dream of indulging in love-affairs on the threshold of a temple and never poisoned their temporary favourites before the eyes of the people who had come to worship them. Lastly, if Cleopatra did keep Greek dancers it would not have been in front of the gods that she would have allowed them to dance the mad bacchanale . . . Yet 'Cléopâtre'

Leon Bakst.
Caricature by Jean Cocteau.

brought the fullest houses . . . Its success surpassed that of Chaliapine.[137]

The power of the miscellaneous music, the décor of Bakst, the choreographic invention of Fokine and the extraordinary talents of the performers made the drama convincing.

Bakst's setting, with its huge columns and pink gods framing a glimpse of the Nile in the purple dusk, was a grand conception and the impression it made on Paris was so powerful that it launched a new age of exoticism.

Following a file of girls bearing pitchers, Pavlova as Ta-hor comes to meet her lover Amoun.[138] This is Fokine, who bounds on with a bow, a splendid, heroic figure. They express their love in a dance and are blessed by the High Priest. A messenger announces the approach of Cleopatra. To a triumphant burst of music a glittering procession winds on to the stage. The rear is brought up by a painted

116

sarcophagus, borne by bearded men. Beside it walk Karsavina and Nijinsky, Cleopatra's slaves. They give the impression of 'two tender and carefree creatures, who, growing up on the steps of the terrible queen's throne, are absolutely devoted to her.' [139] The sarcophagus is opened to reveal a mummy-case, and from this is lifted the swathed body of Cleopatra. Twelve veils of different colours are ceremoniously unwound from her body and the queen with a sweeping gesture throws off the last. The imperious beauty of Ida Rubinstein is revealed to Paris, her pallid features framed by a turquoise-blue stylized wig, bound with gold and jewels. Nijinsky darts forward crouching, and she supports herself with one hand on his head as she moves slowly to a couch. Her court gathers around her and tall fans begin to wave.

Meanwhile Amoun has fallen under Cleopatra's spell and Ta-hor is watching him anxiously. He approaches the queen's couch and Nijinsky snarls at him, baring his teeth like a dog. Cleopatra gives no sign of having seen him and Ta-hor drags him away; then Cleopatra's eyes follow the lovers. The ritual dances begin, led by Ta-hor. Suddenly an arrow lands at Cleopatra's feet. Consternation of the court! – but the queen gazes impassively ahead of her. Amoun is arrested bearing the tell-tale bow, and as Cleopatra rises to face him and he gazes passionately at her, Karsavina as the slave girl 'reads' the message attached to the arrow, in which Amoun declares his love. Ta-hor's pleading is met by Cleopatra with godlike indifference. The queen tells Amoun that he may spend one night of love with her if he drinks poison in the morning. He agrees. Again, as Ta-hor battling with her beloved, Pavlova shows her wonderful dramatic gift. When her pleading proves vain she creeps forth broken-hearted into the desert.

Placing an arm round Amoun's neck Cleopatra draws him towards her couch. They are showered with flowers and their embraces are now hidden, now revealed by the waving draperies of Cleopatra's maidens. It is left to others to express in dance the ecstasies which are being enjoyed on the couch. First, to the Turkish dance from Glinka's 'Russlan', Karsavina and Nijinsky perform a bounding number with a golden veil. As he lifts her from side to side the veil describes a loop or arch in the air. Karsavina runs backwards on her toes, dragging the scarf, then flings it over her as she turns.[140] Then comes Glazunov's 'Autumn' from 'The Seasons', to which Fokine has arranged a Bacchanale embodying all his feeling for classical Greece. In this wild dance girls are pursued by satyrs. Fokina sweeps across the stage like a whirlwind, while Sophie Feodorova freezes into sensual poses.[141] As the pace quickens, all revolve like a maelstrom, and the girls throw themselves on the floor in attitudes of suggestive abandon, while the satyrs hang over them lasciviously. Many people are shocked by this.[142]

Benois, who had suggested to Diaghilev the use of Glazunov's Bacchanale, considered this to be one of Fokine's finest arrangements, on a par with the 'Polovtsian Dances' and the Buffoons' Dance in 'Armide'. He called it 'a wonderful vision of the radiant beauty of the ancient world'.[143] It aroused such enthusiasm in the audience that Tcherepnine, who was conducting, was held up for several minutes. The dancers, in despair of the show being able to continue, thought they had better acknowledge the applause though the drama was not yet over – something quite contrary to Fokine's principles. From the couch, screened by veils, he witnessed the argument going on in the wings. In his own words,

To my horror I saw that the bacchantes of ancient Greece had joined hands with the bearded fauns and, forming a line, were coming out to take a bow. I rapidly disengaged myself from Cleopatra's embraces and pounced like a tiger, running towards the wings to meet these dancers who were destroying the unity of the scene in defiance of my orders. I did not know myself what I was going to do. I did not have time to consider. After a few steps of my 'Egyptian' run, however, the applause ended very abruptly. A tomblike stillness followed. My Greeks, embarrassed, backed into the wings. After holding my threatening position during the pause which followed, I pretended I saw the approaching figure of my weeping fiancée, and then, turning round, I again threw myself into the arms of Cleopatra.[144]

The High Priest brings the poisoned cup. Cleopatra bears it to the centre of the stage, driving Amoun before her. He searches her eyes for a sign of mercy, but she is adamant. He drains the cup; the poison does its work. The Queen raises him by his chin to observe impassively the agony in his eyes, then lets him fall lifeless to the ground. She stands for a moment enjoying her sadistic pleasure, then, motioning to her attendants, leaves the temple, leaning on her slaves. The High Priest throws a black cloth over Amoun's body as he passes. Dawn begins to rise. Ta-hor steals in, in search of her lover, a tiny figure in the huge empty temple. She uncovers his body, kisses his lips, caresses his arms; then, realizing that he is dead beyond recall, she beats her breast and flings herself across him.

'Cléopâtre' was such a draw that Astruc and Diaghilev began to give it after the long opera 'Ivan le Terrible', as if Chaliapine alone could not be counted on to fill the house. There were other changes of programme. Extra performances were announced. Serov's opera 'Judith', as planned, was added to the repertory on 6 June; it was sung by Chaliapine and Litvinne; and 'Le Pavillon d'Armide' completed the programme. Curiously enough, although Glinka's 'Russlan' is music of a superior order to 'Judith', all performances of it were cancelled after the première and 'Judith' was substituted.[145] This must have been because there was no role for Chaliapine in 'Russlan'.

It was Diaghilev's hope to bring a company the following year to appear at the Opéra, so with this in mind he contrived that on 19 June, the day after his season closed at the Châtelet, the Russians should take part in a special Gala performance in aid of the Société des Artistes Français at Garnier's gorgeous theatre, which had seen the success of 'Boris Godounov' in the previous year. There was a rehearsal during the afternoon, to which Pavlova came in street clothes, looking wonderfully smart. As she sketched the movements of her Mazurka, holding up the skirt of her dress, Fokine said to Karsavina, 'I don't know if it's the sunshine, or the success of our season, or her summer frock, but I don't think I've ever seen her looking so elegant before.'[146] Besides 'Les Sylphides' the company danced 'Le Festin' and Chaliapine sang two acts of 'Boris, with the Russian chorus. The performance was naturally a great success, and Diaghilev, pleased that his dancers (who were not yet really his, but the Tsar's) should have appeared for the first time on the famous stage, began negotiations with Messager and Broussan for a Russian season in 1910. At a party afterwards Diaghilev thanked the company in a speech, and a Minister bestowed the Palmes Académiques on Pavlova, Karsavina, Fokine, Nijinsky and Grigoriev.[147]*

There were two reasons, however, why Diaghilev's happiness should not be complete. One was financial and the other was that Nijinsky was ill. Already on the night of the Opéra gala he had been suffering from a bad throat. He was not fit to dance at a private party given on the following day.

This '*soirée artistique inoubliable*' as *Commedia* called it, was at the house of M. and Mme Ephrussi in the avenue du Bois. In the gardens, with their great clumps of trees lit by electricity, the Russians performed character dances from 'Le Festin'; Smirnov sang the tenor aria from the last act of 'Tosca', Rimsky's 'La nuit de mai' and some popular Russian songs; and 'Les Sylphides' found its perfect setting.[148] Diaghilev had arranged that Nijinsky should be paid 1,000 francs for the evening and Karsavina 500. As we have seen, Nijinsky did not appear and Astruc, who never stopped letting fall to Karsavina that she had in Mme Ephrussi 'a fervent admirer', told the ballerina secretly that the hostess wanted her to have 1,000 too, which was an enormous sum for her in those days. Mme Ephrussi's admiration for Karsavina was boundless and the ballerina found her dressing-table festooned with white roses.[149]

Diaghilev called in his friend Dr Botkine to look at Nijinsky, and typhoid fever, probably due to drinking tap water, was diagnosed. The hotel management were afraid of infection, so Diaghilev took a small furnished flat, and set about nursing the invalid. It was in this flat that Diaghilev proposed they should live together and Nijinsky agreed.[150]

Svetlov looked in at the Châtelet to see the company moving out.

The huge deep stage was dark, gloomy and deserted. A few workmen in blue blouses were packing up scenery. At the rear of the stage the *régisseur* [Grigoriev] was paying the artists their final salaries. The critic Calvocoressi, who had contributed so passionately towards the Russians' success, had been so helpful to the dancers† and even contrived with a heroic effort to express himself in Russian by the end of the six weeks' season, was pacing up and down the stage, the prey of a puzzled sorrow.

*Grigoriev omits the name of Karsavina. She always wore the ribbon when she wanted a sleeping-car on the Petersburg train.

†He had even taken Nijinsky to buy a bathing costume. (Calvocoressi, p. 210.)

He was obviously depressed. From all around women's voices were calling 'Monsieur Calvo' or just 'Calvo' . . .[151]

Basking in the dazzling sunshine of Parisian acclaim and in love with Nijinsky, Diaghilev had been for a month under a spell and everything had seemed possible: money trouble was the last thing that could be allowed to spoil his happiness. But already on 15 June Astruc had sounded a warning note. He wrote to Diaghilev that takings to date were 405,000 francs, which made it possible to expect 500,000 or 510,000 by the end of the season in a few days' time: but expenses would total 600,000. While disclaiming all financial responsibility, Astruc felt a moral one as Diaghilev's sponsor in Paris, and asked how the bills were going to be paid.[152]

Pressure from creditors had nearly prevented the Opéra Gala from taking place. Once again Astruc's credit had saved the situation.[153] Enjoying their ovations, not one of the company – not even Nijinsky or Grigoriev – knew about the deficit Diaghilev had to face on the morrow.*

On 20 June, Diaghilev gave Astruc a complete list of outstanding debts and the truth was known at last: the sum to be found was 86,000 francs. One of the guarantors, who was under no obligation to hand over any money since the average receipts per performance had exceeded 25,000 francs, generously paid up 10,000 francs: but Diaghilev's creditors were beginning to appeal to Astruc. The latter acted quickly and took possession of Diaghilev's only tangible asset, the sets and costumes of the Russian season. On these he secured a loan of 20,000 francs from the Société de Monaco, on the understanding that the décors passed to the Casino if not redeemed within a certain time. Simultaneously he carried out a *saisie foraine*, an official seizure of Diaghilev's possessions at the Hôtel de Hollande. Belsacq the upholsterer had already taken this step on his own behalf. Diaghilev owed his hotel several thousand francs. Astruc then set about making Diaghilev bankrupt at the Tribunal de Commerce de la Seine.[154] Finally, Diaghilev signed a bill undertaking to reimburse Astruc 15,000 francs on 7 October.[155]

*And Grigoriev had not heard about it in 1953 when he published his book, for he wrote 'The result of our first Paris season was highly satisfactory, both artistically and financially.' (p. 35.)

Pavlova stayed on in Paris to make another guest appearance in a Gala at the Opéra – a Gala which Kchessinskaya came from Russia to dance in.[156] Karsavina had signed a contract to dance in music-hall at the London Coliseum. Her agent, Marinelli, had asked her to try to bring Nijinsky too, but Nijinsky told her he had already been offered 'thousands' and refused.[157] Karsavina herself had received many offers, including some from Australia and the United States: she chose England because of her love for Dickens,[158] and thus became the first of the Russian stars to shine in London, a year before Pavlova, Mordkine, Kyasht, Bolm and Preobrajenskaya, and two years before Fokine and Nijinsky. Rosaï and Armida's other buffoons were also given a London contract.[159] Benois, though he could ill afford it, had brought his wife from Russia to share the excitements of the season: they now returned home. 'Roaming through the parks of Peterhof and Oranienbaum,' he wrote, 'it seemed to me that I could hear in the rustle of the pine-trees the melodies of the "Camp" or the "Enchantment of Armide", and my stories of how the Polovtsian maidens, headed by Sophie Feodorova, dashed like a hurricane about the stage and of the wild leaps of Bolm, so impressed my children that they would try to reproduce it all – and not without success.'[160]

Diaghilev and Nijinsky left for Carlsbad, and since it is always agreeable to have a third person, an old friend, on a honeymoon,* Diaghilev took Bakst along too. Perhaps he thought he might be bored alone with his new lover. Their hotel, the Villa Schüffler, stood on a hill amid pine-forests next to the Russian church. Vaslav did not take the cure: he did no work, but was regularly massaged. They went on drives through the woods and Vaslav was reminded of a spa called Narzan in the Caucasus, which he had seen on his youthful travels.[161]

After two weeks isolated from the world the friends were parted temporarily. Diaghilev had business in Paris, so Bakst escorted Vaslav to Venice, where, after a few days, Diaghilev would join them. Vaslav loved the train journey through the Tyrol and the Alps and he was glued to the window of their compartment, feasting on the mountain scenery throughout the day.[162]

*Dame Marie Rambert does not agree.

One result of the season's success was that Diaghilev felt confident that it was only a beginning. So without a penny to his name, but feeling like Lorenzo the Magnificent, he had commissioned 'Daphnis et Chloë' from Ravel and a ballet called 'Masques et Bergamasques' from Debussy. He also set going discussions between Cocteau and Reynaldo Hahn, which would result in work being started on 'Le Dieu bleu' the following year. At Calvocoressi's suggestion he asked Gabriel Fauré for a ballet, but the latter was working on his opera 'Pénélope' and the project came to nothing.[163] Now Diaghilev went to Paris to talk to Debussy. In a letter to Louis Laloy, dated 30 July 1909, Debussy excused himself for having stolen a march on Laloy – who was hoping to write a scenario for Diaghilev – and written that of 'Masques et Bergamasques' himself. He summarized the sequence of events thus:

1. You brought Diaghilev to see me. We talked things over without exactly getting anywhere. 2. I met Diaghilev *chez* Durand [the music publisher] and he discussed with me a possible collaboration with P. J. Toulet . . . (a further complication). At the same time he told me that as he was leaving for Venice in three days to meet the choreographer he would like to take a scenario to show him. 3. As we were only talking about a *divertissement* lasting at the most fifty minutes I saw no point in turning the world upside down or bothering you, so I wrote the scenario, providing no more plot than was necessary to link up the danced passages. Diaghilev liked it and at once said that Nijinsky and Karsavina must dance it. You see how easy the whole thing was . . . So things are going ahead. We are dealing with a Russian who speaks our language and who will understand exactly what I want. Naturally I shan't expect Nijinsky's legs to deal in symbols, nor Karsavina's smile to expound the philosophy of Kant. I intend to enjoy myself writing this ballet, which is the right state of mind for a *divertissement* . . .[164]

Three days later Debussy wrote to Laloy: 'Kipling says the Russian is a charming person until he puts on his shirt . . . Our Russian friend thinks the best way to get what he wants from people is to lie to them. He may not be as sharp as he thinks; and this is certainly not a game *I* play with my friends. However, nothing has changed between you and me, whatever chicanery Diaghilev has been up to . . .'[165] Debussy did not like Diaghilev, but it seems clear that he was using him as a scapegoat for his own behaviour towards Laloy, so the chicanery was not all on one side.

'Masques et Bergamasques' never saw the light of day: but the interesting fact to emerge from this correspondence is that as early as the first Saison Russe Diaghilev was intending Nijinsky to be a choreographer,* for of course it was Nijinsky not Fokine who was awaiting Diaghilev in Venice.

Before leaving for Venice Diaghilev took care to get Astruc to return all the Ballet's musical scores.[166] And on 6 August we find him writing to Astruc from the Hôtel de Hollande asking for the return of Serov's original sketch for the Pavlova poster, which belonged to Dr Botkine.[167]

With what pleasure Diaghilev must have looked forward, as he travelled south, to showing Vaslav the beauties of his favourite city! They stayed at the Grand Hôtel des Bains de Mer on the Lido.† Diaghilev and Bakst took Vaslav to the Accademia, the Scuola di San Rocco and the churches. Vaslav swam in the lagoon, and Bakst made an enormous oil sketch of him, sunburnt and naked except for some scarlet bathing pants‡ and a handkerchief knotted on his head, standing with head tilted to observe his outstretched left hand, a golden faun against a peacock sea. Diaghilev never bathed, partly because he was afraid of the sea and partly because he thought only the young and slender should expose their bodies in public. In the evening they would sit outside the gilded café of Florian under the arcades of the immense Piazza San Marco, observing people and pigeons. There were parties at the palace of the flamboyant Marchesa Casati, who led panthers on a chain, and Vaslav met D'Annunzio, who asked him to dance, and Isadora, who suggested having a baby by him, both of which offers he turned down. At night the friends returned by gondola across the lagoon.[168]

The Mariinsky season began on 1 September and Vaslav had to start practising again at least a week before. Diaghilev and he were in Paris on 19 August.[169] Because of the debts Diaghilev left in his wake, which soon became common knowledge in the Russian capital,

*Mme Bronislava Nijinska does not believe this.
†Where Diaghilev was to die twenty years later.
‡No doubt the ones he had bought with Calvocoressi.

it was not such a triumphant return to Petersburg as it might have been. While Nijinsky, whom Diaghilev never bothered about his money troubles, began classes and rehearsals and told his mother about his stay in Germany and Italy, Diaghilev had to try to pay for the past season while planning the next one at the Paris Opéra.

Diaghilev had sensibly but perhaps rather dishonestly concealed from Astruc his negotiations with the Opéra, and Astruc's financial anxiety turned to vengeful fury when he discovered what was afoot. If Diaghilev dealt directly with the Opéra Astruc could be dispensed with: and this transaction after all he had done to ensure the triumph of the Russians in Paris, seemed to him the blackest treachery. What made it doubly serious was that Astruc was planning a season of Italian opera with Caruso and the Metropolitan Opera Company of New York at the Châtelet at the very same time next year; and so as not to clash with the *jours d'abonnement* at the Opéra both Astruc and Diaghilev would expect to give their performances on Tuesdays, Thursdays and Saturdays. They were in direct rivalry and Astruc exerted himself to blacken Diaghilev's name with the Russian establishment in the hope that he would never be allowed to bring artists of the Imperial Theatres to Paris again.

His first step was to try to detach Chaliapine from Diaghilev.

Astruc in Paris to Chaliapine in Moscow, 9.10.09

My dear friend,

I have just received your telegram, and I must admit I am shocked to the core.

It is not only the disappointment I feel as a friend at getting so terse a telegram, when you know how anxiously and even passionately I have been waiting for your answer to a question put to you very clearly five months ago and repeated at regular intervals by letter and telegram. You must have known, my dear Fedia, what importance I placed on this matter, and I should have thought that friendship, apart from practical considerations, would have told you that you should let me know before definitely signing with someone else . . .

The question is: who have you signed with?

I must tell you, my dear Fedia, that if you have signed with M. Serge de Diaghilev without telling me you may have made a big mistake . . . Let me remind you that if the Russian season was able to take place in Paris this *was entirely due to me,* because it was I alone who got Diaghilev the credit in Russia without which the season could not have happened . . .

[Astruc then tells the story of the financial side of the Russian season.]

To show his gratitude to me Diaghilev's sole gesture was to plan a new season in competition with me. He will profit by all the work I put in during the last year to stage performances in Paris and London in an unprofessional way.

Under the circumstances I should warn you that I intend to take the most drastic steps to put an end to this scandal. As you know I possess certain weapons: but there are even more lethal ones which I shall resort to when the moment comes. War has been forced on me and I declare war today.

You have been warned. Make up your mind . . . I should have thought that Boito, Toscanini and Gatti-Casazza, who all played a part in the beginnings of your career and with whom you have so many happy memories in common, would somewhat have influenced your decision. But it appears that all this goes for nothing. I am not trying to influence you, but one thing I will say. Your decision has made both them and myself very sad indeed.

> Yours ever,
> GABRIEL.[170]

Astruc next began systematically to attack Diaghilev through the Russian court. He wrote to Count Friederickx, Minister of the Imperial Court, asking if he might submit a report on the Russian season to the Tsar;[171] and received a reply in the affirmative from General Mossolov,* Head of the Chancellery.[172] In the second week of November he told his story to the Grand Duke Nicolas Mikhailovitch, who was in Paris for a few days.[173] On 18 November, he paid a morning visit to the Grand Duke André Vladimirovitch, Kchessinskaya's lover, at his Paris hotel.[174]

The report to the Tsar,[175] which took nearly eleven pages of foolscap, covered the financial aspect of the story as unfolded above (and indeed is the source for much of it). Astruc takes to himself the credit for making the Russian season financially possible (which he certainly had), and for its success with the press and public; he also points out that he secured a reduction of 50 per cent for Diaghilev with the Société des Auteurs et Compositeurs dramatiques de Paris,

*Author of interesting memoirs. See Bibliography.

thus saving Diaghilev 25,000 francs, and that he himself agreed to take a minimal percentage of 2½ per cent. He accuses Diaghilev of fulfilling none of his undertakings. He observes that in all the documents he signed Diaghilev subscribed himself 'Attaché à la Chancellerie Personelle de Sa Majesté l'Empereur de Russie'. He inserts a little scandal.

One morning when he [Astruc] was on the point of handing over a sum of 10,000 francs to Diaghilev's 'accredited representative' M. Astruc received a letter marked 'urgent and personal' which read as follows: 'Dear friend. Please do not on any account pay money to *any single one* of my secretaries *without a card from me for each payment*. Yours ever, Serge de Diaghilev.' M. Astruc, alarmed at this sudden indication of mistrust, asked for an explanation but failed to receive one. However, he heard a few days later that the confidential associate and *very intimate friend* who acted as accountant and who was trusted with delivery of monies had left Paris suddenly on the very evening the famous letter was sent – a fact which could lead to all kinds of suppositions.

This reference, of course, is to the elopement of Mavrine, Diaghilev's former secretary and lover, with Olga Feodorova.

It is curious – but perhaps typical of the cut-throat world of theatre* – that Astruc, who was to collaborate so closely and so successfully with Diaghilev for several years to come, should have been responsible in the course of this winter of 1909–10 for damaging Diaghilev's reputation at the Imperial Court once and for all. It was conceivable that although the Emperor distrusted him and although none of the Grand Dukes felt the same friendship for him as the late Grand Duke Vladimir had done, and although since her husband's death the Grand Duchess Marie Pavlovna had been influenced against him, Diaghilev might still, as a result of the glory his Paris season had brought to Russia, have received subsidies from the Imperial purse. Astruc made this improbable, if not impossible: so that at the end of his life, jotting down fragmentary reminiscences of the beginnings of his enterprise for the benefit of Kochno and Lifar, Diaghilev was able to state that never at any time had he received a single rouble for the mounting of his ballet seasons from the Emperor.

*This was the comment of Mr Jerome Robbins when I told him the story.

To facilitate his plotting with associates in St Petersburg, and knowing that letters were often opened and censored in Russia, Astruc invented a code for referring to the persons most closely concerned.[176] It is significant that there is no code-name for Nijinsky: he was already considered to be so inseparable from Diaghilev that any attempt to use him as a pawn in the war-game was not even considered. Some of the code-names are less meaningful than others. 'Chemineau', the French word for a tramp, was the role assigned in this code to Diaghilev, in contrast to Astruc's 'Chrysale': Chrysale was the honest man, the *bon bourgeois*, in Molière's *Les Femmes Savantes*.

On 8 December one Jules Martin wrote from St Petersburg about the Diaghilev 'dossier' which was to be shown to Babylas (Count Friederickx). He said he had seen Mélanie (Kchessinskaya) and had long talks with Emile (Grand Duke Serge) and Joseph (Grand Duke André); that he would shortly be seeing Jacqueline (Grand Duchess Vladimir) and would tell her the whole story of Chemineau's (Diaghilev's) behaviour. The latter had failed to raise any money in St Petersburg and was in difficulties because in addition to the 10,000 francs he would have to pay out to the Paris Opéra he was expected to advance a large sum towards the expenses of a projected London season. Martin had heard (erroneously) that Diaghilev's principal guarantor in Paris was the Marquise de Ganay – the Comtesse de Chevigné too, though to a lesser extent. Martin would be seeing Maxime (the direction of the Imperial Theatres) on the following day; Pierre and Babylas (the Tsar and Count Friederickx) would be back (from Livadia in the Crimea) in a fortnight.[177]

However, in the middle of December Diaghilev went to Paris and through the good offices of the Comtesse de Béarn, Mme de Ganay, Mme de Chevigné and Misia Edwards he and Astruc were brought together to discuss their differences. Sert and Robert Brussel were present at these meetings, and in a letter to Brussel dated 23 December Astruc summed up his conclusions.

Astruc in Paris to Brussel in Paris, 23.12.09

Dear friend,

Following the talks which have taken place during the last few days between M. Serge de Diaghilev, M. Sert, yourself and me, and which were due to the kind intervention of a mutual friend* anxious to reconcile two former collaborators divided by a serious disagreement, I now put forward a detailed specification of the conditions which I think will make it possible to arrange matters.

The awkward situation which our friends have been considering is as follows:

1. I am organizing next May and June at the Châtelet Theatre a season of Italian opera in which the company, the chorus and the corps de ballet of the Metropolitan Opera, New York, will appear in their own sets and costumes. This was announced in the Paris press some time ago.

2. M. Serge de Diaghilev, for his part, is giving at the same time at the Théâtre de l'Opéra a season of Russian opera and ballet similar to that which he gave last year with my help at the Châtelet.

The days chosen by me for our performances at the Châtelet, in agreement with the direction of the New York Theatre, are the Tuesdays, Thursdays and Saturdays between 19 May and 25 June. These days were planned to avoid clashing with the subscription days at the Opéra, which would have been definitely detrimental to my season.

The days chosen by M. de Diaghilev are necessarily the same Tuesdays, Thursdays and Saturdays because they are the only days when the Opéra does not perform and can therefore let the theatre.

After reviewing at length the various ways of finding grounds for agreement, it was agreed:

1. That M. de Diaghilev could not get out of his agreement with the Opéra and postpone his season till 1911.

2. That M. de Diaghilev could not put back his season by three weeks because of contracts signed with London for periods preceding and following his Paris season.

The only solution of our problems was that suggested by M. de Diaghilev, namely that I should agree to upset my plans and change my performances at the Châtelet from Tuesdays, Thursdays and Saturdays to Mondays, Wednesdays and Fridays.

In spite of the serious damage this change of days might do me, with the danger of entirely losing the season-ticket-holders [*abonnés*] of the Opéra and of having to subtract the takings of that theatre (22,000 francs a night in May) from my potential receipts, I am disposed to agree to the proposed change.

My conditions would be as follows:

*In the feminine.

1. M. de Diaghilev would undertake to assure me the collaboration of Chaliapine between 19 May and 25 June for three performances of Boito's *Mefistofele* and three of *The Barber of Seville* (in the roles of Mefistofele and Basilio).

2. The administration, *abonnements*, sale of tickets, publicity etc. of the Russian season to be entrusted to me by M. de Diaghilev on the same terms as stated in my contract with the Metropolitan Opera Company, that is that I should receive 5 per cent of the gross takings of every performance, payable nightly in the same way as the Assistance Public and the Droit des Pauvres, plus 25 per cent of the total profits, if any, this sum to be paid within a week of the final performance.

3. Immediate payment today of the sum of 24,711 francs, plus costs and interest, which M. de Diaghilev still owes me from the last Russian season.

4. Messrs G. Astruc & Co. to nominate the Paris representatives of the Russian season, and these persons to be paid by M. de Diaghilev.

5. Financial guarantees to be established which would ensure the carrying out of the above conditions . . .

Yours very affectionately,
GABRIEL ASTRUC

P.S. For your information, after our first discussion I telegraphed to New York: 'Hope to obtain Chaliapine three Mefistofele three Barbers.' I received the following reply: 'Chaliapine affair must be decided within ten days. Later decision would make change of plans impossible. Gatti-Casazza.'[178]

So Diaghilev and Astruc were friends again: their collaboration was necessary for the Russian Ballet to fulfil its destiny. A new associate, Dmitri de Gunsbourg, paid up Diaghilev's debt to Astruc.

Still, the fate of both seasons, the Russian and the American, seemed to depend on Chaliapine. On 5 January 1910 Astruc despatched Robert Brussel to Russia to talk to the great man and ensure his co-operation. Brussel welcomed the opportunity of seeing his beloved Karsavina again, though aware that his editor on *Le Figaro*, Gaston Calmette, would grow impatient if he stayed away too long. The course of negotiations can be followed in an exchange of telegrams between Brussel, in Petersburg and Moscow, and Astruc, in Paris, as well as some addressed to Baron Elter, the chancellor of Grand Duchess Marie Pavlovna, in Petersburg, and to Chaliapine in

Moscow.[179] But Brussel was unable to prevail on Chaliapine to take part in the coming season.

On his return to Paris Brussel sent Diaghilev a letter drafted by Astruc summarizing the situation. Once Diaghilev's debt to Astruc was settled they could go ahead. Astruc was only too delighted to show that his skill and resources were so great that he could make a success of both the Italian and Russian seasons, though they ran simultaneously. It was essential for Diaghilev to announce his repertory so that publicity could be started and tickets sold at once.

In fact there was to be no opera in the Russian season at the Paris Opéra. The first Diaghilev season of ballet alone was largely due to the non-cooperation of Chaliapine: without him it was too risky to transport a large company of singers and several elaborate productions. But, as in the previous year, the exact composition of the ballet repertory would be arrived at only after much trial and error.

CHAPTER THREE

1910

The period of January–March 1910 was no less critical in the story of Diaghilev and his influence on the arts than the same period a year before, when the decision to take the new Russian ballet to the west had been made. We have evidence of the problems facing Diaghilev during these three months. He had to pay the debts of the past season and raise a subsidy for the next one. He was torn between ballet and opera. His desire to make Nijinsky preeminent was very strong – and ballet had been the chief success of the 1909 season: but ballet had been a late-comer in his life and he could not rid himself of the accepted notion that opera was a higher art. Anyway, would the Paris Opéra accept a Russian Season of ballet alone? And was it feasible to take opera to Paris without Chaliapine? If ballet alone was acceptable by Paris, what new works could be taken to augment the previous repertory? Kchessinskaya was a stumbling block. If she consented to go to Paris she would have to be shown in one of her roles from the old repertory. This would probably ensure financial support from the Imperial purse, but Fokine neither wanted Kchessinskaya in his ballets nor did he want anyone else's ballets – Petipa's, for instance – in the repertory.[1] The problem of new ballets and their casting was acute. If Kchessinskaya was important from the point of view of money and prestige, Pavlova, Nijinsky and Karsavina were essential artistically.

Benois, who had first interested Diaghilev in the ballet, and who thought he had been the chief instrument in persuading him to take Russian ballet to Paris, had struck up a friendship with Fokine, and insisted that 'there could be no talk of opera.'[2] We may imagine that Nouvel took the opposite point of view.

Since the first discussions of a new ballet repertory a year before, everyone had thought it desirable to produce a Russian folk ballet, a fairy story – only more magical and less childish than 'The Little Hump-backed Horse'. For months Fokine had been revolving this in his mind. He read through Afanasiev's collections of folk tales and began to combine some of them into a scenario.[3] Benois wrote:

By joint effort we started to search for the most suitable story, but soon came to the conclusion that no single story existed that was entirely adequate and that one would have to be created by merging several together. The music was to be composed by Tcherepnine, the dances to be arranged by Fokine; the fundamental elements of the subject were inspired by the young poet Patiomkin. The working out of these elements was undertaken by a sort of conference in which Tcherepnine, Fokine, the painters Steletzky, Golovine and I took part. Our excellent writer Remizov, who was not only a great crank but a great lover of all things Russian, was carried away with our idea. During the two meetings I had with him, his very tone seemed to give life to our collective work.[4]

Remizov, Prince Peter Lieven recalled,

was a little, odd, extremely ugly man, resembling an overgrown sparrow and forever muffled in warm clothes . . . He bewildered the friends with various tales, incomprehensible strange-sounding improvisations at which he was a master. 'There are also Bellyboshkies,' he would say, 'Evil sort of creatures, some with tails and some without.' What Bellyboshkies were nobody could make out, but this nonsensical word sounded so attractive that the Dance of the Bellyboshkies in the train of the wicked sorcerer was produced.[5]

Fokine, who was certainly the prime instigator of the scenario, and who was ultimately given all the credit for it, does not name these other collaborators in his description of how 'The Firebird' came about.

We met very often, during the evening hours, at the home of Alexandre Benois for tea. During some of these tea-drinking sessions, I narrated the story of the Firebird. Every time some artist visitor appeared who was not familiar with the new ballet, I had to repeat the libretto. . . and I would describe the ballet and be carried away by my own fantasy. With each description I added new details . . .[6]

The recollections of Stravinsky, the 'new boy' on the committee, are different: 'Fokine is usually credited as the librettist of "The Firebird", but I remember that all of us, and especially Bakst, who was Diaghilev's principal adviser, contributed ideas to the plan of the scenario.'[7] Perhaps Grigoriev has a small claim to co-authorship, even if he only borrowed the books of Afanasiev for Fokine, for he wrote many years later: 'I obtained several collections of Russian fairy tales; and between us we evolved a story by piecing together the more interesting parts of several versions. This took us about a fortnight.'[8] Eventually, Benois describes, Tcherepnine, 'who was prone to inexplicable changes of mood, and whose attitude was in those days cooling towards ballet in general', lost interest.[9] It was just as well.

Already, during his holiday in Venice, Diaghilev had written to his old professor, the composer Liadov: 'I want a ballet and a *Russian* one; there has never been such a ballet before. It is imperative that I present one in May 1910 in the Paris Opéra and at Drury Lane in London. We all consider you now as our leading composer with the freshest and most interesting talent.'[10] At one of the early meetings of the 'committee' at Diaghilev's flat in autumn 1909, Diaghilev received Fokine's scenario and announced that he was asking Liadov to compose the score. Liadov was a slow worker. When, a few weeks later, Golovine met him in the street and asked him how he was getting on, he replied 'Fine. I've bought the music paper.'[11]* Diaghilev must have anticipated something of the kind, because, with his usual forethought – which some might call duplicity – he had discussed the new fairy-tale ballet with the young Stravinsky. Liadov relinquished the commission. When in December Diaghilev rang up Stravinsky to tell him he was to compose 'The Firebird' Stravinsky admitted to Diaghilev's surprise that he had already begun it.[12] 'The Introduction,' Stravinsky remembers, 'up to the bassoon-and-clarinet figure at bar seven was composed in the country, as were notations for other parts'. He would finish the composition in March, and the orchestration a month later: the

*He was overdoing the self-disparagement: he had in fact made a few sketches. (Alexander Tcherepnine conversation.)

complete work (apart from a few retouchings) being posted to Paris in mid-April.[13]

Stravinsky was not attracted by the subject of the ballet.

Like all story ballets it demanded descriptive music of a kind I did not want to write. I had not yet proved myself as a composer, and I had not earned the right to criticize the aesthetics of my collaborators, but I did criticize them, and arrogantly, though perhaps my age [twenty-seven] was more arrogant than I was. Above all, I could not abide the assumption that my music would be imitation Rimsky-Korsakov, especially as by that time I was in such revolt against poor Rimsky. However, if I say I was less than eager to fulfil the commission, I know that, in truth, my reservations about the subject were also an advance defence for my not being sure I could. But Diaghilev, the diplomat, arranged everything. He came to call on me one day, with Fokine, Nijinsky, Bakst and Benois. When the five of them had proclaimed their belief in my talent, I began to believe, too, and accepted.[14]

For a composer who had started work on the ballet a month before receiving the commission he was being remarkably coy.

All this time it was assumed that the birdlike Pavlova would dance the Firebird.[15] If Diaghilev had known sooner that Pavlova would not dance it he would certainly have created a new work for Nijinsky instead.

Stravinsky had reason to fear being lumped together with Rimsky-Korsakov 'for Russian export', and it is interesting that at the very beginning of Diaghilev's 'export drive' of Russian colour and folk-lore, one so young should have sensed the danger. (It is almost as if he foresaw with a shudder the excesses of *l'âme slave*, the White Russians in exile, the nightclub 'Schéhérazade' in Paris, staffed by ex-officers of the Imperial Guard, the Russian Tea-room in New York.) Whether because Diaghilev thought the Rimsky numbers in 'Cléopâtre' and 'Le Festin' had been particularly effective in Paris, or because Rimsky's harmony made him appear the most advanced of the Five – the Russian Debussy – or out of piety towards his old teacher, lately dead, or because he genuinely admired his music, he hoped to present not only Rimsky's opera 'Sadko' but also the symphonic poem 'Schéhérazade,' in the form of a ballet, in Paris.

It was because the friends were intending to mount 'Sadko', or part of it, that Fokine agreed to a slight change in the libretto of 'The Firebird'. In the opera the hero charms the inhabitants of the King-dom of the Sea with a magic *gusli*, a kind of zither or psaltery. Fokine had intended that Prince Ivan, the hero of his ballet, should use the same method of subjection on Kastchei's unholy court. Benois persuaded him to substitute a feather from the Firebird's breast.[16] A more important change was made in Fokine's libretto. The choreographer wrote: 'Yielding to the wish of Igor Stravinsky, I agreed to substitute a coronation for the gay processional dances with which I had wanted to end the ballet.'[17]

'The Firebird' has always been quoted as the earliest example of close collaboration between a composer and a choreographer. Many years before Fokine's own memoirs were published (1961), he was telling Lincoln Kirstein – and Arnold Haskell[18] was spreading the story – how the music and choreography had been worked out together.

Stravinsky brought him a beautiful cantilena on the entrance of the Tsarevitch into the garden . . . But Fokine disapproved. 'No, no,' he said. 'You bring him in like a tenor. Break the phrase where he merely shows his head, on his first intrusion. Then make the curious swish of the gar-den's magic horse return, and then, when he shows his hand again, bring in the full swing of the melody.'[19]

Fokine's later description emphasizes his theory of those days (which used so to annoy Stravinsky) that music should be a mere accompani-ment to the dance, but it probably gives an exaggerated picture of his own influence on the score.

Stravinsky played, and I interpreted the role of the Tsarevitch, the piano substituting for the wall . . . Stravinsky, watching, accompanied me with patches of the Tsarevitch melodies, playing mysterious tremolos as background to depict the garden of the sinister immortal Kastchei. Later on I played the role of the Tsarevna and hesitantly took the golden apple . . . Then I became Kastchei, his evil entourage – and so on. All this found most colourful interpretation in the sounds that came from the piano, flowing freely from the fingers of Stravinsky . . .[20]

Flowing freely! Are we meant to think that Stravinsky improvised an accompaniment, then went away and wrote it down? Not very likely. Stravinsky says

I like exact requirements ... To speak of my own collaboration with Fokine means nothing more than to say that we studied the libretto together, episode by episode, until I knew the exact measures required of the music. In spite of his wearying homiletics, repeated at each meeting, on the role of music as *accompaniment* to dance, Fokine taught me much, and I have worked with choreographers in the same way ever since.[21]

It was naturally Benois, with his love for Gautier and the whole Romantic period, who suggested taking 'Giselle' to Paris. It was in Paris in 1841 that this famous ballet on a theme by Gautier, danced by Carlotta Grisi and Jules Perrot, had first seen the light of day. Giselle was Pavlova's great role. Benois pointed out to the committee that, as the Russian school of ballet grew out of the French, in taking 'Giselle' to Paris they would be paying a compliment to France. (Of course, he was longing to design the ballet.) General Besobrasov and Svetlov were both in favour.

But Diaghilev made a face and said 'Shura is quite right, of course. But "Giselle" is too well known in Paris,* and would not be likely to interest the public. I'm quite prepared to consider it, though.' At the next meeting he asked Benois 'What about "Giselle", Shura? Do you still insist on "Giselle"?' 'I do indeed,' said Benois. 'I feel sure that it would give our repertoire variety and show our dancers at their most brilliant. Besides, I should like to paint you a décor for it!' Diaghilev gave a sly smile, and wrote 'Giselle' in large ornate characters in his exercise book.†

Grigoriev thought the question had already been decided in his mind.[22] Probably Diaghilev guessed that if Benois, Fokine's new friend, could be got to insist on 'Giselle' there would be less op-position from the opinionated Fokine, to whom the old ballet with its set dances and conventional mime was a thing of the past. 'Giselle' had in fact been one of the first ballets Diaghilev thought of bringing to Paris, as the notes made by Astruc *chez* Paillard in sum-mer 1908 bear witness.

*It had not in fact been danced there since 1868.

†The word 'Carnaval' appears for the first time on p. 83 of Diaghilev's black book, along with 'Giselle' in fairly ornate capitals, but 'Giselle' had appeared seven times on previous pages.

Calvocoressi was asked by Diaghilev to find out the position with regard to the copyright of Adam's score for 'Giselle'.

We had a lot of trouble . . . and we did not know in whom the copyright was vested. Eventually we discovered the assignee, a music publisher who lived in a side street in Versailles. We went to see him. I believe he had quite forgotten the very existence of 'Giselle'. He gave us the required permission with glee and prepared for the novel experience of pocketing the performing fees that were falling to him from the skies.[23]

The planning, designing and tentative casting of the new repertory went on over Christmas 1909 and well into the New Year: and this strategy was of course dependent on whether or not there was to be opera as well as ballet, on whether terms could be agreed with Paris, on the reconciliation with Astruc, on the payment of debts and other considerations. Contracts with the dancers would only be signed in March,[24] and rehearsals only begin in April.[25] Meanwhile, Nijinsky, Karsavina, Fokine, Grigoriev and the rest had resumed their duties at the Mariinsky. Nijinsky danced nearly every Wednesday and Sunday, his roles being the poet in 'Chopiniana', the Slave in 'Une Nuit d'Egypte', the Slave in 'Le Pavillon d'Armide', Blue Bird in 'La Belle au bois dormant', the Act III *pas de deux* in 'La Fille mal gardée', Vayn, God of the Wind, in a *grand pas d'action* in 'The Talisman' and a number of *pas de deux* and *pas de trois* in ballets of the old repertory.[26] He was also present, this year, at many of the meetings of the 'committee', but he lived with his mother and did not move in with Diaghilev.[27]

Just as with 'The Firebird', the collaborators retained in later years different memories as to the authorship of 'Schéhérazade'. There can be no doubt that the general idea was Benois's. Rimsky's symphonic poem had only hints of a programme based on episodes from the 'Arabian Nights'. Ever since his first experience of the music many years before, Benois, ignorant of Rimsky's name for the turbulent fourth movement – 'Festival at Baghdad: the Sea' – had heard in it 'the voluptuaries of the harem and their cruel punishment'.[28] From the beginning it was agreed that Bakst should do the décor and costumes,[29] but before he or anyone else was consulted Diaghilev had a pianist play over the piano score several times to excite Benois' imagination.[30]

Benois had been hurt during the first Paris season at being given no credit as part-author of 'Cléopâtre'. After all, the ideas for the entry of Cleopatra and for her disrobing had been his. Now, as the scenario of 'Schéhérazade' came to him he wrote down his ideas on the score itself. 'I did this solely to help my memory. One evening, however, as Argutinsky and I were returning home from one of these creative evenings I said to him half-jokingly: "This time my notes are in black and white, which will guarantee that this work will be considered *mine*." '[31] He was not considering the money point of view,[32] although if he had – and he may not have been aware of this – he would have found that as author of the libretto of a ballet he would be entitled, in France at least, to royalties on every perform- ance. The Société des Auteurs were very active in exerting the rights of those they represented. But Benois was too optimistic.

By the time Fokine was called in the friends had discussed the story between them and the choreographer got the impression that Bakst was the author.[33] Bakst wanted the unfaithful wives to be sewn in sacks and thrown into the sea. Nobody else was in favour of this ending. As Fokine pointed out, 'To hide the dancers in bags at this most tragic moment would mean to give up a very effective scene. The bags would be heavy and cumbersome to look at. Besides, to throw them when they contained artists would be dangerous ... A mass slaughter of lovers and faithless wives in front of the spectators presented a much more enthralling problem for me.' This was agreed on.[34] Ida Rubinstein would be the Sultana Zobeïda; Bulgakov, who had been an impressive Marquis in 'Le Pavillon', would mime the Shah; and Nijinsky would be the Negro slave who was the Sul- tana's lover. Nouvel said to Diaghilev, 'How odd it is that Nijinsky should always be the *slave* in your ballets – in "Le Pavillon d'Ar- mide", in "Cléopâtre" and now again in "Schéhérazade"! I hope one day you'll emancipate him.'[35]

All this planning of new works was absorbing and delightful for the friends, but for Diaghilev the months of January, February and March were a time of increasing doubt, struggle and despair. He must continually have been on the point of throwing up the whole idea of another Russian season abroad, and we may imagine that only his love for Nijinsky and the shining hope of giving him greater roles to dance and act than ever before, in ballets yet to be composed by Debussy, Ravel and Stravinsky, kept him going. Karsavina, whom Diaghilev had not warned of his projected season at the Opéra, had returned from London with another Coliseum contract for the spring, which presumably would prevent her from appearing with the Russians in Paris. This was a fearful blow, not only because Diaghilev needed her talent and glamour in the company, but because she was one of the artists whom he was obliged by his arrangement with the Opéra to present. 'The anguish was great on both sides,' wrote Karsavina, who would willingly have given up the financial benefits of her London engagement, but was bound by her signature. She began to dread the sound of the telephone, 'as it was not easy to resist Diaghilev's pressure'.[36] By the middle of January, as we have seen, Brussel had finally failed to secure the co-operation of Chaliapine, so the whole enterprise might very well founder. About 1 February Pavlova told Diaghilev that she could not come to Paris as she was to appear in music-hall at the Palace Theatre, London.[37] So Diaghilev had lost in her his Firebird and his Giselle. Her decision was undoubtedly arrived at for financial reasons and because she felt she could shine more brilliantly in an old-fashioned repertoire of her own choosing away from Nijinsky and Karsavina, but her dislike of Stravinsky's music may have helped to turn the scale. (Diaghilev had taken Stravinsky to a party at her flat, but she was incapable of understanding the new music.)[38] So Karsavina would have to dance the Firebird: but whether she could take part in the season at all depended on an arrangement with Oswald Stoll of the London Coliseum. Without at first breaking this news to Astruc, Diaghilev racked his brains for ways to please him and at the same time make some money. Knowing what a draw 'Cléopâtre' had been, he cabled on 2 February offering Astruc three performances of it at the Châtelet during the Metropolitan season of Italian Opera for 50,000 francs. On 8 February Astruc agreed to pay 45,000 francs for three performances of 'Les Sylphides', 'Cléopâtre' and 'Le Festin', provided that Kchessinskaya, Pavlova, Karsavina, Rubinstein, Nijinsky and Fokine all appeared and provided these works were exclusive to him and not performed at the Opéra. These were impossible conditions. Diaghilev naturally could not eliminate half his repertoire for the Opéra season, and of course he could not produce Pavlova and had come to no firm arrangement with Kchessinskaya, so Astruc called off the deal. On 10 February Diaghilev, who had clearly gone straight to see Kchessinskaya after Pavlova's defection, cabled to Astruc, 'All well here. Giselle replaced by short version of 'La Belle au bois dormant.' On 11 February Diaghilev bravely cabled, 'Everything else is going all right.'[39] But on top of all his other troubles Rimsky's widow and son were placing every possible difficulty in the way of his presenting 'Schéhérazade' as a ballet.[40]

Dr Sergei Botkine, devoted as ever to Tamara Karsavina, used to send his assistant or a nurse to see her daily, to keep an eye on her health and sometimes give her an injection. Karsavina now had a sledge of her own, with a horse and a fat coachman. One cold evening the doctor had tea with her and he told her, 'I am so happy, I have just found a cure for ulcers of the stomach. My whole being is singing with joy.' She dropped him in her sledge at the house where he was dining, on her way to the theatre. Next morning she heard he was dead.[41] Botkine's death was not only a personal loss to Diaghilev, Benois and the friends – and Prince Argutinsky, who had not spoken to the doctor since a row over an antique which they had both coveted and which Botkine had bought, was inconsolable[42] – it was a blow to the prospects of their enterprise. For Botkine, apart from being married to a rich Tretiakov, knew many influential people in the capital and had always been helpful in raising funds and pulling strings.[43] In fact, far from everything going all right with Diaghilev, everything was going wrong. *Les quatre cents coups.*

On 11 February Schidlovsky, one of Astruc's contacts in Petersburg, wrote to him about the possibility of getting him a Russian decoration (Brussel had just received one), and mentioned that Diaghilev was totally failing to raise money in Petersburg, that Kchessinskaya had refused to appear, that the Grand Duchess Marie Pavlovna (Vladimir) had withdrawn her patronage because of all the scandals surrounding Diaghilev's name, and that the Paris season could not possibly take place.[44] What were Astruc's thoughts, after reading this letter, when he cabled to ask Diaghilev to name the dates of his *générale* and *première* at the Opéra?[45] On 16 February Diaghilev gave him two dates without knowing who or what he was going to be able to show. (The suggested dates, 22 and 24 May, were not adhered to.)[46]

Meanwhile, 'The Firebird' was being written.

We have seen how in January Brussel had reason to believe Dmitri Gunsbourg wished to prevent a reconciliation between Diaghilev and Astruc. A dilettante and a lover of ballet, it seems that Gunsbourg saw himself at the head of a ballet-company, another Diaghilev but one with money. Perhaps he thought that if he could prevent Astruc from showing a Diaghilev-led company in Paris, there would be more chance that Astruc might present a Gunsbourg company. Did Diaghilev trust him? The question is academic, because we know that Diaghilev, who admired clever rogues, was quite capable of working with and turning to his advantage people he did not trust or like.[47] His marvellous diplomacy – which could be called insincerity in a good cause – was to sustain a ballet company for twenty years and make possible the creation of many masterpieces. Now he charmed and flattered Gunsbourg, making him think of himself as the joint-Caesar of the enterprise, in order to get his money. He was capable almost of persuading Gunsbourg that the new ballets were his – Gunsbourg's – inspiration; and even if Gunsbourg was too intelligent to be deceived or to deceive himself, he may still have derived a certain pleasure from being treated by Diaghilev in society if not as 'the onlie begetter' at least as someone whose intelligence, taste, name, cosmopolitan Jewish connections, business experience and money were essential to the enterprise of taking Russian art to Western Europe. It must have been Gunsbourg who enabled Diaghilev to pay Astruc 5,000 francs on 14 February and to honour a bill for 17,432 francs on 10 March,[48] for while continually postponing a visit to Paris for discussions with Astruc, after six weeks of shilly-shallying, Diaghilev cabled to Astruc on 10 April that Nouvel and Gunsbourg, his powers-of-attorney (*fonds de pouvoir*), would be leaving on the morrow.[49] However, Gunsbourg had not left on 23 April, when he cabled Astruc he would be 'leaving Tuesday'.[50]

All this time Diaghilev was negotiating with London and New York,[51] juggling with prospective seasons, tours and combinations which might make his projects more feasible financially. He had also arranged that the Russian Ballet (opera having been finally re-nounced in mid-March) would dance in Berlin on the way to Paris and in Brussels after Paris. But with no opera on the programme, Diaghilev realized he needed two more new productions besides 'The Firebird', 'Schéhérazade' and 'Giselle'. The last ballet had not been abandoned on the withdrawal of Pavlova. They counted on Karsavina to dance it with Nijinsky instead, and Benois had designed two charming *pastiche* Romantic sets, which had already been painted. There had been some hesitation in entrusting the great role to Karsavina in spite of her successes in Paris.[52] She had had little occasion hitherto to reveal her genius for mime. Fokine spoke against her,[53] which seems incredible as she was his supreme interpreter. Either he wanted her to appear only in *his* ballets, or, more likely, his marriage to Vera had brought out in him a tendency to decry his former love. Getting to know Tamara Karsavina better, Benois was enchanted with her character: 'Tatochka now really became one of us; she was the most reliable of our chief artists and one whose entire being was suited to our work . . . Tamara Platonovna was not only a beautiful woman and a first-class, highly individual artist, but had as well a most attractive personality, was open to varied interests and infinitely more cultured than most of her comrades . . .' What a relief for the friends to find that 'unlike Pavlova, with whom one could not talk except in a half-coquettish ballet fashion, Karsavina was capable of sustaining a serious conversation'![54]

Karsavina was delighted to find herself admitted to the flat in Zamiatin Pereúlok off the English Quay, where the new Russian Ballet had been born.

In Diaghilev's small flat beat the pulse of his formidable enterprise. Strategic moves and counter-moves of his ingenuity, planning, budgeting, music in one corner, discussion in another. A Chancery and a small Parnassus in the restricted space of two rooms. The lines of each production were discussed there first. Around the table sat wise men; the Artistic Committee drinking weak tea and hatching daring ideas . . . Benois topped the Areopagus . . . He overflowed with benignity, and his erudition was unique. His mastery of blending fantastic with real was the more wonderful because he effected his magic by the simplest means . . . Quite different assets were those of Bakst. He was exotic, fantastic – reaching from one pole to another. The spice and sombreness of the East, the serene aloofness of classical antiquity were his. Roerich – all mystery; a prophet with impeded speech, he could do infinitely more than ever he promised ... While they sat in one room, in the next Stravinsky and Fokine worked over a score and appealed to Diaghilev in every collision over the tempi ... He brought quick, unhesitating decision to every doubt. He had a sense of the theatre to an uncanny degree. Engrossed as he was in his part, he kept a vigilant eye on his collaborators. 'Gentlemen, you are wandering off your point,' came now and then from his corner. Diversions constantly occurred. Tradesmen burst in; alarming news arrived; unless Anisfeld has more canvas at once, he won't be able to finish painting the scenery.[55]

There was evidently a limit to the funds Gunsbourg was willing to put at Diaghilev's disposal, for the latter, having failed to raise money in Russia for the forthcoming season, set out at Easter for Paris.[56] To Benois he sent off such despairing cables describing his set-backs and disappointments that the friends began to fear he might commit suicide.[57] It seemed that the season was doomed.

On 5 March a ball was to be given by the magazine *Satyricon* in the Pavlov Hall. Two young men, Mikhail Kornfeld, later the editor of the mazagine, and Pavel Patiomkin, the celebrated poet who died young, came to Fokine and asked him to stage a ballet to be given at the ball. He suggested Schumann's Carnaval as eminently appropriate and also as something he had long wanted to arrange. The young men were enthusiastic. Let Fokine describe how his delightful ballet came into existence.

We sat down with the German biography [of Schumann] and [Kornfeld] quickly translated to me the part pertinent to Carnaval which had a connection with Schumann's personal life ... From this and from the titles indicated on the music, such as 'Harlequin', 'Columbine', 'Pantalon', 'Pierrot' and 'Papillon' I was able immediately to visualize and construct the picture of the ballet: the series of separate characters linked one to the other – the proverbially hapless Pierrot, the comical Pantalon, the Harlequin always emerging victorious from his escapades; and the light plot around the love between Columbine and Harlequin. The luckless Pierrot and Pantalon were literally improvised during rehearsal. The ballet was staged in three rehearsals, the last of which took place ... minutes before the opening of the ball. The staff of the *Satyricon* magazine were finishing the decoration of the hall, banging with their hammers, shouting to one another, arguing and climbing ladders to hang cloths and garlands. During all this commotion and racket I created the Finale . . .[58]

Apart from the actor Meyerhold, all those taking part in 'Carnaval' were members of the Imperial Ballet. But as it was against the rules for them to appear elsewhere than at the Mariinsky during the ballet and opera season, they danced anonymously and all were masked. Everyone knew who they were, including members of the Directorate of the Imperial Theatres who were present, but because of the polite fiction of the masks, discipline could be said to be unbreached.[59]*

'Carnaval' [wrote Fokine] I composed in the following way: the ballet started and developed on the stage, and continued amidst the audience. . . During the number which Schumann called Promenade the dancers left the stage, and the Finale was done amidst the spectators. At the very end the dancers ran back on the stage. Just before the end Harlequin and Columbine tied up Pierrot and Pantalon with the long sleeves of the former. When the two of them finally managed to disentangle themselves and run towards the stage, the curtain fell right in front of their noses, leaving them alone on the proscenium.

In the final dance everything was built on runs. Florestan pursued Estrella, Eusebius chased Chiarina, Papillon ran away from Pierrot and Pantalon; everyone ran in and out of the audience, the dancers mingling with the spectators. This was novel and entertaining, but not too easy because the dancers, wearing masks, had difficulty in locating and identifying each other.[60]

The enforced anonymity of the dancers meant that their names could not be mentioned in the press: this has led to a confusion over the exact casting which I have had some difficulty in clearing up. In the English-language edition of his autobiography Fokine gave the name of Leontiev as having danced Harlequin; Mme Karsavina says Fokine danced it; Mme Bronislava Nijinska says her brother did.

I wrote to Mr Vitale Fokine, the choreographer's son, about this. He told me that when preparing the fuller Russian edition of his

*For that matter, Meyerhold, who had been working since September 1908 as a producer at the Alexandrinsky Theatre (following his successive breaks with Stanislavsky in Moscow and Komisarjevskaya in Petersburg), was asked by Teliakovsky, shortly after this, to adopt a pseudonym for his private theatrical activities.

father's book for the press, his researchers in Leningrad had found that Leontiev had indeed danced Harlequin, and that Nijinsky had taken the role of Florestan. (In the English edition of Fokine's book, Florestan is given to Vassili Kiselev.) Karsavina was Columbine; Vera Fokina was Chiarina; Ludmilla Schollar was Estrella; Alexander Chiriaiev was Eusebius; Bronislava Nijinska was Papillon; Alfred Bekefi was Pantalon; and Vsevolod Meyerhold, the actor and director (already famous for his experiments), was Pierrot. The ballet was accompanied by the piano suite as Schumann wrote it.*

Time being scarce, Fokine, apart from showing the dancers their moves and timing, left certain details for them to fill in themselves. When Bronislava was practising her Butterfly dance, it was Vaslav who invented and taught her the rapidly changing positions of the arms, now together in front, now behind the back, and the fluttering hands which, with the non-stop movement, seem to us today the essential characteristics of this role in Fokine's famous and much-loved ballet. We can imagine the brother, putting on his coquettish face, flitting about the room and then correcting his sister. Bronia stayed up half the night perfecting in front of a looking-glass the gestures he had shown her.[61] So what was possibly Nijinsky's first effective essay in choreography was embedded in a work of Fokine's, just as Leonardo's angel is said to smile from the corner of Verocchio's 'Madonna' in the National Gallery. Vaslav's mind had perhaps already been directed by Diaghilev since the last summer into thoughts of doing choreography.

It was Grigoriev who told Diaghilev about 'Carnaval'.

Diaghilev looked up from his exercise book and said that he did not

---

*In Beaumont's *Michael Fokine* and in his *Complete Book* he gives the role of Florestan to I. Kchessinsky. In the English-language edition of Fokine's memoirs Florestan is Vassili Kiselev. In his *The Diaghilev Ballet*, Grigoriev gives the roles of Columbine and Harlequin, at the first performance of 'Carnaval' by the Diaghilev Ballet (in Berlin, 20 May 1910) to Karsavina and Nijinsky. But Karsavina was at the London Coliseum and Mme Lopokhova, who in fact danced the Berlin and Paris premières, confirms that her Harlequin was Leontiev. Arnold Haskell in his *Diaghileff* does not make this mistake: on the other hand he states that it was Diaghilev who had Schumann's music orchestrated by the four composers – overlooking the fact that Rimsky would have to have made his contribution posthumously. In his *Complete Book* Beaumont also states wrongly that the first performance of the ballet in Western Europe was in Paris. Nijinsky did not take over the role of Harlequin until 1911.

particularly care for Schumann, and that though he had not seen Fokine's ballet, he had heard that it was arranged for only a small number of dancers and would therefore be unsuitable for a large stage. However, Benois arrived at this point, and, on hearing my suggestion, supported me . . .[62]

By chance Schumann's suite had already been orchestrated by Rimsky-Korsakov, Liadov, Glazunov and Tcherepnine: this was done as far back as 1902 for a concert in memory of Anton Rubinstein.

With a short *divertissement* called 'Les Orientales', for which Diaghilev himself[63] chose music by Glazunov, Sinding and Arensky, and commissioned an orchestration of Grieg from Stravinsky (for which he was paid seventy-five roubles), the repertory was now complete.

Somehow, with the aid of Astruc, Diaghilev contrived to make the season in Paris possible. The financial responsibility was all to be his: he simply hired the Opéra for a number of days.[64] It was hoped to pay for the season out of box-office receipts. Astruc, who was now naturally as anxious as anyone to make this season a success, even though in competition with his opera season at the Châtelet, would have his percentage, but he also helped by raising money on the prospective takings. In all these negotiations, no doubt, Misia, Mme Greffuhle, Mme de Chevigné, Mme de Béarn, Mme Ephrussi and others played their part.

Soon after Diaghilev's return from Paris it was time for Karsavina to depart for London. She had promised to try to get leave from the Coliseum in order to join the Russians in Paris as soon as possible, on the condition that she returned to the Coliseum later in the summer.[65] The young Lydia Lopokhova would dance Columbine in Berlin and on the opening night in Paris; and 'Giselle' and 'The Firebird' would be postponed till Karsavina's arrival.

Diaghilev did not argue with us. He merely went on thinking. On the eve of my departure for London [wrote Karsavina] a more than usually pressing 'come to talk things over' brought me again to Diaghilev's flat. I think he wanted to re-exercise the almost hypnotic power he had over me before I could escape from his influence. There the air was tense, all nerves worn down, as usual nothing ready and time short. He took me to his room, the only uninvaded spot ... Diaghilev reminded me of my promise. We both had outlived the strife, if there was one; mutual anxiety had brought us closer. Diaghilev spoke affectionately; we cried a little. I looked round. The image lamp was lit; Diaghilev looked weary, a mere human. The room was bare of adornment, I had expected it to be fastidious. I could not realize then that the glamour of his personality spent itself in creation of fancy. His gentle words had a touch of resignation. He knew that on his way one obstacle hardly removed another will arise.[66]

On 7 May, King Edward of England died, and all hopes of a London season in 1910 fell through. This was a bitter blow.[67]

The final problem was to find the money to pay for the artists' tickets to Berlin and Paris. More string-pulling, more persuasion. The Finance Minister, Count Kokovtsov,* advised the Tsar to grant Diaghilev 10,000 roubles, the equivalent of £1,000. The Tsar signed the report. The friends heard of this at three in the afternoon, a day or two before the company was due to depart. Diaghilev rushed round to a banker friend and on the security of the Tsar's order borrowed £1,000 for a few days. The tickets were bought. But the Tsar was not a man of honour. Under pressure perhaps from the Grand Duke Sergei Mikhailovitch, who is said to have persuaded him that Diaghilev's ballets were decadent, he withdrew the small subsidy. The banker had to be repaid. Prince Argutinsky and another loyal friend Ratkov-Rognev signed a bill for the sum needed. This was later paid back to them out of receipts in Paris. The Tsar, however, circulated his embassies with the command to refuse all support to Diaghilev's enterprise.[68]

The mild affectionate Benois was subject to occasional fits of temper, sulks – even passion. He had at least one serious quarrel with Diaghilev every year. For Diaghilev, his 'pupil', had now assumed command – by right of having taken all the dirty work on himself in order to allow his painters, composers, choreographer and dancers to get on happily with their jobs – and he was apt to adopt a high-handed manner. On the day before the company's departure Benois called at the passport office to collect his passport for Germany and France and found Diaghilev had not made the necessary

*He became Prime Minister on the assassination of Stolypin in the following year.

arrangements for him, so that he would be held up for two days and deprived of the fun of travelling with the company. Is it possible that in the last anxious weeks Diaghilev had found his old friend increasingly fractious and had hoped to pass a few days without him? Benois returned home, and in an onrush of rage, banged his right fist against a window-pane and severed an artery. He might have lost the use of his hand, but after an operation and a month in Petersburg with his arm in plaster he recovered, and left with his family for Lugano – thus missing Berlin and the Paris opening.[69]

In the middle of May the Russians arrived in Berlin. They were to appear in the Theater des Westens in Charlottenburg, a quiet western suburb grown up around the palace and formal gardens created by the Prussian kings. The dancers from Moscow arrived a few days later. Karalli had not been re-engaged, but Sophie Feodorova returned to dance not only her roles in 'Prince Igor' and 'Le Festin', but one of the three Odalisques in 'Schéhérazade' – which she had already rehearsed in Petersburg. Moscow's most celebrated ballerina, Ekaterina Gelzer, came as a guest artist to dance in 'Le Festin' and 'Les Orientales'. Plump, pretty and excitable, she had a strong classical technique, but very little else.[70] Alexander Volinine, who accompanied her, was the son of a rich Moscow merchant[71] – an unusual parentage for a dancer in 1910: he was quiet, amiable and a good partner.[72]

Of the new ballets only 'Carnaval' was to be shown in Berlin, and, in the absence of Karsavina in London, the role of Columbine would be interpreted by the irrepressibly gay Lydia Lopokhova, whose ingenuous virtuosity was 'tempered by the imperceptible awkwardness of youth'.[73] Leontiev would be her Harlequin. It had rightly been considered essential to show the Schumann ballet to the Germans. It was given on the opening night of the season on 20 May and proved enormously popular.

The setting Bakst designed for 'Carnaval' is so familiar to us today that it is easy to forget how startling it must have seemed in its simplicity to the theatre-goers of 1910. The dark blue curtains have a poetic ambiguity, for they suggest both a tent in which a party is being given and the booth in which the characters of the Commedia dell'Arte entertain their audience. Along the top of the curtains runs a dado of stylized poppies in red, black and gold, which, together with two red and black striped sofas with curly arms, the stage's only other adornment, place the date of the action in the Viennese Biedermeyer period, that is, 1840. For the 'programme' of Schumann's composition, closely followed by Fokine, contains references to his love-life and embodies not only the (gallicized) characters of the Italian comedy, Harlequin, Columbine, Pierrot and Pantalon, but also autobiographical allusions: Florestan, who chases Estrella, representing the headstrong, impulsive side of Schumann's character, and Eusebius, who is shyly and reverently in love with Chiarina, the solitary, dreamy and romantic side. Estrella is Ernestine von Fricken, with whom the composer was in love; and Chiarina the fifteen-year-old Clara Wieck, the pianist whom he later married.

The girls all wear flounced crinolines with bonnets or frilled caps. Some are white and yellow; Chiarina has a white jacket and a royal blue skirt with tassels; Papillon's white dress is shorter, more childish than the others, with little painted wings, and she has bunches of ribbons attached to her wrists; Columbine's big white skirt has cherries painted round one of its innumerable scalloped frills, and she has black silk ballet shoes. The men, mostly top-hatted, sport brown or bottle-green frock-coats with high collars, nipped-in waists and full-skirts in the D'Orsay style, worn over buff or striped peg-top trousers. Pantalon is excessively dapper in ginger, with dyed moustaches and green gloves; and Eusebius, with his long black poetic hair, has a carnation-pink velvet jacket, shorter than the others, and striped black trousers. Pierrot is traditional, in baggy white trousers and smock with a limp black ruff, green pom-pom buttons and long trailing sleeves that hide his hands. The lozenge pattern on Harlequin's tight trousers is apple green, vermilion and white to match Columbine's cherries; he has a floppy white silk shirt, black skull cap, black shoes, and (painted) black domino mask.

The charm of Fokine's ballet is that there is just enough story to give interest to the dancing but no more than the music itself contains – nothing had to be twisted or added. Diaghilev, the archcutter, cut only the brief number called Réplique. The work is delicate, pretty, but also faintly satirical, with a touch of sadness and a hint of cruelty to add spice to the comedy. Harlequin mocks the world and makes love only in jest; and it seems to be through his eyes that we are intended to see the absurd yearning of Eusebius, the Angst of Pierrot and the senile philandering of Pantalon.

After the preliminary stately chords there is a flight of girls, crossing the stage pursued by their lovers – a tripping of feet, an urgency of overtaking, male impatience, feminine provocation. Are they on their way to a party, these dancers to the *valse brillante* of Schumann's Préambule, or merely leaving the ballroom for the secret shadows of the garden? We see for the first time Florestan chasing Estrella, and after the heartfelt sighs of Eusebius for Chiarina the pace quickens from *animato* to *vivo* to *presto*.

Pierrot tiptoes through the curtain, down-sloping eyebrows over tired eyes, to mourn his loveless life. His arms are extended upwards with dangling sleeves, but every glimmer of hope is at once extinguished by his realization of the impossibility of communicating with another human being. To the bounding waltz expressive of his carefree character Harlequin capers on and feigns friendship for Pierrot. He dances round him, points at him derisively, pulls his sleeves, but finally pushes him over and runs off. For the next few numbers Pierrot lies dejectedly by the proscenium arch. There follows a Valse Noble for six couples. Then comes Eusebius to dream of love on a sofa. His languid tune, orchestrated, has seven notes on the clarinet to two on the string accompaniment, which seems to want to trip him up. Chiarina appears to him and gives him a rose, and he dotes on her. How vivid a contrast is Florestan's exuberant onrush to a passionate waltz, his whirlwind flirtation with Estrella! His tune is interrupted in mid-career as he makes his high-pacing exit-run after her. During this dance Pierrot has also been yearning after Estrella and at the end of it he lopes off. To the air called Coquette, Eusebius and Chiarina go through their romantic paces, she throwing him flowers. Then Papillon flits on – *prestissimo* semi-quavers on the flute and piccolo alternating with violins – fluttering hands and tittupping feet. Pierrot stalks her, but she cannot for a second come to rest, and just as he thinks he has caught her in his conical white hat she vanishes through the curtains. To Lettres Dansantes, another fast waltz, we watch the palpitations of Pierrot – his expectation of finding in his hat a butterfly all of his own, his disappointment, as the tune ends in mid-phrase, on finding the hat empty. Chiarina has an *appassionato* solo with a strong rhythmic melody scored for strings. To the tune called Chopin she and her two friends, tip-toeing like three Graces with arms raised and gloved hands meeting, in and out and round and round, impede Florestan's pursuit of the expectant Estrella and 'share with each other the virgin's secret armoury of cruelty'.* Then, having celebrated, as it were, to this solemn and valedictory nocturne, scored for clarinet, harp and strings, the mysteries of girlhood, they back away from each other, still on tip-toe, drawn by fate in three different directions; and we see the extremities of Chiarina's hand disappearing through a parting of the curtains at the back. There follows a short rapid entry for Estrella.

When Columbine and Harlequin enter, linked together, to Reconnaissance, his high-hopping knees-up steps follow the *animato* melody, scored for flute and clarinet, while her rapid *pas de bourrée* echo the staccato semi-quaver string accompaniment. They circle the stage and kiss. Pantalon bustles on in a great fuss and hurry to Schumann's *perpetuum mobile*, afraid to be late for his assignation with Columbine. He looks at his watch, sits on a sofa and re-reads her letter. She steals up behind him and puts her hand over his eyes while Harlequin snatches the note. When Columbine introduces Harlequin to the old man, the latter holds out his hand, but the former flourishes the love-letter, then tears it into little pieces, and scatters them in the air as he executes *entrechats*, wagging his head grotesquely. To the dipping Valse Allemande, Columbine circles round the offended Pantalon and tries to include him in her dance with Harlequin, but at the end they push him playfully off. Harlequin's triumphant solo, to the tune called Paganini, is made up of *cabrioles, entrechats, pirouettes* and rapid hand-claps above the head. At the end he executes a *grande pirouette à la seconde*, spinning gradually more slowly as he sinks into a sitting position, cross-legged on the floor. In Aveu the lovers, on opposite sides of the stage, argue about who should cross over to whom, then to this sigh-heaving amorous tune Harlequin, kneeling, lays a symbolic heart at

---

*I could not resist borrowing this sentence of Adrian Stokes's, although it was applied to a later production of 'Carnaval'. (*Tonight the Ballet*, p. 41.)

Columbine's feet. When the other couples gradually come on and fill the stage to the ambling Promenade, they discover Columbine on the sofa, with Harlequin stretched out on the floor, whispering to her. Congratulations are offered to the engaged couple, and all the men kiss Columbine's hand. General rejoicings. Papillon flits on, pursued by Pierrot. The young dancers march against a group of old 'Philistines' (musical reactionaries in Schumann's mind) who carry umbrellas. Pantalon and Pierrot are spun round in an involuntary embrace and knotted together by the latter's sleeves, but mollified in time to hold hands with Columbine and Harlequin in the final group.

Fokine's 'Carnaval' contained some wonderful ideas and was to provide Nijinsky, a year later, with one of his most effective roles. The virginal *pas de trois* of Chiarina and her two friends, the entry of Columbine and Harlequin and the end of the latter's solo, had the simplicity of genius. Perhaps only in the rather pointless attack on the Philistines can we see signs of the ballet's rapid composition and the transfer of the final number from ballroom to stage.

Vera Fokina with her mannered romantic languor and Bronislava Nijinska with her speed and strength were ideally suited to the roles of Chiarina and Papillon. Maestro Cecchetti was so experienced a mime that he could make even the small role of Pantalon into a masterpiece. That people found Bolm's Pierrot profoundly moving gave an extra dimension to the comedy. As Columbine, Lopokhova was irresistible.

The company arrived in Paris at the beginning of June and Lopokhova was so overcome by the beauty of the Gare du Nord that she fainted.[74]

The Paris Opéra had less elaborate machinery than the Châtelet; the stage staff were as unco-operative as in the days of 'Boris'; it was with the greatest difficulty that the Russians could get the stage to rehearse on; and 'Schéhérazade', of which nobody had yet seen the scenery hung, had still to be finished – and its dress rehearsal went badly.[75] However, it was a satisfaction for the company – as well as an honour – to appear in this great gilded palace, even if it seemed a little shabby and in need of redecoration.[76] The endless wide passages backstage and the large, comfortable dressing-rooms, furnished by their permanent French occupants, each with its private amenities, were superior to anything the dancers were used to in Russia.[77]

Could the Russians, without opera or Chaliapine, without Pavlova – and opening without Karsavina – recapture the Parisian public? If Paris proved fickle and stayed away from the Opéra, or

José-Maria Sert, Jean Cocteau, Misia Edwards (Sert) and Diaghilev in a box. Caricature by Jean Cocteau.

was stolen away by the Metropolitan Opera season at the Châtelet, there would probably never again be a Saison Russe. Fokine, Nijinsky and the other dancers would return to shelter beneath the wings of the Imperial eagle. Bakst and Benois did not live solely by designing for the stage: they had their reputations and livelihoods as painter and art historian to keep them going. But Diaghilev? What would his future be if the season was a failure? He had none in

154

Russia. He would be ruined and there would be many who would rejoice. Outwardly, as ever, he wore an air of supreme self-confidence: inwardly he must have been devoured by anxiety and doubt.

Yet he need not have worried. The Opéra would be sold out. Nijinsky would reveal his versatility in 'Schéhérazade' and 'Giselle'. Little Lydia Lopokhova would be acclaimed. Karsavina would triumph in 'L'Oiseau de feu'. 'Schéhérazade' would astound the public and change the appearance of women and drawing-rooms throughout Europe and America. In 'L'Oiseau de feu', his first very own commissioned 'Diaghilev ballet', the heroic Sergei Pavlovitch would proclaim to the world the genius of our century's greatest composer. What glories after what trials!

The opening programme on 4 June was made up of 'Carnaval', 'Schéhérazade', 'Le Festin' and the Polovtsian Dances from 'Prince Igor'.

Six months before his death two summers earlier, Rimsky-Korsakov had written of Isadora Duncan: 'What I dislike about her is that she connects her art with musical compositions dear to me. ... How vexed I should be if I learned that Miss Duncan danced and mimed to my "Schéhérazade" ...'[78] Diaghilev had had trouble persuading Rimsky's widow to allow him to present the symphonic poem as a dance-drama – it was certainly not a ballet; and we may be almost sure that if the composer could have seen Fokine's production he would have been displeased. When we consider, looking ahead, what shocks Debussy and Stravinsky would sustain when they saw dancing to the accompaniment of scores actually commissioned for ballet, it seems inconceivable that Rimsky could have been pleased with what happened to his 'Schéhérazade' – any more than Chopin or Schumann with the ballets made to their orchestrated piano compositions. When Fokine, taking his cue from Isadora, had arranged dances to Chopin, he was – for a ballet-master – breaking fresh ground. But 'Les Sylphides' had no story: there was one danced number for each waltz or mazurka. By imposing, with the help of Benois and Bakst, a passionate drama on an elaborate symphonic composition complete in itself, Fokine and his collaborators were going much further – and probably in the wrong direction. In view of the numerous compositions, including symphonies, concertos, quartets and parts of operas, which have been 'used' as the basis of story ballets in recent years, it may be of interest to consider the problems facing the librettists and choreographer of this work which was the first of its kind.

Rimsky wote in his autobiography:

The programme I had been guided by in composing 'Schéhérazade' consisted of separate, unconnected episodes and pictures from 'The Arabian Nights', scattered through all four movements of my suite: the sea and Sinbad's ship, the fantastic narrative of Prince Kalender, the Prince and the Princess, the Baghdad festival and the ship dashing against the rock with the bronze rider on it. The unifying thread consisted of the brief introductions to Movements I, II and IV and the intermezze in Movement III, written for violin solo and delineating Schéhérazade herself as telling her wondrous tales to the stern Sultan. The final conclusion of Movement IV serves the same artistic purpose. In vain do people seek in my suite leading motives linked consistently with ever the same poetic ideas and conceptions ... The unison phrase, as though depicting Schéhérazade's stern spouse, at the beginning of the suite appears as a datum in the Kalender's Narrative, where there cannot, however, be any mention of Sultan Shahriar.[79]

Benois, Diaghilev and Fokine, having seized upon the 'unifying thread', a tendrilly *arabesque* for solo violin with slight harp accompaniment, as a theme for Schéhérazade – or rather for Zobeïda, as the Sultana was called in their ballet – could not but use the *pesante* opening theme – which Rimsky calls 'the unison phrase' – for the Sultan, Shah or King.

So the first movement is to be an overture, and the third is to be omitted. The ballet opens with the sinuous blandishment of Zobeïda. The King of India, Shah Shahriar, is sulking because his brother Zeman, the King of Persia (down here on a visit), has told him his wives are all unfaithful. The Shah sits cross-legged on a divan being coaxed by his queen while Persia sits on his left glowering over his *tchibouk* and keeping a suspicious eye on the whispering harem. The fat old Chief Eunuch is in attendance. A dance of three seated Odalisques, who undulate their arms to the *andantino* in 3/8 time, fails to divert the Shah from his gloomy thoughts. At the end of the dance he rises (to brusque chords in the basses), waves aside the beguiling Zobeïda and announces his intention to go hunting. Echoing trumpet fanfares confirm his decision. As the preparations are made he converses with his brother. Zobeïda's begging him to stay will not be her own little *cadenza* on the violin but *roulades* on the clarinet. The fanfares and the marches are varied and prolonged considerably before the Shah's expedition can be lost sight of, so he has to be armed, and huntsmen and soldiers have to be brought on and eventually marched off. A bassoon solo will accompany the Eunuch, whom the ladies of the harem implore to unlock the doors to admit their Negro lovers, and their pleading will be represented by warbling in the higher woodwind. But there is no theme for the Golden Negro, Zobeïda's lover; and a reappearance of the Shah's theme in the background during the movement's final *accelerando* must be explained away in his absence as an imminent threat or a guilty thought at the back of the Queen's or the Eunuch's mind.

The last movement, which Rimsky called 'Festival at Baghdad: the Sea', can be relabelled 'Orgy: Slaughter'. In the ballet it follows the preceding movement without a break. The firm statement of the Shah's theme at the very beginning needs some accounting for when he is away out hunting, as indeed its reappearance twice before the orgy has reached its climax. Perhaps it is a forecast of the Shah's return; certainly it helps to dramatize the tense wariness of the slaves as they enter the Shah's private realm. Zobeïda's solo violin accompanies the embraces she exchanges with her Negro. The surging, terrifying music of the storm and shipwreck will lend itself admirably to the wrath of Shahriar when he returns to find his wives entertaining their paramours, but Fokine will have a problem because hints of the Storm, represented by a suppressed statement of the Shah's theme and distant fanfares, occur during the Festival, so he will have to bring on, as it were, outriders of the Shah's revenge, before the janissaries really set to with their scimitars to slaughter the wives and slaves. The Shah's tune, blasted out by trombones and tuba during the massacre, returns at the end to be played softly on cellos and basses, this final gentle treatment representing, no doubt, in Rimsky's mind not only calm after the storm but also the happy ending of 'The 1,001 Nights', when sentence of death is remitted: but the mildness of its restatement can easily be accepted in the dance-drama as due to the breaking of Shahriar's heart. Zobeïda's final violin cadenza is her pleading for her life. At the end of it she kills herself. As the curtain falls in silence the Shah weeps.

Designing the setting for Schéhérazade', Bakst had given himself up to a vision of the barbaric and voluptuous Orient which was his spiritual home, and in doing so created what was to become the most famous décor of the age. This harem had a kind of architecture – one vaguely related to the mosques and pavilions of Shah Abbas at Isfahan, with their blue and green tiled walls and painted coffered ceilings: but it was rather formless and depended on a debauch of colour to create its Monticellian impression. Anyway, the architecture of the backcloth, with its three blue doors leading to the slave quarters, was lost in purple twilight. The dominant feature of the set was an immense looped curtain framing the top and left side of the stage, apple green striped with sky blue, spotted with pink roses, and with larger circular patterns in black and gold; from this hung golden lamps. Green and blue was the overall colour-scheme but this amazing peacock green-and-blueness (an unheard-of combination in 1910, which inspired Cartier to set emeralds and sapphires together for the first time in history) was challenged by the coral-red carpet painted with blue and rose-pink rugs, and piled with incredible cushions and bolsters. Behind the Shah's raised divan to the left, where the great curtain fell to the ground, was a curious platform supported on the shoulders of highly improbable quasi-Indian caryatids and approached by a steep staircase, the sole purpose of which was to display a feat of daring and endurance by the dancer Orlov, who was one of the Negroes. At the end of the drama he was killed by one of the Shah's guards on the platform and then 'had to hang head downwards, spreadeagled on the steps with open arms, and hold this painful but effective pose till the curtain fell'.[80] To describe Bakst's invention is to belittle it, for this was no mere composition of architecture, furnishing and light, but an Aurora Borealis, a fantastic musical chord, a new and intoxicating smell.

Bakst was probably an even more ingenious designer of costumes than of sets: his invention of pattern and his imaginative juxtaposition of colours has never been surpassed. In the blues and crimsons of his turbaned kings, in the scarlet Eunuch, the orange-vermilion and chrome-yellow high-capped janissaries, in the rose-pink and green Odalisques and the diaphanously clad, speckled and bejewelled ladies of the harem, and in the braceleted Negroes with their strange encrusted *brassières* linked to their bunched metallic *lamé* trousers by ropes of pearls, he showed more even than in 'Cléopâtre' the fantastic profusion of his genius. When the splendours of 'Schéhérazade' were contrasted with the quaint simplicity of 'Carnaval', who could doubt that he was the greatest designer in the world?

Yet Rimsky's music and the setting and costumes of Bakst were only there to give occasion for the drama devised by Fokine and the performances of Rubinstein as Zobeïda, Bulgakov as Shah Shahriar and Nijinsky as the Golden Slave.

Grigoriev wrote of the choreography for the *ensemble* dances in the Orgy:

By means of intricate evolutions for the various groups of dancers woven in with a number of individual moves, Fokine contrived to endow this dance with such rich variety that its climax was tremendous. The strongest choreographic moment came when, having combined all the different groups into one, he used a pause in the music suddenly to halt them, and then, while accelerating the pace still more, as it were to unravel this human tangle. The effect was overwhelming. The audience roared its applause . . . [81]

Here is what Fokine thought of Ida Rubinstein's Zobeïda:

My creation of the role . . . and her performance were remarkable for giving powerful impressions accomplished by the most economical means. Everything was expressed with one single pose, with one movement, one turn of the head. Nevertheless, everything was outlined and drawn clearly. Every single line was carefully thought out and felt. She is displeased by the departure of her husband, and expresses her displeasure with a single movement, turning away her head when he comes to kiss her farewell. She stands in front of a door through which her lover is momentarily due to emerge. She waits for him with her entire body. Then (and to me the most dramatic scene) she sits utterly still while slaughter takes place around her. Death approaches her, but not the horror nor the fear of it. She majestically awaits her fate in a pose without motion. What powerful expression without movement, I consider this one of the most successful accomplishments among my ideas of the new ballet.[82]

The tall, ivory-pale Bulgakov, with his black beard, Benois thought 'a king from head to foot'.[83]

Now, a few opinions of Nijinsky's Golden Slave.

Fokine: The lack of masculinity which was peculiar to this remarkable dancer and which made him unfit for certain roles (such as that of the leading Warrior in the Polovtsian Dances) suited very well the role of the Negro Slave. He resembled a primitive savage, not by the colour of his body make-up, but by his movements. Now he was a half-human, half-feline animal, softly leaping great distances, now a stallion, with distended nostrils, full of energy, overflowing with an abundance of power, his feet impatiently pawing the ground.[84]

Geoffrey Whitworth: From the moment of his entrance the drama takes on to itself a new and terrible meaning. The dark youth flickers here and there among the mazy crowd of slaves, hungry for the faithless wife of the sultan. . . He finds her soon, and his lecherous hands play over and over her body with a purpose too subtle, it seems, to take and hold her once and for all. And presently he leaves her, threading his way in and out of the passionate dancers, to lie at last on a soft cushion, like a flame of lust that smoulders and sinks but never dies. Now he has joined the orgy again. See him leap in the air, no man but a devil . . . [85]

Benois: . . . Half-cat, half-snake, fiendishly agile, feminine and yet wholly terrifying.[86]

Vaudoyer: He was undulating and brilliant as a reptile.[87]

Bronislava Nijinska: From his first bound on to the stage the whole characterization of the Negro Slave was present. He was first a snake, then a panther.[88]

Estrade Guerra: I remember well how he fell forwards, pivoted on his head, then fell back on the other side, his arms and legs completely slack . . . It was like seeing a hare wounded by the huntsman's shot and rising before the final fall.[89]

Francis de Miomandre: The transport of his movements, the encircling giddiness, the dominance of his passion reached such heights that when the executioner's sword pierced him in the final tumult we no longer really knew whether he had succumbed to the avenging steel or to the unbearable violence of his joy in those three fierce somersaults.[90]

Cocteau: He beat on the boards like a fish at the bottom of a boat.[91]

Savage, devil, stallion, cat, snake, hare, panther, fish!

The extraordinary first night at the Opéra which had begun with Lopokhova in 'Carnaval', continued with Nijinsky and Rubinstein in 'Schéhérazade', ended with 'Le Festin' and Fokine in 'Prince Igor'. Gelzer was rather vulgar in a Russian boyar dance,[92] with Volinine, but she had to be shown in something.

Marcel Proust was present to see the first performance of 'Schéhérazade', with Jean-Louis Vaudoyer and Reynaldo Hahn. Writing a few days later to comment on Reynaldo's article in *Le Journal*, Marcel protested: 'I don't see how you could possibly see Nijinsky miming, because there were always two hundred people dancing in front of him'; and he added, 'I never saw anything so beautiful.'[93]

Karsavina, having cajoled the Coliseum management into giving her leave, joined the company two days later, and was delighted with her well-furnished dressing-room, which had 'Mlle Legrand' painted over the door.[94]

It is curious that the ballet which Karsavina had been dancing twice nightly at the London Coliseum with Koslov and Baldina was the second act of 'Giselle' in the Moscow version[95] (though Karsavina in her role followed the Petersburg version), which was billed as 'Gisella, or La Sylphide': and now she had to rehearse the Petersburg version of the whole ballet with Nijinsky and perform it in the city of its origin. It had not been given in Paris since it was danced by Adela Grantsova in 1868.

The old Romantic ballet, conceived by Théophile Gautier and Vernoy de Saint-Georges as a vehicle to show off the wide range of Carlotta Grisi's gifts, had a strong role for the man as well, and we know Jules Perrot had been as vivid a mime as he was agile as a dancer. The artist impersonating the village girl, carefree and loving at the beginning, has, when she finds her young suitor is a count in disguise and engaged to a princess, to go mad and die with the bravura of a Bellini or Donizetti heroine. When she reappears in Act II, disembodied, as one of the sylphlike Wilis, the dreaded '*dames des bois*', she must not only possess a technique strong enough to dance her lover almost to death, but also the ability to convey a tender love which outlasts the grave. Count Albrecht must be both prince and peasant, Hamlet to her Ophelia; he has to perform in the second act an exhausting series of *entrechats, cabrioles, pirouettes* and *tours en l'air* ending in crashing (but not noisy) falls to the ground, while giving an impression of remorse and heartbreak. This must all be done with period style.

It is typical of Nijinsky's seriousness that he was chiefly worried about the conventional mime. To dance an old ballet of this kind as part of the traditional repertory of the Mariinsky was one thing; to make something living out of it in a repertory otherwise consisting wholly of Fokine ballets was another matter. Fokine had abolished the old sign language. True, there was a little of it in 'Carnaval', with Harlequin laying his heart at Columbine's feet, but that was quite in keeping with Commedia dell' Arte characters. In 'Cléopâtre' Amoun did not declare his love for the queen by pointing first at himself, then placing both hands on his heart, then pointing at Cleopatra: he looked at her with passionate admiration.[96] In 'Schéhérazade', when the Shah was battling with himself whether to kill Zobeïda along with all the other wives, his vengeful brother did not embark on a long spiel such as: Listen (hand extended to the Shah). Just think (tapping his forehead) that your queen (pointing at Zobeïda, then sketching a crown over his own head) was making love (cuddling his own body with both arms) to a Negro (making a fierce grimace and passing his hand like a shade down in front of his face to convey darkness). No, the King of Persia, hand on sword-hilt, paced very slowly across the front of the stage and with one foot turned the Negro's body over, so that he lay face upwards.[97] Karsavina could understand very well the charm of the old sign-language – the convention of a past age and a reminder of 'Giselle's origins.[98] But Nijinsky was so carried away on Fokine's new wave that he could not see his way satisfactorily to reconciling old fashions with heartfelt emotions.* One day at rehearsal Diaghilev complained to Nijinsky during Karsa-

---

*The public, on the whole, and particulary in London, would prove to share his confusion.

vina's mad scene that he was standing still doing nothing. Vaslav replied, 'I am acting with my eyes.'[99] He filled a notebook with his reflections on the ballet, and with his analysis of what Albrecht's reactions would be at different moments. And how was he to make the transition from mime to set dances as natural as in Fokine's dance-dramas? The choreographer himself shared Nijinsky's dissatisfaction: he had only been persuaded by Diaghilev to rehearse 'Giselle' when threatened with the engagement of a second *maître de ballet*.[100] After Chopin, Borodin, Schumann and Rimsky, the genuine ballet music written to order by Adolphe Adam in 1841 seemed terribly insipid.

Karsavina had been taught the role of Giselle by her old professor Mme Sokolova: Pavlova, who had made a speciality of the role in Petersburg, could have been extremely helpful to her, but was not.* Karsavina had not had the experience of dancing in the ballet at the Mariinsky, where Pavlova kept it for herself; but she had at least grown used to dancing the steps of the second act in London. She wrote:

So intent were Nijinsky and I on making masterpieces of our own respective parts in 'Giselle' that our eagerness to impose on one another our individuality led to tempestuous scenes. 'Giselle' on our stage was a holy ballet, not a step to be altered . . . I loved every bit of it. I was sadly taken aback when I found that I danced, mimed, went off my head and died of a broken heart without any response from Nijinsky. He stood pensive and bit his nails. 'Now you have to come across towards me,' I suggested. 'I know myself what to do,' he said moodily. After ineffectual efforts to go through the dialogue by myself, I wept. Nijinsky looked sheepish and unmoved. Diaghilev led me off to the wings, proffered a handkerchief and told me to be indulgent: 'You don't know what volumes he has written on that part, what treatises on its interpretation.'[101]

Volumes! an exaggeration of course. And it is clear that *thinking* a role out was not a successful method with Nijinsky, though of course he forced himself to try: he had to *feel* it, and this feeling might only come to him suddenly and at the eleventh hour.[102] The straightforward princely role, romantic or heroic, was not really in his line. Whereas most male dancers spent their lives being just

*When I asked Mme Karsavina if Pavlova had helped, she exclaimed, 'Not her!'

that and nothing more – cavaliers always at hand to lift the ballerina and take a secondary place – he had begun to specialize in roles that were more fantastic. There was also something awkward to him in the normal man–woman relationship in ballet. In 'Schéhérazade', though an embodiment of lust, he had been in a way more feminine than Ida Rubinstein.

'From now on,' wrote Karsavina, 'Diaghilev acted as a buffer between us. We were both inflammable, and the learning of "Giselle" was not without tears and many. Eventually understanding came; and we got well attuned together. "Giselle", according to notices, was a great personal success for the interpreters – nothing more.'[103]

Perhaps Diaghilev had been quite right to doubt whether Parisians would be interested in an interpretation of their old ballet by the Russians. Benois's nostalgic sets – the first an autumn landscape with a distant hill-top castle, beetling on its crag, the second a dark blue moonlit forest – were wonderful evocations of Gautier's dreams – Benois seemed destined to collaborate with *le bon Théo* across the years. When eventually the painter saw his ballet, he thought Karsavina 'almost outshone Pavlova'.[104] Svetlov, comparing her to the dramatic Pavlova, thought that she

took the part in another key. In her interpretation there enters no deep tragedy. On the contrary, it is the lyrical song of a woman's grief, sad and poetic. The pathos is tender, restrained. In the mad scene it is an almost timid complaint. In the act of the Wilis, in all her dances there is something soothing, almost a quiet satisfaction, a submission to fate and a hope for a happier future.[105]

In the photograph of Nijinsky as Count Albrecht his eyes shine and even his wig seems alive.

Now Karsavina and Fokine, Lopokhova and Leontiev alternated in the parts of Columbine and Harlequin in 'Carnaval'. Of Karsavina Svetlov wrote: 'The fine irony and tender smiles of Schumann's Carnaval are blended in her dancing into plastic visions set in an atmosphere of melody.'[106]

Benois was in Lugano with his family, but of course he was longing to share in the excitements of the Paris season, and, in response to 'insistent letters' from Diaghilev, he made the twelve-hour journey. On his arrival his friends Misia, Sert, Vaudoyer and the painter Dethomas made much of him; but a shock was in store.

How great was my amazement when, having taken my seat in the stalls of the Paris Opéra, I unfolded my programme and read under the title 'Schéhérazade' the words 'Ballet de L. Bakst'. I was so amazed I could hardly believe my eyes, but at the first sounds from the orchestra and the raising of the curtain I forgot everything and gave myself up entirely to intense enjoyment of the performance. My enthusiasm was so great that when I went on the stage to embrace Bakst and Diaghilev after the performance I was quite unconscious of having been hurt by them. It was only after I had re-read the programme in my hotel that I became conscious of the real meaning of the words printed under the title, and my heart was filled with bitterness and indignation. This disappointment of mine had nothing to do with practical considerations; they did not enter my head. In spite of my age – forty years – I had only a very vague idea of the existence of 'royalties' ... Next day I was finally flabbergasted by Serioja's answer to my question as to how this could have happened: 'Que veux-tu? Bakst had to be given something. You have "Le Pavillon d'Armide" and he will have "Schéhérazade".'[107]

Never greedy of credit for himself, Diaghilev had made the mistake of overlooking the feelings of his friend, who was already getting a complex about being elbowed out of the new Russian Ballet, of which he was a founder-father. Diaghilev considered that as all the friends pooled their ideas, they might as well pool the spoils. If Bakst – whose décor for 'Schéhérazade', far more than Benois's story, was the epoch-making thing about it – could receive not only credit but also royalties on the work, it would go far to reconciling him to nominal or tardy payment for his many designs.[108] Back in Lugano, Benois wrote to Diaghilev telling him that he was 'breaking with him for good'.[109]

Diaghilev was too busy to be bothered. Like the Pope in Firbank's *Cardinal Pirelli* he probably thought, 'Why can't they all behave?' We have evidence that he not only thought but spoke bitterly against Benois, and ruled him out of his life – until he needed him again.[110] Benois, however, paid generous tribute to Bakst's triumphant décor in an article for the Russian magazine *Rech*.[111]

If 'Giselle' had too subtle a flavour for the pampered palate of *le tout Paris*, it was not wasted on Marcel Proust. From Cabourg in July he was to reproach Reynaldo by letter for calling it 'the celebrated and insipid "Giselle"';[112] and when he began to write *A l'Ombre des jeunes filles en fleur* that summer with the first descriptions of Balbec's (Cabourg's) hotel, casino and *plage*, he gave the name Gisèle to one of the girls in Albertine's 'little band'.[113]

When Diaghilev and Nijinsky and their friends were supping after the ballet *chez* Larue, Proust would sometimes be sitting in a corner drinking chocolate and writing letters. It was here that Cocteau jumped on the back of the *banquette* and climbed over the table (as Bertrand de Fénelon had done in 1902, to be commemorated for his gallantry as Saint-Loup) to put Marcel's fur coat over his shoulders. Proust made a rhyme about the incident.

> *Afin de me couvrir de fourrure et de moire,*
> *Sans de ses larges yeux renverser l'encre noire,*
> *Tel un sylphe au plafond, tel sur la neige un ski,*
> *Jean sauta sur la table auprès de Nijinski.*
> *C'était dans le salon purpurin de Larue . . .*[114]*

Proust found Nijinsky uninteresting off-stage, but he took to Bakst and thought his liking was reciprocated. 'It is true he is charming to everybody, but I thought I detected a *nuance*.'[115] After one of these evenings Diaghilev played a practical joke on Cocteau, who had dropped him home at the Hôtel Mirabeau, by telling the cab-driver to drive on to the Hôtel des Réservoirs at Versailles.

It became clear during rehearsals of 'The Firebird' that Karsavina was going to score a tremendous success. Diaghilev would have preferred Nijinsky to have enjoyed this, and he determined to put matters right in the following year. The ballet which Cocteau and Reynaldo Hahn were devising must have an oriental theme, since this had become all the rage; it must have décor and costumes by Bakst even more striking than those of 'Schéhérazade', and Nijinsky must have a role, like that of Karsavina as the Firebird, which set him apart from and above the other characters, a super-

---

*Literally, 'To cover me with fur and shot silk, without spilling any of the black ink of his eyes, like a sylph on the ceiling or a ski on the snow, Jean leapt on the table near Nijinsky. It was in the crimsony hall of Larue...'

natural being and *deus ex machina*, who, moreover, would not have to support and take second place to any ballerina. In fact, in no ballet by Fokine or himself would Nijinsky ever 'support' – in the sense of acting as a *porteur* – a ballerina again. (In 'Le Spectre de la rose' he would support Karsavina in an *arabesque*, but lift her very little. In 'Petrushka' it would be the Moor who supported the Ballerina. In Greek ballets, because of the nature of their movement, the question would not arise.)

Cocteau asked Karsavina to tell him the story of 'The Firebird'; and he incorporated several of its elements in the libretto of 'Le Dieu bleu'.[116]

Benois thought the story of 'The Firebird' was weak and that the friends had

only succeeded in creating another fairy-tale for children [like 'Koniok Gorbunok'] – not a fairy-tale for grown-ups. The worst of it is, that the hero, Ivan Tsarevitch and the Beautiful Tsarevna are always remote from the audience. One does not believe in them, and therefore it is impossible to suffer with them. The Evil Being, incarnated in Kastchei, is more alive and convincing ... But Kastchei appears too late and perishes too quickly ...

Benois thought that Diaghilev's stipulation that the ballet should last no more than an hour had restricted Fokine and Stravinsky, accelerated the action and made the drama superficial.[117] While admitting that there is a disunity and oddity about the story, I find it hard to imagine the ballet longer or to see what could be gained by drawing the characters more profoundly: as a pageant, a tapestry, the ballet has always satisfied me. The disunity, of course, consists in the Firebird's having her chief dance, one of the longest and hardest solos ever invented, at the very start, when we have hardly caught a glimpse of Ivan and before the action really begins. The oddity is that there are no dances in the processional finale. On the stage these difficulties disappear. It seems wonderful that after the magic introduction we should at once be startled by the flashing apparitions of the bird of fire, who will return later only to lull the powers of evil to sleep; and the wedding procession and solemn immobility of Ivan and his Tsarevna at the very end are grand and moving.

167

Nor did Benois think Golovine's setting helpful to the drama, beautiful as it was. Diaghilev had wanted Vrubel to design the ballet, but Vrubel was dying or going mad,[118] and Golovine was chosen instead. 'Unfortunately,' wrote Benois, 'Golovine, a wonderful colourist and a lover of ancient Russian art, remained true to himself. . .' He meant that Golovine's fine design was just a typical 'Golovine' and unhelpful dramatically. 'A group of poisonous toadstools, not unlike Hindu pagodas, symbolized Kastchei's residence; beneath were layers and outlines of different colours, suggesting overgrowths and thickets that were soft, green, damp and close. . .' There were also the figures of knights, petrified by the evil Kastchei when they had attempted to rescue the captive princesses. 'It seemed like a huge chequered carpet, blazing with colour but devoid of any depth. No one could *penetrate* into such a forest – indeed, it seemed scarcely to be a forest at all.'[119] Benois may have been right, but the design of Golovine, who was a kind of archaic *pointilliste*, seems marvellous to us today – a semi-representational mosaic made up entirely of green, gold and silver beetles.

Golovine's costumes partook of an equal richness and their glitter merged with the set.

Kastchei's servants and followers were elaborately attired, but they were neither frightening nor repulsive . . . The result was that Fokine's choreographic ideas, performed by the artists in working clothes at rehearsals, seemed to be extremely fantastic and eerie, but on the stage everything was submerged in uniform, sumptuous luxury: the Kikimoras looked like page-boys, the Bellyboshkies like Turkish janissaries. Even Kastchei himself (in spite of the performer's terrifying gestures and make-up) was hardly frightening . . . Ivan Tsarevitch would never, as the tale demanded, have spat from sheer disgust in the face of such a Kastchei.[120]

Diaghilev found Golovine's costumes for the Firebird, the Prince and the Princess unsatisfactory, and Bakst made new designs for these.[121]

Thrilled as he was to find himself in Paris, Stravinsky had reservations about the score he had provided and the way Fokine was going to interpret it on stage. The conductor was Gabriel Pierné; and the composer stood in the darkened Opéra throughout eight orchestral rehearsals. One day Pierné put him in his place in front of all the musicians. He had written at one point in the score (no.90) '*non crescendo*', and Pierné said, 'Young man, if you do not want a *crescendo*, then do not write anything.'[122]

At last came the great day, 25 June, when a ballet of Stravinsky's would be given for the first time in the theatre and when his music would be heard for the first time in Western Europe. The composer was always to remember the rival glitter of the stage and of the audience.[123]

The introduction, played before the rise of the curtain, sets the scene. It is the ancient terror of the woods at night, the home of malevolent powers. It is Grendel's Mere in *Beowulf*:

In a doubtful land
Dwell they, wolf-shapes,   windy nesses,
Fearsome fen-paths,   where the force from the mountains
Under misty nesses   netherwards floweth,
A flood under the fields.   'Tis not far from hence
As miles are marked   that the mere standeth,
Above which hang   rimy bowers;
A wood fast-rooted   the water o'er-shadows.
There will, every night,   a wonder be seen,
Fire in the flood.   There is none found so wise
Of the sons of men,   who has sounded those depths.

Lost in this horrible solitude the palace of evil sleeps, but we hear the tread of some of Kastchei's loathsome sentinels. When the curtain rises the Firebird's incandescent music is heard and we see her, apparently luminous, dart across the darkened stage. Karsavina does not wear a ballet *tutu*, but transparent Oriental pantaloons of bluish-green, drifting draperies, gold-braided tresses, flaming ostrich and pheasant feathers in her jewelled headdress. A fragment of the folk tune which represents Ivan steals in as we see his head appear over the wall and realize he is stalking her. Fokine has a medieval Russian prince's costume adorned with gold and jewels, and a cap with upturned brim. The Firebird sports in the garden, picking at the tree of golden apples. Her music is inhuman fireworks. Ivan puts down his bow, deciding to capture her alive. He clasps her in his arms. Karsavina's great dark eyes gaze in terror at him over her shoulder. She flutters, palpitates. Her dance of supplication is a *pas d'action*. He holds her by the waist as her arms are now clasped fearfully across her chest, now spread out as beating wings, now wrapped tightly round her head. Although she dances on point and her movements are extremely hard technically, with many *jetés*, there are none of the conventional coloratura steps of classical ballet – no *entrechats*, no *battements*, no *préparations*, no turn-out. Her pleading sounds very Schéhérazade-like. Ivan feels pity – he is a Christian prince – and this is ultimately to be his salvation: for the Firebird gives him a magic feather. He releases her and she darts exultantly away.

Ivan is alone and looks up as we imagine the bird flashing across in the treetops over his head. The prince's simple downright man-of-honour theme is contrasted with the lurking menace of Kastchei's sinister chromatics played by three bassoons. Down the slope from the castle come, barefoot, twelve princesses in their white embroidered nightgowns, the moonlight falling on their long hair. A thirteenth princess, the beautiful Tsarevna, interpreted by Vera Fokina, is more gorgeously nightgowned than the others. To a sparkling scherzo they dance and play catch with the golden apples. With formal bows and salutes Ivan introduces himself and is greeted with dignity by the Tsarevna. All join in a slow, stately round dance or Khorovod. A brief dialogue of two flutes in canon leads into an old folk-song (from Novgorod), 'In the Garden', played *cantabile* by oboe, then clarinet and bassoon; this is followed by another folk-tune, slightly faster, on the strings, and the dance ends with the prince and princess face to face, and we see that they love each other. Offstage trumpets herald the dawn. The princesses scamper off fearfully, the beautiful Tsarevna looking behind her, longingly. Prince Ivan, in manly desperation, decides to assault the castle single-handed.

As he batters at the castle gate, an unearthly *carillon* breaks forth, beginning with harps and celesta over chromatic waverings by the violas *sul ponticello*. Woodwind, brass and piano join in the movement which is worked up to a *fortissimo* climax, and the trombones play the main theme of the Infernal Dance in canon. No such incredible sounds have ever been heard in the Opéra before. On to the stage crawl, hop or leap the Kikimoras and Bellyboshkies of Kastchei's monstrous court. Ivan struggles but is made prisoner. Six sinister bars played on all the bass instruments of the orchestra (bassoons, contra-bassoons, horns, trombones, tuba, bass) lead to a sharp *staccato* chord as, whiskered, cadaverous, bent double, with bones showing through his golden skin, his shoulders rising into horned humps, with long talons on his skeleton hands, Kastchei enters. There follows a musical dialogue between hero and villain. Kastchei rages, the princesses plead with him in vain, and with loud chromatic scales, up and down, alternating with *pianissimo tremolando* in the strings, the ogre begins the spell which will turn Ivan to stone. Tingling *glissandi* on harp and horn combine with wild upward flourishes in the woodwind, ending on a crash. Before the formula is repeated a third time Ivan waves his magic feather, and with a whirr of wings the Firebird appears. She forces the monsters into a non-stop dance. Quietly at first, cor anglais and violins begin a nervous spinning tune. Wind and then full orchestra take over until Kastchei's retinue, half crazed, begin their Infernal Dance. A low *dies irae* alternates with jagged brass phrases. Snatches of oriental melody are heard from the violins. Xylophone and woodwind join in the *danse macabre*. A flute plays more gently but the respite is short-lived. Ruthlessly the *dies irae* returns. Brass fanfares lead to a diabolical finale for full orchestra with unison strings playing the princess's tune. The dance reaches a height of frenzy. A quiet *staccato* figure for strings works up to a full orchestral *fortissimo*. As the wind shrieks up and down, to a final sharp chord Kastchei's followers sink exhausted to the ground.

Now begins the Firebird's Lullaby – a melody of poignant beauty played by the bassoon with occasional sighs from the oboe. Muted strings quietly sustain, then play a high counter-melody. As the bassoon begins again violins play the Firebird's *motif* in descending chords. The oboe plays, fading into nothingness. As Karsavina circles the stage in *pas de bourrée* with outstretched arms, the whole crowd is lulled to sleep. Kastchei awakens, but Ivan has found the casket containing his soul, which is a huge egg. The ogre sways in terror from side to side as Ivan tosses the egg and finally flings it to the ground. The stage is plunged in darkness.

The music of the conclusion is another folk-song turned into a hymn of thanksgiving which becomes the wedding procession of Prince Ivan and the Tsarevna. The princesses and their knights, no longer petrified, file slowly on; line after line of boyars crowd on to the stage. Ivan and his bride, crowned and sceptred, turn about to display their long encrusted trains, and advance solemnly to take their place like idols in the middle of the crowd; the Firebird flashes by to give her blessing; and with a triumphant swinging rhythm like bells the ballet reaches its happy ending.

With what a glow of glory must Fokine, dancer, choreographer and pioneer, have stood there with his wife beside him and a proud company behind, facing a Paris which rose to acclaim his ballet and Stravinsky's score! And Karsavina, what a triumph for her in the first big role Fokine had moulded on her!

Seated in Diaghilev's box, Stravinsky met all the celebrities, hostesses and balletomanes of Paris. On this and on subsequent nights he was introduced to Proust, Jean Giraudoux, Paul Morand, St John Perse, Paul Claudel and Sarah Bernhardt. 'I was called to the stage to bow at the conclusion, and was recalled several times. I was still on stage when the final curtain had come down, and I saw coming toward me Diaghilev and a dark man with a double forehead whom he introduced as Claude Debussy. The great composer spoke kindly about the music, ending his words with an invitation to dine with him.'[124]

The East was in fashion, just as it had been in the early days of Victor Hugo nearly a century before; and the *divertissement* that followed 'The Firebird' – and which was the last new offering of the season – had the same title as Hugo's second book of poems, *Les Orientales*. Gelzer and Volinine appeared in this, and Nijinsky had two numbers. One was 'Kobold', danced to Grieg's piano piece of that name, orchestrated by Stravinsky.* For this Nijinsky wore greenish-blue all-over tights with patches of *paillettes* – even his face was covered. He was a capering goblin. All that remains of this are three photographs in the Museum and Library of Performing Arts in New York. Of the other number, a more static dance

*Grigoriev attributed the choreography of this number to Nijinsky, but Mme Bronislava Nijinska says it was by Fokine.

made up mostly of poses in the Siamese style – Fokine had seen a troupe of Siamese dancers in Petersburg a few years before – there are numerous mementoes. For Nijinsky was photographed in it by Druet and Baron de Meyer, and drawn or painted in it by Jacques-Emile Blanche, Jean Cocteau, George Barbier and others.

Karsavina took her Firebird costume and Nijinsky took his gold and bejewelled Siamese costume and helmet to the studio of Jacques-Emile Blanche at Passy to be photographed: for the painter intended to save the dancers some hours of posing by working partly from Druet's photographs. It was a sunny Sunday morning and the 'operator', as Mme Blanche called him, arrived at one o'clock.[125]

The garden of Blanche with its chestnuts, catalpa and English lawns had inspired, one stormy evening, Debussy's 'Jardin sous la pluie', which was one of an album of piano pieces dedicated to the sociable painter.[126] Nijinsky posed out on the lawn as well as in the studio, and the poses he took – crouched, half serpent, half tiger on the floor or standing, finger-tips to tilted chin – together with a jump he performed for one of the earliest-ever action photographs, legs crossed in the air and hands joined over the head, are indications of the nature of his Danse Siamoise. Karsavina posed, as he did, in front of their host's fine Coromandel screen. Some of the surviving photographs show her roaring with laughter, which was very un-Firebird-like behaviour. This was the fault of Cocteau, who had arrived to watch the session, and who kept striking poses and making funny speeches from the gallery which ran round above the studio.[127] He also sketched Nijinsky in his Siamese role.

The painting Blanche made of Karsavina *sur les pointes*, with imperious outstretched arms, never got beyond the stage of a sketch, although a vivid one: it is in the Musée de l'Opéra. The big painting of Nijinsky was bought by Princesse Edmond de Polignac and after her death hung for years at Donnington Priory near Newbury, the house of her niece Mrs Reginald Fellowes, who lent it to me for the Diaghilev Exhibition in 1954–5. But Blanche was not the only artist to work from Druet's photographs. A few years later a secret admirer of Nijinsky commissioned a painting of him from Bakst, and the latter copied the crouching pose from Druet's photograph, interpreting somewhat freely the costume he had himself

173

designed (he left the trousers plain *bleu-de-roi*, unadorned by *paillettes*) and subtly varying the face so that it is even more alive than the photograph. This was never exhibited or reproduced – in fact it was hidden from the world – until discovered in Washington in 1969 by Baron Tassilo von Watzdorf of Sotheby's. When it was put up for

Tamara Karsavina.
Drawing by Gir.

sale in July of the same year it fetched £11,400, a record price for any work of Bakst. Such were the far-reaching consequences of that jolly photographic session in Passy, which was followed by a late but delicious luncheon.

Nijinsky and Karsavina returned to pose for Blanche on other Sundays and in subsequent seasons, and occasionally Karsavina brought her friends to witness the sitting. Being at that time very *gourmande*, she described to the assembled company how impressed she had been in the restaurant at the Savoy Hotel by the trolleys laden with varied sweets which were wheeled up for her choice. On her next visit to Passy Blanche had procured a trolley and there was a lavish spread of delicacies to choose from.[128] Blanche painted Ida Rubinstein too, in her Zobeïda costume, reclining on cushions and showing her noble Semitic profile against the black and gold lacquered screen.

Rubinstein also posed for Serov in a building in the Boulevard des Invalides which had once been a monastery:[129] he painted her seated naked on cushions, turning her bony back, head twisted over the right shoulder. She now had not only Montesquiou but also D'Annunzio as *cavalieri serventi*. She liked to attract attention; the admiration of distinguished men flattered her.[130] She bought a tiger cub and told Diaghilev she wanted not only to mime, but also to dance. This was clearly out of the question. People believed that she drank champagne out of Madonna lilies, but this was probably part of a deliberate publicity campaign.[131]

Stravinsky, poor as he was – Diaghilev paid him 1,500 roubles (£100) for 'The Firebird' – was so elated by the success of his ballet and so confident in a golden future with Diaghilev that he sped back to Russia to fetch his wife and children.[132] The last performance of 'The Firebird' was on 24 June, and he was determined that she should hear the music. Already, when he had been finishing his orchestration two months before, the idea had come to him for a new ballet. 'I had dreamed a scene of pagan ritual in which a chosen sacrificial virgin danced herself to death. The vision was not accompanied by concrete musical ideas, however . . .'[133] Before leaving Petersburg for Paris, he had talked to Roerich, the mystic interpreter of ancient Russia, about the scenario and they had agreed to collaborate. Now, at Ustilug, his family house, two and a half days' journey south of Petersburg, he began a letter to Roerich which was to be finished in France ten days later.

Stravinsky to Roerich 19.7.1910

Dear Nicolai Konstantinovitch,

. . . My 'Firebird' was a great success in Paris, but the music proved to be so difficult that it cannot be performed anywhere else this year. It required nine rehearsals, which shows you how unthinkable it would be to attempt to play it with other orchestras. Because of this we had hoped to double the number of performances here, but that was impractical for various reasons, and there will be only two supplementary performances, the 22nd and 24th (next Tuesday and Thursday), after the three alternate subscription performances. I expect to arrive in time only for the Thursday performance, as I said.

Naturally the success of 'The Firebird' has encouraged Diaghilev for future projects, and sooner or later we will have to tell him about the 'Great Sacrifice'. In fact, he has already asked me to compose a new ballet. I said I was writing one which, for the moment, I did not wish to talk about, and this touched off an explosion, as I might have guessed. 'What? You keep secrets from me, I who do my utmost for you all? Fokine, you, everyone has secrets from me.' Etc., etc. I had to tell him, of course, but I begged him to not repeat it. As soon as I said that I was working with you both Diaghilev and Bakst were delighted, Bakst saying he thought our idea was a noble one. They were greatly relieved, obviously, to hear that my secret did not concern Benois: Diaghilev would have been greatly offended if Benois had been involved.

. . .

Later. I have had to complete this letter in La Baule, having found no time in Paris, where we spent only three days. Again the 'Firebird' had an immense success, and I was greatly pleased, but I must say that some of Golovine's work, and some of the lighting, was not very fortunate. I had thought, from the very first, when I saw Golovine's costumes and his beautiful sets, that he had failed to create anything satisfactory for the spooky Kastchei dance, and this opinion was also shared by André Rimsky-Korsakov and Kolya Richter, who came for the final performance. Music and costumes are at odds in this scene, and the dancers look like dressed-up actors. Diaghilev took charge of the lighting himself, but with imperfect results and at times serious mis-synchronizations. In addition to these failures of the company, the Management and Direction of the Grand Opera did everything in their power to hinder and handicap us. To begin with they did not want to rent the house to a company of Russians, and it was only because of the Comtesse Greffuhle and the help of a few others that we succeeded. I do not know the exact reasons for it, but the quarrel between Diaghilev and Fokine began because of difficulties in producing the 'Firebird'. I prefer to stay out of this imbroglio myself, and I regret Diaghilev tattled the remark to me that Fokine's participation in our 'Great Sacrifice' would only be a question of money. (Note that Diaghilev never for a moment considered whether *we* wished to work with

Fokine!) If the Fokine feud is not settled soon Diaghilev thinks we should work with a certain Gorsky, of whom I know nothing. Now it may be that this Gorsky is a great genius, but Diaghilev is bluffing, and is really very upset by Fokine.

As you see, I am living in La Baule, by the Atlantic Ocean. It is a small city, crowded now with children of all ages. I often thought about you during the journey from Ustilug to Paris. How right your advice to go *via* Warsaw and Berlin. Please excuse my last conversation on the telephone.

Now this: I cannot find the paper on which I wrote the libretto of the 'Great Sacrifice'. For God's sake send it to me, registered, and with it the small page of manuscript which I forgot about, as I went away, and left with you. I am using your St Petersburg address as you did not give me one in Hapsal. Awaiting your answer, I shake your hand and kiss you three times.

With love, yours

IGOR STRAVINSKY[134]

Thanks to Astruc's good management and to the popularity of the new ballets, the season had been a much greater success financially than that of 1909.[135] It was arranged that some extra performances should be given at the Opéra. But the Brussels engagement had to be fulfilled first, though it was only two performances; and Karsavina had to get back to do a bit more 'Giselle' at the Coliseum, where the Koslov troupe had been giving an Oriental ballet, 'Salammbo', in her absence. Gelzer was rehearsed in Karsavina's Valse in 'Les Sylphides' and Fokine persuaded Diaghilev with some difficulty to allow Lopokhova, who had already made a success of 'Carnaval', to replace Karsavina in 'The Firebird'.[136] With her fine *élévation* she brought it off, but she was quite different from Karsavina, a hummingbird as opposed to a phoenix.[137]

To guard against any future rivalry with London music-halls, Diaghilev now offered Karsavina a two-year contract to dance for him from 1 May to the end of August, during the closure of the Mariinsky.[138] She hesitated to renounce all holidays, all private life. He raged at her for 'prostituting her art' by appearing in a music-hall. He was possessively jealous, saying, 'I hate your family. It takes you away from me. Why could you not have married Fokine? You would both have belonged to me.'[139] In the same breath he began to complain that Fokine's choreography was old-fashioned and a thing of the past. There had been disagreements between them during the staging of 'The Firebird'. He did not like Fokine, who was so sure of himself and had formulated his new creed without the aid of Diaghilev and the friends. With his greed for novelty (which was to become more and more noticeable as he grew older), Diaghilev had already begun to see the limitations of Fokine's folkloric approach and passion for local colour and period style. He was thinking of re-placing him by someone with newer ideas or someone he could help to mould. There was Gorsky in Moscow; and there was Nijinsky. Karsavina was astounded. It was a year and a month since Paris had been captured by the novelty of the Polovtsian Dances and 'Cléo-pâtre', and here was Diaghilev brushing Fokine aside. At the same time she had the feeling that Diaghilev was trying her out. Would she be faithful and follow him in his artistic adventures or would she fall short like Pavlova? 'What are you going to do with Fokine's ballets, Sergei Pavlovitch?' 'Oh, I don't know. I may sell it all, lock, stock and barrel.' She was shattered, but assured him of her adher-ence.[140]

Bombarded in London by a barrage of Diaghilev's telegrams, the long-suffering Karsavina managed to extract a little more leave from Oswald Stoll and was able to dance at one of the two performances in Brussels. These were attended by the Belgian Royal Family and re-ceived with enthusiasm. Diaghilev welcomed Karsavina like 'a fond father' and 'his joy was touching'. At luncheon with Nijinsky and the ballerina on the day of her performance Diaghilev asked her not to mind if Gelzer danced her Valse in 'Les Sylphides'; he explained that Gelzer had helped him out in Karsavina's absence and he felt he could not now take the part away from her this season. Karsavina, who, a year and a half before, had been almost too shy of Diaghilev to open her mouth in his presence, 'raged and stormed for form's sake meaning all the while to meet his wishes'. That evening, while she was making up, she saw him in her looking-glass. He never knocked on doors. She was no longer angry but thought her dignity required her to look daggers.[141] He said, 'You have slapped one cheek. Here is the other.' Then he added sadly, 'Tata, I am desperately in love.' 'Who with?' 'She doesn't care for me any more than for the Emperor of China.'[142]

After the final Paris performances, the 'Diaghilev Ballet' once more ceased to exist: but its triumphant creator, who was not only negotiating for another Paris season, but planning seasons in London and New York, told Grigoriev as he bade him good-bye that in the following year they would work longer together. As Grigoriev and the other members of the Mariinsky had devoted their whole four months' leave to working for Diaghilev, the *régisseur* found it hard to understand what he could possibly mean.[143] But Diaghilev was dreaming of forming his own company, independent of the Tsar. The trouble was that in return for their schooling, training and the money spent for eight years on their board, lodging and clothes, members of the Imperial Ballet were obliged to dance for a minimum of five years after they left school. This was only fair. Older dancers, if they did not mind renouncing their pensions, were at liberty to leave. Not so Nijinsky and his contemporaries.

Lydia Lopokhova, however, had taken the plunge and cut herself off from the homeland – the first of a long line to do so. She had signed a contract to dance in the United States and would never return to Russia, though she was to rejoin Diaghilev during the war.[144] Meanwhile, Ida Rubinstein, who was tired of miming and was ambitious to dance, speak and if possible sing, was leaving Diaghilev – she had never, of course, had any connection with the Imperial Theatres – to finance with her own money and that of Walter Guinness, her English lover, immense spectacles of her own. From that moment she became ridiculous.

Summer 1910. The friends scattered: when they reunited their 'holidays' would have borne fruit. After a stay with his family at La Baule by the sea in Brittany – from which he declined Diaghilev's summons to Paris, saying he could not afford the fare,[145] and where he composed the setting for two songs of Verlaine – Stravinsky moved to Switzerland.[146] After visiting Benois for a few days, to make up the quarrel, at Montagnola near Lugano, Diaghilev and Nijinsky went to Venice.[147] Bakst and Serov made the longed-for pilgrimage to Greece and Crete.[148] Vaslav was thinking more and more about how to evolve a new kind of choreography: from these thoughts of his and from Bakst's passion for the remains of Hellas would be born 'L'Après-midi d'un faune'. From Stravinsky's stay in Switzerland, where he decided to interrupt work on the preliminary sketches for 'Le Sacre du printemps', begun at La Baule, to compose a *Konzertstück*, would come 'Petrushka'.

The Stravinskys moved from their pension at Vevey to a clinic at Lausanne, where their second son was to be born on 23 September, and the composer rented an attic studio across the street to work in. Here he began his would-be piano concerto, the starting point for which seems to have been a fascination for the discord produced by superimposing the chords of C major and F sharp major, and which developed into a kind of argument or battle between the piano and the orchestra. When Diaghilev and Nijinsky arrived towards the end of the month, after six weeks in Venice, to hear how the music of 'Le Sacre' was getting on, Stravinsky played them his new and almost finished composition, which he had by now decided was 'Petrushka's cry'.[149]*

Both Stravinsky and Diaghilev had known in Petersburg the Butter Week fairs which preceded Lent, when temporary wooden theatres, switchbacks and *carrousels* appeared in the Square of the Winter Palace. They also remembered the Russian equivalent of the English Punch-and-Judy show, in which the adventures of Petrushka would be acted out by puppets. Petrushka was in fact the Russian Punch: he beat his wife, killed people and was finally hauled off to Hell by the Devil. While one man, hidden, worked the puppets, an organ-grinder provided music and dialogue. He would continually warn Petrushka 'Look out! You'll get into hot water', and Petrushka would merely give a shrieking laugh 'He, he, he!' When speaking Petrushka's lines the organ-grinder put into his mouth 'a little contrivance which gave a nasal tone to his voice', and it was the strange sounds thus produced that Diaghilev heard in the new composition.†

---

*According to Lifar it was Diaghilev who associated the music with Petrushka. Mr Stravinsky denied this. He remembered the idea coming to him by the lake at Clarens.

†I have taken the brief description of the Petrushka play from Prince Peter Lieven; but the Prince is wrong in stating that Petrushka's shrieks inspired Stravinsky's composition, for, as we have seen, the music was written before the idea of connecting it with Petrushka occurred to anybody.

When Stravinsky played them a few bars of another piece for piano and orchestra which he was planning as a companion to the first – a Russian dance – Diaghilev at once had the idea – or perhaps it occurred to him overnight – of using the two as the basis for a ballet about the Russian carnival. All agreed that Benois, with his nostalgia for the architecture and traditions of old Petersburg, would be the man to work out a libretto and design the scene; and Diaghilev wrote to him in Petersburg a day or two later.[150] Although, at Montagnola, Benois had been reconciled with Diaghilev, he had still insisted that his collaboration with the ballet was over. Little did he guess that his greatest work was still to come! Now he had to be coaxed. Diaghilev begged him to forget old grudges and create the new masterpiece with Stravinsky. Indeed, the idea was irresistible to him.

Benois reflected:

Petrushka, the Russian Guignol or Punch, no less than Harlequin, had been my friend since my earliest childhood. Whenever I heard the loud, nasal cries of the travelling showman: 'Here's Petrushka! Come, good people and see the show!' I would get into a kind of frenzy to see the enchanting performance ... As to Petrushka in person, I immediately had the feeling that it was a duty I owed to my old friend to immortalize him on the real stage. I was still more tempted by the idea of depicting the Butter Week Fair ... the dear *balagani* [fairground booths] which were the delight of my childhood, and had been the delight of my father before me. The fact that the *balagani* had for some ten years ceased to exist made the idea of building a kind of memorial to them still more tempting ...[151]

So Benois set to happily and began to work out the possibilities of the libretto; Stravinsky moved to Clarens, where in another bohemian attic he completed the Russian Dance;[152] and Diaghilev went to Paris for discussions with Astruc and to London to work out something for the following year with Sir Joseph Beecham.[153] Diaghilev was in London on 10 October, as we know from the date of a cable he sent to Astruc.[154] He had probably left Vaslav at the Hôtel Scribe, but they were together again on the 27th as is proved by the postmark on the following lettercard. After a convivial lunch spent plotting 'Le Dieu bleu', the collaborators were suddenly seized with fear that if the secret of their new work leaked out something might happen to prevent its realization. So they wrote to Astruc from the Restaurant Le Grand Vatel, 275, rue St-Honoré: 'In the name of all you hold dear not a word to *anyone* about the ballet we are planning, and especially about the possibility of including it in the Coronation celebrations, Yours ever Reynaldo Hahn, Serge Diaghilev, Leon Bakst, Jean Cocteau, Nijinsky.'[155] Nijinsky was going to be two months late for the Mariinsky season and would be in trouble for it.[156] Was he deliberately trying to provoke Teliakosvky to dismiss him?

Whereas Fokine had presented Stravinsky with a complete libretto of 'The Firebird' (only slightly modified later) and the music had then been composed to fit it, Benois wrote *his* libretto around music that had already been composed. This applies absolutely with regard to the second scene, in which Petrushka's loneliness and claustrophobic panic in his dark cell were cleverly adapted to Stravinsky's *staccato* and violent 'piano concerto'. It applies partly, but not entirely, to the rest of the ballet: more music was composed and more story was worked out before Stravinsky and Benois met, but there was an increasing degree of give-and-take.[157]

When Diaghilev arrived back in Petersburg in November he told Benois more about the music and discussions began.[158] Bakst was in Paris being 'unfaithful' and planning 'Le Martyre de St Sébastien' with Ida Rubinstein, D'Annunzio and Debussy; and Fokine was not called in till a later stage: but a nucleus of the friends, of which band Nijinsky was now a silent but accepted member, pushed forward with their cosy discussions.

We met daily in Diaghilev's flat in Zamiatin Lane, where at the traditional evening tea with *boubliki* ... 'Petrushka' took shape and fitted ultimately into four fairly short acts, without any intervals. The first and last acts were to take place at the Carnival Fair; the two middle ones were to show the interior of the Conjuror's theatre. The puppets that had come to life in the first act, under the magic spell of the Conjuror, were to continue living a real life in their own quarters, where a romance was to begin between them ...

For Benois had already imagined the pretty, brainless Ballerina, whom ugly Petrushka was to love, and the resplendent Blackamoor whom the lady would prefer. Benois remembered that 'in the street performances of Petrushka there was invariably a separate *intermezzo*, inserted between the acts: two Blackamoors, dressed in velvet and gold, would appear and would start unmercifully hitting each other's wooden heads with sticks'. Benois endowed Petrushka with a soul: he was no longer the knockabout bullying Punch but the pathetic Pierrot, capable of imagination, love and sorrow, a Hamlet among puppets.

If Petrushka were to be taken as the personification of the spiritual and suffering side of humanity – or shall we call it the poetical principle? – his lady Columbine would be the incarnation of the eternal feminine; then the gorgeous Blackamoor would serve as the embodiment of everything senselessly attractive, powerfully masculine and undeservedly triumphant.

In October the Stravinskys had moved to Beaulieu, near Nice. Here more music was written. In December Stravinsky paid a short visit to his mother in Petersburg – finding the city, after his travels, 'sadly small and provincial'[160] – and Benois was at last able to hear the parts which had been composed. The latter wrote: 'Igor played them to me in my little dark blue drawing-room; the piano was my old, fearfully hard Gentsch ... What I now heard surpassed my expectations ...'[161] They conferred about the plot and when Stravinsky returned to Beaulieu* the collaboration continued by letter. Before and after his trip to Petersburg Stravinsky finished the first scene – of which the Russian Dance had been the starting point – and composed both the third, the Moor's cell, and most of the fourth. The ballet would be completed when the friends met in Rome in the spring. Only then was Fokine called in.[162]

As Nijinsky heard parts of Stravinsky's score – and particularly the second scene, which was to be to all intents and purposes a long solo for himself – several times before it was ever played to Fokine, it is probable that Petrushka's typical spasmodic sideways jerks of the hands and perhaps his pattering run were his own invention.†

*Benois mistakenly wrote 'to Switzerland'. (*Reminiscences*, p. 328.)

†I put this idea to both Mme Bronislava Nijinska and Mr Stravinsky. Each agreed separately that it was very probable. But it is interesting to note that – for a day or two at least – the ugly Petrushka was not considered a suitable role for the glamorous Nijinsky. In Diaghilev's Black Note-Book (p. 141) Leontiev is cast as Petrushka. And Nijinsky is even considered for the Magician.

Shortly after his return to Beaulieu Stravinsky fell ill with nicotine poisoning, which bent him double, and he was weak for months. He continued work on the score, nevertheless. Needing the music of a certain popular Russian song for one of the two street-dancers he wrote asking André Rimsky-Korsakov to find him a copy. This was sent, but his friend derisively put some comic words of his own to the song, and asked Igor how he could use such trash. The tune for the other street dancer had a different source. Stravinsky heard it played daily on a barrel-organ outside his window in Beaulieu, was struck by its appropriateness for his purpose and wrote it in. It did not occur to him that the composer might be living, and Maurice Delage, who was with him at the time, thought the tune must be very old. It was not until several months after the première of 'Petrushka' in 1911 that Stravinsky learned that the tune, 'Elle avait une jamb' en bois', was by one Emile Spencer, who was alive and living in France. From then on Mr Spencer and his heirs have received a proportion of the royalties on 'Petrushka'.[163]

In Petersburg Benois set about designing his sets and costumes for the new ballets, the period of which was not to be that of his own childhood in the 1870s, when he had first seen the travelling puppet-shows and the pre-Lent fairs, but a period forty years earlier, in the days of the Emperor Nicholas I, his father's patron. His latest flat was near to the palace of Count Bobrinsky and the room he had taken to work in was directly over the lodgings used by the Count's coach-men. 'Unceasing revels and dancing went on there all day long to the sounds of the balalaika and the laughter of gay ladies. At any other time this would have greatly disturbed me, but in the present case all the noise, shouts and stamping only helped to inspire me. It was almost a gift of providence.'[164]

Winter brought Astruc the usual blizzard of telegrams from Diaghilev. There was a dancer called Dombrovska in Paris – would Astruc engage her?[165] Had Astruc heard from Chaliapine (who denied hotly that he intended to sing in a Russian opera season in Paris in the spring)?[166] If Paradossi would negotiate as instructed without delay Diaghilev knew how to quash all possibility of rivalry from the Argentine opera (probably with regard to Chaliapine).[167] If Reynaldo Hahn did not accept the terms agreed upon by Saturday

Diaghilev would give up the idea of staging 'Le Dieu bleu'.[168] Then, on Christmas Eve,* in reply to some doubts of Astruc about a rival attraction, there was despatched the haughty statement – which by this time was also literally true – 'Am above all competition. Diaghilev.'[169]

*New Style Western Calendar. The Russian Christmas would be thirteen days later.

CHAPTER FOUR

1911

Nijinsky wanted to create choreography and Diaghilev wanted him to. What form was it to take? Just as Fokine had rebelled against the academic dance, throwing out *tutus*, turn-out and virtuosity for its own sake, so were the two friends feeling for different reasons dissatisfied with the results of Fokine's revolution. Their dissatisfaction took different forms and no doubt expressed itself in different ways, if indeed it found an exact definition.[1] Diaghilev foresaw a dead-end to the ballet of local colour and the evocation of past periods or distant lands, and he had a prejudice against stories and drama in ballet.[2] Fokine, brilliantly abetted by Benois and Bakst, had conjured up Versailles and the Romantic era; he had made an Egyptian, a 'Polovtsian', a Persian and a Russian ballet with the help of Bakst, Roerich and Golovine. When Ravel's 'Daphnis' was ready he would no doubt make a Greek ballet, and with Reynaldo Hahn's 'Dieu bleu' he would make an Indian ballet. What had these fairy-tales to say to the people of a world which was beginning to realize it was 'modern'? Better than to *evoke* past eras would surely be to re-interpret them or even to speak for your own. Diaghilev felt a stirring of the new spirit which was moving artists throughout Europe to seek new forms with which to greet a new age.

To Nijinsky, as a dancer, these thoughts probably came in a different shape. There was certainly something to *interpret* in such roles as the Golden Negro in 'Schéhérazade', but this character was just an outstanding figure in a general orgy who had to make love, lie on cushions, cower, somersault and die. Was this dancing? The stilted old ballets had form, if they had nothing else. In gaining expressiveness Fokine had thrown much overboard. The present writer believes that Nijinsky's feelings were similar to those of Cézanne several decades before, when he said that he wanted to make of Impressionism something as solid as the art of the old masters.

But how? Every young artist of talent in this century has been afraid of making or writing something that has been made or written before. The young of this age, more than of any previous one, were and are afraid of the obvious, the *déjà-vu*. In the old days everyone began by copying his master: now this seemed out of the question. To be entirely oneself, totally original, owing nothing to anybody, that was the thing – and a very inhibiting thing too for a young man. What form was the breakaway to take? No wonder if a man has to hesitate for years before allowing himself to put pen to paper. Then the trouble with being twenty-three is that one has nothing to 'say'.

And how was Diaghilev, who had never danced or learnt the secret springs of movement or what the body was capable of or what felt right or wrong or what rhythms the body could accept and what reject or the value of sometimes being heavy and sometimes light – how was he to help Nijinsky devise a new system of movement? He could conduct him to picture galleries, show him sculpture, play him music and hope that some magic process would take place: that was all.

Isadora described how, in the early years of the century, when she first came to Paris and began to evolve her art, she would stand in the dark for hours, with her hands on her solar plexus, plumbing the forgotten sources of natural movement.[3] Like Isadora ten years earlier and like Martha Graham a quarter of a century later, Nijinsky had to put aside all he had learnt and been in order to discover how to tell the truth in his own way.

The great moment of release had happened in Paris during the previous summer. We cannot call it a moment of revelation, because in his first essay in choreography Nijinsky was only beginning to realize some of the things he could do. But release it was. To make a 'ballet' like a moving frieze, to animate Greek and Egyptian reliefs and Greek vase paintings seen in the Louvre, this was the idea that dissolved his inhibitions; for he would then owe nothing to the classical academic dance and would be doing something neither Isadora nor

Fokine had done before. He would find by instinct and experiment a valid way of movement for figures seen only in profile, a way of making his dancers pass from one static group to the next. Did he realize he was taking the first step towards abstraction? He was doing what Picasso had done when he painted his first cubist pictures three years before.

In later years Michel Larionov told the story, repeated from Diaghilev no doubt, and turned into a joke, that Bakst and Nijinsky had agreed to meet in the antique sculpture department of the Louvre; that the painter waited in vain in the Greek section and went away without making contact with the dancer, who was lost in admiration of Egyptian reliefs on the floor below.[4]

Dancer: interpreter: creator. Nijinsky, who had danced the choreography of Petipa as no man ever before, had interpreted the new dance-drama of Fokine like an actor of genius, and who had only to continue dancing and interpreting for the rest of his active life to enjoy fame and fortune and the canonization of posterity, chose instead the hardest, most uncertain road, turned the sharp corner and began to scale the steep and rocky mountain-track of invention.

One of the first events of the new year, 1911, was the arrival in Petersburg of Emile Jaques-Dalcroze, the deviser of eurythmics, who was invited by Prince Volkonsky to give a demonstration with the aid of his pupils during January. This was no doubt the occasion when Diaghilev and Nijinsky, who were later to visit Dalcroze at his headquarters in Germany, became interested in his system.

Bakst had arrived back in Petersburg at the end of December 1910[5] and a few days later, probably at the very beginning of 1911, at their flat in the Street of the Big Stables, Vaslav and Bronislava showed him and Diaghilev what had been worked out in the way of a moving Greek frieze.[6] Fokine had made ballets without brilliant steps, but in Nijinsky's creation there was not only nothing but walking – there was one jump – but this was all done with the torso full on to the audience and the head, arms and legs in profile, and a new heavy way of walking had been invented. The human figure was de-humanized: the dancers were elements of composition. And what story was this choreography in profile to tell, what mood were its patterns to convey, and to what music should it be danced? It was probably Diaghilev, after several possible scores had been rejected, who proposed the use of Debussy's 'Prélude à l'Après-midi d'un faune', inspired by Mallarmé's poem and composed nearly twenty years before. Nijinsky's movement was so little related to the tone-poem, chosen perhaps *after* the style of choreography had been invented,[7] that the score was reduced to background music. A new step had been taken in the history of the relationship between music and dancing. Suddenly it was possible to imagine a dance in opposition to music – or without it.

Diaghilev had asked for something new and he had been given it with a vengeance. Did he get a shock? Was he afraid? If so it was probably the remoteness of music from movement that most filled him with misgivings. If in January 1911 the dance had not yet been tailored in length to fit the Debussy piece and even to coincide marvellously with it in a few crucial places, this operation was soon to be performed, and a remarkably successful marriage would take place.[8] Diaghilev, however, professed himself delighted. Bronia, who had complete confidence in the work her brother had invented, guessed that the right wing of Diaghilev's committee, the balleto-manes, might try to influence him and persuade him to modify Nijinsky's stark new movements – as Besobrasov had formerly begged Fokine not to make such radical costume reforms or to suppress the ballerina's virtuoso solo in 'Eunice', and later to soften down 'Prince Igor'. She said, 'You won't let them make you change anything, will you?' Holding up his hand to show an infinitesimal space between thumb and forefinger, Nijinsky replied 'Not by *that* much.'[9]

Diaghilev may have been nervous about the new work and the balletomanes may have got at him; Debussy may have been raising objections to the use of his music, and anyway, with Fokine's and Tcherepnine's 'Narcisse' on the stocks, there was already one new ballet on a Greek subject to be presented; but the chief reason that 'L'Après-midi d'un faune' was postponed was Diaghilev's and Nijinsky's fear that Fokine would walk out without completing the ballets necessary for their next season.[10]

Diaghilev in Petersburg to Astruc in Paris, 10.2.11
... Debussy replaced by Spectre de la Rose: Théophile Gautier music Weber Nijinsky Karsavina only. Gautier's anniversary.[11]

'Le Spectre de la rose', which was to become so famous, was born from the rose Chiarina threw to Eusebius in 'Carnaval'. While writing some (rather adverse) notes on the latter ballet for *La Revue de Paris*, Jean-Louis Vaudoyer had on a sudden impulse placed two lines from Gautier's poem 'Le Spectre de la rose' at the head of his text.

> *Je suis le spectre d'une rose*
> *Que tu portais hier au bal.**

The article appeared in print in July 1910,[12] at the end of the Paris season of the ballet, and it was then that it suddenly occurred to Vaudoyer to associate the poem with 'L'Invitation à la Valse' by Weber, a composer whom Gautier had much admired. This piano piece had been orchestrated by Berlioz. Vaudoyer wrote to Bakst suggesting that a short ballet might be made of it.[13] Probably Bakst only received the letter on his return from Greece, but on arrival in Petersburg he told the friends about it. Fokine created the *pas de deux* very quickly and spontaneously in two or three rehearsals, working not on the usual stage of the Catherine Hall (also known as The Crooked Mirror) on the Catherine Canal, but on a smaller stage in the theatre's restaurant.[14] Bakst saw the rehearsals and understood what would be necessary as a set.[15]

Now that Diaghilev had resolved to form his own company to perform all the year round it would no longer be sufficient for him to borrow the dancers of the Imperial Theatres of Petersburg and Moscow during their four months' summer leave. Karsavina presented the least problem, for she had now been appointed a prima ballerina of the Mariinsky and could arrange her infrequent performances to fit in with Diaghilev's bookings, and she was devoted enough not only to renounce her lucrative music-hall career in London but to resign herself to continual journeys to and fro.[16]

Bolm, who had graduated in 1904, having served well over the necessary five years with the Imperial Ballet, was at liberty to hand in his notice: being an intelligent man he realized that the new ballets of Fokine offered more interesting opportunities than the Mariinsky repertory; and he gave up the assurance of a pension in order to see the world and seek more laurels such as he had won in 'Prince Igor'.

---

*Most writers, misquoting these lines, make Gautier write '*Je suis le spectre de la rose.*'

The Muscovite Sophie Feodorova also threw in her lot with Diaghilev. Naturally, Diaghilev had to offer more money than the Imperial Theatres.[17] But Grigoriev, who was helping Diaghilev to enlist a troupe and arrange the contracts, considered that the forming of a *corps de ballet* was harder than to secure a few principal dancers.[18] General Besobrasov was dispatched to Warsaw to enlist recruits;[19] and Diaghilev cabled Astruc about a touring troupe headed by the brothers Molodsov, believed to be in Paris, and of whom Fokine expressed doubts.[20] Perhaps Diaghilev realized that whatever novelties Nijinsky might produce, he was a slow worker and could not be relied on for four new ballets a year. So Fokine was to be re-engaged, but in the capacity of choreographer only, since Diaghilev wanted no competition for Nijinsky as *premier danseur*. Fokine fought strenuously for his right to perform, and finally only consented to abandon the Mariinsky in return for a very large salary and for being billed as Choreographic Director.[21] Benois was to be called Artistic Director.[22]

And what about Nijinsky? Of his five years' obligatory service there were still two to run. It was unthinkable that he should not dance with the new Diaghilev Ballet, which centred on him, all the year round, but how was this to be arranged? Fate played into Diaghilev's hands over this matter, but it is not unlikely that Fate was given a gentle push.

At the end of January Nijinsky was to dance for the first time at the Mariinsky in 'Giselle' with Karsavina, and he decided to wear the costumes Benois had designed for his appearance in Paris. The first-act costume was an early-Renaissance tunic of felt ending in a skirt over the thighs, which Diaghilev had ordered to be shortened by two inches. It was very much the costume that Perrot wore in the original production, but ballet fashions had changed in Russia since the Romantic period and it had become customary to wear trunks over the tights in medieval or Renaissance-style ballets. Benois had not included these in his sketch and would probably have agreed with Diaghilev that they spoiled the line. The omission of trunks had the effect of making Nijinsky appear, by Russian standards of the time, distressingly nude. (There was no question, as some writers have inferred, of Nijinsky leaving off his athletic support or jock-strap, an article which male dancers in classical ballet would feel very uncomfortable without.')[23] An official in charge of the production protested to Nijinsky before the curtain went up, but the dancer refused to make any addition to the costume he had worn in Paris.[24]

Teliakovsky was away at the time, but the Dowager Empress was present and so, inevitably, were a number of enemies. During the interval, while Karsavina was sent for by the Empress and congratulated on her success (in music-hall) in London,[25] two friends of Kchessinskaya's did some telephoning and made mischief.[26] Motives are always mixed, and ill-wishers often find that by getting their way they achieve the opposite results to those they had intended: so it is of little importance whether Kchessinskaya, out of jealousy, seized the opportunity to get a rival for popularity out of the way, or whether Krupensky sought revenge on the lover of his enemy Diaghilev, or whether a Grand Duke gave orders, hoping to discredit the Diaghilev enterprise. The next day Nijinsky was told to apologize or resign. He refused to apologize and was dismissed. Almost immediately, it seems, the management of the Imperial Theatres realized their loss – perhaps Teliakovsky on his return disapproved of Krupensky's action – and gave Nijinsky an opportunity to rejoin the company. This he declined to take.[27]

On 26 January, *Petersburgskaya Gazeta* announced Nijinsky's dismissal. The next day they published a long interview with him. He told the journalist that he had asked permission to dance Albrecht in the costume Benois had designed for Paris. This was accorded, but when he was dressed in this first-act costume he was told that it was too revealing. Nevertheless, Krupensky, Golovine and other officials did not prevent him from going on with the performance. Next morning he was summoned by the Direction and told that he was dismissed from the Imperial Theatres because of his first-act costume.

I don't want to discuss the matter [said Nijinsky]. I can only state that if the direction of the Imperial Theatres wanted to retain me in its employment it had two alternative courses of action: either to insist on my changing into the costume which was the property of the theatre, or to give my part to another dancer – either Legat or Andrianov. They were both on stage and both had danced the role more than once. I do not know why I have to answer for other people's behaviour. During my long course of study at the Theatre School and during my three short seasons at the Theatre I have given all my energy to uphold – first in Russia, then abroad – the high standard of my training and the glory of our art. As a reward I was dismissed with twenty-four hours' notice. Personally, I should not dismiss even a servant who had done something much more serious in such a way . . .

Before the year was out Kchessinskaya would be dancing with Nijinsky in London. The Diaghilev enterprise was in no wise discredited. Most important of all, Diaghilev got his heart's desire. Nijinsky was free to conquer the world in his own time.

It would be reasonable to guess that Diaghilev did not finally decide to form his own company until after Nijinsky's dismissal: but this was not the case. He had begun to sign contracts with other dancers as early as 1 December 1910.[28]

Jubilant as he was, Diaghilev determined to wring every drop of indignation out of Nijinsky's predicament and to use it as publicity for his own enterprise. Late on the Thursday afternoon, when it was certain that Nijinsky was well-and-truly dismissed, he cabled to Astruc.

Diaghilev in Petersburg to Astruc in Paris, 10.2.11
After triumphant début presence all Petersburg Vestris was dismissed within twenty-four hours. Reason costume Carpaccio designed Bakst. Monstrous intrigue. Press indignant this morning. Interview director announcing willing take back Vestris who refuses. Appalling scandal. Use publicity. Acknowledge receipt. Serge.[29]

Astruc was naturally incredulous and doubted whether Diaghilev could be telling the exact truth, particularly as he had attributed Nijinsky's costume – the work of Benois – to Bakst. These attributions, such as the authorship of 'Schéhérazade', were becoming a habit. (The only conceivable reason for this was that Bakst's name had greater publicity value in Paris.) He therefore cabled to Gunsbourg. The same evening Gunsbourg replied:

Gunsbourg in Petersburg to Astruc in Paris, 12.2.11
Costume revealing* but responsibility of direction. No difficulty bookings abroad nevertheless foresee possible trouble London Gala.[30]

    *'Costume décolleté' was Gunsbourg's rather odd description in French.

He was referring to the relationship of the Dowager Empress to Queen Alexandra. The direction of the Imperial Theatres had put about the rumour that the Empress Marie Feodorovna had professed herself shocked by Nijinsky's appearance and asked for his dismissal. She later denied saying anything of the kind.[31]

On Friday Diaghilev cabled again.

Diaghilev in Petersburg to Astruc in Paris, 13.2.11
Try to obtain and send me at once letters or interviews with Duncan and Zambelli about Nijinsky and his grotesque dismissal. Reply.[32]

And again the next day:

Diaghilev in Petersburg to Astruc in Paris, 14.2.11
Incriminating costume same as Paris Giselle style Carpaccio. Worried direction invent Dowager demanded dismissal. Let's stir something up.[33]*

An hour later:

Diaghilev in Petersburg to Astruc in Paris, 14.2.11
Whole family present applauded. Mother seeing for first time declared she had never seen anything like it. Next day direction gave out mother shocked insisted dismissal. Acknowledge receipt. Send me press interviews.[34]

Before leaving his office that Saturday Astruc wrote back.

Astruc in Paris to Diaghilev in Petersburg, 14.2.11 (Registered)
My dear friend,
   I enclose all the articles that appeared this morning about the Nijinsky affair.
   I must admit that your telegram worried me quite a lot. I cannot see why you want us to take this Carpaccio-Bakst line when the real reason is Giselle-Benois? You must have your reasons, but I can't give the French press information which differs from what Nijinsky and Benois told the Russian press in great detail in the columns of *Novoye Vremya* and the *St Petersburg Journal*.
   Anyway, you will see that I got going in a big way within half an hour of receiving your telegram. Paris seethed. Every columnist and balletomane in Paris arrived at the Pavillon de Hanovre. So we have [a list of articles follows] . . .

'Moussons.' The French brevity cannot be achieved in translation.

I am very anxious for detailed information about your programmes . . . Let me know also how you stand over your tours and whether you reckon to be in a position to keep all your promises.[35]

Benois was working on his designs for the numerous costumes in 'Petrushka', while in distant Beaulieu Stravinsky pushed on with the score; Tcherepnine was finishing 'Narcisse', for which Bakst had designed a pastoral scene and some striking costumes; Anisfeld, who had painted so many admirable décors by other designers, had now been given the submarine act of 'Sadko', with its ballet of sea-monsters, all for himself.

In Paris Ravel had still not completed 'Daphnis' – although he played extracts from it to the visiting English writer Arnold Bennett on the last day of February[36] – but Reynaldo Hahn had made progress with 'Le Dieu bleu' and Diaghilev now invited him to Petersburg and set out to fête him. On 28 February Diaghilev gave a great dinner for Hahn *chez* Cubat, which was attended by Glazunov, Liadov, Tcherepnine, Davidov, Serov, Bakst, Golovine, Roerich, Karsavina, Nijinsky, Mikhail and Vera Fokine, Schollar, Bolm, Baron Benckendorff, Gunsbourg and other notabilities. (Kchessinskaya, who had celebrated her twentieth anniversary on the stage with a gala at the Mariinsky three nights before, supported by Gerdt and Nicolas Legat and in the presence of the Emperor and both Empresses, was not present.)[37] After dinner Reynaldo Hahn and Baron Medem of the Conservatoire played 'Le Dieu bleu' *à quatre mains* to universal applause. This, incidentally, was the nearest Diaghilev ever got to presenting one of his ballets in Petersburg. It was also probably the last time Diaghilev and Nijinsky were ever at Cubat's together. The evening ended with Reynaldo at the piano singing his own songs, and with Glazunov playing some of the latter's piano pieces. A small apotheosis for Diaghilev the conqueror, who had not only shown Russian art to Europe, but was now commissioning French composers to work for his new company. Surrounded by his friends and triumphant before Nijinsky, whom he had only known for just over two years, how he must have enjoyed the dinner! He who had been dismissed 'without right to appeal' from the Imperial Theatres, who had even been ordered out of a rehearsal of Benois's 'Le Pavillon', who had been thwarted by the intrigues of Teliakovsky, Krupensky and Kchessinskaya and ostracized by the Imperial family, and whose lover had in his turn been dismissed from the Mariinsky, was in fact, and would soon be acknowledged as, the Tsar of artistic Europe. Diaghilev hastened to cable Astruc a report of the banquet, in order to make publicity out of the occasion.[38]

He could not foresee that 'Le Dieu bleu' would *not* be presented in 1911, and that when it was shown in 1912 it would be a failure; nor that his dear friend Valentin Serov, whose enthusiasm for Persian miniatures had just inspired him to paint a fine front-cloth for 'Schéhérazade',* would be dead within the year; nor that within a month Nijinsky would have left Russia for good; nor that within three years he and Nijinsky would have parted company!

Diaghilev had signed contracts to present his Ballet at Monte Carlo, following the annual winter season of opera, and in Rome during the World Exhibition of Art. The Paris season would come next in June; and he was negotiating for a Coronation season in London and a visit to America.

Five weeks before his Monte Carlo season opened and two months before his Paris season, which was to be at the Châtelet as in 1909, Diaghilev's proposed repertory was as follows: 'L'Oiseau de feu', 'Schéhérazade', 'Narcisse', 'Petrushka', 'Sadko', 'Le Dieu bleu', 'Le Spectre de la rose', and a ballet to Liszt's 14th Rhapsody.[39] We shall see how the last, which never came to anything, was still under discussion three weeks before the Paris première.

Another novelty was contemplated. As it was Liszt's centenary as well as Gautier's, Diaghilev planned to play his 'Orpheus' as a symphonic *entr'acte*, while the audience looked at a big decorative curtain by Bakst.[40] This was never realized but a similar project was. An interlude, 'The Battle of Kerjenez' from Rimsky's opera 'Grad Kitej', was to be played, and Roerich was to paint for its visual accompaniment a 'striking red and green curtain, representing a battle between Slavs and Mongols'.[41]†

A company had been assembled; a repertory had been sketched out. Tcherepnine was to conduct in Monte Carlo. Diaghilev still had

*Sold at Sotheby's on 17 July 1968.

†This was later bought back for Russia, and, according to Prince Peter Lieven, was hung in the Kasansky railway station in Moscow.

to find two conductors for the Paris season. He negotiated with Cooper in Moscow and, through Astruc, with Pierné in Paris.[42] In the end it was a newcomer to the ballet, Pierre Monteux, who would conduct 'Petrushka'.

On 13 March Bakst arrived in Paris to paint the décors of 'Le Dieu bleu' and 'Le Spectre de la rose'.[43] On the 15th Diaghilev cabled to Astruc that he would be in Paris on Sunday. Could they lunch together and would Astruc book two stalls for the Colonne Concert that afternoon?[44] On Saturday, 15 March, Diaghilev and Nijinsky set off together in the wide luxurious train and that night Nijinsky crossed the Russian-German frontier for the last time.

They spent only the Sunday and Monday in Paris, but during that time Astruc aroused Diaghilev's interest in a new composition by the French composer Paul Dukas entitled 'La Péri', which he thought would make a good ballet.[45] Perhaps Diaghilev's jealousy that Debussy should have composed 'Le Martyre de St Sébastien' for Ida Rubinstein before writing anything for him – and Diaghilev had given Fokine permission to arrange dances for her production – prompted him to snatch at this work by another eminent French composer. Astruc was to conduct negotiations, and it was hoped to give the ballet in Paris.

Arriving at Nice on the morning of Tuesday, 21 March, Vaslav saw a Mediterranean coastline which was very different from Venice. He and Diaghilev took the train along the coast, tunnelling through the red rocks and passing the as yet unsophisticated fishing-villages and the promontories of Cap d'Antibes and Cap Ferrat on which the villas and gardens were still few and far between. They did not at once go on to Monte Carlo, but got out at Beaulieu to see the Stravinskys and hear the latest parts of 'Petrushka'.[46] Here they remained at the Hôtel Bristol for two or three days, during which time Diaghilev went backwards and forwards between Beaulieu and Monte Carlo, twenty minutes away. He met Raoul Guinsbourg, the Director of the Opera, rented a disused theatre, the Palais du Soleil, for classes and rehearsals, booked rooms for Vaslav and himself – not at the smart Hôtel de Paris, opposite the Casino, where he was always to stay in post-war years, but at the Riviera Palace at Beausoleil, high up on the steep mountain slope above Monte Carlo, which was in France, not Monaco, and only approachable by funicular or by a very zig-zag road.[47]

Then the company arrived from Petersburg, Moscow, Warsaw and Paris; and we can imagine the delight with which these northerners, some of whom had never set eyes on any sea before, beheld the Mediterranean' roads lined with oleander and bougainvillaea, and cascades of pink or red geranium tumbling from the rocks. But they had hard work ahead of them, for their season was due to open in a fortnight's time.

Maestro Cecchetti had to drill into shape a mixed bag of dancers, few of whom had yet worked together, and of whom only the St Petersburgers had experienced the iron rigours of his class. 'These wonderful lessons,' wrote Grigoriev, 'which began from the day of our arrival, were not only of enormous assistance to everyone, but at once imposed a new style and attitude on the dancers not drawn from the Imperial Theatres and were a boon to Fokine by welding the company into a whole.'[48] Fokine had to rehearse the heterogeneous troupe, most of whom were unfamiliar with his ballets, in 'Les Sylphides', 'Armide', 'Prince Igor', 'Schéhérazade', 'Cléopâtre' and 'Carnaval', as well as 'Giselle', which works, together with two of the new ballets, made up the repertory for Monte Carlo.

Fokine was not as happy as he should have been. Although his position as 'Choreographic Director' of the new company ought to ensure him all the scope that had been denied him at the Mariinsky – and on top of this he was to stage the dances for Rubinstein's 'St Sébastien' – he had all too short a time to do what was necessary. He had counted on mounting 'Daphnis' this season, in which he hoped to embody all his dreams of classical Greece, but Ravel had still not finished the score; Diaghilev had obliged him to undertake another Greek ballet to the hastily-composed score of Tcherepnine, and Bakst was diverting to 'Narcisse' some of the ideas he had had for 'Daphnis'.[49] Fokine would start rehearsing 'Narcisse' after the opening of the season on 9 April.[50] 'Le Spectre' at least had been worked out in Petersburg. 'Petrushka', to whose 'non-danceability'[51] he was not completely reconciled, would have to be rehearsed in Rome. And when could he possibly find time to arrange 'Le Dieu bleu' and the other works which Diaghilev was hoping to present in Paris?

'Diaghilev watched all our proceedings closely,' wrote Grigoriev.[52] He was outwardly as confident and imperturbable as ever: what was going on in his mind? Now that he had his own company he must keep them employed. He knew that, in spite of Nijinsky and a few superb principal dancers – and Karsavina and Preobrajenskaya arrived from Petersburg at the end of March[53] – it was not yet so strong a team as he had captained in the last two years. They must be perfected. And they must be paid. At least Dmitri Gunsbourg was by his side in case of emergencies and there were advances to be had from managements who had booked him in Rome and London. His chief interest – apart from watching the interpretations of Nijinsky and Karsavina – was the creation of new works of art; and if he was to be able to continue commissioning scores from Debussy, Stravinsky, Ravel and others life would be worth while.

Most of the telegrams to Astruc over the next two months were about 'La Péri'. The whole trouble with this ballet was that Paul Dukas had a mistress, Trouhanova, who was a dancer – a plump and amateurish one; and Dukas wanted her to dance his music. Even this Diaghilev might agree to on certain conditions. On the day after his arrival in the south we find him telegraphing from Beaulieu. Fokine agrees in principle to 'La Péri', particularly if Dukas will conduct: Stravinsky agrees to play the piano part in 'Petrushka' (23 March 1911). The Dukas question must be settled forthwith – six thousand francs for four performances: the moral effect of this is all-important and the dancers are delighted (25 March 1911). Then from Beausoleil: Trouhanova's conditions are acceptable so long as after the Paris season Diaghilev has the right to give 'La Péri' in every country throughout the world. Nijinsky agrees to dance only if Dukas conducts. If this does not work 'La Péri' must be replaced by the 14th Rhapsody of Liszt (3 April 1911).[54]

Playing over this rhapsody today, which was written first for piano, then for piano and orchestra, then as an orchestral composition (sometimes called 'Hungarian Fantasia'), it is amusing to conjecture what sort of 'Diaghilev ballet' it would have turned out to be. While its brevity (ten minutes) and the nature of the music indicate that it

would probably be a dance for only two people, its veering moods –
funereal, tender, patriotic, capricious, gipsyish, emphatic, vertiginous, trippingly gentle and dazzling at the end – make clear that it
must have been a passionate *pas d'action* with Hungarian colouring,
which Karsavina and Nijinsky would have danced in red boots.

For Nijinsky life was regular, agreeable and not as hectic as for
other members of the company. He was anyway happiest in the
routine of class and rehearsal. He knew the whole repertory, he had
learnt 'Le Spectre' in Petersburg and had merely to perfect it with
Karsavina. He would only have the one role of Narcisse to learn after
the Monte Carlo season opened. So he began working again in
private with Bronia on his Greek ballet, the existence of which was a
secret from Fokine and the company.[55]

Though Bakst was kept busy on Ida Rubinstein's massive production in Paris and would only appear in time for 'Le Spectre de la
rose', a group of the friends had gathered to assist at the *accouchement*
of Diaghilev's own company. Svetlov had brought the contingent
from Russia[56] and Besobrasov that from Poland.[57] Paffka Koribut-
Kubitovitch, Diaghilev's kind and gentle cousin, was there to do odd
jobs.[58] Stravinsky, when he could tear himself away from the composition of 'Petrushka', arrived from Beaulieu to watch the preparations.[59] Benois had come to supervise details of production.[60]
Gunsbourg, gay and immaculate, kept a vague hold on the purse
strings.[61] The Botkine girls, Bakst's nieces, were there to enjoy the
fun.[62] Chaliapine, whose season of opera at Monte Carlo preceded
the ballet season, lingered on to relax in the sunshine and to drink
with his compatriots at the Café de Paris.[63] The Aga Khan, who had
a villa at Monte Carlo and very much admired Karsavina, but who,
in view of her implacable virtue, had to console himself instead with
the blonde and more accommodating Kovalevska, was sometimes
drawn into the conferences, as Diaghilev hoped he would be helpful
financially.[64] The Grimaldis, the princely family of Monaco, naturally viewed the Diaghilev enterprise with a paternal eye from their
neighbouring rock.[65]

The Théâtre de Monte Carlo had been built in a great hurry by
Charles Garnier in 1878. It stands on terraces overhanging the sea.
Approaching it from the town, past gardens planted with palms and

giant magnolias, one sees a cream-coloured rococo façade surmounted by two tiled and pinnacled domes: between the latter is a clock flanked by green bronze seated youths. To one's left, as one faces the theatre, is the Café de Paris, with its *terrasse*: to the right the Hôtel de Paris. The Casino, which is joined to the theatre, extends to the left. Mounting the steps to the triple doors, one enters a rich brownish foyer with marbled columns, serving as an antechamber both to the Casino on the left and the theatre straight ahead. The auditorium, though small, is ornate and golden, with carved oak *fauteuils* upholstered in red plush. As it is rectangular, there are no boxes round the sides, the walls being adorned with huge mirrors.* There is a canopied central box for the Prince. Over the proscenium is the painting of an angel conducting a rather oddly-composed orchestra out-of-doors in a breeze; and the justifiably boastful inscription 'INCEPTUM IULIO 1878–19 IANUARIO EXACTUM'. Four art-nouveau ladies with gilded drapery and palm-leaves support the square dome and there are more beautiful athletes seated round the cornice.

Walking down steps, between the theatre and the Hôtel de Paris, one passes on the left the Prince's private entrance to his box and on the right a fine bust of Berlioz by Roussel, rising from a bed of pink and white begonias, and arrives at the broad terrace overlooking the sea. On the base of the Berlioz bust are reliefs depicting Faust, Mephistopheles and Marguerite. 'La Damnation de Faust' had its first performance as an opera† at the Théâtre de Monte Carlo on 18 May 1893. And this was the theatre where Diaghilev's Ballet was to have its début on 9 April 1911 to be followed by the première of Weber's 'Le Spectre de la rose', which Berlioz orchestrated, ten days later.

Meanwhile, in Paris, Astruc was anxious to have a good poster designed for the Châtelet season and he appealed to Bakst; but the painter was either too busy to make a special sketch or thought his own designs were too detailed or in too many colours to be practical for a poster. He sent another suggestion.

---

*Now covered by curtains.

† It had been composed as an oratorio, and was so performed at the Opéra Comique on 6 December 1846.

Bakst to Astruc. 29.3.1911
Weber,
   rue Royale,
   Paris
My dear friend,

I thought about the poster you need and I have had a good idea. You must get Cocteau to do it. He draws very well and will do you a stunning Nijinsky, for he has often sketched him. I think Diaghilev will agree. What do you think?

See you soon

LEON BAKST[66]

Bakst wrote from *chez* Weber because it was a restaurant and café he frequented, not far from his studio in the Boulevard Malesherbes: that its name was that of the composer of 'L'Invitation à la Valse' was a mere coincidence! Astruc without delay asked Diaghilev's opinion of Cocteau's potentialities as time was short for the colour printing, and Diaghilev telegraphed on 31 March 'Let us use the Russian poster' – presumably meaning the Serov of Pavlova.[67] The logical Astruc, however, who had resisted the attribution of Benois's

'Giselle' costume to Bakst, thought it would be cheating to use a picture of Pavlova to advertise a company in which she no longer danced, so he asked Cocteau to try out some sketches. One of Cocteau's first ideas was to adapt a drawing he had made of Nijinsky in 'Les Orientales' in the studio of Blanche at Passy. He made a bold line drawing of Nijinsky standing on one bent leg, the other crossed over it (as in Druet's reclining photograph) and painted the name NIJINSKI in large capital letters on the right. Not satisfied with the profile, he stuck a scrap of paper over the face and drew it again.[68] Astruc probably advised him that it would be better if the dancer were portrayed in one of the new productions. At this point, doubtless, Cocteau went to Bakst or to the dressmaker to study Bakst's design for the Rose costume. Having made notes of this, he adapted his drawing of Nijinsky in 'Les Orientales', flinging the right arm backwards over the shoulder, and bending the legs back into a classical *arabesque*, but retaining the downward tilt of the head and the backwards extended left arm almost unchanged.[69] It seems clear that the final result of the now famous poster was arrived at without Cocteau going to Monte Carlo and without his ever having seen Nijinsky dance in 'Le Spectre de la rose'. Whether the poster, together with a companion one of Karsavina in the same ballet, was used to advertise the Châtelet season of 1911 is not clear. Cocteau's designs were reproduced in the programme: but the few known surviving Cocteau posters are for the season at the Champs-Elysées in 1913.[70]

On 5 April Diaghilev spent the day with Astruc in Paris, travelling there and back on the night train. Apart from settling a number of problems with Astruc, he was obliged to use persuasion on Bakst to quit his labours for Rubinstein in order to spend two days at Monte Carlo setting up 'Le Spectre de la rose'; and he was probably shown Cocteau's sketches for the poster. He had so much on his mind on this busy day that he left behind in Astruc's office a parcel of photographs by Bert which were needed in Monte Carlo.[71] On Friday, 6 April Diaghilev had his dress rehearsal in Monte Carlo. The programme, to be repeated at the première on Sunday, was made up of 'Giselle' and 'Schéhérazade'. Only ten of the company had been with him at the Châtelet two years before, namely Nijinsky, Karsavina, Bolm, Schollar, Rosaï, Vassilieva, Nijinska, Grigoriev, Alexandrov and Semenov. A few old hands, such as Kremnev and Orlov, would be joining him later. (Alexandra Vassilieva, Besobrasov's friend, and Mikhail Alexandrov had in fact been with him in 1908, and had led the French Opéra dancers in the polonaise in the Polish scene in 'Boris'.) Cecchetti had been with Diaghilev in 1910, but not in 1909.

It was a good programme, the two ballets being well contrasted, and the two stars being able to display their versatility. For Karsavina was dancing not only Giselle but, for the first time, Zobeïda. Diaghilev had expected Ida Rubinstein to travel from Paris for the first two public performances on Monday and Tuesday, 9 and 10 April, but she had cried off on the very day of the dress-rehearsal.[72] (She would turn up on the 23rd, thus saving Diaghilev from breaking his contract, which stipulated that he must present certain artists, including Rubinstein, in Monte Carlo.) There was barely time to have a costume fixed up for Karsavina.[73]

Schollar was Myrthe, Queen of the Wilis; Bolm was Hilarion, the rival lover of Giselle, called on the programme 'Le Garde forestier';

and Giselle's mother was mimed by no less a person than Cecchetti himself. In 'Schéhérazade' Bolm played the Shah and Grigoriev enacted his embittered brother.

Between the *répétition générale* on the Friday and the première on Monday there occurred an accident which cast a gloom over the birth of the new company. A rehearsal of 'Le Pavillon d'Armide' was in progress and the trap-door through which the group of Nubian pages made their appearance with their fans during the transformation scene was open. The theatre's resident stage-manager, Muoratori, an ex-singer, came on stage from the wings, brushed aside Cecchetti, who tried to restrain him, and fell headlong down the trap into the basement many feet below. The shock was so violent that the rings came off his fingers, and he was killed instantly. Diaghilev was profoundly depressed by this useless sacrifice, which he took as a sinister omen.[74]

This was the only cloud to mar the happy spring season, which no one doubted would be the first of many. Diaghilev was worried about 'La Péri' and about Fokine's rehearsal time and he resented the 'treachery' and absence of Bakst, but he only occasionally vented his ill-temper by telegram on Astruc. It was an interlude of hope and construction. After the day's work Vaslav and Diaghilev often supped with Karsavina and Chaliapine at the Café de Paris, whose tables were crowded with their friends.[75] April was the Grand-Ducal season, and one night four Grand Dukes, Serge, Boris, André and George, were seen dining together at the Hôtel de Paris;[76] and of course Kchessinskaya was there too, holding court.[77] Perhaps it was the omnipresence of these potential enemies at the Hôtel de Paris that had made Diaghilev decide to settle further up the hill. Another visitor who was to become a dear friend to Diaghilev, Nijinsky and Karsavina, and who would help to support the company materially in years to come, was Lady Juliet Duff, who arrived with her husband in time to see the first performance of 'Le Spectre de la rose'.[78] And a photograph survives, taken by General Besobrasov after a gay lunch-party at the Riviera Palace Hotel on Sunday, 15 April,[79] of Koribut-Kubitovitch, Nijinsky, Stravinsky, Benois and Diaghilev peering between the immense hats of Karsavina and the Botkine sisters.[80] Vaslav's hair is cut in a fringe once more, as it had been before he graduated; and he is wearing not his mysterious, sultry faun face, but his mischievous little-boy Puck face.

Three days after this luncheon at Beausoleil there took place the first performance of 'Le Spectre de la rose'.

The ballet is set in the romantic 1830s, the furniture imagined by Bakst being the *bois clair* of Biedermeyer rather than that of Charles x. A girl in white returns from her first ball, dreaming of love. She sinks into an armchair, takes the rose from her bosom, smells it, and as her eyes close in sleep, lets it fall to the ground. Then the Spirit of the Rose leaps in at the window, capers round the room, raises the sleeping girl to her feet and dances with her. At last he returns her to her chair and disappears out of the window. The girl wakes, then, finding her rose on the floor, presses it to her heart.

There were several unusual things about this little ballet, which has since become so famous that it is hard for us to imagine how new and original it seemed in 1911. First, Bakst's set, with its wall-paper, curtained bed, open french windows, draped table and urn of flowers, sofa, dressing-table, harp, birdcage and embroidery frame, was more like the set of a Musset play than of a Russian ballet. Second, this *pas de deux*, which was mainly a solo for the man, was about the longest dance ever invented. Third, there was what Nijinsky did with his role as Spirit of the Rose.

To the opening passage on cellos and woodwind, Karsavina walked on – she did not dance. As the first gust of waltz music broke forth Nijinsky flew through the right-hand window, like a leaf blown by the breeze. The rapid swinging rhythm kept him leaping and twirling incessantly round the room. As a gentler rocking waltz unfolded he raised the still-sleeping Karsavina from her chair and drew her across the floor. The whole of her dance with him to a variety of waltz tunes was made up of *pas de bourrée*, that is, tripping steps on the tips of her toes, and performed with apparently closed eyes. At length Nijinsky led her back to her chair, extending one leg in *arabesque* behind him as he bent to kiss her. His first hectic waltz was now repeated. Round and round, to and fro, he bounded with whirling, drifting arms, until as the tune drew to an end he fell reclining at Karsavina's feet, right arm extended back over his shoulder towards her in passionate acclaim. One more phrase and he crossed the stage diagonally at a run and soared out of the left-hand window, appearing to fly up and up into the night. To a quiet slow passage for solo cello, Karsavina then enacted the girl's awakening and finding of the fallen rose.

When Bronislava Nijinska had seen Fokine arranging 'Le Spectre' in Petersburg, she had been depressed by the banality of Fokine's classical *enchaînements*: but in the course of rehearsals her brother completely transformed his role.[81] He instinctively sensed that for a *man* to be dressed in rose petals and to carry on in a giddy non-stop way, waltzing by himself, as he did at the beginning and end of the ballet, was absurd. That a sexless inhuman being should appear and dance thus was a different matter. He abolished the classical correctness of the *port de bras*, curling his arms round his face and holding them, when extended, with broken wrists and curled-up fingers, so that they became art-nouveau tendrils. Bakst had had dyed and sewn to the pinkish-purple leotard the limp silk petals of pinks, reds and purples which merged into each other like the colours of Tiffany glass, abolishing contours and camouflaging sex: but Nijinsky himself devised his make-up. 'His face was like that of a celestial insect, his eyebrows suggesting some beautiful beetle which one might expect to find closest to the heart of a rose, and his mouth was like rose-petals.'[82] As ever, when costumed and made up, he became possessed. As he danced the endless dance, hardly coming to rest for a moment, weaving evanescent garlands in the air, his lips were parted in ecstasy and he seemed to emit a perfumed gaze. This shows in photographs.

The dress-rehearsal was not without its nerve-racking moments. When Nijinsky's costume arrived at the eleventh hour it was found to have been badly interpreted by the dressmaker. Benois later recalled that

important corrections had to be made there and then. There was no other course but to pin the silk rose petals direct to the flesh-coloured *tricot*. Naturally this could not be done without pin-pricks and scratches, which caused poor Vaslav to squirm and cry out in pain. Diaghilev, in evening dress and top hat, looking very pompous and solemn as he always looked on first nights, stood by, giving directions with growing anxiety, while the role of costumier was being improvised by our stage-manager [the scene-painter] O.P. Allegri, as the professional costumier seemed no good at all. Kneeling on the floor with his mouth full of pins, Allegri cleverly performed the complicated and responsible operation of correcting the costume on a living body . . .[83]

Bakst arrived for the first performance to find that his birdcage, which was to hang in one of the open windows, had been removed because Nijinsky said it would inhibit his jump. He wandered round the set, trying to find a place for it. Diaghilev exclaimed, 'Levushka, for God's sake, chuck the canary, the public is growing impatient. Oh, don't be ridiculous; canaries don't stand on the chest-of-drawers.' 'You don't understand, Serioja; we must give the atmosphere.' Bakst protracted the interval alarmingly, Karsavina was to remember, but he finally had the birdcage hoisted high up under a cornice.[84]

'Le Spectre' had been turned out with such ease and was such a slight affair that Diaghilev and his friends, who tended to count on more elaborate or exotic spectacles to excite the public, were somewhat taken aback by its exceptional success. It would gradually dawn on them that this was the most popular ballet in the repertory. In the Rose, Nijinsky, weaving his variations on a theme of Fokine, had created what was to be his most famous role.

Ida Rubinstein tore herself away from Paris to arrive on 23 April for two performances of 'Schéhérazade' and two of 'Cléopâtre', in which latter ballet Preobrajenskaya interpreted Pavlova's old role of Ta-hor.[85] It had been hoped that Rubinstein would be the chief Nymph in Nijinsky's Greek ballet,[86] but these appearances as Zobeïda would be her last for Diaghilev. From now on, a series of annual spectacles, all designed by Bakst, of which the first was 'Le Martyre de St Sébastien', presented a month later, turned her into a rival for Diaghilev – a rich but not a serious one. She stayed five days at Monte Carlo, during which time Fokine invented for her the dance she would perform as St Sebastian.[87]

Somewhat *à contre cœur* Fokine began to rehearse 'Narcisse'. Benois disapproved of the subject, which Bakst had insisted on and which naturally appealed to the paederastic side of Diaghilev (as it had to that of Caravaggio three centuries before), because he

considered it totally unsuitable for ballet.[88] The characters of Echo
and Narcissus he thought were 'the most static in Greek mythology',
Echo being 'imprisoned in her cave' and Narcissus 'immobilized
in the contemplation of his own beauty'. For this and for other
reasons the ballet was one of Diaghilev's semi-failures – in spite of
an attractive score, a good set and the performances of Karsavina
and Nijinsky.

Tcherepnine had written a woodland introduction, reminiscent
of Delibes's 'Sylvia', and there was singing by a backstage chorus
à bouche fermée before the curtain rose. This droning would be used
throughout as the symbol of Echo. Bakst had painted against a blue
sky with dancing clouds a green landscape of weeping willows,
with a stream in the foreground and at the back an arch of rocks
through which a meadow could be seen and across which the
nymph Echo would sometimes move on a higher plane. (She was
not, in fact, 'imprisoned in her cave' throughout nor even confined
to her bridge, but descended to the same level as the other dancers.)
There was a statue of Pomona on the right.

Little green furry creatures with horns, long pointed ears and
tails, wood-spirits, caper about the stage. (The idea of these shy
monsters who only appeared when there were no humans about was
charming, as Benois pointed out,[89] but there is always the risk of
monsters appearing ridiculous on the stage – as we have seen in
'Firebird' and shall see again in 'Le Dieu bleu'.) The creatures are
banished by the arrival of a party of Beotian peasants who celebrate
the rites of Pomona, splash the water of the pool and lie about in
the shade. The bold stripes, spots and checks of their simple smocks
in colours of honey, lemon, orange, rust and garnet, are among
Bakst's happiest inventions. There follows a dance for Bronislava
Nijinska as a Bacchante in coral-pink, with a royal-blue shawl
attached to her wrists, carrying an amphora and cup. She is borne
on at speed by two satyrs, leaning backwards and kicking her legs
high in the air; and her dance, made up of jumps and spins, is
extremely strenuous. Other Bacchantes in periwinkle-blue join her
and at the climax of their dance they all fall to the ground. The
distant voice of Narcissus is heard, repeated by Echo, and Nijinsky
leaps on, followed by two amorous Nymphs. Clad in a white *chlamys*

and wig of long fair hair, he enters gaily to a curving *moderato* in 4 time, with trills, and all the girls on stage follow his movements adoringly. Karsavina, as the melancholy Echo, appears on the bridge with flowing black hair, in purple silk draperies stencilled with silver; she descends and prostrates herself adoringly at Nijinsky's feet. He, who loves to be admired, raises her and gazes into her eyes. Their dance together is an elegiac poem, accompanied by the *bouche fermée* singing. The jealous nymphs, to music reminiscent of the Gypsies in Messager's 'Les Deux Pigeons', explain that Echo is incapable of making an orginal statement but can only repeat

Nijinsky in 'Narcisse'. Drawing by André-E. Marty.

those of others. Narcissus tries her out, and for every few steps he dances Echo repeats the final phrase. He mocks her by improvising faster, more difficult steps and gestures, till, tired of this too-easy game, he runs off with her companions into the woods. Echo, left alone, prays to Pomona that Narcissus may suffer from unrequited love, then leaves the stage. Narcissus returns to drink from the pool and is fascinated by his own reflection. He tries to charm the subaqueous stranger by the beauty of his poses. Echo returns and is ready to love him all over again, but he has no eyes for anything but his image in the pool. (Fokine had had trouble introducing some variety into what Benois thought an 'interminable choreographic soliloquy'. And 'even Karsavina's beauty and her genuinely classic poses did not prevent the melancholy mood demanded of Echo from becoming tedious. Both dancers seemed to be the victims of a strange fancy and one felt sorry for them'[90].) Karsavina goes off. Nijinsky sinks into the pool – that is, down a gaping trap-door; and a huge artificial narcissus rises from the ground to take his place, while the sylvan creatures steal out of their holes to observe the new phenomenon, and Karsavina passes sadly across the bridge to merge with the rocky landscape, as the mournful ululations of the chorus are resumed.

The ballet had so many good elements, but the episodes were 'strung together' and did not achieve unity.[91] There was evidently just too much plaintive posing; and the goblins and the artificial flower did not come off. For once the Diaghilev touch had not worked. But he had given Karsavina one helpful bit of advice, the suggestive power of which she never forgot. 'Don't trip lightly as a graceful nymph; I see rather a monumental figure, a tragic mask, Niobe.' 'In my vision,' she wrote, 'the heavy metric structure of the tragic name became the mournful tread of sleepless Echo.'[92]

Diaghilev was in Rome on Saturday the 5th, ahead of Vaslav and the company.[93] The latter had the pleasure of travelling round the coast of Piedmont and Tuscany. Diaghilev and Nijinsky stayed at the big modern Hôtel Excelsior at the bottom of the busy Via Veneto.[94] Benois and Stravinsky put up at a smaller quieter hotel, the Albergo Italia near the Quattro Fontane,[95] which was between Diaghilev's hotel and the Teatro Costanzi, where the Ballet were to perform; and their rooms overlooked the Barberini Gardens, to the murmur of whose fountains the last pages of 'Petrushka' would be completed. The great ballet, which could be regarded as a culmination of the *Mir Iskustva* movement, had been designed in Petersburg, the city whose life it celebrated, and composed mostly by the Lake of Geneva and on the Côte d'Azur, and it was to be finished and choreographed in Rome, then perfected in Paris. Benois's wife came from Lugano to join him; and to increase the joy of the friends, not only Nourok, their old ally of 'The World of Art' days, but also Serov and his wife were in Rome – Serov being in charge of the Russian section of the International Exhibition.[96] Karsavina found her brother and sister-in-law in Rome: Lev Karsavin was

studying philosophy.[97] Finally Maestro Cecchetti on his own soil
was in his element.[98]

These were indeed wonderful days for us [wrote Benois]. Seen from a
distance they seem as radiant as the happy days of my childhood and as
the most poetical years of my youth. It was wonderful to be working in
an atmosphere of complete friendship and harmony on a task of whose
significance we were all fully conscious. It was wonderful to bring our
work to conclusion in such unfamiliar and beautiful surroundings . . . We
roamed about the town, visiting the churches, the museums and the
World Exhibition of Art, at which Serov had scored a notable triumph, and
where we welcomed the King and Queen of Italy when they came to the
opening of the Russian section . . . Our excursions to Tivoli and Albano I
shall never forget. I already knew those places well, but I was in a state of
spiritual ecstasy and everything seemed fresh . . .[99]

There were, of course, the usual drawbacks. In spite of the friendly
attitude of Conte di San Martino, director of the World Exhibition,
the management and stage staff of the Teatro Costanzi were hostile.
Impossible to gain possession of the stage for rehearsals. (It was the
Paris Opéra all over again.) 'Even access to the theatre was difficult.
The doorkeeper would be outside the entrance; as one approached
the stage-door his gesticulation, usually vivacious, took on a highly
dramatic tenor. In the corridors there would be more "hushers"
and all around walked on tip-toes – Toscanini was rehearsing.'[100]

Fokine had arrived ahead of the company for talks with Diaghilev
about the repertory for Paris, and these put him in a bad temper.[101]
It was a month to the opening night in Paris, and Diaghilev expected
him to produce not only 'Petrushka', but 'Sadko', 'La Péri' and
'Le Dieu bleu', as well as rehearsing 'Firebird' with a company
who were mostly unfamiliar with it. It was a battle of wills between
two extremely obstinate men, which Diaghilev – being the more
persistent of the two – would probably have won had not his
demands been, in fact, impossible. When Grigoriev came to discuss
the rehearsals for the Roman season with Fokine the latter sulked
and refused to speak. When Diaghilev suggested that Fokine should
work on 'Petrushka' and 'Sadko' simultaneously, Grigoriev wrote,

he was still more annoyed and merely said that he would see me about it. I
did my best to calm him down, seeing that he was in no fit state to tackle

the arrangement of a ballet like 'Petrushka', of which not only was the music difficult, but parts of the scenario, and particularly the middle scenes, had not yet been properly worked out. Yet when he began composing, as he shortly did, he turned out to be full of ideas; and the rehearsals went quickly ahead. Only when he reached the third scene, where the Moor is left by himself for a time, did his invention fail him. He could not think what to make him do, and lost his temper, throwing the music on the floor and leaving the rehearsal. Next day, however, he appeared looking happier, and said that he had thought of some 'business' for the accursed Moor: he would give him a coconut to play with – which would carry him at least through the first part of the scene.[102]

Some extra music had to be written in.

Rehearsals took place in a buffet in the theatre's basement, the floor of which was covered in worn, dirty crimson carpeting; and on this the dancers had to dance and even lie. The weather was stifling and ventilation non-existent. Stravinsky, at the piano, asked the ladies' permission to remove his coat.[103] Diaghilev, looking worn out, but immaculately dressed, perched on a hard chair and watched the great ballet take shape. Benois sketched them both, and in the margin of his drawing of the composer, the designer wrote of their choreographer: 'Fokine can make *nothing* of the rhythms of the Coachmen's dance!' and added, 'Appalling heat!'

The Ballet opened on 15 May with 'Le Pavillon d'Armide', 'Les Sylphides' and 'Prince Igor' and was warmly received. Diaghilev lost no time in cabling to Astruc about the elegance of the audience and the sixteen curtain calls. The King of Italy, the Queen and the Queen Mother attended the second performance, which was greeted with 'infinite ovations'.[104]

With his Roman triumph and with the progress made on 'Petrushka', Diaghilev's spirits improved.[105] Karsavina was staying at a hotel opposite the Queen Mother's palace, near the Borghese Gardens.[106] She wrote:

Diaghilev often came round in the morning to fetch me on his way to the Teatro Costanzi. 'Maestro, you say? The old man will wait; it is a sin to be indoors on such a morning', and he would take Nijinsky and myself for some enchanting drive, pointing out here and there an arch, a view, a monument. He would hand us over to the Maestro with a request not to scold his children for being a bit late. Maestro, with unusual blandness, would excuse his unpunctual pupils; he knew he could make up for time lost ... for the sake of discipline, though, Maestro would go through a show of disapproval; twirling his cane, thus giving time for escape, he would sling it at my feet; a well-timed skip cleared the missile ... He was in a frenzy of teaching, and an equal frenzy of learning possessed both Nijinsky and myself.

If, on the other hand, they arrived early for their lesson, the old teacher would still have got there before them, and they would find him 'cracking jokes with the stage hands, making the wise black poodle of the doorkeeper perform his tricks. The dog loved money and knew the use of it. Given a soldo he sedately walked across the road to the pastrycook's, put his coin on the counter and came [back] with a cream bun to eat at his leisure.'[107]

Time was getting on and the Battle of the Paris Repertory was engaged. Diaghilev wanted to give Paris as varied and novel programmes as possible, even though there were only to be two of them, with four performances of each : but by now he realized that in announcing 'Le Dieu bleu', 'La Péri' and a revival of 'L'Oiseau de feu', he had promised more than he could fulfil.[108] Torn between a Fokine who refused to be hurried and an Astruc who demanded that he should present the scheduled ballets, he was to find his diplomatic skill tested to the utmost. While fighting to get as much work out of Fokine as he could, he decided to put all the blame on to Astruc and Bakst for the non-appearance of any ballets he failed to present. On 22 May he wrote as follows:

Diaghilev in Rome to Astruc in Paris, 22.5.11 (typed)

My dear Astruc,

This is the situation: we have a fortnight till the Paris opening, and there are still two ballets we have not even touched for reasons which have nothing to do with me or my company.

First Péri. I have still not received Trouhanova's contract signed. Indeed, you tell me there are still things you cannot agree on with her. You realize that I cannot start working on something which may not come off. Then, Mlle Trouhanova, having given her word to come to Monte Carlo, never managed to do so during the entire two months* we were there.

*i.e., just under six weeks.

Now, having finished her recitals, she still gives no sign of life. Obviously we can't plan a work without the co-operation of its chief interpreter.

I have certainly received the piano score (in which there are some obvious mistakes), but it is of no use to me for the reasons given above and above all for the following reason, which I must now put to you most seriously.

You have followed my work for five years and you know the principles on which it is based. I am not a professional impresario, and my speciality is to make painters, musicians, poets and dancers work together.

Of all my collaborators the most indispensable has always been Leon Bakst, my childhood friend,* who has taken part in all my enterprises. He owes his Paris reputation entirely to the Russian seasons which, as you well know, have cost me such superhuman efforts.

This year I gave him four productions to do. One, Narcisse, we all worked out together. As for the second, le Spectre de la Rose, Bakst watched the rehearsals in Petersburg and saw it arranged choreographically. So he had only to adapt his décor to a ready-made work.

As for 'Dieu bleu' and above all 'Péri' we have had nothing but vague suggestions, possible treatments – nothing more, not even a pencil sketch. I believe there has to be a temple in the set of 'Dieu bleu', but I do not know how or where it is situated. I don't even know if it is the interior of a temple or the square outside it, and I don't know where the pool and the grill stipulated in the libretto are meant to be. In short I know nothing about the construction or the very idea of the décor. And it is under these conditions that Fokine, Benois and myself are supposed to devise a production?

As far as Péri is concerned the situation had become absolutely ridiculous, for we are in total ignorance of whether the action takes place in a palace, on a mountain-top or in the clouds – and this is two weeks before the first night. Bakst claims that we lack confidence in his work, but I must say that I have never seen so astounding a betrayal of every artistic and aesthetic principle as he has shown in his dealings with us. When Bakst took on the production of S. Sebastien he swore to me that it would in no way interfere with our work, which he held much dearer. Now I declare that we have been completely sacrificed to the work of Rubinstein and d'Annunzio. We are the victims of our too great trust in him. Certainly Kchessinska never played us such a dirty trick as you have done over this negotiation, which as you will remember, I was so helpful about. Kchessin-

*When they first met in 1890 Diaghilev and Bakst were eighteen and twenty-four respectively.

ska never obliged us to abandon anything we had undertaken. Now, thanks to you and Bakst, at the last moment we are forced to give up the production of two ballets planned for a season beginning in a fortnight's time, and I warn you that you must take the consequences.

I need not remind you that by giving up the *répétition générale* of Dieu bleu we lose almost a hundred thousand francs. But what hurts me most is not to be able to give Paris the whole splendid repertory we planned – and you know that that is the one thing I really care about.

I leave you to judge who is to blame for what has happened. It was not for nothing that I put myself out to go to Paris to beg Bakst to come to Monte Carlo just for two days. Now I am in the most embarrassing position with regard to Dukas and above all Reynaldo Hahn, who took the trouble to come to Petersburg; and I must ask you to make your excuses for what has happened and to explain to them the reasons for this delay. I have suffered too much from the financial and moral worries that you and Bakst have brought upon me.

Yours,
[signed] SERGE DE DIAGHILEV

P.S. [in manuscript] Copies of this letter have been sent to Bakst and Reynaldo Hahn.[109]

The letter was no doubt carefully timed to arrive on Astruc's and Bakst's breakfast tables simultaneously with the press notices of Ida Rubinstein's 'St Sébastien'. Thus are traitors punished.

Bakst telegraphed at once.

Bakst in Paris to Diaghilev in Rome, 24.5.11

... Protest vehemently against responsibilities you try to place on my shoulders. Two sketches and plantations [explanations?] Péri dispatched last month Monte Carlo remained undelivered returned Paris. Nevertheless began painting backcloth. Costumes sent to Muelle. Costume Nijinsky Péri used cover programme Brunhoff. I telegraphed and wrote accepting Fokine Benois production Dieu Bleu. No reply. In despair adopted Fokine method of staging eve of departure Petersburg. Sketch Dieu Bleu finished costumes designed.

BAKST[110]

Astruc seems to have protested furiously against any change in the programme announced. On the night of the 25th Diaghilev, Benois, Fokine and Grigoriev sat up till the early hours discussing possibilities; and next day Diaghilev telegraphed to Astruc.

Diaghilev in Rome to Astruc in Paris, 26.5.11

After discussion entire night decided definitely renounce revival Firebird in favour following programmes. First Carnaval with Nijinsky Harlequin Narcisse Rose Sadko. Second Scheherazade Péri Kerjenetz Rose Petrushka. Stage director Allegri arriving Paris Sunday with music ... Begin rehearsals Monday.[111]

Diaghilev had entirely abandoned the possibility of putting on the extremely complicated 'Dieu bleu' and he probably thought it would be better to give up 'La Péri' too, but in the letter Allegri took to Astruc that weekend he tried a different tactic.

Diaghilev in Rome to Astruc in Paris, 27.5.11

My dear Astruc.

Your telegrams full of words like disastrous, immoral and deplorable are getting on my nerves. You seem to be willing disaster on our season ... It is obvious that if Bakst and Trouhanova had come to Monte Carlo for a few days Péri would have been arranged already.

Now the unanimous revolt against this intruding ballet has reached its climax. Karsavina refuses to come to Paris to dance alongside Trouhanova. Fokine declared yesterday that to put on Péri with Trouhanova would be the most idiotic thing he had ever let himself in for and something he could never forgive himself. Benois disclaims all responsibility for this inartistic business. The artists are disgusted. I don't speak of Besobrasov and de Gunsburg.

The only thing which makes them entertain the project at all is that I am determined to get Péri on.

Yesterday, after hearing the music Fokine declared that he would need at least twelve rehearsals to arrange it, not counting orchestral ones! !

He doesn't feel ready to start work on it because the libretto is quite inadequate and he has no idea how to produce it.

Under the circumstances I realize that the revival of Firebird, our most complicated ballet and one we have not danced for a year, is a physical impossibility if we do Péri. I had to decide between the two and to give up the work put in on the revival of Firebird.

I made that decision against the wishes of all my colleagues as a result of all the abusive words in your interminable telegrams.

And now I hear from you that the cancelling of Firebird is deplorable too.

Well, I am quite lost and I simply don't know what to do.

I shall have to show your telegram to all these people and the scenes will start all over again and will be worse than ever, since even you don't back me up in a decision come to simply because you say I have given my word and can't go back on it. It's really too much.

There is one thing I must ask you to do. See your friend Bakst and let me know by telegram what you both agree which scheme is likely to be less damaging to my reputation and financial prospects.

I am no longer in control of a season, which will be my sixth in Paris, and since I have obligations towards my company and my backers, I am obliged to submit totally to the decisions of my friends Bakst and Astruc.

If there is a possibility of postponing Péri until another season, the London one, for example, or the American one, I shall resume work on the revival of Firebird.

But I must know by Monday at the latest.

Therefore please cable as soon as you have made up your mind.

Yours ever
SERGE DE DIAGHILEV[112]

In fact there was no necessity to give 'Firebird', and, whatever had been announced, the second programme was quite long enough without 'La Péri'. Admittedly, it was a bit awkward that Trouhanova had already been photographed for the programme, wearing her Bakst costume, and that Bakst's designs for her and Nijinsky were also reproduced. The scenery had even been painted. (It would come in useful six years later, in São Paulo in Brazil, of all places, when the Bakst setting of 'Cléopâtre' was burnt in a railway tunnel!) [113] There would be a few complaints in the press about the changes,[114] but the success of the new productions put these quite out of mind. On the 31st Diaghilev cabled that Tcherepnine would conduct the first and Monteux the second programme; that he needed twenty men, twenty women and eight children as walkers-on (these being for the crowd in 'Petrushka'); that an extra rehearsal room would be needed besides the stage of the Châtelet as there would often be three rehearsals a day; that the company would arrive in Paris on Friday morning and begin rehearsals at the Châtelet at once.[115]

Les Ballets Russes de Serge de Diaghilev arrived for their first Paris season off the night train from Rome on the morning of Friday the 1st of June and began a busy weekend's work. Their opening night was on the Tuesday.

So it was the Châtelet that saw Nijinsky's first performance of Harlequin in 'Carnaval', Fokine's and Leontiev's role, but one Nijinsky was to make inimitably his own. As was increasingly the case, Nijinsky brought to a would-be straightforward role something extra and unexpected which transformed the ballet magically. We have seen how he created an atmosphere even in the classical *enchaînement* of 'Le Pavillon d'Armide', making Armide's Slave appear like the inhabitant of another world. In how many of his roles would he portray a character not quite human! His airborne, knee-lifting, head-wagging, finger-pointing, hand-clapping Harlequin appeared feline – 'an unforgettable figure,' wrote Geoffrey Whitworth,

not at all the blustering, magnificent Harlequin of Italian comedy, but a sly fellow, slickly insinuating, naughtily intimate. He is always whispering subtle secrets to Columbine, and is saved from viciousness only by his unerring sense of fun. Certainly he is the most uncanny and least human of all Nijinsky's creations. For this Harlequin is the very soul of mischief – half Puck – but Puck with a sting and with a body like a wire of tempered steel.[116]

His head [wrote Valentine Gross, a young painter who attended every performance to make drawings in the dark] seemed even smaller in the black skull cap; while the painted black domino mask hid everything but the lower part of his face and the eyes, which were prolonged, slanting up to the temples, and had such a shine and mystery like the eyes of a cat. I have never seen anything to equal the liveliness of his interpretation or the precision of his muscular control – such as at the moment when, with insect rapidity, he tore the letter into innumerable pieces like white butterflies, while wagging his head from left to right so quickly that one could hardly see it . . . The famous *entrechat-dix* executed as he shot up into the air were done so coolly, with such elegance and wit.[117]

It seems incredible to us today that Nijinsky, after dancing his first Harlequin, should have gone on to perform in 'Narcisse' and 'Le Spectre de la rose'. Here is Jean Cocteau's description of him in the latter ballet.

In his costume of curling petals, behind which perhaps the Girl perceives the image of her recent dancing-partner, he comes through the blue cretonne curtains out of the warm June night. He conveys – which one would have thought impossible – the impression of some melancholy, imperious scent. Exulting in his rosy ecstasy he seems to impregnate the muslin curtains and take possession of the dreaming girl. It is the most extraordinary achievement. By magic he makes the Girl dream she is dancing and conjures up all the delights of the ball. After he has bid a last farewell to his beloved victim he evaporates through the window in a jump so poignant, so contrary to all the laws of flight and balance, following so high and curved a trajectory, that I shall never again smell a rose without this ineffaceable phantom appearing before me.[118]

The enchanted evening ended with the submarine act of Rimsky's 'Sadko', which was the kind of exotic spectacle with exotic music that Paris had come to expect from the Russians. Anisfeld's green sea-monsters performed Fokine's ingenious undulations to the marvellous water-music; and the roles of Sadko and the Sea King were sung by Issatchenko and Zaporojetz. This first programme was repeated four times, but at subsequent performances Leontiev took over the role of Harlequin.[119]

In one night the French had seen Nijinsky in two of his greatest roles: but critics like to find something to complain about, and to the charge of blasphemy in dancing to an orchestrated version of Schumann's 'Carnaval', repeated from the year before, at least one critic added that of dancing to Berlioz's orchestration of Weber. He thought it was lazy of Diaghilev not to order new music for 'Le Spectre de la rose'![120]

After the run-through of 'Le Spectre' before its first Paris performance Karsavina had made a new friend who was to become in time her almost official admirer.[121]

Two young men, both tall and both in check trousers, had been to congratulate me after the morning rehearsal; one of them was the author – I only learned afterwards which was which. So I addressed my heartfelt thanks for giving me such opportunity as the part offered to the wrong young man, and for a long time I disapproved of the right one on account of a flicker of a *sourire moqueur*, which on closer knowledge proved to be the most enchanting touch of persiflage in an earnest and refined mind.[122]

This of course was Jean-Louis Vaudoyer.

*Diaghilev imagined as the Girl
in 'Le Spectre de la rose'.
Caricature by Jean Cocteau.*

When the orchestra began to rehearse the score of 'Petrushka' they burst out laughing. Monteux had some trouble persuading them that Stravinsky's music was not a joke.[123] (It took even Fokine many years to appreciate it.) Benois's scenery and costumes arrived from Petersburg: but time for finishing the ballet was short. Fokine only had one two-hour rehearsal with the crowd, including a number of French walkers-on, before the orchestral and dress rehearsals.[124] Diaghilev always remembered one incident which took place during the final rehearsals of the crowd. When Cecchetti as the Magician mimed the playing of his flute solo before animating the puppets, a girl in the crowd was literally 'charmed' by the hypnotic music and strayed unconsciously forward into the clear space in the middle of the stage. Fokine kept this in.[125]

The excitement of staging his ballet was too much for Benois, who was not well, and he made one of his scenes.

'Petrushka' opened the wound that had hardly healed after the 'Schéhérazade' incident [he wrote]. The décor of Petrushka's room was badly crushed during the journey, and considerable damage was done to the Conjuror's portrait, which occupied the centre of one of the walls. According to my plan, this portrait was to play an important part in the drama: the Conjuror had hung it there so that it should constantly remind Petrushka that he was in his master's power, and must therefore be humble and submissive. But it is just this portrait of his master that arouses Petrushka's indignation when he finds himself in solitary confinement: he shakes his fists at him and pours on him maledictions and curses. It was indispensable to have the portrait repaired as quickly as possible, but I, unfortunately, had developed an abscess on my elbow and was obliged to sit at home. When Bakst kindly offered to repair the portrait, I gratefully agreed, having no doubt that he would do it perfectly.

How great was my surprise at the dress-rehearsal two days later when I saw instead of 'my' portrait of the Conjuror a totally different one, showing him in profile, with his eyes looking sideways! Had I been in good health, I would of course have tried to arrange it all in a friendly way; Bakst had probably no evil intentions at all and had only exhibited too much zeal. But I had come to the theatre with a temperature and unbearable pain in my arm, the atmosphere of the rehearsal was tense – in short, I considered the alteration of my portrait an unpardonable outrage against me as an artist, and my whole plan for the ballet. Last year's insult came immediately to my memory. My fury expressed itself in a loud shout across the theatre, filled with a highly select audience: 'I shall not allow it! Take it down immediately! I can't bear it!' After which I flung my portfolio full of drawings on the floor and rushed out into the street and home . . .

My state of fury continued for two whole days. It was in vain that Serov immediately offered to give the portrait its original form and executed it with touching diligence; it was in vain that Nouvel kept coming to explain that it had been a misunderstanding and that both Serioja and Bakst were very sorry about what had occurred. I would not listen, nor give in. Nor would the pain in my arm stop until the doctor operated on it.

I sent in my resignation to Serioja, giving up my post of Artistic Director, and announced my refusal to go to London . . .[126]

The second programme of the Paris season was given on Tuesday,

13 June, a week after the first. It began with 'Schéhérazade', Karsavina replacing Rubinstein. Beautiful, passionate and moving as Karsavina was, the sadistic ballet had owed something of its effectiveness to the cold, inhuman quality of the angular mime, and without Rubinstein it would never be the same again. Once again Karsavina and Nijinsky were to dance in three ballets. The orchestral interlude from 'Grad Kitej', with Roerich battlescape, was played while they changed into their 'Spectre' costumes. 'Petrushka' followed.

Benois's ideas for staging 'Petrushka' must have owed something, though he did not acknowledge the debt in his books, to certain of Meyerhold's productions.* (He and Meyerhold were always criticizing each other.) On 9 October 1910 the latter had presented at the Interlude House, a cabaret-restaurant, a programme including Arthur Schnitzler's 'Veil of Pierrette', renamed by Meyerhold 'Columbine's scarf', with music by Dohnanyi and décor by Sapunov. Like 'Petrushka' this aimed at producing an eerie Hoffmanesque atmosphere; the lovelorn Pierrot who has a suicide pact with Columbine, which she does not fulfil, is a parallel to the tormented Petrushka; the master of ceremonies, a huge-headed Kapellmeister who from his high stool controls the destiny of the characters, and who at the end, when Columbine falls genuinely dead beside Pierrot, flees in terror through the auditorium, as if acknowledging his guilt, presages Benois' flute-playing Magician and his final exit haunted by Petrushka's ghost.[127]

When the curtain rises on Benois's décor for 'Petrushka' the

*But in the ephemeral world of the theatre it is only natural to enrich this year's productions with good ideas from last year's. In Meyerhold's 'Columbine's scarf', the 'flapping white sleeve' of Pierrot, though traditional, appears to be a reminiscence of Fokine's 'Carnaval', first staged in February of the same year, 1910, and in which Meyerhold himself played Pierrot. But was Fokine's 'Petrushka' itself partly inspired by Meyerhold's production of 'Balagan' – 'The Fairground Booth' – by Alexander Blok at Vera Komisarjevskaya's Theatre in Petersburg on 30 December 1906? For this the stage was 'hung at the sides and rear with blue drapes' and Pierrot 'sighs and flaps his arms'. (Meyerhold: *O Teatre*, p. 198, quoted by Edward Braun: *Meyerhold on Theatre*, p. 71.) 'Balagan' was one of the discarded titles for 'Petrushka' (other names considered for it were 'Maslanetsa' – 'Butter-week', and 'Mardi-Gras' – 'Shrove Tuesday'). Its action was heralded by a big drum: no doubt, Stravinsky or Benois or Diaghilev remembered this when they decided to link the three scenes of 'Petrushka' and cover up the scene-changes by a roll of *tambours militaires*.

French audience see before them a picture of the Russian winter – that terrible foe who defeated their ancestors in 1812. But Benois created a scene of colour and gaiety amid the snow. It is Shrove Tuesday, the day before the Lenten fast begins; the period is the 1830s; and Nicholas 1, the younger brother of Napoleon's ally and enemy, Alexander, is on the throne. Over the booths and flags of the fair rises the attenuated golden spire of the Admiralty, beyond which, out of sight, lie the frozen Neva and the islands, where Pushkin has yet to fight his fatal duel. On either side are the *balagani* or temporary wooden theatres, with their painted signs, the left-hand one having a yellow balcony – from which the old man or father of the fair will dangle his long false beard – and red and grey striped curtains below. Just to right of centre, half-hiding a distant merry-go-round and overhung by a helter-skelter, is the curtained booth of the Russian Punch-and-Judy or rather Petrushka show, with a sign showing a devil pitch-forking Petrushka into hell. This is, as it were, the stage within a stage, where the microcosmic drama of the Magician's puppets will take place while the careless crowd orbits around them. But Benois the Master-magician and Puppet-master has, with typical Hoffmannesque (or Pirandellian) humour – and his humour equals poetry – framed the fairground in the arch of a greater theatre, with people looking out of the windows of its painted boxes. Is it by accident that this outer theatre is blue like our sky and that the reveal of a narrow strip of ceiling, painted in false perspective just above the gold-fringed pelmet of its proscenium, is decorated with a yellow sun? Box within box: world beyond world. The artist is teasing us, suggesting that the 'real' people in the crowded fair are as much puppets as the painted saw-dust figures behind the curtain of the booth, or even that we, so safe beyond the footlights, are really puppets too. He seems to be asking, with Omar Khayyam, 'Which is the Potter, pray, and which the pot?'

The stage is filled with a circulating crowd and Benois would later describe what pains had been taken to make them 'live'.

I used to watch carefully during the rehearsals to see that every walker-on fulfilled the part that had been given him. The mixture of various characteristic elements gave the illusion of life. The people of good society showed elegant manners, the military men looked like real soldiers and officers of the time of Nicholas I, street-hawkers seemed really to be offering their goods, the peasant men and women looked like real *moujiks* and *babas*. I allowed nobody to improvise or overact.[128]

There are aristocratic couples arm-in-arm, followed by a cockaded footman carrying an extra coat; grooms and coachmen tipple; cadets salute their officers. 'One admires a samovar, others listen to the senseless chatter of an old man, a youth plays a harmonica, the boys reach for pretzels, girls crack sunflower seeds with their teeth.'[129] The sails of the windmill-like big wheel revolve and children ride on the *carrousel*.

'This merry-go-round,' wrote Benois, 'was a genuine *manège de chevaux de bois* of the time of Napoleon III which we had contrived to acquire at some fair.'[130]*

The stridency and bustle of the fair are represented in Stravinsky's music by a shrill figure on the flute and by an impatient rhythmical stamping which will frequently interrupt the various borrowed tunes that give the score a kaleidoscopic and Shakespearian diversity, and will at the same time serve to bring on a fresh incursion of boisterous revellers. The steady animal panting of the orchestra, simulating accordions, seems to convey the surrounding enormity of winter.

The imminence of Lent and Easter as well as a kind of popular religious element are suggested at the very beginning by the introduction of a tune we recognize at once as Russian, even if we do not know that it used to be sung at Easter by bands of peasants walking from village to village in the department of Smolensk. A street musician enters with a barrel-organ, whose music – the whining tune Stravinsky wrote to ask André Rimsky-Korsakov for – is represented by clarinets. He is here to accompany a street dancer, Schollar, who spreads her little square of carpet and begins to perform to the tune of 'Elle avait une jamb'en bois', to the second verse of which her accompanist adds a cornet *obbligato*. A rival dancer, Nijinska, now appears, her manager turning the handle of a musical-box while she

*It is now at the bottom of the River Plate, having been dropped by a crane when the Ballet's luggage was unloading at Buenos Aires. (Benois: *Reminiscences*, p. 335 footnote.)

executes *ronds de jambe* and strikes a triangle. For a moment the two dancers' tunes overlap as they vie for attention. The stamping rhythms of the crowd and the strains of the Easter song overwhelm them. Two drummers, the Magician's assistants, clear a space for the puppets' performance, and the Magician, Cecchetti, puts his head through the curtains of the booth. After a moment of silence and suspense, he comes out closing the curtains behind him. He wears an astrological cloak and somewhat papal headdress, which hints at his moral tyranny over the puppets whom he is able to endue with life. His sinister aspect is represented by eerie chromatic slides and he proceeds to charm the crowd with a Weber-like flute solo, whose un-Russian nature with its elaborate ornamentations are calculated to seem utterly mysterious and exotic to the unsophisticated merrymakers. Suddenly he draws back the curtains of the booth to reveal the three puppets held up under the arms by metal supports. He touches them each in turn with the magic flute. As the pulsing clockwork rhythm breaks forth their legs are galvanized into life and perform an animated heel-toe dance. To the left is the splendid figure of the black-faced turbaned Moor, Orlov, his emerald-green velvet tunic decorated with gold frogging. In the centre the Ballerina, Karsavina, rosy-cheeked with doll's eyelashes, in a fur-edged crimson tam-o'-shanter, neat crimson bodice, pink skirt and lace-trimmed pantaloons. On the right, Nijinsky's Petrushka has chalky features like painted wood, a scarlet and white bonnet, a white belted smock with a floppy Pierrot collar, checkered red and green trousers, helpless black-mittened hands and turned-in awkward black-booted feet. The puppets get down from their stands and take the centre of the stage. From the crude pantomime that follows we gather that Petrushka loves the Ballerina, but that she is repelled by his convulsive spasms of movement and prefers the gorgeous, brainless Moor.

Tambours militaires maintain suspense during the change to Scene II. This is Petrushka's cell or the box in which he is flung by the old Magician between performances. The black walls of this gloomy room, which we see at an angle, are relieved only by a dado of white clouds round the top and a few stars. The door is guarded by painted devils, so perhaps this is an Arctic hell; and there is a portrait of the Magician – the eye of Big Brother is upon you – on the right-hand wall. The music for this scene is Stravinsky's original Konzertstück for piano and orchestra. Petrushka's dual nature, half-puppet, half-human, is represented by the bitonality of a figure on the woodwind, which is also associated with a gesture of his (fingerless) gloved hands jerked sideways and upwards stiffly into the unpitying air. The trepidations of the creature's heart are illustrated by scampering runs on the piano. 'Several instruments in the orchestra try to console him upon his miserable destiny' and the 'impotent rage' with which he cuts them short, cursing the Magician his master, is a harsh fanfare. He tries to dance, but his knees turn in and his arms shield his awkward body in shame. 'There is a moment' (according to Fokine) 'when Petrushka, being sorry for himself, examines his own pitifully unsightly figure. He picks up his pants to knee level, but when he pulls to the right, both knees move to the right; then in order to see himself from the other side, he pulls himself by the pants to the left.'[131] The Ballerina comes to call on him, entering to a somewhat liturgical tune. Petrushka's transports of passion and hope scare her away. He dances his frustration, darting round his prison, to a piano cadenza, and as his wild fanfare sounds again his flaying arms break a hole in the paper wall of his cell. He falls headlong through; then half in, half out, hangs limp.

The Moor's apartment, in which Scene III takes place, is also shown at an angle, but its decoration affords an extreme contrast to that of Petrushka's. The walls are painted like a garish jungle, with green coconut palms against a scarlet sky and white rabbits scampering on the grass beneath. There is a cushioned divan. The eastern music represents a wild beast sullenly pacing his cage and in the rising arpeggios on piano and strings we can hear the thrashing of the tiger's tail. The Moor, all of whose movements are bold, crude, decisive and turned out, in contrast to Petrushka's, stamps around, knees bent and wide apart, arms held up as if in childish astonishment. This scene is interrupted by an episode, inserted at Fokine's request, in which the Moor, hearing the milk inside a coconut, attacks it with his scimitar. Failing to make an impression on the nut, he kneels down and worships it. A roll of drums heralds the entrance of the Ballerina, who, cornet to lips, dances a stiff little *vivandière* dance to the delight of the Moor. She then performs a waltz, repeats it with variations and breaks into another waltz, played on the harp, whose tune is borrowed from Josef Lanner. The Moor now joins the Ballerina in dancing to the previous tune, his own astraddle stamping, as he grasps her by the waist, forming an awkward counterpoint to her tripping in three-time. Suddenly·Petrushka's cry is heard and the lovesick creature bursts in to threaten the Moor with his ineffectual gestures to dissonant fanfares. The Ballerina stages a provocative faint; the Moor drives Petrushka out with his scimitar, then seats himself on the divan with the Ballerina on his knee. From the way he opens his mouth wide and gnashes his teeth it seems that he thinks she is edible.

In Scene IV we return to the fair, where, as the evening has worn on, the revelry has become more uproarious. The complex music of this scene is a miracle of ingenious orchestration. Out of the initial twangling, piping, tingling and tooting, there emerges the dance of the Wet-nurses in their ornate traditional dress, with their gliding, dipping steps and arms akimbo or folded over their breasts. Their music is based on two folk tunes, 'I was at a feast' and 'Oh my room, my little room'. Next there appear a bear and his keeper. The crowd surround them, half afraid, half teasing, as the keeper plays his pipe, represented by the clarinet, and the bear's lumbering is conveyed by the tuba. A pulsing monotonous breathing as of accordions again suggests the all-enveloping cold. A swaggering drunk merchant, Kussov, appears escorting two Gypsy girls with tambourines, and he throws money to the crowd. Then comes the stamping of the booted coachmen, Rosaï and Orlik, who break into a squatting, kicking dance with a marked rhythm to another folk tune, 'I was going up a hill.' A party of merrymakers burst in wearing over their heads the masks, at the end of long wobbling necks, of the Goat, the Crane and a Devil. With a return of the Easter tune from Scene I, the crowd stamp and beat their arms across their chests to keep warm. They have not noticed that the curtains of the booth are agitated by the Moor's pursuit of Petrushka. The latter's shriek is heard and he shoots from the booth, running on tip-toe, hands clasped between his legs, with the armed Moor in hot pursuit. The Ballerina has her hands over her ears in terror as Petrushka is struck down. The crowd gathers round to watch his brief death scene, hear his last pathetic piping cry, watch

*George Rosaï as a Coachman
in 'Petrushka'.
Drawing by Valentine Gross.*

his final gesture of appeal. A watchman goes to fetch the Magician, who appears, top-hatted this time, from a refreshment stall. There are a few threatening gestures from the crowd. The Magician lifts the limp puppet which has by now replaced Nijinsky (who has run off to the right under cover of the crowd) and shakes it to show it is nothing but wood and sawdust. The crowd disperses and the 'accordion pumping' again emphasizes the bleakness of the winter night. The Magician, left alone, passes slowly across to the left of the stage, dragging the puppet. Suddenly Petrushka's squeaking fanfare is heard and Nijinsky – the puppet's ghost – appears menacing over the booth where he learned sorrow, with 'frantic, waving arms'.[132] Has his soul survived? The terrified Magician slinks off, the ghost of Petrushka falls forward and hangs with swinging arms over the top of the booth and the music ends with a curious question-mark on the plucked strings.

Although he was not speaking to Diaghilev, Benois went to two performances of his ballet before leaving Paris, and 'derived considerable pleasure from them'.[133] 'Petrushka', as we know, was to become one of the most famous of the Russian ballets. But Stravinsky has always thought that Fokine had arranged the ballet all wrong,[134] and that Benois had designed the wrong sort of costumes for the Magician and the Moor;[135] while at the time Fokine did not really appreciate the music.[136] Benois, on the other hand, would look back on the first productions of his ballet as perfect.[137] He was to design five subsequent productions, in Leningrad, Copenhagen, Paris, Milan and London, each being a variation of the original.

Fokine wrote at length about 'Petrushka' in later years. Here are his comments on the performances of Karsavina and Nijinsky.

Tamara Karsavina making up
for 'Petrushka'.
Drawing by Valentine Gross.

The Ballerina must be an attractive, stupid doll. When Tamara Karsavina performed this role exactly and well – as no one has since her – just as I staged it for her, she caused a great deal of favourable comment. I was grateful to her for her efforts, but still could not understand what could be considered difficult in this role. She performed all the required gestures, attached doll-like eyelashes to her eyelids,* and rouged her cheeks to look like two red apples. There was nothing further to create, no personality. It only remained for her not to alter or forget a single movement. Yet I saw many dolls in 'Petrushka' later, and none of them ever approached this first interpretation. I posed this question to myself: 'Why don't they perform the way Karsavina did? It seemed so easy.' But – they simply couldn't.[138]

Of Nijinsky he wrote: 'I sincerely admired his every movement . . . he played his role wonderfully well . . . Never again did I see such a splendid Petrushka.'[139]

Benois wrote:

I was particularly enchanted with Nijinsky at the first performance of 'Petrushka'. He had not been successful in the part during rehearsals and it seemed as if he did not completely understand what was needed. He even asked me to explain his role to him, which was very unusual for Nijinsky. But in the end he amazed us as he had in 'Pavillon', 'Sylphides', 'Schéhérazade' and 'Giselle'. This time also the metamorphosis took place when he put on his costume and covered his face with make-up – and it was even more amazing. I was surprised at the courage Vaslav showed, after all his *jeune premier* successes, in appearing as a horrible half-doll, half-human grotesque. The great difficulty of Petrushka's part is to express his pitiful oppression and his hopeless efforts to achieve personal dignity *without ceasing to be a puppet*. Both music and libretto are spasmodically interrupted by outbursts of illusive joy and frenzied despair. The artist is not given a single *pas* or a *fioriture* to enable him to be attractive to the public, and one must remember that Nijinsky was then quite a young man and the temptation to 'be attractive to the public' must have appealed to him far more strongly than to an older artist.[140]

Robert Brussel praised the new ballet in *Le Figaro*, admired Stravinsky's 'extraordinarily fascinating varied and inventive orchestration', adored Karsavina and thought Nijinsky's puppet was the height of 'naïvety and desolating melancholy'.[141] The public were enthusiastic. In fact, thanks largely to 'Le Spectre' and 'Petrushka', Diaghilev's third short season of ballet in Paris was almost more successful than its predeccessors.

*In fact, I think she *painted* crude black rays radiating from her eyes.

Nijinsky's first night in London (and indeed his first five weeks' stay in England) was spent at the Waldorf Hotel in the crescent of the Aldwych. On subsequent visits he and Diaghilev would always put up at the smarter Savoy, a few minutes' walk away from the Waldorf, between the Strand and the river: but if Diaghilev had tried to book rooms there in June 1911 and failed it was no doubt because London was crammed with Imperial and foreign dignitaries and their suites. Anyway the Waldorf, with its convex back overlooking the roofs of Drury Lane, was as near as you could possibly get to Covent Garden. It had only been open for three years, having been built as part of the Kingsway–Aldwych slum clearance scheme; it is the centre of a pompous stone block with the twin Strand and Aldwych Theatres at either end. Although designed in a mixture of traditional styles of architecture, with French *mansard* pavilion roofs at either end and a colonnade in the middle, it was one of the first steel-framed buildings erected in London and had a spacious Palm Court.[142]*

The Aldwych was the theatre at which the Russians would have appeared in 1910 if King Edward had not died, and where Vaslav's 'Sacre du printemps' would be rehearsed in 1912. Like many London theatres, including the Gaiety across the street, where George Grossmith's *Peggy* was running, and like the Adelphi along the Strand, which was showing *The Quaker Girl*, it was controlled by George Edwardes, a connection of Benois's. Martin Harvey was playing Sidney Carton in *The Only Way* at the neighbouring Lyceum; the Savoy had a festival of Dickens adaptations; and Shaw's *Fanny's First Play* was on at the Little, in John Street, Adelphi.

A more surprising feature of the London theatre and a proof of the extent to which Karsavina's pioneer appearance at the Coliseum in 1909 had changed the whole scene, was that there was a Russian ballerina at every one of the big music-halls except the Coliseum, where the Danish Adeline Genée – for years the unchallenged queen of the dance in London – held the fort. Pavlova was dancing at the Palace; Gelzer and Tikhomirov were at the Alhambra; a 'Mme Sobinoff, Russia's premier singer and dancer', was at the Hippodrome; and Karsavina's old class-mate, Lydia Kyasht was appearing

*In which Ernest Ansermet, three months before his death, received me to talk about Diaghilev and Nijinsky.

with Phyllis Bedells and Fred Farren in a short version of Delibes's 'Sylvia' at the Empire. On her first visit to London in 1910 Kyasht had won the heart of Juliet Duff's uncle Hugh, the sporting Earl of Lonsdale, who had set her up in a comfortable house in St John's Wood.[143]

Karsavina by now was an experienced 'Londoner'; she took a flat with Elsa Will near Baker Street.[144] Gunsbourg was at the Carlton in the Haymarket,[145] in the same block as Tree's His Majesty's Theatre. The rest of the company stayed in small hotels in Bloomsbury. The plain brick eighteenth-century squares and terraces of WC1 amazed the Russians, who were used to the painted plaster of Petersburg, and had taken for granted the grey stone of Paris and the marble of Rome.

> We were surprised [wrote Grigoriev] by the extreme simplicity of the architecture; London houses seemed to us almost excessively plain. We found rooms in the neighbourhood of the British Museum ... but here again the gardens of the squares were all locked up, and only the residents had keys to them ... Something we had certainly never encountered before were the curious two-wheeled vehicles, with the driver seated behind his passengers, known as hansom cabs ... What amazed us above all, however, was the Theatre Royal [the Opera House] in Covent Garden itself. It stood in the midst of a vegetable market and was closely hemmed in by greengrocers' warehouses and vast mountains of cabbages, potatoes, carrots and all manner of fruit ... On the other hand, the interior was excellent ... The stage, to be sure, had one drawback from our standpoint: it was flat instead of raked; and since our dancers were used to a sloping floor, they found this flatness somewhat disconcerting.[146]

Diaghilev, Nijinsky and Karsavina were welcomed as old friends by Lady Ripon and her daughter Lady Juliet Duff. Lady Ripon had seen the ballet in Russia and it was she who had been responsible for arranging that Diaghilev's company should be included in the programme of the Coronation Gala, which would otherwise have been entirely opera.[147] Juliet Duff, as we have seen, had been at Monte Carlo in the spring. Gwladys Ripon was a daughter of the Sidney Herbert (created Lord Herbert of Lea) who, as Secretary for War, had helped Florence Nightingale establish her hospital at Scutari; and as his mother Lady Pembroke had been a Woronzov, Gwladys was a quarter Russian and probably distantly related to Diaghilev. She had married the fourth Earl of Lonsdale, but as he was constitutionally incapable of having relations with women of his own class, it was taken for granted that the only child, Juliet, was by one of Gwladys Lonsdale's innumerable lovers. Some thought the father was the Grand Duke Michael, who lived with his morganatic wife, Countess Torby, in exile at Ken Wood: but Lady Juliet's true father was almost certainly Lord Annaly.[148] After Lord Lonsdale's death (in his private brothel) in 1882, the earldom went to his brother, later famous as a patron of sport, and his widow married Lord de Grey, heir of the rich Marquis of Ripon. It was during her incarnation as Lady de Grey that the exiled Oscar Wilde, in gratitude for her friendship during his troubles, dedicated to her the printed edition of his play *A Woman of No Importance*. On the death of her father-in-law in 1909 Gwladys became Lady Ripon. She was one of the few members of Edwardian society with a real interest in the arts. Queen Alexandra, so beautiful, brainless, deaf, deserted and bored, relied greatly on her for distraction; and the Queen's friendship on at least one occasion saved her from social ostracism after a scandal.[149] Lady Randolph Churchill described her as 'a luxurious woman with perfect manners, a kind disposition and a moderate sense of duty'.[150] In 1911 she had abandoned her vast house in Carlton House Terrace for her big suburban villa Coombe, with what Reynaldo Hahn called its '*jardin de curé*',[151] near Kingston in Surrey, an hour's drive from London. Juliet, who had married Robin Duff of the Life Guards in 1904 and had a daughter and a son, lived in Upper Brook Street between Grosvenor Square and Hyde Park, but was much with her mother.

How would the straitlaced, puritanical, conservative and philistine English react to the Russian Ballet – as opposed to single stars in music-hall acts? How would the exotic Fokine repertory be received in the world of Kipling and Elgar (W. S. Gilbert had died in the previous month), a world which had been shocked by young Epstein's carved nudes on the British Medical Association building in the Strand three summers before? Diaghilev was experienced enough to realize that the enthusiastic Lady Ripon and her daughter were hardly typical members of the audience. He knew that Karsavina,

Pavlova, Kyasht and Preobrajenska had been acclaimed in the music-halls, but they had danced fragments of the old classical repertory and could not therefore, in that context, have seemed very different from Adeline Genée who had been the darling of music-hall audiences for years. Playing for safety, Diaghilev had included neither of the Stravinsky ballets in his London repertory. 'Firebird' he had anyway had no time to rehearse. He could have brought 'Petrushka', but didn't. He would first try the Londoners out on the barbarous Russian music of 'Prince Igor', 'Cléopâtre', and 'Schéhérazade'. With 'Le Pavillon d'Armide', 'Les Sylphides', 'Carnaval' and 'Le Spectre de la rose' he had reason to feel fairly safe. 'Narcisse' and 'Sadko' had also been left behind.

During this first London season the ballet would alternate with Italian opera, and of its sixteen performances six would be shared with the opera company – for instance 'Pagliacci' would precede 'Carnaval', 'Le Spectre' and 'Prince Igor' (24 June), 'Les Sylphides' and 'Armide' (30 June), or 'Les Sylphides', 'Le Spectre' and 'Prince Igor' (3 July); 'Il Segreto di Susanna' would be sandwiched between 'Cléopâtre' and 'Carnaval' (11 July) or between 'Les Sylphides' and 'Cléopâtre' (17 July) or followed by 'Schéhérazade', 'Le Spectre' and 'Prince Igor' (26 July). 'Les Sylphides' would be given ten times, 'Prince Igor' eight, 'Armide' seven, both 'Carnaval' and 'Schéhérazade' six times, 'Le Spectre' five and 'Cléopâtre' four.[152]

The dress-rehearsal was to be held on the afternoon of Tuesday, 20 June, and a small group of Diaghilev's friends had assembled to watch it. But the wardrobe staff had been detained by the Immigration Officer at Folkestone and Diaghilev received a telegram asking if he could guarantee that they would leave the country after his engagement. The director of Covent Garden telegraphed his guarantee, but there was no one to sort out complicated costumes, head-dresses, boots, jewellery and accessories and the small audience dispersed, leaving the Russians to rehearse in plain clothes.[153] The Immigration Officer was no doubt on the look-out for Russian terrorists and revolutionaries. (The fifth congress of Social Democrats, attended by Lenin, had been held in London four years before.)

The Diaghilev Ballet opened at Covent Garden on Wednesday, 21 June with 'Le Pavillon d'Armide', 'Carnaval' and 'Prince Igor'. Karsavina, Nijinsky and Bolm of course danced in 'Le Pavillon'. Elsa Will was the first Columbine the English saw in 'Carnaval', with Nijinsky as Harlequin and with Fokina, Schollar, Nijinska, Bolm and Cecchetti in their old roles of Chiarina, Estrella, Papillon, Pierrot and Pantalon, with Semenov as Florestan and Ivan Kussov, who had just joined the company in Paris as *premier danseur de caractère* (and had been the drunk merchant in 'Petrushka'), as Eusebius. In 'Prince Igor' as at the first performance two years before, Bolm, Feodorova and Rosaï led respectively the Warriors, Girls and Boys, and a newcomer, Anna Gachevska was the principal Captive Slave. Petrenko and Zaporojetz were singing Khontchakovna and Khan Khontchak as in Paris, and Issatchenko took Smirnov's part of Vladimir, the role of Igor being reduced to a *persona muta*. The company had, according to Diaghilev, 'an immense success, though during the "Prince Igor" dances, half the public went home. At least a hundred old ladies, covered with diamonds as though they were ikons, went out past me with a look of disgust on their faces. The business manager came running up, crying "You've spoilt your magnificent opening by this barbarian horror at the end – it isn't dancing – it's just savages prancing about." '[154]* The next day, somewhat stealing the Russians' thunder, King George V was crowned; and there was no performance at Covent Garden.

Diaghilev in London to Astruc in Paris, 23.6.11
Announce unparalleled triumph . . . audience indescribably smart. London has discovered Nijinsky and given a warm welcome to Karsavina, Will, Fokine, Tcherepnine.[155]

But the Russians really were a revelation to the British public. On Thursday, 22 June, the Diaghilev Ballet had its first notice in *The Times*. The anonymous critic was George Calderon.

*Writing in 1926, Diaghilev forgot that his company had given two performances *before* the Coronation Gala. He wrote 'The next evening [after the Gala] came our real opening. . .' Grigoriev made the same mistake. (p. 67.) I have transferred Diaghilev's story of the disconcerted dowagers to the *real* 'real opening' night, from Saturday to Wednesday.

It has been obvious for some years that Russians are the ideal dancers of the world ... the quality in which they all seemed to excel is accuracy of rhythm, as if they were creating the rhythm, not timing their movements according to it ... As for Mme Karsavina ... no words can do justice to her actual dancing; yet her face is so expressive that one forgets all about her feet. M. Nijinsky may possibly not realize the Pheidian ideal quite as perfectly as M. Mordkine, but his technique is even more assured and his leaps are not only of extraordinary height, but his descents from his native element are timed so perfectly that every jump is a separate ecstasy ...

The Schumann 'Carnaval' was an unqualified joy from the beginning to end, with never a moment when one felt that the music had been treated with anything but complete sympathy ... M. Nijinsky dances with incredible virtuosity during the number called 'Paganini', and at the wonderful point where the dominant seventh on E Flat emerges by the deft use of the pedal, the dancer represents the effect to absolute perfection by suddenly sitting down ... The stage-management of the whole was among the most purely artistic things the stage has ever seen.[156]

On Saturday, 24 June, two days after the Coronation, the Russians gave their second performance, and 'Le Spectre' was danced for the first time in England. One critic described the ballet as 'a dream of perfect beauty and all too quickly over'.[157] In 'Carnaval', instead of wearing patterned trousers buttoning above the ankle, which Fokine and Leontiev had usually worn and which Diaghilev had made him put on for fear of shocking the English, Nijinsky reverted to his usual lozengy tights, and *The Times* noticed his dress was 'less conventional and more effective than before'. 'Prince Igor' was given without the singing.[158]

That morning *The Times* had devoted a long and serious article to the 'new and enchanting pleasure' which the novel art form provided. It is interesting that in his very first paragraph the writer envisaged a time when British artists might even 'arrive at some imitation of it on our own stage'. The thoughtful critic went on:

What then are the essential characters which differentiate the art of the Russian Ballet from that which we have hitherto known in England? That they dance better – the simplest explanation – is one of the most misleading, for the elusive differentia does not lie in technique. Certainly their technique is exquisite; all of them can do the most wonderful things with no appearance of effort, and they can do many sorts of wonderful things.

But technique is no more the source of the highest pleasure in dancing than it is in painting, in music, or any other of the arts. It is a channel of communication; it is the means by which the artistic idea comes from the mind of the creator to the senses of the spectator. The Russians, in fact, have so long since brought their technique of dancing, their command of their limbs and bodies, their instinct for balance, for energy without exertion, to the highest point that they have been able to develop the art for which that technique exists – namely, the conveyance of choreographic ideas. Russian ballet-dancing never for one moment escapes from its subjection to ideas – and, moreover, to artistic ideas, ideas that is, conceived at a high pitch of emotional intelligence . . .

Our English ballets have had so little concern with the imagination that even the most pitiful little crumbs of imaginative food, the evolution of recent English choreographic impressionists and mysterious orientals from Montmartre, have caused something of a flutter among us. And now that we have suddenly set before us the abundant fare supplied by the inventive genius of a Benois and a Fokine, inheritors of a great tradition that has been gradually developing, all unknown to us, beyond the Baltic, and the interpretative genius of a Nijinsky, a Karsavina, an Elsa Will, is it to be wondered at that we fall to so greedily? For here we are introduced to a whole range of ideas such as we have never met before.[159]

The critic had a real admiration for Pavlova, but he realized the shortcomings of her presentations.

How much of the work of a ballet-master suffers from being given piece-meal may be seen by comparing the effect of the detached 'turns' of Pavlova and her company at the Palace Theatre before an irrelevant purely 'decorative' back-cloth, with the effect of 'Carnaval' in its entirety at Covent Garden. 'Carnaval' is an exquisitely delicate artistic whole, from the first coy scamperings and hidings of Chiarina and Estrella to the good-natured *grand rond* in chase of the Philistines; and not a detail of it could be spared; least of all the black dado with the giant golden tulips and the two little roguish Pierrots of sofas, crouching against the wainscot, which make one alert from the beginning for the airy mockery of the whole intention. It is the sum of all these details which leaves us in the end with a quite new and brilliant vision of Schumann's work, purged of all possible suspicion of any Germanic seriousness of purpose.

He understood how the Russian art was a collaboration between choreographer and dancers.

In all ballet-dancing there is a dim attempt to represent the spiritual and the fantastic by means of the material: the tip-toeing and the lifting-up of the women is a suggestion of the ethereal; but the perfect ease and grace of the Russians enable them to carry this to a far higher point, so that in their suggestions of things flying, things swimming, things poised, or blown by the wind, the sense of the material passes altogether away. The dancers are able in their turn to create the art of the ballet-master for him by offering him new possibilities, such as Karsavina's instinctive plant-like correlations of balanced extremities, and the contrary movements of head and limbs with which Nijinsky is able to create the grotesque abstract, half-mathematical sensations.

Praising the Russians for their restraint, he even noticed such details as 'the excellently-judged waving of the feather-fans ... in the Armida Palace dances'. He admired in 'Prince Igor' 'the women that crouch, unconsious of themselves, or rise and stretch lazy limbs, and in the end fling themselves prone when their dance is over; the savage-joyful panther-leaping of the men; the stamping feet and quick nerve-racking beat of the drum; and, more threatening than all, the gambolling of the boys, like kittens unwittingly preparing themselves for the future chase'. He wrote charmingly of 'Carnaval'.

A Coquette dancing with two roses at the Carnival shows the graces of the early Victorian period at their daintiest, but all the time you guess that she is making fun of them and of the absurd people who believe in her ... No need to shed tears for your ladies who languish forlorn on the tips of their toes, or for poor gentlemen who die of love for such elfin creatures. Remember that this is an aristocratic tradition, with something of Boucher and Beaumarchais clinging to it, arch, mischievous, *gouailleur*. It is immensely serious as Art, but never for a moment serious as Life.[160]

The next day the critic of the *Sunday Times* wrote of 'the peerless Nijinsky':

It would savour of hyperbole to say of his dancing that the half of it had not been told, but the foreword of him had certainly not been extravagant. He has great charm of personality: the grossness of contour and sensuality of lineament which so often mark the male dancer are conspicuous by their absence; and his every movement is instinct with spontaneity and grace. He seems to be positively lighter than air, for his leaps have no sense of effort and you are inclined to doubt if he really touches the stage between them. His precision is faultless and his technique generally as polished as it is resourceful.[161]

It is interesting to note the effect of the Diaghilev Ballet on at least one English dancer. The seventeen-year-old Phyllis Bedells, who was appearing in 'Sylvia' at the Empire in the company led by Kyasht, had seen Karsavina dance before, but the Diaghilev company was a great new experience, as she was to record many years later.

When the Diaghilev Ballet made its first appearance at Covent Garden with the full company it was maddening not to be able to see them as there were no matinée performances.* All London was raving about their success, and eventually I had to go to the Empire directors and say that as part of my education I must be given the opportunity to see them. Very reluctantly it was agreed that I take one night off which, unless one was ill, was an almost unheard-of thing. I booked a seat in the circle – just one. I could not afford to pay for another seat on my small salary. My father took me to the theatre and collected me when the performance ended. For the first time in my life I heard Grand Opera sung. The ballet programme followed the performance of *I Pagliacci*, with Emmy Destinn, Sammarco, and Robert Martin. Then the curtain rose on *Carnaval*... And afterwards there were the *Prince Igor* dances. As long as I live I shall not forget that night. I could hardly keep still in my seat. Because people who were sitting in neighbouring seats would keep chatting away in a blasé manner I worked myself into a state of fury. It seemed impossible to believe that anyone could behave like that while the magic of those artists filled me with such delight. Several times, young as I was, I asked them to be quiet ... I cannot write about Nijinsky. It is useless. Then he was at the very height of his powers. I was breathless as I sat there in my seat and watched his dancing.[162]

The impression made by the Russian Ballet on one non-professional member of their new audience can be judged by the reaction of the Duchess of Rutland, whose youngest daughter, Diana Manners, was coming out that season. She was a gifted artist and one of the 'Souls', that group of highminded intellectuals – Wyndhams, Horners, Elchos, Grenfells and Asquiths, A. J. Balfour and Lord Curzon –

*But because of the Ballet's success matinées were introduced quite soon after the beginning of the season, as Covent Garden programmes prove.

who reacted against the philistinism of Edwardian society. She had always loathed the idea of ballet, which she considered quite unconnected with art and a mere diversion for the kind of man she most particularly disliked. Her conversion was as sudden as St Paul's. Her very first sight of Karsavina in 1909 had been a revelation, now the Diaghilev Ballet turned her into a passionate devotee of the new art.[163]

For the Coronation Gala on Monday, 26 June, the Opera House was decorated with 'over a hundred thousand roses, and the boxes, according to Diaghilev, 'contained almost as many maharajahs'.[164] Among the flowers were plaques emblazoned with the names of countries over which the King Emperor ruled, with INDIA occupying a central position under the Royal Box. 'The audience began to assemble at seven o'clock, Lady Ripon and her daughter, Lady Juliet Duff, being very early on the scene.' While upstairs, 'the gallery slips were much sought after for their view of the audience.' Queen Mary wore the huge Cullinan diamond and the Star of Africa on her bodice.[165]

Although Destinn and Kirkby Lunn sang the duet from 'Aida', Melba the second-act aria from Gounod's 'Roméo et Juliette', Tetrazzini, Béval, Malatesta and John McCormack part of Act III of 'Il Barbiere', 'applause was restrained.'[166] But what can you expect from a lot of Maharajahs? The critic of the *Daily Mail* was not kept down.

The regal spectacle ended with one of the most enchanting creations ever seen on any stage [this was the second *tableau*, the Gobelins *divertissement*, of 'Le Pavillon d'Armide'] ... Both the King and Queen freely used opera glasses and the interest of the whole assembly was excited. The pauses after the various dances, meant for applause, were at first silent. As the marvellous ballet progressed there was more and more admiration for the delicious Mme Karsavina, M. Nijinsky, who seems the incarnation of youthful joy, the astonishing company of buffoons and the others.[167]

Diaghilev's spirits, however, must have been considerably dampened by the mouselike response of the princely audience. His memory of the evening was gloomy: 'Our reception was icy, and neither Karsavina's variations, nor even those of Nijinsky ... received the slightest applause. It was only after the dance of the buffoons that the strangest of sounds came to us: the public was gently clapping its kid-gloved hands.'[168]

If Diaghilev and Nijinsky were not used to such 'effortless superiority' as the English showed on this occasion, the public's response on other nights was very different; and the box-office returns coupled with the determination of Sir Joseph Beecham to have nothing but the best, regardless of expense, soon made it clear to them that they could plan for longer seasons in London even than in Paris. It was arranged that they should pay a return visit in October.

The newspapers were soon recording that the success of the Ballet had exceeded all expectation. 'There has been nothing like the vogue of the Russian ballet for a generation. So attractive are their performances that many people are postponing their departure from town in order to see them out, and we are getting "tiara" nights to the end of the season, even though we are in the very stew of the dog days.'[169]

On 27 June 'Les Sylphides' was given, with Karsavina and Nijinsky in their inevitable roles, Bronislava Nijinska in Pavlova's Mazurka and Will in the Prelude. Richard Capell, the *Daily Mail* music critic, wrote that although a music-lover naturally looked askance at this 'free handling of the masterpieces of the immortal dead . . . the imponderable Karsavina floats once more across the stage and he is conquered utterly'.[170] Karsavina alternated with Will as Columbine in 'Carnaval'. On 11 July 'Cléopâtre' was given with Seraphine Astafieva as Cleopatra, Sophie Feodorova in Pavlova's role as Ta-hor and Will in Karsavina's as the Slave, Nijinsky's partner. On 20 July London saw for the first time 'Schéhérazade' with Karsavina, Nijinsky, and Bolm as the Shah. On the last night of the season, 31 July, odd as it may seem, 'Cléopâtre' and 'Schéhérazade', sandwiching 'Les Sylphides', were on the same bill. Elsa Will had perhaps been called away and Schollar replaced her in the Prelude, while Karsavina resumed her original small role in 'Cléopâtre' and played Zobeïda in the Rimsky work.

Before the end of the season Nijinsky's name was on everybody's lips, but another Russian had had what was to prove an even more pervasive influence – Leon Bakst. His décors banished for ever from

241

the dress shops and furnishers the favourite Edwardian colours of white, cream, grey and pale mauve. The windows of Harvey Nichols blossomed in purple and red.[171] To be fair it must be admitted that Bakst had been preceded by more than one imaginative theatre designer in England in recent years. Gordon Craig, the starting-point of whose art had been the melodramatic compositions (usually four-poster beds) of James Pryde,[172] with their exaggerated verticals, had designed several productions in the past decade (and would be holding an exhibition at the Leicester Gallery in September). Charles Ricketts, on whom, as on Bakst, Beardsley had been an influence, had made imaginative designs for plays by Yeats and Shaw; and it was he who had devised the production of *Fanny's First Play*, which was running at the Little Theatre, between the Strand and the Thames, and enjoying a big success there. But the stage work of these two artists had been on a small scale, on minute budgets, and for the delectation of a happy few. Ricketts, who, like Diaghilev, had known Oscar Wilde (only he had known him better), and, like Bakst, had just made the pilgrimage to Greece, was a painter, illustrator, printer, connoisseur and collector who would become one of the most fervent admirers of the Russian Ballet.[173]

At the end of the first London season Lady Ripon gave Diaghilev a black pearl stud. Its temporary disappearance in subsequent years would always be a sign of bad times.[174] Vaslav, Bronia and Karsavina also received presents.

Stravinsky, who had not been in London with the company, was working with Roerich on 'Le Sacre du printemps' in Russia.

In July 1911 [he wrote], after the first performances of 'Petrushka', I travelled to the Princess Tenichev's country estate near Smolensk, to meet with Nicolas Roerich and plan the scenario of 'Le Sacre du printemps'; Roerich knew the Princess well, and he was eager for me to see her collections of Russian ethnic art. I journeyed from Ustilug to Brest-Litovsk, where, however, I discovered that I would have to wait two days for the next train to Smolensk. I therefore bribed the conductor of a freight train to let me ride in a cattle-car, though I was all alone in it with a bull! The bull was leashed by a single not-very-reassuring rope, and as he glowered and slavered I began to barricade myself behind my one small suitcase. I must have looked an odd sight in Smolensk as I stepped from that *corrida* carrying my expensive (or, at least, not tramp-like) bag and brushing my clothes and hat, but I must also have looked relieved. The Princess Tenichev gave me a guest house attended by servants in handsome white uniforms with red belts and black boots. I set to work with Roerich, and in a few days the plan of action and the titles of the dances were composed. Roerich also sketched his famous Polovtsian-type backdrops while we were there, and designed costumes after real costumes in the Princess's collection. . .

I became conscious of thematic ideas for 'Le Sacre' immediately after returning to Ustilug, the themes being those of Les Augures printanières, the first dance I was to compose. Returning to Switzerland in the fall, I moved with the family to a *pension* in Clarens and continued to work. Almost the entire 'Sacre du printemps' was written in a tiny room of this house, in an eight-feet-by-eight closet, rather, whose only furniture was a small upright piano which I kept muted (I always work at a muted piano), a table, and two chairs. I composed from the Augures printanières to the end of the first part and then wrote the Prelude afterwards. My idea was that the Prelude should represent the awakening of nature, the scratching, gnawing, wiggling of birds and beasts. The dances of the second part were composed in the order in which they now appear, and composed very quickly, too, until the Danse sacrale, which I could play, but did not, at first, know how to write.[175]

By the beginning of the following year the titanic composition would be complete except for a few details.

Diaghilev, who did not dare to risk frightening off the English with Stravinsky's music, had a hunch that they would take to classical ballet. (In fact, he was to anticipate this appetite by thirty years.) During a second London season which he was planning for that autumn and winter he decided to present not only 'Giselle' but Petipa's 'Le Lac des Cygnes'. Because Karsavina was committed to the Mariinsky for certain performances she would begin the second London season in October, return to Petersburg for several weeks and be back for the end of the season in December: so her role of Giselle must be taken over in mid-season by Pavlova. 'Le Lac' would be danced by Matilda Kchessinskaya. All three ballerinas would be supported by Nijinsky.

Diaghilev had urgent business in Petersburg: he wanted to show his company in Russia. The only available theatre was the Narodny

Dom or People's Palace, a big modern building which was neither attractive nor fashionable: but there was nothing else to be had. On 29 September he telegraphed to Astruc offering him the running of the season of twelve or fifteen performances between 29 December and 1 February, [176] but Astruc could not see his way to take on the job. Nevertheless Diaghilev looked forward to showing Russia the new art to which, with the aid of himself as *accoucheur*, she had given birth.

Grigoriev wondered how Diaghilev would get the scenery and dresses for such a big production as 'Le Lac' – even though it was reduced to two acts: but Diaghilev arranged to buy the whole Moscow production of the ballet, which had been designed as early as 1901 by Golovine and Korovine.[177] Benois was to write, with a touch of jealousy, 'Serioja had decided to include this rather sentimental old-fashioned ballet in our repertoire chiefly to give M. F. Kchessinskaya an opportunity to shine; also because he had a genuine admiration for the sets and "Carpaccio" costumes . . . for the Moscow production.'[178]

Diaghilev left Petersburg on 7 October and was in London by the 10th.[179] There was some trouble over engaging Monteux to conduct the London season, also over securing Zambelli of the Paris Opéra as a possible replacement for Karsavina, if Pavlova let him down.[180] He was in Paris in the week beginning 14 October,[181] but was back – at the Savoy Hotel – with Nijinsky in time for the opening of his second London season at Covent Garden on 16 October.[182] There were a few changes in the company. Elsa Will had departed. Maria Piltz, who was tall and handsome, had been engaged in Warsaw. Vaslav's old school-friend Anatole Bourman had arrived from Russia.* And Max Frohman, whose sister had been with the company since the spring in Paris, came from Moscow. He was extremely good-looking with an oval face and classical features, and it was not long before Diaghilev 'had his eye on him'.[183]

During the first London season it had been noticed that the poor stage lighting had prevented the colours from making their full im-

---

*Bourman's story that he ran into Bronislava Nijinska at the Alexandrinsky Theatre and that she persuaded Diaghilev to engage him is, according to Mme Nijinska, an invention.

pact. 'Great shadows lay across the front of the stage,' wrote one observer, 'amid which the pure reds and greens and blues fought bravely to be articulate . . . while two appalling muddy proscenium wings stood like ogres devouring the colour values.'[184] For the second season a number of improvements were made at Covent Garden. The sides and top of the proscenium were framed with black cloth, the footlights were lowered and the stalls raised to improve sight-lines, and projecting lights were installed in the gallery which, by the use of exchangeable lenses, could be either floodlights or spotlights.[185] A hydraulic curtain was installed, and a new oak stage laid specially for the Ballet.[186]

On the first night Nijinsky and Karsavina danced 'Giselle' and 'Schéhérazade'. London had seen Karsavina in a version of the second act of 'Giselle' with the Koslov troupe at the Coliseum, but never Nijinsky's Albrecht, and the touching old ballet was now seen complete again in England for the first time in living memory.[187]

Diaghilev had miscalculated. London did not take readily to the classic. 'In the first act,' wrote *The Times*, 'M. Nijinsky's solo dance was the most conspicuous feature, and was the most warmly applauded. In the early part of the act the audience hardly seemed to know what to look for . . .'[188] Richard Capell of the *Daily Mail* considered 'Were the dancing anything less than perfect "Giselle" would, truth to tell, be a thought tedious . . . The Russians have for the first time done something incongruous. The dances in every other spectacle they have presented here have been part of a harmonious whole. In "Giselle" we see that even this wonderful troupe of dancers cannot always steer clear of that incongruity which rightly rendered the old ballet a laughing-stock.' He deemed Karsavina 'truly pathetic', admired Nijinsky's flying leaps and *entrechats*, the 'deep-dyed villain' of Bolm's rejected lover, and saw in Cecchetti, who played Giselle's mother, 'an actor of singular and sinister power', but thought the classic style involved motions 'which are acrobatic rather than purely graceful', while the music of Adam 'in an opera or in the concert-room would be wearisomely trivial'.[189] The critic of the *Sunday Times* thought Karsavina 'was delightfully gay and natural in the early scenes' and 'gave a poignant suggestion of a mind distraught in her mad dance'; and Nijinsky 'acted in the final scene with a rare tenderness of feeling'.[190] But, as the *Observer* put it, 'it is difficult to see how these fine dancers were attracted by their parts.' 'Giselle' 'is not a work of art, and can never become one'.[191] 'Schéhérazade' followed. Capell rebuked the audience for talking during the 'overture', though doubtless discussing the 'provocative' perspective of Serov's 'Persian miniature' curtain; but found in Fokine's drama 'not a gesture or motion . . . incongruous in the dramatic scheme. The splendid and cruel spectacle made an overwhelming effect. There is one moment – when a procession of scarlet-and-gold clad youths prance through the harem bearing high-piled dishes of fruit – which seems to sum up all the luscious poetry and pageantry of the Orient.'[192] 'In its wonderful expression of pent-up passion let loose in flood,' wrote the *Sunday Times*'s music critic, 'and in the unity of all its constituents . . . "Schéhérazade" is *sui generis*; its impression bites deeper into you each time you see it.'[193]

On the second night, 17 October, the hard-worked Karsavina and Nijinsky danced all three ballets, 'Le Pavillon', 'Carnaval' and 'Schéhérazade' – but so did both Bolm, playing René, Pierrot and the Shah, and Maestro Cecchetti, miming King Hydraot, Pantalon and the Chief Eunuch. Piltz made her début as one of Armida's confidantes, along with Nijinska, Schollar and Vassilievska, and danced Chiarina.

After appearing in five programmes Karsavina had to leave for Petersburg; and on Saturday, 28 October Pavlova danced once more with the Diaghilev Ballet. She did 'Giselle' with Nijinsky, but in 'Cléopâtre' played not her old part of the despairing, abandoned mistress, Ta-hor, which was taken by Sophie Feodorova, but that of Nijinsky's fellow Slave, the dancer with the scarf. The critic of *The Times* thought Pavlova's roles in 'Giselle' and 'Cléopâtre' 'gave her no proper scope' and was disappointed not to see her as Ta-hor. However, he qualified this with some discerning praise: 'The main thing about Pavlova is that, when she dances, the whole of her dances . . . She dances with her feet, her fingers, her neck (how much expression there is in the various inclinings of her head), her smile, her eyes, her dress . . . She is all dance and all drama at the same time. After the wildest caper she and Nijinsky are instantly poised in perfect balance ready to stand stock still or start off again in any direction.' He went on to wonder how two such expansive people as this Giselle and 'her old mother, Cecchetti' could live in such a very little cottage; and to decide that 'the Wilis ought to be either vampirical or else plaintive and pathetic'.[194] The critic of the *Daily Mail* thought Pavlova 'danced with consummate expressiveness' and that 'her acting in the scene of Giselle's death at the close of Act I was truly poignant.' At the same time the latter critic gave us a hint of how Nijinsky appeared as Loys-Albrecht: 'A young faun from some Slav Arcadia straying here among mortals, was her fantastic cavalier.'[195]

Pavlova continued to perform in these ballets, as well as 'Le Pavillon', 'Les Sylphides' and 'L'Oiseau d'or' (which was the Blue Bird *pas de deux*, called in 1909 'L'Oiseau de feu'); and she danced for the first time Columbine in 'Carnaval' on 6 November and danced it for the last time on the following day. (These two performances might be described as collectors' items!) Her last-ever appearance with the Diaghilev Ballet – or with Nijinsky – was on 11 November, when she danced 'Le Pavillon', 'Les Sylphides' and 'L'Oiseau d'or'.

'L'Oiseau d'or' – or 'The Golden Bird' as Lord Northcliffe's newspaper rendered it – was given in Korovine's setting of an old wooden Moscow palace which had been designed for the opera 'Russlan' and used for 'Le Festin'. In the critic's description of Nijinsky's costume of a 'Muscovite Prince in russet green and barbaric jewels' and Pavlova's 'lemon-coloured tutu and orange corsage, and an audacious crest of scarlet and yellow ostrich feathers, and so many jewels that the dancing was over before one had fully seen them',[196] it is possible to recognize the clothes Bakst designed for Nijinsky and Karsavina in the same dance in 1909.

Gordon Craig, who lived in Italy and was about to mount his production of *Hamlet* at the Moscow Arts Theatre, was temporarily in London and had taken a house at 7 Smith Square, Westminster. Here he set up his large model stage and invited actors and theatre managers to see demonstrations of his system of moving screens. Diaghilev and Nijinsky came with Count Harry Kessler, the German patron of the theatre, but Diaghilev continued talking while the demonstration was in progress, so Craig switched on the lights and refused to go on with the show.[197] This cannot, though, have been the only reason why Craig persisted in animosity towards the Russian Ballet until he saw Balanchine's 'Apollon Musagète' in Paris in 1928.

Lady Ripon took Vaslav down to John Sargent's studio in Tite Street, Chelsea, and the artist made a charcoal head of him in the turban and jewelled choker of 'Le Pavillon d'Armide', exaggerating the length of his neck and recording the curious impression he gave in this ballet (which we have seen Geoffrey Whitworth and others trying to describe) of this being a mysterious but sexless creature from another planet. The head is tilted arrogantly back, the eyes are half closed and the lips parted in Olympian mockery and provocation.

Kchessinskaya had arrived! She was not unaccompanied. She brought her son Vova, a Dr Milk 'for Vova fell ill on journeys', her faithful henchman Baron Gotch,* who used to do female impersonations, her ladysmaid, her dresser and the Grand Duke André Vladimirovitch. They stayed at the Savoy Hotel. She had left the keys of her luggage behind in Petersburg, but 'when they found out who I was the Customs officers very politely, and as a special favour, believed me about the contents of the luggage and allowed us to take them away.' Her jewels had travelled separately.

My diamonds and other precious stones were so valuable that they raised delicate problems. On the advice of Agathon Fabergé, the famous jeweller's son, who was also one of my great friends, I had entrusted the dispatch of my jewels to his firm, the London branch looking after them until my arrival. Two catalogues were made, and each piece of jewellery was numbered: I had only to know the numbers of the jewels I needed every evening, without giving further details. At the appointed hour an official of the firm, who was also a detective, brought them to me in my dressing-room and prevented any unauthorized person from entering; when the performance was over he took the jewels away again. I also had a number of pieces which I wore every day, and these the hotel manage-

*Who, according to Mlle Françoise Reiss, who had it from Kchessinskaya, along with Alexandrov introduced Nijinsky to Lvov. Reiss: *Nijinsky*, (p. 51).

ment had asked me to place in their safe at night. One night there was a big dinner-party at the hotel, and I asked Fabergé to send me my diadem, which was very valuable. The official brought it, but must have told the management of the Savoy, who informed me that as an added security measure plain-clothes police would dine at a neighbouring table; so I was not to be surprised at their presence. Two young Englishmen in tails did in fact follow me like my shadow the whole evening, but so skilfully and discreetly that nobody except the initiated could tell them from the Savoy's elegant clientèle.[198]

On Tuesday, 14 November, Kchessinskaya, 'Dancer of Honour to the Emperor of Russia', made her London début with Nijinsky in the *Grand pas de deux* from 'La Belle au bois dormant', called for the occasion 'Aurore et le Prince'. Diaghilev himself had chosen for her 'a very beautiful blue costume' and discussed the question of the jewels she was to wear. 'I had an undeniable success at the first per-formance,' the ballerina considered, 'but in spite of Diaghilev's claims it was not as great as I had hoped. It was more a *succès d'estime*, due to a famous artist, the prima ballerina of the Imperial Ballet.'[199] The *Daily Mail* described her skirt as mauve and silver, so no doubt the costume was a kind of heliotrope blue: perhaps the bodice was too covered in diamonds to be seen. Nijinsky wore a Russian costume in black and orange trimmed with ermine, which must have flattered her colour-scheme.[200]

At the end of the same programme Kchessinskaya danced Colum-bine in 'Carnaval', which we can imagine was one of the few roles in Fokine ballets which would suit her very well, for a high-spirited bubbling gaiety was her most attractive characteristic. Diaghilev's circle of friends, however, tended not to admire the famous ballerina and used to make fun of her. Bakst was in Lady Juliet Duff's box and so was the Grand Duke André; and the designer looked as if he was missing Karsavina. Kchessinskaya was, after all, forty. Lady Juliet prompted him to say something nice about her to the Grand Duke: but all Bakst could manage was the remark 'Montheigneur, tha robe a l'air bien fraîche'. ('Her dreth lookth very new, Thir.')[201]

That night and on three subsequent occasions the role of Zobeïda in 'Schéhérazade' was taken, in Karsavina's absence, by a mystery lady called Roshanara. She had been doing oriental solos with

Pavlova's troupe at the Palace Theatre,* and the *Daily Mail* judged her 'an accomplished actress, though she fails to express the intensity and pathos of Mme Karsavina'.[202] At these last three performances Kchessinskaya danced 'Le Pavillon d'Armide'. *The Times* compared three Armidas. 'Even with Mme Karsavina it was still a little dull. Mme Pavlova displayed her talent by making this somewhat lifeless affair a thing of real beauty and interest. Mme Kchessinska . . . displays a technical skill which is remarkable, but she has not the personal magnetism of her predecessor. She never makes one forget that she is a *prima ballerina*.'[203]

Since the beginning of their second London season the company had been looking forward happily to showing themselves and being acclaimed in Petersburg after Christmas, but there was a gap in their bookings at the end of the year; so Diaghilev crossed the hated Channel and on 17 November met Astruc in Paris to see what could be arranged.[204] Negotiations were set afoot with Amsterdam, Vienna and Budapest, and three performances were arranged for the Paris Opéra at the end of December. There was also the question of a special gala performance on New Year's Eve in aid of French aviation, and a Berlin season was booked for January.

Rehearsals now began for the first production of 'Le Lac des Cygnes' ever to be seen outside Russia except for one staged at Prague in the composer's lifetime.† This would be given on 30 November. Diaghilev had reduced the four-act ballet to two acts, retaining what he thought were the best passages of Petipa's and Ivanov's choreography. In his version the story could be summarized as follows.[205] Act I: the lake by night. The Prince comes hunting with his companions. They encounter the group of girls bewitched by the Evil Genius, who become swans by day; and the Prince falls in love

---

*In a programme for Pavlova's provincial tour of 1910 (Walford Hyden: *Pavlova*, p. 43) Roshanara is listed as a member of the Imperial Ballet. But the *Sketch* of 7 July 1911 states that she was born in Calcutta and 'picked up her dancing more or less by intuition, for she never received any lessons in the art.' She had danced in Indian palaces but never on the public stage until Oscar Ashe and Lily Brayton brought her to England to perform the oriental dances in 'Kismet' at the Garrick Theatre. Such a background would appeal to Diaghilev in his search for a successor to Rubinstein.

†And a condensed version which Schollar and George Kyasht (brother of Lydia Kyasht) had danced at the Hippodrome, London, in the previous year.

with their leader, the Swan Queen. When the Evil Genius, a gaunt monster, appears among the trees, the Prince tries to shoot him with his cross-bow, but is powerless against his magic. The dancing of the girls is interrupted by the dawn, and they become swans again and swim away. Act II, Scene 1: the castle ballroom. The Prince's mother is giving a party to celebrate her son's betrothal to a neighbouring Princess. After a waltz by eight couples, the Master of Ceremonies ushers in a sinister stranger who is the Evil Genius in disguise; and he is leading the Swan Queen. The Prince, greeting them, is startled to find himself gazing into the eyes of his beloved. But she is led away and he resumes his seat. Neither the Spanish dance, nor the Czardas or Mazurka, which follow, can draw the Prince out of his deep reverie. The Swan Queen reappears and fascinates the Prince anew with her solo. She goes off and the Prince in turn flings himself into an exultant dance, at the climax of which she reappears. When their *pas de deux* ends in an embrace, the court is scandalized, the Queen embarrassed, the fiancée indignant. The Evil Genius snatches the Swan Queen away and carries her off on his shoulder. The Prince, deaf to his mother's pleading, follows them through the crowd. Act II, Scene 2: the lake again. The Evil Genius drags on the Swan Queen, pursued by the Prince. But it is dawn once more, the beloved has vanished and a swan with a crown is seen gliding across the lake. The Prince falls dead.

The chief differences between the version of 'Le Lac des Cygnes' prepared by Diaghilev and that of Petersburg, which was written down by Sergueev and reproduced by him in England in the 1930s, were the omission of the first act and of all the swans' dances, with their elaborate and beautiful groups in the fourth; and the creation of a fiancée for the Prince instead of the Prospective Brides who, in the Sergueev version, are brought to court to compete for the Prince's favour, only to be snubbed for their pains.

Korovine's lake scene was a somewhat wishy-washy landscape, pinkish-mauve, with fir-trees in the foreground and bare hills beyond the lake. For the Prince's companions Golovine had created subtly elegant 'Carpaccio' costumes in velvet and suède, some with short capes. The court scene by Golovine was a medieval Russian palace, mostly golden, with a wide flat arch through which was seen an apse adorned with coats-of-arms. The costumes for the courtiers who stood around to watch the *divertissement* (mostly walkers-on), gowns and tunics in heavy brocade or high-waisted velvet dresses with long dagged sleeves in garnet or russet colours, were magnificent.*

'I firmly decided,' wrote Kchessinskaya, 'to insert my classical solo to music by Kadletz into the ballroom scene . . . counting thus on scoring a true success. Diaghilev agreed with me . . .'[206] Diaghilev had little option. Having bought the Moscow production of the ballet, with over a hundred costumes, simply to show off the famous lady in three performances, he could not risk her walking out on him. To play the violin solo which accompanied the *pas de deux* in the lake scene and for the inserted Kadletz piece Kchessinskaya engaged Mischa Elman, who was in London for some concerts at the Queen's Hall.† He was a pupil of Auer, who used to play the *adage* at the Mariinsky. The *adage* was rehearsed with Nijinsky in front of the company at Covent Garden, but the Kadletz solo, which Elman was 'very anxious' about, was prepared *in camera* at the Savoy Hotel with no other audience but the Grand Duke André.[207] In which suite overlooking the river, one wonders, did this rare event take place!

It is clear from press notices that, contrary to Diaghilev's hopes, the English were not bowled over by the old classical ballets: to present them at this moment when the public had rapturously accepted the new art-form of Fokine was bad timing. In the first act of 'Giselle', we have seen, they 'had hardly known what to look for'. After the passionate acting of 'Schéhérazade' the old sign language in which the Swan Queen told her story to the Prince seemed almost a betrayal. England was not yet 'ready' for the long Tchaikovsky ballets, which would become so alarmingly popular in the middle of the century – and would not even be 'ready' when Diaghilev nearly ruined his whole enterprise by putting on 'The Sleeping Beauty' for a run in 1921. At the end of his life he would write 'Tchaikovsky will

---

*Though they were made in 1901 they are mostly in good condition today.

†The story told by Haskell and repeated in her memoirs by Mme Kchessinskaya, that Elman dashed across London to play for her during the interval of his concert at the Albert Hall, is apocryphal.

never be understood in the west . . . I presented him too soon and in the wrong way.'[208] Could he but have known!

There are very few descriptions of Nijinsky in 'Le Lac des Cygnes' – which, anyway, not many people in England can ever have seen, since it was given only three times in 1911 and twice in 1912. Two accounts survive. A. E. Johnson, author of one of the only three pre-war books to be published in England on the Russian Ballet (Ellen Terry's essay and Geoffrey Whitworth's book on Nijinsky were the others), wrote as follows:

The ballet presents Nijinsky in the kind of role more definitely associated with Adolf Bolm, and it is interesting to note the emphasis which it lays upon the essential difference between the two artists. Bolm is an actor who can dance when occasion demands; Nijinsky, a dancer who seems almost ill at ease when constrained to limit his movements to the actor's pedestrian paces. One would prefer to see the part of the Prince taken by Bolm, and an excuse found (as in 'Le Pavillon d'Armide') for Nijinsky's appearance, in his true function as dancer, in the court scene.[209]

This is an interesting observation. We saw in the previous chapter how hard Nijinsky found it to think himself into the role of Albrecht in 'Giselle'. Princes, cavaliers, manly straightforward lovers – these were the stock heroes of the old ballets, and he was not at home in such conventional roles, in which all that was needed, besides firm support for the ballerina, were a proud bearing and good manners. To become a ghost, a puppet, a half-animal creature, a faun, a character from the Commedia dell' Arte or even a Greek boy in love with himself was much easier for him. He needed a mask.

One guesses that Nijinsky would have felt easier about the role of the Prince if he could have introduced an eerie, haunted element into his character (like Ernest Thesiger, say, in Barrie's play *Mary Rose*, produced in 1920 and conceivably partly inspired by 'Swan Lake'), but that it would be hard to reconcile this with a bounding solo in the ballroom scene is borne out by a description written nearly thirty years later:

The Prince, attended by his friend, entered the glade. Nijinsky wore doublet and hose; on his head was a cap decorated with a long feather. The costume was entirely black except for the hose, which were relieved with vertical pink stripes. Nijinsky's slanting eyes and pale make-up, made paler still in contrast with his dark clothes, gave him a mystic air, the appearance of a man haunted by a vision which he yearns to see again. As he walked near the lake, peering up at the tree-tops or gazing towards the placid water, he made you aware of the presence of mist by the contraction and dilation of his nostrils, and by an almost imperceptible groping movement of his hands, as though he were brushing the mist aside.

In the second scene, I remember his sitting at a table watching the dancers dancing in his honour. But his eyes stared beyond the dancers as though he saw some haunting vision, that cherished form of the phantom Swan Princess, visible to him alone.[210]

The music for Nijinsky's solo was taken by Diaghilev from 'Casse-noisette'.[211] It was the Sugar Plum Fairy's tinkling tune with the celesta; and it is hard to imagine the dance which could have been arranged to this essentially feminine music.* Nothing, indeed, could be more out of keeping with the fey character of the lovesick Prince which it seems Nijinsky was trying to create.

Kchessinskaya was satisfied. 'It was a real feast. Although it was the first time he had accompanied dancing, Mischa Elman did it as a great master, and if the adagio from the swans' scene delighted the public, it was in my classical solo that I secured the resounding triumph I had dreamed of.'[212] This, of course, was followed in the coda by her famous thirty-two *fouettés*. Elman played for her again on 5 December, but not at the last performance of the ballet on the 7th.

Whenever Kchessinskaya danced the stage was covered with enormous bouquets. According to her,

... Nijinsky did not like anybody but himself to receive ovations when he was dancing. His pride was hurt, and he indulged in a scene of jealousy with Diaghilev, threatening never again to dance with me; it was even said that in his fury he tore his costume. But Diaghilev was as skilled in avoiding scandal and smoothing down even the gravest incidents as he was in exciting them, and in the end everything was quickly arranged to everybody's satisfaction.[213]

Although we have evidence that Nijinsky did get rather spoilt as the

*I asked three choreographers at dinner one night if they could imagine a man's dance to this music: Ashton, Taras and Nureyev all replied that they couldn't. Yet the *Sunday Times* (3 December 1911) spoke of Nijinsky's 'characteristic display of his graceful leaps and bounds' to the Sugar Plum Fairy tune.

years went on, his was not a jealous nature and it seems improbable that any young man's jealousy of a famous and favoured ballerina twice his age could have been very violent. More likely Diaghilev, to enhance Kchessinskaya's confidence in the genuineness of her success, invented the story to please her. After all, what could be more flattering than that this triumphant young god should envy her?

And what was the first reaction of the press to this ballet which has now become as regular a feature of British theatrical life as used to be *Peter Pan*, *Charley's Aunt* or the Savoy operas? The famous Ivanov lake scene with the swans' dances bored them. 'Some of the early dances are exceedingly dull and . . . full of padding', thought the critic of *The Times*, while in the music 'there is nothing that quite touches the tiny masterpieces in the "Casse-noisette" ballet until we come to the second scene.'[214] 'The music is of little account . . . It would be unkind to bring this dancing into comparison with Mme Pavlova's magic "Swan" dance' (*Daily Mail*).[215] Kchessinskaya 'did some extraordinary feats of precisely calculated design with *finesse* and a mathematical exactness which suggested a pair of magic compasses controlled by a fantastic philosopher with a taste for humour as well as a sense of beauty' (*The Times*).[216] The national dances were 'fascinating' (*Daily Mail*).[217] 'Nijinsky . . . as usual, combined skilful and delicate mimicry with astonishingly beautiful dancing. In the second scene he made a radiant figure in cream, gold and orange, with peacock plumes waving in his hair' (*The Times*).[218]

Kchessinskaya, with infinite means at her disposal, was always extremely hospitable to her fellow dancers. One Sunday she, the Grand Duke and Diaghilev organized an outing for Nijinsky and the leading dancers to Windsor Castle. An extra coach was attached to the train at Paddington and there were buses to meet them at Windsor station: but when they arrived at the Castle they found, as so many Sunday visitors have done and still do today, that it was shut. It was, of course, raining, but they drove through the Park and observed the Guardsmen at the windows of Combermere Barracks.

She gave a supper for the dancers, with *blinis* and caviare, at the Savoy, and at this Reynaldo Hahn was present; and before she returned to Russia with her suite she had the whole company to luncheon.[219]

Karsavina had returned from Petersburg in time to dance on 28 November with Nijinsky in 'Les Sylphides'. This was the only evening that season that she and Kchessinskaya appeared on the same programme, and she was able to watch her friend dance her part of Columbine in 'Carnaval'.

On 7 December, Karsavina, Nijinsky and Diaghilev, who was just back from Paris,[220] had lunch with Lady Juliet Duff in Upper Brook Street and signed her birthday-book. Diaghilev, after his signature, wrote 'L'ami des dieux' – 'The friend of the gods'. Nijinsky, more modestly and flatteringly, wrote 'Le Spectre à la rose'.[221]

The London season ended on Saturday, 9 December, with Karsavina and Nijinsky dancing 'Carnaval', 'Les Sylphides', 'Le Spectre de la rose' and 'Schéhérazade' – some evening! The applause was so great after the *pas de deux* – the C Sharp minor Valse – in 'Les Sylphides' that Karsavina and Nijinsky repeated it. This was the first encore that had been given during the Ballet's two London seasons.[222] And who led the tumult of applause which produced it? No less an aesthete than the designer of *Fanny's First Play*. Charles Ricketts was to describe the raptures of that evening in a letter to a friend a few nights later: 'I am bitter and melancholy . . . the Russians have left us! . . . On that last night they danced as they dance only in Paradise – Karsavina destroyed utterly all the diamonds which the Tsar had given to the rival lady! (I forget her name), and Nijinsky never once touched the ground, but laughed at our sorrows and passions in mid-air. It was I who got the encore for Chopin's ironical and immortal valse.'[223]

The devoted Richard Capell of the *Daily Mail* reflected that 'the one sad aspect of the Russian season' which had 'revealed to us a new art – ballet-dancing resuscitated and transformed from a decrepit bore into an unimagined joy' was that 'at least a hundred thousand spectators too few have been granted a glimpse of this new beauty.' Of 'Schéhérazade' he wrote, 'There is compensation for some of the depressing conditions of modern life in the reflection that our epoch is alone, in the history of art, capable of producing just such a stage spectacle.'[224] Was he subconsciously echoing Oscar Wilde, who said that yellow satin was a consolation for all the miseries of life?

After the three first ballets there had been 'thunderous applause'[225] but on this electric evening the drama of 'Schéhérazade' almost overwhelmed the spectators. Of the final slaughter Ricketts wrote 'They put such beauty into their deaths that we became amorous of death and a Jew behind me cried out, "Oh! My God." The audience was cowed and applauded silently, one faded round of sound, whereupon that pimple of a French conductor struck up "God save the King", which of course suggests to the Britisher coats, hats, and trains to the suburbs.' Poor Monteux had probably realized that after the prolonged evening his orchestra were impatient to get away. Ricketts was not to be thwarted. 'I was white with rage and, the moment he ceased, I yelled "Karsavina" twice at the top of my voice; there was a pause, then came the roar from the gallery, like the boom of a distant gun, and the house applauded for twenty minutes.'[226] Richard Capell, who should have been on his way to Fleet Street to write his article, stayed to join in the applause and to time it. 'The audience from the front row of the stalls to the dark mass of enthusiasts standing at the back of the gallery applauded, cheered, and waved handkerchiefs for fully twenty minutes. The dancers received many tributes. Among them was a sheaf of flowers and a gold trinket in the form of a ballet-shoe with an inscription for Mme Karsavina, and a huge laurel wreath tied with the British colours for M. Nijinsky, which had been subscribed to by frequenters of the Covent Garden Gallery.'[227]

The next day, leaving Nijinsky behind with his mother and sister, Diaghilev was in Paris for two hours and signed his contract with the Opéra at the Crillon Hotel.[228] While in Paris he cabled to London to find out Pavlova's whereabouts.[229] He then caught the night train for Berlin, where he clinched the deal for his season in January.[230] By the 15th he was in Petersburg, cabling to Astruc to stop Karsavina, who was in Paris at the Hôtel Wagram, leaving for Russia on the following day.[231] He had to find a replacement for Schollar, who presumably wanted to go home for Christmas, and he engaged Nadine Baranovitch.[232] Because Karsavina was a doubtful starter he engaged Elsa Will, who had danced with him earlier in the year, to take the role of Columbine.[233]

Nijinsky in the wings after 'Le Spectre de la rose'. Caricature by Jean Cocteau. From left to right: Bakst, an unknown, Diaghilev, Misia Edwards, Vassili, Sert, Nijinsky.

Diaghilev left Russia in time to be back in Paris for the first performance at the Opéra on 24 December. This and the subsequent three were highly successful, and at one of them Karsavina and Nijinsky actually repeated the whole of 'Le Spectre de la rose',[234] and Karsavina made a speech. 'Diaghilev sent me before the curtain and I delivered my maiden speech to the effect that we would like to please our public by encoring, and that we entertained a hope that a charity collection about to begin would be generously supported.' This was no doubt the occasion which inspired Cocteau to make his caricature of Vaslav being fanned like a boxer in the corner of the ring by Vassili's towel, watched by a benign but anxious Diaghilev. Lady Ripon came over to Paris for the New Year and so did Lady Juliet Duff – the latter thus establishing a kind of record in having seen Vaslav dance 'Le Spectre' in three cities in the first nine months of its existence. The first year of Diaghilev's own company had been a glorious one. Lady Ripon had a party at the Ritz for her friends on New Year's Day, 1912, and Cocteau did a drawing for her of Nijinsky as the Rose, inscribing it: 'À madame la marquise de Ripon, un *dessinateur accidental*, respectueux et charmé'; and Vaslav signed it too.[235] Lady Ripon and her daughter were the first society ladies to follow Vaslav around.

CHAPTER FIVE

1912

January–August 1912

1912, which dawned for the Russians in Paris, was to be the year of the French composers, of Reynaldo Hahn, Debussy and Ravel; the year of Nijinsky's first choreography and the consequent departure of Fokine; the year of Thomas Nijinsky's death and Bronislava's marriage.

Stravinsky had driven himself to finish the composition – but not the orchestration – of 'Le Sacre' because he hoped that Diaghilev would produce it in the spring, but this was not to be.

At the end of January [he wrote], I went to Berlin, where the Ballet then was, to discuss the performance with him. I found him very upset about Nijinsky's health, but though he would talk about Nijinsky by the hour, all he ever said about 'Le Sacre' was that he could not mount it in 1912. Aware of my disappointment, he tried to console me by inviting me to accompany the Ballet to Budapest, London, and Venice, its next stops [presumably Vienna, Budapest and London]. I did journey with him to these cities, all three new to me then, and all three beloved ever since. The real reason I so easily accepted the postponement of 'Le Sacre', however, was that I had already begun to think about 'Les Noces'. At this Berlin meeting Diaghilev encouraged me to use a huge orchestra for 'Le Sacre', promising that the size of our Ballet orchestra would be greatly increased in the following season. I am not sure my orchestra would have been so large otherwise.[1]

Nijinsky was prone to influenza,[2] but one of the factors which was affecting his health was probably overwork. As well as 'Cléopâtre', 'Les Sylphides' and 'Carnaval' which Berlin had seen two years before, the company were dancing 'Schéhérazade', 'Prince Igor'

260

and 'Le Spectre' – which were extremely popular – 'Le Pavillon', 'Giselle' and 'Le Lac des Cygnes'. In the last work Karsavina was appearing for the first time, and Diaghilev was surprised and delighted by her virtuosity.[3]* She and Nijinsky danced in every ballet in the repertory except the Polovtsian dances from 'Prince Igor'.

'Le Dieu bleu' was to be staged at last, and in Berlin Fokine began to build up this complicated work, in which he incorporated bits of Siamese dancing remembered from the troupe which had visited Petersburg a few years back.

Diaghilev had signed with his German impresario to give fifty-three performances in Berlin during 1912,[4] which would be divided into two seasons, one at the beginning and one at the end of the year. His January stay in Berlin was to be followed by the eagerly awaited season at the Narodny Dom in Petersburg, which was due to begin – rather later than had been planned – on 24 February and to continue into March.[5] Early in January Diaghilev was cabling from the Hôtel Kaiserhof to Kchessinskaya in Petersburg about the possibility of once more obtaining the services of Piltz.[6] He was also in communication with two exotic dance recitalists, Napierkovska and Mata Hari (later notorious – and shot – as a spy), whom he wished to create the roles of the Goddess and the Girl in 'Le Dieu bleu', and who would be new to the Russian capital. It was a desperate attempt to repeat the sensation caused by Ida Rubinstein in his earlier exotic ballets. He settled with Mata Hari for seven performances at 3,000 francs plus her journey, but failed to secure Napierkovska's services for six weeks for 6,000 francs.[7] To strengthen his company he also signed a contract with Carlotta Zambelli of the Paris Opéra. She was to be paid 20,000 francs for seven performances, plus her journey, and to dance 'Giselle', 'Le Spectre', 'L'Oiseau de feu' and one other work to be agreed, presumably on the nights Karsavina was on duty at the Mariinsky.[8]

Meanwhile plans were afoot for the Russian Ballet to appear in August at the new resort of Deauville in Normandy, which its sponsor Cornuché was determined to turn into the most elegant and expensive millionaires' playground, with a summer season to rival the winter and spring seasons of Monte Carlo. The South American

---

*Grigoriev does not mention that Karsavina danced 'Le Lac des Cygnes' for Diaghilev.

Ciacchi,[9] whom Astruc with his passion for codes always referred to as Chimène – giving him for a reason now unfathomable the name of the heroine of Corneille's *Le Cid* – was hoping to whisk the Russians off over the ocean as soon as they had finished their stay in Deauville.[10] In the event this trip would be postponed by a year.

Then on 20 January the blow fell. Narodny Dom was burnt to the ground.[11]* All Diaghilev's efforts to find another theatre for his Russian season were in vain. He not only had to get out of his contracts with Zambelli and Mata Hari,[12] he had to find engagements for the company to fill in until their Monte Carlo season opened in April. Some frantic cabling took place. The German impresario went into action. By a miracle it proved possible to obtain at short notice three days in Dresden, eight performances spread over two weeks in Vienna and a week in Budapest. The situation was thus saved.

But Karsavina was due back in Russia, where she had been counting on fulfilling her obligations and taking part simultaneously in Diaghilev's season at Narodny Dom. She relates:

Quite casually Diaghilev said, 'You are not of course going to leave us, Tata; they have made stipulations for your appearance.' – 'My leave will be over, Sergei Pavlovich.' – 'Nonsense, it is carnival now, nobody in the Mariinsky but moustacheless youth, send a telegram asking for prolongation of leave.' Though it was only a matter of matinée performances for schools, my reiterated demands were refused. Through side channels Diaghilev addressed high circles in Petersburg. It was of no avail; Teliakovsky remained adamant. There was nothing for me but to go. Luckily for my shattered fortitude, Svetlov took my side. He followed us pretty often, a faithful friend. No fortitude unsupported could have stood against what I had to stand the last ten days in Berlin, miserable days spent chiefly in tears in the telephone cabin. Diaghilev called me up at short intervals; every evening he got hold of me 'to talk things over'. I realized that he risked forfeiting his contract should I fail him. His arguments exhausted, he bowed to the inevitable, and it was heart-breaking to see his dejected face. On the last night he sat in my dressing-room. My eyelids were swollen with continuous crying, and looked like two little red

*Not only does Grigoriev state that Diaghilev announced the burning of Narodny Dom to him on his arrival in Paris from London just before Christmas, nearly a month before it happened, but he describes the effect of this on Diaghilev's spirits – 'I had quite a shock, he appeared so dejected . . .' (p. 70.)

sausages, Diaghilev sucked the knob of his stick, a sign of depression, and then very wearily, on the off-chance, he said, 'Let us look up the ABC'. He then calculated that starting on the night after the Dresden performance and travelling by the North Express I could arrive at Petersburg early in the morning on the day of my matinée. It seemed a Heaven-sent solution.[13]

It was during their stay in Berlin[14] that Vaslav and Bronia heard from their mother that their father had died while on tour at Kharkov in the Ukraine. They could not be expected to grieve very deeply for the loss of one who was almost a stranger to them, but at least one member of the company was taken aback by Vaslav's lack of demonstrativeness. Bolm crossed the classroom to offer his condolences, and was shocked by the smile with which Nijinsky thanked him.[15] Diaghilev ordered the Bach music for the Mass Vaslav and Bronia had sung for the repose of their father's soul.[16]

Two other deaths that winter which touched the company more closely were those of Serov, over which Diaghilev wept for days,[17] and Rosaï, Nijinsky's classmate, who was carried off by pneumonia.

In almost every town they visited Nijinsky, Karsavina and Bolm found there were artists anxious to draw, paint or sculpt them. Ludwig Kainer made some vivid sketches in Berlin which he subsequently worked up into a series of lithographs.[18] In Dresden, where they performed in the pretty baroque Royal Theatre and went to see Raphael's Sistine Madonna,[19] they were sketched, then modelled by the celebrated Professor Paul Scheurich of the Meissen porcelain factory, and a set of characters from 'Carnaval', brilliant in their modern kind of rococo exaggeration and coloured in a very free variation on Bakst's original designs, were eventually put on the market.[20]

While in Dresden Diaghilev and Nijinsky paid one or two visits to Dalcroze's School of Eurythmics in the suburb of Hellerau.[21] They never ceased to explore opportunities of extending the language of the dance or of studying the possibilities of varying its relationship with music. And it was in Dresden that Grigoriev heard either from Bronislava or Vassilievska – the other girl who worked with Nijinsky – about the secret rehearsals which had been taking place of 'L'Après-midi d'un faune'.

The reason [he wrote] for the secrecy in which this activity had been shrouded was that, owing to Diaghilev's exclusive interest in Nijinsky, he and Fokine had been getting on less and less well, and that before allowing anyone to know about it Diaghilev wished to make sure that the experiment would succeed. I must confess that I was somewhat disquieted by this discovery, foreseeing what might happen when Fokine learnt of it. But I did not let this perturb me for long, since my leave from the Mariinsky would in any case expire in the autumn, when my service with Diaghilev's company would come to an end.[22]*

The train Diaghilev had discovered for Karsavina may have seemed a 'Heaven-sent solution', but, as she found out, he had not taken the elements into account.

I danced at Dresden, rushed off the stage immediately after the performance, threw a shawl over my ringlet wig, a coat over my Egyptian dress and arrived at the station just in time to catch the last train. I washed off my nut-brown complexion of an Egyptian maiden as best I could in my compartment. The express sped on till, on the second day, when a large snowdrift caused a delay, the train was six hours late. From the station I hurried to the theatre. My understudy had been got ready, but there still remained ten minutes of interval. When, in the costume of Sugar Plum Fairy, I came on the stage, the overture had finished and the curtain was going up. Teliakovsky thought it sporting of me.[23]

By persuasive cables Diaghilev was able to lure Kchessinskaya from Petersburg and Kyasht from London to divide Karsavina's roles in Vienna and Budapest.[24]

The Vienna season opened at the Hofoper on Monday, 19 February, and continued for two and a half weeks. The Russian Ballet was well received.[25] Not only was Igor Stravinsky there with Diaghilev to witness the company subjugate yet another capital, but Benois, reconciled once more, was summoned to discuss the project of a new Debussy ballet, 'Les Fêtes', which was to be prepared for Paris. Benois suggested that this should be designed in the sumptuous style of Veronese's decorations for Venetian

---

*Grigoriev either was not told or had forgotten when he wrote his book that 'L'Après-midi' had been more or less completed a year before this: and he was wrong in connecting it with Dalcroze, of whose principles it is the complete antithesis.

palaces. 'Les Fêtes' came to nothing, but, as we shall see, Diaghilev borrowed the 'Veronese' idea for another production – which is one more instance of his high-handed treatment of his old friend. Diaghilev was also talking to Count Harry Kessler and Hugo von Hofmannsthal, Richard Strauss's librettist, about the possibility of getting Strauss to write a ballet for which Nijinsky would arrange the choreography.

Hofmannsthal in Vienna to Strauss at Garmisch, 8.3.12
... will you, my dear Dr Strauss, allow yourself to be inspired by the vision of this central event in ancient tragedy and write a tragic symphony, a symphony of thirty to thirty-five, at the most forty minutes duration, *Orestes and the Furies?* Please read the enclosed sketch and tell me whether this is not an occasion for wonderful, sombre, grandiose music – a synthesis of your symphonies and your two tragic operas. And now imagine Orestes created by Nijinsky, the greatest miming genius on the modern stage (next to Duse, and as a mimer above Duse) – the whole thing, as a panto-mime, as a scene, as a tableau based on your music – just as a symphony of yours would be based on a vision, and growing out of it – think it over and please don't refuse me this ...

... A note is enclosed which contains an outline of the terms which Diaghilev, the artistic director of the Russian ballet, takes the liberty of submitting to you for the composition of these Furies.[26]

But Strauss did not like this idea.

Nijinsky became ill on 5 March at the end of the company's stay in Vienna; however, he travelled on with them to Budapest. Discussions with 'Chimène' kept Diaghilev an extra night or two in the Austrian capital.[27] In Budapest Grigoriev ran into trouble.

The theatre in which we were to perform, though it possessed a very large auditorium, had only a very small and inconvenient stage. The stage-manager in charge of our scenery declared that it could never be used in so small a space and that we could not give our performances. But all the tickets for the latter had meanwhile been sold; and the management would not hear of cancellation. I therefore made a thorough examination of the stage, and decided that with some adjustment the scenery could be used after all and the performances take place. But no sooner was this settled than Diaghilev's secretary, a Pole named Trubecki,* rushed in to

*This is the man whom Romola Nijinsky and Grigoriev call Drobetsky, but I am following his own spelling of his name in telegrams to Astruc.

say that Nijinsky was ill and could not dance – an even more serious blow. Nijinsky had never been known to be ill, and to replace him was practically impossible.* But while Trubecki, on my instructions, was informing Diaghilev by telephone . . . Nijinsky, in fact, felt much better the next morning, and by working all day on the scenery with the *régisseur* of the theatre I managed to adapt it satisfactorily to the small stage, and overcome the many technical difficulties involved, so that we were ready for the performance in the evening . . .

This *régisseur* was a plump middle-aged man with a limp. He wore a shapeless dressing-gown of indefinite hue and had obviously not shaved for days; but he possessed a will of iron. Within an hour of the performance he was still sitting on a high stool in the middle of the stage, being shaved by a barber, while giving last-minute orders to the stage-hands; and every now and then he would get down off the stool and stump about with soap-smeared cheeks; a sight to be seen. After the performance, now properly dressed, he limped up to me and placed a large envelope in my hands, informing me in French that it was a small mark of gratitude from the management of the theatre for the trouble I had taken to make the performance possible. When I politely but firmly declined this tribute, he was quite taken aback. It would have been interesting to discover what remuneration the management considered appropriate to my achievement.[28]

In Vienna Kchessinskaya had already danced her familiar roles in 'Le Lac des Cygnes' and 'Carnaval'. In Budapest she added to these the Girl in 'Le Spectre de la rose'.[29]

It appears, however, that Nijinsky did miss the opening performance.[30] Even so, the artistry of the Russians overwhelmed the audience of smart, rich, intelligent and critical Hungarians. One of these, a girl of twenty-one, wrote later:

On leaving the theatre, I learned that the brighest star of the company had not been able to appear this evening because of a slight indisposition. I determined to attend all their performances. The next evening found me again at the theatre. The programme was composed of 'Cléopâtre', Schumann's 'Carnaval', and 'Prince Igor'. Once again the audience was a brilliant one. Seeing 'Cléopâtre' a second time, I was better able to appreciate the perfection of Astafieva, Feodorova and Bolm's dancing.

*As we have seen, Nijinsky had been ill in Paris in 1909 and in Berlin a few weeks before.

The scenery used for Schumann's 'Carnaval' was a heavy velvet curtain of royal blue, painted with beautiful garlands of roses. The costumes were of the lovely Biedermeier period. The audience instantly grasped its light-hearted gaiety. Pierrot, Papillon and Pantalon flirted and swept across the stage, like so many little whirlwinds. Suddenly a slim, lithe, cat-like Harlequin took the stage. Although his face was hidden by a painted mask, the expression and beauty of his body made us all realize that we were in the presence of genius. An electric shock passed through the entire audi-ence. Intoxicated, entranced, gasping for breath, we followed this super-human being, the very spirit of Harlequin incarnate; mischievous, lovable. The power, the featherweight lightness, the steel-like strength, the sup-pleness of his movements, the incredible gift of rising and remaining in the air and descending in twice as slow a time as it took to rise – contrary to all laws of gravitation – the execution of the most difficult *pirouettes* and *tours en l'air* with an amazing nonchalance and apparently no effort whatever, proved that this extraordinary phenomenon was the very soul of the dance. With complete abandon the audience rose to its feet as one man, shouted, wept, showered the stage with flowers, gloves, fans, programmes, *pêle-mêle* in their wild enthusiasm. This magnificent vision was Nijinsky.[31]

Within a year and a half the enthusiastic writer of these lines, Romola de Pulszky, who had gone on the second night believing that the famous Nijinsky was a ballerina,[32] would be Nijinsky's wife. She at once set about getting to know some members of the company and was introduced to Bolm. 'Bolm', she thought, 'was not only a powerful dancer, but very sociable, extremely cultured, well-read and musical. He was the son of the concert master of the Imperial orchestra. We entertained him, showed him Budapest, and through him I made the acquaintance of many members of the company with whom he seemed to be very popular. I could find no opportunity to meet Nijinsky, nor was I certain whether or not I wished to know him. His genius swept me off my feet, but at the same time I had an uncanny feeling of apprehension. Bolm spoke of him in the highest terms, almost as a priest might speak of divinity.'[33]

The Russian Ballet's first season in Budapest was only a week long, at the beginning of March. If we are to believe Anatole Bourman, there was a scandal because Nijinsky took a call one night after 'Le Spectre de la rose' on his own, without Kchessinskaya, who had gone back to her dressing-room.[34] That he should have done so seems not improbable, besides being symptomatic of the changed status of the male dancer, Nijinsky's genius backed by Diaghilev's force of will having thrust him into extraordinary pre-eminence above the heads of all the ballerinas. Kchessinskaya probably did make a scene and threaten to leave at once for Russia. The absurd frequency with which Bourman, telling his story, turns out to have been on the spot whenever anything of importance happened to Nijinsky – his first meetings with Lvov and Diaghilev, his dismissal, a supposed attempt on his life – need not lead us to assume that he invented *everything* in his book. He took small incidents and, with the aid of his journalistic collaborator, blew them up into sensational dramas. Kchessinskaya does not mention the occurrence, merely recalling that Diaghilev let her miss the last performance of the season so that she could be home in Russia for her name day, 15 March (new style).[35] The Ballet travelled to Monte Carlo without her: but they had three weeks' rehearsal time before they opened and she would be back for the first night.

Diaghilev and Nijinsky returned to the Riviera Palace Hotel at Beausoleil,[36] with its uninterrupted view of the sea. Eleonora stayed down below with Bronia. Puccini had arrived to rehearse 'The Girl of the Golden West',[37] the Aga Khan was at the Hôtel de Paris,[38] and there were a number of distinguished English visitors. Lord Curzon was at the Grand Duke Michael's Villa Kazbeck,[39] Lord and Lady Dunsany at the Jerseys' Villa Capo di Monte,[40] the Joseph Chamberlain family were at the Villa Victoria[41] and Lady Ripon and Lady Juliet Duff, who had been absent from felicity for three whole months, joined their devoted friends at the Riviera Palace.[42]

Although Karsavina was still in Russia and the role of Thamar, in the work planned to Balakirev's symphonic poem of that name, was to be for her, Fokine began rehearsing the Caucasian dances which made up most of the ballet.[43] These involved most of the company and the trouble began when Nijinsky wanted some of the girls to rehearse 'L'Après-midi d'un faune'.[44] Much has been written about the many rehearsals needed to produce this short piece, but Bronislava Nijinska, on whom it had been worked out, is our evidence that it existed complete and finished a year before the other dancers began to learn it, and it was not Nijinsky's uncertainty or stupidity, as has so often been alleged, that entailed such unusually protracted work, but the total inability of the dancers to adjust their bodies to the new form of movement and their minds to the new relationship of dance to music.[45] Admittedly, Nijinsky was far better at demonstrating what they had to do than at analysing it in words.[46] Bronia herself was not to portray the principal Nymph, because Nijinsky wanted a taller woman with a distinctive profile;[47] and Lydia Nelidova was fetched from Moscow to dance the role. She was also to take that of the Goddess, which might have been Mata Hari's, in Fokine's 'Le Dieu bleu'. She had a big nose and was in fact quite plain – apart from being rather stupid and entirely out of sympathy with Nijinsky's experiments,[48] but she fulfilled his qualifications. The other six nymphs were to be Bronia, Tcherepanova, Khokhlova, Maicherska, Klementovicz and Kopyshinska. There was by now no more attempt to conceal from Fokine that Nijinsky's first choreography was taking shape, but rehearsals were still held *in camera*.[49] Fokine could not conceive of the company containing another choreographer besides himself. Even the staging of old ballets like 'Giselle' and 'Le Lac des cygnes' had seemed to him to mar the unity of his new repertory. We can imagine the long discussions with Vera that must have taken place.

Up till now it had been assumed that Fokine would do the choreography for 'Le Sacre du printemps'. Stravinsky wrote to his mother in April:

Stravinsky in Monte Carlo to Anna Stravinsky in Russia, ? 4.1912
... Diaghilev and Nijinsky are mad about my new child, 'Le Sacre du printemps'. The unpleasant part is that it will have to be done by Fokine whom I consider an exhausted artist, one who has travelled his road quickly and who writes himself out with each new work. 'Schéhérazade' was the high point of his achievement and, consequently, the beginning of his decline. I have seen all of his ballets since 'Schéhérazade' (i.e. 'Narcisse', 'Sadko', 'Le Spectre de la rose', 'Petrushka'), and all of them are immeasurably inferior and weaker. 'Schéhérazade' was an inspired spectacle ... New forms must be created, and the evil, the gifted, the greedy Fokine has not even dreamed of them. At the beginning of his

career he appeared to be extraordinarily progressive. But the more I knew of his work, the more I saw that in essence he was not new at all. There is no salvation in *habilité* (mere cleverness). Genius is needed not *habilité* . . .[50]

Soon after the arrival of Matilda Kchessinskaya, who was staying with the Grand Duke André at their villa behind Cannes, her small son fell ill, and her time was taken up nursing him.[51] This meant that she could not stay the night in Monte Carlo after a performance, but was obliged to motor home along the coast, a journey of at least an hour and a half. She did not, however, let Diaghilev down, and her boy gradually got better.

With all these worries, and in the absence of Karsavina, it was a comfort for Diaghilev and Nijinsky to have Lady Ripon and her daughter at the same hotel. They were of course present when the Ballet opened at the Théâtre du Casino on Monday, 8 April. The programme consisted of 'Carnaval', 'Le Spectre de la rose', 'Prince Igor' and 'Schéhérazade'.

While it is understandable that Fokine should resent his authority as sole choreographer and ballet-master of the company being challenged, it is easy to see how Nijinsky would have warmed to a little encouragement from his old master, whose chief interpreter, along with Karsavina, he had been from the start. But this was not to be. The touchy Fokine had brought off one revolution in the nature of dancing: he could not see that in the twentieth century life and art were speeding up. To the liberal in office further reforms seemed mere anarchy. So although in all docility Nijinsky would learn and rehearse his roles in Fokine's ballets, a spirit of resentful rivalry was at the back of both their minds. This, Diaghilev, with his infinite diplomatic skill, could have contrived to dispel: but there was a part of Diaghilev's character which was glad when his collaborators did not get on together. We have seen how he played Bakst and Benois off against each other (and this year the company's Artistic Director was Bakst).[52] He liked to be the only essential link between two colleagues. Divide and rule.[53]

What made Fokine's bad feeling even worse was the realization that his 'Daphnis', which he had long hoped would turn out to be his masterpiece, was taking second place to Nijinsky's Greek ballet

'L'Après-midi d'un faune'. 'Daphnis' meant a lot to him, not least because he considered himself its originator, having planned a scenario on the subject as early as 1904,[54] but Ravel had taken so long over the composition* that 'Narcisse', also on a Greek subject, had been thrust into last season's repertory in its place. Fokine maintained, not quite exactly, that Bakst had used his 'Daphnis' décor for 'Narcisse',[55] thus stealing the thunder of the postponed and more important work. It was at least true that there were statues of gods or nymphs as well as flocks of sheep in each.

Because of Fokine's work on 'Le Dieu bleu' and 'Thamar', and because of the rehearsal time and space needed for Nijinsky's ballet, 'Daphnis' was to be prepared last and given only in the final programme shortly before the end of the Paris season. After long and bitter discussions with Diaghilev, Fokine decided to resign as soon as it had been produced.[56] So Nijinsky would be, after all, the choreographer of 'Le Sacre du printemps'!

Now that Fokine had decided to leave the company in June [wrote Grigoriev], he grew more and more restless and nervy, till it became almost impossible to work with him. He suspected everyone who stood close to Diaghilev of being his enemy, including myself. I was obliged by my work to be constantly referring matters to Diaghilev; and my doing so never failed to arouse Fokine's wrath. He even began accusing me of treachery; and a particularly painful incident led to a final quarrel between us. Diaghilev insisted on Nijinsky having a great many rehearsals for 'L'Après-midi'; and however hard I tried to do so, it proved impossible to avoid refusing Fokine the services of the same dancers at the same time. He flew into a rage with me, and the quarrel that ensued was the end of our friendship, a close friendship of many years. I was so much upset that I asked Diaghilev to relieve me of my duties; and though he, of course, refused, he agreed to provide me with an assistant, in the person of N. Semenov, the *régisseur* from Moscow; and this relieved me of some of my responsibilities.[57]

Meanwhile, on 16 April, Diaghilev was led to believe that an article about the forthcoming Russian Season in Paris had appeared in *Le Figaro*, announcing that among other ballets *Fokine* would be

*The part of 'Daphnis et Chloë' now known as the First Suite was played at the Colonne Concert on 2 April.

creating 'L'Après-midi d'un faune'.* After all Diaghilev's passionate drive to promote Nijinsky's first ballet and ensure him the
maximum of publicity, this was too much. A storm broke out.

Diaghilev in Beausoleil to Astruc in Paris, 17.4.12
After seeing article front page *Figaro* announcing that Fokine was staging
L'Après-midi faune Nijinsky refuses point blank to take part our Paris
season. Have never seen him so determined or unreasonable. Have written
Bakst about replacing him. Situation more than dangerous in view of the
plans of certain people who were just waiting for this. There is no word
too bad for your lack of attention. Diaghilev.[58]

Diaghilev could certainly be extremely rude when he wanted, as
well as hysterical. The 'certain people' may have been Fokine or
Oscar Hammerstein in New York,[59] who had long been plotting to
lure Nijinsky away, or even Gunsbourg or another impresario. But
although Nijinsky may well have made a terrible scene, Diaghilev
must have known that he could calm him down in time, and the
telegram was probably as much inspired by Diaghilev's petulance
as Nijinsky's rage. Astruc was used to these insults. He adopted
appeasing tactics and telephoned Bakst, a fellow-sufferer from
Diaghilev's abuse, to help mollify the tyrant.[60]

Bakst in Paris to Diaghilev in Beausoleil, 19.4.12
All our Paris friends talk of nothing but the eagerly awaited L'Après-midi
d'un faune. Décor going well. Bakst.[61]

Meanwhile 'Petrushka' made its appearance in the repertory, and on
18 April Bronislava Nijinska danced Karsavina's role of the Ballerina.
This was to be followed on 2 May, now that Karsavina was back
from Russia for the season's last three performances only,[62] by
'L'Oiseau de feu'. Diaghilev planned to make a trip to Paris on 27
May in order to see one of a series of Trouhanova's recitals at
the Châtelet, which opened on the 22nd, but he postponed it.[63]
Like Rubinstein, *she* had stolen a march on Diaghilev and got in
before him with French composers. Rubinstein had staged Debussy's
'St Sébastien' in the previous year: now Trouhanova was dancing –
or rather posturing – to Ravel's 'Valses nobles et sentimentales'
(called 'Adélaide ou le langage des fleurs'), to d'Indy's 'Istar', to

*Untraceable. It appears to have been imaginary.

Dukas's 'La Péri', which Diaghilev had failed to put on in 1911, and to Florent Schmitt's 'La Tragédie de Salomé', which he would stage for Karsavina in the following year. Calvocoressi, writing in *Comoedia Illustré*, politely described the rotund Trouhanova as giving first place to the music.[64] Her movements were evidently not too distracting.

Eleonora Nijinsky had enjoyed her stay by the Mediterranean, hob-nobbing with the Cecchettis, whom she had known since the Maestro had been ballet master in Warsaw, and with Diaghilev's new secretary, the Pole Trubecki, the husband of Sophie Pflanz. One day Vaslav took her on a spending spree to Nice, from which she returned with a number of silk dresses and some unfashionable feathered hats, about which her son was tactful enough to make no comment. Nevertheless, remembering her own youthful tribulations she disapproved of Vaslav's life of perpetual touring, thinking he would be better off safely ensconced at the Mariinsky.[65]

The company left Monte Carlo for Paris on 6 May,[66]* and Besobrasov in a white suit waved them off. They were never to see him again, for he died of diabetes at Monte Carlo soon after.[67] He was the third of Diaghilev's committee of friends – those who had planned the first season of ballet and opera in 1909 – to cross the frontier, Botkine and Serov having preceded him.

But Svetlov was still helping Diaghilev to run the company, and a handsome volume of his essays was to be published that year simultaneously in Petersburg and Paris (the French translation being by Calvocoressi). Its cover by Lanceray and decorations by Bakst seem to make it a bridge between *Mir Iskustva* and 1912, its other splendid illustrations, many in colour, bearing witness to what a force the ballet had already become in the field of visual arts in the West. Besides designs for décors and costumes by Bakst, Benois, Roerich, Golovine, Korovine and portraits of these designers and of Diaghilev and Fokine by Serov, Koustodiev, or by each other, and photographs of the principal dancers, there were impressions of 'L'Oiseau de feu' and 'Schéhérazade' by R. Lelong, and drawings of Nijinsky by Dethomas and Paul Iribe. The book was called *Le Ballet contemporain.*

*Grigoriev says 5 May.

For the third time the Russians opened at the Châtelet (it was their fifth season of ballet, if you count the few performances at the Opéra in the winter of 1911, but Diaghilev announced it as the '*septième saison russe*').[68]

It is an extraordinary thing, looking at Astruc's full-page announcement in *Comoedia Illustré* of the season's sixteen performances, divided into four programmes with one new work in each, to realise that the only ballet in the repertory which could be called

Nijinsky and Gabriel Astruc. Caricature by Sem.

classical was 'Le Spectre de la rose'. So far had Fokine's reforms changed the aspect of Russian Ballet since 1909 that all the ballets given were works of local colour rather than virtuosity – Greek, Russian or Oriental. The only female dancer – with two tiny exceptions – who was called upon to stand *sur les pointes* during the Paris season was Karsavina in 'Le Spectre', 'L'Oiseau de feu' and 'Petrushka'. The two exceptions were Nijinska and Schollar as the two street dancers in the last ballet.

On the opening night on 13 May were given 'L'Oiseau de feu', 'Le Spectre de la rose', 'Prince Igor' and – at last – 'Le Dieu bleu'.

How little of what we think of as Cocteau's typical qualities – modernity of spirit and transfiguration of the everyday – can we find in his libretto for 'Le Dieu bleu'! Did he himself realize as he watched it that it already belonged to a period of the Russian Ballet which was past? (Within exactly five years 'Parade', his collaboration with Satie and Picasso, would be given at the same theatre.) And what a mistake it had been to commission Reynaldo Hahn, that most witty and poetical composer of songs which embodied the very spirit of the boulevards and drawing-rooms of Paris, to write an oriental drama, which would turn out at the best to be reminiscent of Massenet and Delibes! Fokine's invention and the performance of his principal dancers were bound to be hampered by the pseudo-Hindu-Siamese idiom. Bakst alone, at the height of his powers, had insouciantly produced an extraordinary décor and a crowd of costumes which exceeded the bounds even of his own high-stepping fantasy.

The sacred place in a cleft between two vast cliffs must have been chosen for the god's shrine because of its spring, which forms a pool in the centre. The steep cliff to the left is in shadow and, between it and the sun-baked orange mountain which fills the centre and right of the stage, the sky descends in a burning azure V, at the base of which can be spied a distant horned pagoda. The orange rock is carved with great heads which emerge from foliage, and springing out from it to the right in exaggerated perspective are two poles from which monstrous snakes hang in trailing loops. Exoticism, mystery and horror can go no further.

As for the costumes, predominantly white, but with varied appliqué patches – triangles, lozenges, zig-zags or peacocks' eyes – of slate blue, purple, magenta, yellow and green, there has never been such an elaboration of gold and pearl embroidery, such luxuriously twined or dizzily towering turbans, hung with such yards of pleated gauze or festooned with such swags of beads!

Entry of the Priests and Temple Attendants – a chromatic oriental music with odd scales. A Young Man (Max Frohman the beautiful) is to become a priest. Over his gorgeous costume* he

---

*As an example of the elaboration of the costumes of this ballet may be appended my description of Frohman's costume in the catalogue for the sale of part of the Diaghilev

wears the initiate's simple white robe. Ritual dances of musicians, the bearers of offerings and the Bayadères of the sacred lotus succeed each other; then as the Young Man stands in wrapt contemplation before the shrine, there breaks out the dance of the Yogis, who are spinning dervishes with long ropes attached to their hats and shoulders which appear to form discs in the air as they rotate.[69] Here, the rites are interrupted. A Girl (Karsavina) in winged headdress and spreading, stiffened skirts, breaks through the guard and flings herself at the feet of the neophyte. She is his mistress and pleads with him not to leave her and the world behind. *Tremolando* strings. The young man rebuffs her gently. Dance of supplication to naïve Adam-like music. Indifferent to the wrath of the priests, the Girl dances the story of their past happiness and as the Young Man watches her his mind is troubled and he begins to doubt his vocation. To a very conventional waltz tune the Girl's movements become faster and more seductive. Scandal! The Young Man is

---

Ballet wardrobe by Sotheby's on 17 July 1968. The costume now belongs to our Theatre Museum.

'The basic garment is a skirted tunic with elbow-length sleeves. The upper part of this is chrome yellow silk with an embroidered collar of mother-of-pearl shells and a large peacock's-eye-shaped brooch on the chest of magenta and silver enamel surrounded by white beads and with a ruby at the centre. The sleeves are flesh-coloured moiré silk with bands of silver braid and shell embroidery; the skirt split at the sides appears as a curved apron of flesh-coloured moiré silk bordered with silver braid and shells with a panel of magenta silk down the front with a rectangle of shell embroidery.

'The coat, worn over this, ends at the waist and has long slashed hanging oversleeves and a knee-length "collar" which hangs in a low loop in the front to reveal the magenta silk panel of the skirt in its opening. The jacket oversleeves are magenta silk repp embroidered with a stylized flower pattern in shells; the jacket terminating in a magenta silk belt with bands of silver braid; the sleeves end in elaborate cuffs of oyster silk and flesh-pink moiré silk with silver braid, silver embroidery and mother-of-pearl raspberries. The "collar" is of chrome-yellow silk edged with silver braid and a fringe of white beads, appliqué with a band of purple velvet encrusted with rings of pearls enclosing mother-of-pearl raspberries on a backing of silver lace.

'Ankle-length trousers in purple satin with cuffs of white silk embroidered with shells, dotted with gold sequins and appliqué with lozenges of chrome-yellow satin bound with gold braid, also hand-stencilled with smaller scarlet lozenges. Indian cap (similar to a Doge's cap) covered in flesh-pink moiré silk with bands of shells and embroidered with a pine pattern and arabesques of gold lace with pearls. In the front a silver crest holds a tassel of human hair and there are tassels of silver thread falling over each ear.

'The costume is marked with Frohman's name and the trousers with that of Bolm as well.'

seized and hustled away, while the High Priest (Feodorov) condemns the Girl to a terrible death. The crowd moves off in procession, leaving the Girl alone. By now it is night. Moonlight music. The Milky Way appears shining aloft. (This is a real Cocteau touch.) The Girl looks for a way out, and on opening a door, releases a stampede of monsters and fiends. (Reminiscence of 'L'Oiseau de feu'.) They circle round her to a trampling music. The Girl flings herself in supplication before the sacred lotus. Change of lighting, the monsters cower, the pool lights up. The Goddess (Nelidova) rises, seated, clad in all gold with a conical gold Siamese helmet, from the pool. She is only the herald of the Blue God's appearance. In a hieratic posture Nijinsky now looms out of the water. His flesh is blue and he wears a glittering crown.* The Goddess indicates to him the plight of the Girl. He proceeds to charm the monsters. In Cocteau's words:

His gestures are alternatively gentle and frantic. He leaps from one to the other with supple and terrible bounds. He glides amid their grovelling mass. Now he fascinates them with cabbalistic poses, now scares them with imperious threats. They try to drag him down, but he escapes them. He crouches as they jump, and flutters in the air when they crouch. At his command the tendrils of jungle plants entwine them and bind them, and the scent of blossom overpowers them.[70]

He shows the Goddess, smiling, what he has done; and she picks him a lotus stem to use as a flute. There follows the dance of Divine Enchantment. The flute solo reduces even the God himself to a state of heavenly intoxication. At the end of it he squats triumphant amid the becalmed and docile monsters.

Lights! Lights! Hubbub. Entry of apprehensive priests. At the

*Nijinsky's costume was sold by Sotheby's on 13 June 1967, and is now on display at the Royal Opera House, being destined for the Theatre Musem. Though equally elaborate it took less words to describe than Frohman's:

'Short-sleeved skirted Oriental costume in yellow watered silk, appliqué with a printed cotton in violet, blue and white, also with white satin; with bands of green velvet studded with green stones; embroidered in green, blue, yellow, black and gold; pink and white stones round the hem of the skirt. Yellow woollen pantaloons with an embroidered white border. Headdress of gold gauze on a wire base, with pearls and an embroidered rose.'

I pointed out to Mme Karsavina that the jewelled buckle over the navel was missing. 'And how it used to scratch me!' she said.

sight of the miracle they fall flat on their faces. The Goddess orders the priests to release the Girl. Terrified, they obey. 'A feeling of Buddhist bliss pervades the scene.'[71] The lovers are re-united. The Young Man tears off his white robe, The Girl describes her ordeal and dances for joy. The Goddess conjures up a vast golden staircase which stretches into the celestial blue, and as she stands in the heart of the lotus, blessing the young couple, the Blue God ascends to heaven.

'Le Dieu bleu' did not receive the acclaim reserved for Diaghilev's outstanding successes, but Brussel could find no fault with it in *Le Figaro*. The composer, a lover of Mozart, 'tended to write increasingly simply'. The designer's work was 'the zenith of decorative art'. Fokine's staging was as fine as that of 'L'Oiseau de feu', and the way he had arranged the God taming the monsters '– a thing which had so often been unsuccessfully attempted in the past – was a triumph of originality, invention and plastic beauty'. He praised Nijinska's possessed Bayadère; acclaimed Nelidova's personality (noting her Paris début); sang Karsavina's infinite variety, observing that her art was the expression of a refined soul; and thought Nijinsky had never appeared more marvellous than in this role, which was worthy of his talent.[72]

The second novelty of the season, performed on 20 May, was 'Thamar'. This gave an opportunity for playing a masterpiece of Russian music, drew from Bakst an extraordinary décor and provided Karsavina with one of her most powerful roles. The scene was the interior of a raftered tower, with crimson and purple bricks rising in giddy perspective. On piles of cushions, surrounded by her attendants, the nymphomaniac queen of Georgia awaited the passing travellers whom she would love and kill. As the music's oriental languors changed to pulsing Caucasian dances – in one of which the whirling men, who danced on the toes of their boots, flung their daggers into the floor – the drama merged with dance. The stranger prince, Bolm, arrived, was loved, spurred on to dance, stabbed and flung down a trap-door into the river below. The queen slumbered until the next horseman came in sight. The vampire beauty of Karsavina, with her white face and eyebrows drawn – at Diaghilev's suggestion – in one unbroken line,[73] has been recorded in a painting by Glyn Philpot.

278

Diaghilev spared no trouble or expense to create a favourable climate of opinion for Nijinsky's first ballet. Following the *répétition générale* – which, according to Fokine, was so silently received that after a hurried backstage conference Astruc appeared in front of the curtain to announce that since 'such a new exhibition could not be understood in a single viewing, the ballet would be repeated' – champagne and caviare were served to critics and supporters in the foyer. This had never happened before.[74]

Bakst's setting for 'L'Après-midi' was much less literal and representational a landscape than his designs for 'Narcisse' or 'Daphnis'. It was as if, in creating this mottled, speckled, stripy, deliquescent composition in greys, russets and greens, he had tried to find an equivalent for Debussy's music in terms of Nabi pattern and colour; and more than any other of his works the design resembles one of those overallish decorations of Vuillard in which a rug, a cat, wallpaper and people are treated impartially as elements of dappled colour. Andrew Marvell's lines come to mind –

> Annihilating all that's made
> To a green thought in a green shade.

All the action of the ballet took place in a narrow strip at the front of the stage, the dancers appearing to move in parallel grooves, so the backcloth was set forward 'on the line of the second wings'. The floorcloth was black as far back as the Faun's rostrum on the left, after that green. The lighting was planned to give an effect of flatness to the dancers.[75]

The characters in Bakst's costumes were not, however, camouflaged: they had to stand out to give the effect of their frieze. The nymphs wore long pleated tunics of white muslin stencilled in blue or rust-red with stripes, wavy lines, leaves or checkered borders. Their feet were bare and white with rouged toes, and on their heads they wore tight-fitting wigs of golden rope which fell in long strands. They wore very little make-up.[76] Bakst painted their eyes 'whitish-pink . . . like those of a pigeon'.[77] Nijinsky wore cream-coloured all-over tights painted round the shoulders, elbows, sides, buttocks and knees with dark brown splotches, like the skin of a calf. He had a small tail and a wisp of green vine leaves round his middle. He wore a woven cap of golden hair like the nymphs, but with two gold horns lying flat on either side so that they formed a kind of circlet.

His facial make-up utterly changed the apparent structure of his face. He underlined the obliquity of his eyes, and this brought out and gave a slumberous expression. His mouth, chiselled by nature, he made heavier. Here also was an infinite languor and a bestial line. His face, with its high cheekbones, lent itself admirably to the transformation. His ears he elongated with flesh-coloured wax and made them pointed like a horse's. He did not imitate; he merely brought out the impression of a clever animal who might almost be human.[78]

Only Nijinsky and Nelidova as the tall nymph wore gilded sandals.

The première of 'L'Après-midi d'un faune' was on Wednesday, 29 May.

Whether Debussy's eddies of sound represent a breeze through birch trees – but there were probably no birch trees in ancient Greece – or sunlight coming through leaves and dappling water, or the light on Monet's poplars, or the youthful euphoria of Renoir's 'Déjeuner des Canotiers', it is beyond question that they are in some sense about the languid ecstasy of a summer afternoon. But it is not an afternoon on the suburban Seine or in Normandy or in the birch forests of Russia, nor even in a wood near Athens, for as the music goes on we hear an exotic strain; and it seems that this must come from Cyprus, or from Crete with its dark pleasures, or from Daphne, the grove of love near Antioch, or from Thessaly, through which the train of Bacchus had to pass, bringing the dangerous gift of wine from Asia.

And in these glades Debussy has placed Mallarmé's Faun, whose pipe, represented by the flute, from the beginning helps to paint the sylvan scene; the following surges of sound conveying the pulse of desire and summer joy in the breast of this pagan creature, just as certain musical scurries suggest little encounters and furtive disappearances among the trees.

Nijinsky had never read Mallarmé's poem,[79] but his animated frieze adapted itself very comfortably to Debussy's score, finding apt cues for entries, confrontations, sudden incursions and panicky exits.

The ballet opens with a breathy warble on the flute and the curtain rises slowly to reveal the Faun seated on top of his bank, supporting himself on his left arm, right knee raised, head tilted back and pipe to lips; as the phrase is partly echoed by the horns against a background of harp *glissandi*, then repeated on the flute, the Faun goes through the action, in his angular, stylized way, of squeezing first one then another bunch of grapes over his face. On the third repeat of the flute phrase, three nymphs enter slowly from the left. They are followed by two more. In the course of a long tendrilly *arabesque* on two flutes with harp then string accompaniment a sixth nymph (Nijinska) walks rapidly to the centre of the stage, and takes up a pose. She then walks backwards and joins in behind the fourth and fifth nymphs as the seventh nymph (Nelidova) comes on. The first six nymphs remain motionless until the tall nymph has crossed the stage at a rapid mechanical walk, one arm across her breast, and undone a clasp on her shoulder to let fall her outer veils revealing a short golden undergarment. Then they move.

The Faun has not stirred during the entry of the first six nymphs. When the tall nymph came on he followed her with his eyes. Now a warbling clarinet sets his head moving and a *spiccato* cello brings him to his feet. Forming interesting patterns as they kneel or stand with elbows turned out from their sides and hands either pointing at their waists or above their heads, the nymphs move in and out as they bathe the tall nymph in the imaginary stream to a wistful tune on the oboe. Violins pick up the oboe phrase. A *crescendo* brings the Faun down his slope on to the same level as the others. The tempo quickens. The fourth and fifth nymphs bear off one veil to the right; and the first, second and third nymphs bear off the other veil to the left. The music subsides into a clarinet solo '*doux et expressif*'. The sixth nymph is stage centre with her back to the Faun. She turns her head and on seeing him raises her hands in surprise to shoulder level, fingers splayed, and scurries off right. The Faun and the seventh nymph are left motionless as the woodwind sing a new theme of quiet exultation. A sudden *crescendo* to the languorous triplet theme. The violins take the new tune over rippling harps. In sharp bursts the Faun courts the nymph with a jump and changes of direction.

His jump is to cross the imaginary stream flowing from the waterfall painted on the backcloth.[80] They link arms, elbows locking, but the tall nymph escapes the Faun, walking off on flat feet to the left. The music surges to *fortissimo* then down again as singly and in pairs the other nymphs return to fetch the remaining veil. A solo violin plays, accompanied by sustained horns and warbles on the flute and clarinet. The Faun tilts back his head and bares his teeth in stylized laughter; then picks up the veil and contemplates it ecstatically in profile. Over an *arpeggio* harp accompaniment the flute plays its original tune. An oboe clucks away. To a downward rush of *staccato* chords in the woodwind three nymphs glide on to mock the Faun. The oboe takes up the tune, and they scuttle off, hands raised. As the cor anglais trills and flutes flutter the sixth nymph (Nijinska) walks on from the right, confronts the Faun with a defiant stare, then goes off abashed. Again, the flutes repeat their tune supported by shimmering strings and the quiet ring of *cymbales antiques* (the playing of which has already been mimed by the nymphs brushing their hands together). The Faun, alone again, nods his head over the veil, and slowly bears it up to his ledge. A solo cello joins the flute over a slower harp figure. Wisps of familiar melodies float by. The Faun holds up the veil, nuzzles in it, then stretching it out on the ground, lowers himself on it, head tucked under, and finally, as muted horns and harp harmonies over a quiet flute chord conclude the choreographic poem, consummates his union with it, taut on the ground, by a convulsive jerk. We are to imagine that this is his first sexual experience.[81]

The audience sat through the new work in silence, but at the end there was a tremendous clamour made up of a mixture of cat-calls and applause. It was impossible to tell whether shouts of praise or abuse predominated.[82] In the past some ballets given by the company had been more coolly received than others – and we have seen that there had been a flight of dowagers during the first performance of 'Prince Igor' in London[83] – but none had ever been booed. Diaghilev was 'visibly put out'.[84] He went on stage. Nijinsky was convinced his work had been a failure. Then through the curtain they could hear that a body of supporters had got together to shout '*Bis!*'[85] (One suspects that this may have been the devoted Valentine Gross and her friends.) Partly to establish a victory, but also perhaps to make Nijinsky happy and to convince him that he had won more approval then disfavour, Diaghilev gave orders for the twelve-minute-long ballet to be repeated.[86]

Paris was of course familiar with the music of 'L'Après-midi d'un faune', and it was to be expected that some critics and members of the public would resent an attempt at dancing to the famous score. Diaghilev had been accused in the past of sacrilege to Chopin, Schumann and Rimsky-Korsakov: none of these had been *French*. That Nijinsky should have imposed so new a kind of dancing on the music – which some people might claim with justification was not dancing at all – while establishing at the same time a freer relationship between dance and music than had ever existed before, might well have made him and Diaghilev apprehensive of a hostile reaction. Even so, they were taken by surprise. There was something for everyone to dislike in the new work – musicians could allege blasphemy, balletomanes deformity and respectable people immorality – that is, if it did not happen to strike them that they were watching a spectacle of transcendent beauty – a kind of masterpiece. How much the adverse reaction of a section of the public was due to musical or choreographic objections and how much to the Faun's final movement of stylized orgasm, it is impossible to know: but it is clear that anyone who had not enjoyed the ballet as it unfolded would like it even less when he had seen it through to the end.

Historians disagree about the exact nature of Nijinsky's final erotic movement, which was anyway slightly modified after the first performance. Grigoriev makes clear that it was shown at the last rehearsals exactly as given at the première and that Diaghilev, warned that it was shocking, refused to have it changed.[87] Prince Peter Lieven's suggestion, based on information from Prince Argutinsky, that the movement was an accident on the first night caused by the breaking of one of a bunch of glass grapes* attached to Nijinsky's tights is certainly nonsense, since what the dancer wore across his private parts was a spray of leaves, not grapes, and they were not made of glass; but the story may have originated in some misleading

---

*His actual phrase in the English translation of L. Zarine is 'vine clusters', which I take to mean grapes.

improvisation of Diaghilev's.[88] In the choreography as handed down to us by Dame Marie Rambert, the Faun, lowering his body on to the veil, slides his arms down by his sides, then makes the last barely perceptible thrust with his pelvis. From the final photograph by Baron de Meyer in the excessively rare book *Le Prélude à l'Après-midi d'un faune*, published by Paul Iribe in 1914, it seems clear to me that on the first night Nijinsky slid his hands *under* his body in such a way as to suggest masturbation. An unpublished water-colour of Valentine Gross shows an even later stage of the movement and confirms this theory. Nijinsky's ultimate gesture could have been slightly out of keeping with the non-representational choreography of the ballet and the subsequent change was probably an improvement.

The press was in the main favourable and *Commedia*, the daily paper which covered all the theatrical events of Paris and the provinces, not only carried on its front page a three-column article by the editor, Gaston de Pawlowski, a keen supporter of the Ballets Russes, with photographs of the dancers, and profuse quotes from Mallarmé's poem with three of Manet's (rather weak) illustrations to it in line, but on page 2 another photograph of the full-stage scene, showing Bakst's décor and the eight dancers, and two more articles by Louis Vuillemin and Louis Schneider. All these were unanimous in praise.[89]

There was, however, one thundering exception to the dawn chorus of approval. Calmette, the powerful editor of *Le Figaro*, professed to be shocked. Instead of printing Brussel's article he denounced the ballet himself on the front page.

Calmette in *Le Figaro*, 30 May 1912:

UN FAUX PAS*

Our readers will not find in its usual place on the theatre page an account by my esteemed colleague Robert Brussel of the first performance of 'L'Après-midi d'un faune', a choreographic scene by Nijinsky, arranged and danced by that amazing artist.

I am not printing that account. This is not the place to assess the value of Debussy's music . . . [etc., etc.]

I am, however, certain that any of our readers who were present yesterday at the Châtelet will join with me in protesting against the extraordinary

*Literally, of course, 'a wrong step'.

exhibition which they had the audacity to serve up to us in the guise of a serious work, decked out with all the refinements of art and imagination.

Anyone who mentions the words 'art' and 'imagination' in the same breath as this production must be laughing at us. This is neither a pretty pastoral nor a work of profound meaning. We are shown a lecherous faun, whose movements are filthy and bestial in their eroticism, and whose gestures are as crude as they are indecent. That is all. And the over-explicit miming of this mis-shapen beast, loathsome when seen full on, but even more loathsome in profile,* was greeted with the booing it deserved.

Decent people† will never accept such animal realism.

M. Nijinsky, ill-suited to such a role, and little accustomed to such a reception, took his revenge a quarter of an hour later with an exquisite rendering of 'Le Spectre de la rose' so delightfully conceived by M. J.-L. Vaudoyer.

That is the sort of show to give the public, with its charm, good taste, *esprit français* . . . [etc., etc.][90]

Diaghilev rallied his forces for the counter-attack. On the same day he was able to have delivered to Calmette his reply with two en-closures, which the editor of *Le Figaro*, out of fairness or perhaps nothing loth to stir up controversy, published on the following day.

Calmette in *Le Figaro*, 31 May 1912:

I had not expected to return to the subject of the Châtelet affair, but among the hundreds of letters which my readers have been so flattering as to write to me, and which have given me so much pleasure, there has come one from M. de Diaghilev, the director of the Russian Ballet Season, which I print in the interest of impartiality.

Paris, 30 May 1912

Sir,

I cannot in a few lines defend a ballet which is the fruit of several years work and of much serious research.

It seems simple in view of the article by M. J.-E. Blanche published by you on Tuesday to submit to the public the opinion of the greatest artist of our day, M. Auguste Rodin, together with that of another master, M. Odilon Redon, who was so close a friend of Stéphane Mallarmé.

---

*Calmette seems to be trying to imply, in the manner of vulgar columnists with whom we are familiar in this country and who titillate while they denounce in the name of morality, that Nijinsky gave some ithyphallic exhibition.

†'Le vrai public' – a meaningless phrase.

First of all, here is the letter I have received from M. Odilon Redon:
Sir,

Joy is often coupled with sorrow. I could not help regretting, amid the delights of this evening's performance by your company, that my illustrious friend Stéphane Mallarmé was not with us. More than anyone, he would have appreciated this wonderful evocation of his thought ... I recall how Mallarmé was always bringing dance and music into his conversations. How happy he would have been to recognize, in that living frieze we have just been watching, his faun's very dream, and to see the creatures of his imagination wafted by Debussy's music and brought to life by Nijinsky's choreography and the passionate colour of Bakst ...

ODILON REDON

Here now is an important passage from the article published by M. Auguste Rodin [in *Le Matin*]:

Nijinsky has never been so remarkable as in his latest role. No more jumps – nothing but half-conscious animal gestures and poses. He lies down, leans on his elbow, walks with bent knees, draws himself up, advancing and retreating, sometimes slowly, sometimes with jerky angular movements. His eyes flicker, he stretches his arms, he opens his hands out flat, the fingers together, and as he turns away his head he continues to express his desire with a deliberate awkwardness that seems natural. Form and meaning are indissolubly wedded in his body, which is totally expressive of the mind within ... His beauty is that of antique frescoes and sculpture: he is the ideal model, whom one longs to draw and sculpt. When the curtain rises to reveal him reclining on the ground, one knee raised, the pipe at his lips, you would think him a statue; and nothing could be more striking than the impulse with which, at the climax, he lies face down on the secreted veil, kissing it and hugging it to him with passionate abandon ...

I wish that such a noble endeavour should be understood as a whole; and that, apart from its gala performance, the Théâtre du Châtelet would arrange others to which all our artists might come for inspiration and to communicate in beauty.

AUGUSTE RODIN

I call attention to these authoritative opinions and to our obstinate experiments, of which 'L'Après-midi d'un faune' is the culmination, in the belief that our works are worthy even of the respect of our enemies.

I have the honour to be, Sir, etc.,

SERGE DE DIAGHILEV

I do not want to argue with M. Serge de Diaghilev [Calmette goes on]: he is the impresario of the business and is bound to find the programme chosen by himself very good. This programme contains beautiful works, I admit, and we have only instanced one 'faux pas'. About this 'faux pas' there can be no argument . . .

After concluding that Redon's opinion could only be his own, since Mallarmé had gone where 'the dead rest in the bosom of the earth', Calmette turned the attack on Rodin, whom he accused of living at the tax-payers' expense in the old Hôtel Biron (which had been given to him as a studio for life) and exhibiting indecent drawings in the former chapel of the Sacré Cœur attached to it, surrounded by swooning lady-admirers and self-satisfied snobs. 'There is the real scandal,' he concluded, 'and it is for the government to put a stop to it!'[91]

The controversy was turning political; and the suspicious Parisians, who love to find fantastic explanations for everything that goes on, leapt to the conclusion that Calmette's real object of attack was the Franco-Russian Alliance. Nijinsky always remembered the excitement of the few days following the première of his first ballet.

Diaghilev's friends, and the balletomanes, as well as the personal admirers of the Russian Ballet, came to the Crillon at once. They had all discussed what would be the right thing to do by the time Nijinsky, who had taken a well-deserved rest, awoke from his late sleep and came in to Sergei Pavlovitch's rooms. All sides of the question were considered. Followers and newspapermen called up, came to the hotel, and tried to talk to Diaghilev or to see Nijinsky, to know what they thought of the Calmette attack. Members of the Russian Embassy came in and explained that they were convinced that Calmette had made his attack, merely using 'Faune' as a pretext, because in reality he wished to attack the policy of the French Foreign Office, Poincaré, and the Russian Ambassador, Isvolsky, who were trying to strengthen the Franco-Russian alliance and friendship. The *Figaro*, and the political group which the paper was representing, pursued a different attitude in politics, and, in attacking the Russian Ballet, the strongest propaganda for Russia in France, they attacked the *rapprochement* with this country itself.

News came that the prefect of police of the city of Paris had been requested to stop the next performance of 'Faune' as an obscene spectacle.

CITY AND ISLINGTON
SIXTH FORM COLLEG
283-309 GOSWELL ROAD
LONDON
EC1

TEL 020 7520 0652

The news went through Paris like a hurricane, and threw the whole city into a great state of excitement . . .

In an incredible agitation, rumours were repeated and grew. The *Gaulois* appeared with an article stating that an apology was due to the public. The anti-Faunists seemed to gain ground. What was to be done in this purely artistic matter which now rocked the whole public? . . . Nothing was definite by evening,* except that they learned that Calmette had obtained from the police an injunction to prevent the further performance of 'Faune'. Inquiries were immediately made, and Diaghilev was informed that the last gesture of Nijinsky, the Faun lying on the veil, was the one to which the police objected. Sergei Pavlovitch and the others devised a subterfuge. They requested Nijinsky to change this last movement, but he refused, saying that he could not see any offence to the public morals in his conception. Nevertheless, for one or two performances the end of the ballet was slightly modified, but without any appreciable difference.

A world-wide controversy exploded. A storm of protest was hurled at Calmette. The admirers of Rodin were up in arms. M. Pierre Mortier, editor of *Gil Blas*, sprang to the defence of Rodin, pointed out that the 'Faune' was the *leitmotiv* of his art, and declared that instead of expelling Rodin, as Calmette had suggested, the State should maintain him in the Hôtel Biron for life, and convert it into a Rodin Museum, providing he could leave his work to France; which was in fact done later.

A campaign to support Rodin was started, in which the names of the most eminent figures of France in the artistic, literary and political world were enlisted . . . Then the rest of the Paris public tried to get in to a performance of 'Faune,' to judge for themselves what this question was that had stirred the intellectual world to its depths. It was a real *tour de force*, however, to get in, as all the tickets for the Russian season had been sold weeks before, and every conceivable influence and political pull was called into play to obtain places at the Châtelet.

Then *Figaro* published a huge Forain caricature[92] showing Rodin, in his studio at the courtyard of the Hôtel Biron. A model enters with a dress over her arm:

'Oh, Master, where can I put my clothes when I pose?'

Rodin: 'Just there, in the chapel.'

This was carefully designed to arouse the clerical animosity of the Faubourg, and a fresh list of adherents swarmed to Rodin's side. The new

*The second performance of 'L'Après-midi d'un faune' was on 31 May; the third and fourth were on 1 and 3 June.

1a.   Theatre Street, Petersburg. In the background the rear of the Alexandrinsky
        Theatre. The entrance to the Ballet School is half-way down on the right.

1b.   The Mariinsky Theatre (Imperial Opera House), Petersburg.

2a.　　Alexandre Benois. Painting by Leon Bakst, 1898.

2b.　　Leon Bakst. Painting by B. Kustodiev, 1910.

2c.　　Anna Pavlova at home, *c*. 1905.

3.   Sergei Diaghilev and his nurse. Painting by Leon Bakst, 1905.

4a. Nijinsky in school uniform, *c.* 1900.

4b. Nijinsky in either 'La Source' or 'Don Giovanni'. Perhaps the first photograph of Nijinsky to be published in the West.

4c. Nijinsky in 'Eunice'.

4d. Nijinsky as a Torero in 'Pakhita'.

5.　　Tamara Karsavina and Michel Fokine in 'The Fisherman and the Pearl'.

6a-d. Nijinsky and Anna Pavlova in 'Le Pavillon d'Armide', first version.

7.   Nijinsky in 'Le Pavillon d'Armide'. Drawing by John S. Sargent, 1911.

8a.   Nijinsky at the time of his graduation from The Theatre School and first meeting with Diaghilev, 1908.

8b.
8c. } Nijinsky and Tamara Karsavina in 'Les Sylphides'.
8d.

9. Nijinsky in 'Giselle', Act II. Photograph by Bert.

10. Nijinsky in 'Schéhérazade'. Photograph by Baron de Meyer.

11.   Nijinsky in 'Schéhérazade'. Drawing by Valentine Gross.

12a.　Framed by the hats of the Botkine sisters, Pavel Koribut-Kubitovitch, Tamara Karsavina, Nijinsky, Igor Stravinsky, Alexandre Benois, Sergei Diaghilev, with Alexandra Vassilieva seated in the foreground, at Beausoleil. Photograph by Nicolas Besobrasov.

12b.　Nijinsky at Isola Bella. Photograph by Sergei Diaghilev.

13a.   Maurice Ravel, Nijinsky and Bronislava Nijinska on the balcony of Ravel's Paris
flat. Photograph by Igor Stravinsky.

13b.   Nijinsky and Ravel at the piano. Photograph by Igor Stravinsky.

14.   Tamara Karsavina and Nijinsky in 'Carnaval'. Watercolour drawing by Ludwig Kainer. Kainer made a lithograph based on it, one of a series published in Leipzig in 1913.

15a.   Nijinsky as the Faun. Etching by Una Troubridge. Done from the same series of sketches on the spot (Chenies Street rehearsal room, London) as the bust.

15b.   Nijinsky in practice clothes. Drawing by Maxime Dethomas.

15c.   Nijinsky on the Lido. Painting by Leon Bakst.

15d.   Nijinsky. Drawing by Oskar Kokoschka.

16, 17. Tamara Karsavina and Nijinsky in 'Le Spectre de la rose'. Details from on-stage photographs by Bert.

18.   Nijinsky in 'Petrushka'. Signed and inscribed photograph given by Nijinsky to Lady Ottoline Morrell in 1913.

19a, b. Tamara Karsavina and Nijinsky in
'Petrushka'. Drawings made in
the theatre by Valentine Gross.

20.   Nijinsky in 'Le Dieu bleu'. Photograph by Bert.

21a.　Nijinsky in 'Narcisse'.
Photograph by Balogh. One of the
only three photographs taken of
Nijinsky in this ballet.

21b.　Nijinsky in 'Les Orientales'.

22. Nijinsky in 'L'Après-midi d'un faune'. Photograph by Bert.

23a.   Nijinsky in 'L'Après-midi d'un faune'. Photograph by Baron de Meyer.

23b.   Nijinsky with Lydia Nelidova and five of the other six Nymphs in 'L'Après-midi d'un faune'. (The missing Nymph is Bronislava Nijinska.) Photograph by Baron de Meyer.

24a-f. Tamara Karsavina, Ludmilla Schollar and Nijinsky in 'Jeux'. Pastels by Valentine Gross.

25a-d. Tamara Karsavina, Ludmilla Schollar and Nijinsky in 'Jeux'. Photographs by Gerschel.

26a-c. Three male dancers in 'Le Sacre du printemps'.

26d.   Six female dancers in 'Le Sacre du printemps', (*left to right*) Julitska, Ramberg (Marie Rambert), Jejerska, Boni, Boniecka, Faithful. Plates 26a-d are four of the only five existing photographs of Nijinsky's 'Sacre'. The top ones were taken against the same wallpaper as the bottom one, but it has been touched out. The actual costumes, however, have survived, and most are in the collection of the Theatre Museum, London.

27a, b. Groups from 'Le Sacre du printemps', Act I (*above*) and Act II (*below*). Pastels by Valentine Gross.

28a.   Josefina Kovalevska, Miriam
Ramberg (Marie Rambert),
Ekaterina Oblokova and Sophie
Pflanz on the *Avon*.

28b.   Romola and Vaslav Nijinsky at the
Majestic Hotel, Buenos Aires,
after their wedding.

29a.   Romola and Vaslav Nijinsky in their car, New York, 1916.

29b.   Romola and Vaslav Nijinsky at Virginia Water, Surrey, 1949.

30a, b. Nijinsky in 'Till Eulenspiegel'.

30c. Lydia Sokolova as the Apple Woman in 'Till Eulenspiegel'. Photograph by White.

31a. Caricatures of 'Till Eulenspiegel' from the *New York Evening Post*, 1916.

31b. Nijinsky making up a dancer for 'Till Eulenspiegel'.

32. Nijinsky reading the score of 'Till Eulenspiegel'.

petition was signed by Isvolsky, the Russian Ambassador; the Senators Dubost, d'Estournelles de Constant, Gaston Menier; MM Edmond Haraucourt and Pierre de Nolhac, and Mmes Alphonse Daudet and Lucie Félix-Faure. Forain, the cartoonist, was attacked by the critic Louis Vauxcelles for his lack of aesthetic self-respect in demeaning himself to draw the caricature in the first place. A Government commission was asked to report, which was favoured both by the President of the Republic and the Prime Minister.

Le Figaro, Le Gaulois, La Liberté, the anti-Faunist papers, were silenced.

The police appeared and witnessed the performance, but they inclined before the public opinion and 'Faune' was not forbidden.[93]

Fokine had been shocked to the core when he had seen, at one of its final rehearsals, the erotic ending of Nijinsky's ballet. His comments on the choreography are interesting. First, he accused Nijinsky of plagiarism. He claimed that the latter had taken three things from his own production of the Venusberg scene in 'Tannhäuser', which Nijinsky had performed so excellently. These were: the Faun's walk 'with the palm of the fore hand extended flat and turned to the audience', the pointing out elbows, when the Faun held the veil, and the slow descent upon the veil at the end. In 'Tannhäuser', though, the dancer had lain down not on a scarf but on a woman.[94] Why the movement should be perfectly permissible with a human partner and 'pornographic filth'[95] – as Fokine called it – when performed on a scarf it is hard to see.

Fokine thought that the style of movement devised by Nijinsky was a deadend, and in this he was probably correct. But he did praise the young choreographer for having the courage to stand still at moments when the music *seemed* to demand agitated movement,* and concluded that 'In general, Nijinsky's archaic, angular choreography suits Debussy's music.'[96] This was quite a concession. My opinion is that although 'suits' is hardly the *mot juste*, implying as it does a quality of matching or paralleling, whereas the angular movement is in sharp contrast to the fluid music, the ballet's magic lies precisely in this contrast, which Nijinsky's instinct, plus a little bit of luck, had marvellously led him to discover.

The first performance of Fokine's 'Daphnis' was to be on 5 June, a week after that of 'L'Après-midi', and the season's fourth pro-

*Such as at the confrontation of the Faun and the principal nymph, no doubt.

gramme, of which it was a part, would be given, like the other three, four times. The season would finish on 10 June. A few days before the première of Nijinsky's ballet, Fokine had already completed the choreography of his new work, all but the final dance of rejoicing. Once 'L'Après-midi' had been got over, there was still a week before 'Daphnis', of which three days were *'relâche'*, that is, without performances.* There was plenty of time – or should have been – yet mysteries, scandals and an atmosphere of disaster preceded the first performance of this ballet whose score was destined to be one of the most famous symphonic compositions by a French composer in this century, and which would contain, besides, the last role created by Fokine for Nijinsky. By Fokine's own account there was so little time left that Diaghilev not only tried to cancel the Ravel ballet altogether, but wrote to Vera asking her to persuade Michel that it was impossible to get it on.

My Vera tried to 'influence me' but was not able to do it. Instead I exploded. 'Are you on Diaghilev's side?' I shouted. 'You want me to drop the work which was my first dream of the new ballet, so that I may never see on the stage what I have created, so that I should watch my ballets staged by another choreographer?'

She replied: 'But you have only three days left, and there still are more than twenty pages of music to choreograph. Besides, the rest needs rehearsing. Wouldn't it be better not to present the ballet rather than show it in an unfinished condition?'

No doubt it was my ballet that was dear to Vera and not the interests of Diaghilev. But at that moment I looked upon her as a Diaghilev advocate. The more she tried to persuade me to agree to a postponement, the more firm was my determination to present the ballet as scheduled. I thought: *Twenty pages of the finale and in a very unusual tempo – 5/4 time nearly continuously. Yes, Vera has a point there!*

I had no idea how I would find a way out of this predicament, but I knew that somehow I would.

'Leave me alone,' I said to my weeping wife, and, almost in tears myself, sat down in front of Ravel's score.

To postpone was impossible. There was no time to sit and wait for an inspiration. There was no time either to console my wife, whom I had offended unjustly.

*30 May, 2 and 4 June.

Soon it would be time to go to the rehearsal and to show the steps as fast as the dancers could learn.[97]

If Fokine was being exact, the conversation with his wife took place on 2 or 3 June.[98] If so, what had been happening during the last few days – apart from newspaper controversy, which should surely not have prevented the company working? And even if, for some reason, Fokine had only three days to complete the choreography of 'Daphnis', twenty pages of the score only represented a few minutes of time. For the man who had arranged 'Prince Igor' almost at one go, who had evolved certain groupings of 'Les Sylphides' just before the curtain went up, and who had sketched out 'Le Spectre de la rose' in a couple of rehearsals, this was child's play.

We can only suppose the trouble arose for one of the following reasons, or a combination of several of them. That Diaghilev, who for months had had doubts about the score for 'Daphnis' – though it was one of the greatest he ever commissioned – genuinely wished not to present it. That he wanted to save it for Nijinsky to arrange at a later date. That he was so elated by the interest 'L'Après-midi' had aroused that he hoped to substitute extra performances of that work. That he did not want to diminish the repercussions of Nijinsky's ballet by following up too soon with another work on a Greek subject which might give critics a chance to say 'Now, *that's* more like ancient Hellas!' That he did not want Nijinsky to have the fatigue of working on a new role so soon after 'L'Après-midi'. Or that he genuinely disliked Fokine's choreography or thought it was in too rough a state ever to be finished in time.

Whatever objections Diaghilev had, one would have thought the ambition to enrich the splendour of his Paris season by adding yet another new work – and one by a distinguished French composer – must have overcome them. It is hard to believe that his wish to cancel 'Daphnis' arose, as Fokine thought, from sheer malevolence. It would have been extremely awkward to announce a change of programme.

But Fokine's glorious talent was equal to the occasion.

When I arrived at the rehearsal I used a unique method of staging the end: I sent one bacchante across the stage, then another, then two at a time, then three together, then an entire group with interwoven arms reminiscent of Greek bas-reliefs. They rushed across the stage again, singly and in groups. I gave each a short but different combination of steps. Each dancer was required to learn only her own brief passage.

Having thus led everyone upstage from one wing to the other, I then had the remaining mass emerge from the downstage wing. The entire ensemble lurched together in a whirlpool of a general dance, and – the biggest part of the most difficult finale was ready! It only remained to stage a small passage for Daphnis and Chloë, a solo for Darkon, and the general end. It was clear that I would make it. I glanced at Diaghilev.

'Yes, you have managed it very quickly and well,' he said obviously disappointed.[99]

Karsavina recalled:

There were many stumbling-blocks in the music of 'Daphnis and Chloë'. In sonority suave, noble and clear as a crystal spring, it had some nasty pitfalls for the interpreter. There was a dance in it for me in which the bars followed a capricious cadence of ever-changing rhythm. Fokine was too maddened, working against time, to give me much attention; on the morning of the performance the last act was not yet brought to an end. Ravel and I at the back of the stage went through – 1 2 3 – 1 2 3 4 5 – 1 2, till finally I could dismiss mathematics and follow the pattern of the music.[100]

The première, however, had been postponed till the 8th. This meant that, since there was a performance on the 7th, there could not be the regular evening *générale*, and that as the 9th was a *relâche* and the season ended on the 10th, 'Daphnis' could only be given twice. Ravel was annoyed.[101]

The worst of the nightmare was to come. Diaghilev decreed that 'Daphnis' should be given not as the middle ballet, which was traditional for a *création*, but first, before 'Schéhérazade' and 'Thamar'. He also arranged that the performance should start half an hour earlier than usual.[102] *Fokine felt sure that he intended the new work to be performed to an empty house.

That was too much. I decided to stop at nothing. In the auditorium, after the last rehearsal, I had a violent argument with Diaghilev. I used

*This is difficult to believe. I have no way of checking whether Fokine's story is true.

words which described his relationship with Nijinsky in plain terms. I shouted that the ballet company was turning from a fine art into a perverted degeneracy . . . and so forth and so forth.

At the end I added that, if the ballet were presented as a curtain raiser, I would come up on the stage and address the spectators and explain the situation. Let Diaghilev have me dragged off stage by force. It would be a beautiful expression of gratitude for my staging an entire repertoire of ballets for him![103]

And so the day of the première of this doomed ballet, commissioned four years before, came at last: and nobody was happy.

When I arrived at the theatre [wrote Fokine] I noticed that the scenery of 'Schéhérazade' was set up. Diaghilev had surrendered. 'Daphnis' would go on second. I was right when I claimed that the audience would pay no attention to the earlier curtain time, as can be substantiated by the following unusual episode.

I was standing on stage dressed in my tails with my opera hat in hand. From nervous tension I kept on toying with the hat, continually opening and closing it. The orchestra was playing the overture to 'Schéhérazade'. It is a long overture, consisting of the entire first part of the orchestral score. Only at its end do the dancers assume their positions on stage. I was talking to someone also dressed in a non-oriental costume. The property men were arranging the pillows and bringing out the oriental water-pipes. Suddenly the curtain went up. By accident someone had given the order. I looked into the auditorium and slowly walked across the stage through the harem to tell a stage-hand to bring down the curtain. I walked slowly, because there was no one in the auditorium. And it was to such an auditorium that Diaghilev had wished me to present the première of my new ballet.[104]*

It seems likely that Diaghilev had made mischief by alleging that Fokine had said something unpleasant about Nijinsky. Anyway, after Fokine's abuse of Diaghilev, any semblance of civilities was out of the question. The company was divided into Fokine and Nijinsky factions, and it did not make matters easier that Fokine had not spoken to his old friend Grigoriev, the *régisseur*, since Monte Carlo.[105] Nijinsky, with his gentle nature, would have longed to part on good terms with the man who had created so many great roles for him,

---

*So, according to Fokine, there was no one in Paris in 1912 who wanted to see 'Schéhérazade' only two years after its creation. This seems incredible. Where was Valentine Gross?

but 'whispering tongues can poison truth . . . and youth is vain; And
to be wroth with one we love Doth work like madness in the brain.'

While the performance was on [wrote Fokine], in the wings, and during
the intermission behind the closed curtain, an uprising was brewing.
Some dancers, followers of Nijinsky, said that I had insulted their director
as well as the company; others, taking my side, spoke about the intrigues.
I heard the words, 'We will not allow . . .' As I later learned, I was to be
presented with flowers and a gift, since this was the last day of my many
years of work with the company. Part of the company was protesting the
presentation. It subsequently turned out that Nijinsky had forbidden the
dancers to present anything to me.*

There was also another altercation during the intermission. I was
surrounded by a group of angry, threatening dancers. Other dancers
formed a ring closer around me, ready to come to my defence if necessary.
At the critical moment, the overture ended and someone called out 'Curtain!' Both factions ran to the wings to take their places. I went to the first
wing to direct the performance.

The curtain rose; the first performance of 'Daphnis and Chloë' began
to a house filled to capacity. The ballet was performed perfectly, by the
dancers loyal to me and by my enemies, alike. A whole herd of sheep
walked across the stage. They were tended by shepherds and shepherdesses. The prayers, the offerings of flowers and wreaths as gifts to the
nymphs, apotheotic dances, pastoral peace, harmony – how far off this
was from the belligerent atmosphere and the narrowly averted riot just a
few seconds before on the very same stage![106]

One reason that Diaghilev may have been averse to 'Daphnis',
apart from the fact that Ravel would not allow the smallest cuts and
apart from the expense of the chorus, was that it was the first work
he had presented, excepting the old classical ballets and 'Le Pavillon
d'Armide' – which was anyway a link with the old kind of ballet –
that did not preserve the unities of time and place. The action did
not take place within the time it took to perform the ballet, nor even
within twenty-four hours, and the scene changed from a sacred
grove to a pirate's camp and back again. Diaghilev liked a ballet to
have as little story as possible,[107] preferring merely to create a mood

---

*I must again emphasize that I am merely quoting Fokine. Mme Romola Nijinsky
put a question-mark against this sentence in the typescript, as if to show her surprise
that anyone should believe Nijinsky acted so out of character.

or an atmosphere, and the story of 'Daphnis et Chloë', with its rival lovers, dance competition, onslaught of pirates, captivity of Chloë, her rescue by the god Pan and restoration to her beloved, must have seemed, in his eyes, too much like the old five-act ballets against which his whole movement in art was a reaction. Then, at least, in the old ballets the hero went hunting for his swan bride or broke through thickets of thorns to revive his sleeping beauty; while the feeble Daphnis lay in a swoon until the raped Chloë was returned to him by supernatural means. The middle scene was all Chloë's with the pirates, and so Karsavina would be sharing the honours un-equally with Nijinsky.

One must also bear in mind how much bigger a work Fokine's Greek pastoral was than Nijinsky's, employing not only the whole company and an orchestra of at least eighty but also a chorus; it was in three scenes and lasted nearly an hour. Nijinsky's 'Faune' had eight dancers in one set for twelve minutes.

The setting by Bakst for the sacred grove is a flat green hollow in a rocky landscape striped by the verticals of innumerable cypresses. Among the trees to the left rear the statues of three nymphs, archaic in style, but with arms improbably extended before them, the rocks beneath them being strewn with garlands and other votive offerings. On a distant hill looms a little golden shrine against a cloudy sky.*

The music begins gently, building up a sustained chord while the stage remains empty. The flute plays an urgent yearning tune while the offstage chorus warble a wordless rocking song – like a lullaby. A procession of young men and maidens crosses from right to left, bringing offerings to the nymphs. The theme of Daphnis is heard on the horn, sounding rather like one in Messager's 'Deux Pigeons'. The music swells to a *crescendo* as the young people kneel before the shrine, then dies away. There follows a stately Religious Dance on strings, taken up by woodwind. Daphnis (Nijinsky) has a wig of fair bobbed hair, bound by a fillet, and a plain white pleated kilt. His entry, with goats, is followed by that of Chloë (Karsavina) in flowered draperies. They go off together. The religious dance tune swells and ebbs. Daphnis and Chloë come on to Daphnis's tune and prostrate

*Above the sky is painted a border of tawny rocks and green bushes, which I have never been able to reconcile with any law of probability, perspective or design.

themselves before the nymphs. A passage for solo violin leads to a more vigorous dance in 7/4 time (beginning on the trumpet), in which Daphnis is involved by some of the girls, somewhat to Chloë's resentment; then, with strings playing alone, the girls drag in Chloë. She arouses the attentions of Darkon, the cowherd (Bolm), who tries to kiss her, but Daphnis pushes him away. Parting the lovers the villagers propose a dance contest between Daphnis and Darkon, the prize to be a kiss from Chloë. Fast timpani and grunting bassoons introduce Darkon's grotesque dance, which Fokine has planned in a more archaic and angular manner than the rounded movements of the other dancers. His outlandish performance, punctuated by trombone *glissandi*, is mocked and imitated by the onlookers, who finally burst out laughing (*staccato* woodwind chords). Daphnis now dances, his arms wound round a staff which rests on his shoulders, to warbling flutes in slow 6/8 time, with harp *glissandi* followed by pauses to allow for Nijinsky's leaps. Daphnis is awarded his kiss to a plaintive oboe solo (Chloë's tune), and Darkon is chased away. The 'Two Pigeons' tune accompanies the embrace of the lovers, and the singers are heard again, humming. Now, to a flutter in the clarinets, enters Lyceion (Marguerite Frohman), a fast married lady from the local town, and she dances to a tripping version of the same tune on the flute over harp accompaniment. She drops veils, which Daphnis picks up with rising excitement as the music gets faster. Then to the same clarinet figure she runs off provocatively. A figure on the cor anglais announces the invasion of a band of pirates, who are seen pursuing the girls. Chloë flings herself before the altar of the nymphs but is carried off by a group of pirates, to the sound of furious *arpeggios* in strings and woodwind. Daphnis finds a sandal she had dropped and curses the nymphs (*fortissimo* crashes by the full orchestra). He faints. Night is falling: the yearning tune from the beginning is heard on flute, muted horn, then clarinet against *tremolo* chords on muted strings. The Nymphs come to life and dance three hieratic solos. Wind machine and general atmospherics in the orchestra. The Nymphs raise Daphnis and lead him to the rock, invoking Pan to horn-calls. The god appears to a slow *crescendo* over a subterranean bourdon on bass horn, and Daphnis kneels before him as the curtain falls.

The keening wordless chorus accompanies the change of scene, and distant trumpet and horn calls announce the pirates' camp. To anyone who has seen Rubinstein's production of 'Hélène de Sparte', which preceded the Russian season at the Châtelet, the orange rocks of the second scene must seem rather familiar (and indeed they are not unlike the rocks of 'Le Dieu bleu'): but this is not a populated landscape with houses and temples, as in 'Hélène', but a bleak cove in which the tawny stones shoot up like gigantic teeth against a dull blue sky with dancing clouds, allowing a glimpse of the peacock-blue Aegean and the black and orange pirate ship moored in the secret bay. The Pirates' costumes are smocks, cloaks, blankets and ponchos of coarse material, stencilled with bold, barbaric patterns – spots, checks, stripes and zig-zags – in primary colours. The Pirates dance a wild measure to a marked rhythm in the basses, whirling woodwind scales and *staccato* trumpets; then, after a quieter passage with an oriental tune in the woodwind, the tempo quickens, the chorus pants passionately, there are three successive *crescendi* ending in crashes, and the men fall exhausted. Chloë is led in bound and Bryaxis, the Pirate Chief (Feodorov), orders her to dance. Harp *glissandi*, then sinister chords. Karsavina's solo is a dance of supplication to a pleading tune on the cor anglais, punctuated by attempts to escape, and coloured by heartbroken thoughts of Daphnis represented by his theme.

The music grows faster and Bryaxis roughly seizes Chloë and flings her over his shoulder (loud trumpet fanfare). Suddenly the scene grows dark and the music sinister, with strings *tremolando* and duets in the woodwind. A harp *glissando* heralds flashes of fire, and fantastic satyrs appear and dart among the Pirates, who are seized with panic and fight each other. An animated *staccato* phrase is tossed around among the trumpets and wood-wind, faster and louder. After a brief pause, a tam-tam crashes, the earth appears to gape open and the great shadow of Pan is seen; the Pirates flee, and Chloë is left alone with a crown on her head, while the harp and strings play *glissandi* against sustained chords.

In Scene III we are back to the sacred grove. With the stage empty except for the prostrate figure of Daphnis, there is heard Ravel's sublime dawn music. 'The murmur of brooklets formed by the dew which has run down the rocks'[108] is represented by *arabesques* on woodwind, harp and celesta. Birds sing and shepherds pass by with their sheep. As the orchestral texture thickens, the chorus joins in this wordless hymn to the rising sun. Shepherds find Daphnis and shepherdesses restore Chloë to him (Daphnis's tune on flute and strings). He understands from her crown that Pan has saved her. The Old Shepherd (Cecchetti) explains that the god has done this in memory of his love for Syrinx. Daphnis and Chloë mime the courtship of Syrinx by Pan, which is brought to a successful conclusion by a solo on the reed pipe, represented by a tender flute solo. The plighting of the lovers' troth is followed by a Bacchanale (reminiscences of 'Schéhérazade') with kicking and tambourines. Finally the music switches into a frantic 5/4 time and the ballet ends in protracted frenzy.

To quote Robert Brussel, who had nothing but praise for Ravel's masterpiece, Fokine's choreography and the artists' interpretation in his next morning's article (which Calmette did not suppress): 'The work was received with acclamation. M. Fokine and his interpreters were recalled several times: but M. Maurice Ravel modestly avoided the ovations.'[109]

Fokine thought his ballet was 'a tremendous success'.[110] If there was a lack of clarity in the choreography, as one critic would complain,[111] this could doubtless have been sorted out, given time. This may have been increased by the use of some Beotian costumes from 'Narcisse', not suited to the new stage groupings of 'Daphnis'.[112] When the ballet was revived two years later, this fault would be put right by some new designs of Bakst.[113]

Saying farewell to no one [wrote Fokine], I left the theatre and my latest ballet, certain that I would never work again for the Diaghilev company and probably would never again see my ballet. My wife and I went somewhere to have supper. We sat in silence, unable to eat.

Very late at night we returned home to the Hôtel des Deux Mondes on the Avenue de l'Opéra. At the entrance to the hotel we were met by a group of waiting dancers. In their arms they held flowers and a vase.

'We, Mikhail Mikhailovitch, were not allowed to bid you farewell on the stage and present you this. So we came here.'

I was deeply moved. I looked. Who were these daring people? I noticed a group of my former pupils who were just recently graduated from my class at the Imperial Theatre School, several dancers from Moscow, several from the St Petersburg troupe. None of the Poles. Serge Grigoriev, my former pal and protégé, whose whole life was intertwined with my ballets, was also not among them. Thus, late at night in front of the hotel entrance, farewells were exchanged between me and a small group of dancers brave and loyal to me, dancers from the company to which for many years I had given an entire repertoire, and with whom I had worked in a friendly, enthusiastic and at times, joyful manner to create the new Russian ballet. And so I left Diaghilev.[114]

Whether this sad parting took place after the first performance of 'Daphnis' or after the second, two nights later, is not clear. It may have been a small consolation to the great choreographer to watch Ida Rubinstein in the dance he arranged for her 'Salomé', which succeeded the Russian Ballet at the Châtelet. The company left for London without him.* After these first two performances of Fokine's ballet, Nijinsky was never to dance Daphnis again.†

The repertory for London was to be more classical than the Paris one. 'Carnaval', 'Les Sylphides', 'Le Spectre de la rose', 'Le Pavillon d'Armide' and eventually 'Le Lac des Cygnes' were to be included; and besides 'Prince Igor' and 'Schéhérazade' there would be the novelties of the two-year-old 'L'Oiseau de feu', the one-year-old 'Narcisse' and the new 'Thamar'. Bolm would be the first Prince Ivan seen in England, and Piltz would take Fokina's parts of the Beautiful Tsarevna and of Chiarina. Karsavina would be seen for the first time as Queen of the Swans. Pierre Vladimirov, one year's class junior to Nijinsky at the Imperial School, had joined the company in Paris and was to alternate with Nijinsky in 'Les Sylphides'. A first-rate classical dancer with a noble presence, he was a dancer of the old school, and – apart from princely roles in the old repertory – there was no other role of Vaslav's he was capable of replacing him in,[115] just as Bolm was only able adequately to understudy him in 'Schéhérazade'.

After the dramas of Paris, there was nothing really to worry about except whether the English would like 'Thamar' and 'Narcisse' or be shocked by their first hearing of Stravinsky's music in 'L'Oiseau

*Grigoriev is evidently mistaken in stating that Fokine left in the middle of the London season.
†I believe no one has commented before on this rather odd fact.

de feu'. In Paris Vaslav felt he was on trial: dancing in London, where his audience was always loyal and appreciative, he found comparatively relaxing.[116]

The season was eagerly awaited by the Russians' English friends and by many others who had to be content with admiring them from afar. Charles Ricketts wrote to the poet Gordon Bottomley:

We both [meaning himself and Charles Shannon] look forward to the Russian dancers, they have been something like a passion during the past seasons; with them the lambent sense of beauty and desire for perfection is so great, that one watches the dancing of Schumann's 'Carnaval', in crinolines and toppers, before a purple curtain, with authentic tears in one's eyes, and with crumpled gloves which are split to ribbons at the end. The Chopin Valse, Opus 64, no. 2, passes into an indescribable twilight world of beauty and tender irony; the rapid portions are played *à la sordina*, to soundless dancing so rapid that it seems disembodied. All that the antique world thought and said about the famous male dancers who were seduced by Empresses, etc., is quite true. Nijinsky outclasses in passion, beauty, and magnetism all that Karsavina can do, and she is a Muse, or several Muses in one, the Muse of Melancholy and of Caprice, capable of expressing tragedy and even voluptuous innocence; the wildness of chastity and the sting of desire; she is the perfect instrument upon which all emotion can be rendered. Nijinsky is a living flame, the son of Hermes, or Logi perhaps. One cannot imagine his mother – probably some ancient ballerina was answerable; but I prefer to believe in some sort of spontaneous nativity, at the most a passing cloud may have attracted some fantastic and capricious god.[117]

When, at Covent Garden, on Wednesday, 12 June, according to the critic of *The Times*, the curtain went up . . .

and disclosed the familiar view of two rococo sofas (red and cream this year instead of red and blue), the sole note of colour against the green of the curtains (green this year instead of purple), a thrill of joy went through the house. The world was once more a world of fantasy, where Pierrot might sob and wave distracted sleeves and Harlequin spin lightning *pirouettes* before the laughing eyes of Columbine, but where neither tears nor laughter were allowed to scratch more than the surface of our emotion . . .[118]

The faithful and appreciative Richard Capell of the *Daily Mail* let out a paean. 'The Russians are back at Covent Garden. This means that the Londoner of 1912 is offered a series of pantomimic and choreographic spectacles of a complete and luxurious beauty such as was beyond the command of Nero and Sardanapalus. These three great arts of music, of painting and of dance contribute to these incomparable shows – all three in their most daring and sumptuous expression . . .' He admitted to having seen 'Carnaval', in Paris and London, about thirty times, and to having been as fascinated on the previous night as ever. He complained of the new green curtain which quarrelled with Estrella's and Chiarina's blue skirts. He wrote of Karsavina in 'Thamar', 'lithe in miraculous lilac clothes and of a dreadful pallor – the victim of her own cruel voluptuousness'.[119]

After a postponement, 'L'Oiseau de feu' was first given on Tuesday, 18 June. Even the *Morning Post*, which had been stuffy in the past about the Russians, being, in a Tory way, suspicious and resentful of anything new, seemed amazed. 'One of the most remarkable things of its kind seen in England . . . perfect harmony . . . intensely pleasing . . . complete novelty . . . instrumental colouring as remarkable as that of the costumes . . .'[120]

The Times thought the music 'extremely vivid and highly coloured, and although not very interesting melodically, [it] is bound together by firm, incisive, sharply defined rhythms . . . Mme Karsavina surpassed herself in agility, grace and sensuous beauty of movement, although she had already taken part in two other ballets.'[121] The *Daily Express*, which had been incredulous a few days earlier that Thomas Beecham was actually going to conduct in person,[122] reported his saying Stravinsky's music was 'the most difficult he has hitherto wrestled with, not excluding "Elektra."!'[123] In the *Daily Mail* Richard Capell wrote that it was 'an enchantment and a jewel of fantasy'. While acclaiming its score as perhaps its chief attraction – 'a little masterpiece of brilliancy, wit and eccentric grace . . . something new in music', he found Karsavina 'incomparable'. 'When the Bird of Fire is captured by the bold Prince . . . there is a fluttering of white arms, a quiver of feathery crest and violated plumage, a bird's beating heart, a wild, would-be escape, with a woman's frightened refusal of caresses.'[124]

That evening brought a newcomer to the audience, a twenty-one-year-old red-head, trained as a research chemist, but with a passion for toy theatres and the theatre. He had already been converted to Russian Ballet by the visions of Karsavina, Pavlova and Mordkine in music-hall, and had in consequence decided to open a small bookshop at 75 Charing Cross Road. His first sight of the Diaghilev Ballet changed his life. His name was Cyril Beaumont.*

He wrote:

'Thamar' was a fine dramatic conception and the opening notes of Balakirev's score set the mood for the ballet. The air seemed suddenly heavy and the darkened theatre charged with foreboding. A half-wistful, half-tragic melody rose above a throbbing undercurrent of sound, a suggestion of a swiftly moving river coursing and churning over a rocky mountainside. Then the curtain rose slowly to reveal Bakst's setting – a great room with walls coloured mauve and purple, and slanting ceiling painted green. The lighting was subdued, save for the dull glow of a dying fire. The scene was dominated by a huge divan set against the far wall, and upon the divan reposed Karsavina in the role of Thamar, Queen of Georgia. Stretched at full length, she occasionally stirred uneasily in her sleep. A waiting-woman sat near her couch, other retainers stood in the shadows, their attitudes strained and watchful.

I can still recall the mood established by that scene. It was just as though some terrible menace had been halted, leaving behind a perceptible tenseness which suggested that the threat was about to be renewed. There was only that silent group of watchers; all was still save for the restless stirring of the sleeping woman. But the curiosity aroused was intense. What was about to happen?

Karsavina was a splendid Thamar, a dangerous, feline creature, as she stretched languorously on her couch, her pale brooding features made sinister by the dark eyebrows which crossed her forehead in a single line.[125]

Of Nijinsky in 'Les Sylphides' Beaumont wrote years later:

Until that evening I had regarded Mordkine, a splendidly virile dancer with a figure that would have delighted Pheidias, as the supreme male dancer. Henceforth, Nijinsky was and still remains my ideal, and nothing I have seen during twenty-eight years of ballet-going has changed my opinion . . . His *pas seul* in 'Les Sylphides' was outstanding . . . In essence

*Mr Beaumont's description of 'Le Lac des Cygnes' was introduced into the last chapter.

its special quality was its suggestion of melody. When you watch a great violinist playing, it is not the violin alone that is a sounding-board for the precious tunes called forth by the bow gliding over the taut strings, the violinist's very body seems to respond to his music. Nijinsky's dancing in this ballet was imbued with the same quality. He danced not only with his limbs, but with his whole body, and the sequence of movements composing the dance flowed one into the other, now swift, now slow, now retarded, now increasing in speed, with a suggestion of spontaneity that had all the quality of melody. So I recall memories such as the billowing of his white silk sleeve as he curved and extended his arm; then that lovely movement when, on extending his leg in a *développé*, his hand swept gracefully from thigh to shin in a movement so graceful and so delicate as to suggest a caress; and then again the end of a *pirouette*, when he came smoothly and with increasing slowness to rest, like a spun wheel which had exhausted its momentum. I always think of Karsavina and Nijinsky as the perfect partners . . . But these two were not mortals. It was the poet's shade visiting, in company with the spirit of his dead mistress, the moonlit grove which had once inspired his imperishable odes.[126]

But the new enthusiast, who as a historian of ballet was destined to add more books to its literature than any man ever before, did not lose his critical faculties. Admiring as he violently did the music of Stravinsky for 'L'Oiseau de feu', the atmosphere of magic and the encounter of Karsavina and Bolm, he still thought that 'from the moment the gates closed upon the princesses, the ballet became stagy. The demons and Kastchei (even though played by Cecchetti), the dance with which the Bird of Fire forced the demons and their leader to dance until they fall exhausted, were all too obvious. It was good theatre, but the ballet was no longer a choreographic poem.'[127]

Nijinsky had met briefly in Paris Lady Ottoline Morrell, who was to become a warm and perceptive friend. With her passionate idealism, love of people, interest in their problems and longing to serve, she was the hostess, confidante and would-be 'mother' to most of the best writers and painters of her time, notably the Bloomsbury set. Many of these – even Lytton Strachey, who most depended on her affection – had an unfortunate habit of mocking her behind her back. She was tall and wore fantastic clothes, in which we have many records of her by Augustus John and Henry Lamb, so she was an outstanding figure and made a strange contrast to the short, stocky

Nijinsky, so inconspicuous in his conventional street-clothes. But she had an eye to observe him and a heart to comprehend, and she has left one of the most understanding descriptions of him that we possess. 'Lytton and most of my friends,' she wrote, 'were such enthusiastic admirers of him, that I, from contrariness, had rather pooh-poohed him, but when I saw him dance I was completely converted, for I saw that anyone who so completely lost himself and embodied an idea was not just a good ballet dancer – he seemed no longer to be Nijinsky, but became the idea which he was representing.'[128]

Lady Ottoline was a duke's daughter, but she felt rather shy as she drove down, at Lady Ripon's invitation, to meet Diaghilev and Nijinsky for luncheon at Coombe. She and Lady Ripon were both devoted to the arts, but the latter still had a foot firmly planted in the palatial, sporting, pleasure-loving world from which Lady Ottoline had broken free. Gwladys Ripon's was the 'smart artistic set', while the liberal Ottoline Morrell's friends were comparatively bohemian. It was the difference between the brilliant and amusing Maurice Baring, with whom Lady Ottoline shared the car to Coombe, and D. H. Lawrence.

Lady Ottoline was placed next to Nijinsky at luncheon, and they got on well together from the start. 'He was very quiet and rather ugly,' she wrote, 'but one at once recognized that the flame of genius burned within him.' She invited him to Bedford Square.[129]

Lady Juliet Duff and Nijinsky were often put next to each other at meals and they managed to communicate although, as she recalled, her few words of Russian

always provoked shouts of laughter, which was one way of making the evening go off well. He literally knew only two words of English: one the name of a London thoroughfare, which he called 'Piccadill' and the other was 'Littler', by which he meant neither Prince nor yet Emile Littler (the theatrical impresario, not yet famous), but Little Tich, an eccentric dancer celebrated in London and Paris ... He wore boots with exaggeratedly long feet, and one of his turns was to bang his forehead on the floor from an upright position. 'Littler' Nijinsky would say inquiringly each time he arrived in London, and if his idol were performing, seats would immediately be booked and he and Diaghilev would sit gazing spellbound;

and one got just as much pleasure from watching their faces as from the antics of 'Littler' himself.[130]

There would be a chance for Vaslav to see Little Tich (and Pavlova) at a Command Performance at the Palace Theatre on 1 July, for it was an opera night at Covent Garden.

Duncan Grant, arriving at Lady Ottoline's full of expectation at meeting Nijinsky and hoping to see him leap over the tennis net, found him seated beside his hostess in her drawing-room and heard her asking, as he entered the room, '*Aimez-vous Platon?*' ('Do you like Plato?').[131]

Nijinsky and Bakst came one afternoon, Lady Ottoline recalled, 'when Duncan Grant and some others were playing tennis in Bedford Square garden – they were so entranced by the tall trees against the houses and the figures flitting about playing tennis that they exclaimed with delight: "*Quel décor!*" '[132]

For years I was puzzled by the house in the background of Bakst's design for Nijinsky's ballet 'Jeux', which was to be put on in the following year.[133] It was not like a French country house, nor even, with its rows of small windows, like the Riviera Palace Hotel at Beausoleil: it had a prison-like plainnness, in spite of the 'dreaming garden trees' which half concealed it. Suddenly, on reading Lady Ottoline's lines quoted above, for the third, or fourth time, I realized that the architecture which had puzzled me was a version of that of a Bloomsbury square, a reminiscence of that summer afternoon in London. And perhaps even the subject of the ballet was suggested by the tennis-party.*

*In his interview with Emile Deflin for *Gil Blas*, 20 May 1913 (quoted on p. 345) Nijinsky is made to say that 'Jeux' originated from his watching tennis at Deauville in the previous summer. The Deauville season, of course, followed immediately after the London one. Perhaps, in giving to the press a French as opposed to an English origin for his ballet, he was merely being diplomatic in the way that visitors to London were formerly supposed to express admiration for our police. In his *Diary*, Nijinsky wrote 'The story of this ballet is about three young men making love to each other. . . "Jeux" is the life of which Diaghilev dreamed. He wanted to have two boys as lovers. . . In the ballet, the two girls represent the two boys and the young man is Diaghilev' (pp. 147, 148). I do not take this very seriously. There is also a story that the idea for 'Jeux' came from watching moths around the lamp on an outdoor restaurant table in the Bois de Boulogne. Of course, every work of art has several origins.

He was very nervous and highly-strung [wrote Lady Ottoline], and his guardian and jailer, Diaghilev, did not allow him to go out into society as it tired and upset him, and I was one of the few people that he was allowed to come and see, as at my house he could be quiet and only meet other artists. 'He is like a jockey,' I laughingly told Lytton, but really I grew very fond of the little figure with long muscular neck and pale Kalmuk face, and the hands so expressive and nervous. He always seemed lost in the world outside, as if he looked on as a visitor from another world, although his powers of observation were intensely rapid. For on entering a room he would see all the pictures hanging in it before he had been there but a few minutes. It was not easy to talk to him as he didn't speak English and his French was very vague, but we managed to understand each other, and he was glad, I think, of real understanding and appreciation of his serious work. I was lamenting one day that I was not able to create anything myself and he quickly answered 'Oh, but you do create, Madame, for you help us young artists to create.'

There were at this time fantastic fables about him: that he was very debauched, that he had girdles of emeralds and diamonds given him by an Indian prince; but on the contrary, I found that he disliked any possessions or anything that hampered him or diverted him from his art. He was incessantly thinking out new ballets, new steps; also he was absorbed by the ideas of the old Russian myths and religions which he wanted to express in his ballets as he did in 'Le Sacre du printemps'. Such ballets as 'Le Spectre de la rose' did not interest him; he said it was *trop joli* and was rather annoyed when people admired it. He gave me a photograph of himself as he was in ordinary life and another to put by its side, as he was in 'Petrushka'.* He said that he made up in this part as an old traditional Russian figure – 'the mythical outcast in whom is concentrated the pathos and suffering of life, one who beats his hands against the walls, but always is cheated and despised and left outside alone.' Perhaps the same myth Dostoyevsky turned into *The Idiot*. Many years later I found in Charlie Chaplin something of the same intense poignancy as there was in Nijinsky.[134]

The worldly Jacques-Emile Blanche, with his flashes of 'impeccable bad taste'[135], was less sympathetic that July than Lady Ottoline to Nijinsky and the creative struggles which were disturbing him.

Chaliapine [he wrote] was one day entertaining Lady Ripon to lunch in the large hall of the Savoy, and I was among the guests. A waiter brought

*These two small signed photographs were sold at Sotheby's on 18 July 1968 for £150 each.

me a note from Diaghilev; I opened it and read: 'Dear friend, we are in the grill-room with Bakst. Vaslav would like to see you; he wants to talk to you about a mad scheme, but you know his fancies – he wants us to collaborate in a "games" libretto and Debussy is to do the score. Come as soon as you leave the table. We have a rehearsal at the theatre at four o'clock.' Vaslav was drawing on the tablecloth when I reached the grill-room. Diaghilev looked as if he were in one of his cross moods, he was biting his fingers; Bakst looked at the drawings on the cloth aghast – but Nijinsky understood only Russian, and it took me some time to find out what was in the wind. The 'cubist' ballet – which became 'Jeux' – was a game of tennis in a garden; but in no circumstances was it to have a romantic décor in the Bakst manner! There should be no *corps de ballet*, no ensembles, no variations, no *pas de deux*, only girls and boys in flannels, and rhythmic movements. A group at a certain stage was to depict a fountain, and the game of tennis (with licentious *motifs*) was to be interrupted by the crashing of an aeroplane. What a childish idea![136]

It is hard, in fact, to imagine a more appealing idea than for three dancers to represent a fountain. As for the aeroplane, it was not until 1926, in 'Romeo and Juliet', that one landed (off-stage) in a Diaghilev ballet!

'I sent the scheme to Debussy,' wrote Blanche, 'who replied: "No, it's idiotic and unmusical; I should not dream of writing a score." Diaghilev pleaded Debussy's cause; Nijinsky was obstinate, and threatened to dance no more in London. Debussy was again wired to; his fee was to be doubled.' When Blanche saw and heard 'Jeux' in the following year he thought it 'a bad score'![137]

Far from Diaghilev leading Nijinsky into virgin forests of experiment, it seems that in 1912 Nijinsky's creative ideas were already leaving Diaghilev behind. The lack of unison and understanding between them made them both nervous. And Diaghilev, Juliet Duff observed, 'was an odd mixture of ruthlessness and vulnerability. He could make others cry, but he could cry himself, and I remember a day at my mother's house on Kingston Hill when he had had a disagreement with Nijinsky, who had refused to come, and he sat in the garden with tears dripping down his face and would not be comforted.'[138]

What other society ladies, in the England of 1912, would a man have dared to cry in front of because his boy-friend had been unkind – apart from Lady Ottoline Morrell?

Off the stage [wrote Lady Juliet of Nijinsky], he seemed in those days like a backward child who sometimes surprises and delights one by sudden flashes of perception and wit. One day at luncheon at the Savoy, Diaghilev embarked on a somewhat lengthy anecdote. Nijinsky bore it with ill-concealed impatience and at the end of it looked up and said with firmness and finality '*Histoire longue mais pauvre*'. On another occasion we were discussing the likeness of people to animals and birds. Nijinsky sat staring at my mother, who had a lovely but aquiline nose, and said '*Vous perroquet*.' My mother, readier than anyone I ever knew to laugh at herself [she was very tall, with a slight stoop], murmured to me 'It's lucky he didn't say "*Vous chameau*".'[139]*

Meanwhile, Hofmannsthal was writing to Strauss.

Hofmannsthal at Rodaun to Strauss at Garmisch, 23.6.12

... At the time of my *Orestes* suggestion, which I sacrificed quickly and readily enough to your objections, I said all that is necessary to broach the ballet question. You were by no means altogether disinclined ... Together with Kessler, who possesses a most fertile, and quite specifically a designer's imagination, I have produced a short ballet for the Russians, *Joseph in Egypt*, the episode with Potiphar's wife; the boyish part of Joseph of course for Nijinsky, the most extraordinary personality on the stage today.

Tomorrow or the next day I shall send you the sketch in typescript ...

... Even if you are not willing to set it to music, I cannot withdraw yet another piece from the Russians (Diaghilev and Nijinsky know the sketch!) But I would endeavour to modify, as far as possible, my collaboration with the Russian or French musician of Diaghilev's choice, so as to make it quite clear that I was concerned to be of assistance only to the dancer, and not to the musician concerned.[140]

Hofmannsthal at Rodaun to Strauss at Garmisch, 28.6.12

... I am very glad that you take to the idea of *Joseph* as an interim work ... Diaghilev will come to see you in Garmisch from London to settle the business side, but will inquire beforehand when this discussion would suit you best. He is a Russian of the most attractive kind, much more like a country gentleman than a manager ...[141]

---

* In Stravinsky's version of the story (*Memories*, pp. 36, 37) Nijinsky *does* say '*Vous chameau*'.

It was arranged that Kessler should take Diaghilev to see Strauss on 3 August.[142]

This fine summer it was the rage to have Russian dancers perform at parties. During July Nijinsky danced with Karsavina and Zambelli at a party given by the Aga Khan at the Ritz;[143] Kyasht and Volinine danced for Lord and Lady Londesborough at St Dunstan's, Regent's Park;[144] Pavlova was partnered by Novikov at Lady Michelham's at Strawberry Hill;[145] and Nijinsky and Karsavina danced at a party Lady Ripon gave for Queen Alexandra at Coombe.[146]

Pavlova was again at the Palace and Adeline Genée at the Coliseum. Genée had opened her season in May with a new ballet, 'La Camargo', for which she arranged the choreography and in which she impersonated the eighteenth-century dancer. The designer, C. Wilhelm, had taken great pains to collect genuine period furniture for the set: but he failed to find an authentic screen and had to improvise. Soon after his arrival in London Diaghilev had gone one evening with Eric Wolheim, his agent, to see the ballet – and immediately spotted the fake screen. But he was very impressed by Genée's dancing, and he took Karsavina and Nijinsky to the Coliseum for a matinée in July. 'There was not a comfortable seat left in the house, and they climbed up into the gallery where they were shown into three seats at the side from which they had to crane their necks to see the stage. But all their exertions were amply repaid when Genée appeared. Diaghilev was as excited as a child, and superlative praises poured from his lips.' He hoped to get the ballerina to dance in his next London season, but in this he was unsuccessful.[147]

'Narcisse' was given on 9 July and received much more favourably than in Paris. *The Times* critic, although he found 'something irritating in the insensibility of Narcissus to the charms of the Nymphs who wreathe themselves around him and literally lay themselves at his feet' and thought the latter part degenerated 'from a ballet into a prolonged tableau', praised the groupings of the Beotian men and girls, the dances of the Bacchantes and 'the unsullied joy of the first dances of Narcissus, a joy which M. Nijinsky portrays perfectly'; these he thought 'as captivating as anything which the

Russians have given us'. The new ballet, he noted, was very well received.[148]

The *Morning Post* opined that Nijinsky had 'not before displayed so wide a command of graceful action as distinct from mere physical exercise'.[149] The *Daily Express* found 'Narcisse' 'an immediate and pronounced success', judging that Nijinsky scored 'a triumph'.[150] In the *Daily Mail* Richard Capell wrote of 'a glimpse of the antique world, a Theocritan idyll made visible . . .' and considered that 'M. Nijinsky's role is the most elaborate of those in which he has been seen here and the performance is curious and wonderful. But he seemed less a simple narcissus than an odd orchid. . .'[151] The critic of the *Sunday Times* said of Nijinsky's performance: 'Every pose, every movement, every gesture was instinct with sexless insensibility and vacuous complacency, and you feel the punishment fits the crime.'[152]

Cyril Beaumont, like everyone else, was struck by Bronislava Nijinska's Bacchante and disliked the artificial flower that rose from the pool at the end. He admired Nijinsky's final pose, when 'crouched by the edge of the pool, he gazed spellbound at his own image, bending down with infinite grace closer and closer to the water, until he disappeared beneath its surface'.[153]

Charles Ricketts wrote his impressions of the ballet to two different friends. To one: 'I confess that the Russian Ballet, with its perfection of dancing and beauty of setting, haunts and enchants me like nothing else. Karsavina as Echo has achieved a new triumph of poetic insight of a touching and lovely order. Her Thamar is also in its way a triumph.'[154] To another:

Karsavina surpassed herself as Echo in 'Narcisse'. She creeps on to the stage, enamoured of Narcisse, and approaches silently, hiding behind trees, she dances in a trance and sinks at Nijinsky's feet at the end of each musical phrase. He leaps like a faun, with such rare clothing on that Duchesses had to be led out of the audience, blinded with emotion, and with their diamond tiaras all awry. On the second performance he wore long knickerbockers, it seems at the request – not of the censor – but of the Russian Embassy.[155]

On 15 July, in the presence of her mother and brother, Bronislava Nijinska was married to the dancer Alexander Kotchetovsky at the

Russian Orthodox Church in Buckingham Palace Road. Diaghilev, *in loco parentis*, gave her away and it was he who bought the ring set with sapphires and brilliants, which he declared firmly was 'to wed her to her art' – rather than to Kotchetovsky. (She had to sell it during the Russian Revolution.)[156]

It is interesting that the English should have felt that in Narcissus Nijinsky had a more extended and demanding role than any other

Nijinsky and Karsa-vina in 'Petrushka'. Drawing by George Banks, from 'Rhythm'.

they had seen him in. Yet, if they had not so far been allowed to undergo 'Petrushka', news of this masterpiece had filtered across the Channel in the form of an enthusiastic article with effective illustrations in the July number of the magazine *Rhythm*, edited by Middleton Murry and Katherine Mansfield.[157] The gifted young Frenchman, Henry Gaudier, who added to his own name that of his twenty-year-older, eccentric and tormented woman friend, Sophie Brzeska, had contributed some drawings to an earlier number of *Rhythm* – before quarrelling with Murry and Mansfield;[158] and he made sculptures this summer both of Nijinsky alone* and of Karsavina and Bolm in 'L'Oiseau de feu'.† (For the latter he was paid by Julian Lousada – whose son, the lawyer Anthony, later became Chairman of the Trustees of the Tate Gallery – the highest price he ever received in his lifetime, £20.)[159] It is hard to resist the conviction that could Nijinsky have been brought together with this lonely, fanatical and hungry pair he might have been united with them in an odd, practicable friendship – but perhaps the Savoy Hotel would have come between them.

The young poet Rupert Brooke fell in love with the Russian Ballet that summer. Sometimes he went to Covent Garden with Geoffrey Keynes,[160] sometimes with the actress Cathleen Nesbitt, whom he loved. The latter would always remember him saying, one night as they left the theatre, 'Do you realize you have seen a miracle? Nijinsky actually stopped still in the air.'[161] A few months later Brooke was to write of the company: 'They, if anything can, redeem our civilization. I'd give everything to be a ballet-designer.'[162] By this he meant choreographer.

It should have been a happy time for Nijinsky. Every night he danced was a triumph. Ahead lay an easy August, with very intermittent performances of 'Les Sylphides', 'Le Festin', 'Carnaval' and 'Le Spectre' at Deauville;‡ a visit to Bayreuth, where with Diaghilev and Stravinsky he would hear 'Parsifal',[163] and then a Venetian September.[164] But he was battling in his mind to give birth to a new language of the dance and the labour-pains made him irritable.

*I have not been able to trace this statue, but Mr Ede, the authority on Gaudier, thinks that it was probably the figure of an imagined dancer to which the sculptor gave the name 'Nijinsky'.

†One casting of this is in the collection of Lord Harewood. I do not know if another exists.

‡Five performances between 6 and 22 August.

CHAPTER SIX

1912-1913

Autumn 1912–September 1913

It has been observed in an earlier chapter that as a boy Nijinsky never had friends.[1] He was by nature a solitary creature and at school circumstances made him an outsider. In 1908, graduating suddenly from boyhood to manhood, he had been, as it were, adopted by Prince Lvov and then by Diaghilev. This kind of relationship with an older man who gave him confidence and a sense of security was obviously ideal for someone of his temperament; and the worst that could be said of it was that the faun might occasionally need to escape briefly from the dominant personality of his tamer, and scamper off into the woods. He might dream from time to time of another kind of relationship, of a flirtation or love affair with a pretty girl. Prettiness, however, was not enough: sympathy was essential, and this included total absorption in the problems of the art of ballet.[2] What girl could feel the holiness of the vocation of a dancer and choreographer enough to give Nijinsky the dedicated understanding he was bound to need and demand? Half measures were worse than nothing.

From the other members of the Russian Ballet he felt utterly removed. They were his colleagues and the raw materials of his art. They worked hard, though nothing like as hard as he did;* and some were even a little intelligent and well educated. Most of the girls were pretty, but most had lovers. Anyway, his closeness to Diaghilev put a distance between him and them. A friendship with one of the men seemed as impossible – however much the rakish

*Mr Vladimirov told me that he had seen Nijinsky doing a *barre* after evening performances. He found this beneficial.

Bourman might push himself forward, presuming on schoolday familiarity – as an affair with one of the women.

There was Karsavina, his partner. In a passage of the *Diary* written in 1918 there would be something about a secret passion for Karsavina.[3] This I do not take seriously, and if it existed even for a few weeks or days the ballerina was never aware of it – and she had been adored by enough men to be alert to the signs of infatuation.[4] For the truth is that Karsavina was unattainable. Just as he felt the rest of the company, judged not from a snobbish point of view but from that of high seriousness, to be utterly below him, so did Karsavina, an artist as dedicated as himself, seem utterly above. To find in a fellow-dancer such natural distinction, such nobility of manner and mind, was as disconcerting as to find the opposite. Then, she was an intellectual, and even if she did not want to create ballets her grasp of ideas was quicker than his own. Finally there was her lustrous beauty. She was loved not only by princes but by poets. In private life he could not compete. Only the dance could unite them.

His sister Bronia was the nearest to a friend that he had ever had. His mother understood and loved him and so did Diaghilev. Bronia alone understood the workings of his choreographic mind and so was closest to his secret heart. They were very much alike in their thoughts about ballet and their attitude to it, conscious of their duty and of a kind of royal prerogative. It was a little awkward that Bronia, with her more downright masculine intelligence, should be the younger and a woman. It was also awkward that Diaghilev's friendship for Nijinsky had removed the latter from daily contact with his sister. They worked together at class and rehearsal, but Bronia's marriage to Kotchetovsky raised another barrier between them.[5] They were not as close as they had been. If Bronia went away Diaghilev would be his only friend.

Now in the winter of 1912–13 something would happen to alter the situation.

The season at Deauville and the summer holiday over, Diaghilev made a flying trip to Paris to persuade Debussy to prolong the ending of 'Jeux'.[6] Debussy had already complained in a letter to Jacques Durand on 12 September that his score had to make a rather improper situation acceptable. But, as he said, 'in ballet, immorality escapes through the dancers' legs and ends in a *pirouette.*' The action must have been plotted in some detail by Diaghilev and Nijinsky by then; and we can imagine Diaghilev being more interested in the 'literary' aspect of the theme – sporting and amorous – which would give Paris '*un frisson nouveau*' and Nijinsky caring most for the ballet's abstract and sculptural side. Now they had decided that the ballet's story must be cyclical and end as it began, with a ball bouncing on to the stage to break up the children's forbidden games: so Debussy was asked on 31 October to reintroduce at the end the chords of the opening Prelude. This he did with subtly varied orchestration, adding a quixotic final cadence.

The German tour opened at the Stadttheater, Cologne, on 30 October. (And, incidentally, the first month of this tour was the only one during which Grigoriev was separated from the Diaghilev Ballet in its twenty years' existence: back in Petersburg he could not make up his mind to resign from the Mariinsky to devote himself to Diaghilev all the year round. He had been continually granted extensions of leave, but the time of reckoning had come. After a period of heart-searching he rejoined the Diaghilev company.[7])

Nijinsky gave an interview to a journalist who reported him as saying: 'Rushing from city to city, we are like Wandering Jews who travel in sleeping cars. We arrive at a station, shake hands with friends and get ready to give foolish interviews. Driving through the town, we catch glimpses of a cathedral, a castle, an old building, a river with picturesque barges or a face in the street we should like to see again. The crowd looks different from that in the last town we visited. We make a resolution to explore the place tomorrow – but. . . We arrive at the Palace Hotel – a big entrance hall, a lift, numbered doors and the inevitable strangers who shake us warmly by the hand. Last year there was a fat lady who rushed at me and showered me with compliments in every hotel. On the third occasion I asked her name and made a note of it. In the next town she was there again with the same compliments – but with a different name. There is one like her in every Palace Hotel. But the most anxious moment is when we inspect a theatre we have never danced in before. This is usually in the morning, when the place is dark and deserted. Only a glimmer of daylight penetrates to the corridors and dressing-rooms. A theatre without light is an invisible beauty, a waterless lake. Then at last we get down to work, we rehearse, we go on stage, we give a performance. We are chained to our eternal task with mortal and beloved fetters: it possesses us entirely, body and soul.'[8]

Following their visits to Frankfurt and Munich, the company arrived in Berlin in November. The Berlin season opened on 11 December with the first performance of 'L'Après-midi d'un faune'. Diaghilev, as ever mindful of publicity, cabled Astruc.

Diaghilev in Berlin to Astruc in Paris, 12.12.12

Yesterday triumphant opening at New Royal Opera House. Faune encored. Ten calls. No protests. All Berlin present. Strauss, Hofmannsthal, Reinhardt, Nikisch, the whole Secession group, King of Portugal, ambassadors and court. Wreaths and flowers for Nijinsky. Press enthusiastic. Long article Hofmannsthal in Tageblatt. Emperor, Empress and Princes coming to ballet Sunday. Had long talk with Emperor who was delighted and thanked the company. Huge success.[9]

On the following day Hofmannsthal reported to Strauss a conversation he had had with Nijinsky.

Hofmannsthal in Darmstadt to Strauss at Garmisch, 13.12.12

... I fear it is the idea of ballet, of the need for accentuated rhythms which has mislead and confused you. Therefore I must make myself the spokesman for Nijinsky who implores you to write the most unrestrained, the least dance-like music in the world, to put down pure Strauss for this leaping towards God which is a struggle for God. To be taken by you beyond all bounds of convention is exactly what he longs for; he is, after all, a true genius and just where the track is uncharted, there he desires to show what he can do, in a region like the one you opened up in *Elektra*.[10]

Gunsbourg was in Paris at the Hôtel Majestic, Avenue Kléber, and active on the company's behalf. On 15 December he telegraphed to London to engage an English girl, Hilda Bewicke, who had presumably been auditioned in London during the summer.[11] She was the first of a number of English dancers who worked for Diaghilev.

Diaghilev was becoming extremely concerned – though he kept it to himself – about the difficulties Stravinsky's score for 'Le Sacre du printemps' would present when Nijinsky got down to composing his choreography. While they were in Berlin in November he had taken the opportunity of re-visiting, with Nijinsky, the Dalcroze Academy at Hellerau, a two hours' journey away. Dalcroze had no intention of training dancers: his pupils were taught to analyse music by a new system of bodily movement. Among them was an intelligent Russo-Polish girl of twenty called Miriam Ramberg, who had previously studied ballet under Slovatsky of the Warsaw Opera. The pupils of Dalcroze despised what they considered the frivolous and pretty-pretty art of ballet, making up satirical rhymes about it and doing comic imitations of ballerinas.[12] Dalcroze himself found that Ramberg, because of her ballet training, tended to give a performance when doing her rhythmical exercises. '*Vous êtes trop extérieure,*' he told her.

None of the Dalcroze students, not even Ramberg, was at all impressed when this heavy imposing Russian gentleman with his small, high-cheek-boned companion appeared in their class: they did not know who they were. Diaghilev was hoping to engage someone to help Nijinsky with the music of 'Le Sacre', and his eye fell on the diminutive Ramberg, probably because she moved more like a dancer than the others. No doubt he talked to Jaques-Dalcroze about her character and background, and satisfied himself that she was likely to take her work seriously rather than indulge in flirtation and frivolity. Apart from speaking Polish, Russian, German, French and a little English, Ramberg was a very well-educated woman. She had stayed in Moscow and Petersburg with relations and knew the masterpieces of Russian literature.

A few days later Dalcroze told Ramberg of Diaghilev's interest in her. She was packed off to Berlin, where a ticket for the ballet awaited her, and an invitation to have supper afterwards with Diaghilev and Nijinsky. So her first sight of the Russian Ballet was at the Kroll Opera House. She saw in that first programme 'Cléopâtre' with Nelidova, barely noticed Nijinsky in the *pas de deux*, but loved the Bakst décor. She next saw Nijinsky in 'L'Après-midi d'un faune' and was puzzled by the dichotomy between music and movement. 'Carnaval' with Kyasht and Nijinsky ravished her, and she was moved by the Polovtsian Dances from 'Prince Igor'. At supper, being (in her own phrase) 'badly brought-up', when Diaghilev asked her opinion she dared to criticize. 'Why don't the women who escort Cleopatra when she is carried on in her litter walk on the beat of the music?' she asked. 'They just slouch on.' It had not in fact been Fokine's intention that these supers should march in time, but Diaghilev appeared to agree with her. 'Yes, they are just like cooks,' he said. Nijinsky sat silent as she complained that his choreography only coincided in two or three places with the music of 'L'Après-midi'. She could not at that time see the point of the extreme contrast between the impressionistic music and the abstract dancing in this work which she would come later to admire so passionately. In spite of her independent attitude, or perhaps because of it, Diaghilev decided in consultation with Nijinsky that she would be useful, and a few days later she heard that she was engaged.

Ramberg joined the Russian Ballet in Budapest at Christmas 1912, and when the new year of 1913 began, she was with them in Vienna. Her first duty was to give Dalcroze classes to the company, but the dancers, being overworked, tended to drop out of these; and Grigoriev suggested to Diaghilev that she should merely be asked to help individual dancers analyse and learn their roles. This was agreed.

So, as the crucial year of Nijinsky's life began, he had a new colleague.

It is extraordinary that within a few days of meeting Ramberg, who grew to understand him very well and who, if given the chance, might have become his wife, Nijinsky also came into the orbit of another young woman who actually did marry him. Romola de Pulszky, who had so admired Nijinsky on the Ballet's previous visit to Budapest, belonged to a distinguished Polish family, which emigrated to Hungary early in the eighteenth century. Her great-grandfather had taken a leading part under Kossuth in the Hungarian revolt against the Austrians in 1848. He represented Kossuth in England, and after the suppression of the rebellion remained in exile there; so that Romola's father was born at Highgate. A great-great-uncle of Romola's was Count Morice Benyovsky, a celebrated traveller and first reigning Prince of Madagascar. Romola's father

Nijinsky in class.
Caricature by Jean Cocteau.

Károly, a godson of Garibaldi, was one of several brothers eminent
in the world of politics, art and science. He married Emilia Markus,
the first actress in Hungary, whom Rostand considered the equal of
Bernhardt and Duse as Roxane in 'Cyrano'. The seventh child of
a button manufacturer, at thirteen she had sat on the knee of Liszt;
at fourteen she had entered the Academy of Dramatic Arts; and at

319

sixteen she had played Juliet. She was known as the 'Blonde Wonder' and was considered by many to be the greatest actress of all time.[13]

With Prince Esterhazy, Károly de Pulszky founded the National Gallery of Hungary and became its Director. Romola, the second daughter, was born in his flat there in 1891. From childhood she was interested in art. When her father told her stories they were not about fairies but about the great painters of the Renaissance, and she grew up with the ambition to be the Vasari of her day. But Károly de Pulszky fell victim to a political plot against his brother August, the Minister of Justice, and was accused of buying fake pictures in Italy. He went to Australia; and it was in Brisbane that he shot himself in 1899 at the age of forty-six. Emilia Markus married again, her second husband Oskar Pardany, a Jew, being converted to Christianity for the occasion, with Romola as his godmother. Romola had two English governesses and also studied at the Lycée Fénelon in Paris. With the second governess, Miss Mabel Johnson, she spent over a year in England, mostly at Eastbourne: but they were staying at Southsea in August, 1909, when the Tsar reviewed the British Fleet. Both Romola and her sister Tessa studied acting, Romola with Réjane and Le Bargy. Tessa appeared at the Burgtheater in Vienna, but gave up the stage on marrying the Danish tenor Erik Schmedes. Romola also had ballet lessons from Guerra at the Budapest Opera.[14] She was pretty, with fair hair, very white complexion and bright Sèvres-blue eyes.

Since the Russians' last week-long visit to Budapest Romola had seen them in Paris, and admired them so much that she longed in some way to be associated with them. She saw the new form of Russian ballet as a second Renaissance and wondered if she could be its chronicler. Some of the company had been entertained at her mother's house in February and Romola had made friends with Maestro Cecchetti and with Bolm: but she had met neither Diaghilev nor Nijinsky. Romola had 'a genuine admiration' for Maestro Cecchetti, she wrote years later, 'but I had to use him in order to achieve my purpose – to become permanently attached to the Ballet.'[15] It was not Cecchetti, however, who first introduced Nijinsky to Romola, but a lady journalist.

At rehearsals [wrote Romola], I always hid in some dark corner of the
theatre, fearing that if I attracted attention I might be sent away. On this
occasion I happened to be sitting in the back of the house with a newspaper-
woman ... She raved on and on about Nijinsky. Impatiently I interrupted her paeans by saying, 'If you really know this "wonder" so well,
then please introduce me to him at once.' We went over to the group of
men where Nijinsky was conversing with Diaghilev. It was an exciting
moment. One would never have thought that this unassuming young man,
with his Tartar face and the appearance of a Japanese student in his badly
fitting European clothes, was the same being as the marvellous apparition
the whole world had learned to admire. The introduction actually occurred. In the ensuing conversation there was a bit of confusion, which
was greatly aided by the diversity of languages spoken. Nijinsky misunderstood my identity, and thought I was the *prima ballerina* of the
Hungarian Opera, whose name had been brought into conversation at that
moment ... It was probably due to that error on his part that he greeted
me with so charming and respectful a bow. For many, many times after
that first introduction I was introduced to him, and never was there more
than a polite, fleeting acknowledgement and never by any chance did he
recognize me.[16]

Compared with the professional dancers who had begun training
at ten years old Romola could not dance at all, so if she was to join
the company it was a question either of bribing Cecchetti or of
bringing social pressure to bear on Diaghilev, who naturally liked
to keep on good terms with influential people in every country.
When the Ballet left for Vienna, Romola followed them. Through
her godfather, who was head of the Imperial Family's Archives,
and her brother-in-law Schmedes, she obtained a pass which allowed
her access to the Opera House at all times.

The Vienna season was a brilliant one, but it was not without its
troubles for Diaghilev. On the one hand Karsavina, who had
rejoined the company in Budapest, was there to add her aura to the
Ballet's radiance, and scored a triumph in 'Thamar'[17]: on the other
hand the Opera orchestra pronounced the music of 'Petrushka' to
be '*Schweinerei*' and at first refused to play it. When the violinists
threw down their bows at a rehearsal Diaghilev went to the orchestra
pit and said, 'Gentlemen, in ten years you will be proud to have
been the first Austrians to play Stravinsky's music.' When they did

play it – only twice – they tried to sabotage it. Thus was Stravinsky, who was present at rehearsals, snubbed in the city of Mozart.[18] Then, Nijinsky was at his most incredible in the Blue-bird *pas de deux* from Tchaikovsky's 'La Belle au bois dormant', which had been called 'L'Oiseau de feu' when included in 'Le Festin' four years before, but which was now billed as 'La Princesse enchantée';[19] on the other hand, 'L'Après-midi d'un faune' was not appreciated in Vienna.[20] Most of the critics were lavish in praise of the Russian Ballet, but Ludwig Karpath, the music critic, had reservations.[21]

Nevertheless, it was Karpath whom Romola knew best and it was him she persuaded to ask Diaghilev for an interview and to take her along. It must have been embarrassing for the kind fat old critic to bother Diaghilev after criticizing his company adversely, but Romola had once done him a service and he could not resist her pressure.

Romola wrote :

I was neither awed nor embarrassed when we went to see Diaghilev. I was determined to obtain my point, and, when my mind was definitely set, nothing and nobody mattered. Diaghilev received us in the middle of the afternoon, in an empty public reception-room at the Hôtel Bristol. As soon as he entered we felt his dominating personality. We expected a cold, a resentful reception. But Diaghilev, who with every gesture and word expressed at the same time the superiority of an emperor and an irresistible charm, confused both Karpath and myself by the warm interest he took in our requests. He made us feel absolutely that nothing interested him more than my intention to be a dancer . . . Apparently a young society girl had come to the great artistic organizer with a request. In reality, two powerful enemies had crossed swords for the first time. Diaghilev held the thing I most wanted – Nijinsky.* And he sensed at once, with his fine instincts, however subconsciously, the approaching danger. I just as quickly realized that he wished to read my mind . . .

'I think Bolm is wrong in advising you to go to the Wiesenthals' [Diaghilev told her.] One thought seemed to follow the other, aloud. 'The

---

*As Mme Romola Nijinsky has always insisted to me that in pursuing Nijinsky she had no idea of the possibility of marrying him, the passages in her life of her husband (published in 1933) which imply the opposite must be put down to romantic exaggeration.

ideal thing for you would be to become a pupil of the Imperial Dancing School in St Petersburg. But of course it is not feasible, even with the greatest possible pull, for you are not a Russian, and you are long past the required age ... I think the best thing for you to do would be to take private lessons from Fokine in St Petersburg.'

With apparent joy I jumped at the idea.

'I would love it.' I misled him deliberately. 'It has always been my dream to go to Russia.'

He then asked my impressions of the different ballets and the artists of his company My answers must have been correct. He smiled approvingly. During all this time I felt gradually that I was falling under his spell. I tried to fight against his almost hypnotic power. With a desperate effort I began to rave about Bolm as a man, not as an artist, like any little 'flapper' would. And then Diaghilev, with unexpected strategy, turned and asked, 'What about Nijinsky?'

Without hesitation I answered, 'Oh, Nijinsky is a genius. As an artist he is incomparable. But somehow Bolm is more human to me' – and I continued my extravagances about Bolm. By this time he was convinced of my good faith, and then said the fatal words:

'I will speak to Maestro Cecchetti. He has taught all our greatest artists. I am sure he will take you as a special private pupil. This way you will have not only a marvellous teacher, but also the possibility of travelling with us and closely studying our work.'

I thanked him gratefully, and so our interview ended. I had won my first battle. I could scarcely believe I had succeeded in fooling such an inconceivably clever man as Diaghilev.

The same evening, when I went backstage, Maestro greeted me from afar with enthusiastic gestures and loud shouts of Italian joy. 'Sergei Pavlovitch has decided that you should study with me. I am overjoyed, *bambina* ...' He embraced me and kissed me on both cheeks. He always liked to kiss young girls ... We finally settled when and how I would start to study. I was to join them on 4 February in London.[22]

On their way to London the company gave two performances at Prague, two at Leipzig and one in Dresden. Diaghilev made a flying trip to Petersburg.[23] From Dresden on 27 January Nijinsky telegraphed to Astruc asking for a stage plan of the new Théâtre des Champs-Elysées,[24] which was to be opened with a production of Berlioz's 'Benvenuto Cellini' on 31 March. In London rehearsals took place on the stage of the Aldwych Theatre, lent by Beecham,[25] and it was here that Nijinsky got down to work on the choreography of 'Le Sacre du printemps'.*

*Tamara Karsavina in
'Carnaval'.
Drawing by August Macke.*

'Petrushka' was shown to the English for the first time on the opening night at Covent Garden. Cyril Beaumont noticed 'the startled expressions on the faces of the audience' and was himself surprised by Stravinsky's music 'which then sounded incredibly daring and uncouth': but he was 'soon captivated'. He admired the way that Nijinsky, when he was supported on the iron stand inside the booth, 'succeeded in investing the movements of his legs with a looseness suggesting that foot, leg and thigh were

*Grigoriev writes: 'After finishing our season in Vienna, and visiting one or two German towns on the way, we arrived in London six weeks before we were due to start performing' (p. 89). As the Vienna season ended on 16 January and was followed by performances at Leipzig and Dresden, this is of course inaccurate – and as Nijinsky was still in Dresden on 27 January there would have been less than a week before the London opening on 4 February.

threaded on a string attached to the hip'. There was 'a curiously fitful quality in his movements, his limbs spasmodically leapt or twisted or stamped like the reflex actions of limbs whose muscles have been subjected to an electric current'. Beaumont's description of Nijinsky's make-up is interesting.

His features were made up a kind of putty colour, presumably a suggestion of wood; his nose was built up to have a thicker base; his eyebrows were painted out and replaced by a wavy line set half an inch higher; his lips were compressed together; his eyes seemed devoid of lid and socket, and suggested a pair of boot-buttons or two blobs of black paint; there was a little red on his cheeks. His features were formed into a sad and unhappy mask, an expression which remained constant throughout the ballet.[26]

The Times found the work 'refreshingly new and refreshingly Russian'; [27] and Stravinsky, who had taken a curtain-call after the performance, told the *Daily Mail* that 'Petrushka' and 'Firebird' had never been better played in France, Austria, Germany or Hungary than by Thomas Beecham's orchestra.[28]

The young writer Osbert Sitwell had fallen under the spell of the Russian Ballet and thought Stravinsky, Diaghilev, Karsavina, Fokine and Nijinsky all partook of the quality of genius. 'The part of Petrushka,' he wrote, 'showed Nijinsky to be a master of mime, gesture, drama. . .' Looking back later, he saw Fokine's work as a portent. 'This ballet was, in its scope as a work of art, universal; it presented the European contemporary generation with a prophetic and dramatized version of the fate reserved for it, in the same way that the legend of the Minotaur had once summed up, though after the event and not before it, the fate of several generations of Greek youths and maidens.'[29]

On 11 February – a day on which was announced the death of Captain Scott* in the Antarctic – Cyril Beaumont saw for the first time Nijinsky and Karsavina dance the Blue-bird *pas de deux*, which had been given so many names by Diaghilev, and was now 'L'Oiseau et le prince'; and he was dazzled by the way in which, during the *diagonale* of the coda, 'he seemed not to touch the ground but to

*Whose widow, then Lady Kennet, introduced me to Mme Karsavina in 1946.

glide forward on air, his feet flashing to and fro in the brilliance of his *brisés* and *cabrioles*.'[30]

'L'Après-midi d'un faune' had its first English performance on 11 February, and, although there were a few hisses, was so warmly received by the majority that, as in Paris and Berlin, it was repeated. The critic of *The Times* considered the work seriously and at some length, deemed Nijinsky's 'stiff poses, and particularly his last action when he lies down to dream beside the scarf ... extraordinarily expressive' and paid the budding choreographer a fine compliment in his concluding words: 'We realized again how apparently inexhaustible are the resources of the ballet, for we had been given a new phase of its art which appealed through quite different channels from those with which anything else in the repertory has been concerned.'[31] Richard Capell wrote in the *Daily Mail*:

The miracle of the thing lies with Nijinsky – the fabulous Nijinsky, the peerless dancer, who as the faun does no dancing. The two inspirations of his subtle and unapproached miming in this piece would appear to have been the Greek pottery at the British Museum and a study of the gambols of chamois or goat. He wears a mottled or rather piebald skin – rather like the coat of a young calf; it is admirable. His movements are at once abrupt and stealthy. He leaps once. This one leap is a surprise and an illumination. It is a full evocation of a being half-boy, half-brute, consummate and also uncanny.[32]

On 19 February Queen Alexandra saw 'L'Après-midi', which was again encored.[33] On the 21st the *Daily Mail* reported that

M. Nijinsky, having telegraphed to M. Debussy, the composer, news of the success at Covent Garden of the new ballet 'The Afternoon of a Faun' – which is now being regularly encored – has had the following telegraphed reply: 'Thanks, my dear Nijinsky, for having sent me that telegram, whose words flame like the gold of victorious trumpets! Thanks to your peculiar genius for gesture and rhythm the arabesques of my "Prélude à l'Après-midi d'un faune" have been endowed with a new charm. Congratulate the English on having understood it.'[34]

One suspects that Diaghilev had a hand in this telegraphic exchange.

The Russian Ballet already had one English dancer, Hilda Bewicke. Now some vacancies had to be filled and Tarasov, a young man who had appeared with Diaghilev in a previous season but was now dancing with the Koslov troupe at the Coliseum, arranged to bring some of his colleagues to be auditioned. An English girl, Hilda Munnings, recorded the occasion.[35]

It was arranged that four of us girls, with Zverev and Tarasov, should be given an audition to show our ability, if any, at the awful hour of ten o'clock on a Monday morning. And so I came to the greatest ordeal of my life up-to-date. We changed into practice dress, and stupidly put on brand new ballet shoes. We had to face a committee more terrifying than any first-night audience: they sat with their backs to the towering safety curtain on the stage of the Royal Opera House, Covent Garden. Diaghilev, of course, was there, and Nijinsky, Maestro and Madame Cecchetti and Grigoriev. We had no music, and nothing arranged. We girls lined ourselves up to do some of our dances from 'Schéhérazade'. Just as we started I caught my uncomfortable shoe in something, and down I went with a crash. The stage was slippery and my feet had not got used to the shoes. Before we finished I had gone down three times. At last Diaghilev suggested that Cecchetti should give us some classroom steps to do, and with these I got on better. I cannot remember how the other girls danced, but Zverev jumped and did his *entrechats* and *pirouettes* splendidly, which seemed to save the situation. Still, we hadn't much hope as we crawled out of Covent Garden and down Henrietta Street to the Coliseum. That same evening during our performance we got the news that five of us had been accepted; Anna Broomhead (later Bromova), Doris Faithful, Zverev, Tarasov and myself.

Miriam Ramberg had already begun to work on Stravinsky's score for 'Le Sacre' with Nijinsky. Even she found it extremely difficult to tell where one phrase ended and when another began – so novel, so unexpectedly interrupted and so strangely superimposed were Stravinsky's rhythms. They could never decide when to call a halt to the day's work. There was no question of Ramberg collaborating on the choreography: she respected Nijinsky's vision of a primitive Russia and admired the awkward unclassical poses in which he planned to group his dancers. Her only suggestion, diffidently recalled (apart from purely musical analysis), was made one day when Nijinsky said 'Here I'll form a big circle. What do you think? Say something'; and Ramberg said 'Why not try several little circles for a change?' – and he did.

327

When he was composing his ballets the idea of virtuosity, of showing off brilliant steps, never entered Nijinsky's head – not even when he was arranging a dance for himself. He first looked for a basic position, then kept to it right through the work. In 'L'Après-midi' it had been that Egyptian combination of a full-on torso with heads, hands and legs in profile. In 'Jeux', the ballet about flirting tennis-players which he was planning – it was the sideways and upwards swing of two arms across the body – a sort of composite sport movement. (In fact, since tennis-players use one hand and not two, this movement was more like golf – but Nijinsky hardly knew the difference between the two games.) In 'Le Sacre' the awkward closed fists half supporting a lolling head, the turned-in bent knees and turned-in feet (reminiscent of Petrushka's) gave the idea of a prehistoric species at the mercy of the weather, the harvest and their own fearful superstitions.[36]

As with 'L'Après-midi d'un faune' Nijinsky had grave difficulty in imparting his intentions to the company, and they resented not only his experiments in movement but his attitude towards them as dancers. When Fokine devised steps, however inventive, they always followed the logic of classical choreography. They had a natural flow. With Nijinsky, the body was no longer one single instrument, but four; and there seemed to be no continuity in his sequences, so that there was no chance of letting yourself go. When composing, Fokine would sometimes take an artist like Karsavina into his confidence and ask 'What do you feel about this?' Dancers could ask him questions and he allowed them a certain freedom of interpretation. Nijinsky was very young[37] – there had never in history been a twenty-four-year-old ballet-master before. Not only his sense of being out on an experimental limb and his curious position with regard to Diaghilev, but also his fanatical dedication to art, made him treat dancers in rehearsal as if they were puppets who had no purpose in life except to interpret his ideas. Human relationships were in abeyance. If Karsavina, when he was thinking something out, asked him the sort of question she would have asked Fokine, he was furious. Then, he preferred to show dancers what to do, rather than explain or analyse a movement. He expected them to copy him.

Considering the unwillingness of the dancers to be the raw material of his experiments, it was a miracle that he and they together really produced such wonderful results. There was the case of Nelidova, who danced the principal Nymph in 'L'Après-midi d'un faune'. She loathed the ballet and it made her long to go back to Moscow. 'Have I come all the way for *this*?' she used to exclaim. But Nijinsky, by persistently eliminating from her technical performance every hint of personal idiosyncrasy, moulded her – in Ramberg's phrase – into a likeness of Pallas Athene.

With all his seriousness, Nijinsky was not unaware of the humour of the situation, as Ramberg discovered. When she asked him if Nelidova wasn't proud to have been turned into a goddess, he replied 'Not at all. She would much rather I invented a little Spanish number for her –' (mimicking in a funny way, hands on hips) 'with a carnation between her teeth and a rose behind her ear.'

Another instance of his sly observation was provided when Ramberg asked him what sort of man Trubecki was. Now, Trubecki was a muddled and ineffectual Pole, who used to get worked up into an hysterical state when anything went wrong. Diaghilev had engaged him as his private secretary and as treasurer of the company presumably because he was the husband of the dancer Sophie Pflanz. 'You can judge the sort of man he is,' said Nijinsky, 'when I tell you he secretly writes stories with titles like [in Polish] *"Fartoushek"* – "Her little pinafore" – for the *Warsaw Courier*.' (This was, incidentally, the only time Nijinsky spoke a word in Polish to Ramberg: they always spoke Russian together.)

No one in the company except his sister and perhaps Karsavina had ever seen this side of Nijinsky's character before. Ramberg found that when she was alone with him they talked quite easily together. She was at his side during the agony of creation, and this led to an ease of intercourse between them. Suddenly, Nijinsky had someone who understood him. But it was an intellectual friendship without warmth.

On the way from London to Monte Carlo the company broke their journey at Lyons, where they gave one performance, dancing 'Les Sylphides', 'Cléopâtre', 'Carnaval' and 'Prince Igor'.[38] By

329

Nijinsky in evening dress.
Caricature by Jean Cocteau.

the time the Ballet reached Monte Carlo on 15 March, Ramberg, whose presence they had at first resented, calling her 'Rithmitchka', had settled down and been accepted. She even had an admirer, Vladimir Romanov, whom she did not find attractive, and she rather dreaded the moment when she had to roll on the cushions with him in 'Schéhérazade'. Her intelligence and vivacity were particularly appreciated by the more educated members of the company, such as Hilda Bewicke[39] and Olga Khokhlova. One evening she was doing an imitation of Sarah Bernhardt in a dressing-room, when an old dresser put her head round the door and exclaimed, '*On dirait Mme Sarah!*' Ramberg's friends called her 'Mimi'.

With Fokine gone and since Nijinsky was a slow worker as a choreographer, Diaghilev decided to go to Russia and enlist the services of Boris Romanov and Alexander Gorsky:[40] Nijinsky was left behind in Monte Carlo, and, as in the last two years, stayed at the Riviera Palace Hotel at Beausoleil, coming and going by funicular or car. Vaslav and Ramberg continued to work together on 'Le Sacre' in the classroom under the Casino. They had three clear weeks before the season began on 9 April. They were alone except for a fat German pianist whom Diaghilev had nick-named '*Kolossal*' – not only because of his size but because he was always using this then fashionable expletive.* During their sessions Vassili would frequently come in on some pretext – to close a window to protect Nijinsky from draughts or to put a cardigan over his shoulders – but really, instructed by Diaghilev, to see that he and Ramberg were not flirting. Nevertheless, because of the absence of Diaghilev Mimi Ramberg did see much more of Nijinsky than she would otherwise have done.[41] Eleonora Nijinskaya noticed the growing intimacy of Ramberg with her son and warned him that she thought Mimi was attracted by him. But Vaslav told her there was no danger.[42]

'Jeux' was to be danced by Karsavina, Bronislava Nijinska and Vaslav himself. Because Karsavina had been obliged to return to Petersburg after the London season, Vassilievska deputized for her while Nijinsky was working the ballet out, which he did with a volume of Gauguin reproductions open before him.[43]

After their afternoon's work together it would often happen that Nijinsky and Ramberg met *chez* Pasquier, the café with a *terrasse* where dancers went to drink chocolate and eat cakes, and they would sit talking until it was dark and the time came to go to their respective hotels. One evening Nijinsky pointed to the trees which had artificial green lighting on them, and said 'That is how I like them and how I want the trees to be in "Jeux".' He also told Ramberg some of his ideas for the ballet about Joseph and Potiphar's wife, the score of which Diaghilev had at last commissioned for an enormous sum from Richard Strauss. In the banquet scene he would suggest the frivolity of this decadent society by making the guests perform a stylized dance with imaginary knives and forks. (This idea was used in 1917 by Massine in 'Les Femmes de bonne humeur', so perhaps it was a legacy of Nijinsky's to his successor, conveyed by Diaghilev.)

---

*'*Kolossal*' was a period word in Germany then – just as '*épatant*' or 'super' or 'smashing' would be in other countries in subsequent years.

His plans for 'Joseph' were much more original than the choreography eventually produced by Fokine.

They discussed Fokine's ballets.

M.R. Don't you think 'Petrushka' is Fokine's masterpiece?

N. (*doubtfully*) Ye-e-e-s.

M.R. You don't sound convinced. What is there that you don't like
about it?

N. The three puppets are certainly very good.

M.R. And the wet-nurses.

N. Yes. But I can't understand how he can just say to one member of
the crowd 'Follow this tune' and leave him to improvise. A
choreographer should oversee every tiny detail of choreography
and leave nothing to chance.

Nijinsky laughed at Fokine's arrangement of 'Schéhérazade'.
When Cecchetti as the Chief Eunuch unlocked the doors and the
Negroes bounded on (as we have seen above), each seized a woman
and began to caress her passionately on a cushion. They were expected to improvise these embraces and did so *con amore*, as Ramberg
had found to her dismay. 'What kind of choreography is that?'
asked Nijinsky. 'Choreography should be precise.'[44] He was indeed
the very first choreographer to give exact instructions in every detail,[45]* and this must have seemed cramping and pedantic to the
dancers at the time. It would be normal practice today.

One day at rehearsal Nijinsky, after demonstrating something
strenuous, looked round for a chair.[46] Ramberg got up and gave him
hers. Later she was mercilessly jeered at by the company for this.
She was told she had no sense of a woman's dignity. It was taken for
granted that she loved Nijinsky, though this had not yet occurred to
her.

Mimi Ramberg was sitting alone *chez* Pasquier one evening when
Nijinsky arrived, white with rage and shaking. He said, 'I have just
nearly killed a man.' He was referring to his brother-in-law Kotchetovsky. 'Bronia is leaving the cast of "Faune" and she is not to
dance in either of my new ballets. That man has prevented her.' To
calm him down Ramberg began to walk him along the gardens and
recited Edgar Allen Poe's 'Annabel Lee'.

*Mme Karsavina, who always defends Fokine, disagrees.

It was many and many a year ago,
In a kingdom by the sea,
That a maiden there lived whom you may know
By the name of Annabel Lee.
And this maiden she lived with no other thought
Than to love and be loved by me.

She translated the poem for him and he became interested. Then she spoke of dance notation and said she had a copy of Feuillet's *Choréographie* at her hotel. He went back to the Hôtel Ravel with her, where most of the company stayed, and sat on her bed to study the book. It was quite normal among young Russians and Poles in those days that a girl should bring a boy back to her room – particularly among students who would not have more than one room of their own: but when he left he was seen by members of the company whose suspicions were merely confirmed that he was having an affair with Ramberg. It was only the next day that Mimi learned the reason – which Nijinsky had neglected to mention – why his sister would not be dancing in his ballets, prevented as he said by her husband Kotchetovsky: she was going to have a baby. Nijinsky could not forgive this when the fate of a work of art was at stake.

'L'Après-midi' was still in the repertory, of course, and a replacement for Bronia as the sixth Nymph had to be rehearsed. This was Bewicke. When towards the end, she had to come on alone to confront the Faun, then walk off with hands raised, she put on a frightened expression. Nijinsky reprimanded her, asking, 'Why do you make that face?' She replied, 'I thought I was meant to be frightened.' He said, 'Never mind what you thought. Do no more than I tell you. It is all in the choreography.'[47]

Meanwhile Diaghilev and Karsavina were travelling from Petersburg together. 'I had a powerful attraction in my compartment,' she wrote, 'an ornamental bucket of caviare, brought, together with chocolates, flowers and a small ikon, as a farewell gift.' Having Diaghilev temporarily in her power, Tamara decided to profit by the occasion.

T.K. Do you say your morning prayers, Sergei Pavlovitch?

S.D. (*after a slight hesitation*) Yes . . . I do. I do kneel down and think of those I love and all who love me.

T.K. Do you ever search your conscience for hurts you may have inflicted?

S.D. (*emphatically*) I do! So often I reproach myself for lack of consideration. I think of how at times I went out in a hurry without saying good-night to Nanny, forgetting to kiss her hand.[48]

On Karsavina's return, rehearsals for 'Jeux' began. Bronia's place was to be taken by Schollar. Nijinsky had been practising in women's ballet shoes as he intended to dance *sur les pointes* in this ballet, as he is shown doing in sketches by Gross of 'Schéhérazade' and 'Petrushka'; but he soon decided this was out of keeping and returned to his ordinary slippers. It was during a rehearsal of 'Jeux' that Ramberg had another sample of Nijinsky's rages. Karsavina asked him a question and he lost his temper and began to rave. She walked out of the room without a word. Nijinsky complained to Diaghilev that Karsavina had the mentality of a *prima ballerina*. Ramberg heard Diaghilev's furious reaction and the abuse he poured on Nijinsky. 'She is not just a ballerina, but a woman of enormous intelligence and distinction, and you are an ill-mannered guttersnipe.' He had seldom been seen in such a fury. Nijinsky was made to apologize and was forgiven.[49]

When Stravinsky arrived from Switzerland, where he and Ravel had been working together on the orchestration of 'Khovanshchina' for Diaghilev's Paris season, and he first saw the work that had been done on 'Le Sacre' there was another tremendous row. Nobody could possibly dance some of Nijinsky's steps to some of Stravinsky's *tempi*, so Nijinsky had slowed the music down. Stravinsky raged and stormed and banged the piano lid.[50] In later years he would write in his book *Chronique de ma vie* that Nijinsky was too ignorant musically to be fit to do choreography: but the *Chronique* was ghosted by Walter Nouvel, and in his old age Stravinsky took back these words. Yet, whatever he thought of the choreography for 'Le Sacre', at the time Stravinsky adored 'L'Après-midi d'un faune'. Perhaps seeing your music interpreted in movement is like having your portrait painted. You admire the artist's gift for catching the likeness of your friends, but are appalled by the caricature he does of you. Debussy doubtless preferred Nijinsky's work for 'Le Sacre' to his choreography for 'L'Après-midi' and 'Jeux', which he detested.

Nijinsky making up for 'Carnaval', watched by Igor Stravinsky.
Caricature by Jean Cocteau.

Maria Piltz, who was to dance the role of the Chosen Virgin in 'Le Sacre' in place of Bronia, was a tall handsome girl with Slav features. Her dance of sacrifice would be the overwhelming climax of the barbaric rite, but, like the *corps de ballet*, she found Nijinsky's new movements so alien to everything she had ever been called upon to do before that she was slow in realizing his intentions. One afternoon Nijinsky rehearsed with her alone, only Ramberg being present. The latter watched in silent dismay, for Piltz could not see what was needed. Nijinsky showed her the dance. If only *he* could have taken the role, thought Ramberg, if only the Harvest God could have been propitiated with a male sacrifice, this might have been Nijinsky's most wonderful creation. With clenched hand across his face, he threw himself into the air in paroxysms of fear and grief. His movements were stylized and controlled, yet he gave out a tremendous power of tragedy. It was a unique rendering of the solo by its

335

creator, something to be remembered for ever. When Piltz came to dance the role in public, she kept the bones of Nijinsky's perform-ance, but according to Ramberg it was a poor copy, a postcard re-production of what he had been that afternoon: even so Piltz made a profound impression on the audience.[51]

The little group of dancers who had been auditioned in London, two Russian men and three English girls, arrived to join the com-pany; and Hilda Munnings has given us an account of her first reactions to the Diaghilev Ballet.

My first impression of the company was one of richness and profusion. There seemed to be such an abundance of everything, whether of ballet shoes and costumes or of the hats, shoes and gloves which the dancers wore in private life. We three English girls felt so dowdy in our blouses and skirts. Most of the girls were exceedingly pretty, particularly the Polish ones. Women all had long hair in those days, and most of the com-pany were dark; but Olga Khokhlova had glorious dark auburn hair. I was one of the few blondes in the company.

Every day began with Maestro Cecchetti's class at nine o'clock ... we wore white tutus and pink silk tights, but for the rehearsal which followed immediately we wore *crêpe-de-Chine* dresses which took three and a half metres of material to make. They were caught in with one bit of elastic under the breast and another around the thigh, and they fell in pretty draperies just below the knee. Although there was a lot of stuff in them, they were easy to move in and as we all had them made in different colours we must have been a wonderful sight. Rehearsals were conducted by Serge Grigoriev, our *régisseur* or stage-manager. He was about thirty, and to us English girls he seemed tall and terrifying. He had a perpetually worried look and seldom smiled, though, when something amused him, he would let out a short, loud laugh. Not understanding much of what he said, I had the feeling that he was usually complaining ... When we failed to understand some explanation, he grew impatient and began to shout, covering us with a shower of spit. Being nervous, I never knew whether to wipe it off or leave it ... I got pushed around a good deal at first, not knowing any of the ballets and speaking no Russian, and the Polish girls used to get annoyed with me and shove me about the stage, saying, 'Pooosh, Meeess.' ... When Diaghilev came for the first time to one of our rehearsals I was scared stiff. His presence was awe-inspiring and he radiated self-assurance, like royalty. Tall and heavy, with a little moustache and a monocle, he advanced into the room, followed by a group of friends.

Everyone who was seated stood up, and silence fell. With Grigoriev following discreetly a yard or two behind, he passed through the crowd of dancers, stopping here and there to exchange a greeting. Any male dancer to whom he spoke would click his heels together and bow.[52]

Hilda observed Nijinsky.

In appearance Nijinsky was himself like a faun – a wild creature who had been trapped by society and was always ill at ease. When addressed, he turned his head furtively, looking as if he might suddenly butt you in the stomach. He moved on the balls of his feet, and his nervous energy found an outlet in fidgeting: when he sat down he twisted his fingers or played with his shoes. He hardly spoke to anyone, and seemed to exist on a different plane. Before dancing he was even more withdrawn, like a bewitched soul. I used to watch him practising his wonderful jumps in the first position, flickering his hands; I had never seen anyone like him before.[53]

Romola de Pulszky had her private lesson with Cecchetti at eleven when the company class was over. Nijinsky and Karsavina came for theirs at twelve. One day Romola sprained her ankle, but the Maestro made her go on working. Vaslav, who had arrived early, took her foot in his hand, felt the ankle and told Cecchetti she should be sent home to rest. He cannot have been unaware of her existence, even if he held aloof.[54] Romola was rather jealous of Mimi's friendship with Nijinsky, but she cultivated her acquaintance in the hopes of hearing useful information about him or obtaining access to him.[55] Ramberg, on her side, found the young Hungarian most attractive and affable.[56] She dressed well, had winning manners and a captivating way of smoking a cigarette. In those days only Nihilists and the most sophisticated people smoked cigarettes, and Romola was certainly no Nihilist. When the company moved to Paris the two women continued to meet; and Mimi would leave her aunt's flat in the old, historic quarter of the Marais to dine with Romola at her Hôtel d'Iéna in the modern fashionable district on the way to Passy. Ramberg was completely innocent of the Hungarian's state of mind. She had no inkling that Romola was in pursuit of Nijinsky: but then she had not analysed her own feelings for Nijinsky either, so completely did her admiration for him as an artist and a creator of genius dominate her thoughts.

The situation was ironical. Romola's friendship with Ramberg enabled her to learn everything she could about Nijinsky's character, his ideals, his method of working, the way his mind functioned, what amused, what shocked and what pleased him. Mimi was flattered and attracted by her sophisticated rival; and there can be little doubt that her confidences went far to helping Romola charm and win Nijinsky away from her when Romola eventually found herself alone with him.

The Monte Carlo season ended on 6 May. Diaghilev would have taken his company to the Opéra for his spring season in Paris, but Astruc wanted him for the new Théâtre des Champs-Elysées, of which he was manager. How much were the Opéra offering, he had asked Diaghilev; was it 12,000 francs a performance, his usual price? 'Yes', Diaghilev had replied, 'but you must understand that people are saying that Astruc invented the Russian Ballet. That, my dear friend, must be paid for.' Astruc was obliged to settle for 25,000 a performance. 'This folly,' he wrote, 'which I had not the right *not* to commit, made possible the creation of "Le Sacre", but cost me the life of my management.'[57]* In fact he went bankrupt shortly after.

The Théâtre des Champs-Elysées was (and still is) not in the Avenue des Champs-Elysées, but in the Avenue Montaigne, which led off it, near the Place de l'Alma and the Seine. It was large, luxurious and magnificently up-to-date. Its architecture was by Perret. Both the sculptured reliefs by Bourdelle on the outside and the painted frescoes by Maurice Denis in the auditorium were inspired by Isadora at her most Dionysian.

Together with his own ballet company – Sophie Feodorova and Ludmilla Schollar were the only guest artists[58] – Diaghilev was to present singers of the Imperial Theatres in 'Boris Godounov' and 'Khovanshchina', but as they could not arrive until 18 May the season was to open with ballet, and the first performance on the 15th was to include 'Jeux'. Nijinsky, however, had not finished 'Jeux' when he and Diaghilev arrived in Paris and put up at the Elysée Palace Hotel. Diaghilev was extremely anxious and said the ballet must be completed without delay. A rehearsal was called in the

*He was over-simplifying. There were other contributory factors. The splendid theatre was not an economical proposition.

new theatre, but it was one of Nijinsky's bad days. 'He stood in the middle of the practice-room,' wrote Grigoriev, 'his mind an obvious blank. I felt that the situation was desperate and suggested a run-through of what had been composed, in the hope of stimulating his invention. This luckily produced the desired effect.'[59]

One of the first visits Diaghilev and Vaslav paid in Paris was to Ravel, and they took Bronia and Stravinsky with them. Stravinsky photographed Ravel and Nijinsky playing *à quatre mains* and also looking down from the balcony of the flat on to the Avenue Carnot, near the Etoile. Ravel was a passionate admirer of Stravinsky's 'Le Sacre', the première of which he thought would prove 'an event as great as "Pelléas" '.[60] According to Stravinsky he was 'the only musician who immediately understood "Le Sacre du printemps" '.[61]

If 'L'Après-midi d'un faune' was a vase painting or a frieze in low relief, one has the impression from the few photographs that survive and from the seven pastels of Valentine Gross that in 'Jeux' the relief had grown bolder. Although 'Jeux' was partly inspired by the paintings of Gauguin it looks as if the choreographer was also aiming at a compact, enclosed sculptural form, the very opposite of the extended *arabesques*, *attitudes* and *port de bras* of classical ballet, which, as we know, does not on the whole lend itself to sculpture. Few painters, of course, have been more flat and decorative than Gauguin: yet it seems hardly less paradoxical that the choreographer, admiring the coloured masses of the painter, should aim at imparting to their realization in terms of human bodies in the round some of the monumentality he had for the last few years been observing in the sculptures of Maillol, Renoir and of his friend Rodin, than that his ballet, pretending to be about sport and triangular love-making, should in reality be abstract, concerned neither with sporting movements nor human feelings, an essay in formal design.

How Nijinsky married his 'stylized gesture' – which was the name for the new kind of dancing – to Debussy's music we shall probably never know. The composer thought it was too literal in some places and totally unrelated in others. Valentine Gross thought that Nijinsky had followed the music admirably, but too closely, and that a certain disparity between the nature of the movement and that of the score came from the ballet having been rehearsed to piano only.[62]

The most sculptural of the groups is that in which Karsavina embraces Schollar.* The latter stands facing us, with right foot slightly advanced, hanging hands curled up – the right just above the left – head leaning over the left shoulder. Karsavina is arrested in a stride on half-point; she leans a little forward from the waist, right arm slanting across the front of Schollar's body to grasp her above the left elbow, left arm placed round her neck so that the curled hand is visible on Schollar's left shoulder. The most striking aspect of this group is the line formed by the underneath of Karsavina's hair, continued by her back and skirt down to her foot. Then there is a kind of interlocking which is highly satisfactory, and the gesture of Karsavina recalls that of the Virgin Mary in the Leonardo painting of St Anne, the Virgin and the infant Christ, in the Louvre.

The group in which the three dancers stand in a row with Nijinsky in the middle is a version of the Three Graces. The composition in which the slightly bending Karsavina addresses Schollar, who sits, knees tucked under her, one hand in her lap, the other at her breast, the head sadly inclined, while Nijinsky watches them both, is, of all these groups, the most reminiscent of Gauguin. In the group where Nijinsky appears to threaten the two girls, his pose with upraised right forearm and left hand clenched tightly to the side of his belt, is like one of those little Etruscan bronzes of warriors with spear and shield, except that the dancer's head is bent, ready to butt faunwise, rather than held back in defiance. In the similar pose where Nijinsky, taking the weight on his left leg, has his right fist to his forehead, he recalls the sculptures of Roman athletes.

At the first dress-rehearsal Bakst's set was revealed. The heavy summer trees are seen at dusk with painted stylized patches of electric light. Behind them looms a big white building with rows of little windows, perhaps, as we have remarked, inspired by Bloomsbury. On the green floor-cloth are painted four circular flower-beds. Bronislava Nijinska thought the setting had too much sense of space, and that the choreography asked for something more confined. Rightly or wrongly, it seems that Bakst's intention was to dwarf the dancers and make them appear more childlike. Diaghilev was sitting

*These few observations on the surviving records of 'Jeux' may be read in conjunction with Plates 24 and 25.

in the middle of the *corbeille*. On the appearance of Nijinsky in his red wig, rolled-up shirt-sleeves, red tie and knee-length trousers with a red border, held up by red braces, and his white stockings with red tops, Diaghilev exploded. 'No, no, it's quite impossible!' Bakst was to the left of the *corbeille*. 'What's the matter, Serioja? It's a very good costume.' 'I'm sorry, my dear Levushka,' came the answer, firm but gentle. 'It won't do at all. He looks ridiculous.' The argument continued in the most affectionate manner, but Diaghilev was adamant. He redesigned Nijinsky's costume himself,[63] retaining the white shirt and red tie, but giving the dancer white trousers which grew narrower below the knee, and gripped the calf, ending just above the ankle. The girls' white dresses with their tight-fitting bodices and knee-length skirts were made by Paquin. Incidentally, it is clear from Bakst's original design that Nijinsky's costume is for a footballer, and the ball at his feet is a football. It was the size of the white tennis ball which began the action of the ballet by bouncing on to the stage that was to provoke mirth in the Paris audience, and comment from the sporting English. And we have seen that a basic movement planned by the choreographer (and of which we have no picture) was derived from golf. It seems that the Russians were as vague about the distinction between one game and another as Sarah Bernhardt, who stopped her car in the suburbs of Manchester to observe a game of football, exclaiming in rapture, '*J'adore ce cricket – c'est tellement anglais.*'[64]

The music of 'Jeux', barely appreciated in 1913, has latterly been recognized as one of Debussy's finest achievements. The composer himself confessed, 'Before I composed a ballet I didn't know what a choreographer was. Now I know – he is a very strong and mathematical gentleman.'[65] Nevertheless, the overall musical plan is more accommodating than Debussy pretends: thinly veiled by the magical sonorities are all the dance-episodes of the scenario.

Orchestral score	Action	Music
Très lent		Against sustained octaves in the strings, harps usher in a dreamily ambivalent whole-tone melody played 'pianissimo, doux et rêveur' by the woodwind.
Fig. [1] Scherzando		Cellos and bassoons introduce the first of the brief snatches of melody which make up the whole work.
[5] Mouvement du Prélude		Return of the opening music, more thickly scored.
[6] Tempo initial	A tennis-ball is thrown on stage. A young man in tennis clothes holding his racket high in the air leaps across the stage and disappears. Two girls appear, shy and inquisitive. They have something to confide to each other and are seeking a suitable corner.	The scherzando proper begins. Clarinets add to the snatch already heard an important two-bar phrase which seems to say 'where is the action?' Curious that the first four notes should be those of the opening of Schubert's 'Unfinished Symphony'. These and other ideas are developed against an infinitely flexible background of sudden glissandos, trills, tremolandos, the subtle stock-in-trade of Debussy's orchestra.
[14] Mouvement	They begin their dance, first one then the other.	
[24] Très marqué	Suddenly they stop, put off by the sound of rustling leaves. The young man has been watching them through the branches. They want to run away, but he leads them back, and persuades one to dance with him.	Loud trumpets, and brusque chords in the strings. The first set-piece dance is over, and is succeeded by Debussy's equivalent of a Tchaikovskian mime-scene. The music follows the action with great fluidity; the score is peppered with tempo indications – 'serrez un peu', 'retenu', 'cédez', 'au mouvement'. Gently insistent melodies alternate with flurries of feminine embarrassment.
[32] Passionnément	He even manages to steal a kiss from her, whereupon the	
[33] Assez aminé, ironique et léger	jealousy of the other is immediately aroused, which	

Orchestral score	*Action*	*Music*
[34] Au mouvement	she expresses in a mocking dance. By this means she wins some attention from the young man who tries to teach her	$\frac{2}{4}$ Spiky pizzicato chords and sneering chromatic tunes in the woodwind.
[38] Mouvement de valse	the steps of a waltz. The girl at first mimics him, but is eventually won over.	$\frac{3}{8}$ Jagged hemiola rhythms in the strings (? Debussy's tribute to 'Daphnis and Chloë'). The clarinet finds a suitable tune after two false starts.
[41] Joyeux	They dance together.	The other woodwinds take it up.
[43] Tempo	Her abandoned friend now wishes to make off, but the other, in a slower passage, retains her.	$\frac{3}{4}$ Downward glissandos. Tremolo in the lower strings sustaining a brief pleading tune.
[44] Revenir progressivement au mouvement de valse	The three now join in a *pas de trois*.	$\frac{3}{8}$ Chattering woodwind introduce the final set-piece number.
8 bars after [48]	Some incident interrupts the dance.	Sforzando violins slither to a pianissimo pause. Clarinets remind us of the opening scherzando tune.
[51] Mouvement initial	The dance continues.	Chattering woodwind over celesta and xylophone. Wistfully, the cor anglais plays the first tune again. With increasing intensity new and old snatches of melody are tossed around. It seems like a gradual fusion of the masculine and feminine elements.
[78] Très modéré	Climax. Another lost tennis ball falls on stage.	The whole orchestra thunders out the first four notes of the opening tune. The energy rapidly evaporates, as the first desk of violins reminds us of 'Schéhérazade'. A final flurry from the woodwind.
[80]	The players flee.	A short section added at
[81] Mouvement du Prélude		Diaghilev's request. Return of the slow opening music, rescored again. Four final bars seem to say to the director of the Ballets Russes: 'This is how "Petrushka" ended, and you wanted to change that, too!'[66]

343

Two days later there appeared in *Le Figaro* Henri Quittard's review of 'Jeux', for which, as he said,

... Debussy had not scorned to write the music ... Even with such a childish libretto, one would think that this haphazard essay in affectation might provide something graceful or pretty to look at. But the new art, of which M. Nijinsky is the prophet, manages to turn even the insignificant to absurdity. What could be more ungraceful than the meaningless, pretentious contortions, dreamt up by this nimble aesthete. It goes without saying that modern dress does not enhance these poses inspired by Greek vase paintings, with which 'L'Après-midi d'un faune' took us by surprise last year. Furthermore this so-called reformed choreography employs the most old-fashioned and conventional gestures and mime, without any attempt to make them less funny.

It is said that M. Nijinsky's intention was to provide, in this ballet, an apologia in plastic terms for the man of 1913. If this is so, we have nothing to be proud of. But it is annoying that he should almost have succeeded, by some evil spell, in turning those exquisite ballerinas, Mlles Karsavina and Schollar, into stiff and awkward puppets. The public, apart from a few quite lively interruptions, submitted good-humouredly to these mystifications. No doubt people would have been content just to listen to the music. Composer and choreographer take absolutely no notice of each other in this ballet. Just as well for the music.[67]

An article signed 'Swift' in the *Bulletin de la Société Musicale Indépendante*, though it may not have reached a wide public, is funny enough to deserve quotation. 'Summer sports. A number of readers have enquired about the rules of Russian Tennis, which is bound to be the rage of country house-parties this season. They are as follows: the game is played at night on flood-lit flower-beds; there are only three players and the net is dispensed with; the tennis-ball is replaced by a football and the use of the racket is forbidden. Hidden in a pit at the edge of the court, an orchestra accompanies the game. The purpose of this sport is to develop suppleness of the neck, wrists and ankles; and it has the blessing of the Academy of Medicine.'

On 20 May, an interview with Nijinsky, signed Emile Deflin, appeared in *Gil Blas*:

You can't just walk into the Debussian dancer's dressing-room as if it were the Moulin de la Galette. I had to use a bit of cunning in order to get into the Faun's cage. My friend Robert de Tomaz, most Parisian of expatriate Slavs, who reads Tolstoi as easily as Stéphane Mallarmé, the lucky devil, scribbled a few words of Russian on his card and the door gaped wide at this Open Sesame as if passwords had been exchanged – 'Toulon?' 'Kronstadt!'

In the dressing-room there is a faint smell of scent, but it is very simple without a hint of luxury. None of the innumerable photographs of the dancer are to be seen – only a few designs by Bakst and some sketches of Rodin. There are no flowers; the wreaths are all in the wardrobe. Sunk in an old divan whose springs have given way, Nijinsky is sponging himself. His white flannel shirt is open to the waist, his tennis belt, undone, is hanging loose. Huge drops of sweat outline the slanting ridges of his cheek-bones. He has just been dancing 'Jeux'. After we have been introduced Nijinsky, with a slight effort, begins to speak French, but Robert de Tomaz comes to the rescue and from then on their conversation is held in the sonorous tongue of our allies.[68]

It must not be imagined from the following interview that so long a speech was typical of Nijinsky. His words have been edited by the journalist and turned into 'prose'.

'I was rather surprised and sad,' the dancer says, smiling, 'at the public's reaction to "Jeux", but I don't despair. I thought they would understand what I was trying to do and didn't expect them to laugh at my experiments in stylized gesture. You probably know that it was while I was watching tennis at Deauville last year that I was struck by the beauty of certain poses and movements and had the idea of putting them together in a work of art, treating them symphonically, so to speak ... M. Debussy's music was a remarkable help in the realization of my aim and, I must say, I went about my work with a good deal of confidence. As I said, the rather unkind reception of the ballet has not discouraged me, because even if most people disapproved there have been one or two whose judgement I value who have liked what I did. I wanted to show my experiment first in France, because it has always struck me that the French public is the most artistic. In England, where I danced for a long season last winter, there is a great understanding of dancing, especially classical dancing. The French, on the other hand, have more flair and I think make better judges of something new. I hope still to interest them in my experiments in stylized gesture. I'm not afraid of hard work; I shall just keep trying to do something really good.'[69]

345

Debussy did not like Nijinsky's ballet. On 9 June he was to write to Robert Godet:

Among recent pointless goings-on I must include the staging of 'Jeux', which gave Nijinsky's perverse genius a chance of indulging in a peculiar kind of mathematics. This fellow adds up triple crochets with his feet, checks them on his arms, then suddenly, half-paralysed, he stands crossly watching the music slip by. It's awful. It's even Dalcrozian – for I consider Monsieur Dalcroze as one of the greatest enemies of music and you can imagine what havoc his method can create in the mind of a young savage like Nijinsky![70]

Listening to Debussy's wonderful score today, our minds boggle at how Nijinsky could have found movements – if not to match or parallel it – at least which would seem acceptable as something to watch while listening to it. It is clear that he sought a most venturesome solution. What would we not give to see revived his choreography to the music of Debussy in Bakst's décor (which is sentimentalized in the pastels of Valentine Gross) and with its original cast! That Diaghilev should have commissioned such a score (which the composer was unwilling to write) and should have made it possible for Nijinsky to rehearse to it his dangerous experiments enhances our awe of him. That the composer of such a score should have been so derisive of pioneering in another medium and that his derision should be shared by both critics and public fills us with such pity for the heroic Diaghilev and Nijinsky that a phrase of Isadora's, written as the postscript of a despairing letter from Turkestan, where she was wasting her sweetness on an unappreciative provincial public, comes to mind: 'Hell of a life anyway.'[71]

Now the time was near for 'Le Sacre du printemps'.

How sure of himself and his innovations in choreography was Nijinsky? Did the cool reception of 'Jeux' give him doubts? Confident or doubting, any artist who has battled all night with his angel and won through to his own satisfaction must be relatively unconcerned about the way his work is received: to captivate the public scores only five points out of a hundred. Of course Nijinsky needed the approval of Diaghilev, of Stravinsky, of Bakst – his earlier mentor, even though it was Roerich who had designed the sets and dresses for 'Le Sacre' – and perhaps of Bronia. The question of

Stravinsky playing 'Le Sacre du printemps'.
Caricature by Jean Cocteau.

having to please the public in order to make money – if it had entered his head as a boy – had long since been something to which he gave no thought, so entirely had Diaghilev isolated him from worldly cares. An anecdote recorded by Jacques Rivière gives a key to Nijinsky's state of mind on the eve of battle, as well as illustrating his puckish sense of humour. An acquaintance asked him what 'Le Sacre' was like. 'Oh, you won't like that either,' said the choreographer. Then, making the angular sideways gesture of 'Faune', he said 'There's more of that kind of thing.'[72] People who are not sure of themselves do not joke about their masterpieces.

Let us consider first the ballet of 'Le Sacre du printemps' itself, its music and choreography; second its rating in the eyes of Jacques Rivière, its most intelligent critic, who wrote a long essay about it in *La Nouvelle Revue Française*; third the reaction of the public on the opening night; lastly its handling by the press.

347

It is impossible to describe in a few words the novelty of Stravinsky's score for 'Le Sacre du printemps', or to judge to what extent its novelties made it the masterpiece it was. A new kind of marvellous monster, it sprang without warning from the forehead of Jove, leaving the doctors a long way behind with their explanations of its conception, birth and magical anatomy. First it was new in rhythm. Stravinsky overthrew the whole rhythmic system – or rather, invented a new one. Bar after bar there was a different time signature. The composer himself was baffled as to how to write out the final 'Danse Sacrale'. Second, the ballet was new in its orchestration, using both string and woodwind in extreme registers, thus producing new sounds – and, of course, at Diaghilev's specific request it had been scored for an exceptionally large orchestra (there were eight horns). A peculiarity was the accumulation of special instrumental effects – such as the use of harmonics, *col legno*, fluttertongue on the flute and *campanella in aria* on the French horn.

Nijinsky's stupendous task was to parallel or find an equivalent for this titanic composition in choreographic terms. But he already had in his mind, as we know, new things he wanted to do, and it must have been a question to what extent his new *plastique* – the chief novelty of which was that it had been conceived as much from a painter's, sculptor's and dramatist's point of view as from a balletmaster's – could be wedded to the composer's inventions. He had to imagine his new kinds of pose, of movement, of grouping – devoid of classical virtuosity, but which would certainly be so hard to execute accurately that only ballet dancers would be able to perform them. Then he had, as in 'Faune', only more so, to overcome the reluctant minds and recalcitrant bodies of these dancers, trained to think, count and move so differently. Finally he had to find the key to the unfathomable score. It was an undertaking to baffle the most experienced choreographer, the most professional musician. Nijinsky was neither. He had only his vision and his genius.

In the Introduction a strange nasal solo on the bassoon playing in its highest register – later joined by the horn – evokes the first stirrings of some primeval Russian spring. Irrupting *arpeggios* on other wind instruments suggest sudden spurts of growth, vegetable or animal, in the womb of darkness. The first violins *pizzicato* set the strict pace of the opening dance which is to follow and lead into the Augurs of Spring.[73] In Roerich's green landscape with its lake and birch-trees beneath a cloudy sky boys in embroidered white smocks are jumping up and down in circles to a steady rhythm of heavy string chords supported by the eight horns in block harmony accenting their syncopated beats. (This percussive effect is achieved without drums.) The boys are being taught by an old woman, represented by an *ostinato* figure on the bassoons shadowed by cor anglais and *pizzicato* cellos, certain spells and divinations which must be performed every spring. It is a question of fortune-telling. Squawks from the upper woodwind are like convulsions of nature (as it were vegetable birth-pangs magnified a thousand times) which happen throughout the human ritual. The groups take turns to dance and sit. A simple almost Greek dance-tune on the alto flute is followed by a Russian chorale-like tune on four trumpets. A variation of the dance-tune is carried on incredibly by violins and piccolos only above the whole orchestra, which abandons itself to a Bacchanalian frenzy, and, as the dancers fall to the floor, spills over into the *presto* of the Ritual of Abduction. Two groups of red-clad girls enter in succession to string chords and syncopated drum-beats. Their sight of the boys induces a sexual panic, represented by vociferous brass and twittering woodwind. The groups of challenging men (frenetic horn calls) and trampling, jumping women confront each other from opposite sides of the stage, as the orchestra emits short *staccato* ejaculations interrupted each time by heavy single punches, with drums to the fore, which later become double and take over the music's texture. To these clashes of brass the men grasp the women in a gesture of stylized rape: this is briefly elaborated on by two pairs of dancers before the movement ends.

Spring Rounds are introduced by an expectant trill which, when heard earlier, seemed a kind of spell, and now played on flutes and alto flutes is extended with shattering effect. Against this clarinets are playing a simple, almost primeval melodic sequence. The dance proper begins with a distinctive dragging rhythmic figure, which is repeated over and over again. When the Russian chorale tune reappears in a slightly different form, some continue to follow the basic rhythm while others follow the melody. As the whole orchestra take up the solemn tune and render it threatening, men and girls form up and revolve in separate circles. Two tribes are established for the ritual games. The dance ends tranquilly with a repetition of its opening bars. The Games of the Rival Tribes open with swaggering martial passages on the brass. These alternate throughout the number with more lyrical dipping sections. Short bursts of warfare between the men alternate with pleading from the swinging, clapping women and competitive dances. At the built-up conclusion a barbaric tune on the tubas serves as a ground bass supporting the orchestral frenzy and runs straight into the Procession of the Sage. To crashing chords the Elders of the tribe lead on their Sage or High Priest with his long white beard. The tribe trembles with religious awe. To a quiet interlude the Sage, supported by the Elders, lays himself spreadeagle on the ground. This is the Adoration of the Earth. Auspices are taken. As the music ends with a held spidery chord on the strings, which somehow suggests the presence of the god, the people run to form a square representing the tribal compound.

The Dance of the Earth, which concludes the first scene, is a frenzied celebration of the people, drunk with spring. A single drum in triplet rhythm is joined by another in quadruplet rhythm: this metric contrast gives the number its wild pulse. *Staccato* outbursts of the orchestra with the brass prominent play snatches of figuration and detached off-beat chords. A quieter passage, dominated by horn colour, is like the stirring of a dark whirlpool. The insistent double drum rhythm is taken up and played with various permutations by the whole orchestra. The whirlpool becomes a boiling cauldron as, to syncopated shrieks on the brass and woodwind, the dancers in separate asymmetrical clumps leap and fall convulsively and the scene ends.

The Introduction to the second part paints a melancholy twilit landscape with small creatures and brooks. A sense of desolation is imparted by the strange colour of the muted trumpets and by mysterious muted horn calls, which seem far away. *Arpeggios* on E flat clarinets and strings suggest water falling among the rocks. A Russian tune introduced very gently on alto flute and solo violin implies that this landscape is inhabited.

Roerich's second scene is a dusky hilltop, with sacred stones and three poles hung with votive skins and antlers. In a number called Mystic Circles of Young Girls one of the virgins will be chosen through the hazard of the dance to be sacrificed to the Sun God. When the curtain rises all the girls stand welded into one group, trembling, facing outward. Their toes are pointed in, their knees bent and their right elbows rest on their left fists, while their right fists support their heads, which are bent sideways. The men and Elders stand watching them. To a languid *legato* tune on six solo violas, against the background of *pizzicato* cello, the ring of girls moves round, and at certain counts the whole group rise on tip-toe, dropping their right hands to their sides and jerking their heads to the left. When one circuit has been completed every other girl leaps out of the ring, then back in again. A spurting clarinet trill and a chromatic *tremolo* passage on violins introduces a romantic Russian tune (reminiscent of the 'Firebird' princesses) on the alto flute. The girls walk with a bell-swinging gesture, start and stop again. One of them is chosen. Guitar-like *pizzicato* chords on violas and cellos provide a new colour; a short passage for two solo violas doubled with flutes adds a further sensuousness. The Russian tune is developed and a *sforzando* chord on muted horns starts a *crescendo* and *accelerando*. Eleven double-stopped string chords supported by four-part timpani chords lead into the next number.

This is the Glorification of the Chosen Virgin, who has fallen into a trance. To ecstatic shrieks on the wind the dancers, divided into five groups, male and female, leap and stamp convulsively to chugging or fragmented rhythms. As they approach and surround the Chosen Virgin her emotions are expressed by a hysterical outburst on upper woodwind and brass.

The Evocation of the Ancestors opens with declamatory fanfares alternating with a three-note figure on the drums and basses, distantly echoed by woodwind and drums. To celebrate the Ritual of the Ancestors the Elders enter covered in animal skins and process round the Chosen Virgin. To an oriental tune, against the steady rhythm of brass drums with off-beat timpani and tambourine, the tribe recall their forbears in a slow reflective dance. A new murmuring dancing tune on the alto flute is joined by a counter-tune on muted trumpets, which takes over and assumes a striding, pounding rhythm. There is a return to the oriental tune and the rhythmic texture of the earlier part. A rhapsodic clarinet leads with little warning into the sacrificial dance.

Maria Piltz in 'Le Sacre du printemps'. Five drawings by Valentine Gross.

To *staccato* shrieks and percussive chords the final ritual begins as the tribe stamp round the Chosen Virgin, whose dance of exhaustion will be the culmination of the dance drama. Then there breaks out a persistent but halting and convulsive rhythm on the strings, and the Virgin is drawn first to assist then to lead her fellows in the celebration of her own sacrifice. Meanwhile, there are heard blood-curdling ejaculations, which seem to be threats or warnings from the erupting forces of nature. These are played first on loud muted trombones answered by two loud muted trumpets, then by a piccolo, E flat clarinet and D trumpet call, twice. A hysterical trill on the violins, augmented by piccolos ascending in a nightmarish way, leads back to the wild, chaotic rhythms of the opening. These are developed and intensified, becoming ever more complex and unbalanced. The mem-

bers of the tribe repeat the same jumps again and again, turning in
ritual despair to left and to right, while the Virgin is galvanized into
leaps of an increasing frenzy. At last she falls exhausted. She tries to
rise, but in vain. Her last breath, which is also the orgasm of the god,
is a gurgle, like the spilling of sap, heard as a little upward run on the

flutes. A short silence, then to a final conclusive chord, not on full
orchestra, but on cellos, basses, horns, trombones and tuba playing
fortissimo, she dies. Six men raise her body at arms' length above
their heads.

Taking a metaphor from the kitchen, Jacques Rivière wrote that
the novelty of both the music and the choreography of 'Le Sacre'
consisted in their lack of 'sauce' or 'dressing'. From a musical point
of view 'sauce' meant atmosphere, Debussyish impressionism,
shimmering orchestration. In dancing it could mean two things:
first the veils and lighting of Loie Fuller which merged the dancer in
a vague coloured haze (Debussy again) – this the Russians, with their
classical geometry, had always eschewed; second, the dazzlement

of the dance itself, such as that of Nijinsky in 'Le Spectre', in which virtuosity and physical magic masked the lack of meaning and inner truth. Rivière rightly imagined – and he had not heard the young choreographer criticizing Fokine as Ramberg had – that Nijinsky, the supreme executant of Fokine's choreography, had begun to feel while dancing it a certain *malaise* caused by a growing consciousness of its soft centre, its lack of inner truth. 'And from that moment he had no rest until he himself had given the final turn to the vice and tightened the screws of the choreographic machine so that it was in perfect working order.' Rivière never doubted for a moment that the twenty-four-year-old Nijinsky had shot far ahead of Fokine and made the greatest of all the Russian ballets.

In Fokine's ballets dancers were disposed in symmetrical groups: this was not the absurd symmetry of the Opéra, but there was a regular distribution of masses . . . this equilibrium did not apply only to static poses, it was carried through the movements of the dance no matter how abandoned that dance might be . . . Every pattern was conceived on the principle of response, of give and take; the dancers seized on a gesture and passed it continually backwards and forwards from one to the other like a ball. No group moved except in response to the movement of the opposite group . . . After a while Fokine had no other way of being original except to vary the subject and the props. In vain that for the golden apples of 'L'Oiseau de feu' he substituted the daggers of 'Thamar' and the crooks of 'Daphnis et Chloë': it was a losing battle. The only way to rediscover the source of all variety was first to forget generalizations and start again from the particular. This is what Nijinsky has done. Taking each group separately . . . he studied its cellular formation and recorded its instincts at the very moment of their birth; he became the observer and historian of its slightest impulse. The dancing of each group consists of movements hatched in isolation from the other groups, like those spontaneous fires that break out in haystacks. The absolute asymmetry which reigns throughout 'Le Sacre' is the very essence of the work . . . There is no lack of composition; on the contrary, there is the subtlest composition imaginable in the encounters, the challenges, the frays and the conflicts of these strange battalions. But composition does not take precedence over detail, does not condition it: it makes the best use it can of diverse elements. The impression of unity which we never cease for a moment to enjoy is like the sensation of watching the inhabitants of a given state moving about, passing, accosting and parting from each other, each intent on his own business, taking his neighbours for granted and putting them out of mind . . .

What advantage did Nijinsky gain by renouncing 'sauce'? To what end has he broken the flow of movement and destroyed choreographic *ensembles*? What kind of beauty is hidden in this spare, restricted dancing? Without insisting further on its marvellous appropriateness to the subject of 'Le Sacre du printemps', it seems to me easy to see in what way it surpasses the work of Fokine. The latter is fundamentally unsuited to the expression of emotion. All one can read in it is a vague, entirely physical and faceless joy . . . By breaking up movement, by returning to the simplicity of gesture, Nijinsky has restored expressiveness to dancing. All the angularities and awkwardness of this choreography keep the feeling in. The movement encloses it, grasps it, contains it; and by the continual changes of direction it blocks every possible outlet . . . The body is no longer an escape-route for the soul: on the contrary, it gathers itself together to contain the soul . . . Fokine's choreography was so inexpressive that to convey to the spectators a change of mood the performers had to resort to facial mimicry, frowns or smiles. That this was added to and superimposed upon their gestures was for that very reason a proof of the ineffectuality of these. It was a reinforcement, something borrowed from another medium to help out the poverty of choreography pure and simple. But in Nijinsky's choreography the face plays no independent role; it is an extension of the body, its flower. Nijinsky makes the body itself speak. It only moves as a whole, as one block, and its speech is expressed in sudden bounds with open arms and legs, or in sideways runs with bent knees and with the head lying on one shoulder. At first sight it seems less skilful, less varied, less intelligent. Yet, with its wholesale displacements, its sudden turns-about, the way it comes to rest only to begin a frantic trembling on the spot, it says a thousand times more than the long-winded, facile, charming chatter of Fokine. The language of Nijinsky is infinitely detailed; it lets nothing get by; it penetrates into corners. No figures of speech, no *pirouettes*, no elliptical allusions. The dancer is no longer wafted by a slight, indifferent inspiration. No longer does he, in his flight, brush lightly against the world around him, he falls on it with the full force of his weight, leaving the imprint of his fall . . . Since he is no longer obliged to run one gesture into another or to consider their relationship with those which follow, he holds nothing of himself in reserve for the transition.

If we can but stop associating grace with symmetry and *arabesques*, we shall find it everywhere in 'Le Sacre du printemps', in the heads in profile contrasted with bodies full-on, in the elbows hugged into the waist, in the horizontal forearms, in the stiff open hands, in the wavelike vibration which runs through the dancers from head to foot, in the minimal and mysterious parade of brooding girls in the second scene. We shall even find it in the dance of the Chosen Virgin, in her quick, awkward convulsions, in her confusion, in her awful waits, in her constrained, twisted bearing and in her arm raised stiffly skywards above her head, calling for help, in threat and in self-protection . . .

This is a biological ballet. It is not only the dance of the most primitive men, it is the dance before man . . . Stravinsky tells us that he wanted to portray the surge of spring. But this is not the usual spring sung by poets, with its breezes, its birdsong, its pale skies and tender greens. Here is nothing but the harsh struggle of growth, the panic terror from the rising of the sap, the fearful regrouping of the cells. Spring seen from inside, with its violence, its spasms and its fissions. We seem to be watching a drama through a microscope . . .[74]

Not since the reception of 'Tannhäuser' at the old Opéra in the rue Le Peletier in 1861, or even since the first night of Hugo's 'Hernani' at the Comédie Française in 1830, had there been such a battle as took place at the new Théâtre des Champs-Elysées on 29 May 1913. At the première of Hugo's play blocks of free seats had been distributed to art and architectural students and poets: these were the passionate supporters of Hugo, the young Romantics with their long hair and exotic attire; and he described looking through a hole in the curtain: 'From floor to ceiling the theatre was a mass of silk, jewels, flowers and bare shoulders. Amid all this splendour, in the pit and the second balcony, could be seen two broad patches of a darker colour marked by the waving of huge manes of hair.'[75] Much the same situation arose on the first night of 'Le Sacre'. Valentine Gross,* a hundred of whose studies of the Russian Ballet (including fifty of Nijinsky) were on exhibition in the foyer, describes it well:

I look back with delight at the uproar of that evening. At that time in the new theatre there was an ambulatory between the boxes of the *corbeille*† and the big boxes – and in those days there were no *strapontins* [folding seats]. It was here that stood all the painters, poets, journalists, and

*Who was to marry Jean Hugo, the great-grandson and heir of the poet.
†A novelty of the Théâtre des Champs-Elysées was that the front of the dress-circle was divided into pew-like boxes. The enclosed boxes of the horse-shoe were some way behind these.

musicians who were friends of Diaghilev, all the representatives of the new ideas and movements of that marvellous period. This band of Apollo was like a delightful river – calm, for the most part – flowing between the ramparts of the boxes, which were ablaze with diamonds and pearls. I knew already that the music of this ballet outstripped in violence and in dangerous experiment anything that had gone before. I also knew that the choreography had necessitated an incredible amount of work and that Nijinsky had shown a terrible determination during the countless and arduous rehearsals – had even, one day at the theatre, lost his temper to such an extent, teaching the ballet to the company, that he had literally nearly hit the ceiling of the rehearsal room – but I was expecting neither so great a work of art, nor such a scandal.

Nothing that has ever been written about the battle of 'Le Sacre du printemps' has given a faint idea of what actually took place. The theatre seemed to be shaken by an earthquake. It seemed to shudder. People shouted insults, howled and whistled, drowning the music. There was slapping and even punching. Words are inadequate to describe such a scene. Calm was briefly restored when the order was suddenly given to put up the house lights. It amused me to see how certain boxes whose occupants had been so noisy and vindictive in the dark quietened down when the lights went on. I must admit that our calm river had become a raging torrent. I saw Maurice Delage, beetroot-red with indignation, little Maurice Ravel truculent as a fighting-cock and Léon-Paul Fargue spitting out crushing remarks at the hissing boxes. I cannot think how it was possible for this ballet, which the public of 1913 found so difficult, to be danced through to the end in such an uproar. The dancers could not hear the music ... Diaghilev thundered orders from his box ... I missed nothing of the show which was taking place as much offstage as on. Standing between the two middle boxes, I felt quite at ease at the heart of the maelstrom, applauding with my friends. I thought there was something wonderful about the titanic struggle which must have been going on in order to keep these inaudible musicians and these deafened dancers together, in obedience to the laws of their invisible choreographer. The ballet was astoundingly beautiful.[76]

Jean Cocteau thought the public's reaction inevitable:

All the elements of a scandal were present. The smart audience in tails and tulle, diamonds and ospreys was interspersed with the suits and *bandeaux* of the aesthetic crowd. The latter would applaud novelty simply to show their contempt for the people in the boxes ... Innumerable shades of snobbery, super-snobbery and inverted snobbery were represented, which would need a chapter to themselves . . . The audience played the role that was written for it . . .[77]

Between the two scenes the police were called in to seek out and eject the most violent demonstrators. But it was in vain. No sooner had the curtain risen on the trembling girls of Part II, their tilted heads propped on the back of their hands, than a voice called out '*Un docteur*', then another: '*Un dentiste*!', followed by another: '*Deux dentistes*!'[78] There was laughter, shouting and whistling; and the battle was renewed. One smart lady in an orchestra box stood up and slapped the face of a man in the box next-door, who was hissing. Her escort rose and cards were exchanged by the two men, who fought a duel next day. Another society woman spat in the face of one of the demonstrators.[79] Comtesse René de Pourtalès* (whose photograph reveals an expression of fatuous pride) rose to her feet in her box, tiara askew, and cried out, brandishing her fan, 'I am sixty years old and this is the first time anyone has dared to make fun of me!'[80] Florent Schmitt shouted at the boxes '*Taisez-vous, les garces du seizième*!', of which the London equivalent might be 'Shut up, you Kensington bitches!' And a woman called Ravel 'a dirty Jew'.[81] Carl van Vechten described how 'The young man seated behind me in the box stood up during the course of the ballet to enable him to see more clearly. The intense excitement under which he was labouring betrayed itself presently when he began to beat rhythmically on the top of my head with his fists. My emotion was so great that I did not feel the blows for some time.'[82] At one point Diaghilev climbed to the gallery, and his voice was heard by the dancers coming from very far away, calling '*Je vous prie. Laissez s'achever le spectacle*!'[83] Leaning from his box, Astruc shouted, '*Ecoutez d'abord. Vous sifflerez après*!'[84]

I was sitting in the fourth or fifth row on the right [wrote Stravinsky], and the image of Monteux's back is more vivid in my mind today than the picture of the stage. He stood there apparently impervious and as nerve-less as a crocodile. It is still almost incredible to me that he actually brought the orchestra through to the end. I left my seat when the heavy

---

*Whom Mme Romola Nijinsky calls 'La Princesse de P'.

noises began – light noise had started from the very beginning – and went backstage behind Nijinsky in the right wing. Nijinsky stood on a chair, just out of view of the audience, shouting numbers to the dancers. I wondered what on earth these numbers had to do with the music for there are no 'thirteens' and 'seventeens' in the metrical scheme of the score.[85]

Bronia was standing beside her brother. Eleonora was in the front row.[86]

Romola had rushed behind the scenes after Part I, to find the dancers on the verge of tears. The passage leading to the dressing-rooms and stage-door of the Théâtre des Champs-Elysées is at the back of the stage, to the left. So great were the crowds of excited Russians in the wings – and there were singers in the theatre as well as dancers, because the programme would finish with 'Prince Igor' – that she could not get through them to return to her seat. Grigoriev and Kremnev tried in vain to break up this throng. There was a similar crowd behind the backcloth, through which Vassili had to force a way for Nijinsky. He was in practice costume, not yet having dressed or made up for 'Le Spectre', which was to follow. 'His face was as white as his *crêpe-de-Chine* dancing shirt. He was beating the rhythm with both fists shouting "Ras, dva, tri" to the artists. The music could not be heard. . . His face was quivering with emotion. I felt sorry for him. . .'[87]

'*Dans l'adversité de nos meilleurs amis*,' wrote La Rochefoucauld, '*nous trouvons toujours quelque-chose qui ne nous déplaît pas*.' Some of the warmest admirers of Stravinsky and Nijinsky, like Valentine Gross, had enjoyed the battle. It was an experience, something to talk about. Even Diaghilev – or one side of him – must have been conscious that the scandal was not without its 'news value'. But Diaghilev and Stravinsky could seek consolation with their friends. Nijinsky had to dress, make up and dance 'Le Spectre de la rose' immediately afterwards. And the *corps* had to get ready for 'Prince Igor'. It could hardly, by the way, be called a well-planned programme.

It was the anniversary of 'L'Après-midi d'un faune', chosen deliberately by the superstitious Diaghilev. Reflecting on the reception of his third ballet, Vaslav must have wondered if indifference was the only alternative to scandal.

After the 'performance' [Stravinsky recalled], we were excited, angry, disgusted, and . . . happy. I went with Diaghilev and Nijinsky to a restaurant. So far from weeping and reciting Puskhin in the Bois de Boulogne as the legend is,* Diaghilev's only comment was: 'Exactly what I wanted.' He certainly looked contented. No one could have been quicker to understand the publicity value and he immediately understood the good thing that had happened in that respect. Quite probably he had already thought about the possibility of such a scandal when I first played him the score, months before, in the east ground room of the Grand Hotel in Venice.[88]

But, of course, whatever his real feelings were, Diaghilev was trying to cheer Nijinsky up, to make him a little proud of the results of his hard work. 'Le Sacre' was the child of their love, even though initially conceived by Roerich and Stravinsky.

Roerich's décor, being less revolutionary, attracted little notice in comparison with the music and choreography of 'Le Sacre'. If all the arts kept in step together to aid the historian's generalizations the designs of Nijinsky's ballet should have been by Picasso. But in the world of Proust, Reynaldo Hahn, Jacques-Emile Blanche and the Russian Ballet the name of Picasso had not yet been spoken. It would not be for four years that, recruited by Cocteau, the young cubist painter worked for Diaghilev. Roerich was not made much of and returned to Russia, feeling he had not been given his due.[89] (He later became a hermit in the Himalayas, dying in 1947.)

After Calmette's attack on 'L'Après-midi d'un faune' in the previous year and the subsequent controversy which Rodin may be said to have won on Nijinsky's behalf, we could hardly expect a critic on *Le Figaro* would dare to give any new creation of the young choreographer's a good notice. Henri Quittard had scorned 'Jeux': 'Le Sacre' he insultingly brushed aside.

I think we can pass over M. Nijinsky's choreography and the inventions with which this frantic beginner gives proof of his newly discovered genius. If we could for a moment doubt his good faith, we might justifiably be angry. To pull the public's leg not just once but again in this heavy-handed way would not be in the best of taste. Unfortunately for M. Nijinsky he is evidently dead serious. He will no doubt persevere and if his creations appear daily more ridiculous he will not be able to help it . . .

*Cocteau's much-quoted story.

This new art form, such as it is, already has its admirers. If only their enthusiasm were less noisy! 'Le Sacre du printemps' was rather badly received yesterday and the public was hard put to restrain its mirth. It would therefore have been in better taste if those who thought differently – and there were not many of them – had refrained from applauding the authors on stage in a way everybody found not only impertinent but absurd.[90]*

Quittard denied Nijinsky's admirers the right to express their approval. Bigotry could go no further.

The turncoat Louis Laloy, who had wanted to collaborate with Debussy and Nijinsky in 1909, wrote: 'Some of us would have liked to rescue the score from the stage spectacle, had not M. Stravinsky opposed this suggestion with all his strength, insisting that the choreography was just what he wanted and surpassed his expectations. His loyalty is praiseworthy. The consequence is total disaster.'[91] He was to elaborate on his views in *La Revue française de la musique*. Repeating the great joke which nearly all the critics made about 'Le Massacre du Printemps', Laloy wrote:

Massacre, firstly because we managed to hear so little of it . . . massacre also because it seemed monstrous to more than one theatre-goer that the spring should be celebrated by the epileptic fits of M. Nijinsky and by so sadly discordant a score . . . The dancing is absurd: to spin out for an hour and a half [*sic*] a choreography of puppets on strings would seem like a bad joke if one had not ample proof of the sincerity and devotion of M. Nijinsky, who is an acrobat of incomparable elevation, but a ballet-master totally devoid of ideas and even common sense . . . The composer has written a score that we shall not be ready for until 1940.[92]

Georges Pioch in *Gil Blas*:

Not once can the strings be heard. Listen to the Prelude, which is dominated by a wind instrument. We ask each other 'What instrument produces these sounds?' I say 'It's an oboe.' My right-hand neighbour, who is a great composer, insists that it is a muted trumpet. My left-hand neighbour, who is no less of a musical scholar, declares 'I should have thought it was a clarinet.' In the interval we ask the conductor himself, and we are told it was a bassoon that gave us such heart-searchings . . . I must persist in thinking what a pity it is that M. Nijinsky, who is such a

*Mr Stravinsky denies that he took a call after the first performance of 'Le Sacre'.

good dancer and jumps better than anyone, should one day have discovered he was a genius – like everyone else in the theatre in these years of plenty. His experiments hitherto have been damaging to the Russian Ballet; and we cannot forget that all the marvellous creations this company have given us were the work of M. Fokine, who was content to be a choreographer . . .[93]

Henry Postel du Mas, interviewing Stravinsky, suggested, 'Nijinsky's production has been criticized as being opposed to the music.' 'That is not true. Nijinsky is a remarkable artist, capable of giving new life to the whole art of ballet. Not for a second have we ceased to think along the same lines. You'll see later on what he will do. He is not only a marvellous dancer: he is capable of creation and innovation. He has played a vital part in the collaboration of "Le Sacre du printemps".' But M. du Mas did not agree with the composer. 'Let him give up . . . making out of the "Sacre" the "Massacre du printemps".'[94]

In *Le Monde Musical* Auguste Mangeot wrote, 'As for the choreography, this time, unlike that of "Jeux", it is far from uninteresting. Although grotesque and absurd it is oddly impressive.'[95]

However, Gaston de Pawlowski, editor-in-chief of *Commedia*, himself wrote a long, illustrated, front-page article on the 31st, castigating the manners of the public and affirming the artist's right to experiment. 'Where were those bastards* brought up?' – he quotes one of the politer remarks heard on 'the elegant and memorable' evening which was not '"Le Sacre" but "Le Massacre du Printemps"'. He thought that Nijinsky's 'ugly' movements had gone on too long, and could have been contrasted, with Romantic antithesis, with more 'beautiful' movements; but intelligently saw in them a kind of reflex action – thus showing that he had caught a glimpse of the new truth, the new way of expressing emotion which Nijinsky had hit upon.[96]

There were four performances of 'Le Sacre' in Paris – and Valentine Gross, among others, went to every one. Her little shorthand drawings in blue pencil, made at the subsequent performances – she could not have drawn at the first – survive. A few

Salauds.

cat-calls were heard at the last three performances but the battle was not repeated.[97]

Chaliapine's success in 'Khovanshchina' followed fast upon. Since Diaghilev was not satisfied with all of Rimsky's orchestration, parts of this opera had been reorchestrated by Stravinsky and Ravel. The Moscow painter Feodorovsky had made some splendid designs; Bolm arranged the Persian dances; and Mussorgsky's second opera, heard for the first time in the west, was acclaimed almost as much as 'Boris' had been in 1908.

The third new ballet of the season was 'La Tragédie de Salomé', with music of Florent Schmitt, choreography by Boris Romanov and décor by Sergei Sudeikine. This had been put on specially for Karsavina, who had reason to feel that she had lately been playing second fiddle to Nijinsky. The most striking part of it was the décor by the young Russian designer, much influenced by Aubrey Beardsley, though not in black and white but in sumptuous purple and gold. Karsavina wore an exiguous costume and a rose painted on her right knee. The latter miniature work of art was recreated for each performance by Dmitri Gunsbourg, who fancied himself as a painter.[98]

'La Tragédie de Salomé' was not the story of Herod, Herodias, Salome and the Baptist in choreographic terms. St John's head was present on a pedestal, but Salome was the only character apart from some Negroes and Executioners. The Princess was supposed to be performing her frantic dance of expiation in limbo. After some preliminary caperings by the Negroes, Karsavina appeared at the top of a flight of steps, and as she descended, an endless black and gold train unrolled behind her. Then followed her bizarre solo: that was all.[99] As a youthful experiment by Fokine's pupil, the budding choreographer Romanov, the ballet deserved some credit: but of all Karsavina's roles it was the one which was least successful in showing off her wonderful qualities. Yet she contrived to give an air of aloofness to her performance, a subtle suggestion that she was not so much dancing as reliving the dance in her mind; and this was no small achievement.[100]

It could not be said that 'Salomé' was a success. That made three new ballets which had failed with the public and the press.

After all the work which had gone into them, particularly 'Le Sacre', this was a bitter disappointment to Diaghilev. While hoping that the new works would meet with a better reception in London, he concentrated his publicity on the opera.[101]

Since 1909, when she was an art student and sat in the gallery, the devoted Valentine Gross had seen every performance of the Russian Ballet in Paris. Scribbling in the dark, then working up her sketches later, then reworking them and producing finished paintings, pastels and pen-and-ink drawings, she had recorded Nijinsky in nearly all his roles.* She was an academic artist, and struggled continually to become less so, but her faithful eye and careful hand

Nijinsky in ' Le Spectre de la rose'. Drawing by Valentine Gross.

*I have not seen studies of him by her in 'Le Pavillon d'Armide', 'Cléopâtre' or the Blue bird *pas de deux*.

have bequeathed us the most extensive documentation of the Russian Ballet. This season, as we have seen, she had exhibited her work in the upstairs foyer of the theatre. She could not know that she was seeing the adored Nijinsky dance for the last time, but she would bear witness to his genius up to the end of her long life. One evening, shortly before the company left for London, she came into the wings immediately after a performance of 'Le Spectre de la rose'. She was amazed to find Nijinsky quite alone, curled up on the floor, panting, like a bird fallen from a nest. His hands were clutched over his heart, which she could hear beating in spite of the distant roar of applause.

He was like a crumpled rose in pain, and there was no one near him. I was so touched that I left him alone and said nothing. Then he saw me and sprang up like a child taken by surprise and came smiling towards me. As he stood beside me in his leotard sewn with damp purplish petals, he seemed a kind of St Sebastian, flayed alive and bleeding from innumerable wounds. In a halting but quite accurate French he began to tell me how pleased he was with some pastels I had made of 'Jeux' and to thank me for the article I had written to go with them in *Comoedia Illustré*. I was almost the only person to appreciate his choreography. When I said good-bye he took my hand in both of his in such a charming way that for the rest of the evening I kept glancing down at it in wonder – this hand which had been covered in dew on contact with the miraculous dancer.[102]

Diaghilev went to London ahead of the Ballet. Nijinsky and Nouvel travelled separately from the company, and Romola went on the same boat and train. During the journey from Paris to London she managed to exchange a few words with Nijinsky, both in the corridor of the train, where she stood outside the door of the compartment he shared with Nouvel, and on the boat, where she braved the wind and weather to settle near him on deck. He still had very little French and she hardly any Russian, but pantomime came in useful. It seems inevitable – though Romola did not realize it – that Vaslav had some idea by now that she was running after him. If in the ensuing weeks he was to give few signs of knowing or noticing her, this may have been partly catlike diplomacy and partly doubt of his own inclinations and of her character and charms. Diaghilev in a straw-hat was at Victoria to meet him and shot Romola a surprised glance as Nijinsky raised his cap on saying good-bye to her. She herself was surprised at Vaslav's courage.

Romola stayed at the Stafford Hotel in St James's Place,* but took every chance that offered to lunch or dine at the Savoy Grill, where Diaghilev held court at a table by the open fireplace.[103]

The London season was to be for the first time at the Theatre Royal, Drury Lane. It was again sponsored by Sir Joseph Beecham, with Pierre Monteux conducting the ballet and Emile Cooper the opera. In the enforced absence of Monteux a newcomer, Rhené-Baton would take over the last evenings of ballet. What made this season historic was that London was hearing Russian opera for the first time. To hear Mussorgsky's epic operas and to experience the Stravinsky–Nijinsky 'Sacre du printemps' – not to mention 'Jeux' and 'L'Après-midi d'un faune' – to be able to hear Chaliapine one night and to see Karsavina and Nijinsky the next – that was something to keep one in London during July! On their side, Diaghilev and Nijinsky experienced a lessening of tension once the Paris season was over; the Savoy Hotel had become a kind of home to them, and they were always happy to see Lady Ripon, Lady Juliet Duff and Lady Ottoline Morrell again.

Hilda Munnings, who had been given the hideous name of Muningsova, which would surely deceive no-one, recorded some impressions of this fabulous season, during which she appeared for the first time with the Diaghilev Ballet in her home town – and on the stage where she had seen Dan Leno as a child.

Every pay-day – that is, once a fortnight – we would line up in the greenroom behind the stage at Drury Lane, and Grigoriev would be sitting there at a table, with piles of golden sovereigns and half-sovereigns, silver crowns, half-crowns, shillings, sixpences and threepenny pieces. In those days, salaries in the Diaghilev ballet were calculated in French francs, and it cannot have been easy for Grigoriev to work out the sums due to different artists. It was quite a sight to see our company, all so elegantly dressed, lining up to receive those piles of gold and silver, and signing the ledger.

*Mme Romola Nijinsky says in her book, p. 172, 'a very smart but small hotel in Mayfair behind St James's Palace.' St James's is not, of course, in Mayfair. She confirmed during conversations with the author that the hotel was the Stafford.

Even I, with my fifteen gold sovereigns, plus a little silver, would feel as rich as Croesus as I walked out into the sunshine of Russell Street.

Classes were held at the Territorial Drill Hall in Chenies Street, off Tottenham Court Road. They always began at nine o'clock, and woe betide anyone who was late. We would arrive to find Maestro Cecchetti watering the floor and whistling an unidentifiable tune. He had a funny way of breaking into a whistle as he was talking to you.

Diaghilev allowed several painters and sculptors to watch these classes. Among them were Laura Knight and Una Troubridge, whose head of Nijinsky as the Faun – the only sculpture of him except Rodin's little sketch* ever done from life – I was to find in a junk-shop forty years later. Nijinsky was certainly the main target of these artists, and sometimes when he worked privately with Cecchetti during the lunch hour they were allowed to stay and sketch. There was one girl who was always sitting, watching in silence, and we were surprised to find that she was allowed to join in our classes with Cecchetti. As she was not a regular member of our company this was exceptional. We learned that she was the daughter of a famous Hungarian actress. Diaghilev, who never let pass an opportunity to make up to influential people, had allowed her to study with us, although she was not really a dancer. Her name was Romola de Pulszka. She spoke English and used to come and sit in the *corps de ballet* dressing-room and talk to me.

Nijinsky, I noticed, even though he was always surrounded by people, seemed always to be alone; he was incapable of mixing in any way. If he spoke at all it was to somebody with whom he was dancing, and then he would talk softly and shyly, without looking at the person, and move away as quickly as possible. Before working, Nijinsky used to walk about a lot on the tips of his toes. He would move a few steps to the right, then a few to the left, holding his hands up in a curious characteristic way with the backs touching his cheeks, his head tilted downward. He used to do a lot of jumps in the first position, gradually jumping higher and higher, then lower in a *diminuendo*. This is a very good way to practise jumping, and I have always copied it.[104]

The London season opened with 'Boris Godounov' on 24 June, and Mussorgsky and Chaliapine were alike acclaimed by a new public.

Each scene [wrote the critic of *The Times*] was so absorbing that one was immediately caught in the spirit of the thing; it was intensely real and even the distressingly long pauses between the scenes and the ineptitude of an

*If this really is of Nijinsky.

audience who would insist upon applauding as soon as the curtain fell and before the music was finished did not betray the sense of reality. It is difficult to say how far Mussorgsky, how far the extraordinarily powerful acting of M. Chaliapine and the other principals, the fine singing, and natural action of the crowds, or the beauty of the scenery were responsible for the effect. They were all fused together in the total result.[105]

On the second night 'Jeux', called in England 'Playtime', was shown. Richard Capell, writing in the *Daily Mail*, seemed mystified, but tried to be loyal.

The new 'Playtime' is disconcerting, delicious and discreetly amusing as is M. Debussy's music . . . The dancing seems inspired by the archaic, but should perhaps be called 'futuristic'. What was the antique stiffness that seemed well in place in M. Nijinsky's first ballet doing here? The piece in effect struck one as a parody of 'The Afternoon of a Faun'. While it was in progress the audience were hilarious in a way not kind; but afterwards there was so much applause that it cannot be denied success.[106]

The critic of the *Morning Post*, likewise, was not sure what side he found himself on. Remarking that there was a fuller house for the Russian ballet than for the Russian opera on the previous night – which was understandable as Russian opera was an unknown quantity – he wrote of 'Jeux':

It works out as a highly impressionistic business enacted in front of a weird green and red background with round splotches of white here and there to represent the electric lights . . . Their [the dancers'] actions are of the quaintest. They suggest that they are suffering from 'tennis wrist' all over. They move with the angularity of clockwork figures. Everything is at an angle. The only thing with a curve in it is the lost ball . . . All . . . is expressed by angles, obtuse, acute, right angle, and, of course, triangle. The business is conceived in the vein of the Cubists. It is a triumph of angularity. It fits M. Debussy's music very well, and the music is wholly suited to it . . . The cumulative rhythms – wholly meaningless – are suited with action of similar character. Mlles Karsavina and Schollar and M. Nijinsky turn themselves very successfully into clockwork figures. The absence of the doll-like costume as found in 'Petrushka' spoils a good deal of the effect, for in a country like this, where tennis is understood, the ridiculous character of the whole thing is perfectly clear. The audience first laughed and then applauded.[107]

368

Diaghilev took pains to make 'Le Sacre' acceptable to the London public. A longer scenario was printed and Edwin Evans spoke from the stage to introduce and explain the ballet.[108] The English received the work with respect, if without enthusiasm.

The first night of 'Le Sacre du printemps' on 11 July was described in *The Times* as follows:

London takes both its pleasures and its pains more quietly than Paris. When 'Le Sacre du Printemps', the latest joint product of MM. Nijinsky and Stravinsky, was produced for the first time in England last night at Drury Lane, the applause was measured, but so were the cries of disapproval. Mr Evans, it is true, was obliged to cut short his preliminary remarks before the curtain, and a certain amount of whistling and half-suppressed laughter was heard during the performance; but that was, perhaps, not very surprising, for Mr Evans forgot that it was for the ballet and not the lecture that people were there, and there are limits to what an English audience can endure when presented with something quite new, especially when it is not certain whether the oddest features of it are purposely or accidentally grotesque. However, M. Nijinsky had not much to complain of in his reception, and both Mlle Piltz, upon whom the heaviest burden fell (amongst those on the stage), and M. Monteux, who achieved a miracle of conducting, were very warmly applauded ... The music, at any rate on the harmonic side, though again perfectly consistent, has moved so far ahead even of 'Petrushka' that it parts company with anything coming even from Paris that one has heard before. This at least ought to convince Mr Gordon Craig that even if the Russian ballet belongs, as he has lately been telling us it does, to the theatre of yesterday, the music is not always exactly retrospective ... Most of the time one seems to be looking at marionettes rather than children or savages, and many of the movements seem to be the result of some stern and invisible hand moving the puppets by an inexorable decree, the purport of which is known to the owner of the hand, but has only at certain moments been declared to others.[109]

The *Morning Post* was antagonistic. 'These early individuals, clothed in picturesque dresses of many centuries later, indulge in gestures that are supposed to be "of the period". They better suggest a physical culture class. .. M. Monteux, the conductor, was called on to the stage at the end, also M. Nijinsky, who seemed relieved at the indifferent attitude of the audience.' [110] There was no notice by Richard Capell in the *Daily Mail*: perhaps he had gone on holiday. After the third performance of 'Le Sacre' on the 23rd, which was conducted not by Monteux but by Rhené-Baton, *The Times* concluded that Stravinsky and Nijinsky 'have achieved something that, in spite of its defects, is a step nearer to a real fusion of music and dancing'.[111]

Writing to Astruc from the Savoy Hotel, Bakst described the 'fantastic success' of the season and reported that the Russian opera was as popular as the ballet. 'That's the difference between London and Paris.' He continued, 'Wonderful weather, hectic life. In fact London is a marvellous place, but alas! very expensive.' He was writing to ask for money.[112] But the gallant and audacious Astruc had undertaken in his Théâtre des Champs-Elysées something which could not possibly pay its way, and by the middle of October he would be bankrupt. For the everlasting glory of having presented Fauré's 'Pénélope', 'Khovanshchina' and 'Le Sacre du printemps' the price was ruin.[113]

So London saw for the last time Nijinsky dancing with the Diaghilev Ballet, which had made him glorious and in whose productions he and Karsavina had raised the art of ballet to a higher plane than it had ever before attained. And the devoted English admirers, who had watched him so often in 'Les Sylphides', in 'Carnaval', in 'Le Pavillon d'Armide', in 'Le Spectre de la rose', in 'Schéhérazade' – the critics, the artists, the writers, the noble ladies – Richard Capell, Cyril Beaumont, Charles Ricketts, Osbert Sitwell, Rupert Brooke, Lytton Strachey, Duncan Grant, Ottoline Morrell, Violet Rutland, Gwladys Ripon, Juliet Duff – would see him in these works no more.*

Nijinsky's 'Le Sacre du printemps' had been given four performances in Paris, and it had three in London: seven in all. When Diaghilev wanted to revive it seven years later no one could remember the choreography and Massine had to start again from scratch. Now that we have the piano score annotated by Stravinsky, with reminders for Nijinsky of the timing of certain movements they had planned together, which came to light in 1967; and with a few hitherto unpublished pastels by Valentine Gross found among her

*But they would see him in a new version of 'Les Sylphides'.

papers after her death; with recollections by Dame Marie Rambert and Mme Sokolova set beside descriptions by one or two historians – with all these added to the tremendous essay of Jacques Rivière we are able to form some idea of what the ballet was like. I am convinced that even Diaghilev and Stravinsky did not entirely appreciate the power of Nijinsky's Blake-like vision or recognize how far ahead of his time he was, and I acclaim 'Le Sacre' not only as a masterpiece, the climax of Nijinsky's career, but also as a seminal work, a turning point in the history of the dance, the ballet of the century. Isadora had asked Nijinsky to have a child by her and he had refused: yet their progeny are legion. The long list is headed by Martha Graham.

However, in July Stravinsky wrote to Maximilian Steinberg:

I am gradually recovering from this hellish disease [of typhus], walking like a fly on two legs. If everything goes according to plan, I will leave for Ustilug on Friday. Nijinsky's choreography [for 'Le Sacre du printemps'] is incomparable. Everything is as I wanted it, with very few exceptions. But we must wait a long time before the public grows accustomed to our language. Of the value of what we have already accomplished, I am convinced, and this gives me the strength for further work.[114]

After this most resplendent of seasons the company had only a fortnight's holiday before sailing to fulfil their engagement in South America. Romola de Pulszky went to enjoy the English sunshine with her old governess in Sussex. Diaghilev, Nouvel and Vaslav travelled to Baden-Baden and stayed at the Hôtel Stéphanie once again. Here they were joined by Benois. A ballet to music of Bach was planned, which was to have 'all the elaborate splendour of Court festivals of the rococo period – the splendour of pageants and fireworks and illuminations'. Benois had already decided on the inclusion of certain pieces, but at Baden-Baden the friends settled down to a systematic perusal of Bach's works, and hired a German pianist to play through the master's innumerable compositions on the modest hotel piano. Nouvel would sometimes replace him, and Diaghilev and Nijinsky joined with the others in discussing which pieces would go well together to make a ballet. In a week the music had been chosen. The selected compositions were from the Englische

Suiten, the Klavierwerke, the Praeludien, Fugen und Suiten and the Wohltemperiertes Klavier. (A complete list with indications as to which number is a solo, *pas de deux*, dance for men, women, peasants or the whole company, is in the Musée de l'Opéra, Paris.) Books were next sought to help Vaslav with the choreography and period style. It was understood that on their return from South America, Diaghilev would take him to the Cabinet des Estampes in Paris and the Museo Correr in Venice. In the meanwhile Benois conducted him on a tour of neighbouring rococo palaces and churches. They visited Vierzehnheiligen, Bruchsaal and the Archbishop's palace at Würzburg, 'places where eighteenth-century music seemed to have been crystallized in enchanting architectural forms'.[115] So the last great works of art Vaslav set eyes on before crossing the Atlantic into the unknown were Tiepolo's masterpieces, the ceiling over the Archbishop of Würzburg's staircase depicting Olympus, and that of the Kaisersaal with the dizzy Triumph of Apollo.

How incredulously Diaghilev and Nijinsky would have received the information, had they been told, as they listened to the music of Bach and craned their necks to study the rainbow frescoes, that they would never be alone together again! But Diaghilev dreaded the ocean voyage; he was totally uninterested in South America, which presumably had no picture-galleries, museums or Archbishops' palaces; he was doubtless drawn to spend the rest of August and September in Venice, where perhaps adventures with pretty dark-eyed boys awaited him; and he decided to stay in Europe.

When the S.S. *Avon*, 11,073 tons, captain C. E. Down, sailed from Southampton on 15 August[116] Romola de Pulszky's dismay at finding Nijinsky was not on board with the rest of the company was only to be equalled by her rapture when he boarded the ship at Cherbourg on the following day without Diaghilev.* There were other absentees. Karsavina, dreading a long voyage, was travelling on a faster ship.[117] Bronislava Nijinska was in Petersburg with her mother, expecting a baby in two months. Piltz was pregnant too,

*Since Nijinsky boarded the *Avon* at Cherbourg, Grigoriev's assertion, possibly arising from a misunderstanding with his editor, Vera Bowen, that Diaghilev travelled to London to 'say good-bye' to the company, which he had only left a fortnight before, is inherently improbable. Mme Sokolova has no recollection of such a scene.

and had stayed behind.[118]* If someone wanted to marry Nijinsky –
whether Romola de Pulszky or Miriam Ramberg – the valet Vassili
was the only person who might be able to stop them, and then only
by cutting their throats.

But Ramberg was in a second-class cabin on a lower deck, which
she shared with Hilda Muningsova. Romola's second-class cabin
was occupied by her maid Anna: for herself she had bought a first-
class ticket, and her state-room was within sight of Nijinsky's.[119]

As the *Avon* sails down the west coast of France in summer
weather, and 'birds of calm sit brooding on the charmèd wave', the
narrative takes on the unreal character of certain kinds of drama,
such as the Barrie fantasies where people change their natures in a
mystic wood or come into their own on a desert island, or the more
prosaic kind in which a group of heterogeneous types are stranded
through a wreck, snowstorm or breakdown in a lifeboat, airport
waiting-room or isolated mountain hotel.

Life on a luxurious ocean liner was a kind of holiday for the
company and one which even the sophisticated Romola had never
experienced. Only Muningsova – in her previous incarnation as
Hilda Munnings – had ever crossed the Atlantic to dance in America
before.[120] The voyage would last twenty-one days, but the *Avon* was
to call at Vigo, Lisbon and Madeira, and until she left European
waters a regular routine of ship-board life would not be established.
There were three constant factors, however, in the company's daily
life. Olga Khokhlova was sick every day;[121] Ramberg, who hated the
heat and sometimes fainted on account of it, intent on self-improve-
ment, did a class alone in her cabin;[122] and Romola de Pulszky made
herself charming to anyone who might be useful in bringing her
into contact with Nijinsky, systematically patrolling the deck – although she hated walking – in pursuit of her shy quarry.[123]

Putting ourselves in Romola's place and banishing from our
minds the knowledge of what came after, we must admit that there
was nothing fundamentally wrong in her pursuit of Nijinsky. After
all, men have been so struck by the beauty or talent of actresses or
dancers that they have followed them round the world in hope of

*Mme Romola Nijinsky writes of her as being on the South American voyage, pos-
sibly confusing her with Pflanz.

love, sex, friendship or even a crumb of attention. They do not even
have to be in love to act in this way, only stage-struck or beglamoured
by the personality of a star. Nobody blames them. To deny a woman
the right to chase a man of genius one would have to be a really
die-hard anti-feminist. That Romola should set her cap at Nijinsky
without being in love with him was odd, but it was not wrong. She
was twenty-three and determined and it was an adventure. She had
the good taste to admire Nijinsky's genius: how could she weigh the
consequences to the Russian Ballet if she succeeded in separating
him from Diaghilev, or foresee the effect it would have on Vaslav
himself? Young people do not look ahead. And of course, she could
not *really* believe it possible, strong-willed though she was, that
she would be engaged to Nijinsky before setting foot on South
American soil. It was a kind of game for her, an impossible test she
set herself. If we admire Alexander of Macedon for marching forth
to conquer India, we must concede a little admiration for the spirit
of Romola de Pulszky (whose grandfather had rebelled against the
Habsburgs and whose uncle had subdued Madagascar) which
spurred her on to connect herself in some way with the artist she
admired above all others.

And what was in Nijinsky's mind at the beginning of this long
hot voyage? Certainly he had no idea of getting married and none of
leaving Diaghilev. His whole life was the Russian Ballet and he
loved his work. He cannot but have worshipped Diaghilev for
giving him such glorious roles and the opportunity to create ballets,
for having made him the idol of the European world. Even if he did
not adore him physically, he must have felt for him the love of a
successful pupil for an inspiring master who has opened a door on
all the wonders of the world. His every action must have been
designed to win Diaghilev's approval. But he was twenty-four; he was
at sea; and the sun was shining. He wanted – needed – to make love.

Whether, as he lay alone in his state-room, he dreamed of a male
or a female partner seems comparatively beside the point. Perhaps
either would have done. (Incidentally, although a relationship of
Vaslav with a woman need not – and did not in the event – make it
utterly impossible for him to work in Diaghilev's company, an
affair with another man would put this out of the question. Diaghilev's

374

jealousy could never rise above that.) I think it is possible that on this voyage, separated from Diaghilev, he could have been seduced by another young man and even fallen in love with him; but it is more likely that his thoughts were of girls.

Girls, however, presented a problem for this reticent, hardworking and secluded young man; and his exalted position placed a barrier between him and the other dancers. He could not possibly, for instance, expose himself to comment, gossip or ridicule by going courting the lovely auburn-haired Khokhlova, or blonde Muningsova, or clever Bewicke in the second class! Then, he was such a well brought-up boy, so sensitive and with such gentlemanly principles that an ephemeral affair must seem sordid and beneath him. Only a beautiful romance would sanctify sexual relations – that or marriage. And even if he was prepared to let down Diaghilev, how could either of these come about? For Nijinsky to make love at all was very difficult.

But Nature, the blind matchmaker, had provided for this exceptional situation. Just as M. de Charlus, in the opening scene of Proust's *Sodome et Gommorrhe*, by paying a call on Mme de Ville-parisis, because of her indisposition, at the odd hour of ten in the morning, had the luck to meet the tailor Jupien, one of the rare homosexuals who only liked old men, and who had not yet left for his office; and just as the bee brought the improbable pollen to fertilize the rare orchid of the Duchess, which would otherwise have been condemned to sterility: so did Nature bring into proximity with this rare orchid of a dancer, who could not seek for love among the members of his company and had little time or opportunity to look outside it, a young woman who was attached to the company and yet not of it, one who was a dancer and yet could be excepted from the rules applying to other dancers, an attractive girl of good birth and yet born into an artistic and theatrical family, and one who had inherited from courageous ancestors the spirit to take the initiative when her prospective partner could not. As Proust wrote about the good fortune of M. de Charlus and of the orchid: it was 'an accident so unlikely that one might call it a sort of miracle'. Viewed either as a sport of nature or as a trick of chance, there was something beautiful about it.

375

Nature was not the sole matchmaker: there were others on board the *Avon* who, once the subject of the play was announced, would be only too willing to fill their appointed roles – Gunsbourg, his middle-aged mistress Ekaterina Oblokova, and a friend of hers in the *corps de ballet*, the chic, pretty Josefina Kovalevska, who had lived with the Aga Khan.[124] If Gunsbourg had already formulated a vague plan to run a ballet company without Diaghilev[125] – and, to give him credit, he had every reason to believe that no enterprise of Diaghilev's would ever attain solvency – it is still extremely unlikely that at the beginning of the voyage he could have imagined it possible to detach Nijinsky from Diaghilev – particularly by means of a woman. For with the naïveté of heterosexuals of that period he probably took it for granted that Nijinsky, because he lived with Diaghilev, was homosexual; and thought that if you were 'like that' you were 'like that' and did not change.

Only a few of the company travelled first class. At meals Nijinsky and the Batons sat at the captain's table; Gunsbourg and Oblokova shared a table with Kovalevska; Romola sat with Trubecki, his wife Pflanz, Bolm and a French-Argentinian dressmaker called Chavez.[126] From the day after the *Avon* left Cherbourg, however, the main body of the company who were travelling second were allowed to come up and visit their colleagues on the upper deck. Romola witnessed the meeting of Nijinsky and the Batons. Rhené-Baton had taken over from Monteux to conduct the last five per-formances of Ballet at Drury Lane, but he had evidently made no contact with Nijinsky except across the footlights. He began to pour out his admiration for the dancer's art, and Mme Baton joined in. But Nijinsky's French was at that time extremely limited, and he shook his head, saying '*Non, non, moi pas comprend, moi parle petit nègre.*' Touched by his simplicity, Baton embraced him and declared that he would be his nurse and look after him during the voyage.[127] On the 17th the *Avon* docked for a few hours at Vigo.[128] The next day Romola went ashore at Lisbon with her friends; Vaslav with the Batons and Chavez.[129] When parties were made up to go ashore at Madeira on the 20th Romola was disappointed not to be included in that of the Batons and Nijinsky. Instead she went with Gunsbourg, Oblokova, Trubecki, Pflanz, Bolm, Kovalevska and Chavez. They nearly got left behind, having missed the last boat back. Romola saw her chances of getting to know Vaslav evaporating. The next ship was in three weeks' time. Oblokova and Kovalevska were in despair at the thought of being stranded without their clothes. Bolm wondered how the company could give 'Prince Igor' or 'Thamar' without him. But a rowing-boat was hired, the *Avon* sent out a launch, and they were saved.[130] They would not sight land again for a week.

Romola found that when she passed Nijinsky, seated with a book in his deck-chair, he never looked up or seemed to recognize her. He was reading Merejkovski's essays on Tolstoy and Dostoevsky.[131] In the afternoons, when most passengers lay with books in the sun or sleeping in their cabins, Nijinsky worked, with Baton at the piano, in a small hall on C deck where a companion-way led to the dining-room. He was working on his Bach ballet. Romola discovered him there and settled down to watch, seated on the steps, but was asked to move by a steward. The next day she returned and this time it was Baton who asked her to go. Suddenly Nijinsky looked up from his notes and gestured that she might stay.[132] Had he been conscious of her admiration for weeks, and was this the first sign of his returning it? Or did the interest she now showed in his work first arouse his interest in her as a woman? Contact of a kind had been re-established.

Baton played the piano and Nijinsky stood beside him. Sometimes he closed his eyes and gave the impression that he did it to concentrate more on a whole choreographic theme. Or with his fingers he danced a full variation, which he composed while Baton played the piece; or he stopped him suddenly, made him play the same bar several times. All the time, as he stood there, one could feel that he was dancing constantly the steps he invented. And so a whole ballet was created before my wondering eyes. Occasionally he searched with Baton for hours for a suitable chaconne or prelude. He stopped Baton often, saying, '*Crois plus vite*' and Baton laughed, 'How true. I made a mistake. It is supposed to be faster.' . . . Baton told me Nijinsky was composing a new ballet on the music of Bach, to be as pure dancing as his music is pure sound. He wanted to lay down the harmony and fundamental truth of the movement . . . Always when Baton failed to make himself understood Gunsbourg was summoned as interpreter. Very soon I tried to make myself liked by them. As I had been educated in Paris and I spoke French like a native, I won Mme Baton's heart easily. But I liked them both. They were kind good-hearted people. Among all the Russians we formed the little western European colony. Of course nobody knew that I was admitted to observe these hours of composition. I often wondered why I was . . .[133]

Vaslav must have thought of Romola when he was alone. If he spoke to the Batons and Gunsbourg about her, would it not be natural that the idea of bringing together the solitary Nijinsky and the pretty Hungarian should take shape in their minds, and would not Gunsbourg discuss it with Oblokova and she with Kovalevska – the two *chic* bejewelled ladies putting their heads together – and would they not enjoy a gossip about the romantic possibilities with Chavez, the dressmaker?

Romola wondered why Vaslav never came on deck (in his usual smart light-coloured suit or navy-blue blazer and white trousers) until about eleven in the morning. Then, waking up earlier than usual one day, she found him practising to starboard, watched by a party of admiring English, with Vassili and Williams the masseur in attendance. She now set about making friends with Williams, who told her that though he could massage the strongest boxer indefinitely, Nijinsky's muscles were so like iron that after an hour's work on them he was exhausted.[134]

Ramberg was trying to avoid the attentions of the handsome Vladimir Romanov, who did not attract her. She had another admirer in a young Polish boy, Loboiko. In Lyons he had proposed that they should take a flat together in Monte Carlo, and when asked why, replied innocently, 'It would be cheaper.' One of Ramberg's friends was a lively little Polish girl, even smaller than herself, Jejerska, who had danced in the same group with her in 'Le Sacre'. They used to laugh together a lot. Jejerska had a lover in Warsaw who was a Russian officer. When asked by Mimi what she would do when she got home, she replied simply, 'I shall go to his house and give myself to him.' Another Polish girl of extreme prettiness was Maicherska. She was the mistress of Feodorov, and when he bit her in an excess of passion, she naïvely explained this away by saying her wash-stand had fallen on her. Ramberg also made friends with Oblokova, Kovalevska and Pflanz, with whom she was photographed on deck. Kovalevska was teased for her simplicity. During the Paris season a group of dancers had gone to her dressing-room and said, 'Have you heard the terrible news? Napoleon is dead.' She put down her hand-mirror, gazed at them in consternation and exclaimed, 'What a misfortune for Paris!' Diaghilev could not prevent the Aga Khan giving Kovalevska money and jewels – indeed, he rather liked his dancers to have grand lovers – but he had steadily refused all pressure to give her roles beyond the limits of her talent. The only concession the Aga Khan ever wrung from him was to allow her to wear a black dress instead of a white in the dance of the Jewesses in 'Cléopâtre'. Now she had been rejected and presumably pensioned off by the oriental religious leader; and she complained tearfully to Ramberg, 'I who have had my clothes from Doucet now have to go shopping at the Magasin du Louvre!'

Mimi saw Nijinsky from time to time and discussed the Merejkovski essays with him. He lent her some volumes of *Mir Iskustva*. She got to know and like the Batons. It was also one of her pleasures to visit Romola in her cabin, because it was so much cooler than her own: they talked while Anna combed Romola's pretty long fair hair. Romola took great pains to look her best. One night she wore a dark blue lace-trimmed dress by Doucet, with a hobble skirt and a big bow, known as a *nœud japonais*, at the back of the waist.[135]

As Nijinsky sat reading in his deck-chair before lunch Romola would make a point of greeting him, yet the voyage was half over before they had any real conversation and it was humiliating for her one moonlight night to find herself being introduced to him yet again by Chavez.

Nijinsky was half leaning against the railing in a 'smoking', holding a small black fan which was ornamented with one gold-painted rose. He was rapidly fanning himself. He looked so strange. His eyes were half closed and oh! so slanted. He conversed in a soft melodious voice with Kovalevska in Polish. I was trembling as Chavez said '*Monsieur Nijinsky, permettez-moi de vous présenter Mlle de Pulszky.*' He did not move; his eyes just closed with an imperceptible *nuance* and he slightly inclined his head. Kovalevska at once began to explain to him who I was.

379

Did not Romola's instinct tell her that he knew very well who she was, and that he was putting on his mysterious irresistible faun face for the woman he had longed for and had been expecting God to send him?

I felt that both Chavez and Kovalevska were expecting me to say something. But suddenly every thought deserted me. I felt a chaos of emotion, saw nothing and nobody any more except the dark graceful silhouette of Nijinsky and his fascinating eyes. I suddenly heard myself speaking. '*Je veux vous remercier que vous avez élevé la danse à la hauteur des autres arts.*' Kovalevska translated. He did not move. Suddenly he looked at the small ring I wore. I followed his gaze and, pulling it off my finger, I passed it to him, explaining: 'My father brought it from Egypt; it is a talisman supposed to bring luck. My mother gave it to me as I left with the Russian Ballet.' It was a green-gold serpent whose head was crushed by a scarab. It had a strange design. Nijinsky held it for one moment and then put it on my finger, saying in Polish, 'It will bring you happiness, surely.' We all four of us began to walk around the deck. Suddenly Nijinsky stopped, looked into the phosphorescent waves. They were more luminous tonight than I had ever seen them before. I saw he was fascinated by the motion of the sea. He looked and looked. For a long time we watched in silence. Then I began to talk in French, choosing the easiest words, about dance, music, and Wagner, whose work I idolized ... Bayreuth and my childhood days which I had spent with my sister and brother-in-law at the Wahnfried at the rehearsals in the Festspielhaus. I don't know whether he understood a word of what I said, but he seemed to listen attentively ... Then Chavez called us. 'Come, come and look at the new constellations, the stars which cannot be seen in the northern hemisphere.' We looked up and saw in all its brilliant splendour the Southern Cross.[136]

Gunsbourg and Bolm were assiduous in organizing amusements. There was a fancy-dress ball. Gunsbourg told Romola that as she had the figure of a boy she should wear a pair of his apple-green silk pyjamas. Was this his idea of the best way to attract Nijinsky? At the last moment she put on a dress by Callot Soeurs, and, making her entrance to cries of disappointment from her friends, saw a look of relief in Nijinsky's eyes. He was the only other person, apart from the officers, not in fancy dress.[137] For him, we may guess, a costume was a magic thing which had to be lived up to and which transformed his spirit as well as his body. There was a party when they crossed the Equator on 28 August,[138] and a ball in the steerage at which Nijinsky enjoyed watching the flamenco dancing.[139] Company classes were held.[140] Kovalevska taught Romola some of the roles she would have to dance in the *corps de ballet*.[141] Life passed pleasantly for everybody except poor Olga Khokhlova, who continued to be sick, and for those like Ramberg, who could not bear the heat.

After the *Avon* had docked for a day at Pernambuco and was sailing down the coast of Brazil,[142] Vaslav and Romola were several times observed to be seated together on deck in 'animated conversation'.[143] Animation was rare with him and his words were usually few and far between, but if Romola provided most of the sparkle and the talk, his few words of French, helped out by gestures, and his pleased expression made it clear to everyone that they were getting on very well together. The company were amazed – Gunsbourg, Oblokova and Kovalevska perhaps less so than the others. If Gunsbourg planned to form his own troupe with Nijinsky at its head, it was now up to him to do everything in his power to bind Vaslav and Romola together. The company began to discuss the surprising situation.[144] Bolm did not believe there could be anything in it.[145]

Nijinsky told Ramberg that he was in love with Romola. She did not take him seriously, convinced that he was as totally devoted to Diaghilev as Diaghilev was to him, and assuming that the love affair was no more than a ship-board flirtation. 'But how can you talk to her?' she asked. He replied vaguely 'Oh well ... She understands.'[146] In his imagination, as usual three jumps ahead of everyone else's, he no doubt already saw himself happily married with a large family.

On Saturday, 30 August, the *Avon*, having put in briefly at Bahia the day before,[147] was sailing south along the coast of Brazil, due to dock at Rio de Janeiro two days later. Romola was sitting before lunch in the bar with the Batons, Kovalevska and a few others when Gunsbourg approached her, saying he must speak to her privately. She was alarmed, thinking that Grigoriev or Kremnev, who took the classes, might have reported her for not being up to her work, but she went with Gunsbourg on deck. 'There he stopped and with a terrible formal face he said, "Romola Karlovna, as

Nijinsky cannot speak to you himself, he has requested me to ask you in marriage." We looked at each other, and then I burst out "No, really, Dmitri Nicolaivitch, it's awful. How can you?" and, blushing, half crying, I ran as fast as I could down to my cabin, where I locked myself up for the rest of the day.'

Romola, unable to believe that her wish had come true, thought her friends had conspired to make fun of her. She remained shut up in her cabin, pretending to have a headache and refusing admittance even to Anna and Kovalevska. In the evening, however, she received a note from Gunsbourg, saying that he could not keep Nijinsky waiting any longer and requesting her answer to the proposal. She dressed and went on deck. It was after eleven o'clock.

Unexpectedly, from nowhere Nijinsky emerged and said '*Mademoiselle, voulez-vous, vous et moi?*' and pantomimed, indicating on the fourth finger of the left hand, a ring. I nodded and, waving with both hands, said '*Oui, oui, oui.*'

Very gently, taking my hand, without a word he led me up to the upper deck. This was deserted. He pulled two deck-chairs under the captain's bridge, and there we sat in silence, hearing the rhythmically recurring steps of the officers on duty, the sound of the waves, following the line of the smoke which rose from the funnels, a dark ribbon against the clear night sky, which was covered by milliards of stars. I could feel the soothing, unceasing throb of the boat, and my own wildly beating heart. Everything was so peaceful in this tepid tropical night. I knew Nijinsky felt as I did. And as this white boat sailed placidly, with an inward hidden tremor, in the vastness of the infinite ocean towards its destination, so did we towards our fate.[148]

Next morning most of the company were up by six to see the fantastic harbour of Rio with its Sugar Loaf Mountain in the morning light. This was one of the unforgettable moments of Ramberg's life, like her first sight of the sea and sense of infinity on the North German coast, and her glimpse of golden clouds on arrival in Switzerland, which turned out to be the summit of Mont Blanc.[149] Josefina Kovalevska arrived in Romola's room on the heels of the morning coffee.

J. K. Ah, Romola Karlovna, I am so happy, so happy! This is wonderful news. I congratulate you will all my heart. Unbelievable.

But somehow I always knew Vaslav Fomitch is not as people say.[150]

Not the most tactful way of putting it, one might think, but indeed the situation was so exceptional that the company would have to draw on every possible reserve of tact in order to react politely to news which must fill them with incredulity and dismay. 'Oh, to see the faces of the others when they hear,' cried Kovalevska. But it was Mme Baton who rushed into Ramberg's cabin with the announcement.

Mme B. Unbelievable news! Nijinsky is engaged to Romola!

And she did not see her friend's face, because Mimi in a sudden flash realized at last, with a sense of loss, that she loved Vaslav, and she bent over and pretended to be getting something out of a suitcase under the bunk in order to hide her tears.

When the bear-like Baton came up on deck to congratulate the happy couple he wrung Romola's hand so warmly that Vaslav was spurred to eloquence.

N. *Peux toucher, pas casser!*[151]

The *Avon* docked at Rio on the evening of Sunday, the 31st, and was not to sail until 5.45 on the following afternoon;[152] so excursions were planned. People are only granted a few days of perfect happiness in their lives. Just as it is a joy to recall one's own, so it is a pleasure to consider those of others. Vaslav and Romola, on the first day of their engagement, not only had the excitement of going ashore after so long at sea, but that of setting foot on a new continent in a New World and of beholding the bay of Rio de Janeiro and exploring the surrounding mountains. Did anything – flies, the heat, shyness, the presence of Kovalevska, who acted as interpreter – mar their absolute content? After six months' perseverance Romola had got her way; and God had sent Vaslav a girl. The hour of consummation was not far off. Before driving out of the city they went into a jeweller's and Vaslav ordered two wedding rings to be engraved with their names and the date. Then they drove up Sylvestre Mountain, where, in a chic hotel in the middle of the tropical forest, they had lunch. This was the first time Vaslav and Romola had sat at a table together. In the afternoon they were driven through the mountains, beneath the orchid-laden trees, Romola feeling like a schoolgirl on a Sunday treat, seated between the God of the Dance and the ex-mistress of the Aga Khan. After calling for the rings, they returned to the boat to receive more congratulations. That night Romola sat beside Nijinsky at the captain's table.

After dinner Bolm took her aside. Many of the company must have foreseen disaster, but Bolm was the only one of those not afflicted by match-making madness whose position and whose friendship with Romola gave him the courage or the right to intervene.

A. B. Romola Karlovna, I have heard – I can't believe it – what is this talk about you and Nijinsky? I never imagined – why, you did not seem to be interested in him. What happened?

R. de P. Well, well, I don't always say what I think and feel.

A. B. But, after all, to get married – to a man you don't know – a perfect stranger – a person you can't even talk to.

R. de P. But I know Nijinsky, I've seen him dancing many, many times. I know his genius, his nature, everything.

A. B. You are a child. You know him as an artist, not as a man. He is a kind young man, a charming colleague, but I have to warn you he is utterly heartless.

Bolm tells her the story of Nijinsky's reaction – or lack of reaction – to the death of Thomas Nijinsky, stating that Vaslav must be without normal human feelings.

R. de P. Not necessarily. No, no, I am sure he has a kind heart. Anybody who dances as he does must be so. And I don't care.

A. B. Romola, I have to warn you. I know your parents. I have received the hospitality of your family. It is my duty. Nijinsky's friendship with Diaghilev, you may not understand, is more than merely a friendship, you see. He can't possibly be interested in you, and it will ruin your life.

R. de P. (*Very determinedly*) I thank you. I know you mean well, but I am going to marry him in spite of everything, even if you are right. I'd rather be unhappy serving Nijinsky's genius than be happy without him.

Bolm bows very low and walks away.[153]

The captain and Gunsbourg were all for a wedding on board ship, but Nijinsky wanted a 'proper service in a church'.[154] Both bride and groom, of course, were Catholic. When Vaslav conducted Romola to her cabin that night she expected him to come in with her. In Hungary an engagement-ring gave the right to pre-marital intercourse. But Vaslav kissed her hand, smiling, and said goodnight. Having come thus far, he wanted to do everything properly. She was not sure whether to be flattered or offended, and even wondered whether Bolm might not be right.[155]

Next day Romola enjoyed the company's congratulations and noticed with a certain satisfaction that Grigoriev, who had become rather autocratic in the absence of Diaghilev, was obsequiously polite.[156] She had not the inkling of an idea that she was going to split up the Russian Ballet. Nor did she foresee how much she would come to love Nijinsky,[157] or the long years of suffering, which were to bring out in her heroic qualities she did not know she possessed.

A cable to Emilia Markus asking for Romola's hand was put into the best literary French by Gunsbourg and sent off by radio.[158]

Gunsbourg gave a gala dinner on board in honour of the engagement on the night of the 2nd, but the *Avon* was sailing through St Catherine's Bay, famous for its storms, and as the ship pitched and tossed, one member of the company after another hurriedly left the dining-room.[159]

Mimi Ramberg stood on the prow looking into the wild waves; and as the wind roared around her, beating her hair and skirt, she howled aloud to herself, 'I want to drown! I want to drown!' In her unhappiness, it was touch-and-go whether she might indeed have taken her life, but she felt a hand on her shoulder. It was her admirer, Vladimir Romanov.[160] Either from pity or hoping to catch her on the rebound from Nijinsky he had come out of the night to save her – for the future.

The *Avon* sailed past Santos and Montevideo and up the Rio la Plata. On Saturday the 6th,[161] at Buenos Aires, she disgorged her passengers, some of whose lives the voyage had irreparably changed, for better or for worse. Nijinsky and Romola both stayed at the Majestic Hotel, he in a suite on the first floor, she in a room on the third. On Sunday Nijinsky went to inspect the stage of the Teatro Colón, which he found large and splendid. Romola went sightseeing in the Palermo Park with the Batons. They rejoined each other that evening at dinner with Karsavina, who had arrived ahead

385

of them. As one might expect, Romola found Karsavina charming.[162] Presented with a *fait accompli*, the ballerina was spared the horrors of a decision whether to interfere – something which would have been profoundly distasteful to her. Now, she had only to be as nice as possible and hope for the best. She wondered whether, had she been on board the *Avon*, she would have tried to persuade Nijinsky that this marriage must prove disastrous to the Russian Ballet; and she could not decide what she would have done.[163]

On Monday, 8 September, took place the company's first rehearsal. Romola was allotted by Grigoriev *corps de ballet* roles in 'Prince Igor', 'Cléopâtre' and 'Schéhérazade'. Then she was given a glimpse of a new side of her fiancé's character.

Nijinsky was practising, and sent over a message that he wished me to keep on my dancing costume as he intended to give me a lesson. I was petrified. I tried to escape, but could not. Trembling, I went up, almost crying, and began my exercises *à la barre*. I looked at him. A strange person stood before me. There was no recognition in his face: the impersonal look of a master towards his pupil. I ceased to be his *fiancée*. I was just a dancer. I expected shouts and cursing *à la Maestro*, but instead found infinite patience ... he always stopped me when I wanted to force any movement.[164]

At first it was decided that the wedding should not take place until Friday, 19 September – for the invitations to the wedding breakfast bear that date. But the wedding was put forward to the 10th. Why? Clearly someone – Vaslav, Romola or Gunsbourg – thought something might happen to prevent the marriage taking place. It is all too obvious what that something might have been. No doubt notice of the earlier date was advertised on the call-board of the theatre after the invitations had gone out.[165]

While Oblokova went shopping for a *trousseau* and wedding presents, Gunsbourg busied himself with sorting out formalities over the wedding, which was to be on the Wednesday. Nijinsky being Russian and Romola Austrian, there were complications. On Tuesday Gunsbourg drove them to church for Confession. Nijinsky confessed to a priest who spoke no Russian or Polish; and Romola was made to promise to try to stop her future husband from dancing in the 'immoral' 'Schéhérazade'.

The civil ceremony was performed, on Wednesday, 10 September, at one o'clock at the City Hall in the presence of only a few friends. Romola wore a dark blue pleated taffeta dress with pink moss-roses at the waist and a black 'Secession' hat with a curved brim and a blue ribbon.[166] The Mayor addressed the happy couple in Spanish. They signed an elaborate scroll and became man and wife.[167]

The whole company attended the wedding breakfast at the Majestic Hotel. Muningsova recalled it in later years: 'It was an extremely awkward occasion, for there was not a single person – except possibly Gunsbourg . . . – who could honestly congratulate bride or groom.'[168] Had Muningsova known how the engagement had come about, she would have had to make exceptions of Oblokova and Kovalevska too. Karsavina, who never did anything without giving thought to it, made a beautiful speech. Bolm spoke too, and said, 'Nijinsky has made many remarkable jumps in his life, but none so remarkable as the one he made today.' Not only was there to be a church wedding in the evening, but this was to be followed by a dress-rehearsal. Some day! Romola was tired, and, leaving the table, asked Mimi Ramberg to go upstairs with her. Mimi was by now calmer and resigned to her loss. Nijinsky soon followed them, bringing a piece of wedding-cake for Romola, which she ate sitting up in bed. Vaslav pecked the crumbs off her fingers, kissing them as he did so, one by one.[169]

And so to the Church of San Miguel, where Romola, in an ivory-coloured silk dress, an improvised tulle turban and white shoes, bought that afternoon, arrived late and noticed a look of disappointment on Nijinsky's face. In this Argentinian church, full of ornate clergy and strange fat fashionable ladies, the Austro-Hungarian bride was led up the aisle to the music of Wagner's 'Lohengrin' on the arm of her Russian-Jewish friend and united to the Russian-Pole, whose language she did not speak, in a ceremony performed in Latin and Spanish, which neither of them could understand. Thence by carriage to their hotel, where photographers were waiting, to be given a yellow-pink pearl. And on to the dress-rehearsal, at which the bride had to dance an Almée in 'Schéhérazade' before the critical eyes of her husband crouching in his role of Negro Slave at the Sultana's feet, and fell flat on her face. Finally, greatest ordeal of all, supper in the hotel bedroom and the awkwardness of silence and the doubt over what was to come later.[170] Journeys end in lovers' meeting. Yes, Nijinsky had got a girl at last (if that was what he wanted) and Romola had achieved her ambition. Could his sexual impulse survive all these ceremonies? For her, would the pursuit have been worthwhile, after all? 'We ate in silence ... He only smiled and served me attentively. We were both so embarrassed that we could not even express ourselves in pantomime. And when, after supper, Nijinsky kissed my hand and left me, I was so relieved that I almost cried from thankfulness.'[171]

Let us look ahead and see what happened to some of the characters who took part in the voyage of the *Avon*, because we shall not run into all of them again. Gunsbourg was sent, during the 1914–18 war, on a mission to the Caucasus, where it was supposed he was killed by revolting Cossacks, since he never returned. Rhené-Baton became Director of the Orchestre Pasdeloup, enjoyed a career as a minor composer and lived until 1940. Bolm stayed with Diaghilev until the second wartime tour of the USA, then remained in America as choreographer and teacher, dying in Hollywood in 1951. Grigoriev and his wife were with Diaghilev until his death, Tchernicheva having become one of his leading dancers. Muningsova became the celebrated Lydia Sokolova. Feodorov, the lover of Maicherska, remained with Diaghilev till the end and mimed the Father in Balanchine's 'Fils Prodigue' in Diaghilev's last season in 1929, but later in Paris had all his savings stolen and hanged himself. Hilda Bewicke married a distinguished Persian soldier and diplomat, General Arfa. Olga Khokhlova married Picasso.

Everyone knows what happened to Miriam Ramberg, who became Marie Rambert: not everyone knows the part that Nijinsky played in the fulfilment of her destiny. In place of the usual reasoning powers, Nature had endowed him with a certain mysterious and magical instinct. On board the *Avon*, going as he was to matrimony, breakdown and madness, he gave Ramberg the advice: 'Don't stay in the Diaghilev Company. This is not the place for you. Your work will lie elsewhere.' She never spoke to him again after the South American tour, but she took his advice. She left Diaghilev; and founded British ballet.

CHAPTER SEVEN

1913–1917

September 1913–November 1917

By the time of his marriage Nijinsky had created all his famous roles, bar one; and I have provided what evidence I could find of the way he danced them. We have remarked his exceptional versatility, and it was Pierre Vladimirov himself who told me that there was only one of Nijinsky's roles in which he was able to replace him, namely the Poet in 'Les Sylphides'. (He might, I suppose, have added, were he not so modest, Prince Siegfried in 'Le Lac des Cygnes'.) But what *kind* of dancer was Nijinsky, judged by the standards of the classroom?

It was Noverre who divided male dancers into the two categories of *jarreté* and *arqué*, which one must translate, though it sounds insulting, as 'knock-kneed' and 'bow-legged'. The tall, elegant *danseur noble*, with his long legs and long line, belongs to the first group; the short, strong, stocky, spinning, bounding character or *demi-caractère* dancer to the second. Since Noverre's day male dancers have been trained in more spectacular techniques and have probably developed wider ranges, so that the two categories have tended to merge, though the distinction still exists. In our own day Erik Bruhn has been an extreme instance of the *danseur noble*, Alexander Grant of the dazzling *demi-caractère* dancer, and Rudolf Nureyev overlaps into both categories.

Nijinsky was an extreme instance of the *arqué* dancer. In spite of the perfection of figure which his wife understandably and romantically attributed to him, he was very short, with a long neck and sloping shoulders, thickset, with enormously developed thighs and bulging calves. His colleague Rosaï was equally short and bulky, but Rosaï was type-cast in grotesque character roles like the Buffoon in 'Le Pavillon d'Armide' or one of the two coachmen in 'Petrushka', and would never be expected to dance anything outside this range. Nijinsky had a quality of grace, flow and style which enabled him to break out of the category which his physique had indicated for him. This was partly because of his long neck, partly because of his superb Petersburg training and partly because of his personal magic, which is ultimately inexplicable. The little *arqué* dancer usually takes secondary roles, the first ones being reserved for the ballerina's partner, the tall prince. Nijinsky's quality made it inevitable that he should dance leading roles, yet his short stature would never qualify him for an ideal partner or prince. Special roles had to be created for him. When he took over someone else's role, as he did Harlequin in 'Carnaval', he made it into something entirely his own.

He had the lightness expected of an *arqué* dancer, but the line of a *jarreté* dancer. Or did he only create an illusion of ideal line through instinctive artistry? Alexander Bland has an interesting theory. He thinks that his smallness and his short thick legs 'merely made him into a sculptural rather than a linear dancer. By continual turning and twisting, by moving non-stop on his toes and by accenting his superb neck and arms he developed a plastic style which was uniquely expressive. It is exactly what have been called his mannerisms which made him great, just as he turned his hang-ups into magnetizing mystery and his bodily handicaps into new aspects of beauty.'[1] Mr Edwin Denby in an essay on photographs of Nijinsky recorded some extremely interesting observations about the way the dancer used his neck differently in different roles.[2]

'The climax of his art', wrote Rebecca West, 'was his jump. He leaped high into the air, and there stayed for what seemed several seconds. Face and body suggested that he was to mount still further, do the Indian rope trick with himself as rope, hurl himself up into space through an invisible ceiling and disappear. But then he came down – and here was the second miracle – more slowly than he had gone up, landing as softly as a deer clearing a hedge of snow.'[3]

Finally, Nijinsky was evidently a most musical dancer. This was not just a question of being 'on the beat' – and there are some distinguished dancers who are so unmusical that they cannot even manage that – but of sensing the shape of a melody which is not measured by staves. Mr Denby wrote: 'To make the continuity rhythmic as he did, he must have had an unerring instinct at which moment to attack a movement, so that the entire sequence of it would flow as continuously and transform itself into the next motion as securely as did the accompanying sound . . . The choreography of 'Faune' proves that Nijinsky's natural musical intelligence was of the highest order. For this was the first ballet choreography set clearly, not to the measures and periods, but to the expressive flow of the music, to its musical sense.'[4]

Buenos Aires seemed to the dancers a town of narrow streets and undistinguished houses. 'The streets were crowded,' wrote Grigoriev, 'but only with men; there were few if any women to be seen at all. We were to discover later that women in Buenos Aires went not on foot but in carriages.'[5] In spite of warnings that walking abroad might result in girls being abducted and sold into slavery, the dancers were allowed to wander about, to the astonishment of the natives, and to find their own rooms. Ramberg, choosing her lodgings, chanced on some sort of brothel, where she was propositioned by a man who had been on the *Avon*.[6]

The company's first performance – in 'Le Pavillon', 'Schéhérazade', 'Le Spectre' and 'Prince Igor' – was on 11 September. Eighteen performances in all were given, of which two were for the benefit of the subscribers to the Colón Theatre's opera seasons. It was the city's first sight of ballet, and the initial polite interest of the fashionable audience soon turned to enthusiasm.[7]

Romola was coached privately by the Maestro and by Kovalevska for her roles in 'Prince Igor', 'Schéhérazade' and 'Cléopâtre'; but her first official appearance with the company was in the mimed part of the Prince's Fiancée in 'Le Lac des Cygnes'. On this occasion her fears were soothed by Bolm, who was dancing the Prince, and who talked to her on stage. But when Nijinsky danced this role, he was 'no longer my husband, but the Prince himself'. There was no communication between them except in the manner of the role. Vaslav's absolute separation between art and life was brought home to her even more forcibly when she found herself gently turned away from his dressing-room before a performance. At such moments, when Nijinsky was 'becoming' a part, Romola was already conscious of 'an indescribable distance' between her husband and herself.[8]

Yet at the hotel Nijinsky was gay and mischievous; and he sent her roses every morning by the frowning Vassili. Progress in communication was slow, but with the aid of painstaking tuition from Gunsbourg Nijinsky laid before his wife confessions and revelations: the nature of his former relationship with Diaghilev, and the story of his brother Stanislav – 'He is insane. You have to know it.' He sent off to Diaghilev a letter announcing his marriage and stressing his unchanged friendship as well as devotion to the Ballet. Diaghilev was so understanding, Nijinsky naïvely believed, that he would give them his blessing.[9] Romola was not so sure:[10] but she could not imagine the Ballet could do without him. It is possible, however, that Diaghilev first heard of the marriage in a telegram from Vassili Zuikov.[11]

Diaghilev was in Venice when he received the news. Misia Sert had been summoned to his hotel room that morning to play for him a score that had just arrived. She found him in nightshirt and slippers. 'Performing elephantine capers across the room, in his enthusiasm he seized my parasol and opened it. I stopped playing with a start and told him to shut it, as it brought bad luck to open it indoors and he was madly superstitious. Barely had I time to utter my warning when somebody knocked at the door. A telegram . . . Diaghilev turned livid. . .'

Hysterically he summoned Sert, Bakst and the others. 'When the council of war was complete, the terrible event was discussed with greater calm. What had been Nijinsky's state of mind when he left? Did he seem preoccupied? Not at all. Sad? Certainly not.' Diaghilev ultimately decided to telegraph and forbid the banns. 'Alas! numerous confirmations continued to arrive: the marriage had taken place, it was irremediable. We immediately took Diaghilev, drunk with grief and rage, to Naples, where he launched himself on a frantic bacchanalia. But he was beyond consolation.'[12]* Apart from his disappoint-

---

*By his own account (*Memories*, p. 135, footnote 2) Stravinsky was present when Diaghilev received the news of Nijinsky's marriage (but he places the event in the Mon-ment as a lover and the crashing of his hopes for the company and for the future of Nijinsky as a choreographer, it was a felling blow for the great Diaghilev to have been tricked by a girl of twenty-three. Even so, Diaghilev – the greatest diplomat of the age – was sufficiently in control of himself not to send any bombshell of a telegram which might terminate Nijinsky's connection with the Russian Ballet in mid-tour. If (as I guess) Romola had hastened the marriage to prevent him hearing the news till it was too late, she had underestimated his business sense and his feeling of duty to the company. If Nijinsky ceased to dance on the South American tour, the Ballet's contract would be broken and the company would be out of work. Diaghilev did nothing.

Reports of Nijinsky's marriage began to appear in the press. '*Un mariage bien . . . parisien*' was a sardonic headline in one French newspaper. '*Le danseur marié*' exclaimed another, jumping to the conclusion that Romola de Pulszky who had been Nijinsky's pupil was now to be his star. Benois wrote from Petersburg to Stravinsky in Switzerland.

Benois in Petersburg to Stravinsky in Switzerland, (?).9.13
. . . Serge is the Devil knows where. After discussing the Bach ballet with me in Baden, he was to have come to see me in Lugano and to have brought Ravel with him. But I have heard nothing from him, and since he has disappeared without a note, I am inclined to believe those charming gossipers (their news has probably reached you too) who say that Vaslav married a Hungarian millionairess and Serge, in his grief, has sold the company to an impresario. Have you any news of our dissolute genius Serge? Valetchka, who went to Paris (cursing his fate, poor fellow), also does not know anything.

Stravinsky confirmed the rumour.

Benois in Petersburg to Stravinsky in Switzerland, 28.9.13
Dear Igor Feodorovitch,
I was in Moscow and found your letter only on my return. The news about Nijinsky's marriage struck me like a thunderbolt. When did it happen? None of our friends is here in town at the moment, and I know of

---

treux Palace Hotel). '. . . I had watched him turn into a madman who begged me and my wife not to leave him alone.'

no one who can give me any information about it, since I do not want to talk to a stranger like Svetlov. I saw Serge and Vaslav almost on the eve of Vaslav's departure for Argentina, and there was no hint then about the coming event. Nijinsky was very attentively studying Bach with us, preparing the Bach ballet. It it possible that he had no idea of it then? Be kind and tell me one thing: was it a complete surprise for Serge, or was he prepared for it? How deep was his shock? Their romance was coming to an end, and I doubt that he was really heartbroken, but if he did suffer I hope it was not too terrible for him. However, I imagine he must be completely bewildered in his position as head of the company. But why can't Nijinsky be both a ballet master and a Hungarian millionaire. The whole story is such a phantasmagoria I sometimes think I have read it in a dream and am an idiot to believe it.[13]

Diaghilev's despair did not prevent him attending to business. Hugo von Hofmannsthal was in Venice and negotiations over the Strauss ballet had to be pushed forward, even though Nijinsky could no longer be considered as its choreographer.

Hofmannsthal in Munich to Strauss at Garmisch, 30.9.13
In Venice I saw a lot of Diaghilev, Bakst and the very charming Lady Ripon and the conversation came round to 'Joseph' over and over again... I entirely approve of Diaghilev's intention to employ Fokine and not Nijinsky as *metteur-en-scène* of this ballet.[14]

In Paris Astruc's great venture at the Théâtre des Champs-Elysées was foundering. The artists he had presented recognized the nobility of his endeavours on behalf of music, opera and ballet. It was arranged that there should be a final performance of 'Boris Godounov' on 6 November, and everyone would perform without payment. Diaghilev, presumably cutting short his Neapolitan orgies, attended this.[15] He then travelled to Petersburg. On 17 November Astruc's company went into liquidation.[16]

Romola was conscious of an improvement in her dancing under Nijinsky's watchful tutelage. He gave her traditional lessons and others of his own invention. 'The most difficult steps became easy if I carefully imitated his movements. The sense of harmony in the movement was the chief factor.' She overcame much of her nervousness, and her rendering of one of the Nymphs in 'L'Après-midi' pleased Nijinsky. But when she danced in 'Prince Igor', in which he had no part, she tried to dissuade him from watching. He insisted that he must see the performance, to judge it as a whole. Romola's fear of Nijinsky the artist returned, and 'as I saw him in the wings, I ran off the stage panic-stricken!' To her chagrin she was suspended for a week: and when she discussed the subject of her dancing with him, he told her that she had started too late to develop a perfect technique: 'But you could dance very beautifully certain dances which I will compose for you.'

Romola made the sensible decision to continue lessons with her husband, but never again to dance in public: she would serve him better by not distracting him with her problems as a dancer.[17] The result of this was to isolate her still further from the life of the company, and as she grew more distant from them so did Vaslav.

Through Gunsbourg Romola now discussed with her husband the question of a baby, and Gunsbourg relayed Vaslav's decision: 'For five years we shall live for art and our love, but the supreme happiness and the fulfilment of life and marriage is to have a child, and after that time, when we will be in our permanent home, we shall have one.'[18]

After a month in Buenos Aires the company moved to Montevideo, where, although the public was even more receptive, only two performances were given. Another sea-voyage followed to Rio de Janeiro, where the first performance took place on 17 October. The tour was to end early in November. Romola had not been well in Montevideo, but in Rio she and Nijinsky went for drives in the forest, delighting in the flowers, the birds, butterflies and especially the ubiquitous little monkeys. They were less fond of the snakes which occasionally penetrated into their hilltop hotel.[19]

One day, according to Grigoriev, Gunsbourg was told that Nijinsky would not be dancing that evening. The Baron pointed out to Grigoriev that the dancer was breaking his contract: and there was the added problem of there being no understudy for the role of Harlequin in 'Carnaval', to be given in this performance.[20] Did neither of them know that Nijinsky had no contract?[21] The *régisseur* immediately got Gavrilov to rehearse Nijinsky's role, and then visited Vaslav and Romola, who were both adamant that Nijinsky should not dance that evening, in spite of Grigoriev's

Nijinsky in 'Carnaval'.
Drawing by Jean Cocteau.

warnings. Nijinsky gave no explanation of his conduct and the next day was dancing as usual. Diaghilev was informed of what had happened by Gunsbourg. Such is Grigoriev's story. Romola Nijinsky denies that Nijinsky missed a performance, and yet the telegram which Diaghilev made Grigoriev send from Petersburg, according to the latter, gave breach of contract as the reason for Nijinsky's dismissal. But Nijinsky had not had a contract since 1909. Grigoriev says he gave this incident, and the question of Nijinsky's marriage, much thought on the boat back to Europe.

It seemed to me that Nijinsky and the Ballet were all but inseparable. It was round Nijinsky that our now considerable repertoire had been largely built up; and the fact that Diaghilev had always concentrated publicity on him had resulted in his being identified with our Ballet in the public mind. Moreover, there was the new movement in choreography inaugurated by Diaghilev's collaboration with Nijinsky, about which so much had been said and written. I could not, in short, conceive how Nijinsky could be replaced; and yet, in the course of my five years' association with Diaghilev

I had begun to understand the complexity of his character. He was not a man to depend on other people, however necessary to him they might appear to be; and now that Nijinsky was married I could not see how their collaboration could continue. Yet such was my faith in Diaghilev's immense resource that I felt sure he would find a solution to this problem . . .[22]

Nijinsky and Romola sailed for Europe with the company.[*] Romola, who had found in Brazil that she was pregnant in spite of everything, felt sea-sick and the thought of childbirth frightened her. Vaslav cheered her by saying that the child, which he named 'Le Petit Nègre' in memory of South America, would be a marvellous dancer. They were beginning to be able to carry on a conversation in broken Russian and French; but to the end of his life even when Romola addressed him in Russian Vaslav answered in French.[23] Romola would speak enthusiastically of the beautiful dresses, hats and jewels and of a brilliant social life which she naturally felt was her due now that that she had married the great dancer. But soon she found out that Nijinsky did not share her enthusiasm for worldly pleasures: he told her 'I am only an artist, not a prince, but anything I can have is yours. If these things make you happy, I will give them to you.'[24] The ship docked at Cadiz and the Nijinskys decided to travel from there to Paris by train, leaving the rest of the company to continue their voyage to Cherbourg.

Their plans were to call at Budapest for a few days, since Vaslav wished to meet Romola's mother, and then to go on a visit to Eleonora in Petersburg, where Bronia's baby Irina had been born in October. But first of all they expected to meet Diaghilev in Paris.

While we passed the frontier, at Hendaye, we were sitting in the dining saloon having dinner when Vaslav suddenly became livid, jumped up, and left. I went after him, and found him in our compartment – having fainted. I tried to summon a doctor immediately, but there was not one on the train. The *chef du train* brought some ice and smelling-salts; and as Vaslav came to himself he complained of intense headache, which he had often when on a long train journey. From that time I gave up smoking, as he could not stand even the smell of cigarettes.[25]

---

[*]According to Grigoriev (p. 99) they sailed on a separate boat.

Diaghilev was not in Paris. The Nijinskys' short stay there, however, was a round of gaiety. The next stop was Vienna, where Romola's sister met them; and so to Budapest, where Emilia Markus had organized parties and press photographers. This lionization Nijinsky found distressing.

Emilia Markus and her doctor begged Romola not to have the baby. At the last moment, however, Romola decided that even death was preferable to an abortion. Vaslav was happy. 'An immense relief and pleasure was expressed in his face. He kissed me gently, and whispered: "Thank God. What He has given, nobody has the right to destroy."'[26] Romola, who had been infatuated with Nijinsky rather than in love with him before their marriage, now began to love him more and more because of his goodness.[27]

Nijinsky was becoming increasingly anxious about the completion of the two ballets on which he had been working, 'Joseph' and the ballet to Bach. All the preparatory work had been finished (some of it on the *Avon*), but rehearsals had been impossible in South America because of the intense heat, and Nijinsky had not been really fit since he left Rio.[28] On arrival in Budapest he had cabled Diaghilev to ask when rehearsals were to start and when he could begin work on a new ballet, and to press for the dancers being relieved of other commitments during the period of rehearsal.[29] While awaiting a reply, Vaslav made preparations to spend Christmas with his family.[30]

Grigoriev and the rest of the company had been greeted on arrival at Cherbourg by a welcoming telegram from Diaghilev. As soon as the *régisseur* arrived in Petersburg he was summoned to Diaghilev who showed him Nijinsky's telegram, then covered it with his hand – which 'he always did with any communication that annoyed him' – and wrote a reply, which he asked Grigoriev to sign. Grigoriev now found his initial fears about Diaghilev's resentment justified. 'By causing the answer to Nijinsky's telegram to go from me, he wished to show that their former friendship now counted for nothing and that their relationship had become purely formal.'[31]

The telegram arrived in Budapest two days before Nijinsky had planned to leave for Russia.[32]

Grigoriev in Petersburg to Nijinsky in Budapest (alleged text), 3.12.13

In reply to your telegram to Monsieur Diaghilev I wish to inform you of the following. Monsieur Diaghilev considers that by missing a performance at Rio and refusing to dance in the ballet Carnaval you broke your contract. He will not therefore require your further services. Serge Grigoriev, *Régisseur* of the Diaghilev Company.[33]

In view of the fact that Diaghilev knew perfectly well that Nijinsky had no contract (and therefore could not break one), even if Grigoriev did not, it seems possible that the latter's story of the missed performance and its being the pretext for Nijinsky's dismissal was a complete invention. Yet a message of dismissal was certainly sent. Nijinsky's first reaction to the communication, whatever its wording, was incredulity; his wife's was to burst into tears. 'Now, for the first time, it dawned on me that perhaps I had made a mistake; I had destroyed, where I had wanted to be helpful.' But Vaslav consoled her: 'Do not be sad. It is a mistake – and if it *is* true, I am an artist and I can work for myself.'[34] He sent a defiant telegram to Astruc:

Nijinsky in Budapest to Astruc in Paris, 5.12.13

Please inform the newspapers that I shall not be working any longer with Diaghilev.[35]

For some time, still refusing to believe in the reality of his dismissal, Nijinsky tried to find out from his former collaborators what was in Diaghilev's mind. A few days later he wrote to Stravinsky (whom he had not seen since 'Le Sacre'):

Nijinsky in Budapest to Stravinsky, 9.12.13

Dear Igor,

I went with my wife to her parents' home in Budapest and there I immediately sent a telegram to Serge asking him when we could see each other. The answer ... was a letter from Grigoriev informing me that I shall not be asked to stage any ballets this season, and that I am not needed as an artist. Please write to me whether this is true. I do not believe that Serge can act so meanly to me. Serge owes me a lot of money. I have received nothing for two years, neither for my dancing nor for my staging 'Faune', 'Jeux', and 'Sacre du printemps'. I worked for the Ballet without a contract. If it is true that Serge does not want to work with me – then I have lost everything. You understand the situation I am in. I cannot imagine what has happened, what is the reason for his behaviour. Please ask Serge what is the matter, and write to me about it. In all the newspapers of Germany, Paris and London, etc., it is reported that I am not working any more with Diaghilev. But the whole press is against him (including the *feuilletons*). They also say that I am gathering a company of my own. In truth, I am receiving propositions from every side and the biggest of these comes from a very rich business man, who offers one million francs to organize a new Diaghilev Russian Ballet [*sic*] – they wish me to have sole artistic direction and large sums of money to commission décors, music, etc. But I won't give them a definite answer before I have news from you.

My numerous friends send me letters of revolt and rage against Diaghilev – and propositions to help me and join me in my new enterprise. I hope you will not forget me and will answer my letter immediately.

Your loving
VASLAV.[36]

The letter was sent to Russia, but Stravinsky was in Switzerland and received it some time later. He felt that it was 'a document of such astounding innocence – if Nijinsky hadn't written it, I think only a character in Dostoevsky might have. It seems incredible to me . . . that he was so unaware of the politics and sexual jealousies and motives within the Ballet.'[37] Clearly Nijinsky's faith in Diaghilev's acceptance of his marriage was unshaken, since he had failed to perceive the connection between it and his dismissal. In spite of his 'confessions' to Romola, the result of his wish that she should know all about him, and despite what he was to write later in his *Diary*, at this stage he did not see his marriage as an impediment to continued friendship with Diaghilev.

In Petersburg Grigoriev was speculating that 'the violence of Diaghilev's reaction was due in part to the failure of Nijinsky's last two ballets. Diaghilev, I thought, must already have decided that Nijinsky did not have it in him to become a great choreographer.'[38] Grigoriev's inability to appreciate the originality of Nijinsky's art, together with his loyalty to Diaghilev, prevented his seeing the issue in its true light: but he was nevertheless astonished when Diaghilev told him that he intended to persuade Fokine to rejoin the company. 'Fokine's an excellent dancer and a no less excellent choreographer. Why not try?' He went to the telephone and the conversation, wrote Grigoriev, 'lasted no less than five hours'. (Karsavina had several telephone calls of four hours or so from Diaghilev at moments of crisis.) Fokine

began by flatly refusing to have anything more to do with the Ballet. But Diaghilev was not deterred. He let him say all he wished, biding his time, and then protested at Fokine's accusations, defended his own standpoint, and embarked on persuasion as only he knew how. The result was that despite all Fokine's stubbornness (and he was of a far from tractable nature), after five hours of uninterrupted talk Diaghilev wore him down and obtained his promise to call the next day. As he replaced the receiver Diaghilev heaved a sigh of relief. 'Well, that's settled, I think,' he said. 'He was a tough nut to crack, though, all the same!'[39]

In *his* account of the incident Fokine makes no mention of this telephone conversation. He records that Svetlov persuaded him to receive Diaghilev at his own flat, and Diaghilev arrived and 'made a most eloquent speech, trying to convince me that he was now wholeheartedly on my side, that his infatuation with his favourite was now long forgotten, and that it was only I who could now save the art of the Russian ballet which I myself had created, and which now faced danger'. Fokine was persuaded, and agreed not only to re-stage his old ballets but to create seven new ones, of which the Richard Strauss work would be the first. He insisted in his contract that none of Nijinsky's ballets should be given under his regime. Fokine was also to be *premier danseur*, and a further clause in his contract specifically precluded Nijinsky's re-engagement.[40]

Despite the fact that Grigoriev and others in the company had been hostile to Fokine when he left in the previous year, and in spite of the choreographer's wish that Grigoriev should be dismissed, which Diaghilev could not agree to, Fokine's return, according to Grigoriev, met with 'everyone's delight'. 'No one had really approved of the Nijinsky period in choreography. It had seemed to be leading us nowhere, whereas Fokine's return gave us fresh hope of success.'[41] Grigoriev's views on artistic matters had their limitations. Much work remained to be done on the repertory for the coming London season of both opera and ballet, but, wrote Grigoriev, 'strangely enough, Diaghilev seemed like someone who has shed a load and can at last breathe freely'.[42]

Later in December Diaghilev went off to Moscow in connection
with work on the operas, and Grigoriev followed. On a visit to the
Bolshoi Theatre Diaghilev was taken by the appearance of a young
dancer, Leonide Miassine, who was dancing the tarantella in 'Le
Lac des Cygnes' and the Knight of the Moon in 'Don Quichotte',[43]
and sent Mikhail Savitsky – a member of the Bolshoi *corps* who had
danced in his company the year before – to tell Miassine that he
wished to meet him. Miassine was flattered, and called on Diaghilev
at the Metropole Hotel the next afternoon. Diaghilev told him that
subject to Fokine's approval he would like him to dance the title
role in 'La Légende de Joseph' – the role which was to have been
Nijinsky's. Miassine was to make up his mind by the following day.
The dancer was 'dazed and bewildered'. He had been on the point
of giving up dancing to start on an acting career, and his friends
advised him against changing his plans lest this tempting offer
should ruin his chances in Moscow. Accordingly, when he returned
to Diaghilev's hotel the next day, he had made up his mind to
refuse. But Diaghilev's magic worked on this as on other occasions.
'I was just about to tell him that I could not accept his offer when,
almost without realizing it, I heard myself say, "Yes, I shall be
delighted to join your company." '[44] Miassine asked for two months'
leave from the Bolshoi Theatre – and left for ever.[45] He travelled
immediately with Diaghilev to Petersburg, where he had an
audition with Fokine: this was a completely formal occasion, during
which Miassine demonstrated his (then not very exceptional) technique, and the next day he was finally engaged.[46] He was eighteen:
Grigoriev thought him 'strikingly handsome'. Diaghilev acknowledged that he was not much of a dancer as yet, and added, 'Of
course, he's rather provincial. . . But we'll soon put an end to
that.'[47] From this moment Miassine became Diaghilev's constant
companion. He was taken straight to the Hermitage to look at the
pictures: his 'education' was begun without delay.[48]

Nijinsky only wanted to be back with the Diaghilev Ballet, but
there was to be no olive-branch from Petersburg. He was determined
that any other offer he took up must have serious artistic intentions:
his art, and his opportunity to create, were all-important, and he
would not consider appearing in music-hall. In vain impresarios

sought his services and offered high salaries: in vain agents wrote to him and visited him in Budapest. Even Rouché, the new Director of the Paris Opéra, who offered him the post of *maître de ballet* and *premier danseur* for 100,000 gold francs a year, was turned down because of the limitations of the Opéra repertory. Romola knew that more than anything Vaslav wanted to create new ballets of abstract dancing – like 'Le Sacre' – as he had been encouraged to by Diaghilev.[49] But he must resign himself to the fact that if he formed a company he must administer it, train it, rehearse it and get engagements for it, besides dancing with it and making ballets.

In order to escape the insistent interference of Romola's mother and stepfather, the Nijinskys left for Vienna: and there the importunings of one impresario succeeded. Alfred Butt, owner of the Palace Theatre in London, offered Vaslav a contract for eight weeks in the spring of 1914, under which he could assemble his own company and plan his own repertory. According to Romola, 'Vaslav believed that this place was not a variety theatre, but one of the most distinguished houses in London, equal to Covent Garden or Drury Lane', and so he signed the agreement.[50] She overstates the case: Nijinsky could not fail to know that the Palace was a Theatre of Varieties – it was printed on the cover of the programmes – and Pavlova had appeared there for years. Nijinsky may have believed that the Palace was the *best* of the variety theatres, and overcome his reservations on being offered for his company £1,000 a week.

Bronia and her husband Kotchetovsky, who had resigned from Diaghilev's company in sympathy, came from Russia to Paris to meet Vaslav and discuss their plans. Nijinsky intended to employ thirty-two dancers, and to create new ballets, in addition to presenting, as requested, 'Le Spectre', 'La Princesse enchantée' (the Blue-bird *pas de deux*) and 'Les Sylphides'.

To carry out his plans Nijinsky needed new scenery and costumes. Bakst was the first to be approached, but he was unable or perhaps unwilling, through fear of Diaghilev, to co-operate.* But Boris

---

*The Nijinskys ran into him shortly after this outside the Savoy Hotel in London and he tried to cut them, exclaiming, 'I'm not allowed to talk to you!' (Romola Nijinsky conversations.)

Anisfeld, the scene-painter and designer of 'Sadko', accepted Nijinsky's commission, as did Mme Muelle who made the costumes for the Ballets Russes. Ravel also took Nijinsky's part and assisted him to choose music as well as providing a new orchestration for a slightly different selection of Chopin pieces which would constitute a new 'Les Sylphides'. The task of recruiting dancers for the company was taken on by Bronia and her husband, who went back to Russia for that purpose. None of the dancers whom Nijinsky auditioned in Vienna or Paris was at all suitable: but Bronia brought back a carefully selected group of Imperial School graduates who were sympathetic to Nijinsky, and these were engaged for one year.[51] The company was peculiar in that it contained only two men, Nijinsky and his brother-in-law Alexander Kotchetovsky. Nijinska was principal ballerina, and the other soloists were Mlles Boni (who had been with Diaghilev), Jvanova, Darinska, Jakovleva, Krasnitska, Larionova, Poeltzich, Ptitsenko and Tarassova.[52]

Meanwhile, Diaghilev had clinched his deal with Strauss.

Hofmannsthal at Rodaun to Strauss at Garmisch, 31.1.14

Many thanks for your letter and for the good news that the *Joseph* contract has been signed. A telegram from Diaghilev in Paris expresses his delight over the same news and informs me that Mme Rubinstein is now apparently certain for the female part. *Tant mieux!*[53]

In February the Diaghilev company gathered in Prague, and many of the dancers heard for the first time of Nijinsky's dismissal and Fokine's reinstatement. During the German tour, which took the company to Stuttgart, Cologne, Hamburg, Leipzig, Hanover, Breslau and Berlin and ended in Switzerland at Zürich, Miassine was rehearsed by Fokine in 'La Légende' and took classes with Cecchetti. Fokine simplified the role of Joseph for Miassine.[54] The future leading dancer and choreographer made his début with the company as a watchman in 'Petrushka'. Fokine was dancing some of Nijinsky's roles, but the company was still deficient in principal male dancers. Diaghilev paid what was to be his last visit to Russia, and while there he re-engaged two notable dancers: Pierre Vladimirov, *premier danseur* of the Mariinsky, who had been with him in London in 1912 to dance two performances of 'Les

Sylphides' in place of Nijinsky, and Alexis Bulgakov, the mime whose association with the Diaghilev company went back to the first night in 1909. He was to play Tsar Dodon in 'Coq d'or'. Not Ida Rubinstein, but Maria Kuznetsova, an opera singer, was engaged to dance the Rubinstein-type role of Potiphar's wife in 'La Légende de Joseph'.[55]

In Paris Nijinsky and his sister began rehearsals for the London season. Romola felt that her sister-in-law disliked her: 'she seemed to resent everything that happened and blame it on me. I was the intruder in the Russian Ballet, in the family.'[56] The Nijinskys' arrival in London in February was much publicized. Lady Ottoline Morrell greeted them at the Savoy with armfuls of flowers, while Lady Ripon congratulated them on their marriage, telling Romola that 'it was always her wish that Vaslav should marry, and that she had tried in the past to introduce him to suitable young ladies.'[57] Gwladys Ripon wrote to Misia Sert that 'Nijinsky's marriage has predisposed everyone here in his favour'[58] – and Misia commented that the event had produced in a society whose memories of the Wilde *débâcle* were still fresh 'a wave of fine Puritan approval'.[59]

There remained two weeks for the completion of preparations, and the season was already fully booked. But things began to go wrong. Some of the trouble was caused by Diaghilev. Though he resented both Bronia's sympathy for Vaslav and her physical resemblance to him,[60] Diaghilev was well aware that she was a valuable artist. He had talked Fokine out of demanding her exclusion from the company, and now he brought a court action to prevent her appearing with Nijinsky on the grounds that her resignation from the Diaghilev Ballet had not been accepted. After much trouble Diaghilev lost the case.[61] Bronia, too, came in for criticism from Vaslav on an occasion when she felt unwell at a rehearsal, and Kotchetovsky insulted him in return. There was trouble with the management. Nijinsky was asked to call on Alfred Butt in his office: but he thought – or Romola told him – that Butt should come to him.[62] This misunderstanding with Butt was the first of several. During one scene Vaslav smashed a table.[63]

To Nijinsky, whose nerves were already on edge, working in the atmosphere of a music-hall was a humiliation. The first night was

405

2 March, and Romola was 'blinded with tears to see Vaslav dance, in his exquisite programme, after a clown's number and before a popular singer's act'.[64] The programme consisted of 'Les Sylphides', with re-arranged choreography to Ravel's orchestration of some new and some old Chopin numbers and a highly inappropriate décor of exotic vegetation by Anisfeld; Sinding's 'Danse Orientale' – the solo originally danced by Nijinsky in 'Les Orientales' and now performed by Kotchetovsky; and 'Le Spectre de la rose'. Cyril Beaumont was in the audience, and recorded the structure of the new 'Sylphides'. 'There was an overture provided by an Etude, then a Nocturne (Nijinska, Nijinsky and *corps de ballet*), a Mazurka (Nijinsky), an Etude (Mlle Boni), a Mazurka (Nijinska), an Etude (Mlle Jvanova), a Mazurka (Nijinska, Nijinsky), and a Nocturne (Nijinska, Nijinsky and *corps de ballet*).'

Beaumont 'anxiously awaited the rise of the curtain, but when the stage was revealed and the ballet proceeded I could not reconcile myself either to the new scenery, the different music, or the changed choreography. And when Nijinsky himself danced I have to confess that I was conscious of a pang of disappointment. He still danced with that rare elevation and feeling for line and style ... but he no longer danced like a god. Something of that mystic fragrance which previously had surrounded his dancing in "Les Sylphides" had vanished.'

Kotchetovsky's *pas seul*, which 'was executed entirely *sur place* and consisted of admirably harmonized, if restricted, movements of the head, body, and limbs, clearly inspired by the Javanese classical dance', was greeted with enthusiasm. Then came 'Le Spectre', danced in front of a black velvet curtain. 'Both Nijinsky and his sister danced superbly, yet something of the old magic had departed.'[65]

The critic of *The Times* praised the dancing of Nijinsky and Nijinska in both ballets, and felt that 'Le Spectre' was quite the equal of the original production: but for him the new 'Sylphides' – though revealing Nijinsky's 'fine taste in figuration and his subtle skill in musical interpretation' – was 'just less than successful' by comparison with the original combination of music, choreography and décor which was an 'acknowledged masterpiece'.[66]

The audience's response, Beaumont felt, was polite and grew cooler as the evening progressed. This was partly due to the fact that during the two scene changes Nijinsky wished the auditorium to remain in darkness, and refused to allow the theatre manager, Maurice Volny, to have music played. Despite the number of people in the audience who had been regular followers of the Ballet at Covent Garden and Drury Lane, there were still sufficient music-hall patrons to resent this deprivation and grow restive. Nijinsky changed in the wings to make sure his wishes were adhered to. On the second night he went to his dressing-room, and on Volny's instructions the orchestra played a Tchaikovsky number from Pavlova's repertory chosen by the conductor, Herman Finck. When Vaslav heard of this, he became hysterical. Eventually 'Le Spectre' went on normally, but Nijinsky continued to protest vehemently in the morning.[67]

For the second week of the engagement 'Danse Polovtsienne' was announced, and for the third a new programme comprising 'Carnaval', 'L'Oiseau et le Prince' and 'Danse Grecque'. But on the evening of the 16th, after rehearsing all day, Nijinsky suddenly developed influenza,[68] and Butt had to announce that he was too ill to dance. A series of vaudeville turns was quickly put on in place of the ballet.[69] Romola had treated Vaslav with aspirin, which according to the doctors called in by Lady Ripon 'almost killed him, as he had an athlete's heart and was in an extremely dangerous condition'. The management of the theatre enforced the clause in the contract which put him in breach of the agreement if he failed to appear for three consecutive nights. He was not well enough to return, and the season ended abruptly, the total cost for properties, music and salaries devolving on Vaslav personally. Negotiations for a new arrangement failed, each side being dissatisfied with the other. Nijinsky had danced for the last time in London. His loyal company declared themselves content with the pay they had received and wanted only their fares to Russia, but Nijinsky would not hear of it and paid all thirty-two dancers a full year's salary from his savings.[70] It may be asked what money he had, since Diaghilev had never given him a salary. The answer is that for dancing at private parties such as the Aga Khan's he had been paid enormous sums. As Diaghilev had always settled his hotel bills, fed and clothed him and taken care of his mother's expenses, these were almost untouched.[71]

The comedian Fred Emney replaced the Russians at the Palace.

While these events were taking place, a reminder of happier times was provided by an exhibition at the Fine Art Society in Bond Street of portraits of Nijinsky in the roles for which he was famous: drawings of him as Harlequin, Petrushka, the Faun and the Spectre by Valentine Gross; in 'Le Pavillon' by Sargent; taking a call after 'Faune' by Glyn Philpot. There were three studies, including that in the costume for 'Danse Orientale', by Blanche; a statuette and etchings by Una Troubridge; and two drawings of him in 'Jeux' by the Beardsleyesque Alberto Montenegro, which the critic of the *Daily Telegraph* found 'repulsive' and 'a blot on the exhibition'. The same critic, Sir Claude Phillips, lamented the absence of any study of Nijinsky by either Bakst or Rodin.[72]

Lady Ripon wrote to Misia Sert about Nijinsky: 'There were some who believed that he did not wish to return to the ballet, but ever since he has been here he has been telling everybody how unhappy he is to be dismissed, and that all he wants is to go back.' Lady Ripon was being pressed by her friends to persuade Diaghilev to re-engage Nijinsky: and although she had divided loyalties, and felt that artistically Fokine augured better for the company than Nijinsky – since she thought that in Nijinsky's ballets 'the *corps de ballet* had become so disorganized that it was unrecognizable'[73] – her personal devotion to Vaslav was great. Clearly she was one to prefer such ballets as 'Le Spectre de la rose' to Nijinsky's audacious experiments. With regard to Diaghilev and his contracts, she wrote, 'he tells you anything that suits him at the moment!' and she was anxious to know from Misia how much he had 'tied himself up with Vladimirov'. She was also conscious of the 'gossip about his new friend' (Miassine). She seemed to believe – or pretended to believe – that Nijinsky hadn't 'the slightest desire to be the choreographer' and was 'ready to dance turn by turn with Fokine'. Unless something could be done to bring Diaghilev and Nijinsky together, Lady Ripon could only 'envisage the coming season with growing anxiety and a desire to go somewhere far away, where there will be no theatre, for when one begins to sacrifice Art to personal matters, it takes away every wish to have anything more to do with it'.[74]

Nijinsky's illness lasted two months, and he was advised that when he was well enough to work again, he should dance but abandon administrative work. During his convalescence he went for long walks with Romola in Richmond Park. As the time approached for the birth of the baby, the Nijinskys travelled to the Semmering in Austria for the privacy which Nijinsky thought essential, and then to Vienna.[75]

The repertory of the Diaghilev company for its seasons in Paris and London – their first without Nijinsky – was approaching completion. In addition to the Russian operas with Chaliapine which would be given in London, Stravinsky's opera 'Le Rossignol' – based on a Hans Anderson fairy-story – was to be produced with *chinoiserie* designs by Benois. The choreography for this work had been given to Boris Romanov, to spare Fokine, and also because the latter was not keen to compose any more choreography to Stravinsky's music.[76] Rimsky-Korsakov's opera 'Une Nuit de mai' had also been prepared. Fokine had arranged four works: the Strauss 'La Légende de Joseph', with flamboyant Veronese décor by J-M. Sert and costumes by Bakst, in which Miassine was to have his first major role; 'Les Papillons' to piano pieces of Schumann orchestrated by Tcherepnine, with a décor by Doboujinsky and costumes by Bakst; 'Midas' with music by Maximilian Steinberg, also designed by Doboujinsky; and 'Coq d'or'. Since Tcherepnine had not completed his score for 'The Red Masks', which it had been intended that Gorsky should arrange, another ballet had been needed for the 1914 seasons. Fokine had wanted to produce Rimsky's 'Coq d'or' as a ballet suite for Pavlova two years before, but the ballerina had not thought it suitable. Fokine writes that he suggested to Diaghilev that 'Coq d'or' should replace Tcherepnine's ballet, and Diaghilev decided to produce the work as an opera-ballet.[77] At Benois' suggestion Diaghilev commissioned the décor and costumes from the Moscow painter Natalie Gontcharova. Benois' part in 'Coq d'or', however, was considerable. He had always longed to produce it since he had heard the work in 1909;

moreover, since singers could so rarely act convincingly, he had the idea of removing them from the stage and having dancers mime the action. His idea was adopted by Diaghilev, and by Fokine (who was to claim it as his own). However, there would not be room for the soloists and chorus of the Bolshoi opera in the orchestra pit, so Benois decided to range them, identically costumed, in tiers at each side of the stage.[78]

The Ballet arrived in Monte Carlo in April, and on the 16th gave the first performance of 'Papillons', with Karsavina and Schollar as the two girls and Fokine as Pierrot. Fokine lost no time in reviving his neglected 'Daphnis et Chloë', which he now danced himself with Karsavina. 'La Tragédie de Salomé' was also revived – unsuccessfully. Diaghilev rejoined the company from Russia before the end of the Monte Carlo season.[79]

Nijinsky was invited to dance, at a fee of three thousand dollars, for the King and Queen of Spain at the wedding reception of Kermit Roosevelt in the American Embassy in Madrid. He travelled there with Romola's step-father and was given a warm welcome. Romola received a letter from him every day, 'of which I was proud, as I knew Vaslav never wrote to anybody, except his mother. He addressed me as "Femmka" or "Roma".'[80] On the way back to Vienna, Vaslav stopped off in Paris to attend the première of the Russian Ballet's season at the Opéra. This was on Thursday, 14 May, and included the first performance of 'La Légende de Joseph'. The newspapers were quick to spot him as 'many lorgnettes turned simultaneously' towards his seat. Though he no longer danced with the Russian Ballet, 'he seemed to me to be perfectly at ease', commented one observer. 'The society of the foyer can be equally attractive.'[81] According to Romola Vaslav went in the interval to Misia Sert's box, where her guests, including Cocteau, gave him a cool reception.[82] Before leaving Paris, Nijinsky had a lesson from Cecchetti. Miassine was sent by Diaghilev to take a class with him and to watch him at work. The *maestro*, using the gold-topped cane which Vaslav had given him years before, corrected Nijinsky's arm positions: 'Not curled up there – down there.' Miassine noticed that Vaslav accepted these corrections without ever answering back.[83]

Richard Strauss conducted the première of his ballet, which was given between 'Les Papillons', which the critics found disappointing (and again they thought the orchestration of Schumann a travesty), and a new version of 'Schéhérazade' with the third movement restored, danced by Karsavina, Fokine, Max Frohman and Cecchetti. 'La Légende' did not have the success which was expected of it: the various collaborators had failed to agree on a number of points and Fokine's choreography was uninspired. Miassine was overcome with nerves, but struggled through the performance.[84] What he lacked in dancing technique he made up for in stage presence and beauty. Hofmannsthal thought Kuznetsova was a failure as Potiphar's wife.[85] The first performance of 'Coq d'or' had been intended for 21 May, but the arrival of the costumes from Russia was delayed and the première took place four days later on a Sunday.* Karsavina danced the Queen of Shemakhan (sung by Dobrovolska), Jejerska was Amelfa (Petrenko), Bulgakov was King Dodon (Petrov), Cecchetti the Astrologer (Altchevsky), Kovalski General Polkan (Belianine). Nicolaeva sang the Cockerel, and Max Frohman and Grigoriev mimed the two princes Afrone and Guidone. 'Coq d'or', with its blazing red and yellow décor, was the real hit of the Paris season, though critical opinion was divided as to the success of the new way of presenting opera. Pierre Lalo thought the dances of Dodon and the Queen were not sufficient justification for imposing on the singers an immobility which detracted from their performances.[86] 'Le Rossignol' was given on 26 May, and the last première, that of 'Midas', which was rather an absurd work, took place on 2 June, Vladimirov dancing Amoun in 'Cléopâtre' in the same programme.

In reviewing 'La Légende', one critic, Alfred Bruncan, wrote: 'With his good taste M. Michel Fokine brings back to the Russian Ballet all the graceful attitudes and harmonious gestures which M. Nijinsky, with his grotesque ideas, sought to abolish.'[87] But this Paris season had proved a disappointment, and Jacques Rivière, staunchly loyal, put the blame firmly on Nijinsky's departure which 'has left a great void. One must say it boldly: the Russian Ballet was Nijinsky. He alone gave life to the whole company.'[88]

*Fokine gives the advertised date as that of the première, forgetting the postponement (p. 233). Grigoriev gives the date as the 25th (p. 271).

When the Paris engagement ended early in June, the company left immediately for London, where the German–Russian opera season had already opened at Drury Lane on 20 May. Performances had been given of 'Der Rosenkavalier' and 'Die Zauberflöte', and of both 'Boris Godounov' and 'Ivan le Terrible' with Chaliapine, as in the previous year. Chaliapine also sang in 'Prince Igor', the first complete performance of which opera in England took place on 8 June. The Ballet made its first appearance of the season with the opera company that night, and Tchernicheva, Fokina and Bolm led the Polovtsian Dances, with Leon Steinberg conducting. The first full ballet programme was given the next day, and comprised 'Thamar' with Karsavina and Bolm, 'Daphnis et Chloë' with Karsavina and Fokine, and 'Schéhérazade' with Fokina and Fokine, Bulgakov, Feodorov and Cecchetti. This season was to be the only one during which Fokine ever danced in London.

The Times, on the morning of the première of 'Daphnis', published a letter from Ravel in Paris claiming that the version to be performed at Drury Lane without the chorus was 'a makeshift arrangement which I had agreed to write at M. Diaghilev's special request in order to facilitate production in certain minor centres'. Diaghilev was putting this version on in London 'in spite of his positive word', and Ravel considered this action 'disrespectful towards the London public as well as towards the composer'.[89] Ravel was always extremely precise in his demands, but music aside, he may, out of friendship for Nijinsky, have been trying to make things as difficult for Diaghilev as possible. Diaghilev replied the next day that the 1912 production in Paris with singing was an 'experiment' and 'it was clearly proved that the participation of the chorus was not only useless but actually detrimental'. He had then asked Ravel to produce the revised version which had been given in April at Monte Carlo with 'unanimous approval': and he felt that he had made 'every effort to present it in the most perfect manner to the London public, to whom I owe a very great debt of admiration and gratitude'.[90]*

Karsavina danced the role of Chloë at this performance: Fokina

---

*Grigoriev states that the Moscow chorus *did* take part in 'Daphnis', 'which made the last scene especially impressive' (p. 110). This is clearly not true.

was to share the part with her, as she did that of Zobeïda in 'Schéhé-razade'. Fokine was Daphnis and Bolm Darkon. The London public was enthusiastic. 'Papillons', given with 'Petrushka' on the 11th, evoked memories of 'Carnaval', the firm favourite of previous seasons, but for Cyril Beaumont 'it remained nothing more than a dainty trifle. It had a definite charm of mood and was invested with poetry and lyricism; but it was too slight, too fragile, too intimate for a big theatre, and consequently failed to make a deep impression.' Karsavina, however, Beaumont found memorable. He had made her acquaintance – and that of Bolm – the year before, and now decided to write a book about her. He visited her at the Savoy where she had already, with typical thoroughness, prepared a chronology of her career for him; and the interview went well. But the war was to intervene, and the book which Beaumont eventually published was Svetlov's essay on the ballerina.[91]

On 15 June, in 'Coq d'or', Karsavina danced the Queen of Shemakhan, with Bolm as King Dodon. Not surprisingly, London found the opera-ballet sensational. Charles Ricketts wrote in his Journal that the novel production delighted him 'beyond all reason' and went on: 'It is a most picturesque interpretation of the principle which obtained at the birth of Greek tragedy, and which still obtains in the Japanese No Dances. The interpretation was magnificent. Karsavina looked like a bewitching Hindu idol, her dancing and miming were incomparable.'[92] Osbert Sitwell felt that this was

a production such as none had dreamed of in the world of opera ... Besides giving us some of the most dramatic and haunting music of the past century, *Le Coq d'or* constituted a great satire. In its stilted, dream-like rhythms, displayed against a background of huge flowers and brightly-hued buildings, was to be felt a mockery of the great, a kind of joy in the doom of lordship. Fortunately for its success, the fashionable audience could revel in the beauty and strangeness of it without concentrating too much on its meaning or implications.[93]

Three days later, after the shared première of 'Le Rossignol' and 'Midas', neither of which aroused much interest, Sitwell noted with a sense of incongruity Stravinsky, 'with an air both worldly and abstracted, and a little angry', bowing to that same audience of 'clustered, nodding tiaras and the white kid gloves, that applauded him sufficiently to be polite'.[94]

In Vienna Vaslav and Romola were thinking of names for their baby, whose birth was overdue. Nijinsky was convinced they would have a son, and wanted to call him Vladislav, which Romola agreed to. Prince Montenuovo, the Minister of the Court, invited them to the première of Strauss's 'Elektra' at the Hofoper on 18 June, saying 'If this modern music won't hasten the baby's arrival, then nothing will!' They went, and the next day the baby was born. Romola's sister Tessa told her that 'as the nurse announced to him, "It is only a girl, but a nice one", for one second [Vaslav] lost his self-control, and threw his gloves on the floor.' But he then consoled Romola for the disappointment, and immediately became devoted to the daughter who was so like him. She was called Kyra.[95]

At the dress rehearsal of 'La Légende de Joseph', Charles Ricketts recorded, 'all little London was present and ... Lady Diana Manners clambered over the balcony from one box to another before an enraptured house.'[96] London had been well primed for this new work as well as for the début of Miassine, and at its première on the 23rd the ballet was better received than in Paris. Miassine's dancing was a disappointment to an audience 'who had been led to expect a successor to Nijinsky', but as an actor – in what was largely a mimed role – he made some impression.[97] Miassine later recalled: 'I was now feeling much happier in Joseph, and was encouraged by the warm reception I was given on the first night.'[98] Karsavina thought that Miassine's performance was 'quite remarkable. His very lack of virtuosity in those days lent pathos to the image he created, an image of youth and innocence.'[99] Karsavina now danced the role of Potiphar's wife for the first time, having 'accepted the part without my usual doubts as to whether I was fit for it'. Strauss, who was in London to conduct his ballet, and whose fiftieth birthday had been celebrated on the 21st by a music club reception which Stravinsky and Karsavina attended, advised the ballerina on her rôle at rehearsals and was sufficiently delighted with her performance to try to get her to dance whenever the ballet was given in Vienna in later years.[100]

Lady Ripon, wrote Romola, 'proved to be the most loyal friend Nijinsky ever had'. She had used her influence as prime mover of the Production Committee of the Russian Ballet Performances in London to oblige Diaghilev to engage Nijinsky to dance with the company, failing which the season would be cancelled. This done, she asked Vaslav to come to London at once, which he was delighted to do, and he set off towards the end of June. It was intended that he should dance three times in 'Le Spectre' and other works. But he found on arrival that only Lady Ripon, Gunsbourg and Trubecki took his part, while most of the company gave him a cool reception. After one rehearsal he could not bear this and wrote his thanks and apologies to Lady Ripon, leaving immediately for Vienna 'as he was afraid that if he saw the Marchioness again he would have to give in to her entreaties'.*[101]

The event which was to precipitate the war – the assassination at Sarajevo of the Archduke Franz Ferdinand on 28 June – had occurred as Vaslav was *en route* for London, and after his return to Vienna at the beginning of July he was pressed with letters and telegrams from Lady Ripon begging him to move to London with his family. The Nijinskys believed that she was still working to reconcile Vaslav and Diaghilev: they were to learn later that her fear of war was the true reason for her communications. But on the advice of Romola's doctor Nijinsky decided to stay in Vienna until the end of July; and then go via Budapest to Russia.[102]

The last night of the London season was 25 July, the ballets being 'Papillons', 'La Légende de Joseph' and 'Petrushka'. The ovations were loud and long, and the dancers brought Sir Joseph Beecham before the curtain and gave him a gilt laurel wreath.[103] After the safety curtain had been lowered, the applause continued, and Diaghilev enticed Karsavina back from her dressing-room, where she had begun to change, to take more calls – or rather to come round the curtain into the auditorium. 'I stood there for a brief moment, oddly confused; feeling as if I had violated the ethics of

---

*According to Grigoriev in a letter to Nouvel (quoted in Haskell's *Diaghileff*, pp. 259, 260) Lady Ripon fetched over Nijinsky merely on the chance of a reconciliation: Fokine's contract would have prevented Nijinsky appearing with the company. It seems likely that the real reason for Nijinsky's swift departure was that he realized this.

the theatre. The excited audience rushed forward: I turned and fled.'[104] 'Overwhelming demonstration of farewell to Karsavina,'[105] wrote Ricketts in his Journal that night: and to Gordon Bottomley he summed up, 'The new ballets have been admirable and have made up for the loss of Nijinsky. . .'[106]

On the first night of 'Joseph' Count Harry Kessler, co-librettist of the ballet, had intimated that the projected German tour might not take place, but Diaghilev had dismissed the veiled warning.[107] It is surprising that so many people failed to hear the threat of war in 1914 – and that even when it did break out, they imagined it would be over in a few months. Karsavina had felt uneasy as the season drew to its close, and experienced an 'acute longing to be home'.[108] But Diaghilev asked her to stay on another day, as he had something to discuss with her. He had not paid her anything for two years. This fact he had carefully mentioned to Joseph Beecham, with the result that the latter had turned up one night in Karsavina's dressing-room and given her £2,000 in notes. Having, no doubt, craftily calculated the result of his conversation with Beecham, Diaghilev wanted to borrow £400. This meant that Karsavina had to postpone her departure by one day in order to go to the bank for him.[109] The company dispersed for their holidays, and were due to gather in Berlin for the German tour on 1 October. When war was declared on 4 August Grigoriev had just arrived in Petersburg, the Fokines were in Paris, and Miassine was in Milan on the way to join Diaghilev and the Cecchettis in Viareggio. Karsavina's delay in London resulted in her being turned back by the Germans at the Russian border. She travelled back via Holland to England; and then finally, after a few weeks, she managed to reach Petersburg 'by means of varied locomotion'.[110] Her description of this journey was euphemistic. Her trials reached the newspapers, and on 27 August Charles Ricketts was to note in his Journal: 'Read in the paper of poor little Karsavina, the exquisite, the incomparable little mime, having to get through Germany with other Russian refugees in goods trucks and being herded in slaughter-houses.'[111]

The Nijinskys were preparing to leave Budapest, after spending a week with Emilia Markus, when they found the Russian frontier

416

closed. The city was filled with marching troops, and Vaslav sighed, 'All these young men marching to their deaths and for what?' Romola, who could only think of their own predicament, wondered at his concern for others. They had missed the diplomatic train, and now their hopes lay in being smuggled into Italy by an uncle of Romola's. Before this could be arranged they were arrested and told that all three of them (Vaslav, Romola and Kyra) were enemy subjects and would be detained for the duration as prisoners-of-war. They were confined to Emilia Markus's house with orders to report to the police weekly.[112]

Diaghilev had signed a contract with Otto Kahn, the Chairman of the Board of Directors of the Metropolitan Opera House, New York, for an American season: and two of Kahn's conditions were that Diaghilev should accompany the troupe, and that Karsavina, Nijinsky and the other specified dancers should lead it. Necessity made a reconciliation seem possible. But Diaghilev did not understand at first that the Nijinskys were prisoners-of-war. Vaslav wrote that he had 'no right to leave Budapest because of the war'.[113]

Diaghilev in Florence to Stravinsky in Switzerland, 25.11.14
Nijinsky behaves so stupidly. He didn't even answer my detailed and, in my opinion, fair letter, and to my modest telegram requesting, 'reply paid', whether he had received it, he answered only: 'Letter received. Cannot come.' I am sure that his wife is busy making him into the first ballet master of the Budapest Opera . . . I will write to him a second, less modest and less reasonable letter and this miserable person will understand that now is not the moment for joking.[114]

Grigoriev was wrong in thinking that Diaghilev had lost faith in Nijinsky's choreography: for in this same letter to Stravinsky Diaghilev refers to another composition on which the composer was working. 'The invention of movement in "Noces" is definitely for Nijinsky, but I will not discuss the thing with him for several months yet.'[115]

After the initial shock, and the failure of various schemes to get out of the country with the aid of Romola's highly-placed relations, the family settled down to what they were convinced would be only a brief restriction of liberty. Hostilities were sure to cease by the end of the year. Romola was told by an official that her wisest move would be to divorce Nijinsky since he was an alien. Emilia Markus, according to Romola, held a similar view: the presence of a Russian in her family and her house was an embarrassment both to her and her husband. She was fond of her son-in-law – he was a great artist and a genius: but he was not working, and had no immediate prospects of work; so Emilia was supporting both her family and Romola's. Pardany tactlessly recounted victories over the Russians, which disturbed Vaslav and irritated Romola. Emilia's concern for Kyra was taken as interference by her daughter, and the Nijinskys gradually withdrew into their own part of the house to escape.

'We were completely isolated from the outside world,' wrote Romola. 'Vaslav and myself had to suffice for each other. I knew that he was happy in his marriage, and that he never blamed me for anything that had happened to him since.' During the winter they read Tolstoy, Chekhov and Pushkin, and Nijinsky explained these works to his wife. As they were reading Dostoevsky's *The House of the Dead* Romola 'could not help feeling ... that I had brought a similar fate on Nijinsky... When I spoke about it, he bravely replied, "Others are dying, suffering far more. I have my art in my soul; nothing and nobody can take it away. Happiness is in us; we take it with us wherever we go."' As spring arrived they were able to go for longer walks, and Nijinsky found solace in nature. He had had little opportunity of exercising his art since internment began: he had been denied facilities to practise and in the summer had to content himself with the hard terrace of Emilia's house. But now Romola's cousin Lily de Markus, a pianist, began to play every day for him. He started to compose a new ballet on a medieval theme – which he had wanted to do for some time – and when Lily played him Strauss's tone-poem 'Till Eulenspiegels Lustige Streiche' (Merry Pranks) he began to get ideas. Vaslav read all he could find about the thirteenth-century Flemish hero – a cross between Robin Hood and Robin Goodfellow – around whom an extensive mythology had grown. In his conception, based largely on the accepted 'programme' of the work, a number of these 'pranks' in which Till poked fun at the rich and exhorted the poor to rebel were to form the choreographic episodes. He planned group movement – 'making twenty people do the same movement as if they were one' – which was a development of his work on 'Le Sacre'. As a relief from his work on this ballet he would dance for Romola and her cousin the gypsy dances of Russia. He would suddenly be transformed into a wild, fierce, savage girl, trembling all over from the tips of his fingers to his toes, shaking his shoulders as if they were independent of the rest of his body. And then he would imitate the different ballerinas of the Mariinsky. 'We often begged him to show us how Kchessinskaya danced. But we loved it most when he showed us how the peasant women flirt whilst dancing. He had an inimitable way of throwing inviting glances, and undulating in such a lascivious manner as to stir up the senses of the spectator almost to frenzy.'

At the same time Nijinsky had begun to devise a system of notation for the recording of dances which was to occupy him for a number of years. He taught it to Romola as it progressed.*

Life with her mother became more and more unbearable and Romola eventually travelled to Vienna to beseech her uncle in the War Council to send Vaslav and herself to a concentration camp. This he could not do, but he advised his niece to be patient, telling her of a plan to exchange Vaslav, through International Red Cross, for five Austrian officers in Russian hands. She returned to Budapest with renewed hope.

Kyra was now walking, jumping, and even dancing to the music of a street organ, and Vaslav was sure she would be a dancer. His devotion to her was his greatest solace. News came from Lady Ripon, and from one of Romola's aunts, that they were working to obtain Vaslav's freedom. Discussing his life with Diaghilev, Vaslav said, 'I will never regret anything I have done, for I believe that all experience in life, if made with the aim to find the truth, is uplifting. No, I do not regret my relations with Sergei Pavlovitch, even if ethics condemn it.' He had begun to doubt his love for Diaghilev, he told her, on the *Avon*, and considered becoming a preaching monk in Siberia. He recounted how he had first seen her in Budapest as she watched his rehearsals so intently, and he had thought

*But she did not remember it.

'A spoilt girl of society, and she possesses a soul.' Nijinsky ended by saying that if Romola ever met anyone she loved more, she was to tell him: her happiness mattered most to him.

Emilia Markus's machinations to rid herself of Romola and Vaslav culminated in a police interrogation: the officials had been informed that Nijinsky was working on a military plan which he was recording in a mathematical code. After days of investigation the police accepted that the 'plan' was Nijinsky's system of notation, and they congratulated him on it. The chief of police was most sympathetic to their predicament. Then, in the autumn of 1915, Vaslav was visited by a Hungarian impresario with the message that Diaghilev was taking the Ballet to North America, and that Nijinsky was needed there. Before long, word came that the police were transferring the three prisoners to Carlsbad in Bohemia: and the police chief suggested that they should break their journey in Vienna for Romola to see her doctor. 'We understood he showed us the way to liberty.'[116]

Meanwhile, in Viareggio, Diaghilev was trying to reassemble his company and make plans for future seasons. Trubecki was dispatched to Poland to find dancers. Diaghilev had in mind new ballets to music of Stravinsky and eighteenth-century composers, with décors by Gontcharova and Larionov. In August 1915 Diaghilev and Miassine went to Florence, where they looked at paintings together.

Sometimes [wrote Miassine], Diaghilev would encourage me to try and reproduce the position and movements of the figures in certain paintings, particularly those of Tintoretto, Titian and Michelangelo.* One afternoon in the Uffizi, while I was looking up at Fra Filippo Lippi's Madonna and Child, Diaghilev said to me: 'Do you think you could compose a ballet?' 'No,' I answered without thinking, 'I'm sure I never could.' Then, as we passed on into another room, I was suddenly aware of the luminous colours of Simone Martini's Annunciation. As I looked at the delicate postures of Gabriel and the Virgin Mary, I felt as if everything I had seen in Florence had finally culminated in this painting. It seemed to

---

*The paintings of Michelangelo would presumably have been seen in Rome, where Diaghilev and Miassine went after Florence. It is in Michelangelo's sculpture that Florence is rich.

be offering me the key to an unknown world, beckoning me along a path which I knew I must follow to the end. 'Yes', I said to Diaghilev, 'I think I can create a ballet. Not only one, but a hundred, I promise you.'[117]

Diaghilev, Massine and the gardener's boy. Caricature by Michel Larionov.

Diaghilev was soon to give him the opportunity.

From Florence Diaghilev took Miassine to Rome, then, together with Sert and Misia, they drove to Switzerland and settled in the

Villa Bellerive at Ouchy near Lausanne. This was to be Diaghilev's headquarters. Grigoriev was summoned from Russia, and after a journey through Finland, Sweden, Norway, England and France, arrived at the Villa to find Diaghilev surrounded by his new 'committee' – Stravinsky, Bakst, Larionov, Gontcharova, Miassine and the Swiss conductor Ernest Ansermet. Grigoriev was immediately despatched back to Russia by the same circuitous route to gather a company.[118] Diaghilev was convinced that under careful guidance Miassine could become a great choreographer. Larionov was appointed to help him with 'Liturgie', a version of the Mass (in Diaghilev's original conception) with no music, but with stamping as in 'Le Sacre'. Several of the episodes were rehearsed, and Gontcharova and Larionov had begun the designs, but Diaghilev soon abandoned the work.[119] He next suggested to Miassine a ballet to music from Rimsky-Korsakov's 'Snow Maiden', and again with Larionov – who was to design the ballet – advising him, Miassine began to compose. The ballet would be called 'Le Soleil de nuit'.

Rehearsals progressed as the dancers arrived in Lausanne: Muningsova and Kremnev, who had been dancing in music-halls in London; a brilliant young Pole, Stanislas Idzidovsky, whom they had met in London and whose audition Kremnev had arranged with Grigoriev as he passed through; Woizikovsky and Slavinsky from Warsaw – Trubecki had got them out of Poland for a 'tuberculosis cure' in Switzerland; Tchernicheva, Bolm, Gavrilov, Zverev; and three pairs of sisters – Vera and Lida Nemchinova, Maria and Gala Chabelska, Luba and Nura Soumarokova.[120] Grigoriev, who made several heroic journeys *via* England and Finland, had been sending his recruits from Russia in batches. He had failed to persuade Fokine or Karsavina to leave Russia in wartime. Since Diaghilev was hoping to have Nijinsky released by the time the American engagement began Fokine's absence did not worry him overmuch; but the company could not do without a leading ballerina. Olga Spessivtseva would not come from Petersburg, and instead Grigoriev engaged Xenia Makletsova from Moscow.[121]

Soon after Muningsova arrived Diaghilev told her that she was to be given solo roles, including Papillon in 'Carnaval', and that he was renaming her Lydia Sokolova, 'and I hope you will live up to the name of Sokolova, as it is that of a great dancer in Russia. Please forget from now on that you have ever been anything but Russian.'[122] By the time Grigoriev got back to Lausanne again most of the company had been assembled. Lydia Lopokhova, who had been in America since she left the company, would be joining them in New York, and she and Makletsova would take over Karsavina's roles. To fill the roles of Zobeïda, Cleopatra and Thamar, Diaghilev looked again for a successor to the exotic Ida Rubinstein: there had been Roshanara, Astafieva, Karsavina, and there had almost been Mata Hari. Although he thought it a makeshift Diaghilev agreed to Bakst's suggestion of engaging Flore Revalles, a tall and imposing French opera singer[123] whom the painter had seen as Tosca in Geneva.[124] She was to become popular in America. Diaghilev now had a company, but, with the exception of Bolm, he had been unable to provide for New York any of the stars Otto Kahn demanded. His only hope was Nijinsky, who he had by now realized was a prisoner of war.

Sokolova believed that the six months which the company spent in Switzerland were the happiest in their history, though the luxurious conditions of pre-war days had ended for good. Diaghilev was happy too, she felt, despite having to make frequent visits to Paris to get subsidies. 'We always knew when Diaghilev had been successful after one of his Paris trips, because Massine would be wearing another sapphire ring on his little finger. Massine, like Nijinsky, collected several of these, but whereas Nijinsky's had been set in gold, Massine's were set in platinum.'[125] Diaghilev's conviction that his new discovery had the makings of an excellent choreographer was his greatest encouragement, and to try out 'Le Soleil de nuit' and his new company he arranged two Red Cross charity matinées for December. On the 20th in Geneva Miassine's ballet had its first performance with Zverev as Bobyl and Miassine as the Midnight Sun. Despite the restrictions of Larionov's colourful but cumbersome costumes, the dancers performed with zest and the ballet was a success. Idzikovsky, Makletsova and Sokolova danced 'Carnaval' and Makletsova and Bolm 'L'Oiseau bleu'. With 'Schéhérazade' in place of 'Carnaval' – and Revalles making her début – the programme was given again at the Paris Opéra on the 29th, conducted by Ansermet. Diaghilev was delighted with the reception of his protégé's first ballet, and remarked to Svetlov: 'You see: given the talent, one can make a choreographer in no time!'[126]

On New Year's Day, 1916, the company sailed from Bordeaux for New York. Vaslav and Romola arrived in Vienna early in January, and they had no idea of how long they would remain prisoners. However, they were treated with exemplary courtesy and accommodated at the Hôtel Bristol, their departure for Carlsbad being postponed indefinitely. The Austrian conditions for Nijinsky's exchange had been prohibitive. Lady Ripon and Comtesse Greffuhle now enlisted the support of Queen Alexandra and the Dowager Empress Marie Feodorovna; the Emperor Franz-Josef of Austria interceded; and through the King of Spain the Pope himself[127] asked for Nijinsky's release – 'The best thing he has done in the war,' wrote the English writer and Churchill's secretary, Edward Marsh.[128] Diaghilev was given to understand that he could expect Nijinsky to be freed, though not before the spring.[129] While they awaited news, Vaslav and Romola were able to live an almost normal life. Nijinsky was given a pass to the Opera, and facilities to practise on the stage of the Theatre an der Wien. Here he worked on his choreographic poem 'Mephisto Valse', classical dances – again in medieval spirit – to music of Liszt. In all there were to be forty-five dancers, and all the roles Nijinsky danced himself with perfect characterization. At the same time, working with Romola's brother-in-law Erik Schmedes, he conceived the idea of composing dances for Wagner's operas, which he hoped to realize in Bayreuth after the war. He met Kokoschka, who made a drawing of him; and he visited Arnold Schönberg – whose 'Pierrot Lunaire' he knew – at his villa in Heitzing and discussed music and dancing with him. Nijinsky also met Richard Strauss in Vienna, who was so delighted that Vaslav had choreographed 'Till Eulenspiegel' that he even offered to make alterations to his score, but Nijinsky had followed the programme minutely. After finishing 'Mephisto Valse', he began work on a Japanese ballet, but this was never completed.[130]

The Diaghilev Ballet had arrived in New York on 12 January

1916, and immediately began a week of intensive rehearsals. The first two weeks' performances in the city were to be at the small Century Theatre on Central Park West. Makletsova was to take the ballerina roles in 'L'Oiseau de feu' and 'La Princesse enchantée'. Lopokhova now joined the company, returning to ballet after a phase of acting, and Massine, whose name Diaghilev had simplified, created a new dance for her in his ballet. Revalles was Zobeïda, and Tchernicheva the Tsarevna in 'L'Oiseau de feu'. Nijinsky's roles were re-assigned: Bolm was to dance the Negro in 'Schéhérazade' (which he had done before), and the Prince in 'La Princesse enchantée' (which cannot have suited him); Massine would perform the Faun, Petrushka, and – later, when he had learnt the roles – Amoun and the Negro. At the last moment it seemed that disaster might strike. Bolm was ill for several days, could barely dance at all in the private performance on the Sunday evening, and had still not recovered his form by the first night.[131]

The opening programme on Monday the 17th was 'L'Oiseau de feu', 'Schéhérazade', 'La Princesse enchantée' and 'Soleil de nuit'. Massine thought the audience's response disappointing, and Diaghilev doubted whether the New Yorkers were going to appreciate his ballet. 'He told me,' wrote Massine, 'that Americans still seemed to think of ballet as light entertainment, to be enjoyed after a hard day at the office!'[132] The reviews next morning were aware of this problem, but highly enthusiastic. The *Journal of Commerce* pointed out that New York's familiarity with Pavlova and her dancers was no preparation for Diaghilev's repertory. 'The present ballet makes its appeal in a different way, to different senses. It is more of a command than an appeal. Those accustomed to the old ballet need education in the new to appreciate it. Abroad, it is said, they have learned to delight in it. Whether American audiences are sufficiently advanced to take to it at once is a question.'[133] A public accustomed to classical dancing, as performed by Pavlova and Mordkine, had to make a great adjustment in order to respond to the totally new experience of the Fokine ballets. In London Diaghilev had had the opposite problem: having brought up his audiences on a diet of Fokine, he found them unable to appreciate his 'Giselle' and 'Lac des Cygnes'. The new music of Stravinsky and the colours of Bakst astonished the Americans, who responded with admiration and respect. But much as Makletsova, Bolm and Massine were admired it was felt that a distinction was lacking through the absence of Karsavina and Nijinsky – and particularly Nijinsky. 'For thousands knew of the genius of Nijinsky,' wrote one columnist, 'where hundreds knew of the genius of the Russian *ensemble*. In a country where "personality" counts most in politics, business and art, the loss of the two chief "names" of a sudden was the most serious mischance that had happened to the Ballet in all its wanderings.' The same writer noted the absence of Nijinsky's wonderful leap in Bolm's Golden Slave, but added that this lack 'would never be noticed this time if it had never been seen before . . .' In all the ballets the company were magnificent in their groupings. This, the American public had been told, was part of Diaghilev's conception of the ballet. 'Try as we may,' said this same critic, 'we can never come away from the Russian Ballet to think of it merely as an achievement of art. It is also a gospel, a philosophy.'[134]

Against the eulogies of the American press might be set the opinion of Carl van Vechten, the music critic who – as Paris representative of the *New York Times* – had seen the Ballet often in Europe and had been present at the first night of 'Le Sacre'. The fact that none of the 'stars' were dancing, he discovered, made a lot of difference. 'Often had we urged that the individual played but a small part in this new and gorgeous entertainment, but now we were forced to admit that the ultimate glamour was lacking in the *ensemble*, which was obviously no longer the glad, gay entity it once had been.' Massine, he felt, was neither a great dancer nor a great mime: he was no Nijinsky. Bolm had 'vitality and abundant energy' but not the skill in characterization attributed to him – and the same deficiency limited the otherwise polished dancing of Gavrilov. Makletsova was accomplished in technical tricks, but she lacked poetry or interpretative power. 'In such a work as "The Firebird" she really offended the eye. Far from interpreting the ballet, she gave you an idea of how it should not be done.' Lopokhova had charm and a 'roguish demeanour', but in her purely 'ballerina' roles, because of deficient technique, 'she floundered hopelessly out of her element.' Tchernicheva made the most of the opportunities – mainly mimic – which she was given. Revalles did less than that: 'Her Cléopâtre suggested to me a Parisian *cocotte* much more than an Egyptian queen.' But in spite of these objections, van Vechten felt, Diaghilev had given New York 'finer exhibitions of stage art than had previously been even the exception here'.[135] This was exactly Diaghilev's view of the situation, and it was also the tenor of almost every press notice.

Besides 'L'Oiseau de feu' (with Massine as the Prince and Cecchetti as Kastchei), 'Schéhérazade', 'La Princesse enchantée' and 'Soleil de nuit', four other ballets were given in the first week: 'Les Sylphides' with Lopokhova, Tchernicheva and Bolm, 'L'Après-midi d'un faune' with Massine, 'Carnaval' with Lopokhova and Bolm, and 'Prince Igor' with Bolm. 'Schéhérazade' was given again at the Saturday matinée together with 'L'Après-midi', and as a result of complaints received after the first performances police witnesses were in the audience. John Brown, the Metropolitan Business Manager, was obliged to order certain modifications before the ballets could be put on again.[136] A controversy over censorship sprang up in the papers. With 'L'Après-midi' the publicity about the Parisian scandal had prepared the ground for the rising of American gorges; but in 'Schéhérazade' the rub came nearer home. It was the idea of 'white' (albeit eastern) women taking negro lovers which was so abhorrent, and, wrote Carl van Vechten, there had even been 'talk of a "Jim Crow" performance in which the blacks were to be separated from the whites in the harem'.[137] While the police were taking *their* action, the Catholic Theatre Movement was busy circulating a private bulletin against the Russian Ballet.[138]*

The production during the second week of 'Le Pavillon d'Armide' with Makletsova, Bolm and Cecchetti, 'Petrushka' with Massine, Lopokhova, Bolm and Cecchetti, and 'Thamar' with Bolm and Revalles, completed the New York repertory and the engagement ended on the 29th. The company then set out on a tour. They spent ten days at Boston – the longest stay of the tour. Here Makletsova

---

*All the obstructions to smooth running during the American tours were attributed by Romola to the disapproval of Gatti-Casazza, the Metropolitan General Manager, and his 'Italian clique', of the engagement of the Ballet by Otto Kahn.

left them.[139] 'Cléopâtre' with Revalles and Bolm and 'Le Spectre' with Gavrilov had their first performances in Chicago, after the company had danced in Albany and Detroit.

The American newspapers printed occasional reports of Nijinsky's vicissitudes in expectation of his arrival in time for the Ballet's second New York season. On 1 February Vaslav and Romola were summoned to the American Embassy in Vienna and told that the Ambassador had been successful in obtaining permission for Nijinsky to go 'on parole' to the United States to join Diaghilev. But there were conditions: Nijinsky should not return to Russia, and Romola and Kyra should remain as hostages. Nijinsky refused the latter, and eventually the condition was dropped in favour of assurances from the Ambassador. The next evening they left for Berne. There was a week's delay on the Swiss frontier, during which they were searched, and then they arrived at the Hotel Bernerhof. A dinner was given in their honour at the Legation, and they received a diplomatic passport. Two days later, in Lausanne, Nijinsky learned of his part in Diaghilev's contract with the Metropolitan Opera House, and although uneasy about the state of his relationship with Diaghilev he expressed himself willing to dance in the country which had worked for his freedom. He also heard that a case had been won for him in London for the money which Diaghilev owed him.*

While Vaslav and Romola were at Lausanne they were visited by Stravinsky, who lived nearby at Morges. They got involved in heated arguments. Stravinsky had a grievance, too, against Diaghilev who had forgotten his promise to secure for him an official invitation to conduct his ballets at the Metropolitan Opera House.[140] Nijinsky would later write in his *Diary* a description of his last meeting with the composer (which Robert Craft, who knew Stravinsky as well as anyone, considered 'as shrewd as anything by Saint-Simon'[141]).

Stravinsky smells things out. He is not my friend, but at the bottom of his heart he loves me . . . Diaghilev loves Massine and not me, and that is awkward for Stravinsky. Stravinsky forces his wife to carry out all his

*According to Romola, the large sum of half a million gold francs. The money would be paid in America.

428

caprices ... His wife loves him. I feel that he does not love her as much, but he does love the children. He loves his children strangely and shows his love for them by making them paint ... He is like an emperor, and his children and wife are the servants and soldiers. Stravinsky reminds me of Tsar Paul, but he will not be strangled because he is cleverer than the Tsar was. Diaghilev wanted to strangle him many times, but Stravinsky is too sly. [Diaghilev] cannot exist without Stravinsky, nor Stravinsky without Diaghilev.

After my liberation from Hungary, I went to Morges to see Stravinsky and ask him, being certain that my wish would not be refused, if he and his wife would take my child while I was in America. He had many children and I felt that my Kyra would be safe with them. I asked Stravinsky to take my Kyra, but though his wife almost wept, Stravinsky said that he was very sorry, but that he could not assume responsibility for the child. I thanked him and did not say anything else. Looking at his wife sadly, I felt the same answer. Being a woman, she knew what it means to drag a child from trains to steamer, from place to place, and she was sorry for me. She did not agree with her husband, but because he spoke so quickly and decisively he made her understand that he did not wish to keep my daughter. I told him that I would pay all of Kyra's expenses, but he did not agree with this either.

Stravinsky saw me off at the station and I gave him my hand very coldly. I did not like him then, and wanted to show him, but he did not feel it because he kissed me. I had a nasty feeling.[142]

February drew to a close in Berne, and then news came in the form of a telegram from Astruc:

Astruc in Paris to Nijinsky in Berne, 1.3.16

Contact immediately Comte Daniel de Pradère, Councillor at the Spanish Embassy, who will facilitate your departure for America.[143]

The final arrangements were made, and on 24 March the Nijinskys arrived in Paris, where they had a day's grace before the boat sailed. Comtesse Greffuhle had done all that was needed, and Romola was able to prepare herself to face New York. With Vaslav she made

a tour of the leading dressmakers and millinery establishments. Nobody would have recognized us twenty-four hours later as we went to the Quai d'Orsay to catch the train. We were elegantly dressed, and followed by sixteen trunks, loaded with flowers, and accompanied by our maid and nurse and escort, Mr Russell [of the Metropolitan]. Many old friends and admirers of Vaslav turned out to say goodbye to us.[144]

At Bordeaux Nijinsky sent Astruc a visiting-card, 'avec tous mes plus vifs remerciments', which was probably accompanied by flowers,[145] then the party boarded the French liner *Espagne*. They took with them Bolm's fiancée whom they had promised to look after. During the voyage Nijinsky found in the ship's doctor, Louis Moret – a famous etcher – a companion who took great interest in his system of notation.[146]

From Boston the Russian Ballet tour had taken in sixteen towns, going as far west as Kansas City. They travelled in a special train of Pullman cars with their orchestra and technicians. On the 'one-night stands', a new and uncomfortable experience for the Russian dancers, they slept on the train: but in those cities where they performed for a few nights – such as Detroit, Chicago, Indianapolis, Cincinnati, Cleveland, Pittsburgh and Washington – they stayed in hotels.[147] The first night at Washington on 23 March was a smart affair in the presence of the President and Mrs Wilson.[148] The news here reached the company that Nijinsky was on his way and would join them for their season at the Metropolitan.[149]

Nijinsky did not, however, arrive in time for the first night at the Metropolitan on 3 April: his ship was due to dock the next day. The programme for the opening performance comprised 'Le Spectre', 'Les Sylphides', 'Petrushka' and 'Prince Igor'. Only 'Le Spectre' was new to New York, danced by Lopokhova and – in Nijinsky's absence – Gavrilov. The sour critic of *Musical American* felt that 'Nijinsky's skill as a teacher does not equal his dancing abilities, for his pupil disported himself very heavily and without perceptible distinction or grace.' The same writer also noted that the two weeks at the Century Theatre 'apparently rubbed a good deal of gilt from the ginger-bread. There were no thronging cohorts at the Metropolitan Monday night and only modified raptures ...'[150] This second New York season had already occasioned some complaints in the press, since it took place during a regular sub-scription opera season. The continual repetition of ballets seemed like cheating to a part of the public – and in fact the repertory was to change scarcely at all with the advent of Nijinsky. Giulio Gatti-Casazza, the General Manager of the Metropolitan, whose Italian operas with Caruso were the staple diet, was unsympathetic to the Ballet, and it now reached the papers that even before the contracts were signed 'a liberal figure on the wrong side of the ledger was expected'. The season was privately subsidized, and even increased prices of admission offered 'no prospect of security against loss'.[151]

The *Espagne* docked in New York on 4 April, and the ship was immediately invaded by newspaper and camera men. Nijinsky was swamped, his muscles were felt, he was asked questions about the war, about his partners, about art, about Rasputin. When he was finally free from reporters and immigration officials he was met by Metropolitan representatives, members of the Ballet, Diaghilev and Massine. Diaghilev greeted Romola with a bouquet and kissed Vaslav on both cheeks, whereupon Nijinsky put his daughter into Diaghilev's arms. They then walked off together.[152]

But now it was Massine who was staying with Diaghilev at the Ritz, while Vaslav and Romola were at the Claridge. There was no real resumption of amicable relations between Diaghilev and Nijinsky: indeed, the first matter to crop up was Diaghilev's debt which Nijinsky insisted on having settled before he would dance with the company. Within a few days a private contract had been drawn up by the Metropolitan by which Nijinsky would dance eleven performances, and each week Diaghilev would pay a part of the debt through the Opera House from receipts.[153] The Press announced the settlement of the dispute, and mentioned that Diaghilev had 'protested that $3,000 a week was enough for even a Nijinsky'.[154] Lydia Sokolova, writing home on 9 April, gave a picture of the disruptions and politics surrounding Nijinsky as they affected the company: 'Nijinsky is here and is making a lot of fuss – won't appear without tons of money, saying in the papers horrid things about the Ballet. You know just how they always turn around on those who make their names for them.'[155] Of course she was not in a position to know that Nijinsky had worked for years for nothing. Edward Ziegler, Otto Kahn's assistant, penned a verse which expressed everyone's frustration:

O Mr Nijinsky,
Where have you binsky?
And if you are here
Why don't you appear
And save the ballet from ruinsky?[156]

It had been settled that Nijinsky should make his American
début on Wednesday, 12 April. Diaghilev had arranged for him to
have as many rehearsals as possible, including one with the orchestra.[157] To his interviewers Vaslav had declared himself 'in the
pink of condition, and he looked it'.[158] But Sokolova thought that
'he had grown heavier and looked very sad. . . He never spoke a
word to anyone and picked his fingers more than ever.'[159] Grigoriev,
too, commented on his 'vagueness and unfriendliness'.[160] The
company, wrote Romola, treated her husband and herself with
great courtesy, but not many were really friendly. Bolm was 'one
of the few who kept aloof from petty intrigue' and who was always
loyal to Nijinsky.[161] During the first week at the Metropolitan,
however, Bolm sprained a tendon, and as a result the programmes
had to be changed. Sokolova's letter home continued: 'Yesterday
Bolm was unable to dance "Petrushka" and so Kremnev rehearsed
half an hour before performance and did the principal part* . . .
We have heard Diaghilev wants to give Bolm the slip now that
Nijinsky's here, and so any part of his that Nijinsky won't do,
Kremnev will get. . .'[162] But Bolm was a considerable attraction
too and was soon dancing again.

Sokolova felt that it must have been difficult – on top of everything else – for Nijinsky to return as *premier danseur* with the young
Massine being schooled as his successor as principal choreographer.[163] But Massine did not feel this, nor was he disappointed in
Nijinsky's dancing. He, too, saw in Nijinsky's reserve the evidence
of his past tribulations. 'But when I saw him dance, I was astounded
at the way his whole personality became transformed on stage. He
had an instinctive effortless control of his body; every gesture
expressed the most tender and complex emotions. . . After seeing
Nijinsky dance, I realized I had seen a genius.'[164]

*Actually the Moor. (*Musical Courier*, April 1916.)

The programme for the matinée on 12 April was announced as 'Schéhérazade', 'Le Spectre', 'Prince Igor' 'and 'Petrushka' – but a slight mishap to Flore Revalles resulted in the first and third ballets being reversed. Mlle Revalles, who attracted much publicity on account of her pet snake which she kept in a cage or twined round her fingers when it was not on stage with her in 'Cléopâtre', received before the performance a letter signed by a cousin of the Kaiser, which, when opened, shot a cloud of talcum powder into her eyes.[165] The rearrangement of ballets allowed her to regain her composure before going on as Zobeïda. Her performance was impressive: but, remarked one critic, had it not been for her accident she would have been 'in direst peril of not having so much as one word in any newspaper on the occasion of the début of Nijinsky'.[166]

Nijinsky danced with Lopokhova in 'Le Spectre' and in 'Petrushka'. 'The Diamond Horseshoe was present in full force,' wrote Romola, 'and the audience was as brilliant as in the great Paris galas.'[167]* Nijinsky's entrance was greeted with a standing ovation and a shower of rose petals (probably organized by the management). The critic of the *Musical Courier* had no doubt that Nijinsky was the greatest of all male dancers: 'Where Nijinsky excels all his fellow artists is in the absolute finish of line in his work. There is never a pause or an angle. Mr Nijinsky's dancing is an absolute and complete realization in movement of the melodic and rhythmical movement of the accompanying music.'[168] Another reviewer, Pitts Sanborn, music editor of the *Globe*, concluded that Nijinsky was 'not of this earth', and added that 'Le Spectre' would have been 'something for the tongue of angels, not of men, had Nijinsky had as partner Pavlova or Karsavina'.[169] In 'Le Spectre' Nijinsky had had little advance competition, but in 'Petrushka', the *Musical Courier* noted, 'he had to stand a very severe comparison because of the superb work of Mr Massine in the same role. Mr Nijinsky paid more attention to the puppet's soul and less to his mechanism than Mr Massine. Those who like this conception will prefer Nijinsky; those who prefer to have the fact that Petrushka is a puppet emphasized, Massine. Both are as fine as can be in their

---

*Though presumably not wearing their diamonds for the matinée.

respective characterizations.'[170] Massine was to write many years later: 'Although I had identified myself with Petrushka, I soon realized that the role came more naturally to Nijinsky.'[171] The music critics noticed that Nijinsky's return to this ballet was accompanied by changes in the action, the *tempi*, and the 'shading in the orchestral accompaniment'.[172]

At the evening performance 'Thamar' was given on the same bill as the New York première of 'Cléopâtre', Revalles and Bolm dancing both. Nijinsky's next roles two days later were in 'Carnaval' – in which Cecchetti (now sixty-six) replaced the sick Bolm as Pierrot – and in 'Les Sylphides', in which, according to the *Musical Courier*, 'his persistence in stroking his curls gave a touch of feminism to his performance . . . which was not relished by many of the audience.'[173] Lydia Sokolova danced Bronislava Nijinska's roles in 'Carnaval' and in 'Narcisse', which was given the following week. (The two performances of 'Narcisse' in New York were the only ones in America.) On the Saturday evening, 15 April, Nijinsky danced in 'La Princesse enchantée' and 'Schéhérazade'. Massine was to write of Nijinsky's 'incomparable' dancing in the former ballet: 'To convey the quivering motion of the bird's wings he fluttered his hands at such a dazzling speed that they seemed to have exactly the pulsating action of humming-birds. I learned later that he had done this by doubling the rate of his wrist movements.'[174] Reviewing Nijinsky in 'Schéhérazade' one critic revealed his racial feelings: 'The part of the negro who makes love to the princess is a repulsive one, but he tones down some of its unpleasantness. The impulse to jump on the stage and thrash him must be suppressed.'[175]

Lydia Sokolova thought that Nijinsky's dancing had deteriorated.[176] Grigoriev wrote that he improved gradually.[177] But Carl van Vechten, who was apprehensive before Nijinsky's first appearance, affirmed that 'it was evident that he was in possession of all his powers; nay, more, that he had added to the refinement and polish of his style. I had called Nijinsky's dancing perfection in years gone by, because it so far surpassed that of his nearest rival; now he had surpassed himself.' Writing of 'Le Spectre', which he thought best displayed the facets of Nijinsky's genius, he said:

His dancing is accomplished in that flowing line, without a break between poses and gestures, which is the despair of all novices and almost all other virtuosi. After a particularly difficult leap or toss of the legs or arms, it is a marvel to observe how, without an instant's pause to regain his poise, he rhythmically glides into the succeeding gesture. His dancing has the unbroken quality of music, the balance of great painting, the meaning of fine literature, and the emotion inherent in all these arts . . . It is not alone the final informing and magnetized imaginative quality that most other dancers lack; it is also just this muscular co-ordination. Observe Gavrilov in the piece under discussion, in which he gives a good imitation of Nijinsky's general style, and you will see that he is unable to maintain this rhythmic continuity.[178]

Nijinsky's performance in 'Schéhérazade' suggested to van Vechten 'exotic eroticism expressed in so high a key that its very existence seems incredible on our puritanic stage': but somehow previous objections were forgotten as

. . . This strange, curious, head-wagging, simian creature, scarce human, wriggled through the play, leaving a long streak of lust and terror in his wake. Never did Nijinsky as the Negro Slave touch the Sultana, but his subtle and sensuous fingers fluttered close to her flesh, clinging once or twice questioningly to a depending tassel. Pierced by the javelins of the Sultan's men, the Slave's death struggle might have been revolting and gruesome. Instead Nijinsky carried the eye rapidly upward with his tapering feet as they balanced for the briefest part of a second straight high in the air, only to fall inert with so brilliantly swift a movement that the aesthetic effect grappled successfully with the feeling of disgust which might have been aroused. This was acting, this was characterization, so completely merged in rhythm that the result became a perfect whole and not a combination of several intentions, as so often results from the work of an actor-dancer.[179]

During the Metropolitan season Vaslav and Romola lived rather a busy social life, and Nijinsky also danced – in a black and gold 'Carpaccio Gondolier costume' – at a special benefit performance of *tableaux vivants* after Italian Masters, in aid of Venice flood relief. Society women stole most of his underwear for souvenirs.[180] This occasion was organized by Mrs Vanderbilt. All the great American families entertained Vaslav. Relations with Diaghilev were now purely formal, and disagreements frequent. Romola remained con-

435

vinced that Diaghilev was intent on ruining her husband by telling everyone that Nijinsky was getting fat and petulant. Also, he showed no interest in Nijinsky's plans for 'Till Eulenspiegel' and 'Mephisto Valse'[181] – partly, no doubt, because they had been composed independently of him, and partly because all his hopes now lay with Massine. A further disagreement arose over 'L'Après-midi' which Massine had been dancing as he had been taught by Grigoriev and others. This was not exactly as Nijinsky had choreographed it, and he offered to rehearse the ballet. He also wished that Revalles should replace Tchernicheva as the chief Nymph. Diaghilev would not consider either of these proposals, and Nijinsky obliged him to cancel the performances advertised for the final week of the engagement, in which New York would have had its first sight of Nijinsky in a ballet of his own devising.[182] On the last day of the season, 29 April, a Saturday, Nijinsky danced in 'Le Spectre' at the matinée, and 'La Princesse enchantée' and 'Schéhérazade' in the evening. Diaghilev recognized the work of the specially selected orchestra of eighty by presenting them with an eight-foot-high floral wreath; and the orchestra was then dispersed.

Diaghilev was anxious to arrange a second American tour, since so many countries in Europe were closed to him in wartime. He took care to be reported in the newspapers as having liked America and wondered why he had never been before, and he praised the appreciation of the American audiences.[183] Otto Kahn wanted a coast-to-coast tour, and, according to Romola, 'even if a deficit were involved he did not mind, as he wished to educate the American public'.[184] In fact, he was trying to get into society.[185] He was determined that Nijinsky should lead the company, but also thought it desirable that the next engagement should not be hampered by continual friction between Diaghilev and Nijinsky. Accordingly he persuaded Nijinsky that Diaghilev's presence was not required, and that Vaslav should be artistic director.[186] The company was thus to be rented from Diaghilev for the period of the tour, on condition that he was to remain outside the United States.[187] 'Everyone except Kahn, Nijinsky and Romola,' wrote Sokolova, 'realized this was madness . . .';[188] but Diaghilev had to agree. He had, however, accepted an invitation from the King of Spain for the company to dance at the Teatro Real in Madrid, and while in Spain he would be able to work with Massine on a new repertory. On 6 May, leaving Vaslav, Romola and Flore Revalles in New York, Diaghilev and the rest of the company sailed for Cadiz on the *Dante Alighieri*. The ship was full of screaming horses, many of which died on the way over.[189]

The Nijinskys moved to the Majestic Hotel, and their leisure time was spent with Caruso and other new friends. But Vaslav's chief pleasures were to walk on Broadway or to go to the 'movies'. On one occasion a luncheon party was given for Nijinsky and Isadora Duncan, and Isadora, just back from a very peculiar tour in South America[190] and temporarily reunited with Paris Singer, who proposed buying Madison Square Garden for her,[191] reminded Vaslav of the time when she had suggested that they should have a child. She said, 'The idea did not seem to appeal to you then; I see you are changed now; you are less intolerant towards us women.' Vaslav replied, 'I did not change. I love everybody, as Christ did',[192] which, if truly reported, was rather an irritating remark.

Nijinsky's presence in New York was a constant source of news and gossip for the papers – some of it fanciful. The *New York Review*, for instance, reported on 13 May that Nijinsky had 'under consideration' an offer made to him by Annette Kellerman, the 'Diving Venus', that they should join forces in a new aquatic production.[193] But Nijinsky was now totally immersed in plans for his two new works and for the next season of the Russian Ballet, of which he was to be sole artistic director. One problem was to find a *prima ballerina* for the company, and the Metropolitan sent to Russia to investigate the possibilities. The next question was the designing of 'Till' and 'Mephisto Valse', since neither Benois nor Sudeikine, whom Nijinsky approached, would leave Russia during the war. Ultimately Rawlins Cottenet, one of the Metropolitan directors,[194] arranged for Vaslav and Romola to go down to Greenwich Village and talk to a promising young painter, Robert Edmond Jones, who had worked with Max Reinhardt in Berlin. 'He was a tall, shy man,' wrote Romola, 'but he inspired confidence in Vaslav. . .'[195] Jones gave a memorable description of Nijinsky at this meeting.

He is very nervous. His eyes are troubled. He looks eager, anxious, excessively intelligent. He seems tired, bored, excited, all at once. I observe that he has a disturbing habit of picking at the flesh on the side of his thumbs until they bleed. Through all my memories of this great artist runs the recurring image of those raw red thumbs. He broods and dreams, goes far away into reverie, returns again. At intervals his face lights up with a brief, dazzling smile. His manner is simple, ingratiating, so direct as to be almost humble.

The conversation took place in halting French, but Nijinsky seemed to be interested in the designs. As they talked Jones sensed

a quality in him which I can only define . . . as a continual preoccupation with standards of excellence so high that they are really not of this world . . . There is in him an astonishing drive, a mental engine, too high-powered, racing – perhaps even now – to its final breakdown.* Otherwise there is nothing of the abnormal about him. Only an impression of something too eager, too brilliant, a quivering of the nerves, a nature racked to dislocation by a merciless creative urge.

Nijinsky's reaction to the drawings was simply '*Très heureux.*'[196]

Vaslav bought a Peerless car which he learned to drive after a fashion, and in which he took Romola and the growing Kyra for rides. The family now moved – by car – to Bar Harbor in Maine to escape an epidemic of infantile paralysis, and there, with one or two friends nearby, they had the advantages of a swimming pool – where Nijinsky's prowess was noted by spectators – a marble theatre on a hill, and a Greek amphitheatre on the lawn. Vaslav played with his daughter on the grass and practised with his accompanist in the Greek temple. Here also he tried his hand – for the first time and with great success – at the game of tennis which he had misrepresented in 'Jeux'.† Once a week there was a concert in the theatre, where distinguished musicians performed. Nijinsky also composed some dances, one of which – 'Le Nègre Blanc' – he arranged to Debussy's Cake-walk.[197]

---

*Jones here seems to be wise after the event.

†I remember another outstanding dancer, Erik Bruhn, being introduced to the game of tennis one Sunday afternoon at the house of Mr William Low at Musselburgh, outside Edinburgh, and taking to it as a duck to water.

Robert Edmond Jones was summoned to Bar Harbor with his designs. The painter was overwhelmed by this commission and thought Nijinsky's conception of 'Till' a masterpiece and the choreographer 'at the very height of his creative power'.[198] Vaslav had asked him to work from books of the period, and was pleased with the costume sketches, which were full of life and colour. Jones's original idea for the décor was not entirely to Vaslav's liking, and Vaslav explained what he wanted.[199] He was to write in his *Diary* that the artist 'worried and worried. . . I used to say to him, "Why should you be afraid? One must not be afraid." But he still worried. Evidently he worried about the success of the ballet. He did not believe in me. I was certain of success.'[200] But as the two artists – each introverted in his own way – worked together, they evolved the final designs. These were described by Jones as follows: the front curtain – 'a huge sheet of parchment emblazoned with Til's device of the owl and the looking-glass, all blurred and worn, like a page torn from a long-forgotten manuscript of the Middle Ages'; the set – the market-place of Brunswick before the city hall and the 'brooding black mass of the cathedral', the buildings leaning towards each other in distorted fashion; the costume designs – 'the rosy-cheeked apple-woman with her big basket of apples, all red and green and russet; the cloth merchant in his shop; the fat blond baker with his long loaves of bread; the scrawny sweetmeat-seller, decked out in peppermint stripes of red and white, like one of his own candies; the cobbler carrying his rack of oddly-shaped shoes; the burghers, the priests, the professors in their long robes and their ridiculous shovel hats; the street urchins and the beggars; the three *châtelaines*, taking the air beneath peaked hennins that tower a full six feet above their heads, their trains streaming away ten feet, twenty feet, thirty feet behind them . . . and Til himself in his varied disguises – Til the imp, Til the lover, Til the scholar, Til flouting, taunting, imploring, writhing in his death agonies. . .'[201]

Romola, in the meantime, was checking Nijinsky's contract, which provided for a forty week tour following three weeks in New York. The Metropolitan wished Nijinsky to dance five times a week: Romola managed to arrange this strenuous schedule so that he danced two ballets three times a week and one on the other evenings.[202] But on top of directing the company and travelling this threatened a great strain on Vaslav.

In June Diaghilev cabled to Otto Kahn from Madrid:

Diaghilev in Madrid to Kahn in New York, (?).6.16
Season ended yesterday admirably. Their Majesties attended every performance. Lopokhova, Tchernicheva, Bolm and Massine were introduced by me to the King, who spoke enthusiastically to them. He wishes us to return next spring. Has twice received Stravinsky, asked him to compose Spanish ballet. His Majesty wants us to give a few gala performances at San Sebastian in August. Diaghilev.[203]

These galas in San Sebastian provided the occasion for the premières of two new works which Massine had created in Spain in collaboration with Larionov. 'Las Meninas' to Fauré's 'Pavane' was inspired by the Velasquez paintings in the Prado: the costumes were by J-M. Sert after Velasquez, and the décor by the French painter Carlo Socrate. The ballet was intended by Diaghilev as a tribute to their Spanish audiences. The first performance was on 21 August at the Victoria-Eugenia Theatre: Sokolova, Khokhlova, Massine and Woizikovsky danced the leading roles, with Elena Antonova as the dwarf. Four days later Massine's other new ballet 'Kikimora' was given, with Chabelska and Idzikovsky. With music by Liadov and décor and costumes by Gontcharova and Larionov, this short Russian fairy-tale would become a year later the first part of 'Les Contes russes'. The third work which the company produced in Spain was a new version of the dances from 'Sadko' which Diaghilev entrusted to Bolm since Fokine's choreography of 1911 was almost forgotten. This was presented in Bilbao, with décor by Anisfeld and costumes by Gontcharova.

Nijinsky was now anxious to rehearse *his* two ballets, but Diaghilev could not dispatch the company to America until five weeks before the New York opening. Diaghilev had decided to retain a nucleus of dancers with him to plan new work, and so he, Grigoriev, Larionov and Gontcharova, the Cecchettis, Massine and some sixteen dancers – including Tchernicheva, Antonova, Evina, Maria Chabelska, Khokhlova, Woizikovsky, Idzikovsky and Novak – went to Rome, while the main body of the company set sail from Bordeaux on

8 September on the *Lafayette*. Nijinsky's biggest mistake, it was generally felt, had been his insistence that Grigoriev – the one person acquainted with every practical question in the management of the company – should not come back to America. In his place as *régisseur* Diaghilev had promoted Nicolas Kremnev, who was impetuous and tactless, and too much 'one of the boys' to have any authority. The business side of management was in the hands of Trubecki, Diaghilev's secretary and Pflanz's husband, and Randolfo Barocchi, who, although the husband of Lopokhova, had little knowledge of the Ballet.[204]

The season was to open at the Manhattan Opera House on 16 October, and when the company arrived in New York only three weeks remained in which Nijinsky could rehearse his new ballets, and the old repertory had to be polished up as well. Nijinsky did not show up to greet his dancers on their arrival,[205] and first met them at a morning rehearsal in the Grand Central Palace.[206] The two most important recruits from Russia were Marguerite Frohman, who, together with her brother Max, had danced for Diaghilev before the war, and the beautiful Olga Spessivtseva, whom Grigoriev had failed to entice to America for the previous season.

'Till' had a difficult birth. In rehearsals Nijinsky left it to Robert Jones to outline the scenario to the company[207] and they were slow to learn the new work. At one point the dancers became so exasperated by what they thought were Vaslav's shortcomings and by the failure of the management to intervene that they organized a two-day strike.[208] This Romola attributed to their refusal to dance to German music, and she remained convinced that the company as a whole – perhaps on Diaghilev's instructions – was intent on sabotaging Nijinsky's work.[209] In Rome Diaghilev and Grigoriev heard of the dissensions in the troupe, and Barocchi confirmed this in a telegram. More cables followed, until even Nijinsky had to wire asking Grigoriev to come to New York. With Diaghilev's approval the *régisseur* replied: 'Grigoriev declines the honour of rejoining the company while under your management.'[210] If Grigoriev's story is true this was rude and unhelpful, but by insisting that Grigoriev should be left in Europe Nijinsky had asked for it.

Despite the collaboration between choreographer and artist on the designs, there was further disagreement in this direction too. The scale model of the set was finished, and the scene-painters had begun their work painting the drops and flats on the vertical 'easel' frames in the scenic studios – the standard method in America, as in England. Nijinsky had wanted the work done the traditional Russian way, with the canvas laid on the floor, the painters walking over it in soft shoes with buckets of paint and long-handled brushes. This conflict was resolved after distress on both sides.[211] Pierre Monteux, who was conducting for this tour in place of Ansermet, now refused to conduct 'Till' because Strauss was a signatory to the Austrian manifesto against France, in whose army Monteux was serving when the Metropolitan got him six months' leave of absence. Dr Anselm Goetzl was engaged to conduct this ballet only throughout the tour.[212] Romola took Monteux's action as a personal attack on Vaslav.[213]

The costumes – which Sokolova thought were 'so striking' that 'they alone might have made a success of the ballet'[214] – delighted Vaslav; not so the sets. They were not high enough to give the effect of exaggeration in the buildings which he had wanted. Jones was summoned to Nijinsky's dressing-room. 'The walls . . . are papered in stripes of two tones of violent red. There is a pier-glass and a chaise-longue. On the dressing-table a number of stiletto-like knives, sharpened to a razor-edge, are ranged in an orderly row. The *maestro* is waiting for me in a flame of rage.'[215]* After his anger had exhausted itself, Nijinsky returned to the stage, and, jumping up to correct a dancer, fell and sprained his ankle. He was taken to a clinic and X-rayed: he was to rest for several weeks.

Confusion reigned. Rehearsals for 'Till' were to go on, but its première was postponed. Nijinsky was told he could dance on tour, but possibly not in New York; and any idea of putting on 'Mephisto Valse' – for which Jones had made the designs – had to be abandoned.[216]

---

*At this point the luridness of Jones's account seems to reflect his own hysterical state of mind at the time: 'Torrents of Russian imprecations pour from his lips. The open door fills with frowning alien faces. Nijinsky switches to broken French. He lashes out at me with an insensate blind hate.'

Mme Romola Nijinsky's comment is 'Not true.' The 'stiletto-like knives', she suggests, could only have been sticks of Leichner grease-paint.

Anna Pavlova sent Vaslav flowers.[217] She was appearing with her company at the Hippodrome in Charles Dillingham's 'The Big Show': it was an engagement which was to last five months – undertaken largely to pay her debts – in which she danced a condensed version of 'The Sleeping Beauty' sandwiched between vaudeville acts of spectacular proportions, including West Point cadets, four hundred minstrels, and an Ice Ballet: 'a jewel in a garish setting', commented one reviewer. As time went on her ballet became more and more vestigial – reduced finally to eighteen minutes – and her costumes by Bakst (the designs for some of which were to be used by Diaghilev five years later) were sewn with spangles to compete with the glitter of the other turns.[218] For Pavlova the presence of both Isadora and Nijinsky in New York at this time made matters worse, and it is perhaps understandable that when Romola told the ballerina that Vaslav's ankle was only twisted, not broken, 'her voice dropped, as though she were disappointed'.[219]

The season opened on 16 October without Nijinsky, whose absence was felt at the box office. The repertory was the same as before, except that 'Narcisse', 'L'Oiseau de feu', 'Le Pavillon d'Armide' and 'Le Soleil de nuit' had been replaced by 'Les Papillons', Bolm's 'Sadko' and 'Till Eulenspiegel'. Lopokhova, Sokolova, Vassilievska and Gavrilov danced 'Les Sylphides'; Sophie Pflanz and Bolm led the Polovtsian Dances; Revalles resumed her roles of Zobeïda and Cleopatra (which Tchernicheva had been dancing in Spain) with Bolm as Amoun and the Negro, and Sokolova dancing Ta-hor; and 'Le Spectre' was given again with Lopokhova and Gavrilov. In 'Carnaval' Gavrilov was Harlequin, Lopokhova Columbine, Pflanz Chiarina, Sokolova Papillon, Bolm Pierrot, Zverev Eusebius, Kremnev Pantalon, and Florestan was taken by a newcomer, Mieczyslaw Pianowski. Lopokhova, Sokolova and Bolm were to dance the leading roles in 'Papillons', whose première was scheduled for the end of the first week, but owing to Lopokhova's illness the ballet was postponed until the night of the première of 'Till Eulenspiegel', which was now to be Monday, 23 October. The only new ballet shown during the first week of the engagement was 'Sadko' with the choreographer in the title role.

443

Nijinsky's doctors decided that he was fit to dance 'Till'. Jones had solved the problem of the set by adding ten-foot-high canvases to the bases of the two flats, and painting them with 'an impression of foliage in broad washes of ultramarine'. Only the top of the scenery was fully lit. (The critics assumed that the effect was intentional, and approved.)[220] The dress-rehearsal was held on the day of the first performance. At this point the dancers knew the first act, which went smoothly: 'Nijinsky danced gaily,' wrote Sokolova, 'and without concern for the future.'[221] As Jones admired his finished set on stage, it was suddenly lit by a shaft of sunlight coming through a *lunette* in the ceiling; he was overcome by the beauty of it, fainted and was carried out.[222]* When the second half was reached, according to Sokolova, 'there was really no more ballet – just a few scrappy bits, under-rehearsed.' There were arguments, and Nijinsky left. And for the rest of the afternoon the company built up the ballet, relying on Nijinsky to know his own role.[223] He was to admit, three years later, writing about 'Till' in his *Diary*: 'It was "taken out of the oven" too soon, and therefore was raw. The American public liked my "raw" ballet. It tasted good, as I cooked it very well. I did not like this ballet but said, "It is good."'[224]

When the audience gathered on the 23rd, Pavlova was among them.[225] The performance opened with 'Papillons', which had as its setting discarded décor from 'Sylphides'.[226] This work made little impression on the critics who found the music in its orchestrated version poor, the choreography weak, and the costumes unimaginative (the 'restored' wings of the butterflies – on which what there was of drama depended – refused to stay in place, putting a jinx on the performance). It was seen as a pale shadow of 'Carnaval'.[227]

Then came 'Till Eulenspiegel'. Monteux had retired to a box, and Goetzl took up the baton.

The music of 'Till', like that of 'Die Meistersinger', surprises us with its un-German humour. Strauss originally intended the work to be operatic: but the spiky themes, the absurd *charivaria* of

---

*Romola Nijinsky wrote: 'When Jones . . . realized his miscalculations, he fainted and had to be taken home.' (p. 274.)

orchestral effects, the flexible construction and the clarity of the story line, coupled with the universal appeal of the hero, provide ideal material for the ballet. The curtain, bearing the owl-and-glass device, rises to reveal the bustling market place of Brunswick on a late autumn afternoon.[228] Peasants and merchants throng the square, at the back of which tower the cathedral and the town hall. 'A species of whimsicality run riot sets before the astonished vision a medieval town that never was in any age and laves it in nocturnal blue touched with a few shafts of crepuscular light which illuminates the inverted cornucopia roofs of tiny houses tiled at crazy angles. . .'[229] The characters – twenty of them – are costumed in exaggerated fashion as a comment on their lives and manners. Here are the notary, the priest, the merchant, the beggar, the lady of the castle, the ragged poor and the children stealing from the stalls. Here is the baker, carrying his bread in a basket as tall as himself, and there the apple-woman (Sokolova) with apple-cheeks and peasant costume, her fruit piled in a bundle on her head. Two policemen prowl suspiciously.

Suddenly a lithe youth in ragged Nile-green costume – tights, shirt and bodice, scarf and sash – and with a mop of unruly hair rushes into the square. This is Till (Nijinsky): he knocks down both the baker's bread and the apple-woman's apples for the poor to grovel for, and quick as lightning has tied up a group of citizens in a bundle with a flame-coloured bale of cloth. He then cuts them free and they fall to the ground. He disappears as quickly as he came, and the angry victims of his pranks march into the town hall to complain.

A little procession enters the market-place: a cowled priest is being followed by the noble ladies, by the learned men, by the poor, all listening to his preaching. To the beggars who ask him for money he counsels patience; then suddenly he pulls out his empty pockets, shrugs back his hood to reveal himself as Till, and darts off. The priests go off to the town hall for justice.

The congregation is leaving the cathedral – among them the Châtelaine (Revalles) and her two companions. They wear the most exaggerated costumes of all: elaborate silk brocade gowns with trains as long as the square is deep, and fantastically high head-dresses, from the tips of which trail endless veils. The Châtelaine is being courted by a rich young cavalier in a cloak, who makes taunting obeisances to her with a hat which is all feathers. She spurns him, but Till's green tights are revealed beneath the cloak and the onlookers are convulsed with laughter. The ladies leave, their retainers entering the town hall to denounce the pretender.

The five robed men who now appear – with long beards, huge square spectacles and weird Don Basilio hats fashioned from rolls of parchment tied under the chin with ribbon – are professors of the university, arguing their abstruse problems. They are thrown into confusion by the arrival of a sixth, similarly dressed: a foreign scholar. As they struggle to understand him, he mocks them and shows them the poor people huddled in the square. Protesting, the professors in turn enter the town hall.

As dusk falls Till is heard singing, and he runs through the streets calling the poor to dance with him. It is a dance of revolution: all are equal. The crowd hoist the hero shoulder-high and carry him to the town hall; but drums roll and soldiers surround them. Till is brought before the Inquisitors who are clad in black with white crosses on their backs, and wear peaked caps. Till is still mocking, but all – priests, merchants, lords and ladies, professors – accuse him and he is condemned. His laugh is stopped only by the noose, and his figure hangs 'high in ruby light among the red lanterns'.

The poor people gather to reproach themselves for allowing Till to go to his death. But suddenly, out of a group of moaning women, springs Till – 'in a flight of toy balloons'. He has cheated even death: his spirit lives on.

Nijinsky had followed the programme of Strauss's music closely: the correspondence between Till's puckish theme on the clarinet and his antics on stage contained the spirit of the piece. But he emphasized the revolutionary aspect of Till's behaviour. In Strauss's programme Till annoys *everyone*, rather than inciting the underprivileged to riot; and whereas the Strauss synopsis ends with the rabble recollecting Till's tricks with nostalgia, Nijinsky chose to introduce an incarnation of Till's spirit in a climax recalling 'Petrushka'.

The ballet lasted only eighteen minutes. As the curtain fell, a storm of applause greeted what was to be the last new ballet by Nijinsky to be performed on any stage, and amid the flowers the choreographer and the designer held hands and took the curtain-calls together. There were fifteen in all.[230] '*C'est vraiment très, très heureux,*' murmured Nijinsky.[231] Even Monteux was applauding from his box. Romola thought 'Till' was Vaslav's best work.[232] The programme continued with 'Le Spectre', danced by Lopokhova and Gavrilov, and ended with 'Schéhérazade' in which Nijinsky, unannounced, danced the Golden Negro.[233] After the performance the reporters clamoured for quotes. Flore Revalles said loyally: 'I like to dance in "Till" better than in anything else, and I adore my costume.' Nijinsky, his magnanimity restored, pronounced Robert Edmond Jones to be 'a greater colour artist than Bakst'.[234]

The patriotic and anti-Ballet Russe critic of *Musical American* attributed 'nine-tenths of the effectiveness and quick appeal' of 'Till' to Jones, whose designs Nijinsky 'with marvellously good judgement' had commissioned. But the choreographic and dramatic conception he found 'inconceivably paltry contrasted with the Rabelaisian comedy which in the concert hall enacts itself on the illimitable stage of the imagination. The spirit of the original has vanished for all the showy medieval accoutrements.'[235] But other critics were more enthusiastic. H. T. Parker of the *Boston Evening Transcript* felt that Nijinsky had 'retained, in matter and in manner, the flavour of the original folk-tale'.[236] Another voice stated that the ballet 'stood in a class by itself as a combination of musical, pictorial and terpsichorean art. The vividness, the depth of colour, was hardly less astounding than the deftness of it all.'[237] Another called this 'a brilliant performance, probably the most brilliant that the Ballet Russe has done in America ... a triumph of stagecraft and choreography'; another 'a complete success'. Nijinsky's performance was seen as a 'fine ... piece of mimic impersonation', a role to which he was 'exactly fitted'.[238] 'The keynote of Nijinsky's interpretation,' wrote Carl van Vechten, 'was gaiety. He was as utterly picaresque as the work itself; he reincarnated the spirit of Gil Blas.'[239] Perhaps the superlatives were partly due to the fact

447

that not only was this a ballet created by Nijinsky and danced by himself but it was also the first Diaghilev ballet to have its première in the United States. 'Till Eulenspiegel' was also the only ballet performed by his company which Diaghilev never saw.

The occasion was notable too from the point of view of Richard Strauss. It was twelve years ago, wrote one columnist, that the city had had a 'Strauss week'. Now it was having another. The following Thursday and Friday the first performance of the composer's 'Alpine Symphony' and selections from his opera 'Guntram' were given by the Philharmonic Orchestra in Carnegie Hall: and a week later 'Till Eulenspiegel' was given at a concert, again at the Carnegie, by the Boston Symphony Orchestra.

The night after 'Till' the performance opened with 'Les Sylphides', in which Marguerite Frohman and Spessivtseva made their American débuts; and then Nijinsky danced 'L'Après-midi' for the first time in America. The newspapers had wondered which version New York was to see, that of Paris or that of London. In this ballet, wrote the *New York Sun*, Nijinsky 'was said to have justified his fame as the most daring dancer on the stage', and much was expected. But 'Mr Nijinsky apparently believed in letting bygones be bygones... At any rate there was nothing in his acting to bring the blush of shame to the cheek of modesty. But it was full of significance and rich in that special art of Mr Nijinsky, which is subtle in its inflections and intangible in its grace. Miss Revalles was the nymph, a part to which her slender and exquisitely drawn figure and her skill in statuesque posing well fit her.'[240] The ballet was performed with the same Bakst décor, less brightly lit than before.[241] The programme was completed by 'Prince Igor', and 'Petrushka' with Nijinsky. Both 'Till' and 'L'Après-midi' were given again before the Manhattan Opera House season closed on 28 October.*

Two days later the company set off on their second American tour, which was coast-to-coast and scheduled to last five months. There were sixty-five dancers and an orchestra of sixty, together

---

*According to Mme Sokolova (*Dancing for Diaghilev*, p. 91) 'Till Eulenspiegel' was not repeated. But press reports prove that the ballet was given twice in New York, and Grigoriev's papers record twenty more performances during the tour.

with a number of technicians. The scenery and props, mechanical equipment and costumes went ahead together with the press agents, so that stages could be adapted and set before the dancers arrived in their twelve-car train. The musicians refused to sleep in upper berths, so the train was twice as long as it need have been. But Otto Kahn was sparing no expense.[242] The Metropolitan management took measures to stir up interest in the Ballet; art and fashion exhibitions reflecting the influence of the Ballet preceded the dancers, and, to Diaghilev's distaste when he heard about it, gramophone records were produced of 'Carnaval', 'Schéhérazade' and 'Les Sylphides' by the Ballet orchestra. There was talk of a film of the Ballet, but this did not materialize.[243] Kremnev became desperate, and tried to get a Metropolitan representative to take over the organization of the tour, but this only happened some months later. He wrote almost daily to Diaghilev and Grigoriev about the deteriorating morale of the company.[244]

The Ballet gave performances in Providence, New Haven and Brooklyn. In Springfield, where the troupe watched a football match, Nijinsky remarked to reporters that football and the Diaghilev Ballet had in common the fact that teamwork counted more than the excellence of any individual performer.[245] The next stop was Boston, where the season opened on 6 November. Barely had Nijinsky settled in than he was told of a rumour that he was a deserter from the Russian Army. This reached the newspapers, who reported him as saying that he was ready to fight, and did not believe that artists had any right to exemption.[246] Among friends in Boston was the painter Sargent who had drawn Nijinsky in London in 1911.[247] H. T. Parker of the *Transcript*, who had produced a thoughtful review of 'Till' on its première, now turned his attention to the Ballet on his home ground. The most notable performance was that of 9 November.

In 'Cléopâtre', wrote Parker, rather turgidly,

Mr Bolm mimed the high-hearted, fascinated, fated slave [*sic*] with large means, with a potent illusion, with a white-hot intensity of suggestion that lifted Amoun almost from melodrama into tragedy. Acting of the spoken word might hardly be more humanly eloquent, of joyous affection, sudden alarm, shrill entreaty and black woe than was the miming, half of the

449

dance as well, of Miss Sokolova. With Cleopatra as with Thamar, there is that in Miss Revalles's personality and poses which suggests the viperous and voluptuous queen but her lack of technical resource and variety sorely limits her impersonation. Yet the acclaimed Rubinstein did hardly more with the part.

Sections of the audience were so inflamed by the passion of Sokolova's performance that they loudly demanded for her the curtain-calls which protocol decreed were for Revalles and Bolm.

In 'Le Spectre' Parker noted Nijinsky's

exquisite *pirouettes* that seem less feats of agility and exactitude than the eddies of an inner elation; the *entrechats* that cleave the air for the flash of an instant as foot meets and parts from foot in gossamer contact; the lovely and adroit play of arm and hand, head and body in flawless and flowing harmony and rhythm; the aroma of fancy distilling from the whole – a dance of the vapours and the gleams of the misty night, a dance of as sublimated a sentiment in girlish fancies. The white sparks kindled Miss Lopokhova too.

And finally Boston saw the other side of Nijinsky's genius, 'the acute and sensitive mind and feeling', in his performance in 'L'Après-midi':

... this strange vision – as motionless, almost, as it has been mute – of pagan and primitive, yet of ultra-modern and a little perverse, fancy. Such feats of imagination, execution, illusion may the brooding Nijinsky, far-ranging and subtly tempered, achieve. The Italians have a word for the quality that shapes and savours them, even though they flower in a strange beauty. It is *morbidezza*.[248]

From Boston the Ballet moved on: Worcester – Hartford – Bridge-port – Atlantic City – Baltimore. Then, at the end of November, the company once again danced before the President in Washington, and Nijinsky was able for the first time formally and in person to express his gratitude for the part America had played in his release from internment.[249] In Philadelphia Nijinsky's first appearance was in 'Till Eulenspiegel'. The sets and costumes made a great impression, while Nijinsky's performance revealed 'a mimetic power which is remarkable and emphasizes the truth of the assertion that "speech was given man to conceal his thoughts."' But this same Philadelphian critic noticed, in Vaslav's dancing in 'La Princesse enchantée', no distinct superiority to either Mordkine or Volinine. 'He has strangely heavy legs for a torso so light and well moulded.'[250]

The tour was proving disappointing: there was no shortage of warm applause for Nijinsky, but to his mind this was simply appreciation of his acrobatic skill, not understanding of the ballet. In November an interesting item had appeared in the *Washington Star*: this pointed out that

The Diaghilev Ballet, which came as a splendid surprise when first brought to this country as the play-toy of a group of wealthy art-connoisseurs, has drifted slightly toward the conventionality of the usual touring theatrical attraction, though still too large a proposition to play out a week stand as a matter of perfunctory custom. It has taken the star system which has of late been reflected so conspicuously in the drama and transferred it to the dance. The name, Nijinsky, is made so prominent that it overwhelms attention. It may be doubted whether American taste is sufficiently discerning in matters of dancing to understand the fine points of expression which would elevate a single interpreter beyond the merits of the picturesque and poetic atmosphere with which he is surrounded in such graceful and proficient co-ordination. The male dancer is still an exception in American attention, save when he appears as the dancing partner of a feminine star.

The author of this verdict concluded: 'So long as the auditor regards the dance as a superficial display, an appeal to the eye, more than an expression of an idea, the male dancing star, however graceful his poses and delicate his shadings in pantomime, is likely to be regarded more as a curiosity than as the artistic marvel which Nijinsky is conceded to be.'[251]

In desperation the Metropolitan management produced in December a publicity sheet disguised as a newspaper, entitled *Ballet Russe Courier*. In this were reprinted past notices of performances, together with advance information on the tour, gossip about the dancers – their exotic pets, their prowess in beauty competitions, the difficulty in pronouncing their names – a series of puns under the heading 'Baksterical Laughter', and an article on Bakst himself. Some of this would have disgusted Diaghilev; but the sponsors of the tour were determined to leave no stone un-turned in order to fill houses and ensure a good reception for the troupe. One item in this paper was doubtless indicative of the situation in a number of towns: Richmond, Virginia, 'may have an evening with this superb organization if ten of our music-loving, artistically-inclined citizens will combine to form a guarantee fund in case the receipts should fall short of the sum pledged to the visiting company. In all probability the guarantors will not be called upon to make up any deficit.'[252]

The citizens rallied and the Ballet danced at Richmond for one night after leaving Philadelphia. Single performances were next given in Columbia and Atlanta – and in the latter town Nijinsky received a summons to appear within ten days before the military authorities in Petersburg. This seemed absurd and impossible, but – after rehearsing Gavrilov in one or two roles – he returned to Washington, where he was able to sort things out with the Russian Embassy. His exemption was re-confirmed, and he rejoined the company in New Orleans early in December.[253] In his absence Gavrilov had danced 'Le Spectre' under his name.[254]

In New Orleans, out of curiosity, Romola wished to visit the celebrated brothels. Though Vaslav was reluctant, from his 'respect for womanhood', she insisted; and Nijinsky was most considerate to the inmates. 'He talked with them and offered them drinks. They were all amazed to see that otherwise he had no interest.'[255] (Nijinsky was to write, later, in his *Diary*: 'I will go to a bordello [in Zürich] because I want to understand cocottes. I want to understand the psychology of a cocotte. . . I will give money to the cocottes, but will do nothing with them.')[256]

The repertory of the Ballet was often determined by what a particular town requested – and that in turn was conditioned by what it had heard. It was hardly surprising that 'Schéhérazade' was not to be performed in the South for fear of offending suscepti-bilities.[257] The dancers moved on: Houston – Austin – Fort Worth – Dallas – Tulsa – Wichita – Kansas City – Des Moines – Omaha. At Des Moines the limitations of the Coliseum prevented the use of the complete Bakst settings – for instance, 'Schéhérazade' was given without its heavy draperies – but the Ballet did not fail to produce 'an impression which will not soon fade, of grace, lightness, litheness, power and a fierce splendour'. The critic of the *Des Moines Register* felt that Nijinsky's Harlequin was necessary 'in order to assure the audience that he is really human', for in 'Schéhérazade' he was 'a lithe and powerful animal . . . a panther . . . the incarnation of something terrible in human nature'. In between these two ballets came 'Les Sylphides' with Lopokhova and Sokolova: 'These two Lydias are as light as thistledown in a breeze.' Though the house was not filled, the second balcony *was*. The price of $3.50 for the better seats had proved too much.[258]

The demands made on the principal dancers were great, and the whole company were exhausted by the conditions of the tour. It had been Diaghilev's practice to 'rest' only Karsavina and Nijinsky – and that but rarely – and understudies were the exception rather than the rule. Gavrilov was now established as Nijinsky's 'second', and Vaslav began to rehearse other dancers in principal roles. Zverev and Kremnev, Sokolova and Nemchinova were given new opportunities in this way.[259] Sokolova, for instance, was cast as the Girl in 'Le Spectre', which she regarded as a great honour. Her regret was that her début in this role followed her performance as Ta-hor, so that she had hurriedly to remove her brown make-up – and take another curtain call in the middle of doing so. The audience was enthusiastic, but she was unnerved. 'Dancing "Spectre" with Nijinsky was very frightening. He was always doing something unexpected. He would throw me in the air and catch me as I came down, or take his hand away at the moment of support in an *arabesque*. If I had come off my point then, the picture and atmosphere would have been ruined. He also puffed and blew.'[260]

The re-allocation of parts may have been partly due to Nijinsky's increasingly democratic ideas. Ever since the rehearsals of 'Till' in New York – and that ballet had had as its theme the rebellion of the under-privileged – two members of the company, Dmitri Kostrovsky, a newcomer, and Nicolas Zverev, both followers of Tolstoy, had attracted Nijinsky's attention. The Pole Kostrovsky, particularly, attached himself to Nijinsky, besides holding forth on his beliefs to the company. Much to Romola's displeasure the two dancers would come into Vaslav's compartment in the train during the company's journeys and preach Tolstoyan philosophy. Nijinsky began wearing the round-collared Russian peasant's shirt in place of a shirt and tie.[261] Romola '*would* rather have seen him with Bolm, or others of the Imperial School graduates than with those *moujiks* – not on account of their origin, but because of an instinctive distrust I had of them'.[262] Whatever the cause, the re-arrangement of roles could be disconcerting. Nijinsky gave Zverev his role in 'Schéhérazade', and then, on account of the illness of the usual Chief Eunuch, took that part unannounced.[263] Romola was surprised by the 'outstanding miming of the old Eunuch [Cecchetti was in Italy]. I was so intrigued that I went back stage and found that the unknown artist ... was Vaslav.'[264] There was some dissension, and a partial strike by the time the company reached Denver, the next stop after Omaha. Zverev occasionally danced 'Le Spectre' under Nijinsky's name,[265] as Gavrilov had done when he was away in Washington.

From Denver the route lay through the snow to Salt Lake City; and then early on the morning of Christmas Eve the dancers set off for Los Angeles, with two extra coaches on the train – a private car for Nijinsky, provided by the railroad company, and a baggage-car decorated for a Christmas party, in which a dance was given with music by the Metropolitan orchestra.[266] The company all received presents from the tree in Nijinsky's compartment. The snow was left behind, orange-trees appeared, and in Los Angeles the Nijinskys took a flat with Fred Fradkin, the concert manager, and his wife.[267] The Los Angeles engagement lasted from 27 December to New Year's Eve, 1917. Nijinsky visited the film studios in Hollywood, where Charlie Chaplin was making *Easy Street*.* Chaplin described Nijinsky as 'a serious man, beautiful-looking, with high cheek-bones and sad eyes, who gave the impression of a monk dressed in civilian clothes'. For several days Nijinsky watched the filming, and never smiled, although he told Chaplin that he admired him and wanted to come again. Chaplin was so unnerved by Vaslav's lack of response to his antics that he instructed the camera-man not to use any film. When Chaplin went to the ballet, he was captivated by Nijinsky's dancing. 'I have seen few geniuses in the world, and Nijinsky was one of them. He was hypnotic, godlike, his sombreness

*Chaplin says *The Cure*, which is apparently inaccurate (p. 205).

suggesting moods of other worlds; every movement was poetry, every leap a flight into strange fancy.' He visited Vaslav in his dressing-room as he was making up for 'L'Après-midi',* and the conversation was halting.[268]

The Ballet arrived in San Franciso on New Year's Eve, and during a party at the hotel, Barocchi, who was reputedly clairvoyant, read everyone's palms. He foresaw for Romola a long and healthy life, but in five years' time some kind of separation from Vaslav. On looking at Nijinsky's hand Barocchi was visibly shocked. Vaslav asked if he was going to die, and Barocchi answered: 'No, no, certainly not, but . . . this is worse . . . worse.'[269]

The San Francisco season lasted two weeks, and for the second week Vaslav and Romola lived in a hotel in nearby Oakland. Nijinsky visited the University of California at Berkeley, and also had his first experience of flying.

The Tolstoyans were now rarely out of Nijinsky's presence: they held long conversations with him in Russian which Romola could not follow, and they resisted all attempts to get them to leave. In the company of Kostrovsky and Zverev, wrote Romola, Nijinsky 'reacted like a sensitive plant and folded himself up. He became silent, meditative, almost gloomy. . .'[270] Kostrovsky induced Vaslav to become a vegetarian like himself – which Romola was sure would diminish his strength for dancing.

January saw the company through the Western States: Portland – Vancouver – Seattle – Tacoma – Spokane – St Paul – Minneapolis – Milwaukee. Now Romola hardly saw Nijinsky who was becoming weak and irritable and whom the Tolstoyans were persuading to give up dancing and work on the land. Romola told him that despite her devotion to him she would not countenance the thought of his leaving dancing for peasant farming. The matter came to a head when they arrived in Chicago towards the end of January and she decided to return to Kyra in New York. As the tour continued (Indianapolis – St Louis – Memphis – Birmingham – Knoxville – Nashville – Louisville – Cincinnati – Dayton – Detroit – Toledo – Grand Rapids – Chicago again) they communicated by telegram and

*According to Chaplin, Diaghilev had this ballet put on specially for him this evening. The management may have done, but of course Diaghilev was far away.

telephone. From Cleveland in February Nijinsky telephoned Romola with the news that Diaghilev had cabled inviting him to join the company in Spain, and to go on a second South American tour. She advised him to defer a decision until he had consulted his New York lawyer.[271]

The next engagements were in Pittsburgh and Syracuse and the last performance of the Diaghilev Ballet in the United States was in the Harmanus Bleeker Hall, Albany, New York, on 24 February 1917, the programme comprising 'Cléopâtre', 'La Princesse enchantée' and 'Schéhérazade'.*

Vaslav now rejoined Romola: to her relief he was wearing his rings and his silk shirts again, and had abandoned his vegetarianism.[272] The rest of the company – with some exceptions, such as Bolm who remained in America for good – sailed back to Europe in various ships. By the terms of his release Nijinsky could only dance in a neutral country, and the United States were about to enter the war. The Ballet were due to give a series of performances in Italy, in which, since it was an Allied country, he could not dance; but their following engagement was in neutral Spain, and it was here that he planned to rejoin them.

He made Romola presents of more jewellery and furs. From fear of being torpedoed they both made their wills.[273] Dining with Cottenet one night, Vaslav placed his American earnings in the form of a cheque under Romola's napkin as a present for her.[274] Shortly after this they set sail for Cadiz.

The main body of the company disembarked at Cadiz early in April, and were met by Grigoriev, who escorted them to Rome, where Diaghilev and the rest of his troupe were waiting to begin rehearsals for a season opening at the Teatro Costanzi on 9 April. Diaghilev, Massine and their friends had been working hard throughout the winter, and a new era of the Ballet had begun. Though there were still works by Fokine and Nijinsky in the repertory, Diaghilev now placed all his hopes in Massine as a choreographer: one whom, wrote Grigoriev, 'he thought capable

*Sokolova (p. 93) says the tour was 'cut short' but the *Ballet Russe Courier* had announced in December a tour of seventeen weeks and it lasted in fact sixteen. There were tentative bookings for Stamford, Connecticut on 14 March and the Princess Theatre, New York, on 15 March.

of becoming the very incarnation of all that was modern in art'.[275] In Rome Massine had been working on three ballets. The first, 'Les Femmes de bonne humeur', was based, at Diaghilev's suggestion, on Goldoni's play *Le Donne di buon' umore*. Diaghilev had also proposed using the music of Scarlatti, and the twenty-three sonatas eventually selected from the hundreds they listened to were orchestrated by Vincenzo Tommasini. Bakst produced elaborate eighteenth-century Venetian costumes and a Guardi set. It was also Diaghilev's idea that the recent one-act ballet 'Kikimora' by Massine and Larionov should be made into a long folk-tale ballet using more music by Liadov. From a wealth of folk- and fairy-tales the stories of the Swan Princess and Baba-Yaga were chosen to be added to 'Kikimora', and the ballet was renamed 'Contes russes'.

The studio in the Piazza Venezia in which Massine and the dancers worked on these ballets had become a *salon* in which not only Bakst, Stravinsky, Larionov and Gontcharova, but a new generation of artists gathered. These included Picasso, who was working with Massine on the ballet 'Parade', and who here met his future wife Olga Khokhlova.

The company gave four performances at the Costanzi, where the première of 'Les Femmes de bonne humeur' took place on 12 April: the ballet was danced by Lopokhova, Massine, Idzikovsky, the Cecchettis, Tchernicheva, Woizikovsky, Chabelska, Antonova and Khokhlova, and it delighted the Italian audience. At the same performance Stravinsky's early symphonic poem 'Fireworks' was played while the stage was occupied by a construction designed by the futurist Giacomo Balla, with lighting effects devised by Diaghilev which flashed on and off.

From Rome the Ballet travelled to Naples to give four performances at the Teatro San Carlo, then to Florence for a single night, and on to Paris for a season at the Châtelet. Here 'Les Contes russes', with Tchernicheva, Sokolova, Woizikowsky, Jasvinsky, Idikovsky and Kremnev, had its first performance on 11 May. 'L'Oiseau de feu' was also given that night, and as a tribute to the recent 'liberal' revolution in Russia Diaghilev arranged that Prince Ivan should receive at the end of the ballet not the crown and sceptre and ermine-bordered cape, but a red robe, the cap of liberty and the red flag. The public showed its disapproval and the former ending was subsequently restored.[276] On the 18th 'Parade' had its première.

'Parade' sprang from an idea of Cocteau's, and he had chosen Erik Satie to compose it because his spare and tuneful music, while being essentially French, was still an antidote to Debussyism. Valentine Gross had introduced the poet and the composer. Then Cocteau had called in Picasso, the founder of cubism. The scene was the outside of a circus booth. The performers appeared in turn to lure spectators inside. First a Chinese Conjuror (Massine) did tricks with an egg; then a Little American Girl (Maria Chabelska) mimed the riding of a bronco, bicycled, danced ragtime, and imitated the flickering of moving pictures; lastly, two beautiful acrobats in blue and white tights (Lopokhova and Zverev) performed a lyrical *adagio*. The numbers of these dancers were punctuated by the antics of two Managers wearing immense cubist constructions and by a comic horse. There had been some disagreements over the creation of the work, Satie objecting to the sounds of typewriters, pistol shots and ships' sirens which Cocteau wanted to impose on the score, and Cocteau resenting the cubist Managers: but Picasso's ideas transformed what might have been a triviality into something marvellous. 'Parade' was a gay work which both dancers and audience enjoyed,[277] and it was unlike anything the Russians had done before.

Vaslav and Romola had endured a cold, rough voyage of thirteen days, and the Spanish ship was infested with rats which so frightened Romola that, braving the weather, she took to sleeping on deck. The Nijinskys decided to spend their holiday and await Diaghilev in Madrid. This city was new to Romola, but Vaslav had stayed a few days there when he had danced at the Roosevelt wedding in 1914: in March they found it cold and windy. They put up at the Ritz Hotel and immediately set out to explore the sights, visiting churches and the Prado, where Vaslav fell in love with Goya. The Los Caprichos etchings particularly delighted him.[278]

When spring came Vaslav and Romola used to sit in the gardens of the Prado and she translated for him from English the poems of Oscar Wilde and Rabindranath Tagore. Vaslav had met Tagore in

London in 1912, and had ideas of doing a ballet to one of his poems.[279] Meanwhile Kyra played among the irises. They were happy; and Romola thought Tagore was a good antidote to Tolstoy. But Tolstoy's influence was not effaced, as Romola found when some of her new clothes hanging in a cupboard were attacked by mice and she began to cry. Vaslav rebuked her gently. 'I give you furs, jewellery and anything you wish, but can't you see how silly it is to attach importance to them? And have you ever thought how dangerous for the pearl-divers and for the miners who provide your jewellery – they also have children, and yet they must endanger themselves daily for the adornment of women.'

They went to see gypsy dancers and Vaslav was very struck by the austere movements of the men. He imitated them and was soon on the way to becoming proficient at Flamenco.

Vaslav was working on his system of notation and practising at the Royal Theatre. Life was regular and peaceful, and the fine weather engendered a mood of optimism. He began to think that his troubles with Diaghilev were over.

One day Romola picked up a newspaper and read of the abdication of the Tsar and the formation of Kerensky's government, which had taken place on 15 March. Nijinsky thought the revolution would be a peaceful one and he welcomed it – as Diaghilev had evidently done in Paris. He believed that it would make no difference to the artistic life of Russia and felt sure that Diaghilev would be appointed Director of the Mariinsky. He envisaged returning home to found his own theatre and school.

At the beginning of June the Ballet arrived.

Sergei Pavlovitch burst into the lobby of the Ritz and embraced Vaslav passionately. '*Vatza, daragoi moi, kak tui pajivayesh.*'

The greeting was as affectionate as if they had only parted a few hours ago, and no misunderstanding had ever occurred. It was the Sergei Pavlovitch of the old days. They sat down in a corner and began to talk. Hours and hours passed, and it seemed that the old friendship was restored. From that day on we were practically all the time with Diaghilev. The contract for South America was just brushed aside, and Sergei Pavlovitch simply said: 'We open in Madrid at the Theatre Royal, and then we will give some performances in Barcelona. Massine has composed

459

new ballets. I want you, Vatza, to look at them and give me your opinion. Have you composed anything new? I want you to do so.'

Recent events in Russia were also discussed at great length, and Vaslav explained to Diaghilev his plans for the school and festival theatre. But Diaghilev objected: 'Why think of the future of ballet? That is not our task. Dance and compose for our company, and leave the future generation to look after itself. I do not wish to return to Russia; I have worked too long abroad – the artists at home would ask what I wanted there. They would say that I wanted to take advantage of the newly acquired possibilities of the liberty for which they had had to fight. They would say, "*Je suis vieux jeu, vieux régime.*" I could not survive in the new Russia. I prefer to stay in Europe.'

But Vaslav did not yet give up the idea of gaining Diaghilev for his plan. 'We can't go travelling about the world forever like a caravan of gypsies; we shall never be able to create real artistic work that way. We belong to Russia; we must go home and work there and make a trip to the West once in a while.'

Diaghilev's little circle, here as elsewhere, was formed of the elite of the advanced guard. He brought Picasso, who was very little known at that time, to us one day. He was reticent and very Spanish looking, and when he began to explain anything, he became full of excitement, and used to draw on the table-cloth, the menu cards, and on top of Sergei Pavlovitch's ivory walking-stick. Diaghilev was to me as a fatherly friend, protective and kind, at this time. Vaslav triumphantly said, '*Tu vois, femmka ; je t'ai toujours dit qu'il sera notre ami.*'

Vaslav had told Romola how Diaghilev had forgiven Alexis Mavrine and Olga Feodorova. Romola observed: 'Vaslav was so happy that he would have done anything to please Diaghilev'; and there was no talk of contracts.

Stravinsky too had arrived.

One evening [wrote Romola] we went to a theatre where Pastora Imperio was giving a recital. To us the name did not mean anything. We were told that she was a gypsy singer from Cadiz, that her fame extended to the Latin-American countries. She was the idol of Spain. As she appeared on the stage, behind the simple curtain, she did not make a great impression. We only saw a rather faded, stout southern woman, but the moment she began to sing, accompanying herself with movement and castanets, we forgot that she had no voice, that she was middle-aged and fat. With a few gestures she offered the history and the soul of Spain.

Vaslav and Stravinsky, as well as Diaghilev, could not keep quiet on their seats, and, like three school-children, applauded, laughed, and cried, according to the mood this ageless marvel dictated.[280]

The Madrid season began and the King and Queen came to the ballet almost every night. Nijinsky danced in 'Schéhérazade', 'Carnaval', 'Le Spectre' and twice in 'L'Après-midi d'un faune'.

*Lydia Lopokhova
in 'Les Sylphides'.
Drawing by
Pablo Picasso.*

King Alfonso was such an enthusiast that he attended rehearsals too – but then, he was in love with Grigoriev's wife, Liubov Tchernicheva.[281] Romola heard from the Duchess of Durcal, a cousin of the King's, that he sometimes tried to imitate Nijinsky's leaps in private. This lady had fallen in love with Vaslav, and Romola, in her desire to bring out his worldly rather than his other-worldly side, positively encouraged her.

Now that the performances had begun, we had less time to go out with our friends, but I insisted that we should not give them up entirely, for I did not want Vaslav to isolate himself from the rest of the world and only live with Diaghilev and the Russian Ballet. I could not trust them after all that had happened in the past. As soon as they returned from their holiday, Kostrovsky and H.* practically installed themselves in our apartment, day and night. They hung around Vaslav after rehearsals. [Zverev] seemed to forget his courting [of Vera Nemchinova] and Kostrovsky his wife. The latter stood, with his shining, fanatical eyes, in the middle of the dressing-room, talking, while [Zverev] pretended to listen with awe. Every second sentence was a quotation from Tolstoy, and Vaslav listened attentively. Either purposely or because he was unfortunately not only fanatical but also unintelligent, Kostrovsky mixed up the teachings of Tolstoy. He preached that art is not justifiable for its own sake, but must have as its end the spiritual development of the individual. He wanted to convince Vaslav that he should work for the Russian Ballet as long as it needed him, and then retire to the land, like Tolstoy.

One evening Romola saw Diaghilev in excited conversation with Zverev in a dark corner near the stage, talking 'not as an officer with his subordinate, but like two accomplices'. She was immediately convinced that the whole object of the Tolstoyan preaching had been to separate Vaslav from herself and that it had been organized by Diaghilev.[282]

This stay in Madrid was a crucial period in Nijinsky's life. Loving his wife and child, being friends with Diaghilev, even admiring the work of Diaghilev's new protégé Massine, he must have embraced the possibility of everybody working blissfully together without contracts for years to come, to the greater glory of art. Perhaps even the principles of Tolstoy could be reconciled with the Russian Ballet and married life. If Romola had not been an exceptionally strong character, this might indeed have happened. But she was a fighter by nature. She would not share Vaslav with the two Tolstoyans, whom she regarded as peasants; and at the thought that they were set on by Diaghilev to separate her from her husband she was up in arms. She has always maintained that Nijinsky was master in his own house and took every important decision himself. Yet she must at this time have decided at least to *try* to stop him going with the Ballet on the next tour in South

*Zverev: Mme Nijinsky does not name him in her book.

America. It was Nijinsky's unwillingness to go to South America which led, as we shall see, to the final breach with Diaghilev.

In her distress Romola was uncertain whether Diaghilev wanted Nijinsky back for the Russian Ballet on the old terms, i.e. without a wife to make trouble over contracts – 'It was all a carefully laid plan to estrange Vaslav from me and restore him to Sergei Pavlovitch's clutches' – or whether he wanted to put an end to Nijinsky's dancing career.

> Sergei Pavlovitch knew Vaslav's character; he realized that only through altruism could he estrange him from marriage, normal life and art, and make Vaslav give up dancing for ever in order to cultivate the earth like a peasant.
> I tried to provide as many distractions as possible for Vaslav, and we often passed the day with the Duchess [of Durcal], who was so obviously madly in love with Vaslav that he objected to going out alone with her, as I suggested. One day, we motored out to the Escorial, a dreary trip through barren desert, but at the last turn of the road we could not restrain an exclamation, for suddenly the grand austere building arose out of nothing, like a mirage, and dominated the whole horizon. The strict, imposing lines of the structure were overwhelming. Vaslav, rooted in admiration, said, 'Spain. Religious fanaticism expressed in granite.'
> As he stood there, so small, so confident in the dazzling sunlight, before entering the gloomy pitiless home of the Inquisition, I wondered how it was that he did not see how the 'teachers' were trying, through religious fanaticism, to seize his soul and destroy him . . .
> At lunch, on the terrace, Vaslav seemed to have regained his mischievous ways. He said to me, 'Please, *femmka*, do not leave me so much alone with her [the Duchess]!' He was too discreet to give her away, but too honest not to put me on my guard.[283]

In spite of Diaghilev, the Tolstoyans and the Duchess, who was beautiful and had red hair,[284] Romola felt her marriage was a success and she loved Vaslav more all the time.

> Our intimate life was ideally happy. Sometimes the strangest feeling would come over me, and I felt that the women of mythology may have felt as I did when a God came to love them. There was the exhilarating and inexpressible feeling that Vaslav was more than a human being. The ecstasy that he could create in love as in art had a purifying quality, and

yet there was something intangible in his being that one could never reach.[285]

Then came Kostrovsky and Zverev, the common brutes, to spoil it all!

Vaslav began to wonder if cohabitation were only justified in case a child is born as the result. Before he had considered the state of my delicate health and the responsibilities of parentage, but now he suggested that either an ascetic life or a child every year was the right way. I immediately understood that this must be Kostrovsky's idea, in order to get me out of the way. One night, when they were discussing this subject, I declared open war.

It was three in the morning. I had listened for hours, seeing how cunningly they were trying to destroy our happiness, and at last, on the verge of tears, I exclaimed, 'Why don't you leave my husband alone? You don't dare to talk about his art, because you know that on that subject you cannot influence him. You are not his friends, but his enemies. If you want to create happiness, do so first in your own homes. Your wife, Kostrovsky, is miserable, your children without shoes, because you give your money away to strangers; and you [Zverev], if you want advancement, why not ask for it frankly? Vaslav Fomitch would help you. I forbid you both to interfere in our married life. Leave us, this place belongs to Vaslav and me.'

Vaslav had never seen me like this before, and for a moment he was taken aback, but then said, 'Please, *femmka*, they are my friends; do not try to withhold our hospitality.'

Kostrovsky and [Zverev] sat waiting, with impertinent provoking faces, to see how things would develop, but I turned round; 'Vaslav, you have to choose between the diabolical influence of these people and me. If within half an hour these people are still here, I shall leave you.'

I waited in the other room, and Vaslav came in to try and persuade me that they were both of good faith, but my determination was unshaken, and, as they were still there when the time was up, I went out into the night.

Next morning, Vaslav found me in the Prado and begged me to return, saying, 'It shall be as you wish.' From that day on, Kostrovsky and [Zverev] never entered our home any more; but in the theatre they still seized opportunities to get at Vaslav.[286]

Massine, as reserved a character as Nijinsky, though in a different way, watched Vaslav rehearsing 'L'Après-midi d'un faune'. 'I was thrilled by the way he demonstrated the most minute details of gesture and movement, correcting each dancer with calm assurance and complete understanding. He was an extraordinarily gifted choreographer.'[287] Vaslav thought 'Parade' showed a straining after modernism for its own sake, but he was fascinated by 'Les Femmes de bonne humeur'. Massine too had invented a quite new kind of movement – a flickering, jerky choreography inspired partly by the harpsichord sonatas of Scarlatti, partly by puppets, by Charlie Chaplin and the silent cinema. Vaslav longed to help and encourage Leonide, and he went to the young man's dressing-room to offer to dance Battista, Idzikovsky's part, in the Italian ballet.[288] He also coached Idzikovsky privately for 'Le Spectre de la rose'.[289]

After their eleven performances in Madrid, the company went to give six more in Barcelona, another city where the Russian Ballet would be performing for the first time. The Duchess of Durcal followed them and Romola was 'rather glad'.

The evenings we spent with the Duchess of X., who was by this time desperately in love, and wanted to become Vaslav's mistress. Jealousy never entered into my head, and I was even rather pleased when Vaslav returned later than usual one night, but this escapade had quite a different effect upon him than I had expected. He was mournful, and told me frankly:

'*Femmka*, I am sorry for what I did. It was unfair to her, as I am not in love, and the added experience, that perhaps you wanted me to have, is unworthy of us.'[290]

Vaslav had resolved to tell Diaghilev he would not go to South America. The reason he decided to give – that he wanted a holiday – does not ring very true: he was only giving sixteen performances in Spain and dancing only in one or two ballets a night – not in four as in the old days – and this after a two months' holiday.

Lunching one day with Diaghilev [wrote Romola] the latter began to talk about our South American trip, but Vaslav said, 'I am not sure I will go, Sergei Pavlovitch, I need a rest, and do not like the idea of being separated from my child in war-time. South America will not be a creative trip artistically.'

Diaghilev, with a freezing smile, returned, 'But you have to go, you are under contract.'

'Have to?' said Vaslav. 'I have no contract.'

'You cabled me from America agreeing in principle. That is a contract.'

'But I also cabled that we would discuss the matter in Spain.'

'That is beside the point. In this country, a cable is a binding contract' – and S.P. laughed – 'I will force you to go.'[291]

Conversation must have been rather sticky during the latter part of this luncheon, which was to be the last meal Diaghilev and Nijinsky ever had together.

There was a rapid *dénouement*.

In the afternoon, Vaslav notified Sergei Pavlovitch that, as no contract existed, he would take no further part in the Russian Ballet, and we left for the station. But as we boarded the Madrid express, two men touched Vaslav's arm: 'M. and Mme Nijinsky, will you please follow us, you are under arrest.' We were aghast.

'On whose authority?' I ventured.

'On that of His Excellency the Marquess of Z., Governor of Catalonia, in the name of the King.'

We were escorted to the police station, where, with the aid of several interpreters, they explained that we had been arrested at the behest of Diaghilev – as Vaslav was breaking his contract. If he did not dance that night, he would be put in gaol. Vaslav was pale, but determined: 'Very well, put me there! I have no contract. In any case, I can't dance now; I'm too upset.' He sat down.

'M. Nijinsky, please promise to dance, then I will not have to imprison you.'

'No, I won't; I can't.'

'Show us the contract which Diaghilev pretends to have, and then Nijinsky will dance,' I said. 'Anyhow, you have no right to arrest me; I am a Russian citizen, and not a member of the Russian Ballet. I will complain at the Embassy at once if you do not let me go immediately.'

The prefect became rather uneasy, but, very much against his wish, released me. Followed by a detective, I dashed to the telephone, called up the Duc de Durcal in Madrid, who informed the authorities there of what was going on. Within an hour an order arrived from Madrid for our immediate release, and Señor Cambo, the eminent Spanish lawyer, arrived to take up our case with Diaghilev.

The Barcelona authorities now realized that they had made a dreadful blunder, and were full of excuses. It was too late to catch the train, so we returned to the hotel, where [Trubecki] and the Spanish director were awaiting us. The director cried out at once: 'The public are disappointed, they are returning their tickets by hundreds. It's you they want to see dance. I am ruined, because I have to pay Diaghilev whatever happens, and now I have not made a peso. My last season was a failure, too.'

Vaslav was sorry for him. 'For your sake, I will dance tonight. Tell the public, please, why I am late.'

Next day, Cambo discussed the situation with us. Spain was the only country in which a cable was a binding contract. So Vaslav was bound to go to South America. He regretted now that he had not listened more carefully to Laurence Steinhardt's [Nijinsky's American lawyer] shrewd advice, and that he had not shown him the cable drafted, word for word, by Kostrovsky and [Zverev]. But Cambo assured us that Diaghilev would have to grant Vaslav the terms he asked. So he drew up a contract, that Vaslav was willing to go to South America, and that his salary was to be the same as in the USA, payable, in gold dollars, one hour before the curtain rose at every performance. I insisted on such a clause. I did not want any lawsuits later on. If this clause was not fulfilled, the contract became void. It was originated by Fanny Elssler after she had been cheated many times by dishonest impresarios. Vaslav agreed to appear in all parts first danced by himself. The penalty for breaking the contract was twenty thousand dollars. Cambo and I went to Diaghilev with the contract. He received us in his drawing-room, with his usual tactics, sitting with his back to the window, and letting others talk while he listened. The contract was so cleverly drawn up that, while it fulfilled all his stipulations, there was no possibility of any trick being played on Vaslav. While Diaghilev's signature was being affixed, my mind went back to that meeting at the Bristol Hotel, years ago – how very different, and yet how very alike, the situation was.[292]

In this affair, even though Diaghilev used the cable as a trap for the unsuspecting Nijinsky, our sympathies are all with the older man, who had the struggle of keeping his company alive in war-time. Thus the famous friendship ended and it was at the Teatro Liceo in Barcelona, on 30 June, that Diaghilev saw Nijinsky dance for the last time.

Vaslav and Romola returned for a few days to Madrid and from there they dispatched Kyra to a sanatorium in Lausanne which specialized in the care of children.[293]

Diaghilev, Massine and their sixteen dancers remained behind once again when Romola, Vaslav and the company sailed for South America on 4 July in the *Reina Victoria Eugenia*.

Romola observed that Vaslav seemed worn out by the emotional upsets of the last few days. He now seemed to be resigned to the impossibility of working with Diaghilev again. He did not allow himself to be idle, however. He discussed his system of notation with Cecchetti and taught it to Kostrovsky and Zverev. One day Kostrovsky's wife called on Vaslav to help her: it turned out that her husband had epileptic fits. Vaslav determined to take him to see a specialist when they arrived in South America.

There was a young Chilean on board called Georges de Cuevas, whom Romola described as 'a typical gigolo, extremely well bred and dressed'. He flirted with her, adored Nijinsky, and begged to be allowed to serve them in any capacity. He was 'completely broke' and they thought he was on the look-out for an heiress, but 'he was amusing, played bridge excellently and danced the tango divinely.' Vaslav, who disapproved of ballroom dances such as the foxtrot and grizzly-bear, which he called *'frotter le plancher'*, was delighted with the tango and learned from Cuevas to dance it 'with incredible elegance and smoothness'.[294] This new friend later inherited a Spanish title, married a Rockefeller heiress and as Marquis de Cuevas for a number of years ran a celebrated ballet company.

Maria Chabelska, one of the Polish sisters who had joined Diaghilev in Switzerland, was seldom seen without a book. One day Nijinsky, patrolling the deck with Ansermet, stopped to speak to her. *'Toujours lire, toujours lire!'* He looked at her book and exclaimed 'Newton! He was the man who saw an apple fall and invented – electricity.' Ansermet thought that it was part of Nijinsky's genius that he could not be satisfied with the everyday, the accepted truth – his mind soared beyond it to more extraordinary explanations or conclusions.[295]

Owing to Diaghilev's having insisted that the dancers travel in a neutral ship, they arrived at Montevideo rather than Rio as planned: and to recompense the impresario Mocchi for the cost of transporting them to Rio, Grigoriev put on a few free performances in

Montevideo. Nijinsky was not allowed to take part in these since he would have had to be paid large additional sums.[296]*

In Montevideo† Kostrovsky was taken to see a specialist. As she spoke a little Spanish, Romola interpreted the diagnosis, which was that the unfortunate man was incurably and dangerously insane. He was to be sent back to Russia.[297] It is curious to conjecture how differently things might have turned out if this diagnosis had been made in Madrid. Romola would have had no reason to fear the Tolstoyan menace and might have encouraged Nijinsky to go to South America. Nijinsky would therefore never have had the difference with Diaghilev which led to their final break. He might have continued with the Russian Ballet for many years and made a number of new ballets. He might have revived his 'Sacre du printemps', with the result that it might have survived intact to

*There are discrepancies between Grigoriev's and Mme Romola Nijinsky's accounts of this voyage and tour – as in many other matters. He says the Nijinskys followed the company to South America a few days later on a Dutch ship (p. 135). She says they travelled on the *Victoria Eugenia*, and describes Nijinsky's conversation with Cecchetti, Kostrovsky etc. (pp. 204–6). She does not mention the visit to Montevideo preceding that to Rio; and the thousand-mile voyage from Montevideo north to Rio on a British ship, *Amazon* (Grigoriev, pp. 136–7), she makes into a trip from Rio to São Paulo (p. 306), a matter of less than two hundred miles – and São Paulo is anyway inland. (Grigoriev says he motored there and the company went by train. p. 137.) Mme Nijinsky places the Montevideo visit after Rio (pp. 308–9). I have accepted her statement that she and her husband travelled with the company – which is anyway confirmed by Chabelska's story – while taking for granted the order of the tour given by Grigoriev. Whether Nijinsky danced in Montevideo or not, and if he did not, why not, remains obscure, for Grigoriev is confusing (p. 136) – apart from being wrong (as I think) about the Nijinskys travelling separately and arriving late. He writes: 'Nijinsky was late in arriving at Montevideo, doing so only after two of our regular performances (that is to say those we had originally contracted to give) had already taken place with outstanding success. Shortly afterwards Mocchi informed us that the ship on which we were to go to Rio had been delayed, and asked us to seize the opportunity of giving our three extra performances at once. On learning that they were to be given, Nijinsky expressed a wish to take part in them. We therefore had to explain that he could only do so unpaid, since they were additional to the number agreed in his contract. The Nijinskys, however, refused to believe this and suspected a plot.' If the company were not meant to be in Montevideo at all, what is the meaning of 'two of our regular performances'? From Grigoriev's papers I deduce that eight performances were given in Montevideo, since about thirty-four ballets were danced.

†It appears from Mme Nijinsky's narrative that this happened in Montevideo, although she places the visit to Uruguay after that to Brazil. In Rio she would have had to interpret in Portuguese.

this day. Continued work within the Ballet might have averted his illness or postponed it.

After their stay in Montevideo the company travelled on the British ship *Amazon* a thousand miles north to Rio de Janeiro. Vaslav and Romola drove straight to the Hotel Sylvestre where they had lunched with Kovalevska on the day after their engagement.

The Ballet were to give twelve performances in Rio. Grigoriev was in charge of the company, and his loyalty to Diaghilev made him regard the Nijinskys as enemies and treat them coolly. Other members of the Ballet followed suit. Vaslav felt that the majority of the company were giving him the cold shoulder, and he who loved his work began to dread going to the theatre.[298] Grigoriev complained that he had to put Barocchi in charge of Nijinsky.[299] When an accident happened the Nijinskys assumed it was a deliberate attack on Vaslav, probably instigated by Diaghilev.[300] This was interpreted by the company as persecution mania.[301] Things went from bad to worse. Grigoriev and others, such as Ernest Ansermet, the new Swiss conductor, who disliked Romola, would in later years and in the light of subsequent events assert that Nijinsky showed on this tour the first signs of mental illness.[302] This Romola Nijinsky flatly denies.[303]

One night Vaslav told Romola that 'L'Après-midi d'un faune' had been announced for performance in two days' time. He had danced it twice in Madrid, but still felt the management should have asked his permission to give it on this tour, and with the help of a friend he devised a way of getting his own back on Grigoriev. The scheme was the idea of Quintana, the son of the President of the Argentine, who happened to be in Rio at the time.

That evening [wrote Romola] the performance seemed to go very smoothly. The *entr'acte*, during which I admired the colourful audience, seemed to me unusually long. 'Faune' was the next ballet on the programme. The public became restless; I wondered what could have happened. Vaslav's friends were smiling like conspirators. I went backstage; everything was ready, the scene lit, Vaslav in position waiting for the curtain to rise. But at one side of the stage there was a gesticulating group. The impresario, Grigoriev, Kremnev pacing up and down in a frenzy, [Trubecki] trying to hide a smile. The impresario was talking to two police officials. What had happened? They told me: 'Nijinsky, the author of "Faune" has brought an injunction to prevent the presentation of "Faune", as it does not legally belong to the Russian Ballet.'

Nijinsky, the dancer, however, stood waiting to begin his part in the 'Faune' according to the terms of his contract. 'But, Nijinsky the author and Nijinsky the dancer are the same person,' said one of the ballet. 'Sorry; have you anything in writing to prove that you have the author's permission to perform it – yes or no?' And 'Faune' had to be cancelled.[304]*

To friends outside the company Nijinsky seemed a delightful companion. In Rio the Russian Ambassador Tscherbatchkoi entertained Vaslav and Romola and drove them to his country house. The American Ambassador Edwin Morgan was another friend. The French Ambassador was no less a person than the poet Paul Claudel.[305] After seeing Nijinsky in 'Schéhérazade' he was in raptures and demanded to be introduced to him. The following night, however, Vaslav was dancing in 'Les Sylphides'. The poet found the old-fashioned romanticism of this ballet repulsive and was delivered of an epigram: '*Il-y-a une chose qui est pire que le mauvais: c'est la perfection dans le mauvais.*' (One thing worse than bad is perfection in the midst of badness.) The young composer, Darius Milhaud, who would become one of the group called 'Les Six', was on his staff, and they had planned together two ballets, 'La Création du monde' and 'L'homme et son désir', which they hoped Nijinsky might stage.[306] These were later realized by the Ballets Suédois, with choreography by Jean Borlin. Milhaud was to compose a ballet, 'Le Train bleu', for Diaghilev in 1924.

Claudel later wrote of Nijinsky:

He moved like a tiger. There was no change of inert weight from one pose to another. His spring came from a buoyant partnership of muscular and nervous energy, like a bird on the wing. His body was not like a tree trunk or a statue, but a complete organism of power and movement. There was not a gesture, be it ever so slight (as, for example, when he turned his chin towards us, and the small head revolved on its long neck) which he did not accomplish magnificently, with a vivacity at once fierce and gentle and with an astonishing authority. Even in respose he seemed imper-

*From Grigoriev's papers (not his book) it would seem that 'L'Après-midi d'un faune' was given once in Rio, once in São Paulo and four times in Buenos Aires.

ceptibly to be dancing, like those luxuriously sprung carriages which used to be called 'huit-ressorts'.[307]

Milhaud noticed 'How beautiful he was when he turned to speak to someone behind his chair. He turned his head, but his head alone, so precisely and rapidly that he seemed not to have moved a muscle.'[308]

The Nijinskys made friends with a young couple in Rio, Estrade Guerra, the composer, and his pianist wife, Nininha, who used to pick them up in Vaslav's dressing-room after performances. Guerra noticed that Vaslav continued dancing after the curtain went down and Romola told him, 'Don't worry. Vaslav isn't mad. He can't stop suddenly after dancing like that; the heart must regain its normal rhythm by degrees.'[309] In later years Guerra recalled

Nijinsky spoke French fairly well, not with complete fluency, but well enough to carry on a conversation. He seemed on excellent terms with his wife. She was likeable and sympathetic; pretty, with delicate features and fine blue eyes. There were two dancers whom he admired above all others, Karsavina and his sister, Bronislava Nijinska. He did not compare them, however, since they were so different. Sometimes one felt there was something mystical about him, but that did not strike me as anything unusual. I assumed it was typical of the Slav character. He was certainly highly strung, but not abnormally so for an artist. Intelligent? Most decidedly so. One of his most endearing aspects was the rather childlike, natural side of his character, without the slightest pretension. He was certainly conscious of his worth and knew quite well what he was about, but he was totally without vanity. Neither in private life nor on the stage was there anything effeminate in his behaviour. He expressed a desire to leave the Russian Ballet to go his own way and said that in any case this South American tour was to be his last ... When I heard subsequently that Nijinsky had become insane, I was unable to believe it. Nothing in our meetings in Brazil could have led me to foresee that.[310]

The journey from Rio to São Paulo was by train, and the costumes and scenery were placed in a van immediately behind the engine. A flying spark ignited this carriage as the train was going through a tunnel and the décors for 'Le Spectre' and 'Cléopâtre' were completely destroyed.[311] Luckily the former was simple to reproduce. For 'Cléopâtre' Grigoriev decided to use the set for 'La Péri', which they were still lugging around with them although the ballet had never been produced.[312]* In São Paulo Nijinsky made friends with the head of the Research Institute, Calmette, a brother of the arch-critic of 'Faune';[313] and Lydia Sokolova, who had been six months pregnant when she last appeared on stage in Madrid – and who was included on this tour, through Diaghilev's kindness, as one of the staff – gave birth painfully and prematurely to a daughter on 1 September.[314]

The Ballet now sailed down the coast to Buenos Aires, where Vaslav and Romola stayed at the New Plaza. They had friends here; they met Pavlova, whose company were also on a South American tour; and on 10 September their fourth wedding anniversary was celebrated with a luncheon given by the priest who had married them.[315] The season at the Colón Theatre opened on the 11th and proved, wrote Grigoriev, 'one of the most trying I ever managed'. This was partly due to difficulties with the impresario, as a result of which Grigoriev refused to go on with one performance, and partly because there was little applause – the audience having become Europeanized and believing that clapping was vulgar.[316] There was also the constant friction between Nijinsky and the *régisseur*. It is clear that they disliked each other. Grigoriev would claim in his memoirs that Nijinsky was already mentally unbalanced, but this is denied by Romola, and from his happy association with Claudel, Milhaud, the Guerras and their many diplomatic friends it seems improbable. Romola accuses members of the company of causing a series of accidents (presumably with the knowledge of Grigoriev, though she does not accuse him directly), and believes they were instigated by Diaghilev.[317] This too sounds improbable.

One night Vaslav trod on a rusty nail on the stage; on another he had to leap out of the way of a heavy iron weight falling from the flies. 'Petrushka' was brought into the repertory in Buenos Aires, and at one of the four performances the puppets' booth was not securely fixed, so that when Nijinsky gestured from the top of it

---

*According to Haskell (*Balletomania*, p. 117, footnote) the décor for 'Contes russes' and the doors of the 'Schéhérazade' set were burnt; and 'Zverev painted a new set that was used for many years.'

at the Magician it collapsed and he had to dive into Cecchetti's arms. Romola was convinced that all these incidents were attempts to get from Nijinsky the penalty of 20,000 dollars which he incurred if he failed to fulfil his contract. Vaslav pitied his enemies, if they existed, and never blamed them. But Romola discussed the matter with her lawyer friend Quintana, who sent detectives to the theatre to watch over Nijinsky.[318]

The audience remained unaware of these goings-on and the season was a success. Nijinsky was dancing his usual roles in 'L'Après-midi', 'Schéhérazade', 'Narcisse', 'Les Sylphides', 'Le Spectre', 'Petrushka' and 'Cléopâtre'; he still captivated the public, and he was always inventing new 'business'. In 'Schéhérazade', which he now danced in silvery-grey make-up, 'the audience rose with a scream' – and Romola with it – at the Slave's death leap. 'In that final jump, Vaslav, with the briefest touch of his head on the floor, flung himself into the air by the action of his neck-muscles, quivered, and fell. I ran backstage, but there was Vaslav practising *entrechats*! So convincing had his execution been that we all thought he was hurt.'[319]

On 26 September, 1917 took place the last of the company's twenty-three* performances at Buenos Aires, and Nijinsky danced for what was to be the last time with the Diaghilev Ballet, appearing in 'Le Spectre' and 'Petrushka'. He had told the Guerras that he intended to leave the Russian Ballet – and according to Ansermet, he and Romola had an idea of staying on in South America to start a school;[320] but they were longing to see Kyra and made plans to return to Switzerland. Before doing so Vaslav helped to organize a Gala matinée in aid of the French and English Red Cross in Montevideo, and this was to keep him in the country a month longer than he intended. He went to the dock to see off the company on their voyage back to Europe.[321]

Determined on his gala for the Red Cross, Nijinsky arranged it with a new diplomat friend, André de Badet. Artur Rubinstein was on tour in South America, and he was called in to share the programme, while a local pianist, Domingo Dente, accompanied Nijinsky. Badet wrote:

*Françoise Reiss says eight (p. 171).

Vaslav had arranged some new dances for the Gala. Since only part of his stage wardrobe was available, he had to improvise his costumes, wearing the black velvet tunic and the white shirt and tights from 'Les Sylphides' with the pink slippers from 'Le Spectre de la rose' . . . How could we have imagined that evening when we saw him bound from the wings, soar diagonally across the vast stage in two prodigious leaps and vanish in full flight on a third, like a sylph whose natural element was the air, that Nijinsky was dancing for the last time in a theatre? . . . His small, rather Asiatic head was poised, proudly and languidly in turn, on the column of his neck, muscular as a sculpture by Donatello. Domingo Dente played for him pieces by Chopin, for some of which Vaslav had composed aerial choreography for that single evening.[322]

So in his last public performance Nijinsky used his God-given talent in the service of the wounded and sick.

CHAPTER EIGHT

1917–1950

November 1917–April 1950

At twenty-nine – though he did not know it – Nijinsky had danced
in public for the last time. His intention had always been to dance
until he was thirty-five, when he would still be in his prime, then
appear only in character roles, devoting himself to choreography
and to the foundation and running of a school where he would teach
other artists to compose ballets. He dreamed of a specially designed
theatre in which great festivals would be held and all performances
would be given *free*.[1] In this, as in so many other ways, his ideas were
ahead of his time. But it was not destined that Nijinsky should be
remembered as a schoolmaster or a festival director.

Nobody would ever see him, with declining years, give a performance which was less than perfect. Although tragedy awaited
him there was another kind of tragedy – that of diminishing powers
and fading inspiration – which he would be spared. He was to be
remembered as the unparalleled artist of the dance and a pioneer of
new forms. Sound in body and mind, he ceased to dance.

There were some who claimed or would claim in the light of
after events, when they wrote books many years later, that Nijinsky
had already shown signs of abnormality.[2] But he had never been
like other people, and it was easy for an enemy or a rival faction to
start the rumours that his nervousness, his reserve and his Tolstoyan
inclinations were symptoms of incipient mania. Grigoriev, writing
in the 1950s, described how, watching Nijinsky's final performance
with the company in Buenos Aires, he 'tried to impress on [his]
memory for the future a picture of his incomparable dancing . . .
being convinced that [he] was never to see him dance again'.[3] This

476

shows almost psychic intuition; and we are justified in suspecting an insertion by an editor and translator anxious to make the fact-crammed Russian chronicle more colourful in English. (It was perhaps this editor, my old friend Vera Bowen, who was responsible for describing the purely imaginary appearances of Pavlova and Chaliapine at the opening of the Russian season in Paris in 1909, the dancing of Nijinsky in 'Carnaval' in 1910, a year before he learned the role of Harlequin, Diaghilev's distress at the burning of Narodny Dom a month before the event, and Nijinsky's breach of a non-existent contract.)

We accept (not having ourselves been on the last South American tour) Mme Romola Nijinsky's account of the various accidents – the rusty nail, the falling scenery[4] – but Nijinsky did not mention these supposed attacks to her,[5] and it was she who enlisted legal and police help.[6] If the accidents were really accidents and not deliberate attacks on Nijinsky, it was his wife who was developing persecution mania and not he – and anyway, persecution mania is a symptom of paranoia and not of schizophrenia, the disease to which Nijinsky was to fall victim a year and a half later.

Rightly or wrongly, Vaslav and Romola felt that it was impossible for him to go on dancing with the Diaghilev Ballet. She thought that all the 'attacks', including that of Tolstoyan philosophy, were planned by Diaghilev. (She is entitled to her opinion, but one finds it hard to see why Diaghilev, however jealous, should set out to kill the goose that laid the golden eggs.) Still, it was Vaslav who took all decisions both regarding his career and his family.[7] He was undisputed master in his own house, and if he decided to leave Diaghilev it was probably mainly because of the latter's total absorption in Massine, not as a person but as a choreographer. When Diaghilev had begun to encourage Nijinsky as a choreographer, Fokine had felt that all the main opportunities would be given to the younger man: now Nijinsky felt the same about Massine. He was incapable of jealousy[8] and admired Massine's talent,[9] but he longed to create new ballets.

If Nijinsky *had* remained with Diaghilev during the last year of the war, spent by the company in Spain and Portugal, it is quite certain that Diaghilev would have been unable to pay him: for the

Ballet was to have increasing difficulty in getting engagements and would be on the point of disbanding out of sheer poverty when they were rescued by an invitation to the Coliseum by Oswald Stoll in 1918. As it was, Vaslav's isolation from the world of ballet may have been the principal cause of his mental breakdown.[10]

While the Diaghilev Ballet remained in the neutral peninsula, the Nijinskys, after sailing back from South America, made for neutral Switzerland to set up house for the first time in a home of their own. But before they looked for a house they had to see their child. On arrival in Lausanne they went at once to the sanatorium where Kyra had been staying, and Romola observed, 'It was remarkable how the child changed the moment Vaslav entered the room. It seemed almost as though they had been one person split apart, and constantly wishing to be reunited. Sometimes I almost felt as if I were intruding on them.'[11]

In Russia the second revolution had taken place. Karsavina, now married to the British diplomat, Henry Bruce, was in Petersburg.

On the morning of the 8th of November I saw cadets marching down the Millionaya towards the Winter Palace; the eldest of them might be eighteen. Sporadic shooting started in the afternoon. Loyal troops had barricaded the Winter Palace Square and the access from side streets. The chief fighting was round the telephone exchange. For several hours I sat holding the receiver to my ear ... I could follow the exchange changing hands many times. . . The other side of the river was cut off, all bridges up; a destroyer [the *Aurora*] faced the Palace from the Neva; the fortress was in the hands of the Bolsheviks ... The wine cellars all through the town were being looted ... It was a ballet night. I started from home soon after five. In about an hour's time I arrived at the theatre by many detours. By eight o'clock there was about one-fifth of the company at the theatre; after a short deliberation we decided to raise the curtain. The few performers on the vast stage were like the beginning of a jigsaw puzzle, a few clustered pieces here and there – the pattern had to be imagined. Still fewer people in the audience. A cannonade was faintly heard from the stage, quite plainly from the dressing-rooms. After the end some friends waited for me outside; we were going to supper with Edward Cunard, whose flat was opposite mine, near the Winter Palace. The square of the Mariinsky was free ... Pickets barred our street ... Cunard's flat was higher up the Millionaya than mine, only a hundred yards from the Palace

Square. Machine-guns rattled with renewed zest; I had an uncomfortable feeling that I might get hit in the shin-bone. At supper we could hardly hear ourselves speak – field-guns, machine-guns, rifle-fire were deafening. Cunard brought out a pack of cards . . . the candles burned down. A grey winter light stole through the curtains. The fighting had died down – only an occasional boom of gun-fire. We broke up, the men escorting the ladies to their respective homes. From my window I could see the barracks. A solitary figure in soldier's uniform crept from the shadow of the gate and started running towards the Champs de Mars; a shot and the figure fell in the snow. I drew the curtain. In the morning we had a new regime – Lenin was Prime Minister.[12]

The Diaghilev Ballet also found themselves in the middle of a revolution in Lisbon that winter: this was soon over, but it had a dampening effect on their season.[13]

Vaslav had never heard of Lenin or Trotsky and wondered that power should be entrusted to men who had lived so long abroad.[14]

In December 1917 the Nijinskys took the Villa Guardamunt in the mountains above St Moritz. Vaslav then returned to Lausanne alone to fetch Kyra. Such a solitary journey was a novelty to him. 'To book a room in a hotel and to buy a railway ticket were experiences unknown to him', but 'Vaslav was very proud, and was full of adventurous feeling starting out on his first trip alone.'[15] While he was away his wife began to arrange the villa.

Our house looked like a real home, with all our personal belongings. The entrance was full of skis and toboggans, as I had decided to take part in all the winter sports. The house overlooked St Moritz, and the lake lay at our feet. Opposite was the beautiful Roseg Alp and the Piz Margna that sheltered us from the eastern winds, and snow glittering, snow everywhere, seven feet deep, that promised us a glorious winter. Vaslav and Kyra arrived, and in a few days we had fallen into our daily routine. I wanted to attend to everything for Vaslav, but he refused. 'A man should not be served by his wife, *femmka*.' The wardrobe of an old maid could not have been more perfectly in order and more spotlessly clean than Vaslav kept his things.

The balcony on the ground floor was cleared. There, every morning, for two hours, Vaslav did his exercises, with Kyra looking on and patiently watching Tatakaboy* dance, and when he leaped she used to cheer and

*Tatakaboy was Kyra's name for her father.

clap her hands, then often Vaslav, forgetting his iron discipline, caught her in his arms and waltzed round singing, '*Votre amabilité, maia Kotyik, maia Funtyiki.*'*

Kyra Nijinsky, who remembers her father dancing at the Metropolitan Opera House, New York, 'flying across the stage in the moonlight, in a dark blue velvet costume with white satin sleeves like wings' (this would have been when she was three), has written the following reminiscence of their days together in Switzerland.

My father leaped and danced joyfully on our terrace at Villa Guardamunt. He used to lift me up on to the terrace balustrade and teach me how to point my toes like a ballerina. My father called me his 'little Camargo', because Camargo was not only a good dancer but also a good actress.

I sat at my father's feet while he painted in his room, and I tried to draw with coloured crayons too. Maybe memories of this later helped me to become not only a dancer but also a painter. I learned at that early age to respect creative art as a sacred activity – but these thoughts only come to me now.

I remember how good my father was to me from earliest childhood, when he used to push my pram, wash me, give me my bottle and play with me constantly. Later on I wondered why my attachment to him was so great. It was more than the natural love of a child for its father – some spiritual force bound us together in a God-given way. It seemed that I had been reared in a hot-house, like a flower which is loved, with my father by my side. His own childlike heart was turned like a sunflower towards God . . .[16]

Romola continued:

This winter was a very happy one. We were constantly together undisturbed, and went for long walks all over the Engadine. I used to practise on the Dimson skeleton run; it was my favourite sport. Vaslav was simply worshipped by the servants. If he met the cook on the way up to the villa, he carried the parcels. If the coal was too heavy to put on the fire, he helped the maid, and he even flirted with the old laundress, brought her chianti, and chatted to her of her native Italy. He would play with all the children of the village. Sometimes we used to meet for an *apéritif* before lunch at Hanselmann's, where everybody goes during the

*Funtyiki was Nijinsky's name for Kyra.

season. Hanselmann, an Austrian by origin, the well-known *confiseur* of St Moritz, quite a personality, played a leading part in the life of the place. He became a staunch friend of 'Monsieur Nijinsky'. Vaslav appreciated his *Käsestängel*, gave him recipes for *Koulibjak*, and sometimes discussed the political situation with him at length.

We often went, too, to Dr Bernhard's. His house was the last word in Engadine style, and was the meeting-place of many interesting Swiss and foreigners. Our neighbour, President Gartmann also entertained us.

Kyra was developing well, and looked lovely trotting beside Vaslav in her teddy-bear suit. They used to *luge* down the hill to Celerina at a breakneck speed. I was scared. 'Nothing will happen to my *amabilité* as long as we are together,' Vaslav used to say. The evenings we mostly spent quietly at home reading.

Vaslav accompanied me when I went skating, and, though he did not take part in any of the winter sports, he gave me remarkable advice on technique and balance. His instinctive knowledge was amazing.

Then Vaslav discovered sleighs that he could drive himself, and twice a week we would go off in the morning, the three of us, either picnicking or stopping at some roadside inn for lunch. We explored the glaciers, passes, and lakes of the Bernina. With the coming of the season many of our friends arrived from Paris and Vaslav seemed to be quite rested and soothed by the light-hearted gaiety of his *entourage*. As a surprise for me, he invited my sister and my brother-in-law Schmedes. Erik was a kind soul, and Vaslav had not forgotten his loyalty.

The spring came, and with it the foreigners departed; we were left alone again with the natives, whose life was quite patriarchal. It seemed remote and five centuries back to us. The celebrated sports centre had become a very quiet Alpine village again. In the evening, at the Hôtel Post, the notary, the Mayor and the doctor would meet to discuss the welfare of their little community. Vaslav loved to listen to their debate; it reminded him so much of Russia. We were so much in love with St Moritz that we did not wish to leave it even for a day.

The first timid crocuses pushed their way up and spring was officially here, but the torrents of melting snow kept us indoors more, and Vaslav resumed my lessons. He seemed lighter than ever; the number of his *pirouettes* and *entrechats* was infinite, and, watching him make his *battements* and *pliés*, it sometimes seemed to me that he was lighter than the snowflakes themselves. But his strength was of steel, and he bounded like india-rubber.

Practice or no practice, it was a strange thing for Nijinsky – no longer a prisoner of war – to spend a whole winter without appearing in a theatre. But his mind was active, and he was inventing.

He was full of ideas for new ballets. He composed a delightful version of Debussy's 'Chanson de Bilitis'. He said, 'I want you to dance Bilitis. I have created it for you. It obeys the same basic choreographic laws as the "Faune".' It was in perfect harmony with the movement of the music, with all its delicate feeling and sweet perversity. This ballet was in two scenes, the first Bilitis and her shepherd, their love, their youth on the green islands of Greece; the second, Bilitis and her girl lover, who shares her sorrows, and her pleasures.

Vaslav's other creation was his own life put into a choreographic poem: a youth seeking truth through life, first as a pupil, open to all artistic suggestions, to all the beauty that life and love can offer; then his love for the woman, his mate, who finally carries him off. He set it in the period of the High Renaissance. The youth was a painter; his master one of the greatest artists of the period, a universal genius, just as Diaghilev seemed to him to be. He designed the scenery and costumes for it himself, modern, and yet correct to the period. 'You know, *femmka*, the circle is the complete, the perfect movement. Everything is based on it – life, art, and most certainly our art. It is the perfect line.' The whole system of notation was based on the circle, and so was this ballet. It was in accordance with Vaslav's previous methods, but, unlike 'Faune' and 'Sacre', it was circular. The scenery was a design in curve, and even the proscenium opening was round. Vaslav worked out the whole design himself to the smallest detail, in blues, red and gold, Raphaelistic in style.

So the spring of 1918 found them isolated in their mountain retreat, while war and revolution raged around them.

Almost overnight our surroundings had changed. The frozen lake began to quiver, the slopes of the Alps, covered with fragrant flowers, had become a riot of colour, the pink alpen-roses, the sweet-smelling purple violets, and the cornflower-blue gentians. The snow retreated to the summits of the peaks, which were now so familiar to us and had each its own meaning for Vaslav. We used to run up to the Alp Giop and throw ourselves down among the flowers. And, while lying there in the scented pasture, we spoke of many things. I told Vaslav about my parents' unhappy marriage, and blamed my mother, but he stopped me. 'Don't be hard. You do not know the circumstances that made her act the way she did. We should never condemn anybody, nor have we the right to judge.' I often complained about the difficult times we were having to go through during the war, but Vaslav said, 'Do not look up to the more fortunate, look down to those worse off than yourself, and be thankful for your destiny.'

Romola had not been entirely well since Kyra's birth and she went into a Berne sanatorium for a minor operation. Vaslav arrived to visit her with his arms full of roses and spent a fortnight by her bedside. While in Berne he saw a dance recital by Clothilde and Alexander Sakharoff and told Romola 'You have missed nothing. It was merely attitudinizing, not dancing at all. *C'est du Munich.*' Romola saw that his artist's hunger to witness some new development was disappointed. But then Nijinsky had never really liked dance recitalists. In 1914 he and Romola had seen a solo recital by a Spanish dancer in London at the Savoy Theatre and commented, 'A dancer by himself is nothing, he has to have a frame. If the Almighty came down and danced from seven till eleven it would be boring.'[17]

In the autumn of 1918 Vaslav's patriarchal interest in household affairs showed itself in concern for laying in a good stock of fuel for the winter, and he helped chop the wood in the garden. He was always in and out of the kitchen, to the delight of the cook, lifting the lids of saucepans, and, if a cake was being baked, cleaning out the bowl with his finger as he had done as a child.

Kyra's Swiss nursery governess was married to a man who worked at the Palace Hotel. One day she was summoned to see him and on her return described with horror how he had been declared insane and taken off in a straitjacket. He had always been quite normal except for walking round the room for hours at night. When Romola told Nijinsky what had happened 'he became strangely silent and his face darkened'. The new governess, though Swiss, had been brought up in England and passed years in India, where she had studied *yoga*. In this, with his exploring mind, Vaslav became extremely interested.

This year [wrote Romola] the winter came early. When the snowing began, it went on for days and nights continuously. It was peaceful and warm; we seemed to be far away from the world, forgotten. The strange fascination of this isolated alpine village grew on us. In this sleepy whiteness, one morning the first news arrived from Bronia and '*Babouchka*'. They were well and did not need anything. They had received the money sent by Vaslav, but when the November Revolution took place they had fled to Kiev.

There was a letter enclosed for Romola, asking her to break the news to Vaslav that his brother Stanislav was dead. He had contracted pneumonia and Bronislava and her daughter Irina had visited him in the asylum a few days before his death.* Romola shirked her unpleasant duty for several days, knowing that Vaslav had loved his brother.

Finally I plucked up courage and went to him. He was drawing at the time. '*Regarde, femmka, ça c'est notre Kouharka* and this is Marie.' He showed me two lovely pastel portraits of the cook and the maid, transformed into Russian peasants, and a striking picture of Kyra. 'This is Funtyiki; you think it looks like her?'
I hated to spoil his happiness. 'Vaslav, I want to talk.' He sat down in the armchair, and I on the edge. Petting and caressing him, I buried my face on his shoulder, and said quickly, 'Stanislav is dead.' A long silence, then Vaslav lifted my face and asked how it happened. I told him, and burst into tears. He looked at me smiling, but with a strange and deep quietness. 'Do not cry; he was insane; it is better like this'; and he bowed his head. The same smile that he had had at his father's death came back again, and now I knew that Bolm had made a mistake, and that Vaslav was not heartless; on the contrary. But I felt it was strange – very strange.

Impresarios arrived at St Moritz with offers for Nijinsky, but they were all sent packing. Nijinsky would not dance until the war was over and he was free to plan his life in the way he wanted. Yet as winter came on, he was always busy composing choreography and designing. 'His drawings were all based on the circle, and he developed an amazing technique of producing portraits out of a few circles.' During the long winter evenings, at the suggestion of the new governess, they tried *séances* of table-turning and got some curious answers to their questions. This amused Vaslav.
Romola and Vaslav had worked out a system of arm signals whereby, as she returned from shopping in the town below, she

*Either Mme Romola Nijinsky did not understand the details of the letter exactly or she had forgotten them by the time she wrote her book. In this she states that the Soviet authorities had opened the doors of prisons and asylums, and that Stanislav, left to himself, had been burnt to death. Mme Bronislava Nijinska assures me that her elder brother died in bed from a liver complaint.

could relay him the latest war news. At last in November she was able to signal that an armistice had been suddenly and unexpectedly declared. Romola ran up the steps of the villa with a newspaper. But when Vaslav read the peace terms he shook his head. 'There can be no peace under those terms. War will go on, but in a hidden, different way.' So, with the instinctive and prophetic gift he had in common with certain other great artists, he saw in a flash something like the rise and fall of the Nazis and a second war – through which he and Romola were destined to live and suffer.

Diaghilev had finally succeeded – through the intercession of King Alfonso – in getting his company out of Spain and conveying them to London, where they had opened at the Coliseum on 5 September a season which was to last over six months. It was the first time Diaghilev had ever allowed his ballet to perform in a music-hall: they gave one ballet at each performance, sandwiched between Grock, the clown, and other turns.[18] Lady Ripon had died in 1917, but Juliet Duff and Lady Ottoline were in London to entertain Diaghilev, and he spent much time in the company of the Sitwell brothers, who were still in the Grenadier Guards. On 11 November Diaghilev and Massine dined with Osbert Sitwell in Swan Walk, Chelsea, and afterwards, before going on to a party in the Adelphi attended by the Bloomsbury group – including Maynard Keynes and Lydia Lopokhova, whom he would later marry – they walked in Trafalgar Square and watched the Londoners celebrating the peace. 'The crowd danced,' wrote Sitwell, 'under lights turned up for the first time for four years – danced so thickly that the heads, the faces, were like a field of golden corn moving in a dark wind . . . there were many soldiers, sailors and airmen in the crowd which, sometimes joining up, linking hands, dashed like the waves of the sea against the sides of the Square, against the railings of the National Gallery, sweeping up so far even as beyond the shallow stone steps of St Martin-in-the-Fields.' Diaghilev, 'bear-like in his fur-coat', gazed on these revels 'with an air of melancholy exhaustion'.[19] Massine later described his own feelings: 'Pushed and shoved in all directions by the ecstatic crowd, I remained curiously unmoved. A sense of calm came over me, and I felt that life could now resume its normal course.'[20]

485

A week later, on 18 November, the Diaghilev Ballet gave its thousandth performance.

That winter Nijinsky read and liked Nietzsche's *Ecce Homo*, which had been written at Sils Maria nearby, and Maeterlinck's *La Mort*. He planned yet another new and original ballet.

It was to be a picture of sex life with the scene laid in a *maison tolérée*. The chief character was to be the owner, once a beautiful *cocotte*, now aged and paralysed as a result of her debauchery; but, though her body was a wreck, her spirit was indomitable in the traffic of love. She deals with all the wares of love, selling girls boys, youth to age, woman to woman, man to man.

'But, Vaslav, how will you be able to express it?' He danced, and succeeded in transmitting the whole scale of sex life. 'I want to show the beauty and the destructive quality of love.'

The part of the old *procureuse* was intended for Réjane.

Nijinsky set about sketching the choreography for this unusual ballet in an even more unusual way. He instructed Romola to stand before him motionless for a few moments, to empty her mind of all thoughts and then begin to dance. She was surprised as he had always regarded improvisation as inartistic. He assured her that this would be different. Vaslav hypnotized her. Romola, who had always been interested in psychic experiments, was a good subject for hypnotism. 'After a certain time,' she wrote, 'I began to dance, strangely fascinated by Vaslav's oblique eyes, which he almost closed as if he wanted to shut out of himself everything else but my dancing. When I had finished, he said that I danced with a wonderful technique all the different parts of his newly composed ballet. . .' Romola was unaware of what she had been dancing, and every time she finished working with Nijinsky in this way she felt as if she were coming out of a trance and was irritable with the people around her. When she asked how he would develop the ballet he would not answer but fell into one of the long silences which were becoming more frequent with him. So the first draft of Nijinsky's last ballet – 'Les Papillons de nuit' he called it[21] – was danced out by his unconscious wife for the eyes of the choreographer alone.

Nijinsky decided that if it was impossible for him to return to Russia he would form his own company based on Paris, and would invite Massine to join it.[22] He asked Romola, who had once aspired to be the Vasari and chronicler of the art of her day, to put on record his artistic views.

They decided to celebrate the first Christmas of peace in style.

The 24th of December was passed in feverish preparations. The pine-tree, which went right up to the ceiling, was brought into the drawing-room and placed near the open fireplace. We adorned it ourselves: it was a beautiful heavily laden tree, full of candies, toys, silver nuts, and garlands, and on the top Vaslav himself placed a shining silver star – 'The tree for Kyroschka'. He looked it over with a critical glance. He wanted it to be very lovely, and so it was. We enjoyed preparing it. Vaslav had helped me to wrap up the presents neatly in silver paper; one for each of the household. Vaslav also remembered many children and sick people in the village, and we went round to take them their parcels.

Our Christmas Eve was a peaceful and happy one. Kyra's eyes opened wide when she saw the beautiful illuminated tree which Tatakaboy, as she called her father, lighted for her. Next morning I slept late, and was awakened by the maid, who came in trembling and as white as a sheet. 'Oh, madame, as I went into the drawing-room I found the Christmas-tree fallen on the floor. It means bad luck.' I shivered. '*Femmka, c'est bêtise*; it only means that it lost balance, was overladen on one side. I can't understand it; I made it so carefully.' We went down to see it. There it lay on the floor, the silver nuts all round and the silver star broken in two. We pulled it up, tied it, and I tried to forget the incident.

In spite of his apparently serene life with wife and child in a comfortable home among the mountains Nijinsky's mind was in a turmoil: it had suddenly become a whirlpool of unanswerable questions. What was the purpose of life? Why had he been born? Why did God allow war? He had no regular routine of physical, professional work in class-room or rehearsal-room or on stage to keep the dark thoughts at bay. Did he miss his mother, his sister, Russia? Did he long for the protective love of Diaghilev? Did the married state give him a sense of being trapped? Did he miss the ballet, the public, the applause? The pleasant trivialities of everyday life seemed meaningless and idiotic. On his long solitary walks and as he sat up late at night by himself gulfs yawned.[23]

My friend Dr Castillo, the Freudian analyst, has given me a

summary of what seems to him to have been Nijinsky's mental state at this time. Briefly, he contends that Nijinsky's schizophrenia had been latent for years (his brother's having developed in childhood). Schizophrenia (or *dementia praecox*, precocious madness) is a disease of adolescence. Diaghilev's care enabled Nijinsky for years to escape from the problems of real life. With the end of youth, with his marriage and with the separation from Diaghilev, Nijinsky was suddenly brought in touch with the realities he had never had to face, and this made him mad. I give Dr Castillo's diagnosis in full in the Appendix.

Nijinsky's mind was frantically busy. He invented a windscreen-wiper and an eversharp pencil. He pondered on mechanical problems and tried to simplify his system of dance notation. He bought quantities of paints and pastels. All this mental activity did not banish the black thoughts. Sometimes his wife would see him running, which she considered bad for the heart at such an altitude. Was he running to escape the horror in his mind?

Violent activity offered temporary relief. One Sunday it was decided that the family should sleigh over to Maloja. 'Kyra was glad,' wrote Romola, 'and Vaslav was very gay that morning.' But the excursion was disastrous and gave Romola her first indication that something was seriously wrong.

As it took us about three hours to get there, Kyra and I got very hungry during the long drive. The road was extremely narrow during the winter as it needed clearing from the heavy snows and in certain parts there was always a space to await the sleighs coming from the opposite direction. Vaslav was as a rule a careful and excellent driver, but on this particular Sunday he did not wait, but simply drove on into the oncoming sleighs. We were in danger of turning over as the horses got frightened. The coachmen cursed, but this did not make any difference. Kyra screamed, and I begged Vaslav to be more careful, but the further we went the more fiercely we drove against the other sleighs. I had to clutch on to Kyra and to the sleigh to keep ourselves on. I was furious, and said so to Vaslav. He fixed me suddenly with a hard and metallic look which I had never seen before. As we arrived at the Maloja inn I ordered a meal. We had to wait. Vaslav asked for some bread and butter and macaroni. 'Ah, Tolstoy again,' I thought, but did not say a word, and bit my lips. Kyra was anxiously awaiting her steak, and, as it was laid before her and she began to eat, Vaslav, with a quick gesture, snatched the plate away. She began to cry from disappointment. I exclaimed, 'Now, Vaslav, please don't begin that Tolstoy-Kostrovsky nonsense again; you remember how weak you got by starving yourself on that vegetarian diet. I can't stop you doing it, but I won't allow you to interfere with Kyra. The child must eat properly.' I went with Kyra to the other room to have our solitary lunch. We drove home very quietly without a word.

Vaslav decided to take part in the winter sports.

We attended the ski-jumps [wrote Romola], the bobsleigh and the skeleton races. We went riding and ski-ing. At the first lesson Vaslav asked our teacher to show him how to brake to stop, and the same morning he made telemarks. 'Well, well, the gentleman only needs a few corrections,' said the teacher, as Vaslav sailed down the slopes. 'He is of course a practised skier.' 'What do you mean! It is the first time he has had skis on.' 'Remarkable, such perfect balance; he bends his knees just perfectly, with the elasticity of a practised skier. You are fooling me.' But I was not surprised that Vaslav was so good; his wonderful training helped him in all sports.

... Vaslav took a liking to skeleton running, though I thought it was too dangerous a sport and told him so, but he was so proficient after a few hours' practice that I could not object. Skeleton running is done in a narrow ice-run built on the slopes of the Alps, with dangerous curves. The speed is terrific, as the skeleton is made out of steel and the person lies head downwards on the skeleton, which is guided by the displacing of the balance. Vaslav became brilliant in its execution. Very soon he asked me if I wanted to go down with him, lying as a dead weight on top of him. I loved it, and I had faith in Vaslav, but, even so, I had to shut my eyes when we went flying through the run. Sometimes he took Kyra down, and I could only stand and pray until they arrived safely in the valley.

But Nijinsky could not for long escape from his inner gloom, because he was in a state of nervous breakdown. Out walking with Romola he sometimes stopped and stood brooding for what seemed a long time, disregarding any questions she put to him.

One Thursday, when the governess and maid had their day off, Romola had an even more alarming experience than the expedition to Maloja.

I was making ready to take Kyra out for a walk when suddenly Vaslav came out of his room and looked at me very angrily. 'How dare you make such a noise? I can't work.' I looked up, surprised. His face, his manner were strange; he had never spoken to me like this. 'I am sorry. I did not realize we were so loud.' Vaslav got hold of me then by my shoulders and shook me violently. I clasped Kyra in my arms very close, then with one powerful movement Vaslav pushed me down the stairs. I lost my balance, and fell with the child, who began to scream. I stood up, more astounded than terrified. What was the matter with him? I was unaware of having done anything wrong. He was still standing there menacingly. I turned round, exclaiming, 'You ought to be ashamed! You are behaving like a *moujik*.' A very changed Vaslav we found when we came home, docile and kind as ever. I did not speak about the incident, either to him or to anybody else.

Nijinsky was turning out drawings at lightning speed until the floors of his study and other rooms were littered. It was no longer portraits or scenic designs that he produced, but strange eyes in red and black. 'What are these masks?' asked Romola. 'Soldiers' faces. War!'

Then he began to put down his thoughts in a diary. This he would not show Romola.

One day Romola went into the kitchen and noticed that the three servants seated round the table broke off their conversation and looked at her oddly. 'What has happened?' she asked. The young man who stoked the boiler said, 'Madame, forgive me; I may be wrong. We all love you both. You remember I told you that at home in my village at Sils Maria as a child I used to do errands for Mr Nietzsche? I carried his rucksack when he went to the Alps to work. Madame, he acted and looked, before he was taken away, just like Mr Nijinsky does now. Please forgive me.' 'What do you mean?' Romola cried; and Kati, the laundress, broke in excitedly: 'Mr Nijinsky is walking in the village wearing a big golden cross over his necktie, and is stopping everybody in the streets asking them if they have been to mass and sending them to church. He just spoke to me.' Romola ran down to the village and saw Vaslav stopping the passers-by.

I got hold of his hands [she wrote]. He seemed embarrassed at seeing me. 'What are you doing? What is this new nonsense? Vaslav, won't you stop imitating that old lunatic Tolstoy? You are making yourself into a laughing-stock.' He looked like a punished child, very sad. 'But *femmka*, I did not do anything wrong. I just asked if they had been to church.' I pointed to Kyra's big golden Florentine cross. 'And what is this?' 'Well, if you don't like it – ' and he took it off. 'The world imitates me; all the foolish women copy my ballet costumes. They make their eyes seem oblique, and it becomes the mode, only because nature gave me high cheekbones. Why can't I teach them something useful, lead them to remember God. Why can't I set the fashion, since I do set fashions, that they should seek the truth?'

Romola could see the logic of this, but felt that he was putting his ideas into practice in an eccentric way.

Returning from another excursion, wearing his cross, Vaslav drove the sleigh so fast that he overturned it and threw Romola and Kyra into the snow. Romola remonstrated angrily with him and went home on foot with the child.

Of course he was home ahead of us. When I entered the house, the servant, who worshipped Vaslav, opened the door and said, 'Madame, I think Monsieur Nijinsky is ill, or perhaps very drunk, for he acts so queerly. His voice is hoarse and his eyes all hazy. I am frightened.' 'Don't be silly, Marie. He never drinks, you know. Artists have moods, but ring up the doctor and say I need him for Kyra, and put her to bed at once.' I went to our bedroom. Vaslav lay fully dressed on the bed, with the cross on, his eyes closed. He seemed to be asleep. I turned cautiously towards the door, and then noticed that heavy tears were streaming down his face. '*Vatza, qu'est-ce que tu as? Vatza, ne sois pas fâché.*' 'It is nothing; let me sleep; I have a dreadful headache.' He had had many of those lately.

On the pretext of Kyra having a chill Romola consulted the doctor, who stayed to tea and had a talk with Vaslav. He diagnosed 'a slight case of hysteria' and sent them a male nurse, who was to pretend to be a *masseur*, to keep Vaslav under observation. Romola noticed that Vaslav gave her 'a long, understanding look' when she introduced this man, but he made friends with him and they went for walks and drives together. For a time he seemed much more cheerful, played hide-and-seek with Kyra, and built snowmen in the garden.

At lunch one day, however, he announced that he had decided to give up dancing for ever and intended to farm in Russia.

I lost my temper [wrote Romola]. 'If you go you go alone. I have had enough; I can't become a peasant. I was not born one. Even if I love you I will divorce you and marry some manufacturer.' And in my bad temper I took off my marriage-ring, the heavy golden Brazilian circle, and ungraciously hurled it at Vaslav. He seemed very surprised. In the afternoon I received a huge bouquet of about five hundred carnations, with the ring in it.

At Nijinsky's suggestion Romola had asked her sister Tessa to stay, and her visit was marked by an increase of social activity. Vaslav spent thousands of francs on scent, shoes and sweaters, and accompanied the ladies to dances, dinners and ski-races. The Durcals arrived from Spain and invited them to tea. Asked what he had been doing lately, Vaslav put on a worldly air, leaned back nonchalantly on the sofa and said, 'Well, I composed two ballets, I prepared a new programme for the next Paris season, and lately I have played a part. You see, I am an artist; I have no troupe now, so I miss the stage. I thought it would be rather an interesting experiment to see how well I could act, and so for six weeks I played the part of a lunatic, and the whole village, my family, and even the physicians apparently believed it. I have a male nurse to watch me, in the disguise of a *masseur*.' Romola was overcome, torn between anger and relief. She was confirmed in her supposition that her fears had been groundless when the male nurse came, after ten days, to assure her from his long experience that Nijinsky was completely sane.

Nijinsky was watching the champion skaters practising, with Kyra seated in the sleigh beside him, when he spoke to a young stranger, Maurice Sandoz (who later became an author), who has recorded the occasion. Nijinsky was wearing a dark suit and a sealskin cap with a large copper crucifix hanging from his neck. He asked Sandoz, 'Can you tell me the name of this skater?' 'He's called Vadas. He comes from Budapest.' 'His skating comes from the heart, which is good.' 'Yes, there are greater virtuosi than him on the skating-rink, but no one so graceful.' 'Grace comes from God; the rest can be acquired by work.' 'But cannot grace also be acquired by work?' 'Grace which is learnt goes so far and no further. Inborn grace has no limits.'[24]

In Nijinsky's mind it seems that *die Gnade* and *die Anmut*, for which in French and English the same word serves, were one: that to him the Grace of God was the same as – or related to – that quality of which Leonardo wrote 'It is the extremities which lend grace to the limbs.' Perhaps he was right.[25]

The arrival of some Viennese friends, and particularly of the pianist Bertha Gelbar, Mme Asseo, decided Nijinsky to give a recital. This would be for an invited audience and there would be a collection for the Red Cross. All the hotel ballroom floors were of course polished parquet and therefore unsuitable, but in the Suvretta House Hotel, which Romola thought looked like an enchanted castle rising from the pine forests, Vaslav found a room which would do. He refused to say what he intended to dance, stating merely 'New creations', and set about making his costumes with the aid of an Italian dressmaker.

Shortly before five o'clock on the day of the recital, 19 January 1919, Vaslav, Romola and Negri, the dressmaker, drove to Suvretta House.

Vaslav was silent, just as before going to the theatre. I knew this mood and respected it. Before arriving at the Suvretta, I ventured to ask, 'Please tell me what Bertha Asseo must play for you.' 'I will tell her at the time. Do not speak. *Silence!*' he thundered at me. 'This is my marriage with God.' A slight uneasiness crept over me. Vaslav looked so menacing, so dark, in his fur-collared coat, with his Russian fur cap.

In this last recital, which began so embarrassingly that everybody remembered it differently, and went on to become so alarming, Nijinsky gave proof both of his genius and his madness. Never, perhaps, in history had an artist demonstrated so clearly how close the two are to each other.

About two hundred people, some uninvited, were seated on rows of chairs facing the empty space where Vaslav was to dance. Bertha Asseo was at the piano.

A little Greek boy staying at the hotel, whose mother had dressed him up to hand round refreshments at this charity performance, was never to forget the alarm and embarrassment caused by Nijinsky standing silent, staring at the audience, for what seemed hours on end. This was Costa Achillopoulos, who later became a distinguished photographer and a friend of mine.[26]

According to one account, Nijinsky first told his accompanist '*Jouez du Chopin*', then stopped her and said '*Non, jouez du Schumann*'.[27] Maurice Sandoz describes it differently. He remembered Nijinsky beginning with an interpretation of Chopin's Prelude No. 20 in C minor.

To each chord struck by the pianist he made a corresponding gesture. First he stretched out both arms in an attitude of defence, the palms of his hands raised vertically; then he opened his arms in a gesture of welcome, raised them in a movement of supplication then, to the fourth and fifth chords, let them fall noisily as if the joints were broken ... He repeated the movements for every sequence up to the final chord.

Then Nijinsky danced a number in the aerial style expected of him, and at the end of it placed his hands on his heart and said, 'The little horse is tired.'[28]

According to Romola

Vaslav entered in his practice kit, and, taking no notice of the public, went up to Bertha, and said, 'I will tell you what to play.' I was standing near the piano. There was an air of great expectation. 'I will show you how we live, how we suffer, how we artists create.' And he picked up a chair, sat down on it facing the audience, and stared at them, as if he wanted to read the thoughts of each. Everybody waited silently as if in church. They waited. The time passed. We must have been like this for about half an hour. The public behaved as if they were hypnotized by Vaslav. They sat completely motionless. I got rather nervous as I caught a glance of Dr Bernhard, who was standing in the background, and his expression confirmed me in the belief that my suspicion was justified. Vaslav was again in one of his strange dark moods. Bertha began as a prelude the first few bars of 'Sylphides', then 'Spectre'. She hoped to call Vaslav's attention to one of his dances. Perhaps then he would begin. I felt quite upset, and wanted to relieve the tension. I went over to Vaslav. 'Please won't you begin? Dance "Sylphides".' 'How dare you disturb me! I am not a machine. I will dance when I feel like it.' I fought desperately not to burst out crying. Never had Vaslav spoken to me this way, and before all these people! I could not bear it, and left the room. Mr Asseo and my sister joined me. 'What is happening? What is the matter with Nijinsky?' 'I do not know. I want to take him home. What shall we do?' We went in again, but by this time Vaslav was dancing – gloriously but frighteningly. He took a few rolls of black and white velvet and made a big cross the length of the room. He stood at the head of it with open arms, a living cross himself. 'Now I will dance you the war, with its suffering, with its destruction, with its death. The war which you did not prevent and so you are also responsible for.' It was terrifying.

Vaslav's dancing was as brilliant, as wonderful as ever, but it was different. Sometimes it vaguely reminded me of that scene in 'Petrushka' when the puppet tries to escape his fate. He seemed to fill the room with horror-stricken suffering humanity. It was tragic; his gestures were all monumental, and he entranced us so that we almost saw him floating over corpses. The public sat breathlessly horrified and so strangely fascinated. They seemed to be petrified. But we felt that Vaslav was like one of those overpowering creatures full of dominating strength, a tiger let out from the jungle who in any moment could destroy us. And he was dancing, dancing on. Whirling through space, taking his audience away with him to war, to destruction, facing suffering and horror, struggling with all his steel-like muscles, his agility, his lightning quickness, his ethereal being, to escape the inevitable end. It was the dance for life against death.

Romola's description recalls Marie Rambert's account of the tragic power Nijinsky showed when he demonstrated the dance of the Chosen Virgin to Piltz at Monte Carlo.

After Nijinsky's last dance tea was served.

That night he wrote in his *Diary*:

I want to live a long time, my wife loves me very much. She is afraid for me today – I acted very nervously. I behaved this way on purpose because the public understands me better when I am vibrating. They do not understand artists who are placid. One has to be nervous. I offended the pianist Gelbar. I wish her well, but I was nervous. God wanted the public to be in a state of excitement. The public came to be amused and thought I danced for their amusement. My dances were frightening. They were afraid of me, thinking I wanted to kill them. I did not. I loved everybody but nobody loved me and I became nervous and excited: the audience caught my mood. They did not like me, they wanted to go away. Then I started to do a joyful, merry dance, and they began to enjoy themselves. First they thought I was a dull actor but I showed them that I could do merry things. The audience began to laugh when I did. I was laughing in my dance. The audience laughed – they had understood my dance and felt like dancing too.

I danced badly; I fell when I should not have. The audience did not care because my dancing was beautiful. They felt my mood and enjoyed themselves. I wanted to go on dancing but God said to me: 'Enough.' I stopped.[29]

From now on Romola foresaw the end. There had been talk of whether she was fit to have another child: they both wanted a son. 'Cannot you find a man like Lombroso to examine us both?' Vaslav had asked. He wanted to be sure their child would be born fit both physically and mentally. And he felt the need of talking over with some wise man the trouble inside his head. Now Romola told him she had found a man as great as Lombroso – Professor Bleuler, the famous psychiatrist in Zürich. She made an appointment. Her mother and stepfather came from Budapest.

I am going away to Zurich. I do not want to do anything before my departure. Everybody is nervous. The maids have become stupid because they do not feel God. I feel Him, but I have not become stupid. I do not want to crack, but to say the truth. Oscar is telephoning to Zurich. He is afraid that people will not understand his name. He feels that nobody knows his name there and so he wants to make them understand it. His name is Pardany, and he pronounces it with an accent on every syllable. I do not care whether people know my name or not, and I am not afraid that people will not love me if they find out that I am poor.

When I was at school I used to shut myself in, pretending I was ill, so that I could read. I used to lie down and read, quietly. I want to write about the departure for Zurich, everybody is nervous because I did not care. I thought this journey was absurd, but I will go because God wants it. But if He did not wish it, I would remain. I am beginning to understand God. I know that he creates movement, and so I ask Him to help me . . .

My wife came to me and told me to tell Kyra that I would not come back any more. My wife's eyes were full of tears and she said, trembling, that she would not leave me. I cried. God did not wish us to separate. I told her that.

I would not remain in Zurich if my wife is not frightened of me; but if she is afraid I would rather be in an asylum, as I fear nothing. Her soul was weeping. I felt my heart ache and said again that if she is not afraid of me I will come home again. She started crying and kissed me, saying that she and Kyra would never leave me whatever happens to me. I said, 'Very well.' She understood me and went away . . .

I will go to Zurich and will see the town, which is a commercial town, and God will be with me.[30]

They travelled to Zürich by train. Romola wrote

I went alone to see Professor Bleuler. Vaslav did not want to accompany me. Bleuler was an old man with an infinite understanding in his eyes. I spoke to him about Vaslav, myself, our marriage, and life for almost two hours. 'Very, very interesting, all you tell me. I can assure you there is nothing the matter with you, my dear. Anyhow, we do not become insane; we are born it. I mean, the disposition is there. Genius, insanity, they are so near; normality and abnormality, there is almost no border between the two states. I should like to meet your husband; extremely interesting. If you spoke of any other man I might be worried, but the symptoms you describe in the case of an artist and a Russian do not in themselves prove any mental disturbance.' I was relieved, and came home happily. I told Vaslav how nice Bleuler was and that he thought I was healthy and that we could now have a son, and that he would like to make his acquaintance. Vaslav agreed, 'Of course, so would I; he seems interesting. I was quite sure everything was all right. After all, *femmka*, I was brought up in the Imperial School, and we were there under constant medical supervision. Since I left there, except for my typhoid, I have never been seriously ill.' In a happy mood, we went out shopping, and I noticed that Vaslav stopped before the window of a great departmental store where babies' layettes were exposed; he smiled, and I knew he was thinking of the son he so ardently desired.

Next day, about three in the afternoon, we drove across the bridge on the Lake of Zurich to the hilly side, where in a wood at a little distance the State asylum is built, a big old-fashioned building with iron-barred windows. But the smiling porter and the flowers which surrounded the directorial building, where Professor Bleuler received, took away the disagreeable impression. We sat for a few moments and then the professor came out. I introduced him to Vaslav, and they both disappeared in his study. Calmly I looked over the illustrated papers lying round: the *Illustration*, the latest numbers of the *Sketch* and *Graphic*. I was relieved that all this unnecessary anxiety was over; at last everything would be all right. We had had such a hard time these first six years of our marriage – the fight with Diaghilev, war prisoners, all the disillusion; but now at last the happy time would commence. The door opened within ten minutes, and the professor showed out Vaslav smilingly. 'All right. Splendid. Won't you step in for a second? I forgot to give you the promised prescription yesterday.' I smiled at Vaslav as I passed him, following the professor; what prescription I could not remember. As he closed the door of his study behind him, he said very firmly, 'Now, my dear, be very brave. You have to take your child away; you have to get a divorce. Unfortunately, I am helpless. Your husband is incurably insane.' I thought the sunray which passed through the window above the head of the professor was curiously full of dust. Why did he have that huge green table in the middle of the room? And those inkstands were irritatingly round – a circle; oh, yes, the Circle. That awful, that merciless circle of misfortune. I was vaguely hearing him ask me to forgive him for being so hard. 'I must seem to be brutal, but I have to be to be able to save you and your child – two lives. We physicians must try to save those whom we can; the others, unfortunately, we have to abandon to their cruel fate. I am an old man. I have sacrificed fifty years of my life to save them. I have searched and studied; I know the symptoms; I can diagnose it; but I don't know, I wish I could help, but do not forget, my child, that sometimes miracles happen.'

I did not listen; I had to get out of there quickly. I felt the place was going round with me faster and faster in a circle. I dashed through the door to the room where Vaslav was waiting. He stood near the table looking absentmindedly at the illustrated papers, pale, strangely sad, in his Russian fur coat with his Cossack cap. I stopped and looked; it seemed as though his face was growing longer under my gaze, and he slowly said, '*Femmka*, you are bringing me my death-warrant.'

Nijinsky's condition was diagnosed as schizophrenia. Romola tried to think of some way in which she could care for Vaslav without having him confined in an asylum.

The idea that Vaslav was pronounced insane made [my parents] lose their heads completely. As they were unsuccessful in persuading me to seek a divorce, they decided to take our lives in their hands. My mother took me out for a walk, and, while we were away – Vaslav being still in bed, waiting for his breakfast – the police ambulance, called in by my panic-stricken parents, came, and the Hôtel Baur en Ville was surrounded by the fire brigade to prevent Vaslav's jumping out of the window, should he attempt it. They knocked at his door. Vaslav, thinking it was the waiter, opened, and was immediately seized. They tried to carry him out in his pyjamas. Vaslav, as I learned from the manager, asked, 'What have I done? What do you want of me? Where is my wife?' They insisted that he should come, and the doctor, seeing his quietness, asked the nurses to release him. Vaslav thanked him, and said, 'Please let me dress, and I will follow you.' When I came back at noon, I found his room deserted.

Desperately I ran to Professor Bleuler, who helped me to find him. He was in the State asylum among thirty other patients, but, by that time, Vaslav, owing to the shock, had had his first catatonic attack. Professor Bleuler deeply regretted this unfortunate incident, which brought on the acute development of the illness, which, under different circumstances, might have remained stationary. On his advice, Vaslav was taken to the Sanatorium Bellevue Kreuzlingen, where he not only found admirable care but kind-hearted friends in the Dr Binswangers.

Professor Bleuler had invented the word 'schizophrenia' in 1911 to describe a certain kind of mental disorder 'characterized by autistic thinking' – that is to say, a condition in which the patient is absorbed in wish-fulfilling fantasy as a means of escape from reality. This term was adopted as being more appropriate than *dementia praecox*.[31]

Diaghilev received the news of Nijinsky's illness in London. From the time years before when he had consulted Dr Botkine about his friend's health, he had believed that the threat of insanity was hanging over Vaslav: but in his usual manful way, he had kept this worry to himself. Now he admitted to Massine that he was not surprised that the blow had fallen, only that it had fallen so soon.[32] Marie Rambert, who had made her home in London since before the war and was married to the playwright Ashley Dukes, heard the news over tea with Diaghilev and Massine at the Ritz, and was surprised at Diaghilev's lack of distress when he told her Nijinsky was 'walking on all fours'.[33] But Rambert had always been emotionally demonstrative, and we can imagine that Diaghilev, having absorbed the shock in private, would be averse to joining in with anyone else's tears.

Leonide Massine, still no more than twenty-four, had developed into a most original versatile choreographer; and his ballets, the fruit of wartime research and work, were being shown for the first time to London, along with works from the pre-war Fokine repertory, as part of the afternoon and evening mixed programmes at the Coliseum music-hall. Diaghilev had been reluctant to present his company under these conditions, but he had no choice if they were to survive, and the Russians proved popular, filled the house and captured a new audience. Lopokhova was now the star, and as Mariuccia in Massine's Italian ballet, called in England 'The Good-Humoured Ladies', and in 'The Midnight Sun', she proved irresistible to the English. 'Children's Tales' ('Contes russes'), which had evolved from 'Kikimora', now comprised three separate episodes to the music of Liadov, with Sokolova as the witch Kikimora and Idzikovsky as her cat, with Kremnev as the demon Baba Yaga and with Massine as the Knight Bova Koralevitch and Tchernicheva as the beautiful Swan Princess. Sokolova, herself a principal dancer now, noticed how whenever Diaghilev watched Idzikovsky as the cat he laughed till the tears streamed down his face.[34] This ballet was so popular that Stoll asked Diaghilev to give it as often as possible.[35]

Although the 'Italian' ballet and the two Russian folk ballets just mentioned were designed by Bakst and the more *avant-garde* Larionov, Diaghilev was beginning to turn to painters of the School of Paris for his décors. Picasso, with his 'Parade' in 1917, had been the first. Now he showed London 'Cléopâtre' in the new set of Robert Delaunay; and Charles Ricketts disapproved. 'The hideous setting was by the post-Impressionist round the corner, pink and purple columns, a pea-green Hathor cow, and yellow pyramids with a green shadow with a red spot. . . Massine dances well. . . He is stark naked save for rather nice bathing-drawers, with a huge black spot on his belly. Two or three idiot girls in the gallery shrieked with laughter when he came on.'[36]

In the spring the Diaghilev Ballet, after a fortnight in Manchester, moved to the Alhambra in Leicester Square for a proper season; and it was here that Massine scored his greatest success to date with 'La Boutique fantasque', danced to the sunny tunes of Rossini in André Derain's *faux-naïf* set, with himself and Lopokhova in the can-can.

Karsavina, having made her last appearance at the Mariinsky – in 'La Bayadère' on 15 May, 1918 – braved exceptional perils to escape with her husband to England. Thence they had gone *en poste* for nine months to Tangier. Re-united with Diaghilev, she told him how the extra day he had asked her to stay in London after the 1914 season had cost her months of wandering.[37] Under the tuition of a Flamenco dancer, Felix Fernandez Garcia, engaged in Spain, Massine had become an expert on Spanish dancing, and he was working on his masterpiece 'Le Tricorne', which it was intended that Karsavina should dance. 'Our first collaboration in "The Three-cornered Hat",' wrote Karsavina, 'showed him to be a very exacting master. . . On the Russian stage we had been used to a balletic stylization of Spanish dancing, sugary at its best: but this was the very essence of Spanish folk dancing.'[38] It is curious that, so soon after Nijinsky had lost his reason, the simple Andalusian Felix, who had hoped to dance his *farucca* in the Spanish ballet himself, but who could neither stick to the strict *tempi* of a musical score nor adapt himself to the regulated life of a ballet company,[39] went out of his mind that summer and was discovered one night dancing on the altar steps of St Martin's-in-the-Fields. Karsavina and Massine danced the principal roles in 'The Three-cornered Hat' in Picasso's wonderful set at the Alhambra on 22 July.

Now began for Romola Nijinsky thirty years of hope, despair, struggle, poverty and heroism. During the six months Vaslav was in Kreuzlingen she and the doctors entertained hopes of his recovery, but this was not to be; at the end of that time he grew worse, had hallucinations, was violent and refused food. The courageous Romola decided to try the experiment of taking him home, thinking it possible that familiar surroundings might have a beneficial effect. This necessitated day- and night-nurses under the constant supervion of doctors, and was expensive. Vaslav had his good days and his bad, but there was no real improvement in his condition.

In Switzerland Romola took her husband to be examined by Professor Jung and Professor Forel. Then, moving to Vienna, she consulted Professor Wagner-Jauregg, who told her that 'as long as a schizophrenic has periods of agitation there is a hope for an improvement towards normalcy.' Sigmund Freud said that psycho-analysis was useless in cases of schizophrenia. Romola kept Vaslav with her at home in Vienna most of the time. Only when he became very difficult to manage did she take him to the Steinhof Sanatorium. Once when she was briefly out of the country her parents committed him to the State Asylum outside Budapest, where he was badly treated. Romola hurried home and took him back to Austria.

On 14 June 1920 Romola gave birth – in the same room in the same clinic in Vienna where Kyra was born, and with the same doctor attending – to a second daughter, whom she called Tamara.[40]

In 1920 Diaghilev decided to revive 'Le Sacre du printemps', of which he still had the sets and costumes, used only seven times before the war. As nobody could remember Nijinsky's choreography Massine worked out a new version. Of this Grigoriev thought it 'lacked pathos, in which it differed notably from Nijinsky's'.[41] Sokolova gave a powerful rendering of the Chosen Virgin, Ansermet conducted; and it was clear the music had become acceptable, respectable and even a classic. Shortly after this Massine fell in love with a pretty, talented English dancer in the company, who had been given the name of Vera Savina. The pattern repeated itself and Diaghilev dismissed him as he had dismissed Vaslav seven years before.[42] This was cutting off his nose to spite his face, for with Russia isolated, with Fokine in New York and Nijinsky insane, Diaghilev was without a choreographer. He determined on an experiment at variance with all his other experiments, namely a return to tradition: he would mount one of the old classical ballets, against which his whole movement had been a revolt. He decided to revive the Petipa-Tchaikovsky 'La Belle au bois dormant', to be called 'The Sleeping Princess', at the London Alhambra in the winter of 1921, and to put it on for a run in the hopes of emulating the success of the musical comedy, 'Chu-chin-chow'. Bakst was summoned, and began designing several sets and hundreds of costumes.

At this time, Diaghilev met a young Russian, Boris Kochno, who became his secretary and was to write the libretti of later ballets.[43]

Bronislava had been running a school in Kiev since the Revolution and in 1921 she escaped with her mother and children to Vienna. Here Eleonora and Bronia saw Vaslav again, but he showed no sign of recognition.

Bronislava then joined Diaghilev in London and set about arranging some new dances for 'The Sleeping Princess', notably 'The Ivans' to the music of the coda of the *Grand pas de deux*.

For three years she was to be choreographer to the company. In spite of the splendour of the production of the big Tchaikovsky ballet, and in spite of the presence of three wonderful expatriate ballerinas, Spessivtseva, Trefilova and Egorova, as well as Lopokhova, who took turns to dance the role of Aurora, supported by Pierre Vladimirov, the regular ballet audience was disappointed and the general public stayed away. 'The Sleeping Princess' was not a success and was withdrawn after 105 performances. Furthermore, Diaghilev had spent so much more of Oswald Stoll's money on it than he should have done that Stoll seized all the scenery and costumes, which made it impossible for Diaghilev to present the ballet in Paris or elsewhere.

It was at this low ebb in the Russian Ballet's affairs that the resilient Diaghilev came to an arrangement with the Monte Carlo Casino which would give his company a measure of security for the remaining years of its existence. Every winter the Russians would provide dancers for the Monte Carlo opera season, and would hold their own spring ballet season there before going on to Paris. These settled periods several months long would give them leisure to rehearse new works.

In 1923 Romola rented a flat in Paris at 50, Avenue de la Bourdonnais, near the Eiffel Tower. The experiment was made of taking Vaslav to the theatre, to the ballet and to watch Cossack dancers in a night-club, but the signs of interest he showed were soon over and he relapsed into his silent lethargic state again. When Romola was away, her sister Tessa kept house for Vaslav. Eleonora and Bronislava took a flat together in Paris.

Diaghilev came to see Nijinsky. This was the first time he had set eyes on him since they had parted in wrath in Barcelona six years before. He was met by a vacant stare. 'Vatza, you are being lazy. Come, I need you. You must dance again for the Russian Ballet and for me.' Vaslav shook his head. 'I cannot because I am mad.'

On 13 July 1923, Stravinsky's 'Les Noces', begun when the ink of 'Le Sacre' was hardly dry on his pen, was presented at last on the stage – at the Gaieté-Lyrique in Paris; and the choreography, instead of being by Nijinsky, as Diaghilev had intended in the old days, was by his sister.

The music which had been an extraordinary conception in 1916 when Stravinsky began to compose it, became even more extraordinary as he scored it between 1918 and 1923, and there has been nothing quite like it since. The preparations for a peasant wedding and its consummation were conveyed in snatches of song, now commonplace, now poetic, and invocations to the saints, drunken interjections and certain conventional remarks by parents and guests so traditional in Russian village life as to constitute a kind of indispensable liturgy. How strange – yet how typical of our century – that Stravinsky felt the need of this banal gibberish as the basis for his solemn music, in the way that Schwitters made grand compositions from a collage of bus-tickets! By this means all the nineteenth-century sentiment and sweetness about the idea of marriage were abolished with one blow. This marriage was like a death. The spoken and sung words had originally been intended to have heavy scoring like 'Le Sacre', but after a long process of brooding and elimination Stravinsky made the work a canata with percussion, four pianos and a great bell to toll at the end. Gontcharova's sets were blank walls, the last with a door through which a bed was seen, heaped with pillows. Her monochrome peasant uniforms in brown and white emphasized the universality of the two families and their friends, whom Nijinska piled up into epic groups and set going in a kind of swaying, stamping and twisting motion which had the inevitability of a cornfield swept by the wind. An original feature of this character ballet was that the women dancers wore point shoes. The result was one of the masterpieces of Russian art like 'Petrushka' and 'Le Sacre du printemps'.

That summer Romola, hoping for a miracle, took Vaslav on a pilgrimage to Lourdes. 'We spent several days there,' she wrote. 'I went with Vaslav to the Grotto. I washed his forehead in the spring and prayed. I hoped and hoped, but he was not cured. Maybe my faith was not deep enough.'

Diaghilev had a new friend, a young English dancer who had been given the name of Anton Dolin. In February 1924, arriving in Paris from Monte Carlo, they went together to visit Nijinsky. The flat was three or four flights up in a block built of grey granite. They were admitted by a Russian man-servant and shown into the drawing-room where Nijinsky was sitting, with Romola and their two daughters. 'Hardly a word was spoken,' wrote Dolin, 'but somehow in this man's face there was something more expressive than a volume of words. There were the same eyes I had seen in pictures, the same beautiful mouth, the upper lip clean-shaven, and dark, hardly any hair on the head at all, white hands that were never still.' Dolin, both happy and sad, contrasted Vaslav's appearance with the Sargent drawing of him in 'Le Pavillon d'Armide', which Lady Ripon had left Nijinsky[44] and which hung among other portraits on the wall. 'Diaghilev tried to make him speak. He wouldn't say a word. He just sat and laughed. I asked him something and he answered, "*Je ne sais pas.*" ... I often wonder what Diaghilev's feelings were; whatever he felt, he succeeded in hiding. During tea Nijinsky would neither eat nor drink. He seemed powerless to do anything. He looked as healthy as any of us, yet somehow his brain refused to work. He sat in his chair, trying to understand. I think he did understand a great deal, but I believe his brain was tired. The visitors left after an hour. 'He came to the door with us, said good-bye in Russian, and then, when Diaghilev asked if we should come again, nodded his head in a wistful way as much as to say: "I am very, very tired."'[45]

Bronislava Nijinska made several new ballets that year: 'Les Tentations de la bergère', a Versailles type of ballet to music of Montéclair in a set by Juan Gris; 'Les Biches' to a commissioned score of Francis Poulenc with designs by Marie Laurençin, which was a masterpiece of frivolity, the very epitome of the 1920s; 'Les Fâcheux', a Molière ballet to music by Georges Auric and with designs by Georges Braque; 'La Nuit sur le Mont Chauve' to Mussorgsky; and 'Le Train bleu', a ballet about sport and flirtation on a beach, with music by Darius Milhaud, Vaslav's old acquaintance from the French Embassy in Rio, a set by the sculptor Henri Laurens and a superb front curtain of running giantesses by Picasso. During rehearsals for the last work, in which Dolin did spectacular acrobatics in a Chanel swimming costume, Romola brought Vaslav to the Théâtre du Mogador. They entered unannounced just as Bronislava was coaching Dolin in his *pas de deux*. Dolin performed his back falls, leaps and a cartwheel: but there was no response from Nijinsky, and eventually his wife led him away.[46]

Benois, who had been curator of the Hermitage throughout the war and revolution, had recently arrived from Russia; and Diaghilev had given him the Gounod opera 'Le Médecin malgré lui' to design at Monte Carlo: but Benois could not bring himself to approve some of the new departures, and Diaghilev for his part found Benois's work old-fashioned.[47] Bakst died in December 1924, leaving a son. Nouvel and Koribut-Kubitovitch still survived to help Diaghilev; and Svetlov was living in Paris, married to Trefilova.

Diaghilev could 'create' ballets through the agency of other people: but he also felt the need, in a sense, to 'create' the people. If he gave his friendship and affection to a young dancer, his highly developed pedagogic instinct made him want not only to educate him artistically, but to turn him into a choreographer. Because he failed to interest Dolin in choreography – and also because the independent Englishman was always running off to amuse himself with friends of his own age – Diaghilev lost interest in him.[48] His eye was attracted to a handsome, slightly-built young Russian with fine dark eyes called Serge Lifar. This boy had recently come out of Russia with a group of dancers from Nijinska's school in Kiev, and although he was comparatively inexperienced, he worked hard and his efforts aroused the interest of Diaghilev – as they were intended to do.[49] When Bronislava Nijinska heard that Diaghilev and Lifar were secretly experimenting with the choreography of a new ballet she was annoyed, having no faith in the creative ability of her former pupil; and just as Fokine had done when he heard of Nijinsky's secret rehearsals in 1912, she resolved to leave the company.[50]

It was not Lifar, however, who was destined to be Diaghilev's next great choreographer. I do not use the word 'great' carelessly: it is an extraordinary fact that all Diaghilev's principal choreographers from 1909 to 1929 had elements of greatness and originality and none was in the least like another. It was Fokine's invention of a more natural and expressive style of dancing, his revolt against the classicism of Petipa, that had made possible the conquest of the West. Nijinsky's mind soared ahead, and his works were fore-runners of all the limitless experiments of modern dance in the age of space. Massine the eclectic, much influenced by the other arts, again found new styles of movement and, among other things, developed the comedy of manners in ballet. Nijinska, the versatile, could produce witty and exquisite trifles like 'Les Biches', but she also had her brother's epic vision and in 'Les Noces' she matched the splendour of Stravinsky's score. The last of the series was a young Georgian, also a refugee from Russia, who joined the company when they were at the London Coliseum in the winter of 1924–5. His name was Yuri Balanchivadze, later simplified to George Balanchine.

Of the varied ballets Balanchine produced for Diaghilev between 1925 and 1929 – comedies, *divertissements*, an English pantomime, experiments in constructivism and surrealism or with cinematic projection – two very different ones were masterpieces and have survived in the repertory of today: the neo-classical 'Apollon Musagète' to Stravinsky's score (1928), and the passionate, eccentric 'Le Fils prodigue' (1929) to Prokofiev's.

In 1926 Bronislava Nijinska went as ballet-mistress to the Colón Theatre in Buenos Aires (to which she was to return in 1932 and 1946) and in 1928 and 1929 she produced in Paris ballets for Ida Rubinstein's company, including Stravinsky's 'Le Baiser de la fée' and Ravel's 'La Valse'.

The dauntless Romola did not give up her hope for a cure for Vaslav. She tried Christian Science; she tried faith healers; and she visited Dr Coué at Nancy. In 1927 she heard that experiments in curing schizophrenia were being made by Professor Poetzl of the Vienna State Hospital, and she wrote to him. He replied that it was too soon to say whether the treatment he was trying might prove successful and that she should inquire again in a few years' time.

Soon after her appearance in 'The Three-cornered Hat' Karsavina had gone with her diplomat husband to Bulgaria. Back in London, they had made their home in Albert Road, Regent's Park, near the Zoo. In 1926 Karsavina had returned to Diaghilev to dance in 'Romeo and Juliet' (music by Constant Lambert; décor by Max Ernst and Joan Miro) with Lifar, and now she was to resume her old role in 'Petrushka'.

Diaghilev thought that to see Karsavina in 'Petrushka' might give Vaslav the shock which would restore him to his right mind. The company were performing at the Paris Opéra. Romola was in America, so Diaghilev made the arrangements with Tessa. At the end of December 1928 he went with Lifar to the flat in Passy. Nijinsky was lying on a low mattress wearing a dressing-gown, 'either biting his nails till the blood came,' wrote Lifar, 'or somewhat affectedly playing with his wrists'. Lifar approached and kissed his hand. 'For a moment his eyes glowered at me from under the knitted brows, with the wild, suspicious glance of a hunted animal, then quite suddenly a wonderful smile lit up his face: a smile so kindly, so childishly pure, so luminous and undimmed, that I fell utterly under its charm.' At first he paid no attention to Diaghilev, but gradually became conscious of his presence, and 'from time to time, like a normal person, he appeared to be listening intently to what Diaghilev was saying. Diaghilev pretended to Lifar that his only object in taking Nijinsky to the theatre was to have him photographed with the company, but Lifar saw through this affectation of heartlessness and realized the intention behind the outing. 'By the way his eyes had lit up, I could see how much he was expecting from it, a very miracle in fact.' Diaghilev measured Lifar against Nijinsky and found the latter was shorter by half a head. Vaslav walked with a stoop. 'His legs were those of a great dancer, with immense globular muscles, though so flabby now that one wondered how they could possibly support his body.' Lifar shaved him.[51]

That evening at the Opéra Diaghilev sat with Nijinsky in a box. Various old colleagues came in the first interval to pay their respects but Vaslav was unresponsive. In the second interval he and Diaghilev went on the stage, which was set for 'Petrushka'. Karsavina described the scene.

Diaghilev spoke with a forced cheerfulness as he led Nijinsky on. The crowd of artists fell back. I saw vacant eyes and a passive shuffling gait, and stepped forward to kiss Nijinsky. A shy smile lit up his face, and his eyes looked straight into mine. I thought he knew me, and I was afraid to speak lest it might interrupt a slow-forming thought. He kept silent. I then called him by his pet name, 'Vatza!' He dropped his head and slowly turned it away. Nijinsky meekly let himself be led to where the photo-graphers had set their cameras. I put my arm through his, and, requested to look straight into the camera, I could not see his movements. I noticed that the photographers were hesitating, and, looking round, I saw that Nijinsky was leaning forward and looking into my face, but on meeting my eyes he again turned his head like a child that wants to hide tears. And that pathetic, shy, helpless movement went through my heart.[52]

The photograph which was taken shows Benois and Grigoriev in dinner-jackets, Karsavina in her costume as the Ballerina with her left arm in Nijinsky's right, Nijinsky in a dark suit with a white shirt and a white handkerchief in his breast-pocket, Diaghilev in tails with his left hand on Nijinsky's shoulder and Lifar, dressed as the Moor. Nijinsky is looking down and sideways and smiling for the camera, and Diaghilev is smiling down at him in a would-be proud, fatherly way. When escorted back to the box, Vaslav grew flushed and hot. At the end he did not want to leave, and exclaiming, '*Je ne veux pas*', was led out.[53] The miracle had not taken place.

Marie Rambert was in the house. After the ballet she hurried backstage and at the top of the steps leading from the long corridor of artists' dressing-rooms she looked down to see Diaghilev helping Nijinsky into a car. She held back and did not approach him.[54] The man supporting Nijinsky by his other arm was Count Harry Kessler. In his Diary for Thursday, 27 December, 1928, Kessler wrote:

In the evening to a performance of Diaghilev's Ballet at the Opera. Stravinsky's 'Rossignol' and 'Petrushka'. After the performance I was waiting for Diaghilev in the corridor behind the stage when he approached in the company of a short haggard youngster wearing a tattered coat. 'Don't you know who he is?' he asked. 'No,' I replied, 'I really can't call him to mind.' 'But it's Nijinsky!' *Nijinsky!* I was thunderstruck. His face, so often radiant as a young god's, for thousands an imperishable memory, was now grey, hung slackly, and void of expression, only fleet-ingly lit by a vacuous smile, a momentary gleam as of a flickering flame. Not a word crossed his lips. Diaghilev had hold of him under one arm and, to go down the three flights of stairs, asked me to support him under the other because Nijinsky who formerly seemed able to leap over roof-tops, now feels his way, uncertainly, anxiously, from step to step. I held him fast, pressed his thin fingers, and tried to encourage him with gentle words. The look he gave me from his great eyes was mindless but infinitely touching, like that of a sick animal.

Slowly, laboriously, we descended the three, endless-seeming flights until we came to his car. He had not spoken a word. Numbly he took his place between two women, apparently in charge of him, and Diaghilev kissed him on the brow. He was driven away. No one knew whether 'Petrushka', once his finest part, had meant anything to him, but Diaghilev said that he was like a child who does not want to leave a theatre. We went to eat in the Restaurant de la Paix and sat until late with Karsavina, Misia Sert, Craig, and Alfred Savoir. But I did not take much part in the talk; I was haunted by this meeting with Nijinsky. A human being who is burned out. Inconceivable, though it is perhaps even less conceivable when a passionate relationship between individuals burns out and only a faint flicker briefly lights the despairing, inert remains.[55]

Such was the last meeting of Diaghilev and Nijinsky, whose friendship had changed the world. Diaghilev died that summer. He had been suffering from diabetes and he neglected it. After a highly successful London season, his Ballet went to give what were to be their last performances at Vichy, and Diaghilev travelled with his latest protégé, the sixteen-year-old composer Igor Markevitch, to Munich. Here on 1 August Diaghilev went to a performance of his adored 'Tristan und Isolde', which was sung by Otto Wolf and Elizabeth Ohms.[56] Seated beside one he loved with the same love as he had given to Vaslav – a driving force in his procreative life – he listened to the divine Liebestod for the last time. So 'Tristan' was the last opera he heard; and it was Markevitch's first.[57]* Going on alone to Venice, he had become ill and telegraphed to Lifar and Kochno, who were with him at the Grand Hôtel des Bains de Mer on the Lido on 19 August, when he died. Misia Sert and Chanel had arrived, and Pavel Koribut-Kubitovitch reached Venice just too late.[58] The company, dispersed for their holidays, were horrified to read the news in the papers. They were out of work. The funeral, organized by Catherine d'Erlanger,[59] began with a service at the Greek church; then, wrote Lifar, 'the procession, wonderful in its solemn, silent beauty, re-formed, led by the

*And the present author, aged fourteen, on his way with his mother and a cousin to see the Passion Play at Oberammergau, heard *his* first opera, 'Die Walküre', in the same theatre, a year later.

magnificent black and gold gondola, bearing the coffin smothered in flowers, followed by that containing Pavel Georgievitch, Misia Sert, Coco Chanel, Kochno and myself, and a whole string of others, full of friends and mourners. Then, over the smooth ultramarine surface of the Adriatic, sparkling with golden sunshine, the body was wafted to the island of San Michele, and there borne on our arms to the grave.'[60] Lifar ordered a somewhat Mallarmean inscription to be carved on the tombstone:

> *Venise, Inspiratrice Eternelle de nos Appaisements*
> SERGE DE DIAGHILEV
> 1872–1929

There was no one able or willing to take over the direction of the Diaghilev Ballet. Neither Nouvel, nor Grigoriev, nor Kochno, nor Lifar, nor Balanchine, had the inclination or the will or the prestige or the social contacts or the authority. After an extraordinary twenty years' Odyssey, steered by its valiant helmsman through an ocean of vicissitudes, the ship broke up, and it was every man for himself. Yet the members of the Diaghilev crew, dispersed or re-grouped in different formations, would in the ensuing decades spread the love and knowledge of ballet throughout the world and promote the founding of national or municipal companies in six continents. Pavlova's company continued two years longer than Diaghilev's: she died in 1931.

In 1929 Romola Nijinsky was given work in the United States and as she could not take her husband with her, since the USA does not allow mentally unsound immigrants, she decided regretfully to install him once more in Kreuzlingen, where she knew he would be well treated. Nijinsky had been ill for ten years: for another ten he would be in the Swiss sanatorium. While Romola was on a lecture-tour in the USA, their latest flat in rue Conseiller Collignon was broken into and among objects stolen was the Sargent portrait of Nijinsky in 'Le Pavillon d'Armide' which had been left to Nijinsky by Lady Ripon[61]* In 1932 Romola heard that Eleonora

---

*For three decades the famous charcoal drawing was lost to the world; then in 1958 it turned up in an exhibition of Sargent portraits at the Bohemian Club in San Francisco. It had been bequeathed to the club by the late Senator Phelan, an old balletomane, who had lived in Paris and who died in 1954. Romola Nijinsky brought an action to recover her property, but was unsuccessful, the club offering her a copy, which she refused.

Nijinsky had died in Paris: she never told Vaslav this, but would occasionally say to him that his mother was well though too old to come and see him.[62]

One of the tasks Romola undertook in order to earn money to keep Vaslav and herself was to write her husband's life. The idea had been suggested to her by Arnold Haskell, then working for the publisher Heinemann, in 1928. She began the book in America in 1930, assisted by Lincoln Kirstein, and finished it in England in 1932. Haskell was by now a literary agent, and he gave the book to Gollancz.[63] Shortly after this, Balanchine had a small company, Les Ballets 1933, appearing at the Savoy Theatre, with Tilly Losch and the young Toumanova. In a dressing-room at the Savoy, the theatre where Vaslav had enjoyed Gilbert and Sullivan with Diaghilev and Stravinsky in 1913, next-door to the familiar hotel, Romola introduced the young Kirstein to Balanchine.[64] Kirstein was eager to advance ballet in the United States, and he invited Balanchine to America. From this encounter was born the School of American Ballet, and a series of ballet companies, the last of which, Balanchine's New York City Ballet, is now one of the foremost in the world.

Nijinsky by Romola Nijinsky, his wife, was published in England by Gollancz in 1933, and in the United States by Simon and Schuster in the following year. It went through several impressions. It was a vividly written and colourful story, in which Diaghilev necessarily played the part of villain. Romola hoped that it might be made into a film. In fact Alexander Korda had the idea of producing a film with John Gielgud as Nijinsky, but this was never realized.[65]

Early in 1936, Kyra Nijinsky married Igor Markevitch, Diaghilev's last protégé, at the Coronation church in Budapest. There would be one son of the marriage to continue the line of Vaslav and Romola.

In 1936 Romola published an English translation of Nijinsky's diary, which she had recently discovered in a trunk. *The Diary of Vaslav Nijinsky*, written at St Moritz in the winter of 1918–19, when the dancer was on the borderline between sanity and mental illness, immediately struck the world as a most extraordinary document.

That year Romola heard that the experiments in curing schizophrenia which had been made at the Poetzl Clinic had produced good results. She got in touch with the young Austrian Dr Sakel, who had invented this shock treatment, and arranged to meet him together with three distinguished Swiss doctors at Kreuzlingen Sanatorium, where Vaslav was still confined. Romola had trouble persuading Nijinsky's official guardians, appointed by the Swiss government, as well as the medical staff of the sanatorium, to give their consent to so novel and drastic a treatment; but the doctors found Nijinsky's physical condition to be good and thought the risk should be taken. Dr Sakel told Romola that if the treatment was not tried the patient's chances of recovery were non-existent: it might produce a cure or at least a partial improvement. 'Many of Diaghilev's and Vaslav's old friends,' wrote Romola, 'thought that it was better to leave him as he was. They were afraid that if he recovered he might be an unhappy man.' Nevertheless, she decided to take the risk, and it was arranged that Sakel himself should administer the treatment as soon as he was free.

In May 1937 Anton Dolin organized a charity matinée at His Majesty's Theatre in London to raise funds for Nijinsky. Lady Juliet Duff and Lady Diana Cooper were on the committee. John Gielgud recited a Prologue, and Martinelli sang in honour of Nijinsky. Lifar danced the 'Blue Bird' *pas de deux* with Prudence Hyman, and 'L'Après-midi d'un faune'; Margot Fonteyn and Dolin danced the Aurora *pas de deux* from 'The Sleeping Beauty'; Maude Lloyd appeared in 'Le Bar aux Folies-Bergère' and Mary Honer and Harold Turner in the *adagio* from 'Casse-noisette'; Molly Lake, Diana Gould, Prudence Hyman and Kathleen Crofton danced Keith Lester's 'Pas de Quatre'; and Lydia Sokolova and Dolin's young pupil Belita Jepson-Turner also took part. Constant Lambert conducted. At the end of the programme Karsavina, who had flown from Budapest, spoke about Nijinsky: for Dolin this was 'the most beautiful moment of all'.[66] When expenses were paid, there was £2,500 for Nijinsky.[67] A trust fund was now set up, known as the Nijinsky Foundation, to which friends were invited to contribute for Nijinsky's treatment.

Shortly after the Gala Dolin was motoring through Europe and called on Vaslav and Romola at the Kreuzlingen Sanatorium. Nijinsky was on the lawn with some of the other residents. Dolin was expecting to find 'a gross, fat man', but he saw 'only a slim, middle-aged man resting in a chair, looking ahead with wandering but far from vacant eyes'. Although at first apprehensive, Nijinsky soon seemed at ease, appeared to understand all that was said and made occasional remarks. Dolin asked him: 'Why do you not dance? You are lazy. Dance for me.' His answer came slowly and not with great conviction. '*Non, non, je ne veux pas maintenant.*' Vaslav showed Dolin his room: there were no pictures because, Romola said, he would break them when he lost his temper.[68]

In November 1937 an exhibition of Vaslav's drawings, water colours and pastels was put on by the Group Theatre at the Storran Gallery off Piccadilly, in aid of the Nijinsky Foundation. Herbert Read wrote in the Catalogue that the drawings – the product of an 'alienated' mind – were, in common with the art of young children or primitive peoples, 'direct or automatic expressions of the unconscious. . . But these drawings have a general characteristic which immediately suggests the fully conscious art of Nijinsky – his ballets. Their rhythm is a dancing rhythm.'[69]

The treatment began at Kreuzlingen in August 1938.[70]

Every morning [wrote Romola] Vaslav was given an insulin shock to provoke an epileptic fit. The treatment was a great strain on the heart and the whole constitution. Every day it was like a major operation. During the hours in which Vaslav was lying in deep coma provoked by the insulin shock, I suffered indescribable anguish . . . But seemingly he stood the treatment well, and when he recovered consciousness he would answer quite clearly and logically questions put to him. This was already an improvement, as for years he had been mute. Dr Sakel explained to me that this treatment was, as it were, opening the way into a pit, but that the real work was to build the bridge with reality by which his inner self, so long buried, might be drawn back into the outer world. The breaking down of his passive resistance and the unifying of his split personality must be done by someone who was near and dear to him. Therefore, I undertook the task myself.

Every afternoon I tried to interest Vaslav in small and simple matters, things which were related to his art, his youth or his hobbies. At first, it was an extremely thankless task. His tendency was to withdraw into himself. But I insisted and forced him to try to be active. One had to draw his attention to something and then sustain it. It might be a rose in the garden, which I would show him and make him gather. Or I would encourage him to listen to the piano or to watch a game of tennis. Later on, I took him out for walks in the town. I would draw his attention to the children. Dogs and cats made him afraid.

Professor Bleuler, who had first diagnosed Vaslav's illness in 1919, and who had long since retired, now came to observe the treatment. The medical staff at Kreuzlingen were impressed that this famous old man who had invented the term 'schizophrenia' should pay them a visit. Romola had not seen him for twenty years.

He arrived early one morning and was present when the insulin shock was administered to Vaslav. Later in the day we were all invited to Dr Binswanger's private house for a luncheon party. Dr Binswanger, the head of the Sanatorium Bellevue, was once Bleuler's pupil, and was naturally pleased to see his former master. Dr Sakel also joined us.

It was then that Professor Bleuler said to me: 'My dear Madame Nijinsky, many years ago I had the cruel task of informing you that, according to medical knowledge as it then was, your husband was incurably insane. I am happy today to be able to give you hope. This young colleague of mine,' and he took Sakel's hand, 'has discovered a treatment for which I searched in vain for over forty years. I am proud of him. And of you, because you did not follow the advice I gave you so many years ago to divorce your husband. You stood by him during those years of mental dimness, you helped him through this terrible illness, and now I believe you will be rewarded. He will once more become himself.'

I turned away to hide my tears.

The treatment was interrupted for a period of two months to give Vaslav a rest; then, as Dr Sakel was moving to America, it was continued daily for three months in the State Asylum of the Canton Berne at Münsingen.

In the mornings, Vaslav was under the care of the doctors. The rest of the day I looked after him, following the instructions of Dr Sakel. Here Vaslav had far more freedom. Dr Müller, following Professer Bleuler, who believed in re-education, encouraged every attempt to lead him back to normal life and to make him dependent on himself. Upon Dr Müller's advice we made longer and longer visits to Berne. The improvement was slow but steady and distinct. We now even ventured to take Vaslav to public places, to restaurants, concerts and the theatre, where we saw a performance by Trudi Schoop, the Swiss character dancer.

515

So marked was the improvement in Vaslav's condition that Dr Müller allowed Romola to take him away to an hotel in the mountains in the hope that he would gradually adjust himself to normal. Romola's devotion was to some extent rewarded and her courage in deciding on the new treatment was justified.

For nearly a year we lived in a small hotel in the Bernese Oberland, once more in the high mountains. Again Vaslav saw the seasons passing in the Alps as he had done in St Moritz. The two places were very similar. Everything went even better than we had hoped, and we seriously began to consider making a home for ourselves in Switzerland.

In June 1939 Serge Lifar, who had arranged an exhibition at the Musée des Arts Décoratifs in the Louvre to commemorate the tenth anniversary of Diaghilev's death, and who was planning a gala performance to raise money for Vaslav's treatment, came to see them.

The last meeting of Lifar and Nijinsky had been when the photograph was taken on the stage of the Paris Opéra. Lifar found Vaslav fitter, more supple and more sociable.

His face had lost its hopelessly timid and downtrodden expression, and he would readily respond to a question or a command. He no longer tore his nails to the quick. The nervous movements of his hands had found quite a different mode of expression. They had something of the dance, of the genuine dance – very beautiful at times. He never ceased playing with his hands, and his movements – especially round his head – were reminiscent, every now and then, of the plastic of Siamese dancers. But gone was his sly and childlike smile, a smile of confidence and good natured benevolence. Its place had been taken by a hoarse laugh, deep and convulsive, which shook his whole body and threw it into sharp and angular plastic poses. In these too something of the dance was subconsciously expressed.

When we entered his room Nijinsky was talking to himself. He is always talking to himself, in a language of his own, quite unintelligible to others – a mixture of the most unexpected combinations of Russian, French and Italian words.

I asked him, 'Do you remember Diaghilev, Vatza?' and Nijinsky instantly answered – his reflexes are exceedingly quick, much quicker than those of normal people – 'Remember . . . yes, yes, he . . . remarkable. . . how he . . .' and suddenly the hoarse, terrifying laugh convulsed his whole body, jerked it hysterically into sharp angular contortions.

516

A *barre* had been installed in the room and Lifar exercised at it in front of Vaslav, who responded by nodding, tapping his foot and counting. When Lifar danced part of 'L'Après-midi d'un faune', Vaslav pushed him aside and corrected him. Other dances he applauded.[71] But when Lifar tried a bit of 'Le Spectre de la rose', as if in reaction to the *entrechats*, Nijinsky, without *préparation* or *plié*, rose from the floor in a high jump, laughing.[72] A photographer was present and recorded this unexpected though hoped-for feat.

Among those who took part in the Gala were the ex-Diaghilev dancers Nemchinova, Dolin, Lifar and Tcherkas, the Spaniard Escudero, the Indian Ram Gopal, and the Opéra artists Lorcia, Darsonval, Schwarz and Peretti. The Nijinsky Foundation benefited by 35,000 francs.[73]

Vaslav began to act and behave quite normally. The insulin shock had decidedly freed him from hallucinations. The only signs of his illness now were his great timidity and a tendency to silence. He very much disliked any attempt to engage him in conversation and got rather excited if anybody persevered. But as even in his youth he was inclined to be silent, the doctor thought it best not to worry about this.

It was only natural that while we were trying to reconstruct a new life among the ruins of our shattered past, we paid very little attention to the outside world and its happenings. When we were sitting on our terrace one day, basking in the sunshine and admiring the mighty peaks of the Alps, our attendant came in with a newspaper. He seemed rather excited. The Germans had concluded a treaty with Russia, he said. It was in August 1939, if I remember right. The Swiss in the village seemed to be disturbed about it. As the days passed, some of the visitors packed up hurriedly and left for their native countries, and there was a certain panic which seemed ridiculous in these calm majestic surroundings.

Vaslav rather enjoyed observing people. As a youth he used to sit with Leon Bakst at the Café de la Paix watching the passers-by. Now we went every morning to the little bar in our hotel. There we sipped our orange juice, looking at the crowds drift in from their walks or the swimming pool before lunch. Beromunster, the Swiss wireless station, broadcast the latest news at noon. One day the chatter ceased and there was silence when it was announced that Germany had refused the plea that it should not occupy Danzig . . .

Then suddenly, as out of the blue, Vaslav spoke.

'So once more they claim "Deutschland, Deutschland, über alles". This is the beginning of the second act!'

The Swiss hotels soon emptied, but Romola arranged with the proprietor of their own that they should stay on indefinitely. Vaslav's male attendant was called up, but Dr Müller undertook to send a qualified woman. This was not a success.

Vaslav did not need any physical care; he needed a companion when I was not present, a person who could also act as a valet, to help him dress and undress, to shave him, and to serve his meals. But most of all he needed somebody with authority whom he respected and who would be able to impose his will and restrain him if necessary. I believed that an able nurse could easily do this, but I was mistaken. Vaslav immediately became antagonistic and did everything in his power to scare the life out of one nurse after another. Being a superb actor and mime, he looked at them so frighteningly and with such powerfully gloomy expressions that they became convinced that their last moment had come. They did not dare to stay with him alone or touch him. So my hopes of help and assistance vanished and my mischievous Vaslav attained his aim. He simply wanted me to look after him day and night; he wanted to be alone with me and to be once more the boss in his own home.

This was a natural and healthy reaction which delighted his physicians and me, as it was a sign of great improvement. But it put a tremendous load on me, as the responsibility was overwhelming. I had to assure Vaslav's bodily safety; but I was also answerable for his conduct towards society. What this means even when you are the guardian of a normal being most people can imagine, but what it is when you have to look after a schizophrenic patient is quite another matter.

Dr Müller, whom I consulted over the telephone, advised me to discharge the nurses, who were only annoying Vaslav by their presence. He very reluctantly said that in the circumstances we would have to abandon for the present our plan of leaving Vaslav at liberty, as he doubted whether I could stand the physical strain of being with him constantly without rest. He felt we could not do anything but bring him back to the asylum until the war was over.

But I was determined not to give up and to try the impossible. So I gave notice to the nurse, who anyway was spending her days strolling in the mountains or reading novels in her room, and took up my duties alone.

At first Vaslav was sweet and docile. He sat quietly when I shaved him, he helped me to tidy the room before we left for our morning walks, he accompanied me when I went shopping, he held the wool when I was knitting; it seemed to be plain sailing. Dr Müller was delighted and congratulated me.

There were, however, more trials in store for the indomitable Romola.

Perhaps Vatza felt that life was too dull here at six thousand feet above sea level and that it was high time to have a little excitement. During one of our walks, when we were climbing, he pushed me unexpectedly and with great strength so that I lost the ground under my feet and landed on the slope. What would have happened to me if Vaslav had pushed me a few moments earlier when we were walking along the precipice, God alone knows. Was his action premeditated, or just a sudden impulse, I wondered. I knew that Vaslav's character was gentleness itself; he was never deliberately unkind to anybody. But I knew also that the schizophrenic patient acted on sudden uncontrollable impulses. That was its danger and what I had to watch out for. Was it possible to control Vaslav or to influence him? To use force was out of the question. Even when in the beginning of his illness those brutal doctors and nurses had put him in straitjackets and iron beds, it needed four male nurses and injections to overpower him. And with what results? He became a human wreck. I was determined that as long as I lived, no matter what he did, this would never happen to him again. I decided not to mention to anybody what had occurred but to watch even more carefully.

At the time of the incident, I stood up and laughed, and patted my skirt clean. Vaslav joined me in giggling as I said, 'Oh how funny, Vatzinko,' and energetically linked my arm into his. He seemed taken aback. I felt that he was wondering how I had the impertinence not to be frightened of him. I understood now he was trying to scare me. I knew that I had to keep the upper hand or my game would be lost.

Many years ago Professor Bleuler had advised me that 'one should never lose one's nerve when a mental patient becomes agitated or violent; on the contrary, then one must show utter fearlessness.' Even in an asylum, in surroundings designed to cope with such cases, with a few and light pieces of furniture, unbreakable windows and automatically closing doors, it is difficult to counter the patient's attack. How far more difficult it is with strangers around, in a hotel where every object might mean bodily harm to one, and not least to the patient himself.

Next day, when as usual I took the breakfast tray into Vatza's room, with one powerful drive he landed the tray on the floor. I was dripping with tea; the scrambled eggs and stewed fruit were all over the furniture, the carpet, everywhere. Vaslav sat up in bed looking at me triumphantly. I bent down to pick up the unbreakable plates and cups, which I was wise enough to use, and to clean up. But Vatza was determined to make a real show. He threw at me first a chair and then the marble cover of the little table next to his bed. When even this did not have the desired effect of making me panic-stricken and of leaving the battlefield to him, with a foreboding expression he made one of his famous *grands jetés* and landed beside me, towering over me with threatening gestures.

At this moment, Vaslav looked very much as Ivan the Terrible must have looked. I saw in his veiled misty eyes that he was beyond hearing or understanding me. He was wild with emotion. But I did not move. I stood steadfast, looking steadily into his eyes with an energetic commanding expression. Vaslav gazed back. A few moments passed; it seemed eternity. Then almost imperceptibly he backed away. It was only a fraction of an inch, but I noticed it. I had won. I knew it, and with great gentleness and firmness I said, 'Vatza, please sit down.' He did so.

After this Vaslav settled down, his hallucinations receded, he seemed at peace and he allowed Romola to guide him. She now came to the conclusion that it would be best for them to move to the United States, where she had many friends and could earn money, and where, in addition, Vaslav would be near Dr Sakel, who was practising there. She applied through her American lawyer and friend, Laurence Steinhardt, for a visitor's visa for Vaslav. Her own visa was valid for another year. While she was awaiting this, she heard from Philip Morrell, Lady Ottoline's husband, that currency regulations would prevent his sending any more payments from the Nijinsky Foundation from England. Romola realized that their hotel-keeper, who had already moved them into two small back rooms on the top floor, would turn them out the moment their bills were not paid, and the American visa became all the more essential.

At Easter 1940, to her delight, she received a cable saying that the visa was granted and instructing her to report to the American Consul in Zürich. Unfortunately the information that Nijinsky was to come to America was released to the Washington press, and it was published in the Swiss papers on the morning Romola visited the Consul. He was annoyed and refused to grant the visa, saying that after their year was up if the war was not over, Vaslav and Romola would apply for an extension, and then he would be blamed by his superiors. Romola cabled desperately to the United States.

But the phoney war was now at an end, and as Hitler's victorious armies spread through Europe Romola felt that before she could arrange for the American visa – *if* she could arrange for it – she and Vaslav would be trapped penniless in Switzerland. With their Nansen passports they could only live in or travel through neutral countries. Hungary seemed to be the only alternative. If Mussolini declared war on the Allies (which he was to do on 11 July 1940) the escape route through Italy and Yugoslavia to neutral Hungary would be closed. Romola was advised to make use of her American visa and to leave Vaslav in a Swiss State Asylum. But reluctant as she was to repeat the experiences of the last war and rely on the charity of her parents, she decided to go to Hungary. Rather than risk cancelling all the good Vaslav's treatment had done him, she renounced comfort and security for herself in America and resolved to stay beside him. This was perhaps her most unselfish and heroic decision.

So on a hot July day, after a long, exhausting journey, Nijinsky and his wife returned to the city where she had first seen him dance in spring 1912.

'Crossing the Danube we saw the outstanding landmarks basking in the blazing sunshine; the chain of mountains encircling the city, the Royal Palace raised upon the hill which dominates the town, the Parliament, old Buda, the Island of St-Marguerite; sights once so familiar to us.'

From the start Romola felt they were unwelcome to her parents. In her book she had, after all, shown her mother in an unsympathetic light. Nobody came to meet the Nijinskys at the station, and when Romola rang up her home from the Ritz Hotel she was told Emilia Markus and Pardany were out of town. Vaslav, noticing Romola's embarrassment, said kindly, 'Don't worry. They did not receive your message in time.' Eventually Romola's parents, caring less, she thought, about being hospitable than for public opinion, came to the hotel and invited them to stay. The Nijinskys were installed once more in the same second-floor suite in the big house in the hilly suburbs that they had occupied in the first war.

Romola still hoped that the American visa might come through and that she and Vaslav might be able to travel through Yugoslavia to Greece and get a cargo-boat to the United States, but, as the weeks passed and she heard of the difficulties her lawyer was encountering, she gradually gave up hope. The Nijinskys resigned themselves to remaining in Hungary.

My family [wrote Romola] did not make life easy for us. They looked on Vaslav with mistrust. Nobody could have been more docile, quiet and good-natured than he was. Nevertheless, he could not disarm them. I was deeply worried, realizing the great mistake I had made in bringing him to my family's home where he had suffered so deeply in the past. It was an error with far-reaching consequences to place him here in this antagonistic atmosphere, charged with discord and suspicion, especially after the insulin shock treatment. Vaslav needed now to be surrounded with sympathetic understanding and kindly people. He was timid, like a child making his first contacts with life and society; he had to readjust himself to reality and his fellow human beings.

In March 1941 Yugoslavia broke off relations with Hitler and German troops poured through Budapest: within a month they would have penetrated to Greece. With Hungary completely dominated by the Germans and virtually ruled by the German Ambassador, Romola had cause to fear for Vaslav's life: the Germans exterminated mental patients. Hungary was still not at war with Russia, and Romola visited the Russian Consul in the hopes of getting visas to travel through Russia to America. But in June, Germany invaded Russia. Romola and Vaslav were in the town when she heard the news.

I stood rooted to the spot [she wrote]. Once more we would be prisoners of war. 'Roma, why are you so silent, what is the matter? What is worrying you?' asked Vaslav. I remembered the advice Professor Bleuler had given me years ago, that one must tell the truth and tell it gently. So I said 'The German Army has attacked Russia. If Hungary sides with Germany, we must face the fact that perhaps we may be interned again. Don't be frightened, we are together.'

To earn some money Romola began to write articles on art, but she was obliged to prove she was 'a pure Aryan' to the Literary Council before she was allowed to publish them. She also prepared a Hungarian edition of Nijinsky's diary.

In December 1941, after Pearl Harbor, Hungary declared war on Great Britain and the United States. When the consulates of those two countries began to pack up Romola begged them to take Vaslav and herself with them, but this they were unable to do. Romola's parents now asked her to leave. Her stepfather, being a Jew though converted, was in danger, and Emilia was hiding other Jews in the house. The ground the family house was built on had been bought in Romola's childhood with money left her by her father, and she refused to budge. However, Vaslav was very susceptible to the unpleasant atmosphere and Romola began to look for somewhere else to live. Through her cousin, Paul von Bohus, she took a cottage in the country near Lake Balaton and for some months she and Vaslav enjoyed a peaceful existence, bathing and making excursions. Then, one day they had a visit from the local police, who searched them and clearly suspected they were Russian agents. They decided to return to Budapest.

Romola rented a small house on Svabhegy, a hill near the capital, and they moved in together with Brindus, a good-natured peasant who had been engaged to look after Vaslav, and who became devoted to him. The Literary Council now withdrew Romola's permit to publish articles. In order to keep Vaslav clothed and fed and to provide fuel for his room, Romola would stop at nothing. She made a list of rich and distinguished people and went from door to door begging them to buy copies of the Hungarian edition of Vaslav's diary. One happy result of this humiliating and selfless task was that she met and made friends with Mr Quand, the General Manager of the National Bank of Hungary, who was able to help her financially in the following years.

All the time she was caring for and providing for her husband, Romola kept to herself her fears that he might be arrested as a Russian or exterminated as mentally sick. What burdens she had to bear! Wilhelm Furtwangler arrived from Germany to give a concert; and he terrified Romola by his description of trains filled with inmates of mental homes on their way to be put to death. She made frantic but vain efforts to have Vaslav sent to Switzerland.

In February 1943 the Nijinskys gave shelter to a young Hungarian officer who had walked two thousand miles from Stalingrad. From his description of Russian endurance and the plight of the German Army, they were more convinced than ever that an Allied victory was only a question of time. But as the German Army retreated, the grip on Hungary tightened. All the able-bodied were called up, Brindus included; transport and fuel grew scarce and Jews had to wear large yellow stars. In April Romola went in the middle of a Russian air-raid to the Palace to see a relation of hers who was a Marshal of the Court, begging for a safe conduct to Switzerland. She was told that the Regent was powerless to help her, being entirely in the hands of the Germans, but received the following advice: 'Get some papers of some deceased relative whose age is about the same as Vaslav's (your Abbé can do that for you), and go towards the Austrian border, towards the lion's den. There you will be safer, there the control of the Gestapo is less severe. Don't go towards the East or Yugoslavia, it would be too dangerous. We Hungarians will shut our eyes.' Romola secured the papers.

Cousin Paul had found an inn in a forest near Sopron, a town on the Austrian border on the shores of Lake Neusiedler, whose proprietor specialized in hiding people and made good money out of it. Here the Nijinskys enjoyed their walks in the pretty country, and Vaslav learned some dances from their gypsy maid. In August 1944 the Russians entered Roumania and it was clear they would soon be in Hungary. People began pouring eastward through the town. On 15 October Admiral Horthy broadcast that Hungary had lost the war and must capitulate; but he was arrested and replaced by Szalassy, the head of the Hungarian Nazi Party.

For fear of being recognized, Romola and Paul decided that another move was essential, and they found lodgings in a nearby villa with a retired opera singer who was afraid of having her house requisitioned. Housework, fetching coal, picking up wood in the forest, and cooking occupied Romola's days. She was once more running out of money, and she decided to go to Budapest and sell some gold objects. As she could not leave Vaslav unattended she reluctantly placed him in a hospital in Sopron which had a department dealing with nervous diseases. When she broke the news to him of the arrangement she had made, he wept.

In spite of constant air-raids Romola was successful in Budapest and returned in a train crowded with fugitives, passing on the way sealed trucks bound for Auschwitz. Back at the inn, she and Vaslav and a group of friends would listen to the 'Voice of America' programme on the radio.

One snowy morning Romola was in the town seeing about a permit for fuel when there was a heavy American air-raid. It was evening before she could leave the shelter, and on her return home she found Vaslav in a roofless room, covered in dust. 'He just gazed steadfastly and silently at me.' Poor Romola took him back to the hospital, so that he should at least have a roof over his head and be near a shelter. The Hungarian Government arrived in Sopron. Now not only Jews but gypsies were to be put in concentration camps. The Nijinskys' maid came to say good-bye. Between air-raids Romola would run out to see if the hospital had been hit.

On 12 March 1945 Romola was hanging out washing when the house was shaken by tremendous explosions. It was an air attack on Vienna, seventy-five kilometres away.

Towards evening [wrote Romola] it began to snow heavily, and there was an uncanny stillness. We were sitting at supper when suddenly we heard knocking at the front door. I went out to see who it was and as I opened the door there stood Vaslav in his old grey winter coat, wearing his little Tyrolean hat and carrying a bundle in which his clothes and belongings were wrapped. Next to him stood the Polish attendant, Stan. 'Vaslav, my dearest, I am very happy that you are here,' I said, and I kissed him and escorted him to the table.

Stan informed us later, 'I had to bring Mr Nijinsky home, even if the danger of bombing is greater here. We have received orders to exterminate our mental patients by tomorrow morning.'

One afternoon Russian bombers were overhead and a bomb fell in the front garden. At two in the morning distant firing was heard. Romola woke Vaslav and together they ran into the woods. There was a full moon. Planes flew over and bombs began to fall. Romola put a plaid rug over Vaslav's head and prayed that he should not be killed by his own countrymen. 'But Vaslav pushed the rug back;

kneeling with outstretched arms, he looked up at the bright sky with its circling Russian planes.'

Now for several days Romola and Vaslav hid in some caves in a nearby hill. There were two thousand others with them, including Cousin Paul, who had measles. This was the most sordid of all their experiences, yet Vaslav endured it. The Russian word for God is 'Bog' but Vaslav had a nickname for Him. Romola could reassure him by saying 'Bundenka is here with us.' Then he would grow calm.

In the early hours of Easter Sunday they thought the Germans must be gone for good and that there would be no more bombing, so they made for the villa.

Once installed at home, Vaslav fell asleep. The others tried to clean themselves while Paul went to bed with his measles, useless and helpless.

In the valley we could see the Soviet troops streaming towards the west like the advance of Genghis Khan, a most gruesome and magnificent sight. Thousands and thousands of tanks, heavy guns and cavalry, covered by hundreds of planes, rolled along through the green smiling spring country-side.

Within a few hours the town was occupied, the forest and all the houses were invaded. The Russian soldiers came into the houses in small groups.

Our gates were broken down and three tall young Russians carrying automatic machine-guns entered our house.

'Nemetski, Nemetski!' [Germans, Germans] they shouted loudly.

In a moment everybody in the house fled, panic-stricken, behind curtains and beds. Only Vaslav remained quietly lying on his couch while I stood beside him. The Russians shouted at me. 'Nazi?'

Vaslav, unexpectedly shouting still louder, replied in Russian. 'Keep quiet!'

The soldiers stood dumbfounded and lowered their automatics. 'A Russian? How does he come here? Is he a prisoner?'

'Yes, he is my husband, an artist.' I did not know that I had pronounced a magic word.

Next morning Romola was summoned before the Russian Commanding Officer, who was no less astounded to hear that she was the wife of the great dancer than that she had had to look after her sick husband for so long without aid from any government. He gave her some official papers.

Every house filled up with Russians and a friendly officer was billeted on the Nijinskys. Romola began to notice a change in her husband.

Vaslav used to stroll around the garden and lie in his garden chair, watching and wondering what was going on. He never asked any questions, just listened and listened, but his eyes became more and more attentive. They were not so dreamy and distant as they had been during the last twenty-six years. It seemed almost as if he was awakening from a long and deep sleep. Shyly, more and more, he approached the soldiers and sat down among them. It seemed that some inward barrier broke down and he seemed to melt towards the outside world. In the evenings, he stood and listened to the plaintive, nostalgic sound of the balalaika for a long time.

For the first time since 1919 people did not stare at him, did not shrink from him because he had suffered from a mental illness. They spoke to him in the same nonchalant manner as they did to us.

At first I warned them: 'Leave Vaslav Fomitch alone, don't talk to him. He might get annoyed and impatient, he is afraid.'

But they just laughed. 'He won't be afraid of us,' they said. 'Let him alone to do what he wants.'

Romola began to wonder if by treating Vaslav as different from other people she and the doctors had made a mistake. She thought it probable that if she had been able to take him to Russia when he had first become disturbed, he would never have been seriously ill. The simple Russian soldiers had a better way with him than any doctor or nurse. Vaslav grew easier in his manner and spoke more. One evening, when the soldiers were singing and dancing, he suddenly stood up, jumped into the middle of them and began to dance. From then on the soldiers took to bringing him presents of food and clothes.

On the night of 5 May Romola was woken by the Russian officer, who said 'Go to Vaslav Fomitch and explain to him why all our planes are in the air; he might get frightened. We are going to fire all our guns. We are celebrating. The war is over.'

Even though Vienna was in ruins Romola felt that it must be the first stage of their westward journey. She and Paul got a lift to the city to reconnoitre the position. All the bigger hotels were taken over by the Russian Army, but the resourceful Paul forced his way into Sacher's, which was barred and bolted. The manager, who was sheltering a few old and distinguished customers, was trying to give the impression that the place was uninhabitable, but at the magic name of Nijinsky he opened his doors. With immense difficulty Romola and Paul returned to Sopron and fetched Vaslav to Vienna. In June 1945 they were installed in a palatial suite of rooms, with fine china and linen: but food was scarce and only available on the black market. Shortly afterwards Sacher's was requisitioned by the Russians. The Nijinskys were, however, allowed to stay on and after that Romola only had to take her place in the line of soldiers to be served plentiful meals.

In August the Russians allowed the Americans, British and French into Vienna, and the city was divided into zones. Russian headquarters was at the Hofburg, the Royal Palace in the heart of the city, the British at Schönbrunn Palace in the suburbs. Sacher's now passed into British hands, but the Nijinskys were given permission to stay until they could make other arrangements.

There now came into their lives an Englishwoman who would prove a precious friend to them. Margaret Power, a widow of thirty-seven, was a passionate lover of ballet, besides being the most generous and warm-hearted of women. She had worked in the Foreign Office and in 1945 was posted to the Allied Commission in Austria. Before she left London, Cyril Beaumont had told her that she should try to find the Nijinskys as there was some money in the Nijinsky fund which they probably needed. One day in August Mrs Power made up a little parcel and set off from Schönbrunn to seek them out. She did not know they were at Sacher's, but remembered from before the war that the hall-porter there was supposed to know everything that went on in Vienna. She was amazed when he said 'They are upstairs. Where else in Vienna would they be?' Romola received the uniformed stranger with some reserve, but soon after Margaret's return to Schönbrunn telephoned to say how touched she had been by the contents of the parcel – tea, biscuits, chocolate and toothpaste – which only an Englishwoman would have been so thoughtful as to put together.

After that, Margaret returned often and was thrilled to meet Nijinsky, whom she found very silent.

One September evening [she recalled] we were sitting in the salon, Vaslav was in an armchair and Romola and I were going through some correspondence, when the lights failed. This often happened at that time; the Russians controlled the only power station and were not very good at maintenance. It was pitch dark as the curtains were drawn. Romola told me to sit quite still while she went to get a candle. She said a couple of words to Vaslav in Russian and found her way to the door. Suddenly I heard a movement, and a hand reached out and touched me on the arm. Vaslav said something soothing and gentle which I did not understand. He passed in front of me and sat on the sofa, taking my hand and patting it. And so we sat in the dark for a few moments until Romola came back with the servant, both carrying lighted candles. I said, 'M. Nijinsky has been taking care of me', and she replied 'He likes you very much. He calls you the English lady soldier.' At this I looked directly at Vaslav, meeting his eyes, which I had never dared to do before, and he smiled at me, murmuring something and again patting my hand before letting it go. We remained on patting terms for a long time after that, but we never had any conversation at any time. I used to chatter to him in French or English, but he never answered. I fell in love with him in Vienna and have remained so ever since.[74]

One winter day Romola and Vaslav were overtaken by a snowstorm in the Imperial Gardens and took refuge in the Hofburg where the collection of the Vienna picture galley was on exhibition. Vaslav ran up the steps as if he felt at home, and Romola thought it must have reminded him of his visits to the Hermitage with his mother when he was a boy. He had not been inside a museum or picture gallery for twenty-six years, but he identified many of the paintings, naming Velasquez, Raphael and other artists. On Sundays, in the Hofkapelle, when he heard Masses by Haydn, Mozart or Schubert, superbly sung by soloists from the Opera and by the Vienna Boys Choir, Vaslav's face wore 'an expression of ecstasy'. He and Romola also went to a performance of 'The Queen of Spades'.

The Russians began to woo the Nijinskys, hoping that Vaslav would return to his own country. One evening a performance was given in his honour. Romola had expected opera but it was the ballet – his own old company – from Leningrad, who had carried on the traditions in which Vaslav had been brought up so many years ago. They danced 'Casse-noisette', a *divertissement* and Fokine's

'Les Sylphides'. Nijinsky 'clutched his hands and followed each step with a perceptible movement of his body.' Chabukiani, Sergeyev and the soulful Ulanova were dancing. Vaslav applauded 'with the abandon of a young enthusiastic student'. Next day, visiting Ulanova at her hotel, he was received with armfuls of roses.

In March 1946, in answer to a letter from Margaret Power, Anton Dolin wrote from Seattle that he had set aside $400 for the Nijinskys and asked if Margaret could find a way of paying them the equivalent. During the year he persevered in collecting further sums of money for them in America, just as he had done in England before the war.

The British were anxious to have Sacher's Hotel to themselves and Romola thought she ought to get Vaslav to the country, as to be continually surrounded by soldiers depressed him. Colonel Yarborough, the American Provost Marshal, offered a pass to the American Zone and arranged for Romola to inspect certain castles which were in the custody of the military authorities. So it was that in July 1946, after an anxious moment at the check-point between the Russian and American Zones, Romola brought Vaslav first for a few days to Salzburg, then to the romantic castle of Mittersill, perched high on a mountainside between Kitzbühel and Zell-am-See. Only now, though the war in Europe had ended more than a year before, could they at last feel that their wartime wandering and privations were really over.

Vaslav's rooms were on the ground floor opening on to the inner courtyard and with windows overlooking the Alps and the Salzach valley. He wandered freely about the ramparts and gardens. Women came from the village to work in exchange for food, not wages; and thanks to American, French and British visitors who began to arrive at the castle, food was never scarce. The village priest celebrated Mass in the castle chapel. Margaret Power came from Vienna and played table tennis with Vaslav. 'Sometimes,' she remembered, 'he would kiss my cheek, always quite unexpectedly – not in greeting or farewell, but just out of affection.'[75]

As one season followed another [wrote Romola], we became so used to this romantic life, and so fond of the place, that we had almost forgotten the past. Once more Vaslav was free to go wherever he liked. For hours he sat in the park or in the courtyard, and we were not obliged to follow or watch him. This was the best thing that could happen to him. For years in the nursing home, he had been watched day and night. Through this constant observation he became very dependent on his companions. Later, during the war, I had to be with him constantly, trying to avert all disagreeable incidents or dangers. Now I was anxious that he should become more and more independent and therefore I let him alone. After a few months my method brought its result. Vaslav, who during the last twenty-seven years had lost the habit of expressing his desires, now very definitely began to say what he wanted or did not want.

During the winter of 1946–7 and again during the summer Romola made trips to Paris and London, where to her great relief, as her father had been born in Highgate and his birth duly registered at Somerset House, the Foreign Office were able to grant her a British passport. With the aid of Duff Cooper, the British Ambassador in Paris, she was successful in obtaining permission for Vaslav to live in England, and procured transit visas for the journey across France. She also arranged for a check-up of Vaslav's physical condition with Dr Rohr, his old doctor in Zürich. This took place in November 1947, and a diet was prescribed for his high blood-pressure.

The Nijinskys and Paul travelled straight from Switzerland to Calais, had a rough crossing to Dover – with Vaslav, the only one who did not feel sea-sick, waiting on Romola and Paul for a change – and motored to London through a dense fog.

They spent a few days in London. Romola felt that Vaslav was not fully aware that thirty-five years had passed since he was there last. He only knew he had been happy and successful there and people had been good to him, so he was delighted to be back. In the few years that remained the English authorities behaved considerately and Romola thought that 'Vaslav at last found a real asylum and complete freedom. Nobody ever worried him. The people who came in contact with him treated him as they would have done if he had never been mentally ill, and he responded with normal behaviour. During his entire stay in England he never became excited or upset.'

531

Alexander Korda, an old friend of Romola's in Budapest days, had made arrangements for them to stay at Great Fosters, a luxurious hotel near Egham in Surrey, just over a mile east of where the London–Exeter road skirts Virginia Water. It was a pretty, late-Elizabethan brick house and they spent Christmas there, very quietly. The rest of the winter passed peacefully, with card-games or chess, walking and going to the local cinema. One film which Vaslav adored was Korda's production of Wilde's *An Ideal Husband*. He admired the Technicolor, which he had never seen before, fell in love with Paulette Goddard, and had to see the film through twice. Romola wrote to Miss Goddard, who sent Vaslav signed photographs.

Tamara Karsavina and Nadine Nicolaevna Legat, second wife and widow of Vaslav's old teacher, who had a ballet school in Kent, came to visit them. He took pleasure in talking to Mme Legat about the Imperial School and the Mariinsky Theatre.

In the spring of 1948 Romola found a small house called Whinmead at Virginia Water on the edge of Windsor Great Park. Vaslav enjoyed driving and walking in the park or sitting in the garden. Romola sometimes took him to London and to the theatre. He saw the Indian dances of Ram Gopal, with whom he felt a close affinity, and applauded the lithe young Mexican Luisillo, who appeared with Carmen Amaya's Flamenco troupe at the Prince's (now Shaftesbury) Theatre.*

The fall of a horseshoe which was nailed over the front door of Whinmead heralded a run of bad luck. Romola fell and tore a ligament. She was laid up for eight weeks, and her illness made Vaslav restless and nervous. 'He took my foot in his hands and was full of attention.' Then Vaslav's attendant, whom he liked, gave notice, and it was hard to replace him. Alexander Korda had been going to make a film based on a story of Romola's and he had promised to get the Nijinskys to America. Now he decided he could not produce the picture and Romola was struck off the pay-roll.

Vaslav sat to a young Polish sculptor who, besides making a bust

---

*It was on his visit to the Prince's that I saw Nijinsky for the only time, seated in a box to the left of the stage. Leon Hepner, the impresario, asked me to meet him, but I was too shy.

of him, took a cast of his foot. With Romola he visited the Legat School at Tunbridge Wells and stood godfather to the daughter of a young dancer. Margaret Power came sometimes to sit with him when Romola had to go out. He took up his drawing again. It was a quiet life, and Romola felt when she came into the room and he looked up at her and smiled 'with such charm and tenderness' that she was married to a rare spirit and all her struggles and sufferings had been worthwhile. 'It gave me the most perfect happiness to sit quietly in the same room with him. One felt protected, content in his presence, he emanated so much tenderness and goodness.'

Romola noticed that on his walks Vaslav would often hold his hand over the small of his back. This the local doctor, Dr Wilson, thought must be due to a nerve pain. He never complained of his health except of an occasional headache. But in the autumn of 1949 he had alarming attacks of hiccups. Romola took him to London to Professor Plesch, a celebrated German physician, then retired, who diagnosed kidney trouble and ordered a stricter diet.

On Christmas Day Romola received news of her mother's death at the age of eighty-nine. Then the lease of their Virginia Water house was due to expire at the end of January and the landlord refused to renew it. On the 30th Romola had still not found another house, and as she packed Vaslav said '*Kak Tsigane!* [Like Gypsies]' They returned for a few days to Great Fosters. 'Then,' wrote Romola, 'out of the blue, a perfect stranger, a Major Wright, who had heard of our predicament through some estate agent, called me up, saying, "I have a house near the sea, not far from Arundel. It has central heating. It is small, but very pleasant in the spring. I would be glad to lend it to Mr Nijinsky."' It was too good to be true, and the offer was gratefully accepted. They motored down to Rustington in Sussex in a howling gale. Moving always made Vaslav nervous, but after a few days he settled down, and when the weather improved went for walks in the Duke of Norfolk's park at Arundel Castle. They were only a few miles from where Romola had stayed and studied with Miss Johnson as a girl. However, Nijinsky seemed to enjoy his walks less than he used to; his face was sometimes flushed and he would take any opportunity to sit down.

Serge Lifar telephoned from Paris to discuss a gala he was planning for June at which he hoped the Nijinskys would be present. This suited them quite well as Romola planned to take Vaslav to see a specialist in Switzerland in the summer. Lifar also said he was coming over with some artists of the Paris Opéra to televise, and would arrive on 2 April. Romola arranged to go up to London with Vaslav to see them. She went ahead to greet Lifar at the airport and on the afternoon of Sunday, 2 April, met Vaslav at Waterloo Station. He waved to her gaily from the train. They stayed at the Welbeck Hotel, where Lifar and his friend Jean Beau visited them. The BBC invited them to watch a rehearsal of the French dancers on the Tuesday.

That morning Vaslav complained of a headache, but wanted to go out. Romola took him round the corner to the Wallace Collection. He looked at the pictures carefully and stood for a long time before Lancret's painting of Camargo. At lunch he was in a good humour and signed some photographs.

We spent the entire afternoon at the Alexandra Palace watching the rehearsal of the Paris Opera Ballet. It all interested Vaslav immensely: he always adored mechanical inventions. Near him the chief engineer had placed a television set on which he could watch the performance while at the same time watching the dancing on the stage.

He was very much taken with Nina Vyroubova, whom he had seen dancing in Roland Petit's version of the old Taglioni ballet 'La Sylphide', a few months before, and who had now joined the Opera Ballet.

Her dancing enchanted Vaslav, who smiled at her all the time.

The rehearsal was interrupted by the tea which Mr Norman Collins, then Director of Television for the BBC, offered us. Serge and a few officials of the company were present. Vaslav seemed cheerful and happy.

When we returned home that evening, Vatza retired at once and had a light supper. He closed his eyes and did not wish to talk to us. Suddenly I noticed that he clutched his hands, and then, with the fingers of one hand, he tapped some dance movements as he used to do many years ago when he was composing and concentrating on new choreography. How strange, I thought. Then with his left arm he began to make *port de bras* round his head as he used to do while dancing the 'Spectre de la rose'.

On the Wednesday morning Romola felt anxious about Vaslav's condition and decided to consult her doctor.

I called him around ten o'clock and asked him to come at once. He was unable to do so. Vaslav had no temperature, but he refused to eat and lay limply on his bed. His pulse was slightly faster than usual. I began to telephone around to acquaintances in an effort to find a reliable doctor. It was already around three in the afternoon. Finally a very good Hungarian doctor was recommended to me. He had been practising in Germany and London lately. I called him and asked him to come at once, and he soon arrived.

He was alarmed by Vaslav's high blood pressure and took a blood test. He told me that until he got the report from the tests, he would be unable to begin any treatment as he might give the wrong medicine. He was not sure what had caused Vaslav's condition, and said, 'If he is suffering from arteriosclerosis, then he will need just a few injections. But if this is not the case, and he is suffering from the kidneys, we will be facing a far more difficult task.'

I begged him to do something at once, but he said he could not. I began to lose faith in all these doctors and phoned to Zürich, but Professor Rohr did not answer. I wired him. The hours passed. Vaslav was lying listlessly while I frantically telephoned around for medical help.

... The Hungarian doctor returned* and said the report was worse than he had anticipated. We decided that Vaslav should be taken next day to a clinic where treatment would be given. The doctor instructed me to dress Vatza the next morning and take him by taxi. He wished to avoid an ambulance so as not to alarm Vatza ...

I still did not realize that Vaslav's life might be in danger. Tremblingly I went to his room. He was sitting up in bed ... and looking at the illustrated papers, smiling and interested. The attendant and I were quite relieved. But he had a bad night and was restless in the morning. His face became small and flushed and he did not react to any of our questioning. He seemed dazed. We were unspeakably worried and summoned an ambulance. Never shall I forget how we took him to the clinic, wrapped up in blankets looking like a new-born baby, listless and helpless.

Throughout Thursday Romola tried to get help from Zürich. She was told that Professor Rohr had left for his Easter vacation and no

*The order of events in Nijinsky's final illness is slightly confused in Romola Nijinsky's *The Last Days of Nijinsky*. With her help Mme Nijinsky's account has been re-arranged here.

535

one knew where he was. 'As I had the utmost confidence in him, I tried to persuade a Swiss broadcasting station to broadcast an announcement that Professor Rohr was requested to fly to London. But my call was in vain.'

During the night a priest came, but Romola would not allow him near Vaslav, in case he should realize he was dying. The next morning – Good Friday – Nijinsky lapsed into a coma. The doctors began to treat him with streptomycin and told Romola that if they could bring him out of the coma within twenty-four hours his life would be saved. Romola called in another consultant who said that Vaslav was 'beyond human help. His kidneys were gone.'

Romola was in a state of shock.

I stood by Vatza's bed while the attendant held his left hand which was bandaged and through which food and medicines were constantly administered intravenously. But he was quite unconscious. His eyes were closed all the time . . . Vaslav moaned constantly and with his free hand he was wiping his face. The night passed. I was trembling. The anguish I felt was inexpressible.

There was a gradual improvement and on the Saturday morning he was better. 'The streptomycin had begun to act. He was coming out of the coma and understood what was going on around him. We all should be careful what we said. . . He opened his eyes. They were clear and lovely. He looked at me with a tender, loving gaze.' Vaslav was able to sit up, looking bright, and his attendant spoon-fed him his breakfast. Everyone felt optimistic, and the doctor now said there was hope of curing the disease. But as Romola was talking in another room to the head nurse, Nijinsky's Swiss attendant, Schneider, called her. Nijinsky had fallen back against the pillow: his expression had changed. Suddenly he sat bolt upright and said '*Mamasha*'.

I don't know if he called his mother or me. And then he stretched out his right hand to me. I bent down and kissed it . . .

I ordered the nurses to give him an injection, some oxygen. Vatza sighed just once. The sun beamed through the window. The nurses stood helpless, while the attendant laid Vatza back. His eyes and mouth closed.

Thoughts and feelings were racing in my mind, but the enduring thought was: 'You were privileged among so many millions of women to share his life, to serve him. God gave him to you. He has taken him back.'

Thus Vaslav Nijinsky died in the presence of the woman who had been for thirty-seven years his wife and for thirty his breadwinner, nurse and second mother.

It was Holy Saturday, 8 April 1950. I was at a matinée of ballet at Sadler's Wells, sitting next to Lincoln Kirstein, the Director of the New York City Ballet, who had helped Romola in 1932 with the book which had changed my life; for I had now for several years been editing the magazine *Ballet*, which I founded, and was the ballet critic of the *Observer*. In the first interval an attendant told me I was wanted on the telephone. An editor of my newspaper said Nijinsky was dead and that I must quickly produce an obituary for Sunday's paper. I went backstage and was allowed to write and telephone in Ninette de Valois's office. It occurred to me that neither I, nor Lincoln Kirstein, nor Ninette de Valois would be where we were or doing what we were if it had not been for Diaghilev and Nijinsky; nor would the Sadler's Wells Ballet (the second of the two companies) be performing in this theatre, nor would the New York City Ballet, under Balanchine, shortly be making their first appearance at Covent Garden.

On the evening of Wednesday, 12 April, I was at Covent Garden, when Margaret Power, whom I then knew very slightly, came during an interval to tell me that Romola Nijinsky was rather upset as no one connected with the English Ballet had offered to be pall-bearers at Nijinsky's funeral in two days' time. I told her to re-assure Mme Nijinsky, because it would never enter an Englishman's head to *offer* to be a pall-bearer; and I promised to arrange matters.

The funeral Mass was held at St James's, Spanish Place, behind the Wallace Collection, on Friday, 14 April. Besides Romola Nijinsky, a number of old colleagues – Tamara Karsavina, Marie Rambert and Lydia Sokolova – were present. The pall-bearers, paired off according to size, with the shortest in front, were Serge Lifar and Anton Dolin; Frederick Ashton and myself; Michael Somes and Cyril Beaumont. Of these only Beaumont had seen

537

Nijinsky in his glory. He confessed afterwards that he had found the weight of the coffin almost intolerable. We slid the coffin into the hearse. Ashton and I did not go to the cemetery.

Two cars followed the coffin: in the first Romola, Karsavina, Dolin, Lifar and Beaumont; in the second, Marie Rambert, Frances James (formerly one of her dancers), Margaret Power and Rupert Doone, a member of the Diaghilev Ballet in later years, and a pioneer of ballet in England. The burial took place at the St Marylebone Cemetery in the Finchley Road. Afterwards, as the mourners moved away, Beaumont looked back to see a new figure standing by the grave. It was the Hindu dancer, Ram Gopal.[76]

But Nijinsky was not to be allowed to rest in peace. *Kak Tsigane*. In June 1953 Lifar arranged for his body to be moved to Paris so that he should lie in the Montmartre Cemetery near Auguste Vestris, where Lifar intended to be buried himself. After disinterment, the coffin was taken to a chapel in the Marylebone Road, where regulations obliged that it should be opened to make sure the body was inside. The inner lead coffin was then placed in a new wooden one and this was conveyed to Victoria Station, where Nadia Legat brought a party of her pupils to adorn it with flowers. Margaret Power accompanied it. The second funeral service was held at about ten in the morning at the Russian Church in the rue Daru. Bronislava Nijinska had insisted that Vaslav be buried with the Russian Orthodox rites. Romola was in America and could not afford to come: Preobrajenskaya and Egorova were present, as well as Lifar and many dancers and singers of the Opéra. The Administrator and the Minister of Fine Arts made speeches.[77] This took place on 16 June 1953, just two weeks after the Coronation of Queen Elizabeth II.

Nijinsky's life can be simply summarized: ten years growing; ten years learning; ten years dancing; thirty years in eclipse. Roughly sixty in all. How long his memory will live in the minds of men we can only guess. As Sir Thomas Browne wrote, 'What song the sirens sang or what name Achilles assumed when he hid himself among women, although puzzling questions are not beyond all conjecture.'

CITY AND ISLINGTON
SIXTH FORM COLLEG
283-309 GOSWELL ROAD
LONDON
EC1

TEL 020 7520 0652

BIBLIOGRAPHY

Agate, James. *Ego*, Vol. III. Harrap, London, 1938.

Alexander Mikhailovitch, Grand Duke. *Once a Grand Duke*. Farrar & Rinehart, New York; Cassell, London, 1932.

Astruc, Gabriel. *Le Pavillon des fantômes*. Grasset, Paris, 1929.

— 'Le Premier Feu d'Artifice', in *Revue Musicale*, 1 December, 1930 (Paris).

Barbier, George and Miomandre, Francis de. *Nijinsky*. Bernouard, Paris, 1912.

Beaumont, Cyril. *The Ballet called Giselle*. Beaumont, London, 1944.

— *The Complete Book of Ballets*. Putnam, London, 1937. Revised 1949, 1951.

— *The Diaghilev Ballet in London*. Putnam, London, 1940. [Beaumont: London].

— 'The Funeral of Vaslav Nijinsky', in *The Ballet Annual*, Fifth Issue. A. & C. Black, London, 1951.

— *Michel Fokine and his Ballets*. Beaumont, London, 1935.

— *The Romantic Ballet as seen by Théophile Gautier*. Beaumont, London, 1932.

— *Vaslav Nijinsky*. Beaumont, London, 1932.

Bedells, Phyllis. *My Dancing Days*. Phoenix House, London, 1954.

Bennett, Arnold. *The Journals of Arnold Bennett, 1911–1921*. Edited by Newman Flower. Cassell, London, 1932.

Benois, Alexandre. *Early Memories of Diaghilev*, introduction to the catalogue of the Diaghilev Exhibition, 1954.

— *Memoirs*, Vol. II. Translated by Moura Budberg. Chatto & Windus, London, 1964.

— *Reminiscences of the Russian Ballet*. Translated by Mary Britnieva. Putnam, London, 1941.

Bibliography

Blanche, Jacques-Emile. *Portraits of a Lifetime*. Dent, London, 1937.

Bourman, Anatole (with D. Lyman). *The Tragedy of Nijinsky*. Robert Hale, London, 1937.

Braun, Edward. *Meyerhold on Theatre*. Methuen, London, 1969.

Buckle, Richard. *In Search of Diaghilev*. Sidgwick & Jackson, London, 1955.

Calvocoressi, M. D. *Music and Ballet*. Faber & Faber, London, 1938.

Carter, Huntley. *The New Spirit in Drama and Art*. Frank Palmer, London, 1912.

Chaplin, Charles. *My Autobiography*. The Bodley Head, London, 1964.

Chujoy, Anatole. 'Russian Balletomania', in *Dance Index*, Vol. VII, no. 3, March 1948 (New York).

Clarke, Mary. *Dancers of Mercury*. A. & C. Black, London, 1962.

Cocteau, Jean. *Cock and Harlequin*. Translated by Rollo H. Myers. The Egoist Press, London, 1921.

— *Opium*. Stock, Paris, 1930.

— *La Difficulté d'Etre*. Paul Morihien, Paris, 1947.

Craig, Edward. *Gordon Craig*. Gollancz, London, 1968.

Dandré, V. *Anna Pavlova*. Cassell, London, 1932.

Debussy, Claude. *Lettres de Claude Debussy à son éditeur*. Durand, Paris, 1927.

Denby, Edwin. 'Notes on Nijinsky Photographs', in *Dance Index*, Vol. II, No. 3, March 1943 (New York). Reprinted in Paul Magriel: *Nijinsky*. Henry Holt, New York, 1946.

Dolin, Anton. *Autobiography*. Oldbourne, London, 1960.

— *Ballet Go Round*. Michael Joseph, London, 1938.

Dumesnil, Maurice. *An Amazing Journey*. Ives Washburn, New York, 1932. Jarrolds, London, 1933.

Duncan, Irma and MacDougall, A. R. *Isadora Duncan's Russian Days*. Gollancz, London, 1929.

Duncan, Isadora. *My Life*. Gollancz, London, 1928. Sphere (paperback), London, 1968.

Ede, H. S. *Savage Messiah*. Heinemann, London, 1931.

Fokine, Michel. *Against the Tide*. Leningrad and Moscow, 1962.

— *Memoirs of a Ballet Master*. Translated by Vitale Fokine; edited by Anatole Chujoy. Little, Brown, Boston & Constable, London, 1961.

Grigoriev, S. L. *The Diaghilev Ballet 1909–1929*. Constable, London, 1953. Penguin (paperback), London, 1960.

Guest, Ivor. *Adeline Genée*. A. & C. Black, London, 1958.

— 'Carlotta Zambelli'. *La Revue d'Histoire du Théatre*, III. 1969.

Hahn, Reynaldo. *Notes: Journal d'un musicien.* Plon, Paris, 1933.

Harriman, P. L. *The New Dictionary of Psychology.* Vision Press; Peter Owen, London, 1952.

Harewood, The Earl of. *Kobbé's Complete Opera Book.* Putnam, London, 1969.

Haskell, Arnold. *Balletomania.* Gollancz, London, 1934.

— *Diaghileff.* Gollancz, London, 1935.

Hofmannsthal, Hugo von and Strauss, Richard. *Correspondence between Richard Strauss and Hugo von Hofmannsthal.* Collins, London, 1961. [Hofmannsthal-Strauss.]

Hugo, Victor. *A Life related by one who has witnessed it,* Vol. II. William H. Allen, London, 1863.

Hyden, Walford. *Pavlova.* Constable, London, 1931.

Jankélévitch, Vladimir. *Ravel.* Grove Press, New York, and Calder, London, 1959 (paperback).

Johnson, A. E. *The Russian Ballet.* Constable, London, 1913.

Jones, Robert Edmond. 'Nijinsky and Til Eulenspiegel', in *Dance Index*, Vol. IV, No, 4, April 1945 (New York). Reprinted in Paul Magriel: *Nijinsky.* Henry Holt, New York, 1946.

Karsavina, Tamara. *Theatre Street.* Heinemann, London, 1930. Revised edition, Constable, London, 1948. Dutton (paperback), New York, 1961.

Kchessinskaya, M. F. *Dancing in St Petersburg.* Gollancz, London, 1960.

Kerensky, Oleg. *Anna Pavlova.* Hamish Hamilton, London, 1973.

Kessler, Count Harry. *The Diaries of a Cosmopolitan.* Translated and edited by Charles Kessler. Weidenfeld & Nicolson, London, 1971.

Khan, Aga. *The Memoirs of Aga Khan.* Cassell and Constable, London, 1954.

Kirstein, Lincoln. *Fokine.* British-Continental Press, London, 1934.

Kochno, Boris. *Diaghilev and the Ballets Russes.* Translated by Adrienne Foulke. Harper & Row, New York, 1970; Allen Lane The Penguin Press, London, 1971.

— *Le Ballet.* Hachette, Paris, 1954.

Legat, Nicolas. *Ballets Russes.* Methuen, London, 1939.

Lieven, Prince Peter. *The Birth of Ballets Russes.* Translated by L. Zarine. George Allen & Unwin, London, 1936. Dover (paperback), New York, 1973.

Lifar, Serge. *Serge Diaghilev.* Putnam, London, 1940.

Lockspeiser, Edward. *Debussy*. Dent, London, 1936. Revised 1951, 1963.
— *Debussy, his life and mind*, Vol. II. Cassell, London, 1965.
Magriel, Paul. *Nijinsky*. Henry Holt, New York, 1946.
Macke, August. *Das Russische Ballett*. Edited by Günter Busch. Philipp Reclam Jun., Stuttgart, 1966.
Manuel, Roland. *Maurice Ravel*. Translated by Cynthia Jolly. Dobson, London, 1947.
Marsh, Edward. *A Number of People*. Heinemann and Hamish Hamilton, London, 1939.
— *Rupert Brooke, A Memoir*. Sidgwick & Jackson, London, 1918.
Martin, Ralph G. *Lady Randolph Churchill*. Cassell, London, 1969.
Massie, Robert K. *Nicholas and Alexandra*. Gollancz, London, 1968.
Massine, Leonide. *My Life in Ballet*. Edited by Phyllis Hartnoll and Robert Rubens. Macmillan, London, 1968.
Morrell, Lady Ottoline. *Ottoline*. Edited by Robert Gathorne-Hardy. Faber & Faber, London, 1963.
Mossolov, A. A. *At the Court of the Last Tsar*. Translated by E. W. Dickes; edited by A. A. Pilenco. Methuen, London, 1935.
Nijinsky, Romola. *The Last Years of Nijinsky*. Gollancz, London, 1952.
— *Nijinsky*. Gollancz, London, 1933. Penguin (paperback), London, 1960. Sphere (paperback), London, 1970 (pagination as in the Penguin edition). [Romola Nijinsky].
Nijinsky, Vaslav. *The Diary of Vaslav Nijinsky*. Translated and edited by Romola Nijinsky. Gollancz, London, 1937. Panther (paperback), London, 1962. [*Diary*].
Painter, G. D. *Marcel Proust*, Vol. II. Chatto & Windus, London, 1965.
Pevsner, Nicholas. *The Buildings of England: London* (*1*). Penguin, London, 1960; revised 1962.
Propert, W. A. *The Russian Ballet in Western Europe, 1909–1920*. The Bodley Head, London, 1921.
— *The Russian Ballet, 1921–1929*. The Bodley Head, London, 1931. [Propert II.]
Proust, Marcel. *Lettres à Reynaldo Hahn*. Edited by Philippe Kolb. Paris, 1956.
Reiss, Françoise. *Nijinsky*. A. & C. Black, London, 1960.
Ricketts, Charles. *Self-Portrait*. Peter Davies, London, 1939.
Rimsky-Korsakov, N. A. *My Musical Life*. Translated by J. A. Joffe; edited by Carl van Vechten. Secker, London, 1924.

Rivière, Jacques. 'Le Sacre du Printemps', in *Nouvelle Revue Française*, November 1913 (Paris).

Rosenthal, Harold. *Two Centuries of Opera at Covent Garden*. Putnam, London, 1958.

Sandoz, Maurice. *The Crystal Salt Cellar*. Guilford Press, London, 1954.

Schneider, Ilya Ilyitch. *Isadora Duncan, The Russian Years*. MacDonald, London, 1968.

Sert, Misia. *Two or Three Muses*. Museum Press, London, 1953.

Seton-Watson, Hugh. *The Decline of Imperial Russia, 1855–1914*. Methuen, London, 1952.

Sitwell, Osbert. *Great Morning*. Macmillan, London, 1948.

— *Laughter in the Next Room*. Macmillan, London, 1949.

Slonimsky, Yury. 'Marius Petipa', edited by Anatole Chujoy, in *Dance Index*, Vol. VI, Nos. 5 and 6, May–June 1947 (New York). [Slonimsky Chujoy.]

Sokolova, Lydia. *Dancing for Diaghilev*. Edited by Richard Buckle. John Murray, London, 1960.

Sotheby & Co. Catalogues of sales of material relating to the Diaghilev Ballet: 15 October, 1963; 26 May, 1964; 13 June, 1967; 16, 17 and 18 July, 1968; 9 and 10 July, 1969; 15, 16 and 19 December, 1969.

Stier, Theodor. *With Pavlova round the World*. Hurst and Blackett, London, [1927].

Stokes, Adrian. *Tonight the Ballet*. Faber & Faber, London, 1934.

— *Russian Ballets*. Faber & Faber, London, 1935.

Stravinsky, Igor. *Chronicle of my Life*. Gollancz, London, 1936.

— *The Rite of Spring, Sketches 1911–1913*. Boosey & Hawkes, London, 1969.

— with Robert Craft. *Conversations*. Faber & Faber, London, 1959.

— with Robert Craft. *Expositions and Developments*. Faber & Faber, London, 1962.

— with Robert Craft. *Memories and Commentaries*. Faber & Faber, London, 1960.

Svetlov, Valerien. *Le Ballet contemporain*. Designed by Leon Bakst. Golicke and Willborg, St Petersburg; translated by M. D. Calvocoressi, Brunoff, Paris, 1912.

— *Thamar Karsavina*. Translated by H. de Vere Beauclerk and Nadia Evrenov; edited by Cyril Beaumont. Beaumont, London, 1922.

Terry, Ellen. *The Russian Ballet*. Sidgwick & Jackson, London, 1913.

Bibliography

Van Vechten, Carl. 'Vaslav Nijinsky', in *Interpreters*. Alfred A. Knopf, New York, 1917. Reprinted in *Dance Index*, Vol 1, Nos. 9–11, September-November 1942 (New York) and in Paul Magriel: *Nijinsky*. Henry Holt, New York, 1946.

Vaudoyer, Jean-Louis. 'Variations sur les Ballets Russes', in *La Revue de Paris*, July 1910 (Paris).

Vaughan, David. 'Pavlova's American "Beauty"', in *Ballet Review*, Vol. 3, No. 2, 1969 (New York).

Whitworth, Geoffrey. *The Art of Nijinsky*. Chatto & Windus, London, 1913.

Wilde, Oscar. *The Letters of Oscar Wilde*. Edited by Rupert Hart-Davis. Hart-Davis, London, 1962.

SOURCE NOTES

My sources are (1) printed books and articles in learned journals, (2) newspapers, (3) theatre programmes, (4) the Astruc correspondence in the New York Public Library, (5) certain unpublished manuscripts such as Diaghilev's Memoirs, in the collection of M. Boris Kochno, Diaghilev's note-book, Grigoriev's note-books, the Romola Nijinsky-Lincoln Kirstein draft of Mme Nijinsky's biography, Nijinsky's copy of the score of 'L'Après-midi d'un faune' with his dance notation, Valentine Gross's typescript and manuscripts and Lady Juliet Duff's essay, (6) questionnaires answered for me by the associates of Diaghilev and Nijinsky, (7) conversations with some of the latter, of which I made notes.

In the list of books and journals in the Bibliography, the date of their first publication in English is given, or if they have not been published in English, their first appearance in French or another language. But the page references in my Notes are, for the sake of the student's convenience, given not to the first edition of a book, but to the latest and most available edition – perhaps paperback – published in England or America. Thus, in the Bibliography will be found: 'Karsavina, Tamara. *Theatre Street*. Heinemann, London, 1930. Revised edition Constable, London, 1948. [Notes refer to] Dutton (paperback), New York, 1961.' (I have made an exception to this rule in the case of the series of Stravinsky-Craft books. Since only two of these have been reprinted as one paperback, I have referred in all cases to the original editions.) Some books referred to have not, of course, been reprinted.

Notes such as 'Rambert conversations' or 'Grigoriev questionnaires' are self-explanatory.

In the Notes, books are referred to by the author's surname, or, if more than one work by an author is used, by the surname and the title (or abbreviated title) of the book. Departures from this practice are indicated in square brackets in the Bibliography.

545

Chapter One   *1898–1908*

1 Bronislava Nijinska conversations.
2 Ibid. Mme Nijinska put the number at between 100 and 150. Bourman wrote 'hundreds' on p. 23 and 'one hundred' on p. 24.
3 Karsavina: *Theatre Street*, pp. 41 and 102.
4 Legat, pp. 51, 52.
5 Bourman, p. 19, lists the class-mates and their fates, but states that Feodorov was killed in error during the revolution. Mme Bronislava Nijinska says that the cause of his death was tuberculosis.
6 B. Nijinska conversations. Mme Romola Nijinsky had been misinformed when she wrote that Eleonora Bereda's father was a dancer, that he was of gentle birth and that he shot himself.
7 Ibid.
8 Ibid. All previous biographers have mistakenly postdated Nijinsky's birth and entry into the school by two years, giving him the dates which should have been Bronislava's.
9 Romola Nijinsky, p. 25.
10 B. Nijinska conversations.
11 Ibid.
12 Ibid.
13 *Diary*, pp. 53, 54.
14 B. Nijinska conversations.
15 Bourman, p. 26.
16 Ibid., p. 27.

17 B. Nijinska conversations.
18 Legat, p. 52.
19 Bourman, p. 34.
20 Slonimsky-Chujoy, p. 126.
21 Benois: *Early Memories of Diaghilev*, introduction to the catalogue of the Diaghilev Exhibition.
22 Benois: *Memoirs* II, pp. 61 and 63.
23 Benois: *Reminiscences*, pp. 187–90.
24 Ibid., pp. 211, 212
25 Ibid., pp. 213–18.
26 Kchessinskaya, pp. 81, 82.
27 Karsavina: *Theatre Street*, p. 133.
28 Karsavina: speech at the opening of the Diaghilev Exhibition, Forbes House, November 1954, quoted in Buckle: *In Search of Diaghilev*.
29 Guest: *Zambelli*, pp. 220–27.
30 Bourman, p. 35.
31 Benois: *Reminiscences*, p. 222.
32 Ibid., p. 187.
33 Kchessinskaya, pp. 86, 87.
34 Karsavina: *Theatre Street*, p. 147.
35 Kerensky, pp. 1–3.
36 Karsavina conversations.
37 Imperial Theatres: information supplied by Mme Natalia Dudinskaya. Also mentioned by Bourman, p. 36.
38 Bourman, p. 36.
39 Ibid., p. 37.
40 Vladimirov conversation.
41 Bourman, pp. 56–9, 94–6. These are two of Bourman's true stories,

confirmed by Mme Bronislava Nijinska, though no doubt some of their colouring has been considerably heightened.

42 B. Nijinska conversations.
43 Doubrovska conversation.
44 Romola Nijinsky, p. 36.
45 Romola Nijinsky conversations.
46 Karsavina: *Theatre Street*, pp. 135, 136.
47 Slonimsky-Chujoy, pp. 125, 126.
48 Teliakovsky Diary, quoted in Slonimsky-Chujoy, p. 126
49 Legat, p. 31.
50 Benois: *Reminiscences*, pp. 229, 230.
51 Kchessinskaya, p. 98.
52 Bourman, pp. 82–4. Also Romola Nijinsky, p. 41.
53 Benois: *Memoirs* II, pp. 221, 222.
54 Karsavina: *Theatre Street*, pp. 153, 154.
55 Bourman, p. 84.
56 Duncan, p. 118
57 Information supplied by Mme Vera Krasovskaya.
58 Duncan, pp. 119, 120.
59 Told the author by Mme Braikeivitch, the donor of the fine collection of Russian stage designs and pictures to the Ashmolean, at the time of the Diaghilev Exhibition.
60 Benois: *Memoirs* II, pp. 223, 234.
61 Sacheverell Sitwell, review of the first edition of *Nijinsky, Books and Bookmen*, November 1971.
62 Benois: *Memoirs* II, p. 234.
63 Diaghilev's speech at the Tauride Palace, quoted by Haskell, pp. 160, 161. Haskell told me he had the text of it from Nouvel.
64 Bourman, pp. 90–93.
65 Letter from Diaghilev to Propert, 17 February, 1926, quoted in Propert II, pp. 87, 88.
66 Fokine, pp. 87–90.
67 Karsavina conversations.
68 Karsavina: *Theatre Street*, pp. 158–60.
69 Legat, p. 45; Karsavina: *Theatre Street*, p. 162: *et al.*

70 Benois: *Memoirs* II, pp. 230, 231.
71 Lifar, pp. 167, 168. Lifar had this account from Mme Greffuhle.
72 B. Nijinska conversations.
73 Vladimirov conversation.
74 Ibid.
75 Karsavina: *Theatre Street*, p. 151.
76 Information obtained by Mme Vera Krasovskaya from the Mariinsky Theatre Archives.
77 Bourman, p. 100.
78 Information obtained by Mme Vera Krasovskaya from the Mariinsky Theatre Archives.
79 Fokine, pp. 90, 91.
80 Facsimile reproduced in Fokine: *Against the Tide*, p. 166.
81 B. Nijinska conversations. Although Fokine tells the story of the painted tights it was Mme Nijinska who told me that it was she who painted toes first on her own, then on the other dancers' tights.
82 Fokine, pp. 93–6.
83 Ibid., pp. 96, 97.
84 Ibid., p. 101.
85 Ibid., pp. 102, 103.
86 Benois: *Reminiscences*, pp. 225–7.
87 Ibid., pp. 106 107.
88 *Petersburgskaya Gazeta*, No. 105, 17 April 1907.
89 *Theatre and Music*, No. 11170, 17 April 1907.
90 Information supplied by Mme Krasovskaya.
91 Schollar conversation.
92 B. Nijinska conversations.
93 Bourman, p. 104.
94 Ibid., pp. 106, 107.
95 Diaghilev Memoirs.
96 Benois: *Reminiscences*, pp. 240–66.
97 Kchessinskaya, pp. 40–42.
98 B. Nijinska conversations.
99 Ibid.
100 Bourman, p. 117.
101 B. Nijinska conversations.
102 *Diary*, p. 74.
103 B. Nijinska conversations.
104 Bourman, p. 131.

105 B. Nijinska conversations.
106 Ibid.
107 Ibid.
108 Ibid.
109 Ibid.
110 Bourman, pp. 133, 134.
111 B. Nijinska conversations.
112 Imperial Theatres: information supplied by Mme Natalia Dudinskaya.
113 Karsavina: *Theatre Street*, p. 152.
114 Karsavina conversations.
115 Schollar conversation.
116 Imperial Theatres: information supplied by Mme Natalia Dudinskaya.
117 Benois: *Reminiscences*, p. 243.
118 Ibid., pp. 245, 246.
119 Ibid., pp. 249–65.
120 Imperial Theatres: information supplied by Mme Natalia Dudinskaya.
121 Fokine, pp. 129–33.
122 Diaghilev Memoirs.
123 Ibid.
124 Benois: *Memoirs* II, p. 246.
125 Benois: *Reminiscences*, p. 268. Also *Memoirs* II, p. 247.
126 Diaghilev Memoirs.
127 Benois: *Memoirs* II, p. 247.

128 Grand Duke Alexander Mikhailovitch: *Once a Grand Duke*, p. 137.
129 Ibid., p. 138.
130 Karsavina: *Theatre Street*, pp. 81, 82.
131 Diaghilev Memoirs.
132 Ibid.
133 Benois: *Memoirs* II, pp. 250, 251.
134 Diaghilev Memoirs.
135 Benois: *Memoirs* II, p. 251.
136 Karsavina conversations.
137 Diaghilev Memoirs.
138 Benois: *Memorirs* II, p. 252.
139 Diaghilev Memoirs.
140 M. Sert, pp. 111, 112.
141 Bourman, p. 140.
142 Reiss, p. 51. Mlle Reiss had this information from Matilda Kchessinskaya.
143 Bourman, pp. 141–4.
144 B. Nijinska conversations.
145 Baroness Budberg conversation.
146 Romola Nijinsky conversations.
147 *Diary*, p. 63.
148 B. Nijinska conversations.
149 *Diary*, p. 59.
150 B. Nijinska conversations.
151 Bourman, pp. 151–5.
152 *Diary*, p. 59.
153 Ibid., pp. 80–83.

Chapter Two *1909*

1 Romola Nijinsky, p. 64.
2 Dandré, p. 206.
3 Fokine, p. 138.
4 Astruc, *Revue Musicale*, December 1930.
5 Ibid.
6 Benois: *Reminiscences*, p. 266; *Memoirs* II, p. 240.
7 Astruc, *Revue Musicale*, December 1930.
8 Astruc papers.
9 Astruc, *Revue Musicale*, December 1930.
10 Astruc papers: the contract is

summarized in Astruc's report to the Tsar, November 1909.
11 Grigoriev questionnaires.
12 Karsavina conversations.
13 Ibid.
14 Ibid.
15 Ibid.
16 Ibid.
17 Grigoriev, p. 17.
18 Ibid., pp. 14, 15.
19 Ibid., pp. 15, 16.
20 Grigoriev questionnaires.
21 Grigoriev, pp. 18, 19.
22 Ibid., p. 20.

23 Stravinsky: *Expositions*, p. 25.
24 Kchessinskaya, p. 111.
25 Grigoriev, p. 23.
26 Astruc papers. Astruc's report to the Tsar, November 1909.
27 Ibid. Pro-forma.
28 Massine conversations.
29 Grigoriev, p. 24.
30 Ibid., pp. 23, 24.
31 Lifar, pp. 181, 182.
32 Astruc papers. Telegram from Diaghilev to Astruc, 12 March 1909.
33 Ibid. Telegram from Diaghilev to Astruc, 14 March 1909.
34 Benois: *Reminiscences*, pp. 280, 281.
35 Karsavina: *Theatre Street*, p. 192.
36 Benois: *Reminiscences*, pp. 281, 282.
37 Grigoriev, pp. 25, 26.
38 Fokine, pp. 149, 150.
39 Grigoriev, p. 26.
40 Astruc papers. Telegrams from Diaghilev to Astruc, 29 March 1909 and 3 April 1909.
41 Ibid. Only Diaghilev's reply to Astruc's demand survives. Telegram, 10 March 1909.
42 Ibid. Telegram from Diaghilev to Astruc, 31 March 1909.
43 Ibid. Same telegram.
44 Ibid. Telegram from Diaghilev to Astruc, 6 April 1909.
45 Ibid. Telegram from Diaghilev to Astruc, 7 April 1909.
46 Grigoriev questionnaires.
47 Benois: *Reminiscences*, p. 283.
48 Ibid., p. 283.
49 Astruc papers. Telegrams from Diaghilev to Astruc, 20 April 1909, 21 April 1909, 23 April 1909, 26 April 1909, 27 April 1909, 28 April 1909, 29 April 1909.
50 Karsavina conversations.
51 B. Nijinska conversations.
52 Astruc papers. Report to the Tsar, November 1909.
53 Karsavina: *Theatre Street*, p. 193.
54 Karsavina conversations.
55 Astruc papers. Report to the Tsar, November 1909.
56 Grigoriev, p. 27.
57 B. Nijinska conversations.
58 Svetlov: *Le Ballet*, p. 86.
59 Benois: *Reminiscences*, p. 287, also footnote.
60 Grigoriev, pp. 28, 29.
61 Karsavina: *Theatre Street*, p. 194.
62 Karsavina conversations.
63 Karsavina: *Theatre Street*, pp. 194, 195.
64 Grigoriev questionnaires.
65 Karsavina: *Theatre Street*, p. 196.
66 Svetlov: *Le Ballet*, p. 86.
67 Painter II, p. 146.
68 Ibid., pp. 17, 18 *et al.*
69 Ibid., p. 10 *et al.*
70 Ibid., p. 3 *et al.*
71 French Press.
72 Ibid.
73 *Le Figaro*, 11 May 1909.
74 Karsavina conversations.
75 Grigoriev, p. 29.
76 Svetlov: *Le Ballet*, p. 87.
77 *Le Figaro*, 17 May 1909.
78 M. Jean Hugo told the author this, but it is no doubt a well-known fact. Proust wrote for these papers.
79 *Le Figaro*, 19 May 1909.
80 Astruc, *Revue Musicale*, December 1930.
81 Benois: *Reminiscences*, p. 289.
82 Romola Nijinsky, p. 72.
83 Benois: *Reminiscences*, pp. 289, 290.
84 Ibid., p. 292.
85 Compare illustration in Benois *Reminiscences*, facing page 297, and Plates 16 and 17 in the hard-back edition of this book.
86 Benois: *Reminiscences*, p. 291.
87 Ibid., p. 291.
88 Ibid., p. 292.
89 The description of 'Armide' is largely based on Karsavina conversations (and, indeed, demonstrations), embellished by quotations from Benois, Fokine and Geoffrey Whitworth. I fitted these accounts of the action to the piano

score, played for me by Brian
Blackwood.

90 Benois: *Reminiscences*, p. 244. I have
changed Benois's past tense to the
present.

91 Whitworth, p. 40.

92 Karsavina: *Theatre Street*, p. 197.

93 Romola Nijinsky, p. 73.

94 Whitworth, pp. 41, 42.

95 Karsavina conversations.

96 Karsavina: *Theatre Street*, p. 198.

97 Fokine, p. 107

98 Karsavina conversations. Her actual
phrase.

99 M. Jean Hugo's description to the
author of how people behaved in
those days.

100 Astruc, *Revue Musicale*, December
1930.

101 Vaudoyer: Introduction to the
catalogue of Lifar's Exposition des
Ballets Russes de Serge Diaghilev,
Musée des Arts Décoratifs, 1939.

102 Kochno: *Le Ballet*, p. 142.

103 Beaumont: *Complete Book*, p. 685.

104 Karsavina: *Theatre Street*, p. 198.

105 Ibid., p. 198.

106 Told the author by M. Jean Hugo.

107 Karsavina: *Theatre Street*, p. 198.

108 Ibid., pp. 198, 199.

109 *Le Figaro*, 19 May 1909.

110 Karsavina: *Theatre Street*, p. 199.

111 *Le Figaro*, 20 May 1909.

112 *Le Figaro*, 15 May 1909.

113 *Commedia*, 20 May 1909.

114 Ibid.

115 Astruc, p. 133; Lieven, p. 104.

116 Karsavina conversations.

117 Lieven, pp. 87, 88, 104.

118 Karsavina conversations.

119 Karsavina: *Theatre Street*, p. 200.

120 Ibid., pp. 282, 283.

121 Karsavina conversations. Mme
Karsavina did not remember at whose
house Nijinsky saw the Gauguin
paintings. It was the author's friend
Mme Jean Hugo who made inquiries
in Paris and found that it could only
have been Emmanuel Bibesco's.

This was confirmed by Princess
Marthe Bibesco, who added that her
cousin, hard-up as he was, used to
make Gauguin a small allowance.

122 It was M. Jean Hugo who described
to the author the attitude of his
father and the Jockey Club to the
ballet.

123 Gautier in *La Presse*, 7 May 1838.

124 Karsavina conversations.

125 Ibid.

126 Ibid.

127 Benois: *Reminiscences*, p. 291.

128 Karsavina: *Theatre Street*, p. 201.

129 Benois: *Reminiscences*, p. 294.

130 Svetlov: *Le Ballet*, pp. 98, 99.

131 Fokine, p. 131.

132 Ibid., p. 130.

133 Stokes: *Russian Ballets*, p. 89.

134 Johnson, pp. 81, 82.

135 Benois: *Reminiscences*, p. 298.

136 Lieven, p. 80.

137 Benois: *Reminiscences*, pp. 295, 297.

138 Description of 'Cléopâtre' based on
Beaumont: *Complete Book*, and
Johnson.

139 Lieven, p. 102. He is quoting
Benois.

140 Karsavina conversations.

141 Fokine, p. 145.

142 Karsavina conversations.

143 Benois: *Reminiscences*, p. 296.

144 Fokine, p. 146.

145 Announcements in French press.

146 Karsavina conversations.

147 Grigoriev, p. 35.

148 *Commedia*, 22 June 1909.

149 Karsavina conversations.

150 *Diary*, pp. 141, 142.

151 Svetlov: *Le Ballet*, p. 103.

152 Astruc papers. Letter from Astruc to
Diaghilev, 15 June 1909.

153 Ibid. Astruc's report to the Tsar,
November 1909.

154 Ibid.

155 Ibid. The bill, which was not
honoured, exists.

156 Kchessinskaya, p. 113.

157 Karsavina conversations.

158 Karsavina: *Theatre Street*, p. 202.
159 Svetlov: *Le Ballet*, p. 104.
160 Benois: *Reminiscences*, p. 300.
161 Romola Nijinsky, p. 80.
162 Ibid., pp. 80, 81.
163 Calvocoressi, p. 136.
164 *Revue de Musicologie*, July–December 1962, p. 34.
165 Quoted in Lockspeiser, Vol. II, p. 169.
166 Astruc papers. Letter from Diaghilev to Astruc's firm, 19(?) July 1909.
167 Ibid. Letter from Diaghilev to Astruc's firm, 6 August 1909.
168 Romola Nijinsky, pp. 81, 82.
169 Astruc papers.
170 Ibid.
171 Ibid.

172 Ibid. Letter from Mossolov to Astruc, 17 November 1909.
173 Ibid. Letter from M. Molodovsky to Astruc on behalf of the Grand Duke Nicholas.
174 Ibid. Letter from F. de Coubé to Astruc on behalf of the Grand Duke André.
175 Ibid.
176 Ibid.
177 Ibid. Letter from Martin to Astruc, 8 December 1909.
178 Ibid.
179 Ibid. Telegrams from Brussel to Astruc, Astruc to Brussel, Astruc to Elter, Litvinne to Elter and Astruc to Chaliapine, between 8 and 15 January 1910.

Chapter Three *1910*

1 Grigoriev, p. 43.
2 Benois: *Reminiscences*, p. 303.
3 Fokine, p. 158.
4 Benois: *Reminiscences*, pp. 303, 304.
5 Lieven, pp. 106, 107.
6 Fokine, pp. 158, 159.
7 Stravinsky: *Expositions*, p. 129.
8 Grigoriev, p. 38.
9 Benois: *Reminiscences*, p. 304.
10 Lieven, p. 106. Benois, who inspired Lieven's book, presumably showed Lieven a copy of Diaghilev's letter to Liadov, for he gives the date, 4 September 1909. If Diaghilev was still in Venice on that date, he had either lingered on after Nijinsky's return to Petersburg, or, if Nijinsky was still there, he had missed the opening of the Mariinsky season.
11 Fokine, p. 160.
12 Stravinsky: *Expositions*, p. 127.
13 Ibid., p. 128.
14 Ibid, pp. 128, 129.
15 Stravinsky: *Memories*, p. 32.
16 Fokine, p. 159.
17 Ibid., p. 159.
18 Haskell, pp. 225, 226.

19 Kirstein, p. 39.
20 Fokine, p. 161.
21 Stravinsky: *Expositions*, p. 129.
22 Grigoriev, p. 40.
23 Calvocoressi, p. 220.
24 Sotheby catalogues.
25 Grigoriev, p. 42.
26 Imperial Theatres.
27 B. Nijinska conversations.
28 Benois: *Reminiscences*, pp. 309, 310.
29 Ibid., p. 310.
30 Ibid.
31 Ibid., also footnote.
32 Ibid., p. 311.
33 Fokine, p. 151.
34 Ibid., p. 152.
35 Grigoriev, p. 42.
36 Karsavina: *Theatre Street*, pp. 212, 213.
37 Astruc papers. My reason for suggesting this date is Diaghilev's cable to Astruc about replacing 'Giselle' by 'La Belle au bois dormant', mentioned below.
38 Stravinsky: *Memories*, p. 32.
39 Astruc papers. Telegrams from Diaghilev to Astruc, dated 2

February 1910, 8 February 1910; from Astruc to Diaghilev, 9 February 1910; from Diaghilev to Astruc, 10 February 1910, 11 February 1910.

40 I have no documentation for Mme Rimsky-Korsakov's opposition, though it is beyond question that she did oppose the production. Evidence for her protest after the event is the letter published in *Rech*, 7 August 1910. Diaghilev's reply to this from Venice was published 17 September 1910. A second letter from Mme Rimsky-Korsakov appeared in *Rech*, 12 October 1910.

41 Karsavina conversations.

42 Ibid.

43 Benois: *Reminiscences*, p. 312.

44 Astruc papers. Letter from Schidlovsky to Astruc, 11 February 1910.

45 Ibid. Telegram from Astruc to Diaghilev, 15 February 1910.

46 Ibid. Telegram from Diaghilev to Astruc, 16 February 1910.

47 Stravinsky: *Chronicle*, p. 52.

48 Astruc papers. Receipt exists.

49 Ibid. Telegram from Diaghilev to Astruc, 10 April 1910.

50 Ibid. Telegram from Gunsbourg to Astruc, 23 April 1910.

51 Benois: *Reminiscences*, p. 312; reference to Metropolitan Opera in Astruc papers: telegram from Diaghilev to Astruc, 18 March 1910.

52 Benois: *Reminiscences*, pp. 312, 313.

53 Lieven, p. 112.

54 Benois: *Reminiscences*, p. 313.

55 Karsavina: *Theatre Street*, pp. 213, 214.

56 Lieven, p. 115.

57 Benois: *Reminiscences*, p. 312.

58 Fokine, pp. 134–6.

59 Karsavina conversations.

60 Fokine, p. 136.

61 B. Nijinska conversations.

62 Grigoriev, p. 40.

63 Diaghilev's Black Note-Book, p. 15.

64 Astruc papers.

65 Ibid. Draft of contract exists.

66 Karsavina: *Theatre Street*, p. 215.

67 Ibid., pp. 214, 215.

68 Lieven, p. 116.

69 Benois: *Reminiscences*, pp. 313, 314.

70 Grigoriev, pp. 44, 47.

71 Stier, p. 237.

72 Vaudoyer, p. 26. Translation by Tamara Karsavina.

73 Karsavina: *Theatre Street*, p. 219.

74 Karsavina conversations.

75 Grigoriev, p. 44.

76 Ibid., pp. 44, 45.

77 Karsavina conversations.

78 Rimsky-Korsakov, pp. 446, 447.

79 Ibid., pp. 292, 293.

80 Grigoriev, p. 46.

81 Ibid., p. 46

82 Fokine, p. 155.

83 Benois: *Reminiscences*, p. 316.

84 Fokine, pp. 155, 156.

85 Whitworth, p. 57.

86 Benois: *Reminiscences*, p. 316.

87 Vaudoyer: 'Variations'.

88 B. Nijinska conversations.

89 Estrade Guerra in an interview with F. Reiss. Reiss, p. 78.

90 Barbier and Miomandre, on the third and fourth unnumbered pages of Miomandre's introduction to Barbier's drawings.

91 Cocteau: *La Difficulté*, p. 70.

92 Grigoriev, p. 47.

93 Proust, p. 188.

94 Karsavina conversations.

95 Ibid.

96 Author's conclusion: see note 97.

97 Fokine, pp. 153, 154.

98 Karsavina conversations.

99 Kochno: *Diaghilev*, p. 48.

100 Grigoriev, p. 43. See above p. 132.

101 Karsavina: *Theatre Street*, p. 220.

102 Benois: *Reminiscences*, pp. 289, 290, 337, 338.

103 Karsavina: *Theatre Street*, p. 220.

104 Benois: *Reminiscences*, p. 313.

105 Svetlov: *Karsavina*, p. 97.

106 Ibid., p. 47.

107 Benois: *Reminiscences*, pp. 310, 311.

108 Stravinsky, letter to Roerich, 19 June 1910, from a copy in the composer's possession.
109 Benois: *Reminiscences*, p. 311.
110 Stravinsky, letter to Roerich, 19 June 1910.
111 Quoted in Benois: *Reminiscences*, pp. 314–16.
112 Painter II, p. 164.
113 Ibid.
114 Cocteau: *Opium*, pp. 163, 164.
115 Painter II, p. 160.
116 Karsavina conversations.
117 Benois: *Reminiscences*, pp. 304, 305.
118 Stravinsky: *Conversations*, p. 96; Lieven, p. 246.
119 Benois: *Reminiscences*, pp. 306, 307.
120 Ibid., p. 307.
121 Stravinsky: *Expositions*, p. 129.
122 Ibid.
123 Ibid.
124 Ibid., pp. 130, 131.
125 Karsavina conversations.
126 Blanche, p. 257.
127 Karsavina conversations.
128 Ibid.
129 Benois conversations.
130 Karsavina conversations.
131 Ibid.
132 Stravinsky, letter to Roerich, 19 June 1910.
133 Stravinsky: *Expositions*, p. 140.
134 Stravinsky, letter to Roerich, 19 June 1910.
135 Lieven, p. 117.
136 Grigoriev, p. 51.
137 Benois: *Reminiscences*, p. 308.
138 Karsavina: *Theatre Street*, p. 221.
139 Ibid., p. 284.
140 Ibid., p. 286.
141 Ibid., p. 285.
142 Karsavina conversations.
143 Grigoriev, p. 52.
144 Ibid., p. 51.

145 Stravinsky, letter to Roerich begun at Ustilug and finished at La Baule, 19 June 1910; and another letter, 27 July 1910.
146 Stravinsky: *Expositions*, p. 67.
147 Benois: *Reminiscences*, p. 323.
148 The book Bakst wrote about this journey has not a single date in it.
149 Stravinsky: *Expositions*, p. 134.
150 Benois: *Reminiscences*, p. 324.
151 Ibid., pp. 324, 325.
152 Stravinsky: *Expositions*, p. 134.
153 Astruc papers. Telegrams from Diaghilev in Venice to Astruc in Paris, 1 September 1910, and on subsequent dates up to at least 10 September 1910.
154 Ibid. Telegram from Diaghilev in London to Astruc in Paris, 10 October 1910.
155 Letter-card formerly in possession of Mlle Lucienne Astruc, 27 October 1910.
156 B. Nijinska conversations.
157 Lieven, p. 142.
158 Benois: *Reminiscences*, p. 327.
159 Ibid., pp. 326, 327.
160 Stravinsky: *Expositions*, p. 135.
161 Benois: *Reminiscences*, p. 327.
162 Fokine, p. 185.
163 Stravinsky: *Memories*, p. 96.
164 Benois: *Reminiscences*, p. 328, footnote.
165 Astruc papers. Telegram from Diaghilev to Astruc, 14 December 1910.
166 Ibid. Telegram from Diaghilev to Astruc, 15 December 1910.
167 Ibid. Telegram from Diaghilev to Astruc, 18 December 1910.
168 Ibid. Telegram from Diaghilev to Astruc, 22 December 1910.
169 Ibid. Telegram from Diaghilev to Astruc, 24 December 1910.

Chapter Four 1911

1 Karsavina: *Theatre Street*, p. 286 ('Diaghilev ... regarded the choreography of Fokine as belonging to the past.'); Morrell, p. 227 ('Such ballets as ["Le Spectre de la rose"] did not interest [Nijinsky]. He said it was *trop joli* and was rather annoyed when people admired it.').
2 Benois: *Reminiscences*, p. 345. An example is Diaghilev's cutting and editing of 'Le Lac des Cygnes'.
3 Duncan, p. 58.
4 Reiss, p. 102. Her interview with Larionov.
5 Deduction from correspondence and B. Nijinska conversations.
6 B. Nijinska conversations.
7 Romola Nijinsky, p. 125. The first mention of Debussy's music in Diaghilev's Note-book was in September, 1910 (p. 123).
8 B. Nijinska conversations.
9 Ibid.
10 Ibid.
11 Astruc papers. Telegram from Diaghilev to Astruc, 10 February 1911.
12 Vaudoyer: 'Variations sur les Ballets Russes', article in *La Revue de Paris*, 15 July 1910.
13 Lifar, pp. 252, 253. He is quoting what Vaudoyer told him.
14 Fokine, p. 180.
15 Astruc papers. Letter from Diaghilev to Astruc, 22 May 1911.
16 Karsavina: *Theatre Street*, pp. 221, 222.
17 Sotheby catalogues.
18 Grigoriev, p. 54.
19 Ibid., p. 58.
20 Ibid., p. 58.
21 Ibid., p. 55.
22 Benois: *Reminiscences*, p. 343.
23 Romola Nijinsky, p. 102.
24 Ibid.
25 Karsavina: *Theatre Street*, p. 226.
26 B. Nijinska conversations.

27 Articles in *Novoye Vremya* and *Le Journal de St Petersbourg*, 13 February 1911.
28 Sotheby catalogues.
29 Astruc papers. Telegram from Diaghilev to Astruc, 12 February 1911.
30 Ibid. Telegram from Gunsbourg to Astruc, 12 February 1911.
31 Romola Nijinsky, p. 102.
32 Astruc papers. Telegrams from Diaghilev to Astruc, 13 February 1911.
33 Ibid. Telegram from Diaghilev to Astruc, 14 February 1911.
34 Ibid. Telegram from Diaghilev to Astruc, 14 February 1911.
35 Ibid. Letter from Astruc to Diaghilev, 14 February 1911.
36 Bennett: *Journals*, p. 4.
37 Kchessinskaya, p. 123.
38 Astruc papers. Telegram from Diaghilev to Astruc, 2 March 1911.
39 Ibid. Telegram from Diaghilev to Astruc, 18 February 1911.
40 Ibid.
41 Ibid. First mentioned to Astruc in a telegram of Diaghilev's from Rome, 26 May 1911.
42 Ibid. Telegrams from Diaghilev to Astruc, 3 March 1911, 15 March 1911.
43 Ibid. Telegram from Diaghilev to Astruc, 12 March 1911 ('*Bakst arrive demain*').
44 Ibid. Telegram from Diaghilev to Astruc, 15 March 1911.
45 Ibid. I assume that it was on this lightning visit to Paris that Diaghilev became interested in 'La Péri', as the first reference to it in his correspondence with Astruc is in a telegram from Beaulieu on 23 March 1911, two days after he left.
46 Ibid. From 23–25 March 1911 the telegrams were sent from Beaulieu.
47 Ibid. On 30 March 1911 Diaghilev

telegraphed to Astruc from Beausoleil, '*Suis définitivement Riviera Palace.*'

48 Grigoriev, p. 59.
49 Fokine, p. 201.
50 Grigoriev, pp. 60, 61.
51 Fokine, p. 188.
52 Grigoriev, p. 59.
53 Ibid., pp. 59, 60.
54 Astruc papers. Telegrams from Diaghilev to Astruc, 23 March 1911, 25 March 1911, 3 April 1911.
55 B. Nijinska conversations.
56 Grigoriev, p. 59.
57 Ibid., p. 58.
58 Evidence as note 59.
59 The evidence that Stravinsky came over to Monte Carlo is the photograph, plate 41 in the hard-back edition of this book.
60 The evidence for Benois is the same as the preceding note. Also see Lieven, p. 154.
61 Astruc papers. At least Gunsbourg was there on 1 May 1911 when Diaghilev telegraphed Astruc that he would arrive at the Majestic Hotel, Paris, on the next day.
62 The Botkine girls are in the photograph mentioned above, note 59.
63 Karsavina: *Theatre Street*, p. 233.
64 Aga Khan, p. 109.
65 Karsavina conversations.
66 Buckle collection. Letter from Bakst to Astruc, 29 March 1911.
67 Astruc papers. Telegram from Diaghilev to Astruc, 31 March 1911.
68 Drawing in Lucienne Astruc collection. Reproduction, plate 35 in the hard-back edition of this book.
69 Design for poster reproduced, *Comoedia Illustré*, 15 June 1911.
70 Poster in Buckle collection and possibly elsewhere.
71 Astruc papers. Telegram from Diaghilev to Astruc, 5 April 1911.
72 Ibid. Telegram from Diaghilev to Astruc, 21 April 1911, quoting telegram received from Rubinstein: '*Regrette mais nécessité de mon travail m'empêche venir dimanche. Pouvez absolument compter sur moi le vingt-trois. Amitiés.*'
73 Karsavina conversations.
74 Lieven, p. 163. Grigoriev calls Muoratori '*régisseur*' (p. 60), and Lieven calls 'Muratore' 'the former singer ... in charge of publicity' (p. 163).
75 Karsavina: *Theatre Street*, p. 223.
76 *Le Monte Carlo.*
77 Kchessinskaya, p. 125.
78 *Le Monte Carlo.*
79 Stravinsky-Craft questionnaires.
80 Plate 41 in the hard-back edition of this book. Referred to above.
81 B. Nijinska conversations.
82 Romola Nijinsky, pp. 114, 115.
83 Benois: *Reminiscences*, p. 340.
84 Karsavina: *Theatre Street*, p. 240.
85 Press; Grigoriev, p. 60.
86 Diaghilev's Black Note-Book, p. 141.
87 Astruc papers. Letter from Diaghilev to Astruc, 27 May 1911. '*Quand Rubinstein a voulu monter une série de danses sur la musique compliquée de St Sébastien elle est venue à Monte Carlo pour 5 jours. Et tout a été fait quoiqu'elle fût tombée en plein dans la période si difficile de la création de Narcisse.*'
88 Benois: *Reminiscences*, p. 341.
89 Ibid., pp. 341, 342.
90 Ibid., p. 341.
91 Ibid., p. 342.
92 Karsavina: *Theatre Street*, p. 212.
93 Astruc papers. Telegram from Diaghilev to Astruc, 5 May 1911.
94 Ibid. Same telegram as above.
95 Benois: *Reminiscences*, pp. 330, 331; Stravinsky: *Conversations*, p. 98.
96 Benois: *Reminiscences*, p. 331.
97 Ibid., p. 331; Karsavina: *Theatre Street*, p. 234.
98 Karsavina: *Theatre Street*, p. 231.
99 Benois: *Reminiscences*, pp. 330, 331.

100 Karsavina: *Theatre Street*, p. 231.
101 Grigoriev, p. 62.
102 Ibid., p. 62.
103 Benois: *Reminiscences*, p. 332.
104 Astruc papers. Telegram from Diaghilev to Astruc, 15 May 1911. The Roman telegraphist relayed the French expression '*ovations infinies*' as '*ovadons infibes*'.
105 Grigoriev, p. 62.
106 Karsavina conversations.
107 Karsavina: *Theatre Street*, p. 231.
108 Astruc papers. Telegram from Diaghilev to Astruc, 26 May 1911.
109 Ibid. Letter from Diaghilev to Astruc, 22 May 1911.
110 Ibid. Telegram from Bakst to Diaghilev, 24 May 1911.
111 Ibid. Telegram from Diaghilev to Astruc, 26 May 1911.
112 Ibid. Letter from Diaghilev to Astruc, 27 May 1911.
113 Grigoriev, p. 137.
114 Adolphe Jullien in *Feuilleton du Journal des Débats*, 25 June 1911.
115 Astruc papers. Telegram from Diaghilev to Astruc, 31 May 1911.
116 Whitworth, pp. 46, 47.
117 Valentine Gross, broadcast on Radio-diffusion française, 1951.
118 Cocteau in *Comoedia Illustré*, 15 June 1911.
119 At least according to a programme in the author's possession, dated 8 June 1911.
120 George Pioch in *Commedia*, 7 June 1922.
121 Karsavina conversations.
122 Karsavina: *Theatre Street*, p. 241.
123 Lieven, p. 143.
124 Fokine, p. 190.
125 Kochno: *Diaghilev*, p. 68.
126 Benois: *Reminiscences*, pp. 333–5.
127 Braun, pp. 113, 114.
128 Benois: *Reminiscences*, p. 336.
129 Fokine, p. 187.
130 Benois: *Reminiscences*, p. 335, footnote.
131 Fokine, p. 193.
132 Unidentified Press cutting.
133 Benois: *Reminiscences*, p. 335.
134 Stravinsky: *Memories*, pp. 33, 34.
135 Ibid.
136 Fokine, p. 184.
137 Benois: *Reminiscences*, p. 335.
138 Fokine. p. 191.
139 Ibid., pp. 194, 193.
140 Benois: *Reminiscences*, pp. 337, 338.
141 *Le Figaro*, 17 June 1911.
142 Pevsner, pp. 314, 315.
143 Juliet Duff conversations.
144 Karsavina conversations.
145 Astruc papers. Telegram from Gunsbourg to Astruc, 3 August 1911.
146 Grigoriev, p. 66.
147 Juliet Duff conversations.
148 Sir Michael Duff conversations, confirmed in a letter by the late Antonio Gandarillas, the popular Chilean who knew more about English society than most Englishmen.
149 Juliet Duff conversations.
150 Martin, p. 151.
151 Hahn, p. 214.
152 Covent Garden programmes.
153 *Daily Mail*, 21 June 1911.
154 Diaghilev Memoirs.
155 Astruc papers. Telegram from Diaghilev to Astruc, 23 June 1911.
156 *The Times*, 22 June 1911.
157 *Observer*, 25 June 1911.
158 *The Times*, 26 June 1911.
159 Ibid., 24 June 1911.
160 Ibid.
161 *Sunday Times*, 25 June 1911.
162 Bedells, pp. 51, 52.
163 Diana Cooper conversation and letter.
164 Diaghilev Memoirs.
165 *Daily Mail*, 27 June 1911.
166 Ibid.
167 Ibid.
168 Diaghilev Memoirs.
169 *Sunday Times*, 23 July 1911.
170 *Daily Mail*, 28 June 1911.
171 Juliet Duff conversations.
172 Craig, p. 84.

557

173 Ricketts, *passim.*
174 Juliet Duff, essay.
175 Stravinsky: *Expositions*, pp. 140, 141.
176 Astruc papers. Telegram from Diaghilev to Astruc, 1 September 1911.
177 Grigoriev, p. 68.
178 Benois: *Reminiscences*, p. 345. But Benois says the costumes were by Korovine. According to the programmes only the lake décor was by him; the palace scene and all the costumes were by Golovine.
179 Astruc papers. Telegram from Diaghilev to Astruc, 25 September 1911.
180 Ibid. Telegrams from Diaghilev to Astruc, 13 October 1911, 10 October 1911.
181 Ibid. Telegram from Diaghilev to Astruc, 10 October 1911.
182 Ibid. Telegram from Diaghilev to Astruc, 15 October 1911.
183 Karsavina conversations. Her phrase.
184 Carter, p. 23.
185 *Observer*, 15 October 1911.
186 Rosenthal, p. 359.
187 Beaumont: *The Ballet called Giselle*, p. 127.
188 *The Times*, 17 October 1911.
189 *Daily Mail*, 17 October 1911.
190 *Sunday Times*, 22 October 1911.
191 *Observer*, 22 October 1911.
192 *Daily Mail*, 17 October 1911.
193 *Sunday Times*, 22 October 1911.
194 *The Times*, 30 October 1911.
195 *Daily Mail*, 30 October 1911.
196 Ibid., 4 November 1911.
197 Gordon Craig's Day book II in the collection of Edward Craig.
198 Kchessinskaya, pp. 132, 133.
199 Ibid., p. 133.
200 *Daily Mail*, 15 November 1911.
201 Juliet Duff conversations.
202 *Daily Mail*, 15 November 1911.
203 *The Times*, 20 November 1911.
204 Astruc papers. Telegram from Diaghilev to Astruc, 15 November 1911.
205 Johnson, p. 226. I have followed his account as it is the only one.
206 Kchessinskaya, p. 134.
207 Ibid., p. 134.
208 Diaghilev Memoirs.
209 Johnson, pp. 226–33.
210 Beaumont: *London*, p. 231.
211 *Sunday Times*, 3 December 1911 (and 28 July 1912); *The Times*, 1 December 1911; *Daily Mail*, 1 December 1911.
212 Kchessinskaya, p. 134.
213 Ibid.
214 *The Times*, 1 December 1911.
215 *Daily Mail*, 1 December 1911.
216 *The Times*, 1 December 1911.
217 *Daily Mail*, 1 December 1911.
218 *The Times*, 1 December 1911.
219 Kchessinskaya, p. 135. But she says Benois was present when he was not in London.
220 Astruc papers. Telegram from Diaghilev to Astruc, 3 December 1911.
221 Lady Juliet Duff's 'Birthday Book'.
222 *Daily Mail*, 11 December 1911.
223 Ricketts, p. 195.
224 *Daily Mail*, 11 December 1911.
225 Ibid.
226 Ricketts, p. 175.
227 *Daily Mail*, 11 December 1911.
228 Astruc papers. Telegram from Diaghilev to Astruc, 9 December 1911.
229 Ibid. Copy of telegram from Diaghilev to Keynote (an agency?), 11 December 1911.
230 Ibid. Telegram from Diaghilev to Astruc, 12 December 1911.
231 Ibid. Telegram from Diahilev to Astruc, 15 December 1911.
232 Ibid. Telegram from Diaghilev to Astruc, 17 December 1911.
233 Ibid. Telegram from Diaghilev to Astruc, 16 December 1911.
234 Karsavina: *Theatre Street*, pp. 240, 241. See also Bourman, p. 212.
235 Drawing in the collection of the late Lady Juliet Duff.

Chapter Five *1912*

1 Stravinsky: *Expositions*, p. 142.
2 Romola Nijinsky conversations.
3 Karsavina conversations.
4 Astruc papers.
5 Ibid. In the telegram from Diaghilev to Astruc, 21 September 1911, the dates had been 29 December 1911 to 1 February 1912.
6 Ibid. Telegram from Diaghilev to Kchessinskaya, 4 January 1912.
7 Ibid. Telegram from Diaghilev to Astruc, 8 January 1912 and another on which the date is indecipherable.
8 Ibid. Draft of contract exists.
9 Grigoriev, p. 87.
10 Astruc papers. Letter from Astruc's office to Astruc in Nice, 21 February 1912.
11 Ibid. Telegram from Diaghilev to Astruc, 9 February 1912.
12 Ibid. Telegram from Diaghilev to Astruc, 9 February 1912.
13 Karsavina: *Theatre Street*, pp. 225.
14 B. Nijinska conversations.
15 Romola Nijinsky, p. 195. Bolm told her the story.
16 B. Nijinska conversations.
17 Karsavina conversations.
18 See plate 49 in the hard-back edition of this book.
19 Grigoriev, p. 72.
20 Illustrated in *Ballet and Opera*, November 1948, pp. 25–27.
21 Grigoriev, p. 72.
22 Ibid., pp. 72, 73.
23 Karsavina: *Theatre Street*, pp. 225, 226.
24 Astruc papers. Telegram from Diaghilev to Astruc, 20 February 1912.
25 Grigoriev, p. 73.
26 Hofmannsthal-Strauss, pp. 121, 122.
27 Astruc papers. Telegram from Diaghilev to Astruc, 6 March 1912; Grigoriev, p. 74.
28 Grigoriev, pp. 73–4.
29 Kchessinskaya, p. 137.
30 Romola Nijinsky, p. 12.
31 Ibid., pp. 12, 13.
32 Romola Nijinsky conversations.
33 Romola Nijinsky, p. 13.
34 Bourman, p. 222.
35 Kchessinskaya, p. 138.
36 Astruc papers. The telegrams from Beausoleil begin on 19 March 1912.
37 *Le Monte Carlo*, 31 March 1912.
38 Ibid., 28 April 1912.
39 Ibid., 7 April 1912.
40 Ibid., 31 March 1912.
41 Ibid., 7 April 1912.
42 Ibid., 14 April 1912.
43 Grigoriev, p. 74.
44 Ibid., pp. 75, 76.
45 B. Nijinska conversations.
46 Rambert conversations.
47 Ibid.
48 See Rambert's anecdote on p. 329.
49 Grigoriev, p. 75.
50 Letter from Stravinsky to Anna Stravinsky, April 1912, quoted by Robert Craft in his review of *I. F. Stravinsky: Essays and Materials* (Moscow, 1973) in *The New York Review*, 21 February 1974.
51 Kchessinskaya, p. 138.
52 *Comoedia Illustré*, the official Paris souvenir programme, 1912.
53 In this assessment of Diaghilev's character the author is not quoting any one person, but summarizing the impressions he received from many.
54 Fokine, pp 71, 72.
55 Ibid., p. 201.
56 Grigoriev, p. 75.
57 Ibid., pp. 76, 77.
58 Astruc papers. Telegram from Diaghilev to Astruc, 17 April 1912.
59 Ibid. Telegram from Gatti-Casazza to Astruc.
60 Author's supposition, based on telegram, see note 61.
61 Astruc papers. Telegram from Bakst to Diaghilev, 19 April 1912.
62 Monte Carlo programmes.

63 Astruc papers. Telegrams from Diaghilev to Astruc, 25 April 1912 and 27 April 1912.
64 *Comoedia Illustré*, 15 May 1912, pp. 638, 639.
65 Romola Nijinsky, p. 135.
66 Astruc papers. Telegram from Diaghilev to Astruc, 2 May 1912.
67 Grigoriev, p. 77.
68 *Comoedia Illustré*, the official Paris souvenir programme.
69 Sokolova, p. 37.
70 Cocteau, note on the musical score.
71 Indication on the musical score.
72 *Le Figaro*, 14 May 1912.
73 Karsavina: *Theatre Street*, p. 212.
74 Fokine, p. 205.
75 The score, inscribed by Nijinsky with his choreographic notation and with indications of staging, is in the British Museum.
76 B. Nijinska conversations.
77 Romola Nijinsky, p. 141.
78 Ibid., pp. 141, 142.
79 Ibid., p. 142, footnote.
80 B. Nijinska conversations. When Mme Bronislava Nijinska gave the reason for this jump I was able to point out to her the relationship of this stream at the right of the stage to the painted waterfall.
81 Ibid.
82 Grigoriev, p. 79.
83 See page 235.
84 Grigoriev, p. 79.
85 Ibid., p. 79.
86 Ibid., p. 79
87 Ibid., pp. 78, 79.
88 Lieven, p. 176.
89 *Commedia*, 30 May 1912.
90 *Le Figaro*, 30 May 1912.
91 Ibid., 31 May 1912.
92 Ibid., 3 June 1912.
93 Romola Nijinsky, pp. 144-8.
94 Fokine, pp. 204-9.
95 Ibid., p. 204.
96 Ibid., p. 209.
97 Ibid., pp. 209, 210.
98 Ibid., p. 209.
99 Ibid., p. 210.
100 Karsavina: *Theatre Street*, pp. 238, 239.
101 Grigoriev, p. 80.
102 Fokine, p. 211.
103 Ibid., p. 211.
104 Ibid., pp. 211, 212.
105 Grigoriev, p. 76.
106 Fokine, p. 212.
107 Lieven, p. 181. Benois told him this.
108 Jankélévitch, p. 50.
109 *Le Figaro*, 9 June 1912.
110 Fokine, p. 214.
111 Pierre Lalo in *Feuilleton du temps*, 11 June 1912.
112 Fokine, p. 201.
113 Dates on certain designs which have changed hands since being seen by the author.
114 Fokine, pp. 214, 215.
115 Vladimirov conversation.
116 Romola Nijinsky conversations.
117 Ricketts, pp. 176, 177.
118 *The Times*, 13 June 1912.
119 *Daily Mail*, 13 June 1912.
120 *Morning Post*, 19 June 1912.
121 *The Times*, 19 June 1912.
122 *Daily Express*, 10 June 1912.
123 Ibid., 17 June 1912.
124 *Daily Mail*, 19 June 1912.
125 Beaumont: *London*, pp. 9, 10.
126 Ibid., pp. 15-17.
127 Ibid., p. 20.
128 Morrell, pp. 226, 227.
129 Ibid., p. 227.
130 Juliet Duff, essay.
131 Duncan Grant, letter to the author.
132 Morrell, p. 228.
133 Illustrated in *Comoedia Illustré*, 5 June 1913.
134 Morrell, pp. 227, 228.
135 Augustus John: *Chiaroscuro*. I have stolen a phrase used by John of Oscar Wilde.
136 Blanche, pp. 257, 258.
137 Ibid., p. 258.
138 Juliet Duff, essay.
139 Ibid.
140 Hofmannsthal-Strauss, pp. 133, 134.

141 Ibid., p. 136.
142 Ibid., p. 139, letter from Strauss to Hofmannsthal, 21 July 1912.
143 *The Sketch*, 10 July 1912.
144 *The Times*, 9 July 1912.
145 Ibid. 18 July 1912.
146 Juliet Duff, essay.
147 Guest: *Adeline Genée*, pp. 125, 129. He is quoting an account by Mme Karsavina.
148 *The Times*, 10 July 1912.
149 *Morning Post*, 10 July 1912.
150 *Daily Express*, 10 July 1912.
151 *Daily Mail*, 10 July 1912.
152 *Sunday Times*, 14 July 1912.
153 Beaumont: *London*, p. 38.
154 Ricketts, pp. 177, 178.
155 Ibid., p. 179.
156 B. Nijinska conversations.

157 *Rhythm*, No. VI, July 1912.
158 Ede: *Savage Messiah*, pp. 138–50.
159 Ibid., p. 191 footnote.
160 Geoffrey Keynes, letter to the author.
161 Cathleen Nesbitt conversation.
162 Marsh: *Brooke*, p. 75. Letter quoted.
163 Stravinsky: *Chronicle*, pp. 66–8 (but Stravinsky does not mention Nijinsky).
164 Astruc papers. A telegram from Diaghilev in London to Astruc in Paris, 30 August 1912, proves that Diaghilev was not yet in Venice. And on 21 September 1912 Diaghilev telegraphs to Astruc from the Lido that he will be in Paris on 25 September.

Chapter Six *1912–1913*

1 B. Nijinska conversations.
2 Ibid.
3 *Diary*, pp. 146, 147.
4 Karsavina conversations.
5 B. Nijinska conversations.
6 Debussy, p. 111.
7 Grigoriev, pp. 84, 85.
8 Interview quoted Macke, pp. 4–6; translation by John Geissler and Richard Buckle.
9 Astruc papers. Telegram from Diaghilev to Astruc, 12 December 1912.
10 Hofmannsthal-Strauss, p. 150.
11 Astruc papers. Copy of letter from Gunsbourg to Bewicke, 15 December 1912.
12 Rambert conversations. The information in the following four paragraphs – and indeed throughout much of this chapter – has the same source. Some of Dame Marie's recollections of the *Avon* voyage were incorporated in Mary Clarke's book *Dancers of Mercury*, but since she is a friend and told me these and

further details I have attributed them to 'conversations'.
13 Szakats conversation.
14 Romola Nijinsky conversations. Some of these facts do not appear in Romola Nijinsky's *Nijinsky*, and some are stated differently.
15 Romola Nijinsky, p. 14.
16 Ibid., pp. 15, 16.
17 Grigoriev, p. 88.
18 Karsavina conversations.
19 Grigoriev, p. 88.
20 Ibid., p. 88.
21 Romola Nijinsky, pp. 19, 20.
22 Ibid., pp. 20–22.
23 Telegram 31(?) January 1913.
24 Telegram from Nijinsky to Astruc, 27 January 1913.
25 Grigoriev, p. 89.
26 Beaumont: *London*, pp. 42–5.
27 *The Times*, 5 February 1913.
28 *Daily Mail*, 6 February 1913.
29 Sitwell: *Great Morning*, pp. 242, 241.
30 Beaumont: *London*, p. 51.
31 *The Times*, 18 February 1913.
32 *Daily Mail*, 18 February 1913.

33 Ibid., 20 and 21 February 1913.
34 Ibid., 21 February 1913.
35 Sokolova, p. 31.
36 Rambert conversations.
37 Here the author interpolates his own observations in the middle of a body of factual evidence by Dame Marie Rambert.
38 Grigoriev papers.
39 Bewicke conversation.
40 Grigoriev, p. 90.
41 Rambert conversations.
42 B. Nijinska conversations.
43 Ibid.
44 Rambert conversations.
45 B. Nijinska conversations. '*Avec justesse*' was Mme Nijinska's expression.
46 Rambert conversations.
47 Ibid.
48 Karsavina: *Theatre Street*, pp. 293, 294. I have rearranged the conversation as dramatic dialogue.
49 Rambert conversations.
50 Ibid.
51 Ibid.
52 Sokolova, pp. 33, 34, 38, 39.
53 Ibid.
54 Romola Nijinsky conversations.
55 Romola Nijinsky-Kirstein MS.
56 Rambert conversations.
57 Astruc, p. 287.
58 Grigoriev, p. 91.
59 Ibid., p. 91.
60 Manuel, p. 74.
61 Stravinsky: *Conversations*, p. 62.
62 Valentine Gross, typescript in collection of Theatre Museum, London.
63 Rambert conversations.
64 Agate, p. 171.
65 Debussy, letter in private collection.
66 Brian Blackwood's analysis, based on his own observations and on a commentary in a 1914 Paris concert programme quoted in Lockspeiser, pp. 202, 203.
67 *Le Figaro*, 17 May 1913.
68 *Gil Blas*, 20 May 1913.
69 Ibid.
70 Lockspeiser, Vol. II, p. 172.
71 Duncan and MacDougall, p. 260.
72 Jacques Rivière, in *Nouvelle Revue Française*, November 1913.
73 In this account the relationship of the choreography to the score is based on notes which Stravinsky made for Nijinsky which have been published in *The Rite of Spring, Sketches 1911–1913*.
74 Jacques Rivière, in *Nouvelle Revue Française*, November 1913.
75 Victor Hugo, p. 274.
76 Valentine Gross, broadcast.
77 Cocteau: *Cock*, pp. 48, 49.
78 Rambert conversations.
79 Romola Nijinsky, p. 166.
80 Ibid., p. 166.
81 Manuel, p. 74.
82 Romola Nijinsky, p. 165, 166.
83 Rambert conversations.
84 Astruc, p. 286.
85 Stravinsky: *Conversations*, p. 46.
86 B. Nijinska conversations.
87 Romola Nijinsky, p. 166.
88 Stravinsky: *Conversations*, pp. 46, 47.
89 Stravinsky-Craft questionnaires.
90 *Le Figaro*, 31 May 1913.
91 Laloy, in unattributed Press cutting.
92 *La Revue française de la musique*, April 1913.
93 *Gil Blas*, April 1913.
94 In an undated, unattributed cutting in the Arsenal.
95 *Le Monde musical*, April 1913.
96 *Commedia*, 31 May 1913.
97 Valentine Gross, typescript.
98 Karsavina conversations.
99 Johnson, pp. 216–21.
100 Svetlov: *Karsavina*, p. 62.
101 Grigoriev, p. 94.
102 Valentine Gross.
103 Romola Nijinsky, pp. 169–72.
104 Sokolova, pp. 45–7.
105 *The Times*, 25 June 1913.
106 *Daily Mail*, 26 June 1913.
107 *Morning Post*, 26 June 1913.

108 *The Times*, 12 July 1913.
109 Ibid.
110 *Morning Post*, 12 July 1913.
111 *The Times*, 24 July 1913.
112 Letter from Bakst to Astruc, Buckle collection.
113 Astruc, p. 286.
114 Letter from Stravinsky to Maximilian Steinberg, July 1913, quoted by Robert Craft in his review of *I. F. Stravinsky: Essays and Materials* (Moscow, 1973) in *The New York Review*, 21 February 1974.
115 Benois: *Reminiscences*, pp. 349–51.
116 Records of the Royal Mail Steam Packet Company, now Royal Mail Lines, Ltd.
117 Grigoriev, pp. 95, 96.
118 Rambert conversations.
119 Romola Nijinsky, p. 179.
120 Sokolova, pp. 14ff.
121 Rambert conversations.
122 Sokolova, p. 48.
123 Romola Nijinsky, p. 185.
124 Rambert conversations.
125 Grigoriev, p. 96.
126 Romola Nijinsky, pp. 178, 179.
127 Ibid., p. 180.
128 Records of the RMSP Co.
129 Romola Nijinsky, p. 181.
130 Ibid., pp. 182–4.
131 Rambert conversations.
132 Romola Nijinsky, p. 181, 182.
133 Ibid., p. 182.
134 Ibid., pp. 184, 185.
135 Rambert conversations.
136 Romola Nijinsky, pp. 188, 189.
137 Ibid., pp. 187, 188.
138 Ibid., p. 188.
139 Ibid., pp. 190, 191. I have slightly rearranged the order of events recorded by Romola Nijinsky to fit in with the dates provided by the steamship company.
140 Ibid., p. 186.
141 Ibid., p. 186.
142 Records of the RMSP Co. Romola Nijinsky does not mention docking at Pernambuco. I have had to follow my sense of probability in placing the events of this voyage, and to reconcile Mme Nijinsky's account of how long it took her to make friends with Nijinsky with Grigoriev's statement that 'After we had been at sea about a fortnight ... [Nijinsky] was often to be seen in animated conversation with Mlle de Pulszka ...' (p. 96).
143 Grigoriev, p. 96.
144 Sokolova, p. 48.
145 Romola Nijinsky, p. 195.
146 Rambert conversations.
147 Records of the RMSP Co.
148 Romola Nijinsky, pp. 191, 192.
149 Rambert conversations.
150 Romola Nijinsky, p. 193.
151 Rambert conversations.
152 Records of the RMSP Co.
153 Romola Nijinsky, pp. 193–5.
154 Ibid., p. 195.
155 Ibid., p. 196.
156 Ibid., p. 197.
157 Romola Nijinsky conversations.
158 Romola Nijinsky, pp. 196, 197.
159 Ibid., p. 197.
160 Rambert conversations.
161 Records of the RMSP Co.
162 Romola Nijinsky, pp. 197, 198.
163 Karsavina conversations.
164 Romola Nijinsky, p. 198.
165 Conclusions drawn from a discussion with Mme Sokolova after I had belatedly noticed the discrepancy between the date of the marriage given by Romola Nijinsky and that on the invitation to the wedding-breakfast reproduced as plate 74 in the hard-back edition of this book.
166 Romola Nijinsky conversations.
167 Romola Nijinsky, pp. 199, 200.
168 Sokolova, p. 49.
169 Rambert conversations.
170 Romola Nijinsky, pp. 200–202.
171 Ibid., p. 202.

Chapter Seven *1913–1917*

1 Alexander Bland, review of the first edition of *Nijinsky*, *Observer*, 14 November 1971.
2 Denby. *Dance Index*.
3 Rebecca West, review of the first edition of *Nijinsky*, *Sunday Telegraph*, 7 November 1971.
4 Denby, *Dance Index*.
5 Grigoriev, p. 97.
6 Rambert conversations.
7 Grigoriev, p. 97.
8 Romola Nijinsky, p. 202.
9 Ibid., pp. 203, 205.
10 Ibid., p. 205.
11 Haskell: *Diaghileff*, p. 257.
12 Misia Sert, pp. 120, 121.
13 Stravinsky: *Memories*, pp. 134, 135. Letters quoted.
14 Hofmannsthal-Strauss, p. 176.
15 Letter from Debussy to Stravinsky, 9 November 1913.
16 Letter from Astruc to the official receiver.
17 Romola Nijinsky, pp. 203, 206.
18 Ibid., pp. 206, 207.
19 Ibid., p. 207.
20 Grigoriev, p. 98.
21 B. Nijinska conversations and Romola Nijinsky conversations.
22 Grigoriev, pp. 98, 99.
23 Romola Nijinsky conversations.
24 Romola Nijinsky, pp. 207, 208.
25 Ibid., p. 208.
26 Ibid., pp. 208, 209.
27 Romola Nijinsky conversations.
28 Stravinsky: *Memories*, letter from Nijinsky quoted pp. 38–40.
29 Ibid., Grigoriev, p. 100.
30 Romola Nijinsky, p. 209.
31 Grigoriev, pp. 99, 100.
32 Romola Nijinsky, p. 209.
33 Grigoriev, p. 100. The date is a guess based on the date of Nijinsky's existing telegram to Astruc.
34 Romola Nijinsky, p. 210.
35 Astruc papers. Telegram from Nijinsky to Astruc, 5 December 1913.
36 Quoted in Stravinsky: *Memories*, pp. 38–40.
37 Stravinsky: *Memories*, p. 38.
38 Grigoriev, p. 101.
39 Ibid., pp. 102, 103.
40 Fokine, p. 204.
41 Grigoriev, p. 103.
42 Ibid., p. 105.
43 Massine conversations.
44 Massine, pp. 41–3.
45 Massine conversations.
46 Massine, pp. 45, 46.
47 Grigoriev, p. 105.
48 Massine conversations.
49 Romola Nijinsky, pp. 210, 212.
50 Ibid., p. 211.
51 Ibid., pp. 211, 212.
52 Beaumont: *London*, p. 78.
53 Hofmannsthal-Strauss, p. 189.
54 Grigoriev, p. 106.
55 Ibid., p. 107.
56 Romola Nijinsky, p. 212.
57 Ibid., pp. 212, 213.
58 Misia Sert, p. 122.
59 Ibid., p. 122.
60 Stravinsky: *Memories*, p. 41.
61 Romola Nijinsky, p. 213.
62 Ibid., pp. 213, 214.
63 Beaumont: *London*, p. 83.
64 Romola Nijinsky, p. 214.
65 Beaumont: *London*, pp. 79, 80.
66 *The Times*, 3 March 1914.
67 Beaumont: *London*, pp. 80–82.
68 Romola Nijinsky conversations; and *Daily Telegraph*, 17 March 1914.
69 Beaumont: *London*, p. 83.
70 Romola Nijinsky. pp. 214, 215.
71 Romola Nijinsky conversations.
72 *Daily Telegraph*, March 1914.
73 Misia Sert, pp. 122, 123.
74 Ibid., pp. 122–4.
75 Romola Nijinsky, p. 215.
76 Grigoriev, p. 107.
77 Fokine, p. 226.
78 Benois: *Reminiscences*, p. 356.

79 Grigoriev, p. 108.
80 Romola Nijinsky, pp. 215, 216.
81 G. de Champdos in an unattributed cutting dated 16 May 1914 in the Arsenal.
82 Romola Nijinsky, p. 218.
83 Massine conversations.
84 Massine, p. 60.
85 Hofmannsthal-Strauss, p. 195, letter from Hofmannsthal to Strauss, 20 May 1914.
86 Pierre Lalo in *Le Temps*, May 1914.
87 Bruncan, in unattributed Press cutting
88 *Nouvelle Revue Française*, 1 July 1914.
89 *The Times*, 9 June 1914.
90 Ibid., 10 June 1914.
91 Beaumont: *London*, pp. 90–93.
92 Ricketts, p. 199.
93 Sitwell: *Great Morning*, pp. 244, 245.
94 Ibid., p. 245.
95 Romola Nijinsky, p. 219.
96 Ricketts, p. 236.
97 Beaumont: *London*, p. 100.
98 Massine, p. 61.
99 Karsavina: *Theatre Street*, p. 245.
100 Ibid., p. 245.
101 Romola Nijinsky, pp. 220, 221.
102 Ibid., pp. 222, 223.
103 Beaumont: *London*, p. 101.
104 Karsavina: *Theatre Street*, p. 305 [1930 ed.].
105 Ricketts, p. 207.
106 Ibid., p. 204.
107 Grigoriev, p. 111.
108 Karsavina: *Theatre Street*, p. 248.
109 Karsavina conversations.
110 Karsavina: *Theatre Street*, p. 252.
111 Ricketts, p. 214.
112 Romola Nijinsky, pp. 222–6.
113 Stravinsky: *Memories*, p. 48. Letter from Diaghilev quoted.
114 Ibid., p. 50. Another letter quoted.
115 Ibid., p. 50.
116 Romola Nijinsky, pp. 226–39. (Source for the preceding six paragraphs.)
117 Massine, p. 70.
118 Grigoriev, p. 114.
119 Massine, pp. 73–4; Grigoriev, p. 114.
120 Sokolova, p. 69.
121 Grigoriev, p. 115.
122 Sokolova, pp. 68, 69.
123 Grigoriev, p. 116.
124 *Ballet Russe Courier*, Vol. I, No. I, December 1916. (Publicity publication of the Metropolitan Opera House.)
125 Sokolova, pp. 69, 71.
126 Grigoriev, pp. 116–18.
127 Romola Nijinsky, pp. 241, 242.
128 Marsh, p. 261.
129 Grigoriev, p. 120.
130 Romola Nijinsky, pp. 242–6.
131 *Journal of Commerce*, 19 January 1916.
132 Massine, p. 80.
133 *Journal of Commerce*, 19 January 1916.
134 *Boston Evening Transcript*, 18 January 1916.
135 Van Vechten, *Dance Index*.
136 *New York Times*, 25 January 1916.
137 Van Vechten, *Dance Index*.
138 *New York Times*, 25 January 1916.
139 Grigoriev, p. 119.
140 Romola Nijinsky, pp. 247–54.
141 *The New York Review*, 21 February 1974.
142 *Diary*, pp. 50, 51.
143 Copy of telegram from Astruc to Nijinsky, 1 March 1916. Buckle collection.
144 Romola Nijinsky, p. 255.
145 Visiting-card signed by Nijinsky. Buckle collection.
146 Romola Nijinsky, pp. 255, 256.
147 Sokolova, p. 76.
148 *Toledo Times*, 7 April 1916.
149 *New York Sun*, 30 March 1916.
150 *Musical American*, 9 April 1916.
151 *Washington Star*, 26 March 1916.
152 Romola Nijinsky, pp. 257, 258.
153 Ibid., p. 260.
154 *New York Telegraph*, 10 April 1916.

155 Sokolova, p. 78. She is quoting a letter she wrote home to her family, which they kept.
156 Discovered and sent to the present author by Mr Francis Steegmuller, the biographer of Cocteau.
157 Grigoriev, p. 120.
158 *New York Evening Sun*, 19 January 1916.
159 Sokolova, p. 77.
160 Grigoriev, p. 120.
161 Romola Nijinsky, p. 261.
162 Sokolova, p. 79.
163 Ibid., p. 77.
164 Massine, p. 86.
165 *Globe*, 13 April 1916.
166 Ibid.
167 Romola Nijinsky, p. 261.
168 *Musical Courier*, April 1916.
169 *Globe*, 13 April 1916.
170 *Musical Courier*, April 1916.
171 Massine, p 87.
172 *Globe*, 13 April 1916.
173 *Musical Courier*, April 1916.
174 Massine, p. 87.
175 Unattributed cutting dated 17 April 1916, in the New York Public Library.
176 Sokolova, p. 77.
177 Grigoriev, p. 120.
178 Van Vechten, *Dance Index*.
179 Ibid.
180 Romola Nijinsky, p. 263.
181 Ibid., pp. 262, 263.
182 Ibid., pp. 263, 264; unattributed cutting of April 1916 in the New York Public Library.
183 *New York Telegraph* 1 May 1916.
184 Romola Nijinsky, p. 265.
185 Romola Nijinsky conversations.
186 Romola Nijinsky, p. 265.
187 Grigoriev, p. 121.
188 Sokolova, p. 80.
189 Ibid., p. 80.
190 Maurice Dumesnil, *passim*.
191 Schneider, p. 203; Duncan, p. 235.
192 Romola Nijinsky, p. 266.
193 *New York Review*, 13 May 1916.
194 Romola Nijinsky conversations.

195 Romola Nijinsky, p. 266.
196 Jones, *Dance Index*.
197 Romola Nijinsky, pp. 266–8.
198 Jones, *Dance Index*.
199 *Diary*, p. 111; Romola Nijinsky, p. 269.
200 *Diary*, p. 111.
201 Jones, *Dance Index*.
202 Romola Nijinsky, p. 269.
203 *New York Telegraph*, 19 June 1916. Telegram quoted.
204 Sokolova, pp. 86, 87.
205 Ibid., p. 87.
206 Romola Nijinsky, p. 270.
207 Sokolova, p. 89.
208 Ibid., p. 90: Romola Nijinsky, p. 270.
209 Romola Nijinsky, pp. 270, 271.
210 Grigoriev, p. 124.
211 Jones, *Dance Index*.
212 *Ballet Russe Courier*, December 1916.
213 Romola Nijinsky, p. 274.
214 Sokolova, p. 89.
215 Jones, *Dance Index*.
216 Romola Nijinsky, p. 274.
217 Ibid., p. 273.
218 Vaughan, *Ballet Review*.
219 Romola Nijinsky, p. 273.
220 Ibid., p. 274.
221 Sokolova, p. 90.
222 Jones, *Dance Index*.
223 Sokolova, p. 91.
224 *Diary*, p. 112.
225 W. B. Chase in an unattributed cutting in the New York Public Library.
226 *Musical American*, 28 October 1916.
227 Unattributed cuttings in the New York Public Library.
228 This description is put together from the accounts of Romola Nijinsky, pp. 275–7, Sokolova, p. 90, a review signed HTP (Parker) in the *Boston Evening Transcript* of 24 October 1916, and an unattributed review by W. B. Chase.
229 *Musical American*, 28 October 1916.
230 Unattributed cutting in the New York Public Library.
231 Jones, *Dance Index*.
232 Romola Nijinsky conversations.

233 Unattributed cutting in the New York Public Library.
234 Ibid.
235 *Musical American*, 28 October 1916.
236 *Boston Evening Transcript*, 24 October 1916.
237 Unattributed cuttings in the New York Public Library.
238 *Theatre*, December 1916.
239 Van Vechten, *Dance Index*.
240 *New York Sun*, 27 October 1916.
241 *Boston Evening Transcript*, 10 November 1916.
242 Romola Nijinsky conversations.
243 *Ballet Russe Courier*, December 1916.
244 Sokolova, p. 91.
245 *Ballet Russe Courier*, December 1916.
246 Ibid.
247 Romola Nijinsky, p. 278.
248 *Boston Evening Transcript*, 10 November 1916.
249 Romola Nijinsky, pp. 278, 279.
250 *Public Ledger*, 24 November 1916.
251 *Washington Star*, 16 November 1916.
252 *Ballet Russe Courier*, December 1916.
253 Romola Nijinsky, p. 279.
254 Ibid., p. 279.
255 Ibid., p. 280.
256 *Diary*, p. 140.
257 Romola Nijinsky, p. 281.
258 *Des Moines Register*, December 1916.
259 Romola Nijinsky, pp. 283, 284.
260 Sokolova, pp. 92, 93.
261 Romola Nijinsky conversations.
262 Romola Nijinsky, p. 282.
263 Sokolova, p. 93.
264 Romola Nijinsky, p. 283.
265 Told to the author by Anton Dolin, who had it from Zverev.
266 Romola Nijinsky, p. 285; *Los Angeles Examiner*, 27 December 1916.
267 Romola Nijinsky, p. 285.
268 Chaplin: *Autobiography*, pp. 205–7.
269 Romola Nijinsky, p. 288.
270 Ibid., p.286.
271 Ibid., pp. 289, 290.
272 Ibid., p. 290.
273 Ibid., p. 291.
274 Romola Nijinsky conversations.
275 Grigoriev, p. 127.
276 Ibid., pp. 130, 131; Massine, pp. 110, 111.
277 Sokolova, p. 104.
278 Romola Nijinsky, p. 293.
279 Romola Nijinsky conversations.
280 Romola Nijinsky, pp. 293–6.
281 Told the author by Mr Anthony Diamantidi.
282 Romola Nijinsky, p. 298.
283 Ibid., pp. 298, 300.
284 Romola Nijinsky conversations.
285 Romola Nijinsky, p. 300.
286 Ibid., pp. 300, 301.
287 Massine, p. 113.
288 Ibid., p. 113.
289 Idzikovsky conversations.
290 Romola Nijinsky, p. 302.
291 Ibid., p. 302.
292 Ibid., pp. 302–4.
293 Romola Nijinsky conversations.
294 Romola Nijinsky, pp. 304, 305.
295 Ansermet conversation; also (independently) Chabelska letter.
296 Grigoriev, pp. 135, 136.
297 Romola Nijinsky, p. 309.
298 Ibid., p. 312.
299 Grigoriev, p. 140.
300 Romola Nijinsky, pp. 311, 313.
301 Grigoriev, p. 139; Sokolova, p. 110.
302 Ansermet conversation; Grigoriev, p. 139; Sokolova, p. 110.
303 Romola Nijinsky conversations.
304 Romola Nijinsky, pp. 306, 307.
305 Ibid., pp. 306–8.
306 Ansermet conversation.
307 Claudel: preface to French edition of Romola Nijinsky's *Nijinsky*, quoted in Reiss, p. 167.
308 Milhaud: *Notes sans musique*, quoted in Reiss, p. 168.
309 Interview with Guerra in Reiss, p. 168.
310 Ibid., p. 169.
311 Grigoriev, p. 137; Sokolova, p. 108.
312 Grigoriev, p. 137.
313 Romola Nijinsky, p. 308.
314 Sokolova, pp. 108, 109.
315 Romola Nijinsky, p. 311.

316 Grigoriev, p. 138.
317 Romola Nijinsky conversations.
318 Romola Nijinsky, pp. 311, 313.
319 Ibid., p. 313.

320 Ansermet conversation.
321 Romola Nijinsky, p. 314; Grigoriev, p. 141.
322 Quoted in Reiss, pp. 172, 173.

Chapter Eight 1917–1950

1 Romola Nijinsky, pp. 294, 295.
2 Grigoriev, pp. 137, 139–41; Sokolova, p. 110.
3 Grigoriev, p. 140.
4 Romola Nijinsky, pp. 311, 313.
5 Ibid., p. 313.
6 Ibid., p. 313.
7 Romola Nijinsky conversations.
8 B. Nijinska conversations; Romola Nijinsky conversations.
9 Romola Nijinsky, p. 297; Massine, p. 113.
10 B. Nijinska conversations. See also Romola Nijinsky: *Last Years*, p. 107.
11 Romola Nijinsky, p. 317.
12 Karsavina: *Theatre Street*, pp. 263–5.
13 Grigoriev, p. 143; Massine, p. 121.
14 Romola Nijinsky, p. 316.
15 Ibid., p. 319. From now on until we reach the beginning of 1919 it can be assumed, except where otherwise stated, that the source for description of the Nijinskys' life is Romola Nijinsky's *Nijinsky*.
16 Kyra Nijinsky, letter to the author.
17 Romola Nijinsky conversations.
18 Massine, p. 129.
19 Sitwell: *Laughter in the Next Room*, pp. 1, 3, 4.
20 Massine, p. 131.
21 Romola Nijinsky conversations.
22 *Diary*, p. 99.
23 Here the author speculates on Nijinsky's state of mind.
24 Sandoz, pp. 66, 67.
25 Here the author speculates.
26 Costa Achillopoulos, letter to the author.
27 Ansermet conversations. But Ansermet had the report at second hand from a friend.

28 Sandoz, pp. 71, 72.
29 *Diary*, pp. 167, 168.
30 Ibid., pp. 151–54, 161.
31 P. L. Harriman: *The New Dictionary of Psychology*, p. 297,
32 Massine conversations.
33 Rambert conversations.
34 Sokolova conversations.
35 Grigoriev, p. 151.
36 Ricketts, p. 301.
37 Karsavina: *Theatre Street*, pp. 247, 248.
38 Ibid., pp. 245, 246.
39 Sokolova, p. 134.
40 Romola Nijinsky conversations.
41 Grigoriev, p. 167.
42 Sokolova, pp. 170, 171.
43 Grigoriev, p. 172.
44 Lady Ripon's will.
45 Dolin: *Autobiography*, pp. 32, 34.
46 Ibid., pp. 36, 37.
47 Benois: *Reminiscences*, pp. 376–82; Grigoriev, p. 198.
48 Haskell, p. 334.
49 Lifar, p. 355.
50 Grigoriev, p. 205.
51 Lifar, pp. 485–8.
52 Karsavina: *Theatre Street*, p. 243.
53 Lifar, p. 489.
54 Rambert conversations.
55 Kessler, pp. 355, 356.
56 Munich programme.
57 Markevitch conversation.
58 Lifar, pp. 511–24.
59 Misia Sert, p. 164.
60 Lifar, pp. 525, 526.
61 Romola Nijinsky conversations.
62 Ibid.
63 Ibid.
64 Lincoln Kirstein conversations.
65 Dolin: *Autobiography*, p. 61.

66 Ibid., pp. 72, 73.
67 Dolin conversations.
68 Dolin: *Ballet Go Round*, pp. 243–5.
69 Herbert Read: Introduction to Catalogue of drawings by Nijinsky, 1937.
70 Romola Nijinsky: *Last Years*. From now on Mme Nijinsky's second book will be, unless otherwise stated, the source for all references to the life of Vaslav and Romola Nijinsky.
71 Romola Nijinsky conversations.
72 Lifar, pp. 529–32.
73 The sum is stated in Lifar's writing on a sheet of Opéra writing-paper stuck in the back of a souvenir programme of the gala which he sent to Lady Juliet Duff, who gave it to the present author.
74 Margaret Power, letter to the author.
75 Ibid.
76 Beaumont, *The Ballet Annual*.
77 Margaret Power, letter to the author.

INDEX

Index

Index